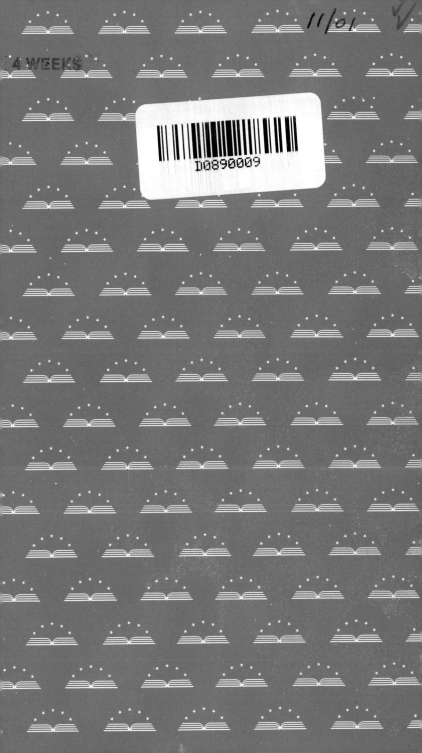

D0890009

DAWN POWELL

Dawn Powell

NOVELS 1930–1942

Dance Night
Come Back to Sorrento
Turn, Magic Wheel
Angels on Toast
A Time To Be Born

THE LIBRARY OF AMERICA

Volume compilation, notes, and chronology copyright © 2001 by
Literary Classics of the United States, Inc., New York, N.Y.
All rights reserved.
No part of this book may be reproduced commercially
by offset-lithographic or equivalent copying devices without
the permission of the publisher.

Dance Night, Come Back to Sorrento, Turn, Magic Wheel,
copyright 1930, 1932, 1936 by the Estate of Dawn Powell.
Reprinted by permission of Steerforth Press, L.C.
This edition of *Novels 1930–1942* has been published
in cooperation with the Estate of Dawn Powell.
Steerforth Press edition copyright 1995, 1996.

The paper used in this publication meets the
minimum requirements of the American National Standard for
Information Sciences—Permanence of Paper for Printed
Library Materials, ANSI Z39.48—1984.

Distributed to the trade in the United States
by Penguin Putnam Inc.
and in Canada by Penguin Books Canada Ltd.

Library of Congress Catalog Number: 00-054595
For cataloging information, see end of Notes.
ISBN 1-931082-01-4

First Printing
The Library of America—126

Manufactured in the United States of America

TIM PAGE
WROTE THE NOTES FOR THIS VOLUME

Contents

DANCE NIGHT

For my sister Phyllis

Dance Night

WHAT Morry heard above the Lamptown night noises was a woman's high voice rocking on mandolin notes far far away. This was like no music Morry had ever known, it was a song someone else remembered, perhaps his mother, when he was only a sensation in her blood, a slight quickening when she met Charles Abbott, a mere wish for love racing through her veins.

The song bewildered Morry reading Jules Verne by gaslight, it unspiraled somewhere high above the Bon Ton Hat Shop, above Bauer's Chop House, over the Casino, and over Bill Delaney's Saloon and Billiard Parlor. It came from none of these places but from other worlds and then faded into a factory whistle, a fire engine bell, and a Salvation Army chorus down on Market Street.

Morry leaned far out the window and looked above and below, but there was no woman in the sky nor any sign of a miracle for blocks around. Girls from the Works in light dresses wandered, giggling, up and down the street waiting for the Casino Dance Hall above Bauer's to open, farm couples stood transfixed before Robbin's Jewelry Store window, the door of Delaney's Saloon swung open, shut, open, shut, releasing then withdrawing the laughter and the gaudy music of a pianola. Everything was as it was on any other Thursday night in Lamptown.

Nevertheless to Morry this had become a strange night and he could read no more. He thrust "Twenty Thousand Leagues Under the Sea" into his washstand drawer, turned down the gas, picked up a pack of cigarettes, thrust them in his hip pocket, and went downstairs. In the dark narrow hallway he ran into Nettie Farrell, assistant in the Bon Ton, her arms encircling a tower of hat boxes. Morry, absorbed in his new and curious quest, had no desire to meet anyone from his mother's shop and he hung back. But Nettie deliberately left the work-room door open and there was his mother, her pale cold face bent over a basket of cotton pansies, a blue-shaded lamp burning intently above her.

3

"You've been smoking!" Nettie whispered accusingly. "I'm going to tell your mother. And now you're going over to Bill's place! You are—you know you are!"

"I wasn't!" Morry denied everything sullenly.

"Hanging around poolrooms! You ought to be ashamed!"

A bell tinkled in the front of the shop and Nettie, hat boxes tipping perilously eastward, backed into the workroom without another word, only her black eyes blinking reproachfully at him.

Morry hurried out the side door into the little stone court where half a dozen Market Street shops ended in kitchen stoops, and half a dozen lights from these dwellings back and above shops united in a feeble illumination of a cistern, old garbage cans, a broken-down doll-buggy, and a pile of shipping boxes.

Where was the song now, Morry wondered, and vaguely he blamed Nettie Farrell and the Bon Ton for having lost it. A freight train rumbled past a few yards from the court, its smoke spread over the Lamptown moon, and then he heard above its roar a girl's voice calling. Though certainly no girl in all Lamptown could be calling Morry Abbott, he was always expecting it, and he tiptoed hastily across rubbish-strewn cinders toward the voice. A flight of steps went up the side of the saloon to where Bill Delaney lived with his mother, and here Morry stopped short for at the very top of these steps huddled a dark figure.

Morry hesitated.

"Did you call me?" he asked uncertainly.

"Yes," said the girl and since Bill had neither sister, wife, nor daughter, Morry could not for the life of him imagine who it was. "I was lonesome. Come on up."

Morry was embarrassed.

"I—I can't." He felt scornful of a girl who would talk to him without even being able to see who he was. If it had been daylight or even dusk a strange girl speaking to him would have meant that in spite of Nettie Farrell's repeated taunts, he was good looking, his black eyes, his broad shoulders, oh something about him was appealing. But it was clear that to the girl at the top of the stairs he might be just anyone.

"Come on," she urged. "I've got to talk to somebody, haven't I?"

The saloon back door opened and the bartender stood there against a sudden brilliant background of glasses, polished brass, and a rainbow of bottles. Morry ducked up the stairs, and the girl moved over for him to sit down. He could see now that she was a stranger in Lamptown, a queer pointed-faced girl, whose hair, black and tangled, hung to her shoulders. He would see if she was pretty when the next engine flashed its headlight down the tracks.

"There's a dance tonight, isn't there?" she demanded of him. In the darkness they eagerly tried to study each other's face, but all Morry could find in hers was a wildness that made him feel oddly older and more responsible.

"Even if I'm not old enough to go," she pursued, "why won't Bill let me go and watch? You ask him."

This terrified Morry. He didn't want to be teased by the factory girls at the dance, and he certainly didn't want to be ragged by the train men in Bill's saloon. Facing their good-natured challenges on his own account was torture enough, but to take on the added burden of a girl . . .

"We don't want to go to any dance," he said. "It's no fun watching. Look, who are you?"

"I'm adopted now," she explained triumphantly. "The Delaneys took me from the Home. This is where we live and I have a room of my own."

"Well." Morry didn't know why you were glad over being adopted but he supposed you ought to be congratulated. "Do you like it here?"

"I like the trains going by," she said. "I like it in my sleep when I hear them whistle way off. And I like it in my sleep when I hear the piano going downstairs and the men laughing. But I don't like to make beds. I can't make the sheets stay under."

Morry lit a cigarette.

"Let me see if I can smoke," she took the one he had lit, made a few masterful draws on it and then gave it back. "Oh well," she coughed, "I guess I can learn."

"What's your name?" he asked her. He liked sitting there beside her but he was a little afraid of her. He must remember, he thought, to hang on to her skirt if she should take it into her head to jump down stairs.

"Jen St. Clair. Maybe I'm Delaney now, but Bill and his mother say they don't care what I call myself." She casually fished in his pocket and drew out a pack of gum, unwrapped it and carefully stuck the wrappings back into his pocket. "But I'm going back to the Home sometime—when I get money."

"Why?" he wanted to know.

"To get Lil. She's my sister and she's still there."

An engine shrieked down the tracks, then a window flew up in the court, a woman thrust her head out and called, "Billy! Oh, Bill- -ee!"

" 'You'll come back for me, won't you, Jen,' is what Lil said to me," Jen went on. "I said I would."

The saloon back door opened again and a quiet scuffling noise was heard,—the engine's search-light briefly revealed Bill in white apron, wrestling with a heavy but feebly organized man in shirt-sleeves.

"There!" muttered Bill. "There, damn you. . . . Oh, Shorty! Give us a hand here."

Bill always handled the toughs but Shorty, the barkeep, had to pick them up afterward and start them home. Morry explained all this to Jen. She seemed pleased to hear of her benefactor's power. She stood up.

"Come in the house," she invited. "I want to show you something."

"But Bill's old lady wouldn't like it." It was Morry's experience that you weren't wanted in people's houses any more than they were wanted in yours.

"Asleep," Jen tersely nodded toward the old woman's bedroom. "Come on, I want to show you this."

She softly opened the screen door and Morry gingerly followed her into the dark vestibule. The rooms smelled of laundry and doughnuts. He caught her hand held out to guide him. It was the parlor, he knew, by the damp, musty air. Jen stood up on a chair and lit the gas light over the mantelpiece. With the flare of light Morry could see that although her hair and brows were black her eyes were sky-blue, he saw the patch of new calico on her faded blue dress. But she did not look at him again. It no longer mattered what he looked like since they were already established as friends. She took some little thing from the mantel and held it out to him in the palm of her hand.

"Look."

It was a tiny gold chair, barely an inch high, an armchair with delicate filagree for its cane back and seat. Morry took it and examined it,—gave it back to her. Jen let it lay in her palm a moment, then with a sigh put it back on the mantel.

"It's so little. . . . I wish I could keep it in my room," she said. "But I suppose it's all right here. I can come in and look at it every once in a while. She got it at the World's Fair in St. Louis."

"I've got to go," Morry decided, watching the door uneasily.

Jen looked stricken.

"No, you can't—you mustn't go yet. Wait."

She tiptoed hurriedly into the next room and came back with a pair of shining tan shoes.

"I've got new shoes with high heels. See? I wanted pumps, black patent leather, but Bill got me these. Look!" She reached down her blouse and drew out a locket on the end of a thin gold chain. "Asafetida. Smell."

Morry smelled. It was asafetida. But he still had to go. He was already out the door. Jen turned down the gas and ran after him.

"There's duck in the ice box," she said. "We could eat it."

Morry only pulled his cap down with more finality. He was amazed at an adopted girl's boldness in entering parlors, and offering delicacies that were undoubtedly reserved by Bill De-laney for his own midnight supper.

"Well, I guess I'm off," he said brusquely.

Jen hung on to the railing and swung her foot back and forth. She wasn't over thirteen or fourteen, he thought.

"I've got folks somewhere," she informed him, rather aloofly now, as if she sensed criticism of her lack of background. "They've got papers at the Home. There's a Mrs. St. Clair somewhere and that's my mother—Lil's and mine."

Morry said nothing, but he was impressed. An unknown mother—a Mrs. St. Clair somewhere who might be a millionaire or an actress.

The window on the court flew open again.

"Billy! Oh Bill--ee!"

And this must have reminded Nettie Farrell to tell something for the next moment Morry heard his mother on their back stoop.

"Morry! Where are you?"

"You're Morry," Jen whispered, and he nodded. Why not Billy, then he wondered. . . . He did not answer and his mother never called twice. He heard her go indoors and close the door.

"Listen!" Jen seized his wrist. From across the street in front of the building came the sound of a drum, presently joined by a piano. Then a man's voice, rich, resonant—on Thursday nights you heard this voice above all other sounds for a block away; it belonged to Harry Fischer, the dancing teacher.

"ONE and two, and ONE and two and ONE and two and—"

"Can't we go and watch?" Jen appealed again.

Morry shook his head. He started down the steps. She said nothing, just swung her foot back and forth, but when halfway down he turned to look back he was startled at the desolation in her face, as if this parting was forever, and as if he, Morry Abbott, meant everything in the world to her.

"What is it?" he wanted to know.

Jen twisted her hands.

"Nothing. Only people last such a little while with me. There's no way to keep them, I guess. Everybody goes away—that's why I've got to go back for Lil because I know how terrible it is to be left always—never see people again."

"I'll see you to-morrow," he promised hurriedly. "I live over the Bon Ton. Probably we'll always be seeing each other."

Jen shook her head. Morry hesitated a moment, then went slowly down the stairs.

"ONE and two and ONE and two and ONE and two—"

The dancing lesson lasted from eight to nine and then the counting stopped and the Ball began. Morry wanted to tell all this to Jen but it was better not to go back once you had said you were going. He looked up. She sat hugging her knees, leaning against the railing.

"Well—goodnight."

She didn't answer. Embarrassed, Morry stumbled over ash-cans and cinders to his own stone-paved courtyard. He wanted to look back again but he did not dare. He went down the lit-tle alley and slipped in the side door. The workroom door was open and his mother was in there arranging her hair before a hand-mirror with deep concentration. He wondered if she was going to the dance. Behind her he saw Nettie Farrell's trim plump figure. She was rummaging through a large pasteboard box of ribbons. Morry went upstairs before she saw him.

The gaslight in Morry's room went up and shadows were chased up the low sloping ceiling. Jules Verne emerged from the washstand drawer. Morry, in bed, smoked as he read and squashed his cigarette stubs in to a cracked yellow soapdish. The short little dimity curtains at his infinitesimal windows quivered steadily with a busy breeze. Below, on Market Street, a group of factory girls gathered about two trainmen just come from Bill's place, and were convulsed by their masculine wit. The Salvation Army moved up a block; its aim was to reach the Casino and save at least a few of those headed for that modest hell. Tambourines clinked.

Morry jammed a third pillow at the back of his head, absently flicked ashes over the quilt, and turned page after page until words again took living shapes and allowed him to enter the book.

He had forgotten the unknown lady singing in the sky.

"Come to me my melancholy baby," sang Nettie, "Huddle up and don't be blue. So you're going to the dance again, Mrs. Abbott."

Elsinore lowered her eyes over the hat for Dode O'Connell. The factory girls always liked flamboyant trimming and she thoughtfully added a green ribbon to the flowers pinned on the straw brim. This was what Charles Abbott would facetiously refer to as a Vegetable Blue Plate.

"There's plenty of time," she answered Nettie. "I don't want to be there first, besides the lesson is still on."

"Huddle up and don't be blue," hummed Nettie. She watched the street door waiting for customers. She was eighteen, she had been in the shop a year and the importance of her work continued to overwhelm her. Other girls in Lamptown worked in the factory or the telephone office, but God had chosen to favor her with this amazingly attractive niche in the Bon Ton Hat Shop. This must be because she was superior, a cut above the factory type, she was on lodge programs, for instance at the Lady Maccabees' meeting she sometimes sang, "When the dawn flames in the sky—I love you———"

"Mr. Abbott ought to be in from the road soon," Nettie said. "What does he think of your going to the dances? I guess he's glad you have a little pleasure, maybe."

"He doesn't mind. He knows I work hard and don't get out much. I don't think Charlie minds." It had never occurred to Elsinore, for ten years self-and-home-supporting, that Mr. Abbott's opinion deserved little attention. She accepted his husbandly domination without demanding any of its practical benefits. If Charles, home for a week from a three months' Southern tour, objected to a gown of hers or a new arrangement of furniture, things were quietly changed to his taste. In Elsinore's scheme a husband was always a husband.

Nettie sat down on a work stool and examined her fingernails. She was a plump, sleek little girl, black hair parted in the middle and drawn back to a loose knot on her neck, her face a neat oval with full satisfied lips. Men followed Nettie on the street but Nettie's chin went up more haughtily, her hips swung more insolently from side to side because Nettie was better than factory girls or telephone operators, she did not speak to strange men, she wanted to get on. Some day she would have a shop of her own. Mrs. Abbott said she was a good worker.

"I don't care about dancing," she observed to Mrs. Abbott. "That's why I never took lessons."

Elsinore held a straw frame out at arm's length.

"I never cared at your age," she said. "It was only this winter I learned."

The echo of the maestro's voice could be heard again—One two three—ONE two three—One———and Elsinore colored ever so faintly. It was easier to wait from one Thursday to the next than from eight o'clock until nine, she thought. She always hoped—yet perhaps not quite hoped, for she was a quiet contained woman, that this night—or next week, then—Mr. Fischer would select her as partner. This had happened once,—just last winter in fact, when she had stayed over from the lesson to the regular dance; Fischer had been demonstrating a new dance and he turned to her, "Mrs.

Abbott knows these steps from the class lesson tonight. May I ask you to come forward, Mrs. Abbott?"

Usually shy, Elsinore had known no hesitation in going straight across the dance floor to him, aware of her own limitations as a dancer she yet was certain that with him all things were possible. If from a raft in midocean this man had called to her, "Now, Mrs. Abbott, just swim out to me," she would have swum to him without hesitation, safe in her enchantment. A few bars of music, two to the left, two to the right, swing, swing, dip . . . "All right, Mr. Sanderson"—then to the musician.

That was all. It might happen again. Always someone was chosen casually like that for a brief demonstration and even if it didn't happen again, there was that one time to remember.

"The girls are beginning to go up," said Nettie.

Elsinore's fingers trembled arranging the trimmings in their labelled boxes but she said nothing. Nettie drew out a nail buff and polished her nails intently. Her hands were plump, white, and tapering. Nettie greased them and wore silk gloves over them at night.

"Bill Delaney's adopted a girl from the orphanage for his mother to take care of," said Nettie. "Imagine."

"That's no home for a girl," said Elsinore, "over a saloon."

Nettie tossed the buff into her drawer and looked toward the front door. Still no customers.

"Fay's coming for her hat tonight," she said, remembering. "She wants it for the Telephone Company's picnic. . . . She said people thought the girl might belong to Bill—you know men are that way, and Bill used to run around a lot."

"Maybe," said Elsinore but she didn't care. In three minutes more she would go over to the Casino. In three minutes. "Did Morry come in?"

Nettie shrugged.

"How do I know, Mrs. Abbott? Morry never pays any attention to what anybody says. He hangs around poolrooms, he smokes, he sits up late reading and smoking. You ought to get his father to talk to him."

Elsinore's straight eyebrows drew together.

"I must, Nettie, that's quite true. He's just at that age."

"Seventeen-year-old hanging around Bill Delaney's!" said Nettie. Talking about Morry Nettie's face always got red, her

eyes flashed, every reminder of this boy's existence subtly offended her.

Two more minutes and Elsinore could stand up and say,
"Well, Nettie, I'll leave the shop to you. Shut it up as soon as
Fay gets her hat and put the key under the stoop."

Now she said, "He's lonely, Nettie,—he goes to Bill's for
the company. But it's not a good place for a boy."

She heard a step upstairs and called Morry's name. A sleepy
bored voice responded.

"At least he's in," said Nettie.

One more minute. The piano from across the street
pounded out the rhythm Fischer had announced—ONE and
two and three and FOUR—Come to me my melancholy
baby, huddle up and don't be blue. . . .

"Oh it's g-r-e-a-t to be f-r-e-e," sang the Salvation Army,
"from the chains of s-i-n that bondage me. . . ."

"Well, Nettie, I'll leave the shop to you," said Elsinore,
standing up at last. "Shut it up as soon as Fay gets her hat—
and put the key under the stoop."

She did things,—rubbed a chamois over her face, patted
her hair, adjusted her dress, but these motions were curiously
automatic for already she was swimming across oceans to a
raft where Harry Fischer stood beating his hands to a dance
rhythm—"one and two and three and four—"

"Here's Fay now," said Nettie, but Elsinore was gone.
Elsinore gone, Morry asleep upstairs,—it instantly became
Nettie's shop and Nettie bloomed. She chatted patronizingly
with Fay's young man while Fay tried on the hat.

"Smile my honey dear," sang Fay softly into the mirror for
the hat was becoming, "while I kiss away each tear——"

Behind her back her young man grasped Nettie's arm. He
slid his hand along her biceps and pressed a knuckle into her
arm-pit.

"That's the vein to tap when you embalm people," he said,
for he was going to be an undertaker.

Two floors above Bauer's Chop House fifty pairs of feet
went slip a-slip a-slip to a drum's beating. Sometimes a piano
melody crept through the drum's reverberation, sometimes
the voice of Fischer emerged with a one-and-two and a one-

and-two, and when this rhythm stopped suddenly there was a clap-clap-clap of hands, a silence and in this silence the clock sitting on the top of Bauer's cash register marked off the hush into ones and twos and ones and twos and ones and twos.

Behind the counter Hermann Bauer, fat, immobile, leaned on his elbows and looked out of the window without stirring for thirty-nine minutes when a lady got off the Interurban and came in to order a fried egg sandwich. Behind the other counter Mrs. Hulda Bauer, fat, immobile, sat on a high stool and crocheted an ugly but innocent device for a counterpane. Parades of girls from the Works went by and tramped up the stairs behind the restaurant to the Casino. Every Thursday night for six years Hermann had turned from the counter to say to his wife,

"Hulda, look how these girls dress! Every cent on their backs. Gott! Silk, satins, and the perfume! I can smell it in here!"

"That will all change when they marry," Hulda answered always, but now Hermann remained silent so that Hulda need not look up from her crocheting. Why shouldn't the factory girls dress well,—they made high wages, living was cheap, and nine hundred girls in a town needed to step fast to compete for the stray men. They went down the street giggling and nudging each other, in pink velvets, accordion pleats, lavender and orange satins, their hair peroxided or natural but always elaborately curled, their faces heavily powdered. In front of Bauer's they dallied, waiting for the saloon door across the street to swing open. From behind that door you could hear men's laughter, the pianola, and sometimes a hearty curse, with so much private fun it was amazing that the men should ever come out for a mere dance. But at nine o'clock when the lesson music changed to Dance Number One, a Twostep, the saloon door swung open and the men came out,—the firemen, brakemen, factory workers, all dressed up to the nines. The girls tossed their heads and hurried up the steps ahead.

"Hello, Jim," a girl leaning out the Casino window upstairs called down to one of the men.

The Bauers had taken in all this play for years but never once had it inspired them to go upstairs to watch as some older people did. It was the duty of one of them to wait for

after the dance couples would come in to this place for coffee
and sandwiches.

In the kitchen Grace Terris, the waitress, having finished
helping the cook with the dishes, hurried upstairs to frizz her
hair. She was a thin blonde with a pale face and glasses. She
was very neat,—her hair and her waist ribbons must always be
just so, her outside garments spotless and starched, even
though out of sheer love of its texture she sometimes wore a
silk chemise three weeks.

Grace brushed past Mrs. Bauer half a dozen times in quest
of pins in the cash drawer, a pocket-book left under a serving
table, a powder puff hidden under the counter. No matter
how busy the place might be on Thursday nights, neither
Hermann nor Hulda would ever ask Grace to stay and help.
Thursday was her night off—nothing could ever alter that.
She couldn't dance but she liked to go somewhere even if she
just sat and watched. Presently in a nimbus of azalea perfume,
a rose-colored scarf wound around her head as a badge of
evening dress, her dark green silk bristling with anticipation,
Grace swept through the restaurant and out the front door.

Dance Number Two, a Waltz. At the dark railroad station
just beyond Bill Delaney's saloon Number Eleven drew in and
a dozen more men from Birchfield, Galion and Ashland
dropped off, and girls leaning out the Casino window hurried
to the dressing-room to powder again. Hermann Bauer nodded to a group passing the window. Upstairs the feet went
slip a-slip a-slip to a waltz, on the stool opposite him Hulda
crocheted a daisy over a waltz foundation.

The Salvation Army stood in front of Hermann's, they
fixed their eyes on his motionless face while they sang shrilly
and mechanically to the dreary jangle of a tambourine. Bill
Delaney's place was silent, a little light gleamed in the attic
above the Bon Ton Hat Shop, the Bon Ton itself was dark.
Now the life of Lamptown had concentrated two floors above
Bauer's Chop House.

Dance Number Three, a Robber's Two Step.

In front of Bauer's a long low roadster stopped. Hunt Russell's. Hunt, by some freak of inheritance, certainly due to no
fault of his languid self, owned the Works, owned Lamptown,
you might say. Now his tall lean person swung out of the car,

followed by the equally lean figure of Dode O'Connell, the factory forewoman,—a proud hard face she had beneath masses of red hair. She was Hunt Russell's woman. No matter whom she had belonged to before, now she was Hunt's. They went up the steps to the Casino. Dance Number Four.

Quietly Hulda Bauer laid down her crocheting, nodded to her husband, and waddled up to bed. It had been quite an outing for her.

"Tonight I am going to demonstrate to you," said Mr. Fischer, "the dance I created for the United Dancing Masters of the World last summer at our convention in Atlantic City. This dance, ladies and gentlemen, is now taking New York by storm. It is called the Duck Slide. If you please, Mr. Sanderson."

One and two and a three and dip. One and a two and a three and turn. One and a two and a dip and turn and two step right and two step left—thank you, Mr. Sanderson.

Elsinore Abbott usually danced first with Mr. Klein the gas man. He was too old for the factory girls and besides he admired a woman who had spunk enough to run a business, always looked trim, always a lady. In the midst of the factory girls' gay colors her dark blue taffeta and black satin pumps seemed wistfully chic, her pale clear-cut face beneath the heavy brown hair gave no hint of naïve pleasure in the dance, her cool grey eyes revealed no vulgar excitement over crowds and music. Over Klein's honest shoulder she watched Fischer, immaculate in evening dress, demonstrating the next movement of the next dance. Fischer had broader shoulders than any man in the room. It was curious that his great muscular body should yield so exquisitely to a dance for it belonged to mighty masculine deeds. He had thick sleek black hair, hard black eyes, a strong-boned heavy face. In a bathing suit at Atlantic City the muscles of his back must have shown powerful and rippling, muscles must have bulged from his shoulders, arms, and legs, his throat must have looked thick and strong like an animal's, like a prize-fighter's. Elsinore followed Mr. Klein's painstaking lead through the second movement.

"In a little while we will pass him standing there," she thought. "In a little while . . . There's no hurry."

When they passed she did not look at him.

In the center of the floor Hunt Russell and Dode O'Connell, cheek to cheek, danced beautifully, silently, as couples do
who are certain of other contacts. Hunt Russell, worth a
quarter of a million, with a background of Boston Russells
and Carolina Blairs, owner of Lamptown, preferred a factory
forewoman to a woman of quality, chose Harry Fischer,
small-town dancing master as his boon companion, lounged
in Bill Delaney's saloon, a billiard cue in one hand, instead of
in country clubs, drove his expensive cars down dingy Lamptown streets instead of on foreign boulevards. There were
men who would not dare be like that, but no one slapped
Hunt on the back, few women dared solicit too frankly the
inquiry of his cold amused eyes. And because for two years
she had been Hunt's woman Dode O'Connell's head was always high, her proud red mouth flaunted the exclusiveness of
her kisses.

After Mr. Klein there were the uncertain young men who
had gone to last winter's dancing class with Elsinore, who
knew that her own lack of skill would make her less critical of
their mistakes. They would learn with her, thought Elsinore
without resentment, but after they became expert they would
choose younger women as their partners. One of these men,
in a waltz, brushed her past Fischer. He stood in a corner
talking in a low voice to Hunt while Dode whirled by with
one of the train dispatchers.

"You'll have to wait till about one," Fischer said looking at
his watch. "Then I'm good for all night. But what about
Red?"

"I'll fix that," Hunt tossed a cigarette in a palm bucket. He
was not over thirty but his temples were already gray.

Fischer laughed.

"Better look out—she'd kill you for less than that. . . ."
and then he clapped his hands. "All right, people . . . one
moment, Mr. Sanderson. I want to announce the date of the
tango contest to be held in Akron two weeks from tomorrow
night. The rules for the contestants, ladies and gentlemen, are
as follows. . . ."

He stood almost at Elsinore's elbow, no more conscious of
her than of the palm on the other side of him. Elsinore did

not mind. She wanted nothing from him, after all, only the rare privilege of being allowed to think about him, as she had thought of him for over a year. Nights after the Bon Ton was closed she had lain in bed wondering where Fischer was now. In Birchfield Mondays, Columbus Tuesdays, Delaware Wednesdays, Marion Fridays. Tonight I am going to demonstrate to you, ladies and gentlemen, the Duck Slide. . . . She saw the young girls of Marion, Birchfield, Delaware looking at him, and saw him selecting this or that eighteen year old for an exhibition dance. With these petal-cheeked young girls surrounding him, why should he remember that once he had singled out Elsinore Abbott for a schottische demonstration? Yet she had been eighteen once as these girls would one day be thirty-six. And he was even older than that. But why should he remember her—why indeed should he trouble her mind, Elsinore sometimes wondered, his ways, his manner, littered her memory as confusingly as a man's clothes in a woman's bedroom. She tried to recall what she had thought of before she saw him, but it was as difficult as trying to decide what she wanted of him now that she did think of him. She was married to Charles. He was married to someone in Columbus. What else could there be?

In the doorway of the Casino two new men appeared, and Elsinore, thinking of her husband at the very moment, saw him invoked before her eyes. The natty checked suit, the flawless necktie, the perfect fedora, the cigar—it was indeed Charles Abbott. His roving blue eyes had found her at once, and quietly she left her partner and went up to him.

"I didn't expect you for another three weeks, Charles," she said following him into the hall.

"No?" Charles looked at her with faintly mocking suspicion. "Since when have you been going to factory girl dances?"

Elsinore flushed.

"You knew I had taken it up," she said in a low voice. "I told you I was taking the course last winter. I go out very little, Charles. You know that. This—I like."

Charles watched the dancers with a fixed smile, tapping his cigar against the railing by the door. He nodded to a dancer now and then whom he knew either as a patron of his wife's shop or as a fellow patron of Bill Delaney's place.

Elsinore's partner looked at her questioningly and she shook her head in the negative.

"Close the shop, do you, to come over here?" inquired Charles with seeming affability.

"I never neglect the shop, Charles, you ought to know that," said Elsinore. The color had not left her face. She turned to him abruptly. "Let's go now. Things are almost over. We can talk."

"No hurry," Charles said. He waved his cigar nonchalantly to Hunt Russell. Elsinore went to the dressing-room for her coat. She passed Fischer again, standing with arms folded beside the palms. He bowed to her, his face a smooth ruddy mask of courtesy.

"Goodnight, Mrs. Abbott," he said.

Elsinore lowered her head.

"All right, Mr. Sanderson, the next dance will be a Circle twostep. A Circle Twostep, ladies and gentlemen."

> "Come sweetheart mine,
>   Don't sit and pine,
>   Tell me of the cares that make you oh so blue—"

Hunt Russell leaned against the exit door and sang the words softly. Charles followed Elsinore with the suggestion of a swagger, an air of being made to leave a gay occasion against his will. Elsinore did not look back. The music, the laughter, had ceased to be once she turned her back upon them. Abruptly she locked away her thoughts of Fischer for these were precious matters not to be dwelt upon with strangers like Charles nearby.

"The good old Bon Ton," Charles observed lightly as Elsinore fitted her key into the lock of the shop door. Elsinore did not answer.

Long afterward Morry was awakened by the dance music stopping. He heard voices in the street and stumbled sleepily to the window. The Casino windows were dark—only one light burned in Bauer's Chop House. Before the restaurant Hunt Russell's car stood, and beside it were Hunt and Dode O'Connell facing each other.

"You cur," Dode was saying in a cold hard voice, "You dirty double-crossing cur."

Morry yawned and went back to bed.

*

Trains whirred through the air, their whistles shrieking a red line through the sky behind them, they landed on Jen's bed without weight, vanished, and other trains, pop-eyed, roared toward her. Trains slid noiselessly across her eyelids, long transcontinental trains with diners, clubcars, observation cars. The people on these trains leaned out of their windows and held out their hands to Jen.

"California, Hawaii, Denver, Quebec, Miami," they chanted, "oh you dear child, New Orleans, Chicago, Boston, Rocky Mountains, New York City."

Then two dark porters made a London bridge and caught her, they said, "Which would you rather have, a diamond palace or a solid gold piano?"

Old Mrs. Delaney finally put on her carpet-slippers and opened Jen's door.

"Well, what's the matter with you now?" she wanted to know. "Waking folks up this hour with your yelling?"

She was irritable, for Bill had been hiding in a closet ever since he came upstairs. He'd been drinking too much and after the big Akron wreck when he'd been the faulty engineer he had spells when every engine chugging by sent him sobbing to some hiding-place. There was nothing you could do with him but sometimes his mother, her withered old face grim and dark, her gnarled hands clenched, sat waiting all night for him to quit moaning and come to his senses again.

"No—no, I've changed my mind," Jen cried. "Not the piano—the other—the diamond palace."

"That'll be about enough out of you tonight," said Mrs. Delaney. Jen opened her eyes and blinked at the old woman in the feeble dawn-light.

"There won't be any diamonds for you, young lady," grumbled Mrs. Delaney. She pulled the cover over Jen, jerked a pillow into place. "Diamond palace my eye."

"All right," murmured Jen as her foster parent slipped out of the room, "I'll take the gold piano."

"Aren't you afraid of the old woman?" Morry Abbott asked one night when they sat out on the steps above the saloon.

Jen shook her head.

"I'm not afraid of her," she said. "That's just the way old

women are. I'm not afraid of anybody. I feel sorry for them, coming to me someday begging me to forgive 'em because they didn't realize I was going to turn out so rich and famous."

"You kid yourself a lot, don't you?" Morry said curiously. He heard voices in the saloon backroom of older boys about town and he instinctively drew his cap down over his eyes. His own place at seventeen was in the saloon downstairs, instead of hanging around kids like Jen. He was old enough to be getting over that queer sickness the saloon smell gave to him, about time he stopped coughing over whiskey, listening frankly awestricken to tales of amorous adventures. He would go down in a little while for the only way to learn anything was to get used to it.

"What did the Delaneys take you out of the Home for?" he wanted to know.

Jen looked at him suspiciously and then brushed back a lock of black hair, stuck it behind her ear.

"What's the matter with me—why shouldn't they pick me?" she demanded.

Morry blushed, at her attack.

"Well, people usually adopt those little yellow-haired blue-eyed dolls—you know—you're all right only—"

"The hell they do," said Jen and Morry was conscious of the same sick feeling the saloon smell gave to him. "They always pick somebody that looks like a good worker. Once in a while some woman that's had her pet cat run over picks out one of those pretty ones. There aren't many of them."

"You don't have to say hell," said Morry. It annoyed him that words which stuck in his own throat should flow so easily from a young girl's lips.

Jen wriggled and sucked her thumb sulkily.

"Well, anyway Lil's like that—she looks like a little wax doll," she went on. "Everybody that visits the Home always wants to hold her . . . but nobody's adopted her. I told the matron not to let anybody because I'm the one to take care of Lil. She's so little—she can't stand it without me. I've got to look after her. Gee!"

She suddenly brushed her sleeve over her eyes. Morry was fired with an aim in life.

"You leave Lil to me," he said. "What about me adopting her myself?"

Jen seized his arm. She was radiant.

"Will you—Morry—will you do that?"

And then Morry remembered the truths that his father mockingly and Nettie Farrell bitterly had so often flung at him. Worthless, overgrown cub, no good to anybody, in everybody's way. If he was going to amount to anything in the world, why was he hanging around talking big instead of hunting a job, why didn't he study one of those correspondence courses at night instead of reading romantic trash till way after midnight? Fellows no older than he was were making money out selling or working in garages or factories and if they could do it he supposed he could stand it. But here Morry shuddered. He couldn't see himself in overalls, he dared not picture himself an agonized applicant for an office job. Somehow he always saw himself a sort of Hunt Russell, a success without callouses and without the embarrassment of however honest sweat. But even Morry could see that this wasn't the way a young man ought to enter the struggle— gasping at the very start. He was miserable remembering the dooms forecast for him by Nettie and his father. Still—Jen St. Clair didn't know all these things about him. On the contrary she seemed to think he could manage anything he promised to do.

"We'll take care of Lil all right," he repeated with slightly less emphasis this time.

"That's fixed, I guess," sighed Jen. "I'll write Lil and tell her. I didn't want to write until I could promise something."

"Does the old woman make you work?" Morry asked, relieved to have the subject of Lil's rescue safely out of the way. "I mean if that's what they got you for—"

Jen looked over her shoulder to make sure Mrs. Delaney was out of earshot.

"I guess they made a mistake," she whispered. "I look bright but I can't seem to pick up anything. The covers stay in little bumps when I make the beds."

She looked gloomy.

"The bottoms of the dishes get egg all over as fast as they're washed," she went on, "even when we haven't had eggs, they do that, no matter how hard I scrub. And when I made popovers yesterday they didn't come out popovers at all. Sort of like pancakes . . . You'd think popovers would be easy, wouldn't you, Morry?"

Jen sunk her chin in her hands.

"It makes it pretty hard for the old woman," she said regretfully. "It was Bill's idea adopting somebody and now they've picked me they've got to keep me."

Morry got up. He thought he might as well go down and get the saloon over with. Jen's black brows contracted. Tomorrow or next day she would see him again and yet it was a lamp going out each time he went away. She wished for some marvellous surprise to detain him with,—a diamond palace or a solid gold piano. "Wait," she would cry and he would come back. She would open the door. "Look," and there would be the palace, its towers glittering, a sapphire light glowing in each window. And so he would have to take off his hat and stay.

Jen didn't answer when he said goodbye. She stood with one hand on the wall and the other on the railing and scuffed the toe of her shoe on the top step.

"Wait," she said when he was halfway down, but when he turned expectantly, she said lifelessly, "Oh nothing."

Diamonds, my eye!

"One beer," Morry said standing at the bar with Hogan, fireman on Number Eleven, and a couple of brakemen from the short line.

The boys of Morry's age usually played pool in the front room and only occasionally joined the older men in the barroom, but now the front room was empty and so Morry went back to the bar. Here Bill Delaney, short, blonde, serious, stood leaning over the back of a chair at one of the card tables talking to three men from the freight yards.

"You've got no kick," he was saying. "You pull down your hundred and fifty smackers every month, you're all right. I'm tellin' you you fellows got it pretty goddam soft."

"You tell all that to the pope," Hogan advised over his shoulder.

"Your dad was here yesterday, Morry," Shorty said wiping up the counter. "Some sport, Charlie Abbott, let me tell you. Some sport even for a travelling man."

"Yeah?" said Morry, whose one aim in life was to keep out of his father's way, or at least out of range of his father's ironic eye.

"You goin' sellin' on the road like your dad?" Shorty asked.

"No," Morry said and then explained, "I'm sort of looking around."

"How about brakin'?" said the brown young man in blue overalls on the other side of Hogan. "You get good pay."

"Don't do no railroadin', buddy," Hogan advised. "We're a tough old bunch, listen to me. You've got to know how to handle your liquor and your women."

"Leave that to Charlie Abbott's boy all right," chuckled Shorty.

"Jesus, when Buck here and me had that seven-hour run out of Pittsburgh—" Hogan drained his glass, banged it on the counter, raised one finger significantly to Shorty.

"Seems to me I get more on the local," Buck said. "Girls in these little towns around here ain't so damned aristo-cratic."

"He ain't goin' railroadin'," Shorty dismissed the whole business. "He looks all right but he's just a kid. How's the game there, Skin?"

"These fellas don't want to play poker they want to crab about life," Bill Delaney shrugged and came back to the bar. "Enough guys come in here hollerin' for jobs you ought to be glad you're workin'."

"That's a lot of bologney from Father Tooey," growled one of the three shuffling the cards again. "You damn micks let him run this whole town."

"Leave Father Tooey out of it, see," Bill retorted. He poured himself a seltzer. "You fellas make me tired always sore about somethin', always crabbin'. You don't have to work, you know. You could get a room in the poorhouse."

"Aw, a guy wants to see something ahead of him, Bill, that's all," the youngest of the three men cut the pack, the oldest silently dealt a round. "Hell, we don't want to be stuck

in this god-forsaken dump all our lives at the same stinkin'
little jobs."

"Have another?" Bill asked Morry but Morry shook his
head.

Hogan leaned back, his elbows on the bar.

"I would rather have been a French peasant and wear
wooden shoes. I would rather have lived in a hut with a vine
growing over the door and the grapes growing purple in the
kisses of the autumn sun," he said in a sing-song voice, his
eyes closed. "I would rather have been that poor peasant with
my loving wife by my side with my children on my knees, I
would rather have been that man and gone down to the
tongueless silence of the dreamless dust than to have been
that imperial impersonation of force and murder known as
Napoleon the Great."

He looked at Morry with bright blue eyes.

"That's old Bob Ingersoll, the greatest man that ever lived,
bar none. Have a drink."

But Morry dropped two dimes on the counter and with a
quick nod to the others, went out the front door. Even two
beers made him feel dizzy. He almost collided with his father
coming in, hat jauntily at an angle, cigar in his mouth.

"Well, well, so you've made the club," Charles Abbott said,
his eyes mockingly on his son's red face. "Isn't that splendid!
Isn't that just splendid! . . . Go on home, there, and see if
there isn't something else you can do to worry your mother."

"I'm going," said Morry.

He dodged the Bon Ton's front door where Nettie stood
and went in the alley entrance.

"I would rather have been a French peasant and gone
down to the tongueless silence of the dreamless dust," he
mused going upstairs. "That's Bob Ingersoll, the greatest man
who ever lived, bar none."

Elsinore knew that Charles Abbott was a weak, blustering
man, but after the day he first kissed her these matters receded, a curtain dropped definitely between her and his faults.
She had worked in a millinery shop when he was a candy
salesman from a Chicago wholesale dealer, she had gone on
working until now the shop was hers, and he still travelled.

Every three or four months he was home for a fortnight. He was a spendthrift, a gambler, a sport, people said, but on the other hand, as Nettie Farrell frequently pointed out to gossips, he was a jealous husband and that always proved something.

When he was home Morry went out early in the morning and hung closely to his room at night for his father held him in complete scorn. Charles slept all morning, drank whiskey quietly and steadily all afternoon, and aware of being drunk, stood silent around the Bon Ton show-room, his hat on the side of his head, always smoking a cigar. He flicked ashes over the workroom table, left his cigar stubs on the show-cases, but Elsinore said no word of reproach. Sometimes he dropped into Bill Delaney's for a card game but he drank mostly at home. In Elsinore's plain little bedroom he lay evenings reading the Columbus newspapers, dropping his cigar ashes over the white bedspread, hanging his heavy suits over her slight woman's things, keeping his whiskey bottle on the dressing-table between her lilac water and her talcum.

In the cities of Charles Abbott's world there were painted little blonde girls who kept his picture on their dressers, there were women who made engagements with him for three months ahead, and all these were gay party women with whom a man liked to be seen. But even now, nineteen years married, there was still for him something curiously chic in Elsinore's manner and dress, something haunting in her white cold face, her isolation made her desirable.

When she closed the shop and came up to bed the night after the dance and for many nights after that Morry in the next room was kept awake by their low voices.

"See here, there's something in this dance business, Elsinore. . . . Some guy there you go to meet."

Elsinore's voice then, cool and tired.

"Don't be silly, Charles, you know there's no one else."

"That's all right, you're not taking up this dance idea all of a sudden for no reason at all. It's some man. Somebody's got you running at last."

"You know how I am, Charles," Elsinore would say wearily.

"I do know—cold as hell, but I always knew if you ever snapped out of it there wouldn't be any limit for you. . . . I know you. . . . Who is the fellow, anyway? Come on, now, let's hear it."

Elsinore would turn out the lights, go to the window in her white night-dress to draw up the shades, stand for a moment to look at the pale far-off moon. She got into bed quietly.

"I tell you, Elsinore. I don't like this business of you starting to run around," Charles' voice in the dark, bereft of his mocking eyes, his jaunty cigar, was weak and querulous. "It's not like you. It means something and I don't like it. I've got to find out, damn it."

Elsinore drew the sheets over her. A freight train rumbling by hushed him for a little while. And then—

"Who is it, Elsinore—come on. Is it Russell? Is it one of those railroad bastards? . . . Elsinore, for the love of Christ. . . ."

"Go to sleep, Charles. . . . I've told you there never was anyone else."

Grumbling still he fell asleep and she put her arm across her eyes.

Where was Fischer to-night,—what young girl's light body was bent to his in a dance, what town was rocking to his one and two and one and two?

When you stepped out of the back door into the alley at night you stomped your feet to scare away the rats. For a moment you heard them rushing over the rotten boards of back porches, scuttling over the ash cans, over the cistern bucket, and into weeds. And then you could proceed in safety to the pump or to the store-house shed where old frames were packed away in trunks, where from a shelf there leered antique window heads with hay-colored pompadours drooping over one eye, or with black bangs madly frizzed and stiff enough to balance any hat three inches above the head.

Nettie came back from this shed with a stack of wire frames on one arm, a flash-light in the other hand.

Morry, about to go out, ducked back in the hall.

"Going to the saloon, I suppose," said Nettie, a little out of breath. "Going over there and drink, you're just a good-for-nothing, Morry Abbott, you ought to be ashamed."

"Well, what are you going to do about it?" Morry retorted sulkily. "What do you want me to do, stick around here and trim hats?"

"Better than hanging around saloon trash and girls out of foundling homes," Nettie flashed back in a low tense voice. "Better than sitting up nights reading books by atheists."

"What were you doing in my room?" Morry demanded, amazed and angry.

Nettie tossed her head defiantly.

"I have a right to go where I please, Morry Abbott, in this house. If you're reading things you're ashamed of I'd advise you to hide them, before your father sees them. I've heard about that Ingersoll man. . . . The idea!"

Morry opened the workroom door for her, angry at his own inability to be devastatingly rude to her. His mother saw him.

"Don't go out, Morry," she said quietly. "Your father's over at Delaney's and he wouldn't want to see you there."

"All right," said Morry.

He heard Jen's voice—"Hoo-oo!" softly calling from outside. He would go upstairs and wait awhile, then go over for a minute to sit on the steps. In the hat-shop he heard the voice of Mrs. Pepper, the corsetiere, and in some alarm he hurried upstairs. But was even his room safe from feminine intrusion, he wondered bitterly, since Nettie's admission of having snooped around? Very likely the next time Mrs. Pepper arrived in town she would use his room for fitting. If only he didn't mind the smell of saloons so much, he thought, he would spend his days and nights all in that safely male retreat.

"Just something to confine the hips, that's all," he heard Mrs. Pepper say, "but darling, if you don't mind my saying so—you really do need that—"

And then Morry hurriedly banged his door shut, while downstairs the female figure came into its own. Every fortnight Mrs. Pepper called in Lamptown and with her headquarters at the Bon Ton fitted the factory girls and shop-keepers' wives who could afford it with marvellous devices in pink and orchid satin-covered steel. She was a short, laughing, fat little woman, with a delicate charm and effect of feminine frailty conveyed by a tinkling laugh, tiny plump hands, jewelled, fluttering in perpetual astonishment to her heavy brassiered bosom.

"Oooh—why Mrs. Abbott!" she would gurgle breathlessly, "Why—why!" and then her tinkling silver little laugh.

A woman's figure was to her a serious matter, and her blue eyes would widen thoughtfully over any dilemma of too big hips, flat chest or protruding stomach.

"I had a lady—Mrs. Forest—in Canton—you know A. Z. Forest, the lawyer, and she was big here the way you are and then thin right through here the same as you. You know Mrs. Forest, don't you, Nettie? Nettie remembers her. She came here for a hat once. I gave her the Nympholette Number 43 and everyone says, 'Why, Mrs. Forest, why you look so *stunning!*' "

Mrs. Pepper made everyone lie down to be fitted for that was the only way she could get their real lines. For this purpose Elsinore had a screened couch in the alcove between salesroom and workroom.

"Now just relax," Mrs. Pepper would say. "Put down 38, Nettie. And 46 for the hips."

Mrs. Pepper sometimes went to the Casino but only to watch for she had never learned dancing. It was only because Mr. Fischer was such an old friend,—they had the same territory, the same towns to cover.

When Mrs. Pepper's round baby face was bent over her orderbooks Elsinore sometimes stole a look at her. Fischer never talked to Mrs. Pepper, except in the formal way he did to every lady in his hall. Yet someone said once they were seen together in the back seat of Hunt Russell's automobile long after midnight, and that those foursomes with Hunt and Dode occurred other times. Was this the woman, then, that Fischer cared for—or had once cared for? Elsinore wondered again and again about it, for Mrs. Pepper with her lace-frilled daintily powdered throat, her little white hands, her tiny silken ankles swelling to heavy thighs, her delicate sacheted underthings, had the air of being desired by men. Yet Mrs. Pepper was a lady, ridiculously refined.

Once Elsinore, driven by her wonder, deliberately mentioned Fischer's name to her but Mrs. Pepper's childish blue eyes never blinked.

"Mr. Fischer is such a gentleman, isn't he," she said. "He must be a lovely husband. Mrs. Fischer is a lucky woman, I'm sure."

"He must see a great many pretty women in his work," Elsinore, faintly coloring at her own tenacity, went on, "A dancing teacher like that."

"And he is so handsome," sighed Mrs. Pepper. "Such a strong man, too, don't you think? Such a big strong man."

And that was all Elsinore could get out of her.

The Bon Ton was in a state of all day excitement when Mrs. Pepper was there. It must keep open until after eleven to accommodate the working girls. Their outer garments hung over customer's chairs while they tried on samples, and Nettie, with both hats and corsets on her mind, fussed about like a hen with chicks. Charles lounged in Elsinore's room upstairs or in the poolroom and ate at Bauer's.

Elsinore alone remained serene as she would if her business suddenly included all of Ohio and two thousand Netties fussed about in the workrooms.

Morry kept upstairs this evening for a little while until a confusion of feminine voices below assured him that he would not be noticed. Then he tiptoed downstairs. The workroom door was open and lying on the table, a pillow under her head, was a girl naked except for a gauze undershirt. Nettie, frowning, was measuring her waist with a tape, which meant that Mrs. Pepper was so besieged with customers that the hat business had been temporarily pushed aside. Morry tried to tiptoe past but the girl sat up and squealed.

"Oh, Nettie—there's a man!" She clutched, rather futilely, a cluster of velvet roses and held them before her protectively. She was Grace Terris, the Bauers' waitress. Before Nettie could answer Morry shot out the back door, quite pale, his ears burning furiously.

The people around her grave were satisfied with their hides because of course they were used to them now, though Jen, in this dream, wondered how they could feel so content when the skins complete were passed out by the public bath house with no regard for individual expression.

These dream people held their handkerchiefs before their

unknown faces and wept; their black taffeta dresses and their black swallow-tail coats and their black cotton gloves holding tall black hats almost hid the white wreaths, and the moth-ball smell of their clothes covered the sweet sick smell of funeral flowers. Mrs. Hulda Bauer in vast black dabbed a crocheted medallion at her eyes, but the other people, Jen knew, were hired funeral people who came with the rented coaches.

Morry Abbott, wandering past the cemetery, came in and saw the name done in red carnations on a white rose wreath "Jennia St. Clair." But he did not cry.

More people in black arrived with faces for funerals handed out to them at the gate, all Lamptown and all the Children's Home came, and their shoulders shook silently, rhythmically beside the grave, but Morry Abbott only looked on, smoking a cigarette, no more than half interested as he always was. Presently, although the singing was about to begin, he pulled his cap down over his eyes and went away.

"Come back, come back," Jen called to him faintly, but even in dreams she could not keep him from leaving, there was nothing she could do alive or dead to make him stay beside her. There was nothing you could do about Morry Abbott. So Jen threw away the graveyard scene and if he wouldn't care, then he wouldn't care.

But sitting on the stairs with him the next evening, Jen remembered her dream and that he wouldn't cry at her funeral, and was very snappish with him. She thought, resentfully, "Some day I'll make him have feelings, I will."

Old Mrs. Delaney was in. She came out and saw them sitting on the stoop, she stood in the doorway, bent and old and fierce, looking at them.

"You'd better get in here, young woman," she said. "Get your socks darned and your towels mended or you'll get what's coming to you."

"When I get ready," Jen answered serenely, and Morry, who was afraid to talk back to even Nettie, cringed. The old woman didn't mind Jen's back-talk, she muttered something and went back in the house.

"I'm going to get out of this town," Morry said somberly. "A young fella hasn't got a chance except to go on the railroad or out selling like my dad, or go in the Works, and stick all his life. I'm thinking about doing things, getting somewhere."

"Working?"

"Sure, working. 'The hand that holds Aladdin's lamp must be the hand of toil'—that's Robert Green Ingersoll," said Morry. "He was a great man. I got the book."

"Going to do something in Lamptown?" Jen asked, worshipping.

"Not a chance. I'm going somewhere where there's something doing," bragged Morry. "This town's run by a bunch of micks from Shanteyville."

"I guess they're better than rich loafers like Hunt Russell," Jen retorted. "The micks work, but what'd Hunt ever do for his money?"

"Hunt's all right," said Morry. "He's a gentleman and that's enough. He could be a barkeep or a fireman but he'd always be Mr. Russell. I'm going to be like that."

Jen dug her chin in her hands.

"Well, what about Aladdin's lamp and the hand of toil? Why don't he do something with his money? Why couldn't he get Lil out of the Home, he could without bothering. I hate him and people like him."

"Will you hush up, you young ones?" Mrs. Delaney's voice complained from inside. "People hear you for miles around with your big talk."

Jen stood up when the door banged shut again and held her finger to her lips.

"Let's go somewhere," she whispered.

They tiptoed down the stairs and then across the tracks to the dark factory road.

"His house cost about a million dollars, Bill said," Jen said. "It's got real marble for steps and it's got solid crystal doorknobs. But *he* never earned it. Hunt Russell never really earned a nickel, and it's not fair."

Hunt Russell's house was no such palace, Morry knew, but he wouldn't have cared if it was. He wanted Hunt to have things and to be a king because in his own mind he, Morry Abbott, was Hunt. Now that he and Jen seemed to be on the way to the Lamptown showplace, Morry was as anxious for

Jen's awed admiration as if the estate was his own. He took Jen's hand and they ran part of the way down the silent dark road.

By day Hunt's home was to the passerby a mile of high iron fence backed by a thick hedge and broken by an arched stone gateway through which one glimpsed a leafy winding drive. At the end of the drive was a huge old brick house spreading out in white-pillared porches and glass-roofed sun parlors. A flagstone terrace sloped into rosebushes and flowerbeds and overgrown grass. An iron deer lifted its antlered head in perpetual fright in the middle of the great shaded lawn, and near the driveway a pair of stone Cupids gazed into a cracked stone fountain bowl and saw that their noses were broken off.

By night the place was a dozen black acres of complete stillness for Hunt lived here now all alone with the caretaker's family. It was far beyond the factory houses, past block after block of empty lots, past an abandoned pickle works and the charred foundations of an old farm.

Jen and Morry clung to the iron fence and peered into the darkness.

"Gee, that's a big house," said Jen and then added indignantly, "Why it's bigger than the Home! He's got no business living there as if he was a king. He's got no right."

"Sh!" Morry squirmed uncomfortably at her resentment because if she belonged to Lamptown's laboring class, he, for his part, was with the aristocrats. He looked on luxury without envy but breathed deep with pride in it.

"You got to give Hunt credit for staying in Lamptown, at least," he argued. "He could have been a big bug in Chicago or New York if he wanted."

Jen, climbing up higher on the iron grilling, was not impressed.

"Well, why doesn't he go there, then," she wanted to know, "instead of hanging around this town aggravating people that have to work for their money. . . . Come on, I'm going on up to the house."

"No—he might see us," Morry protested, but Jen was over the fence and he had to follow. They crept up across the thick grass until they were right by the house. It was dark but for a light in the kitchen and another light in an upstairs room. Jen picked up a pebble and tossed it lightly against the house, and then she and Morry stood looking at each other, paralyzed, for the stone crashed right through one of the dark French windows.

"Gee!"

A light flashed on in the room and before they could move Hunt stepped quietly out of the window. He was in white flannels and Morry could never forget him standing on the porch looking at them, not saying a word, just tapping his pipe on the porch-railing. Then—

"Well," he said looking from one to the other, "Are you just out breaking windows or are you up to some other damage, too?"

Morry's tongue would not move. Jen nudged him and then it angered her that anyone should have the power to frighten Morry—Morry, of all people.

"Aw, you can buy more windows," she answered defiantly.

Hunt lit a match and peered down at her.

"You're not big enough to talk that way, young lady. I might take it in my head to spank you."

"Try and do it!" urged Jen. "I'm not sorry I smashed your window. Go buy stained glass next time, why don't you?"

Hunt whistled. Morry, who had been sick at Jen's outburst, now found himself angry at Hunt for lighting a match again to coolly examine Jen. His grey eyes travelled from her black hair to her checked gingham dress and then to her flashing blue eyes.

"Come on, Jen," Morry's voice came back, hard and cold. "We'll fix up the window, Hunt. It was just an accident."

"I don't know about that. I'm not so sure it was an accident," Hunt said slowly. "What were you doing here, anyway, you two?"

Morry was amazed to find words again in his mouth— smooth, convincing words.

"I was coming in to ask you about a job at the Works, and we—we were walking by and I thought I'd come in."

Hunt gave a short laugh.

"A business call, I see. Not social. I thought when the window crashed it was just a friend. . . . All right, Abbott, I believe you. Come down to the factory next week if you want a job—don't go around crashing my windows. And you—young lady—"

"Don't worry about me," Jen snapped, "I'd like to break every window of your rotten old house."

Again Morry was furious at Hunt's roar of laughter,—it was laughter he wanted to carry Jen away from. He seized Jen's arm to leave but Jen twisted around to shake her fist at Hunt.

"I'll do it, too," she threatened and Hunt laughed again. He said something,—it sounded like an invitation to call again, but Morry did not hear. They heard the sound of a woman's voice and when they looked back from the gateway they could see two figures in the lighted doorway, one of them a woman with red hair.

"You—you workin' for him!" stormed Jen, "I won't stand for it. You're worth ten of him, but you'll have to run errands for him. It's no fair, I tell you."

"It's the way things are," Morry said, "You don't need to start crying about it."

But Jen would cry anyway. They stood outside the big iron gate, Morry sullen and uncomfortable, while Jen cried against his unwilling arm.

"It's no fair, that's what I'm crying about," she insisted. "He lives there like a king—he owns the town, he owns you now, too. He's got everything, all we get is little bits he doesn't want. I'm glad we broke his old window, that's what I am."

Jen hung on to his arm, fuming, all the way home, but Morry wasn't conscious of her. He felt sick and afraid but a little excited, too. For now he had a job. His 'future' had begun and it was no gay golden door swinging open, either, but a heavy iron factory door with a time clock beside it. For a second he was scared, wondering what came after that.

"Ten dollars a week,—fancy!" Charles Abbott smiled charmingly at his son and pushed aside his plate as tactful reminder of the fabulous dinners to which he was accustomed elsewhere. "Next it will be twelve dollars and by the time you're fifty, my boy, you'll be earning sixteen or eighteen dollars a week. Elsinore, I congratulate you on your son."

"That's all right," said Elsinore absently.

When they did not snatch their meals at Bauer's Chop House, they ate in a corner of the workroom. A gas plate and sink was behind a curtain and usually it was Nettie who fixed the meal,—canned beans, soup, and sandwiches, with one of Mrs. Bauer's pies for dessert. Then Nettie pulled out the ironing board and with this as a dining table the meal became a sort of family picnic. Eating together in this way was so intimate that Morry always had to fight against the tenderness he suddenly felt for his family, as if they were like some other family. He wanted to tell about his job, to tell everything that happened from eight in the morning till six at night, what the foreman said, what Hunt Russell said. . . . But you couldn't say these things before your father or Nettie, you had to act as if the whole business was of no consequence to you. If you talked to your mother she listened patiently but never lifted her eyes from her plate, or if she did, made some abstracted reply. It was very hard and Morry ate fast to get out the quicker. After all, when you stopped to think of it, it was sissy for a young man to be eating on an ironing board in a millinery shop.

"I'm surprised he can earn ten dollars," said Nettie. "I'm surprised he could get a job at all, Mr. Abbott, I really am."

Charles broke a sardine sandwich carefully and disdainfully so that, Morry thought, each sardine must apologize for not being an anchovy or a shrimp.

"Oh you're perfectly right, Nettie, Morry isn't the factory type. More of the artist, don't you think? . . . Ten dollars a week. See that you give eight of it to your mother, young man."

"I'm sure he'll give what he can, Charles, stop nagging him," Elsinore said impatiently. She did not see fit to remind Charles that eight dollars a week was more than she had ever had from him and that this solicitude for her, was as a matter of fact exquisitely ironic.

"He ought to give every cent and let Mrs. Abbott give him money when he asks," said Nettie.

Charles nodded approval of this suggestion and Nettie shot a complacent glance in Morry's direction.

"See here," said Charles, "since you're grown up enough to work why don't you take care of your mother—a great lummox

like you sitting up there reading all winter while your poor
mother has to go out to dances alone. You ought to be
ashamed."

"Charles—I—" began Elsinore.

Charles waved her aside.

"It won't hurt him to take you to and from places when
I'm away," he went on virtuously. "I don't like you coming
home alone at midnight from the Casino dances."

"But—Mr. Abbott,—just across the street!" Nettie was incredulous at such beautiful concern. Elsinore kept her eyes on
her plate.

"All very well but my wife can't come three steps alone like
some common woman. I won't have it. No sir. I never liked to
see a woman alone at night. Morry, that won't hurt you, understand, you're to see your mother to and from these dances."

Morry suppressed a groan.

"I can't dance."

"It's time you learned," said Charles sternly. "Seventeen
years old and not able to take a woman to a dance!"

"He might as well learn, I suppose," Elsinore said, weary of
the wrangling. "He really ought to know how to dance."

The horror of exposing his deficiencies in grace made Morry
choke with misery. It was enough getting up early every morning, trying to be as good as hundreds of inferior factory people, wasn't it, without letting himself be the joke of the factory
girls and boys at Lamptown public dances. . . .

"Unless, of course, you'd rather go alone, dear," Charles
added gently to his wife, his eyes on her face. "If you'd like to
have your fun privately of course—"

"Morry will come with me, I'm sure," Elsinore answered
evenly.

Morry, dejected, nodded his head.

"Oh, sure," he murmured.

Suddenly Nettie got up and flounced over to the sink, and
banged her plate and cup into the dishpan.

"Why shouldn't I take lessons, then—I ought to learn
dancing as much as Morry ought," she snapped. "But I suppose I'm to take care of your old shop while Mrs. Abbott and
Morry are over at the Casino having a good time."

Elsinore looked up in amazement.

"I thought you liked the shop, Nettie."

"Oh, I like the shop all right," Nettie sulkily answered. "But Morry needn't act so smart with his ten dollars a week and dancing class. I'm sure I could go to Mr. Fischer myself and he'd be glad to give me special private lessons."

"No! That's too ridiculous, Nettie!" Elsinore's voice was harsh.

Something hot surged in her veins, a swift desire to slap Nettie's young impudent mouth for speaking a sacred name so lightly,—the thought of Nettie smirking through a dancing lesson alone with Fischer angered her.

"Don't worry, I wouldn't go near the Casino," retorted Nettie. She washed her dishes under the faucet, rattling them against each other. "I don't go out with those factory girls, thank you."

The consciousness of having earned two weeks' salary emboldened Morry.

"What about the factory girls? What's so different about them?" he challenged. "They're as good as you are."

Nettie stared at him with horrified eyes.

"Oh you would say that, Morry Abbott—you would! You'd even go out with them, I suppose—that's just your level. Delaney's back room and factory girls!"

Morry's courage, under his father's contemptuous amusement, faded. He choked down the last of a sandwich and made a dive for the door.

"Don't forget you're taking your mother out next Thursday night," called out his father commandingly, as he slid out.

"I think he's just too terrible, Mrs. Abbott!" declared Nettie. "He's getting coarse, that's what he is."

She helped Elsinore fold up the ironing board while Charles, leaning against the sink, lit a cigarette.

"What do you think of having him as a bodyguard from now on, Else?" he asked, tossing the lighted match into the sink. He did not dare look at her.

"A good idea, Charles," said Elsinore gravely. "Very good, I think."

"Morry's going to be a swell dancer, you know," said Grace Terris, beaming at Morry through her glasses. "Mr. Fischer said he had rhythm. This young man has rhythm, he said the other night."

Jen and Mrs. Bauer both looked at Morry critically to see if this odd quality showed, but apparently it only came out on Thursday nights for he looked just as he always looked. Mrs. Bauer resumed her crocheting and Grace and Jen went on polishing silver.

Jen did not really have to help in the Bauers' kitchen, nor for that matter did Morry have to lounge there late at night this way, but Mrs. Bauer liked to have Jen around and somehow Morry drifted in there too, particularly now that the cold weather made Delaney's stairs unappealing.

"I don't care for a dancing man," pronounced Mrs. Bauer. She twisted her chair to get a view through the dining room of Hermann at the cash register. "Dancing men don't make good husbands."

Grace giggled and looked coyly at Morry. Jen laid down a knife and cleaning rag and stared at her indignantly, then at Morry. Morry was smoking calmly. He didn't even know when someone was flirting with him, Jen thought with disgust.

"Hermann is such a good husband," went on Mrs. Bauer. "I've never had a care. When we were first married it was the same. What, doing the supper dishes when you're so tired, he'd say! No, no, Hulda, he'd say, I won't have you worn out like that. You wait and do them in the morning, he'd say."

Morry yawned. Jen and Grace scoured knives silently and diligently. Grace stole a beguiling glance now and then at Morry, and Jen, puzzled, stared from one to the other.

"I'll never forget one day he called me stupid," Hulda's fat moonface became ruddy with sentiment, her fingers dawdled with the crochet hook, "I was hurt—you know how a young bride is—and then lo and behold! That afternoon a wagon came to the door with a present from Hermann to make it up to me. Two bushels of the finest peaches you ever laid your eyes on. As big as your head, Jen."

"But what could you do with two bushels of peaches?" Jen inquired.

"Can them, dear. Hermann always loved preserved peaches. I put cloves in them and English walnuts. I was up till long after midnight putting them up." Mrs. Bauer smiled wistfully at the glimpse through the doorway of Hermann's bald head. "He was a good husband. Always. If he had to go away on a trip he always said, 'Enjoy yourself, Hulda. Let things go. You can do them all when I get back.' That's your good husband, let me tell you, girls."

"I'm not going to marry anyone in the restaurant business," said Grace. "Believe me."

"I guess you'll marry a railroad man," prophesied Jen. "They're always around."

"Don't pick a dancing man, girls, they're no good," warned Mrs. Bauer. "You never find them in a nice business of their own later on in life."

"I don't see why all a man's for is to be a good husband," Morry objected. "Is that all he's made for?"

"Yes," answered Mrs. Bauer placidly, "that's all."

"Morry dances too well, then," Grace giggled. Not even Cleopatra could have had Grace's complacent assurance of mastery over men. Jen glared at her jealously, and Morry squirmed, uncertain of the cause of the curious tension. "You know the class gets to stay over to the regular dance next week, Morry. Won't it be exciting?"

Morry thought of all the older girls sitting in a row waiting to be asked to dance, and he thought of his own inability to control their motions or to synchronize his own with theirs. He mumbled an evasive agreement with Grace's enthusiasm.

"You and I will have to stick to each other," laughed Grace.

At this point Jen got abruptly to her feet. She wasn't going to be left out of things—she'd get out of her own accord.

"Where you goin', Jen?" Mrs. Bauer demanded in surprise. "I thought you was going to help Grace finish."

"Oh, let her boy friend help her," Jen retorted haughtily. "I'm going home."

Morry was embarrassed and reached for his cap.

"You're not going home now, are you Morry?" Grace's pale blue eyes conveyed a coquettish challenge but Morry didn't want to understand it. He couldn't help thinking of Grace's thin white thighs as she lay on the table being fitted for a corset by Mrs. Pepper. He grew red at the mere memory.

"Gotta get up early," he explained and started to follow Jen out.

"See you Thursday night at the dance," Grace called.

"Sure," said Morry and reached the door just as Jen let it bang good and hard in his face. Grace laughed shrilly as Morry pulled the door open again.

"A temper, that Jen," said Mrs. Bauer, and counted four stitches under her breath.

"One, two, three, FOUR, one, two, three, FOUR, one, two, three, FOUR," chanted Mr. Fischer, walking backwards, and the line of thirty wooden figures advanced toward him, one, two, three, steps, then kicked out a stiff left foot on the fourth count.

"Right foot first, one, two three—hold it please. Miss Barry is out of step. One, two, three—now, ladies and gentlemen, we'll try it with music. Mr. Sanderson, please."

> "Will someone kindly tell me
> Will someone answer why
> To me it is a riddle
> And will be till I die—"

In a long even row they followed Mr. Fischer across the floor.

"Dance with the lady on your left!" roared Mr. Fischer.

Stiff country boys placed arms around factory girls' hard little bodies, damp hand clutched damp hand, iron foot matched iron foot, and each dancer kept count under his breath. Mr. Fischer clapped his hands and the music stopped.

"The class is getting on magnificently," he said, "I'm sure you will have no trouble at the regular dance tonight. All you need is confidence. I want each and every one of you to dance every dance on the program. Now we'll try it again. Mr. Sanderson, please."

So Mr. Sanderson's thick hands came down on the keys again and young men danced with the ladies on their left. Morry placed a rigid arm around Grace with a one two three kick, and a one two three kick. He thought if he could lose Grace somewhere he might learn but if you danced you had to have a partner as a lawful handicap. No matter how beautifully you waltzed, you'd never have a chance to waltz alone because it wasn't done.

Grace paid no attention to the commands. She tipped her head to one side and smiled perpetually. When she lost count she said, "Oh, I'm just terrible." Then Mr. Fischer would correct her posture.

"Not quite so close, Miss Terris,—the arm should not go all the way round the young man's neck."

Solemnly then the fifteen couples stepped around the room behind Fischer, and since they were afraid to lose step by turning around on the corners, the dance became nothing more than a march with odd little jerks on the fourth count.

"Fine!" said Mr. Fischer and clapped his hands twice. "The class for this evening is now over. You will please remain for the regular Ball."

And then the rope at the door was let down and the line of people waiting outside were allowed to present their tickets and enter. The drummer arrived and experimented with his instrument, gravely aided by Mr. Sanderson. Crowds of giggling girls, with chiffon scarfs over their curled hair, hurried from the door to the dressing room, and their vivid perfumes mixed intoxicatingly in the air. Mr. Fischer stood by the ticket-man at the door, shaking hands with this or that one, greeting everyone with formal politeness, while his black eyes shot appraisingly from time to time toward the cash-box. Then he tweaked the ends of his white bow-tie and whirled around toward the dance-floor.

"Dance Number One!" he shouted above the excited chattering. "Dance Number One!"

The music began again and men slid from the doorway to the women's dressing-room across the floor to select their partners as they emerged. Morry Abbott stood beside the solitary palm-tree, first on one foot and then the other. His breath came fast and he had to struggle with a feeling that he, too, could sway and whirl with marvellous ease. This assured feeling must be checked, he thought, before he impulsively invited someone to dance and then woke to his inadequacy with a load of responsibility in his arms. So he went into the smoking-room and sat down by one of the brakemen he'd seen in Bill Delaney's often. The young man, dressed up in a much too blue suit and a green tie, was looking through a magazine of photographs. On the paper cover was painted a cream-white

blonde in a very decollete spangled silver dress. The man
rapped the picture with his pipe and looked up at Morry.

"There she is," he said proudly. "That's her. Lillian Russell.
A looker, eh?"

Morry squinted at it judicially.

"All right," he granted. But she was beautiful as no woman
could ever be, at least, he thought, no woman in Lamptown.
Underneath was printed, "America's Most Beautiful Actress."

"You bet she's all right," insisted his friend. "I'd marry her
like a shot, I would."

He picked up the magazine and stuffed it into his pocket.

"Like to cut these out to paste up in my room," he explained, as he started out. "So long."

Through the door Morry could see Grace dancing with
one of the engineers who ate at Bauer's, and he was amazed
that she seemed no different in action than the other girls on
the floor. He had rather expected everyone to stop dancing
and point the finger of shame at her. Since they didn't seem
to notice her errors, he felt encouraged to go out on the floor
again, and when the music stopped he boldly asked Grace for
the next.

"Isn't it swell, Morry?" gurgled Grace. "I'm having a lot of
fun, aren't you?"

Now that the dance had started it was all easy,—easier than
the lesson, for in this crowd your feet were not observed.
Then in his arms Grace changed curiously. She was not the
Bauers' waitress at all, a thin blonde with glasses, but a
stranger, a stranger who belonged mysteriously to dancehalls
and to music and perfume.

"Like Lillian Russell," Morry thought and if he just kept
looking at Grace's curious blue eyes it almost seemed that she
had on a silver dress. When the dance was over Grace kept her
hand on his arm, but Morry thought, "I wouldn't dare ask
her for another dance just yet."

He went back to the smoking room to wait the proper
length of time for he did not dare ask any other girl. The boys
his age who hung around Bill Delaney's saloon did not dance,
they stood in a little group outside the hall door smoking and
sometimes jeering at friends inside. Before this night Morry
thought he would have died at their ragging, but when they

called teasingly to him two or three times he was not afraid to answer back with certain pride. After all he was the one on the inside.

Elsinore was there. Morry caught a glimpse of her slender black-gowned figure without knowing who she was for a few seconds, and then he wondered at the flare of pride he had in her. He tried to puzzle out just why she stood out among the others. Was it because the factory girls were all powdered and painted and wore loud colors, was it because she was his mother, or was it that she looked startlingly out of place without a background of hats and trimmings? She looked over her partner's shoulder from across the room and smiled faintly at her son. Suddenly Morry wanted to do something wonderful for his mother, something to make her glad of him; but what could one do?

"It's almost over, Morry," Grace said, standing beside him. "We ought not to miss this one."

Morry obediently started dancing with her. She pressed against him with a sigh.

"You seem a lot older somehow than some of the railroad fellas," she said. "I don't know why, but you do. More like somebody that's been around, know what I mean?"

Morry wished she wouldn't talk. It made him lose count and it made the picture of the woman in the silver dress fade further away. Couples were dancing very close and very quietly now. Grace kept her head demurely on his shoulder. He wasn't quite sure what was expected of him but knew something was.

"Do you want to stay for the other dance?" he found himself asking her. "It's the Home Waltz."

Grace looked at him thoughtfully.

"We could go now," she said. "If we go down the back-stairs no one will notice us. My room is right at the back—just above the kitchen."

They danced around again. Morry's head was swimming. He saw his mother,—he saw Hunt with Dode and Mr. Fischer, and he wondered if they knew about this spinning in the head, a sort of premonition of disaster, yet you couldn't exactly call it disaster.

"You go first—I'll follow," he whispered, and Grace dropped out of his arms with a sweet smile. Presently he saw her, with her wrap over her arm, going out and he got his hat and followed, after a few minutes. He went along the dirty outside hallway to the back where a staircase went down to the Bauers' rooms on the second floor. Morry fumbled his way down the pitch-dark stairs. On the second floor there was another dark old hallway with a gas jet dimly flickering in the far end. No one was in sight, but Morry's heart stopped at the creaking of the old floor beneath his feet. He passed dark doors with tin numbers tacked on—'27'—'29'—'31'—and the sweat came out on his forehead wondering what would happen if one of these doors should suddenly open. It wasn't likely though, for a lodger didn't come to Bauer's more than four or five times a year. . . .

At the end of the hall water leaked slowly from the ceiling above and made a dirty puddle beneath the gas jet. Morry wanted to drop the whole business and run. He thought with a shock of horror that he was to have taken his mother home, that indeed had been the sole purpose of his dancing lessons. . . . It was too late now—or was it? . . . Then he saw Grace motioning to him from the farthest doorway. She held her finger to her lips warningly. Oh, yes, it was too late now. . . .

Morry, with sinking heart, tiptoed toward her. She reached out a thin bare arm and pulled him coquettishly in, and the door swung swiftly shut behind him.

Old Mrs. Delaney stood inside the Bon Ton's work-room door. She had on her black bonnet and black mitts and a market basket on her arm. It was barely breakfast time, and Nettie had only a moment before she unlocked the shop door. Elsinore was washing the coffee cups at the sink.

"What is it?" she wanted to know in some surprise.

"I want to tell you this much, Mrs. Abbott," said the old woman. "It's got to stop or I speak to your husband. That's all I came to say."

Nettie sat down quickly to her sewing so that she would have an excuse to hear all. Elsinore stood looking at her caller, puzzled and alarmed.

"But what is it? What are you talking about? Is it about Morry?"

"Who else would it be about?" snapped the old woman. "It's about that boy of yours all right. Things have got to stop, that's what I'm telling you."

Nettie tried to keep on sewing casually but she had to look up every now and then, first to the old woman and then to the hall doorway, because she had heard Morry's footsteps outside. He was out there now listening, she thought, listening and afraid to pass the door lest he be called in.

"But Morry's a good boy," Elsinore protested. "I can't see what he's done to worry you, Mrs. Delaney."

"He's going on eighteen, ain't he?" retorted Mrs. Delaney. "Old enough to be getting girls in trouble. I speak out that way, Mrs. Abbott, because an adopted girl's a big responsibility. I'm telling you he's got to stay away from my Jen."

Nettie sewed furiously and kept an eye furtively on Elsinore. But Elsinore just stood there looking quietly at the old woman. Mrs. Delaney sat down on one of the work-stools.

"I don't mean to worry you, Mrs. Abbott—I don't mean you're not a lady," she muttered in a gruff attempt at apology. "Only when you've taken a girl from the Home and she's got old ideas and an older boy keeps hanging around her—well, she's got bad blood in her, that Jen. . . . You can't trust bad blood, you know."

"Morry has never cared about girls," Elsinore said. "He'd never dream of bothering your Jen."

Mrs. Delaney's gnarled fingers tightened over the market basket.

"I'm telling you he does, Mrs. Abbott," she said somberly. "He carries on with the Bauers' waitress—Hulda Bauer told me that. And don't I hear him and Jen out on the steps night after night whispering and talking? Don't I hear her out there cryin' and snifflin' when he don't show up? That's what I'm telling you."

"Oh! Oh!" came from Nettie Farrell's mouth, and Elsinore looked at her, rather surprised.

"That's bad when girls cry over someone," Nettie said hurriedly. "I'm sure Morry isn't as good as you think because you're his mother and you don't see anything. Things right under your nose, too. But he's always going over to that saloon—

I could tell you that much—and when you ask men in there about him they say they haven't seen him. He goes upstairs to see that girl, that's all."

"That's right," confirmed Mrs. Delaney.

"But what harm is there in it?" Elsinore argued gently. "A child like that—barely fourteen,—"

"Pooh!" sniffed Nettie. "That kind learn young."

"She's got old ideas," insisted Mrs. Delaney. "Old ideas and wild blood in her and outside of that I trust no young girl. They're all alike, crazy to get into trouble, always struck on the boys. I've had 'em go wrong with me before and I won't have it this time."

"But Morry's so safe," Elsinore said incredulously.

"I don't trust him neither," the old woman flashed back. "What's his father, I ask? A hard drinker and a fast man. I don't mind coming out with truths once in a while when it's necessary. That boy's old enough to know what he's about and you've got to keep him away from my Jen. Hear me?"

Elsinore could only nod weakly. Mrs. Delaney got up, panting a little. She drew her black shawl over her humped old back, jerked her bonnet down over her ears.

"I said I'd come and I did," she grumbled. "I said I'd put a stop to it and I did. I won't have any more girls in my house going wrong. Won't have it."

She went out the door banging it angrily behind her. Nettie held her needle transfixed in the air and her mouth wide open. Elsinore stood still and thoughtful for a moment, then sat down and picked up a ribbon she was to shir. Suddenly Nettie threw her sewing down and her shears.

"That boy!" she exclaimed. "You can see it's all true—he's running after that girl just because she's wild and now he's working in the factory and dancing he thinks he can do whatever he pleases. What are you going to say to him, Mrs. Abbott? Or will you tell his father?"

"Oh no, I wouldn't ever tell Charles," Elsinore murmured. "And after all, Nettie, Mrs. Delaney's so old she gets funny ideas. Morry isn't a bad boy at all."

"But he's grown up, nearly, and you can't tell what he'd do if girls started getting after him," Nettie rushed on. "He thinks he's so smart, not paying attention to them. He just acts that way to show off. Then he goes and picks some little foundling over a saloon! He would!"

Elsinore went to the drawer for a cluster of satin ribbons. There was a creaking of boards in the hall outside. Nettie jerked her head significantly.

"I knew he was out there!" she whispered. "He heard every word! He was afraid to let on he was out there."

The cloud on Elsinore's horizon lifted with dazzling speed. "He really heard, do you think?"

Nettie nodded impatiently.

"Of course he did. Shall I go call him in for you to talk to?"

"Not now, Nettie," Elsinore said and Nettie's face fell.

Her full red lips pursed into a sullen line. Mrs. Abbott was afraid to talk about things to Morry, it was silly how shy she was with her own son that way. She'd rather let him run wild than speak up to him. It angered Nettie. She got up and walked determinedly to the hall door. She opened it swiftly and was in time to see Morry sliding out on tiptoe, his dark face burning red. Nettie whirled back.

"He did hear! He stood there listening!" she was triumphant. "Serve him right, too. And now's the time for the whistle to blow and he's late to work besides. Oh, you must talk to him, Mrs. Abbott."

"If he heard us, then he knows all there is for me to say," Elsinore said tranquilly. "I needn't go into it any further."

She never even looked up to say this. Nettie stabbed her needle into her straw braid and muttered something quite savage under her breath.

Lamptown hummed from dawn to dusk with the mysterious humming of the Works, the monotonous switching of engines and coupling of cars at the Yard. The freight cars rumbled back and forth across the heart of town. They slid out past the factory windows and brakemen swinging lanterns on top the cars would shout to whatever girls they saw working at the windows. Later, in the factory washroom one girl might whisper to another, "Kelly's in the Yard to-day. Said be sure and be at Fischer's Thursday night."

"Who was firing?" the other would ask, mindful of a beau of her own.

"Fritz was in the cab but I couldn't see who was firing. Looked like that Swede of Ella's used to be on Number 10."

The humming of this town was jagged from time to time by the shriek of an engine whistle or the bellow of a factory siren or the clang-clang of a red street car on its way from one village to the next. The car jangled through the town flapping doors open and shut, admitting and discharging old ladies on their way to a D.A.R. picnic in Norwalk, section workers or linesmen in overalls, giggling girls on their way to the Street Carnival in Chicago Junction. As if hunting for something very important the car rattled past the long row of Lamptown's factory boarding houses, past the Lots, then on into long stretches of low, level hay-fields where farm girls pitched hay, stopping to wave their huge straw hats at the gay world passing by in a street car.

There was grey train smoke over the town most days, it smelled of travel, of transcontinental trains about to flash by, of important things about to happen. The train smell sounded the 'A' for Lamptown and then a treble chord of frying hamburger and onions and boiling coffee was struck by Hermann Bauer's kitchen, with a sostenuto of stale beer from Delaney's back door. These were all busy smells and seemed a 6 to 6 smell, a working town's smell, to be exchanged at the last factory whistle for the festival night odors of popcorn, Spearmint chewing gum, barbershop pomades, and the faint smell of far-off damp cloverfields. Mornings the cloverfields retreated when the first Columbus local roared through the town. Bauer's coffee pot boiled over again, and the factory's night watchmen filed into Delaney's for their morning beer.

It was always the last minute when Morry left his house for work and on this morning he had been trapped into eavesdropping on Mrs. Delaney and his mother. If he only could have gotten out of the house before she said those dreadful things. He slipped out of the alleyway, his hands jammed into his pockets, his cap slouched over his eyes, and he burned with shame thinking of what the old lady had said to his mother. He'd never look at Jen again without remembering,—never! Of course it wasn't Jen's fault but he was angry with her, too. She was the one who called him to come over, wasn't she? He only went because the kid was lonesome, never saw anybody else hardly, didn't seem to make friends in school. Now he was afraid of her. Next time she called he wouldn't hear her.

Along Market Street the shop-keepers were out lowering their awnings, shouting their morning greetings across the street to each other, or peering from behind their show-windows at rival window-displays. Old Tom, Lamptown's street-cleaner, sat on the curbstone in front of the Saloon in dirty white painter's overalls, broom in hand, and held a sort of welcoming reception for all passersby.

"Morning, Mr. Robinson. Morning, Miss Burnett. Howdy, Morry, how's your old lady? Late to-day, ain't you? I just see the last of the girls going in."

Morry crossed the street before he remembered Grace, and there she was in the Bauers' window smiling at him significantly. Morry jerked his head into a sort of nod of greeting and went on. He was ashamed of his winter's affair with Grace. In the saloon the trainmen talked about her. "God's gift to the Big Four," they called her. Morry hated her. She always acted as if he was hers, always beaming at him when he went by and lifting her eyebrows so knowingly. He was eighteen now. He wasn't going to work in the factory all his life, was he, and run with waitresses. . . . Maybe he'd better get a job on the train. You saw cities that way and in the right one you could drop off and start doing things. But do what? Something, this much he knew, that would make his mother very proud of him, because now he felt overwhelmingly grateful to her. He knew she wouldn't say a word to him about Mrs. Delaney's visit and about Jen,—as far back as he could remember she had never said anything to reproach him. She could easily have called him after the old woman left and scolded him, but how could they ever have looked at each other saying such intimate things? . . .

He knew. He'd get out of this town, that's what he'd do. He'd study—but what did you study? Fellows went to college but that cost money and nobody in Lamptown went to college, except a guy now and then who went to Case Engineering School in Cleveland. Fellows in Lamptown went into the Works or into their fathers' stores or on the railroad. If they got on the railroad, they stuck there. It was like the Navy, they said, you had a hard time working into a regular job after you got out. . . . All right then, he'd stick to the factory. He'd work until he owned the Factory, that's what he'd do. He'd work— hell, he hated to work. He hated plugging away at lamps and accessories. He wasn't adept like the girls and he felt perpetually ill at ease around them. They worked faster than he did and made more money, and they kidded him.

Morry could remember when he was only six he was so overgrown that the little girls were afraid of him. "He's so big!" they sobbed into the teacher's lap. "We don't want him to play in our games." Now even when the girls in the packing-room smiled invitingly to him, he was sure they were making fun of him; he didn't know where to hide when they whispered, "Morry Abbott's a swell-looker now, ain't he? Look at them shoulders!"

He would always feel like the unwanted stranger with these factory girls. He wasn't like them—he wasn't like the fellows in the saloon, either. He'd be a big somebody some day, a big gun,—but Morry didn't see himself grubbing away, getting there a little at a time. He saw himself already arrived, a Hunt Russell, a somebody who got there without plugging. Got where, though? . . . Morry saw himself on the decks of great liners, sitting on balconies in tropical cities, always at ease, always secure from Netties and fathers and Graces. He was the master of this fabulous orange grove, he was the manager of this beautiful actress, he was the owner of this estate on the Hudson, stocked with books, thousands of them, and pictures, and liquor, too, French wines and things that weren't so hard to drink as Delaney's Scotch. He'd—but here he was at the factory, twenty minutes late to punch the time-clock.

"Docked again," jeered the office boy in a jubilant whisper. Morry sidled through Door 6 to his table in the packing-room. His foreman came toward him scowling.

"With men out of work all over this country," he began sternly, "it seems a damn shame, Abbott, that a fellow with the luck to have a job can't get to it on time. Now, I'll tell you what's coming to you if this keeps up. . . ."

But really Lamptown was no place for a boy, Mrs. Pepper said.

Take Mansfield or Norwalk or Elyria—pretty little towns they were, every one of them, with nice homes on pleasant boulevards and lovely girls for a young man to marry. But Lamptown! All railroad tracks and factory warehouses and for a park nothing but the factory woods or the acres of Lots which were nothing but clover fields with big signs every few yards,—

"LOTS $40 an acre and up
See HUNT RUSSELL—"

Rows of grey frame factory boarding houses on dusty roads in the east and to the west the narrow noisy Market Street,—choose your home between these two sections.

"Really, Mrs. Abbott, actually you know," gravely said Mrs. Pepper, "it's not the place at all for a young man. Don't you know anyone in Columbus or Cleveland who would board him there—some place where he would have opportunities?"

"If Morry went to the city he'd get a swelled head and never be anything," declared Nettie crossly. "I don't see what's the matter with Lamptown, if he's any good he can get on here. The trouble with Morry is he thinks he's too good for everybody here. He's too good for the girls, he stays upstairs and reads novels instead of acting like a regular fellow."

"I'd hate to have him go away," Elsinore murmured. "I wouldn't know what to do without Morry."

Nettie looked to Mrs. Pepper for sympathy.

"As if he ever talked to anyone or as if he was any company to you," she said sarcastically. "Why, Mrs. Abbott, you know you hardly ever talk to each other."

Elsinore put her hand to her forehead and smoothed it thoughtfully.

"I know, but you see that's just it. We don't need to talk to each other. We never have needed to talk to each other."

Mrs. Pepper tried to assume an understanding expression.

"I know," she sighed. "Indeed I know."

She went to the mirror and daintily replaced a straying lock of hair behind her ear. Nettie watched her with critical eyes.

"Pretty dress," she said.

Mrs. Pepper was pleased.

"I got it in Akron," she explained. She patted her hips and turned around to view the skin-tight perfection of the back. "Cute, isn't it?"

Nettie examined it and urged Elsinore to admire its lines. It was a tight silk dress bursting into irrepressible ruffles at the hem and at the wrist, and yoked with tiny lace ruffling deep on her bosom so that a garnet sunburst was coquettishly lost there. A circlet of tiny pearls followed a seductive line around her fat creamy throat and was matched by a pearl and opal ring on her fat little finger.

"I wonder," mused Mrs. Pepper leaning further toward the mirror, twisting her head a little to one side, "if perhaps my neck is a little too plump for pearls."

Over her pearls and the sunburst her dove-like little hands hovered ceaselessly. She sat down again and the wide silk bows on her tiny kid slippers flopped down like the ears of a sleepy dachshund. Sometimes when she was crossing the freight Yard a young fireman would stick his head out of the cab and yell, "Hello Fatty!" This would make Mrs. Pepper tighten her little red mouth to keep from smiling for after all there was something flatteringly endearing in the term 'Fatty.' But when she kept her lips so sternly from smiling three dimples popped out in her cheeks and the next bold fireman was likely to call out, "Hi, there, Dimples." So Mrs. Pepper, after many such experiences had decided that men were always teases and there was no use being cross with them.

"Lamptown does make the young men rough, you know that," Mrs. Pepper pursued, now doing her nails carefully while Nettie stood in the doorway looking up and down Market Street for possible customers. "If you travelled from town to town the way I do you'd know. People say this is the toughest town on the Big Four."

"It doesn't have as many bad houses as other towns," Nettie said without turning around.

"Well, you see, there are all those factory girls," delicately innuendoed Mrs. Pepper with a blush. "Not that some of them aren't lovely girls, understand, and they do take the best care of their figures. Only last week I took orders from the girls for upwards of sixty dollars worth of corsets."

"This shop couldn't do without the girls," Elsinore reminded her. "We've got no kick, Mrs. Pepper, you and I."

"I know—I'm saying the girls give me my living," Mrs. Pepper hurried to explain, "but I only mean it's not a good town for a boy. I don't see how you ever raised him to be so decent in such a rough place."

"I did my best," said Elsinore and then she thought of Morry.

She thought of Morry consciously so seldom that she came to the subject with almost a shock. Morry—grown up! Morry—old enough to go away just as she'd gotten used to having a baby around the shop. Because even as a baby he'd been a stranger—oh yes, a part of her in some curious way that made his presence always welcome, but none the less he was a stranger. She wondered if other mothers were perpetually astonished at their maternity and secretly a little skeptical of the miracle, more willing to believe in the cabbage patch or stork legend than in their own biological responsibility. She had moved over for Morry as you would move over for someone on a street car, certain that the intimacy is only for a few minutes, but now it was eighteen years and she thought why, Morry was hers, hers more than anything in the world was.

"Don't I know you did your best with that child?" exclaimed Mrs. Pepper. "She had a lonely time of it, too, Nettie, let me tell you—Mrs. Abbott had no easy time."

Elsinore stared at Mrs. Pepper's shoe ribbon flapping on the floor, and for a second she ached for that lost baby with startling pain. The young man Morry they spoke of was hers only because he too could remember the baby. Upstairs in the front bedroom he had been born—with Charles away of course. Charles only came home twice a year then, but Elsinore never complained. Husbands were like that, and Morry and his mother understood.

Whenever Charles did come home Elsinore and the baby moved into the little room, now Morry's, because crying inspired Charles to frenzies of temper. Elsinore's calm protection of the baby annoyed Charles even more than the crying. Both Morry and his mother were relieved when Charles picked up his sample cases and went away. Once Morry, aged two, had gotten into the sample cases and found them full of candies. Usually just before he came home a printed business postcard arrived with the red-lettered tidings—

"The Candy Man will visit you on—"

Then the date was written in by Charles and after digesting this warning Elsinore let the baby have the postcard with its cartooned Candy Man. Charles beat the child after that invasion of his wares so that ever afterward the arrival of the Candy Man's card sent Morry under the bed or downstairs hiding in one of the hat-drawers. Indeed Elsinore suspected that it was the beginning of his learning to read.

Elsinore, thinking of all this now, forgot to sew and the black ribbon in her lap that was to be a turban, unrolled on the floor.

"Do you remember when I used to keep Morry in his baby carriage all day in front of the shop?" she asked Mrs. Pepper.

Mrs. Pepper sighed.

"Oh dear yes. . . . He was such a big baby and you were so small to be taking care of him. . . . I only had one model to sell then, the Diana Girdle. Gracious, what a long time ago. Let's see—he was three or four when I started working . . . hm. . . . I was twenty. Just twenty. Imagine that."

"Think of it, you and Mrs. Abbott were making your own living then just the way I am now," Nettie said, coming back to the counter and leaning her elbows on it, "and you didn't think anything much of it, but all the same Mrs. Abbott thinks it would be too bad for Morry to get out on his own. And he's eighteen. Older than his mother was when she started this shop."

"I need a man here with me," Elsinore said, irritated. "There's no use your talking about it, Nettie, I need Morry. You don't understand these things at all."

"Some factory girl will marry him and that'll be the end of him," grumbled Nettie.

Mrs. Pepper, as always, strove to soothe everyone by switching their interest.

"There are so many of the girls, you can't blame them for going after the younger men," she said. "Nine hundred girls, all young and lively there at the Works with no men's factory around to give them beaux. Why Mr. Fischer tells me half the time they have to dance with each other at the Casino because there aren't enough men."

"There's never enough men. . . . A girl's got no chance in this town," Nettie complained. "There's twenty-five of us for every man. Every time a new man comes to town it's like dividing a mouse up for a hundred cats. If I was a boy in this town I'd almost be afraid to grow up, I would."

"No chance for a girl to marry," Elsinore said, as if marrying were still to her mind the ideal state for any woman.

"Sometimes the girls go away and marry," Mrs. Pepper said brightly. "Dode O'Connell told me they write their addresses on the crates that are shipped out from the factory and they get answers back sometimes from all over the world. That little Tucker girl they say went all the way to Australia to marry a man she'd never seen. He'd gotten her address from the shipment and they started writing each other."

"Yes, they'd all go to Australia at that factory if they got the same chance," said Nettie gloomily. "Those girls do anything to get a man. They hang around the high school freshmen even. They're wild for men. I've seen 'em calling up to Morry's window sometimes after he's gone upstairs, telling him to come out and take a walk."

Elsinore was puzzled and startled too. This was so new to her, considering her son as a potential husband for someone.

"But he doesn't go out," she said.

Nettie laughed sardonically.

"Oh no, only if she's real pretty and then maybe he goes out. Or if he's on his way to go over and see that Delaney kid, that Jen."

Elsinore stared at Nettie.

"But he doesn't go over there any more, Nettie, I'm quite sure."

"They sit on the top stairs still plenty of times," Nettie blurted out indignantly. "That's what they do. And if he isn't with her then he's in the saloon or probably with some little tart from the factory. That's the way Morry Abbott is and that's the way he's always going to be."

"But you said a little while ago that he thought he was too good for the Lamptown girls," protested Elsinore.

"Too good for good girls!" Nettie flared up. "That's what I meant."

Her nose quite red Nettie whirled into the back-room and
for several minutes Elsinore and Mrs. Pepper heard her banging drawers shut and whistling shrilly to indicate how well
under control was her temper.

"How funny Nettie acts about things," Elsinore commented.

She bent frowning over her work once more and the little
chamber of her mind marked "Morry—Private Thoughts"—
swung slowly shut again. Mrs. Pepper picked up her orange-
stick again and coaxed an elegant half-moon on her rosy
thumb-nail.

Mrs. Pepper thought the crying doll was simply sweet, but
Nettie detested it because ever since Charles Abbott had sent
it, the factory girls were constantly running into the shop to
listen to it.

"Wind it up for Ethel, now," they would beg, and Nettie,
with a scowl of resignation would take the doll out of the
show-window, reach under its red satin ruffles and wind it up
again. A thin little tinkle of doll music wailed faintly through
the shop, while the girls listened in rapt silence.

"This is a hat-shop, not a doll store," she complained to
Elsinore.

"Charles says in the city the best hat shops always have a
doll in the window," said Elsinore. "He wouldn't like it if he
came home and didn't see it there. After all he sent it for that
purpose."

"Well, you don't have to wind it, but I do," muttered
Nettie, not really meaning her employer to hear her mutiny,
but always unable to keep her annoyance to herself.

Elsinore was used to Charles sending strange presents. He
sent sea-weed picture frames from Florida, enormous bottles
of perfume from New York, knowing she never cared for
scents; once he sent her a pair of chameleons which alarmed
her so that Mrs. Pepper with many delighted squeals took
them away. He never sent her money or any practical thing.
Usually if Charles fancied an article he bought three, one for
the blonde girl in Chicago, one for Elsinore, and one for the
last hotel telephone operator he had entertained. If Elsinore
suspected this she never said so. She kept his gifts carefully

wrapped up, as a rule, and wrote him polite little letters of thanks.

"The doll must have cost twenty dollars," declared Mrs. Pepper. "What a thoughtful husband, Mrs. Abbott. You are lucky! And letters almost every day Nettie says. Did he always write you every day?"

"Oh no," said Elsinore, "only lately."

Charles' letters. . . .

"I suppose you think I don't know what you're doing while I'm gone. You think because I'm away you can get away with anything you like. Else, old girl, you'd better get that out of your head. I know you too well, and I can tell when things aren't right. Answer me this—why did you get two new silk dresses last fall if it wasn't to show some man? What made you start in powdering your face when you never used to do more than brush it off with a chamois? Think that over, Else, and you'll realize your husband's not so dumb as you think. . . ."

Then a few days later from another town:—

"Well, while I'm lying, here in this rotten little hotel with the grippe, I suppose you're having your good time, going to your dances and dancing with this guy whoever he is! I guess you didn't notice me watching you when you dressed for the dance last time I was home. I pretended to be reading the paper but out of the corner of my eye I saw you put perfume on your hair, the way a chorus girl does when she's got a date. You did up your hair and looked at yourself in the mirror and then took it all down again and did it over. I said to you, why did you do that, and you said, oh it makes me look so old the other way.

"Yes, I went to the Casino and I stood out in the smoking room watching you as I guess you knew because you were too smart for me and knew better than to give yourself away that night. If you've fallen for one of those train men you're a damn fool, Else, and I'll lick the man if I ever see him, I swear I will."

Elsinore wrote her usual brief letter in reply, ignoring all of Charles' suspicions, but this made him write even more insistently. Sometimes she opened a letter, came to an accusing paragraph, and tore up the letter, not angrily, but quite coolly, because what she read might stay in her mind, so she had to protect herself from all disturbing thoughts.

"You said in your letter two weeks ago you were either going to Cleveland or Columbus for some velvets in a few days. Then yesterday in your letter you never said anything about the trip. It's easy to see that you made that trip all right and just don't want to tell about it. It wasn't on any millinery business, either but to meet someone. I can just see you going to some hotel there thinking your husband is far away up in Minnesota and won't know what you're up to, but I got enough brains to read women and I can read between the lines, don't forget it."

If Elsinore herself could read between the lines she would have seen the erasure marks on the crying doll package when it arrived. She might have detected another woman's address written in pencil and then rubbed out and she would have concluded that the crying doll had been originally purchased for someone else, someone with a taste for such novelties. And then inexplicably Charles had decided that his wife should have it, instead. She might, too, have thought from his letters, "No one but a person who has been guilty himself could read guilt in others so well."

But Elsinore would not allow such thoughts to become important. If she permitted Charles' slowly developing jealousy to worry her, then it might creep in her mind when she was dreaming of really vital things, of Fischer, for instance. There had never been a moment that Charles existed in her imagination. Charles—well Charles *was*. He was not real. His letters—his jealousy—these things *were*, and things that *were* could not enter Elsinore's mind except it gave her pleasure. She wondered if Fischer himself were as real as her thoughts of him.

When she sat fashioning a hat silently, there was no room in her for fretting over an absent husband's suspicion; there was room only to listen to the mechanical rhythm of Mr. Sanderson's piano thumping, there was room only to see Fischer at the Casino, or in the Palace, in Marion, or Akron, or Cleveland, demonstrating a pirouette with his shining patent-leather feet. . . . She had no time to wonder over Charles' wanderings, for she was wondering what fresh-cheeked young girl was at this minute being selected as Fischer's partner. Did this fortunate one have blue eyes and yellow hair? Unconsciously Elsinore discarded the red ribbon for the hat under her hand and selected a blue strip more suitable to this blonde image. Did the new love have a baby face or did she have, in spite of her youth and fairness, a strong handsome nose like Nettie's with the same full lips . . . with this new image Elsinore tore the blue strip off of the frame and from the deep drawer beside her drew out a wider model, more becoming to long noses. With thoughtful eyes she tried the blue velvet strip across the front and underneath the brim.

Nettie watched this changing design, bewildered.

"Will you please tell me, Mrs. Abbott, why you threw away the poke for that big milan?"

Elsinore's reply left her assistant completely baffled.

"Because a girl with a nose like that shouldn't wear a poke. You know that well enough, Nettie."

"Like what? What are you talking about?" asked Nettie, still staring, and Elsinore, conscious of Nettie's scrutiny, turned her head away ever so slightly, as if Nettie might read there a whole catalogue of hat designs for Fischer's probable women.

"I was thinking of something else, Nettie," she said. "I was thinking that next week we must make an entire new outfit for the crying doll—something in rose-colored velvet, I think. . . . And remind me to write Charles and thank him."

She wished Nettie wouldn't ask things,—she wished people wouldn't always intrude.

Charles came home late in the summer. He was thinner and without a new line in his face or a single new grey hair he managed to seem ten years older. He walked into the Bon Ton one Saturday afternoon with no greeting but a "Pretty as ever I see, Nettie" for Nettie, an ironic "Well, Mrs. Abbott" for Elsinore and then seeing Morry in the workroom eating a sandwich he scowled.

"Still hanging around your mother's skirts, I see."

Morry never answered. If he lived to be eighty his father's mockery would still make him curl up with hopeless shame and mortification. A mere glance from his father would always be enough to remind him that he was a huge clumsy fellow—with no more business in a house,—least of all a woman's millinery store—than some prize steer. He was taller than his father by at least six inches, but this could only give him a feeling of inferiority. With his father home there was less than ever a place for him here. While Charles took his bags upstairs, Morry quietly dove out the back alley. Where would he go? He didn't think Delaney's was safe because it was a hangout of his father's. Bauer's Chop House had been out of the question for some time, because Morry shuddered at the mere sight of Grace now. She was apt to say whenever she saw him, "When am I going to see you again, Morry? What's the matter—are you afraid of me?"

Morry stood out in the alleyway, lighting a cigarette, looking up and down the street. He wondered if old Mrs. Delaney was in—if it was safe to run up Jen's stairs. But he didn't really want to see Jen. He was vaguely annoyed with her now. The kid was always tagging after him and the old woman glared at him like some old witch every time he had the bad luck to run into her. The only thing—and this Morry would scarcely admit even to himself—was that nobody believed so firmly in Morry's importance as Jen did. She thought he was somebody. Away from her he remembered the old lady's warning, Nettie's taunts, and the factory girls' kidding. But with Jen he fell under the sweet spell of her worship, her reverent, adoring eyes, her perfect conviction that he was incredibly superior to anyone in the world. While Morry stood in the alley weighing these matters he heard Nettie's voice inside answering some inquiry of his father's.

"No, he's gone out, Mr. Abbott. He's probably up on the Delaney's backstairs with that girl of theirs. He always is there."

This decided him. He threw away his cigarette quickly and hurried through the courtyard to the saloon backdoor.

"Kid Abbott!" roared Hogan as Morry sauntered up to the bar. "Don't he look like a prize-fighter though? Say, wait till he gets mad once! Look at the chest on him, will you, Delaney? Got that delivering bonnets for his ma. Look at them shoulders. Say, there's muscle for you. Kid, you're all right. Understand? You're O.K. and I like you. Delaney, another beer for the Lamptown heavyweight."

"What about the factory laying off men, Abbott, anything in it?" Bill leaned across the bar toward Morry but Morry, as usual, had heard none of the inside rumors.

Three men sitting at a card table started grumbling.

"Yeah, Russell would lay off the men before he would the women. That red-head of his would see to that. . . ."

"I seen in the Dispatch that Lamptown Works was cutting out the accessories. Next the Works will go," Hogan said. "You fellows will be out in less than six months, the factory will be closed up unless the girls keep it open for their own private business, eh, Bill?"

"Russell's all right, he's got enough dough," one of the men at the table said. "If the Works gets shaky he can put money back into it. I ain't worried so long as my thirty-two fifty comes in every payday."

"Yeah, and what if Russell ain't all right," Hogan argued, his nose now a bright pink. "Who's going to pick up the pieces of this town, then? As I see it the whole damned town goes round to Russell's tune and if he stops the town stops. What's he ever done but inherit the money that lets things skid along on their own wheels while he sits there on his twaloo or runs around with cookies."

"Say, Hogan, you don't know it all, just because you live in Bucyrus and shook hands once with Bishop Brown. What the hell do you know about Lamptown? You run down the tracks here once or twice on a three-wheeler and you think you saw everything. Who's you, squintin' into beer-steins and spoutin' Colonel R. G. Ingersoll?" The overalled mechanic from the Works spat toward the cuspidor and missed. "Let me tell you this guy Hunt Russell's got brains, he don't have to break his back learning things. He's got the brains of this town as well as the kale."

Hogan went over to the table and planted both hands on it. A couple of chips rolled under the table and were stopped by a big rubber boot.

"All right, he's got brains, has he? Listen, if he had brains, do you think he'd let his town—the town his old man made—be the state honeydump? Do you think he'd sit up there on his pink plush carpets eating his little bonbons while the town around him stood rotting? He's the guy here with the power and he's got the money. Why, if he had any brains he'd wipe out your Market Street there and build a row of office buildings down to Extension Avenue, he'd tear out that street of old boarding houses and build a big swell hotel, he'd get himself made mayor and throw out all these Irish politicians from Shanteyville, he'd have all the sayso and by Judas he'd say something, he'd build chateaux on his lots, yonder, chateaux with gardens around them. He'd make this little mudhole the gardenspot of Ohio, he'd make playgrounds for his employees. But does he do it? Hell, no."

The card-players were impressed, and Hogan leaned back and folded his arms across his blue shirt.

"Why, boys, you don't know things, that's all. You haven't read, you haven't seen. You let one guy run your whole town, a guy that don't give a hoot in hell for any of you."

"How are you going to do anything else?" Morry asked, excited as he always was, by Hogan's fantasies.

"You fellows ought to get your own hooks into that factory so you won't be wiped out when Russell lays down for his beauty nap, and the business blows up. . . . Oh, I don't say Shanteyville will be wiped out—you'll always have your little flower-bed, the priests will take care of that all right."

"What'll it be, Morry?" Bill picked up Morry's glass and Morry dropped another dime on the counter by way of answer. What about a Lamptown such as Hogan described? What about avenues of green-surrounded "chateaux"? Shutting his eyes, Morry could see them now, rows of houses, all different, this one all gables and low-spreading, white, and the next one rough-stone like a little castle. He saw the picture post cards of these places stuck up on Bauer's cigar-counter instead of the perpetual three-for-a-nickel—"The Yards, Lamptown," "The Works, Lamptown," "Bauer's Chop

House, Lamptown." He saw one picture very clearly, a mansion looking like the State Capitol vaguely, and beneath the tinted photograph these printed words, "Home of Morris Abbott, Lamptown, Ohio."

Suddenly he thought he had lived over stores long enough, he wanted some place to stretch his long limbs, some place where he belonged, where he wasn't always ducking to keep out of people's way. Gardens, chateaux—Morry saw them laid out like spangled Christmas cards—vividly colored invitations to a fairy-tale world. He felt homesick for spacious houses set in spreading lawns fringed with great calm shade-trees,—he was homesick for things he had never known, for families he had only read about, he missed people—old friends that had lived only in the novels he had read. Homesick . . . for a Lamptown that Hogan had just created out of six beers. He wanted to do something fabulous, something incredible, that would bring this Lamptown nearer to reality. He'd do all those things Hogan thought Hunt Russell ought to do. . . . But then Hunt had the money, that's what mattered, what did he, Morry, have but two suits and forty dollars in the savings bank?

"Say, if I had Russell's bank account I'd tear up this damned town and go right back to where old man Russell started with it. I'd make it all over again, I would," Hogan leaned one elbow on the bar and became impressively oratorical again. "Why in no time at all I'd have this town a god-damned Utopia, I would. I'd have an opera-house where the Paradise Picture Palace is now, I'd have a business college where kids could learn how to make a living, I'm damned if I wouldn't."

"Say—say Hogan, how would you go about building those chateaux for instance?" Morry edged up closer to the oracle. "How's a fellow going to learn how to plan and build like that? I don't mean like those Extension Avenue frame houses but—well, you know, different houses like you see in the magazines."

"Thing for you to do is to get a job with a contractor," Bill Delaney told him. "Get in with Hogan's wife's old man. He's a builder, if that's the trade you want to learn."

The mechanic at the table scraped his chair around to face Hogan.

"Yeah, Hogan, that's what you'd do with money, is it? What'd you do with the two thousand your wife got from her old lady? Bought stock in a Mexican opal mine, that's what you did, Big Noise. An opal mine,—Christ!"

Hogan wiped his mouth on his sleeve and patted his stomach fondly.

"Well, boys, I'm off. The old horse waits without."

"Hey, Hogan, what about it? How about that there opal mine?" yelled Delaney, and the others roared with laughter as Hogan vanished, grinning, through the swinging doors.

Four Italian section hands strayed in and began dropping nickels in the pianola. An air from "Il Trovatore" rattled out. The darkest, hairiest of the four leaped beside the piano to bellow the words, gesturing ardently to the painting of a fat nymph surrounded by dazzled doves. Morry dropped into one of the big chairs that lined the bar-room walls. A copy of the Cincinnati Enquirer was in the next seat and he picked it up.

"Cut out the opery," yelled Delaney good-naturedly. "Come on, Spaghett, give us Down Among the Sheltering Palms."

"So that was opera," mused Morry enviously. If you were a wop working on the railroad you knew a lot of things like that. What doors did you open to find out these things, where were these doors anyway? Restlessly Morry started reading. A familiar cough at his side startled him. There in the seat next to him was his father, his grey fedora pulled over one eye, a cigar held between two fingers, a faint smile on his lips.

"This is a surprise," said Charles, "and a pleasure. Stand up! Or no, you needn't. I can see already that you're built for big things . . . moving pianos, say, or pitching hay."

"Great kidder, your dad," Bill Delaney, wiping off the table, said. "How's Frisco, Charlie?"

Morry didn't feel that he disliked his father,—he only wanted to keep away from him. He didn't remember ever having thought of his father one way or the other. His only thought had been to keep out of reach, and therefore free from this scalding sense of shame that a look from his father could bring to him.

It was after supper-time and the Saturday night crowd had begun to filter in . . . a few farmers, but mostly factory men or loafers from Shanteyville whose wives did Lamptown's washing. Charles motioned Morry to come to a corner table with him, and trying not to show his reluctance, Morry followed. Charles ordered a highball and Morry was about to take a beer, when Charles called Shorty, Bill's helper, back.

"Two highballs, Shorty," he said. "No beer drinkers in this family."

"Now, isn't this a picture," he chuckled sardonically. "Father and son on a happy holiday."

He tipped his glass expertly into his mouth, set it down, and studied Morry's less finished drinking.

"And now you're a man, what about it?" he said. "Do you plan to spend the rest of your life in a little tank town or is it possible you have ambitions?"

"I was just thinking about planning houses," Morry blurted out, although it was agony for such a secret thought to form in words for a stranger's ears. "I thought I might get in old Fowler's office some day—he's Hogan's father-in-law, and if I was in there I might learn the business."

Charles Abbott bent his head with such an exaggeration of rapt attention that Morry became mute and ashamed again.

"Go on," urged his father kindly. "I am delighted to see that you have such a sense of humor. I had no idea. I hope these houses are to sit a decent distance from the family residence. Fancy such pretty little ideas in such a great big head. Did you tell your mother?"

"No." Morry shook his head.

His father motioned Shorty to bring another pair of highballs, and Morry's throat burned at the mere mention. Charles shook his cigar ashes on the floor with an elegant air of doing the floor a service by this decoration. Then he looked at his son and laughed softly.

"Such pretty little ideas for a young man that looks like a prize bull. A bull with a taste for perfume. A prize bull with a lace handkerchief. Why, if you had any good in that six feet of muscle you'd be supporting your mother by this time."

"I do intend to," mumbled Morry. The bar was filling up and he yearned to bolt outside. A drunken tenor from Shanteyville was singing at the bar, Bill's voice got louder and shriller in an effort at discipline.

"What about her, then?" his father's voice was low and insistent. "You've been around your mother, you've been taking her to these dances. Well?"

Morry didn't know what the other was driving at. He blinked at him stupidly.

"Don't try to look innocent. You know who she meets, you know damn well what she does. Well, who is it? Who's the guy?" Charles rapped on the table with his glass. A kind of horror seeped in to Morry's brain. He unconsciously shoved his chair back from the table.

"Who's her man, I'm asking you?" Charles repeated threateningly. "Don't think I can't get it out of you. You know damned well what I want to know and by God you're going to tell me. Who's she chasing?"

"What?" The question wasn't out loud because something seemed to stick in his throat and no noise would come out of his mouth. Morry wet his lips.

"I'm asking you who's her lover, damn you, that's what I'm asking!" Charles banged the table with a clenched white hand. Morry noted the onyx and diamond ring on his white flesh.

Now he hated his father, hated the false gentility of his voice, the nice perfection of his collar and pearl stick-pin, he loathed the smooth-shaven bluish face with its small correct nose, its even small white teeth, he loathed the scarcely perceptible odor of lilac hair tonic, he hated him, and even with his eyes shut Morry knew every slight thing about his father that he hated. Helpless always in words with him, Morry could think of only one thing to do and that was to get away. The door of the bar to the front poolroom was blocked by a crowd of shouting Italian railroad workers, and there was only the back door into the court. It was toward this that Morry dived, but the minute his two feet were on the stones of the courtyard he realized that his father was there with him, his hand was on the back of his neck in a steely grip.

"Are you going to tell me what she's up to, or aren't you?"

Words finally burst through Morry's chattering teeth.

"I'm damned if I will."

The next thing he knew was a stabbing blow under the chin. Morry, in a flood of rage, swung out on his father, but as soon as his huge fist struck he was ashamed, for his father was such

a slight, soft little man. It was like hitting some kid. . . .
Morry took a step back in the pitch dark of the courtyard with
the headlights of an oncoming engine in his eyes, and the second's hesitation gave the other his chance. His fist tore into
Morry's face and then it seemed to Morry that the engine had
left its wonted track beside the saloon and had come roaring
into the courtyard. Then the roaring suddenly stopped.

The saloon back door opened and Shorty came running out.
"What the hell. . . ."

Charles Abbott was yanking his collar into place. The
shoulder seam of his right sleeve was torn, the bar-keep
noted, and he breathed heavily even while he smiled. The
younger Abbott was crumpled up on the stone pavement.

"Give us a light there, Bill," Shorty called back and the
back-door opened wider. Someone was singing to the pianola's tinny accompaniment.

"Down among the sheltering palms,
Oh honey, wait for me, oh honey, wait for me. . . ."

Shorty knelt down.

"Hey . . . hey, Morry, what the hell. . . ." Shorty lit a
match and looked from the bloody cheek on the pavement
rather curiously at Charlie. "What's the idea here, Charlie?"

"Just teaching," Charles panted, as he dusted off his hands,
"the boy . . . how . . . to fight."

"Well," said Shorty, "they ain't much fight in him now."

Charles left for the road early the next morning. He said
he'd be gone several months this time through the South-
western territory, and he seemed so much quieter and saner
than he had before, that his wife felt relieved.

As for Morry he took good care to keep out of sight as
long as possible and when he finally did try to sneak through
the back-hall, Nettie saw him.

"He's been fighting. Look, Mrs. Abbott!" she cried out,
pointing to Morry's face. "Look at those marks on his eye. It's
a good thing his father's gone or he'd catch it good from him."

"Why, Morry!" Elsinore's clear grey eyes were wide with
astonishment. "Your face is all bruised. What ever happened
to you?"

"That's why he's been eating at Bauer's these last two days, and keeping out of the shop," declared Nettie triumphantly. "Didn't I tell you there was some reason for it? Didn't I tell you he was up to something? And Dode was in last night and said he wasn't at work all day yesterday."

"But you worked today," said Elsinore, her eyes still fixed on the scarred forehead. "What happened?"

Nettie's black eyes glowed with satisfaction as Morry sullenly stared at the floor.

"See, it was a fight! He got into a brawl over at Delaney's Saturday night, he can't deny it. That's why he didn't get up all day Sunday, don't you remember, and that's why he hasn't let us see him. I knew there was something behind all that!"

Elsinore waited for Morry to answer. But he wouldn't open his mouth, just stood there getting red in the face.

"Was it or wasn't it a fight?" challenged Nettie. "Just ask him. Go on and ask him."

Morry scowled furiously at her.

"All right, then, it was," he retorted, "and what do you think you're going to do about it?"

Nettie backed away, pouting. She smoothed her sleek black hair and marched haughtily into the front show-room swaying her hips with each step. Elsinore and her son stood looking at each other. Elsinore knew there was something she must do, something she must say, because this was her son and there was some word you said to sons so that they didn't brawl in saloons. She thought of the saloon smell, of the old tipplers whose obscenities echoed to her bedroom window on Saturday nights, she thought of the hard-eyed young men that hung around the poolroom, whispering of things mysterious and horrible,—and suddenly she shivered.

"Morry," she began, in a funny little voice as if she were called upon to make a speech at a great banquet and her knees shook a little. "Morry!"

Morry looked away. Then because he knew how bothered she was he turned around and rushed upstairs, and his mother breathed a tremendous sigh of relief.

Nettie kept harping on Morry's bruised eye, though, for days. She thought it had something to do with some girl,—it was a fight over a factory girl or maybe over Jen St. Clair.

Morry let her talk and kept out of the Bon Ton as much as he could. He didn't see much of Jen any more, but he knew Nettie wouldn't believe that. After what the old woman had said he felt queer and sick every time he thought of Jen. He'd stay away all right, he'd leave her alone, but every day after work he missed her, at dusk when they used to sit on the steps talking. He knew she watched him from the Delaney's upstairs window whenever he passed, and once when he walked home from the factory with two of the girls he worked with, someone threw a pebble down at him from up there, but he walked on without looking up. But at nights, when he'd be reading in bed sometimes he'd stare at a page half an hour or so worrying about the whole business, about what the old woman had said to his mother, and he felt lost without Jen to talk to.

One Saturday afternoon when his mother sent him in the back-yard for boxes from the store-shed he looked over toward Jen's stairs. Someone was sitting out, sitting so primly that he had to look twice to make sure it was Jen. She had on a hat. Nobody ever wore a hat in Lamptown unless it was Sunday or else they were going away. It struck Morry with a shock that maybe she was going away, leaving Lamptown for good.

He glanced quickly over his shoulder to make sure the Bon Ton was not on watch, and then sauntered boldly over to the stairs. If she was going away, the old lady certainly couldn't kick about his coming over to bid a civil good-bye. He said hello tentatively but Jen only nodded indifferently to him without smiling. He came up the steps with growing curiosity. A blue lace hat sat awkwardly on Jen's head and in her arm was a stiff pop-eyed china doll in a pink satin costume.

"What's the idea?"

"My mother's come to see me," Jen explained drearily. "She went to the Home for me and they sent her here."

"Is she taking you away?"

"I don't know."

"I guess I'd better go," he said hastily, but dying to see what Jen's folks were really like. He looked through the screen door and just inside the parlor he caught sight of the visitor. She looked like one of those actresses, Morry thought, only fatter. She had a voluminous white veil over her stiff straw hat, and a tight-fitting soiled green suit, and white shoes and stockings.

She sat on the edge of her chair and talked to old Mrs. Delaney hunched in her little chair on the other side of the room. Morry sat down cautiously out of line with the old woman's eye.

"She's been talking now for an hour," Jen murmured in his ear. "I guess it's pretty nice to have your mother come and visit you, especially if you never saw her before. She gave me this hat. Look. She gave me this doll. I'd like it if it cried like your mother's doll does."

Morry wanted to laugh at the hat. He'd never seen Jen in a hat and it sat up on top of her head as if it was meant for the doll instead. This was because Jen's mother had no memory for dates and had a vague impression that her daughter was barely eight. As for the dolls, he couldn't imagine Jen ever playing with dolls.

"What'd she come for, then, if she isn't taking you with her?" he wanted to know, but Jen refused to talk. She sat glumly clutching her doll and looking straight ahead while her mother's voice chattered on and on. Finally Jen whispered,

"She said she wanted to see if I was in a good home. She said she couldn't be easy until she'd seen if I was with the right people. That's what she said."

Morry glanced carefully through the screen door. There was old Mrs. Delaney sitting with her shoulders hunched up, her arms folded over her shrunken calico bosom, her thin lips clamped together, rocking, rocking while Mrs. St. Clair went on and on talking, as if she was selling soap.

"I used to be a beauty. I give you my word, Mrs. Delaney, when I was married my waist was no bigger than that. As it is, it's only my hips that are big, and most men like big hips, that's what I say. People say I lace to make my waist look so small. I give you my word, Mrs. Delaney, you could put your hand inside my corset this minute and see how much room there is. I don't have to lace, I tell them. . . . I had beautiful hair as a girl,—thick like Jennia's out there, but that Titian red, you know. My friends say, oh yes, she dyes it. I give you my word people don't think it's real. They think I dye it, and you know how many women my age do have to color their hair, because do what you will, the gray will come out if it's there. But dye my hair? Ha! I said to this friend of mine,

'Look here, I want you to come to my room and I'll just show you the stuff I wash it in.' I showed her. 'Absolutely no dye,' it said on the bottle, 'merely restoring the hair to its natural brilliancy.' Well, that time the laugh was on her. . . . I'm glad to see Jennia in this beautiful home, Mrs. Delaney. I can see you're a good influence."

Now Mrs. Delaney opened her mouth.

"Well, then, who was the girl's father?" she croaked. "If she had one."

"Mr. St. Clair was a gentleman," said Jen's mother. "We had words but I don't deny he was a gentleman. Such hands, Mrs. Delaney! No wonder, he'd never done a lick of work in his life, but I will say they were beautiful hands. He went to Africa. I think he had interests there."

"Africa? Was he black?" exclaimed Mrs. Delaney, and even Morry jumped then, so that Jen put her finger to her lips warningly.

Mrs. St. Clair threw up her gloved hands.

"Mrs. Delaney! God forbid! My husband black!" She shuddered. "That was uncalled for, Mrs. Delaney, that really was. Do you know, Mrs. Delaney, that my husband was considered the handsomest man in our company? The best-looking man in the 'Laughing Girls' company? Not only that but the smartest as well. He had a big future on the stage, but as I say he had interests in Africa, and when Lily was born—that's my youngest, we were staying at a hotel in Youngstown then, the company had broken up,—why Bert just walked out on me with a note. I waited till Lil was a month old, then left her on the Children's Home doorstep right where baby Jennia had been put, the year before. I tell you I cried my eyes out, Mrs. Delaney, because there's nothing like a mother's heart."

Tears now came to Mrs. St. Clair's eyes and she plucked them out carefully as one whose tears had too often had to cope with mascara.

"Oh, I've not had an easy time of it, Mrs. Delaney. When Jennia was born—that was when we were playing in Toledo, so I left her there with a very fine family—my friend said aha, it's only a six months' baby. My own friends said that, mind you. But I could show you the book where I wrote down the dates of my wedding and when Jen was born, and I could prove that everything was just as innocent as I sit here now. I was brought up refined, Mrs. Delaney, I had my education. I was every bit as good as Bertie was but he never would believe it. My people were from Virginia. My mother was an O'Brien."

Mrs. Delaney's thin mouth snapped open again.

"When did you get Jen back from that Toledo family you left her with?"

Jen's mother leaned forward confidentially.

"Mrs. Delaney, you wouldn't believe people would be like that, but when I got back to Toledo that family had put her in the Orphanage in Libertyville. I never would have put her there, and the only reason I left Lily there was as kinda company for her sister, you know. I never saw either of my babies from the time I left them till now when I'm looking them up again. When Lily was born I spent every penny I had to get her to the very same orphanage because I wanted my little girls to be together. You're a mother yourself, Mrs. Delaney. You know a mother's heart."

"Do you want to get Jen back now?" challenged Mrs. Delaney. "Is that what you're after?"

"Do I—oh dear, no,—oh no, not now. Does she sing or dance? Let me hear her sing once. Jennia—oh Jennia, sing me a song, dearie. I want to see if you've got your father's voice."

Jen shifted her doll to the other arm, stood up and with her nose pressed against the screen door in order to face her audience, sang. She sang at the top of her voice and very fast so as to get it over with.

> "Will someone kindly tell me,
> Will someone answer why—
> To me it is a riddle
> And will be till I die—
> A million peaches round me,
> Yet I would like to know,
> Why I picked a lemon in the garden of love
> Where I thought only peaches grow."

Mrs. St. Clair gave a little flattering cry of pleasure.

"You know really that's not bad, Mrs. Delaney, not bad at all. When I was her age I was getting four and five dollars a week singing in my papa's cafe in Newark. Customers would throw the money at me. I had my training all right before I ever stepped on the real stage. Nowadays of course a child performer gets even more than a grown-up,—and a curly-haired little girl. . . ." Mrs. St. Clair studied Jen appraisingly through the screen. "Her legs are good, too, that's a blessing."

Jen mechanically pulled her apron down over her knees, and her mother laughed fondly.

"Never mind hiding them, dear. . . . Now, do you know what I've a mind to do? . . . Hmm mm. . . . Yes sir, I've a good mind to take her along with me to Cleveland. I have my little room there, and we'd manage. Yes sir, I think that's what I'll do, especially since the Home won't let me take Lily. . . . Stand up, dearie, I want to see if you can travel half-fare. She's pretty tall, isn't she?"

Mrs. Delaney got up suddenly and limped over to where her guest sat. She put her arms akimbo.

"You don't get her, missy, do you see?" she spat out her words. "You'd like to put her in a cafe or on the stage and let her make a living for you but you can't do it while old Susan Delaney's alive and I'll tell you that right now. She's here to help me, that's what. You don't get a chance to make of her what you made of yourself, now, take that, and I'll tell you right to your face that I don't like your looks and I'm sorry you came."

Mrs. St. Clair's mouth fell open. Red spots came into her cheeks and her hands clutched the arms of her chair tightly. Outside, Morry decided he'd better leave but Jen clutched him tightly. When he tried to pull away she took both hands and held on to his coat, and the doll clattered down the steps.

"See!" hissed Morry. "You've broken it now. Say, I want to get out of this, hear me?"

"I know you—I know you as well as if I'd borne you myself," went on the old woman shrilly, "you can get away from here and stay away. I got enough to do keeping that wild 'un straight without her ma breaking in."

Words came to Mrs. St. Clair.

"Oh, what an old bitch," she choked. "To think I spend my good money coming all the way from Cleveland just to be kicked out of my child's home. What a rotten old bitch you are! Got no more sympathy for a mother than a snake."

Mrs. Delaney pointed a gnarled finger toward the door and lowering her white veil the other woman whirled around to go. Morry and Jen backed out of the way.

"Here, Jen, give her her hat and her doll," commanded the old woman.

"Oh, can't I keep the hat?" Jen implored.

"Give them back!" thundered the old woman, and Jen hastily took off the hat and picked up the doll to hand to her mother. Mrs. St. Clair gathered her green skirts about her and ran down the steps.

"You'll be sorry for this," she shouted from the bottom of the steps. "I'll get Lily and I'll get Jennia, too, they'll stick by their mother. I only came here for a motherly visit and you——"

"You came here to stay and live off me if you could, don't deny it!" quavered the old woman fiercely. "I tell you I know you like I'd know my own daughter, and you can get out and stay out."

She panted back into the house, stopping to glare at Morry.

"And you, too. You clear out of here, too."

She banged the door shut.

Jen, bereft of doll and hat, hung over the bannister.

"Oh, mother! Goodbye, mother,—come see me again——"

But Mrs. St. Clair was storming angrily up the street to the Big Four depot, a pink satin doll under one arm and a child's blue hat crushed under the other.

Jen turned to Morry.

"Now I'll never see her again," she said despondently.

"What do you care? She wouldn't do you any good," Morry consoled her.

"I know, but it's my mother, Morry, it's my folks," Jen said, troubled.

Morry heard the door rattling ominously.

"I'm going to beat it," he said, "the old lady's on the warpath."

Jen didn't try to stop him. The bar-keeper stuck his head out of the saloon back-door as Morry dashed down the alley. He stepped out and stared upstairs at Jen, shading his eyes with his hand.

"Who was that up there doing all the singing for God's sake?" he demanded.

"Aw, shut up," grumbled Jen. "I gotta right to sing, I guess."

Jen went to the parochial school in the Irish end of Lamptown, the part they called Shanteyville. She played hookey half the time, and lost her books in the woods hunting mushrooms, and fought with the boys in the school-yard. Every few days a black-robed sister would climb the steps above the saloon to old Mrs. Delaney's quarters and during this interview Jen usually disappeared, well aware that the visit had to do with her own waywardness.

Some times when she knew beforehand that the sister was to make a call, she'd stay away from home till nine or ten at night, coming in bedraggled and muddy-booted, with a lapfull of muddy wild-flowers and burrs sticking to all of her clothes. She never quite understood Mrs. Delaney's rage over these night wanderings, nor could she see why they were proof that she'd never grow up into a decent woman. Once it was eleven when she got in and old Mrs. Delaney sat humped up by the kitchen stove waiting for her. Bill was eating a cold supper on the oil-cloth table.

"Well!" said the old woman.

"I been picking flowers out in the Lots," Jen said. "Here."

She laid a clump of sweet williams and johnny-jump-ups on the table.

"Who you been with—that Morry Abbott?"

"I went by myself," said Jen.

"That's likely. Eat supper?"

"I found some green apples. I'm not hungry."

"Look here, Sister Catherine says you throw your books at the boys and that Peter McCarthy had to be sent home today because you bit his hand so hard. She says you swore at Myrtle Dietz."

Jen looked sulkily at her flowers. Bill jerked his chair around.

"Speak up! Tell the old lady what's the idea. We give you a home and then you stay out half the night. We send you to a good school so you can grow up to be somebody that is somebody and you raise hell all over the place. Speak up, kid."

Jen chewed her finger-nails silently.

"What's the big idea throwing books at the boys? What's the idea scratching up this McCarthy boy?"

"I'm not gonna be mauled by any of those smarties," Jen said defiantly. "And I was just getting even with Pete McCarthy. I had a reason."

The old woman pricked up her ears alertly. Bill's fork hung in mid-air. Both looked suspiciously at Jen.

"What happened? What'd he do to you? Speak up there, now, out with it."

"He chased after me coming down the tracks one noon and——"

"I knew it would happen," moaned the old woman, "I said it would happen. Every girl I ever had under my roof, the same every one of them. Out with it, then, what'd he do?"

"Kissed me, that's what!" Jen said indignantly.

Bill and his mother exchanged an unbelieving look.

"And that's all? Now, no lying!" the old woman insisted. "You're sure that was all?"

"I guess that's enough," Jen mumbled, feeling embarrassed that the outrage should be taken so lightly. "I got even with him for it, all right."

"And you beat him up just for kissing you!" marvelled the old woman. "I've a mind to give you a good tanning for it. . . ."

"Leave her be, ma," Bill said. He fished more pickled pigsfeet out of the jar, and stuffed his mouth.

"Wash up those dishes, then, and get to bed," urged his mother. "Wandering around the Lots this hour the night. One of those fresh fellows at the Yard get after you once and then where'd you be?"

"She'd scratch his eyes out, don't you fear," promised Bill. "She won't have anybody around her but maybe Morry Abbott and he don't bother her much, now he's working and going after real meat."

Jen tied on an apron.

"He'd better not show up here any more after I told him not to," said Mrs. Delaney. "No use your sitting out waiting for him, either, because I told his ma I wouldn't have it. And no use your thinking you can meet him nights outside because if I find out I'll give you a hiding."

"I don't care," Jen retorted, banging the dish-pan into the sink. "I can get along without people, I guess. I guess I'm old enough to get along by my own self."

"You bet you're old enough! Next you'll be hanging around dance halls, the Casino and the like——"

Jen clapped her hands.

"Aw, Bill, let me learn to dance, will you? Look, I can two-step already."

She two-stepped around the kitchen, waving the dish-mop in the air. Bill whistled a tune for her.

"Say, what do you know about that? Look at that, ma. . . . Now, wait a minute, and tell you what I'll do, I'll show you the schottische."

He got up and took Jen's hand stiffly in his own fat red hand. He held his foot poised in the air in the third position and Jen raised a muddy shoe to the same angle.

"Now when I say 'Down!' you sachet to your right, and watch now. Down!

> "Don't you see my
> Don't you see my
> Don't you see my new shoe?
> Don't you see my
> Don't you see my
> Don't you see my new shoe?"

"They don't dance that way any more, I've seen 'em," objected his mother. "Things are different now."

"Never mind, she's a fine dancer. What do you say I take her over to Fischer's some night? I'd like to go over some night myself, especially if I had someone to dance with."

Jen caught hold of his arm.

"You wouldn't really, would you, Bill? Take me to the Casino?"

Bill began to regret his offer, but he didn't dare take it back.

"Get to those dishes, will you?" snapped Mrs. Delaney. "You got to do better with Sister Catherine before you go out nights, young lady, yes sir, even with Bill."

"I'll wear my hair up!" Jen was jubilant again. "Like Nettie Farrell does. Give me a dime for hair-pins, will you, Bill?"

Jen couldn't wait to go to the Casino. She could see herself

dancing around amazing Morry Abbott and Grace Terris and
the men from downstairs. She saw Lil there, too, because Lil
was always a part of her ideal dream pictures. She could see
herself grown up, taking Lil across the Casino floor and people crowding around her because Lil was like a little yellow-
haired wax angel. And Lil would be dazzled by all this
glamour, too. Whenever she remembered Lil, back in the
Home, Jen felt guilty. Lil, back there in dark blue calico, always too skimpy, swinging on the iron carriage gate, while
here was Jen having all this fun in Lamptown, with her own
room, and a pair of silk stockings and a box of talcum
powder. . . . Soon the Home would send her out to work
because she was fourteen now, Lil was. Jen'd have to do
something about her, quick, too . . . then Jen skipped all
that and was back again in the Casino with Lil, both in pink
silk dresses, dancing, with Morry watching. . . . Jen turned a
hand-spring joyously across the kitchen floor.

"See, now you've started her," Mrs. Delaney said morosely
to Bill. "Dancing and then what? Mind you, one crooked
move, and out she goes."

Nevertheless the next week Jen started going to the Casino
dances.

On a rainy Saturday night Dode O'Connell strode into the
Bon Ton Hat Shop. Mrs. Pepper was sewing garters on a Stylish Stout model in pink brocade. Elsinore and Nettie sat on
the green wicker sofa watching the rain and waiting for customers. The rain zig-zagged across the show-window in torrents and black gleaming umbrellas with frantic legs beneath
were blown past. Market Street lamps were wet golden blobs
dripping futile little puddles of light that made no difference
to the black, wet night, and the lightning that cracked the
sky showed up Lamptown as such a shabby, lost little corner
of the earth,—it was nothing, just nothing at all for that
dazzling second.

Dode's tall person was wrapped in a man's top-coat, and a
Roman-striped muffler was wound round her red hair. Nettie,
closing the door behind her, saw Hunt's car just beyond, in
front of Delaney's, its curtains buttoned up.

Dode shook off the damp coat and patted up her hair in front of the gilt mirror.

"I want that big hat that was in the window last week,—the one over the doll," she said, and Nettie and Elsinore bustled around with this hat and another like it in blue, because Dode spent good money and besides she usually got her clothes in Cleveland, so that this visit must be quite a compliment.

Mrs. Pepper, sewing on her corset, grew crimson when Dode nodded to her, and she moved a little away as if to avoid any personal contact with this customer. Dode, tilting a hat over one eyebrow, looked over at the corsetiere rather cynically.

"What's the matter, Pepper, you mad at me for that Cedar Point business?"

Mrs. Pepper looked up, confused.

"I—oh no, Dode, I——"

"You and Fischer sore?"

"No—I——"

Now Elsinore's blood began to tingle ominously, in a minute she was going to overhear something she almost knew but didn't ever want to hear spoken out loud. She saw Mrs. Pepper look helplessly from Dode to Nettie. Nettie was busy stretching a hat and pretending not to listen. But Dode paid no attention to the two milliners.

"Well, then, what was the trouble up at Sandusky—did you miss the boat? We waited over at the Point for three hours for you."

Mrs. Pepper puckered up her rosebud mouth very firmly.

"I was too busy. I had a great many customers in Sandusky——"

"Whereabouts—at the Soldiers' Home?" Dode laughed.

"He needn't think I can drop everything and run just because he says so," Mrs. Pepper said tartly. "Besides you know how he is when he's had too much."

Dode's eyebrows went up scornfully.

"Say, that's good coming from you."

Mrs. Pepper tossed her head and jerked her chair around. Dode took the hand-mirror Elsinore gave her and studied the back view of her hat.

"The plumes are five dollars apiece," Elsinore said hesitatingly, but after all plumes did cost. "That makes it eighteen."

"Put another plume over on the other side, will you?"
Dode requested. She lifted up her skirt and pulled a roll of
bills out of her stocking. Her black silk stockings came all the
way up her long shapely thighs, and there were dozens of tiny
ruffles on her white silk drawers.

"I'll come in and get it Tuesday."

She started winding the muffler around her head again.
Nettie shook out the top-coat and held it for her.

"Say, Pepper."

Mrs. Pepper looked around unwillingly.

"Get into your clothes and come out. We're going to drive
over to Marion and pick him up. Come on."

"I might—and I might not," said Mrs. Pepper huffily.

"Hurry up," ordered Dode.

"In all this storm?" Elsinore said because now she knew it
was true about Fischer and Mrs. Pepper, and she couldn't bear
to have her go out to meet him. She'd known about this and
known it was true, she thought, ever since she first heard the
rumor, but it never struck her full in the face until tonight.

Mrs. Pepper, sputtering angrily, got into her coat and hat.

"I wouldn't go over there for a minute if it wasn't that I
have to see a certain party in Marion."

Dode laughed.

"That's the stuff, Pepper. Don't let 'em know when you're
sunk."

The lightning slashed the black sky again as they ran out into
the street. Nettie shut the door and in another minute Hunt's
car rolled through the flooded gutters down the street.

"In all this rain, too!" Nettie said slowly, and then her face
wrinkled up and she began to cry and dab at her eyes with her
tiny sewing apron.

Elsinore looked at her, irritated more than surprised. For
one thing, Nettie or anybody else crying was nothing really in
her life. The only real thing was the terrible certainty that
Fischer belonged to Mrs. Pepper, just as people had always
said, and that they met often, and it was all secret which made
it mean so much more.

"I don't care," Elsinore thought, and in her mind she
didn't, it was only that something sharp like lightning quivered through her chest, and made her want to scream.

Nettie went on sniffling into her apron.

"I get so lonesome sometimes," she whimpered. "People going out on dates in all this storm,—those factory girls always have dates, not that I'd be seen with any man in this town, but when I think of a fat old thing like Mrs. Pepper going out riding . . . while I stay here and work all the time. I never get out, and anyway I'm afraid of lightning. It makes me—so—nervous!"

"Shut up!" Elsinore cried so harshly that Nettie was frightened into awed obedience. Elsinore rubbed her forehead, dazed, as if she had shrieked out some secret in her sleep. Nettie blinked at her, and Elsinore began to be sorry for her, as she was sorry for herself. She was glad when the hall door banged as Morry came in.

"I can't stand people crying," she explained to Nettie. "I never cry myself. If you're so anxious to go out, though, in this storm, why don't you ask Morry to take you to the Paradise to the picture? It's only nine o'clock. There won't be any more customers here on a night like this."

"I'd never ask Morry to do anything for me!" Nettie dried her tears.

Morry stuck his head in the door. He'd been over to Delaney's place and he smelled of smoke and beer.

"Did you call me?"

"Morry, get my umbrella and your old coat and take Nettie to the Paradise tonight. She doesn't feel very good."

Morry and Nettie looked at each other antagonistically. Nettie knew, if his mother did not, how significant it was for a couple to go to the Paradise together. Nobody ever went to movies together in town but engaged couples. Girls went alone and fellows hung around the drug-store outside to take them home afterwards, but to go in together. . . . How he detested her for her smooth, tear-streaked face, her woeful mouth, all the signs of her feminine helplessness, all the appeals for sympathy. . . . What would she care if all the fellows stared at them and snickered when they came in together? That's just what women always liked.

"Well?" challenged Nettie. "See Mrs. Abbott, he won't take me, he'd rather go with the factory girls."

"You'll take Nettie, won't you, Morry?" Elsinore asked him

again. "You can wrap yourself up good. It's the first Saturday
night she's ever had a chance to get out. Go on and put your
things on, Nettie."

Morry scowled down at his wet shoes while Nettie joyously
ran into the backroom to get ready. He hated the Paradise,—
only sissies went to the movies, he was disappointed in his
mother, and he wished somebody would give Nettie's smug,
smiling face a good slap.

"In just a minute, Morry," Nettie called out.

Elsinore caught sight of the pink corset Mrs. Pepper had
left on her chair. She picked it up and threw it across the hall
into the workroom, and banged a drawer shut. Morry's jaw
dropped. He'd never seen his mother in a temper before.

"Leaving her trash all over the place!" Elsinore fumed. "I
won't have it. I've stood it long enough! I won't let her come
here again ever!"

Nettie ran out, pop-eyed, pulling on her hat.

"What is it? What happened?"

"Out she goes the next time she comes to Lamptown!"
went on Elsinore. "I've got no place here for her or anybody
else like her!"

Morry, for some obscure reason, felt the need to protect his
mother from Nettie's curiosity.

"Come on, let's get out of here if we're going," he ordered
brusquely, and shoved Nettie out the front door into the rain.

Nettie raised her umbrella, not at all disturbed by his surli-
ness. Small rivers of rain ran off the shop awning, and two
girls, bent on getting their Saturday night dates somehow, ran
squealing by with newspapers over their heads. Market Street
blurred uncertainly before them.

"Here!" Nettie handed Morry the umbrella, and clinging
very close to his unfriendly arm, she tiptoed carefully along
beside him.

Morry could never forget that walk in the rain with Nettie
Farrell. To be huddled under an umbrella with a woman he
hated, to smell her violet talcum, her scented hair, to feel her
warm, plump hand squeezing his elbow, her body pressing
against his, so that not for an instant could he forget that it
was Nettie, Nettie Farrell, and that he detested her. He said

nothing to her, tramped straight through all the puddles leaving her to scamper along beside him with tight, prim little steps.

He was glad of the umbrella when they passed the drug store, because the fellows inside couldn't recognize him then. He pulled his cap down over his eyes at the gilded ticket window of the Paradise, and pushed Nettie ahead of him into the theatre. The storm had kept people away and for a glad moment or two he thought there was no one he knew in the little scattered audience. He wished Nettie wouldn't make so much fuss getting into her seat so that everybody turned around to stare. Then he saw directly across the aisle the small pointed face of Jen St. Clair. She was with Grace Terris and Grace was nudging her and giggling, but Jen only stared at him as if she'd never seen him before and then, with her chin in the air, turned her attention to pictures.

Morry had spoken to her and now he wished he hadn't. Every time he ever saw Jen he wished she wouldn't show everyone so plainly her worship of him, but now that the worship seemed to be gone he was simply furious with her. He watched the shadowy adventures of Clara Kimball Young and thought of all he'd done for Jen St. Clair, promising to help get her sister and all that, and now she tried to make him feel like a fool by not speaking to him right before Nettie Farrell and the whole Paradise audience. He glowered at the picture, but out of the corner of his eye he could see Grace peeking over at him now and then, and whispering and giggling with Jen.

Nettie kept wriggling in her seat and turning around to speak to people—not to Grace or Jen—but to Bon Ton customers here and there. Morry slid down in his seat a little,— it was no use, though, because everyone knew those big shoulders and the coal black wavy hair belonged to Morry Abbott and to nobody else in town. . . .

It was amazing about girls, how lofty and complacent they became when they got out in public with a man,—any man— while a fellow shrank and felt ridiculous and prayed for the ordeal to end. It was amazing about women, anyway, Grace over there, snickering behind her hand and Jen, stony-faced, remote, and Nettie, bending over his knees to pick up a handkerchief, fussing around in her seat, brushing her ankles against

his and then hastily drawing them back, pressing her plump
arms against him, then moving primly away. . . . God, how he
hated the whole lot of them, Morry thought, the way they
knew how to make a man squirm from old Mrs. Delaney on
down to the littlest girl. It was their function in life, making
men feel clumsy and dumb, that was all they ever wanted to accomplish. . . . He remembered the little girls in big pink hair-
ribbons at parties years ago, looking scornfully at him, twice
their size, until he wished for sweet death to swoop down on
him. Now, in the Paradise, with the thunder growling over the
roof, and surrounded by Nettie, Grace and Jen, he thought of
those smart little curled girls of ten and twelve years ago and
wanted fiercely to be revenged on them. Nettie's hand
touched his carelessly and he boiled with rage and jerked his
own hand away. . . . But what revenge would fit these enemies . . . of course he might leave town forever and go to
Pittsburgh, no sir, New York City, and show them up as cheap
little village hicks while he was a polished city man. This was a
soothing thought, as soothing as if it were already accomplished,—he even saw himself now on the screen before him,
that natty young man in the opera hat emerging from the cafe
door, lighting a cigarette from a silver case while music played.

He saw Hogan dressed up going down the aisle, and wondered what Hogan was doing here. Then he remembered
Milly, the piano-player and a professional lady of joy. That explained everything. He wished Hogan would tell his pianist
girl-friend not to stop dead in the middle of a picture so that
you forget what you were thinking of.

Grace and Jen got up,—Morry saw them and was determined not to look when they passed but Grace said "hello"
and he had to look up and meet Jen's cold, accusing eyes. She
glanced away again and went out, pulling on her coat.

"I wonder who those two are going to meet," Nettie whispered to him and Morry gritted his teeth. Those two! As if
Jen was like Grace Terris! Those two! His vague anger settled
definitely on Nettie now.

Hogan ambled to the back of the theatre nodding to
Morry with an innocently casual air as if no one would ever
guess he was there to date up the town's light woman, the
talented Milly. Cynically the audience watched the pianist, a

few minutes later, get up from her bench, close the piano in the very middle of the heroine's death-bed scene, powder her nose leisurely before the piano mirror, set a large plumed hat reverently over her magnificent pompadour; she jangled bracelets up her fat arms and drew on long gloves; she made an intimate adjustment in her stayed velvet gown; gazing with calm insolence over the audience she finally swept majestically up the aisle. Unwillingly the audience gave up Clara Kimball Young's deathbed scene to watch Milly's exit, reluctantly they conceded the dramatic value of her performance, heads turned to watch her pause at the back of the house to look patronizingly at the picture, exchange a laughing word with the usher, and then a cold draught blew in as the exit door swung open and shut for her departure, leaving the audience to the lesser reality of the screen.

Everyone always knew that of course Milly was joining some man or other outside, and this local passion was more exciting than the filmed one. Some ladies thought Milly's private profession should disqualify her as the Paradise pianist, still the cold facts were that no one else in Lamptown could play the piano that well and you had to have music with your pictures, no matter where it came from.

With the pianist gone the picture seemed dull and people wandered out into the rain again. Morry was impatient to go. He was perfectly conscious of Nettie's bosom rising and falling with each breath so that her lace frill quivered gently. A gold locket on a frail gold chain had a way of sliding down beneath the frill every time she moved forward and Nettie, with a little shocked exclamation, would reach down her blouse and fish it out again. A faint whiff of violet sachet followed this maneuver, but Morry pretended not to notice anything.

"Everyone's going," Nettie whispered. "Come on, let's go."

They went out and stood for a minute in the lobby while Nettie fussed with her rubbers. The storm was over so that now there was no excuse for the umbrella. Morry could see men peering out at him from the drug store window and wished there was some way of dropping Nettie then and there.

"Going back to the shop?" he asked her.

"No," said Nettie primly. "You'll have to take me out to my place, Morry."

There was no getting out of it. They'd have to walk through all the mud of Extension Avenue to the house where Nettie boarded. The maple trees dripped down on them and the pods crackled underfoot. They passed the factory boarding houses with the girls giggling in the doorways or hanging out the windows. A gramophone squeaked out some ragtime to shatter the black gloom outside, and it kept tinkling through Morry's head. Once an automobile slushed through the mud and spattered Nettie's skirt and she went on about that but Morry stalked silently along, his hands in his pockets, his wet shoes weighing a ton. Now they reached the darkest end of the road. Nettie's house was dark,—the Murphys were down-town.

"Bye," Morry said gruffly at the doorstep.

"I suppose if you wanted to," said Nettie, unfastening a glove carefully, "you could come in and get dry. I'm sure I don't care. Only you'll have to take off those filthy boots because I won't have you tramping up Mrs. Murphy's new rug the way you do your mother's rugs."

Once more Nettie became all of the smug little starched girls sent into the world to make mankind feel loutish and immeasurably inferior, and once more Morry was stung with the desire to be revenged on all of them. He followed her into the house. She lit the hall gas lamp, from its brass elbow a string of gilded buckeyes dangled. She took off her wraps and hung them on a golden-oak hall rack and arranged her hair in the diamond-shaped mirror above. Then she saw Morry standing behind her and stamped her foot.

"Look at you, Morry Abbott! Look at you making tracks all over that new rug with your great big shoes! I could kill you for being so clumsy! Look what you're doing!"

Suddenly Morry seized her two wrists and twisted them until Nettie squealed with pain. He held them tightly with one hand, and with the other pulled her into an iron embrace. Nettie's eyes were terror-stricken, her mouth wide open, the pulse in her white throat throbbed frantically.

"I hate you, Morry Abbott! Don't you dare to touch me. See, you're tearing my dress. . . ."

Morry lifted her up and carried her with her heels kicking, to the green satin settee at the foot of the staircase. He had no desire for Nettie, only a fierce antagonism that amounted to a physical necessity. He would like to have taken her by the neck and shook her like a dog would shake a hen, but all he could do was to sink his teeth into her round shoulder and bite as hard as he could. Nettie stopped kicking him and began to whimper childishly. She put up her hands to fix her hair again and to pull her torn blouse back into place. She wouldn't lift her face to look at him, just made funny whimpering noises like a frightened puppy. When she wriggled away from his knees Morry jumped after her and the settee tipped backwards and upset a blue and yellow jardiniere of ferns.

"Mrs. Murphy'll come in any minute," Nettie wailed, fixing the jar on its mahogany pedestal again. Morry might have left her then but she started to dash past him upstairs. He tore after her and caught up with her on the top landing and got one foot inside the bedroom door before she could close it. His fists were clenched as if for a battle.

The upstairs hall lamp shone into the bedroom through the transom after Morry had shut the door tight. The room smelled of violet talcum and scented soap. Nettie was perfectly quiet, he had to fumble toward the bed where she sat, leaning back on her arms, challenging him. He grasped her shoulders and she drooped limply against him, not saying a word, and the familiar detestable perfume of her hair made him grit his teeth again.

A door opened downstairs.

"Now do be quiet about it," Nettie whispered warningly, and didn't even bother to put up her hands in protest when he started tearing her blouse again.

He was astonished and even chagrined at the ease, almost skill, with which she yielded. Somehow he felt it was she who had conquered and not he, after all. Tiptoeing down the stairs sometime afterward he thought cynically, "I'll bet that's the way they all are. Easy, every one of 'em!"

It made him very angry.

Morry was out in the court pretending to fix the lock on the storehouse door but hoping Jen would call him. He could see her dimly through the dusk sitting on the top-stairs. She hadn't called to him since the night he'd gone out with Nettie.

It might be on the old lady's account but he doubted if Jen was really afraid of her. Secretly he was worried about her,—he didn't especially want to see her but he liked to feel sure she was around and lately he'd heard Bill say something about "shipping the kid to some farm where she'd learn to work,— no damn good to the old lady as she was, always getting kicked out of school, always breaking something."

He lay awake nights trying to figure some way out because it would be terrible for Jen to have to go to some farm. He almost thought of asking his mother to let her work in the Bon Ton the way Nettie had started in, then that made him think of Nettie and he thought probably Jen would be better on a farm. If she was taller she could say she was sixteen and get a job at the Works. Then he remembered the way Hunt had laughed the night he and Jen went there and he thought probably Jen would do better out of Hunt Russell's reach, too.

He looked toward the stairs again,—she couldn't help but see him, still she made no beckoning gesture. Ungrateful, he thought, just as if he had already done all those things for her that he had planned. Then reluctantly he started over. He stopped at the foot of the stairs. He wasn't afraid of Bill's old woman any more—or anybody else for that matter.

"Want me to come up, Jen?"

"Sure, come on." She seemed to have gotten grown-up since she'd come to Lamptown, still nothing but a kid, Morry thought, with her eyes always wild and frightened as if she expected somebody to hit her any minute. Now with Morry sitting beside her, she was happy again, but she knew by this time that if she let him see it he would go away at once, because that's the way he was. If she could only keep from speaking to him he'd always hang around her, because silence seemed to mystify him. . . . Or, she reflected, if she could only stay angry with him for all the times he'd hurt her, but when he was here, right here beside her like this, she forgot all the times he'd made her cry all night . . .

"I thought you'd be out with Nettie," she said. "Like two weeks ago Saturday."

Morry sniffed.

"She can't get me to go out with her any more," he said. This wasn't quite true. Nettie still treated him like dirt under her feet in the daytime and this so puzzled Morry that he had to reassure himself at other times that he was really the conqueror. He hated Nettie, though, he never would forget that he hated her.

"Say—say Jen, what are you going to do about Lil? Has she been adopted yet?"

Talking about Lil always pacified Jen . . .

"I wrote her to run away if they started adopting her," Jen said. "I could look after her. I sent her my birthday dollar."

Morry remembered his own brave promises about Lil—he was the one that was going to rescue Lil, he was.

"I've got a job, too," said Jen. "Anytime I want to, I can get three dollars a week waiting table at Bauer's. Grace gets six and her keep but I have to go to school part time."

"Next year you can get into the factory, too," said Morry, "You'll get ten there—maybe twelve."

"I'm not going to work in any factory," Jen told him casually. "I guess I'll go on the stage or be a dancer, maybe. If you'd been to the Casino lately you'd a seen me. Mr. Fischer says I'm a born dancer. So that's what I'll be doing."

Morry was silenced and awed. He saw Jen in a ballet skirt puffed out all around, her picture in some magazine, and at first he was proud, proud because she was his invention, then he was jealous of all the men who would be looking at a ballet-girl's picture. He wanted to be glad of this glamorous future for her and he wanted to be fair, but he couldn't help warning her that it was pretty hard to get on the stage, and besides the Delaneys wouldn't let her, and what's more, who'd look after Lil?

Jen refused to be discouraged.

"I guess I'll do what I please when I'm earning regular money over at Bauer's," she said. "They can't stop me. I could look after Lil, and you said you'd help."

"Sure," said Morry. It was a promise.

The Chicago train thundered by with a fleeting glimpse of white-jacketed porters and lit-up dining cars. Morry and Jen watched it hungrily, they were on that train whizzing through Lamptown on their way to someplace, someplace wonderful, and looking a little pityingly out of their car window at a boy and girl sitting on the backsteps over a saloon. The train went ripping through further silence leaving only a humming in the air and a smoky message painted on the sky.

Morry and Jen looked quickly at each other—this was the thing that always bound them—trains hunting out unknown cities, convincing proof of adventure far off, of destiny somewhere waiting, of things beyond Lamptown. It was like that first time they sat here. . . .

"I'd never go away, Morry," Jen finally said, not looking at him, "not unless you went first."

Morry didn't know what to answer. Windows in the court were slowly lighting up, downstairs the player-piano jangled out "Under the Double Eagle." The kitchen light of the Delaneys' apartment went on—the old lady might come out any minute and chase him off. . . . No, it was different from the first night they sat here because now they were grown up, Jen was old enough to go to the Casino dances.

"Say, Jen, who do you dance with over there?"

He didn't think anyone would ever ask her to dance.

"I dance with Bill and with Sweeney and the men from downstairs," Jen answered. "And last time I danced with Hunt Russell twice."

Morry blinked at that. Hunt was an old rounder. If he got after Jen . . . Well, after all, someone would sooner or later, wouldn't they? Now he looked at her with Hunt Russell's eyes and saw that she was different from anyone at Lamptown dances, she was—yes, you might say pretty, but strange-looking, maybe it was her eyes or something stiff and proud in the way she held herself, yes, there was something here worth hunting down, a man would think. . . .

"It's funny dancing with Hunt," Jen said. "You think he's made different from other people—all solid gold clinking in him instead of lungs and a liver—and it's like his skin was more expensive than other people's, all heavy silk, the very best. It's like dancing with a prince."

"Who—that loafer?" Morry laughed scornfully.

"I used to think so," said Jen, "but you told me how wonderful he was, don't you remember, and I guess I was wrong."

"I don't know about that," said Morry uncomfortably. "Anyway he's not so different as you think from other people."

From far off came the train whistle, an invitation to mystery, to limitless adventure. A few stars showed up faintly. He could see Jen's face on that magazine cover, in a filmy white ballet skirt . . . it was all very far-off, some place where trains went . . . Hunt Russell, there, too, smiling quietly . . .

Morry's arms went around Jen's shoulder, he kissed her hard on the mouth and received as reward a stinging slap in the face. He sat up straight, rubbing his face indignantly. Jen jumped up.

"You leave me alone, Morry! Don't you suppose I know about you and Nettie Farrell? Don't you suppose Grace and I followed you down to the Murphys that night, don't you think I got any sense? So leave me alone, now, will you?"

"Say—oh now say, Jen——"

Morry was crushed by this unexpected attack.

"Go on and kiss Nettie if you've got to be kissing somebody," Jen flung at him. "Don't think I want to have Nettie Farrell's old beaux, I'll get my own, thank you."

She fled indoors leaving the screen to shut in his face.

Morry's face burned at this attack. He was through with Jen St. Clair, that was certain. Nobody was going to slap his face, no tough little kid could tell him anything. With his hands jammed in his pockets he slouched across the alley to his home, angrier at every step with Jen, with Grace for following him that night, with everybody. Inside the hall doorway he bumped into Nettie who was standing there, her finger to her lips.

"I've been waiting for you," she whispered. "The Murphys are out tonight. I'm going to be alone."

It was the last straw.

"Isn't that too bad?" he snorted mockingly. "Now, isn't that a goddamned shame?"

He pushed past her upstairs and banged his door loudly shut. Nettie stamped her foot furiously and went back into the shop.

Mrs. Pepper cried telling Nettie about how Mrs. Abbott had changed, and Nettie answered that it was very funny for Mrs. Abbott to act that way after the years they'd known each other. They stood in front of Robbins' Jewelry Store discussing it.

"I'd hardly got inside the door, Nettie," said Mrs. Pepper tremulously. "I'd just set my grip down when she came out of the workroom, white as a sheet, and she said to me, 'Mrs. Pepper, you've been coming here a long time, too long, in fact, and I just wanted to tell you that it's going to stop right now. I got no place,' she says, 'for your corsets and trash in my shop, and it'll suit me if you take your stuff somewheres else.' . . . Well, Nettie, you know how I am, tenderhearted, and always a good friend to everyone. I didn't know what in the world to say. I said, what is it, whatever happened? . . . And she said, tightmouthed, the way she is, 'It's my place, Mrs. Pepper, I think I have the right to have or not have people here just as I like.' . . . I said who's been talking behind my back, just tell me their names and I'll make them answer for it."

"What'd she say to that?" Nettie asked, thinking over the slurring remarks she herself had often made about the corsetiere, and feeling rather guilty. "Did she say anyone had talked about you?"

"That's just it," answered Mrs. Pepper. "She looked funny and said, oh, so you know there's talk, do you, but she wouldn't say anything else, so I packed up my few little things and went right across the street to the Bauers, and Mrs. Bauer's letting me have a room upstairs for fittings. But, Nettie, what could anyone have said about me? You know I've always tried to be a lady, I've never done anything a lady wouldn't, you know that, Nettie."

Nettie kept her eyes fixed on a gilt clock in Robbins' window.

"Well, she might have heard about you and Mr. Fischer," she said gently. "After all, you know he is a married man."

Mrs. Pepper's little red mouth made an O of astonishment.

"The very idea! If that isn't like a little town. Just because Mr. Fischer and I both travel from place to place and are old friends, people get to talking! So that's what she heard, you think . . . Nettie, that does make me feel badly! . . . But I'm glad you told me. I never thought people would be so wicked saying things, when I've tried always to be a lady in spite of being alone in the world. Goodness, Mr. Fischer would be so upset to know anyone in Lamptown talked like that!"

Nettie said no more. They started back up the street and Mrs. Pepper forlornly left Nettie at the Bauers' front door.

Bauers' rooms were so dark and musty and gloomy. The Bon
Ton had seemed gay with girls chattering in and out all the
time over hats, telling who was going with who, and laughing. . . . But Hermann Bauer never smiled and Hulda Bauer
had stopped thinking and settled into a contented jellyfish the
day she married Hermann. It was not a jolly place at all for a
sun-loving soul, and Mrs. Pepper, lacing a customer into a
lavender satin brocade model in her dingy bedroom, dropped
a few unexpected tears down the girl's back.

"Mrs. Bauer is good to me, of course," she choked bravely,
"and Mr. Bauer is such a fine man that I'd be the last one to
complain—but I think dark places like this ought to be torn
down, I do, really. It would be a blessing if it burned, it's so
gloomy, and when you're in trouble with your dearest friend,
too—honey, are you sure this doesn't pinch your tummy?"

Nettie tried to find out why Elsinore had taken such a serious step but Elsinore gave her no details. She seemed silent
and preoccupied, and all she said was that Mrs. Pepper was a
hypocrite and besides the Bon Ton had no place for all those
corset boxes and trash. Nettie was glad the extra work was out
of the way, she was especially glad because now she was to go
with Elsinore, it seemed, on buying expeditions to Cleveland
or Columbus. Before, Nettie had kept shop while Elsinore and
Mrs. Pepper went off together, all dressed up for a day in the
city. Elsinore said this time they would close the shop and take
an early train, so Nettie sat up half the night sewing a new frill
on her black suit and washing out white silk gloves. She'd been
to Cleveland a few times but this was most exciting because
now she was going as a business woman, a woman of affairs.

They sat in the chair car going in the next morning.
Elsinore, with dark hollows under her eyes from thinking so
desperately of the plan she had for the day, and Nettie,
dressed up and well-pleased with herself, her gloved hands
folded over her new gold mesh purse, a blue veil drooping
from her little hat, lace openwork on her black silk stockings.
This was her real sphere, Nettie thought, going to cities and
wearing little veils and white gloves and perfume, being a
woman of the world and she thought it was funny her living
in Lamptown when anyone could tell she was more of a city
type . . . She was twenty now and she certainly was doing

more with her life than other girls her age were. She was bound she'd be a success, this year she'd join the Eastern Stars, she thought, and she'd read "Laddie" and "The Little Shepherd of Kingdom Come"; she'd get baptized, too, join a church, and whenever she met anyone from out of town she'd always correspond with them so that she'd be getting letters from Cincinnati and Birmingham and St. Louis all at one time. She'd take dancing lessons, too, only she didn't see how she'd ever have the nerve to practice in public with all the younger people. She'd have a hatshop of her own, some day, she'd call it the Paris Shop, or maybe The Elite, Nettie Farrell, prop.

Nettie glanced guiltily at Elsinore to see if this disloyal thought had somehow been overheard, but Elsinore was drumming nervously on the windowsill, watching fields and villages slide past the window.

They went to different stores in the morning buying silks and trimmings and they were to meet in the Taylor Arcade for lunch but Nettie got mixed up the way she always did in Cleveland and waited in the Colonial Arcade instead. She stood at the entrance watching for Elsinore till half past one when a dark Jewish man smoking a cigar spoke to her. Nettie stared him down so haughtily that he rushed contritely into a little cigar store to peer at her over the inner curtains. Nettie, after a minute or two, walked slowly past the cigar store and somehow dropped her purse so he came out to pick it up. This time Nettie thanked him very distantly and when he went on asking her if she was just in town for the day she answered him rather loftily so he could see she was not an ordinary pickup.

When Elsinore finally decided to look for Nettie in the other Arcade she saw her through the glass window of a little tea-room at a table with some stranger. The man was talking and Nettie was sedately holding a tea-cup, little finger flying. Elsinore went in and Nettie said,

"This is Mr. Schwarz, Mrs. Abbott. He used to travel for the same company Mr. Abbott did, isn't that funny, but now he's in the woolen business and he lives at the Gilsey. We're going to the Hippodrome this afternoon while you're seeing wholesalers."

Elsinore had been wondering how she would get rid of Nettie for the afternoon so she was much more agreeable over tea and cinnamon buns than she usually was with strangers, and Mr. Schwarz, at first wary, began to warm up to the idea of a little party for four. He said he'd call up the hotel and get hold of a friend of his named Wohlman, who also was in woolen, and tonight they'd all go to the Rat-skellar and afterwards to a show the Hermits were giving. The idea alarmed Elsinore and she got away as fast as she could.

"Five thirty, then, in the Hollenden lobby," said Nettie gaily, being a woman of the world.

Elsinore took a Woodland Avenue car out to East 55th Street. She didn't dare think of what she was about to do or she might lose courage. She thought of Mrs. Pepper and after three weeks of hating her, even the mental image of the woman was distorted into a fat, lewd beast that deserved an-nihilation. Elsinore wasn't sorry she'd sent her out of the Bon Ton, she wasn't sorry when Mrs. Pepper's blue eyes welled with tears over this broken friendship; she wished she had it in her to be even crueller; she would like to have hurt her as much as she had been hurt herself. . . .

All these years, then, the town whisper about Fischer and Mrs. Pepper had been well-founded. Elsinore felt as betrayed as if Fischer had really been her own husband, she wanted fiercely to be revenged, not on him, but on the woman. Nor was the desire for revenge a spasmodic thought that died out after the first shock of suspicions proved true; she thought of it night and day ever since the rainy night Mrs. Pepper had gone out with Dode to meet him somewhere; she thought of them on Thursday nights at the Casino watching his heavy mask-like face. . . . She had wondered often about his wife and now she felt somehow identified with her, as if Mrs. Pepper had delib-erately wronged them both. What kept her curious indignation at fever pitch was the thought of how long Mrs. Pepper had fooled everyone with her wide innocent blue eyes, her baby face, her dainty lady-like ways, her sweet detachment in men-tioning his name. Worse than a vampire, Elsinore grimly de-cided, worse than the commonest factory girl, because she pretended so much, because she fooled people.

At the other end of the street-car, two girls in white flannel suits giggled over yesterday's moonlight ride on the Steamer Eastland, and the conductor asked them if they were going to

the big brewers' picnic next Sunday at Put-in-Bay. Elsinore
listened to them intently because she wanted to know things
that people around Fischer knew, she wanted to hear and see
the same things he did, she could almost be him, she could
half-close her eyes and admire women and young girls the
way he did. This was what he saw on his way to and from his
house, and now that they were close to 55th Street, that must
be the church over yonder where he sent his children to
Sunday-school, this must be the market where his wife did
her trading, this was his stop. . . .

Elsinore's knees were shaky getting off the car. If she could
only keep in mind how Mrs. Pepper had fooled her and Mrs.
Fischer, she'd be able to go ahead with her plan, but she kept
forgetting and having stage-fright over being so near his place
and so near to coming face to face with his wife. She asked a
street-cleaner where this number was and he pointed out an
old house set far back from the street with a sign in the window in black and white—

HARRY FISCHER
Ballroom Dancing

Oh, she'd never have the courage to walk down that path-
way with someone probably peeking at her from behind the
lace curtains, and perhaps someone following her, too. . . .
This frightened her, she looked over her shoulder, now she
had a distinct feeling of being followed. If Nettie had taken it
into her head to follow her, what would she say?

"I came to arrange private dancing lessons for both of us,"
she'd tell Nettie if it came to that, and she'd say it was always
impossible to get a private word with Fischer about it in
Lamptown so she'd just dropped in. . . .

If it was Fischer himself behind her, though, or Mrs. Pepper, or Charles, or someone from Lamptown. . . . Still, there
wasn't a chance of any such thing, why should she feel guilty
when she was only doing a friendly duty? . . . She walked
quickly up to the grey gingerbread porch. She wondered if he
owned this house, if he had a dance-hall in it the way Mrs.
Pepper had once said, and it made her ache to think of all the
things in his life that she could never guess thinking about
him in the Bon Ton. . . . She was on the porch, in a minute

she'd turn around and run for her life . . . no, she was ringing the door-bell and her black gloved hand was quite steady. She couldn't run now, even if Fischer himself should confront her, her legs were numb, she doubted if she could even speak. She heard steps inside, the sound of a slap, and a child screeching and then the door opened.

"Well?"

Two tow-headed children on a red scooter stared at her with bold black eyes, their mother tried to push them out of the way of the door, she was a large ash-blonde woman with heavy breasts and her voice was deep like a singer's with a vaguely Scandinavian accent. His wife. . . . Yes, she was Mrs. Fischer. The lady wanted to know about dancing lessons? Friday and Saturday were his Cleveland days, if she wanted to sign up for the course and leave a five dollar deposit. . . .

"It's not about dancing," Elsinore said. "It's about him that I wanted to see you."

Her throat felt swollen and tight, talking was like trying to scream in your sleep, driving your voice through your shut mouth with all your might and having it come out only a hoarse whisper.

"There's a woman that wants to make trouble for you and I thought someone ought to tell you so you could stop it."

Fischer's wife just stared stupidly at her. The largest tow-headed child with a little yelp turned his toy car around and scooted down the hall, its bell going tingalingaling, and the littlest one remembered that his mother had slapped him and resumed his wailing, burying his face in his mother's skirts.

Mrs. Fischer pushed open the screen door.

"Do you want to come inside and tell me what you're talking about, missus?" she said, studying Elsinore from head to foot with a puzzled and not at all friendly eye. "What's this about my husband and who are you, anyway, that's what I want to know?"

Elsinore could feel her face reddening, she must be careful now, or Fischer might guess who had told.

"It doesn't matter who I am," she said hurriedly, "but I thought you ought to know—as one woman to another, understand—that there's someone your husband goes with out of town, there's a woman crazy about him, trying to break up your home."

She'd said it now, but Mrs. Fischer's thick pasty face took on an ugly expression. Her pale blue eyes narrowed, under the heavy colorless brows.

"I suppose you don't want to make trouble, too, hey? I suppose I'm to believe a party coming in out of the blue sky and not saying who she is, just bringing tattle tales to see what harm she can do——"

Elsinore backed away from the door, alarmed at the woman's tone. Mrs. Fischer came out on the porch after her.

"See here, what right have you got, coming to my home making trouble for me? If my husband's doings don't suit you, then you don't need to watch 'em, just mind your own step, that's all. Who are you, coming here with your tattle? Where you from, anyway? Who told you I wanted to hear tales about Harry?"

"I didn't want you to be fooled, that was all," gasped Elsinore, and backed down the porch steps with Mrs. Fischer coming right after her, her hands on her hips. "You had a right to know."

"Well, who said you were the one with a right to tell," Mrs. Fischer asked contemptuously. "I've got enough trouble without strangers trying to cook up more. I'd thank you to clear out, and I'll tell you here and now if anybody's got the right to spy on Harry, it's me, and nobody else, understand? So!"

Elsinore, faint with shame, rushed toward the street. Both children now were crying loudly and the toy car bell dingled raucously in her ears. She knew people were watching her, someone was following her again, that much was certain, she felt their distrustful eyes boring through her back, the footsteps behind her were ominous, but when she dared to look back it was only a mail man and further off two women wheeling go-carts, she could not find those watchful eyes. Fog-horns croaked on the lake and made her head buzz, the city noises seemed more than she could bear. She climbed aboard the first street car that came along, it was pure luck that it was going in the right direction. Her face would never stop burning, she was so shamed, yet she was glad in a way because she'd had to do just that thing, she'd simply had to, nothing could have stopped her, and now it was over with, that was all. . . . What would she say to Nettie, she won-

dered, what could she tell her? . . . She sat next to a big colored woman who asked her where the May Company was,
where you got off for the Interurban Station, how you got
out to Gates Mills? She didn't know, she kept mumbling in
reply, and planned what to say to Nettie.

"I went to Halle's for that taffeta, then I walked over to the
Square and sat down for a while, then I went to the braid
place, then I went into De Klyn's for a sundae and cocoa—
no, for a cup of tea, then—then——"

She went into the hotel lobby where she was to meet
Nettie. She was dizzy and faint, for she wasn't used to
crowds and street cars. Suspicious eyes continued to bore
through her, she was certain someone had followed her all
day, she was certain someone was reading her guilty thoughts.

It was long after six when Nettie came. Mr. Schwarz, perhaps a little self-conscious, was not with her, but Nettie
talked about him a great deal on the way to the depot, because she'd never been out with an older man, a man of the
world, before. . . . Elsinore did not breathe easily until she
was finally on the train for Lamptown. No one had seen her.
No one had followed her. No one knew.

"So then we went down to the Ratskellar," Nettie chattered on excitedly, "and Mr. Schwarz asked me what I'd have
since I hated beer so much. So I took a Clover Club cocktail
because Mr. Schwarz said that in Cleveland they were absolutely all the go."

Elsinore didn't dare go to the dance on Thursday night,
she was afraid to face the dancing teacher for a little while.
She closed the shop and sat in the dark watching the Casino
windows, seeing couples whirl past and hearing Fischer's big
voice boom out the commands. She leaned forward on the
wicker settee and wrung her hands each time the music
started for a new dance. If there was a circle two-step
tonight she might have gotten him for a partner for a minute
or two, but now she'd ruined the chances of that. She
wouldn't dare go up again, he'd ask what right she had going to his wife. . . . At least Mrs. Pepper hadn't gone to the
Casino either, because Nettie had seen her get on the street
car going upstate earlier in the day. . . .

The Bauers were in their window peering out at the passing girls, and she reflected bitterly that she might as well be Hulda Bauer now, nothing but a spectator. She saw Grace come out in front of the restaurant and hoo-oo, then the Delaneys' girl, Jen, came running across the street to join her, and they went up the Casino steps together. She saw her own son standing in front of her darkened shop, smoking, waiting for the right moment to go over. When Jen and Grace went up he turned around and stared idly at the dimly outlined hats in the Bon Ton window. Then Elsinore realized that in spite of the darkness, the lights reflected from the street made her faintly visible because Morry frowned and suddenly pressed his face against the pane, staring inside, as if he was seeing a ghost. She stood very still but after all her face probably showed up white and shadowy for Morry shivered and backed away, she saw him toss his cigarette into the gutter and hurry across the street, stopping at the foot of the Casino stairs for a puzzled backward glance at the Bon Ton.

There would be next Thursday night and the next and the next. . . . Elsinore grew dizzy thinking of all the torture in store for her, for how could she ever look at Fischer again after her Cleveland visit. . . . His wife must have told him everything and he had told Mrs. Pepper and probably Mrs. Pepper had put two and two together. . . . Elsinore dragged her feet slowly up the stairs to bed, but she wouldn't sleep tonight, she'd lie there listening to the music and the applause, and think. . . . It was no use, she knew that no matter what the risk she'd go next Thursday night. After all, she hadn't told Fischer's wife her name or even that she was from Lamptown, so how could anyone possibly guess?

She drew a rocking chair up to her bedroom window and huddled there in her nightdress.

"Dance Number Three."

Today some factory girls trying on hats had talked about the chance Fischer had to have a studio in Chicago only he'd refused to give up his Cleveland headquarters. It had been a great chance, they said, and he might change his mind, of course. Elsinore thought of dark, silent Thursday nights going on forever, for the rest of her life, and a Lamptown slackening into a dull shuffle with no Fischer to count out the rhythm. . . .

Well, there was always a chance for a new millinery store in a big city like Chicago, she could get on there, she could always manage her business, Chicago wouldn't be any harder than Lamptown. Now it seemed a question of the Bon Ton moving to Chicago, and she'd forgotten why.

It must be a good dance tonight. Everyone sang softly with the orchestra, they blended into one gay humming voice that might be swelling out of the rickety old building itself though no one could believe it to look at the sleepy expressionless faces of Hermann and Hulda Bauer in the first floor window.

> "Has anybody here seen Kelly—
> K-e- double l-y-
> Anybody here seen Kelly——"

Elsinore sat in the chair and wished she hadn't been such a coward as to stay away. She'd never stay home again, that was certain.

In the smoking-room of the Casino Morry Abbott read a magazine with a red devil on the cover. If he went out on the floor Grace would smile at him waiting for him to dance with her, and he wasn't going to be trapped into anything again. If he looked up from the magazine he would see Jen whirling by with Sweeney, the telegraph operator, or with his own fore-man; if she'd been sitting out by herself he might ask her for a dance but he wasn't going to compete with other men, he'd never do that. Let her have them, but he could tell by the way she flipped her skirts passing the smoking room that she wanted him to be jealous, and it annoyed him. He read on resolutely, all the stories ended in suicide, he wished he knew things so he could read the one story in French. He looked at it wistfully—'l'amour' was love, that much he did know. . . . Something made him lift his eyes and there was Jen dancing with Hunt. Morry threw down the book and went out. Some yellow-haired girl in a red flannel dress was sitting by the door chewing gum. He asked her to dance.

It was a pretty how-de-do, he thought, when people as fussy as old Mrs. Delaney let a kid go to dances and run with old rounders like Russell. He saw now that Jen wore Grace Terris' dress—Grace was wearing a new one—she had her hair fixed up like Grace's as near as she could make it, and she had on high-heeled shoes, surely Grace's, since if you looked closely you could tell they were too big for her, and she seemed unreasonably well-pleased with herself. Morry found himself burning with righteous anger, partly because she seemed able to dance as well as anyone else without having had any lessons, and partly because she giggled too loud and tweaked Sweeney's necktie. He tried to ignore her but she always managed to get right in front of him and when he'd look somewhere else he'd encounter Grace's steady meaning gaze. All right, he'd go home, he wasn't going to stand around here like a fool, but when he put on his coat Hunt Russell was in the coat-room smoking and kidding the fat little hat-check girl. He beckoned Morry.

"Stick around, Abbott, we'll pick up a couple of women and drive Fischer over to Marion. . . . Got a date?"

It was the royal command and Morry obediently took off his coat. Dode wasn't around tonight and he knew Hunt would pick the two hardest-boiled girls in the hall but he didn't care. You had to do what Hunt asked you to—you wanted to, somehow. . . . He went back in the smoking room and read the red devil magazine again. Sweeney and his factory foreman came in and asked him to go over to Delaney's for a beer or two, and Morry said briefly.

"Can't. Going out with Hunt."

He was proud because Hunt didn't ask just anybody. He went with Hunt for ham sandwiches at Bauers' and a pint of rye at Delaney's at the end of the last dance. When they came out Hunt went on up to get Fischer and Morry strolled over to get in Hunt's car. The women were already in—one in front and one in back. Morry took a second glance and saw that the evening was already spoiled, for the girl in front was Jen, and the one in back, swathed in floating scarfs, was Grace.

"Oh, Jen, look, here's Morry!" gurgled Grace. "Won't we have a circus? Wouldn't Dode take our heads off if she knew? Wouldn't she, Morry?"

Morry gloomily got in beside Grace. Jen turned around to give him a triumphant smile. Morry was annoyed, because while he himself was dazzled by Hunt's glamorous position he thought it was ridiculous for a girl to be taken in by all that bunk.

"Thought you couldn't stand Hunt," he challenged her. "Thought you was just about going to burn up his house some day. I notice you've changed your mind."

"I never was in an automobile before," Jen resentfully explained. "I guess you'd go, too."

"Jen's never been anywhere," Grace laughed. "Why, when I was fifteen there was two fellas crazy over me and I had dates every night. I was more like a man's woman, I was. I certainly had a good time and I knew what was what, too."

Fischer and Hunt came down and Morry moved over to let Fischer in beside Grace. With a great roaring of the motor they started. Grace wanted Fischer to be affectionate and she kept leaning against him.

"Look at this, Jen," she'd call and playfully wrap her arms around him but Fischer firmly shook her off. He winked at Morry once and made a wry face, but Morry was only able to manage a half-hearted smile in turn. It was all easy enough to understand. Hunt was amused by Jen the way the men said he always was by every new kind of girl, he asked Morry because he'd gotten the idea she was Morry's girl, that was all. He really didn't give a damn who was in the back-seat so long as he had what he wanted beside him in front there. It made his invitation not so flattering after all, and Morry blamed Jen for this disillusion.

Certainly the ride wasn't any fun with Grace on one hand making a fool of herself over Fischer and Jen in front with her hat off and the wind blowing her black hair all over, not talking, just watching Hunt as if he was some great wonder. She'd get it from the old lady when she got in, Morry thought, and if Dode O'Connell ever found out, she'd get it from her, too. It took two hours to drive to Marion—it would be at least four or five when they got back, and the Delaneys wouldn't stand for that. Jen ought to be more careful. Thinking of this Morry got angrier than ever with Grace for egging her into it, and he was angry with Hunt too. Hunt and Fischer drank the whiskey between them, though Grace, with much tittering took more than a few swigs from the bottle to show she was used to going out. Fischer didn't talk except to call something out to Hunt once in a while; he was sleepy, he said, and leaned back on the seat with his eyes closed most of the way.

It was three when they got to his hotel in Marion and then Hunt insisted that they all go over to the Quick Lunch for ham and eggs. Grace was eager for this because she'd only been a guest in a restaurant twice and she was anxious to be lordly with other waitresses.

"You'd better take those kids back to Lamptown, Hunt," Fischer advised. "You'll have Bill Delaney on your neck if you keep his girl out much longer."

"How'd you like to mind your own business?" Hunt inquired, lighting a cigarette. "This young lady's just about able to take care of herself."

Fischer got his handbag from under Morry's feet and banged the car door shut.

"I'm sure I hope so," he said calmly. "Well, good-night."

"To hell with you," answered Hunt. He drove over to the Quick Lunch and they got out. Morry was sleepy, he'd never been out so late, and much as he wanted to be ranked as a sport like Hunt and Fischer, he only wished he was home in bed, and the thought of the long ride home sickened him, he didn't know why except that he knew Jen would get a good whaling when she got in and she was just a little fool and it was all her own fault. She was excited about being out with men in strange towns after midnight, but she was scared too, you could tell by her eyes, she was scared of what the old lady would say to her coming home in the morning.

"I knew Fischer wanted a date with me," Grace said over the white porcelain table. "He always is looking at me with those big black eyes sort of as if he'd like to say something to me but was afraid to speak out, I suppose on account of his wife. I kidded him to-night about being so bashful and he had to admit that he was, did you hear us kidding, Jen?"

Jen nodded and looked at the big white clock on the wall. It said four o'clock but Hunt wasn't in any hurry and Grace was having the time of her life. She got to talking about all the other swell restaurants she'd been in, and somehow her memory had blurred so that she seemed to have been the most valued patron in these resorts and not an employee at all. Nobody listened to her. Jen kept looking at the clock, more scared than ever now, but afraid to suggest going for fear they'd think she was young and not used to being out.

Grace talked and Morry yawned over his coffee and squirmed restlessly when he saw Hunt stare lazily at Jen.

"Cold, Baby?" Hunt asked Jen when she shivered once. Then when they finally started back to the car Morry saw him put his arm over her shoulder.

"Good kid," he murmured and slid in behind the wheel. "Say, Abbott, anything left of that quart?"

"No," lied Morry, because he wasn't going to be killed tonight by wild driving. "I finished it up."

All the way back driving into the sunrise Hunt kept one arm flung over Jen's shoulders and Grace, after many coy attempts to engage Morry's attention, moved over to the edge of the seat and hummed softly to herself; sometimes she'd call Jen's attention to this house which was just like her Uncle File's, or that railroad depot which was only half as big as the one in Tiffin. Morry saw none of these things, he only saw Hunt's arm around Jen and he thought that it was just as Hogan said—Hunt Russell wasn't so damned much, people in Lamptown were taken in by him only because of the money his old man had made and Hunt was nothing but a sport and a waster with no more guts to him than a jellybean. Dode O'Connell was the only woman that wanted him, he wasn't any matinee idol with his greying temples and his weak chin, what made him so complacently sure he could get Jen St. Clair if he so condescended?

Grace pointed toward Hunt's arm.

"Do you allow that, Morry?" she asked archly.

"Has he got anything to say about it?" Hunt called back, and slowed the car to lean over and kiss Jen. But she didn't slap him, Morry noted cynically, she didn't seem to mind at all, so Morry sullenly put his own arm around Grace for Jen to be sure and see.

It was six o'clock when they drew up in front of Bauer's. Grace rushed in, eager for Sweeney the telegraph operator to come in for breakfast so she could brag about the wild party. Morry and Jen crossed the street together. In the alley between their two homes they looked at each other.

"Well, you're going to catch it," Morry said. "It's Hunt's fault. He had no business asking you out, he knows how Bill is."

"I had a good time," answered Jen, but she looked a little doubtfully toward the saloon.

"See, you're afraid to go up," Morry challenged her. "Do you think she'd have the nerve to beat you up?"

"Pooh!" bragged Jen. "I'd like to see her try. I'd tell her right where to get off."

She was in no hurry, though. Morry wanted to do something big, in a casual, off-handed way to go over and pave the way for Jen, but he knew he was a lot more afraid of Bill's mother than even Jen was. Only the Hunt Russells knew how to have their way, how to get things, all anybody else could ever do was to wish and be afraid. He got his key out for his side door, and still Jen hung back. She took his handkerchief and wiped her shoes off carefully, and straightened her hair.

"Wish I was Grace," she said. "I wouldn't be afraid of anybody then. I'd be on my own and nobody could say a word to me if I stayed out late."

"You're pretty stuck on Hunt, now, aren't you?" Morry said. "I noticed you kissed him and made no fuss about it, either."

Jen looked at him silently until Morry's own eyes dropped.

"I guess you know well enough who I like, Morry," she said. "Well. . . . I might as well go home and get it over with. They wouldn't dare lick me, you bet your life."

She winked at him and walked boldly across the court. Morry let himself indoors and climbed upstairs. His mother was in the doorway of his room, looking very pale and tired in the grey morning light, her brown braids hanging over her wrapper.

"I didn't mean to wake you—I was just out on a little ride," he stammered.

"That's all right, I wasn't sleeping anyway," she murmured. "I only looked in to see if you'd come in."

She didn't wait for an answer, just smiled and pulled her wrapper around her to go back to her room, her long braids swinging. Funny she didn't mind his being out all night. She hadn't even listened to his excuse. Morry was puzzled. Funny her not sleeping. . . . Morry for some reason remembered his father's insistent questioning that night behind the saloon, something hit him sickeningly in the pit of the stomach.

His mother. What if . . . Yes, there was some man. His mother. . . . Morry sat down on the bed and shut his eyes. He heard her moving about on the other side of the wall but suddenly he could see her face before him more distinctly than he ever had—the grey eyes now with faint lines at the corners, the fine hairs of her nostrils, the unsmiling straight mouth, the face of a stranger. . . . He was stiff, sitting there so rigidly, and his eyeballs ached for sleep, but he dared not close them because he had to think about this thing . . . His mother. . . .

On the Delaney back porch Jen rubbed her hand over her eyes to make sure of what she saw. But it was true, no doubt of it. There sat her yellow telescope, packed and strapped, with her hat and coat on top of it. The door was locked. Jen resolutely tugged at the screen door but even that was hooked tight. The old lady had fired her for staying out—that was all there was to it. She sat down on the steps, frightened. She fumbled with the hat,—it was the round sailor she'd worn away from the orphanage and it was too little with a childish rubber band under the chin. She slipped it on. The coat was too tight, too, and the sleeves hardly came below the elbow. Gee, how she'd grown, she thought. . . . She picked up the telescope and went uncertainly down the stairs. She knew the old lady was somewhere behind a curtain grimly watching to see what she'd do. Well, there wasn't anything to do but go.

At the foot of the steps Jen shifted the bag to the other hand and looked toward Bauer's then over toward the Bon Ton. No use looking, nobody was going to look after you but your own self. She looked up toward the screen door again. Bill might come out and call her back. She waited but the door didn't open. She guessed she was pretty lucky the old lady hadn't given her a beating when it came right down to it. Her knees shaking Jen picked her way across the back lot to the railroad. There weren't any trains in sight. She might as well get going. . . . She looked over her shoulder at the Delaney kitchen window but nobody was leaning out there beckoning her to come back. . . . With both arms around the yellow telescope she started grimly walking down the track.

She'd leave her telescope in the Tower with Sweeney, Jen thought; she'd walk east down the tracks and get a ride on a three-wheeler maybe to the next town. If she could get near Libertyville she'd go to the Home and get Lil. Then—then— well, she could get a job like Grace's in a restaurant, couldn't she? She was too ashamed ever to go back to Lamptown. People would know she'd been locked out because she stayed out all night and they'd say, just as old Mrs. Delaney had, that she'd turned out bad the way adopted girls always did. She'd get Lil herself now, so that Lil wouldn't ever be adopted and turn out bad.

It was a foggy morning. In the ditch beside the tracks burdocks and milkweed propped up dewy spider webs, fields were veiled in lavender, in the grey sky a hawk circled lower and lower so that birds were still. Jen hurried to reach the Tower before Sweeney got through because the day trick operators were stricter about visitors.

She was excited because she was going to do something big now, get Lil, and be on her own, but a faint sick feeling came over her when she thought she'd turned out bad the way Mrs. Delaney had always said, and that Lamptown with its dance music and Morry Abbott was behind her. The sun struggled through sooty pink clouds over the Big Four woods, lying under the trees were tramps sleeping with their hats over their faces and newspapers for covers. Two were kneeling by a little bonfire, skinning a rabbit. Jen was afraid of them because once a man was murdered here, they found his head rolling in the ditch and the stump of his cork leg. . . . She got off the track for a slow freight with cattle cars of whinnying western ponies and lambs bleating through their bars piteously. The brakeman waved his cap to her from the top of the caboose and Jen waved back. Names in big letters on the cars tantalized her—CLEVELAND, CINCINNATI & ST. LOUIS,—MICHIGAN CENTRAL—PERE MARQUETTE—LAKE SHORE R.R.—SANTA FE R.R.—DELAWARE LACKAWANNA R.R.— Jen saw the brakeman far down the tracks still waving to her.

"Good-bye," she called to him and waved again.

She stumbled through the cinders on to the Yards. Everything was different, it was a new world today, a world to be measured and appraised with a view to possible conquest. As for Lamptown, it wasn't her Lamptown now, she saw it hungrily from the outside where she belonged. Behind the black fences all along here were the backyards of Shanteyville, there was the spire of the Church of Our Lady. Shanteyville back-yards were different from the boarding house backyards where they sometimes had hollyhocks and grape arbors and swings for the girls. Here were only tumbled-down chicken houses with skinny pin-feathered chickens flapping around, washings always hanging out, grey sheds with dirty children on the roofs screaming and waving to the trains. . . . But even Shanteyville was gay in its shiftless way and people were lucky to live there. . . . Jen wanted to reach the Tower be-fore the factory men from this end of town started down the tracks on their way to work. They'd know she'd been locked out and they'd know it was because she'd stayed out all night.

It was funny about her feet walking along the ties as if they belonged to somebody else. She thought Bill might be fol-lowing her to bring her back, indeed she was so sure that she didn't even turn around for fear of being disappointed. She stepped over rails and humming wires to the Tower stairs. Sweeney was in there alone with his fingers on the little black keys, the room ticked and throbbed with important messages.

"Hey, Sweeney, watch this bag till I come back, will you?"

Sweeney was mad because the day man was late this morning.

"You get the hell out of here before Tucker finds you!"

Jen shoved the bag inside and scurried downstairs again. The factory whistles were blowing for work and the men were coming down the track swinging their lunch pails. The old sta-tion agent hobbled over tracks swinging a bunch of keys and Jen saw him staring at her curiously as he unlocked the ticket-office. She caught sight of one of the freight hands, a young Swede named Davey often in Bill's saloon, pumping a handcar down the track. He sometimes let her ride and today when she got on, his anguish over the English language saved her from any questions. On the handcar you ran off the tracks into cinderheaps every time you saw an engine ahead and you couldn't get very far that way. Davey was going to some sec-tion workers a few miles out, but only a few miles out made Lamptown seem far, far away, it seemed like a dream, last night in the restaurant hadn't happened, or the locked door,—the real thing was the Children's Home where she belonged.

Near the water-tank some Pullman cars were on siding, their names were spelled out in gold letters over their black sides—GRETCHEN—MINNEHAHA—NIGHTFALL—BLACK BEAUTY—. Fortunate people looked out the windows yawning, and Jen saw a woman in a heavenly blue kimona smoking a cigarette. When would one ever get old, she wondered passionately, and know everything and have everything,—if she could only be old like the woman in the blue kimona, and be looking back on all this, perfectly sure of herself, quite unafraid. . . .

The rotten planks on the handcar tore her dress, the old lady would scold her for that—but no,—the old lady wouldn't scold her any more. The tracks went through low fields past an old quarry and here Davey pushed off and Jen said good-bye.

"You know where you're going?" stammered Davey, a little uneasily.

"Sure, I do."

She waded through muddy pastureland to the road. It was the road to the Orphanage at Libertyville, she could tell that, so she wasn't so far out of her way. She'd get Lil, then the two of them would get to Cleveland somehow and find their mother, that was the best thing to do. If her mother couldn't take care of them, why they could work, they were big enough. And nobody could stop you from going to your own mother. . . . She'd get in the back way somehow and find Lil, and even if she did run into the matron she wouldn't be afraid to tell her she'd come for her sister. . . . At least she didn't think she'd be afraid. But now that she was so near the Home the very trees had an air of inescapable authority, the woods, the fields, the houses all seemed busy and complete as if they were all there first and would forever be in command. Jen couldn't believe there had ever been moments when she'd thought herself free of them, when she'd actually planned to defy them and take Lil away. . . . She'd have to be at least ten or twenty years older, very rich, and with a bodyguard of powerful citizens before she'd dare venture inside the Home gates. . . . They'd treat her as if she'd just run away again, the way she used to do, and been caught; they wouldn't believe she'd ever been adopted and out of their hands. She'd never get away again, either, they'd hear from Mrs. Delaney about her and they'd put her to work for the rest of her life in the Laundry the way they did orphans that were too afraid to go out in the world when they got their liberty. . . . Jen began walking slower and slower. No sign of anything like Lamptown all around her, only yards of bushes and then a rain-rusted R.F.D. box. She remembered these bushes for there were berry farms all along here. The orphans were let out to pick berries in the big season, they made six cents a quart and the one that made the most got a silver badge to wear, but all the pennies had to go to the Fund.

It was too late for strawberries but there were currants and gooseberries now, later on there would be potatoes to bug. Jen's heart dropped remembering when that was her world. She looked quickly over her shoulder—if someone from the Home saw her and recognized her she wouldn't stand a chance. They'd never let her get to her mother or to Lil either. She kept over to the edge of the road lingering in the tree shadows when anyone passed. If she was ninety years old, she thought resentfully, she'd never get over the fear of being clapped back in the Home again, made to say prayers out loud, sent out to pick berries. She'd been so certain she wasn't afraid of anything any more, but this one thing she'd always be afraid of.

There was a familiar sign tacked to a post here, "Red Clover Farm," and a muddy lane wound off the main road through a sparse woods. Far down this lane Jen saw someone coming, her hand over her eyes to stare longer and make sure. There was no doubt about it, it was a procession of children from the Home, all in blue calico and straw farm hats, berry pails clinking from their arms. In the lead was the Oldest Orphan, just as Jen had been once. Now it was a girl named Sadie whose folks were in the penitentiary so no one would ever take her. The Oldest Orphan carried the bun basket and behind her somewhere in this line must be Lil. Unconsciously Jen was backing into the bushes as she watched this oncoming procession, and thinking of how near she was to Lil her limbs began to shake. Suddenly she crashed through bushes and brambles for hiding,—she forgot about everything but the fear of being caught again and made to go back. Hypnotized, she watched the line getting nearer, she saw the Oldest Orphan's brown sullen face, she could almost have whispered

"Hoo-oo, Sadie!" but there was a woman in charge at the end. Then she saw Lil and it made her ache to see the sweet little dollface under the big straw-hat; she wanted to rush out and say, "Here I am, Lil, see, come to take you away just like I promised." But they'd only make her fall in line and go back to the Home, too, that's all they'd ever do, she wasn't strong enough for them yet, she couldn't beat them.

The line went on up the road, they didn't laugh or talk, just marched along doing as they were told, and presently they went into the fields and Lil was lost. Jen came out onto the road again, weak and puzzled, too, that there could be something you were so sure you could do and when the chance came you were helpless. . . . So this was the way she was going to look after Lil, was it, always looking out for her own hide first, never able to do the wonderful things she'd planned. . . . Rage swept over her at being young, young and little, as if some evil fairy had put that spell on her. Why must you be locked up in this dreadful cage of childhood for twenty or a hundred years? Nothing in life was possible unless you were old and rich, until then you were only small and futile before your tormentors, desperately waiting for the release that only years could bring. You boldly threw down your challenges and then ran away in a childish panic when someone picked them up. . . . Jen stumbled along the road, glowering down at the dust, sick because she had failed Lil. She'd never get over being ashamed as long as she lived. Lil had been within two yards of her and she'd let her go, she was like all the visitors to the Home who'd promised her long ago they'd come back for her, and they never did, they never came back.

Coming to the Crossroads Jen sat down on a pile of fence-rails. She wondered how far she was from Lamptown and she wanted to erase last night and go back. She thought of the pianola and the little gold chair from the World's Fair, and Morry. . . . She'd let Lamptown go and she'd let Lil go. She'd not been able to hold the things that meant the most to her. Maybe she never would. That was why she liked the tiny gold chair, you could close your hand tight over it and know it was always there.

She was hungry, it must be noon now, but that didn't seem to be the matter with her. The matter was that she'd failed.

She was dizzy, too, trying to figure out where all these roads went. Cleveland? Akron? Columbus? She would like to be on a train named Nightfall going to some place where she'd be twenty-five years old.

An empty hay wagon came lumbering along and Jen hailed it.

"Give us a ride, mister."

"Going east?"

"Sure."

The driver was an old man with a Santa Claus beard, he had a face busy with a tobacco quid. He might have been asleep for all the heed he paid to his passenger. It was a relief to ride, and now if they should pass the Home by any chance, Jen decided she would hide under the burlap bags in the back. They jogged along, and looking about her the old aching years came back to her; going along shady country roads with the low branches flapping against her face. . . . She could remember being as tall as a wagon wheel, the caked putty mud on the wheel, stepping on the spokes and then on the muddy step into the wagon. She could remember being allowed to drive, the black leather reins slipping in her little hands, and her feet not halfway to the floor swinging back and forth, brown mud-caked boots with the buttons off except the first and last; she could see again the horse's black tail swishing back and forth at the flies. She had now the same scratches from brambles that she had then, and here were the same knotty trees that Johnny Appleseed had planted.

Along the road were neat little white and green-trimmed farmhouses with thin scrawny women outside watering rusty geraniums or pansy beds. They were the same women as before, Jen thought, women that would slap you with the backs of their hands so that the wedding ring cut your cheek, if you dared to touch the conch-shell on the parlor mantel, or if you smelled the glass flowers in the vase; those women would make you get up before daylight to help wash, and you wouldn't get any breakfast till the washing was done, either. . . .

Digging post-holes along the road were men in overalls, jolly-seeming sun-bronzed men, but they weren't jolly at all, they'd call up the Orphanage any time to say, "This is R. Mac-Donald on the Ellery Road. I saw a couple of the orphans out by here and thought they might be running away. If you want me to, I'll pick them up and bring them right over." This was because people liked the idea of other people being locked up.

She would never smell hay or blackberries or honeysuckle without that gone feeling of being trapped, Jen realized, while pianola music, saloon smells, engines shrieking and the delicious smell of hot soapy dish-water from restaurant kitchens—these would always be gay symbols of escape.

They were at the pike road now, there was a street-car track crossing it and a big sign reading "Turnpike Dairy."

"Here's where I go, girlie," said the driver. "Somebody else'll give you a lift now, I guess."

Jen got down. She didn't move till the wagon was far out of sight. Then she started limping down the car tracks. Her feet were sore and her eyes were full of dust and sleep. She came to a wide shallow brook and tiptoed over the trestle high above it. If a street-car should unexpectedly come along she'd have to let herself down and dangle between the trestle-ties, hanging by her finger-tips, she planned. . . . She was so tired now she could go on forever without seeing or feeling anything. But this wasn't quite true, for before her was a banner across the road. It said—

WELCOME TO LAMPTOWN

Jen stopped dead. Lamptown had followed her, it seemed. Suddenly she was so happy she forgot her sore feet and started running as fast as she could down the track, stumbling over ties, panting for breath, her hair flying in all directions, but happy, happy, happy—because Lamptown had come after her. . . . She'd go straight to Bauer's and she'd say to Hermann, "I'm going to work for you. I'm going to stay up-stairs like Grace and be a waitress—please, please!"

Happy—happy—

Far back on the turnpike her round straw hat sat on the tracks, crushed to a pancake just as the street-car had left it.

Grace lay on her stomach on the bed and kicked up her heels. She was in a blue cotton chemise and with her glasses off and yellow hair hanging loose she didn't look so bad, Jen thought. Jen didn't want to take off the percale dress and white apron that Mrs. Bauer had given her, so she sat stiffly on the edge of the bed, occasionally stealing a glance at herself in the mirror.

"Men don't respect a factory girl the way they do a girl in a restaurant," said Grace. "I don't know why it is but they just don't. When you've been around as long as I have you'll see."

Jen looked politely interested but to tell the truth she had one worry on her mind and it was not concerned with male respect.

"Do you think Sister Catherine will make me go back to school when she finds I'm here? Because I'll bet the Delaneys will be mad enough to make her do something about me."

Grace snapped her gum.

"Na. You'll get more education right here than if you was in any school. I only went to the fourth grade and I get along, you bet. Some of the smartest men in the world come in this place,—they get to talking and if you keep your ears open first thing you know you've learned something. Telegraph operators are usually the smartest. Take Sweeney. Before I knew Sweeney I used to always say 'me and my friends.' Now I know better. I say 'I and my friend is going to do so and so.' Just keep your ears open and you learn enough all right. 'Who's wrong, too. You should always say 'whom,' but you know how it is, sometimes you get careless, even when you know better."

"I'd hate to go back to school as soon as I get a job like this," Jen said, "with my own room and everything."

Grace's bed took up almost the entire room except for the big golden oak dresser. Jen's room was no bigger, on the other side of the partition; it had a window you could lean out and almost touch the trains as they went by. But usually she was in Grace's room because Grace had her place all fixed up. On her dresser, for instance, was a heart-shaped bon-bon box with a huge red satin bow on it, and beside it a blue painted can of talcum powder smelling deliciously of carnations. A velvet souvenir ribbon say with button photographs and little tasselled pencils hung beside the mirror. Over the bed was pinned a big Silver Lake pennant and a passe-partout tinted picture of a full-faced brunette gazing moodily down at her bare bosom.

"Where'd you get that pennant?" Jen inquired.

Grace tittered and leaned coquettishly on one elbow.

"That's what Morry Abbott was always asking, ha, ha!"
Jen stirred uncomfortably.

"Where did he see it?"

"Never mind, he saw it plenty of times," giggled Grace. "I
used to tease him about being so jealous. Where'd I get this,
where'd I get that, who give me this box of candy and so on.
He wasn't going to let me have any friends at all, he was so
jealous. Can you imagine that?"

Jen twisted her handkerchief, understanding now. That
was why Grace had gotten her to go with her that night following Nettie and Morry. He'd made love to both of them.
She didn't see how she could ever look up at Grace,—she
wouldn't be able to look at Morry again without thinking of
this. She wished she hadn't known, now. Knowing things like
this frightened her. It made Morry seem so far away from
her, somehow.

"It got so bad I just had to stop before it was serious,"
Grace confided, gazing dreamily at the Silver Lake pennant.
"Honestly, Jen, I was afraid he'd do something. Kill himself
or something. Crazy kid. . . . You know how he was always
following me around."

"I never saw him following you," Jen murmured, a little coldly.

Grace was not perturbed by her skeptical tone.

"You wouldn't. But, believe me, I'd never give in. All a
girl's got is her good name and believe me, you got to hang
on to that. The factory girls don't care. Remind me to show
you the place in the Big Four woods where they take their fellas. Gee, but those girls are awful. Sweeney had one of them
up in the Tower during the quiet hour—one to two—in the
morning, and a dispatcher walks in and didn't he almost get
fired, that Sweeney? Only thing that saved him was the girl
happened to have something on the dispatcher."

The fast train tore by and the walls of the house shook, a
chunk of damp plastering fell to the floor.

"Isn't it time to go down?" Jen asked, still anxious to make
good at her new career.

"Never go down till you're called," Grace instructed her.
"Hermann will yell when he wants us. Sunday dinner's always
late anyway."

"Do you think maybe Bill or Mrs. Delaney will try to make

Hermann send me away," Jen asked, apprehensively, "when they find out I'm here?"

"They'd never dare," Grace declared. "Bill's too anxious to keep on the good side of Hermann. If Hermann says you stay, then you stay. . . . Don't you worry, the Delaneys know you're here. The old woman's peekin' out her window watchin' every chance she gets."

Jen stroked her hair and looked at it again in the mirror, because it was done up like Grace's and made her feel very courageous.

"Yes sir, those factory girls are fast, though," Grace went on. "I'd never get too chummy with 'em and don't you, either. . . . You notice Morry Abbott won't go out with the girls from the Works and they're always after him, too. He can't see 'em, he told me. . . . I tried to get him to be friends with other women but he wouldn't do it. . . . Now of course he's sore at me because I never would give in to him. But I'm sure I don't know what he's thinking of. Men are awful when they're so attracted to you."

She wasn't going to care who Morry liked, Jen thought resolutely, she wasn't going to be bothered about anything. She was back in Lamptown, wasn't she, and safe under the wing of Hermann Bauer, so what did anything else matter? But she could not help listening, fascinated by Grace's experience with life, even though whatever Grace said seemed to have a subtle hurt in it. Even when it didn't concern Morry it hurt, because it hinted of a bewildering world unknown to her, it hinted of things she didn't know, it reminded her again and again that she was left out.

"I wouldn't run with those factory girls," sniffed Grace. "I never wanted a chum. You and me could get along, though, Jen, know that? You're young but you're not so dumb. We can go to picnics together and have dates. It's easier for two girls to get dates than it is for one. It makes it more like a party."

Maybe it was a good thing the Delaneys did put her out, Jen reflected, because now it looked as if she was going to see something of the world.

"Grace! Jennia!" Hermann bawled up the back-stairs.

"Oh, all right," answered Grace and slid off the bed to get dressed.

"I'm going to clear out of here one of these days," she grumbled, dumping some powder down her neck,—powder that would daintily shower some customer's soup later on as she bent over. "I'd like a job in a Mansfield restaurant. Out in Luna Park. There's a fella runs the rolly coaster there and say, he's good-looking. He was kinda crazy about me but you know how it is—I only get over there once a year."

Jen had her hand on the doorknob, impatient to go down because it was Sunday and maybe Morry might come over, as he did on Sundays. She hadn't seen him since the dance night and she wanted to see how impressed he was with her earning a living and having her hair done this new way.

"Wait a minute, I want to tell you about this fella," Grace called her back, slightly annoyed. She picked up the hand mirror to study the back of her hair. "I wish you could have seen him. Those snappy black eyes like Fischer's and slick black pompadour. I was walking along there by the rolly coaster at this picnic—The Baptist one, it was. I had on my blue dotted Swiss and a big milan I paid seven-fifty for at the Bon Ton. I was walking along and this fella says hello kid, all by your lonesome? Then we got to talking and he give me three free rides and after that I had a postcard from him with a picture of a girl sitting on a fella's lap. It's around here somewhere, I'll show it to you."

"Girls!" yelled Hermann. "God damn!"

Jen started running and Grace followed reluctantly.

"He had those black eyes, you know the kind," she whispered urgently as they went down the stairs. "Sort of Italian only not so sad."

Waiting table was much more fun than making beds and washing dishes for old Mrs. Delaney. All the time she swung importantly in and out of the pantry door, there was the awed delight of being on her own, getting a salary, looking after herself, there was the thrill of triumphing over the world. When she saw Morry sitting at the counter Jen upset a cup of coffee in her nervousness. It was gratifying to see his amazement. He'd heard she'd run away,—what was she doing here in Bauer's?

"I work here," Jen was proud to answer. "I get three dollars a week and I don't have to go back to school, next fall, either, unless I please."

"Certainly you have to go back to school," Morry said sharply. "Whoever told you you were so bright?"

Jen's face fell.

"I'm tired of being tied to things," she complained. "I want to do things, Morry, instead of just sitting around till I'm old enough. I've been going to school just about all my life and I'm good and tired of it. I want to start in on my own."

"Want to be like Grace Terris, I suppose," Morry sneered. "That's your idea of a great life, waiting table. I thought you were going to be a dancer on the stage and all that. I thought you were going to show this town what you could do. Well, you won't get anywhere quitting school and working in restaurants, I can tell you. Gee, Jen, I thought you had more sense."

Jen hung her head and paid no attention when a man at the other end of the table rapped his fork on his glass for more coffee.

"I only thought if I had to take care of myself I might as well get started," she mumbled.

"Don't you know you can't ever do what you want unless you know things?" Morry scolded her. "You go back there this fall if you know what's good for you."

The man called her then and when she came back Morry had gone without giving her any clue to his indignation. She didn't know that she was Morry's invention, that in some obscure way he expected her to do him credit, her admiration must be more worthwhile than merely flattering worship from a chop-house waitress,—hadn't she promised to be a ballet-dancer-on-a-magazine-cover-in-love-with-Morris-Abbott? . . . Jen understood none of these things, she only saw that he had gone away, the way he always did, nothing in the world could make him stay. She saw him in the street turn back to look and their eyes met. . . . Come back, come back, hers said, but he would never come back for her,—always she would be left because people didn't care for you the way you cared for them. Your hands stretched frantically out to clutch them but they gained no hold, you were brushed aside, you could not hold anyone to you. Come back, come back. . . . Jen's eyes did not leave him until Delaney's door had swung shut behind him. Then with a sigh she took the catsup bottle over to the Ladies Table.

"I've got to go back to school tomorrow," she told Grace in the pantry.

"Why? Hermann says you don't have to if you don't want to."

"I know it," Jen murmured disconsolately. "But I've got to go back."

Dinner was over when Hunt Russell and Dode O'Connell came in. Jen frantically signalled Grace to wait on them but Grace only winked knowingly and shook her head. They were arguing and neither looked up when Jen set the dishes down clumsily before them.

"What'll you bet she's raising Cain because he went out with us the other night," Grace whispered when Jen came back to the pantry. "I guess she's got her hooks into him good. You'd never cut her out, girlie, you're not the type. Say, I'd like to let him know his party the other night got you kicked out of a good home. Maybe he'd do something for you."

Jen was terrified lest Grace should actually tell Hunt all this, and Grace wouldn't promise not to, only laughed teasingly. She put her finger to her lips and beckoned Jen to stand beside her at the little peephole in the door.

"Sh! Maybe we can hear what they're rowing about. Did you see those rings she always wears? Three diamonds and that big Masonic ring. He never gave her that."

At the corner table Dode slumped back in her chair, ignoring the dishes before her. Hunt smoked a cigarette and smiled lazily at her as she continued her low-voiced accusations. She was leaning her chin on her hand sullenly. She was good looking in a hard leathery way, her shoulders looked high and powerful and why not, having pitched hay and done chores till she was old enough to get to a factory.

"She's telling him he don't give a damn about her," Grace whispered to Jen. "Says he'll probably marry somebody else and she'd like to see the little sap he'd pick out. Says she wouldn't marry anybody on a bet, she wouldn't want to be tied up with a house and a buncha kids. I notice he don't say anything. I guess she'd marry him all right if he asked her, that's all that's eating her."

Standing behind Grace Jen marvelled at the intricate design of gold bone hairpins in her hair-knob; she tried to perk out her own white apron strings into the beautifully stiff wings that Grace had achieved. At least she was proud of her own hair screwed up as it was into a tight knob with hairpins torturing her scalp wonderfully.

"Sst!" Grace clutched her arm in delight. "She's trying to find out who he picked up at the dance last week when she didn't go. Can you beat that? He's not even opening his mouth. . . . Go on in and give 'em their coffee."

"What do you care, you never did anything to her!" Grace gave her a little push as she hesitated. "They can't bite you, you know. Go on."

They stopped talking when Jen approached. Hunt's eyes travelled from Jen's new black silk stockings up the blue striped percale dress to her skinned-back hair. Jen colored and fussed with her apron.

"What under the sun have you done to your hair?" he exclaimed, staring at her, amused and bewildered. "You look ten years older."

"Honest?" Jen was radiant. "I had it on top Thursday night, too, but I guess you didn't notice. It's the way I'm going to wear it from now on."

"Where'd you see him Thursday night?" Dode snapped at her abruptly.

Jen looked at Hunt, speechless.

"I—I saw him at the Casino," she mumbled.

"And afterwards, too, don't kid me," said Dode. "I heard about it all right but I didn't believe it. So this is your new girl, is it, Hunt? Want 'em younger now, yeah? . . . This is who you took out Thursday."

Jen picked up her tray and backed away in confusion, but Hunt blew rings of smoke indolently into the air.

"Well, Jen, if you're working here I reckon I'll have to eat all my meals here, won't I?"

"Oh, you will, will you?" Dode flared up and picking up her glass of water flung it straight in Hunt's face. Then she pushed back her chair and rushed out of the restaurant, her head ducked down so that people couldn't see she was crying. Hunt mopped himself with a napkin silently. At the cash register in front Hulda Bauer allowed herself to turn a fraction of an inch to note what was happening. Jen tried to save his

feelings by not watching him but finally their eyes met and
Hunt was grinning a little as if he enjoyed Dode's attack. He
took down his soft grey hat from the rack and sauntered
leisurely up to Hulda at the front counter. In the street a
minute later he didn't even glance in the direction Dode had
gone but got in his car and drove westward.

"Whee!" exclaimed Jen scurrying out to the kitchen. "Did
you see that, Grace?"

But Grace looked at her sourly.

"She threw that on your account,—because he was trying
to flirt with you. That's why she wanted to throw things. It
was your fault."

Then she began bustling about the linen cupboard, quite
aloof. Jen was troubled.

"But they were quarreling about something else, Grace,
honest."

"It doesn't pay to make trouble, girlie," lectured Grace
with a fixed smile. "You'll never get ahead trying to come between couples, just because the man has an automobile, it's
something I've never done, I'll tell you."

"But Grace, I didn't do anything. You saw—"

Grace disappeared into the pantry. After that Jen got used
to seeing that look in other women's eyes, a veiled, hostile,
appraising look. There was nothing to do about that look, Jen
found, but it had something to do with men liking you and
of course for that women never forgave you. Chilled by
Grace's new manner Jen went out in front and sat down idly
at the counter. Hulda pointed a warning finger at her.

"Don't let Hermann see you with nothing to do, Jenny. If
you're through down here go upstairs and fix Room Twenty
for those surveyors. You know your work, child."

She waddled over to shut the piano again; after saving so
hard to buy it she wasn't going to have it ruined by people
playing on it.

Something was happening to the Lots. Surveyors were busy
over it and on the edge of this wasteland men were throwing
up a new house. Its skeleton was a familiar one,—four rooms
down, three up, steep roof sliding off a square indented
porch,—it was Lamptown's eternal new House. Morry saw it

one Saturday noon coming home from work, and he stopped
short, incredulous. That gaunt house leapt out of the horizon
like his name out of a printed page, at first he could not understand its challenge for him, and his feeling of despair. . . .
Why, the Lots were to be turned into a gorgeous boulevard
of beautiful mansions (through the vague genius of Morry
Hunt Russell Abbott)—chateaux, Hogan called them, with
long rolling lawns around them. . . . So long as the Lots
were wilderness all this was possible, but the first dinky little
Lamptown house going up meant that if homes were to be
built, they'd be like all those on Extension Avenue.

The gardens-to-be had become so real in Morry's mind
that he was outraged to see the workmen trampling over
them as if they were nothing more than the weedy mud they
seemed. He stood still, hands shoving restlessly into his coat
pockets, staring unhappily at this apparent signal of his defeat. Each night after he closed his eyes he was used to conjuring the lots before him, acres of tangled clover and
scattered bramble bushes changing on his closed eyelids to
castles of lordly beauty centered in terraced rose-gardens all
magically contrived by Morry Abbott. These pleasant fantasies might have gone on forever if the harsh fact of one
small frame house had not thrust itself before him. It was
unquestionably a challenge, he'd do something about this,
he would—(he thought desperately of his own ignorance
and helplessness)—well, then, where was Hunt,—where was
Hogan,—where were all the people who talked of beautiful
cities. . . . Where was Hunt Russell? After all, wasn't it
Hunt's land? He could stop it all quick enough.

Angrily he looked up at the workmen on the scaffolding.
What right had they to do this?

"Who are you building this for?" he called up.

It was for an out-of-town contracting firm, the foreman
told him. Maybe, he said, the entire Lots would be built up
this year if the factory increased as rumors hinted; two or
three at least would be erected on speculation.

"All just alike?" Morry asked with a sinking heart.

"Sure—all just alike,—maybe some with the porch on the
left, that's all," answered the man. "It's a mighty convenient
little house—a big favorite around here."

Morry walked slowly on, depressed. There was that inextinguishable plan in his mind for the Lots, that ridiculous, fabulous plan,—Hogan's plan, really, only as soon as he'd heard it Morry had made it his own. But somebody else always did these things first,—somebody with money, somebody who knew how to go after things. What were you to do when you didn't know anyone who could help you, no one who could explain the way to the things you wanted,—what could you do,—you couldn't just take a spade, a few bricks, and a geranium and see what happened. You had to be rich, you had to be educated; you had to be powerful to stop contagious ugliness from spreading.

Walking with his head down, thinking feverishly of desperate steps to take, Morry halted at the edge of the fields; still preoccupied he sat down on the running board of a muddy automobile parked there. He was going to do something all right, he'd go to Hogan—but Hogan was all big noise, just as the fellows said, he never really would get down to doing anything. Maybe if he'd gone to college, Morry thought, maybe then you knew just what way to go at things. . . . Maybe he could go to this contracting firm that was building these houses, for instance, and tell them they were making a mistake in destroying Lamptown's only chance for an expensive residential boulevard. . . . That's what he'd do. Morry stood up and looked uncertainly back at the house. He'd go and ask that foreman his boss' address. . . .

An elderly man with grey moustachios and a wide-brimmed black western hat was scowling gloomily up at the building; this was Fowler, the town builder and so-called 'architect,' Hogan's father-in-law.

"He's mad, too, I'll bet," Morry thought, "because they went out of town instead of giving him the job."

He sauntered up to him.

"Look at that house, Mr. Fowler!" he appealed. "They're going to be rows and rows of 'em before the summer's over. When the Works enlarge they'll fill in every chink of land from here to the county land with these sheds. Why doesn't somebody put up a good home for a change?"

"Cheap clapboard!" Fowler puffed morosely on a black briar pipe. "Any good storm would blow them down. I don't see why they didn't come to somebody that knows this land and knows enough not to get stung with cheap lumber. Hunt knows better than that."

He spat viciously at a wilting blackeyed daisy.

"Is Hunt behind this?" Morry wanted to know, incredulously. "I thought Hunt was a smarter man than that."

"There you are,—Hunt's all right," Fowler agreed. "He'd never take a thing out of my hands, but you see Hunt isn't the whole cheese here at all. It's Russell money, all right, but it comes from Hunt's uncles in the East. Smart men, too. Keep out of the picture till it looks like a boom, then they step in and collect a million on their property. They know all right."

"But if there's a boom," Morry stammered desperately, "there'll be rich men in Lamptown, and they won't want to live in these cheap shanties, they'll want beautiful places different from other people's. Don't you see, Mr. Fowler, this was the place to build mansions—like Hunt's, don't you see?"

Fowler sucked his pipe glumly and then recollected a gift cigar in his vest pocket and offered it to Morry. Morry refused it and Fowler stuck it thankfully back beside the Democratic campaign button without which this gentleman had never been seen.

"They'll buy homes in Avon—people with the money. After all it's only twenty minutes out on the car-line and all residential. . . . Damned poor business for Lamptown, though, you're right about that."

Well, why didn't he do something about it, then, Morry wondered, irritated, certainly he was an old man and old enough to know his own trade, wasn't he?

"Somebody could do something even yet," Morry insisted. "Only one house is up. It isn't too late. Somebody could start on the other side of the Lots with a big place kinda like Hunt's—that's what people want to work for,—something different—"

"Say a modified Colonial," mused Fowler, and gazed at the fields beyond where the Colonial mansion was to be, "or maybe a Tudor cottage. I wonder. . . . Come on and walk down to the office, Morry, I'll show you a book I've got down there of what they call these Tudor cottages. And there's some pictures of these Spanish type houses like they have in California."

Fowler's office was a room over the Paradise Theatre, and
as they tramped up the stairs Milly could be heard in the theatre banging out scraps of new songs on the piano.

"A hell of a business building," growled Fowler, fitting the
key into his door. "You'd think it was a conservatory of music, anybody would, with that practicing going on all day.
Come in."

The office was a mere closet cluttered with file cases, their
drawers half-open and papers dangling out; auction sale
leaflets in green and yellow blew frantically across the dusty
floor as the door opened and cowered, quivering, against a
stack of blue-prints rolled up like so many highschool diplo-
mas and tied with yellowing soiled ribbon. The roll-top desk
leaned dizzily forward, gorged with magazines and enormous
photographs of ideal homes, above it a steel engraving of the
Roman Forum was slapped in the face by a large cardboard
poster announcing a foreclosure sale of the Purdy Property.
Fowler dumped the magazines off two chairs and then offered Morry the cigar once more. With a sigh of resignation
Morry took it and chewed on it rather unhappily.

"I'd like to show these people what somebody right here
in Lamptown could do with those Russell lots," Fowler said,
yanking off his coat and vest but keeping on the huge Sheriff's hat. "I'd like to show these people what somebody right
here in Lamptown could do with that property. I'd like to
show 'em we're a darn sight smarter than their fancy city
firms with their cheap little ideas. Maybe I will, too, by golly,
I ain't dead yet.

"Here—look these over." He shoved some photographs
into Morry's hands, and then leaned back in the slightly askew
swivel chair, puffing at his pipe. "I don't know which I'd rather
do out there. A row of Spanish type houses, kinda California
style, see, something to make Lamptown sit up and take notice, or say these Colonial ones like they do down East. Damn
it, I'd like to let 'em know I got ideas, and nothing shoddy,
either. I see other towns, don't I, I keep my eyes open everywhere. Just because I've had to keep to a $1800 house for most
of the folks here, say, that don't mean I don't know how a
$7500 house ought to be built, does it? . . . I'd like to throw
up a string of houses that'd knock their eyes out, I would."

"But not just alike!" expostulated Morry, earnestly waving his cigar. "That's the whole point. Each one a special kind of house, see, so that everybody can feel it's his own special home, not anybody else's but his, see? Something worth saving for, something to show off to his friends. . . ."

"Somebody's bound to get rich in this town on this boom—that's as good as settled." Fowler twisted the ends of his thick gray moustache thoughtfully. "In another year there'll be a demand for better houses than anything we've got here right now, and that's a fact."

He kicked the outer door shut as Milly's practicing became louder, and then with his back to Morry stood before a huge map of Lamptown pinned to the wall. He ran a fountain pen slowly across the letters "Extension Avenue" and made a green-inked 'X' in the center of a large area marked "LOTS."

"Hunt's share of that property is one fourth." He was talking to himself more than to his visitor, Morry realized, but Morry didn't mind because he was learning something, he could almost see a new door swinging open for him. "If we could talk Hunt into the idea, we'd have enough land and backing to start working on. Let the eastern Russells fool around over there on the east side with their factory houses, —we'll begin on the other side of the creek, see, right here, and give the town something to talk about."

"We could call it the Heights," Morry said, and gave up trying to smoke his cigar, allowing it to drop quietly from his fingers into the wastebasket. It occurred to him that it was long past lunch-time and he was hungry, and moreover he'd promised Bill Delaney and some fellows to go to the ballgame this afternoon, but it was too late now. Here in Fowler's cluttered office with Milly's desultory piano accompaniment a new Lamptown was being planned, and it was Morry Abbott's Lamptown, even Fowler must know that, for he went on with the "we" plans as casually as if the name on the door was "Fowler and Abbott" instead of just Fowler. The palms of Morry's hands were wet with tense excitement, he was on the verge of something big, something wonderful. He skipped through the pages of a book called "Long Island Homes,"— some day even these landscaped estates might be possible, too. Then he got up and looked over Fowler's shoulder at the

map. Fowler was marking off a section of the Lots, murmuring, "Lamptown Heights, eh?"

"No—not Lamptown," begged Morry. "Call it Clover
Heights."

"Clover Heights," repeated Fowler and inked it carefully in
green with an air of finality as if the whole plan was settled by
this simple gesture. Then he tapped his pipe on a file-case and
looked at Morry triumphantly. "We'll put it through and
don't you forget it. It gives Hunt a chance to put one over on
the uncles, don't you see? That's why he'll be willing to come
in with us."

"When can you—we—begin working on it?" Morry asked,
struck with awe by the masterful way this man went at things.

Fowler pulled at his moustache with yellow-tipped fingers.

"Well, as soon as we can get hold of Hunt," he answered.
"You're there at the factory all the time, you see him every
day. Get hold of him Monday, say, and give him the idea."

Morry choked.

"That's the thing," continued Fowler with a far-away look.
"You give him the main idea and tell him I'm ready to talk to
him about it any time he drops in. Hunt's a nice guy and he's
not crazy to have his uncles wipe him off the map. You just
get hold of him, say Monday, and outline this Clover Heights
idea to him."

"Sure. Sure, I'll tell him," said Morry hoarsely. He was to do
all the starting, was he, and not Fowler at all. . . . He remembered his father's sarcasm when he told him of just such a plan,
and already he saw Hunt's scornful amusement. It was all right
if Fowler started things but nobody would ever listen to Morry
Abbott,—and worse yet he could never in this world get up the
nerve to approach them. The snappy young Abbott of his fantasies might calmly tap Hunt on the shoulder and tell him just
what was what; but nothing, to the real Morry, was worth the
anguish of going to a man and quite out of a blue sky telling him
your own little private dream of a lovely place to live. Morry
wondered how he'd ever managed to sound so casual to Fowler,
but he thought hopefully he might drop dead before Monday
or the relatives would start building on Hunt's share so that the
whole plan would have to be given up, continuing merely as
a pleasant dream in the night thoughts of young Abbott.

Fowler took out his watch.

"I've got to get to a farm out east by six," he said. "But see here, Morry, what about you coming down here to the office tomorrow—say around twelve—and we'll talk this over some more."

"Sure," agreed Morry again, who usually slept till two on Sundays then wandered out to the factory ball-grounds to loaf away the day.

"There'll be something big in this for both of us," Fowler thoughtfully pursued. "We'll work on it nights for a while till we get everything all set, understand. You're just the boy for this, Abbott,—you've got push and go, not afraid to tackle anybody or anything. That's the right idea."

Morry looked at him alertly to see if he was being kidded, but Fowler's face was serious, almost dreamy. He had push and go, did he?—with his hands already trembling at the idea of approaching Hunt. He wanted to explain to Fowler right here and now that it was all a mistake, the whole plan was just an idea, see, and there was nothing to do about ideas, you just thought about them, that was all. But the big letters in green ink "CLOVER HEIGHTS" across the corner of the Lamptown map made him keep these craven misgivings to himself.

"Tomorrow at twelve, now don't forget." Fowler slapped him on the shoulder. "And you'd better not date up any women for the next few weeks because we'll be working on this every night."

It was dusk when Morry got outside, and the Paradise façade was already lit up, boldly inviting the night to come on. In the drugstore next door and around the barber-shops crowds of men were arguing over the baseball game. The Works team had won its first game and this meant a big night at Delaney's, and celebrations all over town, but to Morry this approaching excitement belonged to him, the town was celebrating because at last Morry Abbott was going to do something about it, he was about to break through cloudy dreams into action. He spoke to men here and there but he couldn't stop, he had to hurry home and tell someone. He had push and go, he was going to be a man of power, like Fowler, like Hunt Russell, he would have an office over the

Paradise and by merely scrawling something with his green-inked pen the whole map of Lamptown would be changed.

At Robbin's Jewelry Store he slowed up his pace, uncertain of where he should take his news. Hogan was the man to tell, Hogan and Bill Delaney, he thought, so he walked on to Bill's place. The saloon was full of the baseball players and men home from the game, they were singing and shouting, while Shorty, perspiration dripping from his bald head, pushed foaming glasses across the bar as fast as his two fat hands could go. Hogan and his fireman were at the bar and hailed Morry.

"Say, Hogan, I'm going in with Fowler," Morry told him, making an effort to sound as if this were nothing at all, really. "Thought I'd learn building—architecture, you know."

"O.K. with me, friend," answered Hogan heartily, banging his glass down. "You're welcome to the old man."

A little dashed, Morry went on confidentially,

"We're planning to develop one end of the Lots,—build beautiful homes like they have on Long Island, you know, these Normandy cottages with two baths and——"

He had to raise his voice because someone was playing the piano and the men were beginning to sing.

"Mansions for the aristocrats!" roared Hogan. "While the honest working-man eats in his simple kitchen in Shanteyville. Mansions for the ruling classes! Why, friend——" his voice became a deep, oratorical baritone,— "I would rather go to the forest far away, build me a little cabin, a little hut with some hollyhocks at the corner with their bannered blossoms open to the sun and with the thrush in the air like a song of joy in the morning,—I would rather live there——"

He paused to wipe the foam off his mouth with a red kerchief.

"Never mind, Hogan'll live in your mansions if the old man gives one to his wife," the fireman winked at Morry. "You don't see him eating in these simple kitchens, either, he's just moved into the biggest house on Walnut Street over in Avon, and he raises hell when his wife doesn't set up the dining-room table."

"That's all right, friend," said Hogan. "You're a single man. You don't understand these things."

It was no use telling anything to Hogan now, Morry thought, disappointed, for Hogan's brightly glazed blue eyes and his rosy nose proclaimed to the world that this was Saturday night and a twelve-hour spree was well under way. As Morry reached the door he pointed an accusing finger at him and bellowed.

"Yes sir, by the Lord Harry, I would rather live there and have my soul erect and free than to live in a palace of gold and wear the crown of imperial power——" and Morry slid out the door on the final impressive whisper— "and know that my soul was slimy with hypocrisy!"

Chagrined at Hogan's lack of interest, Morry turned into the alley to go in the Bon Ton's back entrance. He observed the crouched figure of old Mrs. Delaney on her steps, as if she had been waiting for him. He touched his cap, getting fiery red.

"Well, Morry Abbott!" she bent over the railing and scowled at him, one gnarled hand clutching together the black shawl under her chin. "You're satisfied now, I suppose. Happy now you got my Jen out of a decent home and got her waitin' table where all the men can get at her. God'll punish you, young man, God'll punish you as sure as I'm breathing here. You had no call runnin' after that young girl, now, you've got her started on the road to ruin,—are you satisfied, hey?"

She hobbled up the steps slowly. Morry, hurrying on home, knew she had stopped at the top landing to glare vengefully at him, and he ducked into his doorway, angry again at Jen for putting him into the role of villain and seducer, a role, to tell the truth, that frightened him as much as it ever did any young girl.

Elsinore and Nettie were having tea and sandwiches in the workroom and Morry made himself a salmon sandwich and sat down with them. He wanted to be off-hand telling about his new career but he couldn't help it, he blurted it out the minute after he came in. His mother stirred her tea dreamily and for a while he thought she must be displeased. Nettie dropped her spoon and looked at him as if he had confessed to some tremendous sin. He thought, too late, he shouldn't have told Nettie of any good news about himself, for the only news that would please her, after being scorned, would have to be bad.

"Do you mean to tell me you're giving up your perfectly good job at the factory, Morry Abbott?" she demanded. "After you're lucky enough to get in the Works you'd drop it like this?"

"I'm not dropping it,—not yet, anyways," Morry retorted. "Not till I'm getting commissions or a salary from Fowler."

"Are you out of your mind, Morry?" Nettie cried. "Do you mean to tell me you're going to do all this work without getting any pay?"

"Well, not exactly," Morry defended himself, sorry he had said anything, sorry that wherever he went he had to defend his triumphs since all that people were glad to hear from him was of his expected defeats.

"Come, now, what did he say? Did he or didn't he say he'd pay you for the work?"

"No, he didn't." Morry was stung into the truth. "But it's a chance to learn something I want to learn and I'm going to do it. Gee, Nettie, didn't you ever hear of anybody being an architect?"

Nettie gave him a long, withering glance.

"Don't be silly, Morry, you have to go to college to learn that, and you couldn't anyway, you haven't got the brains. You stick to something you can do, like the factory work, and don't let that old man Fowler make a fool out of you. Don't you think that's right, Mrs. Abbott?"

Elsinore raised her eyes from her tea-cups and smiled gently at Morry.

"What is it, Morry?" she inquired, and Morry looked straight at her, not believing she could be so unkind. She hadn't even listened, she didn't care a bit what became of him. His own mother didn't care, she was so busy with her own life. . . . Well, and what was her own life, Morry asked himself resentfully, if she didn't care about her husband or her son, who, then, occupied her mind? The doubt his father had passed on to him returned fleetingly but he shut it out of his mind firmly.

"No, sir, the thing for you to do, Morry, is to hang on to

your factory job," advised Nettie, pouring herself some more tea. "You'll never get another like it. Mr. Abbott would be furious, too, if he thought you left the Works."

Morry's throat tightened at mention of his father.

"Aw, what's it to him?" he growled. "What does he care what I do——"

"A young man ought never to make a foolish move like you're doing right now, without talking it over with his father." Nettie's lips were virtuously pursed up. "Or at least with his mother."

She picked up her saucer and went over to the sink. Morry stole a sidelong, unhappy look at his mother. She sat there in her low work chair, sipping tea, staring intently into space. Her thick brown hair was loosened a little and in the blue woven dress she wore it suddenly came over to Morry that his mother wasn't old at all, she wasn't even middle-aged; it made him feel unaccountably lonely, as if a white-haired old mother or even a formless, middle-aged mother like Mrs. Bauer would have been his, his very own mother; but this way his mother didn't belong to him, and he had no right to her, no claim to her attention. . . . She glanced up and smiled at him but he was too hurt and lonely to smile back.

"Did you hear about the big Serpentine Ball the end of July, Morry?" she asked him almost lightly. "I hear it's going to be the big dance of the year and I meant to tell you not to miss it."

"I'll get there, all right," he answered gruffly. "Plenty of time for that."

She didn't care that to-day an incredible dream had started to come true, she didn't care that he was going to be more than just a factory hand, he was going to be a figure in Lamptown some day, a somebody that she could be proud of; but she didn't care, she hadn't even listened. It would be a long time before Morry's eyes, ashamed for her, could meet her smile.

There had to be someone who thought you mattered, there had to be someone you could tell things to, somebody who thought you were going to amount to something,— nobody could be left this way all alone. Desperately Morry grabbed his hat and started outdoors heading almost automatically for the saloon backsteps before he remembered that

Jen wouldn't be there, she'd be over at Bauer's. Jen . . .
Jen . . . Jen . . . the only person who believed, the only person who listened, the only person who was sure. He hurried
across the street, afraid to lose a minute now, afraid that
Hogan and Nettie and his mother had so dashed his little triumph that there was none left. He thought it was true that a
thing never happened by itself, it had never actually happened
until it was related for the right person's applause. He saw
Hermann Bauer smoking his pipe and gazing fixedly out the
window and behind Hermann's back he saw half a dozen diners and Jen scurrying around them with a tray half her size.
He'd better go around to the kitchen door, he thought, it
was easier to catch her there than in front with Hermann
watching. Hunt Russell's car was at the curb but Morry impatiently brushed by without waiting to speak to Hunt.

"Hey—hey Morry!"

Hunt had seized his arm jovially.

"Want to pick up the Terris woman later on, Morry?" he
asked in a low tone. "Lots of room in the back of my car if
you want to come along. I'm taking my girl, so speak up if
you want to come."

"Your girl?" Morry asked suspiciously.

Hunt jerked a thumb in the direction of the restaurant.

"The kid in there," he drawled. "Thought you might take
the other one."

"I don't think so," said Morry, the blood swimming furiously in his head. "I'll pick my own damned women, thank
you."

He whirled around and went back home, up the stairs to
his room. His whole body buzzed with hate for Hunt Russell
as if in blocking his way to Jen he'd done him the ultimate in-
jury, using all of his advantages for this unfair blow. His disappointment in his mother and Hogan faded into this final
rage. Very well, let Jen take Dode O'Connell's place as
Hunt's girl if she liked; Morry would never fight for her, he'd
never compete for any girl, he'd never give Hunt the chance
to sneer at a conquered rival. He tramped up and down his
tiny room and when his head hit the sloping ceiling he tore at
it fiercely with his fists, and turned his hate for the moment
on to tiny houses with low ceilings. Jen's blue eyes fastened

worshipfully on someone else . . . Jen listening adoringly to some other hero. . . . All right, he could do without any-body, he didn't give a damn what people thought about him, he didn't care if nobody listened to him or believed in him, he'd show them all a thing or two, he'd make them listen one of these days, he didn't give a damn about anybody.

But in his dreams that night he fought for hours with some enemy, his conquering fists rained on some foe's bent head, a foe who changed under these blows from Hogan to Hunt Russell and then curiously enough took on the features of his father, and ah, what voluptuous ecstasy to blur with his knuckles the significant sneer on this last face!

If Morry was around the shop when Nettie worked late at night, then she made a great fuss about her preparations to leave, locking drawers noisily, calling loud goodbyes to Elsinore and shrilly exclaiming about the darkness of the night and the long walk to Murphy's. Morry deliberately ignored these hints and Nettie would have to stalk angrily out alone.

"I don't mind going home alone," she complained to Elsinore. "It isn't that at all. But after all, any gentleman would see that I got home safely nights I worked late in his own mother's shop, and was going through a dark street into an empty house. Any gentleman would do that much, Mrs. Abbott—that's why I get so disgusted with Morry."

She swung from such dignified reproaches to vehement denunciations of his character—he was just a bum, the town tough, everyone said he was fast, he chased after bad girls, no decent girl would ever want to marry him, he had no nice friends, just lazy good-for-nothing pool-players and Shanteyville souses. He'd rather keep company like that than to walk home with a good girl once or twice a week.

Elsinore did not know how to answer these attacks.

"But when the men want to take you home you won't ever let them," she protested. "I thought you'd rather be alone."

"That's just it!" Nettie sputtered. "If Morry was with me, the men from Delaney's wouldn't follow me, they wouldn't dare come up to me if Morry was along."

"I don't understand you, Nettie," Elsinore surrendered. "You weren't cross with Mr. Schwarz——"

"Mr. Schwarz was very different from Lamptown men," Nettie reminded her. "Very different indeed. He took me to the very best places in Cleveland and our seats at the theatre alone were three dollars. Oh, there's no comparison."

She sat down to the table where the crying doll lay undressed waiting for its summer costume. Nettie had given herself a birthday present of a pair of noseglasses from Robbin's Jewelry Store as most of the girls who could afford it were wearing them, and it seemed to her, stealing an approving glance at herself in the mirror, that this was as nice a touch as a lady could wish. She adjusted them with exquisite care on her determined little nose, and squinting a little, picked up the doll so abruptly that its glazed eyes rattled in its head.

"Never mind, I'm going to go over to the Casino before the summer's over," she declared. "I'm sure I could dance well because everyone says I have such high arches. Morry thinks because I don't dance I'm out of everything, but you just wait. He'll be very glad to dance with me someday, you wait and see."

This set Elsinore to thinking. Fischer had a summer dancing pavilion near Cleveland, and if Nettie learned to dance, then the two of them could go out to this pavilion during the summer. She couldn't go alone, of course, but it looked all right for two women to go places together. She decided it would be worth while to encourage Nettie to learn dancing if only for this one convenient reason. When Mrs. Pepper used to speak of having run out to the pavilion to watch the dancing because she "just happened to be in the neighborhood," Elsinore had yearned to ask if she couldn't "run out" with her sometime. . . . Well, if she ever went now, it would have to be with Nettie, that much was sure.

Sometimes she ran into Mrs. Pepper on the street and Elsinore always dropped her glance before the wounded question in the other's eyes. Nettie told her the corsetiere was often lurking in shop doorways waiting for Nettie to pass so that she could pounce on her and pour out her woe. With the passing weeks Elsinore saw that even if Fischer's wife had told him of a strange visitor he hadn't guessed who it was. It reassured her so that no wounded looks could make her feel guilty, and except for the out-of-town customers occasionally asking for corset fittings, the Bon Ton went on as if these extra activities had never been. She thought that she might even, with Nettie's support, be able to face an encounter with Mrs. Pepper at the Cleveland pavilion this summer. After all, there was no reason why his Lamptown pupils shouldn't drop in at his Cleveland headquarters, was there? . . . Still she'd have to have some excuse for being in the neighborhood. She'd have to invent some business in the city for July or August, some extra business, because two buying trips a year were enough for the millinery stock.

"At least I'm glad there's only one of these darned dolls to dress," Nettie grumbled, pins in her mouth and a scrap of blue lawn in her hand. "It's more work than anything in the shop."

Elsinore had an inspiration.

"But everyone asks about it, Nettie. You know how the girls are always trying to buy it from us. I'd thought of laying in a stock if they don't cost too much."

"No!"

"Later on in the summer—I'll run into Cleveland and get a few as an experiment," she went on meditatively. "I think a millinery store has a right to branch out with novelties now and then. Charles is always telling me about perfumes and hose and extra things they sell in the Chicago shops. I think the Bon Ton ought to be up-to-date."

Nettie's mouth puckered into a disapproving pout.

"Of course," Elsinore added. "I'd expect you to help me buy them. And if we had to go into the city we might have a little extra time for an outing."

Miraculously Nettie's disapproval vanished. If dolls meant a visit to Cleveland for her, then certainly every milliner ought to keep dolls.

"We might happen to run into Mr. Schwarz again," she suggested. She began to hum softly, her little finger curved daintily outward as she sewed, already she had marked another notch in her career as a milliner, and certainly a Mr. Schwarz from Cleveland as a "friend" would put Morry in his place.

Elsinore was writing a letter to Charles that night, explaining her plan for selling dolls when Mrs. Pepper appeared quietly in the Bon Ton. She didn't stop to address Nettie in the shop, but walked straight out into the workroom and shut the

door behind her. Elsinore jumped up, quite pale, and her letter blew unheeded to the floor. Mrs. Pepper looked at her
sadly. Her eyelids and nose were red as if she had been crying,
and she kept dabbing at her nose with a little lace handkerchief as if this gesture somehow gave her courage.

"You've made a lot of trouble for me, Mrs. Abbott." She
didn't sound angry—only tired and pleading. "All I've ever
had is trouble, ever since I lost Mr. Pepper. . . . I—I don't
see why you did it. I can't understand why you'd do that to
me, Mrs. Abbott, it's beyond me."

Elsinore was speechless. She was so sure after all this time
that no one had found out about her visit to Cleveland, and
this belated discovery found her completely without defense.
She rolled her pen nervously between the palms of her hands
and looked at the floor. Mrs. Pepper studied her drearily and
quite without anger.

"As soon as Harry said the woman wore a black hat with a
white feather I knew it was you that had gone to his wife. And
then you'd been so strange with me for a long time. . . . At
first when he told me—things had to stop—at first I couldn't
guess who had told her but then when he mentioned that
black hat it all came over me that it was you. I was so upset I
had to lie right down to get my breath. . . . I couldn't understand. . . . I just couldn't see why you'd do that to me,
Mrs. Abbott."

Elsinore drew a deep breath. Why should she feel so
shamed—after all, she hadn't done anything wrong—it was
Mrs. Pepper who had done wrong when it came right down
to it. *She* was the one to feel guilty. . . .

"It wasn't right for you to go with him," she managed to
say. "You knew he had a wife—you knew you ought not to
try coming between them."

Mrs. Pepper's little white hands flew out in a gesture of
helplessness.

"I know, oh, I do know it's wrong, but I'm not a bad
woman. Nobody could say I was a bad woman. And Harry's
all I've had in my life—those few little trips with Harry—once
we went to Atlantic City. . . . It began so naturally—both of
us travelling through the same towns—but now, I—well, I
just couldn't live without Harry. . . . What made you go to

her, Mrs. Abbott—what made you do it? You couldn't have just
wanted to spoil my life—you couldn't just want that. . . ."

Elsinore kept jabbing the table with the pen and kicking at
a ball of colored embroidery silk lying tangled on the floor.
She had regained her cool detachment as if what she had
done was done, after all, and was no concern of hers any
more. She had eased her own steady torment by hurting Mrs.
Pepper and was rather surprised to find that she had no more
hatred for her. On the other hand when she stole a look at
her, the sight of her plump pretty face screwed up into a pitiful caricature of anguish did not stir her pity at all.

"He's had to promise Her not to see me again," Mrs. Pepper allowed the tears to course slowly down her cheeks. "It's
all right for you—you've got your husband—even if he's
only here once in a while—and your nature's different from
mine . . . but with me . . . I've lost eleven pounds just
worrying over this. I've had to take a 38. See, I've lost it
here." She slapped her hips mournfully. "Worrying about
what I'm going to do without ever seeing Harry. . . . She's
having him watched."

She sat down on a stool and leaned her plump arms on the
table. Elsinore kept her face steadily on the embroidery silk
on the rug.

"I never did you any wrong, Mrs. Abbott, you know that,"
desolately went on Mrs. Pepper. "I can't understand why
you'd go against me like that. I didn't dare tell Harry I knew
who'd told his wife. I didn't want to let him know a friend of
mine had done it. I let him think one of the factory girls—
maybe Dode—or somebody out of town had gone to her,
some woman that was after him."

Elsinore breathed easier and dared to lift her eyes. If
Fischer didn't know who it was that had told his wife, then
nothing was to be feared—nothing had been lost after all. She
had done no harm, really, if she'd merely stopped Mrs. Pepper from being in love with him. That was all for the best.

"If Charles was running with some other woman I'd want
to be told," she said. "I'd be glad if someone came and told
me. That's why I went to Mrs. Fischer. I wasn't thinking of
you at all—I was just putting myself in the position of the
wife."

Mrs. Pepper shook her head sadly. She'd never dreamed of being wicked, she never meant to be at all—it was only that after Mr. Pepper went she was all alone, and travelling through the same territory with the dancing master, always getting on the same trains, they just got so they belonged to each other— they got so they'd meet to talk over business in this town and that, and pretty soon they were terribly dependent on each other, almost like a married couple. And that's the way she was, always dependent on the few bright little things in her life, miserable for months at the slightest change.

"For instance I can't settle down at the Bauers'," she confided unhappily. "I have that lovely big room and all, but I was used to the Bon Ton. I was used to you and Nettie running around and Morry always coming in at the wrong time—and the way we'd sit around gossiping. At Bauer's there's no one to talk to—Hulda—well, you might as well try to talk to a piece of pork. . . . That's what I mean, you see, about being dependent."

Cautiously the work-room door opened, and Nettie tiptoed in, glancing quickly at the two women as if she expected to see them tearing each other's hair. She held out the doll, now completely costumed in a wide lawn bonnet and dress, and held it up to Mrs. Pepper.

"Cute? Dode O'Connell wants one like it, Mrs. Abbott. I told her we were going to carry a few so she might buy one."

Elsinore, glad to change the subject, explained the doll idea to Mrs. Pepper. The corsetiere dried her eyes and listened. She bent forward with a spark of revived spirits.

"Let me tell you, that isn't the only thing you'll have to lay in, Mrs. Abbott. When the Works enlarges, like people say it's going to, you're going to have to carry a lot more things than just hats. Or else sit back and let strangers make the money."

"We'll never carry corsets again, believe me," Nettie laughed arrogantly. "Too much work."

Whenever Nettie became possessive about the shop Elsinore stiffened ever so little.

"We might as well carry corsets as dolls," she rebuked her. "At least we're used to the line."

Nettie, flushing, carried the doll into the front room and kicked the door shut behind her.

"Do you know there's going to be over a thousand new men taken on at the factory next fall?" Mrs. Pepper said. "That means more trade for us, you realize that, with all those families in town. Why, Mrs. Abbott, if I had the running of this shop I'd make the upstairs rooms into shops, too, and sell blouses and all the things girls want when they're making money. I wouldn't let the grass grow under my feet."

Elsinore's eyes caught the sparkle in the other's.

"I couldn't ever do it alone," she demurred. "I wouldn't know where in the world to begin."

Mrs. Pepper pulled her stool closer. Her reddened eyes snapped with excitement, and forgetful of her late wounds, she put a tiny fat hand on Elsinore's knee.

"Let me come in with you, then," she begged. "Let me come back and this summer we can plan the whole thing. I'll be looking around in the other towns, see, and picking up ideas here and there. Let me come back. . . ."

"What about Mr. Fischer?" Elsinore asked in a muffled voice.

Mrs. Pepper beat her hands together nervously.

"I don't know. I'll try to get over it—I know you feel you can't respect me because of that, but I don't mean to be just bad the way you think. Now that She's watching everything I'll have to be so careful anyway. . . . Oh, dear, I wish you hadn't gone to her, Mrs. Abbott, I don't see how you could. If it had been you instead of me——"

"It would never be me," Elsinore harshly interrupted. "And if you come back in this shop I'll expect you to behave differently."

"I've got to," Mrs. Pepper confessed. "That's why I want to put myself into a lot of hard work. I don't want a minute to think."

"As you say we'll have to buy more if the town gets larger." Elsinore looked about the workroom appraisingly. "We could use the upstairs for corsets and say lingerie. I could put a cot down here for Morry so we could start right in using his room."

When Nettie came back she stopped short at sight of the two women talking in low absorbed tones, their heads close together. Something in their attitude made her apprehensive

of her own prestige—after all, she was part of the Bon Ton,
wasn't she, and there was no justice in leaving her out of
things this way. She sat down determinedly at the table and
started threading an embroidery needle, humming a little
tune. Mrs. Pepper turned to her.

"We were just talking of improving the shop."

"Well, we have been improving it," Nettie retorted with no
great friendliness. "Didn't you notice we have electric lights
now?"

Mrs. Pepper exclaimed appropriately as Nettie switched the
lights on and off in demonstration.

"And did you see what Mr. Abbott sent us?" She went over
to the cupboard and brought out an electric fan which she
placed gingerly on the table; keeping her eyes fixed on it to be
on guard against sudden explosions she attached it to the
socket. The fan wheezed and whirred laboriously.

"He certainly is good to you, Mrs. Abbott," said Mrs. Pepper politely. "My, I only wish I had someone as kind to me."

Then both she and Elsinore looked idly at Nettie as if she
were an intruder, but Nettie set her jaw and sat tight in her chair,
sewing diligently. After a few minutes Mrs. Pepper got up.

"Well, I'll see you about that later," she said and reluctantly
left.

Elsinore put the fan back in the cupboard, handling it as if
it were an infernal device, likely to shoot into sky-rockets any
minute.

"Well, now we've got her around again, I suppose," Nettie
ejaculated nodding towards the door. "I'm sure I don't know
where we'll put her and all her junk."

Elsinore looked thoughtfully into space, apparently unheeding. This infuriated Nettie, for it left her outside of
things, somehow. She wanted to say something to remind her
employer of intimate matters between them, to show that she
really wasn't outside at all, but very much in the center of
things.

"You know what Mr. Abbott thinks of her and her old stuff
all over the place, you know how he hates it," she said reproachfully. "You ought to consider what your husband thinks
especially after he sent you that electric fan for a present."

Elsinore whirled around at her almost ferociously.

"I hate that electric thing and you know it!" she blazed. "I hate all of Charles' presents—every single one of them—I'd like to throw them all out into the street this minute!"

"Why—why, Mrs. Abbott!" stuttered Nettie in amazement, so flustered that she dared not utter another word for nearly twenty minutes.

"You're never going to be the drinker your father was," Bill Delaney regretfully told Morry. "You come in here and get green on three beers, a big husky like you, too. Why your pap would sit down there with a quart of Scotch and soak it up without turning a hair. Walk out of this place like a gentleman, too. That was Charlie Abbott."

"Lay off the old man's business partner," Hogan warned Bill. "Don't you know my wife's old man is the biggest finanny on prohibition in this country? Morry can't drink and be in his office."

"The old man's all right," said Morry. "We get along. Did you see the plans for those houses we're putting up?"

"Sure, Fowler's going to make a lot of jack out of real estate," Hogan declared. "But watch out for him, sonny, watch out for a man that won't drink. They'll skin you out of your eyeteeth every time. What's he paying you?"

Morry got red in the face and gulped down his drink. Hogan grinned sardonically.

"Nothing, eh? That'd be the old man, all right—promise big money for next year, get you so dizzy talking in thousands that you'd forget to ask for five dollars to keep from starving."

So Morry couldn't explain about the bonuses and commissions that Fowler had promised. Anyway until last Saturday he'd been drawing pay from his factory job so he wasn't starving. True, on Saturday, the foreman fired him. This was for not showing up one day when he was looking at houses outside of town with Fowler. But the bonuses would begin soon enough and he could laugh at a dinky ten bucks a week.

The saloon was cooler than the July outdoors but its damp fermenting coolness was not refreshing, nor was the smell of sweating laborers crowded around the bar swilling beer. Waves of heat blew in at each motion of the door from the melting asphalt outside, a skinny maple tree sprouting from the cracks in the sidewalk dropped a tiny shrivelled green leaf on the marble doorsill. When the door swung open Morry could glimpse the Bauers' window framing Hulda Bauer, eyes closed, fanning herself rhythmically with a huge palmleaf fan.

Morry wandered into the front room and picked up a billiard cue but it was too hot and too crowded to play, he couldn't play with the other fellows hanging around watching, so he went lonesomely back to the bar. There were strangers in Bill's place all the time now, well-dressed men who asked for expensive cigars and conferred in low voices at corner tables, there were surveyors and gangs of workers from out-of-town who were busy on the Lots. Men dropping in for a drink between trains, said, "Hear you folks are due for a boom. Conductor tells me your factory yonder is opening up a big new line this fall. Is that a fact?" Everyone talked excitedly of the new houses being built, of out-of-town money being put into the Lamptown business, of a boom that was sure to come because it was in the air, but no one seemed to know definitely. Strangers were in town, a little Jew from Cleveland started a branch of a ready-made dress chain store on Market Street and called it "The Elite," the drugstore soda-fountains began to make chocolate frappes, Hermann Bauer raised the price of a meal to fifty cents, and lounging at a table in Bauer's any day you could see a little sharp-nosed sandy man in a checkered suit plunking a mandolin and humming the latest songs, for he was the actor who did a specialty at the Paradise. To most of Lamptown this gaudily dressed figure strolling about town was the symbol of Lamptown's sudden rise, he represented all the glamour of cities and sudden wealth; factory girls merely humming his songs felt rich and beautiful and in the swim, a town had to be pretty up and coming to have specialty actors at its movie house.

Merchants added expensive novelties to their stock when they saw three prosperous strangers in conference with the bank president one afternoon, and after an evening of discussing these mysterious portents and whispers, young married couples decided to buy a davenport or move to a better neighborhood or do *something* to keep in tune with this vague secret progress.

Even without a salaried job Morry moved along on a wave of optimism, planning more and more daring steps in the development of Clover Heights. He was learning now. When Fowler said, "See Hunt" or "See So-and-so at the People's Bank," Morry didn't suffer the same old agonies in collecting his courage. He "saw" people and said, "Mr. Fowler wants to talk to you about something," and then rushed thankfully away. He understood other matters too. He was beginning to see that the big deeds men spoke of were just dares to each other. All of them—Fowler, and everybody—were as afraid of starting something as Morry was, and so as soon as you saw they were all afraid it was easy to step up and be a leader, to say, "I'm going to do this"; these quiet boasts awed other men so that with the mere words power came, the thing magically began to take shape, because other men thought, "Here is one who isn't such a coward as I am," and respected and helped him. Men bluffed each other with brave boasts and then their vanity drove them on desperately to live up to their loud words.

It was as easy, if you had no money at all, to talk in terms of thousands as it was to talk in terms of hundreds. It was as easy to call a bare field "The Heights" as it was to call it "The Lots," and once the numbered stakes were stuck in the ground it was simple for an eager builder to vision mansions behind them. Hunt was easy-going and told Fowler to go ahead with his plans; so while the eastern end of the Lots was cut up in little fudge squares and a second house like the first one started, Fowler winked at Morry and said, "Let 'em get their little chicken-houses slung up there—plenty of time for us. When we start in on the west end this town's going to sit up on its hind legs."

It worried Fowler, though, that when the two Russells from Hartford came on they stayed at Hunt's house. Bauer's was too dingy for them and when any of their associates arrived they took them to Hunt's too.

"It's too intimate. They'll talk Hunt out of his corner, living together like that," Fowler told Morry uneasily. "That leaves us holding the bag. Hunt's too damned lazy to fight for his share. They're squeezing him out of the Works and out of his own home. It's bad for our business to have them all living with him."

Morry didn't tell him he'd been fired because Fowler might think that was bad for business too. He dug out all of Fowler's books on architecture, and it was a relief seated in his cramped quarters in the Bon Ton to let his eyes feast on pictures of terraced gardens with huge spacious houses sprawling over the page. He yearned for wide rooms and tall doorways you didn't bend beneath, he argued doggedly the case for great rooms with high ceilings, the manorial against the "cute" type Fowler rather fancied.

"People want a place to breathe in," he pleaded.

"Listen, breathing costs money," said Fowler, non-committally.

He thought of all these homes as steps to a great manor that was to be his own place, a place for his mother such as she'd never dreamed. The day he told her a little of this plan, she said—

"That reminds me, Morry, I'm going to enlarge the business here, and we're fixing over the upstairs for corsets and lingerie. I guess we might as well start in with your room, so I'll put a cot down here in the workroom for you. You don't get to bed till late anyway, and you're always up early."

Morry didn't mind, he said, and took over one hat drawer for his things. Late on July nights he sat studying at the long work-table, his book propped up in the midst of artificial flowers, and stacks of rainbow-ribboned summer hats. No breeze reached this back room and perspiration would drip from his forehead to the printed page as the hot midnights passed. The room reeked with the dusty smell of long-stored trimmings, of plumes and maribou in mothballs, an old woman smell; but these present irritations were lost in the magnificence of his future. He pored over Fowler's books but when he asked him about complicated problems in them, the older man shrugged.

"What's the idea worrying about anything till you come to it? You know what you want to do in a general way, that's enough. I figure that when you know what you want in this life, all your mind focuses on slick ways of getting that one thing without working too hard at it, and by golly, you get it. But if you plug at it too hard, understand, with your nose stuck in it the way you got yours, then you lose sight of the thing you want. Your mind kinda loses its focus through the drudgery, see, and it's having your mind on it that lets you out of all the hard work. That's my opinion."

"But I want to know the things I say I know," Morry protested. "I want to be sure and safe in my head, don't you see?"

He checked lists of correspondence courses he found in the trade magazines, and struggled hopelessly with their lessons. No one seemed able to explain the Greek of these Simple Lessons.

"Good God, you don't need to know everything!" Fowler exclaimed. "I got along all right without knowing the whole works."

Morry didn't want to tell him that he was going to be more than any Fowler ever was, he was going to do a lot better than that.

Fowler had never had a drink in his life, he disapproved of saloons, but he needed to know what the strangers were up to, so he was glad Morry hung around Delaney's to listen, later on he might lecture him about whiskey and bad company but for the present he was broad-minded. Morry was swelling up a little with the respectful questions asked him in the saloon, he said more than he knew and talked easily of eight and ten thousand dollar homes, of thirty and forty dollar rents. Even Hogan was respectful but his blue eyes twinkled with sarcastic reservations now that he found Morry was to be paid off in "commissions."

"If I was you I wouldn't stick in this town, buddy," he advised. "I'd bum my way to Akron to the rubber works or down to Dayton to the Cash Register Company or take the Ford plant up in Detroit. I'd go where the big money was."

"Listen, there's going to be more big money in this here town next year than you ever saw," interrupted Bill Delaney. "I got my ears peeled, I know what's going on here. It's a good place to stick around, especially if they start floating stock in the new works like I hear, so's everybody gets a slice. You save up and buy there, Morry, you're young, you got time to get rich."

Morry watched Hogan smacking his lips over his beer and thought of when Hogan had given him the idea for a beautiful

Lamptown. There were no two ways about it, he had to do something about that one idea; he had to prove something in the world before he ever dared go to any of those cities. He couldn't ever leave till he'd made a mark here, that much he knew.

"You didn't use to say that, Hogan," he said a little rebukingly. "You said you'd stay here and make over this town."

"That's right," Shorty remembered.

Hogan patted his belly fondly.

"The hell with it," he yawned. "What's a kid like Abbott here want to stick in a little town for? Nothing to do but get some girl in trouble, let her run him to the church and marry him, and at twenty-one he's sunk. Babies, mortgages—what chance has he got? Never dare throw up his job after that and better himself——"

"Well, you did all those things——" someone dared to say.

"Sure, I did. I'm telling my story, ain't I? . . . Married twenty years,—my wife's a damned fine woman, don't misunderstand me. Lost her good looks but like old Colonel R. G. Ingersoll says, God love him——'Though the wrinkles of time, through the music of years, if you really love her, you will always see the face you loved and won.' . . . Old Bob Ingersoll."

Hunt Russell's car obstructed the view of Hulda Bauer's window. Hunt, in grey flannels, shirtsleeves, and tennis shoes, slid out from behind the wheel, and came in. Morry wasn't afraid of Hunt; he'd been fired from Hunt's factory but vaguely this put him on a level with the employer. Lately he'd made a tense, nervous third to the conferences of Hunt and Fowler,—conferences in which Hunt smoked a pipe lazily and said, "Sounds O.K. to me, Fowler,—damned good idea, and if you can do it without getting the family down on me, go ahead,—I'm no good on the details. Figure things out yourself and go to it."

"What about it, Hunt—what about this Hartford factory coming out here to hook up with the Works?" Bill Delaney asked the question no one had dared to ask directly before, and men, hanging around the pool-tables, edged up to the bar to hear what answer Hunt would make.

"That's about right, Bill," he said casually. "Things getting pretty hot in this town all around. We're bringing all the branches of the Works into Lamptown,—taking on fifteen hundred men by the end of October."

"Who runs it, then—you or your uncle Ferd?" Bill asked sharply.

Hunt shrugged his shoulders.

"What's the use of my working myself to death? I'm letting my relatives do the worrying."

"Yeah, and he'll do his worryin' later," muttered Hogan in Morry's ear. "Smarter men'n he is, buddy, you wait and see the big Lamptown cheese king take a spin on his magnum opus, wait till you see what they do to him."

"Where they going to live, for God's sake?" someone yelled from one of the tables. "These fifteen hundred families. Where you going to put 'em, Hunt, eh,—let 'em dig holes in the ground and crawl in, maybe?"

"Looks like a swell deal for Hermann," observed Shorty and sent a highball sliding down the bar to stop exactly at Hunt's elbow. "Hermann'll clean up a nice wad renting out his rooms."

"I've got to turn over my house to my cousins and some of the eastern officials, I know that much," Hunt said, frowning. "No place else for them. But later there'll be plenty of places to stay, what with the new houses on the Lots. Then the Big Four has offered their woods to the Works at a figure."

"Now there's a help," Hogan grunted sarcastically. "Why, the boys can live in the trees as snug as you please and practice birdcalls and sling buckeyes at each other, oh sure, they'll have plenty of places to stay. Why, what d'ye say, Bert, we take a coupla boarders in the coal car, and then there's plenty of room in the Round House. Oh sure, there'll be no trouble about housing the bastards, take any of these swell hotels on Market Street, and there's the old pickle factory building, the Bum's Blackstone——"

Men laughed and then stopped uneasily since after all, Hogan was pretty fresh, trying to make a fool out of Lamptown's big man. Morry didn't take Hogan as such an oracle now, he'd begun to be a little cynical, seeing him back down on his big talk so many times; he didn't kid him the way the other men did and call him "Big Noise" because he was sorry for Hogan, sorry for him because he must despise himself a

little for not living up to his brave conversation. Morry lowered his glance now whenever Hogan talked as if he was president or God or somebody, because he didn't want to betray
the devastating pity in his eyes. No one else listened to
Hogan, either, they were crowding around Hunt, firing questions at him, and Hunt, pouring down his throat one highball
after another, made half-mocking answers in a shrill strained
voice, so that afterward it struck Morry that all this change
was worrying him a good deal for some reason.

"Here, Morry, stick this up in the window on your way
out," Hunt called to him and handed him a cardboard poster.
"There's one for Hermann, too, but I'll take that one over
myself, I told Fischer I would."

"I'll bet you will," Morry thought bitterly.

He reached over the green baize curtains in the window
and propped the poster against the glass.

EVERYBODY'S COMING
TO
FISCHER'S
SERPENTINE BALL!!
July 31.   8:30 P.M.
LADIES 50¢   GENTS $1

The men crowded around Hunt,—Bill ignored orders for
drinks and rapped out questions,—was it true pay was to be
raised, that a guy from Newark, New Jersey, was coming out
to run things, that shares were to be sold to the workers; a
few who were afraid to address Hunt directly even when tipsy,
urged Bill to ask him this and that about whatever worry they
had concerning the new state. Morry lingered at the door, listening, so he could report it all to Fowler, since every sensational new step was fuel for Clover Heights.

In the hot tar-smelling street Morry mopped his forehead
and then was pleasantly cooled by the idea of widening the
creek so that there could be swimming and boating in Clover
Heights, maybe a Country Club, yes sir, Clover Heights
Country Club. . . .

He looked back in the saloon window to see if he'd got the
poster right side up and his mouth curled a little thinking of
how Hunt was afraid to let anybody else take the other poster

over to Hermann's for fear they'd ask Jen to that ball before he did. . . . Bah, let him go ahead and ask her if that's the way he feels!

Hot, sticky nights with no breeze in all Lamptown except underneath the Bon Ton's electric fan or behind Hulda Bauer's giant palm leaf. The night men at the factory worked with their sweating torsos bare, behind the honeysuckle vines on the boarding-house porches the girls sat in their kimonos eating ice-cream, the factory engines with their now doubled manpower chugged steadily through the hot stillness. A lush yellow moon hung over the Big Four woods seeming to send a glow of heat over the fields, in the stagnant creek frogs croaked and mosquitoes buzzed intently, the sultry wind ruffling the damp clover of the Lots was worse than no breeze at all.

In Delaney's the old pianola rattled ceaselessly, its music was worn out, a nickel dropped in hopefully only set the other nickels to jingling like sleighbells for three minutes, but the festive tempo was there still and the hint of devilish gaiety. Morry refused its jangling invitation for Bauer's dining-room. Here, at ten o'clock, he sat at one of the tables with Jen, and pushed a catsup bottle this way to show her where the Clover Heights Hotel was to be, the mustard here was the club, the relish dish was the Normandy chateau that was now under way, and the trail of the fork he pushed across the table was the boulevard track.

Jen's gingham sleeves were rolled to her shoulders, her black hair was kinky with the heat. She leaned half across the table to watch these fascinating maneuvers and could not restrain a sigh of admiration.

"Gee, Morry, how did you ever dare think of it?"

Morry looked bored with such stupidity.

"Good Lord, Jen, did you think I didn't know anything but crating goods at some factory? I'm not like the rest of these fellas. I should think you'd know that by this time. I got ideas."

Jen hastened to soothe him.

"I know—only I can't get over how wonderful it is, that's all I meant."

"Wait. That's all," Morry said impressively. "This is nothing.

Wait till you see our big offices,—maybe headquarters in
Cleveland or Pittsburgh—even New York. Can you imagine
me in charge of the New York business?"

"Sure, you could do it, I'll bet . . . but, it's far off, isn't it?"

Morry laughed scornfully.

"What—New York? . . . Only a couple days' trip. Not even
that. I'd take the morning local to Pittsburgh, catch the limited that night, be in New York the next day."

They were quiet because already he was gone, he was in
New York, and Jen was all alone at the table with a mustard
bottle for a country club, no Morry—nothing. . . . All right,
she would go there, too, she didn't have to follow Morry, but
she could do something.

"And when you're doing all that, I'll be in some show,—a
dancer, maybe, or an actress like Mama. . . . It won't be
long now, will it?"

Morry, not listening, shook his head, and watched the
sandy-haired little actor from the Paradise lounging at the
back table with a frayed copy of a detective magazine. Now
the actor abandoned his reading and tipped his chair back
against the wall. He tweaked idly away at his mandolin,
singing softly to himself—

> "Some of these days—
> You'll miss your hon-ey——"

He was a tenor with a voice of agonizing sweetness, yet
these sugared notes made Morry's spine quiver, they made
him desperately happy and miserable at the same time, so that
he forgot the red pepper tennis court in his hand and surrendered to this drowsy spell. The singer's eyes were closed, his
nostrils quivered holding the high notes, his stiff blue cuffs
stuck out three inches from his tight checkered sleeves. He
slid further and further back in his chair as he played, winding his legs about the chair rungs to reveal every bit of his
purple-striped socks. . . .

Morry sighed. He didn't need to tell Jen any more of his
plans,—she believed so much more than even he dared believe himself. He was exquisitely contented here tonight, he
couldn't imagine why, but it must be the singing. Jen's head
swayed to the melody as if always in the back of her head she

heard whatever music there ever was, but her eyes stayed on Morry's dark face.

"I've been so lone-a-ly," whined the honeyed voice, "just for-a-you on-a-ly——"

Hulda Bauer's fan slowed up for the long-drawn-out rhythm of this song,—if the notes lingered much more Hulda would lose count completely and fall into a doze.

"That's what I'm goin' to do—I'm goin' on the stage," Jen whispered to Morry. "When Lil comes she and I are both goin' to be actresses. Mr. Travers says it's easy. Look here."

She pulled a cabinet photograph from the drawer of the serving table and pushed it across the table to Morry. It was the picture of a young fair-haired girl in graduation dress against a background of painted ocean. Her wide eyes looked straight into Morry's, and his spine quivered again as it had over the song and over the silver-blonde on the magazine. It was her blondness that fascinated him most, except for that she looked like Jen; but he had always wondered secretly what strange things yellow-haired girls thought about.

"Lil," said Jen. "Looks like me, doesn't she?"

"Oh, I don't know," Morry said, and Jen, stiffening a little with unexpected jealousy drew the picture back.

The four legs of the actor's chair suddenly came to the floor with a bang. He threw down his mandolin, stood up and stretched himself elaborately.

"Jesus, what a dump this is!" he addressed the world bitterly. "No place to go—nothing to do—might as well turn in."

Hulda Bauer laboriously got off her stool and approached them.

"That's right, Mr. Travers. Bed's the best place. Goodnight to you."

She waddled somberly toward the stair door, nodding to Jen.

"Better be goin' home, Morry. Jen's got to be up early."

Morry got up. Jen never begged him to stay any more now. Her mouth dropped a little as he reached for his cap. Mr. Travers observed her through half-shut eyes while he put his mandolin in its case.

"Morry, don't you think that's a swell idea—Lil and I going on the stage, travelling all over, seeing everything?" Jen wanted to know.

Morry nodded casually.

"Yeah, that'll be great," he agreed. A flash of irritation came over him that Jen should have plans, too. Part of his own plans was that Jen should always be in Lamptown, always astonished at his great deeds, always breathlessly applauding. He knew a second of cold fear at the thought of this town without Jen, Jen, the one certain thing,—but he'd never let her guess that.

"That sure will be great travelling," he repeated, and Jen said no more.

Morry, aching already for a lost Jen, slouched across the street and Jen traced his name slowly with her finger across the glass cigar counter.

"Stuck on him, ain't you, Kid?" teased Mr. Travers. Jen made a horrible face at him for answer and stalked into the kitchen.

Morry didn't go to bed for hours. He got his cot ready, pulled off his damp shirt and threw it over the screen. He sat down on the cot, one shoe in his hand, and thought of how Jen's arms looked with her sleeves rolled up and who would there be to see how wonderful he was if she left town. She couldn't go away, that was all wrong. He was the one who would go away and always remember to write her about cities and strange lands he visited,—he'd go away and always remember Jen St. Clair and how much a letter from him would mean to her. Since she was only a girl and had to stay home, he'd gladly tell her all about the outside world. . . . But she said she was going. . . .

Annoyed, Morry dropped the shoe and started unlacing the other one. Lil's picture came before him, in startling detail . . . he'd never seen a girl who looked like that except the girl on the magazine. He couldn't get her out of his head. He made a complete mental image of her, made up of what Jen told him about Lil and what he knew about Jen. This confused image was lovely to think about and he could not shake it away. . . .

An eastern wind came up and blew a few drops of rain into the room. Morry went over to close the window and heard singing somewhere; it wasn't from the saloon and it seemed further away than Bauer's. He strained his ears, it was like a woman's voice far away humming to mandolin notes, but he couldn't puzzle out the exact song or whence it came. Even after the midnight fast train roared by he could hear this

music, lingering in the whistle's echo, sweet and far-off like a
promise. Finally he gave up trying to catch it, and sat down
again. He was happy. He didn't know why this was so, but
there it was. He dropped his other shoe. It covered a corner
of a postcard that had fluttered from the table to the floor. It
was a familiar card and the glimpse of it was to Morry like
seeing an evil face peering in the window, destroying every
happy thought, making his stomach contract with sick dread,
almost before his mind had taken in the words—

"THE CANDY MAN WILL VISIT YOU
ON THURSDAY, JULY 31st."

The electric fan hummed and whirred in Elsinore's room, it
sat up on a shelf watching the room, whirring, whirring, it kept
the thin blue silk dresser scarf quivering frantically in its perpetual gale; as she brushed her hair it blew her kimono sleeve
against her pale cheeks. It was like Charles himself, subtly infuriating, quietly goading her nerves, but she was determined not
to let it disturb her self-control. When she picked up her hand-
mirror she knew what the fan was saying, "So you're wearing a
low-necked dress, eh, Else . . . guess this guy's got you running, you never went in for fast clothes before . . . and the silk
chemise, too, eh? . . . Well, why not, all the sporting women
wear them and if that's you, now . . . no more blue or black
dresses, either, I see . . . pink, by George . . . so that's how
crazy he's made you, Else, old girl. . . . Pink silk at thirty-
eight. . . . Pink silk for the Serpentine Ball,—well, well-well."
Elsinore went on brushing her hair, the night was so hot
her kimono stuck to the chair, through the little windows
came the train smoke and saloon stench, the men singing and
carrying on in the street sounded alarmingly near as if they
were in the very room. She could hear the orchestra tuning
up in the Casino, she heard Fischer laughing, and she wanted
to hurry into the new dress but she was afraid of the watching fan. Well, she didn't care now. Let it find out that she
hated her husband, very well, let it know everything. In the
wastebasket beside the dresser was the box in which a silk
chemise had arrived this morning and a note from Charles,
saying, "Thought your new lovers might like this."
She had read the card, stunned, while Nettie tore off the

tissue papers and pulled out the gift in great delight. All
Charles' former taunts had been faint, far-off drum beats leading up to this menacing roll of thunder that could not be ignored. . . . "Thought your new lovers . . ." As Nettie shook
out the silk, admiring its lace edge, the cages of Elsinore's
mind burst open and hatred escaped. There was no way of
locking it back in, there was a fearful joy in facing the truth,
that strange blend of relief and desolation in seeing a jewel,
long desperately guarded, finally lost forever. She wanted to
tear up the note and the gift with it, but her second thought
was a perverse resolve to wear the garment, as if she had carried out his savage suggestion. . . . It occurred to her to spray
perfume on her hair, just as he had told her bad women did.
For the first time in her life she wished for an intimate friend,
a woman who knew her secrets, who would come in now while
she dressed and say, "Elsinore, you never looked lovelier in
your life,—not a day over twenty-eight. If Harry Fischer only
knew you were through with Charles, he wouldn't hesitate a
minute,—Mrs. Pepper's nothing to him, really, just a convenience,—if he knew how you hated your husband. . . ."

Downstairs Nettie sat in the front of the shop, dressed in
prim white embroidery, waiting for Fay and her young man to
call for her. Elsinore wanted them to be gone before she came
downstairs in her new pink dress, so after she was ready she
sat down by her window waiting to see them cross the street
as her signal for leaving. There was a tall, black-haired young
man standing at the foot of the Casino steps rolling a cigarette. He seemed restless and each time the Bauers' screen
door swung open he peered around to see who was coming
out. Finally he pulled his cap down over his eyes and slouched
into the restaurant. This was Morry, his mother saw, and
while his motions stirred no curiosity in her, they irritated the
watchful Nettie downstairs, almost beyond endurance. She
had almost decided to go right into Bauer's after him, and tell
him right before everyone that instead of waitresses he ought
to be taking his own mother to the Casino.

The Casino windows gave out a mellow candy-pink glow
from bunting-shrouded lights, and Elsinore could not distinguish Fischer from his musicians in the dark group near the
window. Then she caught the gleam of a white dress shirt and

a humming in her head joined the humming of the fan behind her. It was difficult to sustain, unfading in her mind, the
black onyx eyes of Harry Fischer, the white eyeballs spread
out and then diminished so that they were now white eyes,
now black eyes, the color flickering and changing with the
electric fan's insistent vibration. . . .

A man and two girls in white crossed the street—Nettie
and Fay. Elsinore took a last look at herself in the mirror. Her
hair was too tightly drawn,—she took the pins out and did it
up again nervously. The pink taffeta dress with its round neck
had seemed too low when she first bought it, she had had to
put a lace ruching across the front. Now she saw that the
ruching was out of place and with her nail scissors she clipped
the threads that held it. She picked up her white silk shawl
and went downstairs through the darkened shop out into the
hot, breathless night.

In her empty bedroom the electric fan whirred and purred,
it kept the dresser-scarf trembling perpetually, the closet door
gently blowing open and shut, the shades on the little windows crackling, and rapidly it flicked the pages of a mail-order
catalogue lying on the bed.

Streamers of colored serpentine fluttered from the Casino
ceiling, men dancing in their shirt-sleeves snatched at it and
lassoed shrieking girls, they kicked through tangles of the
rainbow strips over the dance floor, under the pink lights all
women looked gay and darkly wicked. In the center of the
floor the dancing teacher and Dode O'Connell two-stepped
perfectly, Dode in a skin-tight red dress defying her red hair.
The musicians (Mr. Sanderson at the piano) sang their cho-
ruses, their throats bulged and veins swelled on their foreheads as they bellowed the words, but even so the shouting
and laughing of the dancers drowned them out, only a phrase
now and then soared through the din,—"Some of these
days—you'll miss——"

Morry danced with Jen for the third time running, in this
uproar it would not be remarked, besides she was so light in
his arms he forgot to trade her for someone else. Jen tried to
make herself still and light as a feather so that she could be
close to Morry and not let him notice it, for if he remem-

bered it was only Jen he was holding he'd drop her and go
away. He was so tall he had to hump his shoulders way over
to hold her, and her arm was tight around his neck. All she
could think, dancing, was that this was the way she wanted to
be—always,—fast in Morry's arms. On the visitor's bench by
the doorway Nettie Farrell, watching, her embroidered dress
spread out in stiff petals around her, whispered something to
her chum, Fay, who then stared hard at Jen's feet. Nettie
didn't last very long at the Serpentine Ball for the men were
all hilariously drunk, and they called endearing names to her
as they danced past or chucked her under the chin familiarly,—no one respected a decent girl in this noisy carnival, so
at eleven o'clock Nettie indignantly departed.

"I have an announcement to make tonight, ladies and gentlemen," Fischer bawled through the megaphone. "The Serpentine Ball tonight is the last dance of the summer. The first
dance of the autumn season will be given here in six weeks on
September tenth. I wish to state that I will introduce to my
pupils and members of my studio at that time the Mississippi
Glide. This dance, ladies and gentlemen, is the popular ballroom dance of New York City at the present time, and with
the assistance of Miss O'Connell, here, I will give you a brief
demonstration. The Mississippi Glide. All right, Mr. Sanderson."

Immediately the crowd of dancers backed away, leaving the
center of the floor free for the dancing-master and his partner.
Eyes fastened on the black patent-leather feet (heels never
touching floor) and the red satin ($10) slippers as they traced
an intricate design on the shining oak floor.

"Do you suppose they really dance that way in New York?"
Jen whispered to Morry. It hadn't occurred to Morry to ever
doubt it, but now he shook his head convincingly.

"Na,—they never even heard of it in New York," he answered. Jen's hand was hot in his but he did not drop it for
Hunt Russell was alone nearby, and Morry thought stubbornly that now he was a business man himself he didn't have
to give in to anyone, he didn't care so much about dancing
with Jen but he wanted Hunt Russell to understand he had as
much right to as anybody.

Fischer was the only man to keep his coat on, all the others were dancing with their shirt sleeves rolled up, their wilted collars open, serpentine trailing from their ears and trouser-legs, their sweaty palms making smudgy imprints on the light dresses of their girls. The punch bowl in the hall had been filled three times, strengthened more each time with rum. Couples danced dizzily, wearily around, battered by the crowd; girls' heads, peering blankly over their partners' shoulders, seemed pinned there like valentines, their faces dulled with music, their eyes unwinking, hair stringing damply over their cheeks.

Elsinore danced with a big red-faced drummer from Newark with a silver hook for a left hand. He said, "Just catch hold of that there hook, that's the idea," and he said that when it came to carrying sample-cases a hook was better than a hand, but Elsinore shuddered touching the cold metal. His big tan shoes scuffed her white kid pumps, he held her so tight that her back ached, but this violence strangely pleased her as the clangor about her satisfied some desperate inner necessity. The jiggling crowd tore the sash from her pink dress, in the frenzy of a circle two-step with the music growing faster and faster her head whirled, and the girls, swinging from one hand to the next, kept up a high, dizzy scream that soared above all else.

"Dance with Number Three," roared Fischer and she was swung into his arms. Perspiration streamed from his forehead, he shook out a cream-colored silk kerchief and mopped his head. His heart thumped against her and confused her, even the smell of whiskey on his breath was rare and exciting. She forgot that he was Mrs. Pepper's, that in little railroad hotels those two met and went to one room, she forgot about the big blonde wife in Cleveland, all of these shadows faded under the pink lights and the hard bright gleam in his black eyes. He called a command over her shoulder, "Dance with the lady on your left!" and she was flung into a new partner's arms. She saw that Fischer was dancing with the Delaneys' girl, Jen,—she would always remember that she had been pushed away for that young girl. . . .

She didn't want anyone else to touch her now, so she broke away from the dance and went into the dressing-room. Only two girls were inside, big raw-boned girls with red arms and

necks thrust out of feathery pink and blue organdie, blonde
chickens popping out of Easter eggs. They stood before the
dresser shaking clouds of powder over their faces from huge
powder puffs, trustfully and intently, as if this witchcraft
would instantly compel popularity. Elsinore looked at her
face, white and small in the mirror between their two ruddy
faces. She looked wild, she thought, with her hair flying about
loosely, but she didn't care. Her head was splitting with noise
but she wasn't sure if the noise were outside or inside, so
many strange confusing thoughts crowded through her head
like masked guests at a carnival, exciting, terrifying, shouting
phrases they would never dare whisper under their own
names. There was something familiar in all these suggestions
as if long ago they had briefly appeared and at once been
whisked off to dungeons. There was no guard for them now,
but a fearful exhilaration in the knowledge that they were too
strong for her, that they could overpower her easily.

She saw through the doorway that Fischer was still dancing
with Jen St. Clair and she recalled old Mrs. Delaney warning
her to keep Morry away from this girl. She would, she
thought viciously, or better, she'd tell her to keep away from
Morry. She'd say "Morry" but she would be secretly meaning, "Keep away from Harry Fischer!" Because he belonged
to her, to nobody else. . . . Elsinore looked quickly at the
two girls as if the thunder of her own mind might be overheard. One of them was bending over fixing a red garter on
her white cotton stocking but she caught Elsinore's eye and
smiled.

"If I bring my last summer's hat back, Mrs. Abbott," she
ventured, "could you change the daisies on it for poppies?"

Elsinore smiled back at her but the words seemed no more
concern of hers than the girl's knobby knees above her pretty
legs, and when the girls went out together one said to the
other, "She don't have to snub me twice, believe me." Then
at the door they burst out laughing shrilly to show everyone
they were having a wonderful time. . . .

Elsinore was glad they were gone, she felt sick from their
geranium-scented powder. She opened the window wider and
pulled the moth-eaten velveteen curtains behind her, it was
easier to be here in the next room thinking of Fischer than in

the ballroom seeing him with someone else. There was no air stirring outside, stars and a moon would have looked cool but only the lights from the Works lit up the sky with a soft red glare. She could hear the steady chugging of the factory machines going all night long, and from up here she could see the long dark shadows of freight cars sliding back and forth in the Yard, the emerald and ruby signal lights winking on and off. Through the din of the dance-hall the two-four rhythm of the bass drum throbbed triumphantly and punctuated the swish-swish of the engines outside. They didn't need an orchestra for Lamptown dances, Elsinore thought, holding her splitting head in her hands, the engines and the factory machines could keep two-four time. One and two and a one and a two and a one—this drum-beat that could not be silenced was part of Fischer, all of her fantasies were made to this obligato; they unrolled now automatically,—herself and Fischer on a train going away, away,—away from young girls with smooth throats and light laughter, away from factory girls with hard mouths dancing with fierce grace, away from delicately scented, plump women with tinkling voices,—only Mrs. Abbott, a milliner, and Mr. Fischer, a dancing master. Away to what?—Breathlessly she allowed herself to draw aside this forbidden curtain, to see them alone, he is coming through a doorway smiling at her, the doorway of her bedroom, she is in the pink taffeta dress waiting, and— Crowds of girls burst through the door, abruptly the dream vanished and Elsinore wrung her hands. There could be no torture like interruption, the brutal ripping of cherished tapestries. If she had one wish in the world it would be to be locked in a tower to think of one man undisturbed forever. She was nauseated again by geranium powder, girls battled for place at the mirror, giggling they crowded her away from the window, the room became stifling. She could not endure it any longer. She pulled her shawl from the hook and a dozen wraps fell in a heap on the floor but she couldn't bother with them. If she could only sleep . . . but she hadn't slept for months it seemed to her. The mad circus in her head exhausted her, she didn't want to face Fischer again tonight. Alone, in her room, he was hers completely, here he belonged to all Lamptown. She walked unsteadily down the narrow hallway toward the steps, she didn't look back once to see him. The dance-hall, out of the corner of her eye, was a nightmare of laughter and fluttering colors. She could scarcely wait to get home to think, to plan, to be alone. . . .

In the darkness of the stair landing Morry and Jen and Hunt Russell were standing.

"Well, Jen, how about it, coming with me?" Hunt asked. He was holding Jen's bare arm caressingly.

Jen looked at Morry but Morry wouldn't tell her not to go,—if she wanted to go for a ride with Hunt he wouldn't stop her.

"Should we go, Morry?" she asked.

"Do what you please," Morry said distantly. "You wouldn't go if you didn't want to, anyway."

His mother hurried by without looking at him. He started after her but she ran down the steps in almost clumsy haste, so Morry didn't follow her just then, besides he wanted to see what Jen was going to do.

Elsinore's heart was pounding when she reached the street, she felt enormously elated as if she had escaped her hunters so far and was about to gloat over a stolen treasure in perfect safety. Not a soul was out. As far down Market Street as she could see lights blinked on deserted sidewalks, all Lamptown was crowded under the rose-lights of the Casino; only Hermann and Hulda Bauer dozed in their windows. . . . She fumbled with her key, but her hands were shaking so she could scarcely fit it into the lock. The shop bell tingled sharply in the darkness as the door opened, then stopped short as the door shut. She turned the key quickly behind her again, she wanted to lock out these nameless pursuers who would harry her, for she was going to be alone, alone. . . . Her head and feet were so light, only her heart was thundering away, it could be heard above the Casino tumult or the engine whistles, she was certain. . . . Now she remembered the feel of his thick white hand grasping hers, the sensation was far clearer in memory than it had been in actuality, she could see the fine lines around his eyes, the cleft in his heavy chin . . . she felt so giddy she leaned against the wall for a moment at the top of the stairs. . . . She was strangely happy as if she were on the verge of something beautiful about to

happen, something incredible, she was separated from this triumph by the thinnest of walls, if she could only control the
chaos in her head she would know what this lovely thing was.
. . . In another minute she could think—she'd be alone. . . .
She pushed open the bedroom door and the noise of the fan
made her catch her breath with the shock of reality. . . . The
lovely thing about to happen . . . she clung to its vanishing
shadow, but everything beautiful was fleeing desperately,
there was only Charles Abbott, collarless and red-faced,
sprawling drunkenly over her bed. She put her hand over her
eyes to dispel this bad dream. Charles awkwardly sat up,
blinking at her with blood-shot eyes. It was terrifying, the
spectacle of the immaculate Candyman with his starched
striped shirt rumpled, his black hair tousled and hanging over
his eyes, his thin mouth sagging loosely. His coat and hat
trailed on the floor, his sample cases were open and bonbons
spilled all over the rug. Elsinore shook with blind fury, she
wanted to tear him to pieces with her hands.

"Well, who'd you expect to see here if not your husband?"
He pointed at her accusingly. "You come in here and turn
white as a sheet, cause you see me. Who the hell was you expecting, damn it, stand there shivering away like I was some
burglar. . . ."

She didn't dare to look at him again, hate was burning her
veins, she wanted to kill him, to destroy everybody who outraged her right to be alone. His thick voice, whatever it was
saying, rasped through her thoughts, there surely must be an
end to such torment. She wouldn't look at him for she knew
tears of rage were smarting in her eyes and through this blur
she saw the little heap of silver-wrapped bonbons in the top of
the sample case, she saw how cleverly they formed one curious shape, no use steadying her rioting brain to make sure of
what her eyes saw there, for silver was in her brain, silver shut
out Charles' voice, silver chilled the hatred in her heart, before she touched it she thrilled with the ecstasy of escape that
beautiful metal in her hands could bring, wild happiness swept
over her, the joy, exactly, of finding an opening in the prison
wall too small for her pursuers but for her—final freedom.

On and on the drunken voice droned, accusing her, mocking her, as it had done year after year slowly wearing down

her barriers. Facing him, her hand groped among the bonbons for what she had seen there, as soon as she touched the
revolver she had a vision of a paradise of solitude and privacy
forever. This was one way to shut out words . . . she raised
the gun, closed her eyes and fired.

The awful hush of the minute afterward terrified her. She
was sitting in a chair, tears slowly coursing down her cheeks.
Someone hurrying up the steps, calling out, meant nothing to
her. It meant nothing to see Charles sprawled over the floor,
his mouth still open in his astonishment. A stream of blood
trickled from him across the floor and slowly dyed the little
blue door-mat. The revolver was lost in the candies that had
tumbled over. . . .

She began rocking back and forth in the chair. Her head
ached, it was so empty and numb. Back and forth she rocked.
Someone came in the room but she could not see or hear or
feel, a man lying on the floor was no concern of hers, the only
thing that was oddly familiar was the whirring of the electric
fan behind her.

So Charlie Abbott had shot himself, they said.

No one in Lamptown knew why and no one really cared.
In Delaney's bar they said Charlie Abbott was a bad egg, he
had smooth ways but he was too slick with his women, too
damned slick, never doing a thing for his wife and kid in
Lamptown, they could starve for all of him. In the backyards
of Shanteyville women hanging up the wash, their mouths full
of clothespins, speculated about what fast woman Mr. Abbott
had killed himself for. No good, anyway, running around
spending money while his wife worked her fingers to the bone
keeping herself and the boy. Mrs. Abbott was a lady, as fine a
little woman as you'd care to meet, you'd think after all she'd
done the least a husband could do in return was to shoot
himself in one of those big hotels instead of messing up her
nice little shop.

The reporter from the Cleveland Leader asked Bill Delaney
how the gun happened to be on the other side of the room
after this "suicide," and if it hadn't struck Bill that the wife
might have plugged him on account of his other women. Bill
Delaney fixed the stranger with an indignant eye.

"None of that funny business, now," he curtly advised. "Don't let anybody in this town hear you say a thing like that or they'll run you out of town. I know that's all in your line, but leave Mrs. Abbott out of it, see? She's a quiet lady-like little body that's had her first piece of luck now with her husband kicking off. You just keep your imagination to yourself, because Lamptown people won't listen to a word about Mrs. Abbott. A plucky little woman, that's what she is."

Only Morry knew. He had known when he opened the bedroom door and saw his mother rocking quietly beside the thing on the floor. He was paralyzed with terror and an awful guilty feeling of having wished this very thing until it came true. . . . Then all he could think was how unhappy she must have been to do it, and such pity came over him for his mother that his throat ached and he was ready to face all the rest of her tormenters himself, and to kill them all. It didn't matter about his father, it only mattered that his mother had suffered all these years, it was as if she were the one who had died, and all his failures to understand or to help her loomed in his mind,—too late he would make amends.

But there was little, after all, for him to do now. All Lamptown was taking care of little Mrs. Abbott whose husband had chosen such a tragic end. The Bauers took charge of everything. Hulda slept in the shop and at the last minute there was no place for Morry so he had to stay at Hunt's overnight. He hung around his mother, he wanted her to say she needed him and that Hulda could go home but Elsinore didn't say anything. She stayed in bed, eating nothing, staring at visitors blankly when they asked questions, seeming to recognize no one.

"She's been that way ever since they found him," people whispered.

Hermann knew the story and told everybody exactly how it happened. It seems Bill Delaney was in back of his saloon when he heard the shot, and since Charlie had been in there an hour before, drunk, and waving a revolver, he'd sort of suspected him of something. So he rushed into the Bon Ton and the next minute he was sticking his head out of the upstairs window, yelling, "Hey, Hermann, for God's sake, Charlie Abbott's dead!" Hermann waddled over as fast as he could and by the time he got upstairs Bill Delaney had gone all to pieces,—he was on his knees by the bed sobbing and shivering and out of his mind.

"Oh God, Hermann, it wasn't my fault," he screamed, "I swear it wasn't—but look at them spread out all over the tracks— all bleeding and all dead——" They called in Bill's mother to take him home, he clung to her weakly, sobbing against her bent old shoulder that the wreck wasn't his fault. . . .

Girls ran in from the Casino and Hermann finally had to lock the doors. "Well, Charlie shot himself, that's all, now get back to your dance."

Elsinore, all the next day, sat in her chair by the window, wrapped in a blanket, her hair tumbled down, her face sagging oddly, her eyes stupid. Morry kept patting her hand but he didn't know what to say to her, or anything to do for her except vague magnificent deeds that would somehow make her happy. She cared no more for him than for anyone, and she seemed ten times more remote, never talking, looking dully out the window all the time, never heeding the compassionate questions of the neighbors. She didn't comb her hair or change to night clothes when she went to bed, and this bothered Morry more than anything for he could not conceive of a catastrophe big enough to make his mother neglect her person. He didn't think of his father, all he knew was that a terrible thing had happened to his mother, and he was suffocated with tenderness for her. He thought about her every instant, he was going to do something to make it all up to her, he tried to think of something that would astonish and please her, but all he could think of was a little silver bar pin he'd got her from Robbin's for Christmas once.

"That's it—I'll get her another bar pin," he decided with relief.

The blue veins in her temples and white hands moved him almost to tears, and the marble pallor of her face. . . . He knew what it was like to have it all burning inside of you with no way of showing it. If he could only smooth everything for her. . . . He was enraged at his futility, then the whisper came—"You can't help her because she won't let you,—it isn't your fault,—it's only that she doesn't need you or anybody else."

This wasn't quite fair for her, a woman ought to need her son, oughtn't she? . . . Hurt and troubled, Morry went back to Fowler's office and tried to concentrate on Clover Heights. Everyone he met looked at him reproachfully and said, "Look here, Morry, oughtn't you to be home with your mother?" . . . He couldn't very well explain that his mother didn't want him, so he could only mutter a sullen answer about the demands of his work. He amazed himself by asking Fowler for a salary and getting it.

He was conscious of curious eyes everywhere, and he walked stiffly and proudly so that people would be afraid to talk to him. He'd do something yet, nothing he'd ever planned was big enough, it had to be some colossal achievement now to make Lamptown forget about his father, something so breath-taking that it would swallow up this present scandal, so at the mention of the name "Abbott" the town would not say, "Oh yes, son of the guy who killed himself," but "Oh yes, the young man who owns the Big Four Railroad . . . who built the bridge across Lake Erie . . . the Abbott that put Lamptown on the map." When he read in the paper of some man inventing this or that, or winning a great prize he shook his head and thought, "Better than that . . . it's got to be better than that."

At the moment Clover Heights was all he could work on, and so much depended on other people and money that it seemed not to move at all. He took to wearing overalls and helping out when some carpenter's assistant didn't show up, and found that physical exhaustion soothed his fever to do, to accomplish things.

He fixed up an army cot in Fowler's office because there wasn't any place for him at the Bon Ton. The shop was full of women, and when he would go in the evening to see his mother she didn't talk, all he could do was to pat her hand and finally he shunted off the busy helpers. Hulda transferred herself and her palmleaf to the workroom, and Hermann would bring over great trays of roasts which Elsinore never touched. Nettie and Mrs. Pepper and Hulda and all the visiting women kept the workroom noisy (even though the shop was properly closed) with the rattle of table-setting, and eating, while old Mrs. Delaney washed dishes perpetually for these funeral banquets. The constant activity kept everyone happy and the widow's apathetic silence was not conspicuous, it seemed decent and lady-like.

Four mornings after the funeral Nettie came into the shop and found the wreath off the front door. Elsinore, in a big black apron, was cleaning out the closet in the workroom. She'd hauled out half a dozen boxes and her face was covered with soot. Nettie was unprepared for such a quick return to routine. She herself was wearing a black dress out of deference to her employer's grief, and she was prepared with little consolation phrases.

"Mice have gotten into these felts," Elsinore said abruptly. "We'll have to move everything out."

Nettie looked dolefully at her.

"Oh, Mrs. Abbott, you're so brave to pick up things so quickly again! . . . You've been so brave about it all—I don't see what made him do it! I can't understand! Poor Mr. Abbott! And it's all so hard on you."

"Well, there's so much work to be done around here. Nettie, there won't be time to think," Elsinore said in such a matter-of-fact voice that Nettie couldn't believe her ears. "In another two months we've got to have this whole place ready, upstairs showrooms finished, all ready for business. Mrs. Pepper will be ready to move in as soon as we can have her."

All of Nettie's rehearsed condolences were forgotten in being reminded of Mrs. Pepper's triumphant return. She hung her hat on the clothes-tree and silently pinned on her apron. It was true that Mrs. Abbott looked half-sick dragging herself around with heavy feet, but Nettie wasn't sorry for her any more, not a bit. If a woman showed no more feelings than that after her husband was dead you couldn't expect Nettie to have feelings for her. Why, you might even think she was glad about it.

Elsinore was neither glad nor sorry. The revolver shot had blown out some fuse in her brain. She couldn't remember why it had seemed so important to silence Charles, the thoughts that had made her quiver with fanatic delight a few days back were lost, Fischer ceased when Charles ceased, all feeling died with that explosion. Now, night and day, she was only the proprietor of a thriving millinery store, in her numb memory ran color combinations, arrangements of hand-made lilacs on milan, her heart had become a ribbon rosette worn with chic a little to one side.

"A nice little woman," Harry Fischer said about Mrs. Abbott, "but not very light on her feet."

Mrs. Pepper asked him to be particularly kind to her friend because she'd seen so much trouble, so the dancing master, instead of a mere good-day when he met the milliner, would remember to add, "Is it hot enough for you, Mrs. Abbott?" or "Quite a little shop you have there, Mrs. Abbott, quite a nice little property." It was more than he'd ever said to her before but it meant nothing to her now. She would say over his words afterward in a wistful effort to restore her old romance, but it was gone, it had blown up with its own enemy. She knew that Mrs. Pepper was meeting him again, but she didn't care, it seemed so far away—those years when she had cared. She knew when the affair began again, because for the first two or three months of the enlarged Bon Ton regime Mrs. Pepper had sobbed nightly in bed with her, talked very little, and grew almost thin. Then, after one day on some mysterious business in Cleveland, she began to hum about her work, she no longer wept but chatted optimistically about life, she let out the pleats in her skirts once more and found many important errands out of town, even though she was permanently stationed in Lamptown. She tiptoed radiantly about her showroom over the Bon Ton—(the very room where Charles was killed)—fondly patting the headless dummies in their gorgeous lavender brocaded girdles, peeping out doors from time to time to see if any women on the street were admiring the lingerie display in the window, and in mid-afternoon when business was dull she'd go downstairs and say, "Nettie, I wish you'd sing that thing you used to sing—'Come, come, I love you only—(you know the one I mean)—I want but you——' "

Women from good homes in Avon and neighboring villages began to shop in Lamptown instead of sending to Cleveland or Columbus for their clothes. Two whole new streets were dug up through the Lots by the Lamptown Home Company, twenty-four houses ($2800 apiece) to a street. New families were moving in before the paint was dry on

the walls, dozens of strange children played in the street ex-
cavations and tobogganed down the rubbish heaps along the
torn roads. Officials at the Works rode to and fro in brand
new Fords or even Cadillacs and it was rumored that the
wives of these eastern strangers smoked cigarettes and played
cards every afternoon. Bauer's was crowded with boarders,
young men who wouldn't buy homes or bring their families
to Lamptown till they saw how they liked their new jobs. So
many bigwigs from the east were staying at Hunt's that the
old mansion slipped quite naturally into the hotel class. It was
called the Russell House, and Hunt, running back and forth
to Cleveland nowadays, seemed to think the group of paying
guests was a jolly improvement on his old hermitage. The one
person who looked upon this change as sacrilege was Morry
Abbott, and Morry himself boarded there. When he turned in
at the imposing gate every evening he whispered to himself,
"My home. . . . Now I know how Hunt used to feel walking under these trees." It was his—now, his, almost as much
as it was Hunt's, and the twelve other guests were of no consequence, he swelled with pride of possession whenever he
opened the heavy white doors into the dark spacious hallway,
he scarcely dared think it was true that he, merely by virtue of
nine dollars a week, was able to call this his home. He hoped
his mother would see the importance of this step in his life,
he said, "Well, I got a place at Hunt Russell's now, I'll clear
my stuff out of that bureau." But all she said was, "That's
better than sleeping in Mr. Fowler's office, anyway, isn't it?"

But even the next summer failed to find Clover Heights any
further developed than its original three houses—one complete, the other two arrested in the last stage of their construction awaiting the particular demands of problematical
buyers. On one side of the Lots scores of tiny houses, Model
B, squeezed on to a main road, and dozens of others, neatly
identical, paralleled them behind, waiting trustingly for new
roads to cross their door-stoops. On the other side of the
creek, surrounded by untouched meadowland, three large
houses marked the beginning of "Clover Heights." One of
these was of rough brown stone with a curious rolled roof
and this was known as the "chateau." The other two were
brownish-green frame and were referred to as Normandy

style or perhaps it was semi-Ann Hathaway, though residents of Avon could boast of similar structures which were merely spoken of as a $7500 home. Lamptown's new inhabitants often spent Sunday looking over these three houses, showing them to relatives from out-of-town, but in the eight months they'd been standing no one had ventured to buy or even rent one. Morry was amazed at this apathy, at first, and reassured Fowler that it would only be a matter of weeks; even the bank officials told him that it was a wise thing to show people they need not move out of Lamptown in order to have a better-class home. But Fowler said, "Uh-huh" and looked longingly toward the rival renting office of the Lamptown Home Company where a steady stream of men and women flowed in and out.

"We could rent for forty, maybe," he meditated gloomily, "but we can't meet their twenty-two fifty. . . ."

Instead of a Country Club, the first big building on the Lots was a huge barn-like place called the Working Girls' Club. It stood at the corner, large, blank, square, with a row of little houses stemming from it east and west. A yard of red earth between its front stoop and the cinder walk allowed a few desperate blades of grass to grow, and a gaunt geranium was on either side of the step, but even these decorative touches failed to entice the old factory girls to live there. However, new girls, answering ads put in state papers, poured in here and were given sets of house rules and introduced to a matron who was to help them with their problems. The chief problem of the girls was how to keep from having babies and the new matron's answer to this was a solemn lecture on the wages of sin, so that better paid girls rapidly took to renting the little neighboring houses, four girls to a house, where they could do as they pleased and work out their own problem. The new officials started a welfare department at the Works with a nurse in charge, who sent girls home who had headaches and wouldn't allow them to return till their health was perfect. For these days of angry rest their wages were docked but it was a very efficient service and admired editorially all over the state. Kindly lectures once a week on the dangers, moral and physical, of women smoking and having too close friendships, opened up a new and dazzling vista to

Lamptown girls too busy quarreling over men heretofore to keep up with feminine progress in larger cities.

Lamptown was getting rich. Half the town had accepted the invitation of the directors to buy stock so that you could scarcely find a shoe-clerk or a grocery boy in the place who wasn't a share-holder. When strangers made some ribald joke about old Tom, the drunken street-cleaner, asleep on the curb in the midst of his work, Bill Delaney loved to amaze them by answering, "Looks like a bum, don't he? Well, that bird sold his shanty and bought five hundred dollars worth of shares in the Works not ten months ago. Know what he's worth today? Twenty-five hundred dollars, yes sir, and it'll be twice that before another year's out!"

Careful citizens who were not going to risk their small savings on that dangerous unknown world of stocks bitterly watched improvident neighbors who had thrown everything into this venture roll by in the automobiles they had bought on dividends. The very shyest men accosted fellow travelers with the news whenever they went out of town, in Cleveland hotel lobbies they stared at innocent strangers over their newspapers until their glance was returned, then they drew close and said,—

"Have a cigar, sir? Look here, I want to show you something," and they'd whip a Works prospectus out of their pocket. "Lamptown Works. You know our products, I guess. Well, that's my home town. A year ago I bought a thousand shares in this Works and sir, today, it's worth six times what I paid for it. Why, say, we've got one of the biggest propositions right there in that little town—talk about your Ford plant! Say, what's your name, sir? I wish if you're ever passing through down there you'd look me up. I just want to take you through that there factory. I'd just like to show you something."

Going down Market Street you'd meet dozens of people you'd never seen before, there were four Packards in town owned by men Lamptown never heard of, and when Hunt Russell's car, battered and seedy-looking in comparison to the new ones, drove down town, an old citizen might remark, "Ah—Hunt Russell!" at which newcomers indifferently queried, "Well, who's Hunt Russell?" And after all, who was

Hunt, now? There were Russells on the board of directors but Hunt was only a minor vice-president, he no longer took part in the company's movements. When matters came up needing the signature of a third vice-president Hunt was seldom to be found, unless you wanted to search the grandstand at the North Randall race-tracks or keep an eye on the yellow roadster before a Prospect Avenue sporting house in Cleveland.

The new people didn't know Hunt Russell but they knew young Abbott. Everybody knew the young man who showed you over the 'chateau', who had for an office a tiny sample house at the eastern edge of the Lots, a small house whose roof was lettered in red and white—"Clover Heights Company. See Morris Abbott inside or call Lamptown 66 J." The girls on their way home to the Club went round by this little office and if old Fowler wasn't in they stopped by to kid Morry and see if he wouldn't ask for a date. He seldom surrendered to their laughing challenges however. He smoked cigars like Fowler and was considered a cagey young man with a much better business-head than was strictly true. He talked briskly to strangers, helped all the side issues of Fowler's business as notary public, auctioneer, rent collector, and no one could trace the exact beginning of this crisp aggressive manner, though Morry knew he had adopted it painfully, at first, to protect himself from Lamptown's pity and questioning after his father's death. When it was necessary to refer to that event he could say 'after the old man kicked off' quite casually without that quick fear of someone suspecting his mother that he had once felt.

Nobody could rattle Morry Abbott, he was armored against everything because he knew it was your business to be hard just as it was the world's business to throw javelins into you. He was intensely grateful to Fowler for opening up his life. It was Fowler and he against the rest of Lamptown and Fowler's frequent moods of depression did not discourage him.

"But look at the place, Morry," Fowler nodded toward the desolate expanse of Heights crowned by its three empty mansions. "We can't get another cent to keep on building unless one of these sells—even old Hunt isn't fool enough to advance us any, let alone the bank. And no work going on makes the proposition look like a dud. And if it looks like a dud it might as well be one, see what I mean."

"Wait till people get used to having more money," argued Morry. "They still have the idea that if they get enough money for a swell home they've got to move to Avon for it. Wait. Why, every day I take at least two people over those houses. That leads to something, you know."

"Like hell it does," muttered Fowler. "The damn fools steal the fixtures, we got repair bills on those houses as if somebody was living in 'em already, on Sundays folks have picnics in the gardens and break in for souvenirs to show all their out-of-town friends what swell houses they got. But ask one of them to live there! Ha! It isn't that they cost more, rent or buy, it's because they're different."

"But that's the whole point—they've got to be different!" Morry continued to protest.

Fowler shook his head morosely.

"I got people coming to me all the time asking for houses exactly like this one or that one next door, a man's whole aim is to have a place exactly like everybody's, he feels like a fool being different. Take his wife, she says, 'Oh, but you said this house was just like Traumer's and here is the closet on the left of the landing instead of the right, liar!' I got a hunch we're stung, Abbott, my boy,—not on houses, understand, but on people!"

"Well, we've got to stick it out until we've proved we're right," Morry said.

"Oh sure, sure, we'll stick it out," Fowler agreed without enthusiasm.

Morry refused to believe the Fowler who had been standing with him against the world was so easily scared. He had felt so secure with the older man applauding each new idea for Heights improvement, it was the two of them against everybody else. Now he suspected he was standing alone, and he was bewildered. How could a man change so completely,—the idea was the same idea they started with, wasn't it? . . . Going home, Morry found himself more upset than he had realized. Fowler's misgivings shook the very ground under his future, he hadn't ever dreamed that he would change.

Morry walked down Market Street and in a shop window mirror was surprised to see himself, no use denying it, a big, good-looking young man wearing his new grey suit with an air, his straw hat tilted just so. In this image there appeared no indication of the vague fear in his heart, you would never have guessed that this young man had any doubts as to his own perfection. It was a reassuring image, and Morry was heartened by it. You didn't see a fellow like that out of a job, or working away at some dinky factory job.

He stopped in front of the Paradise to read the bill for tonight. Two vaudeville turns were announced this week, pictures of the performers simpered from the lobby walls. One, a portrait of a slumbrous-eyed Jewess with a guitar proclaimed, "The Singing Salome"; the other photograph showed two blonde girls in white tights and spangled bodices, one holding the other at the waist, both laughing sunnily with an air of incalculable good humor. Morry looked around for other pictures of these "Two Little Clowns from Ragtime Town." He could hear Milly practicing their new songs inside and thought he heard girls' voices, he was almost tempted to go inside and see if the Two Little Clowns were in there, too. He could not get over his old awe of these glamorous stage women, beginning way back with Lillian Russell they were tangled up with his ambition to do great things,—why?—in order to come closer, perhaps to be able to touch them. Men bragging in Bill's bar of affairs with little carnival actresses made these no nearer or more easily attainable.

"When do the Two Clowns come on tonight?" he asked the man sweeping out the lobby.

"Eight-ten and ten-ten."

Morry turned away. He thought fiercely the Heights plan had to prove out, then he would turn into a Hunt Russell, he would have a glittering long automobile at the curb here and when the Two Little Clowns came out he would casually invite them to ride. Still, he didn't desire them, any more than he wanted a gold and white yacht, he only wanted to be equal to these far-off splendors, to have no doors locked to him.

Market Street was crowded as it was so often now, strange women in hats and gloves and plain dark silks came out of shops, you turned to look twice at them for Lamptown girls went around town bareheaded all summer. Sometimes one of these foreign women stepped into an auto at the curb and took the wheel herself. Morry was excited by these dashing gestures. Lamptown was beginning to be a wonderful place, he thought, there was no bottom to it now, you saw new things every day as if it were already a city.

In front of the Elite Gown Shop he saw a girl and even before his eye had taken in the black curly hair, the snub nose and sky-blue eyes, he knew it was Jen. He recognized Jen always by his sudden feeling of embarrassment, here was someone who knew him too well, someone to whom at one time or another he'd told everything, and so when he saw her, his first impulse always was to establish new barriers, to be aloof,—show her that he was not such an open book as he seemed. He was surprised, watching her from this distance, to find her so agreeable to the eye, he so seldom really saw her except in relation to himself, someone whose adoring gaze he must avoid, someone who undoubtedly must be so pleased to find herself getting pretty that he would never satisfy her vanity by looking at her. She had an air, too, of being wonderfully dressed, but even Morry could tell it was only blue-checked gingham she was wearing, her proud delight in its newness fooled you at first. She was talking to the little Cleveland Jew named Berman who ran the Elite but when Morry passed she caught his arm.

"Look, Morry, I'm going to work here!"

"What do you mean—sell dresses?"

She waved goodbye to the Elite's proprietor and walked along with Morry. Isaac Berman, dark, bald, leaned against his door with folded arms, his Oriental eyes following her down the street. He turned to his son inside.

"Nice, hey, Lou?"

As soon as she told him of her plan to work in the Elite Morry was whipped again with envy, for he saw it as she saw it, not merely a job in a dress shop but a step toward great things, —Cleveland—Pittsburgh, New York, dances every night, music all day, Jen in a silver dress on a magazine cover, while Morry's Clover Heights was crumbling, he was alone in Lamptown, waiting for some great thing to come and pick him up.

"I get nine dollars a week. . . . Say, Morry, Lil's coming

to Lamptown. We're going to rent a place, maybe, and keep house."

Morry was always aghast at the things Jen did, he had never ceased to marvel at himself for having got out of the factory, so how could Jen jump so easily out of one thing into another, how could she finally take care of Lil, all of her own doing? His heart beat fast with triumph, as if he had done it, because what he wanted to do and what Jen wanted to do were somehow confused in his head, so this was all his own doing, then.

"What will Lil do?"

"Maybe Bermie will give her some work, too," Jen answered. "Not that what I make wouldn't be enough. . . . Nine dollars a week is a lot of money. I'm taking music lessons from Milly. She's going to teach Lil, too, and I'll teach her to tap dance—Mr. Travers taught me. Bermie's son's got friends on the stage, he said when we get something learned he could fix everything, he said I wouldn't lose anything by learning clothes first. Look here."

She pulled a newspaper clipping out of her pocket. It was a photograph of Maxine Elliot.

"Bermie's going to take me to see her, if she comes to Cleveland. . . . You know those Two Little Clowns at the Paradise this week? Lil and I could do that, easy enough. . . . If Lil wants to, of course."

Morry was dizzy from these swift pictures, he was excited by them, and when they reached Bauer's it was he who was sorry to leave, he wanted to stay near this excitement, he was stirred to immense schemes, Clover Heights, Lamptown was a mere step in this splendid ascent.

"Say, Jen, what about this Berman?" he pulled her away from Bauer's door to ask sharply. "First I hear you're out riding all hours with Hunt Russell,—folks say Dode O'Connell quit the Works and left town on account of you. Now you're in with this Berman fella,—what's the idea?"

Jen looked at him skeptically, her mouth curled.

"What about Nettie Farrell, and those girls at the Club always hanging around you,—what about that girl in Norwalk you always have up at the Casino,—what about——"

"Oh, Jen, for God's sake!" Morry, his face red, dumped tobacco into a cigarette paper and rolled it. It wasn't any of Jen's

business what girls he ran with, the thing about Jen was that
she didn't know men, and somebody ought to tell her who was
all right and who wasn't. Now he was furiously ashamed at being taken personally, as he had been the day old Mrs. Delaney
delivered the warning to keep away from her Jen.

"I'm only telling you to be careful," he muttered, hating
her. "You got to watch out for these foreigners. You've got to
remember you're just a kid, and a crazy one at that. I'm only
telling you to mind your step."

Jen looked down at the pavement.

"You told me to look out for Hunt and for Fischer and for
Mr. Travers and now for Lou. All the fellows I like best," she
said slowly. "Gee, Morry, what do you want me to do? . . .
Isn't *anybody* all right?"

Morry didn't know what to answer. He couldn't tell her
she had no right to like any man but himself, he was ashamed
of his jealousy over Jen.

"You're pretty young to be running around, that's all," he
said finally. "Somebody's got to keep an eye on you."

"No younger than that girl of yours from Norwalk," Jen
answered sulkily. Her eyes met his with a direct challenge and
Morry felt queerly stirred and afraid. He lit his cigarette
silently, and was relieved to see Hogan waving to him from
Delaney's entrance. He dashed thankfully across the street,
and the Bauer screen door slammed.

Walking home from the Elite Gown Shop you had to keep
your fists tightly clenched to keep from dancing, you could
hum softly to yourself but you must remember not to sing
out loud, you could whisper it to yourself but you mustn't shout
it, "I don't have to wait table any more, I don't have to go
to the factory either, I have a real job, next I'll be transferred
to the Cleveland store or maybe New York and there I'll be on
the stage, I'll sing and dance all day and all night. . . . And I
don't have to be helped, I have a home all of my own doing
and I can do as I please, and Lil's coming. The Thing is beginning to happen."

Jen actually only had half a home, she rented the upstairs of
a house way out beyond Extension Avenue for six dollars a
month, she could scarcely wait for Lil to come and be aston-

ished at having a front porch, a yard, a honeysuckle vine and a lilac bush. Each night she ran all the way home from the store because Extension Avenue was pitch dark. She ran down the middle of the road so that shadows behind trees couldn't grab her, even the thrill of having her own latch-key didn't overcome her daily terror of going into the dark house. As soon as she got inside she locked the door and pushed a table against it. She turned on lights in all the rooms and said out loud, "This is my own home," and she was proud of herself, and then sat by the front window wishing somebody, anybody, would come and see her. She visited the old couple downstairs until they ostentatiously made preparations for bed. Then she went up to her rooms and said, "My own home—imagine!" and banged the door quickly behind her so the Unknown following her couldn't get in. It was fun walking back and forth through this solitary magnificence, it was fun so long as she heard the people downstairs, but as soon as they were quiet she was afraid of the silence, of crickets chirping eerily in the clover, of dogs barking far off, she was homesick for engines a yard from her window, they must be missing her, their whistles sounded remote and lonely, yes, when she was alone in the home she'd rented all by herself, she dared to wish for the Bauers' kitchen and the darling clatter of dishes and men swearing, and the smell of fried onions. But this was not to be admitted for then someone would pity her loneliness, and she was not a person to be pitied but a child of luck, see, she was only sixteen and had her own home, she could handle wonderful dresses from eight in the morning till eight at night, she could toss a blue satin dress over a rack nonchalantly as if satin was nothing to her, she could even try on twenty dollar dresses for mothers buying for absent daughters, yes, Jen was a girl to be envied and she was sorry for other women and a little awed by her own good fortune. Whenever she saw old Mrs. Delaney hobbling along the street she wanted to apologize to her for not doing so badly as the old woman had hoped, she was sorry for her but she was still afraid of her, you never could be sure when people who once owned you would clutch you again, and this time you could never, never get away.

But only this old woman and the silent night in her own home could chill her now, only these, for the rest of the time an amazed excitement rushed through her veins, something, something was in the air. She wanted to skip, to clap her hands with delight, because this mysterious something was so close to her she could almost touch it, it was like the first rat-a-tat-tat in the circus parade, any minute now the band would begin to play. She could scarcely bear such perpetual delight, it bubbled over so that old Berman winked at his son Lou, and when Lou pinched her cheek, she had to throw her arms about him and kiss him furiously. When the store closed at night she didn't know what to do but skip down Market Street to see the Bauers, to feast her ears on the music trickling out of Delaney's pianola, to tell a placid Hulda and a jealous Grace every single thing that happened in the Elite that day.

Hulda said she was going to give her something for her place, something nice, you wait, maybe this doily when it was finished, but when it was finished she couldn't bear to part with it, she opened a locked drawer and tried to decide which of these hoarded Larkin premiums she could give away but her heart ached over each decision. When she finally took out a chromo of a white-robed woman kneeling with the printed thought, "Simply to the Cross I cling," Hulda burst into tears because no one, not even her little Jenny, could love any of these tissue-wrapped treasures as she had loved them. After she had given it to her she sat on her stool gazing unhappily at the print now rolled up under Jen's arms, and while Jen leaned on the counter, chattering about what this one said or bought, tears rolled slowly down Hulda's cheek because Jen would not love and save this gift, she would only pin it on the wall where any stranger could look at it.

"I'm going away, too, believe me," said Grace, pausing between the courses of Sweeney's late supper to listen sourly to Jen. "And not to work in any Lamptown dump, either, I'm going to Detroit to work in a big cafeteria. Say, there's a town. A fella was in here the other day, a big bicycle salesman, and he says there's nothing Chicago has got that Detroit hasn't got. He says they got money to burn up there, fellas crazy for a girl with a little life in her, believe me, I'm not sticking in this dump after what this fella told me. He said why a girl with my personality wouldn't have to take nothin' from nobody up there in Detroit, why he says, Gracie, I've seen girls with only half your personality driving their own automobiles in Detroit and you take this Belle Isle, there's nothin' like it this side of New York City, he was sayin'.'"

Hulda smiled tremulously at Jen.

"Gracie's always leaving us," she said. "Always going to some big town, but she never goes."

"Wait!" Grace warned her. "You won't see me slinging this tray around here much longer. Not in this hick town, no sir."

It was the way Grace always talked, she did it, Jen knew, to show her how foolish it was to be happy over the simple triumphs of Lamptown when nothing so trivial would satisfy a high-spirited girl like Grace.

"Seen Morry?" Grace called from Sweeney's table.

Jen nodded.

"Ask him why he never comes in any more?"

"No," said Jen, painfully conscious of that matter between Morry and Grace. "I didn't ask him anything."

"Funny," observed Grace. "You and him never seemed to get on, always bickering when you got together. . . . And you won't see him now 'cause he wouldn't drop into a dress store the way he would in a restaurant."

"Morry's a smart young man, now," said Hulda. "It's got to be a mighty pretty girl to catch him."

Jen tried to avoid looking at Grace who was winking broadly behind Hulda's back as a reminder of the intimacies she had so often confided to Jen.

After a little while with Grace, Jen forgot the terrors of Extension Avenue, a home of her own seemed a refuge indeed, and the dark clover lots she had to pass were nothing if she thought hard about something else. So Jen, running home through the darkness, cinders scattering about her heels, her heart thumping with fear, thought about Lou Berman and the curious lure of dark Jewish eyes and olive skin, she thought of Hunt Russell and the way his oldness held yet repelled her, of the dry things he said which seemed to mean so much more than they really did, of how it must feel to be a dethroned emperor—(in this light of a lost king he seemed glamorous and sweetly sad to her, she almost loved him), she thought of the doughnut smell of the Delaneys' parlor, of the little gold chair on the mantel which she would never see again. A dim light

blinked here and there in an upstairs window, the trees shook
dew from their leaves, a twig snapped under her foot and made
her run faster. Her heart was as big as her chest now, booming
away, it was dreadful to be afraid of darkness, someday she
would go to a great city, Detroit, maybe, where dazzling
golden lights left no corner for night to hide in, where bands
playing day and night crowded out fearful quiet. She remembered that, until then, she must think hard of something else
and so, panting down the last few yards of darkness, she
thought of Morry, and the thought of Morry was so big, so all-
enveloping that there was no wish or feeling to it, it was only a
great name, you said "Morry" and it covered every tiny
thought or wish, it loomed out of the blackness like a great engine searchlight straight in your eyes, blinding you to everything else, even to itself. Morry, Morry, Morry,—you could
put yourself to sleep just saying it over and over.

It wasn't the Elite, as Jen had tried to arrange, but the Bon
Ton that finally took in Lily St. Clair. Morry saw her first sitting on the wicker bench in the show-room when he stopped
in one Saturday night to see his mother. When he went to live
at Russell House he was worried about his mother, he
thought in her quiet way she wanted him near her and he
took care to drop in every evening after he moved. But she
paid little attention to him, talking to Mrs. Pepper or Nettie
about the new decorations upstairs, and forgot always to ask
him about his work or how he liked his new home. If customers came in there'd be no place for him to sit, and after
standing uncomfortably around he'd realize there was no
place for him in his mother's life, that there never had been,
and he'd flush with shame to remember his fierce tenderness
for his mother as a frantic lover might blush who realizes in
cool retrospect that the beloved was always indifferent to him.
    The new independence of his mother bothered him, the
change in her taste in clothes, a certain indefinable boldness
in her manner, a way of glancing sidewise at men that was
disturbingly like Grace Terris. His memory of his mother
as a slight, quiet lady was wiped out by the reality of this
new knowing, politely aggressive personality. When she and
Mrs. Pepper went out together, two well-built, well-dressed

women, their hips swaying, he would redden when men standing near him whistled their admiration. "There go the milliners!" And the more stylish Elsinore became, the more Lamptown women remembered that after all Charlie Abbott hadn't been so bad, a waster, true, but what man wasn't? Morry heard these whispers with fear, but as yet there was nothing definite against his mother except that the Bon Ton widow was always on the go with the corset-lady. What the town whispered did not bother him so much as the sight of someone he knew so well changing under his very eyes into a stranger, a perfectly unknown quantity.

He was worried over other matters, too, for Fowler was persistently sour and silent, hints came to Morry's ears of the Lamptown Home Co. taking over the Clover Heights area, of the three houses being rented out as boarding houses, but these rumors could not be tracked down, nor would Fowler divulge any secret plans concerning the Heights. That he had lost interest in the developing of that community was certain, and with its collapse imminent he had possibly lost confidence in his young assistant. Morry dared not face the fears in his own mind, he smoked restlessly all day and wanted to talk all this over with his mother, always hoping for comfort which reason told him would not be there. As soon as he reached the Bon Ton door, a clear picture of what the call would be rose before him,—his own eagerness to talk, to tell of his gnawing fear of having to go back to the factory for a job, and his mother listening politely but interrupting with orders for Nettie, exclamations about remote matters to be attended to, and leaving him for the always preferable customer. He wondered, since he knew the whole scene so well, why he stopped in at all, but he reasoned when no comfort came, at least then his need for it was chilled and his defenses against an indifferent world that much strengthened.

No one was in the shop but a girl sitting on the green wicker footstool, with her hat in her lap, and when Morry saw her softly curling yellow hair he knew it was Jen's Lil. She was so obviously something to be stared at that Morry dared not look too long. In his room at Russell House he had pictures of actresses, Billie Burke, the Dolly sisters, Anna Held,—and he had never before seen any girl who looked

like these gilded creatures, they were not of the ordinary
breed of women at all, he was certain they had been whirled
dancing and spangled out of some falling comet on to their
stage. And here was just such a girl, her yellow hair, her gold-
tinged, creamy skin, her clear, violet eyes, the very curve of
her lips such objects for wonder in themselves that it was hard
to reassemble them into one complete marvel in his mind.
She was shy and kept pulling down her shrunken gingham
dress to cover her long legs. She must be tall for her age,
Morry thought. Taller than Jen. Her own acute embarrassment put him completely at ease.

"Aren't you Jen's sister, Lil?" he asked.

She nodded, coloring.

"I'm Morry Abbott,—Jen's told me about you."

Then she talked a little, and Morry was enchanted with her
voice, a soft slurring voice using the expressions of the farmers
around Lamptown, but he didn't listen to her words, he was
drinking in her amazing loveliness. Pretty girls in Lamptown
were plump rosy girls invariably handicapped in one way or another, either with thick honest legs, or stringy hair, or an in-
vincible dowdiness, a look of belonging exactly to Lamptown
and nowhere else. But Lil had that quality which had struck
him from the first in Jen, a quality of not belonging to the
place where she was at this moment, of belonging to the place
for which she was reaching. This mystified and held him.

She said Jen had left her there because Mrs. Abbott wanted
a trimmer and she could sew, really, but she wasn't sure yet if
Mrs. Abbott would take her.

"Sure,—you bet she will!" Morry said.

The faint blue shadows under her wide blue eyes suggested
a seductive frailty, the blonde hair curling at her temples and
at the nape of her neck inspired Morry with a persistent urge
to touch it and see if it was true. When his mother came in
and took Lil back to the workroom he stayed in the shop,
smoking and thinking about her, it was as if the silver girl had
walked off the magazine cover, he dared not leave her unguarded, this treasure must not be exposed to anyone else.
He was certain nobody in Lamptown had ever seen anything
like Lil St. Clair, and he had an avaricious desire to set up his
claim first, if it was to belong to somebody, then let it be

known that he had seen it first. He didn't think of her as a girl, or even as a person, but as a desirable possession, almost an achievement. He couldn't think whether he liked her or not, he felt only awe over her goldenness and wonder that such perfection had strayed into Lamptown. He would have been quite content just to read about it.

Presently Elsinore came back in the shop alone. Morry was leafing over a fashion magazine as if this were his prime interest in the Bon Ton. He planned to stroll home with Lil, but it appeared she was going to stay in the store for a while. A beautiful worker, she was, said his mother, seeming to have a knack with hats. Morry swelled with pride as if he had taught her this gift himself.

"She's a good girl to take Nettie's place," said Elsinore reflectively. "I'll need her when Nettie goes. After all she's no younger than Nettie was when I took her on."

"Where's Nettie going?"

"She's starting a millinery store of her own next season," answered his mother. "Some friend has loaned her a little money. She's going to take that little place behind the Paradise. There's plenty of trade for another millinery store. Mrs. Pepper and I don't mind."

At that moment Nettie herself appeared, and Elsinore slipped out. Nettie looked at Morry defiantly.

"Well, I suppose you've heard I'm starting my own business next fall," she announced. "I suppose you think I can't handle it, too, don't you?"

"I think it's great, Nettie," Morry said heartily, for this meant that Lil would be here right under his eye indefinitely. "I think it's just fine."

Nettie was slightly appeased.

"But you'll be too busy with all your real estate funny business to come in and see me once in a while," she said. "You never see me any more as it is."

"Oh, I'll be dropping in," Morry assured her hastily. "I guess I'd want to see what kind of a store you've got, wouldn't I?"

Nettie's gaze tried to hold him to a promise and he looked toward the door, praying for someone to come in before she trapped him into a definite date. His roving look was misconstrued.

"You've seen that St. Clair girl's sister, that's what!" Nettie cried sharply. "The one I'm teaching to take my place. . . . You'll be running after her next. I'll bet you came to see her this minute!"

"Say, now, Nettie——"

"You did!" she insisted bitterly. "A washed-out little blonde. . . . She looks consumptive to me."

This was the meanest thing you could say about anyone, for everybody despises weaklings. Morry hoped Lil wouldn't overhear. He'd better not wait for her, he decided, Nettie's jealous eyes were too shrewd.

"She's just the wrong type for you, too," Nettie went on. "Just the kind you would pick. . . . You know yourself, Morry, you'd never amount to anything if your mother and I didn't keep after you and when you're that type you ought to get hold of a girl with ambition, a girl with enough business head for two. Some good woman."

Morry felt rising the old homelike sense of guilty incompetence and futile hatred of smug womankind. He started toward the door.

"You know perfectly well she's not a lady, Morry. Neither of those girls. Even you can see that."

At least Nettie was a little lady. Nobody in Lamptown could say a word against little Nettie Farrell. Nobody but Morry . . . and possibly a Mr. Schwarz.

Supper in the Russell House was a social event still to Morry. There were two big tables in the dining room and except for Hunt's occasional presence, they were filled with out-of-town men, big men who argued constantly about the Works, about running into Pittsburgh tomorrow or down to the Baltimore branch. America was to these men just an area for developing their product, they never knew there was a Lamptown, it was just a factory, the spaces between factories were not towns but Pullman drawing-rooms where they planned new arguments with brother officials for factory changes.

They talked during meals, drawing diagrams on the table cloth with fat silver lead pencils, they argued their way out to the lawn after dinner waving fat cigars, they sometimes drove in Hunt's car after dinner to some cross-roads saloon where they continued their discussion over beer and came back, still conferring over the same matters. When they left town duplicate officials took their places at Russell House and in the authoritative ring of their voices, expensively tailored suits, and fragrance of black cigars, sustained the same atmosphere in the Russell dining-room.

When the discussion turned to housing problems, Morry often took a part in it and many times talked so forcefully that the strangers removed cigars from the corners of their lips and listened respectfully. Later one would inquire, "Say, young man, I don't think I got your name."

Morry would tell him and the stranger would frown.

"Abbott? Abbott? You're not with us, are you, Abbott? Ah, I don't think I know the name."

Then no more heed was paid to Morry's comments. At these moments he yearned to have accomplished so much, to be such a figure in Lamptown and in all the state that when he gave his name men would start back.

"So you're Morris Abbott!"

Nobody listened to you if your name meant nothing, but on the other hand your name never meant anything unless you forced people to listen. These strangers never heard of Clover Heights, when he said he was in real estate and contracting, they assumed he was with the Lamptown Home Company, part of their own system or else not really in business at all. His three houses at the far end of the Lots had become almost as ridiculous as a full dress would be at a Russell House supper. They meant little enough in the town's development, and only Morry's work on the routine details of the real estate business made him worth any money to Fowler.

But whether Russell House listened to him or not Morry was proud to live there, to dash up and down the great mahogany staircase and tramp casually down the thick-carpeted halls. He had minor panics now and then wondering where he'd go if Fowler's poor business squeezed him out. Supposing he had to live at Bauer's, certainly a comedown, or beg his mother for cot space again in her work-room. . . . These fears could not endure long under the impersonal calm of his new home and the press of his new interests.

There was Lil.

He couldn't explain to himself about Lil. When he went out every night to see her he knew it wasn't because he liked her—you couldn't like or dislike an idea, could you?—it wasn't because he thought she'd be lonely (as indeed her shyness with people was bound to make her), it was for no tangible reason at all, but a certainty that such beauty fell near you only once in a lifetime and whether you wanted it or not you should never let it escape because it was rare. Then the setting Jen had provided for her sister, this little house far out on the edge of town with meadows stretching to the right and behind it, was associated with his dream of a home, somehow, so that Lil was tangled up with the things in life he wanted for himself,—glamour, beauty, freedom, a place in which a man could breathe.

Turning from the noise and clangor of Market Street out Extension Avenue he was conscious of a strange expansion in his bosom, the thick hushed trees drew the houses besides them into darkness, the smell of honeysuckle and white clover haunted the air, the flutter of a white dress on a vined porch stirred vague romantic fancy, then the long stretch of fields, hedges settling darkly over yeeping birds, glimmer of a light way off that was Jen's window, all this scented darkness was an avenue to Lil. Here, too, he was lord absolute, with Jen to listen avidly to his boasting, his opinions on this or that, and Lil, frail and lovely for him to admire. Lil seldom talked, when she did she prefaced her comments always with "Jen says——" . . . She worshipped Jen, and now she worshipped Morry, but he had a disturbed feeling that she would fasten her worship to anybody who was around her steadily.

"Did you hate the Home, Lil?" he'd ask.

"I didn't mind it," she would say.

"Do you like the Bon Ton—is it hard work?"

"I don't mind," she'd answer.

"Are you going away with Jen and try to go on the stage someday?" he'd fearfully inquire.

"I'd rather stay here at the Bon Ton," would be Lil's gentle answer. "I wouldn't want to go away but still I'd want to be wherever Jen was."

He'd hear boys talking about the little St. Clair blondy, he'd ask Lil if she liked this one or that one who had walked home from work with her.

"He's nice," Lil would answer. "I like him all right."

This pale acceptance of life was maddening to Morry, but it kept him constantly intrigued. He suspected that Lil thought he was "all right," too, and he was stirred to more gestures of devotion in an effort to discover some secret intensity in her. She was frightened when he kissed her the first time but after that she turned up her face with the utmost docility. Her intensity came out in her work, her fingers flew over her sewing, they never hesitated over the design of a hat, Elsinore and Mrs. Pepper marvelled over this dexterity, and Nettie, who was supposed to be teaching her the trade, sat back with jealous wonder. Here in the Bon Ton work-room Lil attained the pitch of intensity that Morry hoped to arouse in her. He waited to find Jen's furies in the younger sister, but they weren't there. He needed both girls to make up the one necessary for him. When he found Jen out for the evening he grew restless alone with Lil, he'd start to tell her about something concerning his work, and then he'd remember that it must be told to Jen, he couldn't have the news spoiled by Lil's sweet cool, "That's awfully nice, Morry"; he must have Jen's breathless reaction so that the whole affair became tremendously important and himself, by his connection with it, made more important.

In Lamptown, which had made its own dark conclusions over two pretty girls living alone, Lil quickly became classified as Morry Abbott's girl. Lil knew this and accepted her role as she accepted everything, sweetly and casually. She loved trimming hats and she loved her sister Jen, and the rest of life was pleasantly negative. She was glad Morry liked her because Jen liked Morry. When the two girls were busy cooking their supper, she told Jen everything Morry said and did, until Jen would harshly tell her to keep still and watch the potatoes.

So Jen was no longer lonely in her new house because Lil was there. When she came home from work at night Lil and Morry were always there. At first she was glad that she had something—say it was Lil—to make Morry call every night, but after two or three weeks she somehow didn't want to hurry home, she lagged around the shop, helped Isaac Berman with the books or talked to Lou about the stage because Lou had seen all the plays and all the actors that there were. When Hunt Russell, always slightly intoxicated, always carrying some magic in his insolent lazy manner, drove up to the shop door occasionally and ordered her to drive with him she was glad to go and put off her homecoming a few more hours. But no matter how late she got home Morry would still be there, sitting on the porch adoring Lil.

"I didn't want to leave Lil here all alone," he would say reprovingly to Jen.

"Thanks for looking out for her," Jen would answer in a hard voice and call a gay farewell to Hunt. She said to herself that she was glad Morry liked Lil, but she knew that nothing had ever cut her so deeply as this persistent devotion. When Lil mildly questioned her about Hunt—"wasn't he awfully old and wasn't he bad?" she knew Morry had said something of the sort, she knew he thought she was taking Dode O'Connell's place with Hunt, but she didn't care. Most of the time she thought about places Lou Berman talked about, of what Vaughn Glaser said to him once, of the party a friend of his gave for Blanche Ring, and every detail of her costume, of the time he saw Marguerite Clarke walk into the hotel—("Baby Mine" she was playing), and of so many trips to New York City he never even counted! . . . All these people belonged to her, now, they had places in her brain, and in her dreams they accepted her as a fellow artist, even Lou Berman himself boasted of knowing her. (Why, that little Jennia St. Clair—used to work right here in Lamptown!) Now it changed to Morry boasting of her, but no, Morry must be in the theatre watching her perform, see there he is now. . . . But then that leaves no one in Lamptown to say they knew her once. . . . Dreams were very difficult to control. Anyway she would look into the audience and see Morry . . . no, she would have to be unconscious of his presence for in or out of dreams as soon as she saw him she'd be bound to rush down to him and say "Look at me, Morry, look, see, I did it, just like we used to plan. Isn't it wonderful?" Then it would merely end with Morry reaching for his hat and saying, "It sure is, well, goodbye." And that would be the end of that. . . . In despair Jen decided there was nothing to be done about Morry, and she must sooner or later do things without keeping his possible applause in mind. She went out with Lou Berman sometimes, to the theatre in Cleveland once with him and often to the Paradise. Lou's approval of her became important, because he praised seldom and was scornful of Lamptown girls. When he called to take her out he'd look her over from head to foot critically.

"Are you going to wear that?"

Then she would know it was all wrong, that her new silk dress was not the thing to wear even if it was the prettiest thing she'd ever owned. He was always patting her arm but she learned this was not a caress but a prelude to pulling the sleeve to a tight fit.

"There's the way your sleeves should set, honey. Fix that before you wear it again. You can wear clothes all right but there's things you gotta learn, hey, papa?"

Lou was sleek, slim, foppish, silent, enviably poised. He fascinated her for he represented the City. But when she looked at old Isaac Berman she saw Lou cartooned with age, paunch-bellied, fang-toothed, bald, greasy, only the dark fathomless eyes eternally romantic in silence no matter what price cuts were being calculated behind them. Lou never tried to make love to her, and Hunt Russell was far too conceited to risk a rebuff, but Jen had a waiting feeling inside, a heavy sense of dread, that if either of these men decided to take possession of her she would have no chance of escape, for you couldn't set yourself against Hunt because he was Lamptown, and you couldn't betray your provincial fear to Lou because he was the City. With Morry so enthralled with Lil she was afraid for herself. No longer was the thought of him any protection to her.

She was terrified at the envy she suffered when she saw him sitting with Lil silently on the porch-steps, she had a fleeting lust for revenge, the revenge of throwing herself at Hunt or Lou, of being easy like Grace. But this was no revenge, it was punishment for herself. She listened to Lil's talk of the Bon Ton and when Lil broke out,—"You're cross with me, Jen, you're sorry I came to Lamptown!" she answered carefully, "No, I'm not. Didn't I always say we'd live together, didn't I say I'd send for you to come? I wouldn't have said that if I didn't want you, would I?"

But jealousy was gnawing at her constantly and for this illness there is no rest, day and night veins burn and somehow do not burst with the fever, there can be no peace in remembering a past moment of security, such moments are gone for ecstasy leaves no mark, pain alone cuts deep.

"If I could only see Morry as he really is, then the ache would be gone," Jen reasoned, "because look at him,—he isn't so different from anybody else, when you think of it, he isn't so good-looking, he certainly isn't kind—(yes, he is, remember those nights on Delaney's back steps, yes, he was kind, then)."

If there were only some operation that could destroy this perpetual ache, if you could go to a surgeon and say, "Will you please cut out the Morry section of my brain?" But then what would be left? Because he wasn't just in her brain, he was in her blood, he was part of her. If she could sleep nights instead of thinking, she reflected, then she might be strong enough to wish to be free of him, but wounds from him were better than nothing at all from him, that was the awful part of loving someone. Worn out with thoughts that ran round and round forever in the same little circle, she would at last wearily admit that what she wanted most in the world was to be desired by Morry, but this was not possible because it was so plain to him that he could have whatever he wanted from her and no man ever desired something he knew was his.

She was afraid her mind was getting all crooked, she had to go over the words, "Isn't it fine that I did get Lil out of the Home?" Inside those words she knew the truth, because until Lil came Morry was potentially her property,—Nettie Farrell and Grace and the girl from Norwalk and the little peroxide blonde from the Works, they didn't matter, these women changed but she remained. She thought if she had brains like Mr. Hogan or Lou Berman she would know how to reason Morry out of her life.

At least now she was determined to do something tremendous with her future. If Lil hadn't come she might have waited around Lamptown for Morry all her life, but now—let Lil have Morry and Lamptown! As for Jen, she was going to climb every wall and every ladder until she was so high up that she could look down on loving Morry Abbott as nothing at all. And when she was up there at the very top she would thank him for preferring Lil and she would be glad Lil came to Lamptown. These thoughts passed in clear review in her mind while Lil lay sleeping beside her. Oh she'd leave town, Jen thought, wide awake, you bet she'd go. There'd be no place where trains went that she wouldn't go, no city too big for her to conquer, but the next instant, all the cities in the world conquered, she ached for Morry and buried her face in the pillow. Oh Somebody . . . Somebody . . . Somebody help. . . . She remembered the broken rosary in her top drawer but she made no move to get it after her first impulse. No rosary was going to help you. Nothing could help you but yourself, there was no help from any other person or from any Somebody. This was all right . . . in fact as long as she would live, any unexpected service from outside would be regarded by Jen not as luck but as a sinister unnatural phenomenon to be paid for one day or another in blood and tears. . . .

Along about four o'clock she got out of bed and looked out the window on the clover fields. The sullen grey sky gave no hint of sunrise. It was still smudged with night and a few weak stars. Jen tiptoed to her dresser and got out her manicure box. She sat down by the window with it and in that dull pearl light began earnestly on her fingernails. An actress, Lou Berman said, must have beautiful hands.

"Morry's a fine-looking man," said Mrs. Pepper to Elsinore every time Morry called at the store,—"a fine-looking man, indeed."

They were always saying that about somebody. On their trips to Cleveland, at one time or another during the day Mrs. Pepper was bound to nudge Elsinore and say in quite a dignified low voice, "Isn't that a fine-looking man over there,— that big man in the Palm Beach suit?"

If there were two Fine-looking Men in the hotel lobby or the Union Station or in the parlor car going home, then Mrs. Pepper was likely to lean toward Elsinore and whisper, "They think we're sisters—can you imagine that? It's on account of these hats."

In summer both women wore big milans heavy with flowers set ever so slightly toward the right eye, just as the wholesaler had advised, and in winter they wore big black velvets with two superb plumes curling under the brim. Elsinore, since Charles' death had grown much heavier, her face was full and blankly white, though Mrs. Pepper sometimes coaxed her to use just a touch of her vegetable rouge and her curling iron. The Bon Ton, hats, corsets, lingerie, gloves, hosiery, was prospering steadily and the two proprietors used the cream of their stock for their own persons. When they sat discreetly together on excursion boats to Cedar Point, their dotted veils drooping from their big hats, their long gloves demurely on their laps, men shifted cigars to their fingers and one was bound to observe, "A couple of swell figures, there. Classy dressers, eh? We'll pick 'em up at the Point, what d'ye say and take 'em over to the Beer Garden."

They usually wore rustling black silks, black for smartness and discretion, but certainly alluring enough when cut snugly for a perfect 40, accented with dangling long gold chains, heavy musk scents, and modestly revealed openwork stockings. They went to matinees together in Cleveland to see what new costume touches were in vogue, not so much for the Bon Ton clientele as for themselves, they worked hard for the Bon Ton but they lived for their "trips," the whistles of admiration, the whispers, "Gee—what a figure!" the perfect applause of a man stopping in his talk to stare attentively as they passed. It was always Mrs. Pepper's gay little laugh that answered bolder men's invitations, a silvery little tinkle that slurred over every situation, made the whole business just jolly fun and not at all horrid. If the two women ever got separated by their chance male companions, they never confided to each other details of this interim any more than they talked of their 'trip' when they returned to Lamptown. What they talked over was the success of their new costumes, a new hair-retoucher, and a plan for even more breathtaking ensembles next time. They were two very discreet women, ladies both of them. Even Nettie, jealous and unhappy under the new regime and waiting impatiently for the autumn to launch her own business, could not actually put a finger on anything to talk about except long-distance calls that came from time to time, so cautiously conducted that even Fay, toll operator and Nettie's bosom friend, could not find cause for scandal.

"You know, Elsinore," Mrs. Pepper said as they sat in their pink nightgowns one night patting lotions into their faces,

"Harry Fischer says I've completely changed since we started this new store. He gets so worried about me,—he says you have a bad influence over me."

Elsinore saw herself in the mirror over Mrs. Pepper's head, her full white arms reaching down for a lost juliet, her dark hair flying, her plump breasts bursting through the lace-top of her nightie. The picture was strangely like the image of Mrs. Pepper right beside it, save Mrs. Pepper's bosom, without a corset's support, settled cozily into her 'tummy,' the waistline completely vanished, and Mrs. Pepper's blue eyes, set in the same sort of round white face, were definitely merry where Elsinore's were blank and cold. Sleeping together, though, Mrs. Pepper's fat arm trustingly encircling Elsinore's waist, her cheek confided in slumber to Elsinore's smooth back, they were like sisters, so close to each other under the pink comforter that they needed no words for their secrets.

"We ought to go over more to Harry's dances," Mrs. Pepper said, regretfully. "He says the inspectors have condemned the Casino, so it may be months before he can find a new hall in Lamptown. He and Hunt may build a new pavilion, and that will take time."

"We went over when we could," said Elsinore. "The Casino seems pretty tame, though, after you've been around."

She tried to think what it had been that she used to see in Harry Fischer, but it was no use. That romance was dynamited out of her brain and in the vacuum a strange new Elsinore had grown. When she thought of Fischer she could only recall with distaste how he perspired in dancing and she even shuddered remembering his hot wet hand on her back, and the ever so faint odor of onions from his breath. She listened to the dance music on Thursday nights but it no longer meant Fischer to her. It was only a reminder of a trip to the Hollenden Grill with two B.&O. Officials, or an automobile ride from Cleveland out to a Willoughby roadhouse. When he came to the Bon Ton to see Mrs. Pepper, it was Elsinore who whispered with the latter behind the screen, advising what excuse to give for not meeting him next Wednesday in Cleveland—say they had a dinner of wholesalers to attend, or no—yes, say anything so they could meet those two drummers at the Hofbrau as they'd promised.

"You do make me be mean to Harry," Mrs. Pepper gently protested. "Honestly, I don't feel right about him when I've always been so fond of him. But then I hate to give up a good time and you and I do have good times together, don't we? I'm sure Harry oughtn't to begrudge me a little pleasure after the way I've worked all my life. He surely ought to understand that."

"He does as he pleases," Elsinore answered coldly. "You can't tell me he doesn't with all those young girls always crazy about him. I notice he never got a divorce for you."

Mrs. Pepper's mouth trembled. She still wept over old wounds, over candy denied her as a child, over scoldings remembered from her long-deceased husband, over Harry Fischer long, long ago refusing to divorce his wife for her. So, reminded of this, she became happier in her digressions, not to be revenged on Harry, she was far too gentle for that, but because she thought it wouldn't really hurt his feelings after all.

"That Mr. Kutner from Chicago was so surprised," she murmured to Elsinore, "when Nettie told him you had a grown son. He couldn't believe it, he said."

"Nettie talks too much, anyway," Elsinore exclaimed angrily. "I don't see why the salesmen have to be told all my family affairs."

"She told him about Charles' killing himself, too," said Mrs. Pepper. "Mr. Kutner said he'd read about it but never knew it was your husband."

"I'll be glad when Nettie leaves and gets her own shop," Elsinore burst out in extreme annoyance. "She's much too friendly with strangers. She talks all the time—she's too much of a gossip."

Mrs. Pepper made no reply for in the depths of her amiable soul she was as jealous of Nettie's position in the Bon Ton as Nettie was of hers. And as for her being a gossip, that, to the corsetiere, was her only virtue. She hurried down to the workroom every time she heard Nettie's girl-friend, Fay, come in, for between Fay and Nettie you were bound to get a good hour of fascinating tattle. Fay told everything, every telephone call that came for the Girls' Club, what every vanished factory girl said who called up her Lamptown girl-friend from a tough hotel in Pittsburgh, what women were called up by slightly tipsy visitors in Bill Delaney's saloon. Once Fay stopped her chatting when Mrs. Pepper apologetically stole in the room.

"She'll tell," Fay explained her reticence to Nettie. "I'll tell you some other time."

Mrs. Pepper pouted.

"It's about Dode O'Connell," Nettie told her briefly, "and you'd go right and tell Harry Fischer and he'd tell Hunt and Hunt would get Fay in dutch at the telephone office."

Mrs. Pepper clasped her hands pleadingly.

"But I wouldn't tell! I wouldn't really! I never see Hunt to talk to any more—I wouldn't tell a soul! What's happened to Dode—is it true she got married to a man in Grand Rapids?"

Fay's lip twisted scornfully. She adjusted her turban with a left hand grown much more adept since it flaunted a diamond solitaire.

"Dode isn't married to anybody. Hunt wouldn't marry her and that finished her. Well—you're sure she won't blab, Nettie? . . . it isn't anything. Only Hunt calls up Toledo last night and when I was getting the party Toledo says to me, 'Say, Lamptown, you know the party you're calling, don't you' and I says no, it's a hotel, ain't it, and she says, 'Some hotel,' she says, 'it's Lizzy Madison's, the biggest sporting house in town. Better listen in if you want to hear something good.' So I says, 'Say, Toledo, think I'm so darned dumb you got to tell me to listen in?' Anyway Hunt gets the party and it was some woman answering so Hunt says is Miss Dolores there. All the time Akron was trying to get me, but I let her buzz, I hung on to Toledo, you couldn't have pried me away. Well, this Miss Dolores says, 'Hello, who is it?' then, and Hunt says, 'Hello, Dode, this is Hunt. I want to see you.' She says, 'Who?' and sorta gasped as if she couldn't believe her ears, and he says 'It's me, Hunt. How are you, Dode?' Well, she didn't say another word, so he kept saying, 'hello, hello' and still she didn't an-swer, only sort of a funny noise, I heard, sounded like some-body crying. He kept it up—'Say, Dode, hello, can't you hear me,' he says, 'It's me,—Hunt.' And no answer from her just that funny moanin' sort of, gee, it got my goat coming over the wire that way, and then she clicked off. So he says to me,

'Operator, operator, I was cut off.' And I just told him. 'Oh no you wasn't cut off, Mr. Russell,' I says, 'the lady hung up.' "

Mrs. Pepper listened sorrowfully.

"She was so crazy about him!"

"Well," said Nettie, threading a needle, "she's where she belongs now, I guess."

"I'll say so," said Fay, and flicked a ravelling from her dress with her engagement finger.

Mrs. Pepper told Elsinore about Dode in their room that night while they took turns manicuring each other. Wasn't it a shame, she said, the way Dode turned out?

"There's worse things," Elsinore said.

Coming out of Bill Delaney's Morry heard a "Sss-t!" and saw old Mrs. Delaney at the alley entrance. She jerked her head toward him commandingly. She was in a dry brown calico dress, her shawl pulled over her head, one brown twisted hand grasping an egg basket. She seemed shrinking more each day into old brown goods until some day you could pick up this antique bundle and find no more bones or body to it than to a dried leaf, if you shook it two shrivelled hen feet and a wrinkled yellow mask might fall out but no more than that. She clung to the stair railing as if the languid breeze might blow her away.

"Evening, Mrs. Delaney," Morry said uncomfortably. He could not meet her fierce old eyes, he knew she was ready with accusations and he had no wish to hear them, other things were pressing on his mind.

"I told you she'd turn out bad, didn't I?" she sputtered. "Didn't I say there was bad blood there? Got her own place now, she has, where she can carry on and nobody see, she's a smart one, nobody can deny those bad ones are the smartest and you, young man, you got yourself to thank for it, I could've handled her if you hadn't hung around, letting her think you was soft on her, it's you that's ruined that girl's life and don't you forget it, some day you'll have a daughter of your own and you'll find out, then, you'll be the one to worry then, young man. . . ."

"I never hurt Jen, you're all wrong about that," Morry protested, wishing there was some weapon for dealing with old women.

She sniffed scornfully.

"You can't lie to me. I know my characters. I knew your pa and I knew her mother. Didn't that woman come here time after time trying to find Jen and didn't I run her out of town as fast as she could go—didn't I call the police for her not two months ago when she came to my door?"

Morry hadn't known this.

"Did her mother come again, really?"

"I'm tellin' you right now. She come here not two months ago sayin' she'd heard both her girls was here workin' in town and she was their mother come to make a home for them. You make a home for them, hah, I says, you want their salary and you want them to keep you now you've shirked 'em all your life. Well, she says, they only got one mother and it's my duty to be with 'em now when they need a mother's care. Hah, I says, one mother is one too many and I called Bill up here and he got her ticket right back to Cleveland without her even seeing the girls."

"She'd better keep away from those girls," Morry exclaimed angrily. "Throwing them away when they were born—the way she did . . . she's got no right to them now."

The old woman turned on him.

"If she hasn't who has? You, maybe. . . . I hear things. I hear Jen went from you to Hunt Russell and from Russell to that Jew, but you're responsible, you gave her the start, young fella, and you'll get your punishment, glory be to God."

She hobbled up the stairs and Morry, disturbed, went on toward the Bon Ton. He was always supposed to be Jen's keeper, he reflected, even if he never saw her, Bill's mother or Hulda Bauer would always be giving him old nick for letting Jen do this and that. . . . As if he could stop Jen from doing anything she'd set her mind on. . . . He thought of her plan to go away. He hadn't talked to her much about it because she wouldn't really go, he felt. But what made him so sure? After all Berman had promised to help her go, and there was nothing to hold her in Lamptown. Nothing but Lil. . . . Lil and—well, face it squarely,—himself. He didn't like to think about Jen loving him,—it was such a violent, possessive love, not what he wanted from a girl, such fierce, unreasoning love made a man instinctively cautious and sensible,—somebody

had to be. He could have made love to her, there were times
he remembered, but he was afraid of losing himself. Oh yes,
somebody had to be sensible. As for being in love,—well, he
loved Lil; but loving Lil was like loving prestige or an idea,
not like loving a person. If he allowed himself to be drawn to
a strong person like Jen she would inevitably crowd into the
romance and be equal to the hero,—this was disturbing and
not romantic, romance was between a man and love, not between a man and woman. . . .

Morry found himself caught up in the puzzle of his own
feelings. . . . Could Jen really go away and leave him? Even
here waiting for Lil to come out of the Bon Ton door, he
grew sick with fear of a Lamptown without Jen. The Delaney
backstairs, the Bauers' kitchen, the Casino, the house on Extension, these places were Lamptown and they were barren
with Jen ripped out of them. And Lil, pale and sweet, was
nothing without Jen coloring her. . . . It was silly of him to
be so sure Jen would not leave him, she went around with
other men, he'd never been jealous because he was sure of
her, so certain of her that he had no desire for her. . . . No,
be truthful, there were moments when she was adoring him
that he wanted desperately to possess her, but then he would
be lost, she would know he belonged to her, there could be
nothing casual between him and Jen. . . . But if she should
go away he'd have to go, too. He had to. He couldn't let her
prove superior to him. That was settled. . . .

He leaned against the Bon Ton window and smoked. It
was too early for Lil to go home to supper, he'd have to wait
a little while. He observed the newly painted doorway of the
Bon Ton,—no doubt about it, his mother was a good business woman, she'd done a lot for herself since his father's
death,—all right, call it "suicide." He could certainly use that
word if his mother could so casually. Maybe, if she thought
about that event at all, and sometimes Morry doubted if she
did, she really thought it was a suicide. Anyway the further
back in your mind you pushed those things the better it was
for you.

He stepped back to study the show-window. A gold fringe
ran across the top of it and propped against a little gold silk
screen was the crying doll dressed in black velvet, its blue eyes

staring out under its huge black hat, a duplicate of the life-size black hat on the stand beside it. One hand was held out stiffly with a tiny purse hung on it, the other hand was concealed in the folds of the dress because the fingers were broken. Morry felt curiously guilty before the doll's glassy stare. He wished his mother would get rid of the damned thing. It made him think of his father.

It was a fact, Hogan told Morry in the bar-room, that Fowler had made a deal with the Lamptown Home Co. to continue their little houses all over Clover Heights. When Morry demanded what Hunt said to this, Bill explained that Hunt was selling everything he owned in town, shares in the Works and everything, and that he was going in with Harry Fischer to build a dance-pavilion somewhere in this county.

"Outside of that old Hunt has set up a little drugstore blonde in a swell apartment on Euclid Avenue in Cleveland," said Hogan. "I give him two years to get down to his bottom dollar."

"But I don't understand about Fowler,—why didn't he let me know what was going on?" Morry wanted to know. His head was swimming, he was afraid his face had paled, something stuck in his throat. . . . Fowler had fooled him, everybody had fooled him, there never would be any Clover Heights, but this was not so terrible as finding out how people used you, fooled you, always kidding you along as if they meant what you did.

"If the old boy didn't tell you, then he's got something crooked up his sleeve, Jesus, those Fowlers never had a straight thought," Hogan answered. "Every goddam one of my wife's people, the same. . . . You wait, there'll be a dirty deal in it somewhere, that's why he didn't tell you. Sell you out for a nickel, that man would. Won't touch liquor, won't look at a woman,—say you never can trust an abstainer, boy, if he's abstaining from pleasure it's so he can put all his strength into some shady business deal,—you mark my words."

Morry steadied himself at the rail, he drank fast to dispel that choked feeling in his throat. There was nobody you could believe in,—your father, your mother, nobody.

"I don't see where Morry's stung," Bill had objected. "He's not going to be fired. He'll go over with Fowler and work for the Lamptown Home Company, that's all."

Morry found his voice returning at last.

"I wouldn't do it!" he snarled. "You think I'd spend the rest of my life doing nothing but see how many of those shanties I could squeeze on to an acre of land? Why, I wouldn't work to put a thing like that over on this town, this town's got as much right to be a decent place to live in as Avon has, right next door. I'd feel as if I was spreading small-pox, honest I would. If Fowler's giving up Clover Heights, then I quit Fowler, that's all. You got to believe in what you're doing, Hogan, you see that, don't you? A fella's got a right to work for something he believes in, hasn't he?"

"Maybe," said Bill. "But a fella's got to work at something, believe or not believe."

"The prettiest thing this town will ever have," observed Hogan, "is the Yards. You'll never see anything prettier in this burg than those old black engines pushing up and down the tracks. Boy, you might as well make up your mind now as later that people don't want anything pretty, and damned if they want anything useful, they just want what other people have. You take these cement porches—"

"You never used to talk like that," Morry reproached him.

"I wasn't this old," grinned Hogan.

"All right, then," Morry said, "the hell with Fowler."

He swung out to the street and walked rapidly and dizzily toward Extension Avenue. He forgot about Lil waiting in the Bon Ton. His head buzzed with Hogan's words. Fowler had sold out, gone over to the rivals, he hadn't believed in any-thing but piano boxes for homes from the very first, he only loaned himself to the Clover Heights enterprise because the bank thought it was good business and because the Works di-rectors hadn't asked him to build their workmen's cottages. As soon as they did ask him he dropped everything and went flying over to them like a child going to whoever extended the most candy.

Hogan said the three houses were to be fixed over into a boarding club for the company officials, a big flower garden was to be laid straight across all three front lawns with huge letters in red and white gladiolas, "LAMPTOWN WORKS OFFICIALS CLUB." And Fowler had worked all this out with the Works people without telling him, thinking he'd be glad to go over to them, too. That's the way people were. Nobody believed in the things you believed but yourself, nobody believed that even you were really sincere about it, people believed whatever was good business for them at the time. Nobody believed in anything but good business. Clover Heights was blown up, the world was blown up, by good business. Everybody knelt to good business. No use counting on anybody having faith in an idea for its own sake.

Restlessly Morry walked on. What was going to happen to him, then? Fowler wouldn't fire him, he'd expect him to go cheerfully over to the rival company, but he wouldn't, he'd be damned if he would. Well, what would he do, then—go back to the factory? Give up living in Russell House and beg five dollars now and then from his mother, 'till he got something good enough'? Either he fell in with the Lamptown Home Company for a little while—oh, just a few months, say—and worked to see that every citizen had his rightful portion of ugliness, or he went back to the factory. Damned if he'd go back there. He'd leave town, go to the city. Cleveland—De-troit—Chicago— What would he do there? He'd never dare go. . . . Still, Jen St. Clair wasn't afraid to strike out. He knew a second of despair, thinking that all his life it was Jen driving him to do things, he never did anything without that lash, he never would. He had to do the things she expected of him. She would be a big actress on Broadway, she said, when he was an architect in New York. So that's what he had to do, that was all there was to it. Maybe Pittsburgh first, work it somehow to study at Carnegie Tech . . . then New York. Jen would be there because she always did the things she set out to do, and he—well, he had to be what Jen thought he was. . . . He stopped to roll another cigarette. His hands shook. He dared not think of going away, but if Jen had the nerve to go he wouldn't be afraid, he'd never dare let her see how perilous it seemed to him. . . .

It was nearly six. He could go back to the Bon Ton now for Lil or he could go on to the house, since he was nearing it, and see Jen, who went home earlier. He needed the reassurance of his own voice boasting to Jen about what he was going to do. He needed desperately to be told he was wonderful, that there were far bigger things for him than any Clover Heights, he needed Jen's eyes worshiping him and he forgot Lil.

The sun withdrew and drained all color from the trees, they looked gloomy and ragged, their branches were too skinny, he thought; in the unbecoming twilight the old grey houses of Extension Avenue crowded beside their trees looking dowdy and unloved like the wives of executives. Good-bye, Lamptown, Morry thought, hurrying along, good-bye. . . . This was the moment of curious lull when it was neither day nor night, it was time for the six-o'clock whistle to blow, then warm darkness would smudge these sharp edges and let shadows invent their own town.

The factory siren suddenly shrieked through the air, cutting the day in two, and boarding house kitchens responded with an obedient clatter of pans and dishes, the smell of frying potatoes mingled agreeably with the fragrance of fresh-mown lawns and strawberry shrubs. Good-bye, good-bye to all this, Morry whispered. . . . He'd go straight to the house, then, he decided, and when Jen came in he'd tell her, he'd say, "What would I do in the city? What's there to be afraid of? Don't be foolish, Jen. I'd just walk into an office and get a job, that's all,—there's nothing to that, is there?"

Now the evening fast train roared through Lamptown, its triumphant whistle soared over the factory siren, in its vanishing echoes the beginning of a song trembled, a song that belonged to far-off and tomorrow. Yes, yes, he would come away, Morry's heart answered, now he was ready.

COME BACK TO SORRENTO

. . . Only in fancy—till the tenth moon shone . . .
—FROM SHELLEY'S *The Witch of Atlas.*

For Joe

Come Back to Sorrento

EVENINGS she sat on the porch hidden from the street by honeysuckle and morning-glory vines, through their tangled foliage she watched the sun go down and grey light change to a black screen on which the vine-leaves gleamed in a silvery frosted pattern. She swung slowly back and forth in the hammock, one foot under her, the other rhythmically touching the porch floor, it was swing, tap, swing, tap; one movement released her fancy, sent her soaring through years but the tapping of her slipper brought her back. You are here! here! here! it reminded her.

The house grew dark and quiet, drew the lilac bushes into its shadow, made room in its silence for the creaking of the hammock and the tap of the woman's slipper on the porch-floor. Tonight the smell of burning leaves carried insistently over the fragrance of dead lilacs and drying shrubs. Down the street she caught glimpses of bonfires, the firelight illumining the faces of watching children. She saw the parade of bonfires growing smaller and smaller in the distance, mere blots of gold in the blackness, spangling the honeysuckle vine with their reflections.

The creaking of the hammock came to a gentle stop and with the pause the high shrill murmur of children's voices blended by distance into one long sustained soprano note, crept closer. The eager prolonged note was like a bell, for Connie Benjamin it was a call to Now, to Here, to what was really true. She went to the porch steps and sat down on the stoop. The moss-rosebush she had planted when she first moved here had grown up the porch-trellis beside the steps, its tiny thorns daintily scratched her arm as she adjusted her skirts. One petrified bud remained on its stem but its moment had come for when Connie touched it the very heart fell softly apart, its petals scattered in a little ghostly flutter over the dying bush and over the folds of her dress. She brushed them off and the thorns caught her hand again. She was glad of the sharp tingling pain, it was the tingle of life at least and she had been so far away. Sometimes she wondered if there could be a limit to these twilight voyages, if some day she would stray too far and there would be no bridge nor bell to bring her home.

Bonfires wavered, embers glowed here and there and went out, street-lamps measured the darkness far up the hill and were stopped by the waiting woods, lights blocked out amber windows against the night. Groups of children fluttered past the house in a flurry of breathless laughter, their blurred light figures separated and vanished into different gateways. Connie heard Helen's voice above the others and Mimi's lower-pitched response. It reminded her again that the masks of evening cannot hold for long, no matter how blind one wishes to be. . . . She went indoors and turned on the living-room table-light, then into the parlor and switched on the piano-lamp. The array of music with her own old study book on the rack pleased her as it always did. The page was turned to Lesson XV,—"The Chapel in the Forest." Standing up, one foot on the soft pedal, she tried a few treble bars. The piano jangled gaily, and obligingly carried on a little echoing tune of its own between Connie's fumbling chords. Even Mimi could play better than that for all her square, practical little hands. That was the trouble, either your imagination stopped with the practical limits of your own accomplishment as Mimi's did, or you gave up even trying because you heard the real music, you had inside yourself the feeling for a chapel in the forest, the pure solemn charm of a prayer in primeval wilderness; why destroy a perfect image with the distortions of one's erring fingers?

On the porch she heard the girls talking to someone. Suddenly the thought of her two children made Connie's throat swell, she ached with love for them, love that was like a farewell to some joy gone or soon to be gone forever rather than pride of possession; they seemed almost but not quite hers, hers to touch but not to hold. For that matter nothing in the world ever seemed irrevocably or tangibly hers. This room . . . she had selected the curtains, the oak reading table, the brown rigidly stuffed sofa, even the classic mezzotints on the wall, the flowered brown carpet, the ferns, the hanging baskets in the window, but it was not hers. She took a detached pleasure in its old known comfort, as if she were a visitor doing her best to adapt herself to a strange and not displeasing environment. . . . Gus was not hers, nor any part of her. She was fond of him because he seemed somehow the very kind husband of a dear friend, not her own husband at all. What belonged to her and was hers was the period from supper till dark when she played with her life, shaped it this way and that. The figures of this hand-wrought dream world were drawn from memory and fancy, they fell into whatever roles she appointed like familiar toy soldiers. This was the life she controlled, over which she constantly triumphed. She expected nothing from the other because there she was only a polite spectator and naturally the prizes were reserved for the participants.

She drew the piano bench under her and sat down. As her fingers moved softly over the keys improvising chords and runs she began to hum an air. The humming swelled fuller and then lost itself in a rumbling of bass chords. The piano tinkled resolutely, the keyboard wobbled stiffly from right to left like a concert singer getting the utmost from her diaphragm. Connie closed her lips and the humming went on vibrantly, it seemed not to come from her throat but from one string, her whole body was the instrument. The light soft song soared through the rooms, echoes of it strung out like lanterns through the hall and shadowy corners. It was not a song at all but a gentle lovely purring sound that held to no pattern, and from the street seemed not a human voice but echoes coming from the walls of a haunted house. When Mimi was a baby it had made her cry, this purr, and even at twelve it caught at Mimi's heart, made her lag behind Helen in the shadow of the porch vine, somehow sorry for her mother and wanting to give her some consoling gift, something so wonderful she could not even picture it, something improbable like the last dying bonfire, or the Sunday sun coming through church windows.

Helen turned at the doorway to give Mimi a significant look, a nod toward the street, and Mimi heard the last of the children passing the house on their way home. As they ran they hummed shrilly and derisively, mocking Connie Benjamin's melody with discords.

*

Everyone knew Mrs. Benjamin. They knew she was not snobbish,—she was far too gentle for that and in actual material
possessions had less than her neighbors; her aloofness was not
due to a sense of superiority but very likely to shyness. No one
could blame a woman for natural reserve though often people
speculated on how any human being could live fifteen years in
one village without friends or confidantes. Helen, in school,
heard these comments and reproached her mother more and
more for the cardinal sin of being different.

"I must try and talk to people," Connie would tell herself.
"For the girls' sake I must live more outside the family."

It was bad enough, said Helen, for one's father never to say
more than five words to anyone, but one's mother ought to mix
with the other girls' mothers and know how the Commencement dresses were being made this year, what was being served
at birthday parties . . . a mother, really, Helen said, ought to be
a help to a girl. Mimi, who was only twelve said nothing to all
this, her loyalty to her mother lost in her fear of her sister.

Connie had had spurts of friendliness periodically but since
they sprang from no interest whatever in people but from the
prickings of conscience, her shy ventures came to little. She
was relieved in a way, for the failure of her slight efforts allowed her to bask in her own society without compunction.
She sometimes conversed with Mrs. Busch with the vague
feeling that Mrs. Busch was Dell River and once established
with her she was established with the town.

Mrs. Busch lived up the alley beside the Benjamins' house.
She was a large, silent blonde woman with pale, white-lashed
blue eyes; a wart blighted her nose. She was not really a washerwoman. She just "did a few little things up for Mrs. Tracy" or
someone else; her casual references to her work made it seem
that her long days of laundering were only a gentlewoman's
hobby. Busch drove the Central Delivery and looked exactly
like his wife. When he brought groceries to a kitchen where
his wife happened to be washing, Mrs. Busch would go outside the back door with him and they would confer in low,
grave voices over some great crisis in Central Delivery or a
deep problem in laundry.

When Connie would go downtown or on a walk through
the country she took the alley shortcut and stopped at Mrs.

Busch's gate. A lovely day. . . . Yes, it was, Mrs. Busch would grant, her mouth full of clothespins, her fat red hands hanging up a wet sheet. . . . And warm for September. . . . Indeed, indeed, admitted Mrs. Busch without looking up. . . . The garden looks charming. . . . Why not, after all the work the mister put into it, Mrs. Busch would politely retort, he don't leave it alone a minute. . . . There is a song about a garden, Connie would say,—she wished she could remember the words, but it's so long since she studied. At this point Mrs. Busch would invariably state that her daughter, Honey, sang very well. It was amazing since she and the mister neither one could carry a tune. Connie showed interest—neither of her own girls could sing. Wasn't it a pity when she herself had studied voice abroad and had sung once for Morini himself? Yes sir, she might have sung in grand opera, Mrs. Busch, but it was not to be. . . .

"Is that so?" Mrs. Busch always politely asked, but not surprised since after all she'd heard this announcement practically every time Mrs. Benjamin stopped by.

One morning Mrs. Busch added to their well-known conversational routine by introducing further proof of Honey's vocal talent. The new school music-teacher had said she sang well. He had studied abroad, too, just as Mrs. Benjamin claimed to have done.

Connie felt a rush of excitement at this news. Another artist like herself. Where was he living? What was his name?

"His name's Decker," answered Mrs. Busch, "and he didn't take the house on Mulberry Street that the school music-teacher nearly always takes. He claimed it was too big. So he took those rooms over Mr. Benjamin's shop. Must not have any family."

Mrs. Busch made no further comment on the professor's choice of residence, but Connie knew the cheap little rooms over the cobbler shop were not what the village expected of its music teachers. Even if the man lived alone, even though the rooms were pleasant enough and near the school, they were not suitable, he should have rented a house. Such patent economy looked queer.

"Yes sir, he says, 'that little girl of yours, Mrs. Busch, is quite a singer,' that's what he told me," said Mrs. Busch ad-

justing the clothes pole so that the great white sheets rose
high in the air like a stage backdrop ascending the wings leaving Mrs. Busch the enormous, ugly performer against the
standard over-painted house curtain of green lilac and elder-
berry bushes, grey wood-sheds and chicken houses, and brilliant blue sky peeping through a froth of white clouds.

Connie hesitated at the gate, anxious to say something very
kind and friendly to show that she did not think Mrs. Busch
was almost frightening in her ugliness. She wanted to compliment her on Honey, too, without shivering as she did when
she thought of the poor child.

"I'm sure she must have talent," she finally plunged.

Mrs. Busch showed no gratitude over her neighbor's comment, she was perfectly complacent over Honey and needed
reassurance from no one. Connie never got over her first
glimpse of Honey,—a golden-haired, incredibly exquisite
child then, the loveliest child she had ever seen, dancing
around a group of the other children, thumbing her nose at
them, and finally whirling herself dizzily round and round
down the street, screaming with laughter. Crazy Honey. . . .
Yes, she did have a voice as the new music teacher had said,—
a high, hollow choir-boy voice that soared and glided like
nothing on earth, and hearing that sometimes echoing
through the alley, Connie shivered and did not know why.

"I shouldn't be surprised if Honey ended up on the stage,"
said Mrs. Busch, picking up her empty clothesbasket and
starting for her kitchen porch. "The Mister says he wouldn't
bat an eye if she turned out to be a kinda Marylinn Miller or
something. It isn't as if she couldn't dance, too."

Mrs. Busch's calm ignoring of her daughter's strangeness
was almost as frightening as the antics of the seraphic-faced
girl.

"Well, I must go on down town," Connie said. "Mr. Benjamin expects me."

She felt, as always, slightly dashed that Mrs. Busch merely
nodded a polite acceptance of her good-bye, never urging her
to pause for further conversation or betraying any interest in
her destination. For Connie these interchanges were practices
in friendship and sociability, but each encounter with Mrs.
Busch made her conscious of her own failure, something in

herself must block the way, for certainly she'd seen this curious woman chattering most eagerly with other inhabitants of the village. Her face reddened slightly as she hurried up the cinder-strewn alley to the main street, she restored her poise by the thought of how ridiculous it was to attempt breaking the social reserve of the town washerwoman, as if in Mrs. Busch was concentrated the very heart of Dell River society. Whatever she represented her polite reticence sent Connie flying back into her own shell, unwilling to emerge for contacts with others. She hurried down the main street, smiling back at women who called greetings to her from their doorways or front yards, but not risking further defeat by bowing to them first.

Summer was over once again and all along the street boys were raking up leaves for the evening bonfires; little houses warmed themselves in the scarlet glory of overhanging maples, hydrangeas gloomily cherished their last rusty blossoms, and withering hedges shrunk back from the little white fences they had concealed all summer long. Even after fifteen years Connie was often on the point of exclaiming, "What a nice village you have here, you other people,——" for she did love its quiet streets, its peace, but again as the tourist might. She did not know the names of the streets or more than a dozen of its citizens, for she had vaguely felt that in her brief stay here such knowledge was unnecessary. She always paused at the town square, puzzled until she could decide which turn brought her to Gus' shop.

Crossing the little park she met Mr. Busch, himself, and a few people hurrying home from their morning's shopping with bulging paper market-bags. Some bowed to her and some only stared, but Connie felt them all turning to look after her. She was no longer troubled by this interest. A long time ago she had thought it was because she was a stranger from an eastern city or perhaps because she had almost been an opera star. Now she realized it was only because she wore hat and gloves every time she left her house, whereas other women ran downtown in aprons, bare-headed unless it was a club day or a school or church occasion.

The town buildings in Dell River were old, few changes had been made for decades beyond the new wing on the schoolhouse for manual training and domestic sciences in-

augurated a few years back. Occasionally a modern pink-stuc-
coed cottage popped out among the older shingled residences
but not many, for the town's population had not grown since
it was founded. A small foundry, a few garages, a candy factory, a sawmill and flour mill, these were practically the town's
only industries unless you counted the enormous nurseries
just outside the city limits, whose trading in irises was the
only cogent reason for trains to stop here. As a matter of fact
the newest building was the little two-story brick building
bearing the sign:

AUGUST BENJAMIN
NEW SHOES FOR SALE
OLD SHOES REPAIRED

Benjamin had built the place twelve years ago, but women
sending their children to the cobbler's still directed them to
the little "new" building around the corner. It was squeezed
between the candy sales building and the Gas Company as if
it had no more business being there than a weed pushing up
through the cracks of a city sidewalk. The two large rooms
downstairs were Mr. Benjamin's place of business, while the
three rooms upstairs, accessible by a separate door at the left
of the main entrance had been rented as living and business
quarters to a dentist for several years. That busy little man had
finally transferred himself to Pittsburgh and until to-day Connie had not learned of the successor to his quarters.

She glanced in the show window at the ancient display of
rubber soles, shoe polish, goloshes and the "new footwear"
consisting of four pairs of ladies' stout, high-topped black
shoes purchased eight years ago at a warehouse fire sale and
ever since on display as a concession to his daughter's ambition
for something a little better than a plain cobbler father. Connie
herself obligingly took on a pair of the new shoes every winter
but there were no other customers for the Sales Department.

She saw Gus in the back of the shop bending over his
work-table. In the dark of the shop and contrasting with his
dark brown apron his reddish hair and close-cropped bur-
nished beard seemed radiantly out of place, and from the
gleam of his sea-blue eyes Connie thought he might be creat-
ing some mighty epic instead of a pair of French heels. In his

Sunday clothes, neatly pressed, she often thought he looked less a cobbler than a university professor or a foreign diplomat. August, whether or no he resembled these distinguished figures, considered his own trade quite as dignified as theirs and if he had borne a son would have wished no better fate than a cobbler's for him, so that the line of Benjamins in that trade should not be broken. Seven generations of Benjamin cobblers was a matter of more pride than one university diploma or a single portfolio of public office.

"That is quite true," Connie had thought long ago, a bride eager to be proud of her husband for whatever reasons he wished, and she had sustained this belief in the worthiness of craftsmanship, trying to impress it upon her daughters, who, as they grew up, resented delivering boots to their school-chums, or being asked to mind the store while Papa went home to lunch. If he had only owned the Candy Kitchen, as Mr. Herbert did, endowing his daughters thus with deathless popularity, or the Dry Goods Store, or better yet, the Music Store. . . . What social advantage in school came to little girls whose only fortune was their excellent half-soles?

"The new music professor wants the upstairs fitted out a little more," Benjamin told his wife when she came back to him. "Curtains—cushions—a few things like that. You can see when you go up. He says he has some furnishings of his own, too, but not quite enough. Go up and see what he needs as soon as he comes in."

Connie sat down gingerly on a wooden bench. The smell of leather and polish made her a little dizzy but she had never told Gus. He paid no more attention to her but hammered away at the slipper heels, his red brows meeting in a frown of concentration. Connie looked out the one back-window at the little brick-paved court behind the shop. One fallen leaf was caught in a cobweb spread across the window, through this delicate, silver-threaded wheel she saw the gnarled, rheumatic branches of the old apple tree, no longer making any pretense of pushing toward heaven but curling its roots in comfortable resignation to age and fate. Its mighty gesture had been made, after all, years ago when it pushed its roots up through the brick paving. Now the grey blighted roots were humped into a semblance of grey toes bursting out of

their worn old boots, a fitting monument to Benjamin's establishment. Wooden stairs went from this back court to the
apartment upstairs, though the regular entrance was through
the tiny vestibule in front.

Keeping her eyes fixed on the cobweb, Connie did not
mind the musty odor of the shop. She did not talk to Gus,
partly because he believed in silence and partly because there
was so little they had to say to each other that they must
spend their words very cautiously if they were to last them a
life-time. Sometimes Connie had a rush of reminiscences,
confidences, and hopes,—she would talk feverishly for hours
to Gus' quiet "That's right. . . . Sure . . . oh, sure . . . you
bet . . . uh-huh . . . yeah . . . sure . . . that so? . . . well,
well." Worn out finally by beating against this calm wall Connie would fall asleep, consoling herself with the thought that
however inarticulate he was Gus understood, his silence was
not a cold barrier but fundamental understanding. . . . She
remembered the music teacher.

"What's his name, Gus?" she asked.

Gus wrinkled his brows and then answered, "Decker's the
name. Blaine Decker. Professor Blaine Decker."

She was thinking of the blue curtains she could put in his
living room when the music teacher appeared in the shop.
He was a slight, brusque little man with a tiny moustache
which he twisted constantly; his grey suit needed pressing
badly and this, with his longish thin fair hair gave him a surprisingly unkempt appearance. But his eyes and manner were
so perfectly confident, his voice so assured, almost commanding, that one ended by being vaguely impressed that
here was a somebody, there was no mistaking that. Let him
be shabby, let him live over the humblest cobbler shop, this
man was sufficiently a personage to do as he jolly well pleased,
so Connie thought.

He bowed to her in a curiously foreign manner, clicking his
heels, then devoted himself to a discussion with Gus of keys,
ventilation, hot water heating, and all the time his brilliant
blue eyes strayed absently toward Mrs. Benjamin, until, unconsciously her head drooped and her face grew scarlet. A few
minutes later she was guiding him through the upstairs apartment, discussing blue curtains and bed linen.

"I won't need much," he explained carefully. "You see I have all my own things,—bits of tapestry, all the little things you pick up abroad. I studied in Leipsic and Paris, you see. . . . I intended to be a concert pianist . . . however. . . ."

At his words Connie's heart swelled with unknown excitement, for a moment she had the curious sensation of having invented this character for her evening fancies, it was almost too difficult to bring him from her ideal into her actual world. Now it was like meeting another exile in a strange land, a fellow countryman, and all the treasured experiences locked away from the blank gaze of the world could be freed for these familiar understanding eyes. Phrases of the old language came stiffly to mind, so stiffly that all she could do was to stand in the sunporch—(to be curtained in yellow, he decided)—and smile at him.

"Your husband is German, isn't he?" he inquired. "And you—you belong to Dell River?"

"Indeed no—I'm a stranger here, too, Mr. Decker. You see I am—or was a musician, also," Connie confessed in a rush. "I studied in convents in the East, then I sang one day before Morini, who was to teach me. I might have gone into grand opera, perhaps."

"No! Is it possible!" The professor's violent amazement was not at all like Dell River's skeptical acceptance of the same words and Connie's heart pounded in gratitude.

"Girls are foolish. For instance I—I ran away instead. I was confused, only seventeen, and such a great man to compliment me. . . . I was trapped by my own excitement, don't you see? . . . I ran away . . . married . . . and . . ."

"You ran away with Benjamin, eh?" He did not wait for an answer, assuming that of course this was the case so Connie did not set him right. It was too complicated for explanation, the story of herself and Tony. Easier to let people believe there had never been anyone but Gus. . . .

"That's the way with women as artists," he said, "always throwing their careers on the rubbish pile for some man. . . . So now, here you are. . . . Never hear an opera—or concert——"

Connie was made bold in her excitement.

"How about you. What about your career, too? You talk

about women, but after all what are you doing teaching music in a public school?"

"A different story." He turned abruptly away and then, as
Connie flushed, feeling rebuffed, he smiled at her. "I'll tell it
to you, some time, don't worry."

He opened a packing case and took out some china carefully wrapped in rags, a battered copper samovar, a cracked
terra cotta dancing figure, a moth-eaten Paisley shawl. He
proudly held out a small satinwood box for her to examine,
and twisted the key in its lock.

"There's nothing like having one's own things, is there?
Look." He pulled some bits of yellowed lace from the interior of the box and waited for her cry of admiration, but
Connie was obliged to beg his forgiveness for not knowing
lace—lace or glass. His face fell. That was the way with
women, he complained, they never appreciated their own
subjects. It was outrageous, all the things they might and
should be but *would* not. Even his mother—here he pulled
out a silver-framed photograph and placed it on the little oak
desk beside the sun-porch doorway—yes, even she neglected
the charming opportunities of a woman's life to raise dogs.
Dogs, according to his mother, probably the most unreasonable person in the world, were more fascinating than old
china, and an automobile road map was more beautiful than
an opera score. . . . All the time he was adjusting the pictured profile of the handsome woman so that it would show
to advantage. He wiped off the glass with his sleeve.

"Why did you come here?" Connie found herself asking
him. "There must be better places than this near New York,
—if you must teach school."

He bent over the packing-case and drew out a blue cream-
pitcher with a broken handle and set it with infinite care on
the table.

"Wedgwood. . . . I did have the tea-pot once but a maid
broke it. . . . Why, bigger schools want better teachers,
Mrs. Benjamin. After all I'm not trained in the teaching end.
I bluffed a few years in a Southern high school, that's all
—good enough experience for here but not for city schools.
It's not bad, after all, because I gave up the great concert
hero idea long ago. When one has a mother to support——"

"It was a baby that stopped me from going on," Connie said.

"You poor child! Then stuck forever out here in the woods, eh?" The pity welling in his bright compassionate eyes was so much that it frightened Connie. She had never wanted pity, she only wished to explain. Pity? Surely she was too fortunate a woman to warrant that, she was not lost, and pity was for lost souls. She was so unprepared for the understanding in his eyes that her own eyes blurred unexpectedly and there was an ominous tingling in her head as if old thoughts long stored in the attic were being creakily dragged out for this season's use.

"It's a lovely town,—you'll like it," she said, striving for safer ground. "After all I've been very happy here, Professor Decker, for nearly sixteen years. People are kind. And I have my children."

"I know. Goodbye to everything but house and food and family,—that's what you mean." Connie flushed, bewildered at his sharpness. He went on, without noticing her. "Can I get a piano up here? The school promised me one—I saw the music store on the Square, didn't I?"

He was unpacking great piles of music, torn manuscripts, worn study books. Connie got to her knees and picked them up as they slid from his arms, merely handling them gave her indescribable happiness. She studied a page here and there eagerly, though what she had once known was long forgotten, she pronounced the composer's name to herself, as if the burning love for all music would magically endow her with knowledge, as if before the jumble of black notes and strange names a light would miraculously flare up in her mind, gates would swing wide, all would be known and long familiar to her. Sitting on the floor, arranging the scattered pages she began to hum softly, then stopped suddenly to look up at him.

"When I finished singing that day for him he said, 'Bravo! A glorious voice, Manuel,'" she said. "Manuel was my teacher. He had known Morini before, you see. I was only seventeen—and I'd never really applied myself. But after that I knew I must. All the way going back to my grandfather's— Manuel and I talked of nothing but my future. I couldn't sleep for days. It was ghastly coming down from being treated

like a great star to being treated like a child by my grandfather. . . . So, a week later I eloped and——"

It seemed so natural to be telling all this to him, for they
knew each other, they seemed to have always known each
other. Connie got to her feet and put the music on the study
table. The stranger lit a cigarette thoughtfully and leaned
back against the arm of the one easy chair.

"And you're sorry?"

Connie shook her head.

"No—I don't see how I could ever have done any differently. You know the way a person's made . . . I've gone over
the whole thing dozens of times and I always come to the same
goal . . . there never is any real choice about your life . . . just
the one door open to you always. . . . You can't say you're
sorry."

"Well, of course Benjamin is all right," he agreed, then feeling that this was almost rude in his understatement he hastened to add, "You can see he's unusually decent,—the quiet
protector type, the refuge after a terrific disappointment."

"That was it." Connie nodded and hesitated over the implied lie, but somehow she couldn't tell him that it had
been Tony, not Gus Benjamin that she'd run away with. She
couldn't—after telling him of her high youthful ambition—
tell him about the street carnival in the little New England
town and Tony in silver tights, how they'd run softly over the
great moonlit lawn, remembering to keep his dark coat over
her white dress, pausing in the pointed shadows of the little
balsam trees to catch their breath and look back toward her
grandfather's window, then stumbling on to the main road,
waiting in the glare of automobile headlights for the bus to
pick them up, clutching each other's trembling fingers. . . .
No, Connie couldn't explain to Decker about Tony. After
eighteen years she couldn't explain it even to herself . . . there
are no alternatives in life, that was all she could say, one does
the thing there is to do. . . .

Going downstairs back to the shop her lips moved unconsciously continuing an imaginary conversation with Decker,
telling him all about Grandfather, about Manuel and the convent, changing the truth into suitable words, pouring her
thirty-five years into sentences that would explain her life

complete—(except for Tony) so that they could begin afresh with this day. Her mind leaped to furnish Decker's own life up to this moment. She saw him in foreign cities,—Munich, Leipsic, she saw him in stiff little German parks and then on sidewalk cafes in Paris, in casement-windowed salons playing the piano so beautifully she could weep for thinking of it. Little adventures unwound marvellously before her, composites of motion pictures she had seen, books she had read, and she even saw herself in these pictures, herself and Tony. Yes, Tony. She was surprised to find Tony here, willy-nilly, but why not, since though it was Decker's past, these were familiar scenes to her imagination, they were built years ago with Tony and there was no getting him out now.

In bed the two girls whispered of school, of the music teacher, of the new boys. In their stiff cotton nightgowns, their thin young arms under their heads they lay, careful not to touch each other, only in sleep tumbling unconsciously into each other's arms. They went to bed at ten but whispered until twelve, remembering through all their confidences to tell each other nothing for they were sisters.

Helen, at fifteen, resented her parents, collected little grievances against them and spread them out at night like so many trophies and Mimi, being twelve, was torn between loyalty for her parents and dazed admiration for one who escaped such unconventional feelings. It was Mimi who stayed awake long after Helen had drawn her long legs up and fallen asleep. Mimi, wide awake, stared at the dim shadows the mirror helped the intruding starlight to create and wondered if Helen really would run away some day to Cincinnati or Chicago or New York as she threatened, if she really would ask Papa for twenty dollars for dancing lessons as her right, if she really would demand that Mama remain upstairs when some boy came to see her. Then would come the wave of love for Mama, stronger than any feeling for Helen or anything in the world. She was not jealous of Helen for being the pretty Benjamin girl, she did not think much about her own square homely little face, she did not mind so much walking home from school alone while Helen ran with a laughing admiring crowd.

Mimi's romance concerned her mother and not herself at all. She had made up a glamorous past for her mother, she swelled with pride over the little triumphs of Connie's past, made new ones to fill out the gaps. Beauty, to Mimi, meant her mother's face, clear, wide-apart brown eyes, sharply cut nose and oddly full lips, a rather thin pointed face softened by rich chestnut hair. There was to Mimi something fine, soft and perfumed about her mother, she was fascinated by the operatic gestures of long white hands, the throbbing excitement of her voice, the ever-present hint that some day the witches' spell would be broken and the Snow Queen herself, no longer disguised as Connie Benjamin, would emerge gloriously triumphant. Mimi saw her mother always on a swell of music, she saw her on a stage in a magic circle of light with swaying figures holding out their hands to her, she could hear her mother humming through it all, while radiant maidens floated over rainbows of heavenly music. She was ever dazzled that the enchanted one should be her mother, she could not understand how Helen could be so casual, often so cynical about this miracle.

"That old picture of her in the ermine jacket," Helen complained. "She wasn't much older than I am. Why don't I have fur coats then? Maybe if she'd had to wear an old sweater under a blue serge coat for two winters when she was a girl she'd understand more about me. And if she went away to boarding school, why shouldn't I?"

Mimi, not at all offended that this injustice did not extend to her but was only directed at Helen, whispered logical explanations.

"She should have thought of all that and about her children when she quarreled with her family," Helen retorted gloomily. "I get just furious thinking of all the things we might have had if she'd had more common sense. You too, Mimi,—you could have had your hair permanent waved like Estelle Mills and be quite pretty."

This was a stab in the dark but it went home, for Mimi's private theory was that curly hair would have made up for all other defects of feature. For Helen to guess this startled her and made it seem an absolute fact instead of mere theory. A brief resentment came over her for the mother whose magnificent gestures cost her daughter personal beauty, but Mimi dismissed it at once as a wicked idea. Even Helen relented a little on second thoughts. Today the new music-teacher (freak though he was, all the girls said so) had singled her out from the whole class to be leader of the school chorus. She was to have charge of the class music every day except on the lesson day the way Rena Blake had done last year. Miss Murrell, the old dumb-bell, had said, "but Professor Decker, Helen isn't one of our strongest voices, you know," and he said right to her face and before the whole class, "That's all right, Miss Murrell, her mother is musically trained and I trust to background in these matters." Miss Murrell had plainly wanted Rena Blake for leader again. It was a come-down when old Decker spoke up that way.

"It was all because Mama was almost a great musician," Mimi told Helen breathlessly. "You've got to admit that, Helen. And maybe he knew her in those days."

"No, he didn't," Helen answered and then turned over toward the wall, punched her pillow into the right shape and prepared now for sleep. "How would he have known her then?"

Mimi lifted her head, leaned on her elbow.

"Why not when they were both abroad? Maybe he heard her singing for that great man—Morini?"

Helen yawned and pulled the covers up to her chin.

"Don't tell me you really believed that story," she said sleepily, and then added, while fear froze in Mimi's wondering heart. "Nobody else ever did . . . and certainly not me."

The dinner for Professor Decker was a problem. Connie wanted a touch of formality about it but this was hard to achieve in Dell River where one was not invited a week ahead of time unless it was a holiday banquet. Usually dining with friends was impromptu and nothing more than taking pot-luck with neighbors before an evening at cards. Connie had taken no part in these casual entertainments so that Gus was surprised to find her so concerned over the proper way to entertain his tenant. Why should he be asked to dine, they never had mixed with the teachers before, what was the idea of it now? Connie ceased to discuss the occasion with him but planned it carefully in secret. She had never had any good table linen or china, so she decided to use the batiked piano scarf as a table cloth and by having a Sunday night supper she could use her yellow china tea set. She had no new clothes for years but finally she dyed her old pink lace and satin negligee a deep grey, it looked quite like the tea gowns one saw in the magazines. She was never a good cook but Helen could fix things very nicely and had promised to make chicken à la king.

For days Connie worried about this great occasion. Mimi and Helen insisted on demanding the why and wherefore of it, they were mystified at Mama asking strangers in and Helen bitterly complained that their house was too shabby for those out-of-town teachers to visit. Old Decker would tell the Herberts and the principal—(Helen liked Don Marshall, the principal's son)—that the Benjamins had no glassware, just used old jelly glasses at the table, and he would make fun to everyone of their having overhead glaring lights instead of floor-lamps and bridge lamps the way other people did. These shortcomings were all Connie's fault even more than they were a question of economy, for Connie was blind as a man to little household touches outside of color and light and general effect. It had never occurred to her, as it did so often to Helen, that there was much difference between her own home and other Dell River homes aside, of course, from Laurie Neville's great barren mansion out by the nurseries. That was what one should have, but between that Victorian museum and the simplest workman's cottage Connie saw no gradations, one had one or the other and she saw no way of softening the contrast, nor any reason to bemoan it before now. One was what one was and one had what one had. But now she saw everything with the stranger's eye and was vaguely dissatisfied. She was sorry she had made no friends in Dell River, for it made her gesture toward Decker seem too important to the family. She ended by inviting Helen's English teacher, Miss Murrell, since she had called twice about the girls' school work and had talked to Mrs. Benjamin confidentially about her own desire to write. She had even showed her the letters she had written home from France during the war when she had been a canteen worker. Connie, to whom writing was an almost impossible and not very important art, had been impressed by the other woman's ease in expressing thoughts and facts, and when she showered her with the sincerest praise the guest suddenly burst into tears. Connie stood helpless while the teacher, tears streaming down her face and hiccoughing little sobs, gathered her beloved letters together and fastened them in the gold-trimmed blue leather notebook again. At the door Miss Murrell had, after a final dab at her red eyes, squeezed Connie's hand and murmured, "I can't tell you how much this has meant to me—your saying that. No one ever—I mean—you know—here away from everything you might say—and—I thank you—oh I do thank you."

Then, bursting into tears again, she had run out of the house. That had been last spring. Connie hadn't seen her after that. The teachers usually went away in the summer, and somehow they had not met again. Connie had been more than a little frightened to see such a pale, quiet little person torn by such dreadful sobs, they were not like ordinary cries at all, not the gentle moans of a woman used to weeping, but hoarse, horrible noises like those of an animal in pain. By this time the memory of the awkward occasion was decently dimmed for both women, so Connie issued and Miss Murrell accepted the invitation without undue embarrassment.

"I wish," Connie said at breakfast, "that you girls would try to talk about classes as little as possible because that's what Mr. Decker wants to escape. And Gus,—if you'd try to talk just a little——"

"Why?" asked her husband. "And what about? Shoes? No one wants to hear about my business and I've got no time for anything else, you know that."

"When Papa came to the school exercises and the principal talked to him," said Helen, "he didn't answer a single word, just nodded and then when the principal finished Papa tipped his hat and walked away."

She fixed cold, rebuking blue eyes upon him.

"What the hell," growled her father. "What do I know about education? Let him do the talking, that's his business."

"But he thought you couldn't understand English," explained Helen, flushed with shame at the recollection. "He asked Miss Murrell if you were foreign."

Gus was not disturbed. He left the table for his low leather chair in the kitchen corner, the Sunday paper in hand, lit his pipe calmly and adjusted his spectacles.

"I've got my work—let him have his," he answered.

Connie hurried to fix matters since Helen always would hang on to an argument until it was in shreds and Gus in a quiet fury.

"All right—all right, Gus, don't bother to talk to the company. But please stay at the table until they've finished eating instead of going off to the kitchen to doze right away. I would hate that, honestly, Gus."

"Don't worry about me," Gus answered impatiently. "Have your party. I can look after myself. I've never disgraced anyone yet."

"You wouldn't know it if you did," muttered Helen but subsided at an imploring look from her mother.

Miss Murrell came half an hour before the expected time. She lived with the two other high school teachers in the town's only hostelry—"The Oaks." She was seldom asked anywhere and usually was left on the Oaks' porch reading with the greatest absorption the "Atlantic Monthly" or Harper's while the pretty newest teacher went out driving with the town bachelor, Matt Neal, and the other in her best blue suit and white kid gloves went out for an evening of bridge (which Miss Murrell looked upon as unintellectual) with Laurie Neville or her secretary-companion, Miss Manning. Tonight she was forced to leave the house before six if her friends were to witness her departure and note that she too was sometimes invited out. They helped her into the blue crepe de chine (drapes flying from waist to neck) which Miss Neville had sent down to The Oaks for whichever of the teachers it would fit. It was almost too small for Miss Murrell but if she didn't bend her elbows it was all right.

"It's only a little supper at Mrs. Benjamin's," she explained carefully. "But Professor Decker will be there and you know how a new teacher will talk if he sees you aren't gotten up properly."

The other teachers were not envious of Mrs. Benjamin's invitation but their eyes met in mutual envy of Miss Murrell's opportunity with Decker. The only man teacher in town beside the married principal,—not bad-looking and possessing a shy reserve always challenging to women even when complemented by age, gout, or stupidity. . . . In Laurie Neville's huge home one never saw a sign of a man unless it was one of her doctors from the city or the snobbish husband of some bored house guest. After Miss Murrell left the teachers looked at each other, more friendly than they had ever been.

"You know, Louise isn't bad looking,—she's almost pretty, but not quite," said the young, pretty teacher, suddenly making the other young and pretty, too, with her air of including her in a secret. "Being not quite pretty is worse than being ugly, I think."

"Anyway, Louise isn't a man's woman," said the older one, and then was silent, thinking of a certain "man's woman" she had in mind who was practically wasted in Dell River.

Miss Murrell felt excited and flattered by the formal air of the Benjamin dining-room due perhaps to the rigid bouquets of asters which Mimi had placed on table and cabinet. She revelled in the discomfort (always associated with high social functions) of sitting alone in a dimly-lighted room waiting for the hostess to make an appropriate entrance. One imagined that soon doors would open and witty, delightful people would saunter in and talk of books, plays, poetry,—talk of these things easily and charmingly instead of rolling them out like great ugly boulders into the conversation, handicaps that people of character gave themselves to conquer, no matter how painful it might be, before they could go on to the unworthy business of having a good time. Even Miss Murrell could not talk of books or poetry lightly, it was like taking out one's very heart and playing bean-bag with it. When she thought of Swinburne or of Galsworthy her head swam, blood pounded in her throat, so that she could barely speak, and when she wanted to talk in class about "Un Bel Ami" her hands shook and her eyes filled with tears, so she had to pretend to be reading from notes, and when she managed to force her words out of her trembling lips her voice was strange and harsh, so strange that pupils stared at her open-mouthed. That was what came of being shy, of caring too much for things, and of keeping them to yourself instead of getting accustomed to airing them in public.

Mrs. Benjamin, in trailing grey silk, fitted in with one's dream of a Sunday night salon. Miss Murrell felt a wave of gratitude to her for fitting in so well, she was moved further by

Professor Decker in a wing collar and tie that seemed almost formal, so magnificently did he wear it, bowing over Mrs. Benjamin's hand,—it was all so fitting that Miss Murrell did not mind that he merely nodded, clicking his heels, to her.

"That's why I can never be happy with simple, *good* people," she thought. "It isn't enough to be honest and good—to be happy they must pretend. They really must!"

Helen was angry because the milk curdled when she made the white sauce, so she passed the plates with a face black as a thunder-cloud. This was the privilege of pretty girls, they could always be rude or angry and were forgiven because tantrums accented their beauty. Mimi, tongue-tied before teachers and Helen's rage, sat at table and could not eat. She was tired of seeing everything with Helen's eyes, then with mother's, then with father's. She knew Helen resented the whole business, especially now that they were eating the soured chicken and politely saying nothing about it. Mimi knew Helen wanted to shout, "See how poor we are, we don't even have soup spoons or bread-and-butter plates, why don't you come out and say so, you teachers that have been everywhere and know the way things ought to be, you make me sick pretending not to see and not to care, talking all that rot. Come on and say what you're really thinking,—that the chicken's sour, the napkins are all ragged even if you do call them serviettes!"

Mimi saw her father hurry through his portion before anyone else began, then push his plate back, and she looked quickly at her mother and the guests to see if they looked revolted. But they were laughing and talking in formal, slightly foreign accents, begging each other's pardon, thanking each other, and if-you-please-ing each other, passing their cups and dishes with elaborate ceremony, their voices quite changed with little tremors of excitement.

"They're pretending it's a party," Mimi finally decided and was awed by her discovery for she could never pretend very well, even when she was little mud-pies were mud and dolls were dolls, not babies. When she grew up perhaps everything would change and for her then Professor Decker and Miss Murrell in for supper would be a party, not just extra dishes and the strain of good manners.

Connie saw none of the things that Helen saw, she could even forgive Gus for dozing in his chair and did not mind when in the after-supper confusion Mimi and Helen started chattering about classes and wrangling excitedly not because they disagreed but because it covered their self-consciousness.

"I think we will have a little music now," said Connie, and led the way to the front room. Both ladies flushed and were happy when Decker offered his cigarette case, and each shook her head hesitantly as if on this one occasion she would deny herself. Decker sat at the piano and tried a few chords, acting as if the resulting noise were not half-bad, and remarking that undoubtedly it had been a good piano once.

When he sat down the old-fashioned cut of his suit was apparent, the heavily-padded shoulders, slightly raised pinched belt and the shining greenish seams. Miss Murrell watched his foot on the pedal, first because it was a small foot for a man, though he was undoubtedly no giant, and then because the tan oxfords were patched and the heels run over, and she could not help wondering how he could be so gay, quite as if he had new patent leathers on, though perhaps, she reasoned, new shoes would only have accentuated the ravelling edges of his trouser cuffs. She felt guilty for taking notice of these trivial points.

"It's because I hear Marian and Stella talking so much about people," she mentally excused herself, "so I've begun to notice the things they are always on the watch for. I must stop it."

Gus had silently gone upstairs, having uttered only two words during the evening, but the guests appeared not to mind, as if the only decent way to treat such afflictions in society was to feign not to see them. In the beginning Decker had tried to talk to him but Gus had answered very briefly. Connie felt disturbed, and had a sudden passionate hatred for him, but the feeling vanished as if hatred were too big a word for such a little man. She thought of how hard Gus worked, she was moved, as always remembering that he had been left an orphan when he was only ten,—ah no, she couldn't hate Gus. Certainly, if he must sleep, it was better to have him upstairs than right here where everyone could see and hear him snore.

Listening to Decker, by some magic, conjuring music out of the old tin piano, Connie grew dreamily happy. Now it seemed to her she had always led a charming life among charming people,—this was not one evening in a thousand, it was the way all her evenings were spent,—indeed her evening voyages of fancy were very like this reality in essence. She was about to ask Decker to play the Liebestraum but Miss Murrell did and he smiled so scornfully that Connie looked with reproach on the poor woman. Then he offered to accompany her and she sang "Come back to Sorrento" but she had forgotten the words so she hummed the air while Decker improvised runs and trills so cleverly that she had the sensation of giving a marvellous performance. But it made her sad to think of how much she had forgotten, how much she loved music and how little she knew about it, her blind ecstasy over a mere chord made it appear irreverent to inquire what made up such rich beauty.

"I think," said Decker, "we might learn to hate music if we had to fulfil its demands. This way we can play with it, as if it were our toy. If circumstances were different—" they sighed and thought of their lost careers— "we could not play with it, for we would be its slaves."

"Yes, yes," cried Connie, happy just to hear the word "music" as women are happy to hear a lover's name mentioned.

Mimi stood in the doorway shyly listening for a while, too awed to sit down, too embarrassed to leave, conscious of her freckles, her chewed fingernails, her new budding breasts. She was afraid to speak lest she make a grammatical error before the English teacher, and she was afraid to call herself to Decker's attention lest he recognize her as the pupil he scolded yesterday for singing off key. Presently Helen's voice, calling her from the kitchen, released her and she stayed out there pretending to do her home work on the kitchen table long after Helen had stolen out with the Herbert boy who had whistled to her from the alley.

"And do you know," Professor Decker said, "actually when I accepted the Dell River position I said to myself, 'My dear fellow, this is the end for you,—you are going into the wilderness. No one will have heard of Debussy or Ravel. They will think Brahms is a disease and Moussorgsky—a mineral water!"

Connie laughed joyously, her cheeks flushed, her eyes radiant. Miss Murrell laughed, too, and fixed the names in her mind so that in the library tomorrow she could find out if they really were mineral waters. Decker spraddled the piano stool as if he were quite at home, he looked boyish running his fingers through his thinning hair in a shy way, and he stammered a little before he said something amusing. Miss Murrell could not keep her eyes from Mrs. Benjamin who sat on the edge of the chair, her hands clasping one knee, her coral ear-rings quivering with each move of her head, sometimes they fell against her brown hair and sometimes against her slim, creamy throat.

"Why, she is beautiful!" thought Miss Murrell and tried to think wherein she had changed since last spring. For a moment it struck her as shocking for this woman to be a cobbler's wife, —how could it have happened? And then she thought wasn't it better to be an "old maid school teacher" than to have people wondering how you came to be the wife of a cobbler or a brick-layer or a butcher, but the answer, alas, was no . . . and especially in Dell River where it was merely being decent that counted, regardless of butcher's aprons or workmen's overalls.

"It shows that everywhere—no matter where you go," Decker pursued, seriously, "you find your own people, your own kind. Isn't that true, Mrs. Benjamin?"

"Indeed it is," Connie agreed and it seemed to her that the last fifteen years had all been like this night when actually this was her first party, even the walls of her house with their old-fashioned wallpaper looked different now that they had absorbed a dozen allusions to glamorous places—"A funny thing happened to me once in Bremen. . . ." "A friend of mine in Vienna, a perfectly charming widow—" (immediately Connie and Miss Murrell blushed with pleasure as if a man who knew a "perfectly charming widow" would only associate with women he considered equally attractive so this was indirectly a nice compliment to them)— At "Of course I found Berlin at first a frightful place, simply frightful" they looked complimented again and a little benevolent as if they knew all along that Berlin was really splendid and were amused at his tourist's first impressions.

Connie felt herself swelling with joy, this lovely, lovely evening must never end,—the concert pianist, the opera-singer and—well, call Miss Murrell a writer, then. . . . But the evening was hers and Decker's. Miss Murrell was outside. Poor Louisa, so nearly pretty, so almost clever, what a pity not

to be downright ugly rather than forever tantalized by the
hairbreadth between herself and happiness. Her diluted
charm made her so easy to ignore yet she was so sweet . . .
too bad that with only three persons in a room you could still
forget her as if she were a pale pink little ghost.

Miss Murrell kept looking at her watch. It was eleven. She
would not be home till after twelve, the others would say, ah,
a wild party. Her heart beat fast and her throat ached the way
it did when she was about to mention poetry or her own writing. She did not know how to bring it up but she wanted to
say something, to show that even if she did not understand
music, she did have her divine yearnings. In a sudden pause
she was so unprepared for her opportunity she could only
gasp out "Swinburne" and then when they looked at her, surprised, she blurted out in a strange, breathless voice, "I mean
music is like Swinburne. Like 'In a Garden.' 'Ah, God, that
day should come so soon.' . . . And 'Oh Dolores, mother of
pain.' So beautiful, so—so like music."

"It is beautiful!" Connie agreed and her whole body grew
warm with love and sadness for the poet who could say such
things.

"You know Swinburne?" Decker asked Connie, taking him
away from the English teacher and giving him to his hostess.
Connie nodded eagerly, for it seemed to her she did know
his work, surely she did, not that it mattered, one needn't
know poetry, it was only loving it that was important. Miss
Murrell was reciting "In a Garden" in a dry, breathless voice,
sitting upright, her face red and queer-looking, her fingers
tearing her handkerchief. Connie was not conscious of never
having heard this poet before, something inside her rushed
out to all lovely things with a "I know! Oh, indeed I know!"
The only things she really knew were the names of trees and
flowers, for even in music which she loved best she had a
vague superstition that exact knowledge cancelled sensuous
pleasure.

"I used to write poetry," said Miss Murrell, choking at her
own boldness. "I only write occasionally—little essays—little
—little prose poems. . . . Then I teach. . . ."

"Oh yes, teaching," sighed Decker. The word seemed a dis-
enchanting one for he looked at his watch.

"Don't go," begged Connie. "At least come in the back-garden and see what's left of my flowers. And we can look down the river."

"River's such a big name for such a little brook," Decker laughed.

Miss Murrell, suddenly sad and silent, got her hat and coat. They went out through the kitchen door and saw the dishpan piled high with their dishes and the cat reluctantly licking the remains of the soured creamed chicken. Mimi had fallen asleep over her study books, but jumped up quickly as they came out.

"Oh no, don't go out there," she begged her mother in a frightened whisper, but Connie paid no attention so there was nothing Mimi could do but follow them out, wringing her hands because everyone immediately saw Helen lying down in the backyard hammock with the Herbert boy. So, laughing as if this were quite—oh quite—usual, the two teachers said goodnight and Connie stood in the yard, watching them walk away together as if they were to be gone forever. . . . She did not say anything to Helen, who was merely angry at the intrusion, and not at all humiliated. Instead she went into the living-room and closed the piano as if it were a rare old instrument whose exquisite mechanism would be easily affected by the raw night air. She started to arrange the music again and then decided to leave it the way it was. In the kitchen Mimi set to work on the dishes. Helen came in, her hair tousled, her eyes flashing, and grumbled loudly of the outrageousness of her home which wasn't a home at all where a girl had to entertain friends in a hammock instead of on a decent sofa. They clattered through the dishes together.

From the east bedroom of The Oaks the youngest teacher looked out the window, holding her nightgown over her bosom, and saw that a man was seeing Louisa Murrell home and she had the unpleasant sensation that this was a shocking insult to herself for *she* was the pretty teacher, the one who had beaux.

Connie went upstairs and her heart sank thinking of the episode in the backyard, almost spoiling the evening. She knew Helen was stronger-minded than she had ever been and far wiser,—no use telling her of the dangers of life. What could she tell a daughter, anyway? She thought again of Tony and those summer nights. . . . As she sat on the bed, undressing in the dark so as not to waken Gus, it came to her that she had been contented then as she was tonight, and that if tonight had never happened she might never have known how utterly, completely, hideously unhappy she had been for these many years.

Dell River was changed. Connie saw it now as if she were here for the first time, still not a part of it, but an amiable visitor who finds many dull places and characters delightful since she won't see them again anyway, and they heighten her complacence over her own far different life. When Mrs. Busch came to do the washing she no longer was disturbed at her haughtiness but smilingly indulgent. Poor quaint Mrs. Busch, she thought, and her beautiful idiot child, for that was the way Decker had spoken of them. After the girls had gone to school in the mornings she sat down to the piano and went through Mimi's "Parlor Pieces for the Piano," enchanted over a chord here and there, marking the piece in her mind so that she might speak of it later to Decker. "Don't you love that Cyril Scott thing—that one that goes this way. . . ."

She got out her three operatic scores, "Traviata," "La Boheme" and "Martha" and hummed through them, picking out a struggling accompaniment. She thought of Decker not as a man but as the creator of a personality for herself, a beautiful role into which she gratefully stepped. No, he himself was not a person at all, but a symbol of cities, of fame, of magic. She could not think of the way he looked but of the curious way his mere presence in the town flattered her, assured her of very rare cosmopolitan qualities. Her evening fancies changed from the past and the unreal to the possible future—talks with Decker, tea on the porch or in her rock garden, serving Gus' dandelion wine when next he came to dine, making a dozen little special plans so that every day should be an event. She saw her moss-rose bush wither into its dry brown winter and was sad, then at once wanted to share this sadness with Decker. She listened carefully to the girls' tales of school, of the preparations for Christmas exercises, selections of a chorus, reports of arguments over the program.

"And what did Professor Decker say?" she would ask and if he had insisted on "Toreador" instead of "The Pilgrims'

Chorus" as an opening number or an arrangement of "The Spinning Song" instead, she would nod her head in admiration of such exquisite judgment. Yes, oh yes, she could see exactly why he had decided that way. . . .

She thought of Gus in a kind, detached way as Decker did,—dear old Gus, a dear good friend of "ours." . . . To this point of view Gus was comfortably oblivious. Her days were arranged to lay before Decker, they became the pretty pattern of a cultured woman's life, with the window-washing, curtain-mending, cooking, marketing, as amusing little side issues of an artist's career, all quite in the category of his teaching.

When she went down town she was always prepared with some light greeting in case she should meet him coming out of the school building or out of his apartment. Once she saw him in the music store, so after that she often went in there. Old Mills kept nothing but the prescribed pieces for young musicians, but usually a sample of the latest gramophone was on display and Connie took to playing records over and over here. For the first time she was angered at having no pocket money, she wanted to buy a record once in a while, it was so childish to have only a few pennies in her pocket, twenty-two cents for tonight's hamburger, seven cents for bread . . . nothing for "Caro Nome!" Then this very poverty became an adventure when Decker, passing by, saw her through the show-window and came inside.

"Isn't it silly that we can't buy these things?" he sighed. "I come here every day and rage that a grown-up man should have no more pocket money than a child for his candy. . . . Look at that damn instrument—only thirty or forty dollars. . . ."

"Two hundred," came Mills' voice from the desk in the corner of the store. Connie and Decker looked at each other and laughed. They started out of the shop together.

He had a slouching swagger that seemed the ideal carriage for a man of the world, and Connie wondered, when she saw men look at him a little oddly, if they were not envious of the casual jaunty way he wore his ragged clothes,—shiny, greenish-blue suit with the sleeves too short, run-over patched shoes, frayed shirt, faded green necktie that was never thrust into his vest like other men's but appeared to have complete freedom to fly wherever it pleased,—and that shapeless green felt hat. . . . It was provincial for a man to be neat, she decided, all very well for Gus, since it suited his German idea of system, but how charming to be above system! She knew, however, from his glances at her own costume, that it was certainly the thing for a woman to be neatly groomed.

Walking across the Square with Decker became a promenade through the Bois, they exchanged comments on the quaint design of flower-beds, found something remarkable in the whole plan of the town, so that actually some of the most intelligent people in the world would have excellent cause to settle here.

"Sometimes I wonder," said Decker very seriously, "if a man with his own work,—a writer, say, or composer,— wouldn't do far better working alone in a pleasant spot like this, rather than in the confusion of Paris or New York where he is the prey of every fad, and often forced by his envy into some tawdry success."

Connie nodded in complete agreement.

"Isn't it better, I've often thought," she said, "for me to be here keeping up with my interests in music, keeping my ideals, than to have failed as an opera singer and been trapped into cheap musical comedy work?"

"Singing Red Hot Mama blues," Decker added, "with Mr. Blaine Decker accompanying you on the sax."

They laughed radiantly together, a little complacently, as if, try though they would, they could not help gloating a little over the poor souls trapped by their art, in stuffy concert-halls or pitifully pretending to enjoy the hollow success of second-rate fame. Connie felt young and buoyant, a great artist taking a holiday from her public in a little quiet inland village, romping away as if she were a perfectly ordinary woman.

"I want to come and see you again some evening." They stopped at the corner of the Square. Decker stood swinging his hat, his head slightly bowed, his heels together, so sensationally chivalrous his attitude that a passing automobile slowed up and some women in the back seat leaned far out to stare. "But you ladies with your homes and your luncheons, and your teas,—always so busily idle. I dare not interfere."

Connie dismissed her supposed occupation with a pretty shrug. Why didn't he drop in again Sunday,—she would get in touch with Miss Murrell, too. Immediately her mind began working on plans for this "dropping in." Pimiento sandwiches, she thought, this time, and chocolate cake.

"Ah yes, little Miss Murrell," Decker said, and they both smiled indulgently, granting that she was a good little soul, no doubt unusually gifted in her quiet way, but lacking in that god-like ruthlessness so necessary to the genuine artist. By implication they granted each other this rather brutal but Olympian quality, and even while admitting that Louisa Murrell was not up to the cosmopolitan mark, they agreed to include her because she tried so hard, and things which they took as a matter of course,—intelligent conversation and all that,—meant so much to the poor little thing.

"I hope to have a beautiful new wardrobe to dazzle you next time," Decker promised gaily. "The good principal, Mr. Marshall, took me aside today and suggested that a new suit would enhance the dignity of my position. Something in black or blue, he thought, as if he suspected me of some Scottish plaid intentions."

They roared with appreciative laughter again, and the dreadful twenty minutes this morning was almost forgotten when Mr. Marshall, large, blue-shaven, immaculate in carefully pressed blue serge, shiny black gunmetal shoes, neat black tie, stiff white collar, had stopped Decker as he swaggered jauntily down the high-school corridor.

"Parents have commented," Marshall whispered hoarsely. "Trustees have asked me to speak of it. It doesn't look well, you know, to the taxpayers. They say on a hundred and sixty a month you really should dress better, nothing fancy, understand, just black or blue, that always looks dignified and neat— I always wear blue myself—and perhaps a fresh shirt every day. I wear a shirt two or three days myself—just fresh collars—but I notice you wear the attached collars—so——"

Decker could feel the blood swirling through his head. He, who spent an hour over bath and shave every morning, who had such irreproachable standards for grooming, even though he had to compromise on style, economize on laundry and tailor repairs. . . . As if he were a child come to the table with dirty nails! He found himself raising his hand to show that no matter what else Marshall might criticize he must surely see

how impeccably manicured he was, but the ragged cuff thrust
out of the frayed coat sleeve was all that Marshall's eye took in.

"A new suit wouldn't be more than thirty dollars—possibly
forty, and you've just been paid," Marshall said, looking away
from Decker. He hated the whole business as much as the
music teacher did.

Decker would not speak of the hundred dollars a month
sent to his mother. It was no one's affair but his own. When
speech came back to him he found his voice, in very Oxford
accents, saying, "My dear Mr. Marshall, do you know I wear
nothing but linen as underwear? The very purest, the very
finest linen!" Almost like a drunken man he wanted to show
Marshall the London label on his underwear, the label that
enabled him to swagger in any company no matter what his
outward apparel might be. . . . Someone,—Louisa Murrell,
in fact, approached the principal, then, and Decker swung
haughtily away, looking whatever pupil he passed ferociously
in the eye as if no matter what that pupil may have overheard
the real triumph had been his, Decker's, for he had proved
that he was the true exquisite, he wore linen, pure linen next
to his skin. Ten years before on his trip with Starr Donnell
through Switzerland, that immortal precious summer, Starr
had cast aside two suits of underwear as too small, and
Decker, pretending to give them to the valet, had secretly
kept them. Threadbare but elegant, he was still instructing
laundresses wherever he lived in the special process necessary
to the preservation of the rare fabric, storming when they
were scorched or torn, mending them himself when they fell
apart. Like a magic ring these garments kept him above all
failure, all despair, they represented foreign culture, and that
year in his life when he had been on the brink of spectacular
fame. Thinking of Starr, as he would be thinking of him forever, he knew that his heart again seemed torn out of his
body, it was impossible that two people who were one person
should be ripped apart, the only way he could heal this anguish of remembering was by thinking hard of the perfection
of that brief year, thinking of it proudly as a triumph rather
than dwelling on the end of it which meant defeat.

How would he get a new suit, how, he thought, beating
time for "The Soldiers' Chorus" that afternoon. . . . How

could he live with Marshall thinking he was a tramp, a filthy tramp when he shaved every morning and night, too, sometimes, pumiced his hands so meticulously, bathed himself, heating the water while he dusted the apartment. Rather die than tell Marshall that he laundered his own three shirts now to save two dollars a month for his piano rent. Rather die than admit anything that appeared the shoddy dreary poverty of the ordinary teacher instead of the ascetic simplicity of a true aristocrat. Aching with shame as he had been all day, now he marvellously recovered his dignity by chatting with Mrs. Benjamin as a gentleman to a lady.

He saw that her gloves, her black kid gloves, were to her what the London label was to him, they made of Dell River a center of wit and culture as a monocle and lorgnette might have done. And when he humorously told of Marshall's suggestion, Mrs. Benjamin's amusement made a blundering provincial ass of Marshall, made of himself a charming but absent-minded artist, a helpless child about fashions as all artists were, at the same time wearing his rags with such genuine distinction that it brought out the blind, futile envy of dubs like Marshall.

"Of course I shall forget to buy the damned suit," Decker chuckled. "I'll buy some etching instead. There's a nice McBey in a shop in Pittsburgh. I told the man I might send for it when I changed cars there."

"You really are quite hopeless," Connie scolded him admiringly. "I'm sure Mr. Marshall is never going to understand you. . . . And I am quite as likely to spend the grocery money on 'Caro Nome' for my poor squeaky old victrola."

They laughed again and being poor became a mere youthful whim, being not quite what they once planned became a purely temporary compromise, or at worst a philosophic adjustment which superior people made with a gallant shrug of their shoulders.

Decker, his tie flying over one shoulder, swaggered busily eastward, still swinging his hat in his hand and throwing his head back as if he had an unruly mop of hair instead of not quite enough; he continued to smile slightly, thinking of poor, stupid old Marshall and his thirty dollar suits,—as if one could get a really decent suit such as Starr always wore for less

than a hundred. He'd rather wear these old rags than the
ready-made sort of thing men like Marshall wore. The hot
shame of the morning had vanished into a warm glow over
Mrs. Benjamin, in whose clear hazel eyes he saw himself a
witty talented fellow who found it more amusing to be a
vagabond than a gentleman. He glanced back before turning
toward his doorway, and saw her looking backward, too. She
looked slim and discreet in black, adjusting her close-fitting
black velvet hat ever so slightly to the right, her gloved hands
twisting it delicately as if it were a priceless import. A beautiful and cultured woman, Decker pronounced her, an extraordinary woman who evidently appreciated almost to the full
his own rather extraordinary gifts. Catching each other's eye
in this backward glance they experienced a sudden guilty embarrassment for each was so warmed and stimulated by their
brief intimate exchange that they almost ignored the source
of this self-gratification. Each, on second thought, had looked
back to fix in mind a clear image of this understanding friend,
and each saw the picture made up of the actual and the desired. For years this was to be their habit, turning back a few
steps after parting to fix that final image, and always they saw
the pleased smile or flush that was a tribute to their own conversation; always Connie would be caught adjusting her hat
or veil to make sure she was as soignée as Decker's eyes had
proclaimed, and always Decker would be glimpsed twisting
the end of his meager moustache in a debonair way. Always
Decker, as he did now, would bow, waving his hat with a
magnificent flourish, and always Connie, blushing a little,
would raise her little gloved hand gaily, charmingly.

Connie was not jealous when Laurie Neville invited Professor
Decker with the two teachers from The Oaks to dinner, but
Louisa Murrell suffered for her, for herself, too, since she was
not invited, and it was humiliating to have the other women
speak mockingly of Decker's mannerisms, his elegant gestures
and adopted accent warring with his ragged clothes, when she
had made so much of the privilege of consorting with the brilliant man at Mrs. Benjamin's "Sunday evenings." The other
two had been so plainly impressed all season with Louisa's

private social life, the sophisticated conversations reported and the fascinating mystery surrounding Mrs. Benjamin. Louisa had not boasted, she could not boast, she had only referred to these occasions as modestly as possible, but always implying their sacredness. Miss Emmons and Miss Swasey after their dinner at Miss Neville's, giggled mockingly while Louisa dressed for Mrs. Benjamin and Decker. He was so shabby, they said, and even shabby, he needn't be such a freak, he might get a decent hair-cut and some new shoes. Say what you will a man has no business talking of the grand opera in New York and his titled friends in Paris, the different names of wines, when he is sitting in a lovely home with mud caked on his old shoes and his trouser cuffs trailing ravelled edges. No, now really, you could not expect people to do more than smile at such an outrageous contrast. Laurie Neville and Miss Manning had been interested in the way they were in all freaks, but Miss Manning had assured the two teachers that he was the strangest creature she'd ever seen and pray why on earth didn't he do something about that little moustache of his,—one side drooping and the other twisted up from that nervous habit of his? Why, asked Miss Manning, couldn't he direct his nervousness into twisting both ends evenly?

Louisa Murrell tried to be merely amused as she listened to them but her head swam with futile indignation that women who knew no more than the elementary subjects which they taught should be so armoured in self-assurance, so certain of their superiority that they could, by their smug ridicule poison the simple triumph of a really intellectual person like herself. She hated to believe that she could be even slightly influenced by their chatter. If she could only look with patronizing de-tachment at them as they chattered, the way, in fact, that Laurie Neville's companion looked at them if they but knew it, —if she could look on with cool, faintly cynical eyes until Miss Emmons would be obliged to redden and Miss Swasey would be silent or burst out defiantly—"Well, what are you looking so superior about?" Then she would give a little embarrassed start, as Miss Manning sometimes did, and say, "Oh dear, nothing—nothing! I was only thinking how perfectly killing you two would be in a big city! Just like children disappointed to find that Bernard Shaw doesn't look like a movie idol!"

But in place of this easy annihilation *she* was the one who lowered her eyes and blushed, and made snappish defeated little retorts. No more could she silence their arguments about stories in the daily papers by saying, "Well, Professor Decker said at Mrs. Benjamin's the other night——" Miss Emmons and Miss Swasey only exchanged veiled but significant glances.

She continued to go to Mrs. Benjamin's every Sunday night, however, choking a little when she was allowed to quote poetry. Always she took along, concealed in her purse, the little album of letters she had written home from France, and sometime she hoped the moment would come when either Decker or Connie would ask if she'd brought them, and she would read them to Decker. But whenever painfully she worked up to this subject one or the other would swing it around to something else. Once Connie said, "Oh yes, Professor Decker, you should see how beautifully Louisa writes! A genuine talent! She should write novels!"

Louisa saw her opportunity then but Decker blocked it.

"By all means she should!" he exclaimed heartily. "A friend of mine in Paris is a novelist, although I've not seen any of his books recently. Starr Donnell. I remember his first novel which he wrote while we were rooming together. It's the only one I've seen published. In that he used a rather striking theme. A man, in love with his sister, actually goes through life believing he hates her, and always in his amours seeking her direct opposite,—and then breaking off when a little gesture, a lift of the eyebrow, or tone of the voice, reminds him of Estelle, his sister. Now, Mrs. Benjamin, I appeal to you as a sensitive, intelligent woman, do you believe such a state of mind is possible?"

So they would talk about Starr Donnell's first novel. Louisa, instead of being angry, was secretly relieved, even in her disappointment, for those rare moments when she betrayed her secret self to anyone were frightful agony and left her shaken and weepy for days; it was such torture to bring out this self, and she was always puzzled at its occasional insistence on breaking through to the shrivelling light of day.

Sometimes Decker spoke of Laurie Neville,—a curious woman, he said. Why, with her money and looks, had she elected to stay in Dell River? An unhappy woman, he said, who could be so much happier in Italy or Cornwall or an Eastern city. . . . Louisa explained about Laurie's parents, her careful boarding-school training, her chaperoned world tours, her return to Dell River where all the men were too awed to approach her, how this diffidence in men had given her a frightful inferiority so that she could scarcely speak to a man, feeling she was repulsive, how she went to psycho-analysts and tried to find liberation, ended in a sanitarium one whole year, how she had to have a nurse-companion as Miss Manning was because she was so given to hysteria. . . .

"Remarkable," said Decker, and Louisa's heart quickened with pleasure that she should have contributed something to his thoughts, for she could hear him telling about Laurie in other cities, when he returned to his little group in Paris, he would take Laurie's story, he would discuss it with his friend, the novelist who would put it in a book, and all this would come indirectly from Louisa Murrell. He would even think of her as he told it. . . .

When Laurie Neville's invitations were for Sunday, Decker refused them, considering Connie's invitation a standing one; and when he went on other evenings it made his return to Connie more flattering, and made life richer by giving Dell River the temporary lustre of a gay, social center.

Louisa did not know for many weeks that Decker served tea to Connie alone in his apartment over the cobbler shop. Connie had formed the habit of stopping in the shop during her Saturday marketing. Decker was usually there, sitting on the old oak table beside Gus' work bench, smoking cigarettes, talking constantly about Germany to Gus, who would nod his ruddy blonde head over his work and say, "Sure . . . Sure . . . That's right . . . Sure, I remember going to Leipsic when I was seven years old. Visited my father's aunt. . . . A big woman, not like the Benjamins at all. . . . A big woman with hair on her lip like a man's and strong . . . almost break your back when she squeezed you. I was a little fellow. Just seven. . . . And the opera. . . . Of course . . . Tristan . . . Der Frei-schutz. . . . Sure, Mr. Decker, oh sure. . . ."

Connie would come in with the Sunday roast sticking out of her market bag, and Decker would jump down from the table, take the bag out of her hands, and they would burst into laughter at the absurdity of Connie Benjamin shopping for meat like an ordinary housewife. Gus never talked much after Connie came in, for he believed that only a ladies' man would have much to say to a woman. He let Decker do the talking, refused his invitation to drink tea upstairs while Decker played the piano, though he did accept a glass of wine Laurie Neville had sent Decker. At six Gus went over to the Dutch barber's— Hans Feldts', had his hair cut and beard trimmed, and he and Hans drank beer and ate leberwurst and zwiebelkuchen made by Hans' wife in the back room of the barbershop, and Gus forgot all about his wife and Decker. He was glad they did not oblige him to keep up with their constant play of talk. When, having vanquished Hans both in beer capacity and argument, he opened the shop once more, it was often eight o'clock and the upstairs windows dark. This meant that Connie had gone home to be with Mimi while Helen went out with her date, and Decker had gone, malacca stick in hand, brave in Piccadilly collar topping badly fitting suit, to Neville's or Marshall's for dinner or even to a Bridge Club supper. This was as it should be, but as time wore on Gus returned to see the light burning long after eight above his shop and heard the piano thunder-ing, while in the shop he sometimes found the Sunday roast still lying on the work-bench, the brown paper wrapping moist with blood. And above the piano's magnificent noise Gus would hear a woman's voice sometimes singing out the words but more often humming, so that if he had not known better he would have believed it came from a violin or cello. Tying on his apron, preparing for work once more, Gus would listen a moment, frowning, he would think of the girls alone at home while their mother stayed here. Ah well, the girls were old enough to get their own supper once in a while. Decker was a harmless freak,—let them make their uproar if they must. It was only once a week, like his own festivals with the German barber. So Gus shrugged his shoulders and dismissed the whole business.

Professor Decker brought his servant problem to Mrs. Ben-jamin. Someone, he said, he needed to dust his bits of foreign bric-a-brac, to polish his samovar, and occasionally to wash his real lace dresser-scarf. Someone, he said, who knew how to handle rare things,—nothing of value, of course, but all those little things one picked up traveling and could not replace in this country. The work would require two or three hours a week and Decker stated that he was prepared to pay a few cents above the average for this rather special work. Mrs. Benjamin arranged with Mrs. Busch to take on the responsibility in return for a dollar a week or two dollars if he included his two other shirts, bed linen and the linen underwear.

After that arrangement was made part of every Sunday was spent in telling amusing anecdotes about their mutual servant. She reminded Decker of the fat Felice he and his friend Starr Donnell, the novelist, had employed in Paris, though her somber pride in her half-witted daughter made him think of Marthe, the strange little old chambermaid in that Leipsic pension. Presently Mrs. Busch, all unknowing, became the rock on which innumerable layers of moss clung, upon her hinged legends about all the handmaidens of history and fiction, and her simplest word or gesture was feverishly watched so that the legend might be kept constantly alive. Mrs. Busch personally referred to Decker's effects as "trash" and hung quite as many legends upon him as he did on her, but these stories eventually reaching Decker's ears, served as further evidence of Mrs. Busch's quaintness. Connie, at first shyly and finally quite brazenly, asked Mrs. Busch about Decker,—there was not so much new that Mrs. Busch could tell her but she wanted to hear his name, hear another Dell River woman, even poor Mrs. Busch, speak with awe of his foreign background and cosmopolitan tastes until she thrilled with proud knowledge that this rare creature should come to her for understanding. Mrs. Busch no longer had the power to make her cringe. Decker's arrival had changed that, had made of Mrs. Busch a character rather than a sinister symbol of Dell River.

Mrs. Busch sensed something amiss in the growing tender amusement of these two clients and frankly resented it, not exactly sure of what she disliked beyond the fact that this fond possessive attitude did not fit in with her idea of herself as an independent gentlewoman whose hobby was laundering. She became to Decker and Connie of more vital importance than

Louisa Murrell or anyone in town for she represented that
doting old retainer who figures in the background of all aristocrats. "Dear, quaint old Busch," they thought of her with
tears in their eyes, gratitude for her blind, gruff devotion to
their interests. Mrs. Busch regarded the two of them with
profound indifference and a high measure of patronage, but
everyone has the privilege of construing the attitude of others
to fit in with his own philosophy.

Decker seldom called during the week, and it was on these
lonely evenings, once devoted to a real and then a fancied
past, that Connie thought about him. The girls would sit in
the dining-room, heads bent over their home work. Often
Mimi studied alone for Helen was popular and free to make
her own engagements. Connie sat in the porch hammock,
thinking of Decker. Frost nipped off the vines, left the lattice
naked, and Connie, wrapped in an old shawl, sat in the chill
of early December, shivering but unconscious of discomfort,
till Helen or Gus, irritated or puzzled by her queer behavior,
would call her indoors.

Connie thought not so much of Decker as of herself talking
to Decker, of this little childhood episode to tell him, of this
opinion of Debussy to mention to him, tasting in advance his
flattering amazement. One thing troubled her. Why did the
image of Decker perpetually give way to the image of Tony, so
that even naming the hero of her fancy "Decker" his face was
unmistakably Tony's. . . . She seldom faced the idea of Tony
but suppressed it raged up and down her brain, up and down,
or lay in wait behind other thoughts, dark, ominous. . . . It
seemed to her that she had never thought of Tony until now as
a person, for when she knew him he represented only a
tremendous catastrophe, so appalling that one could not analyze it, one could only accept as they came the changes it
wrought, shutting doors behind one as the future dwindled
down to a mere thread of day to day existence. Now she saw
his shallow black eyes, the thick girlish lashes, the beautiful
straight nose and the short muscular body as clearly as if he
were before her. Each day, reluctantly she allowed herself to remember another chapter and thinking of it always in terms of
conversation with Decker try to mould it into a perfectly un-
derstandable situation. If she said they had been lonely . . . if

she said that no one had ever kissed her before . . . if she said that she was deliriously blind because Morini had said she might be a great singer like Melba or Patti . . . if she said they had been so much in love . . . not that they were, they were both far too carried away by their illusions of great careers . . . if she were only to say she was so young. . . .

So young. . . . In her white net graduation dress she must have looked lovely. She recalled that it had been plain, the trimming was all on the under slip, bands of pink ribbon, blue rosettes and forget-me-nots. She wore it when Manuel took her to the great man because it was her prettiest dress, and she sang "La donna é mobile——" and "Torne a Sorrento." She had told Decker of that moment, of the sudden holy feeling of being divinely selected for great deeds.

"The throat of an artist!" she remembered the exclamation and afterwards the long wait seated on a gilded Venetian chair in the vestibule while the two teachers discussed her in feverish Italian. A natural voice, but in need of training. She knew again that awed sensation of being in the hands of fate, for her voice and future seemed to be none of her concern but matters to be decided by Manuel and the great man. Driving back to her grandfather's house she had been ecstatically silent while Manuel planned for her, how he would approach her grandfather,—already she was invoking those golden-mirrored salons for her future dreams. . . . Then alone at dinner with Grandfather, trying to tell him of the wonderful thing that was to happen to her, and unable to risk losing its joy by hearing his cold "Interesting! Interesting!" The story wanted to rush out but a childhood of chilling experience reminded her that it was better to keep her joy secret than to fling it to the frosty indifference of that bitter bloodless old man. Manuel would talk it over with him, but somehow she felt she must tell someone just for the telling. She was tempted to rush down the road to her old convent and tell the sisters but they were not enough, they too were indifferent. She thought of the cook but she was old and cross. Who was there to listen to a young girl telling that she was to be famous, she was to be a Jenny Lind, a Patti . . . who was there in the whole countryside to listen? Connie had wandered about the old unkept gardens of her grandfather's park, watching through the grilled iron fence the passing automobiles. She thought exultantly, "Someday they will come back here and say, 'This is where she walked the day Manuel told her.'—'This is where she was so lonely as a young girl, seeing no one but tutors and the girls at the convent day school,—no one to talk to,—this is where she lived' they will say!"

At the edge of the estate she heard sounds of a brass band. There was no night-life in the village so, curious, she walked down the lane to the town center. She had told Decker about that,—how the whole village was jewelled with colored lights, a carrousel and an illuminated ferris wheel glittered through the trees. A little shy, she kept in the shadow till she came to the Square where the crowd was collected, waiting for some special performance. As Connie looked around she was jostled by a young man in a spangled tunic and white tights. "Look—there—that's Tony, the Daredevil! Look! There he goes!" She heard the whispers from the crowd about her and caught their excitement. She was glad when he turned back and smiled boldly at her. She pressed forward and saw him climb the torch-lit ladder to the balcony from which his wire stretched across to a warehouse roof on the other side of the brook. His smile had made his performance somehow her special responsibility, she blushed at the crowd's rapture. That would always be her picture of Tony,—that first glamorous impression, red torch-lights illuminating a hundred upturned faces, a band playing, and high up the glittering figure of a boy in spangled tights, dancing on a silver thread. When she thought of herself singing in some great concert hall later she could not untangle the dream of her own fabulous triumph from this triumph of Tony's. Because this was the day a golden door had opened to her Tony seemed the messenger of the gods who was to lead her into worlds of fairy-tale splendor. There was no explaining this in after years to any-one else,—Tony himself was the only one who understood.

The Silver Daredevil had climbed down, the crowd moved on to the Sword-Swallower's tent, and Connie Greene turned slowly homeward,—slowly because she knew the hurrying feet behind her were those of the glamorous dark performer, and she knew in a little while he must catch up with her. . . . Sitting in the shadow of her grandfather's hedge late that

night they talked of the magical future that each saw so
clearly,—applause, glittering lights, the Champion Tight-rope
Acrobat of the World, the greatest coloratura. Tony was eighteen, too, and in a loose tweed suit, collar open and tie carelessly knotted he was unbelievably beautiful. Perhaps she was
beautiful, too, she must have been to have strangers stare so,
but she had cared only for the marvel of her voice, she could
scarcely remember how she looked then.

The second night she went again and saw him dancing on
a huge shining ball across the wire and agonized at first with
fear for him, she finally wept with joy in his arms when he
came down once more.

The third day—Connie could no longer understand the utter blackness of that third day, she could weep a little in sympathy as over a daughter's grief but understand?—that was no
longer possible. She could only be grateful for the numbing
process of the years. That black day after Manuel had approached her grandfather and found that his consent to her
career would never be given and backing was out of the question. Even Manuel, once money was withdrawn, looked
vaguely past her, promising a little sadly to do what he could.
The curtain dropped on the triumph of Constance Greene,—
the lovely gate swung back and became a bleak door which
heard no prayers, a calm, relentless door as final as her grandfather's austere brow. There was no other door for Connie,
once this one closed, her world was at an end. At eighteen it
was hard to believe one's world was at an end.

Dimly, in memory, she saw herself wandering to the carnival grounds that day and remembered the men packing up
the Talking Doll concession just beyond the merry-go-round.
She remembered the dull shock in her heart—"Tonight the
carnival leaves." After the eight-o'clock performance Tony
came to her and for hours they talked in that hidden hollow
shadowed by the hedge. It was not important to remember,
as it had been unimportant then, that they lay in each other's
arms. What was important was that the gate was not closed.
Tony, the Silver Messenger of the gods held it open for her,
they would fly through together. She was saved.

It was hard to recall, since she had esponged it once so willingly from her mind, the girl crying alone, her cheek against

the mossy pine trunk, crying for sheer exultation because the
miracle, after all, was to happen. Tony was to lead the way.
And there was Tony running down the middle of the street to
change into tights for his twelve o'clock performance. In an
hour he would be back for her. She could not remember now
that it was once herself, this slight girl in white stumbling
across the great lawn to the house, for even then the girl had
whispered, "This is where Constance Greene once lived. This
is where the great singer almost stayed her days till Tony
saved her, took her to New York, to a manager——"

Then an hour later, backing out of the hall door, her eyes
fixed on the back of her grandfather's head,—he mustn't
turn, he mustn't turn and see her. Tony's hand clutching hers
reassuringly in the shadow of the summer house, then flying
across the lawn, speechless, to the Post Road, and waiting for
the bus. One thing she could never forget, the little light of
the westbound bus far, far down the road, that round, shining eye growing bigger, bigger, soon she and Tony would be
swallowed in its golden immensity, her breath still caught remembering the splintering golden rays, the doorway to a new
heaven. Wider and wider the glittering circle grew until she
shut her eyes with a little sob, and then they were welcomed
into its magic brilliance.

Seventeen years were wrapped around that Constance Greene,
like rags around a mummy. Within these bandages the mummy
breathed, she saw, perhaps heard, but no new pain could scar
her, no new passion could stir her veins for the motif was gone,
once lost in the sun no failure could touch her, no further destruction was possible. Seventeen years of kind numbness and
now there was light and dark, music and silence, joy and nothing. The mummy came alive and linked today with that runaway day seventeen years ago as simply as if no dreary years
came between. Connie Benjamin was Constance Greene and
Tony—Tony was Decker, yet Decker was more than Tony, he
was Manuel believing in her, too, and more than that he was
her public. No, she decided, she could never tell Decker about
Tony, even while she was preparing the way for that confession,
she knew it must not be told . . . so few pretty ways of telling

it, yet there it was, the final justification for her being Mrs. Benjamin of Dell River rather than Constance Greene, the singer. Her pride and sense of fitness held her back, but her desire to prove that it was fate, nothing but fate that had blocked her, was too much, and one day Decker knew.

Connie thought he might pity her, he might despise her a little as weak, but she had never dreamed that he would rage and fume like a jealous husband. He sat on the piano stool in his living room and though she had made the story quite a naive girl's idyll looked upon through later sophistication, she observed that Decker's face grew quite grey as she talked.

"You say this Italian circus performer then left you penniless, about to have a child, helpless, in this cheap hotel?" he inquired in a strange thin little voice.

Connie frowned at the blunt summing up.

"Yes, but you see he was just a child himself. He hated having me or anyone dependent on him, so that instead of his being the great performer with applause, he had to be a waiter in a restaurant, just to keep us both alive. Oh, you can understand that. When the chance came he had to run away with the show again. Don't you see? He had to?"

Decker shut his eyes and leaned his head on his hand.

"I can't. No. . . . He promised you an introduction to this singer who was to help you get started——"

"It wasn't his fault the man wasn't in New York, and he was too young, too gay to be bothered with marrying. He wasn't the type," Connie protested.

"He left you half-starving for days! I understand why you couldn't go back to your grandfather's. But that you, a delicate, gentle girl,—an artist——"

As he spoke Connie felt the stab of that old anguish. . . . Day after day watching from behind the torn lace curtain in the Atlantic City hotel, watching for Tony to come back, the heavy ache of her own body, her heart a dull metronome of pain, ticking out the days till doom came. She shivered remembering with awful clearness the days walking up and down the Board Walk, huddled in his discarded overcoat, her mind dulled to everything but the thundering of the waves. Who was she, why was she here, what was to happen to her, these things were lost in the rhythmic beat of the sea, but back

in the dreary little room, waiting behind the lace curtains——
A drowning person, Connie suddenly snatched Decker's hand.

"But then Gus came, don't you see? Quite out of the blue
this perfect stranger came and took me away. I'd never dared
even hope for such a thing but he came,—don't you see how
splendidly it all worked out? Even if I did lose the baby—who
but Gus would have been so kind, no one but a simple, good
person like Gus would have tried to talk to me and seen at
once what was to be done. . . ."

"It's outrageous!" Decker cried out. "I could kill that circus ape. Connie, how dared you be so weak, so common, as
to go away with him? How could you do it? I hate it, I wish
I'd never known. Why tell me now?"

"But we've told each other everything else," Connie said
faintly. She was frightened now for they were losing Decker,
the cultivated stranger and Mrs. Benjamin, that delightful
artist in a mere man and woman; she couldn't bear to feel
them slipping into these simple, ordinary moulds. "I went
with him because he was mixed up in my mind with my career, my future—don't you see?"

"Ah, you were crazy about him!" Decker shouted at her.
His hands gripped the piano bench, and she couldn't help seeing that for a pianist they were such small hands. A lock of hair
dropped over one eye, his mouth quivered, and Connie was
shocked that he did not seem conscious of this lack of poise.
"You were like any other woman when a big brawny brute
came along . . . why tell me? Why tell me about it at all?"

His fist beat the keyboard unexpectedly and a thunder of
bass chords roared support. Connie saw that for some reason
it had been a mistake to tell him. She heard the water boiling
in the samovar for the tea and she glanced regretfully at the
two china cups waiting to be filled, but now she could not stay.

"Well—say something, go on, tell me of this deathless love
of yours," Decker challenged her, trying to control the break
in his voice. "Tony the Daredevil. Go on, let's hear more of
the little idyll."

"There's nothing more to say," Connie said dully. She was
putting on her hat. She didn't look at him, for fear the picture of an angry, blazing-eyed little man would insidiously replace the other portrait of the suave, poised man of the world.

She knew he was looking at her accusingly, waiting for her to say more but it was quite true she had nothing to say. You can not talk about real things, there are no words for genuine despair, there are not even tears, there is only a heavenly numbness for which to pray and upon that gray curtain words may dance as words were intended to do, fans and pretty masks put up to shield the heart.

So Connie did not want to look at Decker now, unshielded, nor, since he was tearing down her own curtain, dared she remain; without their words between them she was frightened. She saw her sad but rather charming story of young love ripped down to its grim skeleton,—betrayal, hunger, bleak agony,—this was not what she had wanted Decker to see, this was not what she had wanted to remember. It was amazing to find that no matter how well she had dressed the facts the bones of tragedy still emerged, and she, as its heroine, became a weak little object of common pity, an ordinary human being, not Mrs. Benjamin, the artist, just as Decker had changed into a jealous, ineffectual little man, with the glamour of foreign places receding from him ever so gently, leaving what might have been the real man but a stranger to Connie, a stranger who was marring a structure built with infinite care. She went to the door, not allowing herself to think or to face the destruction he was wreaking in their design, not daring to wonder if this was the end, if their little game of words could ever be caught up again.

Decker watched her, his eyes glassy, as if he were drunk, Connie thought, and when she put her hand on the doorknob, his voice, shrill and cracked like an old man's came to her——

"Like any other woman, falling for the first big truck-driver that comes along, not caring about anything else. Music— bah—it was nothing for you but something to mark time till a lover came." He tried to make his breathing more even so that his words would have the power of restraint. Automatically he picked up the purse Connie had dropped and handed it to her, the habit of chivalry was stronger than anger, for struggle though he would against the impulse, he could not help holding her coat for her the next minute.

"Women put no value on themselves,—no matter how cheaply you hold them they themselves would sell for less,

and you—that you, of all women. . . ." Connie silently buttoned her coat and he opened the door for her, clicking his
heels in his farewell bow as if his body with its training in polite gestures were at the command of someone else, operating
smoothly, while he quite apart, led an independent, undisci-
plined life. Still Connie did not want to look at him, she
could not bear to lose any more than she had already lost and
she could feel it slipping from her, the precious conviction
that her life had been a charming one, the anguish and despair of eighteen was before her again and the sudden complete horror of seventeen blank years. She couldn't bear to
lose what he had given her, better to blunt every other feeling, even pride, than to lose that lately-won faith in a pretty
destiny, so Connie pulled her forces together and threw out
both hands in an operatic gesture of resignation.

"What is one to do with so much temperament? It shows
the artist isn't quite dead, doesn't it, for us to scream like two
children at each other," she tried to smile into his white angry face. "I can't stay another minute or we'll be actually
quarrelling,—you and I of all people,—quite as if we were
Dell River itself——" She managed quite a gay little peal of
laughter and drew gloves on her trembling hands, adjusted
the little veil on her hat,—with gloves and a veil it was easier.

She held the laugh till one foot was on the stairs and chattered in a light trembling voice as she went downstairs, one
hand groping the banister, her eyes straight ahead. "I'm afraid
that Mozart you heard at Miss Neville's this afternoon un-
strung your nerves,—the way it always does me. My teacher
used to tell me that Mozart was soothing——" Her voice
shook and she dared not look back—"but you know I agree
with you, perfection can be as disturbing to civilized persons
like us as primitive music. I—I never liked primitive things.
Those Oriental songs, and those African motifs—they leave
me—quite cold. Some people—some people——" she was on
the last step now and she was saved, her creation of a Mrs.
Benjamin was saved,—"some people prefer them——"

"Constance!" He hadn't meant to call her but her name
slipped out. She looked up quickly and saw him, clinging to
the side of the door, weak and spent and grey.

"We'll have tea some other day," she said, her voice bright and convincing, "Very soon, Blaine."

The vestibule door closed softly, she must have gone straight into the street without waiting for Gus in the shop. Decker stumbled back into the room, brushed his hand over his eyes and dropped into the chair by his desk. He sat still and dazed for a long time until his body slumped gently forward and he spread his two hands over his face, covered his burning closed eyes.

"Starr!" he groaned. "Oh my dear Starr, where are you now?"

They dared not see each other for Decker could not recapture the enchantment. He knew this, puzzled over it constantly, why had he set out to break this delicate thread, knowing well enough how little it could bear. . . . Perhaps for the same reason a child deliberately breaks a rare vase, merely to end that intolerable fear of breaking it.

But, if this was finished, what was there left in Dell River? Without Connie to hear his interpretation of life it became a poor teacher's dull routine in a dull village. Laurie Neville's occasional musicales were no longer, as they appeared in properly described retrospect, gay cosmopolitan events but amateur programs by third-rate musicians, the frantic efforts of a neurotic lonely heiress to warm up her bleak life. Teaching selected groups in high-school the "Soldiers' Chorus," or "Toreador," was of itself dreary mockery. He met Louisa Murrell in the gloomy corridors every morning and thought, "The day may come when I'll think I'm no more brilliant or extraordinary than she is. I may think I fit in here as well as she does." Thoughts, which up to this time, had arranged themselves in the shape they were to be presented to Mrs. Benjamin, in little bouquets of wit and philosophy, grew morbid and self-flagellating with no destination in view. Memories, even memories of Starr, were dangerous under their dust, one needed an eager audience before a delightfully impersonal patine could be attained for them and the flavor of elegance put into one's past. The artist's and gentleman's past which Connie Benjamin had invoked for Decker could not support him without her constant encouragement. His shoulders drooped a little. Louisa, watching him from the girl's cloak-room as he strode down the corridor, observed the disappearance of the swagger, and wondered if Mr. Marshall had spoken to him about the way he walked, or worse, if he'd at last noticed the students imitating him on the streets.

But he couldn't see Connie yet, he had to be quite sure he could command the old casualness, he had to be certain tears would not come to his eyes as if he were some Dell River farmer, thinking of a young girl's trouble eighteen years ago, thinking of Mrs. Benjamin as a crippled human soul instead of a gratifying impersonal invention. The habits of walking down certain streets at certain times, harmless little tricks for meeting each other unexpectedly now had to be abandoned, though every moment one ached at the loss. In Decker's mind this unfortunate afternoon with Connie grew inevitably into the memory of his last afternoon with Starr Donnell. Each time he had desolately seen himself destroying the thing he loved, powerless to control himself, watching himself air a burst of pride or small vanity at the risk of his whole life. That hotel room in Geneva . . . the unconquerable feeling that he must be recognized as Starr's equal, Starr must know he was a person, but why? Hadn't he had a glorious year worshipping, adoring Starr, happy in sheer proximity to such a dazzling richly-favored figure? Was it not compliment enough that he, of all people, should be Starr's preferred companion and confidante—he had been flattered many times in Paris and on the Mediterranean steamer when whispers reached him, "That's the friend of Starr Donnell, the writer. They say his name is Decker." Why should this same whisper suddenly enrage him so that he must assail Starr with unforgettable insults, break irrevocably the thing between them? Content, nay flattered to be the slave for so long, the moment came when the position infuriated him, the pride in his own talents which Starr's flattering friendship had created must needs overreach itself and repudiate the very relationship that had inspired it. There was no place in Starr's life for an equal and no adjustment was possible after the roles of master and slave had once been assigned. Decker had known this was the end even while he was denouncing Starr. He knew, as one committing suicide must know, that this was final. Yet they could not withdraw the rare intimate things they had given each other, they could not—once having bared every vanity to each other, look each other in the eye and deny their so generously confessed weaknesses. What demon of self-destruction had seized him then as it had with Connie . . . it had been the end so far as Starr was concerned; how could it fail to be final this time?

He found himself hurrying past the cobbler's door, starting like a guilty lover when Gus called to him, avoiding his eyes as if actually he had some secret to hide. In the school auditorium, waving his baton for sophomore girls to sing "The Spinning Song" his preoccupied glance would suddenly fall on Helen Benjamin and he would be faint with nostalgia for the old self-assurance, his cheeks would redden and girls in the front row would nudge each other and look slyly around to see if Miss Murrell had come in the room for this was the romance Dell River had invented for him.

By some miracle the two did not meet each other for an entire week, but when Sunday night came Decker knew that another week could not pass like this, no matter in what state he went back to the Benjamin house go he must. There was no use waiting for a return of the old easy manner, that would come after the meeting, not before. He could not beg forgiveness, he only hoped she would pretend to forget. Brooding with shame over his own hysteria he never thought of Connie's possible reaction to the scene.

Where had she lost their thread, Connie puzzled, lying in bed beside Gus' heavy, sleeping figure, at what exact instant had the amused deference in Decker's blue eyes changed to curious suspicion, then to angry accusation? How blind she had been to miss that turning point when balance was within saving. . . . She had said—what? . . . Again in sharp detail Tony was invoked, she tried to recall just what words she had used concerning him to make her few months with Tony appear such a degradation. She could not for the life of her remember, yet she dared not analyze too well lest she come upon some naked reason more perilous to face than this bewilderment. What had she said, or was it some way she had looked?

Sunday without Decker was intolerable, as if the week were lost without this bright marker. She could not get out of bed,

she seemed actually ill all day and Mimi brought her a breakfast tray, delighted to display her training in Domestic Science.
Late in the afternoon, with no one to look forward to seeing,
a frightened feeling of deprivation came over her. She looked
out of her bedroom window and saw behind the seared garden hedge, the thin rusty trickle of Dell River now laid bare
by the lost foliage on either bank. Beyond this creek a series of
hills swelled out past the town border to farmland and far-off
woods. Connie closed her eyes as if this were a dreary nightmare to-day, though often she and Decker had commented
with pleasure on the mysterious shadows on these hills. The
street, too, depressed her, viewed through the opposite window, even though at this hour it was brightened with little
strolling groups of citizens in Sunday clothes, families
crowded into automobile back-seats. Where would Decker go
to-day—to Laurie Neville's perhaps or to a bridge party in
The Oaks' living-room? Languidly she dressed and trying not
to think of Decker or the aching present, found herself thinking of Tony. She knew that in some curious way they represented one and the same thing to her, a belief perhaps in the
Constance Greene legend that she had herself created.

Where was Tony? A little fearfully she examined details of his
desertion, permitted herself to remember the soiled, elaborate
red silk scarf he left behind, the half-used bottle of hair pomade on the dresser, yes even the torn Irish crochet bureau-
runner and the deck of gilt-edge playing cards with the dark
girl's rosy face printed on the backs. Connie saw the cards
again scattered over the red-flowered carpet, a dozen girls with
left shoulder bared, forever smiling with a champagne glass
lifted to their lips, all the little things that made her wait one
day more and one day more in spite of Gus' blunt advice, for
surely Tony, wherever he was, was incomplete without his
cards, his loosely knotted red scarf, his violet pomade. . . .

Afraid for so many years to think of these things Connie now
sought them out as protection, for the thought of Decker was
an uncovered live wire, too dangerous to approach un-
equipped. At last she could think of Tony and wonder if there
had been more real love in that adventure than she had hitherto guessed. Thoughtfully she pulled on a kimono and went
up to the attic. Downstairs Gus fidgeted, waiting for supper,

afraid to voice his increasing hunger lest his wife be ill in earnest,—occasionally he went to the hall door and called upstairs, "Connie! Say—say Connie!" and when no answer came he would glance frowning at his watch—6—6:30—6:45.

In the attic the candles could no longer cope with the increasing darkness and Connie got up stiffly from the floor by the trunk. She was too tired now to put back all these old relics, the dress in which she'd run away, the program of "Louise" which Manuel had taken her to hear the day before her audition. She carried downstairs to her bureau drawer the pictures of Tony in tights, the red scarf, moth-eaten and frayed, and the two clippings she had put in the Billboard.

> "Tony:—Waiting for you in same place.
> C.—"

Waiting too long, Gus had said. Doing her hair Connie stopped to look at the pictures again. She remembered the landlady had recommended the Billboard as the only way to reach him. She thought of him after she went downstairs, through the girls' conversation, she thought of him all night and the next day, putting him together once again with a hundred tiny pieces until the shadow of Tony, complete, had almost obliterated Decker and had filled the barren hills of her exile with a rich warming glow. Afraid to lose this protecting image she barely spoke to anyone but held it fast, a golden shield. The next night she sent a notice to be published in the Billboard:

> "Tony: C. wants to hear from you again
> after eighteen years.
> No. 672 Billboard."

She was frightened after she'd sent it, but she could think of what might come of it, and she wanted to be prepared with thoughts in case Decker should slip out of her life.

Days dropped in the wastebasket, blank pages from a meaningless calendar. Connie saw nothing before them, nothing following. She heard her voice discussing market errands with Helen and arithmetic with Mimi, and wondered curiously what divinity operated these superficial motions of a person after the essence had vanished. No word came from Tony and she realized she had neither expected it or been prepared for any further step had news come from him. It was Decker's notion that Tony had been the great thing in her life, she had never thought of him as anything but a means of escape, nor had she ever reproached him in memory for being gaoler rather than liberator.

Mrs. Busch came in and must talk of Professor Decker until Connie was desperate, trying to devise some means of mending their broken chain. Helen told of the boys mocking Decker's clipped, precise English, and Gus commented on a certain strangeness in his tenant's manner of late. Even the most disparaging news of him excited Connie. The children telling her he was mocked, Mrs. Busch questioning his sanity made her think proudly, "Everyone talks about him—in less than a year he's made himself a unique figure in this neighborhood. No wonder he is so important to me—he is to everyone." On the second Saturday Connie found herself in the music store watching the street cautiously from time to time to see if he would pass. She could not face a second Sunday without him, for even her thoughts of Tony were empty with no audience to hear them translated into fascinating revelations. In her mind she repeated over and over what she would say if Decker should appear. "Decker, my dear! How nice to run into you again. I've been meaning to drop you a note but you know how busy we housewives are!"

She saw Laurie Neville's car drive up and Laurie, in a great bearskin coat that made her sharp handsome face look pinched and hungry, got out with her efficient tweed-garbed companion. She heard them call out Decker's name and saw him hurrying across the street. He looked strangely little and cold in his badly-fitting suit with no overcoat, yet he would not of course betray himself by pulling up his collar. Connie kept her back to the window and her lips moved in repetition of her lines. The shop door opened.

"But I never wear an overcoat—never!" Decker was protesting. "It's such a nuisance, really. I have to have one on hand, of course, but I'm always forgetting it, so why bother with one?"

"But don't you freeze?" Miss Neville begged to know.

"I love the winter," Decker answered. "I never feel the cold."

He saw Connie.

"Decker,—my dear!" she put out her left hand casually as if her right were far too busy fingering the records. "How nice to run into you. I've been meaning to drop you a note——"

"Oh you busy women!" he interrupted, shrugging his shoulders in despair. "It's a marvel to me you have any time at all for us poor unfortunate males. . . . What are you buying now, you extravagant creature. Not that Schumann Concerto!"

"Just wishing for it," Connie said.

Laurie picked up the book containing the Concerto and then put it quickly down, not daring to buy it before someone who confessed not being able to buy it.

"Perhaps Mrs. Benjamin can come to your Sunday evening," Miss Manning said quite clearly to Laurie. "It's next Sunday and there'll be music,—some musicians on their way to Detroit. Can you come?"

"She must come," Decker said. (They were getting back again, he thought, but did not dare exult too soon.) "Old Gus, too, and perhaps the girls."

"I'll try to come," Connie said brightly as if she would have to consult a crowded engagement book first. Then she lowered her head smilingly to all of them and started out. Decker leapt to the door, held it open with almost reverent courtesy. She nodded, smiling to him, and carrying herself as one accustomed to having all doors held open and canopies thrown up for her. They had achieved the right tone once more, he thought joyously, hastening back to Miss Neville and Miss Manning.

"A sweet woman," said Miss Manning, looking out the window rather curiously after the vanishing figure.

"Charming!" declared Decker and squinted down his cigarette as if thus to find a more exact word for his description. "Yes, a thoroughly charming person!"

It could not be helped, Decker finally decided, pacing up and down his living-room, smoking furiously, and conscious of himself as a man with a dilemma pacing and smoking as if he were Lou Tellegen or John Barrymore. This idea made the dilemma itself bearable. Here it was January and here was he with no overcoat, croaking and sneezing, calling

for "Doreador" and "The Sbidding Zong" which young
fools of course loved to mock. Croaking and shivering, not
even daring to wear his rain coat, a plain confession of
poverty, and sounding insanely ridiculous when he barked out
his explanation, "No, I never wear an overcoat. I never feel
the cold. Hot weather—ah, then's when I suffer—" winding
up this remark invariably with such a fit of sneeezing and
whooping that people stared as if he were mad. Well, he
probably was. At this point, lighting a fresh cigarette, he saw
himself Ilsa Darmster, the goddess of glamour. Thank you,
oh, thank you again, dear Decker, she thought, for Mozart
and Rimsky-Korsakoff, for St. Julienne and Lachrymae Cristi,
for all the beautiful names to shine in dark minds.

Connie Benjamin kept nodding in sympathetic understanding. The musicians had gone to their train and guests were
gladly going home. Laurie Neville kept a tight hold of
Gertrude Manning's arm and did not scream as she so much
wanted to, because no matter what she did, no matter how
she tried, Dell River would not have her, she must always be
its freak, someone to be pointed at, exploited, or at best
soothed as if she was a sanitarium case, well she was, she was,
she WAS, and she was going to scream—scream—but she
couldn't scream after Gertrude had decided to sing and that
was what was happening.

Professor Decker, very red and very strange-looking, sat on
the piano bench and varied his accompaniments with a spontaneous vibrato in the treble chords and occasionally was
moved to impromptu trills while Miss Manning bravely held
a high note to which she was not accustomed. "Jeune fil-
lette—profitez du temps" she sang. She did not really think
she could sing but she could read music and music of any sort
kept Laurie Neville's hysteria in check. Laurie had joined Mrs.
Benjamin and Louisa on the staircase. Louisa said that she
had never realized how well Professor Decker played and Mrs.
Benjamin agreed, adding that she herself had studied music
years ago, that she had been at one time on the verge of a
great career.

"I sang in English and a little Italian—my teacher was an
Italian," she whispered confidentially. "For instance that song
tonight—'Sorrento—' that was an old favorite of mine."

"Amazing!" replied Miss Neville and then Decker and Miss Manning left the piano since the latter was deeply concerned about Laurie's desperately white face. Decker helped himself to another glass of wine at the buffet-table and then glanced up to meet the sad understanding look in Connie's eye, her tired amused smile—"My dear, think of it,—you with your genius, here playing for a handful of stupid provincials who refuse to even listen, when actually you belong in Carnegie Hall! My poor precious Decker,—lost here—completely lost!"—Her smile said all this and more.

Helen had vanished long ago. Vaguely Connie remembered seeing her hurry out the door with a tall boy some time ago. She must follow her home, so Miss Manning went with her to the big damp upstairs bedroom where the coats had been piled on a great walnut four-poster bed. In a cracked gilded mirror Connie adjusted the white chiffon scarf about her face, as the mad genius, tearing his hair and muttering to himself. The mad music-master. . . .

But if he used next month's salary for a coat then he could not send his mother the money for her three weeks down South. Which was the worse pain, shivering before Dell River, or confessing to his mother that quite as she suspected all these years, he was incompetent. . . . Even before he put it into words Decker knew which of these two situations he could never meet, even without pausing to look at his mother's handsome superior face, without remembering her letter—"Everyone's going down to St. Augustine again. These women who have broker-sons! (Stupid creatures of course with no more notion of who your Debussy is than I myself have, but they do appreciate how dreary middle Massachusetts is in winter.) I sometimes wonder, Blaine, if I didn't emphasize the artistic too much in your childhood, encouraging you and perhaps forcing you beyond your real capacity in music. It was only because you did so poorly in school, dear, and I was so glad to find something in which you could excel. Anyway, it's all too late now and I'm willing to say it's much my fault. Your town sounds beautiful and your apartment so luxurious that I look on my own modest cottage with great discontent. However, one must make the best of things. Certainly I shall loathe the place during February when Alma Trent and Mrs. Ford are in the South. . . ."

He could see the crisp note he would write, ignoring her challenge, enclosing his check for $100 and at the same time confessing that he meant to make it more but new suits, coats and all the paraphernalia that his rather amazing social position here required forced him to be niggardly. Much better that she should accuse him of selfishness and extravagance than of incompetence or failure. . . . Much better that he should teach Dell River to sing America through their noses, sneezing every measure, than that his mother should say, "It's quite all right. I never expected you to succeed anyway, dear boy." A wave of violent hate came over him, thinking of her lovely cold face, her correct mouth, her faint violet perfume—he saw the bottle on her bare dressing-table, the same violet essence, expensive—(one drop on her handkerchief was enough) from the same parfumeur every year at Christmas as far back as he could remember. The rage passed as it always did leaving him depressed, with the certainty that nothing, nothing would ever erase the faint contempt from that mouth, no sudden expression of admiration would ever be surprised in those eyes. She knew her son very well, was devoted to him as wives are sometimes devoted to their husbands as inadequate, futile blow-hards whose occasional triumphs prove not superior wit but fool's luck. But his brother Rod—ah that was another matter. He could lie and cheat and bully his mother and draw nothing but a soft, fatuous smile of adoration. Why Rod had only to rumple her hair and she was ready to give him the world,—take away Blaine's share if necessary, but darling Rod must not suffer. Decker's fist clenched remembering how many, many years this jealousy had nagged at him, even after all these years of absence from both of them the pain of thinking of their understanding glances could still draw childish tears to his eyes.

So he must write the note to his mother, possibly even the score by some patronizing question as to whether Rod was on his feet yet or still loafing on his rich wife's money. To inflict that hurt would ease his own a little.

But nights in Dell River were frigid in January, once chilled no fire could thaw you out and Decker could see himself calling on Mrs. Benjamin next week (for that was understood once more) paying his compliments to her and Louisa Murrell with nose blue and teeth chattering. And Laurie Neville's musicale next Sunday night, the function of the season, you might say, for Dell River. He would arrive wet to the skin with snow,—of course it would be a blizzard,—the colors of his best tie would be damply running over his best shirt, and he would be wheezing like a steam calliope. They would ask him to play accompaniments for Miss Manning to sing her little Weckerlin songs and his fingers would be so stiff that he would fumble and how impossible his wet, mussed suit would look there at the piano . . . Marshall, blue-shaven, immaculately dressed as befitted a school principal, would be watching him, taking it all in . . . Decker, thinking of Marshall's cold grey eyes, weakened a little, then his glance fell once more on his mother's picture and he sat down to his desk. Winter—Laurie Neville's Sunday evening—Mr. Marshall—all these things would pass (in his mind he jumped lightly into April)—but his mother's cynical smile was fixed, all other struggles must be abandoned for combatting this permanent foe.

It frightened him a little, as miraculous demonstrations are bound to do, when leaving the house to mail his note to Mrs. Elsie Decker, Shaler, Mass., he encountered Marshall outside the shop door hunting for a bell.

"Oh hello, Decker,—there doesn't seem to be any way of getting in here."

"There's no bell," Decker said a little coldly, sensing the implied criticism of his living-quarters. "After Benjamin goes at night you call out or throw something against my window and I have to come down."

"Rather complicated," said Marshall. He avoided Decker's eyes guiltily and—after taking in the other's light clothing he pulled his own coat up under his chin securely. "Unless of course you don't want guests."

"I enjoy company," Decker answered. "I have always entertained constantly until—of course—this year. In the towns I've taught I used to take a huge place and have my evenings regularly."

Then he saw that the reason Marshall was embarrassed was that he was carrying a huge box, its string and tissue paper trailing on the frosted sidewalk, and he knew at once that this was a coat for him. He knew, too, that they would have to talk about a dozen other things before they got to winter, colds, and overcoats, and both would get more and more confused every minute until finally Marshall would blurt out something like, "Oh by the way, Decker, speaking of the Easter exercises, here's an old coat you can have." And he would have to be amazed and say, "Coat? Coat? Oh yes, coat—why so it is. Of course I never wear one but as a favor to you I may accept. . . ." No sooner had Decker recognized the principal's mission than Marshall saw that he did, so they stood under the dim street lamp looking uncertainly at each other, Marshall trying to hide his enormous parcel and at the same time indignant that Decker should make him feel like an ass instead of the benevolent overlord he fancied himself. Decker sailed into the silence, waving the letter to his mother, chattering of her winters down South, of her beautiful home just outside—(by 200 miles) of Boston.

"He might at least ask me inside," Marshall thought angrily while Decker with shaking fingers tried to light a cigarette in the gently falling snow since a cigarette always gave him opportunity for grand gestures. He was warmed already by the prospective coat, and saw himself swaggering past Marshall in it, making vague mention of his English tailors and almost forgetting that the swaggering could not be done safely before the donor. He wanted to rush down to Connie Benjamin's house at once and show her the coat, show her the beautiful stitching, speak of the excellent work on the lining as a connoisseur of tailoring would speak. It didn't matter that the coat wasn't his yet or that he hadn't seen it. But finally Marshall shoved the box at him.

"It's not mine, really—it belonged to my wife's brother, but since you haven't got yours yet and you're about the same size as George Almon——"

"I wish I could use it but I never wear a coat," Decker heard himself saying, "of course in a storm I might, but I use one so seldom it's hardly worth while taking it. However I will keep it—thanks, of course,—as a matter of fact I'd already sent to my tailors in London—on Bond Street, you know. I instructed them to send samples and I sent my measurements, of course it's terribly expensive but I don't believe in sparing a cent when you're after the best tailor,—but then there's the delay—and the mails went astray—in fact my order only reached them a few days ago—I can cable a cancellation——"

"A cable's expensive, too," said Marshall, stamping his feet partly because they were slowly freezing and again because he hated Decker and his sudden change to a British accent, and he wished he could take the coat back and rush to his own fireside with a to-hell with you and your fine tailors, go on and freeze to death.

"Only a few dollars," Decker smiled and went on wildly—now he was clutching the box with one arm. "I was just writing my mother to send me a few of my old winter coats that I left in her attic. Among them I should find one or two adequate——"

"I thought you never wore them," roared Marshall, unable to bear more.

"I don't—or seldom do," Decker answered quickly. "But one always has a coat of course, wearing it or not. As a matter of fact I've never been satisfied with any of them since I had my Scotch woven ulster, the one I wore tramping through Brittany. The work on that coat! The sheer beauty of its worksmanship,—actually, Marshall——"

"If you're getting all these other coats, then give this one back for God's sake," Marshall wanted to say but instead he only growled, "Yes, of course. Then you don't want this one?"

Want it? Decker was crushed for a moment.

"Oh, I can find some use for it," he said limply, and then, his arms clutching the package he dropped his letter in the mailbox on the lamp-post and started back toward the house.

"Won't you come up, Marshall?" he asked rather patronizingly. "I could give you a little touch of wine, or tea if you prefer?"

"No," grunted Marshall. Decker felt a jarring note somewhere. He wanted to say something light and casual to show that he saw the quaint humor of one gentleman presenting another (and that other Blaine Decker of all people) with a coat, but something rather ominous in Marshall's eye restrained him. He hesitated in the doorway.

"Then goodnight, Marshall, old chap," he called out genially, for merely holding the coat gave him the advantage over Marshall. Good old Marshall, he thought, stupid, blundering, well-meaning old Marshall, so puzzled and yet underneath it all so unquestionably impressed by the brilliant savoir-faire of his music-teacher.

"Poor old boy." Decker, back in his room, tipped up the lamp-shade to examine his new coat. A chocolate brown wool with padded shoulders and pinched back and extra buttons, slightly worn at the elbows and a tiny patch under the arm. Decker tried it on and having nothing but a shaving mirror held this at different angles before and behind him to get the effect.

"Not bad, not bad at all," he murmured. "A little snappy, but fortunately I can carry that off. . . ."

Poor, stuffy old Marshall. He must do something for him sometime, show him that he didn't look down on him just because he was a small-town school principal. Yes, he must do something for the poor old boy.

Mimi thought about her mother when she went to bed every night. It was pleasant when one knew one was plain and dull and would very likely be a plain dull old maid for everyone prophesied this, to know that one's mother at least had been beautiful and glamorous, that one's mother from infancy on had walked in an enchanted path, and one could cling to this victory of one's own blood at least. Mimi thought about her mother's near-career until it became real, for hundreds of nights she had continued in her mind a story of unending triumph for her mother. She shut her eyes and the pictures obediently unwound before her, her mother beautiful as the dawn in shining white satin and a golden halo receiving ovations before a red plush curtain, bowing this way and that. The picture varied only as Mimi changed the costume from white satin to delirious blue jewel-studded velvet, and the setting from a stage to an enormous drawing-room like Miss Neville's only ten times as large. Gentlemen resembling Blaine Decker in opera hats and tail-coats kissed the beautiful creature's hand and threw bouquets of fabulous roses at her. This was Mimi's private life, an imaginary spectator of her mother's imaginary career. Imagination stopped here, it could perform no such miracles for Mimi herself. Present or future she saw only the facts of her plain, stout little body, her slow anxious brain, stolidly she accepted her limitations, even in fancy she could not make herself a heroine. Boys ignored her, though sometimes at birthday parties one rejected by Helen would take Mimi home just to be near the sister, and Mimi, knowing this, would be tongue-tied. They would walk from the party to the Benjamins' very door without Mimi being able to utter a word. Her escort would carry on a conversation with Helen and her preferred companion walking in front of them, and at the door Mimi would scuttle inside leaving Helen to say the good-nights.

Mimi's feeling toward Helen who was complacent with beauty and shrewdness that passed for brains was not envy but astonishment and alarm. In the main girls' cloak room Mimi stood twisting her handkerchief in a dull hopeless panic while Helen urged a little cluster of girls to cut the physics class until the teacher gave up her new system of weekly examinations. Helen played truant with Bessie Herbert and they went skating on the pond by the Nurseries.

"But what will you do if Mr. Marshall finds out you weren't sick,—if someone at the Nurseries tells on you?" Mimi whispered anxiously when Helen told her that night.

Helen shrugged her pretty shoulders.

"He can't do more than kick us out."

"Expel you? Oh, but Helen, if he really should expel you——"

"I wouldn't care," Helen declared calmly. She was undressing before the mirror, pausing occasionally to study herself critically with infinite appreciation. "I'd like to know what good all that bunk is anyway, especially if a person's going on the stage the way I intend to do. Believe me, I'd get out of that old school as fast as they would let me,—glad of the chance. I'd go straight to New York or maybe to Hollywood and go straight on the stage."

"You wouldn't have the money!" Mimi's heart was thumping furiously. She was ready to cry at the mere thought of the disturbance Helen was planning.

"I'd get it out of Papa. He's got some salted away, the old tight-wad. I heard the boys talking about him once and they said he had money, he was an old miser, they said." The idea had evidently held Helen. "Miser, mind you. Can you beat that? With us wearing the same winter coats the third year running. . . .

You bet I'd get out of this place if I got a chance. Let old Marshall expel us. I don't care. Bessie might mind but I wouldn't."

"It would be awful for Mama," Mimi reminded her. "Mama wouldn't know what to do. And with Miss Murrell and Professor Decker always coming here, they'd talk about it and Mama would just die!"

Helen braided her hair in two thick bronze braids and then sat on the edge of the bed in her white cotton nightgown polishing her finger-nails. Mimi, lying in bed, watched her, aghast at her and eternally puzzled. How did Helen think of these wonderful things to want, for instance, why should she—any more than Mimi—be gifted with such fierce desires for silk underwear, a sequin evening dress, ocean voyages, a stage career,—and why should it be such rotten injustice for her to be deprived of these things,—after all, none of the other Dell River girls had them or even felt entitled to them? Mimi tried to reason this out but found no answer. Helen was the victim of a terrible conspiracy, there was no use arguing about it or even consoling her, and, above all, was it futile to compare Helen's lot with her own or any other ordinary girl, since it must be distinctly understood that Helen was ineffably superior and the service she had done the humble Benjamins years ago in allowing herself to be born to them instead of to the great families she might have selected was a favor that should be properly paid for.

"Mama's got no right to talk to me about what I do," Helen went on,—she rather enjoyed and was whipped to further defiant attitudes by Mimi's wide alarmed eyes. "Just because she was a failure is no reason I should be. She can't stop me. Dad can't stop me. If I want to be something they can't stand in my way. What'd they ever do for me? Might as well be an orphan. No clothes—no pocket money,—I can't even have my own room, but have to sleep with my kid sister."

Mimi said nothing though she thought vaguely that Helen had a rather crushing way of listing her injustices. Helen pulled out the chain of the blue-shaded lamp and yanked up the window. She got into bed and lay tensely beside Mimi.

"Mama!" she repeated the name scornfully. "I'd like to just hear her try to talk to me. I'd like her to try just once."

She gave a bitter little laugh.

"Some of these days I'm going to jump in and tell her just what I've been thinking all these years."

"Oh Helen!" Mimi pleaded in a little gasp.

"You wait," said Helen. "Just you wait."

Louisa Murrell knew that the other teachers at The Oaks thought Professor Decker was her suitor, and therefore it hurt all the more to know it was not so. She was not in love with him but one has to have something, and Decker was the only strange man in town, the only man she saw outside school except when she went to Mr. and Mrs. Marshall's and the principal, though handsome enough in his way, was not really a man; he was a husband and a school. Decker was, on the other hand, culture. He was also eligible. Like most women, married or single, Louisa's first impression of a man was an appraiser's impression, and as the years went by and she met fewer and fewer men this impression was invariably favorable. Yes, he would do. Not, of course, anything like her ideal, but the imagination was always, thank God, adaptable and could, after a little coaxing, make romance of very little. She did not want definitely a husband, indeed she was frightened at the idea, but she wanted something special in her life if it was only a blighted love, something to which poetry could cling. So now public opinion was forcing her to cling to Blaine Decker, obliging her to feel as hurt and wretched over his coolness as if she actually did love him. When he passed her absently in the school corridors the students winked to indicate this indifference was just a pose, but Louisa, torn between what she realized they were thinking and what she knew was true, scarcely knew how to act. Most of the time she resented Decker's failure to accept the role allotted to him and though he was undoubtedly a marvel of wit and brilliance, nevertheless it did seem a little stupid of him not to know what was being said about him and either play up to his reputation or be properly embarrassed about it.

In her bedroom at The Oaks, dressing with the other teachers for Laurie Neville's party she blushed at the allusions to Decker.

"Will you go with us or is the boy-friend calling for you?" Miss Swasey wanted to know. She and Miss Emmons had spent the afternoon giving each other facials, manicures and shampoos, and having admired themselves in their own mirrors now completed examinations of their evening toilettes before Louisa's long mirror. Not that it made any difference how they looked, Miss Emmons observed, since whatever new men there were present would be delegated to Laurie herself or to Miss Manning. Miss Swasey looked complacently at her pretty throat in the mirror, trying her curly brown hair back over her ears, then pulling it forward again.

"I think we should look nice on account of the parents," she said gently. "After all a lot of trustees and board members will be there and they notice if we don't look right. That's all I care about."

Miss Emmons was silent, reminded that it had taken her twelve years of teaching in Dell River to get over delusions such as the younger teacher cherished. Now she was able to speak out openly and with a bitter gaiety about "getting a man." She could boast of the school janitor's compliments to her, she whispered of farmers who stared at her legs when she got on the Cross-State bus, she loudly proclaimed her devotion to the primitive types, and what she would do if she ever had the money to go on a Polynesian tour. This frankness more insistent and more unnatural than her original shyness made Miss Murrell shudder. Louisa thought, "I would rather never see a man than admit it mattered so much to me; and to go screaming around that you like someone just because he's a man—instead of a—well, a *person*—is frightful . . . The way she jokes about the football boys . . . How awful if Professor Decker should hear her sometime."

If he should hear them asking about him as if he were her property he'd never dare to even speak to her again, Louisa thought, and if Mrs. Benjamin knew what everyone said—but it occurred to Louisa that Mrs. Benjamin heard only what she wished to hear, a marvellous device for converting all sensations to pleasure. Sometimes, as now, vaguely hurt because Professor Decker did not know she existed yet she must blush and lower her eyes every time Emmons or Swasey mentioned him—sometimes Louisa wondered why she had agreed so unquestioningly with Mrs. Benjamin's and Decker's estimates of themselves as great figures. Certainly neither Swasey nor

Emmons would be trembling with pleasure at the prospect of a Sunday evening at the Benjamins' simple home. Nor, Louisa reflected, pinning down the neck of Laurie Neville's black crepe with her pearl bar so as to make it more of an evening dress, would they feel as she could not help feeling, that for Mrs. Benjamin to appear at Laurie Neville's musical evening gave the affair a certain professional stamp.

Connie's own feeling was the same. She was glad to show Laurie that she approved of her gallant attempts to make Dell River a music center; it seemed to her there had been a touch of deference about the invitation, as if Miss Neville and her companion scarcely dared hope that their simple entertainment could interest a genuine artist. Connie wanted to assure them that she was not at all proud, that indeed she thought Miss Neville's interest in music a very encouraging sign in this section and in this age. She would show this opinion, of course, by her mere presence. She thought of seeing Decker there, of talking it over with him, and there in the crowded drawing-room capturing their rhythm once again. She saw tonight as something upon which they would fasten next Sunday night,—he and Louisa and she. So eager was she for next Sunday's discussion of tonight that the present seemed endless, she could endure it only by marking each detail for future description, the walk through the frosty blue night to the mansion seemed unending, the thought that this was only the beginning of the occasion was hardly to be borne. Helen took quick excited steps beside her,—there had been no use inviting Gus to come, he was interested neither in Miss Neville or society. Helen wanted to go because the Marshall girls had gone there once with their parents and she had never been there; she thought there might be dancing and Laurie Neville's city friends would undoubtedly be there doing all the latest steps and she could learn just by watching and astound the girls in the Domestic Science kitchen tomorrow by demonstration.

They hurried up little side-streets and where lights were shining in windows Helen would say, jealously, "They must be going, too! Why were *they* asked." Next Sunday, Connie thought, she would tell Decker how exquisitely the crescent moon decorated the bare twisted branches of the huge oak on the hill, this tiny rim of silver caught, like an antique brooch, in the deep velvet of the winter sky, could not light the Dell River night, yet the houses and their hedges were outlined in a frosty phosphorescent glow that came from the sky somehow, perhaps from millions of invisible stars massed behind the curtain, burning it through with their collected radiance. She pulled the white chiffon scarf over her hair so that the occasional wandering snowflakes would not disarrange her and absently slipped her hand through Helen's hard little arm.

"There!" said Helen and they were at the carriage entrance of the old Neville mansion. For a moment Connie had a curious feeling of being in a play, of being that lost daughter who returns on a winter night with her child to weep at the family gates that once closed upon her. Already she reduced the feeling to words for Decker, saw his appreciative amusement in advance and then shivered, for it struck her for the first time how much this huge iron gate revealing the gay lights from the house with an involved lace pattern was like her grandfather's iron gate. She thought if she were Laurie Neville with that great estate she would tear down all gates for they did not keep trespassers out, they only made the dwellers prisoners.

"Poor Laurie Neville!" she thought. "She never had a Tony to free her from those gates."

They walked up the snow-sprinkled cinder path to the square brick house. In the glare of a dozen automobile headlights, bereaved of its ivy vines, it looked bare and unfriendly; any stranger would know that here was a house accustomed to being boarded up, any passer-by would guess that the chill of many funerals would cling to these walls, that in a stupendous gilded what-not inside the door would be tiny jade and ivory figurines, Rogers' groups and painted Italian fans brought home by travelled ancestors, that upstairs visitors would be amazed by an old parlor organ and would inevitably experiment with "viola," "vox humana" and all the beautifully named stops that seldom worked. A sad familiar house, Connie thought, known all over the world with little variation in either architecture or history. She wondered if somewhere in middle Massachusetts there might not be a Decker family house like this, but there had never been for the Deckers anything but a small decent home with its women complaining of it.

"This is like my old home, dear," Connie said.

Helen turned her skeptical, pretty little face away.

"Sure," she said enigmatically.

She thought, in a little burst of rage, that she wouldn't mind Mama talking so affectedly all the time if she would only come out and be natural at least with her own daughter. She wouldn't care, Helen thought, if the whole Greene family had lived in a barn (very likely they had)—but why couldn't Mama come out and say as much? She, Helen, would have said so and if people didn't like it they could lump it. What bothered Helen was not where her ancestors lived but where she herself lived. The present was the important thing. And right now she hated her mother for being so complacent about where *she* had been brought up, when she made no attempt to give her own children the same luxury. She might have nagged Papa, at least, into being something besides a shoe-maker,—say he ran a dry goods store or something that would give his daughters free silk stockings. . . .

At the front door they rang the bell and waited. Helen felt her resentment diminishing in the noisy excitement released with the opening of the door, but even with her mother's fingers gently pressing her arm she would not relent completely. The idea whirred around in her head, "I could have lived in such a place as this instead of only visiting it. I would have had a chance if Mother hadn't been so hot after her own chances. And she's happy and satisfied instead of being ashamed of her selfishness!"

They went in together and Miss Manning, standing by the piano, commented to Laurie Neville and Louisa beside her, "Mrs. Benjamin and her daughter, Laurie. Don't look right now, but doesn't it seem sweet and old-fashioned to see mother and daughter coming in together, arm in arm, perfectly at ease with each other?"

"A perfect picture," agreed Laurie, glancing in their direction.

Louisa Murrell blushed as if any compliment for her dear friend was a compliment for her, too.

They were safe at last, their old ground once more restored. Happily they shivered in the window-seat of the Neville drawing-room, sipping their glasses of California wine, nibbling their lettuce sandwiches, chatting in rather high-pitched tones of matters they thought suitable to this occasion. Louisa Murrell fluttered near them and shut her ears to the others. Here in this little corner by the glass miniature case one could believe in civilization, she thought gratefully, just being near Mrs. Benjamin and Decker one could swear that most people were fine, sensitive souls, that in Dell River beauty could thrive as well as in great cities. If one looked around one saw Dell River, stiff, uncomfortable, harassed by the thought of listening to music, wistfully looking toward the card-room or openly suggesting a rubber of bridge to escape the tedium of a set program. There was Helen, reduced to wandering drearily about the house with Hank Herbert, a lanky chinless boy she had passionately hated for years but what could one do, —he was the only other young person present . . . and he did have a dandy plan for skipping out to the back dining-room with the portable victrola later on; he figured the musicians would drown out the sound of the victrola so no one could catch them in the other room dancing. . . .

"They're fair entertainers," Decker explained to Mrs. Benjamin. "Not bad musicians, really, but not first-rate by any means."

"Of course not!" agreed Mrs. Benjamin and they both laughed a little sadly thinking of days they could have revelled in first-rate performances. Decker offered her a cigarette and as always Connie hesitated, as if, inveterate smoker though she was, she would reject the temptation this once, so she gently shook her head.

"You look amazingly well tonight, my dear lady," observed Decker—eying her with the air of a connoisseur. She wore her old blue embroidered Spanish shawl over a black silk dress. "That shawl's a rather rare design, isn't it? I had a friend once—you've probably seen her picture in the paper a dozen times—Ilsa Darmster?"

"I know the name," said Connie politely.

"She had a similar shawl. She used to say, 'Blaine, there isn't another shawl like this in all Spain.' I must tell you about Ilsa sometime. A curious woman—but fascinating." Here

Decker blew a ring of smoke in the air and gazed meditatively after it. "Ilsa was a very strange character indeed."

Louisa, leaning on the back of a chair, listened eagerly, rapidly throwing together in her fancy an Ilsa Darmster, like a stage carpenter building a set from a playwright's limited description. Tall, long-nosed, with dozens of gold bracelets, long antique ear-rings that clinked against a jewelled comb thrust in her sleek black hair—that was Louisa's Ilsa Darmster,—a drawling voice punctuated with a low, rather sinister laugh, a green velvet, excessively low-cut dress, and a volume of Baudelaire in her long, coral-tipped fingers. Ilsa Darmster. Oh, thank you, thank you, Blaine Decker, Louisa sighed under her breath, for this new invention, this lovely new person to find in Dell River. The four musicians began to play and dreamily Louisa leaned on the chair, thinking of the new, fascinating friend Decker had given her.

Decker whispered to the two ladies that Laurie had heard the quartette in a Lyceum program near Pittsburgh and thought, since they were touring nearby, it would be a good chance to bring them to Dell River. Decker lounged back against the window, smoking with half-closed eyes, listening, Louisa thought admiringly, with his whole body. Mrs. Benjamin's chin was in her cupped hand, she gazed so intently at the musicians that the dark violinist muttered something to the 'cellist, but Connie did not see or hear, she was thinking of Ilsa Darmster and for her Ilsa was built majestically, a Brunhilda with glorious golden hair and blue eyes, she walked up and down the deck of the ocean liner with a man's coat and hair streaming, she looked like a Viking princess and when she spoke there was a husky, vibrant quality in her voice that made everyone know she was a singer, or perhaps an actress. Ilsa . . . A wave of gratitude to Decker for the lovely dolls he gave her, swept over Connie. She smiled absently at the violinist and saw the sea beyond him, blue tumbling waves that crashed into the faery music of a Chinese wind bell—but no, that was the violin. She caught Louisa's eye and they smiled vaguely at each other, their Ilsa Darmsters met somewhere on a Mozart phrase and bowed, dissolved once more into music.

"Not bad at all, you know," Decker commented to the ladies, applauding with the rest of the guests, most of whom felt that bad or good, it was all exceedingly dull and with a big room like this, and musicians a dance would have been so much nicer. He looked for approbation toward Mrs. Benjamin. Connie inclined her head thoughtfully to indicate that after proper deliberation she might approve this program but would not rush into a hasty condemnation or approval. Miss Manning, in a severely cut black velvet unobtrusively filled Decker's glass once more and moved away. Decker moved the glass about under his nose and closed his eyes appreciatively.

"Excellent wine," he whispered to Connie. "I'll venture it's as good as the average table wine in the best foreign restaurants. Miss Neville is a marvel, the way, quietly here in Dell River, she maintains a perfectly cosmopolitan standard. Take this wine,—I must ask her if it isn't left over from her pre-war stock. I'm positive it's at least ten years old."

Mr. Decker illustrated his point by finishing the glass deftly, in a silent toast to Miss Neville who was passing. Laurie wandered among the guests, fully aware of their discomfort, trying to speak to groups knotted here and there, but conscious of the chill she spread she caught Gertrude Manning's arm and whispered desperately, "Why do they always stop talking when I come up? They make me feel like Teacher spying on them while they cheat. . . . Why must people treat me this way as if I were a plague? I'll never have another party—never."

"A lovely party, Laurie," Miss Manning said firmly grasping the other's elbow. "I was just thinking we must entertain more so that the town people get to know you better."

"Always I must make these mistakes," Laurie rushed on in a little sobbing whisper while her companion smiled fixedly to show that they were merely having a friendly chat. "I open up to people and they hate me. I tell you they all hate me. Dell River will never take me in,—look how stiff they are—just look——"

The musicians were playing some Italian songs and the violinist put down his fiddle and sang. Connie listened with a rapt face.

" 'Come back to Sorrento,' " she whispered to Decker. "You know that's the song Manuel used to sing. Imagine hearing it after all these years."

Judicially they discussed the man's voice, decided he was rather good, though Decker deferred to Connie on this point. They did agree that it was possible to find as many good things in this little village as anywhere in the world.

Decker saw Marshall and his stout wife approaching and waved his hand patronizingly.

"Marshall's not a bad sort, you know," he confided in Miss Murrell who prayed for the day to come when she would no longer be terrified of the school principal. "A man without background, of course, but not bad for here, not bad at all. Impossible socially but that's only the fault of his training."

He was sorry now that Miss Manning had decided not to sing for he felt like showing Marshall how much more at home he, Decker, was in a salon than the principal himself. He was radiantly happy with Connie and the reverent Louisa hanging upon his every word. He could face any situation with these two ladies' perpetual testimony that Blaine Decker was a most extraordinary man.

He observed Mrs. Benjamin going up to the singer as they picked up their instruments to close the program. He heard her grave compliments to the singer, the carefully considered praise of one great artist to another. The musicians beamed but the violinist's eye roved speculatively over Connie's rich, graceful figure. Connie saw that they were not as impressed with her approval as they might be so she added, with a smile, "You see I know good things for I'm a musician myself. I sang for Morini, —in fact I once sang the song you gave this evening—'Come back to Sorrento'—I've forgotten the words now but——"

The 'cellist, a pallid grey blonde, pressed eagerly toward her. "You say you were a concert singer?"

Connie hesitated.

"Not exactly," she admitted finally smiling reassuringly as if she had dismissed that particular role as inferior. "Hardly that."

"I didn't catch your name," the 'cellist insisted, for so often in just such little places as this one discovered fallen stars. Again Connie hesitated and twisted the fringe of the blue Spanish shawl.

"Benjamin—Madame Benjamin," she said softly.

She saw Decker and Miss Murrell wandering restlessly to-

ward the door so she broke away, leaving the men with hands
to their foreheads trying to place the name "Madame Benjamin" in concert history. The violinist gave it up with a shrug
and looked after Madame Benjamin's departing form.

"Not bad," he muttered to his companion. It was his theory
that there was a practical base to feminine musical appreciation.

Connie saw herself in a long gilt hall mirror and now
that Decker had admired the shawl she saw herself as a very
distinguished-looking woman; these musicians had unquestionably recognized her as someone of importance and she
was glad she had been able to congratulate them in perfect
sincerity, for who knew better than herself the necessity to the
artist of intelligent appreciation? She recalled the 'cellist's face
as she had told him her name—Madame Benjamin; it was difficult to believe that he would not eventually place her as a
famous Isolde of former years. She stood beside Decker and
Miss Murrell in the chilly hallway. Decker leaned against the
stair newel-post, his arm negligently around it, the other
clasping his wine glass. He was flushed and perfectly content
for he was telling Miss Murrell of the first time he had heard
Paderewski, of fabulous musicales he had attended in Paris
and Leipsic in the company of Starr Donnell, the novelist, and
Ilsa Darmster, who never wore stockings; he referred in passing to the satires of Mozart, the unfinished opera of Rimsky-
Korsakoff, and then, finishing off his glass of wine with a fine
gesture, he listed out of sheer splendid extravagance a dozen
composers, giving them their full names and hyphens.

Louisa was dazzled and so happy that she was afraid Miss
Swasey or Miss Emmons might see the tears in her eyes from
across the room. Her ears hummed with Decker's voice, her
lonely mind eagerly collected his jewelled allusions, decorated
itself with the names of Russian composers, arranged a permanent altar for—a sweet face, Miss Manning thought, a
sweet gentle face like a child's.

Decker waited downstairs and it was after they had said
goodnight that he remembered his coat.

"Let me get it," Miss Manning begged. "What was it like?"

Decker described his raincoat, described in particular the
London label although his coat could more easily have been
identified by its shabbiness. Miss Manning could not find such a

coat anywhere. She sent others in quest of it, even Mr. Herbert, the candy store man, who was slightly intoxicated and intended to stay till he was more so. But no London coat could be found.

"It seems a little odd," said Decker in restrained indignation, "that any of Miss Neville's guests would take a coat. After all it's rather hard to replace a London ulster, you know."

"It is indeed," said Miss Manning, and searched again, while Laurie went upstairs for a double bromide,—in a little while she might burst into tears but at least that was more discreet than screaming. . . . The coat was not to be found. The only one left was a brown one with a belted back and a patch under one sleeve. A sickening wave of recognition came over Decker.

"Does it have a London label?" he asked weakly.

No. Instead of a London label, Miss Manning laughed, there was the mark of the People's Big Store in Lima. Moreover a man's name was sewn on the collar—"George Almon."

"Not mine," Decker said. "Oh, dear no."

Everyone was looking at him and after he had been so fussy about that London trademark he could not claim this one.

"But it doesn't matter—" he said with a wan smile.

So Mrs. Marshall's brother's coat was left indefinitely at the Neville house, thrown over the gardener's head on a stormy day, used as a cozy bed by the dogs, worn by Mrs. Busch when she hung up the clothes and all in all made a familiar note in the Neville back hall. Decker, a little drunk, pulled up his jacket collar and walked with Connie Benjamin on the left and Louisa on the right through the still cold midnight. The light dry snow crackled under their feet while Decker, with chattering teeth, told them of the time Ilsa Darmster astounded Vienna or Munich or possibly Berlin by dancing her New World dance right out in the snow, clad only in one brilliant green veil.

The second notice in the "Billboard" read:

> "Tony: Please let me hear from you through this paper. Still have your scarf after all these years. Constance."

Connie had sent this paragraph because the violinist had reminded her of Tony, and the notion had somehow taken hold of her that Tony was near her, else why did she think of him so persistently? She began adjusting her memories to fit in with Decker's theories that she had been madly in love with Tony. A career lost because of a great love, she thought, and wondered if after all it hadn't been worth it. As a photographer erases unflattering lines and defects in a portrait so Connie revised her recollections of Tony, changed the brutality of his desertion into a sensitive boy's anguish over being unable to support a wife. She had never been resentful of his actions any more than she had felt bitter toward her grandfather,—these defeats had crushed her so completely that they lost all personal quality and became part of the relentless routine of a grim destiny. She remembered well the fatigue in her ankles and in the balls of her feet after walking blindly up and down, anesthetizing her mind with the rhythmic clock-clock of her high heels on the Board Walk, she remembered the blank ache in her head, the curious weight on her chest that made her bend her head as if it were a real burden. But the actual shocks were forgotten.

She remembered the day she reached Marblehead when the ocean wind became too much for her and her legs quietly folded up. She was neither grateful nor surprised when the round-faced little foreigner—German or Jewish, she was uncertain which—helped her across a frosty field into someone's house. She did not care when he explained to the woman, "My wife just fainted," though later on she marvelled that such a stolid man as Gus should be so discreetly efficient, taken it for granted that she was sick and in trouble, ready to accept any direction, kind or cruel. In her life all events seemed final and pre-arranged. It was arranged that some man should save her, marry her, and so it developed, bring her to Dell River to peace, a peace in which past years were drowned, sensations past and present lost. After that first baby miscarried, Tony himself was erased, he was only a name until Decker had decorated him with the glamorous garlands of first love. So she had not only missed by a mere hair's-breadth, great fame—she had also known a great love. Tony. Without Decker she would never have realized this.

The violinist at Laurie Neville's party had reminded her of Tony. His image replaced Tony's vaguely in her mind and both were lost when a poster went up in the Music Store carrying a picture of one Tyler Stewart, whose "Colonial Days" entertainers were coming to play in the school auditorium. The school children were urged to attend these two performances partly for its cultural value—(some singing, a one-act operetta, a "reading" or two)—and also because half the proceeds went to the school board in lieu of a fixed rental.

Decker spoke of this affair at Connie's on Sunday night.

"I understand this fellow Stewart sings fairly well," he informed her. "Old English things and all that. It might be well for you to drop in. I'd seriously like to know what your opinion is. Of course I've heard him rehearsing but—well, I'd like a really professional opinion of his work."

Mimi and Helen went to the matinee but Helen would not let Mimi sit with her after they arrived because none of her crowd wanted younger sisters tagging along so Mimi sat alone, reasonably content, and Helen with the older students crowded in the front rows, laughed, waved to friends in the balcony, popped paper bags, stamped their feet rhythmically till the curtain rose and all in all enjoyed to the full the jolly privileges of age.

Connie arrived only for the songs, as Decker had recommended. She wore the little worn sealskin capelet that she'd worn as a girl, and a little turban to match, its bald spots disguised by a dotted veil. She slipped in the dark hall and sat by herself in the back though even in the shadow she recognized Decker's figure standing in the back of the house, his arms folded. Mr. Marshall, present in his capacity of official manager of the auditorium but always slightly alarmed when it took on the gay aspect of a theatre, saw Mrs. Benjamin enter and was so impressed by her late arrival and the suggestion of quiet importance in her bearing that he hurried to where she sat and whispered apologetically to her, his program discreetly held up to his face, "It's really a very good little company, Mrs. Benjamin, —no one could possibly take offense,—and very instructive— many schools and women's clubs have had them purely for educational reasons. They tell me Tyler Stewart is a great favorite in the West, where he used to play in light opera. I think you'll be interested in his songs,—of course he's no Caruso but I heard him rehearsing this morning and actually you could hear him all the way down to the Candy Store. I was astonished!"

"Really!" said Connie, and then the artist made his appearance in Colonial costume and Marshall tiptoed hastily back to his seat and found himself watching Mrs. Benjamin anxiously across the hall to see how she took the performance. Afterwards he wondered why this lady's reactions seemed so important, after all she was not a Board member or a Miss Neville . . . it must be the way she came into the hall, her dignified air of authority and then there was all that talk of her being musical.

Connie felt that aside from the school children who naturally would not know, the audience was as conscious of her presence as Mr. Marshall was, and the subdued gratification this gave her made her only dimly alive to Tyler Stewart. In his white wig and red sateen coat he looked darkly beautiful, far more handsome than his poster in the Music Store, and Connie thought if it had been this man instead of Tony who carried her away everything would have been different, their ambitions would have united them and made them both stronger, they might have been concert singers together. But no sooner had she conjured this picture than she was tired of the weight of success and lonely for Helen and for Mimi whom she saw now watching the stage with a resigned bored little face; she thought it was nicer to be listening with Decker to someone else sing than to be the solitary performer.

"My love is like a red, red rose," sang Tyler Stewart, holding his palms together as in prayer and swaying from side to side, "that newly blooms in June. My love is like a mel-o-dy——"

Tears came to Connie's eyes and she bent quickly over the program for she did not want the watching Mr. Marshall to suspect that the song reminded her of the great love that had been in her life, she wanted him to believe that her attitude toward music was more gravely critical. She did not mind so much that Decker should guess her emotion, for it was Decker who had made of her early mistake a great love, and she knew intuitively that no matter how angry her feeling might make him it was really what he wanted to see, the very thing he expected of women with great loves in their past. . . . She would put a third notice in that magazine for Tony, she decided, but when he did come back to her she would never dare let Decker know she had summoned him, he must believe it was Tony who had done the seeking. Still, the other way revealed how weak she was in a romantic, feminine way and she knew this angered and flattered him curiously. . . . She did not applaud the song for she would not decide till the end whether this singer was really worthy of her praise.

Mr. Stewart sang operatic airs, he sang *La Donna é Mobile* and Connie allowed herself to bend forward on this, intently critical, he sang old English songs and many a spirited ballad with a chorus of staccato "la-la-la-la-la-la's," while the profiles of Mr. Marshall and Decker were turned in Mrs. Benjamin's direction to see if the way she now leaned back in her seat indicated disapproval. In the interval of applause while a smiling girl in a pink shepherdess costume played "The Rustle of Spring" Mr. Marshall hurried over to Mrs. Benjamin again and Decker, twisting his moustache, followed.

"What's the verdict, Mrs. Benjamin?" whispered Mr. Marshall anxiously. "He is really excellent, don't you think? After all we have so little music here, you know, that we ought to be grateful for a gifted fellow like Stewart. He does very well, don't you think?"

Connie nodded her head judicially.

"Quite well," she answered with a kind smile. "It's hard to judge a man's voice unless you've heard him in other things, as well."

"A different type of program," agreed Decker. "I think as Mrs. Benjamin does, Marshall. The man is fair but the upper tones——"

"The upper register, exactly!" Connie said. "Still he does have feeling . . . a great deal of feeling. And that counts for so much."

She sighed thinking that it was so true that love was like a melody.

"It makes up for everything," stoutly asserted Marshall, looking savagely at Decker. "And wait till you hear his next group. I tell you we're very fortunate in getting him."

He was ruffled and his spirits a little dashed by Mrs. Benjamin's quiet little answering smile. He might not know music but he was the one who ran the hall, he heard the rehearsals of everything that came to town and if it weren't for him these superior people like Decker and Mrs. Benjamin wouldn't hear anything at all, he'd like to tell them that, too. . . . He resumed his seat and was aware of Decker standing behind him with folded arms in that irritating Napoleonic pose of his.

"On the road to Mandalay—" sang Mr. Stewart after the scene from "Eugénie Grandet" had been acted out thoroughly by the company, "where the flying fishes play——" whereupon the highschool boys stamped their feet, whistled and shouted their applause. Marshall twisted his head and motioned Decker to lean forward while he whispered "Might be a good thing to have in the Boys' Chorus for Easter Exercises."

Decker smiled dubiously—he hated the implication that he needed any outside suggestions in his own department.

"Hmmm . . . Possibly. Quite possibly," he answered and Marshall ground his teeth at the arrogance of his tone, as if what was good enough for a fellow like Tyler Stewart might not be up to Professor Decker's musical standard. Conscious of having impressed the principal, Decker drew back and leaned against a pillar while the artist with imploring eyes and a slight sob in his voice sang, as encore, an old love-song so tenderly that Connie shut her eyes to guard the tears and pictures of Tony flickered on the insides of her eyelids, though, to tell the truth Tony had never spoken of love, being inarticulate about all his emotions but anger. At the end of the performance Connie knew that Decker was waiting to walk home with her but she could not resist an impulse that had occurred to her when the curtain dropped. Before the lights were on she hurried quietly out and around the building to a back-door leading to a school store-room used as dressing-room for the stage performances. She had stumbled into the cast dressing-room where the three ladies and two men (sensibilities assuaged by a battered burlap screen used for segregational purposes) were throwing white wigs and tarnished metal cloth costumes into a great open trunk. There was no sign of Stewart.

"He's in the furnace room,—the star's room," said one man, looking rather curiously at Connie. "Does he know you're coming?"

"No," said Connie. "Will you be good enough to tell him—ah—Madame Benjamin would like to congratulate him?"

She was getting used to the sound of Madame now and regretted not having thought to use it years ago since there was
no harm in it and it did give one a sense of dignity impossible to find in a simple "Mrs." She saw the actor look curiously
at her and then he went down two steps to knock at the
furnace-room door, planting his knuckles firmly on the black
chalked letters "KEEP OUT." He stuck his head inside then
motioned Connie to go on in.

Gravely Connie entered the furnace-room and saw Tyler
Stewart in a black velvet dressing-gown that had unquestionably seen many and better days standing in a corner
where the twilight filtering through the basement window
could mistily enhance his failing beauty. The grey furnace
sending huge grey arms across the ceiling gave her a slight
chill, it was like a giant octopus and in the dim light aug-
mented by one small blue electric bulb Tyler Stewart seemed
more sinister than beautiful. She saw that he was older than
he appeared on the stage and his hair was dyed so black and
curled so rigidly, even his black roving eyes must have been
touched up with some unknown chemical. His costume
hung on a hanger attached to a water-pipe and the vivid blue
suit he was about to wear hung on another pipe. A small
mirror was propped up on a ledge by the narrow barred
window and a tin of cold cream was beside it. He was lighting a cigarette as Connie came in, and looked at her
obliquely over the flaming match.

"Madame Benjamin?"

Connie inclined her head. Now she felt completely at ease,
the gracious patron of the arts.

"I came to tell you how much I appreciated your work, Mr.
Stewart. We hear so little first rate talent, you know, here—it
was a perfect performance."

Mr. Stewart disclaimed perfection with a wave of the hand
and a modest smile.

"You see," pursued Connie with a sigh, "when one has
been so close to professional singing as I have—ah yes, I sang
for Morini at one time—'The throat of an artist' was what he
said. But it was not to be. . . . However, you can understand
that I have the professional point of view and know a real
singer when I hear one."

"Thank you," said Stewart and studied his visitor with frank curiosity.

"You still sing?" he inquired.

Connie lifted a shoulder with a deprecatory smile.

"I keep in touch with things, of course," she said. "I might go back into it again though I'm afraid I'm needed far too much at home."

"You do give occasional concerts then?"

Connie frowned.

"Not exactly," she said and added quickly, "I act as sort of musical advisor to my friends—I'm by no means out of the music field just because I live in this odd little place. One can keep up, you know."

"I see."

Connie was vaguely disturbed by his unresponsiveness, and by his roving eye which seemed to be waiting for some cue, as if what she was saying was not convincing and he expected the real cause of her visit to be revealed any minute. She tried to say something, something to sustain her original feeling of assurance and polite superiority but Stewart's expectant attitude was not helping her. Someone knocked on the door and Stewart hurried over and spoke to someone outside in a low tone. The door closed again and then Connie said as he came back to her, "I sang 'My love is like a red rose' at one time myself, but I really enjoy the arias more, don't you, Mr. Stewart? If I had kept up with my career nothing would have satisfied me but opera."

"Is that a fact?" said Stewart and poured himself a drink of water from a china pitcher on the stool. He drank it leaning back against the grey stone basement walls, his eyes on Connie with a quick calculating look that made her feel curiously defensive. She said, "I hope you will forgive my intruding but I wanted you to know how much your singing meant to me. I—I thank you for it."

Tyler bowed stiffly and murmured something she did not understand.

There was nothing more to be said so he stood waiting either for her to continue or to leave. Dissatisfied and embarrassed Connie turned to leave. Stewart followed her to the door, smoking his cigarette. He took the hand she extended in farewell and held it a moment.

"When do you want to come again?" his voice was so low and silky that the meaning did not penetrate her mind at first. "I think we understand each other, don't we?"

Connie put her hands out frantically against him but he caught them and kissed her mouth lingeringly, smiling a little because he knew so well the favor he was bestowing and because women were so transparent. . . . Someone turned the knob of the door and Connie stumbled out as the actor entered. She remembered to smile brightly at the players dressing in the gymnasium and not to reveal by the horror in her eyes the quite dreadful thing that had happened to her. When she came out on the street it was dark and she ran down the nearest byway crying out softly "Oh . . . oh . . . oh" then remembered to put her hand over her mouth so that no one could hear. In the unexpected glow of a street corner lamp she recognized Decker leaning against the post waiting for her. She couldn't see him now, she couldn't possibly talk to him lest he should suspect that Madame Benjamin, the artist, had been so hideously mistaken for Mrs. Benjamin, the woman. She turned quickly up an alley and ran.

In the shadow of Mrs. Busch's house she saw a man embracing a girl. Her heart pounding and her whole body aching as if bruised merely by a sensual look, she reached her own door, the refuge of her own living-room. She pulled the gloves from her trembling fingers and sat down to the piano. Desperately she began to play in the darkness, singing in a choked and shaking voice——"La donna é mobile—la-la-lala——"

Connie was ill. Gus wanted to call in the doctor but she would not hear of it for she did not know how to describe her symptoms. Was it a disease to be afraid to face people, was there a prescription for terror, for shame so intense, so fatiguing that she could not stand on her two legs? The third day in bed she received a note and roses from The Oaks' own hothouse from Louisa Murrell but no word came from Decker. Connie knew he must have seen her go into Tyler Stewart's dressing-room and evade him afterward, and no matter what he may have thought of this she was grateful to him for staying away. She could not have faced him and confessed—"I went to him to discuss music and he thought I only came to be kissed."

Shame poured through her body when she recalled Stewart's eyes as she talked of songs. How could she have mistaken that look for deference? She could scarcely face Gus who sat patiently at the foot of her bed every night while she tried to drink the hot milk Mimi prepared.

"No cough, no headache—just a little fever—I don't understand this," Gus shook his head in great perplexity. "If you can't get up tomorrow I'm going to send in the doctor no matter what you say."

Connie patted his hand reassuringly. She could not explain that this weakness must persist until her mind came upon some philosophy that would banish shame. In the darkness it grew worse, for Stewart's avid eyes became the violinist's eyes, then Tony's eyes, then changed into Blaine Decker's eyes, none of them looking up to her admiringly as an artist but hungrily as if she were any woman.

"Only Gus," she thought sadly. "In all the world Gus is the only one who knows what I might have been. To the rest I'm like any other woman,—Mrs. Busch—or Louisa——"

Her veins burned, her eyes were hot aching stones from unshed tears, it seemed to her for the first time she was conscious of her body, a body that was Connie Benjamin in some curious way almost as music was Connie Benjamin. The consciousness grew out of the remembered look in men's eyes translated into meaning now for the first time. But it was not in Decker's eyes, strive as she might to collect the entire damning evidence she could not fairly credit him with desire. Yes, there was a difference in his admiration, he did see the Madame Benjamin, she gratefully admitted, and strength seemed to flow back into her with this quiet revelation. He did not think of her as accessible or desirable but as the artist—dear, dear Decker. . . .

She lay facing the window watching the clouds blow over the moon, they played with different arrangements of gossamer as so many costumes for a spoiled prima donna. Connie dozed and when she opened her eyes a chilly shell pink stained the pale eastern sky. The dried brown rambler vines rattled against the window in the frigid dawn winds. Shell pink merged into amethyst and lemon and presently these shy colors shivered into a winter sun. Connie thought, "I am well—I can get up." Because of Decker, because he saw her as she wanted to be seen.

To Decker she was without gender, she thought contentedly. But why did he find her undesirable? Were there other women—say Laurie Neville or Ilsa Darmster whom he considered beautiful, women a man could love rather than revere? Connie could not remember her own face or form as she had never looked in the mirror for anything but the impression of dignity she wished to give. What did she really look like? What had Tyler Stewart seen—and the violinist and Tony—what had they found that was not enough for Blaine Decker?

Still a little uncertain of her legs Connie groped her way to the dresser and tipped the mirror so that she could see herself. What was it Stewart saw? The pallid daylight made a grey shadow of the mirror and she saw only dimly but it seemed to her that this was the first time she'd ever looked upon herself. She peered closer at her face and thought, "Why, I am beautiful." So this was Connie Benjamin, the woman. All these years she might have been happy in merely being beautiful, but she had never known. She tipped the mirror further back to see the outline of her body,—richly curved yet slim. Her face in this light had the pearly translucence of a ghost, her dark hair tousled and uncombed looked wildly strange, her full mouth curiously brilliant. A ray of sunlight suddenly annihilated the misty perfection of this picture and with a contraction of pain in her heart she saw that the verbs describing her beauty must be in the past tense for there were lines near her eyes, the droop of lost youth in her mouth, in the contours of her cheek, her throat that a moment before seemed so indestructibly firm was circled with fine threads. She was overwhelmed with sadness to think these remaining charms were passing, and that all these years she must have been lovely without knowing it. She was old. Thirty-seven was old. In five more years more lines—in ten years what Tyler Stewart or violinist would look at her with disturbing appraisal . . . was it possible that any man, however crude, would glance at her ankles as she talked of music? And at forty-seven . . . Connie ran a finger slowly over her cheek. Even now the doom of age was upon her. She was saying farewell to a woman she'd never known, a woman, once beautiful, her beauty congealing into years until presently a man could only pity her as an Hellenic fragment no longer able to provoke tumult, admired only for its vanished loveliness. . . . The sun crept through the gnarled branches of the vine and cruelly found more signs of ruin, each reluctant ray brought a chill to the woman at the mirror, pointing out relentlessly the faults of age. So she had been a woman, a desirable woman . . . and now that was over and the chill of approaching winter was to slowly creep over her as hemlock might steal slowly through her veins, the victim conscious of her fate, yet even up to the moment the hemlock reaches her heart she knows and suffers, she still can weep for her forlorn doom.

Now shame was lost in fear that this degradation would never happen again. And Decker who saw only the artist, who did not know her throat was white or her bosom charming . . . was he not stealing youth from her? And Gus who had never told her she was alluring. . . . After all had not Tyler Stewart done something kind for her in revealing her own vanishing treasures to herself? She had a feverish wish for day to come that she might send for Decker and watch him, just to see if she might not surprise that look in his eyes too before the sun betrayed her with further evidence of lost years.

Here was something again that could not be told to Decker. It puzzled Connie that no matter how swiftly they cleared the way of all secrets between them new reserves formed automatically, there could never be complete understanding between two persons, new barriers were built as fast as the old were torn down. She could not tell him of this change in her, this bewildering consciousness of her body, she could not explain the sensation of guilt she experienced whenever Gus referred now to his tenant.

When they met for the first time after Stewart's performance there was a certain restraint between them. Decker called on his way to a Saturday night buffet at Laurie Neville's. He could not explain to himself why he had not called during her illness but somehow he could not bear to see her disarmed. He had no interest in a sick woman, de-

manding of pity, her very weakness a disillusioning proof that
she was only human and not the rare immortal he fancied. He
felt bewildered and a little ashamed that for an invalided Mrs.
Benjamin he had no tenderness but rather impatience that the
dear routine of their companionship should be interrupted,
indeed his own life thrown quite out of key for the moment.
He could not imagine sitting beside her couch discussing
physical disabilities with her, it would be impossible to assume
more than a polite pretense of concern over her pains. The
Mrs. Benjamin he reverenced was their joint invention and
not subject to the infirmities of God-made beings.

"Perhaps I have no real sympathy for anyone," Decker
mused and was rather proud of being above such sentimental
limitations until he thought of a week years ago when Starr
Donnell was in the hospital and he, Decker, sat at the foot of
the bed, the heart torn out of his body with anguish, listening to Starr's tortured delirium. Yes, then he had believed in
human afflictions and suffered for someone else.

So now he waited for the return of his Mrs. Benjamin, impatiently marking time for her vacation from Olympus. When
he called he felt a wave of pleasure at seeing her almost as before, so well that there was no necessity for referring to her
sickness. Indeed she wore convalescence as a lady should,—a
touch of spirituality in her pallor, a certain fragile delicacy
combined with poise so that, Decker thought with relief, one
was pleasantly conscious of one's masculine strength and,
better yet, assured that no demands would be put upon it.

"I wanted to talk over Tyler Stewart's songs with you," he
said, sitting on the arm of a chair, unwilling to allow himself
the permanent commitment of a comfortable seat. "There
were so many things that were good, for instance, his lyric
quality—I looked for you afterward."

"Yes," said Connie and looked steadily at the jar of
Jerusalem cherries Mimi had placed on the library table.

"Someone said you had gone back to speak to Stewart but
I knew they were mistaken," Decker went on. He lit a cigarette and smiled at her,—after all it was rather charming and
in a way flattering for her to succumb to the usual feminine
vapors, and the brief separation made him realize how comforting, how actually necessary this relationship was to him.

Connie returned the smile queerly, holding tight to the arms of her chair.

"Yes,—I did go back to see him," she said in a strained voice. "I wanted to compliment him, of course. . . . You know how important that is. People here never think to tell the artist what he's meant to them. . . ."

It was nothing but she looked at him with such odd, frightened eyes, her face turned questioningly toward him as if waiting for a verdict, and Decker's heart seemed to stop, he swallowed two or three times but no words would come, and a shocking sensation of hatred for her overwhelmed him. He saw the feeling come up as one might see the approach of a huge steam roller, powerless before it, knowing this must be the end. Little doors opened, one, two, three, all along his brain . . . something had happened at that interview to upset her, that woman hurrying up the alley in the darkness that night had actually been Connie just as he first thought and she was running from him for some reason . . . lastly there was no escape from the rack of jealous, stabbing, frightful humiliating pain that she should have had some intimate experience, however innocent, with that man, particularly someone so nearly glamorous. He saw it all coming, the jealousy, hate, love, like a dreaded but inescapable sickness, and afterwards this premonition was vaguely connected with a green flowerpot of Jerusalem cherries on a lace table-runner . . . his eyes fastened desperately to each external detail as if to distract him from inner revelations . . . he studied the scars and rings on the walnut veneer of the table, took in the red and fudgy-brown of a magazine cover and then stopped at the old unpainted door leading to the upstairs. It was when his eyes reached this door that the entire sensation struck him irrevocably,—no protection from jealousy or suspicion, no longer any armor against feeling. He could almost have wept at this defeat. Instead he said, "Isn't that strange, I've never noticed that the stair door is crooked. See? The whole door is at least three inches off the line."

"I never knew that," said Connie and they both studied the door intently. Then Decker remembered seven o'clock supper at Miss Neville's. For the first time Connie did not urge his staying or dropping in later in the evening. She examined the hall door as if nothing had ever been so vital as its dimensions. Decker got quickly to his feet, trying not to look at her or show his mounting indignation at the unexpected betrayal of their friendship.

"I felt that Stewart had a very slender talent," he said, and was angry to find he was stammering a little, "a very slender talent, indeed. I'm surprised you thought him important enough to visit. A very poor voice and a very poor program indeed."

"Yes, I know," said Connie simply and her face looked so pale and her mouth so weak that it was hard not to strike her, Decker thought. It was all very well for women to be fragile but to be deliberately so pliable and at the mercy of any stronger will was not decent. There was nothing one could do about such a woman, as quickly as one built her up she collapsed into a jelly,—worse, far worse, than being definitely wanton, Decker reflected, at least there was something hard and dependable in a wanton. Then, too, one could hurt and be revenged upon a wanton but there was nothing to be done about a delicate, changing shadow.

"I suppose this man Stewart reminded you of your first romance," Decker said, fixing a smile on his face to indicate how amused he was by her poor little romances. "The same cheap theatrical type, doubtless. Once a taste is formed in women they invariably run true to form."

He saw that Connie's head drooped a little, evidently there was one way he could return wound for wound, but he knew there was for him not enough satisfaction in these feeble blows. Physical violence would be inadequate as well, and as for this shaming of her, there was a guilty confidence in her eyes, once fleetingly meeting his, that made a virtue of shame.

He left the house confused and angry. Now he saw his life fretted with desire and warped with jealousy, he saw the delicate threads of their friendship tangled with the new consciousness and now, leaving Connie, he could not sustain the warm, flattered knowledge that he had been brilliantly extraordinary, instead he carried a brutally distinct image of the blue of her gown against her disturbing white throat.

Abruptly Decker turned from the Neville gate and went back the street to his own rooms. The corner was dark as it

always was on Sunday night and he fumbled for the keyhole
in the dim starlight. He stumbled up the staircase and turned
on his living-room light. The one light with its bluish shade
made the room incredibly dreary and lonely. Decker dropped
his hat on the table and leaned against the piano, his hand
rumpled his hair in a vague, bewildered gesture. Something
vital was slipping away, if he concentrated now he might win
it back, he must regain it, for God knows there was little
enough he could lose now. In the queer blue light his eyes
found the portrait of his mother. There, that was one thing,
though his heart rejected even this as being completely his.
And Starr. With a twist of fear in his breast Decker thought,
"In this room I have nothing, not even Starr. Starr never was.
Paris never was. There was never anything but this village hidden far off alone and Mrs. Benjamin. She made the other
things for me,—she gave me myself with a past . . . but there
was never anything but this present. . . . The Pilgrims' Chorus and this quiet room . . . this tomb. . . ."

He slowly went into the bedroom and lay face down on the
bed, but even with his eyes shut he saw the blue light of the
other room blurring shadows into chairs and tables. Never anything but this room to be furnished now with futile suspicions,
a queer dull desire for something his real self rejected, a desire
whipped by the insistent memory of a curving white throat.

Vacations were always a problem to Decker, but the present
prospect of three months' freedom was unusually frightening.
After Teacher's Meeting which was held in the Chemistry Laboratory he saw Louisa Murrell edging toward him and knew he
must have answers ready for the current query, "Are you going
to the seashore for the summer?" One could say simply, "Indeed
no, I must go up to Ann Arbor and work on my M.A.," or there
was the perfect answer, "I plan to spend the summer abroad."
Decker wished for some wretched farmer cousin who would
hide him for the summer, no matter how desolate the place, just
so he might vanish from observation, so that the possibility of
three months in Dell River would be definitely cancelled.

In April and May teachers were gentler to each other and
respectful to Marshall for even though they complained

bitterly during the year of Dell River limitations, they were in a panic at the thought of some far-off strange, even smaller post next year or worse yet, no assignment at all. Louisa was not afraid, she knew quite well she had never mattered enough to any superintendent to be discharged, it was always the outspoken, free-thinking sort that had to be fired. She had saved money for years and had almost enough to buy a little place on Cape Cod where she could live quietly and write. She thought about this often but she feared the realization. There she would be a lonely stranger among the dunes with no one to wonder who she was, no one to witness her romantic solitude. And if someone should come to see her in her little house this some one might ask, "How do you spend your days, Miss Murrell, what do you do?" how could she ever hope for courage to answer, "I write all day long. I am a poet, you see, though I do prose quite as easily." She could never come right out and say it even though that was the sole purpose of the venture; however she saved money and some day when the school dismissed her she would find herself, horror-stricken, on a train bound for that little place on Cape Cod.

Marshall enjoyed those last two months of deference, when the instructors who had been rather superior, as Decker, for instance, during the year, now knuckled under and all but begged for recommendations for next year. He stood at the desk after the teachers left making notes busily on a pad and trying to hear the conversation between Miss Murrell and Decker over by the blackboard, not because he really wanted to eavesdrop or expected to hear anything of moment, but because spying gave him a grateful feeling of authority and power.

"You'll be going abroad, I suppose," said Louisa with a sigh. "How I envy you!"

"Not this year, I'm afraid," Decker answered, frowning a little as if his important affairs were in such a prodigious state of complications that he could scarcely leave them for a pleasure trip. "I planned the trip of course, but——"

"The university, then?" Louisa inquired eagerly. "I went to Normal last summer you know in Michigan."

Decker shook his head.

"No, I shan't bother with any more degrees, I must confess. My mother, of course, will be at her place in the mountains and insists that I join her, but I honestly prefer the sea. . . . Of course my ambition is to own a little place on the coast somewhere—not too far from concerts——"

"Of course!" Miss Murrell agreed.

"——a little place where I could work occasionally, if I should want to do a bit of critical writing, or get into my music once again . . . a little place where I could hear the ocean. . . ."

"Cape Cod," said Louisa softly.

"Exactly . . . Then it doesn't matter if I must teach in winter, for at least I have my retreat in summer."

"Yes," said Louisa in a choked voice. "A little place on the Cape where you can hear the ocean."

She looked quickly around to see if Miss Swasey or Miss Emmons were near, for they would be sure to guess why she could not wink back the tears in her eyes. She wouldn't be afraid in that little retreat with Decker. When people asked her what she did she would not need to answer, "I'm a writer," for Decker would be on hand to say, "No, she doesn't write, but I have a friend who does. Starr Donnell, the novelist. My very best friend."

She was frightened that Decker wanted the very same thing she did—it seemed like Fate. She hoped, no matter how intimate and revealing the midnight confidences at the Oaks became she would not tell about this conversation, no matter how much Swasey might tell of men's approaches or Emmons tell of the time she was engaged to the Hazelton widower. She hoped she would be strong enough to lie, saying "Nothing very thrilling has ever happened to me, girls."

Marshall collected his records and tidied the desk. He smiled remotely at the other two, as if in his benign omnipotence he had heard nothing of their "crush."

"Glad to get away next month, Decker?" he said briskly.

It had to be faced sooner or later so Decker braced himself.

"Certainly not, old man, you forget I'm new to your charming little inland towns. We haven't anything in the East as pleasant as this—a real place for a vacation. I couldn't find a better place for a summer of work—getting my music in order—enlarging on some of my notes—that sort of thing. If I can get out of leaving town I'll be delighted. May run up to my mother's place or take occasional week-ends at the Lake but—well, frankly, I'm looking forward to a fine summer right here in the village."

"Well," said Marshall with all his dislike for Decker returning now that Decker had made Dell River so attractive there was no triumph in mentioning his own family plans for a motor trip through Washington, D.C. and Mt. Vernon,—he sensed that Decker might be superior even about that.

"I may be here a good deal of the summer," said Louisa suddenly as they went down the dark corridor. "I haven't any plans—nothing definite."

"I see," said Decker absently. He thought of the hot sticky summer nights over the cobbler shop, the blue light burning and the hot droning days and his thoughts all prepared themselves in advance—jealousy over his mother and Rod's family so content in that mountain boarding-house without him,— oh quite as if he were dead,—and that dumb hurt over Starr and now the endless fretting over Connie.

"I shan't mind it myself at all," he said helping Louisa into her new spring coat. She saw it had paid to get the one with the pretty lining even if it had cost more. "I shan't mind anything, you know, so long as I have my own things about me."

"Your music," sympathized Louisa.

"Yes," said Decker, "my music."

If you bathed your face in sunrise dew on May Day you became beautiful; this was an old saying and every May Mimi meant to do it but no matter how firm her desire the dew was always long gone when she opened her eyes. This year Helen had promised to go out with her to the meadow beyond the river and in case beauty failed to come they could gather mushrooms and violets. It was dark when Mimi wakened and shook Helen, but Helen only muttered, "Let me alone! Don't!" and pulled her blanket over her head protectingly.

"You promised," whispered Mimi. "You can't back out now, Helen, honestly you can't."

Helen could back out of any promise that made her uncomfortable as her sister very well knew and no recriminations could move her. Mimi shook her once again but Helen's long slim body was dissolved into covers, there was no more to grasp here than there was in her entire nature. Depressed,

Mimi sat up in bed and faced the fact that if she was to be
made beautiful in May dew she must be brave enough to go
through the dark meadows alone, for certainly there was no
hope of Helen as companion.

Shivering a little she pulled on her stockings and shoes, then
drew on her underwear under her thick, cotton nightie as a
Sunday school teacher had once taught her to do and finally
struggled into the woolen middy suit she had inherited from
Helen as her winter school costume. She heard her father's
heavy breathing as she tiptoed down the stairs and tried to
keep the boards from creaking for there was no explaining this
early pilgrimage to her father. The kitchen seemed darkly alive
as kitchens do in early morning as if they kept guard while the
house sleeps. The cat brushed against her legs and Mimi took
the pail of milk from the outdoor pantry and poured some in a
saucer. She found some doughnuts in the breadbox and ate
two, stuffing a third in the already crumby pocket of her skirt.
She thought, "Of course I don't actually believe in this dew
thing but what a grand revenge on Helen if it actually does
work out. And Bertha Marshall says it did cure her of freckles."

The tea-kettle lid fell off and clattered to the floor, a pile of
muffin tins slid into the sink, a wooden bowl slid off the rack
somewhere overhead and spun gaily around the spice shelf,
releasing a strong aroma of cinnamon and sweet marjoram.
Mimi, sneezing desperately, was almost convinced that there
were evil spirits about and certainly all hope of slipping unobserved out of the house was gone for already footsteps
could be heard descending the stairs. Her mother appeared in
the doorway, her brown hair swinging in rich braids over her
faded blue wrapper.

"What is it, Mimi? Are you ill?"

It was too much for Mimi's nerves to bear.

"Bertha said it made her freckles go—I don't believe it but
I only wanted to try," she babbled. "Then Helen wouldn't
come so I'm going alone." And then she burst into loud sobs
and hid her face in her hands against the cupboard. "It was
just for the fun of it," she wept. "I don't see why Helen has
to spoil it all by backing out. She'll be good and sorry if I find
some mushrooms."

Connie gently patted her shoulder and went to the window. Day was coming up softly beyond the river. The silver of early dawn hung over the meadow and tinged the marshy river banks with unearthly lavender. This early light seemed to come not from the sky but from the earth, a dull, smoky radiance exuding from gently opening flowers and wakening grass. The world was lonely and macabre in this glow, this half-lit world belonged to strange nightmares, to prehistoric beasts, fantastic flying things. Connie shuddered and then saw her vague terror dispelled by a shaft of sudden sunlight.

"Wait, Mimi," she said. "I'll go with you."

She twisted up her braids and pulled on a coat over her wrapper. They walked swiftly down through the back alley, the cinders beneath their feet crackling protest in the morning silence. Houses sagged drearily with sleepers, cold little red chimneys made a ragged fringe on the pale sky. The winter had drifted away untidily leaving a scanty patch of stale snow here and there in hollow stumps beside which violets dared to peep. When they came to the river the sun burst out, birds shook themselves and celebrated with shrill joy.

"We'll have to hurry or the dew will be gone," Mimi said breathlessly. "And it doesn't work except with the first dew."

They found the little dam to cross the shallow river and made their way over it. The wind shaved the water, whipping up tiny swirls and ripples as if it were a real river instead of barely more than a brook. Mimi waited for her mother on the other side. She remembered her third doughnut and munched it happily.

"I'm so glad you came," she couldn't help sighing.

They hurried through the meadow across the damp soft earth until they were out of sight of the village. Mimi ran ahead and impulsively knelt, burying her face in the wet weeds. Connie knelt too and there did seem magic in the tingle of the icy drops on her cheeks for when she lifted her head she felt divinely happy. She sat down on a fallen log near the woods and watched Mimi scurrying around for mushrooms, occasionally finding a stray violet or crocus and dropping it into her outstretched lap with the mushrooms. Without being conscious of it Connie hummed softly, her body swaying to and fro and then her lungs seemed overwhelmed with the morning air, she opened her mouth wide and sang, hardly knowing what she sang, something she had long ago forgotten but now remembered. This was the way she had always meant to sing, freely, splendidly, but she must never have given hint of such power for Mimi came running up, wide-eyed and dazzled.

From a path in the woods a man appeared. He stood still listening and then took off his hat. When the last note died, birds sang furiously for an instant and then Connie held out her hand for Mimi to start homeward. She was flushed and trembling and had to look twice at the man before she saw it was Busch.

"Lady," said Busch in a choked voice, "I swear to God that's the most beautiful music a man ever heard. I'm telling you the truth and I thank you."

He vanished in the path across the woods and Mimi whispered, "It was—oh, it was beautiful, mother."

Holding her treasures in her lap Mimi balanced herself across the brook once more and Connie followed, her heart thundering in her breast, a thousand voices in her ears saying, "The most beautiful music a man ever heard"—the very words she had always wanted to hear and now due to the magic of the May dew she actually heard them. This was her great premiere, the sunrise and flushing clouds her audience, the grocery man's praise her triumph.

It was enough. Connie's feet scarcely touched earth on their way back to the house and Mimi, in her scurry to keep up with her scattered a trail of violets and tiny ferns.

Mr. Busch told Mrs. Busch and Mrs. Busch told Decker. He stood on the front-steps of the Busch home and Mrs. Busch talked to him through the gingerly-opened parlor door, thrusting her head out and occasionally waving a fat, red forearm, but keeping the rest of her body safely behind the door so that Decker had a delirious impression of a Punch and Judy show, ending with Mrs. Busch's head and shoulders attached to limp sawdust legs being jerked suddenly out of sight. The few inches Mrs. Busch allowed to open permitted a chilling picture of the dreadful parlor behind her, the polychromed pink floor lamp (too good to be used) the gaudy red and pink roses of the carpet, the shiny mahogany veneered table, the Busch wedding picture,—indeed, Decker thought, the whole room looked like a 1905 wedding present and it was. He was deeply relieved that he did not have to sit in it, though he did wonder who in all Dell River was considered worthy of an invitation inside the sacred sill.

"He said, 'Mrs. Busch,' he says to me, 'I never heard anything like it in my life, never, I only wish you could have heard it, he says, coming right out of her throat that way.'"

"Of course! Of course!" Decker nodded and felt so exultant that he wanted to rush at once over to Connie's and congratulate her upon her success quite as if it had been her metropolitan debut.

Mrs. Busch was obliged to open the door a few inches more to receive the bundle of Decker's laundry but she quickly adjusted it again to the proper angle. "As if I were a book agent," thought Decker.

"The way I say is, she may have sounded just as good as the Mister says, but do you think that's natural, Professor Decker, for a body to go out singing in the fields at crack o'day? My Honey does it but she's just a child, things like that is natural for a child."

She was alarmed when Decker threw back his head and laughed.

"Well, I only mentioned it to you, her singing, I mean, on account of your being friends and the Mister being so tickled with the whole business . . . I didn't see it was so funny as all that . . . I'll get these things back to you Friday."

Decker found the door closed firmly in his face and the next moment the stiff lace curtains of the upper half of the door were parted to permit a fair little girl's face to grimace out at him, thumb her nose and vanish as her mother had done. Decker walked down the front path uncomfortably aware of Honey darting from one window to another to thumb her nose at him. When the gate clicked behind him he heard her singing at the top of her lungs a mocking travesty of "The Spinning Song." Where Mrs. Busch had concealed her own figure he could not guess but he was conscious of being watched and not by the fatuously adoring eyes of an old retainer, either.

"Still, she gets a thrill out of us, I suppose," he thought contentedly. "We probably give her more to puzzle over than all Dell River put together."

He could hear himself telling Connie this after they had first laughed over poor old Mrs. Busch's questioning the sanity of one who sang outdoors instead of at funerals. It was so characteristic of Mrs. Busch to doubt superior intelligence and be proud of her own half-witted daughter. Once Decker had cautiously tried to find out if Mrs. Busch really was unaware of her daughter's deficiency or knew it and was proud of the distinction. Neither was the case. Mrs. Busch felt that she had given birth to a capricious little beauty with the most amazing ways and as unlike as she was superior to every other child in town.

"Isn't she a card?" the mother would fondly exclaim as Honey screamed foul epithets at her little friends. "But that's the way children all are nowadays. And she picks up every little thing she hears, smart as a whip. Oh, she ain't smart in the usual way, I mean, being still in the third grade and nearly fifteen years old, but I never asked for smartness. I was bright and what'd it get me? I like a pretty face. I never had one and Mr. Busch, God knows is no picture, so I said, there ain't nothing I wouldn't do, Lord, for a pretty little girl. I went to church and cooked Church suppers every week and prayed and when my baby came people came for miles around to look at her, she was that pretty. If you work and pray, Mr. Decker, in the end you get what you want like I did."

Dear, quaint old Busch!

By the time he had turned the corner he was smiling fondly at the good soul, forgetting the vague sense of inferiority her daughter's caprices had given him. The little town smelled of spring, of wet turf, sprouting grass and geraniums. Underfoot the cinder paths were damply elastic, flower-beds with white-pebbled borders were arranged or being arranged on every lawn in crescents, stars and simple ovals; spades and hoes leaned against porch lattices and elderly relatives, up to this season of the year nuisances to their families, were happily put to use white-washing young trees or dropping potatoes in tiny kitchen gardens. Decker dashed jauntily along the street, breathing deep of the raw spring air, with a sensation almost of contentment.

"Not a bad place to live, really," he thought. "Of course if one were tied here for life it would be frightfully dull, but for a year or two it's charming. Good friends, my nice little place—I couldn't have a better one in the Bohemian quarter of any city, Starr would love the idea of living over a cobbler shop!—I'd hate to leave it, really!"

Leave it? Where was he going? It was true each fall he planned to go abroad the following summer, but in the spring he knew it was impossible, as a winter in New York or Boston was, too. And as for this coming summer he could do nothing but stay above the cobbler shop, all vacation money must be sent to his mother for the mountains, God knew Rod would never take care of that expense. His mother and Rod seemed further and further away, as if he had never belonged to them, as if he had always belonged to Dell River, the five or six years in that little Virginia town had slid out of his memory. How nicely memory could be made to serve one's happiness, erasing all the things that tended to obliterate the great moments, leaving a Swiss summer with its original colors unmarred even though a dozen summers in American coal towns or hot Midwestern villages came between! Now Decker found himself making room in his mind for a cottage on Cape Cod, the ocean side, he thought. Quite selfishly he took over Louisa's dream cottage. So real did this cottage instantly become that when Laurie Neville stopped her car just then to pick him up he told her at once that he was hoping to get down to his place on the Cape next month.

Miss Manning was driving, her hat stuck on the back of her graying head and one little square-toed boot planted tentatively on the brake. Decker sat in the back of the coupé with Laurie. Laurie's eyes were red, as indeed her nose was too, but the obvious cause of this condition was a mystery to Decker beyond a casual suspicion that Miss Neville probably had a cold. She spoke in a slightly English voice, a product of her foreign schooling and further cause for Dell River men's terror of her, and Miss Manning's accent was distinctively Bostonian so that Decker's own curious accent became, after five minutes' exposure to theirs, more alarmingly Oxfordian than Starr Donnell's had ever dared to be. It was true that even

Mr. Marshall, a stickler for good pure Hoosier inflections had caught himself saying "my paunts and vest" in a brief conversation with Miss Neville so that Decker's susceptibility was not to be wondered at.

"I didn't know you had a summer home in the East," said Laurie.

Decker laughed self-consciously. He was never able to feel at ease in an automobile, it still represented aristocracy to him, even though many teachers—even Marshall—owned one. To Decker the conversation of people in limousines was that of men in dinner clothes and that of people drinking special wines, it must be rare and studied, a touch theatrical in its cadences; certainly it must deal lightly and wittily with luxurious subjects—vacations, property, opera, decorations, and all material beauties. In the comfortable purple cushioned seat of Laurie's car it actually seemed to him he was a man of property and position.

"The place is not exactly in my hands yet, it is true," he admitted. "I'm not satisfied at the price they're asking."

"Where is it?" Miss Manning asked, without turning her head and without really wanting an answer since she could never drive and listen at the same time.

"Wellfleet," said Decker, capturing the name from somewhere far back in his memory. "Of course, the real drawback is that I'm expected abroad in June. My friends are there—Starr Donnell, the novelist——"

"Yes," said Miss Manning.

"I sometimes think," said Decker musingly while the little houses of Dell River appeared one by one on the window of the car, each one modestly inviting his mind to return to reality. "I sometimes think it would be wiser to give up the plan for the cottage, give up Europe too, and stay here in this little town and get to know it. With my work I've never had a chance to study the place, get the feel of it, don't you know."

"Don't stay," said Laurie abruptly. "Go where there's music and people who aren't afraid of you."

"Laurie thinks Dell River is afraid of intelligent people," said Miss Manning in the cheerful, hard voice she used to balance growing hysteria in her friend.

"Paris would be ideal, of course."

Decker flicked ashes of his cigarette out the window, bowed briefly to Louisa Murrell just coming down the front steps of The Oaks.

"I'm afraid I'm something of a snob, Miss Neville," he said. "I can't bear travel except under first-class conditions. I must have my little luxuries, you know, and I can't do the way my friends there would expect me to. So I'll be perfectly contented here in Dell River. I've always wanted to investigate those woods over there and walk out beyond those hills by the Nursery."

"There would be the festival at Salzburg," said Laurie Neville. "All the things you love . . ." She suddenly leaned toward him. "Let me take you. It would be so easy for me to do. Let me . . . I assure you we would make it as comfortable for you as you'd like. . . . Do let me do that for you, Professor Decker."

Decker was stunned. He had no answers ready for kindness or for reality, his words, like Mrs. Benjamin's were for protection from people, not for communication with them. He met in the little crescent-shaped driver's mirror the quizzical eye of Miss Manning and its gentle cynicism braced him, it seemed so sardonically certain of his greedy acceptance.

"My dear lady," he answered with a little laugh, "if I really wanted to go abroad I'd go—it isn't a question of money, oh dear no!"

"But you said—" Laurie flushed and her lip trembled.

"Don't misunderstand me," Decker said with a wide flourish of his cigarette. "Fortunately I'm not dependent on teaching as poor old Marshall is, for instance, and if I really wanted to travel——! I was only trying to be judicious in my spending, that was all. Sorry I gave you the wrong impression."

Laurie looked mutely out of the other window and Miss Manning drove hastily around the Square and stopped the car before the cobbler shop.

"It would have been nice to have you with us, Laurie thought," said Miss Manning as Decker got out. "One needs a man travelling."

Decker bowed over Laurie's outstretched hand.

"I wish I could be there to take you around among my friends," he said. "Fascinating people. I miss them constantly. Artists—then there's Ilsa Darmster and Starr——"

Laurie drew her hand away and dabbed savagely at her eyes with a handkerchief. Miss Manning silently released the brake and the two women drove home in silence.

Decker dropped in on Gus, feeling as exhilarated as if he had just returned from actual visits to Paris and his Wellfleet house. Seeing Gus gloomily bent over the work-table he called out, "I hear your wife has a wonderful voice,—the whole town's talking about it. They've waked up at last."

"Maybe," said Gus. He raised his eyes to Decker and said bleakly, "I had the doctor for her this time. It's in her chest. She had a hemorrhage this morning."

Gus put a day-bed in the front living-room downstairs so that Connie could watch people out of her window during the long days of convalescence. At night Mimi slept on the dining-room sofa so that she could wait on her mother if anything happened. Helen was frightened at first into keeping house without a murmur, and once she broke into hysterical sobs at her mother's bedside because at school they said it was tuberculosis. For Dell River the word was like leprosy, and nice people did not have it. After a few weeks the business of getting the family breakfast, even with Mimi's help, restored Helen to her normal resentment and by Junior Prom time with no one to help her make her party dress, Helen was convinced the whole thing was part of the family's determination to ruin her life. When she came into the front room to take away Connie's supper tray she always pulled down all the shades and arranged the curtains carefully so that her own privacy on the porch might be maintained. Sometimes Helen studied her mother's face shrewdly to see if she could detect any guile there, for Helen wouldn't have been surprised to learn that her entire family deliberately peeked through walls at her whenever she had a boy friend. That was the trouble with this family,—a girl had no privacy and now that all the house sofas were in practical use a girl might as well have no home at all.

Mimi felt embarrassed about Helen for the sake of her mother and Professor Decker and Miss Murrell—none of the lovely, gracious, far-off people they discussed would ever act as Helen did. But when she hinted as much to Helen she realized that however she felt over her sister was nothing to her sister's humiliation over her. It appeared that the high school crowd disapproved of Mimi.

"You might as well walk in from Bluff Corners every day carrying your lunch-basket with hay in your hair," Helen informed her in exasperation. "It's all over school every time a boy tries to kiss you, you scream——"

"I never!" Mimi was scarlet with shame.

"You did so. And they only do it then for a joke to see if you'll scream louder," Helen went on. "You don't know as much as I did when I was ten and here you are—nearly fourteen. You can imagine how I feel having everyone talk about you—calling you a sap!"

So Mimi was crushed with the knowledge that the only crime was to be a sap and in this respect Helen looked upon her family and their friends as utter criminals. When the girls would come home from school with the Marshall boy in tow Mimi would skip along beside the other two, trying to give the watching villagers the impression that they were just three school friends but most of the time neither young Marshall or Helen spoke to Mimi and at the front door Helen would say peremptorily as if, Mimi thought indignantly, she were a baby—and right before a boy, too, "Go on in and fix supper. Don doesn't want to have to talk to the whole family."

Mimi could not help thinking of the world of politeness and pretense to which her mother and Professor Decker belonged. "People ought to pretend," she thought, "Don ought to pretend he came to see the whole family even if he didn't."

Connie was no longer ill but lay quietly day and night waiting for Decker's afternoon calls, marking off the Saturdays and Sundays when he was there all afternoon. She cried softly when she was alone, thinking of how good Gus was, how kind Mrs. Busch was, how very kind everyone in the world was. She could hear the girls quarrelling over the housework but it seemed to her to arise from the fine spirits of youth and not from any ill temper.

Heretofore she had loved best the night hours, the drowsy modulation from wakefulness to sleep when she painted her own life in richer colors, but now she had all day to dream. Her body, no longer in pain but drained of all energy and purpose demanded nothing from her, so fancies flowed through her mind lightly, warmed her veins, filled her with perpetual excitement and a sense of approaching joy. The sound of Decker's quick steps on the porch was almost unbearably thrilling—ah, what things she had to tell him to-day! Little childhood impressions tenderly resurrected, new meanings read into suddenly remembered advice from Manuel, a compliment from the nuns about her flair for musical criticism. With no present and only a vague happy confidence in the future she had nothing to do but elaborate upon a re-created past until even her senses seemed not to respond to the sensations of the moment so overburdened were they with their remembered reactions. If Decker was late in arriving Connie would talk to Mimi or if possible to Mrs. Busch on these fascinating shadings in her past. One day she thought of the strange way fate justifies itself after many years.

"Supposing my grandfather had allowed me to go on with a career," she said to Mrs. Busch. "Then on the evening of my debut I had this very attack! How humiliating to have my career ruined on the very eve after perhaps months of hard preparation,—how much better never to have gotten into it at all! Because now, though I won't be able to sing at all for awhile, at least I have no manager to scold me, I don't *have* to sing!"

"Yes, and you shouldn't talk so much either," said Mrs. Busch practically. "You save your breath, let me tell you."

"But it only shows how wisely everything works out in life, Mrs. Busch, don't you see?" Connie explained eagerly.

"Yes, I know," Mrs. Busch responded briefly and returned to the kitchen to finish her washing. Now that she was giving two or three mornings a week to the Benjamins, their house reeked perpetually of steaming soapsuds, damp woolens and ammonia. Connie longed to be outdoors in the fragrant early summer air and even though the doctor summoned from the big hospital at Greentown through Miss Neville recommended the outdoors Gus knew better and was certain fresh air was death to a weak chest. So Connie lay propped up on pillows in the front room, her eyes wistfully watching the leaves thickening on the porch vine until they had made a glistening green barrier between her and the street, and the sunlight appeared merely in tiny triangular apertures through the leaves, unable to send more than a few weak rays into the sick-room.

The day after Commencement when Decker had so many gay stories to tell, including that of the renewal of his own contract, he could not bear to sit in this sad sunless room, so without consulting Gus he arranged the cot in the back-garden and helped Connie out there. After the weeks indoors the garden seemed unbelievably beautiful and her heart choked her. Gus, usually painstaking of his garden, had been paralyzed by her illness into neglect so that tulips fought for survival among the ragweeds, and hyacinths, stunted by crowding strangers, cowered together like little girls in party dresses frightened of big boys; the tall larkspur had been beaten down by the rain and the brilliant blue ruined blossoms peeped through matted clover and sourgrass. The vines had died on the summer house and it looked brightly ugly in undisguised saffron paint, its broken rail and crippled bench no longer concealed by kind Nature. But to Connie this stretch of ground, so long desired, was perfect, she dared not at first risk the ecstatic shock of lifting her face to the wide June sky and when she did the light puffs of clouds seemed as festival as a birthday cake, the very day a jewel set in celestial blue seemed a gift from someone who loved her deeply.

Propped up on cushions, her faded silk scarves tied loosely about her hair and throat she looked more beautiful than Decker had ever seen her. As he talked to her sometimes the blue transparency of her long hands adjusting their blankets made him frightened as if this illness was real, not just a pretty little accident to vary the monotony of their lives. People do get really ill—they die—but not us, not anyone like us! . . . He pulled the broken wicker chair from the summer house and placed it near her to get a view of the river though the modest little stream was obscured now by tangled bushes, all that could be seen from the garden was an ancient locust tree that dropped thick fragrant blossoms lazily into the water and with every breeze released a heavy, tantalizing perfume.

"In one way it's lucky you never went on with your career," Decker said. "Supposing this illness had come on the eve of an important concert engagement——"

"I know! Exactly what I said to Mrs. Busch," exclaimed Connie marvelling again that Decker should have her identical thoughts. "Doesn't it make you frightened to see the way Fate works out? There might even be some meaning in my being in Dell River instead of—well, say Indianapolis—or Iowa—or Flint, Michigan!"

"In my coming here, too," added Decker. "And that reminds me I'll be staying here this summer. Fuss about with my music and brush up a bit on the piano. So I shan't be able to go to the mountains or shore as I rather planned."

"Too bad," sighed Connie and then had a terrified moment trying to realize what would happen if Decker had had to leave for the summer,—or for good. What meaning would her days have then, how could one live without some interested listener to give importance to the little details of one's routine? Pain had been bearable, even exciting, because it was a new experience to be described to Decker and thus tenderly shared. Without the assurance that sensation was impossible, without a later audience in mind pain could only be a barren avenue to death.

Louisa came around the corner of the house as Decker was telling of his yearnings for a place on the Cape. She wore the blue printed foulard dress and blue glazed straw that Dell River had last summer associated with Laurie Neville, but in accepting Laurie's cast-offs Louisa had the conviction that they looked far smarter on a woman of her own type so that the town would not recognize them on her at all. "And what if they do?" inquired Miss Emmons who was indeed envious of being too large for cast-offs herself. "They know you're not so rich you can refuse clothes,—if you were you wouldn't be teaching here, would you?" This was the sort of thing that irritated Louisa beyond endurance, this bald facing of unfortunate facts. One couldn't even say—"Dear me—another grey hair!" without Miss Emmons laughing shrilly, "Well, good Lord, what do you expect at thirty-five!" From these good-natured interchanges Louisa emerged bruised and hurt, frantically eager for the soothing contact with Mrs. Benjamin and Decker. Here, of all places, no one would remember Laurie Neville's old clothes or observe the sad signals of middle-age, here in this magic circle one was known by words and Louisa's word was "poetry."

She blushed seeing Decker lounging in the chair smoking, there was always something alarmingly intimate in meeting him out of the classroom, for one thing he wore glasses in school and these spectacles were a stern barrier to human interchange; with this uniform removed they became only human, almost, Louisa thought—naked, no longer Professor and Teacher but two gentle creatures, defenseless against the world, orphaned of blackboard and spectacles. Louisa felt such a rush of protective warmth for Decker that it seemed incredible he could himself be unconscious of their bond. Certainly there was nothing but formal gallantry in his manner as he rose, clicked his heels and offered her his chair.

He sat at the foot of Connie's bed.

"I'm going to be Miss Neville's guest at their place on the Lake this summer," Louisa said the instant Decker allowed her to speak. "I was afraid I'd have to stay at The Oaks—except for my usual two weeks at my sister's in Monessen,—but now I can spend a whole week on the shore. A real vacation!"

"Splendid!" said Decker kindly, not really caring.

"Miss Manning said Laurie wanted you to go abroad with them as a sort of escort," Louisa went on with an inquiring inflection. "I can't see why you don't go, I really can't, Professor Decker."

Connie put her hand slowly over her heart, the pain that shot through her was too acute to be only mental. Afterward she wondered why the reactions to an emotion should come before her mind had even registered the fact.

Decker ground his cigarette into the earth with his heel.

"After all, dear Louisa, I'm not a tourists' guide," he said patronizingly. "I think Miss Neville understands that. Besides I'm not at all sure I care about leaving America this summer. France in summer with all the tourists—oh no, I don't think summer is the time for foreign travel."

"A dreadful time!" agreed Connie breathlessly. "I don't blame you!"

"If I went I should want to spend the winter," mused Decker.

"It was kind of Miss Neville, I thought," Louisa timidly suggested but both Connie and Decker looked blankly at her as if the kindness had been on Decker's side in merely listening to the proposition. Thinking of a year abroad Decker's face became set, he was silent, and Connie looked at the locust tree yonder, her heart beating frantically . . . Decker to be gone a year? . . . Laurie Neville arranging all this so a charming dream should become a nightmare of reality . . . Decker gone. August—September—October—without Decker. . . . She pulled the blanket up about her shoulders, cold with fear. In the silence Louisa Murrell pulled a little book out of her bag.

"This is the one you asked me to read again,—the Blake one—" she moistened her lips,—"the one about the Garden of Love.

> " 'I laid me down upon a bank
> Where love lay sleeping.
> I heard among the bushes dank
> Weeping, weeping.' "

Decker's eyes left the snowcapped Jungfrau he was seeing beyond the river and met Connie's as the gaze of two drowning people might meet above the waves,—farewell to me, the eyes said, oh farewell. . . . Louisa coughed and went on—

> " 'Then I went down to the heath and the wild
> To the thistles and thorns of the waste——' "

Why had Laurie Neville, Connie wondered passionately, made Decker that offer, why unless she wanted him? She was free and wealthy. She could marry him. She could support him forever in Paris where he would be happy. A spasm of hate for Gus came over Connie, it was Gus' fault, standing like a stone wall, like her grandfather's stone wall ready to crush anything beautiful. . . . She closed her eyes, tired out from the unaccustomed feeling, but when she opened them again Decker was looking at her and he seemed suddenly very little and shabby and forlorn, a stray begging to be released from its chain for pity's sake. . . .

"I'd better go in," she whispered faintly. "You and Louisa can stay here——"

"We wouldn't dream of it," said Decker quickly. He took her arm but their flesh shrank curiously from each other's, rejected the contact as yellow and white flesh rebel against each other.

Connie thought dizzily, "I must find Tony, I must try some other way to find Tony."

Drowning, drowning . . .

"I'll leave the book for you," Louisa suggested after she had fixed the living-room couch once more for Connie. "You always loved that one so much. I think it should be set to music, don't you, Professor Decker?"

"Yes," said Decker. He was afraid to stay in the room now and looked slyly beyond Louisa as if he expected doors to lock themselves and forbid flight. He did not want to look at Connie but it could not be helped. How shockingly naked her arm looked curved under her head! Some women could wear a dozen wrappings and still their eyes would be undressed, he thought, fighting this sensation of chains tightening, the trap closing in on him, definitely, ominously. He fought the veiled word in his mind, beat it back into the darkness as a monster foe who must not kill that precious toy, the magic world of Decker, the genius and Madame Benjamin, artiste. . . . The word shone almost slyly in Mrs. Benjamin's brown eyes, it lay in the curve of her arm, it hovered in polite ambush in Louisa's puzzled frown as she looked from Decker to the sick woman. Like a masked beggar in an opera it crouched in shadows ready at the final curtain to drop mask and rags and stand revealed in shattering splendor.

"I'll walk to The Oaks with you, Louisa," he said. "We may be tiring her, and she mustn't get tired, the doctor said."

Both Connie and Decker smiled gratefully at Louisa as if her pale presence had for once fully justified her. Connie patted the little books on the table.

"It's so good to have this. When one can't keep at one's singing, poetry is a real refuge."

"You'll be well enough for the Chautauqua concerts," Louisa encouraged her. "We can go together, unless of course it comes while I'm at the lake. Those summer concerts are sometimes excellent."

Professor Decker smiled and was able to meet Connie's glance with an amused smile.

"Of course they are," said Connie kindly. "Especially when you have so little chance at real music."

"So many Dell River people have never heard anything else," Louisa apologized hastily. "Naturally to a professional musician they wouldn't seem very good. I only thought——"

"Oh Mrs. Benjamin and I are both enormously grateful for even an echo of 'Il Trovatore,'" said Decker benignly. "Beggars can't choose, you know. And sometimes a real talent turns up in just such places."

"A Tyler Stewart," said Louisa. "That type."

Connie flushed and Decker frowned. Louisa, ready now to dawdle over her departure since they seemed to be getting into a discussion of their favorite sort, was surprised to find Decker holding the screen open for her. Connie said goodbye weakly and turned her face to the wall. The wheels of her brain were too tired to deal with the immense word, she could only follow carefully with her eyes the formal pattern of the wallpaper, stiff rows of brown bell-shaped blossoms twined in faded yellow leaves. The failing sunlight filtered through the window vines, the back garden was still there with the trampled larkspur, Connie mused, and the locust tree, but Louisa and Decker were on the outside with real gardens while she must lie here indoors afraid to think. She must not think of Laurie Neville or of what life would be without Decker . . . she mustn't think of what might happen—impossibly enough—if this weakness of hers grew worse instead of better, if for her summer would be only the distant croaking of the bull frogs, the fluttering of humming birds in the porch vines, if for her gardens would be a conventionalized lotus on wall-paper.

"If I only were allowed to sing a little," she thought fretfully, "then nothing would matter."

For ten years Commencement Day had been for Decker an empty day of blank sky and pointless sunshine, a gay mask for a great Nothing; a day of echoing auditoriums, bleating of young voices, a screen of noise through which his despairing ear detected the dreary monotone of another year exactly like the last. A day of unexpectedly fond farewells to other teachers and young men as one realized that hollow as these relations had been, they were at least warmer than those impending. Decker found himself clinging to Louisa's hand in the little station by the Nursery greenhouses, as if the few weeks she was to be gone were as important to him as they were to her.

"I'll visit my sister's family for two weeks and then go to Miss Neville's cottage," Louisa explained in a high excited voice. "It won't be anything thrilling of course, nothing more than staying in Dell River——"

"But it's the going away," Decker interrupted wistfully. "It's the change. And besides there won't be anyone left in the Village."

"Except Mrs. Benjamin," said Louisa. "It's really a good thing you're being here with her sick. It will be so nice for her. You can talk over so many things in three months."

Decker saw the summer months approaching as three gay dancers, hands clasped, closing in on him, drawing him tighter towards Connie until there would be no space between them, no escape; fantastically the dancers grew larger, their flying draperies swelled to huge dark clouds enormous, suffocating, no spoken sonnet could break this dreadful magic nor the resolute fortissimo of a favorite Prelude. Louisa was moved by his weary, pale face, and looked hard at a truck laden with brilliant flowers emptying its frivolous burden into the dingy maw of a freight-car, she winked away tears thinking that this rare, delightful man was actually sorry for her departure. She gripped his hand passionately and then as abruptly dropped it. She would do anything in the world for him, she thought, anything—anything. If he were sick, he did look so frail, she would take care of him, she would feed him delicate broths made by her own hands,—she was a wretched cook in reality, nevertheless for him she would excel, she would hold his sad charming head against her frail breast, she would write great tomes which would be sold to motion picture companies for millions and with this she would surround him with the grandeur he missed, she would scrub, unless perhaps something really needed scrubbing, a hopeless business, then, as a matter of fact. . . . She wanted nothing from him, nothing, she thought, but to suffer hardships for him, to have her whole body tired with work for him, and when she was so spent with sacrifices for him that she could only smile a frozen blessing on him from her coffin then he would notice her and say, "Dear little Louisa! No one was ever so good to me. No one!"

Then this bold fancy alarmed her, she fumbled in her purse for tickets fearing that these flying images were imprinted shamelessly on her face for Decker to read. Decker's thoughts however were so far away from her that he started when the distant whistle of an engine brought him back to the slight little creature at his side.

"A few weeks with your family, eh," he repeated her words. "A few weeks of being spoiled, of course, but it will do you good. You should have a little pampering."

"Thank you," said Louisa with a hysterical impulse to laugh wildly. Pampering? In the brief interval of watching the far-off smoke materialize into approaching engine she pictured the weeks of "pampering" which in all the years of vacations with her family had varied so little. The small house which her arrival threw uncomfortably out of joint, the dingy, busy little town with its perpetual soot cloud from the factories, the house smelling of sour milk and baby clothes, the endless whimpering of the latest baby as obbligato to the staccato arguments of Eleanor and Dale, their affectionate bossing of old Mr. Murrell who only asked to be left quietly alone . . . Louisa already prepared the defensive smile with which she would answer Dale's genial "Well, back again, Louisa! And not married yet, I'll be bound! Well, never mind, while there's life there's hope, ha ha, as the old man says!" Each year,—seven on this very platform—she had tried to strengthen herself before she got on the train so that her return to her family would be triumphal rather than the sad homecoming of the defeated, but the complacency of her sister's family always disarmed her. No use pointing out to Eleanor or Dale the advantages of her single career, they, even in their quarrels and economies, were certain of their own enviable position, their smiling pity made her discontented, their proud flaunting of connubial intimacies made an old maid of her. Pampering . . . Two months of squeezing out of her the last vestige of vanity, affectionately demonstrating how pitiful were her personal charms, how inadequate her gifts, how much they loved her for being so sweetly inferior to them, until on her departure she wept to

think of leaving this tender patronage for a world more aus-
terely just to such defections as hers.

"This year at least I can hold on to the idea of visiting
Laurie Neville," she consoled herself. "I never had any place
to go before except other relatives', the convention, or summer school. And they can't do much to me in four weeks,
they're rather sure to be impressed with such a grand invitation. Dale is stupid but he knows a place like Belmeer Lake is
pretty swell. That will keep him down . . . No, this year it
will be better, the way it was that first year after the war when
I was the only one in the family who'd been over . . . They
thought I was wonderful then. I almost was, too—with all of
them believing it . . ."

"I wish," said Decker picking up her bags so masterfully
that Louisa was sorry the other teachers weren't there to see,
"that I could join my own family this year but once in three
years is all I've ever done. . . . It's impossible, anyway, to do
one's work with a family fussing over one."

"I'm sure yours spoils you," said Louisa.

Decker raised his shoulders modestly.

"An older son always is over-rated . . . I realize that, but
how could I tell my mother I'm not the genius she thinks I
am?"

Louisa wanted to say, "Oh, but you are a genius, you are,
no matter what you actually do, you're a great man!" but
there was no time. She found her seat in the train and when
she wanted to say some special word to him, something that
would spread out delicately in his memory after she left recalling her to him as a definite fragrance might, she saw such
a cool, politely remote smile on his face that her own warmth
was checked; she had the startled conviction that no matter
how deftly she built farewell words into a bridge across their
separation it would signify not the slightest thing to him, she
might as well just say "Good-bye" and forget him as easily as
she herself would be forgotten. This fear chilled her but as the
train slid out the old tenderness returned. She rubbed a clean
triangle on the window-pane and watched his slight but, she
felt, arresting figure swagger across the station tracks, his
thick walking stick synchronizing so neatly with his stride that
to Louisa at least here was masculine power at its finest.

Straining her eyes she watched him as he swung across the station green and turned buoyantly at the corner in the direction of Mrs. Benjamin's cottage.

Laurie brought her doctor to see Mrs. Benjamin after Gus had told Miss Manning in the shop of the danger.

"Of course I'll see him," Connie had said when Miss Neville hesitatingly proposed her specialist from the city hospital. Miss Neville had been afraid Connie might consider it an officious suggestion but Connie assumed she was doing Miss Neville a favor in accepting. She had reached the stage where perpetual languor would be hard to surrender, what would she do with a return of vitality? In health she had little excuse for slurring her household duties, for being an indifferent mother and wife. There was relief in being absolved from domestic responsibilities, a forlorn joy in being set apart even by misfortune.

Laurie Neville had seldom called on her before but now the little grey roadster often stopped before the Benjamin house and Laurie, usually accompanied by Miss Manning, sat in the tumbled garden with a gracious but wan hostess. Laurie talked of operas, of concerts she had heard last year in Pittsburgh or New York, of this or that new conductor just over from Holland, of a Viennese singer who had dazzled New York, and Connie would nod, smiling, as if all these matters were old news to her so close was she to the real center of music that she needed to be told nothing, the progress of music was not to be marked by newspapers but by her specially appointed sensory system. When Laurie left musical weeklies or magazine clippings with her Connie barely glanced at them, these guides were for the outsider and uninitiated, there was nothing she needed to be told. Moreover, the world these journals described was at no point tangent to the Decker and Benjamin world, it was a world of trade talk, catalogues of definite names and works and this was not the music that sang for Connie and Decker. Connie felt gently superior to such outsiders and believed that Laurie called on her in a deferential spirit.

The day the city doctor came it rained and Connie waited in the living-room, dressed but exhausted with the fever which seemed never to leave her. To her surprise Gus closed the shop in order to be home when the visitors came and he sat by the door gloomily looking from Connie to the street. He was only a few years older than she but in the last year he had shrunk into a bent hunched little old man, bright blue eyes glaring morosely under shaggy graying brows. He would look like this for the next thirty years, perhaps, bending over more ever so slightly each year arriving at seventy a grizzled Wagnerian dwarf.

"But I'm getting better, Gus," Connie protested. "There's no use your staying here. All he will do is give me a tonic or diet and there's no need your being here for that."

"I don't know," said Gus. "He might say you had to go away."

"Go away?" exclaimed Connie. "But why should I? I couldn't get any more rest than I get here. The girls and Mrs. Busch do everything for me . . . Why should he send me away?"

Gus pulled at his pipe silently and watched the street. It was raining lightly and steadily, the vine leaves glistened and fluttered in the fresh eastern wind, a wet robin perched on the porch rail shaking his feathers luxuriously, two little girls ran squealing past, their light frocks drenched. The smell of wet nasturtium leaves came to Connie's nostrils and she wished at once for Decker who would catch this bitter fragrance at the moment she did and one of them would say, "Nasturtium is really the flower for rainstorms,—better than violet, I think," and then the other would very likely say, "More earthy."

She was growing more and more weary of the hours when he could not be there. Since her life centered so completely around him it was ridiculous that they should have so little time together. Two or three hours a day,—it was nothing when the other twenty-one were spent vacantly wishing for the meeting or fondly spreading out past discussions in mind as line drawings to be colored at leisure with one's own crayons. It had been many months since her conversations with Gus had concerned anything but his tenant, though it was hard to draw anything but monosyllabic answers from him. Had he heard Decker's piano lately? was it a concert piece or something for the school chorus? or did it sound hesitating and broken as if he might be composing it himself?

Gus would shrug his shoulders. He had heard the piano—wasn't that answer enough? And had he heard voices upstairs, had Miss Neville called, if she had did she bring flowers or papers resembling new music as she used sometimes to do? Connie was impatient with Gus for paying so little heed to the details of Decker's life, though she knew in a few hours Decker himself would tell her all these things, decorating each point as if it were an after-dinner story. It delighted her, however, to be able to surprise him as he entered her house with, "Ah, so you did go riding with the Marshalls after all! You see how scandal spreads!"

Decker would smile, surprised and flattered that his busy social life should be the talk of the town. One day Mimi reported the great news that he had been seen in Mills' music store purchasing one of the new portable gramophones and Connie was able to gayly accuse him of this shocking extravagance when he called that same afternoon.

"But how did you know?" he demanded, his face clouding. "I told Mills not to tell you. It was to be a surprise for you."

"For me?" Connie raised herself on her elbow to stare at him. "You got it for me—oh, my dear Blaine!"

"I thought we could take it to my place when you got better," he explained, "but keep it here the rest of the time."

The gift was so important to her, so close to her heart that she could not thank him at first. Later when Gus brought her a record—a gay Bavarian dance tune played on an accordion, the instrument Gus had once tried to learn, the dark thought struck Connie that she must be going to die to meet with such a conspiracy of kindness. It was not like Decker to do more than wish for such luxuries as this, and she could not recall ever receiving a gift from Gus beyond a great clock for the house on one birthday and at Christmas an occasional new petticoat or woolen kimono, never anything to indicate a knowledge of her real tastes.

"I must have some disease they won't tell me about," she thought, frightened of death already, a long, black wait for Decker it seemed to her, shuddering. It was not the picture of herself, silent, shut in the earth that made her cry aloud with fright, but the thought of how many times Decker's footsteps would pass her and she would not know, how many things he would have to tell her and she would not hear. The quick familiar rap-rap on the loose screen door on summer nights, the cigarette smoke curling in the air after he left, that gentle modulation from presence to absence; the perpetual feeling of suspense, waiting for him to call, and now that he was here waiting for tomorrow's visit. Connie wept for the death, not of herself, but of all these things . . . She saw Gus' staying home for the doctor a further dark proof, and scarcely dared ask for Mimi and Helen lest it prove they too were staying home from their planned picnic. She watched Gus' silent, inexpressive face and was heartened to see no sign of worry there in spite of the evidence of his actions, she heard the girls at last moving furniture about upstairs and thought, "Of course they didn't have the picnic because it was raining." And if this were so serious wouldn't Decker have been here instead of playing chess with the German barber? Of course, Decker would not fail her, for one afternoon if she were in danger, and at once his defection to-day which had disappointed her so much, seemed the most delightful gay gesture he had ever made. He was not here—therefore her fear was preposterous.

"You say Professor Decker was in the barber shop when you came?" Connie asked Gus to make sure and when Gus nodded she exclaimed, "I'm so glad he couldn't come."

Gus removed his pipe.

"Well I should think so," he said with a depth of honest feeling. "You've been too nice to that young man, Connie. Just because he rents our place is no sign you got to keep him from getting homesick. I should think you would get tired hearing him talk."

"I didn't mean that," Connie laughed a little.

"What then?" Gus inquired, vaguely angry with her as he was with his daughters and women in general for having secret laughter. Seeing that Connie had no answer but lay there smiling at the window he resumed his pipe and the gloomy wait for sight of the Neville car. Her fright had vanished and now she thought it would not be long before she was completely herself. She traced with her forefinger the pattern of lotus on the wall, then turned, still smiling, to watch the rain trembling on the window-pane.

When Laurie finally appeared with the doctor Gus stood awkwardly in the doorway of the living-room looking so morose that Connie was embarrassed.

"My husband is a coward about doctors," she explained to the visitors. "He thinks they're as final as undertakers, so please tell him I'm getting better. Anyone else could see it."

The doctor was a heavy-jowled dark man with tangled greying eyebrows, his rimless spectacles seemed designed to protect the world from his steely relentless black eyes. It was incredible that women should fancy a caress might stir momentary tenderness in these eyes, yet some believed in the miracle. Laurie Neville stood beside Gus trying to talk to him but her glances kept straying hungrily toward the doctor.

There seemed nothing extraordinary to Connie in Miss Neville's interest in her health. After all were they not the two leading figures in Dell River cultural life and though their previous contacts had been only pleasantly accidental, Connie would have said they understood each other. The visits from Miss Neville's doctor seemed more of a social call than a professional one. She was annoyed at Gus' silent refusal to offer them any of his wine, to make any hospitable gesture.

"You know this attack has been so inconvenient for me, Doctor," she said brightly. "I had planned to do a great deal of work this summer."

"Out of the question," said Doctor Arnold brusquely. "Let someone else take care of the house."

"I meant my singing," Connie explained gently. "I've been rather lax with my practicing,—there's so little to encourage me in the Village as you can see. . . . But I really intended working at it this summer. You know, Doctor, I was started on a musical career years ago but—well, things happened to stop me." She shrugged sadly. "Perhaps I wouldn't have been strong enough to stand that life."

"Probably not," answered the doctor absently. He ignored Laurie's beseeching look and studied Connie thoughtfully.

"I sang before Morini. He said—'The throat of an artist'," Connie went on. "I had no one to help me so—— Even now I live only for my music. I suppose I might take it up professionally once again if it comes to that."

"Doctor, she ought not to talk so much," Gus broke in roughly. "I've told her."

"That's true," said the doctor. "All unnecessary exertion is bad."

Connie flushed deeply. She saw so few strangers she wanted to make an event of this occasion but Gus' rudeness had spoiled it. She saw the doctor preparing to go and tried frantically to think of ways to detain him. It was such a relief to find someone so interested in her work,—at least that was the way she construed his absorbed attention. Gus must understand that a woman with a career is not a mere wife, but an artist first and foremost. She felt her eyelids burning and futile excitement mounting in her as it did every afternoon as if something unbearably delightful was about to happen. The succeeding letdown each day was increasingly hard to endure, and by her bedtime she was trembling with exhaustion. Gloomy dreams would assemble vaguely in her mind, dreams of pain or sorrow which made her sob and moan in her sleep. She saw no reason to speak of this state of mind to Doctor Arnold but his hard black eyes seemed to read it all from her tired face.

The doctor and Gus went into the dining-room out of hearing. Connie was quiet, trying to collect her energy for a last plea for him to stay, just to take the visit from its almost brutally professional tone. She smiled at Laurie Neville who had drawn a chair to the side of her bed but was looking past her toward the two men with intent interest. Connie thought with surprise that Miss Neville was an exceedingly handsome woman, so striking with her vivid eyes and coloring as to seem almost exotic. She gripped Connie's arm suddenly and nodded toward the dining-room.

"Isn't he marvellous, Mrs. Benjamin?" she whispered. "When I watch him talking to a patient, measuring him with those eyes, my heart almost stops. Actually I feel myself melting away. I think—'How strong he is, how completely sane—how sure!' I could die of admiration. Sometimes when I go to him with all sorts of things wrong with me he tells me—just by a glance at me—exactly what's the matter. Then of course he thinks as Manning does that I'm hysterical, but it isn't that. Really it isn't that. Is it hysterical to worship strength, do you think, Mrs. Benjamin?"

Connie was surprised by the unexpected rush of confidence and by Miss Neville's strangely intense manner.

"Have you known him so long?" was all she could think to ask.

"Seven years."

Laurie watched his big broad back as she whispered and occasionally she would glance out toward the rainy street as if she expected Miss Manning to appear and march her off as if she were a child staying too long at the birthday party.

"I went to him first for my father's last illness. Then I was often sick but he is so busy now that I can't get him to come over to Dell River except for other people's illnesses. Never to my house for dinner—not even when I ask his wife, too."

She rose abruptly and went to the porch door, her nervous fingers beating upon the screen. The low voices of the men in the other room dropped a word or phrase clean-cut on the air and Connie tried to piece them together as fragments of a picture puzzle. "Mountains"—"recurrent attacks"—"expenses"—. . . The words were as puzzling as Laurie's curious actions and her fears of earlier in the day had worn her out so much that she was now too tired to worry. Her eyelids fluttered dryly over her hot eyeballs, she only wanted things to be clear and simple, these furtive whispers and shadowy corners defeated her.

"Doesn't he make you feel strong—just his being here?" Laurie demanded huskily. She returned to the chair beside the bed and leaned over it. "Sometimes Manning makes me feel the same way—but not much any more. Have you ever thought how few people there are who can make you feel completely unafraid? They terrify me—alone or in crowds. Their eyes say—'Who are you—what is your excuse?' I have no excuse for existing. Nothing. If I want to be kind their eyes accuse me again. 'So you want to bribe us into liking you, make us admit you have some excuse.' . . . Before I was sick I used to travel alone, dine alone in restaurants, talk to no one on shipboard. At my table would often be some famous person I would give my soul to talk to. But I was afraid. Their eyes made me afraid. . . . 'Who are you? What is your game?' . . . Just as now you're looking at me—why have I brought Doctor Arnold here? Yes, you are wondering."

"I never thought of such a thing," Connie answered in astonishment. "It was very good of you. Gus and I know so little about doctors. We wouldn't have known what to do without you."

Laurie colored.

"You needn't be polite. I know the whole town talks about it. They knew as soon as Doctor Arnold came to town that summer seven years ago. It was all my fault—I knew I was acting like a fool. I knew they said I ran after him—they still say it, you needn't bother to smooth things over. Well, what of it? I never was brazen about anything in my life before,—but you have to be about the things you want. Can't expect people to just hand them over. And this mattered too much to me. I'd have run all over the world crying for him. Wouldn't care who saw."

"I didn't know about it," Connie said weakly. She didn't want to hear more. It hurt her to see naked feelings. She recoiled from them as she would from an indecent picture, frightened, a little sick, as a too civilized tourist might look on a primitive dance.

"But he won't let me now," Laurie whispered fiercely. "And so far as that goes there's nothing between us now. Do you know what he says? That I'm the type who runs after orchestra leaders, gets crushes on the riding-teacher or the captain of the steamer—that that's all I feel for him. . . . All right. Does it make it less real—less painful?"

She turned to the window as Gus and the doctor came back in the room. The doctor did not look at her but picked up his hat quickly and took Connie's hand.

"You'll be getting along," he said. "A few things to be settled first—that's all—whether Dell River's the place for you——"

Go some place without Decker?

"I couldn't leave Dell River," said Connie and shook her head decisively.

"I see," answered the doctor amiably. "Well, Laurie?"

"Tell her she's got to be careful, tell her she mustn't talk or sing," Gus begged the doctor.

"I'll be very good," Connie answered them both. She was no longer annoyed at Gus treating her like a child. It was dear old Gus who was the child. She and the doctor understood. Gus and Laurie were the children. She watched the two callers scurry out to the car, their outlines blurred in the slanting rain. Gus sat on the chair, gloomily watching her, trying to find proof in her face somehow of the doctor's diagnosis.

"If you should have to go away——"

"We haven't the money, Gus. Even if I would consent to go. Where does he suggest? The South? Doctors are always suggesting the South."

"No," said Gus heavily. "A sanitarium in the Southwest, he says."

Connie frowned.

"Oh, no," she said. "They can't take me there. Oh, no."

Then her momentary fear vanished again in the consoling reflection that here was something amusing to tell Decker when he came. "Great specialists must have their great names for the simplest diseases. Even laziness has a name and a most imposing treatment." She wondered how soon he would come. She wanted to talk to someone civilized to break the troublesome memory of Laurie's shocking bluntness and the Doctor's brutal eyes. The raindrops on the window trembled, swelled into eyes, dripped tears, and were whipped off by other raindrops that in turn, swelled into eyes. Doctor Arnold's.

Connie shivered.

Laurie, driving the doctor to the Benjamin home on his weekly Dell River visit, was hard-eyed and defiant.

"Let them talk," she said to Miss Manning. "It can't make them like me less. If gossip makes them think about me, so much the better. At least they know I exist."

But Dell River knew little and cared less about Laurie's connection with the doctor. He was one of those smooth-acting city men often seen about the old Neville home in summer, people Laurie picked up probably on her travels and occasionally introduced at some Dell River gathering to make the natives feel uncomfortably crude. In their indifferent politeness Laurie thought she read suspicion, even certainty. They saw, perhaps, that when she first fastened her violent adoration on this man she did not dream of a wife back in Baltimore, and they laughed, perhaps, at such naïveté in the Neville girl for all her fancy education. They suspected,—oh, Laurie was sure they did!—her hysterical insistence on an affair, they probably saw how angrily he tried to retreat and finally the furtive desperate moments in his office, on lonely roads between Dell River and his hospital. They knew of his final breaking off with her because of his perfectly stupid complacent little wife and they must have said, "See how little money and French schools can get a woman, even a handsome one, in our little closed respectable community. Her money could help a doctor's career but instead he chooses a dumb little plain wife— not through love but through pure respectability." . . . They must see now how eagerly she pounced upon any professional excuse to see him again, how wretched it made her to know he was still attracted by her but was stronger than steel against her. She sensed—and so the town must, too—she thought— how quickly some appeal from her could change him into ice and she knew—if she could adopt this controlled ease herself he might come back to her. Yet this knowledge never helped her to control her hysteria, she saw herself at each meeting ruining each shred of hope by eagerness. Now that Mrs. Benjamin's illness was an excuse to bring him often to Dell River she was constantly in a state of tension, and Miss Manning's power to still her nerves was diminished. The little routine of her days since her parents' death several years before,—the little duties invented to make believe life was not so futile as it seemed were rushed through carelessly as the silly time-markers they were. Letters to girls she'd gone to school with——

"MY DEAR ELIZABETH—
    I have not heard from you for months but Bella writes your trip to India was a heavenly experience. I wish you would write me about it—Manny and I might go over next year. . . ."

"MY DEAR ELEANOR—
    So sorry not to get to the Foxdale luncheon when I was East and see all the girls but I was shopping and——"

It wasn't that these old school-friends, now busy matrons and not as anxious to correspond as Laurie was, were so dear

to her—indeed she'd almost forgotten how they looked,—
but letters were all she had to look forward to from day to
day. They came on the morning breakfast tray, were slowly
read and discussed with Manny and then put away to be taken
out after dinner as they sat before the fire with their coffee
and cigarettes and so little to talk about! . . . Now such answers as came were wasted for Laurie paced up and down the
rooms, flushed and nervous, ready to scream if Manny even
attempted to distract her.

"It's no use, Manny," she exclaimed. "When a person has
just one thing to think about she's got to think until her brain
wears out, that's all."

The only thing that helped Manny's final surrender to the
one subject was her theories as to how all this misery could
have been avoided.

"The advantages my parents gave me—that's at the bottom
of everything!" Laurie said savagely. "Bringing me up to be
different from the people I was to live with—so that they hate
me——"

"They don't!"

"—and despise me and I'm afraid of them. So I'm afraid of
everyone. Only with him I feel strong. Sometimes with you—
but always with him——"

But no one in Dell River knew the things Laurie thought
they suspected. They didn't care. Even Connie Benjamin finally decided that the reason Laurie had interested herself in
her illness was someway related to Blaine Decker,—perhaps
Laurie was in love with him, and therefore concerned about
his friends.

A dreadful summer, Decker thought, each day to be balanced
on the nose cautiously to keep from spilling its incipient
disasters in all directions. In the thick sultriness of Middlewestern August it took god-like energy to preserve the pleasant insanity necessary to happiness. No breeze stirred the blue
curtains of his apartment by night and by day the sun beat
down with savage diligence. Decker would be in bed feeling
the night's humidity modulate in the dry morning heat and
he would think, "Today I must work,—practice the Sonata,

plan a new course for—say a history of music or a study of instruments,—talk it over with Marshall—send for books. At
least if I must teach I might show how much better I can do
it than the average school teacher. I could do that."

But the plan for a new course usually ended in being discussed—as a cast-off idea—with Connie later in the day. A
brilliant plan and—"So like you," Connie admiringly observed, "giving yourself away completely to students who
don't half appreciate what you've given up for them." The fact
that these plans went no further did not detract from Decker's
courage in Connie's eyes but these unfinished ideas, discarded
the day they appeared, worried Decker as a sign of approaching age and resignation. When he finally got out of bed in the
morning he pattered about the place in frayed dressing-gown
and slippers for hours making coffee and toast, tidying up,
making tasks to delay the actual work of the day. He sat at the
desk giving up all idea of a cool breeze at either window, and
with different colored inks played at his old game of arranging
concert programs. No Debussy if there was Brahms, was his
theory of programs, and no little group of French moderns if
he began with Bach. Years ago he had played this game according to rules,—no number he couldn't play well, but now
he was lazy, listing pieces he had only heard about in newspapers. When he sat down to the piano it was usually to play
the opening bars of some old favorite then to stop dead as his
memory collapsed, too upset by this failure to look up the
piece in his cabinet. His fingers were stiff, they moved wood-
enly about the keys, strangers to music, and Decker after the
first bungled chords, was too angry to practice. The only consolations were the little songs such as Miss Manning sang, and
he would dwell tenderly on these simple accompaniments and
sometimes take the books over to Connie's to play in the afternoon. "This was probably one of your favorites," he would
say and play a little bergerette. Connie, who might never have
known of the song's existence till that moment, would smile
sentimentally and murmur, "I'm not sure I could do it now. It
suited my voice once but now——"

"Too light for operatic shadings," Decker would say understandingly. "You're quite right. But it is charming—let me
play it for you again."

As Connie grew better they sometimes went on leisurely walks across the river into the fields and sometimes Mimi would follow them later with a picnic basket. They sat in the clearing in the woods where Connie had once sung to the May morning, and they talked of music until the careers they once planned were the careers they actually had had but had given up for the superior joys of simple living. Mimi sat, cross-legged, on the grass, eating sandwiches, her round eyes moving respectfully from Decker to her mother, and as Decker's voice grew more and more British and her mother's more silvery in their mutual appreciations Mimi would blush, thinking of Helen's mockery of these very affectations. When her mother would sigh, "At least it's something to know one could have had fame—we should be grateful for that, for so many people never have even that assurance"—Mimi would try not to remember Helen's caustic remarks, "Listen, nobody has to give up anything unless they really want to or are too darned weak. If Mama really could have done anything she would have—if anybody wants something all she needs do is go and get it. There aren't any excuses."

Decker ignored Mimi and Helen though he managed a smile of fixed politeness when they interrupted his discussions or when their mother called upon them to perform some errand. He disliked young girls just as he did household pets, they were always upsetting things or brushing against you, ruining a well-turned phrase with some unfortunate interruption. In school he saw them without prejudice in groups but too often one of these girls would stop at his desk to ask questions. If they concerned music or were inquiries into future professional work Decker forgot they were silly little girls and expounded on foreign and domestic teachers, on the Thorners and Witherspoons and on teachers long dead or settled definitely in Berlin; he loved explaining the differences in their various methods, this one had a tendency to overstrain the upper register, this one pushed the student too fast into public engagements,—he went over all the musical patter of his first student years, enriched it with anecdotes about a certain director in Milan, an impresario in Munich, and allowed a hint to enter here and there of his own former advantageous connections. Meantime the girl, who had only wanted to

study with some good cheap teacher in Pittsburgh or Columbus so that she might some day teach privately in Dell River
or sing solos in the church, would squirm uneasily and grow
so appalled at the magnificent picture Decker was evoking
that she could only murmur a faint, "Oh, thank you—thank
you"—and scurry away, thoroughly disheartened.

Boys were not so bad for they were, underneath their rudeness, sensitive and mentally alert, so the music teacher felt,
whereas girls were callous and futile, designed only to weaken
the male. Decker thought very little about his students indi-
vidually unless as happened sometimes one betrayed an unusual intelligence about music. He had overcome to some
degree his early terror of sheer youth, though he still could
not face the main auditorium on a crowded Friday morning
without a shudder of pure distaste for such uncontrolled energy as was here massed, the air always seemed charged with
the dangerous electricity of youth, any moment a volt might
strike you. But he enjoyed the effects of their mingled voices
and in so far as these young people represented instruments
of sound he almost loved them.

The Benjamin girls were tolerable only because of their
mother and once in a while he studied them with detached
curiosity to find points of resemblance. Mimi's eyes for instance—and Helen's profile. . . . There were times when he
was distinctly annoyed at their mother's fugitive bursts of interest in them, but this was not jealousy so much as surprise
that so intelligent a woman as Constance could find any fascination in the hopeless gropings of youth. Unless they were
actively jumping about or noisy, they did not bother him, but
the occasional proofs of their existence—a squeal from Mimi
over a nest of field-mice or a snake if they were outdoors—
made him impatient. Connie, even in their finest discussions,
did not mind having the children about since she had learned
long ago to shut her ears to whatever might not harmonize
with her private thoughts.

In many ways Connie's illness had been an advantage to
both of them for she was reading more. Laurie Neville had ordered different musical monthlies sent to her and now both
Connie and Decker pored over them from cover to cover,
discussed even the advertising and constantly exclaimed over

some concert they would love to hear or some modern song they would most certainly—if Connie's health had only been better—have tried out. Before her sickness they had felt that they knew by instinct everything to be known about music and everything that was going on. If at Laurie Neville's someone had mentioned a new artist's sensational debut in the East, Decker would have said patronizingly, "Oh yes, of course—but he's very likely just a flash in the pan—" for to betray curiosity would be a confession of his isolation from the cosmopolitan world, as he always assumed both to himself and others that he caught all these little rumors and many artists' secrets in the ordinary course of his professional life. He was by no means, he tacitly assured them, cut off from the centers of culture just because he taught in Dell River. Ah no, indeed.

As for Connie she had ruled her life on the same principle of being instinctively in touch with music without being forced to study any current chronicles. Now that sickness excused her from any pretense of practising she began to talk to Decker of private recitals she might have given—now alas, impossible!—in Dell River and eagerly Decker mapped out programs she should have given. Miss Neville would gladly have given her an afternoon at her home; he, of course, would have accompanied her, playing an opening number himself,— say the Waldstein Sonata. He had not played it for years but if Fate had not so cruelly intervened once more, he would certainly have played it at her recital. They began to look at other singers' programs listed in Musical America and they would smile sadly at each other as if—"The very things we would have done! The very same things!" It really seemed that these plans for a series of recitals not only in Dell River but in Greentown and surrounding towns, had been on the very verge of completion when the illness had ruined all.

"It almost seems," mused Connie, "as if there were some definite god working against us——"

"It does indeed," agreed Decker in a low grave voice and both were silent and humble over the gifts which had so excited the fear and envy of the gods.

"It must mean we would never have been happy if we'd won out," pursued Connie.

"Exactly," said Decker solemnly. "Success would have destroyed us."

As school days once more approached Decker grew irritable and confused as a banker might who has lost, through his own carelessness, a fortune and with only himself to blame must hurl recriminations at the whole world. In such a way the summer was lost, he had not practiced, he had not planned new courses, he had not taken soul-refreshing weekends at the lake, he had not read, but drowsing through the hot days he had used over and over the same old thoughts; he had, for Mrs. Benjamin, turned his mind inside out and upside down, evoked and embellished memories of his past until they were thin with repetition, he had examined each microscopic detail of his past, selecting bits for Connie's afternoon as the Papa Robin might choose bits for his nest. The days, pointed toward those afternoon hours together, had seemed to some purpose but with the school year close before him and time laid out in terms of accomplishment, these vacation months seemed to have been waste, sheer waste.

Decker liked to think of himself as someone, unlike the provincials with whom his life was cast, who was constantly at the spring of things, living a rich, full sort of life. But September always loomed bluntly before him saying, "Well, here you are, at the same place you were last year, sentenced for another year."

Through the bars of September he saw the monotony of another year, the definite death of the improbable hopes always lurking in his mind. Despairingly he saw the great drastic moves he should have made in June to free himself. How wastefully he had allowed the days to slip past, raising no hand to stop the certain prison they were building for him! He might have written to New York bureaus,—of course concerts were out of the question for him now but at least he would be in touch with the main offices and be able to say to Marshall or anyone else, "I've just had a letter from Hartzell and Jones,—they manage most of the big artists, you know." . . . It wouldn't matter what they said, the point would be that something might be stirring, something might happen to leave a gate open in that September prison.

Louisa Murrell, even, seemed to have had a most amazingly rich summer, merely because she'd spent a week or two at the Neville shore cottage with a room of her own and candles on the table at dinner. She fluttered in and out of The Oaks with such an important air that the rumor got abroad she was engaged to be married. And Marshall! His ten-day trip around the national capital had given him the assurance that a season or two in Legislature might have given better men. He came back with a greater sense of the dignity of his own position, and one of his first deeds on arriving in Dell River was to send for Decker to discuss improvements in his department.

They sat in the glass-enclosed porch of the Marshall home, a rather staid Victorian house painted a dull pink by a light-minded tenant and left nakedly in a great stretch of lawn with not one tree to hide its shame.

"What Mrs. Marshall and I planned," said Marshall, offering Decker a cigar, then leaning back in a gaudily cretonned chair, "was a sort of historical pageant on Thanksgiving with all the old camp songs, don't you know? That's the idea this trip gave us around Mt. Vernon and up the Potomac."

"I should imagine it would," said Decker with polite sarcasm.

"It was really Mrs. Marshall's idea," admitted Marshall with not a little pride and a jerk of the thumb toward the interior where the noise of a carpet sweeper could be heard. "She has a lot of ideas that way."

"Indeed!" Decker commented and then said with a sweep of his hand. "Of course if that's the sort of thing you want I can take charge of it very easily. True, it's often been done and I like to think we have a little more originality here in Dell River but then the conventional thing is simpler—of course."

Slightly stung by Decker's lack of admiration Marshall puffed silently at his cigar.

"I think we should have examinations in general music," he said. "I talked to some other teachers at the hotel in Washington. And I think you're too lax with rehearsal cutting, —lots of those boys never show up except for the Friday roll-call."

Decker, who had often suspected this but was too preoccupied with the difficulties of teaching to go in for individual discipline, grew very frigid at this accusation.

"I think you exaggerate, Professor Marshall," he said stiffly. "I believe I can handle my rehearsals as well as an outside observer."

"Hardly an outside observer, Decker," said Marshall, irritated. "Anyway there are a great many changes I'd like to suggest in the music department. Say a history course in music, for instance."

"Impossible," said Decker as if he had not in his more active moments planned just such a course. "The school isn't ready for it. The casual way we'd have to teach it would not be worth while. No, Marshall, I'm distinctly opposed to these so-called popular courses in serious subjects."

"Well, of course, if you're too busy," said Marshall, a little alarmed lest his talk should lead Decker to feel too much the importance of his department. "Mrs. Marshall talked to the teachers and got the idea,—a lot more in fact."

Decker was still ruffled by the implied criticism of the way he conducted his department.

"I think I explained to you when I took this position," he said, "that I had very carefully laid out my plans for the next three years. I felt that I made that quite clear. Not that I don't appreciate Mrs. Marshall's suggestion. It must be splendid to feel you have such a clever little wife."

"Oh, Mrs. Marshall herself used to teach, you know—she had the English classes," Marshall grew more amiable. "Nothing like having cooperation right in your home. Frankly, Decker, I got along twice as fast after I married. I don't suppose I'd ever have been anything but a history and chemistry teacher if I hadn't met Mrs. Marshall."

"Amazing!" said Decker, not at all interested in the romance of his superior.

"That's why I'd hoped you'd get married,—maybe this summer," Marshall continued confidentially. "You'd be a much better teacher, Decker. Mrs. Marshall and I figured out that was what was the matter with you. You need a wife. You'd have more ambition then. Take more interest."

Decker felt as if Marshall had genially placed a large boot right on his solar plexus. He was outraged at this insulting suggestion of marriage, and that such inferior people as the Marshalls should feel it their privilege to weigh his situation and prescribe. As if his case were a "problem" instead of cause for envy and admiration! He could not speak for indignation.

"Yes, you'd find yourself a lot more adaptable if you married," pursued Marshall, mistaking his silence for docility. "And there's no getting around it, a man as close to forty as you are ought to be settled. It's all very well living alone but nothing like a few woman's touches around a place."

Decker's stomach did a rapid contraction, something like a somersault as the kaleidoscopic picture of what having a wife involved sped across his brain,—corsets on the piano, nail files and combings all over the place, awful women's magazines mixed up with his music and in his bed a soft, pliant creature, —merely imagining the obscene softness of the female skin gave him gooseflesh,—the hint of intimacy with this mythical wife made him shudder with horror and revolt. He glared at Marshall wishing there were some easy annihilation for such busy-bodies.

"Have you seen Louisa since she's gotten back?" asked Marshall slyly but the connection was lost on Decker.

"I don't think so," he answered stupidly.

"Looking splendid!" said Marshall, the matchmaker, heartily, but now a little afraid if he pushed the matter too far he'd have to get a new music teacher in the middle of the term. "Did you have a good summer?"

Decker shook off his momentary nausea and rose to go.

"Simply delightful!" he announced. "Long walks through this gorgeous country,—I assure you it's much nicer than Brittany!—and occasional runs up to the Shore, some business meetings with a chap from the East who wants me to accompany artists again, but of course I'm much too contented here,—and then working constantly at my piano! An ideal summer, thank you!"

"I suppose Dell River isn't as bad as some places in summer—especially if you can't get away," said Marshall sympathetically.

Decker twirled his hat.

"When you've travelled as much as I have, my dear fellow," he said with smiling superiority, "you will realize how rare a

charming spot like Dell River is, and nothing could persuade
you to leave it for any of the usual tours. Well, I must be off!"

And he swung gallantly down the cinder path to the street.

Marshall stared after him, his mouth still slightly agape, not
sure just where he had been wounded but certain that he disliked his music-teacher with an undignified intensity.

Laurie Neville's doctor was helping Connie but Gus hung
around the house gloomily each time he called, often interrupting the light chatter of his wife with, "Don't let her talk
so much, Doctor. She makes herself worse that way."

Lately he would bring up the subject of the doctor's fees
too, insisting that this was none of Miss Neville's affair and he
would not allow anyone to help him with his family troubles.
Connie was more indignant at this humiliating candour than
she had ever been before, and could find no words to ease the
awkward situation Gus invited. It took longer and longer each
time to restore her old reassuring thought, "Gus is so true and
simple! He only acts that way because he cares so deeply. And
after all he's been so good to me in his kind natural way. No
one else in the world would ever have been so kind."

Once she took him to task for dickering over the bill the
minute the doctor entered the house.

"Well, by God, I can't go on paying it forever," Gus finally
shouted angrily. "More money for six months of doctoring
than I make in a year."

"But it's almost over," said Connie, surprised that the actual financial worry was at the bottom of Gus' frankness more
than bad manners or concern over her own condition. "Remember we've been well for years,—most people have doctor
bills every year."

"Almost over!" exclaimed Gus. He shook his finger at her.
"Do you know what that man says? That you'll never get
well. It's going to be this way and maybe worse from now on.
All he can do is to keep you from getting worse! The best
food—no work—no worry! That costs money! I've got a
right to ask him where we stand!"

Connie looked blankly at him. To herself and Decker she had
referred to her disease as her "breakdown" as if it were the

result of acute intellectual labors and a fine nervous maladjust-
ment. She had succeeded in ignoring the doctor's hints, invariably adopting the tone that his calls were more social than
professional, and gliding as quickly as possible over the ruder
details of his visits. The few times actual pain had forced her to
face reality she had been in such terror of death that she was
glad to banish both truth and fear when the pain left her. Of
course she would not die and of course these little disorders
were not to be worried over. But Gus' bluntness frightened her.

"You mean I won't ever be able to take care of the house—
to play the piano—to sing——"

Gus was shamed by her trembling voice.

"Well, he says you mustn't tire yourself. The girls can do
the work anyway. Mimi can cook and Helen can work when
she's a mind to."

"Yes, the girls are good," Connie said in the queer strained
voice of someone in a dream. "But what about the money for
the treatments and all the things he says I must have? We
haven't much."

Gus looked down at his thick-soled boots.

"We can manage."

"But how—Gus, tell me. . . ."

He raised his eyes.

"We've got the shop," he said. "I guess we could make out
in those three rooms upstairs. That way I can look after you
more when the girls are in school."

Live over the shop? She looked at him blankly.

"Decker'll find a place," Gus said gruffly. "It's the only
thing to do as long as this goes on."

"But what about this house?" Connie asked limply. "We've
always lived here."

"Sell it," Gus said. He got up and came over to her chair,
patted her on the head. "We've got to have the money to get
you well, you know. I don't say we'll have to move but we always can. You just wondered how we'd manage the bills
and—well—I had to tell you. So there you are."

"Yes," said Connie. "I see."

She went to bed, keeping the danger and confusion away
from her mind; her head was empty and dull. For the first
time the effort to keep out fear kept out Decker as well.

*

Gus said no more about financial worry and Connie dismissed
it from her thoughts. The doctor came less often for her improvement depended not so much on his treatment as the
daily precautions against excitement. Laurie Neville and her
companion continued from their shore house to New York
for their annual fortnight of shopping and theatre-going, and
Louisa Murrell could not resist showing the note Laurie
wrote her from New York as against the picture postcards she
sent to the other teachers at The Oaks. The old Sunday teas
at Mrs. Benjamin's were resumed with Louisa preparing the
supper assisted by the girls and sometimes by Decker, which
gave the parties a gay bohemian touch offsetting the dampening effect of Connie's illness. After tea the little new victrola was placed on the library table and Decker fussed over it
as jealously as if only years of training could enable one to
operate this very special instrument. Now, although he possessed very few records he liked to believe they were the vital
ones and certainly had persuaded Connie and Louisa of this.

"Which shall it be first tonight?" he would ask after the
records had been carefully dusted off, the machine adjusted
to his taste. "Shall we begin with the Pathétique or save it for
the last?"

Connie, lying back in her chair, would see that his fingers
were on the Fifth Symphony so she would say. "Let's begin
with the Fifth,—I'm not in a Russian mood just yet."

And Decker would play the Beethoven as if he had not
planned to do that first no matter what was said. Connie
closed her eyes, each record might have had cut into it the
separate dream it sent Connie. On the Beethoven she thought
of Tony and transformed their love by this pure music into a
Lancelot-Elaine legend and slowly it grew into the fable that
Gus had appeared not so much as her saviour but as Duty, a
worthy figure for whom she had renounced the too ecstatic
pleasures of ideal love. In the Tchaikovsky record were the
invisible grooves where the dream story of her triumphant
career unwound and so each piece became known to her only
by the definite images it evoked. Gus stayed in the kitchen or
went up to bed during these concerts but he kept the bedroom door open for the music soothed him the same way the

barber's beer did, gratifying his stomach in the same rich way. Sometimes his voice would be heard as he leaned out the front window to hail his daughter.

"Helen! Where are you going?"

"I'm only going for a walk," was the sullen response.

"Who's that with you?"

"Just Hank."

"Well, see that you get back here before dark."

These clearly heard exchanges did not interrupt the pleasure of the three downstairs, least of all Connie who usually smiled gently as if the impulsiveness of youth was charming to observe. Louisa tried to give an answering smile but hers was often rather strained since Helen's independence was regarded with more alarm in the school than it was at home. But one couldn't very well speak of a daughter's misdemeanors to a mother, dewy-eyed over Beethoven, even if one was—as Louisa definitely was not—that sort of helpful friend. The nearest she could get to the subject of Helen was to speak, from time to time, of the troublesome case of Honey Busch, who had taken to running away from home every few days and was brought home by officers when Busch himself couldn't find her.

"That must be so hard on poor Mrs. Busch," said Connie.

"Oh, no," said Louisa. "She chuckles over it. She says, 'Isn't that Honey of mine a card? And don't the boys just run after her? They never looked at me, the boys didn't when I was a girl!' That's the way she takes it."

"Funny old Busch," mused Decker and he and Connie nodded their heads fondly.

Decker sat up late nights with catalogues, checking the records he would buy if he had the money, and stayed in the school office on Saturdays to type in neat classifications the list of this prospective collection. The pages were then placed in a leather notebook, its title page inscribed—"Blaine Decker Collection." He spent as much time weighing the eligibility of each piece as if he were actually putting out money for it and many times, after judicial consultation with Connie, decided that such and such a piece was too light to be included in a permanent collection. When Laurie sent him some foreign catalogues he was enchanted though—as he explained to Connie—these imports were likely to ruin him!

Louisa was pleased with this new interest for she had more spending money than her two friends and could often, after listening to a discussion about some piece, appear later in the Benjamin parlor with the coveted record under her arm, her face beaming with pleasure at being able to provide such a surprise. Louisa had a new source of strength in her summers' fortnight at Miss Neville's. At The Oaks she could put down any insult from Swasey or Emmons with a casual reference to her gay evenings at the shore, all the charming little ways Laurie had shown respect for her opinions. If Swasey laughed at the diary Louisa was keeping in verse Louisa had only to say, "Goodness, Laurie and Miss Manning were so embarrassing the way they insisted on showing my diary to the friends from Chicago who drove down,—that newspaper editor you know, and that University of Wisconsin professor. They seemed to think it ought to be published as a sort of calendar. Goodness knows I try not to be too personal in case it *should* be published."

Louisa knew this vantage ground could last only as long as some mystery surrounded the two weeks and daily new facts were grudgingly put out so that in due time every little incident would be known to The Oaks, no dark horses of suitors, or unreported conversations with Laurie could be mentioned for The Oaks would know all. She could put down Swasey's impudent references to "the Professor" as they called Decker by saying, "Laurie says he's easily the most interesting man we've had stay in Dell River."

One evening the two other teachers got the upper hand. They were sitting in The Oaks' dreary living-room, the table under the forlorn light of the green chandelier littered with papers to be graded, a plate of apples and a slim box of chocolate peppermints. Miss Emmons occasionally smoked a cigarette but it kept her awake and always gave her a headache so she forgot it when unobserved. Louisa had turned from one theme paper to the next until the mere sight of the day's title, "A Day in the Country" gave her a chill, so the papers lay idly in her lap while she stared at the bright blue gas logs in the grate.

"Thinking of your sweetie?" teased Miss Emmons. "Look at her, Swasey, you can always tell by that dreamy look who she's got on her mind."

"Which is it he likes best—you or Mrs. Benjamin?" asked Miss Swasey. "He's more of a ladies' man than I ever gave him credit for being."

Louisa drew her mouth into a line of disgust.

"You people don't understand the simplest things," she said coldly. "You don't even know there's such a thing as intellectual companionship, that's much more important than a silly love affair."

"I'll bet he's in love with the Benjamin woman," speculated Swasey. "I think they're just using you as a blind, Louisa. If I were you I wouldn't stand for it."

Louisa was exasperated.

"Oh, can't you see they're friends because they're the only two people in Dell River who could have been something else? She could have been a great singer—you've heard all about that—and you know that he started out studying to be a concert pianist. They can talk over music and careers and no one else in Dell River—except myself—knows what they gave up."

Miss Emmons decided to light a cigarette to give more distinction to her own speech.

"I didn't ask them to give up anything," she said lightly. "My theory is that if a person has the stuff he can deliver it—he doesn't let anything else come first."

"He certainly isn't modest about his talent," agreed Miss Swasey. "Every time he opens his mouth he lets you know how good he is."

"Why shouldn't he?" blazed Louisa, the most modest of women. "What's so fine about modesty—except for it making other people feel superior? A person can afford to be modest after he's got everything he wants. When everybody knows you're good you don't need to brag. It's like generosity—it's easy to be generous after you've had plenty—but it's no credit to you. Modesty's no credit to anyone—it's just a social grace."

"Well, well!" ejaculated Miss Emmons, wide-eyed. "I hadn't asked for that. Is 'Modesty' your class subject for tomorrow?"

"Come down to earth, Louisa," advised Miss Swasey. "You know if Blaine Decker or Mrs. Benjamin were really good they wouldn't be here in Dell River just talking."

"How can you be sure what anyone would do or be under other circumstances?" Louisa angrily retorted. Her papers had slid to the floor, the corrected mixed with the uncorrected, and her face was flushed with unaccustomed indignation. "When someone doesn't accomplish what he set out to do it doesn't mean he hasn't enough talent. Maybe he hasn't the character, maybe he's too fine to cut people's throats and step on them the way you have to do to get on the map."

"You can't expect me to believe in such a person until I've seen him at least make a try at what he claims to do so well," defended Miss Emmons mildly.

"You might believe in his ideals," sputtered Louisa. "All I'm saying is that a man might be too fine for success—instead of not being good enough he might be too good. That's all I mean."

Sulkily she picked up the papers. Miss Emmons shrugged her shoulders and passed the peppermints to Miss Swasey. They exchanged a look. Louisa stared fixedly at "A Day in the Country" trying to get calm enough—as she never could in speaking of Decker or Mrs. Benjamin—to make some telling dispassionate remark that would completely crush her audience, something to the effect that it took more than average intelligence to recognize genius when it passed, anyway. But the amused silence of the other two women made her suspect that anything she said would only entertain them.

"All the same," said Miss Emmons in a low voice, "there's more than intellectual companionship between Decker and the Benjamin woman, and I'm only surprised more people haven't noticed it."

"Not really!" exclaimed Miss Swasey, highly pleased.

Louisa sat very still with her mouth in a prim tight line. She was so angry at the two women that it was all she could do to compose her mind later on for her nightly poem in her diary, —eight lines this time on "A Woodland Path."

Early spring found the Benjamins installed over the shoe-shop. Mimi was enchanted with the little flat, its tiny kitchen, the porch where her mother sometimes slept, the sound of victrolas and pianos being tried out in the Music Store nearby, were all advantages not obtainable in the ordinary home. Since Helen disliked housework and her mother was not equal to it, the place was practically Mimi's play-house, and the girls in the Domestic Science kitchen envied her this responsibility. Helen herself was pleased over the excuse now provided her for being constantly in touch with whatever excitement the town could offer,—certainly no one could scold her for "running the streets" nights when she lived in the very heart of town. With no place to entertain boy friends she had excellent reason for late automobile rides and constant visits to girl friends' homes. Her mother could not blame her for not spending an extra minute in the home for every move she made brought forth sharp rebukes from her father. She could not run down the steps to slip out without Gus calling from the shop, "Helen! Why must you paint your face so to go to the butcher shop? You, not sixteen yet!"

"I'm past sixteen!" Helen would retort.

"Wipe that red off your lips! Pull your skirts down! What's the matter with your eyes, you look like a damn movie girl! Let's see what it is you've done to yourself. What've you done to your eyebrows, hey? What's that stuff on your eyes, hey? Go right back upstairs and make yourself look like a decent girl."

With such constant heckling it was surely no wonder Helen was in a perpetual sulk, venting her righteous wrath on Mimi when her father was out of hearing and allowing her gloomy face to indicate prodigious dissatisfaction to her mother. Connie refused to let Helen's discontent affect her, for it was hard enough as it was to get accustomed to the change in their lives. If the past few weeks of trips to Doctor Arnold's hospital for fluoroscoping, X-rays, serum injections of one sort and another,—if all these expenses had made it wiser to sell the house to the first bidder and take over the shop's upstairs then hers was too serious a condition to bear much scrutiny. She was crushed with fear but the doctor found her really improving after the move and of course it was logical that the nearness of Gus made it possible to do without a nurse.

Decker had moved to The Oaks where Louisa, in secret triumph, saw this male intrusion change Swasey's and Emmons' cynicism into fawning respect for his every mood. Decker dared not tell Connie how uncomfortable his new quarters made him lest she reproach herself for her inconsiderate illness, but he hated the feeling of being in the "teachers' house" as if he were no longer Decker, the individual, the man about town who did a few hours' lecturing in the schools, but the drab, doomed schoolmaster. The Oaks' living-room with its table piled high each evening with school papers, text-books, educational magazines, made his heart sink, though for the three women the room had now become almost wickedly gay with music notebooks shining amid Latin papers and English themes, as significantly masculine as the soft fedora hung on the hall-tree among the women's wraps. Miss Emmons no longer sat down to the old upright piano after supper to fumble through last year's song hit, or inspired by Sunday dinner try to struggle through "The Rosary" to Miss Swasey's falsetto obbligato. No, the piano was turned over to the maestro, copies of "St. Louis Blues" and "I'm Sorry, Dear" were hastily concealed in Miss Emmons' bottom drawer and the piano rack left free for a more musicianly display.

Decker was made uncomfortable by this expectancy. If he wanted to play when the room was empty he heard their footsteps tiptoeing respectfully past the door and his fingers made ridiculous mistakes. If, at dinner, he referred lightly to this or that prelude he was bound to be requested to play it later on and it irritated him that he must so abruptly face the results of his words, that he must privately acknowledge that this piece, once so familiar to him, was more than he could even attempt now. So, for weeks the silent piano held proudly on its rack a worn Beethoven collection and opened out over this, as if constantly practised, a frayed "Fantasie Stücke."

Louisa had a quiet revenge in seeing the deference paid to Professor Decker by his detractors. She was cynically amused when Decker's table talk of his friend Starr Donnell, the novelist, sent both teachers to the little library with requests for Donnell's works, and stories about Ilsa Darmster, that strange, exotic woman, kept the Misses Swasey and Emmons in a whispered argument upstairs lasting half the night on just what Ilsa's fascination had been and if Professor Decker hadn't been a little more involved with her—oh naughty, sophisticated man!—than he cared to reveal.

Louisa visited Connie often and on the latter's good days they walked together around the Square or sat down on a bench near the fountain. For Connie after a while the little flat had a compelling charm merely by its association with Decker. She found a certain satisfaction in living behind walls that had known his shadow, that had shielded his secret thoughts. Sometimes this new intimacy made her feel shy with him, afraid that her face should reveal some guilty admission. There were days when her thoughts of Decker in a hundred different aspects whirled in her head like a color wheel, her heart raced, the fever carried her to a pitch approaching ecstasy. There was the familiar sense of something audaciously wondrous about to happen, then, as these premonitions of joy proved unfulfilled, symptoms of physical weakness rather than of psychic power, a weight of sickening fatigue would drop upon her, it seemed to her that to weep or to smile was labor beyond her strength. The next day, however, the same anticipation would mount once more, images of Decker would speed through her brain and after a while she no longer tried to keep them within the bounds of reason but allowed and even watched with tired curiosity the distortions of face and deed.

As spring grew she thought of the rosebush by the porch and the bleeding hearts by the hedge. She missed the fresh smell of wet, tumbled earth and lilacs—her garden in May. Louisa brought her a canary and this she hung in the front window over a box of geraniums, conjuring an imaginary forest of birds from its fluttering solo. Through the rainbow window at the back of the apartment she could look across the court to the fields surrounding the church and school. This picture varied magically according to the glass and Connie used to grow absorbed in these changes like a child with a stereopticon, watching the fairy-tale brilliance of Dell River change to ghostly chill through blue glass and to a candy heaven through crimson. This pastime held her more and more after Decker told her the village under ruby glass seemed to him a stage Valhalla, so that, added to her own pleasure was the conjecturing as to how this would appear through Decker's eyes.

Louisa too, was amused to compare the shifting moods induced by the rainbow panes. It seemed to her that Decker and Connie were a little like these tinted panes, and she did not want to look at life except as transformed through their colored light. It was the same way with love,—a dreary—often ridiculous business when studied realistically but what a heavenly lustre it had when viewed through her poets!

Louisa was almost able to see Helen with Mrs. Benjamin's eyes, who sighed sentimentally, "Ah, youth, youth!" when Helen banged all the doors shut or refused to speak because Papa forced her to spend an evening at home. Secretly Louisa was terrified of Helen, she felt tired and used up merely seeing Helen's fine hard body swinging vigorously through the school halls as if the will and even the mind behind that physique were sharp and splendidly cruel, unsoftened by innocence. When there were examinations Louisa was afraid to flunk Helen, she could not stand up to the storm of righteous indignation from this pupil who had answers for every criticism. Even Mr. Marshall felt the same having once encountered her wrath. Louisa would have been frightened merely by her clean-cut ruddy beauty,—she was always dashed by physical perfection in women as if no weapon in life could equal the consciousness of beauty. She envied Connie for being able to dismiss this young symbol of power with a shrug.

"What else could a mother do with a girl like Helen?" Miss Swasey wanted to know when Mrs. Benjamin's nonchalance was discussed. "She couldn't ever discipline her so she might as well pretend she sees wise old Nature working behind all those high jinks. Just what old Mrs. Busch does with Honey only of course Honey's bound to get in wrong and Helen's too shrewd for that."

One day Honey Busch came down town wheeling a baby carriage. The rumor of this event had gone about before and Mrs. Busch had in fact hinted of it to Connie for it seemed to Honey's mother that girls would be girls and there was no difference between Helen Benjamin petting in parked autos and Honey Busch staying out all night in a barn with some farm hand. An unexpected baby now and then could only be put down to unusually high spirits and Honey's misadventure did not dismay her mother but made her child seem unusually precocious.

"She always was a caution!" she sighed to Connie with baffled pride. "Never could tell what she'd do next. . . . And
the boys after her every minute. I only wished I had the beaux
Honey has. That's what makes the women in this town talk
about her—they're jealous. Anyway it's the prettiest baby I
ever laid my two eyes on."

Honey looked pale and angelic wheeling the baby up
and down slowly and looking eagerly about for people to
admire it.

"Look!" she would say, plucking the sleeve of some embarrassed passer-by. "A baby!"

It was the first time she'd ever done anything unusual, and
now she was proud because none of the children who teased
her for not passing the third grade had babies. They still followed her up the street shouting "Crazy Honey! Crazy
Honey!" but Honey was too weak and too happy to answer
back, she only smiled and silently pointed to the carriage.

Connie wanted to be sympathetic but Mrs. Busch seemed
to feel that Honey was only proving how normal she was
after all.

"It seems funny to me," she said, "that your Helen hasn't
got into trouble before but I guess she hasn't got as much life
as my Honey and boys like a girl to have a little life."

The young farm-hand appeared at the Busch home asking
to marry Honey but Honey kept herself locked upstairs during his visit and instead of having any tender feelings for her
suitor, jeered at him from her front window, calling out, "Hay
foot! Hay foot!" until he whirled around at the gate to shake
his fist at the unseen taunter. The sight of the sixteen-year-old
Honey wheeling her baby proudly up and down the town
made Dell Rivers take their daughters into grave confidence
on the facts of life and fathers roared their disapproval of all
beaux, springtime, and school dances.

Connie had never scolded her children beyond a gentle,
"Now, now, dear!" when Helen insisted on new dresses or
pocket money to go to a theatre in a neighboring city. It gave
her actual pain to hear Gus berating his elder daughter,
though she did not object to Helen's defiant replies, certain
proof, after all, that Helen was well able to handle her own
wrongs. Sitting at her window she often heard their quarrels

in the shop as Helen was detected coming in late or going out with her face rouged. Connie's eyes would fill with tears at Gus' harshness.

"Well, when a mother's not strong enough to handle her girls," Gus retorted, one day when she rebuked him, "the father has to take hold. We don't want her getting into Honey's fix and that's what happens when girls get their head."

Connie had no answer. Even if she had been well she would have allowed the girls to go their own way, preferring the gentle course of seeing only good in them to the disagreeable task of correction. She too had been in "trouble" as a girl, but she had not learned through that what warnings to give to daughters. She only learned that there were veils that became Truth as the stained glass window became Dell River. But even this philosophy could not be handed to one's children in a concise form. One could not say to them, "Life is a dragon certain to devour you, but if you keep your eyes shut you won't mind so much." So perhaps it was better to let Gus manage the problem in his way since she had no alternative to suggest.

Helen looked as Connie believed she herself must have looked at that age. Helen was more robust, with more color to her, but their profiles and bodies were the same. It was the resemblance that made Connie believe she knew Helen. She would not worry when Mimi reported that Helen was threatening to run away, or to go on the stage, to get married, or to quit school and sell tickets in the motion picture house.

"Helen's just talking," Connie said indulgently. "She'd never do anything to make us worry. I know my little girl."

When Blaine Decker called at his former home Helen made a point of leaving the room with a glance of silent contempt, and this unspoken criticism annoyed Decker because it could not be answered. The look seemed a complete catalogue of reproaches,—he was conscious of growing baldness, of shabbiness, of age, of every weakness in his armor, though Helen's frown only meant that his presence in the living-room deprived her of the opportunity to entertain any of her younger friends there.

The place was unquestionably far too cramped for the family and compelled unaccustomed intimacy. Connie realized with full force what a stranger her husband was to her, and

here there was no disguise or means of retreat from their lack
of mutual interests. She felt helplessly cornered by the hard
facts of her daily life, there was no porch or garden where she
might escape. Gus' constant presence, the sight of his square,
uncompromising back, even the sound of his hammering in
the shop downstairs were dreary, sickening reminders of the
poverty of her life; they came to stand more and more sternly
between her and her own amiable world until she wept not
for luxuries or conquest of fate but only for the privacy to
dream of them. As her illness made her weak it made Gus
strong, there was no forgetting him for a moment, and Connie felt bruised before his stiff, unyielding mind. She began to
think of it not as a kind machine for grinding out wisdom but
a rigid trap for platitudes. Decker grew further and further
away, a storybook hero colored by the rainbow window, and
the thought that Gus might come in any minute tempered
the joy of their visits. It was as if Gus were allied with her illness in imprisoning her, and this quiet force could only be
offset by clinging tight to Decker's hands. She needed more
than spiritual understanding now, she wanted to touch him,—
to be sure he was as solidly near her as was Gus.

The whole town was talking about Helen Benjamin's disappearance before the news finally got to the cobbler shop. So
far as the family knew she'd spent the night with the Marshall
girls but Hank Herbert's confidences to his friends were soon
known and Mimi, excited and frightened by turns, had to inform her parents.

"Helen told everyone in the school but me," she said.
"They were married in Greentown and then they were going
on to Detroit so that Hank could get a job in an automobile
company, where his brother works . . . Helen told all the
girls but me. . . ."

"You'll have to go after her, Gus," Connie kept repeating
helplessly. She thought of Helen as that pretty little child of
years ago who danced to her mother's singing; she was staggered to find that that very child could be so indifferent to
family feeling. This independent gesture was a betrayal of a
fond illusion, it said in essence, "See, I have my own life and
you are nothing to me. I can leave without a pang, without

even hinting my plans to you, for you're nothing in my life but a handicap, not even as much to me as my school chums. It's all none of your business."

But Gus was a stone wall. Helen had made her own plans, let her see them through alone. He washed his hands of her. If she wanted to make a fool of herself over that young smarty—only last week she'd declared she loathed him!—let her do it. He wouldn't raise a finger to save her. She had complained of her home, let her see how she liked the home her nineteen-year-old groom would provide.

"But we can't let her go without making some move!" Connie feebly protested.

"Why not?" asked Gus. "You did the same thing yourself. Nobody stopped you. Nobody looked for you. And you got along all right."

Connie was surprised. Gus seldom referred to her life before she met him or the circumstances of their meeting, yet now something in his tone made her suspect he had thought about it often.

"But my grandfather was different. He wasn't human, Gus! He would never have forgiven me or taken me in again. I've told you all about that."

"Maybe that's so," said Gus irritably. "I never saw your grandfather or that big home you used to tell about. All I know about you is where I found you."

In the silence that followed his words something quietly died in Connie's brain. It was the image she had built of a kind, adoring Gus, the man to whom she owed so much for all these years of quiet understanding. She looked at him with her brows knit.

"I'm only glad she's made him marry her," said Gus. He filled his pipe somberly. Connie dully watched his stained thick little hands moving about the bowl. "She won't have so much to explain to the next one that comes along. Might not have been lucky enough to find a man willing to give her a home."

"The way you did for me," Connie whispered. "Why did you do it for me, Gus? I've sometimes wondered."

"I needed a wife. I was thirty and Hans Feldt wrote me to come on here. Why not?" Gus shrugged. "I helped you—you helped me."

"But you never forgot how you found me, did you?" Connie pursued. "That's all you are sure of about me—I was just a stray to you——"

"It's all right," Gus dismissed the remark impatiently. "You've been a good wife. I got no complaint."

Connie said no more. The days and nights she had eagerly poured into his ears the stories about Manuel, about her grandfather, the Sisters . . . all the time rejoicing in his tacit sympathy . . . he had believed none of it but what he had seen with his own eyes, for the rest he shut his ears to her. She looked at him carefully almost expecting his face to change now that his inner nature was revealing such unexpected and unfamiliar traits. A sense of having been brutally betrayed grew in her reluctantly,—she'd been believing in a support that was not there, had never been there.

"Women always talk a lot. I thought there might be something in what you said," Gus said laconically. "It didn't seem likely a girl brought up with the chances you talked about would have been wandering around the country all alone, half-starved. . . . But what's the good of talking about it? You never needed to put on airs with me. I would have understood if you just told me the plain truth."

"But I did," Connie said, knowing how futile her protest was.

"Sure you did—sure," Gus soothed her. "You tell me anything you want to, that's all right. I don't hold anything against you. You're a fine girl. . . . No need to wear yourself out now talking, though."

He smoked thoughtfully for a few minutes, ready to argue about Helen if his wife spoke of the runaway again but Connie did not speak. Several times she opened her mouth as if to say something then shook her head silently. There was nothing she could say to Gus. She should have known that many years ago.

After Gus went back down to the shop Connie pressed her hands to her head as if the resulting pain would waken her mind and show her some plan of action in regard to Helen. She must scheme alone, she knew, since no help from Gus was possible. She walked up and down the little living room angry with herself for being weak, for being exhausted by even these few steps, and frightened at the unguarded thoughts that rose before her,—Helen wretched and deserted as she had been once,—Helen alone in a hotel room, penniless, hungry,—for certainly the Herbert boy was as slim a hope as even Dell River could have provided.

"I must go to her," Connie made up her mind. "Perhaps I can't make it alone but Blaine will help me. He wouldn't fail me, no matter if Gus should."

Decker was horrified at first that she should risk the journey, but she was quietly determined. Mimi heard from the Marshall girls of the place in Greentown they were staying though there was a chance they had gone on to Detroit. Connie did not dare to tell Gus she was leaving for she was too uncertain herself how much action she could stand and knew he would not hear of her making the trip.

"But I can't let her go through all the dreadful days I did,—no matter what happens," Connie told Decker.

Greentown was three hours away from Dell River on the street car. It was drizzling, the car was damp and smelled of stale pipe smoke. Decker and Connie were depressed into long silence as if this were a funeral ride and Helen a corpse rather than a bride. Connie watched the green country through the rain-stippled window and dabbed at her eyes occasionally because she felt helplessly unequal to the adventure. All very well to try to find Helen and offer help but already her body was trembling, the most stubborn determination could not whip up her strength. She wished she could cling to Decker's arm but he always drew away from her touch. As for Decker he had given little thought to their mission, he was only concerned in supporting her, but when they arrived at the huge, gloomy Greentown Depot he realized his position and would gladly have turned back. Intruding on a honeymoon,—asking two of his students to return to their homes as if he were the dean of morals, as if, indeed, he gave a continental whether they ruined their wretched little lives or not. Only Connie's pale resolute face kept him at her side and there was, too, an abstract satisfaction in playing a role in a romance or scandal—whichever it was.

It was noon when they arrived but Connie would not stop for lunch until they had found Helen. The busy streets with their tangle of automobiles and street cars dazed her and Decker found the mere business of crossing the Square and hailing a local street car a ticklish task that required all of his attention. The address Helen had given her school-chums turned out to be a rooming-house in the middle of town, its ground-floor given over to a grimy little millinery shop. A sign over the front-door announced flamboyantly that this was the home of "La Belle Hats." The elderly proprietress of the shop was the landlady as well, for she came out when they rang the house-bell. Connie sat down on the oak bench by the stair-case. The sight of the thin old lady with her grey, rapacious old face reminded her queerly of the old landlady in the Atlantic City boarding-house, the same landlady—eyes showing the struggle to make allowances for all humanity and the itch to profit by its failings. Connie found herself arranging the same fixed nervous smile on her face she had used then, a smile to show she was not afraid at all, she was, oh, quite at ease, a smile that immediately defeated its purpose and drew a guarded answer from the other. Connie's head felt dizzy and light, she tried to keep her mind from going back to her own runaway but everything in this dim, musty-smelling hallway sent the old sensation of helpless desperation shivering down her spine. She would scarcely have been surprised to see Decker change to Tony before her very eyes, certainly being with him in this place gave her a strangely guilty feeling. She was afraid to meet his embarrassed glance.

"She's up there but the young man is out," said the old woman and added fretfully, "I knew somebody'd be after those kids as soon as I took them in. They showed me their license but I knew there'd be trouble—they had that look. Either somebody'd be after them raising Cain or I'd have to feed 'em myself."

"There won't be any trouble," Decker said with dignity. "I can assure you of that. We only want to talk to them."

He had hoped to stay downstairs while Connie went up, but she clung to his arm so he reluctantly accompanied her to the room at the head of the stairs. Helen's voice, sharp and suspicious, answered their knock.

"Who's there? Is it you, Hank?"

She opened it a crack and her face grew set at the sight of her mother.

"So you followed me. . . . Well. . . . Come in."

She wore a new red dress, Connie saw, and she had her hair lacquered to her head in an attempt at sophistication. The bed was unmade with the paste-board dress box and tissue paper wrapping scattered among the covers.

"At least you have a big easy chair and blue silk curtains," Connie commented, half to herself. "I didn't have anything that nice. . . . And you have a real closet instead of a clothes-tree with cretonne over it."

Yes, Helen's room—so like in spirit the room in which her mother had once lived—was not so dreary in its actual details. Helen was taken aback by the remark. She relented a little and even beamed at her callers.

"And the curtains slide together by this cord—look!" she demonstrated looking eagerly from one to the other. "And I got this dress and another new one—no, I won't show it to you, you'd say it was too old but I guess I can pick my own clothes now."

She sat down on the edge of the bed and crossed her legs. Connie could only stare at her, not knowing what to say or how to begin.

"You don't need to look at me that way, Mother, and there's no good expecting me to come home 'cause I won't," Helen said belligerently. "Nothing could get me back to that hole. I'm married now and I can do as I like. You can't annul the marriage, either, because if you do Hank promised we'd run away again the very first thing. I don't see what you came for—it won't do you a bit of good."

Connie put out her hands appealingly.

"But, Helen, I wanted to tell you things you didn't realize. What if——"

"There's nothing you need to tell me, Mother,—don't be silly."

"You may have to go hungry, you may be wrecking your whole future, Helen——"

"Wrecking my future!" Helen laughed sarcastically. "Stay-ing in that dumb town would have wrecked me if you want to know. How could I ever get near a theatre living in the backwoods? How could I ever learn to act there? Never see anything, never hear anything! I suppose you expected me to sit around the rest of my life talking about things that never happened the way you and Miss Murrell and *he* do! Believe me I'd call my life wrecked if I had to do that——"

Decker was stung into defense.

"My dear girl, you're not on the stage yet, you're just on your honeymoon. What's eloping got to do with this career you speak of? I'm afraid I don't see the connection."

Helen planted her hands on her hips.

"Everything! Can't you see that's the only way I could ever get away from home?" she cried. "I got to make things happen when they don't happen of their own accord. Hank had money saved up to get us on our way—it was really to go to college but Hank doesn't want to go to college, he's sick and tired of school. Pop would never give me a nickel so I had to get married to get out, see? You can't just sit around and wait, you know, and talk about things; I want to be doing them. I hate talk."

"But, Helen——" Connie said feebly. She was already defeated, more than that, she saw that here was no shy, sensitive Constance Greene but someone she could not understand, a cruel and curiously fortunate creature who demanded envy rather than pity.

"Yes, and I've got a job, what's more," Helen flung at them triumphantly. "I went around to the stock company playing here and I got a job right off—leaving for Chicago next week."

"What about Hank?" Connie asked in astonishment. Helen sulked and was silent for a minute. Apparently this consideration had worried her a little.

"Oh, Hank'll be all right. He can go on to Detroit like he wanted to. He thinks it's great for me to go on the stage. He'll understand."

"You haven't told him?" Decker asked, hating her for her assurance, her easy mastery of fate.

"I thought I'd see how he felt first," Helen admitted, twisting her wedding ring. "I thought when he came in I'd hint around and see—after all it's a job and he knows we've got to make money."

"Supposing," pursued Decker, "after you've—ah—hinted at your plan Hank shows he doesn't want you to go. You'd have to give it up then."

"Don't be silly," said Helen impatiently. "I'd just have to go and leave a note, that's all. I wouldn't want to fight with Hank. He'd get used to the idea of my going. Hank's all right."

Connie wanted to laugh, the idea of coming to Helen with help or with warnings was so ridiculous. Helen marrying, not out of foolish infatuation, but by shrewd calculation, knowing each step of the way what to do. And after all—hadn't she run away with Tony, herself, for the same reason? Yet in Helen she saw some strange alloy that made her strong where she had been weak, made her blind to all pain and all pity in the march toward her goal. She knew almost for a certainty that Helen would climb the heights she herself had only glimpsed. She could climb because she had no respect for those heights —only respect for herself, and she was not to be stopped by considering where her heel went. For the first time Connie had a sickening realization of her own failure. She looked around and met Decker's eye, knew instinctively that he had been struck by the same thought.

"We were too kind," she murmured to him sadly. "Too kind to everyone."

"Perhaps to ourselves," Decker answered morosely.

"Well, what about it?" demanded Helen. "Honestly, mama, there's no point in trying to get me back home because I'll never go there. I've got my chance right now and some day when you see me a leading lady you'll see I was right."

"I think I see it now," said Connie wearily. "I suppose you'll want us to go so you can tell Hank about your job— alone."

Helen was softened by her mother's surrender.

"I have to see the manager first. And you might take me to lunch. I told Hank I'd just have a sandwich but if you're going to a restaurant. . . ."

She pulled on a little velvet hat—new, too, Connie saw,— and hurried them out.

"There's a rotisserie down the street. We went there last night."

Decker held Connie's arm for she was trembling visibly as they walked down the street. They were quiet while Helen, now assured of peace so far as her family was concerned, chattered of her interview with the Stock Company manager, how he complimented her on her looks, what a fine way she carried herself, how well she could wear clothes, what a fine dramatic quality he detected in her voice. . . .

In the window of the rotisserie an enormous chef stood, and Connie watched him fastening the chickens to the spit with his great hands. As they ate she dimly heard Helen's boasting and her great plans against a background of this revolving spit and the smell of frying chicken fat. She felt sick and unhappy as if someone had shaken her by the shoulders and shouted, "See, you weren't good enough! Say what you will about Fate and all that you just weren't good enough. Too soft."

She saw Decker through a blur of tears and without touching him knew that they were closer than they had ever been, that he, too, was glad at least they were together. . . . He wanted to tell her about the rotisserie Ilsa Darmster had discovered. He wanted to talk about the difference between French and Italian cooking, what wines were best served with fowl, but Helen's chilling presence intervened, her hard, cool voice came between them like the cold nose of a revolver, ominous, real. . . . He wanted them to be back again in Dell River so that they could really enjoy this strange expedition and he hated Helen for her savage self-sufficiency.

As they went out Connie lingered behind to watch the chef impale a new batch of broilers. His hands fascinated her, their routine movements soothed her nerves. She saw that he was looking at her with a half-smile and she gripped the counter-rail in sudden recognition.

"Tony!"

"Sure," he nodded toward Decker and Helen now at the door. "Better go ahead,—your friends have gone."

"Did you see the notices I put in the paper? I wanted to see you."

"Sure, I saw 'em." He salted a pail of French-fried potatoes. He had grown enormously fat, Connie afterward could not understand how she came to recognize him except for the great brown eyes and perhaps the special delicacy of his great hands.

"You didn't answer."

He shrugged.

"I been too busy. . . . Too busy then . . . too busy now. . . . Look—your friends——"

Connie hesitated.

"I'm glad you're happy . . . glad I saw you again. Do you —do you miss the carnival life?"

He frowned at her and leaned forward confidentially.

"Say, that was no life. . . . This is the business. Wish'd I'd started in it earlier. . . . My wife helps, too. . . . She's in the back. . . ."

There was nothing more to say. Whatever she had ever wanted to know was answered now.

"Well,—goodbye—, Tony."

He was relieved.

"So long, signora."

He had forgotten her name, Connie reflected, hurrying after Decker and Helen. Helen announced that she was going to go to the building next door to see her manager again and was ready to say goodbye immediately.

"What were you saying to that awful man, Mama?" she wanted to know.

"I only asked how the machine worked," Connie murmured.

Helen burst into a peal of laughter.

"Mama, you are such a ninny!" she exclaimed almost affectionately. "Here's where I go. Goodbye . . . Oh, say, you can give my green pocketbook to Mimi—all my new clothes are red."

She darted into a doorway. Connie and Decker walked slowly back to the depot, both of them tired out, as if they had been on a long, long journey.

On The Oaks' front porch Miss Swasey and Miss Emmons whispered their conjectures about Professor Decker, while Louisa pretended to read. He ran in and out of the place like a man possessed, speaking to no one, half the time not even recognizing friends who addressed him. It was all very well to diagnose all this as "genius" but his nervous condition was far too obviously related to Mrs. Benjamin's illness. She had collapsed after her expedition to Greentown, the doctor from Greentown was there every day and Mimi was kept out of school to take charge of the house. There were even days—the whole town knew this—when the sick woman was allowed to see no one and on such days the music teacher might be seen rushing through the streets swinging his cane, his necktie flying, his hat askew, his face so desperately pale that no one had the heart to take him to task for his eccentric behavior. He waited in the cobbler shop hours for Gus to come downstairs and report on her condition; his hands unconsciously went through the "Campanella" on the worktable. Rehearsals for the Commencement music were forgotten and students waited in vain for their special lessons.

He would not talk to Louisa about this dark disaster in the air for even Louisa was morbidly pessimistic about the outcome. He, Decker, was certain that Connie Benjamin could not die but the thought held such frightening possibilities that he could not sleep. In one way he resented the illness—a charming game carried beyond the bounds of good taste; after all one may vary friendship with separations, quarrels, and sickness but at no point is it permissible to prolong worry to such an agonizing pitch. At night he could not endure the intimate living-room of The Oaks with the Misses Swasey and Emmons so anxious to discuss the Benjamin family with him. He would scarcely touch his supper and would leave abruptly to call at the cobbler shop upstairs, if possible, then to roam in the darkness along the river bank, swishing at the bushes with his cane, stumbling blindly over stumps and broken fences. Night after night Louisa threw on a dark cape and slipped out of the house to follow him, alarmed by his haggard appearance. She would stop at the church gate seeing him go on into the fields, then strain her eyes to follow him in the moonlight. She knew he always lingered by the old Benjamin house now occupied by a young married couple given to noisy card parties and much entertainment. When he was back in sight again she could breathe easily and slip quietly back to The Oaks again.

"What was there between them to make him so upset by her being sick?" Miss Emmons pondered aloud more than once.

"Nothing," Louisa was almost despairing of making people believe. "They were only friends—it was because they both loved music."

"But don't I love music too?" Miss Emmons loudly argued. "Didn't I take lessons all my life and don't I go to concerts in Cincinnati every time I visit my cousin? And haven't I told him so a dozen times? That doesn't make him friendly with me does it? No, sir, there's something more."

She caught Miss Swasey's eye and Miss Swasey nodded complete agreement.

"Then I don't know," Louisa surrendered but her heart was heavy. Now they no longer teased her about the music teacher and first she was relieved, then a dreadful empty sensation followed. If she had not the town's belief that Decker was rather specially hers, then she had nothing, certainly she had no private assurances to sustain her. All she had had was the reputation for being in love with him; now that reputation was vanishing and she felt as deprived as if it had been a real love. She could hear him muttering to himself at night in the room adjoining and sometimes she got up and crouched beside the wall whispering, "You poor darling—there—there!"

One night she was out in the hall when he unexpectedly opened the door and saw her there.

"I heard you walking about," Louisa apologized in a whisper. "I thought you might need a bromide."

Decker blinked at her as if trying to remember just where this little woman in a brown wrapper, her braids down her back, could possibly belong. He brushed a hand over his forehead.

"I don't want to sleep, thanks," he said. "There are too many things for me to think about."

Louisa sought to distract him.

"Arrangements for your summer?"

He seized upon the idea gratefully.

"Exactly," he said. "I'm making some important decisions."

She waited till he closed the door before creeping back to her room. She could not think of Mrs. Benjamin except through him,—even while she tried to imagine Connie's pain she knew she was thinking for Decker, loaning him her heart and her own pity as if his were not enough for this major assignment. Here, take my strength to put with yours, take my heart to relieve yours. . . .

"Poor, poor darling," thought Louisa, because his swagger had vanished and he was such a shrinking, forlorn little man. She loved him for being so plainly not a romantic figure, not a hero.

Footsteps going up and down the stairs, up and down, creaking tip-toe, cautiously hurrying, sounded in Connie's head as if they were connected with the painful beating of her heart. She could lull the pain by staring fixedly at the rainbow window until the colors raced after each other in a dizzy blur, but a look in this direction meant a contact with Mimi's white little face, and this required a reassuring smile almost beyond her strength. So Connie kept her eyes fixed on the wall before her where a diamond-shaped mirror hung and so she waited for the peaceful split second between the agonizing heart-beats. The mirror swung to and fro like a pendulum and shrunk from the size of a house to the size of a tiny jewel, yes, a diamond, whose corners were intolerably sharp, a diamond that was lost in her chest somewhere, its tiny points stabbing her with each breath. This was not true, of course, it was only that she was so in the habit of transforming what she saw into amusing images for Decker. When he came in the room she knew she had only to point to the mirror and he would know what she meant, he would perhaps put it into the very same words she would have used. Another thing about the mirror was the way it presented faces to her before the owners of these faces came into the room. There was a door in this mirror, for instance, a door that was somehow familiar but it was too tiresome to connect it with a real door so it was just a magic one. Sometimes it opened just a few inches and a terrified face would look silently down at her,—Mrs. Busch, Laurie Neville, Louisa, Gus, Doctor Arnold. The face would remain just a moment or two with alarm and pity shining in its eyes, then it vanished and the real face would appear, smiling, complete with owner, at the head of the bedside. Connie thought, "When I get better I must re-member to laugh at this. It's such a joke my spying on people before they put their faces on. . . ."

She must tell Decker. She was glad she had so much to tell him now. There were her impressions of physical pain. There really was such a thing, it appeared, and when you had it you could not help knowing that that was what you were meant for,—a body was marked like a baking measure for how much pain it could hold and then it was efficiently filled to the brim. Decker, Decker, where are you? . . .

He was there and she could smile at him but breath was too priceless to risk speaking. She was getting used to the pain—at first it had been accompanied by surprise; it was undignified, people should not have diamonds in their chests for hearts to stumble upon in their frantic beating. . . . With Decker be-side her and his expression revealing that he forgave her this unfortunate error and was as sure as she was that *we* do not die,—parents, friends, yes, but *we* do not die, though it would make a fine discussion sometime (she must remember every little detail of the fear to describe to him). She had so many things to tell him,—she couldn't think of them now, but new things kept popping up in her mind,—the way her grandfather's hand shook lifting a tea-cup, the clear-cut profile of a nun—Sis-ter Bertha!—fancy that name flying through space to her. It had been years since she'd thought of Sister Bertha . . . her very voice came to her . . . her first singing lesson. . . . Connie looked at Decker eagerly but she could not spare the breath to tell him about Sister Bertha or the diamond, she must use it for something more important, something she'd just thought about Gus;—yes, she could almost laugh at it now and Decker surely would,—that Gus had never believed in her, he only knew he'd picked her up, a girl in trouble, in Atlantic City, and he was willing to overlook her past since she made him a good wife . . . that was really funny, wasn't it? . . . Tony would have been like that too. . . . She should have told Decker about Tony in the cafeteria. That was funny . . . oh, it was amazing how much she had to tell him. In a minute she would speak—she'd save enough breath to tell him.

When Dr. Arnold's face flashed on the mirror she thought, "This must be the way one dies. People collect on

a mirror like dust and something rushes through your mind
emptying all the drawers and shelves to see if you're leaving
anything behind—a Sister Bertha or a Mrs. Busch." . . . Do
you remember, Decker, the day Busch said, "That was the
loveliest music I ever heard?" . . . That was the day I sang—
"See the waves of fair Sorrento,—What a treasure lies beneath
them——" Manuel's song. . . .

Now Dr. Arnold was sitting on the side of the bed but she
could see Decker behind him. There were other people near
but there was so little time for anyone but Decker, so many
things to tell him. When she caught his eye she knew he understood, he forgave her for not telling him all at once, he understood about the mirror, about the diamond, about Sister
Bertha. . . . In Dr. Arnold's black eyes she saw herself tiny,
tiny enough to fit into the mirror at its very smallest, dwindled away to nothing. So this was the end. What a pity, she
thought, no one will ever know these are my last thoughts,—
that Dr. Arnold's mouth was so small. . . . *And* so little—
(very different from small)—and his necktie was so blue, so
amazingly blue. You couldn't breathe for the pain of looking
at such blue. Please, oh please, please not so blue. . . . And
a bell tingling somewhere was a sensation further off than the
sharp agony in her chest, the soft splintering of rhythmic
bombs in her heart, splintering into stars of almost perfect
pain. . . . Her body was not big enough to hold such feeling. How do birds die, Decker, when they have such little
hearts—not big enough really for more than a few beats and
certainly no space left for pain. . . . The doctor's little
mouth—his teeny, tiny mouth—how perfectly ridiculous! She
would like to tell Decker these last thoughts, these sudden
revelations. My dear, she would say, you've no idea how perfectly ridiculous. . . . But that was not what she wanted to
say to Decker. . . . She must not waste words, especially
when there was that one very important message for him.
She'd forgotten what it was but it buzzed about in her
head—she almost captured it once when she met Decker's eye
and then the Doctor came between and it was lost. . . . She
detached herself from her body, it was so riddled with bombs
one might as well leave it, but already she ached with missing
it. The pain of separation was exactly like the real pain in her

heart,—perhaps that was what she meant to tell him, but that
was wrong, she knew it when she saw his blue eyes again and
felt him groping desperately for her hand as if at last he must
find something tangible about her to hold. . . . She felt the
words forming in her mouth—she could not be sure they
were her words or his words, but they were exactly what she
wanted to say, that most important thing——

"Dear—my dear——"

That must have been right for he bent over and kissed
her hand,—Deckers do not do that except for the right
words. . . . Now his blue eyes again. Blue that broke your
heart, that made your ragged breath catch once more, that
stabbing blue that would not relent but swam nearer and
nearer until there was no escape. Connie saw her thin white
fingers flung out frantically against it, a thin little white fan
caught in the blue, fading into it and then quite lost in it—
quite lost.

He was on the steamer. He was not the village music teacher,
he was Blaine Decker, cosmopolite, that young man who
showed such promise at the Conservatory and who later—as
the intimate friend of Starr Donnell, the writer, played charmingly in one or two important drawing-rooms in Paris. Once
he had not been able to enjoy a situation until he had put it
into its best form in his mind, but now—with no fascinated listener in mind he could see no advantage in his position, he
was just a dazed man going through the motions of a long-
familiar dream,—a dream that had been so dear that the reality was hopelessly dull in comparison. He was not happy in the
fulfilment—he was lonely for the dream. He missed the little
apartment over the cobbler shop where he could wish so much
finer wishes than this. He could not feel properly grateful to
Laurie Neville for arranging the trip; it was clever and kind of
her to make the gift so simply as if it were a loan,—he had been
too crushed by the last few weeks to refuse, but he was not
grateful. Here he was on his way to two years in Europe and all
he could feel was a hideous sense of loss and resentment that
his private life had been invaded,—he was being forced to
make good a promissory note. Vaguely he knew that his own

far country—which Laurie Neville could know nothing about
—was tangled irretrievably with Connie Benjamin's; it was
not Paris or Munich or Milan—those were only the working
names for this charming place. It was not fair to be asked to
check up on it. Connie would have understood.

He wandered around the deck, his muffler flying in the
breeze, his new topcoat flapping about his knees, his tie—as
always—flying gaily from side to side. In six more days he
would be in Paris—oh terrifying thought! It was no longer a
city of dreams set in the silvery mist of romantic memories
but a strange unfriendly place that had once found him not
good enough; it was only back in Dell River that Paris belonged to him completely, a tender place that loved him, that
perpetually held out arms to him. . . . And Starr. . . . He
had discovered that Starr was living in Paris again. In the
steamer dining-room an Englishwoman he did not remember
came up to his table and reminded him that they had met
abroad years ago. She'd seen Starr last winter in Italy.

"You'll be staying with him?" she inquired.

"It's possible," murmured Decker, feeling pushed by this
woman into something he was not at all sure he wanted just
as Laurie had pushed him. Did he want to see Starr? . . . Of
course he would call at the old address. He would stand in
the downstairs hallway waiting for the "Who is it?—Come on
up!" with that same old feeling of not being equal to Starr's
friends . . . he would take a deep breath on each landing to
brace himself for the plunge,—keep guard on himself so that
no naive spontaneity should escape. . . . How could he look
up Starr when he had forgotten the Waldstein Sonata, his fingers stumbled over the Military Polonaise, how could he explain he'd been teaching the Pilgrims' Chorus?

"So you're back," Starr would say with his queer restrained
smile—decently bred people never betrayed childish joy. "Well,
well! Here you are, everybody, here's old Blaine Decker back
from the American jungle. He'll play for us presently. . . ."

No, he wasn't prepared for Starr, he wasn't prepared for
Europe or leisure, either. He was being rushed into all sorts
of things with no chance to savor them. Laurie had hurried
him into this trip, the woman yonder was pushing him back
to Starr,—Starr would force him back into his old professional

ambition for you must do—do—do—to justify Starr's friendship. Starr was bored by amiable nobodies. He drove you to
agonizing ambition.

Aimlessly Decker drifted down to his cabin and closed the
door. On the wash-stand lay the books from Miss Manning.
He picked them up and examined the titles. Novels. He'd
never liked novels but probably Starr's crowd would talk
about them so he'd better read them. . . . On the bed was
the package from Louisa Murrell. A volume of Swinburne.
He sat down and turned it over in his hand, fighting back a
wave of unutterable loneliness, a nostalgia for Connie Benjamin's soothing flattery and the sweet drug of their mutual
consolations. Now that he was on his way to Paris he could
think only of Dell River, the lazy little Park, the twisted tree
behind the cobbler shop, the Benjamins' ragged garden, the
haunting fragrance of locust blossoms. . . . No, Connie Benjamin was not gone. Nothing could ever happen to him that
he would not know exactly what she would have said about it.
He would never be alone again for he would have her in his
brain, in his very veins,—to every song he ever heard there
would be two people listening.

The fog-horn blew harshly and Decker looked about the
little room, puzzled for a moment. Ah yes, Paris. . . . But
Paris wasn't the real place. That was now Dell River,—the
place he had just left.

TURN, MAGIC WHEEL

"Turn, magic wheel,
Bring homeward him I love."
—THEOCRITUS.

For Dwight Fiske

I

. . . the little words of the rich . . .

SOME FINE DAY I'll have to pay, Dennis thought, you can't sacrifice everything in life to curiosity. For that was the demon behind his every deed, the reason for his kindness to beggars, organ-grinders, old ladies, and little children, his urgent need to know what they were knowing, see, hear, feel what they were sensing, for a brief moment to *be* them. It was the motivating vice of his career, the whole horrid reason for his writing, and some day he warned himself he must pay for this barter in souls.

Always as he emerged late in the afternoon from a long siege of writing, depressed by fatigue, he was accustomed to flagellate himself with reproaches and self-inquiry. Why had he come to New York, why had he chosen this career? though to tell the truth he could not remember having made any choice, he just seemed to have written. But if a Muse he must have, he reflected, why not the Muse of Military Life, or better the Muse of Advertising? . . . Actually I should have gone out to South Bend, he decided, into my uncle's shoe factory and made a big name for myself in the local lodges; but there again was the drawback. Did my uncle invite me? No. He said, "You'd be no good in my business, Denny. Here's a hundred dollars to go some place way off." "Thank you, uncle," I should have said briskly, "I prefer to take over the factory and with the little invention I have been working on all these years for combination shoe-stocking-and-garter I propose to make the Orphen shoe known the world over. Allow me, uncle," I should have said, "to put your business on its feet or at least on its back." Then I would have married Alice or was it Emma who lived next door? We would have had a cottage at a respectable Wisconsin lake in summer and in winter fixed up the basement with chintz and old furnaces to be a boys' den. I would have satisfied both my intellect and my ego by sitting up nights reading thick books Alice couldn't

possibly understand, and for my cosmopolitan urge I could
have winked at stock company actresses. Even if it was Emma
and not Alice I should have done that. But no, I am a born
busybody. Curiosity is my Muse, lashing me thousands of
miles across land and sea to study a tragic face at a bus window, not for humanity's sake but for the answer's sake. Have
I no finer feelings, he begged his stern inquisitor, look what a
loyal friend I have been to Effie Callingham, for instance; was
there ever a truer friend? . . .

The answer to this query was not gratifying for his speculations on Effie, her emotions, her past, her future, had resulted in his latest book, so that if this was loyalty it worked
hand in glove with his major vice. Face it, then, curiosity was
the basis for the compulsion to write, this burning obsession
to know and tell the things other people are knowing. Unbearable not to know the answers. Behind those blank faces
on the subway, *what*? In the spiritualist parlor on Seventy-
third and Amsterdam what casual guess sums up this one,
what blind prophecy outlines another's future; in the reading
rooms of the Forty-second Street Library countless persons
absorbed in books (Why absorbed? What do they read? Why
do they read it?) look up and away; what sentence stirred
what memories so that interlacing thoughts float through
glass and steel to faraway, to places you will never know,
dwell familiarly on faces you will never see. At the Dolly
Raoul Studio of Stage Dancing, Inc., Acrobatic, Ballet, Toe,
Ballroom, Tap, Radio, Fourteenth Street and Second Avenue, what does the little peroxide Jewess leaning out the
window feel or know, what perhaps beautiful plan is shaping
in her little head for a break from Avenue A to Carnegie
Hall? On paper you can fill in the answers, be these persons,
transfer your own pain into theirs, remember what they remember, long for what they desire. Spread out in type, detail added to detail, invention added to fact, the figure whole
emerges; invisibly you creep inside, you are at last the
Stranger.

Words, sworn testimony cannot help here; between the
candid phrases stands the Why, the Why *she*, why not some
one else, so that Effie's own story known in sum so well to

him could only tantalize him, make him forever intrigued by her sweet ravaged face, her simplest gesture. Thinking of Effie without ever being able to be or fully know her, filling in her past as he walked so that his own story became more real than hers, Dennis followed the little blonde down Second Avenue, at first absently then deliberately as she came out in green hat and astrakhan-trimmed jacket from Dolly Raoul's Studio of Stage Dancing. He watched what she watched but again he was lost; before the millinery window which hat delighted her, the red feather toque or the black taffeta, did the push-cart of Persian figs tempt her that she glanced at it twice or was it the tray of St. John's bread, the stand of Kolomara grapes and pomegranates, or was it that she was really hungry? Perhaps in the rhinestone-stippled velvet purse there were only a few pennies, her tuition at school took all her money; she must remember, perhaps, that this ten cents is for carfare to a casting office. Below Seventh Street she glanced up at the banner flaming across the street—"THE FOURTH ANNUAL DANSANT OF THE RIDGE STREET BOYS"; of course she wanted to go there, show how marvelously well-trained she was. In the corner of the dance hall she would teach her partner a few fancy steps and would astonish and delight the other dancers with her professional execution; here she paused before a gown shop and saw herself in the blue velvet evening dress she would wear, dreamily she opened the purse to powder her nose, saw Dennis' inquiring eyes reflected in her pocket mirror, looked him haughtily up and down, angry that he had seen her in the blue velvet at the Dansant dancing with Irving.

She hurried on down Second Avenue, high-heeled gray suède boots, Russian style, clapping firmly down on the pavement, head with its firm yellow curls exploding beneath the green felt hat, but Dennis found now a conscious coquetry in the rhythmic swirl of her skirt, and disillusioned, he stood for a moment at the Fourth Street corner watching her swish right, left, right, left across the street. What called her to the other side—surely not the Church of the Nativity, bare edifice of pilgrim simplicity, simplest crucifix looming above surrounding Yiddish shops and symbols? She was

gone, perhaps into the side gate where a sign in black and
red letters said:

YE OLD BARN DANCE
COME YE CHICKS AND YE HICKS
OLD NATIVITYVILLE BARN DANCE

Now she was lost, he could look in vain upward at Dolly
Raoul's windows as he passed on his way home, pause at every
pushcart of figs, look in the millinery shop to see if the red hat
was still there, no, the girl was gone, he would never see her
again, never, though already the next encounter flickered on
the screen—The Paradise or possibly the Folies-Bergère, and
the cigarette girl leaning her tray on his table. *"Haven't I seen
you before, sir?"* A little Turkish cap on her head this time and
embroidered trousers, but the same girl, the same sharp nose,
same galaxy of tight blond curls. So you weren't a dancer, so
you weren't ambitious East Side but nostalgic Broadway all the
time, so the answers were never in the book.

A light mist was rapidly turning into snow, and chilled, he
pulled up his collar to his ears. This would be a deuce of a
time to get pleurisy again and be pitiful, winter just over, a
joyous spring in bed with no money, no fireplace, just magazine editors encouraging him to finish stories not yet begun.
He would be damned if he would ever be pitiful again, better
be arrogant, vulgar, boorish, cruel, anything rather than be
soft, sick, weak, poor, pitiful. The mere fancy made him wince
just as a loaded pistol could still make his brave blood run
cold, yes, he was still afraid of Fate, the cruel stepmother.
Would a day come, he wondered, when his fame and living
would be assured, when a stroke of good fortune would not
make him speculate uneasily what subsequent string of failures would be required to pay for it? Ah, to sit pretty, he
thought, to fold hands over stomach with a smug smile and
accept confidently, and not mistrustfully, the homage of the
gods! On the other hand, the ability to sit pretty was glandular and not in his make-up, success must be mysterious, evasive, unfaithful, to allure him.

In the mirror of a street weighing machine he saw how
thin, narrow-chested, unimpressive he looked, unlikely seducer of Fortune, the Lorelei. Here was a man, he would

swear, who would never be a homeowner, a shoe-factory president, a car-owner, a steady jobholder, here was a man who could be nothing but possibly a ticket-owner, and in fact, studying his image with detached even hostile eye, it struck him that he had a Passport face, one that could be placed on anybody's papers and not be entirely wrong; such a face could justifiably sweep through the world passionately examining other faces but exempt from the curious second glance itself. This was only justice in exchange for an injustice, he concluded, and wondered if it was possible that he was getting increasingly partial to himself since there were fewer and fewer negative reflections on his charm, ability and superiority that he could not flout with two minutes of judicial analysis. As a matter of fact he was a mighty personable figure of a man, a fine commanding physique (if he just remembered to stay away from tall women), a rather nonchalantly Prince of Wales way of wearing his clothes (if he just stayed on Fourteenth Street or Second Avenue), and a manner all his own that he got by combining Clark Gable and Wallace Beery. Going back up the Avenue with a more confident swagger, he stopped near St. Mark's to buy a bag of roasted chestnuts from the old man shivering before his charcoal oven. He would take them to Effie. It was the one charming unconquerably childish thing about her, that question, "What did you bring me?" It never mattered what it was, but it pleased her to have tangible proof that, absent, someone had thought of her.

Chimes clamored through the distant roar of the elevated trains, the Metropolitan clock cut through the giant music box with five authoritative strokes. He should be home now, for Effie had promised to come in. Curious how behind his back in ten minutes Fourteenth Street had changed. An old barge captain, red and bearded, in oilskins and sweater, had sprung up before the Tom Mooney Club, a pocked old woman invited him to choose between white parrots and white mice as fortunetellers, here was a Gypsy Tearoom, Tea Leaves Read Gratis. In front of the shooting gallery the Princess Doraldina from Tasmania, golden-haired figurine in a glass cage, for five cents breathes, moves, passes a wax hand over cards, sighs, and releases the card of your future. *"You*

*will meet with one who will love you. That love will be returned
by you. The first name of this person begins with M and you will
be introduced at a place of amusement."*

Magically the five o'clock people came to life, bounced out
of their subways, jumped out of their elevators, bells rang,
elevator bells, streetcar bells, ambulance bells; the five o'clock
people swept through the city hungrily, they covered the sun,
drowned the city noises with their million tiny bells, their five
o'clock faces looked eagerly toward Brooklyn, Astoria, the
Bronx, Big Date Tonight. They enveloped Dennis, danced
about him, sang I-sez-to-him in a dozen different keys, whispered he-sez-to-me, they whirred off into night and were
gone like the blond Jewess in the Russian boots, they were
nothing to him, he was less than nothing to them, a young
man with a passport face on his way to meet Effie Callingham,
one-time wife of the great man Andrew Callingham, one-time
companion to the Four Hundred's Mrs. Anthony Glaenzer
. . . and this was the part of her life Dennis knew least about,
must guess at in his novel about her. He did know that
through all those years in the Glaenzer household New York
had been only a dream around her, this present confusion
which he loved, these masks flung out of office windows,
these wax Doraldinas with printed fortunes in their hearts,
these pretty puppets were only a dim noise outside the Glaenzer coffin doors, a cry, a wish, a dream. Sometimes he thought
of Effie as part of that rich fat enemy world of Glaenzers, he
saw her with them peering out at New York through Fifth
Avenue lace curtains, listening to the Help! Help! of the city
through symphonic arrangements of Stokowski; he saw her
with the Glaenzers swimming in their goldfish bowl, observed
rather than observing, swimming in and out of their skeleton
castle, pressing their little blind noses to the glass, blinking,
aware of only light or dark. Effie could not, in fairness, be
blamed for Glaenzer fat, but there was no denying that contact with this fat polluted subtly, the golden germ made delicate havoc wherever it went. In a sudden burst of rage he
damned all Spode, Genoese lace, Haydn, Rosewood, Hollandaise, Clos Veugot, Stiegel, Ispahan, Schiaparelli, Picasso,
Rosenkavalier, and all the little words of the rich, the little
baby fingers reaching out, the little golden curl clutching the

sterling heart, sweetly softening the brave. How charmingly Effie wore her little rich words thefted from the Glaenzer fatness, weaving a spell about her present despair, throwing out splendid marquee and rug to lead to her bare closet.

Yes, he despised her gallantry, he informed himself even while he hurried to meet her, despised her for not fighting like other people. Why couldn't she call Callingham a swine for deserting her, why couldn't she row over the Glaenzer luxury while she had so little, why must she be noble, frail shoulders squared to defeat, gaily confessing that life was difficult but that's the way things were? Pity for her taxed him, held him bound to the strange gentle woman in something so like love, so like lust, that often sleeping with his little Corinne he was tormented by conscience—he was being unfaithful to Effie, Effie the brave, splendid, unhappy woman who was nothing to him, nothing more than the tender object of his passionate curiosity. Yet she could command this odd fidelity of him, so that for days he would keep away from Corinne, deny himself the pleasure of his jealous suspicions, refuse the delicious agony of dining with her and her complacent husband, write her a dozen notes to say he was through—through, do you hear? It was all so impossible, bad for everyone all around, and it certainly was fine to be a free man again and get back to honest work. So all because of Effie, goodbye, goodbye, Corinne. Goodbye, oh excellent wife to excellent Mr. Barrow. Goodbye, love for these four, five years, torturing, maddening, stupid, unfaithful, wicked little love. Goodbye, cruel darling, sweet, soft, curly, dear little love, I'll be over in ten minutes.

. . . page four . . .

SURRENDERING then to Corinne he must justify himself by looking on his friend Effie cynically, reluctantly worshiping he must make his sardonic asides, must in fact make her an amusing character in his book, to show that, bound as he was by his infantile, damnable romanticism, he still had his wits about him. Admit he was on his knees, kissing the celebrated hem, say at least he knew what was going on, he could count out more flaws in his princess than any enemy could. There was her ridiculous adoration for her ex-husband's triumphs, for instance. Look at page four "The Hunter's Wife, Mac-Tweed, Publishers, $2.00——"

"She wears his name as if it were a decoration from the King entitling her to the profoundest consideration; she wears it for evening like a jeweled wrap which catches mirrored light so it cannot be ignored. Without referring to his achievement she boasts of them by keeping his full name on her mailbox these fifteen years since he deserted her. Crushed and mystified by him when they were together, now at last she can understand and interpret him with the exquisite lens of long separation, or more probably she has in that fallow period created a hero she can understand, a hero who cannot deny her interpretation as the original might. Indeed, poor soul, while grieving for him she has become him, and observe how neatly she rules her life by what would please him. The friendship she bestows is his favor, the books or music she prefers are his preferences, the crown for every newcomer is 'The master would have loved you.' What fragment, then, is left of the person who once lived in this body, before he came—is there one exclamation that comes from the buried woman, or must all be strained through the great man's cloak? Is there indeed a living soul behind this monument to him, does it breathe of itself, does it of itself weep over 'Tristan' or are these *his*

beautiful tears? Rebelling against him when they were together, she surrenders utterly after his leaving so that if now
he were to hunt for her throughout the world he would find
her only in his own mirror.

"Past youth the sweet creature lies about her age, not
through ordinary female coquetry but in the way men lie,
men who having failed to do the great deed by the given
hour, ease their desperate fear of failure by cheating with the
calendar. Fifteen years and he has not come back to me, she
says, perhaps never, then, and this cannot be borne so she
swears she is only thirty-nine, this year the miracle must happen, he will come back, the hunter will return, and see the
wise gentle wife she has become in his long absence. How
resolutely she has borne her honesty through a sophisticated
world until it has the shabby sheen that comes from long
usage, it gleams in its artificial setting as the one false note!
Tired Truth barks at her heels as stylishly as any other thoroughbred on leash."

When he came into the apartment he found Effie already
there, the book in her hands, and Dennis had his first swift realization of what the words must mean to her. Why, he
thought, meeting her stricken eyes, this was not merely writing. This was a living woman he was putting on the market,
the living Effie. He felt guilty and angry. She was sitting on
the sofa in his room, stiffly erect, one finger in the book as if
she had held that pose for hours, frozen by what she had
read. He could imagine her hurrying up the stairs at one second to five—she was always on time in spite of his own defections—very probably she paused at the landing outside his
door to pull the brim of her blue felt hat lower over her shadowed, fine gray eyes, he almost saw the half-smile as she
tapped lightly on his door once—twice—nobody home, very
well, try the knob, he will be here any minute since it's unlocked. . . . Then the book, fresh from the printers, on the
table, her little exclamation of delight, the jacket examined,
—not bad, the title page—by Dennis Orphen, author of *No
Defense*. He saw her settle herself among the cushions, still
smiling with pride, to read the first page, the second, third
page—smile fading into faint bewilderment, page four—page
four—suddenly straightening up, reading carefully each word

once again so that there could be no mistake, page four, page five.

How clever I was, how damnably clever, Dennis thought, furious with his own demon now that made him see so savagely into people's bones and guts that he could not give up his nice analysis even if it broke a heart, he could not see less or say less.

"I'm late," he said, throwing his hat into the corner where it landed arrogantly on the plaster bust of some visiting Venus modeled and deserted by the former tenant. "I see you found the book. Won't be out till next month, you know. The tenth."

Sometimes, in candlelight, Effie's slender face had the delicate sad charm of a very young girl, her rare smile was appealingly youthful, but now he saw her face frankly old and tired, and his heart turned sick; he could find nothing, nothing in the world to justify this crucifixion, good God, no, not even if he was Proust or Homer or Hemingway himself, no, there could be no excuse for telling the world about Effie.

"I can see it's about me," she said finally. "You never told me that. All the time you were writing it, you never said it was about me."

"No, it isn't really, it's a—a——"

"A composite?" She smiled faintly. "Yes, I know."

There was really so little to be said when you came right down to facts. It made him all the more angry.

"Well, what if it is about you?" he challenged her, standing in front of her, hands jammed into pockets. "Good Lord, Effie, you've been a writer's wife, you ought to know how little it means—a few words here and there which tally with a real object—what of it? You've been around, you know there's no Emily Post rule as to what's legitimate copy and what isn't. I tell you it doesn't mean a thing——"

Effie looked at him quietly and put the book back on the table. He wished she would answer but she sat twisting her gloves, the cape she always affected slipping from her fragile shoulders. How slight she was, he thought, and shivered for what had once seemed an eternally slim, youthful figure, today seemed frail shrunken age, a frailty to be protected rather than shrewdly analyzed.

Suddenly Effie laughed and he turned gratefully toward her, for in the moment's silence shutters and curtains were being drawn on confidences, doors locked that were once wide open, walls barricaded so softly, so subtly that in another moment no crevice would be left through which two one-time friends could call to each other. But now Effie laughed and a door once more swung open between them.

"I was going to ask you to go to the Gieseking recital, tonight," she said, "but I knew you would say—'she goes to concerts because Andy used to like concerts.'"

"Applesauce. Certainly I'm going with you," said Dennis. "Let's go get a cocktail some place first."

His mind sped on through the book—what else would she find there for her torture? Clever, clever Mr. Orphen with his nice little knack of thumbnailing his dearest friends. Honest Mr. Orphen who gave up the big money in Hollywood and the lazy life of southern France for the brave duty of annihilating Effie Callingham.

Effie hesitated as he held open the door for her.

"You say the book isn't out yet?"

"Not till the tenth. Why?"

She drew a breath of relief.

"Because I wouldn't dare go anywhere with you if it was already published. Everyone would know then that it really was about me—everyone would laugh."

Laugh at her . . . Dennis did not know how to reassure her, so he followed her silently down the stairs. His fingers fumbled in his pocket and found the paper bag.

"Roast chestnuts," he said and handed them to her. "Present."

"Darling, that was sweet of you."

She was plainly touched and pleased by his thinking of her on his walk. Nice Dennis. They went out the front door and across Union Square, friends again, the "interesting older woman" and the strong young man, the red-haired strong young man who had written the amusing book about her.

. . . the little French figure . . .

In the Brevoort Café they found their favorite corner table, or rather Dennis' favorite table, for if he sat here he could watch all the mirrors for Corinne and if some day she should come in the next room with another man, that actor for instance, he could watch them from here and next day when he asked her where she'd had tea and she answered "Oh, I was at Olive's" he would say "Liar, I saw you at the Brevoort with that man." Already his heart thumped in preparation for the shock of seeing the little fur hat, the new leopard coat, the plump little figure—("I'm not really fat, you know—I have what they call a French figure")—but she never came unless the mirror lied, and it was worse for her not to come, now he must wonder where she was and if she really did meet that actor as his cruel mind was always suggesting. Nor was this curiosity, he brutally told himself, this was wrinkled old Knowledge itself flirting behind a coy veil of decent doubt to seem more endurable.

"It must be a great comfort to be so handsome," Effie said, watching his survey of the mirrors.

"It is," Dennis assured her. "I spend hours here studying my profile and pitying poor women."

"It must be satisfying to be so clever, too," Effie said. "How cozy to know that all the world is performing solely for you, and any minute with your shiny little pen you can make everybody laugh and laugh."

"Oh yes," said Dennis guardedly. "It's a great consolation to feel that you're a perfect scream. Are you trying to revenge yourself, Mrs. Callingham?"

"Couldn't I have just a little revenge?" She smiled at him. "After all, it is my birthday."

Dennis was dashed.

"I knew I'd forgotten something. Do you mind wearing my Martinis instead of my gardenias?"

"I wear a Martini beautifully," Effie said. "And I hate wearing flowers. They depress me. 'See what fun I'm having,' they say, and after that, of course, I don't have any fun."

Louis, the favorite waiter, came up and bowed.

"Well, Mrs. Callingham. Quite a change here from the old days, isn't it? Mr. Callingham still in France?"

"Oh yes," Effie said graciously, as though naturally Mr. Callingham was far too superior a man to be anywhere but in France.

"Someone said he had flown to China or Japan——"

"Yes—oh yes," Effie said hastily and Dennis pitied and hated her for not saying "Look here, I haven't had a word from that man for over fifteen years and I don't know anything about him except what I read in the papers."

"Is everything all right, Mrs. Callingham? Some hors d'œuvres, perhaps?"

"No, thank you, Louis."

This was what happened to Effie wherever she went, and Dennis, though contemptuous of her pleasure in these salaams, could find no real reason for her not sharing a crumb or two of her ex-husband's glory. Callingham had given her a hell of a break years ago and if this gave her a kick, this whispering that followed her entrance—"That's Mrs. Andrew Callingham"—then welcome to it. He had known her three years, as a matter of fact it was that very whisper in a crowded room that had made him look at her twice. Confess now, Mr. Orphen, you would never have escorted her home, never have urged her to drop into Reuben's for a sandwich and beer, never, never have pursued the acquaintance if it had not been for that awed whisper—"not the wife of Andy Callingham, *no!*" Easy enough now to make fun of people's wide-eyed reverence for that name, no doubt about it, he had been as impressed as any one else, as eager to find out intimate details from someone who had been close to the man. Maybe he was just another one of those ambitious young men who snatched up ex-wives and ex-mistresses of the elect, saw in this dim contact a personal promotion in line with their ambition, even whipped up love, though the romance was not with the woman but with the success she had once lived with. . . . No, considering this point carefully, he could plead not guilty; his own infatuation had been with her story, her laboratory possibilities.

It was getting late so they ordered dinner, carefully talking about small things so the matter of the book would not come up. If the book was not to be discussed then the references to Andy—always a part of their talk, as if Andy were their mutual dearest friend, must be checked, and if Andy was to be left out, then even inquiries as to Andy's old friends and Effie's present ones, the Glaenzers, must be omitted. This was difficult going, for so much of their fun together was in Effie's reports on the latest Glaenzer outrage, Belle's decision after all these years to be beautiful and her sweep through beauty parlors, Tony's taking up with Harlem, the servants put on the reducing diet of their mistress since she couldn't go through with it and smell a chop anywhere in the house. But the Glaenzers were Effie's only link with her past romance and Andy's name was bound up with theirs; he'd been their friend first and met Effie at their house. These subjects taboo made the sequence of Martinis ineffectual in relieving the tension of the dinner, and Dennis found himself desperately recounting stories of his boyhood which Effie must have known by heart by this time, so often had he told them. Once he thought he really did see Corinne and his mouth fell open.

"What in the world are you seeing, Dennis?" Effie asked curiously.

A fine two-timing husband he'd make, he thought, paling every time his honey's name was mentioned, probably carrying silk panties home in his brief case, leaving blond hairpins in his wife's bedroom—oh, he would be a suave old sinner, all right. This reminded him that while Corinne knew about Effie—anyone over thirty was no rival of Corinne's so she never gave the relationship a thought—Effie had never heard of Corinne. If Corinne should walk into the café this minute—he wished she would, he could not deny that leap in his heart every time he saw her sullen little face—send her here, God, even with that actor!—Effie would be astonished, bewildered, that here was an intimate friend whose name she had never heard, never in the three years they had seen each other every day. Transferring himself into Effie, he saw that this was a strange reticence considering that every other thought he'd ever had was in her confidence. Here they were, inseparable friends, confidants, and if he were to cut his throat tonight Effie would tell the police, "Whatever the motive I know there was no woman in his life." How little boon companions knew each other, he marveled! No reason, too, why Effie herself shouldn't have a love life unknown to him. Supposing that fat man now eyeing her across the room—for Effie did look young and piquant by electric light—should come up and say, "Well, Effie, tomorrow as usual?" Why not? But the idea of Effie having secrets from him was annoying and he would have none of it. The only thing that kept his spirit up, Dennis reflected, was the childish hope that other people at least were honest. Other people were sincere, transparent, candid. So he must know everything about Effie and Corinne, even though he budgeted his own confessions most cannily.

"How about it?" Effie asked. "Concert—yes?"

"I want to talk," Dennis stated. "Either I talk during the recital with everyone pointing at us or we sit here over our expensive brandy and talk a cappella."

"I'm afraid to talk," said Effie and he saw the hurt still in her blue eyes. "I'm afraid of you now. Every word I say you will be thinking—Andy taught her that, that isn't her own phrase. I'm even afraid if I drink any more I might snivel and try to be brave. You know how you hate that."

"God, yes. All right, come on." Dennis pushed his chair back abruptly. "To the concert, quick."

. . . under music . . .

Not such a good idea, Dennis thought, listening to music when you had things on your mind. The music simply drove the worry out in the open, made it race around the brain to varying tempos, induced the saddest of endings. During the Debussy he saw Effie drowning herself because the futility of her life had been pointed out to her by her dearest friend, Dennis Orphen. He reached for her hand and held it tightly, rings cutting his palm, so that if during the Ravel she tried to float gently and sadly up to heaven like Little Eva as the music urged everyone to do, he could hold her down. He stole a look at her face to see if, as she had threatened, she was really sniffling, but her profile was calmly musical, quite proper, quite controlled. He thought again of what her brief connection with Callingham had done for her—given her a confident way of holding her head, a consciousness of her public, so to speak, and this sweet arrogance affected people, even crowds, —"Who is she? She must be *somebody*,"—and even when the illustrious name was not recognized as it seldom was in musical circles it was thereafter remembered because it must be fine indeed to bestow such dignity on the wearer.

He wished, though, that some day he could persuade her to a definitely stylish outfit so that she would look less a personage and more a person. Dressed by Hawes or Bergdorf she would be a devilish sight more attractive than that scrawny little Kansas girl Andy was now with. But no, she must wear capes and flowing sleeves, Russian jewelry, Cossack belts on velvet smocks, costumes deserving an escort with a black beard, black Homburg hat, opera cape, ribbons of honor and a tiny medal or two twinkling on the lapel. Come to think of it, Alfonso of Spain was the man for her, he thought, like a producer doing type-casting. Wonder if we could get hold of old Alfonso? Call up Packards, Browns, all the agents,—what?—in Hollywood? Take a wire to M.-G.-M. Studios. Dear Alfonso, would you consider a return to stage in role particularly adapted——

Effie drew her hand away from his suddenly and when he lifted his eyebrows——

"I don't like my hand held just because somebody's thrilled over music or a sunset," she whispered.

"You want it to be sheer lust, eh?" he accused her, quite shocked.

Gieseking, the pianist, looked too big to be bullying such delicate melodies, he thought, though he tried to be very gentle with them. He crouched over the piano with his big hands cupping the keys as if a mouse might peep out of his fist once he relaxed. Softly his fingers in ten little bedroom slippers tiptoed up and down Schumann, music became so diminished under his microscope, made so tiny and perfect that it could be neatly placed in a baby's ear.

"He plays as if the piano was his valentine," Effie said as they walked down Seventh to her apartment, "and little white birdies with tiny envelopes marked 'I love you' might come twittering out any minute."

Little white messages, yes, flying across oceans, over green Spain, pink Alps, lavender Saar, fluttering over Persian temples, high over missionary-colored China, into the longest bar in the world, paging Mr. Callingham, is it true he's in Shanghai, was his picture in yesterday's *News* beaming out of aviation hood or was that only Malraux or the merest Halliburton?

Effie's apartment was the top floor of an old Chelsea private house because she—or was it Andy?—liked neighborhoods with a history, she liked to feel that Lillie Langtry had often passed, perhaps even entered this house, that H. C. Bunner, Clement Moore, O. Henry, Poe, anybody once glamorous, might have lived here or next door. Dennis thought, too, she selected her rooms always for their quietness and suitability to a writer, as though, supposing Andy did come back to live with her, he wouldn't be displeased with her home. In the doorway Dennis hesitated, for Effie made no move to invite him in but started fussing with the fireplace silently.

"Look here, Effie, you don't mind that book, really? You know it has nothing to do with you. You may have started the idea off in my head, of course, but the rest is all my gorgeous imagination. Give me credit for originality, please."

"Of course, darling. You don't mind if I hide for a few days after the book comes out, do you? I mean—you know—I hate people finding out that Andy deserted me, that's all. I'd rather they just went on thinking we—well—were temporarily away from each other."

Dennis stared at her in absolute bewilderment. She actually thought people didn't know! Or did she?

"Is that all?" he blurted out in amazement. "Why everyone's always known that he walked out on you, if that's all that worries you about the book. Hell, Effie, that's no news to anybody!"

Now it was too late. Now there was nothing more to be said. This blow was final. Effie, quite pale, sat down abruptly on the desk-chair, staring at him blankly. He'd done it now, if he hadn't before.

"I'll run along," he said, angry at the whole mess.

He walked hurriedly down the stairs, his cane, as always, clattering down ahead of him. Now he'd done it, now he'd said it, now he'd fixed it, but how could one dream what fantastic lies people's egos fed on? Here was Effie, a balanced, intelligent woman nourished for years on the pretense that people believed her solitude was accidental circumstance, not her husband's own selfish choice. What made a woman like Effie so blind, or was it perhaps not rosy veils but healing bandages she wore, and was it not tonic but ruin to destroy them? Behind them what did Effie really think, did she love Andy truly all these years or was that loyalty, did she hurt when she saw his name or did she swell with possessive pride? He wondered if now she was up there—yes, she probably was—flung down on the black sateen-covered couch under the Van Gogh print; or no, she was staring into the fire not sad over Andy, but storing bitter, vengeful thoughts against Dennis, each resentful memory of tonight a fresh stone for Andy's monument, loyalty to him enhanced by the detractor's sarcasm, words erased by anger at the speaker . . . or perhaps this was only what he would feel and do in her situation and instead was she—

. . . becoming the Stranger . . .

—WAITING quietly till the slamming of the front door
showed he had gone, hands clutched together in her lap, a
little hole in her mind where the bullet had gone through—
"everyone has always known he walked out on you"—and
nothing to put in its place but an old swimming pain, that
same almost-forgotten pain of smiling gaily at the party, eyes
fixed on companion—don't turn, don't wince, don't pale,
don't show you see Andy pulling the blond girl out onto the
balcony with that veiled excited look in his eyes she saw only
for other women,—yes, this pain was blurred like that old one
had been and flowed outside as well as through her, tingled
like frost in the air about her. Slowly phrases jumped into
place in her brain—"Tired Truth barked at her heels"—say
rather it tore at her heart. She stood up astonished that legs
could support this heavy stone, legs marched out the door,
one, two, one, two, downstairs one flight, see the picture of
the landlord's graduation class 1911, Brown University, under
the hall lamp, down one flight more into the vestibule, and
stop, turn, look. There was the card on her mailbox:

MRS. ANDREW CALLINGHAM

It had been there and on all her other mailboxes for years,
secretly shaming her before the world. It was incredible that
she had not realized its mocking pretensions before, somehow
it had seemed only loyalty, it was to show Andy she bore no
grudge, see, she really did understand him after all and was
proud of the little while she had held him. . . . "A buried
woman." . . . "What fragment is left of that buried woman—"
She pulled the little white card out of the mailbox and turned
it over. On the back her trembling fingers printed in pencil—

MISS EFFIE THORNE

—and put it back in place.

. . . lifting the lid . . .

BECOMING other people, leaving this gray suit of Wanamaker
tweeds, black ties, favorite therefore always soiled green shirt,
incredibly stained, fantastically misshapen, chewed-up, tram-
pled-on brown hat, leaving this pretty ensemble bodiless in
the Trayful for a Trifle Cafeteria, bemused before a mug of
coffee and chop suey, this flight into other souls had dis-
advantages. There were moments, for instance, when all findings were annulled by a blank, unpredictable act, and then
there was the infallible law that simple souls were insoluble by
this magic. You could listen and look and wonder, but there
was no solving of simplicity. It was as baffling as nobility. Very
well, you say, granted there is no artifice here, no trickery,
what motive has this man for having no motive? Put him
down then, at his best, as merely smug, what secret knowledge does he treasure to give him this complacence? Let him
be candid, let him fasten to your lapel and declare, "You want
to know about me—what I'm really about, eh? Listen, I'll tell
you everything, every deed, every thought, there's no puzzle
here." All the more puzzle then to know if these are lies, or,
if truth, why so willingly revealed? In the end one gives up
these transparent but baffling cases for those more complicated; at least there are recognized rules and categories for
neurotics.

"Just the same I would like to lift the top off Effie Thorne's
head and see what is really there," Dennis mused. "How was
it like living with old Andy, how does it feel hearing people
pant and gasp over his name, how does she feel remembering
when he used to sleep with her just like the king and the Jersey Lily—was that the secret then of all these years' regret,
that he was so fine in bed? But then women fight and lose all
pride to hold such men. In that case there would be no self-
sacrifice, even for an Effie."

Out in the street he saw that tiresome red-faced fellow who was always after him to write a 'piece' for the weekly he ran, the man who knew everybody and said "okie-dokie" to everything. Okie, as one instinctively thought of him, was with a gay party just leaving the Irving Place Burley and Dennis, now entering a seventh plane of being that one-armed sailor on the corner trying to roll his own cigarette, wished only to be unnoticed. No use.

"Hi, Dennis Orphen!" Okie always used one's full name as if it were a title and would fill hearers with awe—not *the* Dennis Orphen, as if he were Al Smith or somebody. He enjoyed knowing everybody in New York and said he did whether or no. He liked knowing the 'Greenwich Village Bunch' and it was no use telling him that East Sixteenth wasn't Bohemia and for the matter of that neither was Bohemia. Okie lived with his family somewhere in the Bronx—(though here Dennis recalled Okie always was insisting East Ninety-first Street was *not* the Bronx)—and it was no good telling him that one room on the fourth floor within gunshot of the Rand School wasn't deliriously racy bachelor quarters. Okie, in his envious remarks, seemed to feel that Dennis lay in bed all day in an actor's dressing gown while glorious coeds from the Rand School and teasers from the Burley paraded in and out in a never-ending orgy.

"You writers down here in the Village!" he would jovially exclaim, as though all you needed to do was wave a manuscript at a girl and she had a baby. No. Okie was a man to be avoided when possible as it was apparently not tonight.

"Come over to Lüchow's with our gang," he insisted. "We're all tight as ticks and tomorrow's Saturday."

"Work," said Dennis.

Okie breathed a blast of gin confidentially in his face.

"Theatrical people," he whispered. "Two fellows just got here from London—they're like that with Cochrane—they know Dame Sybil Thorndike personally. The girls just got back from Hollywood. They're bridge hostesses."

"Great," said Dennis. "So long."

They were all tipping over each other more than was necessary and after a look at the two blondes and the two long-faced chinless young men, Dennis, with his wonderful new prescience, knew everything they were going to say from now on into infinity.

Okie's hand dropped cajolingly on his shoulder.

"One beer?"

"No."

"How about a little bock? You know this fella's a big shot, let me tell you, Dennis Orphen—he got a prize once—"

"Oh, for Christ's sake, Okie, leave me alone."

As soon as he'd said it Dennis realized he'd gone too far but you had to with a person like Okie. As the others pulled him away it was not pleasant seeing Okie's red embarrassed face. One of these days he'd need a hundred dollars and want to write that article for Okie, and Okie would remember being insulted. Dennis heard one of the two girls call out to Okie.

"Do you mind if Tony Glaenzer meets us over here? Lucille called him up and he said he would come."

Dennis suddenly turned around and caught Okie by the arm. Tony Glaenzer, part of Effie's past. That was different.

"Sure, I'll come along, old boy. Let's go."

Okie was mad. If he'd been sober you could have insulted him all night and he wouldn't have noticed but now he was offended.

"Oh yes, you'll have a beer with us all right," he sneered. "Okie-dokie. I get it. You got to have some Park Avenue in it before you'll join. Got to work right up to the time you hear Tony Glaenzer's coming along, then it's okie-dokie. Come on, then, phony."

His round red face in a ferocious scowl looked like a magazine-cover baby about to bawl. Dennis despised him.

"Can't blame me for wanting to get ahead a little socially," he said amiably. "I like a nice contact now and then."

Now he became Effie again, meeting Tony Glaenzer, discussing old times at the Beach Club on Long Island twenty years ago, evoking the old buried life, the buried woman. At the same time he was Dennis tomorrow telling Effie about Tony and his two blondes.

"Is he a Jew?" asked one of the girls pointing to Dennis.

"No, he's a Turk," Okie sourly answered and as this went over big he forgave Dennis for being a snob and slapped him on the shoulder fondly. "Good old Dennis Orphen. The red-headed Turk."

Lüchow's was filled with a lodge banquet and in every room middle-aged men grimly wore paper hats and clinked glasses with their big wives. The orchestra played polychrome waltzes and a fat man was stirred to get up and holding his stomach in, danced marvelously with a thin toothy girl who arched her scanty behind the way her crowd at Montclair always did.

"Geschichten aus dem Wiener Wald," said Okie as they found their table. "My favorite piece."

Dennis looked around for Glaenzer, wondering if he could spot him from Effie's description.

"Four bock, Herr Ober," Okie shouted and then cupped his hand close to Dennis' ear. "Theatrical people," he whispered significantly. "Actors. Actresses."

The two girls were obviously not happy in their evening's outing, nor for that matter were the two young men from London. These narrow-chinned fellows carried on a private discussion about one Wylie and whether Wylie really meant things when he said them and funny experiences each had had with Wylie both here and abroad. Wylie was one of the most inscrutable, brilliant yet brutal characters Dennis had ever heard of. The chances were he would never meet Wylie. Supposing he did, at Caroline's for instance—it seems he was always at his cousin Caroline's parties; in fact, Caroline's were the only parties Wylie ever attended—he, Dennis, would march right up to him and say, "What did you mean that day on the *Bremen* when you gave Thurman that terribly strange look and said, 'Thurman, you can't go on like this, you know'?" No, he would never meet Wylie nor Caroline either, for that matter; he was fortunate indeed in merely knowing young Thurman. The two blondes kept exchanging glances of veiled meaning and took turns borrowing nickels from Okie to telephone wonderful men somewhere else. The messages were then relayed to the other on her return to the table, rather rudely, Dennis felt.

"Says call in about an hour," Ethel told Lucille. "We'll go up. Unless you want to call Van first."

Then Lucille went to telephone and came back, giving Ethel a meaning look as she resumed her seat.

"Something funny to tell you," she said quietly smiling, but did not say what it was Van had said, obviously something far too good for the rest of the crowd.

"Let's all go up to old Van's and have a good laugh," suggested Dennis.

"You don't even know who we're talking about," said Lucille with a superior smile.

Okie conducted the orchestra from his seat, waving both hands.

"*Sari,*" he announced. "Dum de dum de—that's *Sari.*"

Then Tony came in, walking right through the baronial beer parlors out of Effie's past, carrying in his head, which would never reveal these pictures, memories of a young radiant Effie, Effie in the formal gardens of the great Long Island estate Dennis could never quite paint, and as he saw him approach their table Dennis suddenly knew something Effie had never told him or else never known—that Tony had been in love with her.

"How do I know that?" he wondered but he would have sworn it was true; his heart beat fast as though he had found something of terrific importance to the world, something that must be telegraphed at once to all the papers—stop, press, stop, Winchell—

Tony must now be near forty but he was as slim and as weak-faced and beardless as Effie had described him years ago. Dennis felt annoyed with Effie that apart from this weak youthfulness he would never have recognized the man from her description. Obviously, in her preoccupation with Callingham at that time, she had never noticed that Tony was extremely handsome in a hungry, girlish, petulant way, that he was tall, lean and rubbery as though he might snap back to the little spoiled child he was at any minute, that his hands were large, frantic, futile, crazy hands. It was plain to Dennis that Tony had not wanted to come out on a party, but it was also plain that he was always doing things he didn't want to because he was afraid some day something real might happen and he wouldn't be on hand to see it.

"Always wanted to meet you, Mr. Glaenzer," said Okie, beaming. "I run a little magazine, you probably have heard of it—*The Town*, and somebody's always writing in—'Why don't you get pictures of Tony Glaenzer's home,' they say, 'give us some pictures of that Tudor barn or whatever the hell.' This is Dennis Orphen. That's Victor Herbert."

"How do you do, Mr. Herbert." Tony sat down, sniffed at Ethel's drink. "Scotch and seltzer, thanks."

"*The Fortune-Teller*," said Okie, conducting again but with his knife now instead of a forefinger. "Dada da da da. I'll get them to play the *Rosenkavalier*. They'll do anything for me here. Hey, Herr Ober."

What if he, too, should go telephone, Dennis speculated, what if he should ask Effie to come over to be surprised by the two extremes of her life spending a jolly evening together over bock? No, it would be more fun tomorrow.

Ethel and Lucille made a great fuss over Tony. The two actors thought they had run into him once at Caroline's. Did he know Wylie Meigs? Yes, Caroline was a friend of his wife. Mentioning his wife made Dennis wonder how this handsome fellow could have lived with Belle Glaenzer all these years, even with her fabulous fortune to ease the pain. Dennis could visualize Belle, as Effie's stories had built up the image—a moonfaced mountainous woman padding through the handsome plush corridors in the silent hours of the dawn up to the maids' quarters trying to still her heavy panting breaths and to keep the house from shaking with her Olympian tread, listening for her young husband's amorous whispers in this or that bedroom, sniffing for his cigarettes near this door and that, and occasionally being certain of her clues but uncertain how to stop whatever was going on, so up and down the hall she must wander, sniffling and moaning like a sick old hound. How could Effie have stood such a household? Dennis wondered. Even if it was her livelihood, trotting around with a rich old woman, how did she do it, how could she endure them?

It seemed the two girls knew Tony as the boy-friend of their chum, Boots, who was coming in from the road tomorrow. Tony was candidly bored except when discussing Boots and Boots' plans with her friends. When the talk shifted and became general he merely smiled fixedly at the tablecloth, and dabbled his long white futile fingers in the sugar bowl like a rich nursery child who knows he must not play with the sugar lumps but his silky fingertips enjoy the rough crunching of the sugar against them almost as much as he enjoys spoiling them for other people, surely a rich young man's simple, just prerogative. He shot an occasional sidelong look at Dennis and when Okie shouted or made flamboyant gestures of conducting, his face lit up as if active bad taste stirred his admiration.

"You were with Callingham in Lipps' one day in Paris," said one of Wylie's chums, deciding that here at least was someone worthy of an Englishman's friendship. "Andrew Callingham."

"Oh, he's a great friend of old Callingham," Okie explained with a lordly wave of the hand. "Nice guy, Callingham. I know him personally. Or rather I know Wife Number Two. A Kansas City girl. Marian, that was."

"I heard he backed that Swedish dancer in Paris last year," said one of the young men. "There was quite a little talk."

"He brought her on a cruise once with us while Marian had dysentery in the American Hospital," said Tony. "Asta Lundgren."

Hm, thought Dennis, that's a new one Effie hadn't heard about, Asta Lundgren, eh?

"I read everything he ever wrote," said the dark actor, the one who had actually spent a whole fortnight with Wylie on a cruise. "I daresay I'm the only person who ever read his *Little Hazards*, his first. Wylie had a copy of it, you know. Quite rare now."

Little Hazards. He wrote it on his honeymoon with Effie. She still thought it was his finest book. Her blue eyes always filled with love for anyone who spoke of it, for then she could explain how every phrase came to be written, how funny Andy had looked in that dreadful shooting outfit in which he worked. She had typed it three times and even then there were so many mistakes—she was no typist after all—that they had to get a secretary in. It was Effie's book, really.

"This Marian is Wife Number Two, did you say?" asked Dennis, playing a game with himself—no direct questions, no admissions, all information must come out casually in the course of the conversation, and whether this information was for himself as a check-up on his speculations about Effie or for Effie herself, he could not have said.

"Who was Number One?" asked Okie. "What was she like?"

"Coldish," said Tony briefly, making a fortress on the table out of the sugar lumps. "Might have worked out only she was too noble. Forgave Andy every time he ran out on her."

"Is she alive? Did she fuss when he ran away with Marian?" Okie asked. "Marian had some good-looking pins, let me tell you."

"This first wife was my wife's companion when they met. That was Effie," said Tony and mussed the fortress into a heap. "Andy visited me. He was a big hairy roaring sort of guy—he-man. Loved trying out every woman he met, especially the difficult virginal type. Effie was that and of course he fell all the harder. He could never make her out. Still talks about her. He said to me, 'You know, Tony, a man can never tell the difference between the reserves of a deep, forgiving, all-understanding love and the polite indifference of a well-bred casual attachment. They act just the same.' So when Effie was noble about letting him go he couldn't figure out whether it was martyrdom or plain indifference."

"What was your guess?" asked Dennis.

Tony looked at him a little curiously.

"I've thought about it. You know I don't believe Effie gave a damn," he said. "She was unhappy all the time with him. She's happy now—lives her own life. We see her now and again. Has an apartment somewhere around here. Has a lover."

"Oh, she has a lover, has she?" Dennis pricked up his ears but Tony's next words explained.

"Another writer," said Tony. "Cares more about him than she ever did about Andy. Talks about him whenever we see her. Young fellow. This one's an æsthete, I guess, no he-man."

"Oh, is that so?"

Dennis saw the light suddenly. So *he* was supposed to be Effie's lover, that was the story. So Effie cared more about him that she ever had about Andy. So *he* was not the big he-man raper Callingham had been but just a little petered-out æsthete, eh? Angrily Dennis' legs stretched out under the table until his feet caught the ankle of the nearest blonde, Lucille. She looked at him inquiringly, and then smiled a little.

"What are you laughing at?" asked Ethel after a moment. Tony had lapsed into a bored, austere silence.

Lucille took out her vanity and made a new mouth over her old one, then glanced over the little mirror at Dennis with increased interest.

"Nothing," she said airily and hummed with the orchestra. "What is that thing, Okie?"

" '*Dein ist mein ganzes Herz,*' " said Okie, waving his menu in authoritative rhythm. "Dein-ist-mein-ganzes-Herz—dum-dee-da-dum—"

"I thought we were going to Harlem," Tony said to Lucille.

"We hate Harlem," said Okie disagreeably.

"That's the truth," said Ethel.

Tony got up.

"Well, I hate German waltzes and beer," he said. "I'll run along. See you at Boots' tomorrow, Lucille."

They watched him run along, his lithe elegant figure hurrying through the tables as if they might pursue him and bring him back.

"Doesn't like waltzes!" repeated Okie. "Why, he's married to an old Coney Island waltz!"

"Anybody that could stand that old woman of his all these years needn't be so fussy about what they like or don't like," said Ethel, personally insulted by his departure.

"He married her to get on with his music," said Wylie's friend. "Boy, is that irony! He marries her to get to Vienna and when he goes it's only with her to the spas for her varicose veins. Ha, ha."

"Tough," said Dennis.

"Yeah," said Okie, "a snob like you would stick up for him."

"I'm not a snob," insisted Dennis. "Would I be out with you folks if I was a snob?"

Everyone laughed but on second thoughts got a little mad. Even Lucille withdrew her foot and slipped it back in her shoe as silent evidence of disapproval.

"Where'll he end up?" asked Ethel. "He can't lift a finger for himself. What happens to fellows like that?"

"He'll end up in a flophouse on Third Avenue," said Dennis dreamily.

Okie was terrified at the mere words. He shook Dennis' arms pleadingly.

"Don't say such things," he implored earnestly. "Why

should he end up in a snobhouse on Third Avenue? Not un-less there's a revolution. Why should he?"

"It's the snobhouse for all of us quicker than that," said Dennis dourly. "The system's failing, the game's up."

"Oh, let's go, Lucille," Ethel urged her friend. "I can't stand it when people talk like this. And Van will be waiting—"

Lucille had permitted her foot to be won back again and was being appeased by Dennis' rather serious attention under the table.

"Van can go to hell," she suggested casually. "Who does Van think he is for Christ's sake—Mervyn LeRoy?"

. . . the little nest itself . . .

THE PALE lovely city morning, thought Dennis, and was
sorry for the country with its poor morning sky bereft of clangor blended into its blue. From a house across the court—
and it amused him never to know what street those houses
faced, came the sound of a piano; it trickled through the
backporch trellising, sounds light and dark like shifting sunlight. Scarlatti, a laundress in the basement yard singing over
her clothes-hanging, the swish of a broom on stone and hy-
drant splashing over cement court, the endless flow of trucks
and streetcars and fire engine all translated into a steady throb
in the walls of his fourth-floor room, a perpetual dynamo that
operated the life of Manhattan. The walls throbbed night and
day like a cabin next door to the ship's engines, and the silver-
framed picture of Corinne in her bathing suit at Asbury Park,
with Phil cut out of the background except for a white shoe,
quivered out a Morse code against the wall.

So that was Tony. So he had a Boots who was on the stage.
A little toots named Boots. So Callingham's new wife wasn't
much. So Okie was afraid of the revolution and the snob-
houses. So Wylie was the way he was. . . . Dennis looked
over the *Mirror*, a stale one as it was only today's. He read
Barclay Beekman's sprightly reports of the six hundred dollars
raised for the Free Milk Fund by Mrs. Ten Bruck's brilliant
Firebird Pageant and Ball at the Waldorf. It seems the costumes alone cost over fifty thousand dollars, but the rich spare
no expense when it's to help the little babies of the slums.
Nor for that matter, reflected Dennis, do the Communists
even without a Mrs. Ten Bruck as La Flamme. How nobly do
these hundreds put their little half-dollars together for a
Webster Hall–Mercerized Firebird Pageant and Ball to help
miners, all in order to break nearly even. There was direct action
for you. Sacrifice upon sacrifice. However, looking on the

bright side, both affairs are always well-publicized and it would be an ungrateful baby or miner who would prefer a bed to Mrs. Ten Bruck's Tropical Float or a sandwich to a program of hillbilly songs sung by loyal comrades.

He read Gladys Glad and was astounded to find that the secret of little Sylvia Sidney's success was in twisting her torso fifteen times right and left with deep breaths and an ounce of camphor dissolved in your witch-hazel. . . . Ah, here we are. MacTweed will publish on the tenth *The Hunter's Wife* by Dennis Orphen. It is rumored that this novel concerns the ex-wife of a well-known literary figure. Of Mr. Orphen's last book Lewis Gannett said, "Orphen knows New York like a fish knows water." So Mr. Gannett called him a fish. O.K., Mr. Gannett. Effie would see that. There would be more of it every day and there would be nothing for him to say, no excuse, no denial was possible. Probably the name itself would come out in some gossip column and reporters would call up and ask Effie how she felt about it. She would be hurt at first, then freeze up the way she had over that biography of Andy someone had written in the *Atlantic*.

"Rather cheap," she would finally say, chin raised in a superior smile, "a little cheap after all. But then Dennis never did have any breeding. Not that I mind what he said about me—dear me, no—that's only to be expected from that sort of person."

She would take on her English accent the way she did in referring to people she disliked. She would turn into Lady Diana. At the thought Dennis' love rushed out to her—oh dear, lovely person, understand and forgive and be happy again, but don't be brave, don't be gallant or noble, it's far too heartbreaking.

If people, thought Dennis, only came right out and called each other an s.o.b. when they were just that, it would make the world a much finer place. It was these martyrs, these silent sufferers, these decent fine people, these chin-uppers that gave selfishness and crime its head start. Why, he thought, I ought to be tarred and feathered for telling all in this book. It would teach me to pick my material with more care, more decency. As it is, Effie will be noble; and next year, spoiled by this, I will write about Corinne, so Phil Barrow will divorce her and she will starve but be noble, and noble bodies will be stretched from here all the way up to the printers, just because nobody called me a s.o.b. at the right moment. People are too well-bred, so on with little crime!

Somewhere on the mysterious street beyond those houses across the way a German band was economizing on *Wien, Wien, Nur Du Allein*, and when the combined notes of all four bronchial instruments failed on the 'glücklich bin' a lamed flute eked out the last bar. The piano across the court left Scarlatti and went into polite accompaniment for a frantic soprano, her shrill wings beat futilely against the locked octaves of a treble paradise and fell short a good half-note. The pianist is really good, thought Dennis, he has to accompany her for his room rent and how he suffers, for his fifteen a week. She'll never make a concert stage any more than she'll make high C, and for that matter neither will he—(but I alone know that)—because he won't have the money, and even if he did find a Belle Glaenzer to marry him she would only tie him up for life like old Tony, so wherever he turns he's wrecked.

The winter sun pulled aside a grimy negligée of clouds, a bit consumptive, this Manhattan sun, giving nothing but a pallid glow to windowpanes and a sickly fever to bare streets in summer, perpetual slush in winter. Instead of giving it went about its own racket of drawing life and color from city streets as it drew rainfall from mountain streams.

Dennis made himself coffee on the electric ring in his bathroom. Once a friend of Corinne's named Walter had nearly electrocuted himself that way. This fellow Walter was taking a shower while his coffee, or in this case his whistling teakettle, was on the electric plate. He reached out with his wet hand to turn it off when the whistle began to whistle and just then the shock came and there was Walter, great hulking fellow, captain of a team once, too, unable to let go, shaking away with shock after shock, but meantime the old whistle on the kettle was whistling so somebody came in from the bedroom—Dennis always suspected this little somebody was Corinne but she wouldn't admit it, it was just a nameless but very kind intimate somebody—and she did all the right first-aid things and fixed everything. Walter was saved, the shower was finished, the clever little heroine—(Corinne, you can't fool me)—poured the whistle water out of the whistling teakettle on to the drip coffeepot, a pleasant breakfast of delicious Maxwell House Coffee and last week's brioches from Longchamps was soon had by all, and that was why Dennis would never have a whistling teakettle, even though they cost only eighty-nine cents and were terribly funny.

"But they saved Walter's life, darling," Corinne protested.

"That's just it," said Dennis. "They'd always be reminding me of the bastard."

. . . keep him guessing . . .

"Every day of my life," wrote Dorothy Dix, a kind-faced gentlewoman in the New York *Journal*, "girls write in to me that their boy-friends for no reason at all are turning cold to them. 'I have loved John dearly for two years,' writes one, 'and have never given him a moment's doubt of it. Yet lately he seems to avoid me and seems annoyed by my gestures of affection.' Oh, my dears," continued Dorothy Dix, "don't you understand that nothing is so deadening to a man as certainty, that to keep a man mystified is the secret of holding his love? Don't let him be so cocksure, let him sense the possibility of losing you to someone else—keep him guessing if you would hold him."

So it was that when Dennis telephoned, Corinne put down the paper and answered that she really couldn't say when she'd be free to see him.

"Lunch, eh?" suggested Dennis, the cocksure.

"I couldn't possibly," said Corinne briefly, mystifying him.

"Why not?"

Corinne's chilly, polite silence proclaimed the insolence of such a personal question.

"You come over here at five, then," said Dennis, but again Corinne made it clear that she had important other plans. It was the same with tomorrow and next day. In fact Corinne politely implied that she was a very busy and popular woman for the next few weeks but if any of these fabulous engagements should fall through she would be most happy to give Mr. Orphen a ring. Goodbye, and thanks terribly for thinking of me.

What's up now, speculated Dennis, she must have seen me at Lüchow's last night or somebody told her, and anyway where had *she* been? He'd called up her house a dozen times in the evening changing his voice every time he got Phil and always Mrs. Barrow was out. There was no chart to the simple but cockeyed course of Corinne's emotions so, thoroughly mystified and even more annoyed, Dennis went back to the piece he was writing on Old Yorkville for Okie, taken from his last article on the same subject but with the tenses changed, to give it a fresh note.

Pursuing her role as suggested by Miss Dix, Corinne immediately taxied over to the Algonquin to lunch with Walter himself, just this moment arrived from three weeks in London. At least he was supposed to have been in London on business but Corinne understood and all the people Corinne knew understood that Walter had really been in Paris with Mrs. Bee Amidon. Walter's own wife had stayed home in the beautiful Larchmont home she had heckled him into buying. Walter was Phil's best friend but it was Walter and Corinne who really understood each other, who whispered in the kitchen over the cocktail-shaking while Phil and Mary played bagatelle. Walter knew all about Dennis and Corinne, knew all about Bee Amidon, and often Walter and Corinne stayed out all hours of the night confiding in each other the anguish of finding true love too late. For Walter had never loved as he loved Bee, and Corinne would never love anyone the way she loved Dennis. Bee Amidon had other affairs and even ran around with her husband more than was necessary and all in all made Walter miserable, while Corinne told stories of Dennis' casualness when her own feelings were so eternal and deep. Once these mutual confessions of great love unrequited had ended up on Walter's studio couch—he kept a room in town—but this episode was regarded as a foul and stricken promptly off the records and Corinne could not help feeling wounded when Dennis suspected her in the whistling tea-kettle business. Walter was always surprised that Corinne and Bee were not chums, but his confidences and expressed suspicions about his love had established such a hideous picture of the woman that he did not realize that in relieving himself of this monster he had given her to Corinne for keeps.

Nor did Walter think Dennis Orphen was anything but a big phony. He did not for a minute think Dennis gave a damn about Corinne as she herself once in a while darkly intimated. In spite of these mutual reserves, Walter and Corinne gave each other an amazing amount of reassurance. Concerning Walter's suspicions of Bee, Corinne said, "Why, darling, you just don't know women, that's all. Bee's simply crazy about you and she wouldn't dream of that dumb lawyer you're so afraid of."

Privately Corinne thought Bee was sleeping with ten dumb lawyers but Walter never guessed.

"Dennis never asks me to leave Phil," Corinne then complained to Walter. "Sometimes I think it's because there's some one else in his life, but really the only serious friend he has is that woman Mrs. Callingham, and of course she's much too old."

"He's too decent to ask you to give up a good home for the ups and downs of a writer's life," Walter told her as Corinne had wanted him to, though as Walter told Mary and Bee and all the other unknown repositories of Corinne's secrets, Dennis was really scared to death Corinne would plump herself down on him one of these days and try to trap him into something serious. As for this 'old' Mrs. Callingham— ha-ha—she was a damn fine-looking woman and not over thirty-four or so—not much over anyway and you could bet your sweet life a man wouldn't tie himself up with a little nitwit like Corinne when he could get a glamorous, famous woman like this Mrs. Callingham. He'd seen her in the en-tr'acte of *Biography* and you could tell right away she was a keen person. She was with Dennis and had her arm through his, talking and laughing. Walter has just given Dennis a quiet level look as if "No, I won't tell Corinne, you bum. What kind of a fellow are you anyway? Haven't you any decency at all with your women?" Because, the way Walter felt was that there was a certain code about intrigue the same as anything else and Dennis didn't measure up, though when Walter mentioned this to Bee Amidon she said men were always having very high codes for other men to follow and nobody ever measured up, but she noticed they all seemed to do about the same things.

"I met this Callingham one night at the Dôme, Bee and I did," Walter told Corinne. "He's a big good-looking guy. He'd flown over Persia and people were fussing over him like mad. Bee knew him. I told him there was this book being written about him. He was sore as the dickens."

"You shouldn't have told him," said Corinne. "He might sue Dennis."

She was having a pernod and having said so many nasty things about Dennis her heart was filling with love for him and a slight indignation at Walter. It was *his* fault she'd said Dennis was phony and shallow and insincere. Why did men let people say such things about another man?

" 'Who is this Orphen, anyway?' says Callingham," said Walter and leaving out the deprecatory description he and Bee had eagerly furnished at the time he continued, "so we told him he was a very good writer and got a prize once."

Walter poured a brandy into his coffee the way Bee liked it. He missed Bee now but sometimes he thought it was more fun talking to Corinne about how he loved Bee than really being with Bee, for Bee never seemed to want to be alone with him, she was always asking every one else to join them. In fact the affair from her point of view was just loads of fun and that was all. She never cried or talked about divorces or any of the normal things, she just had a fine time as if it wasn't serious at all.

"What'd Whosis say when you told him who Dennis was?"

"He said Erskine Caldwell was the only writer in America worth anything," Walter finally recollected.

"That's because he's something like Callingham," Corinne deduced.

"He said America was dead anyway," said Walter. "He said we hadn't really produced anything he could dignify by the name of literature since *Three Soldiers*. He kept saying America is dead, dead and drinking straight whisky. I say, Corinne, let's get tight and cruise through the city all day. Mary's coming in tonight and if I'm sober I'll feel guilty about Bee and won't be able to carry the thing off."

It seemed a good idea to Corinne. That would show Dennis he couldn't be sure of her if she spent the day celebrating with Walter. Be cool, be aloof, don't let him be sure of you, Corinne went out to phone Dennis and show how cool and aloof she was.

"What's up?" he said. "I'm working. Want to come over?"

"Come over? Certainly not," said Corinne with a light tinkling laugh. "I just called to ask if you could come to our house for dinner the fifth of next month."

Dennis was plainly astounded by such a formal message.

"Good heavens, next month? How do I know what I can do next month? I'll let you know when the time comes. What kind of party is it anyway that I got to be asked so far ahead— a masquerade?"

"Just you alone. No party, I'm afraid," said Corinne stiffly.

"Well, I'll let you know when I see you."

Corinne allowed a significant pause to take place.

"In case we don't see each other till then I wanted to be sure, that's all," she graciously explained. "It's a Wednesday. Can you make it?"

"No," he said in tremendous disgust and the receiver banged up.

Corinne went into the ladies' room and made up again. It was always fun making up after a few pernods because they made your face freeze so it was like painting a statue. She went back to the dining room which was rapidly filling with witty wonderful characters and they were all drinking and eating like anybody else. Walter was entering his third brandy when she got back to the table. Walter was really terribly sweet. He understood about Dennis, too, that Dennis was too fine, too decent, to ask her to give up Phil's protection for his small earnings. Even if this new book was a great hit it wouldn't be as much as Phil made and she loved her nice little house on Sixty-fourth Street with its little garden and Dennis wouldn't want her to leave that particularly after she'd just fixed it all up. Walter understood how Dennis felt. It was the nicest thing about Walter, the way he understood about Dennis. She put her arm around dear Walter, standing behind his chair and pressed her mouth to his ear.

"Walter, I can't stay," she whispered. "I have to go over to Dennis' right away. You understand, darling."

Walter was, nevertheless, as mad as he could be, watching the cunning little figure in the leopard coat and green beret patter out of the room. It was all very well for wives to fail you or for your true love to fail you—they had some excuse, but for a friend—and after all he'd done for Corinne, too, fixing it up with Phil a million different times, and letting her weep on his shoulder, and not telling her all he'd heard around town about Dennis and Mrs. Callingham. After all he'd done as her one true friend the least she could have done in return was to help celebrate his return. What kind of pal was she, anyway?

Walter ordered another brandy, this time with soda, and sat gloomily thinking of all the things he'd done for Corinne, and for Bee too for that matter. After a while his mind saved him a lot of trouble by making the two into one woman, a wayward, double-crossing, lying little tramp. He wished he hadn't bought Bee that hat, though in another way he wished she'd asked for diamonds so he could accuse her of being plain mercenary. In crises like this, being left all alone at noon in a café with all day to waste, Walter's Michigan morality suddenly came out in full force to sustain him, and he wanted to see his wife and thank her for being a good woman. Someone you can believe in, that's what you needed, someone you could trust—

. . . Mrs. Callingham lying down . . .

—Someone in fact like Effie Callingham who had never lied to a living soul, who had never betrayed anyone, had committed no crime in her whole life save for the crime of one Great Renunciation Gesture, but like many renunciations she had not fully realized at the time how great and how final it would be.

Lying down on the black sateen couch, a guest-towel soaked in cologne over her eyes as if this might relieve the ache that rippled through her whole body, Effie remembered saying it, saying the sentence, to Andy that day years ago. The scene unrolled itself again in the private projection room of her mind as if through seeing it so often she might learn where the mistake had been made, how else she could have acted. There they were, young hero, blond heroine, setting out in Andy's launch. The old launch, Andy's pride and extravagance, had been their refuge ever since their first meeting, a refuge from the Glaenzers, from Andy's increasingly insistent public, and finally it had become a means of recapturing their own romance in crises, but after three years the tranquil shores once the background of their idyll had become tainted with their misunderstandings, their long patient talks, the patient, civilized talks that, if one only knew it, are the end of love.

This reel, labeled 'The Last Week-End,' viewed always through headaches, pointed out only one lesson, Effie decided now: She should never have tried to be modern, she should never have tried to be generous. Her instinctive horror of Andy's infidelities should have expressed itself in natural ways—rage, or flight, rather than the philosophic, tolerant front utterly foreign to herself. When Marian appeared she had been no different than a dozen other little affairs he'd had, it hadn't been necessary to step out so nobly.

But then remember she was tired after three years of it, tired of entertaining her pretty rivals, tired of talking to husbands to distract them from Andy's admiration of their wives, frightened of the subtle shift in their relationship from lovers to good sports, tired of the stiff smile on her face. Yes, something undoubtedly would have had to happen, Effie realized that now. But it need not have been separation. And she need never have brought things out in the open. She should not have mentioned knowing about his feeling for Marian. She should have been discreetly obtuse. She knew how he hated to feel guilty or selfish, and he hated to promise faithfulness when he had no such intention. So it was her fault. When they had their little week-end together she should have made it theirs and theirs alone, instead of allowing Marian's name to come between them.

She remembered the fog as they slipped out of Cold Spring Harbor, the croaking of the foghorns far out, the tinkle of the bellbuoys, and the tiny lights of the village trailing over the hill. They stood together at the wheel, wrapped in sweaters for the mist was chilly. Effie, sick with love for him and utter despair over his remoteness, slipped her fingers into his hand once and was stopped by his utter unconsciousness of her touch. Presently he turned and patted her shoulder and that too, Effie reflected, means the end of love.

Late that night they anchored somewhere near Port Jefferson for here was country they knew and by day they could row ashore in the dinghy and walk through woods and beachlands. Andy was soon asleep but Effie could not sleep for wondering about the other girl, if indeed he really loved her, and how she could bear it if it was true. A damp stinging wind blew through the portholes and kept the cabin's screen door rattling on its hook, she could hear the gulls squalling over their fish, could smell the marshes. She sat up in her bunk, staring out at the few pale stars that pinned together the shawl of night. Just before dawn she watched clouds being torn by the wind, bits of gray blown furiously across the black, massed into monstrous grisly shapes and ripped again. A loon cried out from the pine-fringed shore, and the foghorns sounded steadily. She clung to these sounds and to the steady beat of the waves as all that was hers, for Andy asleep was the enemy, the stranger, her cry could never reach him though his face was so near. She drew deep breaths of the salty night air, each second of this night must be remembered, it was this night against years. She caught his hand and held her lips to it desperately, but even while she held it this moment was gone; there is no present in love, only past and future, so that kissing him she was far away lonely for him.

All the next morning they did not speak of Marian. In the dinghy they rowed out of the harbor toward Setauket and Conscience Bay. They drifted into a little cove where the sea floor changed to curiously tropical vegetation and glittered and bloomed with scarlet sponges. Horseshoe crabs trundled about carrying their ugly shells clumsily like great false heads in a Venetian carnival; these creatures paraded in a body awkwardly, a little ashamed of their ridiculous costumes; once masked they could think of nothing to do but attach themselves to fellow sufferers, crunching over pebbles and weeds, finding soothing anonymity in crowds. A few fishermen sat in their rowboats farther out and a sailboat flaunting orange sails fluttered back and forth across the horizon.

Andy and Effie carried the thermos and rye on to the stony beach by the lighthouse. They lay back on the Sunday newspapers, Effie in her blue bathing suit, beach hat pulled over her face, Andy in trunks, brown body sprawled straight out, arm thrown over his face. Effie's eyes were fixed on the back of his hand, a strong large hand, fingers wide apart, spatulate. She touched it gently.

"Look," she said, "the hair on your hand is turning red, darling."

Andy suddenly chuckled.

"I know," he said. "Marian swears it's a toupée."

So there was Marian. Neither said anything for a moment now that the name had been spoken. Then Effie said slowly:

"You *are* crazy about Marian, aren't you?"

Andy did not move. The arm stayed over his eyes.

"I imagine so, Effie," he said.

Effie pulled the hat down farther over her face, turned away from him, heard her voice saying it, "Why don't you find out for certain? It might be the big thing in your life, you know."

Andy still did not stir.

"Do you really mean it, Effie?"

"Certainly. Why don't you go away with her for a while? See how you feel about each other. . . ."

Andy withdrew his hand from his eyes and regarded her curiously. She smiled reassuringly at him.

"I might at that," he said thoughtfully and then suddenly reached over and squeezed her hand. "Effie, you know you are a swell person. I don't deserve you."

A swell person. Words to remember while he packed his bags the next week, words to dwell on when he wired weeks later that he and Marian had decided to stay abroad a year. Swell person. Words to hug for years and years, extracting some meager balm from the hollow praise, words to ponder as you lay, head swimming with pain, heart wrenched with dull loneliness. Yes, thought Effie, better to be selfish, wanton, evil, vain, better for your own happiness. Let somebody else be the swell person while you cling to your happiness. Marian had done that. There was even something a little brave, a little gallant, about fighting selfishly for your love. It did show a fiery metal that was more appealing to a man than the martyr spirit. But if you didn't have that fire, if decency was stronger in you than passion, if the beloved's happiness was to you the object of love— One did what one could, Effie thought. One did what was in one to do, and then waited. Waited for what? Her mind turned the pages of Dennis' book . . . "waiting always for him to come back"—"the hunter will return, he will see the wise gentle wife she has become in his long absence."

A twinge of real anger at Dennis came over her. He had no right to peep into her heart, there was no secret thought safe from him, even now his wicked lenses might be directed at her, cynically analyzing her reflections. There were no longer private shutters against the world, the dearest friend, spying, becomes a foe. But who was there left now to be her friend, who but Dennis, the enemy? They two, offender and victim, must stand alone against the world, must be seen together, must cling together, he to show there was no malice in his work, she to show she bore no grudge.

She got up and drenched her face in cold water, stared at herself in the mirror, surprised as always to find that the tired lines in her face were still there, unwilling to admit to herself that these lines were more than temporary. She was to dine at the Glaenzers' tonight and she had promised Belle to come early in time to help with her letters. She suddenly put her face in her hands, sick at the thought of the Glaenzers, sick of the front she must always present to them, sick of her own face growing old in the mirror.

When the doorbell rang she thought it might be Dennis and she let it ring a long time while she made up her face, rouging heavily as though the bold color would transfuse courage into her blood. But it was a messenger boy with a note for her. She had a crazy conviction that this note would be from Andy, that the end of waiting might be here. She was so certain of it that she had an almost uncontrollable desire to tear up the message without reading it lest her instinct should disappoint her. You did not escape defeat so easily, though; it ran after you through your dreams, through fields and crowded streets, paging you. You could not escape by postponing it. Effie tore open the envelope.

MY DEAR MRS. CALLINGHAM:

If you are any connection of the Mrs. Andrew Callingham now in our hospital under treatment for a cancerous condition we would appreciate your getting in touch with our patient. Her condition is grave and she is without friends in the city. You would be doing a service by calling on her or letting us know, if possible, what branch of the family to notify in case of a crisis.

Sincerely yours,
A. WARING.
Secretary to Dr. Bulger, St. Ursula Hospital.

. . . the press . . .

Andy "Little Hazards" Callingham of Paris and Cannes will learn in this column that his wife Marian is seriously ill in a New York hospital.

New York *Evening Journal.*

The famous love-birds Andrew and Marian Callingham "pfft" over four months ago in Paris. Marian walked out leaving her keys to a Garbo from Sweden. Paris friends say Marian is hiding in New York.

Daily News.

An orchid to Dennis Orphen for his forthcoming tome showing up what famous novelist.

Daily Mirror.

. . . an orchid to Mr. Orphen . . .

CORINNE cut it out and pasted it in his mirror.

"You act so funny," she said plaintively. "Sometimes you say I don't care about your work and the next minute you make fun of me for clipping things out of the paper about you. I don't know what you expect of me, honestly I don't, Dennis."

Dennis shook cigarette ash on the floor. He was lying on the couch, studying a dark stain in the ceiling which had shaped itself into a Gibson girl profile, pompadour and all. It occurred to him that he was facing a nice problem, whether to complain to the little Communist upstairs about his leaking pipe and be robbed of this pleasant work of art, or to let the matter slide and watch her gradual transformation into an elephant or an eagle. In the final triumphant moment when the whole ceiling was painted by little drops of water into a Winslow Homer battlefield or a Machine Age mural, who should leap through the plaster in a cloud of pamphlets but the little Communist himself, accompanied no doubt by all his furniture.

"Look," said Dennis, pointing to the Gibson girl.

"Silly."

Corinne was fussing about with a feather duster, her round little white arms thrust prettily out of blue apron sleeves. She loved wearing an apron around his room, she loved cleaning it all up although she was not in the least thorough and nests of pussies were always left undisturbed under his bed or quite blithely swept into closet corners. Anyway the little task, half-done though it might be, gave her an enjoyable sense of possession.

"Really, Dennis, what do you want me to do? One minute you call me a dumb cluck—you did, you know—and the next I'm trying hard to be clever."

"Be yourself, that's all, my pet," said Dennis. "Stay as sweet as you are, da da da da, and throw away all those clippings. Already the publishers are afraid of a lawsuit. I don't want to be reminded of it, see?"

"See what, Dennis?"

"See my darling."

Corinne sat down on the blue leather ottoman she had bought for him last Christmas at Bloomingdale's. She put her chin in her hands and gazed steadfastly at him.

"I wish you wouldn't call me pet names when you're just kidding," she said somberly. "I've wanted to talk to you about it ever so long. It's the way you kiss and make love, too, as if it didn't mean anything. I don't like it. Don't bother about me if that's all it means to you, just something to kid about."

Dennis raised himself on an elbow and looked at her, eyebrow lifted.

"Oh, I mean it, Dennis," she repeated gravely. "You've got to be more serious about us. It hurts me."

He could never imagine how it would feel to be Corinne. She made seemingly banal remarks, but they were really opaque veils behind which her complex little female nature dressed itself. Another thing was that no one in the world ever looked like Corinne. Maybe, as he sometimes suspected, the only really mysterious thing about her was her looks. Her hair was reddish, silky straight hair cut in distinct lines away from her temples, her skin clear white, high cheek bones, quite lovely brown eyes, far apart, sharp little nose, nostrils cut in high arcs, short full red lips, even little white teeth, a sulky charming little face it was in its odd little way, a face perpetually about to burst into tears so that even strangers felt impelled to offer a shoulder with a "There, there, little girl, cry it out," though a shoulder would not really be enough, one felt, she would burrow in the neck, in the armpits, under the skin like a cunning little beast. Dennis decided to take her seriously this time. She had not made any scenes for several days and it needed only a little argument, or today a little levity, from him to start one.

"The point is I'm worried about the damn book, Corinne. I don't want to hear about it. I wish I hadn't written it. It's making things very hard for my friend, Mrs. Callingham. She's had a tough break in her life and now this——"

"It looks as if her husband would come back to her," said Corinne unexpectedly. "He's free now. His second wife has walked out. You can't tell. I'll bet he comes back to his first."

Dennis digested this thought unwillingly. It had never occurred to him. He was annoyed with Corinne for suggesting it, he could not explain why. After all, there was some logic in it. Effie, too, had probably considered it a possibility. Andy may have sent for her. It wasn't likely that the Garbo mentioned was anything more than temporary. That must be the Swedish dancer Tony Glaenzer had referred to.

"Say, I wonder," he speculated aloud.

He felt an irresistible impulse to get over to Effie's at once and find out what this was all about, see if she really was involved in it. Maybe, with her successor gone, she might even have taken it into her head to go over to Andy of her own accord. Women were like that. Dennis got up briskly and pulled Corinne to her feet.

"You've got to run, my—er—Corinne. You simply can't take these chances. What will you say to Phil when he asks where you've been?"

"I'll just say I've been to Olive's," said Corinne, placidly enough. She slipped off the apron and powdered her nose. She kept a box of powder and some cold cream in Dennis' dresser and once when they were found elsewhere she made a terrific scene, suspecting quite shrewdly that somebody else had been visiting him lately. "I *always* say I've been to Olive's."

Dennis smiled a little wryly.

"That's what you told me yesterday when you wouldn't come down," he remarked.

"Yes," said Corinne and giggled a little. "I see a lot of Olive."

Suddenly Dennis had leapt up and was shaking her furiously by the shoulders. His jealousies were so obscure that even he was never aware of them until he found himself screaming or trying to choke her. Corinne could not stop laughing. It was Dennis, after all, who couldn't see anything funny in things, who took love seriously. You only had to make a light little crack and he was furious, ready to kill you.

"Goodbye, sweet," a little flushed but still gay, she blew a kiss to him from the door.

Dennis sat down after she left, angry that she had got a rise out of him. His nerves were in bad shape. He was afraid about his book, mainly, afraid of everything connected with it as if it were dynamite he had lit and now it was too late to withdraw the match. If Effie had gone back to Andy, which was highly probable in this improbable age, it was the book's fault. Well, he had to see her. He had to find out how she felt about an Andy who was free once again, free to take her back. He couldn't wait for a taxi but must feel haste in his own legs so he walked swiftly westward, across Union Square, up Broadway to Twenty-second and over to Sixth, Seventh, Eighth. Of course she wouldn't be idiot enough to go back to Andy, just because his second marriage had broken up. What did Corinne know about such things? But as soon as he thought of it a dozen such reunions came to mind, revivals of first loves. He had not called on her for two or three days because of the tension between them, but now he wished he had. It would most certainly have saved him these silly apprehensions. He grew angry at Corinne for putting them in his head.

On the doorstep he paused a moment, to calm his nerves, anticipating Effie's quiet laugh over his fantasies. Then he rang. He rang three times with no answer forthcoming. He called out the superintendent of the building. Mrs. Callingham—or rather Miss Thorne as she now wished to be called—was out, said the superintendent firmly. As a matter of fact, he added, Miss Thorne—or Mrs. Callingham, as you liked—had been gone since night before last.

"But where could she have gone? She must be home," Dennis stood there ridiculously arguing, for her absence seemed unquestionably final to him and not a mere night out as the superintendent implied. Effie was certainly upstairs as always, or perhaps the superintendent had misunderstood the name, or perhaps they both were dreaming, the whole thing was a dream, yes, that must be it, the the whole thing was nothing but a dream—

. . . the dream . . .

I wish I could find myself, thought Effie, in the shadowy corner of the bedroom at St. Ursula's Hospital, it's not true I'm here beside Marian, hearing her breathe, it can't have been me myself who just sent the cable to Andy begging him to come to her, it can't be me whispering to her every time she opens her eyes that of course he loves her, of course he will come back to her, of course he won't let her die, of course he loves her, of course he does, it can't be me saying these words to her, any more than that thin worn body on the bed can be Marian, the gay dancing girl in the pointed hat and Columbine ruff at the masquerade ball, the eager little infatuated creature forever feasting her eyes on Andy, hanging on his words long ago while I smiled. It cannot be true, said Effie, it cannot be true; and the heavy breathing of the woman on the bed drowned out her thoughts as soon as they were born as the drums of Santerre drowned out Louis XVI's dying words.

I wish I could find myself again, but I hunt in vain for a familiar clue through every door of my mind and there is nothing of me there, nothing. There is no inside to me, nothing but tactile sensations—this momentary presence is tolerable, its absence pain, but why I do not know. It is as if a blowtorch had gone through me and left me outside the same but no furnishing within except a fear, a little fear left behind like an abandoned pet, an utterly cowardly deathly fear of being hurt more, but even that is not a human reaction but a mechanical one, shrill static in the empty cavern of the body, and hollowness hurts more than live quivering guts. Life, or even wonder about life, has vanished, my brain has broken up like an old wedding present into a thousand bits, I can put together only a few of them to spell out the anagram of my own misery. Repeated pain cancels itself, so that instead of details, facts, adding up, a blank appears at a given suggesting word or deed, and this blank, this mask, is more terrifying in its bleak impenetrability than any careful picture; it appears like a No Sale signal in a broken cash register when you know there was a sale, but it repeats the sinister blank inanely, endlessly.

This must be Marian, this must be the letter itself in my hand, this must be my own heart beating at the thought of Andy again on the fringes of my life. . . . What happens inside people like me who are braced for certain challenges and then spoiled a little, dikes weakened through lack of use, is that the storm, the ocean breaks in and we have nothing but our sheer shock, we have no emotional equipment to handle it, nothing, so that the lightning plays over naked heart and bowels, the blowtorch burns us out, and no pain is left, nothing but the numbed nerves, the broken will, the broken pride.

From a person one turns into a sick dog, defeating itself and its own recovery with every feeble whine. To wake and find myself gone, no part of me left, terrifies me, where am I?—is this Effie Thorne here in the chair, or is it Effie Thorne there on the bed breathing her last few hours away? Look, my hand, veins so clearly outlined, the turquoise on the engagement finger, my ring, my hand, but how quaintly remote, and my body, this very chair in which I wait, this heavy antiseptic air, all are part of another person's life, not of mine, for I am not real, it is as if meeting Marian again had changed me from human to vegetable and I can be conscious only of the sun, of light and of shadow.

Marian's body twitched restlessly and Effie armored herself with a smile to greet her waking, a glittering unbreakable smile that should cut through dusk and suffering.

"Effie."

"Yes, Marian."

"You know I never meant—I mean—I did like you, Effie. It wasn't really taking advantage of your house at first—I mean—it was just that Andy and I——"

"I know, Marian."

"When this new girl came along a few months ago, this dancer, I realized things for the first time. I saw how you must have felt. I hated her—the way you hated me——"

Effie forced herself to interrupt the dry weary voice.

"I never hated you, Marian."

"Well—I couldn't stand their looking at each other and laughing. Can you understand that? Just that, I mean? I couldn't bear their eyes suddenly meeting over a joke. It sounds silly, something got into me—I was sick, too—and I—well, I bought a ticket to America. I wanted to show him. Then I got sick as soon as I landed and I wouldn't let anyone tell him. I thought I'd die just for revenge, but—oh, Effie—I——"

"I know." How well she knew!

"She never meant anything to him, not the way I did. You know he told me he never could write decently till he met me. He needed me, he said. He started the triology as soon as we settled down together—his best work, too——"

What's the matter with my lips, they won't open, why can't I say something to her, why can't I say that's fine, that's dandy? Effie wondered. The nurse came in, a sharp white line in the gray of the room. She turned on the light and adjusted the pillows.

"Isn't it nice we've found your friend?" she murmured. "Now if we can only get hold of your husband and tell him to hurry right over."

"Yes," said Effie.

"This naughty girl wouldn't let us tell anyone she was here for weeks and weeks. She said she didn't want anyone to worry about her, so finally we just had to do a little detective work of our own. And now she's glad, aren't you, dear?"

"Terribly glad."

The nurse picked up the water carafe and left.

Marian had not changed much, Effie thought. Thin and gaunt as she was, her body scarcely more than a long fold in the blanket, her face still held the eager hunger it had possessed at twenty-three, the heavy dark hair and thick lashes were the same, the same narrow pretty mouth.

"What did you say in the cable, Effie? Tell me again. You're quite sure you didn't say I was too—too sick, you're quite sure you didn't ask him to come out of pity?"

"I said 'Marian ill,'" said Effie, "and the name of the hospital."

"You do think he will come?"

"Yes, yes."

Marian was silent, smiling a little to herself.

"I know he will," she said presently. "I know he'd come to the ends of the world for me. I'm the only person he ever loved. He's told me. Even after this girl came along. I'm the only person. So he'll come to me."

Effie got up and looked out the window into the gathering night, twin churches in twin duncecaps of illuminated spires across the street, a skyscraper emptied of workers now threaded with a single row of hall lights, and far off flaming red sky over Broadway. Outside blurred suddenly into a shadowy reflection of herself in the windowpane, herself with churches, skyscraper and red sky spreading over the ghostly outline of her head.

"Yes," she said, almost inaudibly, "yes, Marian."

. . . the Glaenzers' Effie . . .

Two eyes stared at Effie from the other side of the shop-window. The eyes, black, close-set above a Semitic nose and suave delicate mustache, traveled questioningly from Effie's face to brown oxfords labeled 'Snappy' in the case, up again to Effie, and down to green antelope pumps named 'Chic,' hopefully back to Effie and over to silver sandals named 'Classy,' all three reflected in a mirrored floor edged with green velvet and carelessly studded with silver stars. The eyes, persistently persuading, roused Effie's numb senses. How long she had stood there staring at shoes she never saw she could not guess. She must have walked endlessly after leaving the hospital for she seemed to be somewhere in the Sixties and under the El Third or Second. With the black eyes still challenging her, she pulled her coat together resolutely and crossed the street, hurrying close beside a big man in gray coat, paper bag in his hand. She was afraid to be alone, and the big man did not mind her scuttling along beside him, he pulled her back so roughly before an oncoming truck that her arm hurt. "Thank you," she murmured. In a little while the mist in her head would clear, she would remember where she was going, why, and this year, this moment would drive out the too vivid past. She would remember Marian. Yet Marian would not shape in her mind as the sick woman in the hospital but the Marian of old, and with that girl came the rest. Already the familiar dreadful figures assumed possession of her brain, the cast of the endless comedy were on the stage ready again for her aching memory to feed them their lines. But for that last hour or two of blessed amnesia Effie thanked the gods.

The dismal blue lamp of a corner coffeeshop reminded her that she had scarcely eaten in the two days with Marian. She had slept on a cot in Marian's room. "I'm so afraid alone—

426

really," Marian had pleaded with the nurse. As if Effie, too, now that they had presented each other each with her half of the magic ring, did not feel the same desperate fear of breaking apart again. What was that rule of the sea when a ship was rammed—keep the prow plunged in the split vessel, withdrawing brings on the wreck. . . . Keep the hurt close to you, then, stay with it, live with it, till all else is lost in this immediate urgency, mind and heart numbed. . . . The doctor had commanded her to go for the night. Go where? Step from the past into the bewilderment of the present, collect the bits that made up Effie Thorne of this year to present to the world, to Lexington Avenue, to the big man in the gray suit with the bag of oranges, present this assembled figure to the world of no-Andy? No-Andy. But Andy was coming back, coming back, leaving beautiful young Swedish girls for Marian, the only woman he ever loved. Drinking coffee and crumbling up a slice of dry pound cake into its cellophane wrapper at the lunch counter, Effie was alarmed to see her face in the mirror between the glistening percolator and the giant green ginger-ale bottle. Her felt hat was tilted back from her worn face and tears tracked aimlessly down her powdered cheeks as if someone inside her were weeping, weeping, though all she was conscious of herself was her aching spine, as if each tiny bone was a hot little ball, a little cranberry, she thought, exactly that, a hard little cranberry.

Supposing Andy did come back as Marian was so sure. . . . Dim shots of jealousy after all these quiet years frightened Effie; it frightened her to find a vengeful sardonic hope that Andy would fail Marian now as he had failed Effie before. Let Marian find out what heartbreak really was—after that her pain would be welcome! Desperately Effie captured and annihilated this rebel wish. Poor Marian, poor Marian, she repeated, poor, poor Marian, she could never stand what I did.

She paid her check and walked westward. She would call on the Glaenzers. If Andy was to return the Glaenzers would know, he would be certain to go straight to them. Moreover she wanted to be with them, she longed for the gloomy security of the dark old house as she had longed for it years ago only because Andy so often graced it and here were those who remembered. Here were people who could say, "Yes, it

was true he did court you here, he did pursue you, he did
love you, we saw him, we saw it all." Entering the old cage of
thoughts the present was sloughed off as a mere inanimate
shell protecting the living organism that was the past. Andy
about to return, not for her, no, but for her rival, but nevertheless Andy, Andy, Andy, rose and swelled before her as the
one reality till it lost all proportion like a heroic statue viewed
too closely. Vainly trying to hold his image constant it kept
changing before her eyes like a Coney Island mirror—wide,
thin, long, squat—all she could recognize was the shaking in
her knees over his mere presence in the room. In these long
years his picture had dissolved into all the strangers she had
mistaken for him, a man glimpsed briefly at a Pullman window, a waiter, janitor, actor, a little boy in Prospect Park on a
tricycle, all the people she had glanced at twice because something about them reminded her of Andy. So she had lost his
image in her anxiety to preserve it, and the defection of her
mind so angered her that sometimes in her dreams she had
shed real tears. Real tears when she had learned long ago that
there was no one on earth who could afford to weep, no occasion worthy of it; or if there was, what reason, then, once
begun for ever stopping?

   She looked at her watch. Ten o'clock. If she could only find
Belle alone, for Tony's faintly sarcastic manner would be too
much for her tonight. Sometimes she could ignore it, his half-
smile looking at her, see, it said, see what happens to women
who lock their bedrooms against me, who push *me* away from
their arms, see, their lovers leave them, they grow old and
poor, they pay for spurning me in their brief youth. See,
happy lover, his smile said, you come back to us for comfort,
we enemies alone remain to you. . . .

   Belle's dignified brownstone house resolutely pushed its
way out of the shadow of penthouse apartments on either
side, just as her respectable old limousine raised its body a few
haughty inches above the gutter instead of slithering along,
daschund style, like the newer models of the penthouse tenants. A high iron grilling separated this decent-person's-
dwelling from the unworthy passers-by. There was something
about the solid mahogany door, good lace curtains drawn
taut over the narrow windows at each side, brass knobs

scrupulously glistening, that made the occasional women callers wipe off their lipstick, pull down their skirts a little more.

Effie paused at the gate, bracing herself to be casual. The Effie of the Glaenzers today was the same Effie as of old, naïve, shy, blushing, target for sarcasm, apologetic, inferior to all in wit, beauty or intelligence, as ready to be astounded at any Callingham's protestations of admiration as to be abused by Belle's caustic recrimination. Outside, as the former wife of Mr. Callingham, as Mrs. Callingham, woman of the world, Garden Apartments, West Twenty-second Street, it was different. Outside the iron-grilled gate on East Seventy-first Street she had grown, become a figure in a small Bohemian world, living quietly but always admired by a few sensitive young men, earnest artistic fellows as a rule who talked breathlessly of Andrew. The absent Andrew was the focus of this modest salon, though when Dennis Orphen appeared in her life this little group had fallen quietly away. Effie wondered about it a little, for the little circle of admirers had been something. But then Dennis was enough; egotistical, violent, loyal, he brought her the best of the active world like a papa robin bringing home the cream of the bait. Dennis was enough. Changed under his influence as she knew herself to be, gayer, happier, more integrated, her Glaenzer self still remained the same, uncertain, shy, girlish.

She found herself tonight mechanically adjusting her hat as though this futile gesture was a fairy wand transforming her from a harrassed shaken woman into the nice untouched youth demanded by the Glaenzers.

"I'll have to tell her about Marian being here and Andy coming over and I mustn't be shaky about it," she thought. "I ought not to let them see me this way but I've got to talk to somebody."

Somebody—but not Dennis. Not after the book. There must be more of a front for Dennis than even for the Glaenzers. A front for Everybody, the enemy. A special public face decorated with a smile, a special manner. Trying out a smile tentatively, she saw a man slip beside her through the iron gate. It was Dennis, and in the sudden pleasure at seeing him she almost forgot for the moment that he was Enemy.

"I looked everywhere for you," he said, quite angrily. "You've got no business worrying me this way. I've got work to do, damn it, I can't be chasing around morgues and police stations hunting for you. It's too childish running away like this, never telling me, never even a note! How was I to know you'd be coming up here to the Glaenzers'? I just took a chance, and as soon as I got here I wondered what I'd say—where's Effie? and they'd say who the hell are you and what's it to you?"

His battered hat was set sidewise, Napoleonically, on his tousled sandy hair, his tie was over his shoulder somewhere, his vest was buttoned up wrong, his eyes furious, and he smelled strongly of Scotch.

"I was worried." His bombast collapsed quite simply. "What happened? I couldn't find you. I couldn't imagine what happened."

"Do you want it for a new book?" Effie asked wearily. Exhausted herself, his tired hysterics did not move her.

Dennis was crushed.

"I got feelings," he said. "I'm a writer but I still can feel. Don't run off again, please. Let me stay with you here—I can't stand thinking of you alone and upset. I was afraid it was the book that started it and it was too much on my conscience."

He followed her up the steps and in the dark vestibule caught her arm urgently.

"All right, come in with me," Effie said, beaten.

She rang the bell. Now her Dennis world and her Glaenzer world would merge and for her hereafter there would be no refuge in one from the other. Her two little spheres would combine against the two Effies to laugh, to study her pretensions; the Glaenzers would smile at the proud Effie Dennis knew, and Dennis would despise the hesitant apologetic Effie of the Glaenzers. Between them they would leave her nothing. It seemed to her that in the last few days she was being steadily relentlessly stripped of all armor, all retreats were being cut off, no mystery was left her for pride's sake, no person but would know her story and her poor excuse for living. Let her die, she begged, let her be the one instead of Marian. She was too tired to struggle for herself.

As for Dennis, his anger at his own weak-minded worry over her now expressed, he was relieved, but there ensued an embarrassed sensation of being caught unawares by an unexpected emotion, and now his vanity came back, he didn't want to visit her damned Glaenzers if it was to them she turned in her hours of need instead of to him. Besides he knew them, knew them too well from his own story of them written without ever having seen them; he didn't want to live over his own novel. So, reluctantly he entered the hall behind Effie, afraid that his description of the 'Glasers' as he had named them would seem pale by contrast with the original. He had a nauseating sense of entering the looking-glass, of dreaming true, and once inside the door of horrid magic to follow. Even the gnarled old dwarf butler he had plagiarized from Effie's anecdotes, though only the other day leafing over the first printed copy he had complimented himself on inventing the character. He saw himself stepping into a living material world of his own mind's creation; here was the dark tomblike hall he had described with the little round stained-glass window over the first stair-landing. Through the open carved oak doors on the right he saw entwined bronze fauns upholding candelabra over the alabaster mantelpiece of the reception room, saw the blurred pouting face of an ancestor in oil on the wall, the formidable blue brocade sofa, the gloomy electric logs in the fireplace. This was all in Chapter Nine of his book, and a faint chill crept up Dennis' spine that his literary shadow should have investigated so truly, or worse, that his so-called creative process was sheer Pelmanism, careful records of other people's conversations. His eyes stole up to the niche at the head of the stairs, not daring to believe that here would be a terra-cotta madonna. He breathed a sigh of relief to see in place of his own guess a large hideous Chinese vase filled with gloomy lilies.

"Belle likes lilies," Effie said. "The house always smells like this. Like a funeral."

They followed the old dwarf upstairs.

The rich, the good, solid old rich, live in wretched style, reflected Dennis. These ponderous old mausoleums with jail windows, moldy walls, dark high hallways, heavy dark consoles or carved chairs crouching in every corner like rheumatic old watchdogs ready to pounce on intruders, heavy-padded floors, these houses were to haunt and not to dwell within or visit. Poor Tony Glaenzer, Dennis thought, poor bastard, he should have picked a jolly phony rich woman, a penthouse nouveau, a flashy marcasite oil heiress with a nice dash of bad blood; that would be a gay vulgar prostitution, but never this substantial, true-blue Bank of England type.

The upstairs hall was a large rectangle with two crystal wall clusters dimly illumining an enormous Venetian oil painting, framed with alarming solidity for eternity. Three dark mahogany doors were stonily closed to view but double doors opened at the far end and from here voices could be heard. In here the dwarf vanished, carpets so deep, the walls so silent that you could hear his old knees crack as he walked and his wheezy asthmatic breathing even when he was out of sight. Effie walked on in without heeding Dennis' hesitation. He stood still in the hall with his eyes shut tight, fearful again that the voices he dimly heard in there would belong to the creatures whose story he had so cleverly told, not told, he corrected himself, but imagined, built up from nothing but the sticks of a few chance remarks, for now it seemed to him Effie's anecdotes had been not the base of his novel but the merest springboard for his own original imagination. If here and there reality fitted fancy so much the finer fancy, the artist brain outguesses God. True, he granted grudgingly, once a story begins in the hidden cellars of the brain, a thousand little thievish atoms steal out automatically raiding friends' confidences, woes, loves, desires, to build and furnish complete the edifice which the artist, erasing all other sources and signatures, canceling all debts, believes his own magnificent sorcery. Bewildering to find the structure laid brick by brick of simple facts filtered cunningly through sleep or memory. No magic here at all, alas, but a tale reflected again and again in a dozen mirrors, shadows and gaps filled by conjectures, and even the prophetic gift operated by a secret statistical mechanism. So here was Dennis Orphen, entering Chapter Nine of a book by himself, disturbed by the growing conviction that his genius was no more wondrous than an old file. He shouldn't have come in here, anyway, he thought, for there was in his novel no role for Dennis Orphen; he had no business following his heroine brazenly through her own secret story. Wells wouldn't do such a thing. Proust wouldn't have. No decent author would step brashly, boldly into his own book. He hesitated outside the drawing-room door again, heard his name asthmatically creaked, and a distinctly rude, "Who? Who, Milton? Oh, hello, Effie." No getting out now. He would throw salt over his left shoulder, murmur an incantation, before subjecting himself to further necromancy.

. . . salt over left shoulder . . .

IN A HUGE black plush chair, in a ring of grisly bluish lamplight contributed by a great silver lampshade, sat Belle Glaenzer, a vast dough-faced shapeless Buddha in black velvet that
flowed out of the chair and spilled its inky folds into the du
Barry roses of the thick carpet. There should be an emerald in
the middle of her forehead, thought Dennis, and a great
cabuchon ruby glittering in her long-lost navel; like an automatic traffic policeman they would direct stop-go-stop-go-
stop. This vast blob of female flesh was nothing he could ever
have imagined, thank God, thought Dennis, setting his own
creation down beside her for favorable contrast. Behind the
throne the room seemed surprisingly small and inadequate,
though this, on second glance, was actually not true. The ceilings were so high that the rococo splendors of the cornice, dividing as it did green tapestried walls from a ceiling-pool of
cupids, was lost in shadows. On the walls were further pow-
erfully framed visions of Venice by Canaletto and, appropriately enough, a gentle Van Cuyp cow waded across a pastoral
brook over the fireplace to examine jealously an ivory miniature of Belle at twenty. A great lionskin spread from one of
Belle's large sandaled feet to the divan that faced the fireplace.
This beast's great jaw was smugly closed in a gentle simper,
though not because a fanged open mouth might terrify the
guests but, as Effie had once explained to Dennis, because
stuffing the tongue cost fifteen dollars extra at the taxider-
mist's and Belle was not going to have this gift—from Andy
himself—run into money. This passive beast was all that Dennis
recognized from Effie's many anecdotes, but the room, apart
from that, depressed him hideously, made him want to run
quickly before he was caught as Effie was in this life. Awful,
he thought, awful, and his desire to hang on to Effie now that
he'd found her again melted before his rebellious hate of

434

settled houses, nailed-down carpets, murals, all investments that smacked of permanence, of long live the home, long live property, long live this cancerous, highly-respected ménage, oh stuffy-stuffy-stuffy detestably, inalterably fixed, smug, fortunate, blessed-by-the-church property.

I must move from my room tomorrow, thought Dennis, before I too get trapped. Never let me be party to the fetish of permanency, the snug-as-a-bug-in-a-rug fetish. Possessions need camphor balls and in time the possessor reeks of the musty smell himself, his brain smells of bank vaults. And save me from Fat, too, prayed Dennis, repelled by the monument to Hollandaise in the black velvet chair, though, he reflected, fat people never go crazy. Come to think of it, all the nuts were skinny beggars, there were no fat ones—or were there? . . . A great ball of dough, Belle Glaenzer, thought Dennis, not woman at all, her huge breasts were as sexless as Earth itself. Caught between dobs of pasty flesh, her little black eyes darted restlessly about, lively little squirrel eyes, imprisoned in fat.

"Well, Effie," said Belle without stirring. Her voice was a shock, a deep hoarse masculine voice that seemed to come from somewhere quite apart from the squirrel eyes or the body, from somewhere behind her. Perhaps a priest stood in the velvet curtains behind her and spoke for the oracle. Effie bent over Belle and kissed her white passive cheek, crossed eagerly to the divan where a bald, ruddily plump little man sat. He banged a sherry decanter abruptly down on the coffee table as Effie approached, and seized both her hands.

"Not my little Effie," he cried. "Not my dear, dear little Effie. It must be fifteen—no, sir, by God, twenty years."

Effie sat down beside him, her face suddenly relieved and radiant.

"I needed someone to talk to," she said. "I don't know why I didn't think of you before, Dr. MacGregor."

That's a new one, thought Dennis, she never mentioned him to me, but I knew the story needed him and I put in the Jesuit priest. That at least I did make up. . . . Watching Effie change in this room, he compared the group and background with his own printed description.

I had the same atmosphere, the same feeling, he thought with complacent triumph, and what's more I got it with entirely different objects. The feeling of the place, the mothball mummified quality I caught as truly as if I'd been here. Yes, I do have a psychic gift, not mere journalistic memory. . . .

Intent on his observations, Dennis as usual forgot that he was not invisible. He was made conscious of himself, the man, not the curious literary prowler, by Belle's direct antagonistic scrutiny.

"Who's this man, Effie? You can't leave him dangling over there like a dummy just because you see MacGregor again?" she boomed out. "Anyway you didn't ask if you could bring company. You might have spoken of it."

Effie, hands still in MacGregor's warm grasp, drawing friendliness, protection, strength from this contact with the old man, leapt away at the reproach, made her introductions.

"Dennis Orphen," she said. "He lives near me."

"In Chelsea?" asked Belle.

"No, no—near Union Square," Effie stammered and flushed as if, just as Belle suspected, the fellow was a dubious connection indeed.

"Union Square?" repeated Belle, examining critically Dennis' none-too-impressive figure. It seemed to him that his always askew tie jumped naughtily even farther behind his ear at her hostile survey. All very well for a writer to examine the world but damned unjust for the world to examine the writer. Dennis scowled at her. He wished he dared make a face. "Union Square never recommended any visitor yet, young lady. Is he one of those radicals?"

"No," said Dennis flippantly. "Not even a fellow traveler. Just a window-shopper as we say in the Party."

"We saw some kind of demonstration down there last week as we were driving," said Belle. "Disgusting."

"Dennis isn't dangerous, Belle," Effie said and smiled at Dennis, conscious of him as a stranger, awkward and foreign in this part of her life. This was her Andy-life, and for that he was an enemy, a spy.

"Sit down," said Belle.

Dennis sat down.

"That's not to sit on," roared Belle. "That's a very old, very valuable Venetian chair. I paid nearly five hundred dollars for it. Four eighty-five. Sit over there."

Dennis hastened to obey and dropped down cautiously on the ottoman indicated.

"Five hundred for a chair and not a penny for my Babies' Hospital," said MacGregor gloomily. He appealed to Dennis. "Mrs. Glaenzer is the meanest, stingiest old woman of all the mean stingy old women in New York. Furthermore she's eating herself into the grave. That's her second box of candy tonight, Effie. At least you kept that away from her when you were around."

"She gnawed up all the sugar lumps instead," remembered Effie. "Where's Tony?"

"Tony went to a musicale at Caroline Meigs'," said Belle. "They were to play Haydn. I hate Haydn."

"I remember," said Effie.

"Effie's changed, hasn't she, MacGregor?" said Belle, fat white fingers fumbling among the silver-wrapped bon-bons on the arm of her chair. "Lost her looks. I look younger than Effie and I'm over fifty."

"I should say you were over fifty," said the doctor mildly. "You know perfectly well you'll never see sixty again, and if you think all that face-lifting makes you look anything but horrible, just you take a peek at yourself in a well-lit mirror."

"I've got a new cream, Effie," confided Belle, unperturbed. "Made of porcupine livers or something. Thirty-five dollars. You ought to buy yourself some—take away that drawn look."

"We get that drawn look trying to make thirty-five dollars, don't we, Effie?" said MacGregor dryly. His eyes, small and guarded, kept darting inquisitively toward Dennis, but Dennis balked this examination by fixing his eyes boldly upon him. "Well, well, Effie! What have you been doing? And what do you hear from Andy? You know this is the first time Belle's let me call since she ordered me out—let's see—that was just after you and Andy separated."

Dennis was aware of the bleakness that descended on Effie at the name. Her slender shoulders slumped, incalculable weariness was in her face and body. Stabbed with sympathy and love for her, Dennis looked away uneasily, tried to fix his attention to Belle's tapering hand fumbling among the chocolates so lovingly, choosing her pet very slowly, very carefully, as if she were in no greedy haste, no indeed, as if it were nothing to her, that rush of ecstasy to the tip of her tongue the instant sugar touched it. The robber fingers withdrew reluctantly from the candies with only one treasure but with it in her mouth her eyes continued to keep passionate watch over the others. Be happy, little cocoanut fondant and almond paste, Belle's adoring tongue will soon appreciate you too, all in your turn.

"Effie never hears from Andy," said Belle bluntly. "He never even sends her his books, though he has them sent to Tony. Effie has to go out and buy them."

Effie did not reply for a moment, clinging to MacGregor's hand tightly. Look at me, Effie, Dennis silently pleaded, you've got me. I'm here. Don't count on these wretched mummies.

"Andy's coming back any minute," said Effie, trying to sound casual. "You see Marian's here, sick, cancer they say, at St. Ursula's. I sent for Andy."

"Marian here! Where's Tony? Tony ought to hear this. Effie, it can't be true."

Dennis looked at Effie's drooping shoulders, downcast face. So Andy was coming back. Corinne had guessed right in a way. Why couldn't she have come to him, wasn't he her loyal friend, stanch supporter these three years, why couldn't she have come to him with her news? She needn't have come to this smug, smothering house. He was angry at her for leaning against the little doctor's broad shoulder—ah, here, here, her sad body cried, here is refuge, here is friendliness, here is sweet neutral ground between Belle's placid brutality and Dennis' too-sharp, too-inquisitive sympathy.

"If he comes," said MacGregor, "if."

"I doubt if he does," said Belle. If I was at all shy, thought Dennis, I'd be mowed down by that horrible old woman. She might at least offer me a nip of the old boy's sherry. California, at that, I'll bet. I know these stingy old connoisseurs. Has her imported bottle in her own room but the ninety-cent bottle out for company. Sure I know her, I invented her, didn't I?

"He won't come," said Belle, voice rasping and hoarse as if words were pumped from a dry rusty old well. She makes it sound that way on purpose, thought Dennis shuddering, like a nasty spoiled little girl. She should have been smacked down in kindergarten for it, except that fat little rich girls were always analyzed instead of smacked. Fleetingly he saw himself at five, undersized, sandy little squirt with freckles and no eyebrows and two front teeth out, scratching raucously with a fine new red-white-and-blue-wrapped slate pencil on red-braid-trimmed slate. . . . Miss Hough giving him a good cuff on the ear for his nerve-racking noise, and his outraged explanation bawled out to the whole class—'But all I was doin' was makin' a pine tree!' Belle Glaenzer's larynx scratched a pine tree on slate every time she opened her mouth, and no Miss Hough to slap her for it, either. Dennis heard her leisurely scratching off a pine tree to Effie——

"No, I doubt if Andrew Callingham will come back to America. He doesn't like us here—he made his big name in Europe and he'll never forgive us for that."

"But if Marian is here seriously ill——" expostulated Mac-Gregor, still patting Effie's hand. Now what was there about a few feeble pats to make her feel better? Dennis wondered, annoyed. Next she'll be cheered up to hear that it's all for the best and it's always darkest when it's darkest.

"Andrew hates scenes," Belle boomed out, rolling her cocoanut fondant about in her cheek at last. "Deathbeds and all that. Andy's not at all sentimental. He won't come for any woman in the world, dead or alive, if there's going to be a lot of crying, not if he's the man I know."

"He will," Dennis heard Effie say firmly. "Oh, he will come, Belle. You'll see."

Effie's eyes met Dennis' haughtily. You, too, you'll see. So certain had her spoken words made her, so sure, that Effie drew away from MacGregor's friendly arm and sat upright, chin lifted, looking calmly from Belle to Dennis. The words made her know what she had not known before, that she wanted Andy to come, that to come for Marian's sake was for her sake too, for love's sake. Inextricably she and Marian were bound together, waiting for him to come to them across the world, waiting for him to prove he did care, he did love— which woman was not the issue now. Demanded now was proof of love stronger than his own ambition or his present lust. For Marian, dying, and for Effie, long believing, there must be testimony that here was a man worth death and

endless fidelity. A short hour ago Effie had been frightened by
the flicker of passionate jealousy for Marian; now she was surprised by her sudden knowledge that she and Marian were
one, their fates were entwined, Marian's last desire was hers
also. . . .

She looked past Belle's dark shadowy bulk to the alcove beyond where the French windows led down into the stone garden; she could see herself dimly in that garden, iron balcony
rail patterned in lamplight on the garden floor, she could hear
Andy imploring her to love him.

"But how can I say that this is love?" she had patiently asked
him. "How can I know? How does anyone know? If it's something that fills you up, that gives no place for any other
thought, something that rolls you out like a—like a machine so
there's nothing left of you, no wish, no sense, then this is love,
but it doesn't make me happy, it's like doom, like melting into
eternity and I don't want to lose myself—I don't, Andy, I
don't. How do I know this is love? It couldn't be love, darling,
to make me so lost, so lonely, so blind and deaf. I can't see St.
Thomas' spire—I can't see trees in the park or the sky—I can't
read—I can't hear Tony playing, for you're outside, everywhere, all about me. Is that love? Isn't there some way of
loving and being oneself too? I don't like to be so lost, so
drowned—no, darling, if this is love, then I don't want it, I
don't like it, I'm afraid."

Lost . . .

"If he comes," Belle's voice scratched out another pine tree
for Miss Hough's nerves, "if he comes he can stay here. You
know how fond he is of Tony. They've always got on. Tony
helped you two pull the wool over my eyes, naughty boy,
after I told you both you were making a mistake. I was right
too, wasn't I, MacGregor?"

Wool indeed, thought Effie. They had told Tony everything
from the start, partly to gain his support in eluding Belle's antagonistic barriers, and partly because Tony was then a lonely
miserable young gigolo-bridegroom, just finding out how bad
his bargain with Belle was to be. At nights he would knock
softly on Effie's bedroom door. "If you don't let me in, I will
tell Belle, I'll tell about last night and about your staying on

Andy's boat. Let me in or I'll tell Andy you belonged to me—let me in, please, please, Effie." . . . Each night she pushed the dresser against the door, not trusting the lock, each night for months till the day she slipped away with Andy. Pulled the wool, indeed, Effie thought now, as if Belle had ever asked for anything but wool.

"Andy owes Tony nearly four thousand dollars," Belle said, turning to Dennis politely at last as if in such small talk he might justly be included. "He's made plenty since he borrowed it, too. I'll certainly talk to him about that. With stocks going down and our Long Island place costing more than ever, we can't afford having big sums out. What do you think, young man?"

"I think it's too goddam bad," said Dennis, jumping up suddenly. He could not bear rich people complaining of their poverty, and since that made up most of their conversation he might as well face the fact that this class was poison to him, he'd be sick for a week just thinking of Belle Glaenzer. How Effie could endure it! . . . She was looking at him at last, eyes widened as if his voice had brought her out of a dream. Like Flip, I am, he thought bitterly, to her Little Nemo; I wake her out of it but she doesn't want to be wakened.

"Effie," he cried out—he had the floor now, after that incredible Madame Chairman had gaspingly dropped the gavel—"come on—let me take you home—you're tired—"

Effie quietly rose.

The red-faced little doctor got up, looked curiously at Dennis stalking to the door without so much as a goodnight. I look like some little pest from Greenwich Village, Dennis thought angrily, some lousy little Stewart's Cafeteria poet, they're thinking, what has Effie come to running around with a squirt like that with no hair on his chest, no foreign hotel tags plastered on his behind, he doesn't even look like Max Eastman, that would be something at least.

"Come on," he muttered fiercely, jerking his thumb toward the door.

"Ring me up at the hotel any time you want to see me, child," he heard MacGregor say, "any time, my dear. If Marian needs me, if you want to talk over anything just as we used to—anything, anything in the world——"

"Well, well, well!" Pine trees on the red-braid-trimmed slate, scratch, scratch, scratch, dark ancestor in oil glowering farewell from the downstairs fireplace, gnarled hand of the humped old butler on the outer door. Then they were outside—free.

Dennis kept her arm as they walked over toward Fifth. It was going to storm soon. Papers blew down the Avenue, ash cans rolling over in areaways clattered against stone walls, the few midnight pedestrians, hanging on to their hats, hurried for shelter. The sky was a coat of mail, the bright gray twilight that precedes the night storm. Taxicabs with steel antennae scavenged the city looking curiously transparent in this false light. A few large raindrops fell and a discarded newspaper scurrying before the wind blew frantically against Effie's skirts. Dennis, sheltering Effie with his coat, held up a finger for a cab.

"Thank you for coming," murmured Effie, clinging to him. "I didn't know how much I needed you."

It began to pour. A taxi slid to the curb and Dennis pushed Effie into it before another couple running up the street behind them, could steal it. Someone called out his name.

"Why, it's Dennis. Hello there!"

Dennis jumped into the cab, banged the door shut behind him. As they drove off he saw Corinne and Phil Barrow staring after him in blank astonishment.

"She knew you," said Effie in surprise. "What a pretty girl. Why, Dennis! Who was she? Why—why *Dennis!*"

"Mistake," said Dennis curtly. "West Twenty-third Street, driver, and stop at the Eighth Avenue uptown corner, the liquor store. What we need, my dear Mrs. Callingham, is a stiff hooker of Johnnie Walker."

The rain poured down blindingly, it drove slanting tears across the windowpanes.

"Did I ever tell you how I learned to skate?" said Dennis. "I was visiting my aunt in Vincennes and it was Christmas."

Effie, wrapped clumsily in his topcoat, dropped her head against his shoulder and fell asleep.

II

" 'So LET'S call it a day and be glad we knew when to end things,' " Dennis read aloud from a cream-colored note. " 'I hope you realize the whole affair has been no more important to me than it has to you and certainly right now won't break my heart any more than it will yours. So goodbye—' " here Dennis choked and flourished the note in the air, tore open his pajama collar to beat his chest dramatically—" 'and so goodbye.' I would have liked farewell here—the whole paragraph is lousy with redundancy anyway. And there's more— dear, dear! . . . 'So goodbye. You have never cared for anything but your work and apparently for that Mrs. Callingham, judging by the way you were hanging on to her the night you refused to speak to me. As for me'—always talking about herself—'I am happily married. I love Phil dearly and should never have mixed up with you. Damn everything.' Tut, tut, we're losing our head a little. 'Anyway, this is goodbye. P.S. You can keep my cold cream and apron and negligee but please return my copy of *The Wind in the Willows* as it was a present to me from Phil.' "

Dennis sat up in bed, letter falling from his nerveless fingers.

"I've lost her," he cried. "I've lost my little Honey Bear, my little Honey Lou."

Corinne leaned across the bed and slapped him smartly on the mouth.

"Will you stop kidding about that!" she said resentfully. "Give me that letter. I did mean it, too, every word."

Dennis tweaked her nose.

"I apologize for reading my mail before guests. Get up and get me a cigarette, my angel."

Corinne did not budge. She lay with arms clasped under her fine tousled head and stared sulkily up at the Gibson girl on the ceiling so cunningly devised by the leak in the little

Communist's sink. Leprous spots had appeared about the famous face and the pompadour was chipping off, flakes of the plaster snowed over the bed occasionally, and the one eye was casually spreading off toward the window in the shape of a crocodile. One of these days I will look up there, thought Corinne, and the crocodile will have devoured the Gibson girl and very likely changed itself into a hippopotamus.

"Isn't it funny how contrary I am, Dennis?" mused Corinne. "As soon as I say something out loud I mean just the opposite. I take sides against myself. I can't help it. I suppose it's me."

"Fascinating."

"Dennis, are you happy—really happy, I mean?"

"Deliriously happy, pet." Dennis got up to find a cigarette on the table, returned and sat on the foot of the bed and reflected that as a matter of strict fact he was happy. There was nothing in the world he wanted or any place he wanted to be but here. Happy happy Orphen, protected by azure cellophane from misery, pain, terror; nothing, no sir, nothing could destroy this bliss, this perfectly idiotic ecstatic peace. The little Communist might tear his heart out over sharecropper woes, Okie might snivel over his inability to find a wife—a wife, mind you, not a pleasing mistress—he, Orphen was at peace.

"Why?" demanded Corinne cajolingly. "Because of me?"

Dennis blew a happy little ring of smoke into the happy air. He stretched out his bare feet—beautiful arches, he observed with pleasure, and hooked the exquisitely matched toes over the bottom rung of the chair.

"Because of you, because of your undying faith in me and in my work."

"I never said as much," said Corinne. "I can't even finish reading what you write. It doesn't hold my interest somehow, darling."

"Sweet! You're spoiling me. Well then, I must be happy because I am young, beautiful and rich, because I am the darling of New York, the toast of Paris, because at any moment in a million and two homes all over the world fascinated readers will be opening up their copies of *The Hunter's Wife*——"

"See," reproached Corinne. "You don't even think of me. Only your work. I don't see what you like about it so much. Darling, why were you squeezing Mrs. Callingham Tuesday night on Park and Sixty-fourth? Why wouldn't you speak to Phil and me?"

"I do think of you," said Dennis, carefully ignoring her final query. "Every day, I think—why is Corinne so hopelessly infatuated with me? Why me? Am I so wonderful? I daresay."

Corinne sniffed.

"Well, I'm happy too," she said. She reached for his cigarette, stole a puff and handed it back. "I have a nice husband who loves me—and I love him, too. I do love Phil, Dennis. That's something you wouldn't understand but it's the truth."

She hugged her bare knees up to her chin, looked somberly off into space. Dennis shook his head.

"I don't see how you can possibly be happy, Corinne," he said frankly. "You're crazy about me—no, darling, your life is horribly botched up."

"I've had a very happy marriage," Corinne repeated and suddenly began to cry a little, drying her eyes on the edge of the sheet. "I shouldn't be here. I shouldn't. You don't love me. I don't even like you as a friend—how could I?—there's not a thing about you for a girl to admire. That's what my common sense tells me."

"You must learn to distinguish between your common sense and your conscience," Dennis told her placidly. "No, you're a very, very unhappy little girl, Corinne. You're all messed up about life. I've done something for you. I've allowed you the freedom of my apartment and furnished unstinted the beauties of my personality. But that isn't enough, odd as it may seem. I'm worried about you."

"Phil loves me. We're perfectly happy together. You don't need to go worrying about me, you big liar," quavered Corinne. "Phil and I drive out to Long Beach every Sunday in summer. We swim—he still likes to dance with me better than any one else he knows. We've had lovely times and never quarreled. I'm lucky, I tell you."

Dennis looked at her thoughtfully. It did not seem, in fact, the ideal spot in which a happy little wife should sing of her good fortune. The cream-colored note, of course, peeping out from the tumbled folds of the comfort, was the logical voice of the loyal little Mrs. Barrow, but the plump, ivory little bare shoulders and the arms above the covers were definitely none other than Dennis' own naughty little Honey Bear.

"When Phil saw you he said—'so that's Orphen's girl-friend, is it—that Mrs. Callingham?' Because you didn't speak to us and acted as if you were in a hurry to get away. Oh, darling, when he said it I thought my heart would break. I cried. Phil had to hold me all night."

"Oh, really?"

Dennis jumped to his feet and began to dress quickly. Whichever one got out of bed first showed character, showed he or she at least was loftily unaffected by mere sensual indulgences. It was always a mild insult and Corinne's face fell proportionately.

"O.K., you're happily married, then! Your husband holds you all night long, does he?" he snarled. "How about my little heart breaking, too, one of these days? Right in the middle of a Barrow family dinner, right in the middle of the salad, that wonderful goddam salad of that wonderful husband of yours . . . '*Oh, Phil always makes the thalad dwething with hith own hanth!*' Why, Mrs. Barrow, is that a fact, *and* how perfectly delicious. How in the world do you make it, Mr. Barrow? . . . '*We don't like to tell*—'" he mimicked the female voice, "'*but weally it's a secwet. It's not wegular wine-gar, it's tarragon!*' Why, why, Mrs. Barrow! Not tarragon! Why, why, Mrs. Barrow, you don't mean to tell me tarragon! . . . '*And a dash of wokefot and sasson oil*—' oh—oh—oh, Mr. and Mrs. Barrow, what a secret, what a surprise, what a salad dressing and what a happy, happy, happy little couple. Now if you'll just add a soupçon more bird oil, Mr. Barrow, just a soupçon mind you, while I give your dear little wife a nice little buss under the table. . . ."

"Stop!" screamed Corinne, leaping out of the covers. "Stop."

Dennis stopped. He examined his belt buckle intently.

"To be absolutely honest," he said quietly, "I haven't the faintest idea why I didn't speak to you the other night. I can't tell what makes me do things—I can tell about other people but not about me. Let's see, now, supposing I was my hero in a book . . . I think it was the way Effie said—'she's a pretty girl' as if she'd been bitched by every one else and by my writing that book, so that she wouldn't be surprised to have me leave her there in the rain just like Callingham would have for any pretty younger woman. So I—well, my mouth wouldn't open—I just didn't say, Good evening, dear friends. I—just—didn't—speak. So."

"So," said Corinne. She wriggled into her girdle. "Hand me my dress, please."

Corinne, silent, was someone to conjure with. A little tentatively Dennis kissed the back of her neck. When she didn't whirl around at once and fling her arms about him, when she imperceptibly moved her head away, he knew something was wrong again. She fastened her garters, eyes resolutely downcast.

"Do you understand that, Corinne? You're so intuitive you probably do," he said cleverly. "You know more about me than anyone, don't you, Toots?"

Corinne looked at him with odd thoughtfulness.

"There's something between you and that Mrs. Callingham," she said. "I know, because this is the first time you've ever explained anything to me. Any other time when I ask you where you were, who she was, or what you did, you just kid me and say 'never you mind.' This time you explained. It shows it's pretty serious."

Dennis' mouth dropped open.

"She's used to famous men," said Corinne. "Maybe she knows how to talk to you better than I do. I don't mean you're famous yet but you will be. Even Phil says so. And she probably knows what to say."

She tied the orange scarf around her neck, fastened it to the blue wool dress with a crystal clasp with the tiny dog's head preserved in it. Dennis watched her, wanting her to say more, but he was afraid to ask her any questions. Corinne would be sure to jump to some jealous conclusion.

"Applesauce," he said.

"You must not be quite sure what it's all about yourself," said Corinne and shook out her skirt carefully. "You wouldn't be doing all that explaining just for my benefit. It's more for yourself. Look, is it true the book's about her?"

"More or less," admitted Dennis. "I exaggerated—made a real heroine of her, I daresay with a dash of malice, so they tell me."

"You used her for a heroine then fell in love with your heroine," said Corinne. "You act as if you were married to her, as if she came first because she was your work. You act worse than I ever did about my marriage."

She suddenly snatched up the little white note, nestling in the blanket folds like a little white bird, and read it over.

"It is so sad, darling, isn't it," she said mournfully. "I did mean it all, too. I do love my husband—he's so kind to me and you're so beastly. What makes me act this way to him— why do I come here at all—oh, damn, damn, damn!"

She ran out of the door, handkerchief to her eyes, the note fluttering to the floor behind her, saying goodbye. Dennis went to the head of the stairs after her.

"Hey!"

He heard the front door close wheezily on its heavy hinges. She'd be back in a few minutes. He stood in the doorway waiting to click the downstairs entry door for her return, he stood several minutes but she did not come back. Dennis finally closed the door and picked up the note from the floor. "I hope you realize the whole affair has been no more important to me than it has to you." Without Corinne beside him the words did not seem so funny, after all.

"I shouldn't have laughed about it," Dennis reflected uneasily. "I really shouldn't have laughed."

The telephone rang and he picked it up with relief. That would be Corinne saying hadn't she been silly—would he come out for a cocktail. But it was only the publicity man at his publisher's asking if tomorrow morning would be all right with him for photographs and an interview. And did Orphen know where they could get in touch with that Mrs. Callingham so they could get her to deny that the book had anything to do with her?

"No," roared Dennis and hung up.

. . . 'twixt truss and bras . . .

THE JACKET for Dennis Orphen's new book was lousy, said MacTweed to his young partner And Company. What was more it was inadequate. He would go a step further and say it was only so-so. The last modest adjective, being unfamiliar to And Company's blurb-conditioned ears, struck him as the most sweeping condemnation one could hope to hear. He could not keep the admiration out of his eye.

"In fact," said MacTweed, banging on the desk willed to him by old Pat Negley, that 'beloved' dean of publishers, that name used by a thousand authors for years to frighten their children, "in fact," said MacTweed louder, and banging on this same desk so that the Children's Book editor in her little dimity-deviled room next door spilled red ink all over proof sheets of *A Book of Valentines*—"In fact I'm not at all sure of this book, anyway."

"Not at all sure it will sell, perhaps," said And Company, eyes twinkling, for a source of quiet amusement around this temple of art was old MacTweed's old-fashioned interest in profits. "There can be no doubt about it's being good. No doubt at all."

"Why no doubt?" parried MacTweed, lifting his horrendous piratical gray eyebrows by specially developed muscles at the top of his skull—certainly no ordinary temporal muscles could undertake such a mighty task very frequently. "Why no doubt? I doubt if Walter Scott is any good. I doubt if H. G. Wells is any good. I doubt if *any* author's any good. As a matter of fact, Johnson, I look forward to the day when all our books will be written by blurb writers."

"Ha," said And Company obediently for he was not so long with the firm he could merely smile nor so new he need have hysterics, so he merely said Ha with taste and restraint. The last And Company had decided to pull his money out of

449

the firm and take up some safer career like backing musical
shows, but for some reason the money seemed to have taken
root in the fertile MacTweed spring list so that it wouldn't
pull up without pulling up a great many lawsuits and other
liabilities with it. So the withdrawing member had been presented with a great many papers all signed and notaried and
highly non-negotiable, and had allowed his partnership to be
resold to another promising young fellow, namely Johnson.

MacTweed had seen his young partners' faces change so often in his time that in order to give an air of stability to the
office he had refused to alter his own style of sideburns, soup-
mustache, pepper-and-salt Norfolk business suits, dog-headed
ebony cane, and high Walk-Over black shoes (for fallen
arches) in forty years. The changing faces got on his nerves
once in a while but the solid old firm could always use 'new
blood'—publisher's argot for new investors. Johnson was
more ambitious than any of his predecessors since he came
with far less backing. Already he was reputed to be one of the
most brilliant of the younger publishers. He had discovered
more young proletarian writers than MacTweed could shake a
stick at. He was so brilliant he could tell in advance that in the
years 1934–35 and –36 a book would be hailed as exquisitely
well-written if it began:

> 'The boxcar swung out of the yards. Pip rolled over in
> the straw. He scratched himself where the straw itched
> him.'

Johnson hoped for the day when 'And Company' would be
'Johnson.' He hated And Company. He often looked about
him at the Travers Island Athletic Club and saw all the other
And Companys. They seemed to be stamped permanently
'And Company' for they all looked alike. Good God, he
looked alike too! Keen, long-jawed, tallish young men with
sleek mouse-colored hair, large mouths filled with strong big
white teeth good for gnawing bark or raw cocoanuts but
doubtless taxed chiefly by moules or at the most squab,—
nearsighted pleasant eyes under unrimmed glasses that might
be bifocal, large ears set away from the head like good aerials,
large carefully manicured hands, a bit soft, and agreeable deep
voices left over from old Glee Clubs. As for dress, they wore

well-made loose English clothes with the pants sometimes, as in Johnson's case, coming up almost to the armpits, English style, the pleats making a modest bust, and the long stylish fly tastefully and unobtrusively operated by a zipper. These And Companys, many in publishing, some in their uncles' devious businesses, were all men of good taste, and if Semitic were decent enough to be blond and even a little dumb just to be more palatable socially. But they all looked and talked alike and it had Johnson by the throat. He tried to break away from this insidious chain. He married a chorus girl, instead of a Bryn Mawr girl, a very pretty one from *Face the Music*. But all the other And Companys that year had married chorus girls from *Face the Music* and furthermore, like Mrs. Johnson, the girls were all private-school products and all wrote an occasional poem for F.P.A. or the weekly magazines dealing with the curious effect nature had upon them and how, in sum, it made them feel alone.

Johnson decided to throw his fellows off the track by lunching at the Vanderbilt or 70 Park instead of the club but they all went to lunch with him—indeed, they were there first, their fine clean-cut jaws uttering well-bred baritone remarks, never too personal, never too witty for good taste. In summer, instead of going up to Woods Hole, Johnson stole by night with his wife and the little blond baby everyone was having that year over to Martha's Vineyard. But there they all were again on the ferry, their spectacles adjusted keenly over their copies of *Men of Good Will*, their pleasant deep voices politely deferring to their decently un-made-up little wives. Johnson, anxious to have one gesture of individuality, took to drinking applejack instead of Scotch. They all ordered applejack. He saw them all over the country clubs and town restaurants, he saw them in bar mirrors, rows of clean-cut, spectacled, somewhat adenoidal young men drinking applejack, hats at the same angle, eyes never quite blue or never quite brown but compromise shades between the two, they were all the same except for one who had a boil on his neck. Johnson envied this pioneer, this rebel. Not being gifted with boils he must differentiate himself intellectually, he felt. So he went to Communist meetings, he heard lectures at the John Reed Club, he went to a dinner for John Strachey—they were all there, their *New Masses* in their pockets. He discovered Forsythe. They all discovered Forsythe. Johnson was going mad. "Am I the mass mind?" he asked himself. "If I have a thought or an impulse does it mean that at that very minute ten million other men of my education and background are having it, too? Isn't there a chance of my having one atom, one little hormone different from the others or do our metabolisms all work together like Tiller girls?"

One night, late in leaving the office, he was cheered up by a rather simple incident. He had often passed an Oriental wholesale house on Fifth Avenue called MOGI, MOMONOI & CO. The name held his fancy. He had even thought of it as an ideal motto beneath some splendid heraldic device for future publishing purposes. Mogi (I live) Momonoi (I conquer) and Co. (and forever). The translations he made up himself but they soothed him. All of the shops in this neighborhood, which was the wholesale clothing district, were closed on this evening, for it was nearly eight, and he had Fifth Avenue to himself, a delightful sensation for a man doomed by birth and instinct to Westchester. He was going to a performance of *Sailors of Cattaro* that evening feeling reasonably assured that the majority of And Companies would be at the Beaux Arts Ball, when he saw the front door of the Oriental house open and two short little Japanese gentlemen come out. They stood on the sidewalk quietly waiting. They were, oh, beyond a doubt, Mogi and Momonoi themselves. A third was locking the door. Johnson waited eagerly. The door locked, Number Three joined the others; unquestionably he was And Company himself, but how unlike any And Company Johnson had ever seen! He was smaller than his partners and he had a mustache. Johnson could not remember a Jap with a mustache but what elated him most was the daring, the insolence of an And Company with a mustache. The very next day his electric razor, Christmas gift, skirted his upper lip in its swift flight. In less than three months Johnson boasted a mustache as large as an anchovy, but its undersize was made up for by its rich emphatic black color, particularly since Johnson's own hair was only hair-colored. The mustache was distinguished, smart, and only Johnson knew that the pallid reddish bristles from his native follicles were heightened daily by his wife's eyebrow pencil. So this visible badge of a unique personality gave him the courage now to argue with his master, MacTweed, to insist that Dennis Orphen's book was exactly what Gannett, Hansen, and Isabel Paterson had been waiting for all their lives.

"The truth is," said MacTweed, and when MacTweed prefaced his remarks with the word 'truth' or 'fact' Johnson suspected the worst, so he looked discreetly down at his finger-nails now, "I don't like the idea of one author satirizing another. This would be downright libelous, this book, if Cal-lingham was fool enough to sue. Naturally he won't want to bring such attention to it since he's so savagely ridiculed in it. But still is it right, is it ethical, I ask?"

The word ethical was a masterpiece. Johnson was moved by it. It sounded like the deep choked voices of all the clean-cut And Companys swearing loyalty to their ivy-covered alma maters. It was a word for seniors to use, hallowed by cap and gown. Ethical. It said, framed as it was now by the tobacco-stained fangs of MacTweed's generous mouth, boys, it said, there's something more to the game of life than just drinking and wisecracking and wenching; there's a gentlemen's code. There's ethics. Ethics the white flag that went up when you saw you were licked, ethics, the rules for other people, ethics, the big King's X. Through the momentary glamour of MacTweed's ethics Johnson perceived a cablegram lying under the chromium Discobolus paperweight. He had a dim hunch.

"Yes, Johnson," said MacTweed. "You think I'm just a hard-headed businessman, an old Scrooge. Well, let me tell you I've got a sense of professional ethics and, by God, I don't see where this guy Orphen gets off raking over a giant, a titan, like Andrew Callingham."

"Callingham's last book sold nearly a hundred thousand," agreed Johnson.

"Yes," said MacTweed, consulting a memorandum before him, "one hundred and fourteen thousand. And now in seven languages. If we should ever be in a position to publish Cal-lingham—he wants an unearthly advance—how is it going to look for us to start off with a satire on his love life? I ask you, Johnson. It's simply a problem of publishing ethics."

Johnson felt depressed. He fingered his mustache ner-vously. He looked out the window over the tops of Fourth

Avenue and saw the tugs on the East River breathing out
sooty puffs of smoke, chugging along on their little ethical
duties of carrying oil or coal or canned beans some place else.
It was too bad. He, Johnson, had been the little father of
Dennis Orphen, he felt very proud of his discovery, picking
him up out of the gutter, you might say, and making literature of him. He had seen his first Orphen in a woodpulp
magazine eight years ago, a full novelette it was, sandwiched
between ads for bust developers for wallflowers and designs
for a stylish truss. This, said Johnson at the time, reading eagerly from bust to truss, is it. It's literature. For it began:

'The freight slows up just outside the yards. As she jerks
round the bend by the tower Spud gives Butch a kinda push
and out they rolls outa the side door onto the gravel. Wot the
hell, sez Butch, take it easy, take it easy. Ya wanna kill us?'

He had nursed Orphen along. All the other And Companys
were nursing promising lads and lassies along and Johnson
thought he might as well nurse talent as the next one. The
trouble with this nursing was that it involved a lot of pocket
money and not the firm's either. Orphen, for instance, had
never felt properly nursed without a half dozen or so Man-
hattans and lunch besides, a good lunch. Presently, in due
course, the first full length novel was ready for publication.
Johnson read it and was chagrined to realize that in the case
of Orphen he had overnursed. Orphen, instead of staying in
the box car of his woodpulp days had, at the first kind word,
leapt to the past tense and grammar of satin pages. Johnson
was worried, not only for the immediate author but for future
nursees. It was an age of the present tense, the stevedore
style. To achieve this virile, crude effect authors were tearing
up second, third and tenth revised drafts to publish their simple unaffected notes, plain, untouched, with all the warts and
freckles of infancy. The older writers who had taken twenty
years to learn their craft were in a bewildering predicament,
learning, alas, too late, that Pater, Proust and Flaubert had
betrayed them, they would have learned better modern prose
by economizing on Western Union messages.

So Johnson saw future nursees, like Orphen, encouraged
out of their native gold mines into the sterile plains of belles-
lettres. Very well, he said, I will learn something myself from

this and hereafter discourage virile young writers till they get tougher and tougher out of sheer bitterness and become incorruptible. Too late now to save Orphen, however. A seeming dyed-in-the-wool hard guy, he had become in Johnson's nursing school a coddler of fine phrases, a figure-of-speech user, a master of synecdoche. He had been compared to Huxley and Chckov alike, and Louis Bromfield had retired to the south of France to do a blurb for *The Hunter's Wife*. 'Fine,' it said, and was placed by Johnson himself on the back page of the jacket under Hugh Walpole's own words, just above what the women of England in *Time and Tide* had said and the women of America in *Books* had said about the earlier book.

MacTweed had liked this change in Orphen for his part, having never got over an old apprenticeship in throwing out any manuscript whose first page smacked of illiteracy. His committee of judges, consisting of himself and his chromium Discobolus disguised under five other celebrated names, had awarded Orphen the MacTweed Prize for 1933. Orphen became a minor property. But now, as Johnson saw, MacTweed had scented big game. MacTweed, plucking at a fertile eyebrow reflectively, admitted as much.

"Frankly, Johnson," said MacTweed, "we *are* publishing Callingham. Foster visited him in Saint-Cloud and contacted him constantly. It sounds to me as if Foster contacted the pants off him. He outcontacted Doubleday and Harcourt and Macmillan. He certainly did his job. I like Foster." MacTweed chuckled, offered Johnson a Players' Club cigarette from his lizardskin case, gift of his wife and embarrassingly initialed Y.M. so that everyone must guess his unfortunate real name could be nothing but Yuremiah.

"Has anything been settled yet?" asked Johnson uneasily. He saw a bad month ahead explaining to Dennis why his book was not being pushed, and grasping at straws desperately, he decided he'd have to say it had offended the Church or would the Chase National sound more powerful? But ah the distinction, the glory of being Callingham's publisher over all the other And Companys. He brightened a little.

"Foster's sailing here on the *Bremen* with him right now." MacTweed beamed. He lit Johnson's cigarette generously. "It's in the bag."

"Callingham on his way here?" Johnson gave a start. "With *The Hunter's Wife* coming out tomorrow, and with all the gossip about it being Callingham's own life—the reporters all meeting his boat and getting his denials that the book is about him—what a break for sales!"

MacTweed's eyes half-closed under the grizzled brows. He toyed with the Discobolus. His hands were tobacco-stained, calloused, the nails ripped off and appallingly unkempt due largely to his passion for tending his own garden at his place up the Hudson. Johnson tactfully withdrew his own large, beautifully tended white And Company hands from the desk.

"That is something," muttered MacTweed and smiled appreciatively. A nice problem in ethics here. The book with its scandal base would probably sell as much as Callingham's last one. It would get all the Callingham foes as well as his fans. And wouldn't it in a way stir up interest in Callingham's own future work? Wouldn't there be controversies back and forth that would aid sales? That's the way it could be put to Callingham. It could be handled. Foster could handle it. Mac-Tweed banged on the table suddenly and once more the Children's Book editor in the next room must grab the toppling vase of jonquils and calm the storm-tossed ink bottle.

"We'll make that young Orphen yet," said MacTweed. "We've got a real property there, Johnson. Let's get behind him on this book. Let's get Caroline Meigs to give a tea for him. Let's get all set before the *Bremen* lands."

He swung his chair's front legs which had been patiently poised in the air during the conference down to the floor and thrust out his hand. Johnson shook it eagerly. This was a step forward.

"Congratulations, sir, on getting Callingham," he said.

MacTweed stood up and faced the picture of old Pat Negley standing in a trout stream, rod in hand, an inscription running across the grassy bank in the right lower corner— "To Mac, Ever, Pat."

"We'll be bigger publishers than you ever were, you old sonofagun," said MacTweed. "By golly."

He slapped Johnson on the back. It was all very amiable and jolly, a real esprit de corps. Johnson saw And Company changing into Johnson almost before his eyes.

"By the way, a new young man is coming in on Monday to learn the trade," MacTweed said casually. "Just out of Harvard—a connection of the Morgans on his mother's side. Seems to be a hell of a clean-cut fellow. Wants to learn the ropes ha-ha."

"Ha," said Johnson with a sinking feeling.

"Building up the way we are we need all the new blood we can get," said MacTweed.

"New blood, yes," said Johnson.

MacTweed dropped back a step and studied his young partner's face with concern.

"You look peaked, Johnson. I wish you'd let me put you on a Hay diet. All proteins at once, all starches—well, hell, you see what it's done for me."

"Yes," said Johnson and went rather gloomily back to his dark room under the filing cabinets.

. . . announcement in Publishers Weekly . . .

OUT THURSDAY, APRIL 11

THE HUNTER'S WIFE

by Dennis Orphen

What they say . . . .

"Fine . . ." Louis Bromfield
"Significant" . . . Hugh Walpole
"Timely" . . . J. B. Priestley

Statement on the first page of
"The Hunter's Wife":

"All the characters in this novel are highly fictitious"

. . . from a letter to MacTweed and Company: . . .

. . . inasmuch as his bringing suit would only convince the public that this was indeed Andrew Callingham's own story I believe the publication of "The Hunter's Wife" to be without danger to the firm. A number of features in the story coincide with facts in Callingham's life, but we can show point for point where they coincide with eight other well-known writers' lives including Dreiser, Lewis, Hardy, Wells, Zola, Hawthorne, Galsworthy and Ford. Callingham would be deliberately wooing ridicule by a suit or an injunction. I would advise getting in touch with the former Mrs. Callingham and smoothing her over in advance. Some trouble might come up there, particularly since the characterization here is unmistakable according to all report, though here again we can cite a dozen famous authors' wives whose portraits conform to this satiric outline.

> Yours faithfully,
> JOHN LAMBERT,
> *Lambert, Arnst and Bing, Attorneys.*

. . . I remember . . .

"I REMEMBER the first time I met Andy," said Marian, lying on her left side where it did not hurt so much, "it was at Caroline Meigs' tea for him just after his first book came out. She had a little house over by the river with a big garden. There were trees and we were all so surprised at weeds and trees in a New York back yard. There was a table of sandwiches and fruit punch. It was just before we got into the war."

"Andy hated going to that party," said Effie.

"I was terribly excited about meeting him. I'd been in New York a year at the League and I hadn't met anyone famous. Andy of course wasn't known much then but at least he had been published," said Marian. "He was sitting on one of those rustic benches she had around, glowering at everybody. His hair—it was terribly thick and there was something noble about his big head——"

"Everyone always spoke of it," said Effie. "Sculptors were always after him to pose."

"He had on the dirtiest blue shirt I ever saw in my life and no tie and he was tight as a tick," said Marian.

"He started when that bad review came out in the *Times* and got worse because he detested Caroline Meigs," said Effie.

"I was crazy to meet him," said Marian. "I'd bought a new hat, a red one, with the money my mother was sending me for my League expenses and a red jersey silk coat. Then when I saw you I thought, oh dear, if his wife dresses so quietly that must be his taste so I turned the blue side of my coat out—it was reversible, but there weren't any buttons on the blue side and it must have looked funny. You stood in a corner with a big fat woman and very young pretty boy with such a white face and charcoal eyes——"

"The Glaenzers," said Effie. "He wasn't over twenty-one or -two then."

"I met them later," said Marian. "There you were with everyone around saying 'Isn't that Mrs. Callingham distin- guished-looking?' and you never took your eyes off Andy, though he was yards away. No one introduced me to him—I guess I wasn't important enough, just a friend of a friend of a friend. Presently I couldn't stand it any longer and I went up to Andy, 'Let me get you a sandwich,' I said. He had very odd gray eyes, sea-gray. He looked me over very sourly—he says now he was only trying to figure out whether my breasts were as fine as they seemed. 'No, I don't want any more of those goddam sandwiches or any more of this swill to drink,' he said. I was so startled. Caroline could hear him. She was right beside us."

"He never cared who heard him," said Effie. "He was al- ways perfectly honest."

"I sat down beside him. He hadn't asked me to and it was pretty bold of me," said Marian, "and before I knew it I was saying 'My, it must be wonderful to be a writer.' I said how much I admired his work, and did he write at night or in the daytime and did he write from life or imagination. I really did. I said all those things. And he gripped the arm of his chair as if he was going to throw something but all he said was 'ex- actly.' 'Exactly,' he'd say. I was so thrilled. I thought he was brilliant. And he thought I was. Actually. Finally he said, 'Thank God, there's one intelligent woman here, what do you say we clear out and go someplace decent?' Can you imagine?"

"It was odd I didn't notice you that day," said Effie. "I was only wondering if he would run out after a while with that tall blond girl and how I could make it look perfectly natural so people wouldn't talk. I was always doing that."

"Later on that summer I got to visiting a girl from the League who lived out at Cold Spring Harbor where he kept his boat," said Marian. "I would see him at the station some- times or when we were out sailing. He always looked like a tramp, bearded, dirty dungarees, sometimes a battered old sunhat with the crown kicked out, likely as not shelling peanuts on the village streets and eating them as he went along, some detective story sticking out of his pocket. I thought he was wonderful. Sometimes I saw you out on the deck of the launch on Sunday mornings when we sailed by. You'd be washing your hair or just lying in the sun. You had lovely hair, Effie. Every time I'd see you out there with your yellow hair flying about I'd go back to town determined to have my hair dyed or get a permanent wave or something. You know it's still lovely, too—no, don't put your hat on yet, please. Andy still speaks of your hair. He loved it."

"I know," said Effie.

"Do you know I remember Andy so clearly before we got to be friends, isn't it funny? I mean I remember the wanting to know him, the terrible hoping I'd run into him, the wondering what I'd say to him and what he'd say to me next time we met, much clearer than how it all finally happened?" said Marian. "Isn't that extraordinary? Pretty soon you and he and I were going places together, and on Sunday nights back in town eating at Mouquin's, both of us laughing at everything Andy said and me drawing pictures of Dubois, the waiter, and trying to hear what the Pennells were saying at the next table. Andy always had a favorite waiter—not Dubois—but—I've forgotten the name now——"

"Ernest," said Effie.

"You were the serious one, always," said Marian. "You didn't see how we could be so silly with war so near. Andy was a ferocious pacifist. I was shocked at first but afterwards of course I respected him for daring to be one. I sometimes wonder what would have happened to him if we'd stayed in America till war was declared. He would have been jailed or killed. And there wouldn't have been any me in his life. It was lucky our deciding to go to China instead of to Europe as we first planned. You stayed right on in New York until the Armistice, didn't you, Effie?"

"Yes," said Effie. "There wasn't much else for me to do."

"Do you remember the three of us that Fourth of July at Coney Island, Effie? The astrologer . . . the description she gave of our true mates . . . Andy's and mine fitted," said Marian, "and I was so thrilled over that till I looked at you——"

"I hadn't even noticed it," said Effie. "I didn't pay any attention to those things."

"But I felt so guilty over being thrilled, you see, and I suddenly hated Andy for being so wonderful that two fine girls had to fight and suffer for him, so all the rest of the day I stayed beside you and I wouldn't dance with him or go in the loveboat or do any of the things I wanted to do most. He got angry, remember, and left us and at Feltman's when we were eating later on he came up with two awful little tarts and a sailor he'd picked up on the Boardwalk. They all came back to town with us and we could never get rid of them."

"Andy was always doing things like that," said Effie.

"We did have good times," said Marian, closing her eyes. "Wherever we went we had fine times. I never knew who Andy would bring up to our room in Shanghai or Tokyo—" she went on, leaving Effie alone now in New York and taking Andy far far away forever, "some British earl or some Viennese dancer. At first he was always in the dumps thinking maybe you were having a bad time of it alone and you never wrote——"

"There was nothing to say," said Effie, "and I was getting along all right. I was perfectly all right."

"I told him that. If it had been me in your place," said Marian, "I would have died. I would have killed myself, I would have jumped out a window. My heart would have absolutely broken, but, Effie, you were so calm, so sane, so marvelous, you were such a swell person, we always said that, Effie, Andy and I always said so. And you had told him to do just as he thought best, go if he must. I couldn't have said that. I couldn't say it last fall when this new woman came in—I couldn't bear it for a minute, oh, I couldn't stand it, it killed me, it did, it killed me. I had to run away just seeing them laugh at each other across the room or saying silly things to each other the way we used to do at Mouquin's—I went out of my mind. And I hurt so—this thing hurt me so. . . . Effie, do you believe he's still with her? Don't you think when I ran away he got afraid of losing me altogether and sent her off? I'm so sure he did. I can't stand thinking about it—but after all he does love me—we did have good times, he will come when he hears I'm here sick, and he will laugh at me for being so silly as to run out. You sent the cablegram?"

"He'll come," said Effie. "Don't worry, dear."

"He will. But when? Where is he now?" She was silent for so long that Effie, turning toward her, saw that her cheeks were graying and rang for the nurse.

"She's gone again," she whispered.

The nurse shook her head gravely.

"It can't be long now. If her husband could only get here in time!"

IN THE DRUGSTORE a block away from the hospital Effie
stood in the telephone booth staring at the dial face, as if
some of its own blank unconcern might pass out to her. It
could not be that to roll back two decades she had only to
turn the dial, a voice would answer exactly as it had answered
then. Thinking how incredibly simple was this contact with
another age, Effie wondered what had restrained her from
performing the miracle before this. What a comforting game
it would have been, pretending his absence was only for the
day, the hour, and not forever. Just a twist of the wrist as the
magicians said. Hello, Bruster Company? Is this Tom? Mrs.
Callingham speaking. Has Andy got there yet? When he
comes in will you ask him to call the apartment? Thank you.

Effie found herself trembling as one should tremble before
such miracles. She dared not risk it. Scientists must have felt
the same primitive terror before bringing their robots to life,
terror of the unknown world about to be released. Put up
your right hand, dial up two down one. She looked again for
the number in the book, mind balking on the side of fear. So
easy. Bruster Company, Literary Agents, Graybar Building.
Would the same Miss Hupfel be there, efficient, moderately
friendly, later moderately patronizing. . . . 'We are instructed
to deposit the March royalties to your account in the Guar-
anty Trust. . . . Why, no, Mrs. Callingham, the new novel is
late in being delivered. Mr. Bruster just had a letter from
them. They're in Singapore now. Yes, Singapore. They seem
to be having a wonderful time. No, the last book didn't do so
well . . . he lost a good deal of his public by those pacifist articles of his, Mr. Bruster says, coming as they did right in the
heat of the war feeling. . . .'

Effie's hand darted up quickly, swung the dial around,
swung it round to the year 1916, heard the calm answer on the

phone, as calm as if there were no nineteen years between the two telephones. Long distance, thought Effie. It would be long distance, too, to take a train—quite possible, no reason why not—out to Cold Spring Harbor, walk along the harbor, see the *Violet II* there at the dock, perhaps, a launch really might survive that long.

"This is Mrs. Andrew Callingham"—how brave she was speaking out loud with only the dial face to mock her—"and I wanted to know if your office had heard from Mr. Callingham. Is he expected in America this month?"

"Mr. Callingham arrives on Saturday," said the cool voice. No, it could not be Miss Hupfel, of course. Launches might last but not Misses Hupfel. "We've had a cable. You can reach him through this office if it's important. What name was that again, please? Mrs. What?"

Thank God.

"Thorne, I said, Miss Thorne."

"Thorne, did you say? I understood you—"

The receiver on the hook. Suddenly Effie took it down again, dropped in another nickel. Dennis. She must get back to Now, to the little Present that did not matter. She heard the buzz repeating dully, rhythmically. No answer. No Dennis. No one. It was hard to believe you had no one. Yet Marian, too, had no one. Still, that was not true, she had her belief in Andy and Andy was returning for her. Marian did have her Andy. She, Effie, had no one. She turned to the telephone book, fumbled desperately through its pages. Did she look so strange, for the boy at the soda fountain was peering at her intently? Did it matter? She found the number.

"Dr. MacGregor, please . . . Effie Thorne . . . Oh, doctor, I thought I'd call to see how you were. It was lovely seeing you last night. How have you been—oh, yes, you did say you'd been splendid. Andy's coming on Saturday. I thought you'd like to know. Yes, I just had a cable. Yes, it will be nice seeing him—we've been in touch constantly of course. He always liked you so much. Yes . . . What? Oh, I'm fine. Yes, I'm fine. I sound funny? That's strange, because I feel perfectly fine. No, there's nothing else, I just thought I'd give you a ring. No, I'm fine. Goodnight. Goodnight, Dr. Mac-Gregor. Thanks so much . . . What? Did you say thanks for *what?* . . . I don't know, really, it just slipped out, I guess. Goodnight."

Without warning, tears streamed down her face, she leaned her face against the telephone, mechanically pulled the booth door slightly open so the light would go off and hide her, she stood in there, receiver dangling from its hook, her body shaking. The soda fountain boy was looking at her. The marcelled blonde at the Helena Rubinstein counter was looking at her. The customer was looking at her. They could see through both glass doors, dark or light. They could see through long distance to Bruster Company, Literary Agents, to Dr. MacGregor in the Hotel Rumsey. They could see through everything but she could not stop crying. She picked up her pocketbook, left the receiver still hanging with I'm-fine-I'm-fine-I'm-fine and ran outdoors into brilliant sun.

. . . family dinner . . .

"To the book!" said Phil Barrow, lifting his cocktail, third
gin, third vermouth, third cold tea *and* a dash of bitters
shaken up and if you-have-any-cucumber-in-the-refrigerator-
I-usually-soak-it-peeled-of-course-in-the-cold-tea-say-for-half-
an-hour—"To the book!"

"To the book!" said Corinne, lifting hers, and staring defiantly at Dennis don't-you-dare-make-a-face-when-you-taste-
this—don't-you-dare-say-what-is-this-mess—don't-you-dare.

"Thanks," said Dennis and politely drank it down. "It's
mighty nice of you people to celebrate for me this way. Say,
that's a fine drink you've made here, Phil, how did you tell
me you made it?"

Corinne rewarded him with a grateful smile because it was
no fair hurting Phil, it was strange but she simply could not
bear for Phil to be hurt in any of his little vanities, whereas she
was almost vengefully pleased when shafts were tossed in
Dennis' direction. But no one must tease Phil about his recipes
or his anecdotes or his pleasure in his own good sense, no one
must make a fool of him, no one, that is, except his little wife.

"I use cold tea as the basis for all my cocktails," said Phil,
eyes behind his spectacles faintly contemptuous of his guest's
ability to appreciate nuances of taste. "Iced tea and applejack,
for instance, makes a darned fine highball, or a good punch
base for the matter of that."

"Dennis can't make a decent cocktail to save his soul," said
Corinne proudly, and turned to Dennis—now *you*, now *you*
say something.

"It's the truth. Nor a salad nor a soufflé nor a gingerbread
man. It's mortifying," agreed Dennis readily. The evening was
on. Now we all join hands to build up Phil. What-a-cook—
what-a-swimmer—what-a-financier—what-a-thinker—what-a-
man-Phil!

"Let me give you another," suggested Phil. "Pass his glass, Baby."

"Here you are, Baby," said Dennis maliciously, and passed his glass to Corinne. She kicked him under the table. Over the centerpiece of African tulips—lecherous-looking posies for a family dinner, he thought—he caught Olive's significant, sarcastic half-smile. He wondered what would happen if one of these days he would shout out his hate for Olive, his hate for all women's girl-friends. Must every woman in the world have some other woman best-friend, always hovering in the background, voicing wisdom very bad for the sweetheart's naïve ears, advising, reporting, knowing, always knowing so much more than the sweetheart herself? Olive, dear loyal Olive! If women were only as deceitful to their female friends as men hoped and said they were! But no, wherever a man went he must be annoyed and frustrated by sex solidarity. Olive, for instance, knew all about Dennis because Olive and Corinne had gone to Miss Roman's together. Corinne always told Olive absolutely *everything* and Olive told Corinne everything, especially little things she'd heard here and there about Dennis, odd places she'd run into him. Olive was an old peach, that way. Every time he saw Olive's smooth, rather handsome dark face across the table he thought of how much Olive knew about him and he shuddered, how much more she knew about Corinne, too, than he did. She probably knew of plenty little escapades Corinne had confessed only to her, little infidelities that made a stalwart true lover like Dennis seem a rather ridiculously romantic figure. Olive knew all, she knew—no use pretending she didn't—exactly how Dennis made love, how he first did this, then he did that, how he looked in his B.V.Ds, his every weakness. Infinitely more detached than Corinne she could weigh the evidence coolly, check this against that, and balance all with her own sour philosophy. Dennis, as seen through the eyes of the girl-friend's girl-friend, could be Romeo only to some feeble-minded Juliet, not to shrewd Miss Olive Baker. He could see himself reflected in her clear dark eyes, very, very diminutive and extremely upside down, and in her quiet smile he read how decent she was in not telling Phil, in comforting Corinne in minor crises, in never revealing to a living soul except by a slight sneer what a two-timing Casanova she happened to know Dennis really was. Ah there, decent square-shooting girl-friend's girl-friend, he saluted her silently across the table, what was your private opinion of that last lovers' quarrel you've just been hearing about upstairs, and didn't you think the little episode concerning my new azure-blue shorts was enormously entertaining, and how did you explain my kissing Corinne right smacko in the Snack Bar—kinda sweet and spontaneous of me, wasn't it? . . . One thing to count on, old chummy, you won't ever quite dare crack down hard on me because I know such wonderful people and you're crazy to meet them, because you never yet have met anybody except the people the Barrows pass on to you and they're not hot enough. How long has it been now since I promised we'd get hold of Okie-Dokie, the big editor, and have a party, just the four of us? Ever since that promise Olive had read Okie's magazine from cover to cover with curious loyalty to this future friend. She'd cut out a picture of him in a tabloid paper where he was one of five men asked a question by the Inquiring Reporter, and she always referred to Okie with a positively possessive smirk. Dennis could not imagine why he'd never brought about this meeting or come through with some elegant party, but having it always in the air, the brilliant unknown Okie always hovering in the background gave him a certain hold over Olive, much more than if he had ever produced the too-too-average Okie of reality. Honestly, though, Corinne protested time after time to him, Olive did think a great deal of Dennis, she certainly admired his courage sticking to his writing after that bad review of his last book in *Time*, for most people, Olive felt, would have given up after that, and she *did* think in certain lights he had sort of a sweet profile. Dennis knew all this because Corinne had often told him so, just as she had told Olive how much Dennis liked her and how he couldn't understand why a girl with her personality had so many free evenings.

In taxis going home from the little dinners at the Barrows', Dennis and Olive would be alone, silent, detesting each other, he trying to remember his sweet profile, she striving to sharpen up on her personality. There were bad hours indeed, these rides through the night in love-scented taxis. Once

Dennis had had a horrible temptation to make a grab at her virgin thighs just to see her triumphant smile—aha! didn't-I-say-that's-the-way-he-was-Corinne—just to see what she would report later to Corinne. But the fear that he would only have her calling him up every morning instead of loyally tattling all to Corinne, kept him from this experiment in female-friend psychology.

"How about it, Orphen, does MacTweed think this book will go at all? What does MacTweed say about it anyway?" inquired Phil, arm-and-arming it with MacTweed, two big businessmen sticking together against their wives' artist friends. The closest Phil could ever get to Dennis' work was an interest in MacTweed's overhead. Dennis warily tried to duck this snag familiar in his talks with Phil. If he commented unfavorably on MacTweed, Phil would at once patiently explain to Author Orphen what MacTweed, a brother financier, was driving at. He would smile patronizingly at Goodfornothing Author Orphen while he interpreted the farseeing wisdom of MacTweed to Corinne and Olive, as if, Dennis thought resentfully, he was his personal friend, a pal, a buddy, instead of being a stranger known only through Dennis' descriptions. Naturally Phil felt warm toward any unknown party who was kind enough to get in Dennis' hair, that was only to be expected, but he needn't take this Olympian bow every time the Big Interests were mentioned.

"Corinne read some of the book, Phil," said Olive, the fixer. "She says it's quite interesting and it may catch on."

"Is that so, Baby? You read it, did you?" Phil deferred eagerly to Baby's intellect, as if her having read it showed far more brilliance than merely having written it. "Interesting you say, hey? You know, Orphen, Corinne reads everything, whatever the reviews suggest. She saves those little lists of different authors' favorite books in the *Tribune* and goes through every one."

She does? She *does*?

"I trust her judgment, too. If she says a thing's interesting, I take her word for it, don't I, Baby? Another thing, she's saying, oh dear, she says, I certainly wish Dennis could write something that would make money like *So Red the Rose* or those things."

She does? She *does?*

"Hm," said Dennis, very red, very angry, glaring across the African tulips at this strange Corinne of Mr. Barrow's, glaring as if she did not look unusually sweet in her simple little yellow dinner dress, ruffles modestly falling over pretty arms, friendship bracelet, of all things, jingling silver hearts over her wrists.

"I think it's really good," she said, unconscious of this baleful scrutiny. "You know, Baby, I think there's a picture in it. It would suit Ann Harding."

"Ann Harding! You don't say! Well, well, Orphen, congratulations, that's fine!"

Dennis strove vainly to force Corinne's attention so she might see his scorn. *Baby!* So, not only did her husband call her Baby, but she called him *Baby,* too! You'd think people could think of something fresher than that to call each other, something that would exhibit more flamboyantly their feelings for each other. Why couldn't they call each other Butch, for instance? Good God, what was he doing here between these Babys! And Olive smirking down at her plate, pleased with the whole nasty situation, something to talk over tomorrow, or, no, by Jove, tonight. After coffee the girls would rush to Corinne's bathroom and stay in there whispering for hours while he, outsider, stranger, must sit in the living room with Phil and cognac, disliking both, and hear how bright Baby was, what a head, what a brain!

"And if I hadn't spoiled everything by rushing her off to get married she would have had a career herself!" said Phil, for suddenly there they were, the two of them, in the living room, brandy bottle between them on the glass-and-silver coffee table, girls whispering furiously away in corners upstairs. "She wrote pieces for the school paper and had parts in plays. I'm to blame for keeping her just for myself."

"I wouldn't blame myself too much," said Dennis. All right, now, let's get on with the build-up. That was the legitimate tax on bachelors; wherever they stole their jam they must build up the rightful owner. Briefly looking back over the last ten years, Dennis could not remember a single husband he had not spoiled for life by his flattery, many of them so set up that they felt they were too good for the very wives

Dennis was testing out. "By George, you know how to pick a nice brandy."

"Marie Brizzard," said Phil. "More? Sixty-five years. Yes, one thing you can't economize on is brandy. Either it's good or it isn't."

"Brandy and neckties," said Dennis, watching the door frantically. Where were the little women anyway? "I never spend less than four-fifty for my ties."

He fingered his Woolworth tie delicately as if it were something infinitely rare and fragile.

"That's the truth," said Phil, looking toward the stairs. "Oh, *Baby!* Hey, we're waiting! Did Corinne tell you I'd just made the University Club? Sort of embarrassing for me in a way as the head of the firm doesn't belong, so naturally I'm a little on edge as to how he'll take it. Did Corinne tell you we're planning a world cruise this year? Poor Baby, she's had her heart set on it for so long. Her one aim in life."

Corinne wanted a world cruise?

"That and a mink coat. Well, it's one or the other, I told her, maybe the mink next year."

Corinne wanted a mink coat?

"Olive may come along on the cruise—make it more fun for Corinne, another girl, of course. More brandy? No, I just have one myself. Corinne got me a bottle eighty years old for my birthday. Smoothest stuff you ever tasted. By the way, Orphen, does MacTweed pay you a straight royalty or a stated amount? Not much in a book of that type, is there?"

"He pays plenty," said Dennis mysteriously. "Plenty. Through the nose."

Phil was impressed but skeptical.

"I've been thinking of a cruise myself," said Dennis dreamily. "Not with a crowd. Just private. On a yacht. Friends of mine. Glaenzers. Anthony Glaenzer—she was the Cody daughter, you know—Stuyvesant Cody, all the other children put away in asylums here and there so she has everything. Yes, we have some fun together, the Glaenzer bunch and I, laughing and kidding back and forth."

There. Behind Corinne's back the boys might fight as much as they liked. Nice little Phil could brag and Dennis could lie. Me and the Glaenzers, now what put that in my mouth? . . .

"What is it girls tell each other that's so important?" fretted Phil, looking toward the hall door. "Olive's been here all day and Corinne was with Olive all last night but they still got things to say. Like boarding school."

Dennis' eyes narrowed. So she told her husband she'd spent last night with Olive, eh? Well, she'd told Dennis she'd spent it with her husband at Radio City Music Hall. One answer to that—a new lover in the offing. How stupid Phil was not to guess this. Almost irresistible not to prick his smugness with a hint or two, a doubt of Olive planted here right now. Then have Phil on guard, keeping careful watch on these little Olive nights, protecting her from cads, keeping her safe and true for Dennis!

"Did Corinne seem a little upset to you tonight, Orphen? She's such an emotional little creature. Even a movie upsets her. The other night she saw Jean Harlow in something or other—*Reckless*—and she cried her eyes out. Terribly sensitive."

Sure, she cried her eyes out over Jean Harlow, thought Dennis, intensely disliking this man's wife, this sensitive little Mrs. Barrow who was upstairs giggling over that man last night—could it have been Walter, the teakettle man? . . . Sure, she cried over *Reckless*—just a little bundle of emotions. She could see plays or read books on revolution, poverty and starvation with a detached "Tough luck" as if among the oppressed further misfortune were the rule and left her unmoved. But when she saw hearts really break, as only hearts under ermine can break, then tears by the gallon did she shed, did Mrs. Baby Barrow, her whole exquisite nervous system bathed and sublimated in sympathetic anguish over Harlow's diamond-studded woe, Harlow gallantly wearing her sables, chin up before the servants, smiling at the cruel Four Hundred, while her brave heart broke in the back seat of a Rolls-Royce. That would upset Phil's Baby, all right, that would be the gamut of her feelings, all passed on later in whispers to Olive.

How can I stand such people, marveled Dennis, how can I do this man the honor of sleeping with his clever, booky little wife? How can I endure them, and say what you will there must be a streak of that fudgy respectability in her to enjoy this man's company, she must have something like that in her. . . . I mustn't have any more of this cognac, he thought, Phil's face drops an inch every time I pass my glass, but he has to keep on asking because he's a perfect host if it kills him. Then, too, I might go a little screwy and tell him to make Corinne wear more underclothes while she's got this cold, and watch out for the little rascal when she says she's with Olive. . . . Hello, here we are on our feet, the girls all whispered out back in the room, Olive with lowered eyelids, abulge with secrets Dennis would never, never know.

"Gossiping again, you two!" accused Phil none too merrily. "We've been here hours."

"Why, Baby!" murmured Corinne.

"We were not gossiping," said Olive, smoothly crossing a very good leg for a girl-friend over a handsome knee. "Phil thinks women don't have anything to say to each other but gossip. We have ideas, too."

Ideas! Dennis looked with vast scorn at Mrs. Barrow's ivory valentine face. Ideas! Why, this creature's whole nature recoiled when she came smack up against anything as cold and repellent as an idea. A turtle in my bed, she would scream, a cold turtle! A statistic poking its clammy nose into my face! Away! Oh, nasty, nasty Idea!

"We were discussing Captain Anthony Eden, if you must know," said Olive proudly. "It happens we both admire him."

"He's doing a lot for England," said Mr. Baby.

"For all of us," said Dennis morosely, "and for Finland too. Captain Eden represents Virtue and Right all over the world, for he represents England."

"That's so," said Phil. "England is England and if any country has high ideals, it's England."

"What a nice couple, England and Eden," said Dennis thoughtfully. "I wonder if they call each other Baby."

Ah, there the resentment was revealed! Corinne flashed him wounded astonishment—you-*are*-you're-making-fun-of-Phil! Olive laughed goody-goody-goody-a-scene-a-show-down. Phil drew back, insulted, then managed a sour smile and lit his cigarette very carefully with his beautiful birthday lighter.

"Very good," he said. "Excellent."

It's very strange, thought Dennis, apparently my insides are as old-fashioned as a White Steamer, no matter how modern my top is. Can it be true that these old insides shudder at something so simple and everyday as a triangle situation, can it be they recoil from an up-to-date Family Dinner? Why, you funny old insides, you, operated by Federal instead of local laws, so that all local actions are canceled out by this invisible G-man.

"I'll say this, *my* Baby is looking mighty pretty in the new dress this Baby bought her today, ha ha ha ha ha ha ha!" said Phil.

"Ha ha ha ha ha ha ha!" said Olive and Corinne gratefully. Into the doghouse, you go, Orphen.

Phil reached across Corinne's lap, placed a hand comfortably on her knee. Dennis looked at the ceiling, out the window, up the stairs. He stared so sternly at the walls that it would seem the mortgages must pop out in very shame.

Detestable Babys! Hateful Olive! Horrid House! Raw searing rage seethed through him, a little dinner celebrating his book, a little family dinner, don't dress, just wear your armor, just a little family dinner. Rage left and he was sad, far worse to be sad, too, to wonder why love today came to people in fragments like a jigsaw puzzle and no one person had all the pieces, nothing whole was left any more, nor was this England's fault, nor could even Captain Eden fix it up. . . . This sadness, this ache, jealousy, whatever it might be, must be what Effie Thorne carried always with her, this was what it was like, this was it when she saw Marian, this unbearable tormenting bewilderment. Effie, Effie, he thought, I understand, so this is what stays with you always and no one can help, no one. Only you and I know, we understand.

. . . the trousseau . . .

"Buy me a pink bedjacket," Marian had implored. "Could
you get someone to curl my hair—only how can I lift my
head when it's so tired and heavy? Effie, isn't there something
to be done about this room—but never mind, there's no
money, is there, and anyway Andy won't let me stay here long
as soon as he comes. Oh, I do hope it stops hurting when he
comes. When it hurts there's really nothing else, nothing but
pain, pain. . . . A pink bedjacket, Effie, not woolly but that
lacy kind."

But the boxes now scattered about the Chelesa apartment
did not contain bedjackets, even Mr. Hickey, the janitor,
could guess that much, piling them up one after the other
outside the door. Effie could not explain it even to herself.
Reason had fled before this sudden urgency, years of discretion and economy were wiped out in hours of mad shopping.
Pride could get in no word, or fear of Dennis' cutting analysis. Effie shook out her purchases in her room, laid the dresses
out over the couch, piled the dainty lingerie, price tags still
modestly fluttered from shoulder ribbons, on the window
seat. In a daze she wandered through Fifth Avenue shops, ordering this and that, never asking the price, though certainly
these long-dormant charge accounts, once gracefully sponsored by Belle Glaenzer, could not bear such demand without
investigation sooner or later. This new wardrobe was one she
had treasured in the back of her mind, something she had
planned half-asleep through the long lonely nights. It had
nothing to do with her present needs or tastes, it was definitely a wardrobe for the Effie of long ago, a recostuming of
the glamorous scenes of her honeymoon. Let other women of
her years prepare for age, here was one who was building for
her youth. Useless to bring common sense to bear when she
saw the blue-flowered hat in Saks, useless for the saleswoman

to hint that it was a little too on the bridesmaid side, for this was the hat Effie should have worn to Caroline Meigs' garden party so that Andy could have looked at no one else. Remembering the plain dark blue taffeta she had worn running away to Connecticut with Andy on her wedding night, she corrected herself now by buying a rose-colored print, and here too on the black couch were the elaborately strapped French slippers Andy had wanted for her but which she would not have. Here were the ridiculously fragile underthings Andy was always suggesting for her, the chiffon stockings, all the feminine extravagances she had laughed at him for admiring. Ordering two insanely expensive chemises from a Madison Avenue shop Effie was brought to a pause by the suspicious interrogation in the salesgirl's eyes. You can't pay for these, said the look, and for whom do you buy these bridal treasures, surely not for your old poor person, modest finances betrayed by ready-made coat, counter hat, bargain gloves, pawnshop antique silver necklace, basement pocketbook. Effie drew up her shoulders haughtily at this inquisition, flung out Mrs. Anthony Glaenzer's name as the charge's name, and then she thought, Why it's true, she's right, I can't pay for these things, I will have to explain to Belle soon, and for that matter when and where will I wear them and for whom? She examined her mind curiously as if it were something inanimate, detached from her, studied it to see what strange secret hopes might be betrayed there lurking, yet when she caught a faint shadow of an answer she withdrew, terrified, from the word, the articulate wish. She called in the janitor to help hang her new curtains and as he stood on the maple highboy, heavy shoes planted on a Sunday paper, he uttered his own private astonishment.

"These ain't like you, missus—excuse it, Miss Thorne. Kinda loud-like for you, they don't seem just right somehow."

Effie straightened the folds at the side of the window, ivory glazed chintz splashed with bright scarlet flowers. She saw herself walking through Lord and Taylor's with Andy behind her, heard his occasional exclamations—"Here it is, Effie. Look! Isn't that great? How many yards do we want, say about fifty?" She would turn from the blue denim counter to her husband so hopefully planted at the gayer counter two aisles back, beaming over a pile of red and yellow flamboyant cretonnes, so outrageously wrong for their little place that she would shake with laughter.

"Darling! Please not that! And eight yards is all we need whatever it is."

Andy stood beside her, hands gloomily thrust into his pockets, complaining all the while the plain blue was being wrapped.

"What's the good of buying curtains if they aren't any fun? Who wants to live in a dark blue house? I'm damned if I'll go shopping with you again, Effie. I'll bet you five dollars you're going upstairs now and buy a dark blue dress."

Effie thrust the packages into his unwilling arms.

"I am, but, Andy, we can't get wild colors because we'd get sick of them, and when you're as poor as we are we have to get something that will wear. Dark blue *wears!* There, is that clear?"

"I hate things that wear," shouted Andy wrathfully. "I've always hated them ever since I was a kid and got three woolen union suits for Christmas instead of roller skates. I'd always rather have roller skates."

"Even in winter?" asked Effie, smiling because he was always the child, always the little boy.

"Especially in winter," he said firmly. "Another thing, Effie, I hate houses in good taste. My aunt's house was in good taste and so I never dared asked the bunch in to play. I like red."

So, holding the chiffonier steady for Mr. Hickey to climb down, boot on the white window seat first and then secure on the light oak floor, Effie said to him, "I know it doesn't seem like me, Mr. Hickey, but tastes do change, you know."

"That's right," conceded Mr. Hickey amiably, shoving the chest over to the next window and once more adjusting the protective *Tribune*. "I never used to eat rice no matter how it was fixed. Now you can give me rice any time o' day, any time at all."

He was a square, broad little man and looked alarmingly apelike with his hat off, for his round bullet head was blue-shaven, and his wide flat nose spread out loose and moist and pinkish above the blue-stippled grayish skin. His eyes were red-rimmed and suspicious, his chin large, outthrust, antagonistic, but this manner melted before the least kind word, the least sign of friendship, the least mention of his crippled son. The eyes became weakly docile and doglike, the pugnacious chin hollow and defenseless. Nor was this his own chin, literally. It had been made for him only a year before by our good government after the mustard gas left in his system by the war had eaten away the old chin. He talked about this good fortune proudly as he hammered the little gold prongs into the window frame, his flat down-East apologetic voice punctuated with surprising violence by the staccato hammering, while Effie sat below on the window seat, the gaudy material engulfing her as she hurriedly basted hems.

"No, sir, I got no kick against the government," said Mr. Hickey, whack, whack, whack at the curtain nails. "They certainly treated *me* all right, givin' me this new chin without leavin' a scar as you can see for yerself, takin' care o' me free o' charge every year in the hospital the last eighteen years. See that mustard gas done somethin' to my lungs way back in 'eighteen so somethin' has to be done every year about that, then my stummick where the bullet went through, it gets bad, and every time I get those attacks, say, the government looks after me, no expense at all, months on end, you know yourself, ma'am, how I'm allers goin' back to the hospital. I been lucky at that, though. See, I was a naval gunner, we were on this ship outta Saint-Quentin and there was this mistake in the command the way I figure it we loaded the guns twice with powder and no shell at all, 'cause eighteen of us was blown straight to pieces. I was the only lucky one and acourse I was outa my head, even so, and lost my speech and all for two years, but the government hospital worked on me and I concentrated the way you have to do, and in a few years I was just fine, exceptin' for the way the mustard gas keeps eatin' away and nachally my wife and Tom lame that way has to shift along while I'm gone but with the Relief and people chippin' in here and there like you and the folks downstairs and the church, I certainly got no complaint, we certainly been pretty lucky, savin' Tom when he got the paralysis, and then I got some good care, *some* care, I'll say, and I got this new chin out of it. My wife says it's better than the old one, got more character, she says, *she* likes it better for my type o' face."

The hammer ceased, the boot came gingerly down again on the newspaper, the other boot followed on to the floor. Mr. Hickey stepped back to look at his handiwork and again a faint bewilderment came into his eye, staring at the flaming curtains, then at the slender faded woman beside them. The curtains swayed gently, poinsettias swelling out to full pattern, then withdrawing into their white shiny folds; they were alive, blood-red flowers leaping out of a gleaming shroud, and in between their flowing lengths the body of the woman, oddly graying into the shadows beyond the window, fading into the smoky clouds far in the distance, far over the river and the Jersey shores; and the room belonged to the curtains, they swelled and bellied in the river breeze, bleeding blossoms moved barely perceptibly, they blew over Effie Thorne, concealed her. Whee, they said, blowing out and in, wheee, and Effie's face returning, brilliant blue eyes wide, seemed strangely pale and frightened so that Hickey suddenly shouted out, "They don't suit you, missus, I'm tellin' you, they don't suit you, they ain't right for you. The old ones, the blue ones, were better."

Effie's hand fluttered up, startled.

"Really?" she said, staring at him as if he had never been there; then she collected herself and smiled wearily. "But I've had blue so long, Mr. Hickey, in every apartment I ever lived."

Mr. Hickey mopped his forehead, read in her protest an excuse to resume the chip-on-the-shoulder expression. He looked curiously at the bright dresses spread out on the studio couch, was frankly amazed at the silver and crystal perfume atomizer set out amid its wrappings on the table.

"You going away, Mrs. Callingham?" For the room cried out, *something's happened, something's happened*, and he was an unconquerably curious fellow. "Or is somebody movin' in? If it was anybody else I'd think they was gettin' married."

The question, articulate, brought a flood of color to Effie's face, a sudden dizziness to her head. No one had the right to make these direct challenges, she herself had never made them to the world, the world should not make them to her. Before her Hickey, ape-faced, muscled arms swinging low from great shoulders, Hickey the janitor, pitifully coughing in the basement winter nights with his mustard gas lungs, proudly carrying his crippled boy upstairs to the roof on summer mornings, beaten proud little man, changed to Enemy, slipped quietly over to the hostile ranks of Dennis Orphen, Glaenzers, World.

"Thank you for helping, Mr. Hickey," she said coldly, and following his bold stare longed to fling acres, seas, fields of dark decent blue over the gay ruffles and silks scattered over her bed, over the leering curtains, over her own heart, dark limitless smothering blue to hide her shame before the Enemy's knowledge of her secret folly.

If there were some way of legalizing friendship, of compelling confidences by law, of waving a contract at the sulking friend, saying "Look here, you can't leave me this way, it's against the law. You can't turn cold and hostile as simply as all that, ah no, indeed." But there is no binding of friends, no redress when one vanishes into new circles or into quiet sulks, the deserted companion can wait in vain at the accustomed rendezvous, can burst with curiosity over the withheld secrets, there is no compelling the desired one's presence or confidence, no guarantee of the ten-, twenty-, thirty-year-old bond being credited one more minute. It's not fair, you scream, he cannot do this, we've been friends too long, quarreled, revealed ourselves in every horrid light to each other, there is no justice in his suddenly breaking off forever because I called him—what was it I called him—a 'dumb reactionary,' perhaps, in last night's argument? After all, haven't I called him worse than that, haven't I cheated him at cards, done him out of his best girl, borrowed and never returned his best shirt, haven't I called him liar, coward, thief, haven't I belittled his favorite work, cried down his ability, as he in turn has me? How can it be fair, then, that a modest epithet like 'reactionary' should put him away from me for life? A law should be made forcing justice here as it does in marriage courts, a law should be made, thought Dennis desperately, requiring certain formalities to be observed in breaking up a friendship. Effie Thorne, for instance, should be required to telephone him and explain definitely if the return of her ex-husband meant the exit of friend Orphen. Certainly it would seem that way for she had not called him once since the news of Andy's returning, and when he had managed to get her at her apartment her tone had been as politely remote as if he were her grocer instead of last week's dearest companion.

"How's Marian? Are you at the hospital every day?" he asked.

"She's conscious most of the day, thank you. I'm there during the afternoons usually."

"Don't you need some cash, Effie? You must have to buy her things and probably Callingham hasn't sent—I mean—"

Ominous pause here on Effie's part as he floundered, pause saying, my dear young man, aren't you being a little presumptuous in your generosity? Then—

"Thank you, we manage quite well." Yes, we wives of Mr. Callingham are always well taken care of, my dear impudent young fellow!

"I only asked because you said something last week about running low—and I just got my check from MacTweed—it's more than I expected, so you're welcome to any or all of it—" Dennis stammered.

"How nice for you," Effie smoothly evaded.

Dennis racked his brain for some word, some suggestion that would break down this wall of politeness, something that would fasten the oddly broken links again.

"Could I meet you at that garden place near the hospital today for a drink when you're through? I want to talk to you. Or perhaps I could run in to see you tonight."

Run in and see the new curtains, the fresh flowers, the gay new rugs, the proof of her insanity, and smile at her quizzically, say without words 'ah so you really did expect him to come back to you, you poor creature?'

"No, no," said Effie frantically. "I can't say when I'll be home. Perhaps later—oh please, Dennis, please!"

Please? An appeal to the ogre, the Enemy, a startling betrayal of her fear of him, her dearest friend. Dennis gave up, stunned. Consider we are enemies now, her frightened voice said, consider that in our battle you won, your book conquered me and now we may follow our different destinies, and please, oh please, have mercy on me now that you have won. . . . Deeply hurt, Dennis sat back in his desk-chair and smoked, glared at the six free author's copies of *The Hunter's Wife* piled on the table, hated himself for writing it, hated himself at this very instant for the sly return of the author-mind, the sly little annotations being made concerning wounded friendship, the sly little speculation twinkling through the hurt feelings. Now he would not hear firsthand how Callingham behaved, he would not hear details of the hunter's return for checking up on his own artistic intuition, he might never meet Callingham and be able to attack him for the way he handled the final chapter in his last book.

Furious at this opportunistic Second Self, this Bounder, or rather call it Artist-Self, Dennis savagely turned to his type-writer. Time he started work again on the new book, but each time he faced that Page 1 it seemed incredible he had ever got beyond it, he could not imagine ever having finished anything, ever having gone on to a Page 2. It was unbelievable that he had ever been able to shut off these incessant problems of his own life for the creation of imaginary problems. Now he would never be able to write again, he declared fiercely, he would be afraid of each written word now that words had destroyed Effie Thorne. This discouraging thought gave way to helpless indignation at Effie, the futile indignation of the male when the female collapses in tears right in the middle of the game. He was angry at Effie for having made herself so important to him, more important than any mistress he had ever had or any love or any family or any friend. He jeered at his blind foolish sense of safety in getting himself so deeply involved in another person's life, entering it with all shields down, weaponless, joyously secure because here was no marriage threat or permanent entanglement in the air to be dodged, since Effie was so much older, so obviously not in the arena, getting into the safe strange affair deeper and deeper, with his cocky self-assurance—here at last the perfect relationship, the feminine friend with no hooks out. . . . For the first time he realized how completely Effie had grown to fill his life, how after meeting her he had somehow dropped away from all other friends except for casual diversion or matter with which to amuse her later. She was the first friend he'd ever had who was unfailingly, dependably, satisfying, to be counted upon for whatever odd mood his day's or night's writing had left. Curious how he, in turn, had taken the place of the circle of 'interesting people' who had once drifted about Effie's life. He remembered how intensely they had talked, argued, agreed, laughed, with such undivided attention for each other that others in the room would slip away unnoticed, and presently they would be left alone like two absorbed lovers, not one person to each other but a complete circle. And now Callingham returning—or was it merely his book revealing him?—had ruined this relationship. Whatever was to blame for the breach, Dennis was aghast at his desolation without Effie, the one friend, the one firm peg on which his days had hung. Vengefully he wished he could have annihilated Callingham with his pen, but here again he would have ruined the thing he wished to preserve. . . . There was, of course, Corinne. . . . Here Artist-Self, or Bounder, suddenly suggested that Effie's greatest importance had been as buffer against his need for the feminine wife-touch, the touch that once creeping into the ordinary armor spells danger, marriage, promises, the trap. From behind Effie's skirts he had wooed his women, said his Artist-self, the Bounder, the Cad, safe in loyal, tender understanding, all he needed from any other woman was a sweet little lust that need have no trailing ties. . . .

Impulsively Dennis rang up Corinne. Mrs. Barrow was out. Mrs. Barrow had gone for a little ride in Miss Baker's new car. So there was no Effie now and no Corinne. Miss Baker's new car indeed. The very innocence of Mrs. Barrow's simple pleasure made it suspect. In a minute, thought Dennis, astonished, I'm going to cry because nobody will play with me. Yes, sir, now he was going to be hurt at every little thing people said or did, he was very likely going to be jealous again of Corinne as a release for his other frustrations, very likely indeed judging by the sudden passionate rage at her being out. His jealous spell came, as a general thing, once a year about the time he'd finished a book and was feeling restless, nothing else to do with his imagination. It lasted about a month as a rule like influenza or spring cleaning. It had nothing to do with causes but had as germ some casual phrase from which it grew enormously, vining in and out of his nights and days, feeding itself on its own roots, tainting every thought and word. There was no explaining the start or equally unreasonable end of these seasonal furies, for real cause might pop up any other time to be most nonchalantly brushed aside. But now, thanks to Effie's desertion, thanks to Corinne's willful absence from her home at this needed hour, thanks to being unable to begin Page 1, the disease was on. He was jealous of Callingham, of the Glaenzers, of that little doctor, of all the people Effie now leaned upon, as well as jealous a trifle more logically of his little Corinne. Very well, very well, he would go out and make a new circle of friends, he vowed, he would drive off the fever with an army of Tom Collins'. Wonderful new friends, welcome to Dennis Orphen, he cried, welcome, new bunch, welcome, let's call each other up all the time. Why, thought Dennis angrily, there is absolutely nothing left for me to do but to call up Okie.

But Okie, too, was busy but say—how about joining them after the theater at the Alabam—a marvelous new place on Fiftieth—and wonderful girls in the party? At this moment, appropriately enough in the midst of his destructive thoughts, a large segment of ceiling fell down on the bed, followed by a shower of snowy plaster. Dennis was about to rush upstairs and find blessed relief in tearing down the whole house when the phone rang and it was Corinne. He was a little chagrined at his jealous suspicions having gone wrong. He would really have preferred being right, pride in his excellent intuitions outweighing vanity in commanding fidelity.

. . . the paper dolls . . .

"MY HAIR ought to be done," grieved Marian. "I don't want Andy to see me this way. And a manicure."

The nurse had turned her over on her side facing the white dresser, and for some time she had lain there staring unhappily at her image in the mirror. Presently she closed her eyes so as not to see the greenish shadow creeping over her, blocking off into sharp angular segments her face and the narrow throat which, curiously shaded into definite planes, seemed transparent and no more than the esophageal skeleton itself. The always smooth-textured shining skin was drawn taut over the frame, flesh whittled by disease down to essential bone. Breathe deep, Effie thought, breathe long and deep now for these few hours must last you for eternity. Lifted up slightly against the pillows, Marian showed more plainly the devastation of her illness, and her long still body, sheet-covered, seemed already ready for its coffin. Effie felt herself drawn with pity and love for her, it seemed to her she had never loved anyone as she loved Marian for Marian was her own self and Andy and Andy's happiness all in one and now she was dying, all of them were going, going, their little pattern was dissolving like a pretty formation of twigs and leaves floating down a river, separated and forgotten at the first obstruction. Marian was her child, too, hers and Andy's, she was her sister, the two of them helping each other to stand before the storm, the hurricane, that was Andy's love and Andy's love withdrawn.

In her pink bedjacket the abnormal greenish pallor of the patient was more pronounced and with her blue eyelids drawn over glazing eyeballs the face spelled out the imminence of death. Effie looked beyond this out the window across the church spires, into the clouding sky for relief from the presence in the room, she looked down the street below, intently watched a man and woman wheel a perambulator of twins, all four alive, breathing, years, decades ahead of them somewhere up Lexington Avenue there. She watched a girl and boy dallying before the corner store, laughing because they, too, were triumphantly alive, each one hesitating to break the spell of each other's presence yet with nothing more to say they merely stood there laughing, swinging a foot, inarticulate, wondering why they were held and with each moment increasing the secret fear of a pattern breaking up, fragments lost, plan forgotten.

"I'd like my fingernails painted red," mused Marian, "as if I was all ready to go someplace. Oh my God, I'm going to die!"

Effie jumped, heart pounding.

"I'll die, Effie," screamed Marian, "and Andy will marry some one else, he'll marry that Asta and they will laugh at each other and forget me!"

Her eyelids flew open, wild eyes begged Effie for denials, thin fingers pressed against mouth to hold back the cry of terror. Effie's heart turned slowly over in her, the fear of death was loosed like a bat in the room, even the nurse, entering at the moment, took a sudden step backward as if blown back by the blast of dark terror that raced through the room. Effie's throat locked with this freezing word, she could not speak nor could her widened eyes break away from Marian's fierce inquiry, breathless, unable to look away or to smile, she gave back fear for fear, knowledge for knowledge. Yes, you will die, yes, yes, and no one can save you, no Andy, no lover returning, nothing, and he will be lost to you, murmuring in other live, vibrant arms, laughing in bedroom darkness, secretly exulting, your ghost forgotten as mine was once, is now. . . . But as soon as this swift certainty flashed between their fearing eyes denial surged forth and Effie burst out, "No, no, Marian, you won't die, oh never, dear, and Andy's coming, he's coming only for you, so rest now. I'll bring a manicurist, I'll get someone to do your hair, I'll be back."

The nurse beckoned her into the hall, and shook her head. "She can't lift her head for any hairdresser, Miss Thorne, she couldn't stand it. No use."

"Then what will I do?" Effie asked her, helpless, unwilling to disappoint the woman in the bed.

The nurse lifted starched white shoulders.

"Talk to her about her husband. You were related to him, weren't you? That seems to be the only thing that pleases her. Maybe you've got some pictures of him she's never seen— you knew him long ago, didn't you, before she met him?"

"Yes," said Effie thoughtfully, "I have some pictures."

"Pretend you're going for the hairdresser and run home for the pictures," suggested the nurse, and added quietly, "Hurry."

In her apartment later Effie went through her desk, collected all the photographs she had saved of Andy, snapshots, postcards, studio pictures as a boy, little celluloid medallions, showing a curled, round-faced baby lying on a bear-rug, a shy four-year-old in a sailor suit, six years old in tight velvet kneepants, ruffled shirt, sulky mouth, leaning against his mother's shoulder in Berman's Studio, Cincinnati, or standing proudly beside his first bicycle, cap pulled down over radiant eyes. There, yellowed and carefully folded up, was his first poem, "A Boat Ride by Andy Callingham, age 8 years" . . . *"I like to ride in great big boats. . ."* here, in a drawer, was the letter he wrote to his mother from Aunt Bertha's cottage in the Adirondacks, "Dear mother, we have not seen each other for a long time. there is a boy here named Fred. I had the nosebleed and I asked Fred for his hakerchef but he wold not give it he said it was new then he ran away from me and I could not catch him till Wilbur Street and the nosebleed got all over my new pants. I am mad at Fred. I hope you are well. Your sincere son Andy."

There was the wedding picture of Charles and Alma Callingham, Andy's parents, and the second wedding picture of Charles and Estelle, the newspaper picture of Charles Callingham, new history head at the State University. Here were school diaries, clippings of early school triumphs. The boy Andy, thought Effie, belongs to me and to no one else, and then suddenly she knew she must take all these treasures to Marian, paper dolls to amuse the little sick girl.

"There!" whispered the nurse, nodding toward Marian's feverish joy in these relics. How happily and how completely

Marian appropriated them, how possessively she forbade the nurse to touch them as they sprawled over the counterpane and slid to the floor. Even closing her eyes with drugged pain now and then, her greedy hands groped about to assemble all within her touch.

"He never told me about that poem," she murmured, puzzled. "And look, Effie, look at the face with his first bicycle. The funny little face of him!"

"And here all dressed up except the stocking falling down," Effie eagerly offered the Fauntleroy photograph. "This is his fifth birthday here, sitting on his Aunt Bertha's lap; that was in Boston the year his parents went abroad and left him there. His aunt had just punished him for scraping all the frosting off his cake. Look how scared he looks!"

A smile, tender and wishful, played about Marian's fine bluish lips, it sang through her eyes and the hands so lovingly lingering over these mementoes, a little lullaby of a smile, an emanation from the small scraps themselves, for it fluttered across Effie's lips also, delicate, fleeting, an odd little ghost of lost happiness, a butterfly blown about by death. Effie, returning from this enchanted dreamland first, was flicked with pain by the quiet proud possessiveness of Marian's hands on the boy's pictures. Mine, mine, Effie cried inside herself, oh, surely these are mine if nothing else, and then, surrendering, frightened, defeated, hunting for some other solace, "If I had had a baby, if I had had a son *that* would have been mine, that at least she could not share, Andy's and mine it would be—" she thought, desperate, defeated, pushing the scattered pictures toward Marian.

"If I had only had a baby," said Marian, "something of Andy always with me forever. Ah, Effie, I should have had a son!"

Effie could only nod bleakly, heart numb. There are words that cannot be borne, suggestions so burning with anguish and despair that no heart can endure them, so Effie, her lover stolen, her dream of a son now stolen, got to her feet and motioning, speechless, that she was leaving, found her way out of the intolerable room.

. . . the erlking . . .

"No," Andy had said firmly—she could still see him idly stretched out on the porch of the Glaenzer boathouse where they had docked for the week-end, though Belle had still not forgiven them completely for running away without her authority—"we both had too unpleasant childhoods ourselves to want any kids. Not till we can give them more than we ever got. There was I, for instance, batted from Aunt Bertha to Mother to Dad to Uncle Tom—all detesting each other and taking it out on me in obscure ways. Then at school with the headmaster having written a history not as well-received as my father's, so again I was the goat— Oh no, Effie, we don't give the world any whipping boy. Even if we had some sort of security to offer him—"

"Can't you just see those little embryos shopping around for security?" gloomily asked Effie. She had been hurt by his attitude as if her baby were already born and heard his father's insults. She didn't want to discuss it again, but brooded, and was surprised to remember her savage bitterness later when he played on the beach with two little towheads so gaily that their pretty mother said sympathetically, "What a pity Mr. Callingham has no little ones of his own!"

She remembered her desperate fear after he left her that he would in no time at all be the proud, even fatuous father of Marian's child, for if Marian wanted it she would get it willy-nilly, and then everyone would say, 'Only natural and rather splendid for a man to leave a woman who won't give him a child for one who will'. . . . Trying vainly now to find the clear path she should have taken then as if finding it now would make her any happier, she thought, Yes, that was the answer, I should have had a child no matter what he said. If she had been less in love with him, less generous, and more concerned in clinching her own future happiness than his, she

491

would have gone against his expressed wishes calmly and deliberately. Other women did, God knows, and were richly rewarded for selfishness. Wayward males, declaring violently against paternity, were forever being touched and flattered by some girl's really not so romantic determination to express her own ego at any cost, they were flattered into permanent loyalty, finding a strange source of pride in the lady's willfulness, as if this proved that their own charm was stronger than they realized if it impelled this urge in the woman. Their male independence once boldly expressed they were secretly well-pleased to be led back into the conventional haven.

For a long time after Andy had gone Effie thought, Thank God, it is only I who must bear this loneliness, there's no one I need comfort when I have no comfort to give. But now she felt differently. She should have had the child. She would have had something, someone, her life would have been more complete, no one else could have claimed this trophy of love, either, it would have been hers, blind or crippled or lame, it would have been her very own as Mrs. Hickey's little Tom was Mrs. Hickey's own, someone to cherish while Hickey was in the hospital with his mustard gas lungs, someone, yes, little Tom, even with blue-veined hands, halting speech, lost blank eyes, braced hips and shriveled legs, even so he was Mrs. Hickey's own.

"I had it when I was fourteen," Dennis said one day, watching Tom from Effie's window. "I dragged my leg for a long time, but it's not so noticeable now except when I dance. I always do a rhumba or some sort of stylish dip no matter what the music calls for. Maybe Tom'll get over it."

Tom was Mrs. Hickey's, hers and no one else's. White, thin-lipped, defiant little Mrs. Hickey waited for him outside the public school, stood outside beside the Special Bus when the first dismissal bell sounded, and a sudden high shrill shriek, many children's voices blended into one cry of freedom, sounded louder and louder till the big doors burst open with it and all the little broken children stumbled out, on crutches, in braces, limping, fumbling, stuttering, the little Specials, their leaping cry at liberty as loud as the Regulars to be released ten minutes later. Mrs. Hickey, standing to one side of the gate so as not to embarrass Tom by betraying his need of her support, could single him out at once, swinging books along by a strap, twisted leg in silver brace dragging; she could see a bigger boy push him back and knock his head, laughing, against the wall, and she had to keep herself from rushing to his defense, she could see his lost blank smile, bewildered, uncomprehending, but she must not interfere, this was boy's play, make a man of him, though so far as that went, he would never hit back, never, he was too gentle, and he only looked dazed at taunts. Not normal, the teacher had firmly told her, sub, she added briskly, and for the mother, facing clear-eyed skeptical educator, there was no use telling about the poem he wrote, a drawing he made, the toy airplane he built with his own weak little hands, but some of these days the teachers would be sorry, some day they would see how wrong they were.

"Let's go home now," said Mrs. Hickey as she always did, and took his hand. He blew along beside her skirts, frail, spindly leg dragging; passers-by looked curiously at his blank little face, they turned eagerly to watch him drag the distorted foot. His mother stared somberly ahead, oh, some day he would be a great poet, a great composer, an engineer, a president, look at Roosevelt, he would confound all the starers, the teachers, the cruel other children, he would astound them all, but for the present there is no kindness or understanding in all the world for a mother to beg or buy for those moments she cannot utterly surround him with her love, and hurrying along the street, half-carrying him, her fierce lonely love for the sad child flowed out of her and all around him and made her strong, Olympian, heroic, made the erlking himself, riding ever so close behind them, fade away into a dream, a legend only.

And Effie, at her window with the new curtains blowing, watched them unfastening the basement gate and she wished that Tom was hers, broken little boy that no one else would want or could take, something from Andy for her alone. She caught Mrs. Hickey's quick proud smile as he locked the gate behind him without falling, and she envied Mrs. Hickey, envied her for a woman who had someone, something that no one else would ever claim.

III

. . . to a wild rose . . .

"TELL ME," said Corinne, "who was your very first love and how old were you and was she like me? Tell me."

"Of my awakening?" pondered Dennis. "It must have been Minnie. Yes, by Jove, it was Minnie. I was twelve."

"Then you lived in Yonkers," said Corinne with satisfaction at her fine memory.

"I hadn't moved to Yonkers yet," corrected Dennis. "My mother was still alive so we were in Terre Haute. Anyway all the older boys talked about Minnie with a knowing leer. My chum—Cliff Riley was his name by the way and now he's a big judge in Washington or maybe that was his older brother Chester; that's right, Clifford never turned out very well. Anyway my chum Cliff and I were devoured with lust and a dreadful curiosity about sex which never seemed to get us anywhere. We tagged along with the judge who was of course only fifteen or so at that time but anyway he did know Minnie, and how. Cliff and I nearly went crazy wondering about Minnie. Cliff was eleven and we both were small for our age and cursed with short pants, a big handicap in luring women to your rooms. As a matter of fact, we were about the two most lureless lads in the whole damn town."

"It can't be true, darling," said Corinne.

She sipped at her strawberry soda, making a funny little noise through the straw which appeared to please her mightily for when the straw broke down under its musical burden she took two fresh ones and began a note higher on her piping, a simple enough pleasure after all for Empire State Tower visitors which they were, though Dennis for his part preferred to accompany the view with a perfectly noiseless coca-cola. Clouds as white as if the sky was baby-blue instead of black swam softly about them, stars were below and above, glittering through the plumes of the moon, listening for compliments from the Tower visitors.

"Are you going to put this story in a book?" interrupted Corinne suspiciously. "If you are, don't tell it to me now. I hate having things tried out on me. Let's just talk instead."

"Hush," suggested Dennis. "Grampa is reminiscing. Yes, it was Minnie who awakened me. Cliff and I had heard about this boy and that boy taking Minnie out behind the church, for in this town the boys were cads and told. Cliff and I, frustrated by our short pants, just hung around looking wise and snickering evilly at the older fellows' fun."

"With me it was my music teacher," said Corinne. "He was forever teaching me *To a Wild Rose*."

"Interesting," said Dennis. "So finally Cliff and I decided that we had to find out and two small boys were just as good as one big one, so we waited together for Minnie to come along one day. She was about six feet tall but our taste hadn't formed yet and anyway she was all there was to be had. Pretty soon Minnie came down the street. Cliff and I—"

"The judge and you," said Corinne.

"No, that was Chester and another kettle of fish. Cliff and I clutched each other and stepped boldly out in front of her. She stared at us, not realizing at first our plan. 'Hello, Minnie,' we said together, giving her a big leer, 'how about it?' With that she picked us up by the scruffs of our necks and knocked our heads together. That was my first big experience and that was sex in Terre Haute."

"The music teacher wasn't so terribly handsome, it was just that he was the only man in school," answered Corinne. They walked out on the terrace and eighty-six stories below them the city night spread out in a garden of golden lights; trucks, trains, ferryboats crawled soundlessly in and out of the island puzzle. They sat down on the steel bench, their arms about each other. "All the girls at Miss Roman's were crazy about him, but he fell for me, he really did; as I look back on it now I realize he was pretty crazy about me—considering that he was over thirty and I was only thirteen. We called him Ducky."

"Ducky, hmm," said Dennis. "Very refreshing."

"I started on *To a Wild Rose* in September and I couldn't play it by June," said Corinne. "I still can't play it. Ducky would just talk to me and once he snatched my hands and kissed them madly. He would stare at me with great burning eyes in the mirror over the pipe organ—he played for the chapel service, see—and I was the first girl in the procession and coming down the chapel aisles I would see him staring at me in the mirror and I'd get the giggles, really, right in the middle of *Crown Him the King of Kings.*"

Dennis kissed her.

"Poor old Cliff never got anywhere, it was always his brother," he said. "Chester was the big shot of the Riley family, he had push and another thing he was a very steady boy. Worked nights in the telegraph tower as an operator to get money to go to Notre Dame while Cliff and I were wasting our time on Minnie."

"Getting your heads cracked," said Corinne. "Darling, do you ever see that Beverly girl you used to run around with before me?"

"I've told you a million times I never see her any more," Dennis, exasperated, exclaimed. "I promised you I'd give her up, didn't I? You don't think a man of my caliber would go back on his promise, do you?"

He was aggrieved. Corinne moved away from him as a little boy in plaid plus fours ran away from his father and dropped a coin in the telescope in front of them. Then, as the machine recklessly ticked off the precious minutes, he spent his dime in staring at the couple on the bench with scientific concentration.

"I know you promised. I was just asking if you ever saw her."

"What can you do with a woman who won't trust you?" Dennis invited the sky and the curious little boy to make answer. "Anyway she lives in London now, so how could I see her?"

"That's the only reason men ever keep promises like that," observed Corinne. "The girl has either moved away or died."

"I'm afraid there's something in that, Honeysugar," agreed Dennis politely. "Vows of abstinence are valid only when supported by a major inconvenience, biological or geographical. Old saw."

"Thank you," said Corinne. "I'm crazy about you, Old Sawmaster. You're so attractive to me. I suppose any other woman would wonder what I saw in you. If your book is a success you'll start cruising around again, won't you, dear? Society women will take you up."

"Let those society women just try to get me, let them just try," boasted Dennis.

"Some of them aren't so bad-looking," Corinne said jealously. "They all wear triple-A size seven and have bad knees but they do have plenty of teeth. I'll bet you fall for them. You'll get white pants and a hat with a front and back to it and you'll run around with next year's debutantes."

"Only for material," said Dennis with the quiet smirk of conquest already on his face. "A literary man has to go a great many places and do a lot of queer, often disagreeable things for his material, my dear. It's the artist's cross. I'll have to endure all those rotogravure beauties just to learn a few society songs and dances, something for my notes."

"I'm going to write, too, Dennis. I really am," said Corinne.

Dennis looked uneasy.

"Not those sad little glad-I'm-sorry poems that women always write when they're nervous?" he asked.

"You know I can't rhyme things," said Corinne. "No, this is little prosies, little glad-I-see-things-quaintly ones. I sold one already to the *Manhattanite*. I didn't want to tell you while you're so wrapped up in your own success, your book coming out tomorrow and all that."

"You sold a story? No!"

"It was easy." Corinne waved her cigarette. "I studied their style. It's just a trick. Olive and I figured it out. You take an Uncle Wiggly story and change the animals to quaint old bachelors or dear old ladies who economize. You use very tiny words and all the adverbs you can use are 'rather' and 'quite' and 'very' and 'really.'"

"How did your story go?" inquired Dennis, still impressed and thinking of Phil boasting all over the club of his wife's artistic triumph.

"I took 'Sticky-toes the Tree-Toad was really quite cross,'" said Corinne. "I changed it to 'Mr. Wootle, the funny old bachelor, was really quite cross' and so on."

"Damn clever," said Dennis, astonished.

"Olive is working on Buddy Bear," Corinne added. "It begins 'Buddy Bear and Mrs. Bear hadn't been asked to tawny Tiger's birthday party. Buddy Bear did not mind so very much but Mrs. Bear really felt quite cross.' Olive changed it to 'Mr. and Mrs. Wuppins had not been asked to the Major's birthday party which made—' "

"I get it, I get it," interrupted Dennis hastily. "I still think writing is a man's work."

"I suppose you're afraid it will make me a little horsey," said Corinne scornfully. She jumped up and walked over to the stone balustrade, leaned her face on her clasped hands and sighed. New York twinkled far off into Van Cortlandt Park, spangled skyscrapers piled up softly against the darkness, tinseled parks were neatly boxed and ribboned with gold like Christmas presents waiting to be opened. Sounds of traffic dissolved in distance, all clangor sifted through space into a whispering silence, it held a secret, and when letters flamed triumphantly in the sky you felt, ah, that was the secret, this at last was it, this special telegram to God—Sunshine Biscuits. On and off it went, Eat Sunshine Biscuits, the message of the city.

"Darling," said Corinne.

. . . you will meet at a place of amusement . . .

"WHATSA matter, whereya been, here we been waitin', whatsa idea callin' up if you arna gonna be here, issen atso, Gracie?" Okie was tight so that his basic resentment against all his magazine's contributors, particularly those he needed most, was floating to the surface. He glared at Dennis defiantly above the smile of good fellowship mechanically placed on his mouth, he was about to say more but obviously nothing devastating enough rose to mind, and he must content himself with, "You writers! All the same! Oh, dyah, I had to finish my second act. Oh my, Red Lewis and Teddy Dreiser and Maxie Reinhardt dropped in and I couldn't get rid of 'em! Oh, Bee Lillie and Gingie Rogers were kiddin' me about never givin' 'em a buzz—always some excuse."

Dennis slid on to the chromium-plated bar stool beside Okie. He knew Okie was reaching a pitch of rage where his only relief would be for someone to be a Jew. Oh, if only everybody could be Jews or women, was Okie's silent prayer, so that in times of stress one could hurl the name, one or the other, at them, with all Christianity, all masculinity behind one, and then once spoke, the shot fired, to relax proudly victorious! There was, to be sure, some pleasure in other classifications but these were less satisfying. There was modest fun in You Swedes, You Catholics, You Yankees, You Wops, You Southerners, You Methodists, You Harvard Boys, You Dekes, You Artists, You Lawyers, etc., but these were not real destroyers, and often as not a certain envy crept into Okie's voice as he flung out these names, an envy which naturally was not in his two major classifications. He made up for this sense of inadequate epithet by whispering a suspicion of Jewish ancestry or feminine characteristics in You Swedes or You Harvard Boys. He had, as a matter of fact, only a moment before Dennis' arrival hinted that no one knew quite where old

Orphen stood, you never saw him with any steady girl, but he was suspiciously devoted to an older woman, someone old enough to be his mother. Old Orphen was foxy enough to disguise all other traces of his weakness but there was always something mighty suspicious in that older woman racket and he got that straight out of Freud. As soon as Okie had made this insinuation Gracie on one hand and Boots on the other had given him a sound kick in the shins and Lora, Okie's own girl for the past few years, looked vaguely down at her drink and then toward Tony Glaenzer beside her, so Okie, reminded of the glass house so near, quickly gulped down his Scotch and ordered another one as Dennis came up.

Dennis looked around the place. It was like all of the wonderful little secret places Okie discovered in the Broadway district, little places with their own special crowd, tail ends of the theater, fringes and pale copies of more celebrated circles. There was the same modernistic silver and glass bar, the same glittering mirrors with liqueur bottles stacked in geometric design invariably crowned by the beautiful Fiore d'Alpi, sugar-frosted tree in the green bottle promising exotic surcease from the harsher realities of gin or Scotch. A few chromium-trimmed red tables were crowded around the little dance floor and in the middle, flanked by unbelievably bushy, fiercely tropical palms, was a tiny poppy-colored piano spraddled by a lean, chinless, pompadoured pianist who smiled vaguely and not too promisingly at the eager lady customers as his long competent hands collected handfuls of sprawling sugary chords. A large policeman-type tenor walked slowly about the floor singing in a rich honeyed whine and this was really the proprietor, easy enough to guess for even while he was somberly whining, "A boyuh—ahnd—ah gurrul—war dahncing—" he kept a keen eye on the bartender to make sure no cheating was going on, and when he was not warbling this shrewd fellow (called 'Sammy' to suggest the affectionate esteem of the Broadway crowd) stood in the outer vestibule bowing welcome to new arrivals but fixing eyes on an innocent mirror upon which the bar activities were remirrored, all of which the bartender knew perfectly well, having been warned by the Cuban hat-check girl.

Dennis recognized Tony Glaenzer between the two new blondes Okie's genius had provided. These blondes, Gracie and Boots, were surprisingly like his last pair, though Okie seemed as proud as if he had just uncovered a fresh race.

"Boots is Tony's girl-friend," Okie whispered, "just back from her show."

That Boots was Tony's girl-friend was patent from Tony's all-enveloping princely possessive air and from the girl's discreet manner, a special arrogance that could pass for 'class' and small wonder she should adopt this, for Tony, with her, became doubly the aristocrat, triply the aloof patrician; his pointed absorption in her declared defiantly her worthiness for the honor, and permitted her to share in his own private privilege of snubbing her friends, just as it gave these same friends, excluding them as it did, their own privilege of rather bitter class consciousness.

Boots raised heavy-lashed pretty eyes to Dennis in greeting and then lowered them modestly to her seventh stinger. She was very tiny but rounded and wore severe little tailored dresses to offset her essential cuteness. When she got up to dance with Tony she stretched herself stiffly erect and took long swooping steps to match his while he bent, bored, Byronically gloomy, over her. She looked haughtily over the heads of the lone men ogling her at the bar. Men? the look said, I never even heard of them, and in her demure acceptance of Tony's polite rather than amorous absorption she seemed to proclaim her resolute unchallenged, decent, high-class virginity, and even to the bartender whom she knew quite well and to Sammy and the other acquaintances who had seen her many nights before Tony Glaenzer discovered her and made her respectable through isolation she employed a new manner of speech, something that was not quite Southern nor yet British but more genteel and more wonderful than either, certainly far more intriguing since the refinement in accent was perpetually questioned by the deep-blues voice.

Gracie was another matter, and since there was no talking to Tony, Dennis applied himself to her.

"She's the artist Gracie Kessel I told you about," Okie breathed excitedly in his ear. "She's the nymphomaniac."

"Thanks, pal," said Dennis.

Gracie smiled at him over her Tom Collins and pushed a salami sandwich toward him.

"Go ahead, I don't want it, honest."

Gracie's pure beautiful blue eyes in her calm fair face and her dewy baby skin, her sincerely naïve expression, challenged her sinister reputation. Her matronly figure with accompanying good-natured sentimentality—*Aw, Sammy, why don't you let me have that little kid of yours, honestly, Mr. Orphen, Sammy's got the darlingest brat you ever saw*—and then her sudden bawdy exclamations followed by gusty uproarious laughter were more like a healthy, sensual young village bride chuckling with the other village wives of their new knowledge. Drunk, she talked so much and so pompously of her art that it was hard to believe she was regarded as seriously as she actually was in that world. Anxious to be friends she sympathized with Dennis over the success of other writers as if it were axiomatic that every writer or artist automatically detested every other worker or work in his own subject, and every success in any line was legitimate enemy for no other reason but his success. Egotistically enough, Gracie was more jealous of men than of women and apt to dismiss her female competitors with a large gesture. She accepted the kisses, lingering strokes and whispered flattery of the men who wandered in and out of the place with a gracious, proud complacency as if this were homage indeed, these ex-hoofers, gamblers, small racketeers, friends of friends of celebrities. These big shots knew their business, knew a great artist when they saw her.

"That's the way it is everywhere Gracie goes," Okie boasted. "You can't walk in any place without somebody coming up—it's hi, Gracie, *good* evening, Miss Kessel, hello there, Gracie, wherever you go."

"Ah, they only think I'm in the money," disparaged Gracie, smiling, not really believing her words. A complete peasant type, reflected Dennis, enormous vitality and lust combined with shrewd narrow bigotry. With each drink her voice went a pitch higher, words lingering on the air, whining, coaxing, often bitter words, but excused by the childish little girl whine. They lingered on the air like stale tobacco smoke, and her infrequent pauses were grateful whiffs of clear mountain air through which Dennis could watch, fascinated, enchanted, Okie's girl, Lora. No, he had never seen anyone like Lora, never, captured as always by a cool mysterious face no matter how banal the secret it concealed. The only thing against her was Okie, but he must dismiss this objection as another proof of man's basic conventionality, unconsciously baited or repelled by the quality of a lady's previous lovers. Again, only a half-hour removed from Corinne's goodnight kiss, he must question the validity of this sudden warm interest in Lora. Was it his practical literary curiosity once again, the constant buzzard at work rather than the man, or could it be due to that odd little instrument located somewhere near the heart that gave warning signals when the organ itself was getting dangerously involved, instructed the master to flee, shift, break, do something quickly before the sudden avalanche of pain that was real feeling? These last few days without the protective hedge of Effie Thorne's all-sufficient friendship—a friendship that had been worn by both as an armor against the rest of the world and against all other contact, without this buffer Dennis had felt himself drawn, sucked into bondage to Corinne, he glimpsed aghast the unamusing sinister face of scandalous, unreasoning, ruinous, self-destroying Love, and this must not be. With or without her husband, with or without her gratifying but on the other hand suspect passion, with or without obstacles, there was grave danger for Orphen the individual, Orphen the independent, heart-free fellow.

"Now why must I always get hysterical when I see a Big Moment ahead?" Dennis asked himself, "as if a Great Love as we used to term it were a supreme faux pas? Is it because I doubt my qualifications for the Great Lover role, is it that I realize what a ridiculous figure I would cut, infatuate, easy victim for gulling? Is it because all the persons I ever loved as a boy died or left me or in some way taught me not to let myself in for too much feeling? I wish to God I was some one else, say, Okie there, so I could analyze myself, find out of what this strange barrier consists. How do I know, maybe it's mere gypsy blood, or claustrophobia, or—the hell with it."

"What I don't understand," said Gracie loudly, nodding toward Tony and Boots, "is why if they're so darn wrapped up in each other they always have to go out with a crowd. They don't really want to be alone—you'd think so to look at 'em—but it's not so. They could go someplace else if they wanted to. But, oh no, they got to have an audience, got to have people around to snoot."

"Don't let Gracie have any more, Bill," Boots primly instructed the bartender. Tony looked idly at Dennis.

"Haven't I seen you before?"

"Apparently not," said Dennis rather sourly.

Okie pulled Dennis' ear toward him and hissed, "Glaenzer gives me a pain in the pod. These playboys always being such big shots with the girls just because there's millions in the offing! In the offing is right. I'll bet he ain't got more'n two bits in his pants right now, his old woman thinks that'll police him. Say, you can't hold back an eel or a sponge either, eh, Orphen, just holding out on their pennies? Watch him now. Every time the check comes round he's all of a sudden on the dance floor or in the can, and as for Boots, why, nobody can touch her since she made this swell catch. All the girls envyin' her—wishin' they had a big moneyboy too so they could have the privilege of payin' his way everyplace and passin' out the taxi-money. I'll betcha Boots has borrowed a thousand bucks from her friends so she could afford this so-called wind-fall! Hell, his old lady will never die and never let him go—he'll cut his throat waiting for her! Ssst! Lora's my girl, understand, but Boots there is my type. Get it, Orphen? Get the picture? Ah, you old sonofagun, sure you do!"

Dennis looked at Lora. She never spoke but sat on the bar stool quietly sipping her highball. She was frail, exquisitely thin and smart in a gray nunlike gown with high collar, a capelet chastely fastened to the shoulder with a diamond clasp. Her small bonnet drooped a narrow veil over her forehead and her blue-black hair lay in stiff sculptured scallops against her narrow white face, an almost abnormally narrow Madonna face with glowing dead-black eyes, delicately cut nostrils, lovely red mouth. In her fine little ears tiny jewels gleamed and on her wrist from the nunlike white cuffbands peeped a slender diamond-studded platinum chain. Now just where, reflected Dennis, does she get those?

"Dance?" he asked.

Okie stared gloomily at them over his glass as they moved to the dance floor. Dennis was bewildered to find that this silent, controlled sphinx could scarcely stand on her feet, must grope at chairs and tables for balance as she passed, but he could not really believe she was tipsy. Taking her in his arms gave him a disturbing sensation of holding absolutely nothing, of clutching only the floating scarves of her demure French gown and no woman at all. A faint halo of Oriental perfume swam about her, yet this carried no more hint of sensuality than her narrow frail shoulders or inconsequential body, seemed rather incense from some mystic temple, as elusive as a dream not quite remembered. Cheek to cheek, dancing, Dennis drew back, puzzled and vaguely repelled by her unearthliness, he seemed to the touch the sawdust torso of a boudoir doll, and the cellophane glaze he now detected over her eyes and the waxy perfection of her immobile face, these were the charms of embalmed queens, virtues for the historian rather than the live, questing male. She floated numbly through the dance, her eyes never blinked, when he addressed her she smiled beautifully, idly, and by her silence and the lingering smile gave an irresistible impression of intelligence nicely muffled for masculine appreciation. She swayed from him finally toward the red-curtained Ladies' Room, and when Dennis returned to the bar Gracie whispered, "Lora's a dip, you know, we'll probably have to take her home pretty soon."

"A dipsomaniac? Lora? *Lora?*"

Gracie nodded.

"Drinks all day long but always the lady. The only way you know is when she starts falling down. Nobody can pick her up. Just like a piece of wet soap. Okie and I had to drag her by the fanny all the way home the other night. Just folds right up."

"Lora does that? *Lora?*"

"Hears everything going on, though, don't kid yourself about that, even after she's passed out," warned Gracie. "Remembers every crack and hands it back to you later on. Okie runs around with her because she's the only person in town that'll stay up all night any night and go anyplace any time."

"Where does Okie get with her?" Dennis asked.

"Nowhere." Gracie snickered. "Lora's always half-unconscious and such a lady besides, so Okie just has to burn up."

Dennis asked so many questions about Lora and watched the curtained door for her return with such obvious interest that Gracie became annoyed. She confided her annoyance to Okie. They danced and Dennis uneasily saw them whispering, exchanging their unfavorable thoughts about him, the snob, the pansy, the phony. It occurred to him that he was bound to Okie by a chain of insults. Each meeting, either in the magazine office or in a restaurant, began on a fairly jovial friendly basis and ended with Okie wounded, sat upon, insulted. Unwillingly apologetic, Dennis would call up again, proffer an invitation, assume the jolly pal pose, let's have a drink, and then the insult popped out again, the subtly snobbish remark, the vaguely patronizing implication, and once again Okie had to be mollified by a phone call, another comradely gesture. Now, openly yearning for Boots as he had confessed, he was nevertheless offended by Dennis' interest in Lora.

"So this place isn't good enough for you, eh? So this is just a cheap Broadway joint, eh?" he loudly inquired, coming back to the bar stool beside Dennis. "It's good enough for Anthony Glaenzer, I guess, and he could be in the best club in town right now if he wanted to be. That right, Boots? Look at those eyelashes, will you, on that kid, Dennis, lookat! Don't tell me they're real, now honest, Boots."

"But they are," said Boots and she and Tony changed a quiet superior smile. Boots couldn't endure Okie, but if Tony thought he was such a card she could take it, particularly since he paid the check. A young actor's agent, swarthy, handsome, shifty, occasionally came up and talked to her but Tony was not jealous of this intrusion, it gave the added luster of her profession, an added importance, making her doubly worthy of his haughty favor.

"No, sir," Okie called to the bartender, "this guy here thinks the Alabam's not good enough, he's the big prize author, y'see, he thinks that means somethin'. Listen, bud, that little pen of yours means very little to the Alabam, eh, Bill, eh, Sammy? You can kid about my magazine all you want but they know about that here and not about that little prize of yours. Well, Sammy, old boy . . . Sammy owns this place, a great character, Sammy, if you writers had any literary sense at all you'd put him in a book, but, oh no, the proprietor of the Alabam isn't good enough for your high-class books, you got to write about Lady Agatha and that old blueblooded family. No kidding, Sammy, don't these writers give you a pain in the pod? Great old boy—Sammy, there. I know him personally. Hell, I been in here a hundred times. I know Sammy all right."

"And now Sammy knows me," said Dennis, none too amiably.

Okie slapped him on the shoulder.

"I was just kidding, boy, don't you know good-natured fun when you hear it? Why, say, Bill,—hey, bartender, another drink all around and give Lora a stiff one."

"A stiff one knocks her out so it saves her drinking all night," Gracie explained laconically to Dennis.

The bartender was a thin concentrated little man, facial contours tight, black hair slicked back in a neat side-part, trim little wrestling body, a young man at first glance judging by his nimbleness and young face but a second look revealed the mass of tiny furrows, the sailor's weather-beaten face masked in healthy tan, with age only briefly betrayed by fanged old tobacco teeth, weary yellowed eyes, scant hairs too black and too cautiously arranged for careless youth. Arrogantly he mixed his drinks, flipped the tips into his hip pocket, slid the glasses down the marble counter to the bidder, contempt for the Alabam, the customers, their tips, and for alcohol in the large betrayed by every gesture of the wiry competent little hands. You call this a job, you call this a life, you call that good music, you call *her* beautiful, you call this New York—Say! As he passed the highball to Dennis he yanked words out of the side of his mouth like a ventriloquist, as secretly and cautiously as if Gay-Pay-U men were all about and the message itself was highly political.

" 'At true you're a writer?" he asked. " 'At true about the prize and the books—whatsat name again, chief?"

"Orphen. Sure it's true."

The bartender smiled secretly, craftily, attended to some call at the end of the bar and then came back, still smiling mysteriously.

"Wanta know something, chief? I'm a writer myself. Sure, I write stories. I got a book. Sure. Goin' to be published, too, so no wisecracks. Say, I don't have to work here. When this book comes out—listen—here's the payoff, it's about that guy there, about Sammy. Nah, he don't care, he's tickled to death. He tells everybody somebody's made a book about him, all puffed up about it. He don't say I did it, he wants all the credit himself. It's about this place, right here, the Alabam. A writer's got to write about what he knows, don't he? That's what this guy tells me, 'at's goin' to publish it. Sure, I got a publisher. He comes here all the time, just to get the feel of the place, check up on my story. Damn nice guy, not a bit stuck-up. We get along. There he is, over there at the table, over there by the palms."

Dennis looked around the tables in the general direction of Bill's wide gesture. Then he blinked to make sure his eyes were not deceiving him. No mistake, however, about that pleasant well-bred face, that sharply etched mustache. It was Johnson himself, no less.

. . . *the blue hours* . . .

JOHNSON was not too glad to see Dennis. He made no pretense of smiling a welcome as Dennis drew up a chair at his
table, but that his gloom was not personally directed at his
client was soon evident. It was a despondency stimulated, as
he well knew, by the perfectly unreasonable competency of his
new rival at MacTweed's, unreasonable because the least a
wealthy young man buying his way into a firm can do for his
less fortunate coworkers is to be dumb. But, oh no, young
Hiller had to be bright, shrewd almost to the point of
crookedness—oh, happy MacTweed! . . . In a way Johnson
held it against his unsuspecting author that *The Hunter's Wife*
had not sold out its first printing in advance of publication as
he had so generously prophesied, and he was out of sorts with
his protégé, the bartender, because the type of literature he
represented, the type religiously encouraged by Johnson heretofore, was imperceptibly retreating before the avalanche of
Old South novels. His new rival had practically sold
MacTweed the idea that no novel was acceptable or publish-
able unless it registered a dreamy, high-class nostalgia for the
Old South; and such sagas were springing up by the hundreds, proud answers to *Tobacco Road*. There were already
half a dozen on the MacTweed list and Johnson morosely
doubted if he could squeeze in even one hard-hitting monosyllabic pastiche of the People. Looking about the Alabam, he
thought, A year ago I would have sworn there was a natural
in each of these hard-boiled Broadway figures. Now, since
that young snort has come into the office I doubt my own
hunches and believe in his—they're all the last of old Southern families. He could shut his eyes and read their stories, he
saw the old mammies and their violet-colored sons who
looked so strangely like young Marse Jephthah, he sensed the
magnificent decay, the cud'ns, the cun'ls, the haughty revela-

tion that these splendid old aristocrats were the author's own family.

Embittered by this in general, Johnson was depressed over more immediate woes. He was blue but blue with a sour greenish nimbus that spread out and tainted all who came near, a veritable poison gas emanated from him which he would gladly have used to destroy his own protégé behind the bar as well as the group with Dennis Orphen, a group he had been observing with acute dislike, from the loud red-faced fellow to the smallest, prettiest blonde. By way of minor revenge on the world, he resolved to nag Orphen about writing what he wrote the way he wrote it, he would, he reflected with a ghost of mild pleasure, make him feel like a cad for being a Northerner, and as preparation—seeing Dennis approach—he fastened on an obscure uncle who had settled in Coral Gables as his own claim to a Dixie flag.

"How's the advance on the book?" asked Dennis, with a slightly patronizing nod toward his friends at the bar—have your fun, wastrels, the nod implied, I'm putting in a few swift strokes of business.

Johnson shrugged and looked mysteriously down his nose.

"Has any of the critics reported yet—or any word from the out-of-town dealers?" Dennis urged.

"It isn't the kind of book," said Johnson carefully, "that we can expect everyone to like. Not really."

"Oh, it isn't?"

Johnson smiled.

"After all it's no *Bellamy Bountree*, you know."

"Hm," said Dennis thoughtfully. "That's true, of course."

"In a way," pursued Johnson, gently sadistic, "it's a sort of a tour de force."

A tour de force! Dennis winced at the slighting words. No-Bellamy-Bountree was bad enough but sort-of-a-tour-de-force was even more devastating. Seeing Dennis as crushed as he could wish and some of his own azure mood creeping over his companion, Johnson felt a faint glow of friendliness. He leaned across the table.

"Do you know, Orphen, I've gone home from this damnable joint three times tonight and each time had to come back? I have no place else to go. I hate it. If that man sings *Trees* again I'm going to chop him down myself."

"Apparently you don't realize that these simple gangsters and chorines have hearts of gold," said Dennis. "They love and laugh like any one else and when they part they sue. Just like Park Avenue."

"Who are those awful friends of yours?" asked Johnson.

"Come over to the bar and meet them," suggested Dennis, not too warmly. "You won't need a place to stay, then."

Johnson shook his head with violent revulsion at the mere fancy.

"I detest people, Orphen, everybody!" he cried savagely. "Do you realize that I have been turned out of my home— not just tonight but any night? Wait till that happens to you and you'll laugh on the other side of your face, too. . . . No, no—it isn't the sheriff turning me out, it's just old Bing."

Seeing Dennis' blank bewilderment at this information, Johnson went into angry explanation.

"You see my wife's gone to the Vineyard to open our house so I took an apartment with old Bing. You probably know him, he's the junior partner at Lambert and Company. What happens? Every night when I go home there's Bingy's girl in my bed. Sometimes her clothes are in the living room, sometimes in the bathroom, sometimes she's even in my pajamas, but she's *always* in my bed. I have to back out. 'Sorry, Bing old man,' I say, and go out. 'Quite all right, Johnson, old chap,' he says. I come back to this dreadful hole—I drink— presently I go to Thirty-ninth Street again. She's still there. 'Terribly sorry, old man,' I say and out again. 'Quite all right,' says Bingy. Do you realize that I haven't had a night's sleep since I plunked down my half of the two hundred for rent? Do you realize—" his voice rose to a wail and for a second Dennis thought he might burst into outright tears—"my pillows, my bath towels, my very toothbrush, by God, have been so saturated with Chanel Five for these last ten days that every time I pass a poolroom the boys start to whistle? Is it any wonder I lost my temper to MacTweed today? Is it any wonder I wish I hadn't encouraged that wretched fellow behind the bar there to write his story? And for God's sake,

Orphen, why do you hang around a place like this? Haven't you any pride?"

"Me hang around this place?" Dennis retorted in resentment. "This is my first trip here. *You're* the old habitué, my friend."

Johnson ignored this simple truth and looked at him firmly, reproachfully.

"The idea! A man of your talents—I don't say genius because yours is not a gift to be mentioned in the same breath with, say, that of titans like Wells and Callingham—but a man of your abilities—"

"Make it a man of my limitations, if you like," offered Dennis genially.

Johnson waved this aside.

"—to waste your creative hours in a cheap Broadway dive, frankly, Orphen, shocks me. I don't know what MacTweed would say to it. Here you are, mind you, I'm not moralizing, Heaven forbid, I like a dash of wild oats as well as the next one—" This, Dennis, thought, was an out-and-out lie, for no one disliked wild oats or even tame oats more than Johnson; oats were his hayfever and no use boasting any other reaction. —"but for you, right on the eve of a significant event—no use denying *The Hunter's Wife* coming out tomorrow is a significant event—here you are, roistering like any ham crooner. I don't like to see it, Orphen."

"Maybe you'd like the Havana Bar better," suggested Dennis. "It's just a few blocks down."

Johnson was disarmingly delighted at this idea. On the way out Dennis introduced him to Okie and Lora and Gracie,— Boots and Tony were swooping about the dance floor—and Gracie flung her arms wildly about Johnson.

"I love this man, honest," she cried. "I adore that little mustache—oh *cu-ute!* No kidding I love this fellow. Where's he been all my life, Sugarpie? You don't mind my calling you-all Sugarpie, do you? That's what my old mammy used to call me."

Johnson drew back stricken.

"He wants to stay, doncha, Sugarpie?" crooned Gracie, suddenly ineffably Southern, even to her soft innocent gurgle as she snuggled Johnson's reluctant face in her neck.

"Do you?" asked Dennis.

"No!" yelled Johnson, struggling out of her clutches. "Let's get out of here."

The bartender shoved a glass of whisky into Gracie's hands.

"Here, woman, bear down on this," he commanded, "and lay off my publisher."

Okie, with his arm around Lora, smiled quietly and significantly at Dennis. On the other side of Lora two young men in derbies slipped into a tap dance and drinkers all around the bar were reminded of their routines. Lora alone sat quiet, unmoved, beautiful white face frozen into a gentle oblivious smile, chin resting on narrow jeweled wrist.

"I knew you'd run out on us as soon as anybody better came along," chanted Okie above the rhythm of the tapping feet all around him. "You big phony, you wanted to get my girl, didn't you? I saw you looking at her. You and Tony. Look at him dancing. Sticks his neck over like some zoo bird, expect him to dive for a fish any minute. The big snob. You and him both. Goodbye is fine with me."

"See you soon, Okie," Dennis put out his hand, eyes on Lora, but instead of shaking it Okie thrust both hands into his pockets and somberly essayed a waltz clog.

"I'm going mad! Come on!" screamed Johnson in Dennis' ear, and his pale eyes actually did flash a maniacal fire as Sammy, fan-spread fingers meeting beneath his chin, heels together, and feet squared to nine o'clock began to croon in clear bell-shaped melodious tones——

> "Ah know thaht Ah shall nevah seeah-
> Ah theeng ahs luvlee ahs ah treeah—"

. . . the night thoughts . . .

"So I WENT to tea at her place and we talked it all over," said
Johnson, for now they were in the Havana Bar and the bartender's name was Joe. "She says she knows you, you're a
good friend of hers. Why didn't you tell us that to begin with,
Orphen, so we wouldn't have had to worry about libel? We've
been trying to contact her for days. You could have given us
a tip."

"I don't know. I didn't think of it," said Dennis, but he did
know why he had not spoken of knowing Effie; it had seemed
a way of protecting her once his own damage was done.

"Do you know, Orphen, a woman like that can do a lot
for a fellow," Johnson said somberly. "As a matter of fact,
Orphen,—I'm speaking absolutely frankly and confidentially,
understand—I could fall in love with a woman like that. Not
that I mean any disrespect at all to Mrs. Johnson, but—well,
take Mrs. Callingham. Say she *is* older than I am, what of
it? It's the quality underneath, understand, that sad, sympathetic quality. And lovely hands. Did you ever see such hands,
Orphen? White tragic hands—delicate, expressive. . . . Ah,
she's a special person, Orphen, a very special person."

"Effie has nice hands," agreed Dennis guardedly. He felt
his usual unreasoning resentment at another's patronizing appreciation of Effie, and wondered why it was he could write a
book about her but would certainly avenge such betrayal if
any one else had done it. He paid the check and they were
out again in the street. In the quiet of three o'clock the
Forties looked dingy, deserted, incredibly nineteenth-century
with the dim lamps in dreary doorways; in these midnight
hours the streets were possessed by their ancient parasites, low
tumbledown frame rooming houses with cheap little shops,
though by day such remnants of another decade retreated ob-
scurely between flamboyant hotels. A ferret-eyed little street-

walker in a black beret scuttled past, thin childish buttocks outlined sharply under black satin biased skirt, skinny legs in sleazy silk stockings, large bony feet bulging out of flimsy strapped sandals. She vanished into a battered door marked 119, eyes flinging a sidelong contemptuous invitation at the two men as she turned the knob. Beside her door a dim blue light burned in a costumer's window, shadows built a face for the suit of armor and eyes for the hideous African masks. From a dark alleyway a lean powerful gray cat sneaked out with thievish caution, laid its ears back guiltily at the suspicious clatter of garbage cans behind it, warily it darted between the two men and into another shadow from which came a snuffling sobbing noise, a faint female whimper, long-drawn-out, tired, complaining. An immense cavern suddenly yawned before them and from out this sinister darkness a great clumsy bus snorted and roared into the street, a small warning printed on its side—"LOS ANGELES–SEATTLE"; resigned transcontinental faces were appliquéd on the windowpane, straw suitcases, sample cases, honeymoon luggage loaded in the back. Dennis and Johnson waited as it wheezed out, strange clumsy monster thanking night for cover. A few steps to the left and a flaming "BAR" sign hypnotized them as if here indeed were a fresh thought, and here the bartender's name was Steve and a Martini only twenty cents. A tight trim little hennaed woman in turquoise lace with a rather unbelievable bust sang *Isle of Capri* so nasally, so convincingly and withal so energetically that the languorous isle seemed to have undergone some potent glandular injection if not revolution itself.

"The way she talked," continued Johnson dreamily and Dennis closed his eyes to invoke the memory of Effie's light broken contralto tones, a feat indeed with so much tumult in his ears—"the odd gracious little expressions, oh, I don't know how to describe it, Orphen, but let me tell you that Effie Callingham is an amazingly compelling personality."

"You should know her better to really appreciate her," said Dennis jealously. "Why did you have to see her, anyway?"

"We wanted to make sure she was taking your book all right after we found out you had real people in mind. MacTweed thought it best to smooth her over. And I'm glad

I met her. Why, come in for a cup of tea, she said, I should be very happy to see you as soon as I get back from the hospital. We talked a little while—she told me some amusing stories about Callingham, showed me some pictures—it seems that once—"

Dennis' lips slipped into a sardonic smile. Effie courting a new audience now for her Callingham connection. Then he thought of how desperately she must fear and hope for his return, how the thought of Andy must be in her head night and day, wondering what he would say to her, wondering how she must act, and his heart filled with hot burning pity and despair that she refused his friendship now that she needed it most, feared him, found hurt wherever she turned. Yet she welcomed Johnson, or anyone who allowed her a few rags of glamour.

"I asked her about the wife, the one now sick here, you know," said Johnson. "We had thought of getting in touch with her since we signed up Callingham, but they tell me they don't give her more than a few days or weeks to live. Here's the problem, Orphen, as it struck me—you're up on this situation so maybe you know,—is Callingham coming home, detesting America as he does, as a favor to Wife A who cabled him to come or for the sake of Wife B who is desperately ill? Which would you say pulled him over?"

In the brief moment it required to slip out of Steve's domain around the corner into a little red-checkered tablecloth barroom named Hannah's Place, Dennis pondered this question.

"You see what I mean, don't you?" urged Johnson. "How would any man react in the same boots? After all he couldn't have been around a marvelous woman like this first wife I was telling you about without having some little hangover of feeling for her. Remember this is the first word he's had from her since he left. It says 'Come.' Supposing it's the very word he's been waiting for all these years, some sign that she wants him back no matter for what reason."

"But it's for the second wife—"

"Never mind her being sick," interrupted Johnson, blinking a little to adjust his alcoholized eyes to the smoke-hazed blue of Hannah's Place. "Never mind that part, the excuse for the cable doesn't matter, the point is, the man gets his first hint of being needed and he comes like a flash. I swear I think it's for Wife A and not for Wife B's sickness at all."

"I wonder," said Dennis, and as he stared into space, space materialized in its orderly way into a large square windowcard tacked on the bar wall, with its simple tidings neatly printed in bright red:

GARDEN FOLLIES
OPENING MAY 10 AT THE GARDEN THEATRE
WITH TOMMY BENDER, FREDDIE CARVER,
AND THE
DANCE SENSATION OF PARIS
ASTA LUNDGREN, PREMIERE DANSEUSE

"This is April, isn't it?" Dennis thought aloud. He pointed to the sign. "Had it occurred to you, Johnson, that Callingham might be coming over for no other reason than to launch his latest girl-friend, Asta Whosis, in her American debut?"

"By Jove!" said Johnson, staring. "Well, by Jove."

He paid the check and they walked out into the sickly still gray of the Broadway dawn, the grisly ghost that waits outside barrooms to remind the merrymakers of their lost day, their misspent laughter, their ill-chosen companions.

"I hadn't thought of that new girl at all," said Johnson, blaming Dennis vaguely for this new disrupting thought, this unpleasantly plausible destroyer of romance. "I declare! That is the girl, isn't it? Oh, confound it, Orphen, can't the man have some loyalty, some deeper feeling than the lust of the moment? I know what a bounder you make him out in your book but, look here, would a woman like Effie Callingham, a fine woman like her, would she fall in love with a plain bounder?"

"Why not?" said Dennis with a shrug. "When did women ever fight over a Galahad?"

Johnson scowled, unwilling to grant approval to such heresy. He was annoyed that his adoration for Effie Callingham should be affected by her husband's indifference to her. He thought of Benjamin Constant's bitter words about a woman—"people were against her because she had not inspired her lover with more consideration for her sex." He followed Dennis to the steps of a taxi.

"Get in, I'll drop you," said Dennis.

Johnson drew back, face sinking abruptly into passionate despair.

"I can't go home yet. I told you!" he cried plantively. "Bing's woman'll still be there. I have no place to go. Old Bing'll run me out again sure as you're alive. I might as well be dead."

"Come to my place," suggested Dennis with a large gesture. "There's a folding chair—plenty of room, old fellow, glad to have you."

Johnson brightened. They rode downtown and at Dennis' door Johnson breathed a sigh of happiness. "If you only knew what a relief it is to crawl in someplace with no fear of a perfumed handkerchief jumping out at you! This is damned decent of you, Orphen. I won't forget this."

Inside Dennis switched on the lights. An exotic perfume tainted the air, and on the bed sprawled a limp gray figure, the head falling slightly off the edge gave a curiously doll-like unreality to the marble face. The velvety shallow eyes rolled toward the intruders.

"Lora!" Dennis said, dumfounded.

"The man upstairs let me in and I came down his fire escape," her voice floated out of the red lips languidly, and her arm, drooping from her shoulder lifelessly, did not move. "I thought I'd come and stay with you. Okie was so mean."

Johnson stood rigid gripping the back of a chair, his eyes in speechless reproach on Dennis.

"To tell the truth, Lora," said Dennis rapidly, "this isn't my place at all. It—er—it belongs to old Johnson here. I'll be running along now. So long. Sorry, Johnson, old man."

"Quite all right, old chap," Johnson muttered mechanically and sat down, wild-eyed, on the bed as Dennis dashed down the stairs to the street.

. . . the negative . . .

MOMENTS return, Effie thought, surprised, and half-closed her eyes that this one returning, so near, so exquisitely clear even to the pungent marshy fragrance should not elude her. Without memory appearing to function at all a long-lost scene complete may appear, colors unfaded, the very expectations in one's breast reincarnated, the fear, the sense of one's young awkward body, perhaps the tiny threads of a dotted Swiss graduation dress unraveling under one's nervous fingers, the sound of cowbells, of an engine switching, of white clouds frosting the sky in odd broken little fragments, all unobserved at the time but faithfully recorded on dark negatives behind the conscious mind; without these unnoticed minor properties the moment itself fails, a word, a sigh, striving to emerge from the picture, retreats elusively without the whole, and you may beg in vain for some consoling fragment to return. It is not memory, Effie protested, thrusting the slow delight drugging her senses far back so as not to injure the frail bubble of time now within her reach, not memory but the very moment itself, more perfect by framing. Then the perfection of its detail frightened her, as one might have a spasm of fear the last second before surrendering to ether, or to the opium dream, the fear that the gate to reality was locking behind one, and to drift unquestioning into this languorous death was farewell to all else.

"I don't care," Effie whispered, surrendering, and was surprised again at her sly elation in floating thus unseen over the unsuspecting heads of the other passengers on the bus; an almost greedy satisfaction, she thought, astonished, in being the fortunate receiver of this rare work of art, inhaling its antique incense while those other poor creatures beside her were permitted merely the rumble of immediate Madison Avenue traffic; for interpretations they had business firm names lettered on passing trucks; for anesthetic they had only the thick fumes of motor exhaust; a bludgeoning acrid odor that would allow no rival sense to function. But I alone, Effie chanted silently, am away from all this, I alone can escape because of this frail, incalculably lovely moment caught like a wild bird in the palm of my hand.

Time fell away and magically became a long-ago summer. She could even see the sky above this captured moment bright azure blistered with tiny white clouds; bus changed imperceptibly to canoe, stone walls to water, and as the canoe slipped through the avenue of weeds she and her dream companion could watch in the water these clouds diminished into tiny popcorn balls bubbling beneath the surface. A light western wind thrummed the ragged marsh grass, shadows sloped down the hills from the Glaenzer castle high up on the peak, and along the winding hill road the bright shield of a warrior caught the sun and would not let it go, the shield or actually the aluminum fender of an automobile winked radiantly in and out of trees, it outdazzled the sun. The dream figures, Effie and Andy, slipped along the fringe of the beach, where magenta-roofed little cottages punctuated the shore line, a great heron fluttered heavily over them, sinking into marsh without sound, gulls and quail squawked and circled the blue, mudhens, dowdy middle-aged birds, sat on old marking posts, immovable, ugly. A black-and-gold butterfly danced suddenly out of the beachplum trees, essayed a tiny sea voyage, followed what seemed the fractured reflection of a dear playmate in the water, then was gone in sunlight. The canoe slid through the bushes, the tall, stiff, salt-tanged grass, it brushed the shore where wind whooshed through the balsams, where bee and blue-bottle fly whirred low over the brown toasted earth. They were here at the Glaenzers' to talk it all over away from Marian and the friends of town, for they agreed such calm intelligent people as they could not fly into a new romantic experiment without discussion, plan, consideration. Yet such talk of separation had become impossible with everything about them reminders of their elopement, their first meeting, their secret kisses. Here were the same servants as before assisting them to be alone in the pavilion or the lodge or the boathouse, the same sympathetic winks, and here was Belle Glaenzer ever in the background with her disapproval of their love a whip, as it had been before, to rebellion. Here were the same two lovers, the hushed charged atmosphere of love but fraught now with the sweet deathly fear that this was the end. This quiet deep certainty of each other would vanish, thought Effie, this moment of understanding silence would evaporate in future years like a drop of perfume and nothing she could say would hold it or him. There was no talking it over for them, he was leaving, and with his new love, and what more was there to be said, what more to be done but this still summing up of the old love intensified now beyond the new because it was the end, the end—

"Ah, don't go, don't leave me," she heard a voice cry sharply, and then thought, astounded, but I didn't say it really, thank God, I didn't say it. . . .

"I'll never leave you," he said, "never," but had he said it, was it in words or was it only in a sudden agonizing grasp of her arm as he helped her out of the canoe? And if they had spoken would he have stayed? . . .

"Andy's going to town," Effie said to Belle the next morning. She could not bear to tell Belle the truth, hear her complacent I-told-you-so, I-knew-you-two-would-never-get-along.

"Is he coming back tonight?" asked Belle.

"Oh yes, I'll be back—but not tonight," Andy muttered, looking away from Effie.

It was a day indeed for parting, different from the serene June of yesterday when no sorrow could happen, trouble was fleeting, love must return. Today fog rolled in from the ocean, it webbed the trees and distant hills, flung slender bloodless tentacles into the bushes, fuzzed the pine-stabbed horizon, breathed warnings on window and wall; through its dim glass one saw houses suspended in vapor, cattle in fields transfixed; a sailboat floated lightly in a blurred nimbus through space, long-forgotten fairy-tales posed in gray dream backgrounds, old calendars swam briefly past hill, house and pool. Stay, stay, Effie cried silently, as they got into the car to drive to the station. Oh stay.

"The sun'll be out soon enough," said the chauffeur—the very Daniel that Belle had now, but there would be no sun with Andy gone, never any sun nor fog nor star nor meaning to any day. Oh stay, stay. Even getting on the train he did not speak, did not say goodbye, only put his arm around her for a minute, patted her shoulder . . . oh stay, stay, stay. . . .

"Any shopping in the village, Miss Effie?" asked the chauffeur, opening the door once more for her, the train retreating behind her back but she would not turn around.

"No, just drive around the shore road, Dan, until it clears up," said Effie.

The sun presently struck through the mist a baton of radiant gold, a red farmhouse leapt out of the dazzling blare of color, sustained this dominant shrilly while cattle bellowed, catbirds squawked, an automobile siren sent out a round curving note, A major—he was gone, gone. . . . The fog thinned swiftly, faces at farmhouse windows in the valley road, on fishing boats moored to the shore, assumed eyes, noses, special mouths; the far-off train ruled off a single line of sound, a vanishing point for all sensations—oh come back, come back, come back!

He *was* coming back . . . why, of course. . . . Effie shivered, fell through the dream to the reality, from the distant prayer to the answer. He had come back. It was true. The broken brown feather on the woman's hat directly in front of her, her own gloved hand grasping her purse, the glimpse of gray tweeds sitting down beside her, these immediate sharp impressions broke through and dispelled the illusion. She thought, why, this very man beside me might be Andy, don't look, don't move, but it *was* possible. The *Bremen* had docked. The newspapers had carried his name as an arrival. There—a dark man with a Gladstone bag hurried out of a bank at Madison and Forty-second, even that might be he, or wait—the bus lurched to a stop for a gray, heavy-set bearded man, mightn't he now be gray, heavy and bearded? Desperately Effie shut her eyes, tried to push hope away; now it would be worse than ever, the frantic wooing of coincidence, the eager fantastic hope that each passer-by, each distant footstep, each opening door might reveal him. At the hospital street she stumbled out, walked hurriedly toward Lexington, her new black suède purse held awkwardly up over her chest, gold initials E. T. C. gleaming out boldly as if to conceal the quick frantic beating of her heart.

. . . Marian's trousseau . . .

MARIAN looked ghastly. The nurse's eyes met Effie's gravely over the bed.

"I told her the rouge made her look worse," said the nurse, following Effie's bewildered glance, "and I thought she should have worn a plain gown—"

"They don't understand about Andy," Marian breathed patiently as if this were an explanation she had made again and again, "he likes things gay. He always liked me in red. Pretty, isn't it?"

Her feverish fingers fluttered over the scarlet velvet evening cape wrapped about her shoulders, stroked the torn lace of the nightgown beneath.

"We've had no word yet from him," the nurse whispered to Effie.

Marian caught the whisper.

"But they don't know Andy, do they, Effie?" she protested. "Andy doesn't cable, he just walks right in the door, *right* in the door, there he is now, what did I tell you, see? See him there? He's hiding behind Effie. No one can see him but me. *Right* in the door . . . what time is it? It's almost noon, isn't it, what will he think finding me still in bed? Oh dear, someone's put something heavy on my legs—please, mother, take the suitcase away, Andy's coming—"

Effie tried to speak but her tongue would not move. She sank into the chair, felt the nurse's reassuring fingers on her shoulder. Marian's drugged eyes fluttered open again, the drowsy murmur went on.

"I'm not asleep, Andy, it's the medicine . . . I'm not even sick, you know, just this—this pain . . . and don't be frightened, dear, don't run away. I know how you hate sickrooms, but this isn't a hospital really, darling, it's only the American Club. I just came in to write a letter and I saw we were

523

posted, why didn't you tell me? Darling, why didn't you use
the Cosmopolitan check to pay the dues instead of buying
me this evening coat? . . . You're too good to me, you are,
you know. . . . Do you know, dearest, I think you're good to
me to make up to your conscience about Effie. . . . You feel it's
a little for *her*, too, don't you . . . aren't you funny . . . but
I'm that way, too . . . I guess all lovers are that way when they
hurt some one else to be together . . . I keep saying I mustn't
be too happy with you, because it isn't fair to Effie . . . Effie.
. . . She was here, wasn't she? . . . Effie!"

Effie choked out an answer. Marian's glazed rolling eyeballs fastened to her resolutely, clung to a moment of consciousness.

"Effie, when he comes, will you let me see him alone first?
Will you make everyone go away? I want us just alone, so I
can make him understand why I ran away from him . . . why
I was so silly when of course there was never anyone but
me. . . . I want him to walk in and see me looking perfectly
well, because I do, don't I, in my red jacket,—because the
poor boy mustn't be worried about me, and he does get upset over sickness. He *hates* it. He'll be so relieved when he
sees I'm almost out of the woods . . . almost . . . ah, here he
comes . . . mustn't smoke that cigarette, darling, that's your
thirtieth today. . . ."

Her voice trailed into the pillow as she turned slightly to
sink her teeth into the muslin as if this gave relief to the
flicker of pain. The doctor slipped into the room, stood at the
window beside the nurse silently looking over the chart. Effie
got to her feet.

"All right, Marian, I'll wait outside," she said, "so you can
talk everything over."

"Don't stay away long," said the nurse.

Effie walked slowly down the hall, a dreadful fear shaping
itself in her mind. Andy might not come at all. Women might
die of love for him, yet he would not pity them or ease their
doubts, for he despised weakness in others and in himself, he
would not come for death itself; and here were both love and
death beseeching him, not for their sake but that their ideal of
him should not crash into dust, years lost on a worthless
dream. . . . How heavy her slight high-heeled slippers felt, as

heavy as riding boots, it was like walking underwater against strange powerful currents. . . . She heard herself answering the good-day of the nurse at the reception desk, heard her footsteps dawdling slower and slower over the marble floor of the entrance hall. Supposing he did not come. . . .

"You look very pretty today, Miss Thorne," said the reception clerk. "Violets, too!"

Flowers and a rose-colored dress—for what? Rouge and red velvet on a dying woman—for whom?

"Have you seen the paper, Miss Thorne?" the girl asked and came over to her with the newspaper. She was a pretty girl, fair and petite, with unusually fine teeth. Effie found herself noting these details desperately, the pretty ankles, the coquettish sway of the crisp white skirts, here was something that would bring Andy quickly—if she could get word to him to come to the hospital quickly, not for duty's sake or for pity's sake or for love's sake, but because there was a remarkably attractive nurse at the reception desk he would come, he would rush. . . . Why, she thought aghast, if that is what I know of him how could I care for him, and yet it's true. . . . Her shaking hands turned the paper to the shipping news— yes, the *Bremen* was in . . . she looked for interviews with famous passengers but a prime minister took the honors, sharing them with a film couple. Andy's name wasn't there, unless it was A. Carrington . . . though she had seen it someplace else. A name leapt familiarly out of a neighboring column . . . HUNTER'S WIFE . . . THE HUNTER'S WIFE. . . ."

". . . study of a genius and a woman who lived on a great lie, one of the romantic lies upon which women in bourgeois society are persistently nourished. Such a woman as this Edna Banning of Dennis Orphen's creation could not possibly find root in Soviet Russia where sentimental love as the primary food for the feminine soul is not tolerated. The book is interesting as a picture of romance under capitalist Cupid, in a society where nostalgia is regarded as more beautiful than a wise destruction of a rotten foundation. This woman's life hinged on a sentimental lie, on false individual expectations, so she was dead. . . ."

Effie dropped the sheet, saw it flutter to the floor, wondered a little bewildered at the reviewer's signature, for it was that of a Russian woman, a dead poet's wife, whose memoirs and biography of him as well as brave use of his famous name were her main appeal to the Party and reason for existence. "Her life hinged on a lie." What did that mean? Fleetingly Effie thought of a new system of obituaries in which the lives recorded were criticized, mistaken steps pointed out, structure condemned, better paths suggested. . . . All of these reviews of Dennis' book would be like that, critical obituaries for Effie Thorne who was dead, whose life was a lie, for its glory depended on believing in a man who was worthless, cruel. Effie was aware of a strange hollow agony in her body, an obscure insistent fear that cried out to be named and flouted, that if the dream failed her as the man had, life would be intolerable. A bleak glimpse of the next years came to her, years without hope and without the pride of memory, only shame for wasted tears, misspent adoration. Forty-five, fifty—sixty—no, she could not face a future so barren, a final curtain as Marian's might be with only the bitter knowledge of his indifference, his unworthiness.

"He must come," she cried aloud, not only for Marian's sake but for hers. It could not be true he dared stay away, that nothing mattered but his present pleasure.

Luncheon trays were being wheeled out of distant rooms down the eastern corridor. Nurses chatted in the hall clearly, loudly, as librarians do, insolently proud to be above their own rules. Andy might at this very minute come running up the front steps—Effie folded up the newspaper and returned it to the desk. Footsteps running up the marble steps, don't turn, don't look . . . they passed on into the business office. Effie went out the swinging doors into the street. A taxi-door opened and a man got out—not he. Someone was running behind her—caught up, ran on, a hatless young man, not he. A streetcar stopped, a man with a suitcase got off, not he. Suddenly she knew that she must find him, must beg him, force him, to come, must swallow all pride, all the desperate plans she had been making to seem aloof, independent of him and his actions, only politely interested in his attitude toward Marian—all this pattern for her conduct must go, she must surrender all defenses before the plea for Marian.

"How—how?" she whispered to herself. Dennis would know. If she could find Dennis he would help her. He would go to the *Bremen* offices, call the hotels, Dennis would help her. But he was at Caroline Meigs' party. . . . Hesitating a moment to see where she was, she turned back and began walking rapidly eastward toward the little pair of blue spruce trees that marked Caroline Meigs' home.

IV

. . . the gypsy camp . . .

In Caroline Meigs' garden Dennis stood by the bird-bath
where silly stone dolphins feebly sprayed a cracked bowl. He
could watch both doors for Effie from this point; she might
come from the balcony stairs or the basement hallway that
opened directly on the garden. He hated this anxiety over her,
scorned himself for finding his life somehow lacking without
her. He thought she might come since she had sometimes
spoken of Caroline Meigs and had, he surmised, often basked
here in the respectful adulation of intellectual young men.
Curiosity had led him here as it had into Belle Glaenzer's, to
see how nearly the picture Effie had given checked with the
original. Moreover, today's party was for him. Mrs. Meigs insisted on a focus for her afternoons, preferably the freshest of
public names which she ordered from publishers or producers
or senators as she would order other decorations from florist
or caterer.

Mrs. Meigs herself seemed to be nowhere about though
she had screamed down to the butler from an upstairs window, "Be careful of that sandwich plate, Yama, it's Belle
Glaenzer's." Nor was her famous yachting cousin Wylie present. There were in fact no familiar faces among the lonely
guests wandering about clinging to their red rooster cocktail
glasses as if these glasses were protective aprons for their shy
miseries, so Dennis went indoors to see if there might be
some sign of Effie or word of her. He recalled rumors that
Mrs. Meigs prided herself on a perfectly delicious punch made
of pure alcohol and grape juice, which she declared fooled
everyone, and enabled her to entertain at very little expense.
The result of this shrewd fooling was that guests were always
prowling about the basement in a game she had never
thought to invent but which was the life of her parties,
namely the Scotch Hunt. There was invariably some old family friend or an intuitive type who knew the hiding place and

528

since her private stock was very good indeed little groups of guests were always clustered in the laundry leaning over the electric mangle or in the coal cellar or the cook's bedroom, contentedly sharing a glass with no gaily embossed red rooster on its rim at all but more likely the plainest jelly glass or even a half pint cream bottle.

Dennis wandered through the downstairs hall eyeing these groups disagreeably. Some young men with startlingly broad-shouldered suits returned his examination with equal hostility. These gentlemen had elected the pantry as their clubroom, and their adenoidal voices with accompanying flashes of prim-itive dentistry proclaimed British culture nobly upheld by Cinnamon, Paprika, Curry, Ginger and Bread.

"Has Mrs. Callingham been here, do you know?" he in-quired.

The tallest, thinnest, palest young man with the boniest skull and the narrowest jaw, appraised Dennis.

"I've never met her so I can't say," he said civilly. "I know Callingham, of course—he's a great friend of Caroline's cousin Wylie, you know. Look here, aren't you the chap we met at the beer-place with Glaenzer a fortnight or so back?"

"Possibly," said Dennis and added as a bright afterthought. "I meet so many people."

"She might be upstairs," ventured another. "Women always are mulling about up there."

Dennis went up the narrow creaking staircase wondering idly how soon the entire house would fall to pieces or be re-turned to the horses from whom Caroline had obviously stolen it. Women were hovering in a raftered bedroom around a handsome silk-canopied bed upon which a large bullish man in somewhat premature Palm Beach was reading palms. No Effie here. Dennis crossed the hall, bumping his head on a low-hanging Moorish lamp, and saw in another bedroom, definitely Turkish in spirit, or at least Turkish tea-room, his hostess, judging from the dressing gown and mules she wore to match the damask hangings. She was seated at her desk, a plumed pen in hand, scanning a sheet of paper.

"I'm looking for Effie Callingham," he said. "Is she coming, do you know? I'm Orphen."

Mrs. Meigs absently looked up from the paper. Her face was quite young if a trifle leathery in texture, but the years like relentless moths had revenged themselves on her neck, shriveling almost visibly by the minute under its heavy Oriental jewelry.

"Effie? Was she in a leopard jacket—oh no, that was Carol. Did you have your hand read yet, Mr. Orphen? Mac— MacTweed, you know, told me you were interested in palmistry—"

"I beg your pardon?"

"—so I had Vinal Turner come to read, just on your account. You must let him do you."

Dennis saw she had a great list of names printed on the paper in hand, evidently her guest list, for she read aloud gloatingly: "—the Argentine ambassador, the second cousin of the Duchess of Kent, a Russian film director, the Southern senator—oh, it's a grand party I'm having for you today, Mr. Orphen!"

Unlike most guest lists, Mrs. Meigs had not only the names of her company but the reason for their invitations beside them in case the name conveyed nothing. She thought of people in their categorical terms so completely that she sometimes startled them by her absent-minded greetings,—"How do you do, Mrs. Charles B. Tody, wife of the Paramount director?" or "Are you having a nice time, Mabelline Emma Foster, first white woman to breakfast with the Sultan?"

She was, Dennis thought, having a much better time up here alone with her glamorous paper guest list than with the stupid people themselves downstairs. She had been giving parties for years and aside from once having been a showy debutante who rode her ponies straight onto the ballroom floor and other such pranks seemed to have no other career than that of a resolute salonnière, a woman sought by the art set because she was in the Social Register and was rich besides, and approved by the Registered because she knew artists and was rich besides. She drew aside the curtains to peer down into the garden.

"There's Tony Glaenzer. You must get to know each other. I wonder if he brought Callingham. Do make Vinal Turner read your palm, darling."

Dennis retreated, leaving her to her reading, and heard the earnest voice of the palmist. "You have a well-defined sense of taste. I'll bet you're a good cook." Then, as the lady demurred he amended with a hearty laugh, "At any rate you do appreciate good cooking. Ha ha."

Coming downstairs he was almost pushed back by the rush of ambassadors, film directors, politicians and other titles all rushing to have their hands read in the tiny bedroom. Sentences floated through the air like autumn leaves, voices said they did or did not believe in palmistry but on the contrary did not or did believe in astrology. An ex-Central American president and an ex-Metropolitan singer noisily agreed that they did believe in black cats and Friday the thirteenth because of certain curious experiences they were only too happy to relate, and a gray little woman in pince-nez held up a group outside the bedroom door by whispering that she had just driven in from Danbury and that she herself read palms in an amateur way, and this news spreading down the crowded halls and stairs stirred Yama, the Filipino butler then in the pantry to take on a few of the well-tailored young men in actual crystal gazing, the ball being conveniently on hand over an opened jar of Major Gray's chutney, so that out in the garden the other guests were forced to wait on their own sandwich and punch needs in the most uncivilized fashion. Dennis struggled through this mob to the end of the garden but voices fluttered out from all directions and hushed exclamations of awe as an omen struck home. "Courage and endurance but no aggression." "I see a woman making trouble," stated Yama in a flat singsong voice, "a red room on a hill by a sea—" and from the woman with the pince-nez— "Either that hump means a great musical talent or a good sense of order or else you're terribly sensual," and again the earnest Turner voice, "A fine sense of taste here. Hm . . . I'll bet you're a good cook. . . . No? . . ." then once more the hearty laugh though having waded through so many palms the tone was tinged with desperation now, the laugh had a tinny quality, "at any rate you do appreciate good cooking."

Dennis nervously dipped into the punch on the long iron marble-topped garden table, and gulped down the potion. It burned the throat, tasted feebly of grape juice and left the tongue stiff and suddenly enormous and misshapen in the mouth while the recipe divided inside his chest and stomach into its singularly uncongenial ingredients, this one stinging, that one burning, and another merely throwing the entire intestinal system into reverse. That, deduced Dennis, must be the cucumber, that fine cucumber base, and it reminded him of Phil Barrow's punch recipes, which, like Mrs. Meigs', had no antidote but straight Scotch for the two days following. He put down the glass quickly, felt a gloved hand on his wrist and saw Olive Baker of all people smiling pensively at him from under a large rather flattering black hat.

"You didn't expect to see me at such a celebrated party, did you?" She laughed triumphantly. "Now really, don't you wonder how I came here? Don't worry, Corinne and I never expect *you* to ask us anywhere with your famous friends. Is that Tallulah Bankhead over there in the wool hat?"

"It's not my party. Where's Corinne?" Dennis felt his customary unreasoning annoyance at Corinne's popping into his private bachelor life. He wanted her to be on call for him in his depressed moments or between other engagements but when she unexpectedly appeared at a party he became automatically *her* man, someone he must watch to see she had a good time and watch also to see she did not have *too* good a time. If Olive was here then Corinne must be around. Olive raised her brows at his questioning glance around.

"I'm all alone," she said coquettishly. "I came with Vinal Turner—he's Mother's palmist and he knew I always wanted to meet people like this, and that I knew you. Imagine having all these wonderful people here just to meet you. Doesn't it make you feel proud?"

Dennis looked at her narrowly and detected a faintly sarcastic twist to the lips. She would tell Corinne and Phil that there was poor Dennis without a soul to talk to; no wonder he never took Corinne to those marvelous places, the poor fellow didn't know anyone. And Phil would say with great satisfaction, "After all, Orphen is *not* the man to attract friends. I could never see how he appealed to Corinne here, but I daresay some maternal instance came out in her. Why don't you let me buy you a dog, Baby, a dachshund?" Yes, that would be exactly the discussion Olive would stir up. He saw she was smiling at him with arch significance, the girl-friend smile he classified it, the smile that telegraphed we've-always-understood-each-other-better-than-you-and-she-have. He poured her some punch silently and she gracefully arranged herself on the arm of the one chair in the place and pulled her hat impulsively down to cover the tiny but study-provoking birthmark over her left eye.

"Now let's talk," she commanded playfully. "We've never had a really nice talk, have we, Dennis? Tell me how you came to write. I suppose you had to make money so you just started writing, didn't you?"

Dennis sighed. He looked uneasily at the man in the chair who after all had been there first and was now forced to cower in the shadow of Olive's fine derrière. The man returned Dennis' look pugnaciously. Dennis bowed. There was something familiar about the fellow. Of course. It was none other than the young man who lived above him, the young agitator.

"Mr.—er—Schubert, Miss Baker," he said, and Olive turned quickly to meet the great man. It was useless to explain to Olive it was not *the* Schubert.

"I know you," the young man said sourly to Olive. "I let you in Orphen's apartment about daylight the other morning."

Olive gave a gay laugh.

"Not me. And Corinne doesn't look anything like me, so it must have been another lady. . . . Never mind, Dennis, don't look so worried. I'll never breathe it to Corinne."

The hell she wouldn't. She beamed reassuringly at Dennis and then set about being charming to Mr. Schubert. The way Olive was charming was to part her lips breathlessly, throw her head back, eyes wide and glazed, intent on her vis-à-vis, a trick she had got from the most popular girl at Miss Roman's school. The most popular girl had astigmatism as her excuse, but the squinting, the difficult focusing, the voluntary dilation of the pupils, the sudden shake of the head like a wet puppy as the vision blurred, all these were somehow connected in Olive's mind with being the Prom Queen. To this trick she had added a quick incredulous, "Oh no! NO!" to register eager astonishment combined with a dash of intellect. Her social manner thus displayed appeared to be the flag of the class war to the young man Schubert, who watched her performance with narrowed eyes and a sardonic superior smile, answering her bright sallies with a meditative, "Yes, that *would* be your point of view. . . . Yes, a woman of your class *would* say that."

There, reflected Dennis enviously, is a young man sitting pretty, and literally too since his politics dismissed bourgeois etiquette and allowed him to relax at ease in the one chair of the place while ladies fumed. His sharp face wore the veiled and justifiable satisfaction of a man with a secret formula for destroying society. How simple his life was, reflected Dennis, no demon of wonder or curiosity over each separate human being; he was a wholesaler as against the artist retailer. Olive, for example, could be dismissed without study as our Number 742 Bourgeois Virgin; he, Dennis, was our Number 549, Bourgeois Realist, who fairly enough satirized his own class but then, with reprehensible bourgeois honesty, even satirized the Party itself and the Revolution, subjects alone out of all human life to be treated purely mystically. Our Number 549, Bourgeois Satirist, envied our Number 1, Complacent Communist, for he had the answer book, he need not work in the laboratory where the experiments so often refused to prove the premise, he could wear his political blinders like any romantic old lady in the midst of sordid testimony to human behavior, he could wear them and receive a bright little red button for his lapel in reward. For our Number 1 no individual woes need disturb, but only Wholesale Conditions and this made life pleasanter, for then Society could be blamed for the poverty of one's friends and no gift from one's own pocket was necessary. Five answers to everything, Vegetable, Mineral, Animal, Fish, Fowl. Happy Mr. Schubert, now placing Olive as Fowl, eliminating all the remarks that made her Olive and heeding only those that made her Fowl. As a matter of fact Mr. Schubert belonged definitely in Caroline Meigs' class, those who dealt not in persons but in categories, and this was the making of Snobs, people who believe the world would be more beautiful if it were made up not of blundering human beings but of lovely paper guest lists.

"Tell me, Mr. Schubert, or you, Dennis," begged Olive brightly, "which is Anthony Glaenzer? I saw his picture in the rotogravure and he looked so terribly attractive. You know him personally, don't you, Dennis?"

"Yes, indeed," said Dennis and thought of all the boasting he had done at Barrow dinners to offset Phil's smugness and Olive's distrust of him, and it served himself right, he thought, for Tony Glaenzer to come up from the kitchen at that moment with an eager young man on either side. Caroline Meigs' red face appeared at the upstairs' window, frantically waving a bony hand cuffed with antique jewels.

"Tony!" she screamed above the hum of mounting confusion. "That's the guest of honor there by the snacks. Say something to him."

Tony's weary eye fell on Dennis and he graciously obeyed his hostess.

"Haven't I met you before?"

Dennis bowed.

"Thank you," he said gratefully.

He felt Olive prodding him in the back with her forefinger but he ignored this hint for introductions. He saw the young Communist quickly take a pad out of his pocket and make a rapid sketch of Glaenzer's profile. Bored Bourgeois, Dennis deduced, and thought, surprised, his neighbor, aside from being a radical and dropping plaster into Dennis' room, was undoubtedly the Schubert whose suave caricatures appeared in all the smart magazines. As the artist leafed over his pages, he saw a disheartening sketch of himself, fantastically unkempt hair and tie, wild, shrewd eyes slightly crossed, an ahah smile pulling at the left side of his face, and he thought with alarm that it was true, other people had realized he had a Passport face with even distinct criminal features.

"Dennis," said Olive urgently, but Dennis did not hear her for her saw Effie pushing her way through the crowd about the basement door, a fixed party smile on her face. She caught his eye and there was such dazed appeal in her glance that Dennis forgot everything in hurrying to her side.

"That," said someone beside him, "is Mrs. Andrew Callingham—the first one."

She kept smiling, conscious of this stir whenever she appeared in public, straightened her shoulders to appear more worthy of bearing the great name, a gesture that had become second nature to her.

"Will you come with me?" she whispered. "Oh, please. I do need you."

He took her arm silently and hurried her through the basement door. In the front hall it occurred to him that his hat was somewhere upstairs but it didn't matter, and he had a flicker of apprehension about Olive's reaction to his rude desertion, but nothing mattered. The Danbury lady, her hat pushed on the back of her marcelled hair, spectacles askew, was being read by the master himself, though by way of impressing a rival he was now throwing in a dash of astrology. "You are a One person," he was saying, "and in another week you will be entering the Fourth Vibration."

"Is that good?" someone asked.

"Perfect," promised the seer.

"Andy's back," Effie whispered to Dennis. "We've got to find him for Marian."

"Isn't that Mrs. Callingham?" someone said, but this time Effie did not smile or turn. They hurried out into the street, Dennis bareheaded, hat and Mrs. Meigs' party for his book forgotten in his elation that Effie needed him, he was as necessary to her life as she was to his.

. . . the hunter returned . . .

No MATTER what happens I will never let it take me this way, vowed Dennis, outside Callingham's bedroom at the Madison, I'm damned if I'll have a bedful of literary agents, movie magnates, lawyers, brokers, Spanish and Russian translators, editors, gossip columnists, and old college roommates. The hotel valet with a suit of evening clothes over his arm emerged from the sacred bedroom and the open door allowed the chatter, the clink of glasses, the typewriter clicking out statements to the press and other inner sanctum noises to nourish for a brief moment the hungry ears of those awaiting an interview. No, resolved Dennis, I won't put on this act, not for a minute; I may have naked ladies jumping out of Easter eggs and drinking out of my slipper, I may have an extra suit and a watch with two hands and a charge account at Bellows, but this prima donna act, this big business ritual that obliged ex-wives to wait their turn with tailors till the big affairs were attended, contracts signed, checks deposited, broker called up, dinner arrangements for the next fortnight made . . . oh no, never. Dennis looked at Effie on the sofa beside him and wondered how she could endure this delay. She had spelled out her name and repeated it three times to the secretary—E-f-f-i-e—T-h-o-r-n-e—and finally said, "Just tell him Effie." The awful delay that followed this announcement sickened Dennis though Effie seemed undisturbed. Maybe after a lifetime of keeping up a front the front ossified and a little of the stone seeped through the veins. Then Dennis saw her hands and looked quickly away. He studied the rug, the little whispering groups, the pictures on the wall, but all he really saw were Effie's hands gripping the gloves in her lap, twisting them, rolling them, crumbling them, smoothing them out again.

The secretary opened the inner door and called in the film

reporter. Effie pretended not to notice, kept her eyes on a picture.

"Hotels have their own art, don't they?" she said.

Just Effie. But the tailor, the film reporter came first. Dennis passed her a cigarette.

"I've always felt there ought to be a museum of hotel art," he said. "It hardly seems fair that only the great or rich can enjoy these masterpieces, the living-room sunsets and forest fires, the little pastel bedroom quainties, the old tavern on the parchment lampshade. Do you think the twin prints over the twin beds in there will be Godey's or something from the chambermaid's own palette?"

Effie smiled, turned to the man just entering the suite, and Dennis knew she was thinking this newcomer would be admitted before she was.

"About the launch," the new caller informed the secretary.

The bedroom door closed again on voices.

Andy was buying a new launch, then. The launch came before Effie, before Marian dying. . . .

"I'm so glad you came with me," she whispered. "I could never have found out where he was."

It had been easy enough to get the address from Johnson, though Dennis dared not explain the cause of his request, knowing how stanchly the author's world unites against wives and mistresses, readier to protect the darling from these catastrophes than from bill collectors and minor nuisances. It was easier, however, to prepare the way for Effie than it would be to explain his own presence to Callingham. He found himself growing slowly enraged at the situation. He was mad because he had no hat, because his shoes had suddenly become conspicuously muddy, his shirt cuffs frayed, his fingernails black; his beard leapt out of his face, his tie's white flannel stuffing wiggled out of its decent cover, his garter broke and dangled down, all the things happened that would put him at a disadvantage with Callingham, made his anger with the man seem nothing more than the futile envy of the failure for a successful rival.

"There," said Effie, nodding toward the table and he saw a copy of *The Hunter's Wife*. "Dennis, tell me why you wrote that book. You *are* my friend, then why—*why?*"

"I wrote it for you," Dennis answered and for the first time he knew he was speaking the truth. He had written an annihilation of the man Callingham, but whereas only last week his conscience had reproached him for this betrayal of Effie, he saw now with illuminating clarity that he had done it *for* her. Somewhere, unconfessed, inside him was the St. George who would free the princess from a dragon and for no other purpose than this had his pen lashed out. The truth will free, he had cried, and then was remorseful when the truth only destroyed the princess in the telling.

Effie looked at him curiously, trying to understand. Someone in the room asked the time and another answered that it was half-past six. Effie gave a start of fear. Marian. It might already be too late. She would almost at that moment have braved everything and run straight into the other room to Andy, but this courage fled when the secretary beckoned to her from the door. She shrank back, looked beseechingly at Dennis. She had never really expected the meeting to come true, he thought, the man in the doorway summoning her to step from a long dream into reality was a shock. Dennis handed her her bag, gloves, cigarettes.

"I'll be waiting," he said, and drawing a deep breath she walked slowly, numbly, away from him into the open door.

. . . from the World-Herald . . .

If Andrèw Callingham were a less modest artist, as indeed all great men are truly modest, he would have had reason to crow over his native land this morning. It was America's indifference to his genius eighteen years ago that sent him roaming the world, from China Seas to the Mediterranean until, decorated with literary prizes and an international reputation as one of our greatest living authors, he returned yesterday to these soils. MacTweed, his latest publisher, told reporters in the author's suite at the Madison, of the artist's early struggles, the mean little attic in Chelsea, the brave solitary fight for publication and fame. He told of his efforts to earn a bare living against the skepticism of his family and friends.

" 'It is to this country's everlasting shame,' said Mr. Mac-Tweed, 'that England was the first to recognize his genius.'

"Callingham appeared to be a tall, bronzed, healthy specimen, in the prime of life, gray mustache and sparse gray hair, keen dark eyes under unrimmed spectacles, speaking with the unmistakable twang of the Yankee. He waved his hands disparagingly at photographers and the autograph-hunters outside the hotel, and only shook his head at the flattering remarks on his last novel.

"Asked what he thought of the work of the newer generation of American writers, Wolfe, Caldwell, and Faulkner, he answered that unquestionably they had something. He was equally spontaneous in praise of Dos Passos, Hemingway, Lewis, and Ellen Glasgow.

" 'Where do you think you stand in American letters?' he was asked.

"He laughed and shrugged his shoulders.

" 'Some critics would put me at the bottom of the ladder,' he said good-naturedly, and added with a twinkle, 'I do hope they're not right.' "

. . . out of the dream . . .

"I'm the best goddam writer this country ever turned out, yes, or France or England too for that matter," said Andy, lying on the chintz counterpane, English tweed dressing gown pulled across his trousers. "I know you and the Glaenzers think it was easy but let me tell you I worked hard, Effie, I earned whatever kudos I got, I never had anything just handed to me."

It was Andy, of course it was Andy, Andy caricatured by that unkind cartoonist Time until he was Uncle Henry Callingham from Syracuse, so that Effie had to keep staring at him trying to find some familiar gesture or expression, but whatever was familiar was some trait of that uncle who used to come to New York to visit them. Even his voice had taken on a brittle nervous quality unlike the lazy drawl she remembered. She tried in vain to combine in this present figure the young Andy, the Andy of her imagination, and the great man Callingham. It was preposterous that Marian's dying or any other mere human trifle would matter to this stranger. She looked helplessly from him to the young man with fair mustache who was unpacking duffle bag and suitcase, occasionally rushing in and out with telegrams and messages. Would he, she wondered, take a message through this Andy-façade to the Andy she knew, or where could she reach that vanished person?

"Get out those snapshots, Jim, I want to show Effie the places at Cannes," said Andy. He poured a drink from the cognac bottle on the night-table but Effie shook her head. "Effie, I've got a grand place, right there on the Mediterranean. And a yacht. A beauty. Pass them over here, Jim, I want Effie to see that set. And say, I wish you could see the cottage at Cornwall. I had such a good summer there I went right back and bought it so I could always have it when I wanted it. I like to own the place I stay—I'm buying here, too, did Tony tell you, maybe stay here six months a year. Ah here, here's our party in India, that's me, and that's the Duke of Malvern, a hell of a nice fella. Here's the château, rear view, you can see the sea right there in the corner, and here's me receiving the International Novel Prize in Paris, that's the prime minister—here's me and Lloyd George,—here's my stable—"

She knew she should have exclaimed with admiration, made questions, but she was utterly overcome with shyness, wonder that she had dared burst into this perfect stranger's life. There was an odd buzzing in her head, a sense of not being really there, of being in a confused nightmare, and it reminded her of a childhood dream in which the cruel ogre was her father even though he had another name and another face. So this big gray man had once been her husband, the pattern from which she had cut her real lover, the dream Andy. If she only looked and listened she might get accustomed to him, as one might accustom one's eyes to darkness, but she could not speak. What link could she and Marian ever have had with this legendary hero? How presumptuous of women to think their life or death mattered to a legend? Observing with surprise the pouches and deep wrinkles about his eyes, she pushed her chair about so that the light was behind her, shadowing her own face and hiding the hollows of her throat. She looked over the photographs, records of a life she could only dimly grasp, definite proof of how far afield her own conjecturings had been. She had, it is true, pictured an adventurous life, but these pictures were not proof of adventures, they were history, and there was something chilling in that. All of the imagined dialogues fled from her mind, for they were for lovers reunited, not for embarrassed guest and a great name. Why, she thought, groping for reasons for her shattering bewilderment, there was no Andy left, he had been wiped out by Callingham the Success as men before him had been wiped out by the thing they represented. Her knees quivering, her disobedient, paralyzed tongue were evidence enough that she was in a royal presence; she might better kiss his hand and flee.

"You've only a few minutes to dress," said the secretary.

"Mr. MacTweed is calling in half an hour. I've told the reporters you can't see any one else today, so they're cleared out."

She must go at this hint, go, or make her demand for Marian at once. She was disgusted with herself for her sweating palms, her chattering teeth, as if she were about to make of this great Name an outrageous request, beg some incredible favor as if he were a mere human being instead of already an immortal, a god she had once presumed to love. She was even surprised that he remembered her at all, flattering her by sending away the other guests, and by showing her trophies of his triumphant journeys. Yet second thoughts were more cynical; his tone had the forced heartiness he might use on a poor relation, the desire to share his successes with her warring with the fear that too glowing a story would only remind her of her own poverty. Her head swam with conflicting resolutions, she would beg him to come with her to Marian, no, she would not dare be so bold. But time was short and she plunged.

"Did you get my cable, Andy?"

He frowned and glanced in the direction of the secretary rather significantly as if this was coming to a problem often discussed between them. The photograph in his hand of the gay gardens of his château dropped to the floor unheeded.

"I was sorry Marian was ill," he said stiffly. "Thanks for wiring me."

"She wanted you—"

"It was lucky I had already booked passage for America. I wrote the hospital of course that I would attend to all the expenses. I was very fond of Marian."

"She loves you," said Effie. Now her eyes were hot with tears and her voice sounded utterly strange to her as if in command of some one else, certainly it seemed to her of her own volition she could never have spoken a word.

"Effie, is she really sick?"

Effie started. "Why, Andy, she's dying."

Andy stared at the floor.

"She used to send word she was dying or about to commit suicide whenever she was upset over something I'd done," he said. "Marian is a lovely person, but she is not the wife for a man in public life. I can't work and soothe hysterics, you know; no man can. She made herself miserable with needless jealousies—whoever I talked to or danced with—you were never jealous, Effie."

It was the first reference he'd made to their old relationship. He paced up and down the room nervously.

"Damn it, you can't work with a wife always screaming for attention," he said savagely. "You can patch up scenes for a while but finally you give up, no matter how much you love her. She ran away. I was worn out. Let her run, I said. I can't go on with it—right in the middle of a new trilogy. I always admired you, Effie, you knew a man doing high-keyed work breaks out in a high-keyed way—a little flirtation, a binge—just a form of nerves, but you understood it, Effie."

Effie nodded, silent.

"I know women," he went on rapidly, "I'm the best writer on female psychology in the world today but, by God, that doesn't help you to know how to handle a woman who wants to make jealous scenes, wants romantic love at the expense of everything else. You had common sense, Effie, there was no romantic nonsense about you. Our marriage busts up, O.K., you say, that's that. No spilled milk. You knew it was the best thing."

Effie fumbled in her cigarettes to hide her face.

"It was a fine thing for both of us," she said then. She thought, of course, you lose him because you don't make a scene, and you lose him because you do make a scene; at least I know now there's nothing you can do either way to hold a man once he's going. He would have gone no matter what I did or said.

Andy rushed to her and took her hands impulsively.

"Effie, it's worth coming back to the States just to hear you say that. You don't know how I felt, running off the way I did, never knowing whether I was breaking your heart or what. But all this time you knew it was for the best. Oh, Effie, Effie, thank you for that. Sometimes I've almost hated you thinking of you over here, so goddam noble, still loving me, forgiving me, waiting for me—"

"Ridiculous," said Effie. "When it was over, it was over."

"Exactly. I knew you felt that way, too."

"It was swell while it lasted," she said, smiling. Swell. That was it. She was to be the swell person still, mustn't let anyone feel ugly. That's that. O.K. Over when it's over. Swell while it lasted. No romantic nonsense. Those were the words to remember, the vocabulary for the swell person.

"Gee you're great, Effie," he was beaming at her now, radiant. "It's been the one thing that bothered me—feeling like a bastard about you. And all the time—let's have a drink."

This time, because her hands were shaking so, she took the glass he offered and drank with him, hoping the brandy burning into her blood would give her courage, to keep smiling while he looked at her, looked at her for the first time since she came into the room.

"Do you know, something strikes me that never did before? I'll bet the reason you let me go off with Marian was that there was somebody around you liked? I know women and I know you don't send a man off that easy unless there's some one else."

"You are clever, aren't you?" Effie answered.

"I thought so," he exclaimed gleefully. "I always held that nobleness against you. I see I needn't have. Who was it? Tony? He always was around."

"No secrets from you, are there?" said Effie.

"We should have stayed together, Effie," he said and poured himself another drink. "We understand those little strayings. I'll bet you've run through a dozen lovers since my day. Who is it now?"

"Well—"

"Come on, you might tell me that much. What does he do?"

Effie hesitated.

"He's a writer," she said and glanced quickly toward the door to make sure Dennis wouldn't suddenly walk in. "Dennis Orphen."

"Orphen?" Andy drew back, offended. "That's the man who wrote that attack on me. I shouldn't think you'd like him—I don't think that's very sporting of you, Effie. A man who's lampooned me brutally—after all, Effie—"

Effie got up.

"I can't help what he writes, and then I never did feel any romantic nonsense about you, you know." She pulled on her gloves. "Now you must go to Marian's. Dennis is waiting for me."

"I've got this dinner tonight, I'll go tomorrow—"

"There won't be any tomorrow!" Effie cried, unable to bear more. "She's dying—she loves you—you've got to go to her."

Silently he got into his clothes. She felt ghastly and her heart seemed torn with her betrayal of it. She thought, how did people live to be old, each year betraying themselves more, crippling themselves with lies until the person herself is lost, she is only a whisper saying hear, hear, this is the real me, don't listen to what I say and don't look at what I do, this is the real me beneath all that changed into nothing but a little unheard voice, and if this wicked witch's body flays you don't be hurt for it isn't really I, don't heed it, only listen to my voice saying I love you. Finally even the voice is killed and all that is left is the ugly deed, the cruel word. When it's over, it's over, she had said, so smilingly cut out her own heart.

She saw Andy talking to the young man but there was a din in her head, a ringing in her ears, echo of her own voice shouting, *when it's over, it's over*. When they finally left the bedroom only one person was left in the living room, Dennis, and Effie beckoned to him.

"Andy," she said, "this is Dennis Orphen."

Andy held out his hand stiffly.

"Congratulations, Orphen," he said. "Effie has just told me."

The three rode down in the elevator, Effie quite scarlet.

. . . Baby's birthday party . . .

"To Baby's birthday!" cried Phil Barrow, and Walter and Mary and Bee Amidon and her husband (present at Walter's secret request to Corinne) and Olive all clicked their Martini glasses a little too gamely, Corinne thought, as if, for crying out loud can't we ever get a cocktail in this house without toasting the queen or a brandy without an anecdote?

"My birthday isn't till Tuesday," said Corinne. "You know it, Phil."

She thought of how many times guests would have to drink to Baby's birthday before she went crazy with boredom, and she thought this is the good-wife feeling, this teeth clenched, controlled screaming-boredom feeling. The guilty-wife feeling is better for the whole family, she reflected, that remorseful tender understanding, the seeing all his good traits because your badness has cancelled his bad ones. The bad wife was far pleasanter around the home; she could stand a lot from a husband because it eased her conscience. "Why, dear, of course I understand," she said day after day indulgently. "Don't let it worry you for a minute, darling."

Darling. This darling business was getting on her nerves. There had been more darlings in the drawing room tonight than had ever been in one room before. There was Walter darlinging his wife Mary so that Mr. Amidon would be reassured about Walter's feeling toward Mrs. Amidon; there was Bee Amidon darlinging Mr. Amidon for the same reason; there was herself darlinging Phil very very conscientiously just to keep from knocking that ever-raised-aloft drink out of his hand. And Dennis hadn't come, hadn't called up, hadn't been in his house when she went down to see him, had vanished, and if she never heard from him there was no way she could find him, nothing she could do, nothing she could say, she could only cry all night and pretend to Phil it was something else. She couldn't even tell Olive for Olive was too obviously thinking, my dear girl I always said he was no good, this is just what I always told you, you wouldn't believe me when I said he dropped me like a hot cake and ran out of his own party with that Mrs. Callingham but everyone knows about it. . . . No, she couldn't tell Olive.

"I'm spoiling the whole dinner party," Olive said gaily. "Since Dennis deserted us, I'm that awful thing, the girl without a man."

Everyone laughed although Mr. and Mrs. Amidon, Walter and Mary, and Olive and Corinne all knew it wasn't Olive but little Mrs. Barrow who had been deserted, and all, particularly Mrs. Amidon and Walter, felt a certain moral satisfaction in this.

"I don't see why Baby is so surprised at Orphen," said Phil and broke off a piece of bread in his soup slyly in the way he had that most irritated Corinne. Why didn't he break the whole piece boldly or dunk it and say this is the way I like it, but no, he just sneaked a little bit now and then into his soup or gravy when he thought no one was looking. "Orphen is a crude sort. I understand he was brought up in a cheap little railroad hotel. His father was a traveling salesman. Not that I don't admire the lower working class. And mind, I don't criticize Orphen for not being a college man. But I do object to rudeness. The sonofabitch might have telephoned at least. Olive here—"

"I could have brought a very nice neighbor of Dennis', if he'd only given us warning," said Olive archly. "Mr. Schubert. The one who draws all those things for the *New Yorker* and *Vanity Fair*. He's going to Hollywood next month to do sets for that Joan Crawford picture. A thousand a week. I had tea with him at a little place over on East Fourteenth named Kavkas. Oh, *terribly* interesting. He's a Communist."

"There you are," said Phil triumphantly. "I'd like to know how these Communists can reconcile themselves to Hollywood jobs. That seems to me just the same as being a capitalist."

Olive gave a condescending smile.

"No, Phil, the way they feel is that until the Revolution they might as well avail themselves of their capitalistic opportunities. They have to sacrifice themselves to the present system."

Now Olive would be radical, Corinne thought wrathfully, she would have to listen to Olive's big thoughts on Russia and economics, and anything she hated was an economical bore. Olive would be going down to that apartment—up until the Hollywood moving—spilling things in the sink to make more plaster Gibson girls for Dennis' ceiling. She wished she had never told Olive anything. She wished she had never cried on Olive's shoulder. She wished Olive would move to California and never write to her, so she could have a really good reason for being mad at her. Looking about the table she thought she really detested everyone there; Walter particularly, who was always bellyaching to her that Bee Amidon didn't love him enough, was now—right in front of Bee, taking tender care that Mary, his wife, didn't get in a draft. Bee Amidon, bold-looking, dark, hearty woman, with a fine bouncing figure, was getting tight pretty fast without waiting for Phil's organized toasts. She was stroking Mr. Amidon's madly curly black hair and talking baby-talk.

"Wooty wooty wooty," she said. "Mama's toy poodle."

I can't bear it, I can't bear it, Corinne screamed inside herself, how can you love two people at once, well, she ought to know, but no, she only loved one at once, the one she wasn't with at the time; or was love for Phil only being sorry she didn't love him, sorry he was so good to her when she was so bad, sorry she loved Dennis who wouldn't even call her up any more, who wouldn't write or phone her, who probably didn't love her, who wouldn't even carry her suitcase or help her across the street. Now she was sorry that Phil loved her so much, while Dennis just not calling up made her want to die, she wished the wine was poison, she could not bear sitting here laughing and drinking with Dennis vanished from her life. She dabbed at her eyes, pretending to listen to awful Mr. Amidon tell jokes. Awful maybe-you've-heard-this-one-Mr. Amidon. What was worse was that the Amidons were a story-telling couple. They boned up for parties. Then each whispered a story to the partner on their right, then to the partner on the left, then one told the whole table, and it wasn't funny anyway, but just very long with a bad word as the point. How

could Walter stand a storytelling sweetheart? In the middle
of the kiss—Oh-I-just-heard-a-good-one! Corinne saw that
Walter and Mary were not laughing much at the Amidon
jokes. Walter, beside Corinne, whispered nervously to her,
"I've told all of Bee's jokes to Mary and now Mary smells a
rat hearing Bee tell them all. For God's sake, pretend to Mary
they were all in a book!"

"Orphen's novel is getting big reviews," said Walter aloud.
"They say it's all about Callingham. Looks like a hit."

"That's good. I'm glad to hear that. I'm sincerely glad,"
said Phil. He turned to Amidon. "This book, *The Hunter's
Wife*. My wife knows the author. He's a great personal friend
of Baby's."

"Yes," said Corinne sarcastically. "I know him personally."

That's the way it was going to be. Dennis was going to be
famous and forget all about her. She was going to hear Phil
brag a thousand times a day—my wife used to know him personally! She put her napkin up to her face and ran out of the
room. Why, Baby! Why, Corinne! Why, Mrs. Barrow! She ran
upstairs, ran into the maid.

"I'll be all right—don't let them come up," she said, thinking of Olive ghoulishly rushing up for confessions.

She ran into her bedroom, breathlessly snatched the telephone, dialed Algonquin 4—— No answer. Try the Havana
Bar. No Mr. Orphen here. Try his house again. No, send
telegram. Worth 2-7300. Telegram for Mr. Dennis Orphen—
D as in darling, E as in ever, N as in never, N as in never, I as
in Ink, S as in Sugar . . . O as in— I hate you hate you hate
you hate you hate . . . is that ten words? . . . Now Phil was
coming up. She would jump out the window. Poor Phil. He
loved her so. He would die if anything happened to her. His
whole life centered about her. That's why she couldn't run
away to Dennis. It wasn't the mink coat or the world cruise
or the diamond wrist watch, it was Phil not being able to live
without her.

"Baby, what is the matter? Are you sick?"

"Just something in my throat . . . Phil, dear—" No, no
dears. Walter calling his wife dear all the while playing footy
under the table with Bee Amidon finished that for her. "Phil,
what would you do if I should die?"

"Why, Baby!"

"I don't mean anything, I was just wondering. You'd probably give up this place and stay at the Harvard Club, wouldn't you?"

"I should say not," said Phil promptly. "I'd take a north apartment at Essex House and get that Jap houseman you fired last year and every March I'd go to London and stay six weeks."

Corinne stared at him as if he were a monster. He had actually made plans. He probably had already signed up for a lease. So that was your loyal, faithful Phil, that was inside that toast-making head, plans for what fun he'd have when she died.

She went down with him and had a few brandies with the others, thinking about Phil, until people's dishonest voices cracked in her head and their horrid private lives came out from behind their darlings and their dears. Bee and Walter had to go out in the kitchen naturally to make a stinger in a very special way, and Mr. Amidon and Phil had to brag. The way Phil boasted was to tell about the big bank presidents' doings and Andrew Mellon and J. P. Morgan as if this were more or less his outfit and in a quiet way he could take bows for their achievements. Mr. Amidon, on the other hand, did his social climbing by picking out just such big figures for his personal rivals, told tales that insinuated that Stalin, Roosevelt, and the Pennsylvania Railroad had a powerful enemy in B. J. Amidon.

Olive didn't seem to be having much fun. She sat in a corner with Walter's wife, Mary, and they talked about their Schiaparellis of which they each had one, and whether the *Normandie* did or did not have a throbbing worse than the *Ile de France* or the *Conte de Savoia*. Once in a while Olive would give Corinne a sympathetic smile, an I-know-what-you're-thinking-you-poor-kid—you've-been-stood-up. He might be at the Glaenzers', Corinne thought frantically, if people would only leave so she might run through the streets looking for him. Why didn't Olive go hunt for him, perhaps he was sick, why didn't Walter help her out, but oh no he had to make stingers in the kitchen with Bee Amidon. Supposing Dennis was sick, at death's door, who would tell Mrs. Philip Barrow, no one, or if she found out and went to nurse him how would she explain to Phil? . . . She slipped up to her room again. Worth 2-7300. Telegram for Dennis Orphen. D as in darling— Darling darling love you love you please come love you. . . .

She must be going out of her mind. It could not really be Phil standing in the bathroom door, horrified, gaping at her. Why hadn't she looked in there?

"That was Orphen," Phil said mechanically. "You said you loved him. Orphen."

Corinne burst out sobbing.

"Yes, I do. I love him madly if you want to know," she screamed. "Get a divorce or kill me, I don't care. Now you know the truth. I love him—oh I do!"

She was torn with wild sobs, leaning over the bedpost.

Phil shook his head.

"Poor Baby," he said. "Poor Honeybaby."

"Honeybaby! That's right. Put it on my tombstone," she cried. "Go on, carve it on a monument for me—Poor Honey-baby—"

Between Phil and Olive and the maid they got her into bed with an icepack and a dose of luminal. Olive was frightened that when she and Phil tiptoed out of the room together he'd want to have it all out with her and she didn't know what she could say. He stood at the head of the stairs and took off his glasses, wiped them off carefully as if this would help him to see things straight.

"Don't say anything about this to the others," he said in an undertone. "Let them think she was just tight."

"That's the idea," said Olive quickly.

"As a matter of fact, Olive," he said gravely confidential. "This has me pretty worried. For a few minutes there the poor kid went clean out of her mind."

. . . some fine day I'll have to pay . . .

DENNIS STOOD at the window beside the scarlet curtains and watched the rain twinkling over the city, drops like golden confetti quivered over street lamps, they dribbled over the window ledge, made quick slanting designs across the pane, blurred the illuminated letters across the street—HOTEL GRENVILLE. On the glittering black pavement legs hurried by with umbrella tops, taxis skidded along the curb, their wheels swishing through the puddles, raindrops bounced like dice in the gutter. Foghorns zoomed on the river two blocks away, they croaked incessantly, the storm, the storm, they warned, beware, so beware; their deep note quavered and blurred like ink on wet paper, so be-e-e-wa-a-a-r-r-e—so—be-e—

He was acutely conscious of Effie in the room behind him, conscious of the new intensely personal quality in their relationship, a perturbing modulation from author and heroine to man and woman that made their conversation now strained on his part but far more confident on hers. He was glad of the swelling and diminishing screen of radio music that separated him from her. A rich soothing voice advised the use of Barbasol, an announcer gave the time—ten o'clock—in tender fatherly tones as if it were the facts of life. . . . Where was Corinne now? She was probably a perpetual ringing of his telephone over at his apartment, a why-didn't-you-meet-me-yesterday, why-aren't-you-ever-in — what-is-this-about-you-and-Mrs. Callingham — oh darling-why-did-you-run-out-with-her-so-that-Olive-says-says-says—says—

"When I saw you there in Andy's room that day," Effie said dreamily, "I knew in that moment you were closer to me than anyone in the world, and all the time I had talked of Andy it was you were nearer to me. The Andy I knew went long ago with his first success. Do you know, Dennis, I would never even have known him—his very voice, his walk, his gestures, and of course his hair?—he had turned into the Uncle Henry who used to visit us. I couldn't get the two separated in my mind. Isn't that fantastic?"

"That happens," said Dennis.

He walked over to the radio and dialed till a soprano flew out as if she had been imprisoned for years in this ugly form waiting for the magic touch of the prince. Released now, her song flooded the little room, set the two fat goldfish in the bowl on the mantel to waltzing furiously through their miniature cosmos; another soprano joined in, the two voices floated idly through the air, high silvery bubbles of light; l'amour, ah l'amour, they sang, l'amour, a balloon bounced lightly from high C to F, slid gracefully down to B. Now other feminine voices came winging to the aid of l'amour, balancing their delicate balls of sound on the end of magic wands—there— there—ah there— The goldfish, side by side, swam rhythmically round their coral castle, their tiny green undersea forest undulated ever so faintly, oh l'amour, l'amour. . . .

Effie was silent and Dennis thought, now she was thinking of Marian, of Marian's dying eyes flickering with dim joy because Andy did come, he loved her, he came all over the world for her, oh l'amour, l'amour, and when he saw her lying there he had slipped suddenly to the floor, buried his face on the pillow beside her and so she had died. "Gone," Effie had telephoned Belle Glaenzer. "But Andy was there." "Dead," she told Dr. MacGregor, "but Andy came. It was in his arms—" And Effie forgot, but Dennis never would, that Effie had left the hospital with radiant transformed face, walked through the streets, through crowds, smiling and murmuring, as if she were the one who had died and this was not her body but her spirit that was wafting invisibly through the city night, triumphant after death because her lover had returned, had held her sobbing in his arms as she passed, oh l'amour, l'amour. Dennis had unlocked her door for her, saw her vague beyond smile, and had sat down on the stairs of her hallway a little afraid of what she might do. Mrs. Hickey, coming up to open the skylight door in the morning, had found him there.

This week Effie was marvelously serene, but it was Dennis who was upset for he could not understand her quiet air of consummation. Was it that Andy's arrival had freed her from the myth or was it that meeting him, she found him worthy of all her secret tears? Losing her as a character under his control, Dennis was alarmed; now she was as baffling to him as himself, unpredictable, unanswerable, and he feared she was becoming too much a part of himself.

"You made me see things, Dennis," Effie went on. "Now I know that the Andy I loved was the Andy I made up after he left, and when I loved him most was talking him over with you, for I put part of you on him, till he was more than you or Andy. I know it all the more because in your book you wrote about him just as I see him now. I was the one who didn't see my own picture straight. Thank you, my dear, for truth."

Her blue dressing gown trailed on the floor, her arms were clasped over her head, her hair hung in long braids over her shoulder and about her sad lovely face . . . like Melisande, Dennis thought, and there was nothing he would not do for her, nothing, his throat felt choked with his deep love for her, with sad l'amour drifting in cigarette smoke about the ceiling, with raindrops beating on the windowpane. Yes, he would give his life for her, he thought, for this high devotion was more than any carnal contentment. He thought of how fretted his life had been, how wickedly trivial, and he vowed that Effie would be his life from now on, chivalry for lust, beauty for pleasure.

"I didn't tell you one thing." Effie hesitated a little. "Andy thinks you are his successor with me. I—it seemed to make him feel better, so I let him think so. In case we ever run into him around town—"

"Oh, I'll act the part," promised Dennis. He knew Corinne must have already heard this same rumor. He had not seen her, or called her, for there was no explaining why his first duty always lay so curiously with Mrs. Callingham; no explaining that it was not an affair nor that this deep bond with Effie was stronger than any love he had ever known. Corinne seemed nothing to him beside Effie for Effie was not only a person, she was his book, just as Andy had been to her not only a man but her dream. He felt exalted and strangely bodiless around her, filled with vague high purpose. He would do something magnificent for her, something beyond mortal power.

"Tea tomorrow?" he asked, taking his hat. "Say fiveish."

Her hand stayed in his.

"You are a dear, Dennis." He thought, a little startled, that if it were anyone but Effie he would have sworn the lingering tone and gesture belonged to a woman in love. Could it be that with Andy materialized she was unconsciously turning to a new romantic ideal, to him, Dennis, because he had vanquished the dream Andy? . . . He walked back to his apartment in the rain, wondering at the new Effie that was being born, and disturbed at the hint of his own responsibility. With each moment's consideration he slipped a bit from his high mood of selfless ambition. What he wanted, suddenly, was the clean-cut brutality of the Havana Bar, of Toots and Boots and Lora. A row of news trucks lined up before a red traffic light on Union Square bore glaring posters across their sides.

START ANDREW CALLINGHAM'S DARING LOVE
STORY IN THE DAILY MIRROR—JUNE 15TH.

"I'll have to get to work on my new book," thought Dennis. "I'll make it about Lora. The story of a woman with the soul of a statue, animated only by rum. How Johnson will hate it!"

On the steps of his apartment house a little figure in a white raincoat loomed like a ghost in the dark. It was Corinne.

"I've made up my mind," she said, "I'm going to leave Phil and live with you."

"The hell you are," said Dennis.

But he was enormously glad to see her. She took the burden of high resolutions off his back and he drew a great breath of relief. He kissed her.

"Come on in out of the rain," he said.

ANGELS ON TOAST

To Max Perkins

I

THERE was a bottle of Robinson's B.E.B. right in Lou's bag but Jay Oliver wasn't interested.

"The hell with cooping up here in the compartment," he said. "Let's go down to the club car. I like to see people."

"I don't," said Lou. "I got things on my mind."

The porter brought the ice, glasses and soda.

"Okay," sighed Jay. "I might as well stick around a minute."

He sat down and kicked his shoes off. They lay on the floor jauntily toeing out, reddish brown, sleek, very much Jay Oliver. He crossed his stockinged feet on the seat opposite and viewed them complacently, marked the neat way the crimson clocks in the gray hose matched the herring-bone stripe in his blue suit.

"Paid four fifty for these socks," he stated briefly.

Lou took his suit coat off and hung it in the closet. He had put on about ten pounds in the last year, but there was something about a little extra weight that gave a man a certain authority, he thought. All right so long as it didn't get him in the middle and he'd have to watch it so that he didn't blow up like his old man had. One ninety was all right for five-eleven—he could carry it because of his big shoulders—but two hundred was the beginning of the end. Even this ten pounds made him a touch short of wind and made sitting around in his clothes uncomfortable. He undid his collar—he wore a separate white with his new imported colored shirts, —hung up the tie, a Sulka clover-leaf pattern, over the hanger, then sat down beside Jay's feet.

"Some shirt there, Lou," said Jay. "What'd it set you back?"

"Eighteen bucks," said Lou. "I swore I'd never wear a pink shirt but it was the goods that got me. Feel that material."

"Say!"

Jay leafed over the *American* and folded it at the sporting page so that the crouching figure of a Northwestern star, football under arm, seemed ready to whiz past Lou in a perpetual touchdown. Jay was still a little sore because Lou wouldn't wait over for the fight that night and plane out the next day, but he'd get over it. Lou hadn't told him that he had his reasons for booking the General. You don't have to tell all you know.

"If we got to take a train, why couldn't we have taken the bedroom train on the Century?" complained Jay. "Give me the New York Central any day. I took the Commodore Vanderbilt out of New York last month and slept like a baby. Not a jolt."

"Ah, you can't beat the General," said Lou. "You got to admit the Pennsylvania's got a smoother roadbed."

So far as he was concerned Jay could get out if he wanted to and let him do some thinking. Jay was all right, Jay was his best friend but a little bit of Jay went a long way. Lately, although their businesses were not the same, they seemed to be in everything together, and you can't have even a best friend knowing every damn move you make. Or was Jay his best friend? Jay was Whittleby Cotton and Whittleby Cotton was really his best friend. If Jay was ever eased out there his successor would be Lou's best friend.

"What's your wife think of your opening a New York branch?" Jay asked.

"What would I be telling her for?" Lou wanted to know. "I don't go round looking for trouble."

He was still disturbed by Mary refusing to say good-bye to him. He had been jumping in and out of town at a minute's notice for years, hell, that was his business, and she had never uttered a peep until this morning. What did she know? What did she suspect?

"You just got back from New York three days ago," she had said. "We've scarcely had one evening together since I got back from my cruise. I can't understand why you can't handle these things by telephone the way other men do."

"Honey, you wouldn't understand even if I told you," he answered breezily. "I'd be wasting my time."

"I really believe," she said in a low voice and then he realized she was serious about it, "you *prefer* being away from home."

So he explained how tricky his New York contracts were and how he had to keep feeding them in person,—telegrams and telephone calls were never effective, but while he was talking she quietly rose and left the table, her coffee and the toast she had just buttered, untouched on her plate. He had always been glad Mary had been so well brought up that she wouldn't dream of making a scene; but this silent indignation could get your goat just as much as a couple of plates flying through the air. He started to go after her, then shrugged, you can't let these things get you. When he called out good-bye to her a few minutes later there was no answer from behind the closed bedroom door. The baby had been sick so he did not dare stop to say good-bye to her either, for fear she might be sleeping. Outside he looked up at the bedroom window, half-expecting Mary to be there waving good-bye, but the shade was drawn to shut out the sun,—that meant she had one of her headaches,—those headaches, he suspected, that came from controlling her feelings too well. It annoyed him now that such a little thing as his wife's unusual parting mood should cross his mind when he had so many important things to think of,—a lot more than old Jay could ever guess. There was the matter of his ex-wife showing up in Chicago, old Fran whom he'd never expected to see again. As long as she hung around town there was the danger of Mary finding out he'd been married before. He was a close-mouthed man and after he and Fran broke up, so long as she seemed unlikely ever to bob up again, he saw no necessity for going into all that business with the new friends he made in Chicago. By the time he and Mary were married it would have been senseless to bring up the matter. No reason why not, but it would be hard to explain that the sole reason for his keeping it secret was that he liked to forget the ups and downs of his life before he settled in the West. With old Fran running around Chicago, goodness knows what Mary was likely to hear. Smart man that he was he had certainly outsmarted himself in not making some deal with Fran last time he saw her to keep out of his territory. It was not like him to make such mistakes.

What really was on Mary's mind, he wondered. A little fleabite, that's all it was, but that closed silent door of hers leaped out of the page of Jay's newspaper where the touchdown hero should be. It stuck out of flying Indiana villages, diminished, it winked at him from the highball glass in his hand. Lou clenched his fist and socked the green plush cushions. He could handle anything if he only knew what it was, but he hated being tormented with these trifles he did not understand. His wife not saying good-bye to him and then Judge Harrod, his wife's uncle, cutting him, sitting back there in the club car this very minute smoking a Perfecto and reading *The Atlantic Monthly* as intently as if it was the stock closing news,—so intently that he did not see Lou's outstretched hand.

"Nuts," said Lou clearly and finished his drink.

Jay freshened up their glasses.

"Flo will tell Mary you're getting N. Y. offices," he said cheerfully. "Flo can't keep her trap shut five minutes."

Sure, Flo would tell her. That is, if Mary gave her the chance. Flo had met them at the Drake for lunch and heard them talking over the plans. Jay's main office had been in New York for years so he had plenty of suggestions, and Flo put in her oar now and then, as if she was an old New Yorker. Mary wouldn't mind not having been told the business details, she never showed much interest in the office anyway, but what would hurt her would be the fact that Lou hadn't asked her downtown for lunch when Jay had his wife down, especially when she loved eating in the Cape Cod Room as Lou well knew. Those were the things that hurt Mary, and the things that were least important to Lou. The point was that Jay took care of those little matters because he had a guilty conscience, but you couldn't explain that to Mary or she'd remember it someday when he, Lou, might have a guilty conscience himself and be fixing it up with a nice luncheon. Jay figured that if he buttered up his wife before every trip and brought her a present afterward it gave him his freedom.

"Personally, Lou, I'd take the Rockefeller Plaza office," said Jay. "It's central, and you got your address. Unless you think you'd get more prestige out of the Empire State building. Personally, I don't think you will."

Was anybody asking for advice?

"You don't need a whole floor, you know," pursued Jay. "You don't need a lot of antique furniture. All you need is a desk, a telephone and a good-looking receptionist."

"I suppose you'll pick her out," said Lou.

"I could," said Jay. "I know how to pick."

"I was thinking of a nice older type," said Lou with a straight face. "Lavender gray marcel, lorgnette, class, yes, but the mother type."

Jay gave a snort of laughter.

"Get a blonde and let me age her," he suggested. "Listen, Lou, no kidding, though, you don't need to set up a palace suite like you've got in Chicago. In New York when they see a swell suite of offices they think Chase National's just about to take over. Keep it simple."

How about letting Lou Donovan take care of his own business in his own way?

"I got my eye on a log cabin," said Lou, "unless you think I could do with one of those Hudson River coal barges."

"Indiana is a lousy state," said Jay looking out the window. "Take South Bend. Or Terre Haute. Flo wants to buy a melon farm down by Vincennes but I say if we buy any farm it'll be in Pennsylvania. That's a state."

"You going straight to the Waldorf?" asked Lou. "I got a suite reserved if you want to bunk with me."

Jay took out a pearl-handled knife and began paring his nails.

"Can't stay at the Waldorf," he said. "That's where I stay when I'm with Flo. I'll be at the Roosevelt."

"Looking for a little party?" Lou asked.

Jay shook his head.

"Ebie?" Lou asked, getting the idea finally.

Jay nodded.

"Getting on at Pittsburgh," he said.

Lou shrugged.

"Give me a hand with her if any of Flo's relations pop up, will you?" Jay asked.

Lou didn't say anything. Jay made more trouble for himself taking chances that way, saying good-bye to his wife at one station and picking up Ebie at the next. And like as not he would go into the club car any minute now and try to promote the first skirt he saw till Ebie got on. If he, Lou, was as scared of his wife as Jay was of Flo he'd give up running around, or else get out and stop making excuses. Lou used to run around but since he'd been married to Mary he kept out of trouble, still doing what he liked when he liked but in

out-of-the-way sectors and on a strictly casual basis. Jay was
forty, all tied up by Flo, but so afraid he'd miss something he
could never enjoy what he already had. He said it was because
he'd been in a t.b. sanitarium once for six years and always felt
he had to make up for lost time. He couldn't say good night
to a hat-check girl without getting all messed up in something, though. His friends were always fixing up Flo so she
wouldn't walk out whenever she found out things. She never
found out anything she didn't want to, though, she knew
when to play dumb and get a booby prize of a new car or
bracelet. It annoyed Lou for Jay, a pal of his, to never learn
any technique, to go on that way, walking into trouble.

"All right, say it, you don't like the idea of Ebie," Jay said
when Lou was silent.

Lou shrugged again.

"Ebie's a good egg," said Jay. "I always go back to Ebie.
Don't get the idea she's a tramp just because she's an artist.
Ebie's all right."

"Ebie's all right, then," said Lou. It was nothing to him
what his friends did, but it irritated him to see a smart guy
like old Oliver, a guy who pulled down between twenty and
forty thousand a year, let any one woman get a hold on him.
Ebie was a commercial artist, she hung on to her job, but
how, nobody knew, because she skipped all over the country
at a telegram from Jay. Jay thought she wasn't a gold-digger
because she had gone to Art School and made her own
clothes and asked for loans instead of out-and-out presents.
You couldn't tell him anything.

"Oh, I admit she's not F.F.V. like your wife," said Jay, a
little nastily just because Mary was not friendly with Lou's
office connections, "but she's good-hearted. She'd give me
the shirt off her back."

"I'll bet," said Lou.

"I think a hell of a lot of Ebie," said Jay. "Ebie's done a lot
for me. Ebie's a darn good egg."

No sense in making him touchy.

"Ebie's all right on a party," said Lou. "You can have a
good time with Ebie."

He was willing to bet money that *anybody* could have a
good time with Ebie, if Jay only knew it.

"Ah, but there's more to Ebie than that," insisted Jay. "Ebie's got a deep side. Everybody sees those blonde curls and gets the idea she's a featherbrain, but I wish I had her mind. The other night we were sitting around listening to 'True or False,' and Ebie could answer four out of every five questions just like that. Reads everything."

"I'm surprised you don't cut loose and marry her," Lou said drily.

Jay Oliver was visibly shocked.

"Marry Ebie? Listen, you can't marry a woman that makes love as well as Ebie," he said. "You know that, Lou."

It was warmish in the little room in spite of air-condition and fans. Lou got up and propped the door open. It was one of those unexpected impulses he often had at certain moments that made him think he was born lucky, for a minute before or a minute later would have been wrong. This was the exact instant that a tall stooped man in loose gray suit was making his way down the corridor and Lou's hand was immediately outstretched.

"Well, Judge Harrod," he saluted him, "I didn't get a chance to speak to you in the club car. Why not come in and have a highball?"

The tall man shook hands without smiling. He was well over six feet and the sagging folds of flesh in his neck as well as the slow careful walk indicated that he was a man used to carrying a great deal more weight. His eyes, gray and almost accusingly penetrating, were deepset under a thick hedge of white tangled eyebrows and these with the high-bridged commanding nose and stern straight lips gave him a dignity that the wide, unmanageable ears and pure bald head bones, as openly marked as for an anatomy lesson, must have enjoyed mocking. His teeth, strong and yellow as field corn, were bared in a momentary smile, none too warm.

"You've heard of Judge Harrod," Lou waved a hand to Oliver. "My wife's uncle. This is Jay Oliver, Judge, Whittleby Cotton, you know."

"I see," nodded Judge Harrod gravely. "How do you do?"

Jay made a reluctant motion to rise but was waved back to ease by the Judge.

"No, I can't join you, Louis," said he. "I have some papers to attend to in my compartment. I didn't know you were going to New York. Mary didn't mention it at lunch."

So Mary had been to the Harrods' for lunch.

"I guess she and Mrs. Harrod were going to a matinee," Lou ventured easily.

"A recital," corrected the Judge. "Myra Hess was the soloist, I believe. I understand she was to be guest of honor at cocktails later at our house."

"Oh, yes," said Lou, reddening, for this was another matter that annoyed him, that Mary should be an integral part of the Harrods' social life except when he, Lou, was home. He didn't really give a damn and, of course, Mary knew how musicales, contract, and formal dinners made him squirm, but he would have liked to have all his customers see him making himself at home in the Judge's pleasant garden, large Tom Collins glass in hand, the Judge's blue ribbon Scottie sleeping trustingly at his feet, the Judge's big shot friends—governors, bank presidents, bishops, all hanging on to Lou Donovan's sound analysis of business conditions. If such pictures could have been distributed without the actual boredom of listening to an evening of musical baloney or highbrow chit-chat, Lou would have been quite happy. But after half a dozen efforts on both Mary's side and the Judge's to include Mary's husband in the Harrod social life with nothing but embarrassment on all sides, the contact dropped back to a family matter between the Harrods and their favorite niece, Mary. Lou suspected that he was barely mentioned, even, during these family conclaves. He found he could make use of the connection conversationally without the bother of going through the actual meetings, and this suited him fine, except for the increasingly rude attitude of both Judge and Mrs. Harrod when they met him. They knew well enough that Mary was crazy about him, but they acted when they met him alone, as the Judge was acting now, as if Lou Donovan, in speaking of Mary, was presuming upon a very slight acquaintance to refer to this intimate member of the Judge's private family. The fact that he happened to be her husband did not lessen the outrage.

"Sure you won't have a quick one with us, Judge?" Jay Oliver asked hospitably. Jay knew of only one way to dissolve his faint uneasiness with either superiors or servants, and that was to get drunk with them very quickly, and it was this simple formula of his that probably accounted for the hot water he so often found himself in, because it was during these ice-breaking friendly drinks that he was most easily taken advantage of. The Judge did not respond to the friendly offer.

"Hmm, I seldom drink in the afternoon, hmm," said the Judge, and then decided to soften the rebuke with a worse one. "It seems to me unnecessary to my mental processes,—hmm, as well as to my pleasure, hmm. I daresay other men are differently constituted, and possibly depend more, hmm, on, hmm."

His sentence trailed off into a final cough.

"I'll say I depend more," laughed Jay comfortably. "I can't think without a shot first, then I can't relax without another."

Lou was embarrassed by Jay's easy assumption that his own brain processes and the Judge's belonged in the same conversation, even though in any argument with Mary on Jay Oliver's intelligence he was always quick to say the advantage was Oliver's. Oliver's business took more brains and common sense than the Judge's, Lou always declared.

"I drink to think and think to drink," chuckled Jay.

"I see, hmm," said the Judge. "That, of course, is one way of, hmm."

His voice, earnest, unctuous, and benevolent, was a pat on the head, a well-son-are-we-sorry-now-we-smoked-the-cigarette voice, and his "hmm" was a kindly purring growl that finished off a vague sentence, punctuated a phrase, a stroking soothing lullaby to suspicion; and in sterner, more official conversations it was an official seal on the basic authority of his statement. His voice was always prepared with this apologetic butter, though if it had been unmasked and not keyed to the inferior class or age of his listeners it might have been a harsh whine of intolerance. It was as if his highly exaggerated pharynx, romping up and down his throat like a busy bell-boy, was a jack-in-the-box, and this little lurking demon, as each phrase clicked shut, sprang out with a gurgle of "Yay, bo, amen!"

"Mr. Oliver and I were discussing the opening of my New York office, Judge," Lou said, and as usual when he talked to the Judge he oiled up his own voice.

"A New York office, eh? Ah," said the Judge. "That ought to please Mary. I heard her saying just today how sorry she was to miss the fall concerts again. There's one she spoke of only this week—could it have been the Modern Music one? Something at Carnegie Hall. Too bad she wasn't able to come along with you."

"Oh Mary hears plenty of music right there at home. We've got the finest radio, she doesn't need to miss anything," Lou assured him confidently. "Naturally on business trips like this I wouldn't have time to take her to any musical affairs. I have to be on the job every minute."

"After all, Judge, you haven't got Mrs. Harrod along, have you?" Jay put in with a guffaw, and was that the wrong tack, for the Judge did not smile.

"I see, hmm," he said. "And of course Mary's having a big dinner party Thursday, that's true. I suppose you have to rush back for that."

"Oh sure," said Lou, who had forgotten all about that party.

"Well, good day, Mr. Oliver, good day, Donovan," said the Judge.

"One of the richest men in the country," said Lou as the door closed. "He could buy out the Gold Coast if he felt like it. Has his own plane, keeps a three hundred acre estate in Maryland, pays three thousand bucks for his hunters, has a bass lake and camp in Wisconsin, Christ, he's rich. Pretty close to the White House, too. Like a father to my wife and me. They brought her up, of course."

"Looks like an old buzzard," observed Jay, yawning. "I wouldn't want him nosing around me, I can tell you, and sounding off to my wife."

That was the kind of dope Jay was; he never took in any connection outside his immediate business that might be needed in some other way.

"I don't need to worry about that," said Lou shortly. "I don't fool around, not in his precinct anyway." Then, as this sounded a little too pious, he added more amiably, "Never do anything you can't deny. That's the old Donovan motto."

"You're a smart guy, Lou," Jay said with a sigh. "You and Ebie ought to like each other more."

Now Lou was willing to go into the club car, feeling that it would give him another chance at the Judge, so they went back presently, but the Judge was not there. Instead a fellow in a threadbare greenish plaid suit got them into a conversation about the difference between English and American business methods. He was a bronzed leathery little fellow with scrappy sandy hair and bleached eyelashes, buck teeth, long humped nose, and tufts of fuzz sprouted out of his ears and nostrils. Lou could not make out from his speech whether he was a genuine limey or just wished he was.

"Take the Duke of Windsor," said the stranger. "A personal friend of mine. My name is Truesdale, here's my card, T. V. Truesdale, originally an old Nebraska family, migrating from South Carolina, and incidentally the present governor is a connection on my mother's side. For the past eighteen years, of coss, I've lived abroad, personally representing the royal families of England and Europe. My wife, of coss, is Eldorana May, the operatic singer, here's a picture of her, a clipping I just chanced to catch in *The London Times* a few days ago. Of coss I read all the foreign papers, German, French, not Russian of coss,—'wife of T. V. Truesdale,' you see the caption there."

Lou examined the clipping, yellowed, with the faded picture of a sumptuous looking brunette of at least a twenty-year-ago era, checked on the caption, passed it on to Oliver, who studied it with interest.

"What do you mean you represent the royal families?" he asked.

Mr. Truesdale, who had whipped out the picture like magic from a bulging scuffed brown briefcase, replaced it now in a large manila envelope which he handled as tenderly as if it was a valuable second mortgage.

"Did represent, did, did," he corrected in his nasal sing-song voice. "Europe is to me a dead country. Look at this Spanish situation, that will spread, don't you see, there'll be no business left in Europe. That's why I'm in America once more. America's the only country. And don't think they don't know it over there. I am not a Communist, though I was at one time a member of the Socialist party, voted for Eugene Debs, believe it or not, and personally I feel that there are many things to be said for Joseph Stalin, though I can't say the same for Mr. Chamberlain. Not after what he did to my friend Windsor. One of the nicest fellows you'd hope to meet. I said to him, to Windsor, that is, I said, 'Look here, sir,' I said, 'I don't understand the way half of these Britishers talk, it's not our language at all, do they have to mumble and squeak as if their mouths were full of hot marbles?' and he said 'Truesdale,' he said, 'it's the bunk, they don't have to at all, it's purely an affectation.' "

He paid for his beer very carefully from a frayed ancient pigskin wallet, and this too he fondled as he had his briefcase, as if these were all that had been rescued of his priceless treasures when the palace was destroyed.

Oliver was having a fine time listening to the stranger, winking at Lou over each anecdote. This was the real music of the rails, some eccentric stranger popping up telling his life story, it passed the time while Indiana slid past the window, towns popped up, announced their names with a placarded station momentarily thrown on the screen, then dissolved into fields, forests, hills. The brown stranger swept through a score of countries, his story was mounted on the wind, it sweetened their drinks, it mingled in Lou's mind with a picture of Mary's closed door and the house in Winnetka.

"What was your royal racket, sir?" Lou asked.

The stranger's pale eyes moved suavely from the perfection of Lou's gray suit to the ravelling cuff of his own shirt, and he looked down at this cuff now with astonished concern.

"I must apologize for my shirt," he said. "My laundry did not arrive as I left the coast so I was obliged to borrow from the porter. Disgraceful looking. I hate that sort of thing. I like the best clothes, always have, always will. Well, as I was saying, when I was travelling in Africa I bought for the royal family. If any member of the royal family was about to make a tour of Africa or India or possibly even Canada, I'd go ahead, investigate the private tastes of all the biggies he would be likely to meet, get dossiers on all the leading families, find out maybe that the Chief of the Kenja tribes has a musically inclined daughter, suggest a harmonica as a gift on the royal visit. The man before me, as I happen to know, on a previous royal tour, suggested an accordion as a gift, a tremenjus mistake, of coss, in the tropics, since the thing's nothing but glue, so it fell apart in the heat of the first day, and did not create the right international goodwill intended."

"Pretty smart," said Lou, pleased at such a complicated job. "Look here, maybe I could use you in my business."

He ordered a drink for the man and was even more impressed when the stranger refused, insisting on drinking only his own beer which he paid for himself from his worn wallet. Lou was sorry Oliver was there to hear the guy's story as he would have liked to present him as someone he had long sought for his staff of superspecialists.

"I may look you up sometime," said Truesdale, without eagerness, but efficiently slipping a calling card into Lou's hand. "You can usually get me at the Ellery, in New York, or the Knickerbocker in Los Angeles, or the Lafayette in Havana. I was stabbed in Havana last October. Look."

He was rolling his pants leg above the knee, showing a scar on his knobby calf when Judge Harrod beg—hmm—pardoned himself past them and brought Lou up short. He went back to the compartment, leaving Jay to the stranger, and indeed did not see Jay again till they reached Penn Station, for Ebie had gotten on in Pittsburgh. Ebie was in the corridor beaming when he got out in the morning, and the three of them got together for an eye-opener, Jay, glassy-eyed with a terrific hangover and Ebie still a little tight from all night drinking and inclined to giggles and squeezing both their arms. Lou was more than ready to drop them both when they got to the station but just as they stepped into the waiting room Jay clutched him.

"My God, Lou, look!" And there coming at them out of the crowd was Flo Oliver, no less, laughing triumphantly, and hanging on to some old lady who looked as if she must be her mother.

"I caught the plane to surprise you!" Flo screamed. "Didn't I put one over on you!"

She was upon them before either man could think what to do about Ebie, until Lou was inspired to quietly take Ebie's arm and say, "Well, Jay, so long. Ebie and I have got a day ahead of us. Oh, Flo, this is Miss Vane. Jay, you remember my speaking of Miss Vane—the artist who's going to handle the decorating of my new office."

"I just came down to meet Mr. Donovan," babbled Ebie.

"Just like me," Flo giggled and snatched Jay's arm. "Mama and I couldn't wait to see your face when you saw me here."

"Nothing like a little surprise," Lou said. "Come on, Miss Vane. Good-bye, Flo."

He firmly manipulated Ebie away from the happy little family reunion, leaving Jay still mopping his head in a daze, still paralyzed from the shock of danger. The poor sap just stood there, not having sense enough to make the most of his miraculous escape, gaping after his loyal friend and Ebie as long as they were in sight.

"Now, what, for Christ's sake?" Ebie muttered in disgust as they got into a taxi. "Good Lord, what a squeeze that was."

"Waldorf," said Lou to the driver.

"I'm still shivering from the shock," Ebie confessed. "Honestly, you don't know what a thing like that does to you. So that's his wife."

"That's Flo, all right," said Lou. Ebie really was shivering and Lou put his arm around her shoulders. He hoped to heaven she wasn't going to start his day off with a little womanly hysteria but she soon had herself under control. Looking out through the back of the cab he was suddenly aware of a familiar figure standing by the curb waiting for a cab. It was Judge Harrod and he was looking straight at him with an expression of unveiled contempt.

II

THE STUPIDITY of having a wife who could spring a surprise like Flo's on you! The stupidity, Lou kept repeating to himself, of allowing yourself to be so nearly trapped by her when a few simple precautions in advance would have cleared everything. And above all the stupidity of permitting yourself to be rescued by a business friend who would always have that on you!

Ebie was disgusted, too, that was the first thing she and Lou had ever had in common. They stopped in the New Yorker for a quick shot to brace their nerves after the shock of seeing Flo, then rode uptown in silence since there was only one thing to say and that was what a dope Jay Oliver was, can't he manage anything like a grown man! The picture of his baffled docile face looking pleadingly after them while Flo and her mother encircled him with gay chatter was not an impressive one, but if that was the kind of guy Ebie fell for, all right, so Lou said nothing.

"God-damn fools," Ebie said suddenly with a bitter laugh. "Both of them, I mean. Thanks for pulling us out of that. God knows what Jay would have done if you hadn't stepped in pretending I was with you."

"I'd expect the same thing from Jay in the same situation," said Lou. He was beginning to admire himself for the instinctive good sense he had shown in saving his friend's face. He felt a little fonder of Jay (though still a little contemptuous) for permitting him to give this faultless exhibition of sterling male friendship.

"Ah, he would never have done the same thing," said Ebie. "It would never have even occurred to him."

Of course it wouldn't, Lou reflected; though Ebie looked dizzy she did have sense enough to know that much.

"I'd set aside the next forty-eight hours for him," she said.

"Want to have dinner with me?" Lou asked. Ebie shrugged a might-as-well. He could stop by at her apartment that night around seven. He dropped her at Saks Fifth Avenue and went on to the Waldorf.

When he came back to the hotel that night to wash up, Jay had called twice, and Lou knew what he wanted was for him to fix things up so Ebie wouldn't be sore. There was one urgent message to call Mr. Oliver back at Jack Dempsey's place by six or Suite 26B by seven, but Lou tossed the notes in the wastebasket. If you were signing up for a New York office, seeing bankers and realtors all day—in fact taking one of the biggest steps in your business career, you certainly didn't have time to help some poor dumb-bell out of a wife-trap. Lou felt he had fixed up the front for Flo, now let Oliver do his own fixing with Ebie. He had a laugh when finally a telegram came "Please take Ebie to a show or something and explain situation to her but not to Rainbow Room or Victor Moore show."

Taking a shower Lou thought how well things had gone for him that day. He'd clinched a swell suite of offices on Fifth Avenue in the Fifties, he'd lunched with and made a good impression on one of the biggest hotel men in the country, he'd started a whale of an idea on a kind of hotel survey, and so far as he was concerned, he was J. P. Morgan. He often in the past had dated up a red-headed hostess in a near-by nightclub but tonight he felt more like bragging than he felt like sex, so the date with Ebie was okay. There was no attraction there so it made it sort of homelike. He thought they'd go down to Cella's for a steak and some old-fashioneds, maybe drop in the Plaza later for some highballs and talk. Ebie seemed to have more sense than he'd given her credit for, so it was all in all a rather cheerful prospect. He tried two ties with the newest shirt, finally picked the dark red. Going down in the elevator, he thought it would be funny if he ran into Oliver or Flo in the lobby but he'd brush them off. It was ten to seven, and Ebie's apartment was only a dozen blocks off.

The elegance and respectability of the apartment house when Lou finally reached it stumped him. First there was the Park Avenue address when he had expected some West Forties rooming house, then there was the courtesy of the doorman at mention of her name, a courtesy reserved as he well knew only for the solvent. He found himself vaguely shifting his plans for the evening to something more pretentious—

Voisin's, he thought, or the Persian Room, but still he wasn't sure. Once in her apartment he was even more baffled. The fact that Ebie wasn't ready and that a quiet elderly maid had him wait impressed him as favorably as the obvious expensiveness of the apartment. There was a something or other about the place that he could not quite classify or duplicate in his own home though God knows Mary certainly had a better background than Ebie. Maybe it was all the pictures, though he had a half dozen much bigger oil paintings at home that he'd paid at least fifty or sixty dollars apiece for at Marshall Fields. There was her drawing table, easel, and desk that might have looked freakish anyplace else but in this de luxe background, with grand piano, Persian rugs, odd bits of sculpture, these artists' tools seemed a charming decoration since they had so obviously justified their use. Lou sat down and lit a cigarette, oddly pleased with this surprise about Ebie, and still puzzling over the quality in the place he couldn't name. Maybe it was the casualness without disorder of the gadgets lying around, or the aura of good address which gratified his senses like a specially fine cognac, and he kept rolling it over on his tongue in the same sensuous way,—Park Avenue duplex, must be at least four thousand, and for the first time he felt a little jealous of Jay. It made him look at Ebie more closely when she came down from the balcony bedroom. To tell the truth he'd never had a good unprejudiced look at Ebie.

Of course lots of women look better in their own places. Once in a while you get a stunner who knocks them cold in a restaurant but back in her own living room takes on the second-rate lifelessness of her own handpicked ordinary background. Still the majority of women come out better in their own homes, so it wasn't really so surprising that Ebie should look quite dignified, and unusually pretty, coming down the staircase to music, for the radio was playing a Paul Whiteman recording of "Afraid to Dream" as sumptuously soft as the white bear rug in front of the great fireplace. Ebie was a girl who changed at every appearance from pretty to chic to naïve to plain tart, but this was a good night, the socko from Oliver had challenged her. Her hair was reddish gold tonight—Lou dimly recalled it as platinum at one time—and instead of the

cutie-pie curls it was arranged in two plaits around her head
so that her small naughty face with knowing hazel eyes looked
not the least tartish. She wore a long-sleeved brownish-gold
dinner dress and the amber jewelry on that with her hair and
coloring was something that struck an odd new chord in Lou,
something that didn't seem to stem from Ebie herself but
from some new force Lou had never struck before.

"I know I'm too dressed up, Lou," she said guiltily, "but
that's what I always do when I'm mad."

"You're still mad at Jay?" Lou asked.

"Raging," she said positively and this for some reason
struck Lou as extraordinarily amusing for he roared with
laughter.

"He's such a fool," she said plaintively, "he never plans
anything right."

"He was lucky this time," said Lou.

"Oh, he's always lucky," said Ebie. "Jay always comes out
all right except it's always somebody else that has to wangle
him out. I'm crazy about Jay, of course, but I do despise a
fool. If he wasn't such a natural born genius in business I'd
have been through with him ages ago, but he isn't a fool in
everything, thank God."

"Jay's a good business man," agreed Lou.

"He ought to save his money, though," said Ebie. "I try to
tell him that."

Lou wondered just how much of the grandeur of Ebie's
place was due to Jay Oliver's money. Jay would be fool
enough to think he had to pay for an apartment, buy the
works, when all any intelligent guy needed to do in these
cases was to buy dinners and birthday presents. Ebie poured
out two highballs.

"Nice place, this," Lou said. "I guess there's some good
money in commercial art."

Ebie shrugged.

"I could make more if it wasn't for Jay," she sighed. "I
throw up any assignment when he's in town. I'm a fool, you
don't need to tell me."

"He don't appreciate it," Lou said. "I doubt if Jay knows
what you do for him."

Ebie looked gloomily into her glass.

"I'm always a sap," she said. "I'm a sap for all my friends. I'm a sap for that louse that handles my stuff, too, Rosenbaum. He says to me, 'Do me a favor, Ebie, put up a friend of mine for a few days will you, you got a big place.' So for six weeks I put up his friend. It looks to me like I've got her for life."

"So it's a woman," Lou said.

Ebie tried to look insulted.

"I don't let any men stay here," she said haughtily. "No, this friend of Rosenbaum's is a foreigner. She doesn't want to go back because of war. Rosenbaum can't have her at his house on account of his wife. I'm always being a sucker for somebody."

"German?" asked Lou.

"A little of everything," said Ebie. "White Russian, mostly, I guess. You'll meet her if you stick around. She's always here. Trina's all right, only why is it always me that's got to be the goat?"

"You only got yourself to blame, girlie," said Lou. "Same as Jay. You can't blame anybody else for trouble when you walk right up and shake hands with it."

"I wish I had somebody like you to talk good horse sense to me once in a while, Lou," Ebie said. "As you say Jay's as bad as I am."

It was a surprise to find how really intelligent Ebie was. They had a few highballs and by the time they got out of the apartment it was too late to take in a show so they went over to Leon and Eddie's and ate a steak watching the floor show. They didn't talk about Jay after a while except to wonder where he went and whether Flo was smart enough to catch on. Ebie didn't see why Jay didn't send his wife to Mexico for the fall and Florida for winter like other men did. Then you knew where they were and could relax.

"A fellow doesn't need to do anything that drastic," said Lou, smiling. "A little common sense is all anybody needs."

Ebie was bitter about all of Jay's weaknesses now but Lou didn't say anything because of Jay being his best friend. There was plenty he could complain of but a pal was a pal. Ebie was a good sport, Lou had to admit it. She didn't try to put on a big show of being as smart as a man, the way Flo was always doing, and she didn't put on an act of being a pure young thing before she met Jay. She was on the level, told him about a couple of other affairs she'd had and then she asked him if he'd ever been mixed up with anybody. He was on the verge of telling her about his secret first marriage and about Francie popping up now to hound him, but pulled himself together in time.

"Men don't discuss those things, girlie," he said.

For some reason that made Ebie rather sore.

"Oh, they don't, don't they?" she said. "Then why are they always asking me about things like that? All right, I wish I hadn't confessed anything to you now if you're going to turn into a gentleman."

Lou tried to kid her out of her sulks because he did like her, especially after the apartment had shown him she was no tramp as he had once thought. He took her over to La Conga where they danced, something she said Jay didn't care about but she did. They bumped into a man just leaving the place with a trim-figured little woman who smiled at Ebie.

"My house guest," Ebie whispered to Lou. "The Kameray woman. She's with Rosenbaum."

"Not a bad figure," Lou said looking after the undulating movements of Mrs. Kameray's hips appreciatively.

Ebie turned out to be a good dancer and they danced and drank till the place closed. It had been the best evening Lou had had in New York for years,—friendly, restful, altogether what he needed. He said so to Ebie in the cab.

"I'll bet we had a better time than Jay," she said, her face darkening. "I damn well hope so anyway."

"Listen, don't be so hard on Jay," Lou laughed. "You can't be that mean to a fellow's pal. Have a heart."

He put his arm around her. The sun was shining in her bed-room window when he woke up.

III

B UT WHY Maryland?" Jay Oliver wanted to know. He had been summoned to the Waldorf by a phone call from Lou with the insinuation that there might be a nice bit of business waiting there for him. Lou had had luncheon on the roof with Rosenbaum, the advertising and promotion wizard, and then taken him to his suite for completing their deal with Rosenbaum's multi-millionaire backer. The project involved a big order from Whittleby Cotton so Lou was glad to do his friend Oliver a favor. Unfortunately Jay had the shakes so badly from his last night's celebration that he didn't half-appreciate this piece of luck and in fact didn't seem to be able to get anything through his head.

"What's the matter with Maryland?" Rosenbaum asked.

"I don't say anything's the matter with Maryland—I just wonder why Maryland," Jay feebly explained. "You got Virginia—the Carolinas—take Virginia Beach. Ever stay at the Cavalier there? If you want swank, I mean."

"Oh, take another bromo and forget it," Lou called curtly from the serving pantry. "What the hell's biting you today, Jay?"

He came out of the pantry with a bowl of ice-cubes and set it down on the low table before the sofa, where Jay was sitting. Through the windows, curtained in heavy pink toile de Jouy, the afternoon sky seemed marvellously blue, with bubbling clouds stiffly whipped, looking as if the great chef Oscar himself had shot them out with a pastry-gun. This serene vista seemed to be no comfort to Jay Oliver for he stared out gloomily.

"I hate this damn town," he said. "No offense to you, Rosenbaum. I realize it's your home town."

Rosenbaum shrugged.

"We New Yorkers don't care what anybody says. Maybe we don't have civic pride like other cities. Maybe we're just smug. Anyway go ahead and hate it."

"I don't like Maryland, either," said Jay. "I put in the worst

week of my life at the Lord Baltimore one summer. A dame
had put detectives on me."

"Will you get over that grouch?" Lou exclaimed. "Maryland or California, what the devil do you care? You're in. It's
the sweetest contract you've seen in many a moon, old boy."

"I just don't seem to get the idea," Jay said. "I know it's a
big deal or Rosenbaum here wouldn't be in it."

"Call him Syd," said Lou. "We're all friends here."

"If you don't mind I'm going to call him Rosenbaum,"
said Jay. "I mean if we're going to be personal friends. I always call my personal friends by their last names—first names
are just for business purposes."

Jay was getting into one of his nasty moods, as usual at the
wrong time and with the wrong people. It was a mystery to
Lou how Jay could do the business he did when he was so
careless with his contacts. Lou was especially nice to Rosenbaum now to make up for his friend's rudeness. He started to
fill his glass but Rosenbaum put a warning hand over the top
of it. Drinking was the one feature of business that he heartily
disliked. He was a big loose-limbed man with pale gray pro-
tuberant eyes, gnarled heavy features, loose mouth and curly
graying brown hair. His big shoulders and build made him
appear athletic which was far from the truth, just as the
humorous curve of his lips and the alert twinkle in his eye
libelled his somber brooding nature. If he resented Jay's
irritability he did not show it.

"Mr. Oliver missed the Major's explanation," he said.

"Call me Jay," Jay said.

"The property we're dealing with is that big stretch of
woodland along the Chesapeake that the Van Duzers started
to develop in 1928 then lost to the Chemical Bank. Well, the
Chemical Bank is the Major. What we're doing now is building it up into one of the most exclusive resorts in the country. Stables, fox-hunting, health baths, thirty beautiful manors
serviced by one great hotel or club."

"You say you can rent these houses for a week-end or a
month," Jay said.

"We want your finest goods, Jay," Lou said. "The Major's
crest on all the linen."

"Everybody is the Major's guest, you see," said Rosenbaum.

"Be a millionaire for a week-end, see, that's the idea," said Lou, genially. He clapped Jay on the back for he was in a fine mood. The very air of the room seemed charmingly alive with little floating dollar signs and fat little ciphers, commas, more ciphers, all winging around happily, waiting for a mere scratch of the pen to call them into action. The Major's conversation had left this agreeable effect, and although Lou had put in three hard days in the City to say nothing of his nights, and had, right up to the noon conference today, been worn out with nerves and other complications, the final settling of the proposition had left him miraculously refreshed. Like the colored porter on the Pullman, too tired to do anything till the five dollar bill galvanized him into a perfect frenzy of efficiency. "Thought you were tired, George," Lou had teased him. "Nothin' rests me like money, suh," George had grinned back.

"Sounds like a big job," Jay admitted.

"There's a fortune in it for all of us," said Rosenbaum. "If you knew the Major like I do you'd know he's a cautious bastard. He won't put a nickel into anything unless he's going to get fifty back."

"I suppose we'll have to put a lot of time from now on sticking around Baltimore," Jay said. "Baltimore or Washington. You can have them both."

"Don't kid yourself, this place is one of the best locations in the country," said Lou. "Look. Catch a plane at two-thirty—you're in Baltimore at 4:15. Car meets you and takes you straight to Castles-in-the-Woods. You meet the richest men in the country. The cream of society. You're the Major's personal guest. Don't tell me that isn't good stuff."

Rosenbaum went to the table and opened up his briefcase, fumbling in it for photographs which he silently passed to Jay.

"We're going to modernize the whole place," said Lou. "Wait till the natives see what we make of that state."

The pictures reminded Lou that he had not showed Rosenbaum the photographs of his house in Winnetka, so he went in the bedroom and brought back the snapshots of the place, the picture of the kid playing with her poodle in the backyard, and the snapshot of Mary in her sable coat standing beside the Packard.

"My wife," he said.

Rosenbaum glanced politely at the pictures, made appropriately flattering comments.

"I'll bet Mary's sore you're not home for that dinner she's giving tonight," Jay observed.

Lou looked at his watch.

"I'd better call her," he said. He had gotten over his disturbance over her strange behavior at parting and in the exultation of his unexpected good fortune today remembered only how proud he was of his high-bred wife and the excellent way their marriage was conducted. He remembered he had not told Rosenbaum about his wife's connections yet, though he had mentioned them casually to the Major. Both their wives were from the Lucerne convent, then a year at the Boston Conservatory, the Major's father-in-law was a judge, Lou's uncle-in-law was a judge. These little coincidences had been mentioned casually by Lou, that was all, but they had helped. No less a private authority than the recent train acquaintance, Mr. Truesdale himself, had furnished Lou with these little personality tidbits about the Major, at eleven o'clock that very morning, by telephone.

"Speaking of Maryland," said Lou, "did I tell you my wife's uncle has a big show-place down there, not far from your spot? Judge Minor B. Harrod."

"Oh, yes," said Rosenbaum, impressed. "I know of him, of course. Your wife a Harrod?"

"Mary Harrod, she was," said Lou, "Boston originally. Are you married, Rosenbaum? I'd like Mary to meet Mrs. Rosenbaum."

Rosenbaum smoked a cigar impassively.

"If they meet it will not be in the Castles-in-the-Woods," he observed, sardonically. "Part of my job is to protect the guests from non-Aryan intruders."

"Well, if you're ever in Chicago, then," said Lou. He went in the bedroom and called up for more seltzer and put in his call to Mary. He had left word with the operator not to disturb him for the last two hours and now she told him that Ebie had called twice. He had figured out Ebie as good enough sport not to regard last night as anything but a momentary lapse, but he might be mistaken. Sometimes these girls that talked like such good sports were more trouble than the other kind. Even while he had the receiver to his ear the operator said, "Will you take Miss Vane's call now?" and there was nothing to do but say yes. He went to the living room door and nodded to Jay.

"Long distance," he said and closed the door between the two rooms.

"Listen," said Ebie's voice, "do me a favor, will you?"

All right, now it was coming. Buy me some Tidewater stock, please, and I'll send you a check later. Lou braced himself.

"Rosenbaum's there with you, isn't he?" she asked. "Don't be so damned cagey, this isn't going to hurt you. The point is that he's going to suggest my little permanent guest to you for some promotion work and for God's sake say yes to it, will you?"

Lou was slow getting it.

"Who? What do you mean promotion work?"

Ebie was impatient.

"This Kameray dame I have on my neck. She knows too damn much—especially after last night."

"Oh."

"She doesn't know it was you. She only knows it wasn't Jay. Anyway it's getting me. You know. Not knowing when she's going to pop out with something when he comes in."

That was easy. Lou was relieved.

"What do you want me to do?"

"Get her out of town, keep her in the West, I don't care. Rosenbaum's sort of afraid to push her into something for fear you'll catch on to his position, so you help him out."

"That's a cinch," said Lou. He was glad of the tip. Some way to please Rosenbaum, who after all, represented the Major. "How do you feel today?"

Ebie groaned.

"Awful. Butterflies in my stomach, you know. I had to turn in two drawings to the agency this morning. That's where I saw Rosenbaum. I shook so I could hardly hold a pencil. We drank a whole bottle of Hennessey after we got back here, you know."

Lou hadn't remembered that.

"You kept telephoning everybody," Ebie said. "God knows who. Then you passed out."

The operator cut in and told him his call to Chicago was ready so he told Ebie he'd call her back and waited.

"Hello, Mary," he said briskly, "I thought I'd better let you know I'm tied up here. Some things have turned up and it will take me a few more days to get them cleaned up."

"Yes?" Mary said coldly.

It reminded Lou they were not on warm terms, so he tried to think of something personal to tell her, the sort of thing he seldom told her but which she loved to hear.

"Oh, by the by, I had a nice talk with your uncle on the train," he said. "He was on the same car."

There was a silence and he rattled the receiver.

"Mary, are you there?"

"This is the third time you've called me and told me all that in the last twelve hours," she said quietly.

This stunned Lou.

"You called me twice last night," she said. "Once at four o'clock and again at four thirty. It seems to have left no impression on you."

Lou mopped his brow. That was something he had never done before. Must have had his conscience working overtime.

"I forgot to tell you about seeing the Judge," he said.

"The conversation has been exactly the same all three times," said Mary.

Lou pulled himself together. If she was trying to get his goat he'd show her.

"Supposing I call you when I get back in town, then," he said coolly. "No use my wasting long-distance dough. So long."

At that he'd forgotten to ask after the kid. That would burn her up. It was funny, too, because he was fond of the kid. The only thing was that Mary had sort of taken it over from the minute it was born and made it her special personal property, none of his, until he had gotten out of the habit of even taking it on his knee. He occasionally surprised himself wishing he had a child of his own, and then he'd remember why he really had one, only it was Mary's and he didn't dare touch it. Some women took their children that way. It didn't matter, really, and it filled her life all the time he was on the road.

He was about to call Ebie back and get more dope on Rosenbaum when Jay opened the door.

"Flo and her mother went to Atlantic City," say Jay.

Who the hell cared?

"Nice for you," said Lou.

"I didn't have a chance to thank you for pulling me out of the jam there at the station," said Jay. "I sure appreciated it. Flo didn't bat an eye."

"Flo know's what's good for her," said Lou. "I'll bet if she didn't know what was up yesterday she did today when you handed her that hundred dollar fitted bag."

"She didn't say so," said Jay and then astonishment lit up his ruddy tan face. "How'd you know I gave her a fitted bag?"

Lou laughed.

"A shot in the dark," he said. "I ought to know how you work by this time. A woman would have to be mighty dumb not to notice your tracks."

Jay sat down on the bed, and lit a cigarette.

"Bring your drink in, Rosenbaum," Lou called. "We're holing in, in here."

"Listen, Lou, you didn't pull a fast one on me with Ebie, did you?" Jay muttered in an undertone.

Lou was hunting for a fallen cigarette and did not answer at first.

"She said you took her out, and I was wondering," Jay said slowly.

"What the hell are you getting at?" Lou exclaimed, and then Rosenbaum came in.

"I was just wondering if a good smart girl couldn't help us interest the right people in the Castles," Lou said. "Not just the pushing average looker, you know, somebody a little different, higher class, maybe, different."

Rosenbaum went over to the window and looked out.

"I could get you a very competent young woman who answers your description," he said. "Part German, part Russian. Exiled here. She brought my cousin's little girl over from Germany last year and we feel grateful and of course very responsible for her. As I think of it she would give the right continental class to the thing. Discreet, smart—a very unusual personality."

"Sounds perfect," said Lou easily. "Let's hire her. What's her name?"

"Mrs. Kameray," said Rosenbaum, still not looking around. "I'll have my office get in touch with her and send her here."

It struck Lou as funny that Jay Oliver sat there, knowing who the woman was but not speaking up for fear Rosenbaum would then know about him and Ebie, and Rosenbaum, who knew perfectly well through Mrs. Kameray all about Jay Oliver and Ebie, did not dare mention where Mrs. Kameray was staying for the same cock-eyed reason.

Jay lay back on the bed smoking, shading his eyes with his hand.

"What's eating you?" Lou upbraided him. "Here I give you a nice bit of business and you act as if you'd just lost it."

"I feel lousy, that's all," said Jay. "Can't a guy feel lousy?"

Rosenbaum picked his hat and stick from the dresser-top.

"You people will want to celebrate at some hot spot, I suppose," he said with a sigh. "I'm a family man. I stay home tonight with my family and my little Hilda, and listen to the Jello hour."

Lou saw him to the elevator. When he came back he winked at Jay.

"Family man, oh, yeah," he said. "You should have seen him doing the rhumba up at La Conga last night."

"Oh, was that where you and Ebie went?" Jay asked.

"It's a good orchestra," Lou said lightly.

"I should take Ebie dancing more, I suppose," said Jay.

His tone was so mournful that Lou was annoyed.

"Go ahead, but don't act as if it was such a chore," he said. "After all I see you dancing with every other chippy in town."

"So Ebie's a chippy," said Jay.

"I never said any such thing," said Lou, and that was the way it went on till finally Lou called up Ebie to show how much he respected her and he asked her and Mrs. Kameray to come out and have a cocktail with Jay Oliver and himself.

"Wherever you want to go," he added.

"Trina would like to go to the Rainbow Room," Ebie said with a patient air. "She says she's never seen twilight come over the Rainbow Room."

"For Christ's sake, isn't that too bad?" said Jay, when this message was relayed to him. "Tell her to hustle herself up there then right now before it's too late."

Jay took a shower and borrowed one of Lou's ties and they were pals again.

"We can shake 'em at eight or so and go have a good time," said Lou. "We don't want to get into anything."

IV

THE KAMERAY woman wasn't bad. She wasn't bad at all, Lou told Jay in the men's room.

"That phoney accent throws me," said Jay.

"I think it's cute," Lou said.

"Sure, that's why she hangs on to it," Jay said. "She's a liability if you ask me."

Jay was still worried because he hadn't been able to get back on Ebie's good side. Just as she was beginning to mellow and was hinting at lunching with him tomorrow, Jay recollected that Flo would probably be back by then and he didn't dare commit himself. So that made it worse. It was the longest Ebie had ever been mad with him. All through the cocktails at the Rainbow Room and the dinner at the Trouville she had been high-spirited and charming, always a bad sign in a woman who has every reason to be sulky. She had been brightly interested in everything Jay said, exclaimed "How amusing!" after his anecdotes, and all in all showed such a pointedly polite, agreeable side of her nature that Jay feared the worst. As a feeler he made some remark about wives popping up in unexpected places, but Ebie merely laughed gayly and said, "My dear man, if you'd known as many married men as I have you'd know they all have to jump when the little woman appears." And she added parenthetically to Mrs. Kameray, "After all, you can't blame the wives—it's not their fault they're always getting left at home."

"I'll bet Rosenbaum would do a burn if he knew we had the Kameray woman out tonight," Jay said to Lou in the johnny. "He was saving her to spring on you tomorrow, wasn't he? Poor leetle Meester Rosenbaum."

"Her accent isn't phony," said Lou. "She's foreign, isn't she?"

Jay made a face.

"Nuts, she spoke English perfectly when she got here," he said. "Then she caught on to this accent business and how it gets the guys. So she's been doing this-how-you-say-in-English, and-eet-ees-zo-how-you-say stuff ever since."

"She's got a right to an accent if she is foreign, hasn't she?" Lou said. "Anyway, she's a darn smart little dame, if you ask me."

Jay brushed his hands over his coat.

"What she says with that cute accent would sound dumb if she said it straight," he said. "Don't be a goddam fool. The dame's a phony of the first water."

"Phony or not she'll be okay working on Castles-in-the-Woods," said Lou. "Snap out of this, will you? I throw a nice bit of business your way, and here you are, griping."

Jay did not smile.

"I got worries, Lou. Flo popping up all over the place. If it was anybody but a wife it would be blackmail, because she never comes right out and accuses me, she just sort of hints until I give her a check to shut her up. And now Ebie's sore. I know you don't like Ebie but——"

"All I got against Ebie is that she's too good for you," Lou interrupted. "What do you want to mess around with somebody like Ebie for?"

"I don't know," said Jay, dolefully. "I'm not messing. It's just that I like to go back to Ebie, that's all."

"That's the trouble with you, Jay," Lou told him frankly. "You're always getting into fly-paper. Take me. I drop in the Spinning Top, pick up Tessie or Fifi, slip them a fifty-dollar bill and that's the end of it. I can meet them on the street with my wife, they never bat an eye."

"Ah, they got no feelings," Jay argued. "What's the fun of sleeping with some little tart with no feelings?"

"Once you got feelings you're in trouble," Lou warned him. "Those girls are all right. No talk. Nothing. But what do you do? You get some dame that's restless, mad at her husband, maybe, too high-class for a fifty-dollar bill so you got to give 'em a diamond pin. Then the trouble begins. Oh, Jay, this is Mrs. Friedman——"

"That's all washed up," Jay said.

"Never mind, it's always somebody like her. Oh, Jay, she says, I'm here at the fur storage and I'm so embarrassed, I'm short a hundred dollars cash for the alterations on my mink. Do be a lamb and loan me a couple hundred—send it over, will you? . . ."

"Ah, shut up," said Jay.

"Or else she has to get her car out of hock, or she wants to pay her dues at the Golf Club," Lou went on relentlessly. "Too high-class for fifty bucks a night. It's just five hundred a shot, that's all. And then she talks, and her friends are your wife's friends and then you're in. Don't you ever learn anything, Jay, for God's sake?"

Jay looked sorrowfully in the mirror at his brown face, now a little haggard from a combination of hangovers and woes.

"Can I help it if I like high-class women?" he asked. "I like a looker, sure, but I like a little class to them, a little intelligence. To me it's no fun unless the woman has a little intelligence."

"They got more than you can use, believe me," said Lou. "It's that intelligence that costs you money, boy."

When they got back to their table Ebie and Mrs. Kameray had their heads together whispering about something furiously, but drew apart when the men sat down.

"How you women dish!" said Jay. "Clothes and men, that's all you women think of."

"I suppose the subject of clothes and sex never came up in the forty minutes you two have been in the little boys' room," said Ebie snippily.

Lou took charge of that one.

"Men don't have the time to discuss sex when they're alone, I assure you," he said.

"Well, then, I don't know where they picked it up," Ebie said. She turned to Mrs. Kameray. "Wonderful, isn't it? They never talk sex and they never listen to sex talk. They just learn it by Braille."

Ebie getting nasty was a good sign, so Jay cheered up. No man was more miserable in the doghouse, than Jay, Lou reflected, and no man in the world did more to get himself into the doghouse. Figure that one out. They danced a little more happily together this time, but Mrs. Kameray was too tired so Lou sat with her, wondering what to talk about that would keep her seductive accent going. He couldn't imagine why that got him so, but it did, just like Ebie's apartment had got him. Some quality there he had never encountered.

"We were talking about our fren' Meester Rosenbaum," Mrs. Kameray explained. "The feeling about Jews is so strong I say he should make his name Gentile, like Rosetree or Rosebush."

Lou laughed loudly.

"Is it fonny?" Mrs. Kameray inquired innocently. "Meester Rosebush, he laughed too, but I say I am going to make the start until everyone will think he is a good Meester Rosebush and not a bad Meester Rosenbaum."

Lou laughed until the tears came to his eyes. He looked around for Jay and Ebie to come back so he could repeat the story but could not spot them on the floor. They must have gone out to the bar for a private quickie. It was just like Jay Oliver,—here he could easily seize this momentary break in his relations with Ebie to cut it off for good, but no he had to get his head back under the axe again, in a good position so that Flo or Ebie could take turns whacking.

He looked at Mrs. Kameray and wondered curiously why Ebie disliked her so much. Here was a lady, definitely a lady, you could tell that, nobody to be a nuisance around the place, yet Ebie was catty about her. She was different from American women he had known, about twenty-eight, he thought, or less, but tricked out to look like a dainty little woman instead of the youthful college girl type that the twenty-eight-year-old American girls tried to imitate. She had brown sleek fine hair parted in the middle with a little bun at the back, a fine bust, tiny waist, rounded thighs and slender legs, like old-fashioned women, he thought, and small in stature like old-fashioned women. Her little flowered hat dripped a silvery veil over her smooth white forehead and even over the nose—a strong New England nose like his mother's with the same full high cheeks and rich full lips, pouting a little but all the more provocative. He liked her slender sloping shoulders, the long slim forearms, he liked her slim ankles with their slow breath-taking ascent into plumpness, and more seductive than that was her poise, her calm acceptance of her own charms, the cool glaze over her dark brown eyes. He had been a long time trying to figure out what gave the piquantly artificial air to her person, and decided it must be the foreign flavor of her clothes, smart with lacy jabots, and the painted ivory ear-rings must help, for to his surprise she wore no make-up at all.

"Don't you wear lipstick?" he was impelled to ask.

She smiled deprecatingly.

"Everyone looks at me so when I wear leepsteek," she said. "I don't like it when everyone looks at me so. And my eyes are so beeg I cannot put on the stuff they put on."

"Ebie certainly lays it on," said Lou.

Mrs. Kameray lowered her eyes.

"Ebie is so nice," she said. "Ebie is a very nice person."

Lou couldn't help thinking how decent this girl was, nothing catty about her, when Ebie had put *her* on the pan all right behind her back. You didn't often run into women with any loyalty to each other. He saw Ebie and Jay standing out by the bar talking earnestly. They were getting along now, he could tell by their faces.

"Ebie's all right," he said, "when she isn't drinking."

Mrs. Kameray did not reply.

"I wonder what Rosebush would say if he knew you were out with Jay and me tonight," Lou kidded her. "He's arranged for me to meet you tomorrow, you know."

Mrs. Kameray's eyes danced.

"We wouldn't want to disappoint Mr. Rosebush, then, if he's made himself so much trouble about the introduction. Let's pretend tomorrow we don't know each other," she suggested.

Lou laughed again and agreed. He could see Jay and Ebie craning their necks to look at him and thought they were probably surprised to see him laughing so much. He was usually pretty deadpan, but then he didn't get a girl with such a dandy sense of humor often.

"What's your business like, Mr. Lou?" asked Mrs. Kameray, earnestly, hands locked beneath her chin. "I so want to know."

"Take a hotel," said Lou. "Or take a tavern or a resort. It's got to have equipment, hasn't it—furniture, orchestra, cigarette girls, maybe palm trees? And it's got to have good roads leading to it, good neighborhood around it. All right, I'm the man they consult."

"You do all that?" she was wide-eyed.

"I have small office staffs, sure, but I got investigators all over the world, people making maps, people shopping for equipment, people wangling local politics to clean up bad sections around a hotel,—they report to me. I keep a finger on everything, I'm the works."

"Like an emperor," sighed Mrs. Kameray wonderingly. "Oh, how you must be a genius! Yes, like a czar!"

Jay and Ebie had disappeared for a long time before Lou realized it and even then, he went on explaining his business to Mrs. Kameray for hours, sipping brandies to her Rhine wine and seltzer, glowing in the unexpected pleasure of talking business to a woman, and though he did not even touch her hand he felt more disloyal to Mary than he had ever felt in his six years' married life.

V

ON SUNDAYS Ebie lay in bed and thought what a mess she'd made of her life. She had been in the habit of thinking this every Sunday for years and it struck her that she hadn't run through these Sabbath meditations for weeks. Why was that? By Sunday she still had done enough things to be sorry for, she hadn't stopped making a mess of things, that much was certain. It must be she had turned off the routine during Trina Kameray's long stay. That was it. All during Mrs. Kameray's stay she had waked up, at first irritated and finally furious at the mere sound of somebody breathing in the next room. The shower running made her think jealously—"my new red-and-silver shower curtains, damn her hide!" The smell of coffee reminded her that it would be made in Trina's way with a twist of lemon peel which Ebie loathed. The phone ringing made her snatch the receiver and snap "Wrong number" before the person had a chance to ask the infinitely grating question, "Is this Mrs. Kameray's apartment?" All these little things had made Ebie irritable and continuously filled with Christian intolerance. No one could have been more unobtrusive than Mrs. Kameray around the house, and after all it wasn't as if it was a tiny apartment, there really was room and to spare for two people. Nor was Ebie a selfish person, she told herself, she was perfectly candid with herself, if she'd been a selfish person she would have been the first to admit it. It was just that what was hers was hers.

All right, she'd brushed the woman off. There wasn't a shred of her around, she had been shipped off on a three months' tour of the country for Castles-in-the-Woods, representing the Louis Donovan Service. Therefore now Ebie hadn't any hates and Sunday rages. She had doldrums. The same set of doldrums she'd had for ten years,—ever since she had started being twenty-four, in fact, an age she had loyally stuck to socially for these ten winters. Professionally she admitted twenty-eight, and a maidenly fear of thirty. No reason why not, she looked better than she ever did, that is, dressed up. A commercial artist got a lot of graft, especially when she did clothes, as Ebie did. So even if her income hadn't been enough to dress her handsomely her graft would have. And presents. One thing and another.

The chimes from St. Thomas' told her it must be around eleven so she rolled over and checked this with her little musical alarm clock which had been tinkling "Lazy Mary" for the last half hour. It was the chimes' fault she had such bad Sundays, Ebie decided. They nipped into her sleep, dimly reproaching her for being late to Sunday school at the M. P. Church on Elm Avenue, Greenpoint, Iowa. She would struggle to wake up because although she didn't care about Sunday school she did want to wear her new pink dotted Swiss with the toast-colored straw hat so that the little boy who played in the yard next to the church would see her. Finally she would manage to wake up. And here she'd be in New York and not Greenpoint, and then she'd think of what a perfect mess she'd made of everything since those dotted Swiss Sundays, and that had been, roughly speaking, ever since she'd been ten. No sir, she thought mournfully, she hadn't had a pink dotted Swiss since her tenth birthday, unless you counted that dotted Swiss kimono with the china blue silk lining. Nothing Sunday school about that, of course. Still, it was dotted Swiss.

She threw off the cover—it had been a warm night but there had been a little cool breeze with a pleasant hint of autumn and burning leaves. The kids in Greenpoint used to burn leaves on September evenings, she recalled. On Sundays, too. She wondered why anybody wanted to burn leaves but anyway it was fun and smelled wonderful. She must tell that perfume company to put out a Burnt Leaf fragrance. They'd say women didn't want to smell like a small-town bonfire, but she would say look at Russian Leather. People had said women didn't want to smell like Russian Leather but it turned out they did. Well, there was a constructive thought. Burnt Leaf Parfum. Only you couldn't say "parfum" any more unless it was made in France, because of that new law. All right, call it Burnt Leaf Smell and see where you got. She got out of bed and walked into the adjoining room, barefooted in her new high-necked nightgown, the one with the train, the one she had been presented with after drawing it for the manufacturer. She wanted to see what the work-room looked like, being a work-room again and not a guest-room. It looked wonderful, the couch a couch again instead of a bed, the table a desk instead of a dressing-table.

"My God, I really am getting selfish," she admitted, and then she decided this joy in the house to yourself was not self-ishness but just pleasure in self-preservation, a New York characteristic. In a town full of people the New Yorker's only haven was home, she thought, pleased at being so clever and philosophical with just her own thoughts, and then she wondered if that was what she really thought. That was another angle to her Sunday soliloquies, this thinking things then wondering if that was what she really thought or what she had made up her mind to think, and if so, what was she really thinking behind her thoughts.

Ebie had two small rooms, the bed-room and the work-room, opening on the balcony over the living-room, but the work-room was so dark she usually worked in the sunny living-room below and used the upstairs room just for storing and filing. She had had this apartment for five years and was still amazed and delighted with its magnificence. A woman cover-designer had first had the place, it was a co-operative apartment, and it was still filled with the little touches that had finally bankrupted her,—the concealed lighting, the built-in cozy corners and trick bookshelves on the balcony, the specially made door-knobs, wall fixtures, ventilating gadgets, all things the poor owner could not take with her or resell. Moving in here had represented a big change in Ebie's life, a definite decision to play the commercial game, drop the old artistic crowd downtown and the Village nonsense. She'd spent enough time sitting at the feet of somber soon-to-be-great painters having them lecture her about taking her talent seriously, urging her to make good the promise of her Art League days, and decrying the advertising art she was making a living at and incidentally which they couldn't do. She was a sap for some of those boys, no doubt about that. She used to cook midnight supper for them while they kept her up all night talking art and she was flattered that they allowed her around. Then she met Jay Oliver with one of the advertising men she knew at an Illustrators' Ball and it was a moment in her life all right. The change from art talk to hard-boiled Middlewestern business talk seemed marvellously refreshing. Her ten years with Art seemed a long expedition into a foreign, fuzzy, phony world,—it was fine stepping out of it into straight commercial world, hearing Jay's straight talk. Money. Money. All right, there it was, the thing everybody wanted, artists, too, only it was wonderful to have people come right out and say so. It was like the simple dotted Swiss days, all one, two, three.

Ebie reflected now that she had begun thinking life was a mess ever since she'd made up her mind not to be kidded any more about life or to kid herself about it, for that matter. So here she was, not knowing when she was kidding herself and when not, whether she liked this handsome independent plush life her income brought her or whether she had had more fun, while she had it, out of the old rowdy-serious Bohemian life. The thing she had decided was that a girl alone had to have an above-reproach background in which to be Bohemian. You could slide down banisters yelling "Whoopee" in a palace and you might and could be a gay visiting duchess, but a little gay solo dance in a Greenwich Village basement made a girl out either a nut or a tramp. A good address was a girl's best mother in New York. A man saw a place like this and thoughts of marriage came out on him as obviously as freckles.

Not that Ebie wanted marriage. She'd had chances enough but where would she get off, marrying somebody and then scramming out every time Jay Oliver called up? Still she'd like a little affection, she thought with a modest dab at her eyes with her kerchief, maybe you didn't want a husband or a mother or a father or a child or a dog but you did have to have something. You did really have a right to have something belonging to you, something you could kick around and say, now that, that is definitely mine and nobody else's, and nobody has the right to kick it around but me, and that's security. What did she have secure in her life? I mean tender, true security, not financial security. That set her thinking some more.

Ebie put on the taffeta housecoat and slippers that Hannah had laid out for her and turned on the radio. She felt like a little companionship. If you could only skip Sundays! Her bed-room was rather bare in comparison to the heavy-carpeted luxury of the living-room and it was not so much that she had run out of money by the time she had furnished the downstairs as that she did not like to wake up in a clutter of ruffles. She couldn't quite explain this but if you waked up to bare walls, uncurtained windows, Venetian shades of course but no drapes, you could map out the day's work with no interfering images. The little white radio on the night-table bleated out a sonorous sermon and again Ebie shivered and turned it off. She might as well go down and get breakfast. Hannah never came on Sundays so she got her own.

In the kitchenette off the living-room, shelves were prettily stacked with black-and-white checkered canisters, a glass cabinet of all manner of goblets, tumblers, ballons, liqueur glasses, all betraying the old Southern hospitality standards, and the shelf of fancy canned goods, pickled walnuts, brandied peaches, smoked salmon, pickled mussels, shredded cocoanut, black and red caviar, teas—oolong, jasmine, mate—revealed a nice imagination in food.

"And to think," Ebie reflected, "I'm the girl that used to eat sugar and vinegar on my lettuce."

As a matter of fact Ebie, when she cared to, could whip up a nice little dinner, a gift that had made her quite popular as a Sunday night hostess for her father back in Greenpoint, and later on as an art student living on Washington Square. She wondered now, as she plugged in the percolator, whether Lou Donovan ever let on to Jay what had happened the other night. Men were always such gentlemen with each other that any dope could tell what they were hiding. She wasn't mad at Jay, as he thought, for the stupid mess about his wife,—though she had let him think she was still mad. She was really mad at herself. There was the telegram on the table cancelling one job, all because she'd delayed it by rushing out to Pittsburgh to meet Jay. She could blame Jay for that if she wanted to be unfair but of course it was all her own fault for being such a fool about him. Here she deliberately sets out to be a success instead of an artist and then lets a married man make a mess of both things! All right, that was bad enough, but then she ought to keep the love part secure, since she messed up her life for it, but no, she had to make even a mess of that by letting the man's best friend stay all night.

"How did I get to be such a louse?" she wondered out loud. "If it had to be somebody why did it have to be his best friend?"

So she decided to blame it on the brandy, but then there were more self-reproaches there. That meant she was making a mess of her life by drinking too much. Drink ruined a girl's looks in short order, Rosenbaum had told her that much. On the other hand, as she had pointed out to him, she could show him girls who had never had a drink in their lives and yet were no balls of fire so far as looks were concerned. She turned the downstairs radio on to WQXR and got the Fifth Symphony. She always got the Fifth Symphony. She could almost write it herself now,—boom boom boom, begin the beginning over and over till every instrument has got in a few well-chosen remarks, then begin again, and again, ah now we're getting into it. But no, just where the middle should be the end begins with each little instrument saying a few last words, then altogether, amen, amen, good-bye,—ah but wait a minute, just a last minute suggestion, then good-bye, but wait, one more final nightcap of finales, boom da da boom, then another (now I really mean it this time, we really must go after this last one). That was the Fifth Symphony and that was what art and culture finally rattled down to—too much spinach, take it all and say you like it, or else throw your weight with people like Lou Donovan and Jay Oliver who made fun of culture because they didn't have any. She had kidded the pair of them the other night at dinner, the night she brushed off Mrs. Kameray.

"What'll you have, baby, a steak?" Jay had asked.

"A steak for God's sake," she had mocked. "These two bums clean up a fortune today and they can't think of anything better than a steak to buy for us."

"Anything you say, baby," Jay said. "You can have quails on toast just by lifting a finger."

"That deal today is nothing," Lou said. "By the time we're through, old dear, we'll be buying you angels on toast."

The waiter stood at attention and Jay looked up.

"Four angels on toast, waiter," he said, "nothing too good for us."

Angels on toast, my eye. Ebie sat eating toast and sausages with sliced pineapple, listening to WQXR and looking over the Art Section of the *Sunday Tribune*. Whenever she got disgusted with her affair with Jay she cried a little over the art columns. That helped along her Sunday doldrums as much as anything. Here was Royal Cortissoz or Jewell approving "Dunes," "Kansas Dirt Farmer," "Apples and Bible," "The Old Captain," "Upstate White Church"—(as if she hadn't practiced them all herself ages ago)—by her former art school colleagues. She too might be in that blessed company— "heavily influenced by Kenneth Hayes Miller," or "under the domination of the Midwest School," or "reminiscent of Cézanne but lacking of course both his gusto and his inspiration." Yes she could be among those contemporary immortals instead of here in this elegant apartment, last night's orchids and tomorrow's breakfast all on ice, her life a mess,—yes there could be no doubt of that, though her gift for prostituting her art had always made those old companions strangely jealous. She dried a tear again, and turned to the society page, for no reason, except that there could be nothing certainly in those small periodic sentences to make her think of either the futility of love or of art. Or so she thought until she was idly glancing down "News of Resorts" and after "White Sulphur Springs" came to the first item under "Atlantic City":

"Mr. and Mrs. Jay Oliver and her mother Mrs. MacAlister are at the Hotel Traymore."

Ebie put the paper down and lit a cigarette. After the way he had tried to make it up with her. After the way she had almost forgiven him and really intended to at the right moment. Then he goes down to Atlantic City with his wife and mother-in-law of all people. No reason why not. A wife was a wife. She shouldn't flare up at Jay. The fault was her own for giving up her simple old life as a real artist—(work away at it even if it takes years! That's what she should have done)—and started distorting all the decent things in life with commercial art, married men, Rainbow Rooms. Hopping all over the country at a word from the man. Kicking her work over. Kicking over her ideals. Her little old dotted Swiss ideals, she thought sadly. Served her right that he should pass her up

now for his wife and a little family stroll down the old Boardwalk. Served her right for picking up with a fellow like Jay.
Visiting fireman. That's what fellows like Jay and Lou were
called. Fellows the old crowd would have laughed at. Fellows
you took to Luchow's for dinner then to Jimmy Kelly's for
the midnight floorshow and they shouted "Greenwich Village—whoopee!" And your crowd sneered at them and didn't
appreciate that they might be smart in their own line to make
all that money, and the visiting firemen looked at your
friends' and your own art works and said, "How long did it
take you to copy a picture that big?"

You fell for them for a while of course, the firemen, because
maybe you got a little too much art talk, a little too much literary conversation, a little too much brain work instead of dancing and fun. But a person was a fool to let them get you. Here
Ebie pulled up the shades and saw that the day was fine, it was
wearing its finest Sunday clouds, white, calm, substantial, and a
stern blue sky, and the sun was all polished up and glittering,
throwing eye-stabbing reflections on windows across the court,
shining away fiercely, working hard to make a good impression
so that it needn't come back after lunch. No, nothing to prevent her picking up her old life, she could always go back to
it, just as Jay and Lou could always go back to their wives. Jay
and Lou with their big respect for marriage. Doing anything
they pleased on the side but keeping up the great marriage
front. The Show Must Go On. That was the phony part of the
visiting firemen. And just as Ebie had gotten very suddenly fed
up one day with artists' life in Greenwich Village she now got
fed up with her present. She dialed the garage for her car and
then raced upstairs to dress. She rummaged through a drawer
till she came upon a dotted Swiss dance set with blue ribbon
bows. If you couldn't wear it outside you could at least wear
it next you. Then she turned on the radio full blast to a recorded program and sang with it, "I Can Dream, Can't I?"
softly along with Bing Crosby while she hurried into a suit.
She suddenly felt like kicking over every trace of the present.

"I'd almost go back to Greenpoint," she thought, "only it
wouldn't work out because I'm not ten years old any more."

Outside the apartment the doorman opened the door of
her little blue Plymouth for her.

"Glad to see you can get away such a fine day," he said heartily. "Sure fine weather for getting out in the country."

She must certainly have had the look of going some place all right.

The little blue Plymouth with the red wheels rolled down Park and over the Grand Central ramp and down Fourth. On Sundays Fourth Avenue below Murray Hill was a deserted street except for the little comings and goings of the Vanderbilt Hotel. There was a nice hotel, Ebie thought, it had Wedgwood medallions all over the doors and a dark mezzanine where you could lunch with one man and see over the balcony rail the man you were going to dine with that night being a big shot with the boys—(cigars, brandy, do-you-know-the-one-about-the-derby-hat-and-the-plumber)—at a table down in the dining-room below. A nice hotel, the Vanderbilt. Caruso had a floor there once, but there were other things about the place, too, Ebie recalled with a reminiscent smile. She had forgotten to salute the old Murray Hill Hotel a few blocks back, but there were memories of that, too. Brass beds, for instance. Bay windows. In the dining-room, publishers, agents, travelling salesmen, and Hartz Mountain canaries, a pleasantly out-of-town flavor to it that made you able to guess the type of man he was if he suggested this restaurant.

A little blue car is very becoming to a young woman as every young woman knows, so the casual pedestrian today turned to look after Ebie as she drove on down and over to Irving Place where the Sunday hush fell on old well-kept brownstones, handsome old apartment houses;—people really lived here, there was even a father out wheeling a baby, a rare spectacle in Ebie's life so she leaned out to see whether the pram really contained a baby or a publicity stunt. Now the lights changed and stopped her directly in front of the house she had once roomed in with her girl friend from the League named Honey. Ebie was surprised to see the house still there, an old brownstone, one of Stanford White's designs (she remembered the landlady pointing out the house around the corner on Gramercy Park where Mr. White had lived before his murder),—oh, yes, and it was there that young musician had shot down the author, David Graham Phillips. It was a romantic murder belt, this section, sometimes famed as the home of Washington Irving though he had never been murdered so far as she knew.

From a fine old mansion this house Ebie once knew had deteriorated into "Furnished Rooms" with an Armenian restaurant in its basement. Odd spacious black walnutty rooms, Ebie recalled, with dark mahogany stairs up and down from one wing to the other, elaborate balustrades, little balconies in the great foyer as if for a small orchestra, so that the bleak rooming-house atmosphere blended with the dim fragrance of long-ago balls. You could almost shake out echoes of "Kiss Me Again" from the dark velvet hangings. Oh, yes, it was an old waltz house, Ebie thought, definitely that. She wondered if Honey still lived there and looked at the door intently, half expecting the old girl friend to walk out as big as life, but there was no sign of her. Just as well since they had parted on very chilly terms for no reason at all except that they either disliked each other's men friends or else liked them too much. At any rate they had a habit of spending the last hour before retiring, the Stocking-washing and Cold Cream Hour, in snarling at each other over each other's dates. Honey was a virgin (at least you couldn't prove she wasn't), and was as proud as punch of it. You would have thought it was something that had been in the family for generations so that no matter what the circumstances she could never quite bring herself to hock it. Honey took courses in oil at the League and modelled for a commercial photographer for money, and Ebie took black-and-white courses and did fashions and illustrating for money. They had a living-room with quite nice furniture, at least like Honey's virtue you couldn't prove it wasn't, since it was always encased in bright chintz slip covers. There was a fireplace with fires forbidden, a little bedroom and bath and kitchenette, all for eighteen a week. Since all they ever cooked in was breakfast or a canned hash supper their expenses were very little, unless they were being rushed by League boy friends at their own expense since the boys there were usually poor. Ebie and Honey used to try to break even by taking out a Visiting Fireman one night and a League boy the next. They even had their moments when they had no dates at all but just went on a girls-together-spree. They'd wait around till almost eight pretending they

wanted to finish a detective story, or that they weren't hungry
really, then face the fact that there was no dinner date coming
up tonight, so they would go round the corner to a tavern
where O. Henry used to go, and they'd sit in the dark smoked-
wood booth drinking old-fashioneds and telling each other
things they certainly wished later they had never told, and
bragging about their families, sometimes making them very
hot stuff socially back home and the next time making them
romantically on the wrong side of the tracks. The families must
have been on wheels back in the Midwest, whizzing back and
forth across the tracks at a mere word from the New York
daughters. The thing about this restaurant, too, was that there
was nothing tea-roomy about it, so they felt very sophisticated
being the only women in it often. Honey loved literary men so
other times they went to a literary hangout on Eighth Street
where you could see your favorite author in the sidewalk café.
Honey usually carried a magazine with her "work" in it to impress the strangers who usually barged up trying to promote a
date. They drank Planters Punches here, a specialty of the
place, one that usually brought all the men's eyes to their table,
and eventually the "Pardon me, I hope I'm not a nuisance, but
would you mind telling me what the name of that wonderful
drink is? . . . Planters Punch? . . . Thank you. Look, you
won't think I'm fresh I hope, if I suggest buying a round of
them. Seriously, I'm just curious about them."

What a drink! The waiter bore the glass with snow a foot
thick all around the glass and a mountain above it topped by
a miniature fir tree of mint, and extra long straws through
which you drilled for rum, and it seemed to come up from
the damp bowels of the very earth, you could almost get
Floyd Collins on a clear day as somebody had once remarked.
After things got going Honey would whip out the magazines
and show her Work. She was the girl on page 98 in the nightgown holding her hands to her head and remarking in capital
letters right beneath the picture, "Oh, why didn't I take a
Selzamint and Wake up Happy?"

"There," Honey would cry, "would you believe that's me?
My other profile is much better—the right side of my face, I
mean, but they liked this side for a change."

Then she'd eagerly leaf through the next magazine. There she was on the back of the cover page in three colors in three different poses. ONE: Ball gown. Dancing with white-tie man who averts his face. Balloon coming out of her mouth saying, *Let's go home, dear, no one will dance with me, yet I look every bit as nice as Emily.* Balloon from white-tie man says, *Yes, dear, but why not see our family doctor?* TWO: Doctor Troutman's office. Honey in street clothes. Balloon coming out of Honey's mouth saying, *But, Doctor, is there nothing I can do about Body Aroma?* Doctor balloons back, *Fortunately, Mrs. Flashman, there is a secret formula known to physicians for many years but only recently made available to the public. It is* ——" THREE: The Ball. Different ball dress for Honey and this time surrounded by half a dozen men all holding out their hands as she is wafted triumphantly into the dance by her proud husband. *Well, dear,* he balloons at her, *I notice you had every dance tonight. What has changed you? Bodyjoy,* she radiantly balloons right back. *Ever since using Bodyjoy my pores have been breathing properly and I am once again the girl you used to know.*

The strangers were always impressed and usually told Honey that her acting in these three little vignettes from real life was so good she ought to be in pictures, and she always had the snapper ready, "But I AM in pictures, only not the kind you mean. I'm an artist."

Honey was such a feeb Ebie couldn't understand how she'd stuck it out with her those two years. It got so just the sight of Honey on a Sunday sitting around painting her toenails and brushing her red hair one hundred strokes was enough to drive her crazy. When the hairdresser burnt off a big hank of this prized hair in a permanent wave, Ebie did feel sorry for her and tried to comfort the poor girl as she lay sobbing on the bed, the handmirror face down beside her.

"Never mind, Honey," Ebie had said, "you never were the conventional type of model anyway, you're not dependent on a glamor-girl haircut. You've got a different style, see, not the regular model type of face."

At this Honey sat up and looked eagerly into her mirror again.

"I know," she agreed with satisfaction. "I'm more the elfin type. My face is a perfect heart-shape, isn't it?"

Even if it was kidney-shaped Ebie didn't want to hear about it and she moved out almost at once before she started screaming. She took a place then on Washington Square North East with a back door on the Mews. An enormous, high-ceilinged room it was, panelled walls, great windows through whose perennially dirt-stained panes the sun threw a stingy little light. There was an oil-heater to combat the strange blasts and drafts that wolfed around the baronial room on winter nights, whistled through locked doors, walls, closed windows, barred fireplaces. But a great cathedral chair, a vast sofa all bought at auction around the corner and ready to crumble at a glance, and her easel, drawing board, and reproductions of Daumier, Steinlen, Breughel, Grosz, and a few of her own sketches, pinned on the wall, gave the place quite an atmosphere. In fact the studio was so romantically Bohemian, so much the artist's dream, that Ebie did less and less serious art here and more and more discussion of it. The more commercial work she did the more of her old studies did she pin up with pride, and the more money she made the more she enjoyed the company of the arty boys and girls. "My God, but I was bright then," she reflected now with astonishment, "I certainly threw away a good brain when I started up with Jay and Lou's crowd." But of course it was her own fault, she knew that.

Further down the street the blue Plymouth drew up before an entrance labelled simply "BAR and GRILL." It was the tavern entrance to a somewhat mediæval looking hotel, whose time-and-soot-blackened façade was frittered with fire-escapes racing the dingy windows up to the ugly gargoyles on the roof. For Ebie this hotel too held certain associations and for a minute she looked out of the car thoughtfully at it, wondering whether to rouse these sleeping memories. Even on a bright noon like this the BAR and GRILL was a sunless cavern, its dark oak wainscoting rising high to meet grimy black walls, its ship-windows covered with heavy pumpkin-colored chintz, so that entering the room you seemed at first in a cellar fog till a feeble ray of gray light from a window above the door permitted you to grope your way down the long somber bar. Once in you were in for no mere moment, and Ebie, aware of this legend as she was, gave a slight start on seeing that same ruddy but glum man in the derby at the foot of the bar who had been there five years ago day and night, his coat always over his arm as if in the act of flight, a flight that never took place.

It was after twelve, the hour when the bar opened on Sundays, and the elderly lady residents of the hotel were without too much obvious haste taking their places in the grill-room, nodding and smiling to the waitresses, carrying their knitting and a slender volume of some English bard, anything to prop against their first Manhattan. If you ever had asked yourself "What ever became of that famous old suffragette who chained herself to the San Francisco courthouse? What ever became of that lawyer who saved Killer Mackay? What ever became of the girl who survived Niagara Falls? What became of the author whose one book sold so many million copies he never wrote again? What became of the first wives of these now famous men?" the answer would be—"Look at the BAR and GRILL." Here they dwell, as remote from life as if they were in Bali. Coming out at noon to the Grill they retreat at dusk into the even dingier caverns of the upstairs, grope their way through narrow silent hallways to their small dark respectable rooms. Seldom speaking to each other they are comforted by each other's presence and if in the night the lady who had once sung with Caruso should feel once and for good that wild pain in her left auricle she could always rap on the wall and thus summon the ex-eminent architect who had been freed of the charge of strangling a whole family twenty years ago near Albany.

A stained-glass window behind the bar gave a saintly glow to these resident lunchers as they sipped their drinks and dipped into literature. It was sip and dip, sip and dip, until cocktail time was proclaimed by the arrival of the little cocktail sausage wagon, and by that time the barriers that prevailed at noon would be brushed aside, privacies violated, discreet bits of personal information exchanged, letters from absent nephews or far-off celebrated friends read out loud while Music by Muzak played Songs From Cole Porter Hits. Another curious thing about these small, venerable, respectable hotels, there seemed no appeal here to the average customer. BAR and GRILL for instance, appealed to seemingly genteel widows and spinsters of small incomes because there was an air of musty piety about the management, a lady could be a dipsomaniac here under the most genteel conditions,—very quiet, very hushed, this place; then there were these tired flashes in the pan, the one-shot celebrities, and on the other hand there was a gayer younger group whose loyalty to the BAR and GRILL was based on the cheapness of its martinis. Over their simple dollar lunches (four martinis and a sandwich) this livelier set snickered at the old residents, whispered nifties to each other when the small very, very fat little old resident waddled in and was assisted with great dignity to a bar stool by two courtly gentlemen near-by who appeared unable to get a real hold on the gelatinous little creature and must scoop her up by handfuls.

The sight of the smart little blue car drawn up outside joined all groups in a common excitement, heightened by the unusual spectacle of such an uptownish and well-turned-out specimen as Ebie Vane coming in to this ancient cavern. Not that many of the residents did not have friends as splendid as this in other quarters of the city, but these friends were understandably loath to contact them in this dark hole. Who was she meeting—what brought her here instead of to the Lafayette, the Fifth Avenue, the Brevoort or one of the other more expensive and certainly more suitable rendezvous?

Ebie, after a brief glance around, took a stool at the bar and ordered a Dubonnet with a dash of brandy by way of eye-opener.

"What happened to Willie?" she asked the bartender, a beaming rosy young man, a chain grocery store clerk, she thought.

"Willie? Willie's been gone these five years," he said in a pleasant Scotch brogue.

The glum man in the derby with his cane hooked over the bar-rail, the fat lady, and the two gray-haired men drinking Scotch silently at the other end of the bar all were eyeing Ebie in the bar-mirror. She saw their eyes reflected between the mirrored stacks of bottles, their quietly questioning faces. She certainly must look out of place, there, the only normal-looking visitor in the whole joint. She looked around more carefully and then saw in the dim little stall in the corner where the livelier set was lunching the person she was seeking. She paid for her drink and walked over.

"Hello, mama," she said.

"Why hello, Ebie," said her mother pleasantly. "Sit down— these are friends of mine—I didn't catch their names. I was just telling them how perfectly ridiculous this article on Edgar Arlington Robinson was, so don't interrupt."

Ebie nodded to the others and sat down on the end of the bench beside her mother. The others, who had been sitting with resigned, unhappy faces, exchanging hopeless looks with each other, up to this point, now brightened. No good deed of hers was ever more appreciated than this simple appearance at the table, for her natty plaid suit and simple good looks gave point to her mother's endless anecdote as well as excuse to her mother's mere existence, something the group she was now entertaining had doubted could be done. To tell the truth the lively set had just about decided to give up Ye Bar, in spite of its twenty-cent drinks, because of Mrs. Vane. The three of them, two men and a girl, had been hilariously comparing notes on last night's party, burying their heads in their hands as they were reminded of the perfectly awful things they had said and done, and to so-and-so of all people; they had reassured each other that it didn't really matter since the so-and-sos had been known to misbehave themselves on occasion.

"But at Mrs. Whitney's!" the girl kept exclaiming. "At Mrs. Whitney's of all places! Oh, Foster, you shouldn't have! After all, you can't go around tweaking every Van Dyke you see."

"How did I know it was General Vanderbilt?" complained the young man, and then he sighed. "But what hospitality! Two footmen to each guest, pouring up your glass as fast as you could down it till finally they kicked us out. Why aren't there more homes like that?"

"You can't say anything, my dear," the other young man chided the girl, "after you pushed that dealer into the chocolate cake."

They buried their faces again, roared with laughter, reproached themselves, roared, and then Mrs. Vane appeared,

as indeed, she appeared to almost every guest in the Bar and
Grill at some inopportune moment, and for this reason was
known as The Haunt. A tall gaunt woman of sixty, she looked
like a witch, black eyes, dyed oily black hair, and strange
drapes pinned together somehow on her person with little
oddments of jingling jewelry and bracelets which served to set
off her amazingly long fingernails. As a wit-butt Mrs. Vane
had served her purpose more than well in Ye Bar and Grill,
but it was her flair for society that was ruining her and in fact
almost ruining the hotel. Mrs. Vane loathed the lonely
women of the hotel and yet a literary woman of violent opinions has to have someone to talk to, and frequently Albert,
the bartender, was too busy to listen. At those times she
would raise her lorgnette and examine the room for suitable
companionship. Today she spotted the intelligent young
group in the end stall and at once descended upon them.

   "I love laughter," she said by way of introduction. "May I
join you? I am so outraged by this article on Robinson,
Robinson, the poet, you know—let me read you what this
absolute fool has to say about him—hmm . . . let's see—
here . . . listen to this."

   She was in, the young lively set was crushed, and there she
sat, ordering her dry sherry, very very dry please, Albert, one
after the other because she was not a drinking woman and
could only take a dash of sherry or in cold weather a medicinal
dose of brandy. Of both these liquors she drank very little but
all the time. Her companions were imprisoned, their laughter
stopped, gloomily they foresaw hours passing with this sort of
thing and no decent escape. Ebie's entrance at least permitted
them to watch curiously the smart stranger at the bar, without
having to fasten their eyes on Mrs. Vane's witch-face. Then to
their amazement the handsome stranger walked up to their
very table and was Mrs. Vane's own kin and they respected
Mrs. Vane, then, and listened eagerly to her, lest she take their
pretty guest away. In a pause during which Mrs. Vane lifted her
glass to drink, one of the young men said, "Are you and your
mother in town for long?" hoping to draw Ebie in and freeze
mother out but it proved to be the opposite, for Mrs. Vane
hastily set down her drink and switched at once from reminiscences of Robinson to her own life story.

"Goodness me, young man, I've lived in New York ever since I found I couldn't get a decent psychoanalyst in Iowa. I've been here since 1924, off and on. A few years in Europe, of course. I met Freud. Speaking of Freud, Ebie, what do you hear from your father?"

"I got a Christmas card," said Ebie. "Nothing since then. It was just signed Father and Daisy."

"Probably married again," mused Mrs. Vane but the subject did not seem to interest her for she immediately launched into her life up to a treasured evening she had spent with Gogarty, the great Irish writer, who, she stated, definitely was the wittiest man she had ever had the pleasure of meeting. The young people looked curiously at Ebie, trying to fathom her connection with the weird old bore, and Ebie looked at her watch. Mrs. Vane described in detail the violent prejudices she had mentioned about George Moore, James Joyce, Bernard Shaw, and other great figures to the sparkling Mr. Gogarty on her great evening with him.

"What did he say?" politely inquired the girl.

Mrs. Vane's yellow face lit up.

"Gogarty? He didn't say a thing," she exclaimed triumphantly. "Not a damned thing all evening! Where was the card from, Ebie?"

"Greenpoint," said Ebie. "He still lives in Greenpoint. He still has the store, you know. Look, mama, how would you like to take a house in Connecticut with me?"

The inquiry served to silence Mrs. Vane's monologue as nothing else could. She lifted her lorgnette and frowned intently through it at Ebie.

"Connecticut? A house?" She was suddenly aware of the amenities for she turned to the three now embarrassed young people and said graciously, "I don't believe I introduced myself. My name is Mrs. Vane. You must excuse my daughter for bringing up personal matters at a public luncheon. What kind of a house, Ebie, do you mean a boarding house?"

"No, not a boarding house, nor a bawdy house, either," Ebie exclaimed, exasperated. "A house."

Mrs. Vane now rested her chin on her hand and studied Ebie seriously.

"I suppose you mean a salt-box. That's the kind of houses they have in Connecticut. Salt-boxes. No, Ebie. I don't see why I should have to live in a salt-box. Not at my age."

The girl saw an opportunity now to escape and nodded significantly to her companions.

"Mrs. Vane and her daughter want to talk family matters, boys," she said. "They don't want us intruding."

"No, no," protested Mrs. Vane reaching across the table toward her escaping companion, "it's my daughter who is the intruder. I had no idea she was coming in. Why didn't you telephone me, Ebie? After all, one doesn't just drop in on a person."

"I've left messages," Ebie answered, "but you never called back."

"Probably had nothing to say," said Mrs. Vane. "I see no reason for using the telephone just because there's one handy. If I had had something to say, naturally I would have called. Don't go."

She urged this last in a most hospitable voice as if it was she who had arrived early to snatch this prize corner and had graciously permitted these strangers to join her. The Lively Set, however, climbed over her draped knees with alacrity, the men with a last wistful glance at Ebie. As they hurried out into the little oblong of light that revealed the mouth of the cave Ebie heard the girl say clearly, in answer to some murmured comment from the man, "Yes, but don't you think a little too, too Harper's Bazaar?" All you needed to be Harper's Bazaarish down here was a tweed suit and a loud muffler, she thought.

"Who were they, mama?" Ebie asked.

"I don't know their names," said Mrs. Vane, with controlled ill-nature regretting her loss of public, "After all, Ebie, I have lived around here for some time. It's natural that a great many people should know me without my knowing them. Now what is this about a salt-box?"

"I was just thinking today," Ebie explained patiently, "that here we are, the only two Vanes in New York and we ought to see something of each other. I thought we might have a house in some little village the way we used to out in Greenpoint, and go there when we're sick of New York."

It sounded so perfectly foolish after she said it that Ebie was not surprised to see her mother twist her mouth into a wry grimace and examine her sidewise, with head cocked, like some curious old barn-fowl.

"I'm sick of New York, right now," Ebie added.

"I'm not," said Mrs. Vane. "I'm not a bit sick of it. Why should I want to live in a house again? I was analyzed out of a house once, I don't want to get back in one. Do you realize what a house means, Ebie?"

"I've got some money, that's all right."

"It isn't money," said Mrs. Vane with a certain amount of passion, "it's the grocery list, the bread-man, the coal-man, the garbage-man, the children."

"I haven't any children," Ebie said desperately.

"There are always children," said Mrs. Vane. "I've never seen a house that children didn't get into sometime or other. A salt-box. That's characteristic of you, Ebie. Typically, typically Vane."

As Ebie had never made any suggestion in her life that even approached the fantastic normality of this one, she let her mother's remark pass.

"We could have a station wagon and on a Sunday like this we could even go to one of those little churches, the kind you used to make me go to when I was little," Ebie said.

Her mother was still looking at her as if expecting a more actively violent evidence of insanity.

"The only reason I sent you to church was to have a little quiet in the house," she said. "That's the only reason people send their children to church. Besides, my property's here in New York. I take a great deal of interest in my property."

Mrs. Vane had used "the property" years ago as an excuse to stay in New York and Ebie recognized the argument now. She had in fact traded her house out in Iowa for first payment on a made-over tenement in New York, and this deal had obliged her to make her first trip to New York, a trip which turned out to be one-way. The "property" was in back of a bakery in the Italian quarter and was tenanted by impoverished artists and writers who seldom paid rent and who left word constantly at the BAR and GRILL for Mrs. Vane to please fix the hole in the roof, the rats in the wall, the boiling

water in the toilet-bowl, the two old panhandlers who slept
on a newspaper every night in the vestibule, the explosions in
the furnace, the roaches, the bugs, the boys playing baseball
in the court, and other minor matters. These little messages,
written on the hotel's pink memorandum slips as the calls
came in to the operator, were brought one by one by the lone
hotel bellboy, an elderly negro of sixty, to Mrs. Vane every
day at twelve when she reported for her first sherry in the bar.

"Goodness me, Albert," she would say, examining these
pink slips with the complacency of a star looking over fan
mail, "Two B says the girls up in Four A are streetwalkers and
wants them either thrown out or a carpet put on the stairs so
the tramping up and down all night is hushed."

"Better throw them out," Albert advised at this point.

Mrs. Vane was astonished.

"Indeed not, I shall throw out Two B instead. They're the
ones that are always complaining."

"You can't throw 'em out if they paid their rent," Albert said.

"That's the nice part," Mrs. Vane responded. "They
haven't. I can always throw anybody out I want to because
nobody ever pays their rent. Except Four A."

Even Four A complained one day. They wanted Mrs. Vane
to come over right away and see about the roof. They did not
so much object to the hole in it as to the bricks falling
through it. God knows whom they might hit. Mrs. Vane decided to regard this summons and, arrayed in her most splendid vestiges of rabbit and imitation leopard with a green scarf
wound round her head to set off her long hooped ear-rings,
she went over to her Property and rang Four A's bell. But
every time the door opened a crack and a girl peeped out she
cried out, "Go way, go way." Mrs. Vane, mystified, finally
went downstairs into the little courtyard between the bakery
and her house and made noises till the girl looked out the
window and again made frantic gesticulations of dismissal.
Mrs. Vane shrugged and went home, found a call waiting to
come over to see Four A's room at once.

"I was just there, my dear girl," she said. "You wouldn't
permit me to enter."

"Oh," said the girl weakly, "we thought you were a gypsy."

It was this very property that was now holding Mrs. Vane in the city and keeping Ebie from living a fresh wholesome family life in a simple village far from Jay Olivers and commercial art. It was not the first time her mother had disappointed her, but Ebie was still able to be surprised.

"My life is here, my dear child," said Mrs. Vane. She tapped her magazine pointedly. "I was just reading this article when you interrupted with this salt-box notion. I like to keep up. I read everything, no matter how mad it makes me. You ought to read more. You're always chasing about. You ought to read and find out what life is all about."

There didn't seem to be much more to say. Every few years Ebie remembered her mother and tried to revive the acquaintance but it was always the same. There was nothing to say to each other, and definitely no need of each other any more than there had been years ago when Mrs. Vane was the leading clubwoman of Greenpoint.

"Now, why," asked her mother, suddenly interested in Ebie's fingernails, "would anybody have fingernails like that?"

"Because I like them, that's why," snapped Ebie.

"I'm glad it's a matter of choice, then," said Mrs. Vane. "For a moment I thought it was doctor's orders. I must go upstairs and see if that little snip that does my hair has come. Good-bye, my dear."

"Are you having your hair dyed again?" asked Ebie.

Mrs. Vane looked pained.

"Not dyed, Ebie, restored. There's a great difference."

She rose and wafted away, her magazine under her arm, and Ebie gave up. She thought she might as well have a drink to revive her spirits and stood at the bar after her mother had floated into the hall.

"We met on the General out of Chicago," a voice said at her elbow. "I believe we have a mutual friend in Mr. Donovan, Mr. Louis Donovan."

Ebie started and drew back. Beside her at the bar was a middle-aged gentleman in the newest-looking suit imaginable, soft gray hat pulled jauntily down over a weather-beaten face now illuminated by an ingratiating toothy smile. Ebie didn't remember ever having seen him before.

"My name is Truesdale," he said, and lifted his hat briefly. "Here's my card."

Bewildered, Ebie looked at the card thrust into her hand.

"T. V. Truesdale," it said, and down in the lower left-hand corner, "Personally representing Louis Donovan, Pres. of the Louis Donovan Service."

"Well, for God's sake," said Ebie. It was quite true as her mother had pointed out, you never knew who knew you until it was too late.

VI

M R. TRUESDALE had been nipping in and out of the
Hotel Ellery for many years without attracting either
the respect or the interest of the management. He had a seventy-five-cent room on the first floor, that is the floor above
the Bar and Grill, and since this was the only seventy-five-cent
room in the whole place and was originally intended for the
colored elevator boy, its possession by Truesdale did not automatically endow him with great prestige. He knew this, of
course, and did not draw the manager's contemptuous eye by
entering the palm-riddled lobby, but instead scuttled in and
out by the delivery entrance in back, over ashcans and stray
cats, and whisked through the court up the back stairs to the
little dark hole over the kitchen. Steerage, that was what it
was, and he was used to it, you could hear the hotel machin-
ery throbbing all night, dishes rhythmically clattering, cooks
fighting, ashcans rolling about, milk bottles clanking, delivery
trucks backfiring, trunks galumphing up and down stairs, and
hearing this you felt you were really going some place, if only
into another tomorrow.

The fact that Mr. Truesdale was not a drunkard or woman-
chaser or a noisy guest with pets or violins, that sort of thing,
did not particularly enhance his position. Sometimes those
abstinences from the ordinary vices merely indicated the man
was a pauper or possibly a law-avoider for obscure and sinister reasons. Honest, yes. But even this was not too much respected ever since the time he had doled out his two-nights'
bill with a dollar in dimes, thirty-eight pennies and twelve
cents in postage stamps. The dollar and a half was paid, all
right, but supposing one of the fancier guests had seen the exchange offered! It would make the Ellery seem like a flophouse, and decent guests would run like mad.

The manager of the Ellery had a selection of greetings for his
customers. For the old gentlemen permanents he had a gravely
respectful, "Good day, sir. How's the arthritis today, sir?" Usually he leaped ahead of them to hold open a door and on icy
winter days looked out the door after them, calling out "Are

you all right, sir?" and none of the old gentlemen permanents thanked him for this apprehension that they would drop dead any minute. With the old lady permanents he was fatherly, humorous, kidding them about their flirtatiousness, complimenting them on their spryness, patting them a good deal, scolding them lightly for not wearing their mufflers, and pleasing them mightily by his assumption they were all feeble-minded. He was especially concerned over his old ladies, though they were a niggardly lot and wanted everything for their money, but he had sense enough to know that women were the ones with the money, old women, anyway, and nobody minds miserliness in guests that have it tucked away in a sock. It's when they don't have another cent that stinginess is a vice. The manager—his name was Mr. Lowry,—had another greeting for the neighborhood husbands who put up at the Ellery when their wives were away or their apartments being done over; these were business men, family men, with daughters in college, and Mr. Lowry treated them as equals; shaking his head over business, the fate of the Dodgers, European conditions, the damn Reds, and gravely making it clear that he too had a home, a family, a Buick, and a cocker spaniel like any other law-abiding citizen, he was not to be mistaken for a fly-by-night whippersnapper just because he was in the hotel business; with these equals Mr. Lowry often had a beer or two in the bar, and if they were really solid men he occasionally got drunk with them on a summer night; you could safely bet on his companions' good bank standing if you ever saw Mr. Lowry weaving about in glorious abandon; with such good men Mr. Lowry even permitted himself to get drunk in his own bar, but he never drank with a drunkard, that is an ordinary drunkard, and he made it a rule never to drink for pleasure. For Mr. Truesdale, who was relentlessly remembered as having paid his bill in three-cent postage stamps once, Mr. Lowry had a democratic nod, or more exactly a half-nod, unaccompanied by a smile or direct gaze, a preoccupied busyman's nod, but at least it was something, better than his brusque half-nod to debtors. Mr. Truesdale, however, stalwartly refused to accept any nod, marching past the manager when they did meet, with a stony face, though afterwards in the hall or in the privacy of his room his lips moved soundlessly in a brief imprecation. "Bastards! I'll get the bastards!" Mr. Truesdale, by throwing Mr. Lowry in the plural, indicated that he was not so much a solitary enemy as a mere private in an army of enemies.

The Hotel lobby was even darker and drearier than the Bar and Grill, not a whit brightened by its palms or circulating library stand that was rarely open for business and when it was only had twenty or less books. A stand of picture postcards, five cents each, showing the Hotel Ellery did not require any attendant inasmuch as the Ellery residents obviously were never tempted to advertise to the folks back home their present fortunes. Through an avenue of palms the guest strode or crawled to the desk for mail or bills, and here Mr. Lowry usually stood checking on the work of his employees, or handling the guest himself. For ordinary routine he placed himself behind the mailboxes and frowned out at his telephone operator or the room clerk as if it was his frown that did the work, not the assistants at all. Occasionally Mr. Lowry laughed, a booming fine laugh that made everyone feel better. He had his fond chuckle for the old residents, his good sport laugh for equals, but these were nothing to his laughter when he heard a genuine bit of wit, a good story or a snappy comeback. People were often telling him anecdotes or some merry fellow would toss out a good crack and Mr. Lowry laughed and laughed, that is if the guest had paid or was paying his bill. If the fellow was in arrears Mr. Lowry shrugged at the jest and muttered "Hmm. A wisecracker" sarcastically after him. But what could be wittier or more refreshing than the remarks made by a man paying his bill? Mr. Lowry had a dandy sense of humor and did not consider it his fault that nothing witty was ever said by a party that owed you money, or passed out a rubber check.

In Mr. Truesdale's scuffed Gladstone bag under his bed there was—and this would have astounded Mr. Lowry—a large index card with brief bits of information about Mr. Lowry and indeed in the same package of cards were snippets of news about other figures in the hotel, about Mrs. Vane, for instance. Mrs. Vane was listed, with a few personal remarks about her tastes, under "Automobile Prospects." Mr. Truesdale had been able, on occasion, to turn an honest dollar by selling a list of "Interested" Prospects to an auto company salesman. Mr. Lowry, it would have embarrassed him to know, was a potential toupée customer, being a self-conscious bald man instead of a debonair one. Under "Suggested Approach" Mr. Truesdale had jotted "Toupée would add dignity necessary to hotel manager besides making youthful appearance attracting younger clients, also relieve L.'s tendency to head colds." It can be seen that Mr. Truesdale, even when seeming to be unemployed, was in reality never idle, profiting by any overheard conversations as well as by his own sharp little eyes. Mr. Truesdale never forgot a face nor anything about its owner that he'd ever known. This was not really so remarkable since his bread and butter so often depended on this memory, aided by his dossier of tidbits. It was not that Mr. Truesdale was a lover of humanity or an observer of the contemporary scene, either. If he ever got two cents he could rub together, he often mused, he would rejoice in never speaking to anybody, he would shrug his shoulders when anyone asked for recognition and say, "I meet so many people!" He'd have the great pleasure of minding his own business and telling everybody else to go mind theirs. However, he was fifty now, and the chances of ever having two pennies to rub together were less and less. Twenty years ago he might have been optimistic over his little finger-hold on Lou Donovan. Now he accepted it as a bit of luck for today but tomorrow it might vanish. While it lasted he was playing it for all it was worth, never mind about that. There was always a chance of a bit of permanent luck. Within the last three days he'd made more money than he had in the last two months. He'd had a couple of tens and three fives in his worn wallet—in fact he'd gotten a new genuine pigskin wallet at a chain drugstore for ninety-seven cents, ten cents more with his initials. Lou had prescribed a decent suit of clothes, advanced forty bucks on it. Forty bucks for a suit of clothes! Truesdale hated to spend money on clothes, but it was an absolute fact that the trouser seat of his present suit was worn to such gossamer thinness that he had to rise with the utmost caution. So he went down to Division Street and selected a natty extraordinarily aquamarine-colored suit for fourteen-fifty.

"I wouldn't pay a penny more than twelve for this quality suit any other time," he told the salesman sternly, "of coss, as you see my bucket's out in my old suit so I can't bargain with you."

He bought a Paisley-patterned shirt, ninety-four cents with tab collar and came across a rare bargain in bow ties, three for fifty-nine, blue polka dot, green polka dot, and a more severe black polka dot, all absolute rayon. Shopping further at a "PRICES SMASHED! BUILDING COMING DOWN! FORCED OUT OF BUSINESS!" place down by Brooklyn Bridge he was able to pick up half a dozen colored handkerchiefs with "Lawrence" embroidered in the corner for nineteen cents. He could have gotten three with his own initials for the same money, but economy prevailed over egotism. Very few people looked at the name on your handkerchief, and if a manufacturer's mistake about the popularity of the name "Lawrence" could be profited upon, then by all means proceed to profit.

No doubt about it, the new outfit did give him quite a kick. He went to the stationers on Fourteenth Street and bought a new brief case, eighty-nine cents, a beauty, zipper style; he also bought a handsome fountain pen and pencil combination, one buck, a brand new set of index cards, and four bottles of ink named "Aztec Brown," "Patrician Purple," "South Sea Blue" and "Spanish Tile." These were business improvements, for he had decided to use each color on a person's dossier to denote certain things, the blue, say for automobile prospects, the purple for piano or radio possibilities and so on. He placed the ink bottles in a neat little quartette on his dresser-top and laid the two ties with his old one in the top drawer, and felt the first genuine thrill of possession he'd had in years.

"Of coss, it's only a beginning," he reminded himself.

On the Sunday he met Ebie Vane he paid his week's bill with a twenty and was rewarded by Mr. Lowry telling him a joke. He rewarded Mr. Lowry by saying calmly, as he picked up his change, "Yes, as I recall it that anecdote was quite a favorite with the old Maharajah—quite a favorite, as a matter of fact. He's told it for years."

He left while the manager muttered "So. A wisecracker, eh!" quite disgruntled at the rejection of his good-will offer. The good-will was not offered solely because of the new show of affluence on Truesdale's part, it was due also to the sudden series of phone calls, telegrams, incidental indications of a guest's rise in the world. Mr. Lowry was even willing to suspect that the three-cent stamps episode was the gesture of an eccentric rather than a pauper. But if he was prepared with friendly overtures, Mr. Truesdale on the other hand was not, stalking into the Bar and Grill with head high quite as if Mr. Lowry was merely a servant of the hotel, as was indeed the case, not the owner as he liked to imagine himself.

In the Bar and Grill this Sunday Mr. Truesdale found the conversation between Albert and the glum man in the derby going on about houses in the country, a conversation which Mrs. Vane's raised voice on salt-boxes had given the cue. The glum man wished to God he could get rid of his farm near Danbury, Connecticut, speaking of farms, and this one only raised chickens and taxes. If he could get rid of the place he'd take the dough and buy a forty-foot tub, a sea-goer, and by golly, he'd never get off it. He'd fish from Newfoundland to Bimini and the Keys, he'd go after every damn fish there was. He'd never do a stroke of work, he'd call in his insurance policies, he'd lie on every beach from here to hell-and-gone, and for food he'd eat fish, it wasn't bad, and he'd wash it down with beer, or, if he had it, some plain old Dago red. Albert, the bartender, however, never could see a thing in fishing. So far as he was concerned fish was only something that came in cans and could stay there. He had a lot at Northern Beach, Long Island, bought with newspaper subscriptions and a hundred bucks down, and if he saved some more he'd turn that over with his old Chevy and buy a double house in Bensonhurst, rent out the top floor, keep the bottom, make it pay for itself. Mr. Truesdale made a note of these two desires for his dossiers on each of the men, exchanged cards with the glum man, who was a Tompkins of some paper manufacturing company. Even while his ears were picking up this information his eyes observed Ebie Vane, the lady he spotted on the train with Lou Donovan, and the other fellow. She looked a darn sight better than she had the morning he saw her get off the train; he had marked her then as a high-class tart. Maybe he was wrong. She looked fresh as paint today. What she was to Donovan he could not figure out, whether a train pick-up, a regular secretary, an accidental encounter, or an old friend. Being in the Ellery Bar made the pick-up theory seem the strongest, since Donovan was certainly not the kind of man to park a genuine lady friend in such a dump. After a few minutes' observation, however, Truesdale marked the car, the mother, and the comments of the other customers indicating that Ebie was a stranger here. The old dame was her mother, that was made clear. Mr. Truesdale, always loyal to his many employers, observed everything with the greatest care in case there might be something here Mr. Donovan might care to know. No matter what her connection was with Donovan, friend or employee, there might some day be some complication that a word or two of straight data might clear up. No harm, certainly, in speaking up to her. His new turn of luck gave him confidence, for he was not one ordinarily to accost strange young ladies; on the other hand Ebie's gloom made her more receptive than was usual for her. She looked at his card and then looked over the man curiously. Lou's promotion activities she knew had strange wires out all over so this man was probably all right. Not that she cared much about the references of men she met in public places. The world after all was not a private club, thank God. You could talk or not as you liked with any stranger unless they started making passes or being a pest.

"I didn't know Mr. Donovan had a representative in this hotel," she said.

"I'm in and out here," said Mr. Truesdale. "The cuisine, of coss, is not of the best."

"What is the cuisine?" Ebie idly asked. "I don't eat here, thank heaven."

Mr. Truesdale pondered this only a minute.

"Irish," he stated finally. "Personally, I find East Indian cooking the finest in the world."

He signalled Albert for a beer.

"You're having Dubonnet, I see. May I suggest another with this time a dash of Campari bitters, a favorite of my old friend, the Duke of Malleywell, at one time a resident of Calcutta?"

"I'll chance it," said Ebie, with a shrug.

It struck her that the man might be a detective. He might be a detective for Jay's wife, using Lou as an opening wedge.

That was it, of course. The wife flying to New York with her mother, trying to get the goods on Jay, planting this fellow on the train even, so as to have further evidence. Probably right now he was checking up on Lou's alibi that she was an interior decorator doing his office, no connection of Jay's at all. She tried to remember what else Lou had said that day in the crisis. That she'd met him at the train. Well, this man knew differently so she'd have to fix that up a little if he should ask any questions.

"I dassay most of you New Yorkers think you know curry," said Mr. Truesdale. "But what do you get for curry here? A cream sauce with a sprinkle of the powder! No Bombay duck. No shredded cocoanut. A touch of Major Grey, perhaps, perhaps not. Depending. Have you known Mr. Donovan long?"

Ebie braced herself for the witness stand. She was, she decided, a very old friend of Lou's. She had gotten on the train in Pittsburgh, since he must have checked that. She was a commercial artist, since he must have checked that also, but was hoping to branch out in decorating, hence the opportunity to do Mr. Donovan's New York office. She had met Mr. Oliver for the first time on the train with her very dear friend, Mr. Donovan. She was now calling on her mother at the Ellery to discuss settling in the country.

"But why is it me that has to be on the spot?" Ebie's resentful second thought came. "Why don't I get the goods on Jay's wife, instead? But oh, no, it's me that's the criminal. It's me that has to save the home for Jay. Lou Donovan and me. The old marines."

Mr. Truesdale, using a little running sideline of comments on Siamese versus Ceylon dishes, as a siphon, managed to painlessly draw off Ebie's prepared information. The declaration of her friendship for Lou verified his feeling that she was the girlfriend, her mother explained her connection with the Ellery. The matter that interested him most, however, was the desire for a farm. It was a long shot that the lady who wanted to buy a farm would want to buy the very thing the glum man wanted to get rid of and indeed Mr. Truesdale had never known of a case where such a pat deal ever came through. But it was worth a gamble. A word here, a private tip to Tompkins, and there might be ten or twenty bucks in it for the informant. Mr.

Truesdale had no lofty notions of his value, a few dollars picked up here and there, no responsibility about further complications, no duties, no ties. Pick up any time and move on to the West or East, unless he had something that looked pretty steady like his Lou Donovan contact.

"A commercial artist makes a lot of money," said Mr. Truesdale, eyeing Ebie thoughtfully. "Maybe more than a decorator."

"It's too high-pressure," Ebie said. "You can't ever catch up. And I never save. No matter what I make."

"Best thing for a type like you, then, is to put it in possessions," advised her new companion, authoritatively. "Cars. Diamonds. Of coss, you ought to safeguard your future, roof over the head, and all that. It's a tremenjus comfort to a New Yorker to know he's got a little place out somewhere he can retire to if bad times come."

"It sure is," said Ebie. She looked at him suspiciously. Was this a quiet warning for her to get out of town? Maybe Jay's wife was out with a gun. Sometimes wives did get hold of a gun and the first thing they wanted to do was shoot down all the other women, never the guy that needed shooting. Maybe this little dick was tipping her off. Of course she had given him that lead about wanting to settle down somewhere in the country with her mother. He certainly picked it up fast, though. There was some reason for that. Calling her bluff, maybe.

"Of coss, it's a matter of finding the right place," said Mr. Truesdale judiciously. "You might want a showplace—or you might want a self-supporting sort of place. Of coss, if you aren't dependent on your own salary, if you have other resources to count on——"

"I haven't," Ebie nipped that one in the bud. Jay's wife wanted to see if Jay was passing out any of the family silver, evidently.

"I happen to know Mr. Donovan's business is very good so the decorating of his office is bound to be well paid," said Mr. Truesdale with a large gesture, as if the emolument was to come from his own pocket.

"If I should take the job," Ebie said cautiously, "I know Mr. Donovan would be generous. Particularly to such an old friend as I am."

She thought she'd better clear up everything now so she added, "Perhaps all Chicago people are generous, I don't know. Lou is the only person I know really well out there."

Mr. Truesdale blinked and then recovered himself. Ebie thought it was from surprise that she only knew Lou, but then reflected that he might assume she was out to get Lou. It struck her as funny. One on Jay and the little woman. She would not let Truesdale pay for her drink, which she gulped with considerable distaste for the overdose of bitters. She was relieved when the old bellboy came in with a message that if Mrs. Vane's daughter was still there her mother would like her to step upstairs and see her for a moment.

"If I should hear of a place in the country, I'll get in touch with you," Mr. Truesdale offered, affably. "Sometimes I hear things. Not my business, of coss. But sometimes I hear of things. I dassay I can always contact you through Mr. Donovan's office. That is, if you're seriously in the market."

"Oh, I am," Ebie assured him. "Indeed, I am."

"A genuine pleasure to meet you again," Mr. Truesdale said, bowing. "It would be a privilege to be of any assistance."

Ebie gave him a friendly nod and departed into the interior lobby. Mr. Truesdale paid for his beer and glanced around alertly to see what had become of his other friend with the boating desires. Mr. Thompson was at that moment seated in a booth having the dollar steak luncheon. He did not encourage Mr. Truesdale since it is one thing to mix at a bar and another thing at one's board.

"Just a word about that property of yours, friend," said Mr. Truesdale. "Is it in good condition?"

"Forty run-down acres, house leaks, garden gone to pot, chickens dying off," said Mr. Thompson readily, without slowing up the terrific eating pace he had set for himself, eating being merely a necessary stoking of the body to strengthen it for further drinking. "My wife sold all the decent furniture in it before we separated and the rest my daughter took when she got married so it's half-bare. Damned uncomfortable. I stay here mostly but there's the place. Yelling for repairs. Got a nigger out there, shiftless cuss, but he half-tends to it and makes a little, gardening."

"How much would you sell it for?" asked Mr. Truesdale.

Thompson looked more friendly. He thought a minute.

"Four thousand five," he said. "It would cost me that much to fix it up. I'd rather get rid of it."

Mr. Truesdale looked around.

"How much would it be worth to you to know of a good prospect?" he asked in a low voice.

"Not a damn cent," said his friend readily. "Unless they bought it."

"Supposing they bought it?" asked Mr. Truesdale.

"Sit down," said Thompson. "Have a beer."

VII

Mrs. Vane had a seventeen-dollar-a-week room and bath at the Ellery. It was a fair-sized room on the fourth floor front with two big windows and a respectable bath. Through these great windows the sun, at certain glorious moments around noon on certain days in December and late in the afternoon during the summer solstice, flooded the apartment across the street with its radiance and the grateful house at once flung the radiance back by reflection into Mrs. Vane's fortunate chamber. It was a time worth looking forward to, and the lady was always disappointed if a little errand kept her out during this magic interval.

"Oh, dearie!" she'd exclaim poignantly. "I've missed the sun today!"

The furniture was imitation maple, with a day-bed to give a sitting-room effect. This desirable effect, however, was at once offset by the piles of hat-boxes, bulging battered suitcases, and one open wardrobe trunk which took up most of the room and the huge Victorian walnut dresser with pier glass mirror, and marble top, an item Mrs. Vane had salvaged from a country auction somewhere and which she said was worth a perfect fortune if the right person came along. It had cost a small fortune already to have it crated and delivered and hauled to her room at the Ellery, that much Ebie knew.

"Is that you, Ebie?" called her mother. "Come in."

The old lady was in the bathroom, draped in Turkish towels, seated before the washbowl while the "little snip" from the next-door beauty shop worked the dye into the ancient scalp, with dabs of cotton. The snip nodded to Ebie and winked.

"This ain't a dye, you know," she said naughtily, "it's just a tint, if you please."

Ebie pulled up a chair to the bathroom door and lit a cigarette.

"Why don't you have it brown, mom?" she suggested, "it's more softening. I mean, if you must dye it."

"What do I want to look softened for?" irritably asked her mother.

"See?" said the snip.

The snip was a wiry little Irish girl with a big pretty doll's head, blue-eyed and curly-haired, attached to her small, tough little body.

"The old lady's got a bee, today," she whispered to Ebie. "Look out."

"I feel low, mom," said Ebie, "got any brandy around?"

"Now, Ebie!" upbraided her mother. "How did you know I had any? Besides I'm saving it."

"I sent you some not long ago," Ebie said defensively. "Where is it?"

Her mother heaved a sigh.

"I can't keep a thing," she said. "Look in the closet behind the shoe cabinet."

Ebie found the bottle and some glasses.

"Want some?" she offered the girl.

"A half one," said the snip. "I learned that in Ireland. I went back last year, and my dad thought it was awful I didn't drink. 'Come on, Maureen,' he'd say, 'a drop'd do you good, just a half one.' He'd put away a dozen half ones. I'd say, 'Why don't you take a full one, pop, you want it, and he'd say, 'No Maureen, I only take a half one, I'm no drunkard, my girl.'"

"So long as you're passing it out, I'd better have a touch," said Mrs. Vane. "After all it's my brandy."

"Soon as the old boy'd get a snoot full he'd start telling me the stories," said the snip, smacking her lips with pleasure over her glass. "All about the little people, not like your fairies, but little people with beards, dressed up with red shoes, all cocked up. There's a little man dressed up like that in Queenstown in the church, a real little one, he plays the chimes."

"Yes, and you never brought me back the colleen cape," Mrs. Vane remembered reproachfully.

"Your ma's always asking for a colleen cape like she seen once in the pictures. No good telling her the colleens don't dress that way. Like dad wanting me to bring him over an Uncle Sam suit, like the Americans wear."

"Never mind, get busy on my hair," Mrs. Vane ordered peremptorily. "I want to speak to my daughter."

"Fire away," said the snip.

"What's on your mind, mom?" Ebie asked.

"It's that antique," said her mother. "Look at that, Ebie. That's a beautiful thing, isn't it? You ought to know, getting around, what a thing like that is worth. It's genuine antique."

"It's old, but that doesn't keep it from being a pain," said Ebie. "What do you want with a thing like that? It looks like a ferryboat, all bulging out on the sides that way. All it needs is a whistle."

"That's the God's truth," agreed the snip.

"How do you know about antiques, my dear girl?" coldly asked Mrs. Vane, as the snip wrapped a towel around her head.

"My boy friend," said the snip.

"That upholsterer?" Mrs. Vane inquired, then added sternly, "I should think he would have asked you to marry him by this time, Maureen."

"Now, mama!" Ebie scolded. "Girls don't have to be getting married every minute. Times are different."

"I'm not an octogenarian, my dear," Mrs. Vane snapped.

"Sure, my boy friend and I figured we'd just live together," the snip giggled, with a wink at Ebie.

Mrs. Vane struggled to turn around and wither the girl with a look but it was too much with the firm hands now holding her head in a vise.

"A nice Catholic girl like you!" she exclaimed, outraged.

"What's the harm?" innocently asked the snip.

"I wouldn't do it, that's all," Mrs. Vane said, trapped. "I wouldn't do it. He'll leave you, sure as fate. And what if you have a baby?"

"I won't," said the snip.

"Leave her alone," said Ebie to her mother. "I'm the person to worry about. I'm your daughter."

"I hate young people," said Mrs. Vane sincerely. "You two seem to think any older person is someone to be mocked, and ridiculed. Neither one of you has a dime's worth of intellect. Ebie, about that tea-room you were planning . . ."

"Not a tea-room, mom," Ebie protested, now beginning to feel tired of the whole idea of the country what with everyone pressing her about it.

"Whatever it is, I begin to think it's the best idea you ever had," Mrs. Vane went on, surprisingly. "I'm only surprised it didn't occur to you before."

"You kicked it out when I suggested it downstairs," Ebie said.

Her mother dismissed this.

"I've thought it over. I think it could be a gold mine."

"A gold mine?" Ebie was startled at this angle.

"Certainly. Take that beautiful old dresser there. I have a flair for that sort of thing. I'd like nothing better than whipping about the country picking up a piece here and there. I'd make a mint."

"Like you do on your apartment house," jeered Ebie.

"Never mind about that," said Mrs. Vane. "I can do two things at once. Or I might even sell the place and put it into antiques. You run the tea-room, say by some old mill stream, and I handle the antiques."

Ebie got up.

"That's a perfect whiz of an idea," she said, "and I can see right off where you make a million, but skip the tea-room part. The place I want to get is to use for a home, see, a home."

"A home," Mrs. Vane repeated, puzzled.

"Well, skip that part, too, then," Ebie said with resignation. "I just made the suggestion because I'm fed up with New York. I'm tired of the works. I want to lie around the porch all day like decent folks and dig in the garden and read serials in the *Cosmopolitan*."

"Ebie, you're not yourself," said her mother, shaking her head. "But I'm serious. We'll find a place and I'll take the piece out as a starter and snap up a few bargains here and there and make a profit."

"Isn't she a one?" the snip marvelled, working away at the old head as if her manual operations over the brain centers were helping this wave of inspiration.

"It's the first genuine inspiration I've had in years," stated Mrs. Vane proudly. "I'm really excited for once."

"I guess the Ellery'll be glad to get that thing out of the hotel," said the snip with a nod toward the dresser. "You don't need a house, Miss Vane. Just park that thing on a lot somewhere and move in."

"When will you find out more?" eagerly Mrs. Vane inquired, ignoring the girl. "I'm really intensely serious about this venture."

Ebie felt weak and as if fate was pushing her into something
she had no right to fight. Once, in her early days with Jay
Oliver, she felt like slashing up her wrists and ending the
whole mess. Since then worse things had happened than mere
lovers' quarrels, and she only felt now like running away, not
poking her head in an oven or anything like that, just walking
out of her present life quietly with no fuss, no good-byes, no
quarrels. First her mother hadn't liked the country idea, all
right, then, that was out. Then that funny little man at the
bar, undoubtedly somebody hired by Mrs. Jay Oliver to watch
her, challenged her about the country idea again, as if it was
either that, or else. She didn't much care. But now her
mother was hopping on the idea. The antique gag would oc-
cupy the old lady, maybe, but she'd get over it when it was
time to really work on it.

"Don't let this old girl bully you into buying her a house,"
advised the snip jocularly. "I know how your folks are. Believe
me, I stopped mine. They write me from the old country and
they say, 'Maureen, we miss you, send us your picture and p.s.
you might put a bit with it as times is hard here.' So I send
'em pictures of breadlines here in New York and I say,
'There's me, third from the end, with the tin cup up high.'
That stops 'em."

"I don't blame you, Maureen," Mrs. Vane said. "You'll
need every cent you make for your baby. But Ebie here——"

Ebie and the snip laughed.

"Okay, mom, I'll look around," said Ebie. "We'll see about
the antique business when we get the place. I don't care what
you sell so long as I'm not in it."

"You'll miss New York, believe me," said the snip.

"The hell with New York," said Ebie and went away, even
more depressed than when she had come.

VIII

WHAT a week, what a week, Lou thought, yodelling "ya-ya-ya-ya-dee-die-dee-ya" in the shower bath, what a perfect honey of a week he'd had. What a town, New York, he thought, lathering his head with the piny-scented suds, what a beautiful, big-hearted honey of a town. No place in the world like New York. Everything had gone tick-tock, not a hitch. Call it the town, call it maybe a little bit Lou Donovan knowing how to handle it, too. That was the kind of guy he was, big town stuff. Little things floored him, but give him a big problem, give him a big town, the biggest, and he could swing it with his hands tied. People, for instance, the same. Little people, small fry, they only got in his hair, but give him the presidents, the managers, the thoroughbred women—(take Mary, for instance, his own wife)—and he knew just where to scratch.

He stepped out of the shower and doused himself with cologne. He had decided to plane out at one but first there were some matters of office equipment to settle (the receptionist really did turn out to have white hair, premature, sure, but it did give a high-class touch to the place) and arrangements had to be made to send Truesdale down to Maryland to look things over for him, quite sub rosa. The man could be valuable to him. Then there was the luncheon Florabella Cosmetics, Inc., was throwing for its officials and the press at the Ritz, at twelve. He promised to take a peek in and say hello to the boys before he took the car to the airport. Florabella was in the class with Elizabeth Arden and Rubinstein, and Lou was happy at being able to recommend such high-priced products to his clients. Most of them couldn't afford the prices wholesale but for Castles-in-the-Woods nothing was too good. Florabella Arbutus Soap and Florabella Arbutus Bathsalts in every bathroom, Florabella Make-up and Arbutus Tissue in every powder room, a fountain of Florabella cologne in the Tea Garden of the hotel. He'd already signed the order and it was a pip. A joy indeed on such a fine September day to have an unlimited treasury to dip into, not your own.

He whistled as he selected a gray tie with a small yellow dot, eight-fifty, a gray suit with the merest flicker of a darker stripe, one forty he paid for that suit, gray silk socks,—he looked all right, maybe a little tell-tale crinkling around the eyes, still he looked better than the run of men you'd meet. Nothing flashy, just quiet good taste. Mary had taught him that, she hated loud clothes, it was all he could do to sneak in an occasional pin-stripe.

"I don't know why it is," she said once, shaking her head humorously, "Lou always *looks* as if he had on a plaid suit even if it's the plainest dark blue."

He knew what she meant,—that he could give anything a certain air as soon as he put it on his back. Even in the old days when he paid twenty-two fifty for a suit he could wear it as if it was something.

In the florist's downstairs he selected a neat freesia for his buttonhole, ordered a batch of chrysanthemums, twenty dollars' worth, sent to the Major's wife with his card—ah, those were the touches that counted!—whom he hadn't met but who had just arrived on the *Normandie* according to his informers. He went to the telephone operator's desk to put in a call to Jay Oliver, find out if he was back yet from Atlantic City but he wasn't, so he called his Chicago office and told Miss Frye out there what to do and what to say.

"I'll be back tonight, but better tell Mrs. Donovan I'm not expected till tomorrow," he said, thinking ahead that he might want to date up Mrs. Kameray when he got in town, since she was already in Chicago. There it was, he thought, the difference between him and Jay Oliver,—he paved his way in advance for any little adventure, so he always had an out.

"The first Mrs. Donovan came in again," said Miss Frye over the phone. "She's still on your tail."

Francie again. You'd think you could brush somebody off after fifteen years, and true enough she hadn't crossed his path for ten years till this last month when she and her consumptive husband had hit Chicago. He had nothing against Fran, she was all right, only she made him feel so damned uncomfortable, always reminding him that once they did this and that, and there was always the danger of her spilling the beans to Mary. Why couldn't the past stay in the past quietly?

"What did she want?" he asked.

"Said she was broke," said Miss Frye. "You know. Wants to take the husband to Arizona. Hocked the car here for hotel rent."

"Arizona, hell, I'll bet he wants to get to Santa Anita," Lou growled. "That guy never learns. Dropped all his bonus money at Hialeah in two days, all right, so now he's set for Tia Juana and the West Coast tracks. No wonder he's broke."

"Well, she said she wanted to get him to Arizona for his health," Miss Frye said non-committally, "I don't know what's on the level with her. She's coming back in later."

"How much she want?"

"Enough to get the car out and a couple weeks' board. Sixty—seventy bucks."

"Seventy bucks is a lot of dough," said Lou. "Give her twenty and tell her I said scram. I'm no Rockefeller."

He was feeling too good this morning to be bothered by Francie still hanging around. He remembered there was a hotel men's convention at the Stevens this week and some business friends might be around.

"Line up whoever calls up for a little party tonight," he said. "I'll be in late this afternoon. Open house. You might check up on the Scotch."

"Mr. Oliver was in," she said. So Jay was home already. "He helped himself to the bar a while ago and left on a high note."

"If he calls again tell him to drop in around sixish," he said.

"He will," said Miss Frye. "He says he's got to check stories with you as soon as he gets in. What goes on there in New York anyway?"

"Never you mind," Lou laughed. Smart kid, Miss Frye.

He paid the telephone operator, a cute trick with bangs. On her mark every minute, too. A kidder, but no funny business. At least that was Jay Oliver's report. Jay never could see a telephone operator without trying to promote.

"Don't you look grand with the posy!" she said. "You certainly do look happy. Is it the flower?"

"Sure, it's the flower," he said. "What else would I have to be happy about?"

"If that's all it takes!" she sighed. "Maybe I ought to wear a flower myself if that's all it takes to be happy."

Smiling, Lou went back to the flower shop and ordered ten dollars' worth of red roses and a spray of gardenias sent to the hotel telephone operator.

"Not the blonde one," he specified, "the one with the bangs and the Southern accent."

"That's the one that likes sweetheart roses," said the boy wrapping a corsage in waxed paper standing near.

"All right, send her sweetheart roses, too," said Lou. "Let the girl be satisfied, by all means."

He wrote "Now, will you be happy?" on a card, signed it with his room number and "Donovan" and slipped it in the envelope. On second thought he slid a twenty into the envelope, too. That kind of thing gave him a big kick. He could never understand stinginess. These fellows that figured out ten per cent for tips, never tip unless you have to, and all that. All right, he had to figure close that way twenty, even fifteen years ago, but Christ, he was only making fifty or sixty bucks a week then. He was playing the horses then, too, and they certainly were doing him dirt all right. That was another thing. Some men never learned. Some men, like the punk Francie was living with right now, went on following the races year in, year out, losing and never knew when to stop. After three or four years of bad breaks he pulled out. Give him a wheel, the bird-cage, roulette, or even poker, at least there was some fun in the game itself. He usually managed to walk out with a little more dough than he went in with. But the horses—well, horses just didn't like him. The hell with them.

He walked up Park, holding his stomach in, feeling so fine that he was surprised to see so many glum faces about, glum-faced doormen in uniform walking tenants' obstinate little dogs on leash, grim nursemaids holding yelling little boys in sailor suits and little girls with a mere ruffle for a dress above little knock-knees, holding them by the hands but plainly wishing it was by the necks. What was the matter with people all so glum today?

He felt fine all morning, approved his receptionist, ap-proved the rug, sofa and chairs that had come for the inner office. Not much was really needed,—just a front, an address. He probably wouldn't see it more than two or three days a month, if that. Unless the Castles-in-the-Wood thing took more time than he expected. He thought he'd drop in the Florabella Show Room over on Madison and pick up old Florabella himself, otherwise Bill Massey, and go on to the lunch from there. The Florabella Show Room was a sweetheart all right, you had to hand it to these guys, they knew how to dress up a cake of soap till it looked like the Hope diamond, all encased in jewelled tinsel paper in a satin box, and the rest of the stuff the same, all displayed in a satin-walled scented showroom with beautiful girls in different flower-colored satin play-suits making you order more than you ever intended. Lou sat down on a dainty pink sofa while Florabella products, exquisitely mounted on little gold stairs, revolved slowly under a glass bell in the middle of the room. Bill Massey came in from the rear offices, which were a far cry from the elegance of the front, but nobody cared. The pretty girl who had summoned him for Lou smiled at them both and departed gracefully. Massey, a big Irishman built like a prizefighter, thick neck, big nose, red curly hair, looked after the girl frowning.

"Was she giving you the eye?" he asked.

"Why the hell not?" Lou wanted to know. "I'm a customer, ain't I? Doesn't the customer get any breaks around here?"

Massey sighed.

"I hire these girls for their sex appeal but I'll be goddamned if I'm going to let them use it," he said. "I got a problem on my hands, believe me. They make the business, but they aren't supposed to make the customer. After all some customers got women in the family. It wouldn't be the first time if a wife walked in right now and started bawling hell out of me for selling her husband a bill of goods. That was Nettie, I'll tell her to lay off, you got a wife."

"Ah, leave her be, she didn't give me the eye," Lou said.

"It was a double take if I ever saw a double take," Massey said firmly. He sighed and rumpled his red hair. "I give 'em a pep talk every morning. Just gave 'em one now. 'Get in there and fight,' I said to 'em. 'It's for Florabella, your old alma mater. But for God's sake, kids,' I said to 'em, 'slow up the hips once in a while.' I said, 'Can't you take your mind off it for say just an hour a day?'"

He went back to get his hat and Lou started talking to the

girl who had now come back and was going through her
little routine of passing around a silver tray of samples, prettily
boxed, stepping about prettily with the rhythm of the professional model, carefully toasted legs very appetizing against her
aquamarine satin play-suit with its advantageous little flare-
ups at front and back.

"Too bad you've only got two legs," said Lou.

"Thank you," she said courteously with a little bow.

"Don't thank me, thank God," said Lou. "Would you
mind loaning me the pair of 'em to pin up in my office?"

She giggled, and wriggled her foot in its silver sandal.

"Yes, sir," said Lou, "if you were a centipede, by golly, I'd
marry you."

"Don't be silly, I *am* married," she giggled.

Lou shrugged.

"Okay, you turn me down. How old are you?"

"Nineteen," she said.

"Hell, what would I be doing with an old hag of nineteen?"
he wanted to know. "You'd only be good for a couple more
years. I'd be out time and money. Make out I didn't say anything."

"All right, Mr. Donovan," she tittered. "I didn't know you
were looking for a wife."

"I'm always looking for a wife," he insisted. "I'm fresh out
of wives today. Too bad you're not my type."

Massey came back, hat on the back of his head.

"We're early for the banquet," he said, looking at his watch.
"Let's drop in the Men's Bar and I'll match you for drinks. I
could use a whiskey sour after the helling I did around town
last night. Remind me to bump myself off next time I go up to
Harlem, will you? Make a note of that, Nettie."

"All right, Mr. Massey," she obediently said.

Lou tucked a ten on her tray and lightly flicked her chin
with his forefinger.

"You're in," he said. "Next time I'm in town I'll shoot it
out with your husband. How big is he?"

"Six feet," she said, "he was a fullback at Dartmouth."

"Six feet? Then I'd better make friends with him," Lou
said. "The way I pictured him was about four feet two. You
can tell him it's all right. Come on, Florabella."

"You slay 'em, don't you?" jeered Massey. "A killer-diller. If you had as many of them around as I have day and night you'd be so sick of glamour girls you'd hunt down the plainest fattest woman in the world just for a thrill. Or turn nance. Why, I heard a story just the other day that I—me—mind you, was supposed to be a queen."

"Well?" Lou asked. Massey banged him on the shoulder.

"That'll be enough," he said.

"I don't have to flatter you, boy," Lou said. "I threw you an order, now I can sit back and insult you all I damn please."

In the Men's Bar at the Ritz they ran into Rosenbaum reading the *Journal* and waiting for some client of his. He offered to buy a round but Florabella insisted on matching for it.

"Christ, the match game is the only exercise I ever get," he pleaded.

Rosenbaum shrugged. He didn't know the match game so Florabella patiently explained it, you guessed how many matches the other guy had in his hand and if you were right it was a horse and when you got three horses you won the round.

"Listen," said Rosenbaum, "do you mind if I just buy the drinks and save us all that trouble?"

Lou and Florabella wouldn't let him, however, so he regretfully won and it was Florabella's check. When Florabella went out to see if the guests were coming to the luncheon yet, Rosenbaum drew Lou aside.

"I want to thank you for giving our family friend, Mrs. Kameray, that job," he said in an undertone. "She was very happy about it, and I think will be darn good at promoting. I was especially flattered that you took my recommendation without even bothering to interview her. That's confidence, all right."

"If you say somebody's all right, they're all right," said Lou heartily. "That's how much I think of your opinion, Rosenbaum."

The little rascal! She'd never even peeped to Rosenbaum about being out all hours with him that night.

"I think you would have been very satisfied with her if you had met her," Rosenbaum continued. "She has poise and charm—all the stuff."

"Hell, fella, I can't meet everybody that's recommended," Lou said heartily. "She may be Helen of Troy but when a guy's only got four or five days in New York he doesn't have time to meet all the people he'd like. You say she's okay—all right, then, she's okay."

Florabella came back and said they had to go in to their luncheon party. Nobody was there yet but as host he had to be there. And if Lou could only stay a few minutes he'd better come in now.

"Wish you could join us, Rosenberg," said Florabella.

"Rosenbaum," corrected Rosenbaum.

Florabella waved his hand carelessly.

"Rosenberg, Rosenstein, Rosenbaum—it's all the same, pal, so long as the old heart's in the right place."

"Call him Rosebush the way I do," Lou chuckled, but he ended his guffaw by clearing his throat for a sudden startled expression had come to Rosenbaum's face. Lou was uneasily aware of Rosenbaum's eyes following him thoughtfully as he went out with Florabella. He could have kicked himself for the break. It was just the kind of fool break a fellow like Jay Oliver might make, a dead give-away if the other man was even half-smart. From the reflective look in his eye Lou was rather afraid Rosenbaum was more than half-smart.

"Now why did I have to pull that Rosebush gag?" he lamented. A fine crack to set a guy thinking, all right. As bad as being too quick knowing a wrong telephone number. Lou was so annoyed with himself for spilling Mrs. Kameray's little Rosebush joke that he did himself no credit with Florabella's early guests. He stood around for a few minutes with the bunch, laughing perfunctorily as Florabella wowed them with anecdote after anecdote, shady limerick after shady limerick. Usually Lou jotted down any new gags in his notebook for future edification of clients, but today he only half-heard. Later, on the plane, he tried to remember some of them but couldn't think of a single one.

IX

I N THE dead of night wives talked to their husbands, in the dark they talked and talked while the clock on the bureau ticked sleep away, and the last street cars clanged off on distant streets to remoter suburbs, where in new houses bursting with mortgages and the latest conveniences wives talked in the dark, and talked and talked. All over the country the wives' voices droned on and on about the bridge prizes, the luncheon, the hollandaise sauce, the walnut surprise, the little defeats, the little jealousies, the children, the grocer, the neighbor, and husbands might put pillows over their heads or stuff their ears with cotton, pretend to snore, sigh loudly with fatigue, no matter, the voices went on and on, riveting the darkness, hammering into the night hush, as ceaselessly and as involuntarily as cricket noises.

Jay Oliver sometimes comforted himself with the thought of all those other husbands, and he forced himself to admit in all fairness that perhaps he would not be so dead tired when he spent a night at home if he hadn't been up to plenty mischief elsewhere lately, so that listening was a just penance for past defections. Flo's nasal voice went on in the dark from her bed on the other side of the night-table while she worked Helena Rubenstein's tissue cream into her relaxed pores and laughter lines; Jay could almost tell now by the changes in her tone whether she was working on chin or nose or throat. Tonight through his dozing there ran something about a Tossed Salad. Eleanor, it seemed, whoever Eleanor was, and God knows he'd heard enough about her so he should know by this time, Eleanor had insisted on a Tossed Salad. Everyone else had wanted Waldorf at the club luncheon but Eleanor had absolutely insisted on a Tossed Salad. Sleepily Jay pictured this Eleanor Whosis stamping her feet in the middle of the dining-room, throwing the Waldorf apple-and-nut concoction smack on the floor and screaming, "A tossed salad, or else! I insist on a tossed salad!" He pursued this melodramatic scene in dreamy fancy, half-asleep so that the images changed from normal size to dream proportions and

just as Eleanor herself had become a Statue of Liberty in a
dining-room as big as the Grand Central Station, in fact a
dining-room that was exactly that with trains shooting around
under the table on two levels, just then he heard another familiar cue, a phrase that on innumerable other occasions had
threaded Flo's bedtime monologues.

"If I could just set foot in that house, just once," she was
saying. So then he knew she was on her perpetual grievance
about the Lou Donovans, and the cool way Mary Donovan
kept her at a polite distance, and of course there's never anything a husband can do about this, even though he harbors
the same secret grudge himself.

"Oh, I've passed the place plenty of times, I know the outside," Flo went on mournfully. "It's all right, it's a nice house,
if you like Normandy Cottage style. Personally, I think Southern Colonial like ours is a lot prettier and more American
looking. And even if this neighborhood is falling off a little at
least it's nearer town and that's what I like. I mean I've seen
the place outside, but I just want to know for curiosity's sake
how she's fixed it inside. She's supposed to be so darned cultured and have such wonderful good taste and being a Harrod, my goodness, you'd think it was royalty the way Lou
goes on about 'My wife, of course, is a Harrod.' I guess my
folks are just as good as anybody's. My grandfather owned
the biggest store in Taylorville, I could have gone to Vassar if
I hadn't been fool enough to fall for you. I could have gone
to Europe. What I mean is that it seems funny that all of your
business friends have had us at their homes for dinner or cards
except the Donovans, and here he is supposed to be such a
pal of yours. I'd just like to set foot in that house, see what's
so wonderful about it that they won't let anybody in. Not
that she snubs me, she was just as nice as pie today at
Eleanor's, and she asked me all about the petit point I made
for Eleanor's dining-room chairs. I must say it is unusual,
whether Eleanor appreciates it or not, so we talked about
that, I mean Mary Donovan and I, and then I told her all
about our trip, and do you know she didn't know a thing
about Lou having an interior decorator to do his New York
office? I said, 'My yes, she met him at the train in New York,'

you know, that hard-looking girl with the pink veil over her hat, that Miss Vance or Vane or something."

Jay's eyes and ears opened so sharply at this last name that he felt as if they must have made a terrific noise. He was suddenly wide awake, and gripping the covers.

"Vance?" he said hoarsely.

"Well, Vance or Vane, anyway, believe me, Lou is in bad about that, I could tell by her expression," Flo went on complacently. "As soon as I mentioned her and how Lou said she was decorating the New York office for Lou, Mary Donovan pricked up her ears, so I knew something was up, and then she said, 'Oh, yes, that must be the one Uncle mentioned meeting with Lou. I'm sure I hope she does as nice a job on the New York office as Marshall Field did on his Chicago office.' Just like that, you know, very smooth, very easy, only you can't kid me. I could tell right away that I'd spilled something that was on her mind already. I could tell something was up right there at the station. So could Mama. Mama said the same thing, when she saw how funny Lou acted. She said, 'That girl's no decorator, she's Lou's girl friend.' "

"Oh, I don't think so," Jay's voice sounded so faint that Flo said, "What?" and he said, "I just said you might be right but I hardly think so."

This irritated Flo so much she sat right up in bed and raised her voice.

"You don't think so, oh, no, of course you don't think so, you men always stick together, you stick together instead of sticking to your wives, you know damn well Lou has a girl friend in New York, you're just afraid to tell me. Well, you don't need to, Mama and I are smart enough, we caught on. An interior decorator doesn't have to meet the customer's train, does she, if you ask me I'll bet she was on the train all along, probably came all the way from Chicago with him. Lou gets away with murder just because Mary is too refined to keep her eyes open. But you wouldn't admit it. You men are so darned afraid to tell anything about each other. Believe me, you don't even need to. Mary Donovan's no fool, though, she's on to him."

Jay lay very still, afraid to trust his voice, wondering irritably

what was the matter with him that he couldn't stand up for
Lou and defend him the way Lou had for him, and he felt
mad at Lou for showing such superior guts in a crisis.

"You won't admit she's his girl friend," Flo said resentfully,
"because you do the same thing, probably, and you're afraid
I'll find out. Well, listen, old thing, you don't hide anything
from me, at all, at all. I have a pretty good hunch about things
like that. Now what's the matter? Where are you going?
What are you getting out of bed for?"

"I'm going to get a drink," Jay said patiently, sliding his
feet into bedroom slippers. "I'm thirsty, that's all."

"It's that ham we had," said Flo. "We had ham at Eleanor's
for lunch, too. Baked with pineapple, like a casserole, and
mashed sweet potatoes with marshmallow whip along the
edges. And then the tossed salad and banana-almond ice
cream with strawberry sauce and fudge cake. I was so nervous
when one of the girls dropped some sauce and it nearly
stained the petit point seat but fortunately it went on her
dress instead. Eleanor says when she has men for dinner she
protects the petit point on the dining-room chairs by putting
an oilized napkin over the seats the men use so they can't
drop stuff on the petit point between their legs; of course
with the women their skirts protect the petit point. Mary
Donovan said they were the most attractive chairs she's seen,
and I offered to show her how to work them, so maybe she'll
ask me over there sometime. I feel kinda sorry for her, so big
as you please and so darned sure of herself, and all the time
Lou keeping that Vance girl in New York and pretending it's
business. Believe me, if I was in her shoes I'd have it out with
him, I'd march myself right along to New York next time he
went and I'd follow him wherever he went till I got the goods
on him. I'm going to tell her so, too, if she asks me."

"I wouldn't," Jay wanted to say but no sound came from
his lips so he gave it up and pattered out the bedroom door,
relieved to stumble over a hooked rug in the doorway so that
he could relieve his feelings by cursing and upbraiding the
stupidity of the maid, and even the mistress for overwaxing
floors and having rugs skating all over the place. The coun-
terattack successfully silenced Flo.

"I'm too tired to argue with you, Jay," she complained.

"I've been flying all over the country for the last four days and then the lunch today and I'm honestly dead. It's just mean of you to start something when I'm trying to get a little rest. Go on, get a drink, if you can't sleep, but let me get a little rest, for a change."

He heard her turn over and he drew a breath of relief. In the sunroom he found the drink he was looking for and it was not water either. He sat in the wicker chaise longue, smoking and sipping a brandy for an hour or two, gloomily reflecting on how miserably he was repaying Lou for saving his life. All right, he was a bastard, but what could a man do once his wife sets out to make a bastard of him? God damn fool, that's all he was, he muttered to himself a dozen times, fool of the world, ought to have a rousing good kick in the pants, serve him right. Lou, though, was the regular fellow, a real friend, a pal, the man who saved him when he was on the spot. Well, the least he could do was to tip him off about what Flo and Judge Harrod had told Mary. In a way, though, he didn't see any real reason why Lou Donovan shouldn't get in a little hot water now and then. Other men did. Other men got caught every time they tweaked a stenographer's chin or snatched a kiss behind a kitchen door. A fellow—even a smart one like Lou Donovan—couldn't expect to have everything work out like velvet every minute. It wasn't normal to go through life with never a slip-up in the arrangements. Lou was a fool to expect his luck to always hold. Still, he'd tip him off to watch his step as soon as he got back in town. He owed him that much.

X

A T SIX O'CLOCK who should show up but old Francie. She would! Lou, back in Chicago, was in the "office bar" shaving himself and getting a kick, as he always did, out of the elegant little hideout he had created out of a dirty old file-room. One of these days he'd put a bartender on the payroll, boy would that be something! More like a yacht than a business office! He had a small handmirror rigged up against a highball glass on a card-table; his coat and vest and gray shirt hung over the chromium chair-back. He was in his stocking feet, because he'd handed his shoes over to Mike the building bootblack so he wouldn't lose any time.

"Well, she's in again," said Miss Frye, closing the door to the office behind her. "What do I say now?"

What could anybody say?

"Now, how did she know I just got in town?" asked Lou. "I get off the plane at five forty and in fifteen minutes she's right on my tail."

"I told you," said Miss Frye. "I warned you."

"Did you give her the check I told you?"

"She wouldn't take it," said Miss Frye. "She said she had to see you personally. I couldn't say anything."

"What she want to hang around Chicago for?" groaned Lou.

"You men," said Miss Frye. "You want to step out of your past as if it was an old pair of pants."

"I wish it was that easy," Lou sighed. In a way it was a relief to have Miss Frye know about all his private affairs, even to that old marriage. She knew how to ward off trouble, then, and she was dependable. No sex there, nothing but hard-boiled efficiency. If he ever got into trouble, he could count on Miss Frye all right. It was worth sixty a week to him to know that.

"Anybody with her? What was the situation, anyway?"

"Well," said Frye, "she's still got the Ford; that means she's not so hard up. I saw her parking it across the street."

"How's she looking—the old girl, I mean?"

Miss Frye's sharp little pixie face went up, sniffing the air, hunting the right word.

"Tacky?" prompted Lou. "Weepy?"

"No," said Miss Frye. "On the make."

On the make. Worse yet. Miss Frye seemed to think so too for she shook her head sympathetically.

"I'll give her ten minutes," said Lou. "She can see I'm rushed, and then when the fellas come in it'll be easy to brush her off. That convention crowd will scare her off."

"Are you sticking around here all evening?" Miss Frye asked.

Lou shrugged. One thing Miss Frye didn't know and wouldn't if he could help it, was that he had fixed up a date with Mrs. Kameray for that evening. Let the fellows use the bar, let them have a good time there, do as they pleased with nobody in town to spy on them. He'd give them the keys, let Jay Oliver be host, and he'd slip off to the Stevens and pick up Mrs. Kameray, get acquainted.

"Maybe, maybe not," he said. "Anyway, if my house calls up I'm not back yet. Give me some cash, too, before you go. Get it in fifties."

As soon as Francie came in, Lou saw what Miss Frye meant. She had taken off ten or fifteen pounds since the last meeting ten years ago, and had a bunch of cornsilk curls sticking out of a black satin lid that looked like an opera hat with an extravagant veil floating around it. Her flaring plaid skirt was way up to here (her legs stayed good and did she know it, for she took one of the bar stools right away where she could swing them to good advantage) and if the swirl of her skirt showed more knee than was necessary they were good enough knees to justify it. A chiffon scarf was tucked around the neck of her black velvet jacket with polka dots to match her poppy-red lips and fingertips. She must have put in some stiff work on her face because it did not look old, not even thirty, only it had that desperate set look that a woman's face always gets when she's decided to show the world she's not afraid of it. It was a brave thing to see, but pretty grim as an invitation to the male. Or maybe he just felt that way, knowing Francie so well. It was a blind spot. Maybe she'd never look or be anything but five hand-to-mouth years, 1920-to-

1925, Newark, N. J., to Coral Gables, to Coney. God, he almost forgot that Coney Island rooming house! Maybe to him Francie would never be anything but Lady Bad Luck. Even if she hadn't had a thing to do with his bad luck he still thought of her that way because as soon as he broke with her his luck sprang high. Not her fault. Couldn't really blame old Fran. Still she was always Friday the thirteenth to him, and you couldn't laugh her off.

"Excuse the undress, Francie," he said, deciding to take it very natural. "Just got off the New York plane and rushing right into conference with some big restaurant men."

"Never mind the undress," said Francie, laughing. "An old married couple like us!"

Socko. Just like that. Always bringing up that they used to be married, that so far as that went they still were. Lou couldn't help shooting a look around the room as if Mary or the Harrods might be somewhere behind a curtain, listening, horrified. You'd think he and Francie had never even had the divorce to hear her talk. Just as if he didn't have Mary and the kid now and Francie herself had the punk, but Francie had always managed to take a line somehow that would embarrass him. He really had nothing against Francie—they'd had a couple of good years and three bad ones, but why in the name of heaven did she have to pop up right now in his life? Why did she have to take in Chicago after all these years? Why did she have to walk across his path like some black cat just as he was having the biggest break of his life? Sure, he felt sorry for her, his luck coming and hers going as soon as they broke up, but he'd been decent enough there for a while, sending her a check once in a while when she wrote, not as much as she wanted, maybe, but hell's bells, what was the matter with the punk supporting her?

It would have made him more comfortable if she raised the roof or bawled him out now, but instead she just sat staring at him, smiling and managing to remind him of old intimate things. It was indecent and he could feel his neck getting red. Undressing him with her memory, that's what it amounted to. He wished she would get down to brass tacks and say what she'd come to say—that she was broke again and she hated terribly to ask but this was just a loan, she'd get it back to him the tenth of some month or other. He braced himself for defense against this, he braced himself to remind her that he'd handed out a check twice in the last month to her, after all he'd better make it clear he was no sucker. He knew damn well it was the punk putting her up to put the bee on him.

"This is a new angle," she said, looking around the cozy little lounge. "Bar right next the office. What's the idea? Can't you wait to get to the one downstairs?"

Lou looked at his lathered face in the mirror.

"This is a convention town," he said. "Visitors like a little hideaway where they can drink and talk deals over privately. Have some fun without some big customer watching them. It's all good business for me. I had it fixed up last year."

Francie walked around and looked over the tables.

"Roulette, even," she said. "And look at those bottles!"

She pointed to the glistening array behind the Chinese-red bar.

"Reminds me of the time we had getting enough dough to buy brandy for that Senator who was going to let you in on a deal. He never came through, anyway, that was the joke. I knew he wouldn't all the time."

"Yes," said Lou quietly. "You always knew they'd never come through, didn't you, Francie?"

That stopped her. Without turning his head he felt her grow very still.

"I know what you mean, Lou," she said in a low voice. "If I'd had sense enough to believe in those wild schemes of yours we'd be together right now and I wouldn't be broke while you're riding high. We'd both be in the money. And we'd be—together. Like we ought to be."

Lou finished his shaving, folded up the mirror and put it in his bag on the chair. He didn't look at her because he knew well enough she had her handkerchief to her eyes.

"Still shave twice a day?" she said a little shakily.

"I got up early," he said coldly. The only way to stop this sentiment-fest was to get tough right away and he did.

"O.K., let's hear it," he said. "What's the punk let you in for this time? I told you I got big expenses on my hands, the kid's got mastoid trouble, Mary's had to cut short her cruise, the income tax people are after me. Money's mighty scarce."

He saw her stiffen and turn her head away. She was trying to pretend this was just a social call for old-times' sake, and if money came into it the idea was just casual, on the spur of the moment.

"Too bad about the kid," she said, and there was that again. All the time they had been together, he recalled now, she had wanted children—one, anyway,—and they used to fight about it. If he could put two hundred down on a car he could afford to pay for a baby, that was always her argument. His line was that he couldn't stand kids, they'd break up the marriage. And the crazy life they lived, rooming houses, a jump ahead of the sheriff or the landlady,—no, he said, no kids for him. So now he was crazy about the little girl Mary had presented him with. What was wrong with that? Was it his fault he had human nature?

"Like a drink?" he said. "Oh, no, that's so, you never could take it, could you?"

He was glad he could remember something that wasn't too personal.

"One drink and you hit the ceiling, remember?"

"I'm different, now," she said. "Sure I'll have a highball."

He went behind the bar and mixed her one. Where the hell was Jay Oliver or somebody, somebody to break this thing up?

"Look, do you mind not saying anything about being my ex?" he asked, trying to act offhand about it as if it hadn't been on his mind ever since she blew in to town. "I mean there's no point in bringing it up now. You're Mrs. Thomson now and there's a new Mrs. Donovan. You know. Might look funny."

She nodded slowly. Her eyes travelled around the room, studying the silver Venetian shades, and the nudes outlined in silver on the scarlet walls. Through the gleaming silvery curtains you could see the lake, blue and cold and smooth as metal.

"Pretty swell place," she said. "It's a wonder you don't stay here every night instead of going home."

"Lots of times I do," he said. "The out-of-town fellas are keen about it, naturally. Gives 'em a sort of private spot to drop in between trains, put in some phone calls, catch a few drinks, do business or line up a hot date. Like an old-time speakeasy, that's the charm of it. I had a crowd of advertising men here couple weeks ago and they were shooting craps up here till Sunday afternoon. Never left the place. Boy, was it a shambles! Shooting for five hundred a throw. I won three grand but I was the host so I had to let 'em take it off me."

She was sipping her drink and he could tell the way she went at it that she still didn't know how to handle it. Small-town, that was Francie, even to the devilish way she smoked a cigarette, little finger crooked, head cocked, like a stock-company vamp. The Girl from Rector's—that was Francie with a drink and a cigarette and her legs crossed. It had once rather tickled him, he recalled now with amazement. Maybe it was because he could in those early days measure how much he was learning in the world by what Francie was; she stayed exactly where he started, and once this had pleased his ego, now it embarrassed him to think he was ever that much of a hick.

"I'm planning to do a little branching out on my own," she said. "It's this way, Lou. I know you don't think much of Frank——"

"Right!" Frank was the punk she married.

"But honestly, Lou, he isn't well! He's got that bad lung and there isn't much work a guy with a bad lung can do. A little cold and he's laid up all winter. The climate's bad."

Now it was coming.

"Why didn't he go out West with his bonus money instead of dropping it all at Hialeah?" barked Lou. This was the same old fight. "I got no sympathy."

"Listen, Lou, the race track is all he knows. He can lie in bed and study it, and that's all he can do. Gee, that boy knows all there is to know about horses and tracks. You did once, but, honest, you'd have to take your hat off to him, if you could hear him. He knows every stable, he knows which horse likes mud and which likes sand; he has everything fig-ured out. Everybody in the neighborhood comes around wherever we are to hear what he has to say."

"Maybe they didn't hear how he come out at Hialeah," said Lou sarcastically. "Seven hundred bucks in two days."

"Lou, you know you can't do much with seven hundred," said Francie plaintively. "You got to have something to play with. If he'd had a thousand now——"

Lou laughed harshly.

"Seven hundred bucks is a lot of money, baby," he said.

"Can I have another drink?" Francie asked suddenly.

Lou looked at his wrist watch.

"These fellas ought to be here any minute, but O.K. Same?"

"Maybe I'd like it better straight," said Francie. "Or look, maybe you got some absinthe. I got crazy about absinthe in New Orleans. And then in Havana I always drank ojen."

"Been around a lot, haven't you?" said Lou. "You'd better stick to Scotch."

He poured two fingers in a glass. Every minute seemed torture. He didn't want to see her, no reason why he should have to, it downed him, somehow, brought back every bit of the old desperation under which they had lived. If she just would stand up, act as if she was going. Anything. And it made him suddenly see the perfect awfulness of Mary or the Harrods suddenly finding out about a previous marriage. Nothing criminal in it. But why in God's name hadn't he ever mentioned it? How would he ever be able to explain that?

"So your marriage turned out all right, then," Francie said slowly. "I read about it in the papers, of course. She was a somebody, I guess. What'd it say—adopted by her uncle, old Judge Whosis? Anyway I got the idea that you'd married into some class."

Lou started talking hastily, trying to keep her off this tack. He talked about the new house in Winnetka, how the decorator soaked him, how the electrical fixtures alone cost ten thousand, it was criminal, but in this business you had to make a show, entertain the boys, put up a front. You had to look like big money to make it, a funny thing that was, and besides he dealt direct with the big shots, the presidents, the general managers, why only yesterday he lunched in New York with Major—well, not to mention names, but later on the world would be hearing about Castles-in-the-Woods, one of the biggest—Lou stopped as suddenly as he had begun, for in his anxiety to get away from personal matters into business he was making his business so prosperous that he was letting himself in for a bigger touch than ever. Francie, however, did not press it then.

"I should think those convention boys would go some place where they could get girls instead of just drinking here with no fun."

"I get girls for them all right, never mind about that," said Lou shortly. "Never let it be said! I date up a half dozen live numbers from the Spinning Top down the street or a couple of dancers from Giulio's Grotto. They drop in between floor shows over there and keep things moving. Most of them leave with a hundred-dollar bill stuck in their pocket. These guys are the real thing, you know, and do the babes know it!"

Talk to her as if she was a man, that was it! Forget the personal thing entirely. Don't let it get you!

Francie kicked her slippers off.

"I don't know why liquor always makes me do that," she said laughing. "All of a sudden I got to take my shoes off."

Miss Frye opened the door and Lou jumped.

"I'll betcha it looks funny coming in and finding us both with our shoes off," Francie giggled.

Miss Frye smiled uncertainly. Lou tried to signal her to try getting rid of Francie but Francie kept her eyes on him so he dared not try anything.

"Mike brought your shoes back, Mr. Donovan," said Miss Frye, and the dwarfed old bootblack crept in behind her and set the shoes down on the chair.

"Is there anything else before I go?" she asked.

"Can't let you go yet, Miss Frye, sorry," Lou said hastily. Good heavens! Leave him alone with Francie? God knows what she'd do. Cry. Scream. Anything was possible. "See if Mr. Oliver's left his office. Or try him at the store. Or the Drake. That's right. He might be at the Drake with old Whittleby. Tell him I'm waiting. And phone the café to send over canapés, olives, chips—get plenty of everything. There may only be half a dozen of us and there may be twenty."

"Some conference," said Francie.

Lou shrugged.

"Just a routine, that's all. All right, now, what's on your mind?"

And Francie plunged.

"I was figuring if you could let me have sixty-two dollars we could get the car out of hock and drive to Arizona next week," said Francie, all in a breath. "Don't say no, Lou. I know you've been good to me and I realize how you feel about Frank, but this time it'll work out. I'll leave him in Arizona with his aunt and maybe he'll get his health back. Then I'll go on to Los Angeles to pick up a job—I don't mean pictures, I realize I'm too old for that, but maybe in some church or something. They must use organists somewhere; you hear 'em all the time on the radio. After all, when you knew me first I was getting seventy-five a week there in the picture show—more than you made taking tickets."

If there was one stage of his life he wanted to forget it was his ticket-taking days in that lousy movie house in Jersey. Next she'd ring in the stuff about his being pin boy at the bowling alley when he was a kid, all the stuff he wanted to forget—not because he was ashamed of it, hell, anybody might have to work their way up the ladder, but the days it brought back were so wretched, days of being kicked around, days when he was dumb, too, afraid to speak out, even, just remembering them gave him an inferiority. Oh, sure, she'd have to bring all that up. She couldn't let a fellow be happy in his present. That was Francie for you.

"I was a darn good organist," said Francie. "You said yourself I could get more out of 'I Love You Truly' than anybody you ever heard."

Now the old organ stuff was going to come out, about how long she studied to be a movie organist and had that swell job just a year when sound came in and threw everybody out. It was too bad, sure it was too bad, he'd said so then over and over, day in, day out, but women and elephants never forget anything.

"I hear that in some of the high-class restaurants they've started using organists," she said. "So far as that goes I got my figure back now and might get a hostess job some place. Maybe in a night club."

Lou didn't say anything. If she thought she could compete with the glamour girls he wouldn't remind her how old she was. Two years older than he was.

"How do you make it sixty-two bucks exactly?" he asked. "Why does it have to be sixty-two?"

He was being nasty, all right, he knew it, but there was something about her coming in and hanging around this way that made him feel that way. Coming in, spoiling his wonderful week, his top moment, reminding him that once he was a small-town dumb-bell, taking the rap from everybody, afraid to call his fritter his own.

Francie fidgeted with the chiffon scarf.

"I figure a dollar fifty a day for food for the two of us, forty to get the car out of hock and we're set for about two weeks, long enough to get West. Something'll turn up in Santa Fe, maybe."

"You just might drive on to Santa Anita or Caliente, too, mightn't you?" Lou inquired softly. "Race tracks handy there, for the punk. And supposing you didn't have the car in hock at all, supposing you had it parked around the corner right this minute, you could put that forty bucks on a horse, couldn't you?"

She was trapped and she knew it.

"Okay, I lied about that," she said, looking down at the floor. "A person's got to lie about things once in a while. God knows you ought to admit that. Anyway, you're so down on Frank I can't talk straight to you. Honest, Lou, I can't be mean to a guy that's only got a year or two to live. If talking track makes him feel like a big he-man when I know damn well he isn't one—well, gee, I can't explain, but if you heard him crying sometime because he can't take care of me right——"

"You can't expect me to keep some guy just because you happen to be crazy about him," said Lou, and was sorry he said it right away.

Francie looked straight at him, very solemn.

"You know I was never crazy about anybody but you," she said. "You knew it when you walked out. You'll always know it. Frank was sick in the house and I was low—well, that was all there was to it. You got to have somebody. Look, Lou, take it this way. If it hadn't been for my marrying him, you'd have had to put up alimony. I ain't ever bothered you much, you got to admit that, I never let out a peep since you been married, not till now. I ain't bothered you."

Those "ain'ts" made him squirm as much as her sorrowful eyes. You'd think women would get over a thing after a while, but no, by God, they hang on to every damn thing in their lives, hoard every little ancient romance as if it was a Liberty Bond. He tried not to see how her eyes followed his hands as he buttoned up his shirt, and he reddened, knowing what she was thinking, that this was like old times, old times she was always remembering, and he was always trying to pretend never had happened. It was funny how a man was so ashamed of having cared for somebody once and funny how a woman never got tired talking about it.

"Sixty-two dollars is a lot of money, Francie," he said briskly. "Maybe not if you don't have to slave for it, the way I do. You can just go back and tell the White Man that Red Feather says if he had to pay the government what I do he wouldn't be shelling out sixty-two bucks to every mug that wants to put the bee on him."

Yes, and that was another thing that made him detest this whole scene, himself, and Francie and everything about it. The little reminder that he had ever had anything to do with a dame that could go for a down-at-heels mug like that dope she finally married. That was the kind of thing that got a man down.

Francie stopped swinging her legs and wriggled the toes in her stockings. Her silence rattled him. Then she spoke in a very low voice.

"You talk about your house," she said. "I've been past there lots of times. I've seen the baby. I've seen her, too. Mary."

Lou's blood ran cold. Had she talked to Mary? And the thought of the eyes watching him, watching him and Mary when they didn't know they were being observed. The sad jealous eyes of old Francie.

"Oh, I never went in," Francie said bitterly, as if sensing his uneasiness. "I never said anything to her. I just wanted to see, that was all."

Lou suddenly felt he could endure no more.

"Miss Frye!" he bellowed. "Miss Frye, where the hell are those things from the café?"

Miss Frye hastily opened the door and the boy from the restaurant was right behind her with a great tray of hors d'œuvres and a basket of tidbits to spread out in little silver dishes along the bar. Lou mopped his brow.

"Your house just called," said Miss Frye.

"Call back and say I'm expected on tomorrow's plane," said Lou. "And call the Colony. Maybe Mr. Oliver dropped in there."

"Okay," said Miss Frye and again Lou could not give her a signal because of Fran's watchful eyes.

The door to the office closed.

"So you're brushing Mary off, now," said Francie. "Through with her, eh, through with her, too."

Lou gave his necktie a furious jerk.

"Certainly I'm not through with Mary, too," he snapped. "What put that in that little pin head?"

"Staying here nights with all those girls," said Francie. "What kind of woman is she, allowing you to do that?"

"Allowing me!" Lou shouted. "How would she know about it?"

"Lying to her," said Francie. "That's one thing you never did with me. You thought too much of me for that, I'll say that for you."

Lou gripped the table with both hands.

"I'm not lying to her," he expostulated. "I'm merely saving myself explanations, that's all. Explanations take time and I'm a very busy man."

"You never did that when *we* were together," said Francie. She said "together" as if it meant everything. "Honest, Lou, you were happy with me, then, you got to admit that much, you really were happy. I used to call you 'pussy,' remember?"

"Every man that's called 'pussy' isn't the happiest man in the world," muttered Lou. "Can't you drop this, Francie, for God's sake?"

"We were never even separated," went on Francie dreamily, looking out the window over the lake, "except the time you went to Toronto about that advertising job and the time you and your brother went to Texas for that oil deal."

"I've never been in Toronto in my life," said Lou grimly. "And this is the first time I ever heard of my having a brother."

He realized what he had done the next minute, but it was too late.

"Oh!" gasped Francie, clutching her heart. She looked straight ahead for a second then carefully stooped over and picked up her shoes. She wiggled her feet into them silently. She looked pinched and stricken.

"Good Lord, everybody has to alibi once in a while just to save a lot of talk, that's all it means," Lou bumbled along.

Francie straightened her skirt out now and fussed with her scarf. She gave a little laugh that was like cracked ice in a glass.

"I don't know what could have been eating me," she said. "I knew you did a lot of things I didn't like, but I was perfectly certain you never two-timed me. That was the nice thing. I just *knew*. I used to say to myself, never mind how things turned out in the end, at least when they were right, they *were* right. A person has to have something to kinda go on, you know, especially. . . . The brother in Texas. . . . How dumb I must have been. It's a laugh. It was right when we were really crazy about each other, too. I—I—I mean. . . . Funny how you hang on to some things no matter what happens, then it turns out those are just the things you should have skipped."

So now she'd have to cry a little.

Lou scowled and folded his arms. Where were these fellows that should have come in now to save him?

"Snap out of it, Francie," he growled.

"Oh, it isn't that I care so much about that forty dollars," she sniffed into her handkerchief. "Maybe he would lose it right away like he did at Hialeah, but in a way it's your fault. I keep remembering that if I had believed all your talk about buying up hotel concessions, then selling them, and all those other wild notions of yours, you and I would never have split. Now I make it up, see, by believing what Frank tells me. I think maybe if I walked out on him it would be just the time for him to strike big dough just the way it was with you. I don't want to make the same mistake twice."

"You would compare a business genius with a turf tramp," said Lou sarcastically.

He kept himself from screaming at her to get the hell out and stop making his insides squirm this way. He felt like half a cent. He might as well never have made good since the movie house days. Francie could do that to him in just ten minutes.

"Here," he said, inspired, and rummaged through his pockets. "This is all the cash I can spare right now. The checkbook's in the safe for the night. This will help."

He put three tens on the table. Francie looked at it a minute without touching it, then suddenly brushed it on the floor and stamped on it.

"Say!" he blazed at her.

He was so surprised and indignant that he could say no more.

Just as unexpectedly Francie the next moment bent over and picked up the three bills, straightened them out carefully and put them in her pocketbook. He saw a nickel and an aspirin and two one-cent stamps in the coin department.

"Even if it was only a penny," Francie said wearily, "I'd have to end up scrambling for it."

She powdered her nose and fluffed the new blonde curls over her ear. At least she was going. At least that. Thirty bucks was enough to get her out of town. He could have given her more, he would have only she made him so boiling mad the way she got his ego down. It was a gift with some women. But he shouldn't get mad, not show it, anyway.

"So long, Francie," he said. "I'm sorry about things, but you can't blame me, considering everything. It's a tough world, some of us got the touch and some haven't, that's the way I see it."

"Got it all figured out, haven't you?" said Francie. "Mr. Dale Carnegie."

He saw she was looking at him in a sorrowful, still way, and he might have guessed something was coming, but somehow he didn't expect her to do this, fling her arms around his neck and kiss him wildly. It was the worst thing that had happened so far, and of course that was the exact moment Miss Frye chose to open the door and let some men barge in.

"Hot dog!" yelled Jay Oliver.

Lou pushed Francie away from him and tried to grin, wiping lipstick off his face.

"Will you look at old Lou," jubilantly cried Jay. "Damned if he isn't in conference!"

There were the two promotion men from Denver and the Canadian whiskey baron. They beamed and waited for introductions which Lou mumbled through, conscious of Jay's gleeful enjoyment of his embarrassment. Francie quietly picked her bag up.

"I'll be with you fellows in a sec," Lou said, trying to act casual. "I got to see this lady to the elevator."

"Thought you were having some babes in," said the Canadian.

"Oh, the babes will be along any minute," Lou reassured him. "Come on, Francie."

"Why do we lose this little lady?" Jay demanded genially. "What's the matter with keeping her here for a little drinkie or two? Or is she your private property, Lou you old rascal?"

"No," said Lou, "only she's got to——"

His eyes fell before Francie's sardonic smile.

"Look, you can stick around, can't you, Halfpint?" Jay caught Francie's arm jovially. "What's the matter with playing around for a while? We're all good guys. You tell her, Lou."

"Sure they are," said Lou with a sickening sense of defeat. Outside he heard the shrill giggles and scampering of the girls from the Grotto just getting out of the elevator and it sounded to him like the marines coming. He breathed a sigh.

"Ah, here they come. Here come the babes, now, no need holding you any longer, Francie, if you've got to go. The lads will have company."

"Ah, come on, anyway, and stay," urged Jay, thoroughly happy now that he sensed Lou's uneasiness. "Can't you stay?"

"Sure, I'm staying," said Francie. She yanked off the opera-hat lid and threw it playfully at the big Canadian. "I'd like to play with a good guy for once in my life. Set 'em up, Lou, let's get going!"

Friday the thirteenth, Lou thought numbly, trying to smile, black cat cross your path, new moon over wrong shoulder. Lady Luck. Lady Bad Luck. Okay, shrug your shoulders, take it on the chin.

"Don't I get any caviar?" complained Francie reaching for the tray. Lou passed her the caviar canapés.

"Angels on toast if you ask for them, sweetheart," he said easily. That was the way. Chin up. Always leave 'em laughing.

XI

IN THE MIDDLE of the morning after a party Lou always got a craving for creamed marinierte herring and breakfasted on it at the Old Heidelberg, with a glass of beer. He felt depressed and it wasn't just the hangover, either. A little ammoniated bromoseltzer had fixed that an hour ago over at the Stevens Hotel where he had spent the night. Little things, little things again. He'd muffed the date with Mrs. Kameray last night, simply because, believe it or not, he was afraid to leave the office party last night for fear Francie would tell something she shouldn't. She'd been all right about not mentioning their old marriage, but what was so good about that discretion, after all? Her doting glances and embraces, the little clubby cracks about past intimacies, made the thing look even worse. They all ended up at Giulio's, but it was too late then to meet the little Kameray. When he called her up to explain she was sore as the dickens. That was all right, when he had time he'd smooth her down. She wasn't the type, as he figured her out, to stay mad. But it was simply plans going wrong that irritated him. And old Francie. She'd gone off finally with Jay Oliver and that was safe enough, he thought he could count on Jay even if she told him the whole business. Jay wouldn't tell, but the mere fact that he even knew was disagreeable enough. Well, he'd just have to keep reminding Jay of how he fixed up the Ebie business for him. On days like this the least little thing could set him up or throw him. The waiter fussing around, giving him the "Mr. Donovan" this and "Mr. Donovan" that, was soothingly satisfactory, but then there was the little encounter with old Grahame, the head of a hotel chain and friend of Judge Harrod. Lou had waved genially to him as he passed him.

Grahame, who was about to squeeze his two hundred and seventy-five pounds behind the wheel of a Packard coupé, actually got out of the car and waddled back to the restaurant door to shake hands with Lou. It was the warmest greeting he had ever given Lou and Lou's flagging spirits soared.

"Great seeing you, Mr. Grahame!" Lou said happily.

"Great seeing you, too," said Grahame in his panting breathless squeaky little voice, "and doing fine, now, I can tell by your looks."

"Thanks, Mr. Grahame," said Lou. "Nice of you to say so."

"Always glad to see one of our old bellboys make good in the world," said Grahame, still pumping his hand. "Good luck, Cassidy, and if you're ever around the hotel look in and say hello to the old crowd."

He had waddled back to his car, happy in his democratic little interview, before Lou could think of anything to say. Of course he really had only seen Grahame a couple times at the Harrods' and the old boy was over sixty and probably stone blind. Still that "Cassidy" was a burn. He was glad to see one of Grahame's managers, a fellow named Pritchard, having a late breakfast at the next table, so he could take out his wounded feelings. Pritchard was all right, he thought a lot of Lou and they'd had some deals together.

Today Pritchard, too, was gloomy.

"How do I know what makes the old boy say things like that?" he said, when Lou complained. "Imagine you or me being able to get away with a crack like that! 'One of our bell-boys'—can you imagine it! The only thing is that he isn't smart enough to have meant it as an insult."

"He's not so dumb," said Lou. "You don't pile up four million by being dumb."

"The hell you don't," said Pritchard. "Old Grahame's typical old-time success. When he was twenty-five his old man handed him the business. He married dough, and so now he gives a sales talk once a week on how kind hearts and coronets are all you need to get to the top. It's a pain."

"He could have been an ambassador," said Lou, still smarting. "He's travelled all over."

"Not all over. Only where there's a Ritz," said Pritchard sourly. "Why, that old bastard hasn't been off his fritter in twenty years. When he goes to Paris he drives straight to the Ritz and then he has his meals sent to his room till it's time to go to London. Same there. 'Where's the Ritz?,' he says when he comes out of his stateroom, and then they shoot him there and he says, 'Where's my suite?' and then he's done London. Why, he won't go any place there isn't a Ritz.

'Where's the Ritz?,' he says when he gets off the boat or the plane, 'take me straight to the Ritz.' If there isn't any he climbs back on the plane. Oh, sure. The brains of the business and all that. From the bottom up and bottoms up and all that."

"What's wrong with the Ritz?" said Lou. "It's a good hotel. Or wouldn't a bellboy know?"

It seemed funny now, or sort of funny.

"What's on your mind now?" Pritchard asked when Lou was silent.

"I was just thinking I might move to New York," Lou said reflectively. "I don't know. As soon as I get back home here something comes up, some little thing, that throws me. I'm not the small-town type. I'm at home in New York or travelling around."

"Chicago's a small town, then, all of a sudden," Pritchard mocked.

"I mean I care about things here, as soon as I get off a train, that don't matter any place else," Lou explained.

"Nuts, it's just your conscience," Pritchard said. He sighed. "Nobody has their conscience around much away from home. It's like a garage. It ought to be handy to your house. Believe me, I know."

Lou didn't encourage the confession he was pretty sure was coming up for the simple reason that it was his experience that men were always sore at you after they opened up their hearts. As if you'd asked them. He didn't want to find out. He never asked. But try and stop them telling you.

"Last night, for instance," said Pritchard, true to form. "What a mess that turned out to be."

"Yeah?"

"I took my wife and daughter, you know Barbara Lucy, you met her at the races, well," Pritchard took a gulp of beer, scowling, "here it was Barbara Lucy's sixteenth birthday so we took her down to the Chez Paris. I was dancing with the kid or trying to, I'm no dancer, and who should I bump into on the floor but Jay Oliver with a floozy."

Francie, thought Lou. So that's where they went.

"I was kind of high, you know how you have to brace yourself for the old family outing," continued Pritchard, wiping his moustache, "I'd have one with the little woman—the kid only has sherry—then I'd have a couple of quick ones at the bar. So Jay and I make a few cracks, just good-natured you know, on the floor, and end up switching partners, Jay with Barbara Lucy and me squeezing up the floozy."

So Jay didn't even have sense enough to take Francie to a little out-of-the-way spot. No, it had to be Chez Paris. Why he might even have had Mary there—that is, if Mary would ever have been willing to go out to night-clubs or for that matter, if he himself had been anywhere near her last night.

"Well, of course the wife was sore at Jay, because she knows Flo, and she thought it was laying it on for him to bring a floozy out in public like that. I was too high to care, and the kid got a kick out of changing partners on the floor that way, so I was squeezing up the floozy—I can't dance worth a damn, all I do is sort of march around and love 'em up a little if they're the type, and all of a sudden my wife prances up to the dance floor and calls Barbara Lucy off first, then she tries to catch me by the arm as I'm floating past with the floozy. Well, you know me. I was feeling no pain by that time, so the upshot was that the wife took Barbara Lucy home and left me with Jay and the floozy, and when I got out to Evanston I was locked out. So I spent the night at the Stevens. What the hell I do next I don't know."

Lou lit a cigarette, admiring the way his fingers hardly shook at all. Two up for old Francie, then.

"Wonder where old Oliver stands now at his house," was all he said.

Pritchard shook his head sorrowfully.

"He hasn't got a chance. Not if Eleanor has anything to do with it. I said, soon as we spot the floozy, I said, look, now Eleanor, I know you know Flo and I know how women stick together so far as telling each other any bad news goes, but skip it this once. Let's have a gentleman's agreement, that you don't tell Flo. So she said okay, I'm mad, she says, but at least I'm no troublemaker. So we had a gentleman's agreement she shouldn't say anything."

"Think she said anything?" Lou asked.

This was all old Francie's fault. Typhoid Mary if there ever was one.

"Listen, the thing was all over town by ten o'clock this morning," said Pritchard gloomily. "That's what comes of my wife not being a gentleman."

"I'll hear more about it from Jay, then," Lou said. You bet he would. He'd have to fix it up with Flo again. And Flo would bully Jay until he'd say he was only taking one of the girls home from a party at Lou Donovan's office, and then Flo would say, why I understood Mrs. Donovan to say he wasn't home yet. Or no. There was one salvation. Mary, his dear, dear wife, snooted Flo, thank God. Mary snooted all his business friends, Mary was too high-class to be a little helper to her husband and what could be sweeter than that? She never saw Flo except at some card club they all belonged to, thanks be to good breeding. He suddenly felt safe again and it was all because of Mary. He was glad now that things had turned out so he hadn't had the date with Mrs. Kameray last night. At least that was one thing he needn't feel guilty about. He thought now he'd better fix up the whole business before he went out to the house that night.

"I got a man from New York coming in at twelve," he said. "If you see your boss tell him his bellboy wants a new uniform, will you?"

"Ah, don't mind what that old fathead says," said Pritchard. "I swear to God I've worked for him fifteen years and he still calls me Mitchell. Listen, I was out taking some visitors through my brother's paper mill one day, by accident, when who should I see sweeping through the place but a Chamber of Commerce delegation led by old man Grahame. He didn't even know me. I spoke. He gives me the old handshake and then he says, 'Well, Mitchell,' he says, 'the working man has a better time today than when I was a young man.' I burbled something or other and then he says, 'Are you satisfied with your work here, Mitchell? Have you got a good foreman?' Hells bells, you're bellboy crack is nothing new. Forget it. You're in."

Lou laughed. The hell with Grahame. Next time he ran into him he'd let him have a little bit of the old stuff right back.

"If you see old Oliver tell him we're not friends any more," Pritchard called after him.

Back at the office the sun was pouring in the great windows as if nothing had happened. The false book-cases that formed the door to the bar looked innocent as could be, never for an instant hinting that a mere push of the button could make them swing open into a world of unlettered temptation. Miss Frye was busily typing at her huge oak desk, reading goggles perched on the tip of her sharp nose. Lou tossed his hat in the closet and got on the phone. He got the Building Superintendent.

"What's the matter with this water cooler? Get more ice in it, will you? Right away. Donovan's office."

"How do you know?" Miss Frye queried, looking up from her typewriter. "You haven't even tried it yet."

"Never mind, I go by hunches," Lou said.

Miss Frye looked him over thoughtfully.

"So that's the way it is," she said. "Maybe you should have gone to a Turkish bath."

Lou made an impatient gesture.

"Don't argue with me, Miss Frye," he begged. "I got things on my mind. What's new?"

He went to his own desk, a large kidney-shaped handsome affair in the corner, set between two long windows hung with heavy blue. This blue frame against the oak-panelled walls was a fine spot for a blonde, Miss Frye had often remarked, and had prophesied that one of these days that was just what would happen. Lou picked up the telegrams. One from Rosenbaum advising him to check up at once on Mrs. Kameray, one from the New York office girl advising that the office furniture was now in. Telegrams from his personal scout, old T. V. Truesdale, Personal Representative of Louis Donovan Service.

"PERSONALLY INVESTIGATED MARYLAND VENTURE STOP WHOLE COUNTRYSIDE ANTAGONISTIC STOP FEEL TOO COMMERCIAL VIOLATING SOUTHERN IDEALISM JEOPARDIZING EXCLUSIVENESS OF LOCAL CLUBS AND RESIDENCES STOP ALREADY LOCAL MERCHANTS PREPARING RESISTANCE BY RAISING ALL COMMODITY PRICES STOP PARTICULARLY HOSTILE TO ROSENBAUM STOP WOULD SUGGEST HE LEARN TO RIDE OR DRINK

BEFORE FURTHER SOUTHERN PROMOTION WORK
COUNTRYSIDE FEARS CASTLES WILL CHEAPEN LOCAL
REAL ESTATE STOP WOULD SUGGEST GOOD WILL SWING
THROUGH THIS REGION. SIGNED T. V. TRUESDALE."

"Sweet," said Lou and tore open the next one.

"HOW ABOUT DREAM ANALYZER AS FEATURE OF CAS-
TLES COCKTAIL ROOM? JUST MET UNUSUALLY GIFTED
ARMENIAN PRINCESS HALF EGYPTIAN ADAPTABLE TO
SOUTHERN SOCIAL LIFE ALSO READS CARDS HANDS AND
STARS AND DOES CLASSICAL DANCING AS POSSIBLE DIN-
NER FEATURE IN GRAND HOTEL BALLROOM. JUST A
SUGGESTION. SIGNED T. V. TRUESDALE."

"Isn't that just ducky?" Lou exclaimed. The old boy was
jumping right into it. And still another one.

"RELIABLY INFORMED MAJOR AND WIFE TIFFED OVER
SECRET ADMIRER SENDING TERRIFIC FLORAL GIFTS
WIFE MOVING TO AMBASSADOR GO SLOW IN CASE OF
DOMESTIC RIFT. SIGNED T. V. TRUESDALE."

"Would you mind telling me who that screwball is that you
took on in New York?" inquired Miss Frye, observing Lou as
he read the Truesdale works.

"He may turn out handy," Lou answered judiciously.
"Right now he's just found out about Western Union."

"They've been coming in every ten minutes," said Miss
Frye. "They don't make sense to me. Not unless you've got a
syndicate gossip column that I don't know about."

"I got no secrets from you, honey," said Lou, "except a few
little things I keep to myself."

There were three phone calls from Mary. That was funny
since she'd been told he wouldn't be in town till this afternoon. Somebody must have told her something. Something
had slipped up.

"Did my wife say anything about what she wanted?" he asked.

She hadn't. But she must be worried about something to
have made three calls in one morning. Mrs. Donovan wasn't
one to call up the office much. Lou frowned. A horrid suspicion crossed his mind.

"Look, Miss Frye, do you think Francie might have called up my wife? I'd like your guess on that."

Miss Frye gave a whistle, screwed up her little face in an intense effort at concentration, then shook her head.

"I doubt it," she decided. "She was feeling too good last I saw her."

"Where'd you see her? You left here before seven and she wasn't off the ground till around nine."

Miss Frye tossed her head.

"Listen, I go places like anybody else. Boy friend and I dropped in Chez Paris after the movies and there was the old girl with Mr. Oliver."

"What was she doing?" asked Lou.

"They were trying out a new kind of rhumba, looked like," said Miss Frye. "Mr. Oliver stood still and clapped his hands up over his head and she was doing the bumps."

Why in heaven's name hadn't he given her a couple hundred and told her to leave town? Lou groaned. He called the house. Better not experiment with any fancy lies if Mary was worried. He wouldn't tell the exact truth, of course, but he would shoot around it.

Whenever he heard Mary's cool agreeable voice on the telephone he had an exultant pride in having won her. There it was, sheer class and no mistake about it. It was in the way she walked into a room, in the clothes she wore, in her simple reserve, a man didn't need to say a thing, just "This is my wife" and his stock went straight up.

"Hello dear," he said briskly before she could say anything. "Got in so late last night didn't want to disturb you, so I parked at the Stevens. How's the kid?"

"That's what I wanted to ask you about, Lou," Mary said. "The doctor says she's perfectly well but a little rest would help her. So Aunt Felicia wants to take her with her to Arizona next week."

There it was, as usual. His wife and his daughter belonged to the Harrod family. Aunt Felicia and the Judge were in charge of them. He, Lou, was just a sort of chauffeur, so far as they knew his name was Cassidy. If he hadn't shelled out so much on his home and family it would be different. Then they could rightfully step in and say, "that bastard husband of yours doesn't treat you right, he's not taking care of you, but we'll see that you and the kid get three meals a day." Sure, then it would be all right. He'd still be mad, but at least they'd have a right. But no, they have to nose into a perfectly well-to-do happy family that he's looking after up to the hilt. But there was never any use talking to Mary this way. She never understood or, when she did, understood wrong, thinking he didn't appreciate family feeling because he himself never had any. She sympathized with him but said he must learn that other people did have strong family feelings reaching out even to fourth cousins and even to old servants of fourth cousins. He must recognize his narrowmindedness there as a forgivable fault but nevertheless a fault.

"What does the doctor say?" he asked after a pause.

"The doctor thinks it would be splendid. He thinks it will build her up."

"Too bad he couldn't have suggested it to me, then, when I paid the bill," snapped Lou, but never mind that, he mustn't get mad. "How long will you be gone?"

"Not more than three or four weeks," said Mary. "Of course Baby is perfectly happy with Aunt Felicia if you think I'd better stay here. I'll send the nurse along, of course, and she won't miss me at all, really."

"Oh, no," Lou said. "You'd be worried without her. I wouldn't want you to stay home and be worried."

"You're sure you'll be all right?" Mary asked.

"Oh, sure. I may not go out to the house. I may stay at a hotel in town."

There was a pause and then Mary said, "Oh."

"When do you want to go? I'll get tickets and make arrangements."

"No no, dear, it won't be necessary. Uncle will attend to everything."

The usual brushoff. Old Cassidy, the bellboy, mustn't try to muscle in on the Harrods' exclusive family affairs.

"You're quite sure you'll manage all right alone?" Mary asked.

"Oh, sure. You do when I'm away, don't you?"

"Of course, dear."

There seemed to be something else she wanted to say but whatever it was she hesitated. Lou was afraid to ask, for it might be something he didn't want to hear. She might explain what troublesome news had made her so unusually cold to him when he left town. It was better for both of them not to have these things out in the open. He admired her far too much to give her direct lies and it was not becoming in a person like Mary to descend to the nagging, niggling questions that wives like Flo were always putting to their husbands.

"That all?" he asked.

"Yes. . . . You had a nice time in New York?"

"Nice time? Listen, do you think I go to New York for a nice time? My dear girl, I'm on my toes every minute there. I've been working like a dog. New things in the fire. I'm dead tired."

"We'll have a quiet evening tonight, then. It's Aunt Felicia's Chamber Music night but I'll stay home with you instead."

Ordinarily Lou would have taken the opportunity to line up a date on the side since his wife was going to be busy. But now he thought it would be a good thing for the Harrods to know that when he was home Mary preferred his company to theirs. Let them know who was running the Donovans.

"Want some people in for cards?" he asked.

"No," said Mary. "I'd rather we talked. I'd like to talk to you alone. Some things that are on my mind. You know."

So there was something. So now it was coming. He stared out the window after she hung up, beating the desk with his fingers.

"Miss Frye," he called out finally, "I want you to get out all the Castles-in-the-Woods material, pictures, everything, and order all the Florabella samples you can get, and give me copies of the orders we've given out in the last month."

Miss Frye looked up surprised.

"I want to take them out to the house tonight to show Mary," he explained.

"I didn't know you talked business with your wife," she exclaimed.

"Tonight I will," said Lou.

XII

LATELY Mary had thought more and more about going to a psychoanalyst. Something was going queer in her mind, but the trouble was she was not having hallucinations, she was having facts. What could the doctors do about that? Well, doctor, she would say if she went to one of Them—(she always thought of the psychoanalysts as Them) I was perfectly normal for the first twenty-nine years of my life, I lived on a normal diet of hallucinations; an unusually intelligent and cultured upbringing enabled me to conduct my life decently blindfolded, but lately my mind seems to be shaking. Doctor, I think I'm going sane. Then the doctor, of course, would say, Nonsense, Mrs. Donovan, you can't tell me that an intelligent woman like you is beginning to doubt your insanity. Why, Mrs. Donovan, he would say, smiling indulgently, I assure you on my word of honor as a medical man you are as insane as anybody in this room. Forget it. You're tired, perhaps, you've been worried about your child's illness, that mastoid operation, natural, perfectly natural, you've overdone your music, gotten yourself in an emotional stage about it, that's all. These Truths, which you describe as disturbing your night dreams and your day thoughts, will soon pass. Why not go to New York on a shopping binge?—forget yourself, don't think about your husband for a few days, don't wonder about these problems; I'll guarantee you'll be your happy smiling insane self in no time.

The difficult thing about Truths was that, unlike Hallucinations, they could not be shared with anyone else. Truth came in little individual portions and that was all there was to it. For instance she had always been able to talk to people about her husband's shrewd business genius, his great reserve of wisdom, his generous heart, but there was absolutely no one with whom she could discuss the sudden blow of doubt, of genuine distrust, that had come to her. Doctor, she would say, though of course she would never in the world dare go to a psychoanalyst, Lou would be horrified, but just supposing she did, Doctor, she would say, can you suggest some harmless

powder to restore Hallucinations? Is there some dietary cure
for loss of complacency, is there some hypodermic needle to
inject self-deception?

For the life of her, Mary could not understand exactly what
moment had brought this unwelcome blaze of perceptiveness
to her life. It may have been a glance intercepted, a word overheard, but whatever the starting point was it had happened and
now everything she heard or saw in her day's routine had significance. There was his calmness, of course, in leaving her for
a week or two weeks, any time business called. She was calm,
too, about those absences, but she had thought till recently
that they were calm in the same way, with their unhappiness
locked up inside. Well, his was calmness inside, too, it seemed.
There was his lack of responsiveness, the cool kisses, the casual
love-making. She was not responsive exactly, perhaps, she too
gave cool kisses, but then that was all an impetuous man demanded. It was when he was no longer impetuous that the
anemia in their relationship became apparent. Certainly both
could not be passive. But what else could she be? It would be
more than she could do to confess that she could never sleep
when he was away and that she often got up in the night, quite
lost without him, and played phonograph records till daylight.
And she could never say love-words the way other wives did or
hold hands, but it seemed to her Lou would not have liked that
anyway. It had always seemed perfectly suitable to her and she
had assumed—to him—the man to be the lover and to voice
their love, the lady to be acquiescent and shyly passive. But
what did you do when there was nothing to acquiesce to, no
stormy advances to be passive about? Well, she would never
know, for she would never dare ask. Maybe someone could
teach her how to kick down her own reserve. Maybe, instead
of the psychoanalyst, she should go to a School for Etiquette.
Professor, she would say, I should like to know how to forget
good breeding. Is there a short summer course in forgetting
the gentlewoman's code? Is there a little home study extension
course in how to operate like a human being instead of a lady?
But then she did not *want* to shout her feelings to the house-
tops. That was the trouble.

Perhaps it was a surgeon she should consult. Surgeon, she
would say, how long would I have to be in the hospital for a

minor mental operation? How serious is it to cut out that little section behind the brow that separates what a Nice Girl Sees and Hears from What Really Happens? The night that the woman called up for Lou, for instance, and left word for Mr. Donovan to call her.

"Is this his mother?" the lady had inquired in a foreign accent.

"This is his wife," Mary had answered. "Is there anything I can do?"

There was a brief pause and then a "No, thank you" that sounded almost embarrassed. That was how she guessed he was already in town, though he had said he would not be in till next day. But she could not for the life of her bring herself to mention this, no, you could not deliberately accuse someone of deceiving you. She had wanted him to insist on her staying home and letting the baby go West alone with Aunt Felicia, but she could not propose it herself. And he had merely said, "How long will you be gone?" Then one of the women at a bridge party had declared Jay Oliver had a mistress in New York, and in a flash she was certain this was true of Lou too. But she knew she would never mention it, she could never ask him, she could never spy, whatever suspicions she might have would have to freeze up inside her along with the evidence.

Now that everything about him had new meaning Mary was astonished to realize that her aunt and uncle had never for a moment liked or trusted Lou. She knew they had reservations about him, but she had thought it was merely their disappointment that he was not their sort. She did not dream it was active dislike. He had been new to Chicago and no part of Aunt Felicia's Eastern background, either. He had seemed to Mary just the rugged hearty salt-of-the-earth American that her uncle had always publicly praised and privately patronized. She had discounted their coolness to Lou as just the natural jealousy of the man who took their darling niece away from them. And Lou's loud pooh-poohing of the Judge and Aunt Felicia she took with loyal understanding, as his perfectly unnecessary feeling of social inferiority. She assured him over and over that he was more brilliant, more admirable in every way than anyone in the Harrod circle, he mustn't have a chip on his shoulder about them, he must only understand that they were spoiled, fortunate people who could never match his self-promoted achievements. Now, suddenly, she saw how genuinely they despised him, when Aunt Felicia said, "Your uncle doesn't encourage divorce, my dear, but he often says that if you suffer too much from your mistake he would do anything in his power to get you free."

Mary was too surprised to be angry. It happened the very day after Lou had told her about the friendly meeting with the Judge on the train. She mildly spoke of this now to her aunt.

"Oh, then he told you about that," said Aunt Felicia with a peculiar smile. "The Judge didn't think he would want it mentioned."

Aunt Felicia meant something, and the obvious implication was that Lou was in company he should not have been. Mary dared not ask. Her aunt would have said no more, anyway. Instead they listened to the Simon Barere records that had just come from England, until time for Aunt Felicia to go to her fitting.

When Lou called up later in the afternoon to ask if she wouldn't like a little company for dinner, she did not remind him that they were to have a talk alone that night. It was another mark of change in him that he disregarded their old taboo against unprepared entertainment, at home. Unexpected social demands on him he nearly always took care of by staying downtown and excusing Mary from the picture. She had always taken this as consideration for her shyness and dislike of crowds. Now, he was considering only his uneasiness at being alone with her.

"If you like company, by all means let's have it," she said.

"It's the Olivers," he said. "You know. He's Whittleby Cotton. I do a lot of business with them. You've met her. Sure it's all right?"

"Perfectly," she said.

It was the night of Aunt Felicia's Chamber Music group, which she loved but always gave up when Lou was home. She knew she would be thinking of this and the peace of music all the evening when she would be straining to be gay or merely friendly with Lou's friends. Already her head began to pound with its constant ache of thoughts, feelings repressed. Sometimes she thought she would like to take off the top of her own head just to see what was really in it. All she was certain of was her own trained reactions.

"Everything all right, then," Lou said, with the faintest doubt in his voice. It was almost, she thought, as if she was expected to ask him the questions that bothered her.

"Oh, quite," she said.

XIII

THE HOUSE at Winnetka was really Lou's house more than Mary's. He had spent a great deal of time and money on planning it and furnishing it, and once done, he forgot about it and left it up to Mary to finish. First he wanted a bigger house than Judge Harrod's, where Mary had made her home before. Since the Judge, in spite of his superior fortune, was not a showy spender, it was fairly easy to get a bigger house. Next, he wanted a larger living-room, since the Judge prided himself on his large living-room, so Lou's was two feet longer. The extra floor used for Aunt Felicia's little concerts did not interest Lou so he skipped that. The Judge's fresh-air obsession with sleeping porches all over the back of the house, also did not excite Lou's envy. However, the Judge's bar and game room in the cellar was only half as well equipped as Lou's and had but one ping pong table, whereas Lou had two, both usually ignored for the bar. Lou, through his wholesale rug connections, had fine Orientals through the house instead of the worn carpeting the Judge deemed sufficient. And if the Harrods prided themselves on the thick stone walls that made their house so cool in summer, Lou countered this with air-conditioning. At least his wife was not going to complain of being deprived of former comforts, nor could she boast of having left a more expensive home. Lou saw to that.

There was a quiet and bare peace about the house that seemed to Lou, always happy in his connection with the Harrods, the very epitome of class. Mary loved her music room and the baby's sleeping and play quarters and whatever whimsicalities of taste she possessed were expressed here. The rest of the house was as impersonally well-done as any other interior-decorating professional display. Mary bowed to Lou on this as she had bowed to Aunt Felicia before on home decorating. She did like flowers and collected beautiful vases wherever she could and on drives with the nurse and baby through the country she would often stop to gather appleblossoms, pussywillows, or other decorative branches for the house.

Lou was almost prouder of Mary's lack than he was of her virtues. The thing he admired most in her and counted on the most for his own happiness was her reserve. He never had to listen to what went on in her little mind, and she never asked him what went on in his. If she cried about little things now and then, and he supposed she did, he did not know what it was and certainly did not want to find out. If he himself felt sunk he didn't want anybody asking what was the matter with him, and Mary, even if she noticed, did not ask questions. If he suspected she disapproved of something he said or did—he was forever doing something wrong about her aunt and uncle—all she did was to stay in her room with a headache for a couple of days. It couldn't have been a more agreeable relationship.

Another thing that had won Lou, besides her good breeding, her name, and her discreet passivity, a quality he'd never found in any other woman, was her youth. She was twelve years younger than he and it seemed to give an added piquant flavor to the conquest, as if her youth was a rare diamond that he was able to buy and show off. He spoke of her youth oftener than necessary because, to tell the truth, she seemed older than himself with her restraint and dignity, qualities he was still struggling to master. At twenty-one, when he met her, she even looked a good deal older. She was no beauty, even then, unless fragility could be considered a beauty. Whatever was pleasing about her appearance was certainly nothing he had ever admired before as seductive. Hers was no full luscious body, radiating tropic passion or even the natural vitality of youth. Instead her tall frail frame radiated nothing more than an ingrown anemic sickly spirituality. She had grown too fast as a girl, everyone said, but it was fortunate that her motions were sufficiently graceful to give an air to her lanky limbs. Her face was full, however, and her slender bones seemed well-enough covered. She had heavy drooping eyelids, enormous gray eyes, full wide mouth with fine teeth, an appealing quite angelic face, the luminous dead white skin striking against the short coppery curls. Her face and the mat of casual curls was so pure and childish it was always a shock to see her standing, see the long thin body, too long and too thin, the delicate neck, the incredibly thin wrists, the almost papery white fingers. The upper arm was rounded enough as were the hips and thighs, but the ankles again were unbelievably delicate. Up to the time he met Mary, seven years ago, Lou had been attracted by the very opposite of every one of Mary's bodily characteristics, it seemed to him. But then he fell for her and he found something quite devastating in her dreamy sexless charm. One thing he had guessed—was that here was a woman he would never tire of, because there was not enough of her to tire of. Nor would he ever leave a mark on her, so that would make him keep trying. That pale virginal quality would remain, and even after he had slept with her for six years—a not too satisfactory business because he was still afraid of her—he never felt that he had really made the complete conquest. Her eyes had no different glow than before. He learned something, and that was that while he had dismissed much more satisfying women from his life, the challenge of the too cool woman went on forever with him, as it did with many men, the virgin challenge, and sometimes he reflected that the great courtesans of the ages must have been like that,—cool, unmoved, perpetually unawakened, giving less than nothing to tease the lover into further bondage, instead of being the hot babies history assumed they were.

He came home about six, his brief case full of the material Miss Frye had gotten together for him. Mary was in the bedroom dressing and he went in and kissed her. As soon as he saw her sitting in her slip, thin shoulders bare, brushing her hair before the vanity-table, he realized with a shock how lost he would be without Mary. He still wondered how he had ever had the courage to go after her, how he had ever braved that other world for even a little while, but here was permanent evidence of his bravery, he still did not understand just how or why unless his very effrontery had pleased her. It gave him new confidence in himself just to see her, part of his home, like this. Whatever had been on her mind these last few weeks he was determined to override. This was not so difficult for him, because as soon as he came in the room Mary's doubts lightened, his vigorous presence threw such a dust of general confusion in the air that it was hard to remember what little headaches his absence had caused.

"So you're walking out on me," he said, grinning at her in

the mirror. "Leaving me to shift for myself while you run around with those dude cowboys."

The little reproach showed that he really did mind her going so her face lit up eagerly.

"It's only for Baby, dear," she said, "and even now I wouldn't go if you wanted me badly—I mean——"

"The kid comes first," he said firmly. "You and I don't count. It's the youngster. Wait a minute—I haven't seen her for a month—is it all right to go in?"

This, too, lifted a burden from Mary's soul, for it showed he was interested in the baby, and words of her aunt had insinuated that Lou was an indifferent father. She slipped on her robe and followed him down the hall to the nursery.

Baby was sitting at her small table on the porch eating her supper in the company of her two favorite friends, an enormous Easter rabbit on one small chair, and a black and gold Krazy Kat in the doll high chair. The nurse was straightening the bed in the nursery.

"She's still a little pale," Mary said, though the little girl was like her mother, naturally pale and underweight.

"Well, how's daddy's girl?" Lou asked and lifted her up.

"Please don't disturb her supper, dear," Mary protested, "and it always frightens her to be lifted up."

Lou put her down.

"I don't mind," said the child politely, "if daddy wants to play that way."

Lou laughed, embarrassed. Baby was a Harrod just as Mary was and even though she was only four Lou felt afraid of her quiet, gray eyes, he was uncertain what the Judge and Aunt Felicia may have taught the child, at any rate it was completely theirs, not his. Mary stroked her head, copper-curled like her own.

"Perhaps daddy had better visit you in the morning when it won't make the little head ache," she said tenderly. "Nurse says company at night always gives her a headache."

Lou left the room while Mary gave some instructions to the nurse. That was the way it had been from the time the baby was born, there was no beating that situation, he knew that. Baby was Mary's, just as his business was his. All right, if it made her happy. But he was glad that none of his business friends saw how badly a good mixer came off in his own child's nursery.

"What about dressing?" Mary asked him.

Lou shook his head.

"No, hell, this is just a little home evening, we want Jay and Flo to feel at home, friendly, you know," he said.

Nothing could have alarmed Mary more than the thought of a friendly get-together with Flo Oliver, but she braced herself.

"I thought we'd have mint juleps," Lou said. "It's late for them but there's nothing like them for icebreakers. Have them down in the game room, see."

The new set of silver mint julep mugs was a Christmas gift from the Judge and always made a good anecdote, would show Jay Oliver that the old boy was friendlier to Lou than his attitude on the train would indicate.

"It's all right for me to wear a long dress, isn't it, dear?" Mary asked.

Lou was firm about that, though. It had been an informal invitation, Flo was scared to death of Mary anyway, and the only way to handle that was to show that although the Donovans had a little more dough they were not putting on any dog about it.

"I suppose bridge would be the best thing later," Mary said with resignation.

"No bridge," said Lou. "I've got a little surprise for the evening's entertainment. Leave it to me."

Mary was glad to. It was such a relief to see Lou bustling noisily all over the place again that she began to think perhaps the evening would not be so hopeless after all.

XIV

THE OLIVERS had started their fight at a brisk tempo at four-thirty—the hour when Flo had summoned Jay to Marshall Field's for ominous reasons—but by six-thirty they were running out of material and on the ride to the Donovans it looked as if there would be no photofinish at all, merely whimpers and "Oh, is that so?"s, and "That's what *you* think!"s, and "Oh, for crying out loud!"s. As the Donovan house hove into view there was one brief moment of complete rapport when both Olivers joined in a vast rage at the Donovans and a mutual silent vow to get stinking as fast as possible. Flo was looking singularly warlike in the brand-new gold-embroidered red evening dress she had bought that very day for the occasion, and had smartened herself up with one of the grimmest permanents her beautyshop had ever turned out, every curl seemingly made of purest iron. She was in the habit of using more rouge than was advisable and had gone to town this evening with a brand new shade, which Jay sorrowfully begged her to wipe off.

"Listen, everyone wears rouge," Flo had snapped back. "You don't like me in red, you don't like me in jewels, listen, I'm not an old lady, yet, I got a right to a little gayety."

The little ermine jacket Flo had purchased at the last minute had started the fight, since the Oliver bill at the store was already steep enough, and Jay didn't see why a little family dinner at the Donovans' should cost him three hundred dollars. Besides Lou had said nothing about dressing. He kept protesting about this point all the while he was putting on his dinner coat.

"Listen, dope, people like Mary Donovan always dress," Flo expostulated. "They don't say anything about it because they take it for granted. Or else maybe they think we're the type that wouldn't know anything about that. They give me a pain."

"Keep your shirt on," Jay said. "Wait till you're insulted, for God's sake."

"What's so special about that house, I'd like to know," Flo sourly observed as they approached the driveway. "I suppose they thought it would be a real treat for us to see their lousy place."

"You asked for it," Jay grumbled. "You've been bellyaching about it from the first time you met them."

"Oh, is that so?" Flo said.

"Oh, for crying out loud," said Jay. "You jump on me every minute I'm home, is it any wonder I hate coming home? I'll betcha there isn't another married man in town that has to put up with what I do every damn minute."

"That's what *you* think," said Flo and permitted herself to be helped out of the car. "You don't know how lucky you are."

The ice was not immediately broken by the homey spectacle of Mary Donovan in a knitted sportdress and Lou in loose collar and sport jacket of vivid green. Lou had spotted the magnificent spectacle of Flo in trailing red taffeta and ermine as she got out of the car and he groaned.

"How nice of you to dress!" Mary said. "You needn't have, of course, but——"

"Well, we did," said Jay. He avoided the lightning look from his wife's eye, for even though it was she who had insisted on dressing he knew that would not save him from blistering reproaches for her own error.

"It's just us, you know," Mary said desperately as she took Flo into the powder room.

"Not really!" Flo said in such frank dismay that Mary was even more confused.

Downstairs in the game room Lou was having no better time of it, for Jay was in a state of profound gloom. If he had ever been a man to admit defeat Lou would have confessed that even a straight heart-to-heart talk alone with Mary about all of his past sins would have been easier than this craftily planned evasion of such privacy.

"What's Flo beefing about?" Lou jovially asked. He was getting out the handsome mint julep service and carefully making his preparations with the help of the fat black maid, Annie, who knew better than to volunteer too much help on this sacred chore of Mr. Donovan's.

"Nothing the matter with Flo," Jay said testily. "What's *your* wife beefing about?"

This was going a little too far, and Lou almost lost his temper. Mentioning his Mary and a battleaxe like Flo in the same breath.

"I was just wondering if anything came up about Ebie," Lou said.

"No, that's all right," Jay said guiltily, wondering just how soon Flo would be tight enough to say something about her own misconception of whose girl Ebie was.

"I was going to get her to do a little mural for the New York office," Lou said. "Not her line but no reason why she shouldn't take a whirl at it. Called her couple of times but Rosenbaum's office says they haven't been able to locate her for two days."

"Can you blame her?" Jay queried indifferently. The wives came in then, Mary looking unusually pale and skeletonic compared with Flo's flamboyant aggressiveness.

Lou hastened his julep ritual, keeping up a genial flow of conversation, all about how the Judge had paid a small fortune for the julep set and had taught him his own special way of making the drink, inverting the glass first over the powdered sugar, and so on, till Flo said, "Isn't it too bad your uncle couldn't be here to make them personally!"

"That's an idea," said Lou. "We may give him a call on that."

"We were hoping we'd have a chance to meet them tonight," said Flo.

"Do you mind making mine just plain Scotch, old man?" Jay asked. "I started on that and I'm afraid to switch."

"That's a good idea," said Flo. "I always get sick on juleps. They look wonderful, too, but I think it's the Bourbon. I never can take Bourbon."

Silently Lou nodded toward the Scotch decanter on the bar, and Jay happily poured a couple of drinks for himself and Flo. Mary was about to ask for her usual sherry but the collapse of the mint julep experiment was too much for her and to Lou's gratification she took a julep.

"I thought Lou was lying when he said you didn't drink, Mrs. Donovan," laughed Flo. "I guess you're one of those women who just drinks in the home."

"Oh, sure," Lou said. "Mary can carry quite a little package with nobody noticing a thing. You ought to get her to teach you, Flo."

Cooled her off with that one, he thought with satisfaction. He thought no wonder Jay goes for a swell girl like Ebie, anybody would with a hellion like Flo swinging the axe around every minute. He had thought this little friendly dinner would fix up the whole little unpleasantness between himself and Mary and between Flo and Mary, for Flo's wound at being so consistently snubbed by Mary was no secret. Instead it looked as if they were all going to end up in a free-for-all.

Jay and Flo helped themselves to the Scotch again, Jay getting gloomier and gloomier and Flo gayer and gayer. They seemed bent upon outdoing each other and in showing their host and hostess that so far as they were concerned the party, the house and everything in it was no treat to them.

"Go on, show Flo the upstairs," Lou urged. "Show her that mirror we got for the blue Bed-room."

"Is it an antique?" asked Flo.

"Antique, nothing," said Lou. "That antique stuff is nothing but a fad anyway. That's the trouble we had with Castles-in-the-Woods, Jay. Got a man down there, friend of the Major's, wants to load the whole place up with antiques. Bought out the neighborhood, I guess. I put my foot down. Modernistic, I say. Stream-line. Stick to your period."

"I think antiques are such good taste," said Flo, to Mary.

"Yes," said Mary helplessly.

"What's Castles-in-the-Woods?" asked Flo.

"Now you're asking something," said Lou. "After dinner tonight I'm going to show films our Baltimore man took of the whole property, then I've got colored pictures of our plans, the whole proposition. That's what Jay and I have been working over in New York when you girls thought we were playing around."

"I didn't hear anything about it," said Flo.

"I never ask about Lou's business because I know I shouldn't understand it," Mary said apologetically.

"Well, this will give you an idea," Lou said.

Dinner improved Jay's spirits slightly and when the wine came out Jay decided to make amends to Lou for his former rudeness by asking for one of those old mint juleps. Flo decided she would change her mind and try one herself. Lou no longer cared what happened and left the soup course to go downstairs again and throw a few juleps together, not such a delicate operation when performed without an audience, chipped ice, a couple slugs of Bourbon in each glass and some mint poked around in it for a second.

In the dining-room Flo complimented Mary on her china service, her linen, her cook and her complexion and Mary squirmed in her seat unhappily, not having the faintest idea whether Mrs. Oliver was mocking her or flattering her. Flo adjusted each compliment so that it would have a boomerang effect and fly back and hit Jay. All of the things she admired were things she too would have if it were not for Jay's indifference to nice things, his inferior business head which prevented him from making the money Lou did, and his never listening to his wife. If Jay had listened to his wife they would be living in a house bigger and better than the Donovans' and instead of Jay coming to Lou that time for the loan it would be the other way round. But oh, no, Jay was just like his whole family, a good-for-nothing don't-care lot, you couldn't blame them, it ran in the family.

"Oh, is that so?" Jay asked.

"You bet it's so," said Flo.

"That's what *you* think," said Jay.

They were really having a splendid time, but Mary could not know that and looked helplessly from one to the other, smiling politely till the full import of the remark would hit her, then looking with wide grieved bewildered eyes down at her plate. Lou, coming back bearing the mint juleps, saw that Jay and Flo were rattling down to their usual act, no harm in it, and was only annoyed that Mary seemed to be giving them the freeze. He thought resentfully that it wouldn't hurt once in a while for her to loosen up for his friends, God knows he loosened up to her crowd when he saw them; the only thing was he probably loosened up too much with them judging by the way they snubbed him. He was annoyed at her, too, for not mentioning the friends he wanted her to mention, so it left him with the clumsy task of working her contacts into the conversation.

"I read that speech your uncle gave at the college festival," Flo said to Mary. "Believe me I think that old boy knows what he's talking about. These foreigners trying to run this country. I could tell him some things about that."

"Why don't you give him a call, Lou?" Jay asked.

Lou looked him in the eye.

"All right, why not? Go ahead, honey, call up the Judge. He'd be interested in the Castles-in-the-Woods pictures. We're showing the models at the World's Fair next year, Jay."

"No kidding!"

"Why not?" Lou begged to know. "Jay, you old buzzard, you don't seem to realize this Castles-in-the-Woods is the biggest thing since Boulder Dam. For anybody that's getting as nice a cut as your company is out of it———"

"Maybe I'm not getting as big a cut as I should," said Jay, which was not quite cricket, as the little extra cut he turned back to Lou on these deals was strictly confidential.

"There's other firms, my lad," said Lou, dead pan. "There's Cannon. There's Lady Pepperell."

The gentle little threat straightened Jay out and he shrugged.

"When did the World's Fair thing come through?"

"I started it before I left New York," Lou said airily. "Put it up to the Major and Rosenbaum and now it's practically in. The hotel itself, in miniature, serving nothing but Chicken Maryland and coffee. And mint juleps. Then the working models of the whole project with leaflets and photographs. An agent in charge."

"You're a fast worker, all right," said Jay.

"It'll take a few more weeks to get set, of course," Lou said. "I'll have to run back to New York oftener."

"Oh," said Mary involuntarily.

"I guess you don't care much about Lou's work, do you?" Flo laughed. "I was in business myself once in New York, so I understand. I ran a tea-room."

"For six months," said Jay. "Lucky I came along and bailed her out."

"That's all right, I know what business men do in New York," Flo said roguishly.

"For crying out loud, you'd think all we did was chase, from the minute we leave this town," Jay said indignantly.

"That's all right, I can see where Flo might get that impression from some of these fellas," Lou said judiciously. "Take some of these fellas, they get to New York and make fools of themselves."

"It's the high buildings," said Jay. "You got your neck out from the time you leave the station."

"The point is that it's tough on the rest of us," Lou said earnestly. "We got a job to do, we haven't the time to play around."

"Oh, oh," said Flo. "I could tell Mrs. Donovan something about that."

Jay gave her a quick kick under the table.

"Do that, will you?" Lou said. "Give her an angle."

The loud voices, the wrangling, and the new doubts she had of Lou, made every moment seem intolerable to Mary. She had wanted to please Lou but she did not know how, and Lou with these friends was not the Lou she knew. The allusions they made to their common interests made her feel desolately left out and again filled with the odd fears Aunt Felicia had started. She made a desperate try to salvage the evening, when they started in to the huge living-room for their coffee.

"It's Aunt Felicia's night for Chamber Music, Lou," she suggested. "Perhaps the Olivers would like to go over there and listen to some Haydn."

"Say, now, doesn't that sound ducky?" Jay said.

"Shut up, dope," reproved Flo. "A little music wouldn't hurt you. You might learn a little something."

"It's all right with me," said Jay. "I can take it or leave it alone."

It was Flo's turn to give him a nudge.

"If you folks don't appreciate an invitation to one of the most high-class homes in Chicago, then the hell with you," Lou flared up. "If my wife's willing to take you into her Aunt's private musicale, by golly, you ought to be proud to go."

"I thought we were asked here," said Jay. "What's the idea? Trying to brush us off?"

"Now, Jay," Flo complained, "I don't see why we can't drop in the Harrods' for a while. I've never been there. I'd like to see the house even if there is music."

The fat colored maid produced brandy and benedictine, and Lou poured them out.

"Pardon me, just a minute," he said, suddenly. "Is there anything you have against my showing my friends the Castles-in-the-Woods films? That was my original suggestion. Apparently the idea bores you, my dear."

Mary blushed.

"No, no, I—I mean, of course, I'd like to, but——"

"That's all right," he said with elaborate indifference. "We'll go to your uncle's. A little music at your uncle's would be so much finer than your husband's business pictures. Oh, sure."

"It's all right with me," said Jay. "I can take anything."

Mary rose quietly.

"I'll call and tell them we're coming," she said. "I'm sure Mrs. Oliver would enjoy it."

"You bet your life I would," said Flo, loyally. "Personally, I'd rather listen to some good music right now than anything in the world."

"Personally, I'd rather sit around and get cock-eyed," stated her husband. "That's the way it is with me."

Lou was still looking with silent anger after Mary's proud exit when the maid called him to the extension in the hall.

"You didn't call me back," said a charming voice. "I am so cross. You're a naughty boy."

It was Mrs. Kameray. Lou was delighted.

"You don't like me," she pouted. "Here I am, a stranger, and you are too busy to see me."

Lou closed the door and talked to her in a low voice. When he came back he was beaming.

"Hold your hats, kids," he cried. "We're going back to town and fix up the Spinning Top."

"Thank God," said Jay.

Mary came back in.

"Aunt Felicia will expect us in about half an hour," she said. "She says it's always a pleasure to have guests who really enjoy music."

"That's off," said Lou briskly, still angry with her. "The Donovans have to meet some friends at a restaurant downtown. We can drop you at the folks', since that was your suggestion. I'll show the pictures to Jay and Flo at the office sometime where it won't bother you."

"Isn't he mean?" exclaimed Flo, happy always in a little misunderstanding.

"Excuse me while I change," Mary murmured, flushed and head bowed.

"Oho, she changes for the Harrods, then," Flo said triumphantly. "I knew that was how it was."

No one said anything while Mary was gone. Flo tinkered with the piano, playing "Begin the Beguine" with one hand. Jay tossed off a couple of brandies silently. They were sorry for him, Lou thought indignantly. They had stopped kidding him because now they saw how it was about his wife waving her fine family over him all the time, freezing all his business friends and brushing off his business interests, making a cheap tramp out of him by showing off her superior taste. Barely saying ten words during the evening. Making him a laughing stock before Jay and Flo.

"Doesn't Mrs. Donovan care for nightclubs?" Jay asked.

"They give her a headache," said Lou, and then as she came in he thought he'd add for good measure, "just the way my business does. And the way the Harrod family does me."

Everyone laughed.

"Jay, you drop Mary in your car and I'll take Flo on down," said Lou, as they got out to the driveway.

"Oh, but I'm going on down to the Spinning Top with you," Mary said in a low voice. Lou glanced quickly at her but her eyes were staring straight ahead. It suddenly struck him that she had been on the music-room extension when Mrs. Kameray had called and had not hung up.

"That's great," he said. Never let them get you. Ride it through.

XV

"MAYBE we'd better go to the Colony," Flo suggested to Lou. "Maybe the Top is too rough for Mary. Maybe the Chez Paris."

"The Top's all right," Lou said easily. Flo was trying to be a pal, show how well she understood a man's problems. The trouble with a "good egg" was that you had to talk to them all the time, you couldn't just drive along, thinking your own thoughts in silence, the way you could with a girl like Mary who wasn't and never could be a pal. Flo squirmed around in the seat to see if Jay's car was following.

"I wonder what Jay's talking to her about," she mused aloud and then chuckled, as if she and Lou and Jay were one kind and Mary another, instead of Lou and Mary being of a piece. Even if they weren't Lou preferred to keep the knowledge to himself.

"I sure feel sorry for her," said Flo sympathetically.

"Just why?" Lou asked, but getting it just the same.

"Oh, I don't know," Flo said. "She doesn't understand you at all. She doesn't get one thing about you."

"Maybe I don't want to be got," Lou said, sore, but trying not to show it. He wished it had been possible to ride with his own wife but of course that was out of the question. Even mad at each other and the slip-up on the Kameray dame's call he was sure they wouldn't have had to talk it out, anyway. Talking things out was what made people so sore at each other. They were madder at the things they said talking it out than they were over the original misunderstanding. He and Mary, thank God, could misunderstand each other and never have to speak of it. Right now he was appalled at the idea of Mary in the Spinning Top, but he certainly was not going to talk it over with Flo. Flo was the type that fifteen years ago after a few drinks would have welcomed a pass driving out like this with the other guy. Now that she was forty and bulging in the wrong places she took it out in a good heart-to-heart pal talk. Lou stepped on the gas to shorten this intimate little chat.

"No, seriously, Lou, you've never had a woman who really understood you," Flo went right to it. "I mean, you're ambitious, you've got a lot more guts than Jay, you get an idea and go right to town on it. Jay never has any ideas. He just does his job and sells Whittleby Cotton."

This was all okay with Lou but it made him mad to hear it from Flo, especially with the little sideswipe at Mary.

"I don't blame a man like you—I mean I *wouldn't* blame you if you had a little hideout in New York," Flo went on knowingly. "You're too big a man to be tied to one woman."

"I'm satisfied, never mind about that," Lou cut in.

"I mean your wife doesn't understand you the way I understand Jay," Flo explained. "There's no excuse for a man running around when his wife understands him like I do Jay, but in your case——"

"Why should I want a woman to understand me? Just to have the b'jesus balled out of me all the time?" Lou asked. He gave a short laugh. "That's why a fellow runs out; so he won't be understood."

"Well, if you're going to be that way," said Flo. "That's the way I'm going to be," said Lou, and that cooled her off till they got to the Spinning Top.

If Jay and Flo thought there was anything funny in Mary deciding to come along, as indeed there was, Lou was determined not to show it. He wanted to show Flo, damn her hide, just how Mary could be a good egg without making a fool of herself. A woman didn't need to get so fried she had to be carried home in order to be a good egg. She could be a good egg by just keeping her trap shut and letting other people enjoy themselves. She could be a good egg by meeting the husband's girl friends and not throwing a plate at them.

The Spinning Top was not one of Chicago's better spots; its chief charm for its customers was that it was not popular and was no place to take a wife. It was a jolly combination of seedy Hollywood glitter and old-time honkytonk. It was near enough to the station so that a busy man could nip over for a drink and the show between trains, say hello to the girls, maybe, and then, after he missed his train, could even be put up in the little adjoining hotel. The girls were good-natured, not bad-looking graduates of various exclusive burlesque wheels, and they sat around at the bar in little fig-leaf costumes, fluttering their blue-greased eyelids at strangers, and on dull nights at least keeping up a semblance of gayety by their perpetual squeals and chatter. It was said, with authority, that a favored customer could toss his coat to Marie, the hatcheck girl, for repairs while he drank, and he could even send her out to do his wife's shopping, if necessary, while he downed a few at the bar. Homey, that was the way a traveller described the Spinning Top, and it was fine dropping in a place where they didn't snub you, a place where the waiters all called you by your first name, and the girls kidded and scolded you and took care of you, and took every nickel you had. All right, it was a clip-joint, but if you passed out the manager himself took all your valuables out of your pocket to look after till you came to, so that at least nobody else would steal them. It was your own fault if you forgot next day where you'd been.

It was a dull evening tonight and the girls had listlessly walked through the dinner-show with little more than the orchestra and waiters for audience. Since their gifts were little more than walking under any circumstances the performance was not too much worse than usual. As soon as the Olivers and Donovans arrived, however, the place sprang into action. Two girls who had been slumping at the bar wrangling with the bartender now rushed to attach a cigarette tray and flower tray respectively to their persons; Tessie, the accordionist, struck up "Give My Regards to Broadway," a roguish reminder that on Mr. Oliver's last appearance at "The Top" he had obliged with a simple timestep to that tune. The headwaiter, a punch-drunk ex-fighter, who was making himself feel like a crowd with a series of short brandies, snapped to his heels, with an almost reverential bow.

"Good evening, Mr. Donovan," he said. "And Mr. Oliver. Well, well!"

He had fortunately learned to take no chances on calling the ladies by name, but men customers sometimes wondered whether the flattery to their ego of the bow and their names remembered was really worth while, since the lady was often not impressed so much with the regard in which her husband or boy-friend was held as by the deduction that he must spend a lot of money here.

Lou saw that Mrs. Kameray had not arrived yet and he had a moment to plan. It was foolish, he thought, to be alarmed at any meeting between Mrs. Kameray and Mary, since there was nothing between him and Mrs. Kameray. That is, nothing as yet. Nothing but a level look exchanged at their last meeting and her eyes dropping, an electric hint that when the time was right would be time enough. It was these little promises without words, not the conquests, that gave zest to a man's life.

"My goodness, those girls don't have much clothes on," whispered Flo.

"Some women get along better without clothes," said her husband.

Lou could tell by the lift of Mary's head and the cool look in her eyes that she was hanging on to herself, she hated the place, the noise, the gaudiness, the company she was in. But he was not sympathetic. She asked for it. When she got that frozen Harrod look he felt either hopelessly inferior or mad as hops. Tonight he was mad. He could do a freeze, too, in his own way. They didn't bicker like the Olivers but they knew how to give it to each other without an unpleasant word. She was continuing to be graciously attentive to the Olivers, with dampening effects on their spirits. When Jay used a bad word or Flo passed out an off-color joke Mary's polite laugh was worse than a rebuke. She had decided now to show Lou that these people were really not her sort and so she was giving an exhibition of correct, thoroughly irreproachable behavior that was more disagreeable than anything that could happen in "The Top." To punish her Lou motioned Jay to come over to the bar. More people were coming in and the girls' voices keyed a little higher with expectation, Tessie started moving around kidding the newcomers and the orchestra took over with a deafening, drum-thumping rendition of "Oh, Mama, please get that man for me," which the leader sang through an amplifier and his own nose.

"The Kameray's coming in later," Lou notified Jay.

Jay whistled.

"Boy, are you in a jam!" he exclaimed with delight.

ANGELS ON TOAST

Lou took a pack of Luckies from the girl, waved away the change for a dollar, offered Jay one.

"What do you mean—jam?" he said. "I got nothing to worry about. Just an extra woman, that's all."

Jay shook his head.

"I wouldn't trust that little baggage," he said. "She's looking for trouble and not for herself, either."

"She's working for me, that's all."

"I hope," said Jay.

"I was just thinking we'll have to look out for her, on Rosenbaum's account," said Lou. "Don't let the women ride her too hard. You know how they go for a new dame."

"Oh, sure," said Jay. "Only hang on to your watch, fella."

"Never let it be said," said Lou, and then he saw Francie and the punk walk in. He might have known that a fourth-rate joint like the Top would be about the punk's speed. He might have known, too, that they'd hang around town till they made trouble. Francie was dolled up to the gills in an olive green fall suit with a pair of supercolossal silver foxes swinging to her knees and a green Robin Hood cap jauntily tilted over the doll-hair. If you hadn't known her of old she wouldn't have looked bad.

"The little floozy's back in," Jay muttered to Lou. "Don't let her speak to me, for God's sake, or Flo will start throwing."

"Is that all?" asked Lou. "I would have said Flo was about ripe for a good hammer murder right now."

"Well, Mr. Thompson," said the bartender and reached in his pocket for some bills. "You're in luck again. She came in third today."

"Better than nothing," said the punk and took it. Thirty bucks.

So he was playing the Pimlico races from here. He glanced up while he was counting it and caught Lou's sardonic eye. Francie followed the quick flush on Thompson's face back to Lou and she gave a little gasp. It was the time to clear up this headache, for good, Lou thought. He would never be in a better position to do it, even with Mary and Flo watching, they could not hear the conversation above the orchestra din. Jay had quietly slipped out to the john.

"Hello, Francie," said Lou quietly. "Glad to see you're in the dough again." He looked over the foxes thoughtfully. "Spend much time at the Top?"

Francie was flustered, looking from Lou's impassive ruddy face to Thompson's pale sullen one.

"Frank won about forty dollars in bar checks here the first night we came here," she explained breathlessly. "We sort of stayed in town to spend them. No good any place else, of course. And then we got a little extra——"

"So I see," said Lou. "Well, I was glad to be of help."

He nodded to Thompson and started away but Francie grabbed his arm.

"Give me that thirty, Frank," she commanded the punk, and as he reluctantly drew it out of his pocket, she pressed it into Lou's hands. "Here's the thirty you gave me. Thanks."

"Wait a minute——"

"No, no, take it. Take it, Lou, you've got to. Feeling the way you do about it—no, no——"

He managed a laugh, for the sake of the ones watching, and took the money to keep her from yelling any louder. Thompson looked down into his drink and didn't speak to him at all. Lou wasn't jealous of him, how could he be when he hadn't the faintest feeling left for Francie except annoyance, but somehow every time he saw the haggard, weak little blonde face of his successor he wanted to take a poke at it. He did the next best thing.

"What kind of a gambler do you call yourself, Thompson?" he called over to him with an attempt at a grin. "With all your expert information I should think you could play more than two bucks. No use being a piker. Why don't you branch out?"

"I bite," said the punk bitterly. "Why don't I?"

"Lou, please—" Francie pleaded.

Lou brushed her aside and walked over to Thompson.

"Tell you what I'll do," he said. "Here's a hundred. If you can make that pay fifty to one, it's yours. If you can't you owe me a hundred. Of course if you're out of town there's no way I can collect. But——"

"Don't take it, Frank," Francie begged. "Don't take it, honey, he just wants to humiliate you."

"Nuts," said Lou, "he'll take it."

He did, too, slowly, but he took it without a word. Just stuffed the bill in his pocket with a queer look.

Lou started back to his table, with Francie still tugging at his sleeve, and to make it look better he swung her into the dance floor, pretending that was what she had asked him.

"All right, he took it," Francie whispered. "I know you've got that on him just like you wanted, but honest, Lou, the reason he acts so terrible with you is he's so jealous——"

"What for?"

"Oh, Lou, you know. He loves me, don't you see, and it hurts him to know I stay crazy about you, he's not a fool, he knows, I can't hide it, I'm so happy just this minute with your arms——"

Lou stopped.

"Thanks for the dance," he said. "As for the hundred nothing would please me more than to hear I lost it. Night."

He managed a big laugh again, as if they were kidding, but Francie's yearning look after him was no corroboration.

"What a pretty girl!" Mary said when he sat down.

"He can pick 'em," agreed Flo. "If he can't, Jay can. Kinda hard boiled, though, I would say, and certainly no chicken."

"I wouldn't know," said Lou. "Women nowadays can trick themselves out any age at all."

More people were coming in and the orchestra was playing louder, the crooner was going to town on "Tonight We Love" and Flo was blowing the little whistle the waiter left as favors to the ladies. Francie and the boy-friend were doing some fancy steps and whirls that would have finished off a healthy man let alone a guy supposed to have only one lung. Jay came back with an uneasy glance at Francie but she seemed bent on drowning her sorrows in the dance so he got back safely.

"Too bad you can't find a girl-friend like Lou's," Flo shrilly cried. "Then Mary and I can go home and leave you to your fun."

"How do you like the place, Mrs. Donovan?" Jay politely asked.

Mary turned a pale bright face toward him.

"Oh, terribly amusing," she said. "I had no idea there were places like this."

"I knew it, all right," said Flo. "The only thing is try and get your husband to take you to one."

Ha ha ha, laughed everyone, and then the drinks came, and Lou saw that Mary was having plain soda, and to add to this exhibition of good sportsmanship she was taking a couple of aspirin with it to help endure the pain of having a good time. She looked at him apologetically but got no sympathy from his hard smile. It was really the worst thing that could have happened to either of them, this little introduction into his business life, for he could feel not the faintest remnant now of his old-time pride in her. If she had only gone to the Harrods', as he had thought she would, then he could have excused her chilling out the dinner guests by the thought of her later being at ease with much bigger shots. It was the thought of her, that he loved, and how can you have the thought of anyone if they're around your neck at the moment complicating everything? He would have liked to sit here with the Olivers—yes and maybe even with Mrs. Kameray—and brag about how his wife never went to night-clubs, never drank, loved music and culture and riding, that sort of thing, a real lady, and talking he would have sold himself all over on her. But here she was being a lady in person, and away from her own background, a lady was just a dud on a party, a liability, a wet blanket. He could not feel even the slightest admiration at this moment for her wide gray eyes and the gray dinner suit, all he thought was that every aspirin she took was a martyr's silent but public reproach to her brute husband for bringing her out with such people to such a place, and he felt an icy indifference to whatever torment her suspicions of him must be causing her.

"What's the woman's name?" Flo teased. "I mean the blonde. Jay, do you know?"

"Me? Why should I?" Jay asked.

"I thought she kind of looked at you," Flo said, and Jay slid further down in his seat.

"I believe it's Kameray, isn't it, dear?" Mary said, but Lou did not bat an eye.

"No, dear, this is Mrs. Kameray coming in," he said. "The other lady is Mrs. Thompson. I used to know her in Dayton."

Mrs. Kameray looked wonderful to him, coming in at that minute. Her trim little black suit, the simple fur bow at her

neck, the charming calm face, not childishly sweet like
Mary's, no, this was young but dignified. Lou and Jay got up
and brought her to their table. No give-away here, either,
thank God, Lou thought, for her little hand-clasp to each
man was accompanied only by the most gracious little smile,
any watching wife could see it without a flutter. Lou, without
looking at her, could see Mary preparing herself.

"My husband has often spoken of you, Mrs. Kameray," she
said.

Mrs. Kameray looked in pretty amazement at her.

"But Mrs. Donovan, how could he?" she said. "It is true I
work for him, yes, for him and Mr. Rosenbaum, but even
though I call up and call up, Mr. Donovan will not let me see
him in person until tonight. Isn't he naughty?"

Lou mentally doffed his hat to this superb job of fixing. It
was as if she sensed the telephone extension eavesdropping
and was covering every angle. Mrs. Kameray looked appealingly from Flo to Mary.

"But it is naughty, isn't it? I have to see the man, I call up,
I tease, I flirt, and when Mr. Rosenbaum calls me up long distance to ask, I say, I cannot talk until I have seen Mr. Donovan and that naughty Mr. Donovan will not meet me.
Tonight, I caught him, yes?"

Mary, drawing a long breath at this unexpected solution of
her fears, looked at Lou, wanting him to forgive her her suspicions, wishing she had never doubted, longing for the old look
of admiration, but Lou, cleared, at least momentarily, was arrogant. He must take Mrs. Kameray to another table for a little talk on Castles-in-the-Woods, a matter which had proved so
boring to the others at dinner that he was sure they would be
glad not to hear it mentioned again. Mrs. Kameray obligingly
drew notes and pencil from her bag and gave every indication
of being nothing more than a dutiful, attentive secretary, and
her little bottle of white wine was further proof that she was
only here in the line of duty. Proof, that is, to Mary. To Flo it
was a case for exchanging winks behind Mary's back with Jay,
and to Francie, watching from the bar, it was cause to down
half a dozen drinks quickly and insist on playing the drums
with the orchestra, her hat on the saxophonist's head, her husband Mr. Thompson passed out slumping over on a corner

table. The spectacle of Francie at the drums was too much for Flo, and in a huff at Jay for not dancing with her, she joined a lone wolf at the bar, a swarthy Spaniard, and cajoled him into doing a tango. Mary looked at Lou, then at these women he knew and it seemed to her her head would split with the din and the strangeness of this side of his life, the effort of understanding him. She knew that to leave was another hideously wrong step, but tonight had been full of wrong steps anyway.

"Mr. Oliver," she said, "I mean Jay—would you mind taking me to a cab? I feel—I've got to have air. I'd like to go home, so much."

"Cab, nothing, I'll drive you home," Jay said. There was nothing here for him. He'd had the good luck to miss the floozy's recognition but the way she was acting up there with the orchestra it wouldn't be long now before she started the stuff on him, and then Flo would take over. Flo came dancing past with the Spaniard, showing off. She could take care of herself all right. Or Lou could. He got Mary's cloak, and piloted her past Lou.

"We're driving out for some air," he said, and Lou nodded. Mary smiled a little too eagerly at Mrs. Kameray and Mrs. Kameray smiled a little too sweetly back. Jay was glad to get out before anything started. At least Flo was busy with the stranger and she wouldn't be jealous of Mary.

But that was just exactly what Flo was. In fact Flo never took a chance on anything. It was no fun showing off her powers with other men without Jay to see it so she snatched her ermine cloak and ran after them.

Lou and Mrs. Kameray were so busy going over their data, scribbling addresses and other inspirations in their little notebooks, that they were remarkably oblivious to this last departure. All the more wonder then that they stopped talking at exactly the minute the door closed on Flo and looked at each other. It was the same look that Lou had remembered with heightened excitement, the slow measuring promise of complete surrender. He quietly signalled for the check and when they got up they did not even bother to collect the valuable data they had been so busily exchanging. They did not speak as they got in Lou's car and they did not even hear the special drum roll from the Spinning Top orchestra as they left.

XVI

"Yᴏᴜ'ʀᴇ sure Mr. Donovan's coming back today?" Jay asked.

He sat at Lou's desk drumming on it till Miss Frye thought she'd go nuts. She looked up from her typing.

"Look," she said. "Would I tell a lie?"

"I don't know, sister," said Jay. "All I know is you said he'd be back last week, then you said Monday, then Tuesday, now today. Where'd he go anyway?"

Miss Frye had only told him that about five times, too.

"He's been making a swing through the West," she said. "The way I told you before. Do you want his itinerary?"

Jay saw his persistence was getting on the busy woman's nerves.

"That puts me in mind of my old man," he said. "He was a regular old-time travelling salesman, quit school in the eighth grade and started canvassing right outside Taylorville here. Got to be head of his own business and put me on the road soon as I got out of school. Called me in one day when I got back and he says, 'What's this here?' and I said, 'Why, dad, that's my itinerary.' 'The hell with this itinerary stuff,' he says, 'after this you send us in your route.' That was the old man for you."

"That's darned interesting," said Miss Frye.

"Do you want me to tell more?" asked Jay. "I got a million of 'em."

"Put 'em in a book," said Miss Frye.

"Hell, money means nothing to me," said Jay. "I'm glad to give you a little family history free of charge. You can mull over it while wrassling with the boy-friend."

"I don't 'wrassle,' " said Miss Frye.

"Fine!" said Jay. "That's the kind I like."

Miss Frye got up and giving her caller a measured look, laid a sheet of paper before him.

"There," she said, "is Mr. Donovan's itinerary."

"What's he doing at the Knickerbocker in Los Angeles?" read off Jay. "I thought he stayed at the Ambassador. And what's this about the Park Plaza in St. Louis? I thought he used the Statler."

"Look, Mr. Oliver," said Miss Frye, patiently. "Would you like to wait in the bar? I'm sure Mr. Donovan would rather you made yourself at home."

"I'm at home anywhere," said Jay. "Any old place I can hang my head is home sweet home to me."

"I know," said Miss Frye. "I heard that one."

"I never promised my script was new," said Jay. "All I said was I'd keep sending."

He looked over a stack of telegrams idly.

"All this on Castles-in-the-Woods?" he inquired but Miss Frye pretended the noise of her typewriter deafened her. "Did he put it through with the Frisco Fair people, too? He did! Well, well. And here it says the station wagons are to be maple with a Dubonnet trim, hospitality lights flood every driveway leading to the Castle Hotel, male help is Filipino— what does he want down there—race riots?—wearing white silk blouses with red sashes, pardon me, Dubonnet sashes."

"I know," said Miss Frye patiently.

Jay picked up another piece of paper.

"What was he doing at the St. Francis in San Francisco?" he inquired. "He's a Mark Hopkins customer."

"Mr. Oliver, I don't think Mr. Donovan wants you going over his mail," said Miss Frye. "There's a lot of stuff there in the bar. You look as if you needed something."

Jay got up with a sigh and strolled over to the bookcases which swung open showing the bar.

"In case Mr. Donovan wants my itinerary," he said, "put down that I'm going from Canadian Club to Ballantine's and will spend a short time in Martel. How come the boss stayed so long?"

"It's a big country," said Miss Frye. "It takes three weeks for that Western trip. I admit he's delayed, though."

"Maybe he's having trouble with Indians," said Jay.

Lou walked in and threw his hat on top of the safe.

"Well, son," he said to Jay, and shook hands. "Let's see your report card."

"Thank God, you're back," cried Miss Frye. "Everybody's calling. Mrs. Donovan has called from Arizona a half dozen times, that Mr. Truesdale has telegraphed for all kinds of information, Mr. Oliver here——"

Lou started leafing over the stack of mail.

"Lou, I got to see you," said Jay. "I got to. Just a minute. It's——"

Lou looked up, surprised at the odd tone in Jay's voice. Jay looked terrible. Hollow-eyed, miserable. Lou, staring, walked into the bar behind Jay and closed the door, leaving Miss Frye to throw up her hands in despair.

"It's Ebie," said Jay. "I can't find her. I put in a couple of calls to her apartment and no answer. I called Rosenbaum about something else and slipped in a little inquiry about Miss Vane. No Miss Vane. Severed her contracts. Can't be located."

"That's ridiculous," said Lou.

"Wait. I flew to New York two days ago. No Ebie. And not a word anywhere about where she is. God, Lou,—what am I going to do?"

Lou lit a cigarette.

"Just have to replace her, that's all," he said.

"Lou, this isn't funny, supposing something's happened to her, maybe she's another Dorothy Arnold——"

"Sure, maybe I'm another Charlie Ross, too. I'll bet I can locate her in ten minutes."

Jay poured a small brandy. He was torn between genuine anxiety and his natural desire to believe in Lou's ability to fix everything.

"Lou, I'm crazy about Ebie. It's been going on for years. You know, I chase, and I keep Flo going, but it's always been Ebie with me. And mind you, not a note, not a letter, not a call. It's not like her." Jay saw he was beginning to impress Lou. "Ebie tells me everything she's doing. And if she was mad she'd want to fight, she isn't one to pick up and walk out, without a fight-talk. I thought of everything. I thought—well, she was sort of worried last month, maybe she went to a bad doctor, maybe she passed out and he stuffed her in a furnace—you know those guys are liable to twenty years if they're caught——"

"Good God, Jay, pull yourself together!" Lou exclaimed. "Now, sit down. Let's look this thing over. Last time I saw

Ebie was—well, the time Flo pulled the cute trick and beat you to New York. All right, Ebie was sore as the devil at that."

"I know," groaned Jay. "And if I had the guts I would have kicked Flo out as soon as I met Ebie. That's when I should have done it. First time I ever laid eyes on Ebie, I should have broken with Flo. Ebie's worth ten of Flo."

"Check," said Lou. "All right, Ebie isn't the type to walk out, you say. Look. There's the type that walks out and walks out and walks out, know what I mean, round the corner and back, it's a habit. Then there's the type that walks out. That's how I classify Ebie. Just once she walks out."

"But why this time?" said Jay. "She's caught me fussing with other women, and I'm always dropping her as soon as Flo gets in the picture, not because I like Flo better but because Flo raises such hell."

"This was just once too often," said Lou. "You know how it is. You excuse a fellow putting the bee on you a dozen times but all of a sudden it's that one time too often. And you're through. Maybe Ebie's through."

"I got to get her back," said Jay. "I mean I can't get along without Ebie."

"Don't talk like a fool," Lou expostulated. "There's a dozen Ebies in every block. Nobody has to have just one particular dame, you know that. But we'll track her down."

He stepped to the door.

"Get me Truesdale at the Hotel Ellery, New York," he said to Miss Frye, and closed the door. "I'll put my man on her trail."

Jay drew a breath of relief.

"Gee, old boy, you take a load off my mind. It was getting me. Couldn't talk about it, of course."

"We'll find out what there is to know," said Lou. "Now, if you don't mind, I've got a month's stuff to clear up out here."

"What was the idea your changing hotels?" Jay asked.

"Don't you ever change hotels?" Lou growled.

Jay whistled.

"I get it."

Lou scowled.

"Nothing to get. Just trying out different services. I can't be too partial to one place, in my business."

"You put on some weight, too," said Jay, looking him over. "You must have about ten pounds more on you. Must have had a good trip."

"I did," said Lou.

"You old son of a gun," said Jay. "That's one thing I never could get away with—taking a woman along on a business trip."

"I never tried it myself," said Lou, offhanded. "If you want to know I was so damned busy this trip building up the Castles-in-the-Woods I wouldn't have had time for any women."

"I saw Rosenbaum in New York," said Jay. "He said the Kameray was working out all right at the job. I had to laugh. She called him up while I was there."

"Oh, she did?" Lou exclaimed.

"The secretary had given it away, so he couldn't gloss it over much, just said she made a daily report to him from wherever she was, by phone or wire. I got her little phony voice squealing, oh Wosebush, darling——"

"Where was she talking from?" Lou asked.

"St. Louis," said Jay. "Old Rosebush went into his other office to give her the babytalk back. How was she in St. Louis, old boy?"

"Mrs. Kameray is a wonderful person," said Lou sternly. "If you make any more cracks about her I'll have to poke you right in that mush of yours."

"She's a two-timer, pal," said Jay. "I'm warning you. Old Rosebush has ten times the dough you've got."

Lou was irritated at having betrayed himself.

"Mr. Truesdale can't be located," Miss Frye came in to say. "The Ellery is leaving him a message."

"Go on, now, worry about Ebie," Lou recommended Jay with a nod. "I'll worry about me getting two-timed."

XVII

YOUR LIVES, said the analyst to Mary Donovan, are drifting apart, it is up to you to join them again. Make an effort, he said, to draw your husband into your life, above all do not show him you can have a perfectly pleasant life without him; make him feel that your social and musical life is flavorless without him. And in the relations between your family life and your husband do not act as if it was you and your family versus a stranger husband, but you and your husband against even your own family. An egotist like your husband demands this assurance.

So here they were at the Harrods' intimate little dinner party where for two hours Lou had been glancing at his watch and wondering how long it had taken these people to get this way. The ladies were fluttering about the fireplace in the great living-room while the gentlemen dallied over coffee and brandy in the dining-room, chewing at their cigars and their memories. There were Grahame, the big hotel man, Carver, an ex-governor, Sweeney, the old banker, the Judge, and Mr. Donovan, promoter. Mrs. Harrod had sent the butler down four times to get the gentlemen upstairs, but old Mr. Grahame always had one more story to tell, and after he finished that Governor Carter had a now-defunct state secret to reveal, and Mr. Sweeney, a stern gentleman with a trim Vandyke, threw out some secret statistics on world affairs with prophecies on how these figures would affect the war in Spain and the progress of Russia.

"Do you realize," said Mr. Sweeney, turning to Lou on his right, "that in the city of San Francisco there are over two hundred thousand Chinese, a city in itself, with its own telephone exchange? Now what would you say would happen there in the event of the Japanese and Hitler forces combining?"

"I don't bother much with Chinatown there," said Lou. "I usually stay at the Mark Hopkins."

"No prettier spot in the world than the roof of the Mark Hopkins," said Mr. Grahame, sucking at a cigar. "Look right out over the prison across the bay. Top of the Mark, they call it."

"I know," said Lou and thought of Trina Kameray and wondered how long before he could get away. He had assured her he would be out by ten-thirty since he was known to be a busy man and had half a dozen sound alibis at his disposal. Besides, there would be music and Mary knew how he felt about that, she would excuse him and come home later herself in her uncle's car. He nodded to have his brandy glass refilled and looked glumly down the long table to where the Judge was benignly puffing away at a cigar, a large glass of water in front of him with a small vial of his after-dinner medicine beside it. The dinner had been distinguished, as many of the Judge's dinners were, not only by the powerful names of the guests but by the display of medication. Both the Judge and Mrs. Harrod had small medicine bottles beside their plates and Mr. Grahame, before gorging himself on the roast beef, popped two large alka-seltzer tablets in his glass. Mrs. Sweeney, an angry gray woman of sixty, had denied herself every course but the salad which she attacked with the grim determination of a person finishing once and for all a persistent old enemy.

It rather surprised Lou to find himself noticing all these disagreeable features of the occasion. Usually he was so impressed with the magnitude of the combined fortunes and power present in the Judge's house that he noticed little else, and there were always his untiring efforts to show them that he was as good as they were, a conversational effort that took up so much of his time and energy that he had little opportunity to observe anything else. Tonight Mary had told him that if he didn't go, she wouldn't; she had added that her uncle was very eager to hear more about that new project of his on Chesapeake Bay, and that Aunt Felicia particularly had asked for him.

"No kidding," he had said, not really believing it, but half-pleased at the same time. In the veiled arguments he and Mary had been having ever since her return from the Southwest he had for the first time hinted that she had allowed her family to snub him, that they had used his indifference to music as an excuse not to ask him to their most publicized entertainments, and it was very nice, very nice indeed, that in guest lists in the society columns she was referred to as Mary Harrod Donovan, instead of Mrs. Louis Donovan. It was very nice, too, that Mary never had the Harrods to dinner except when Lou was out of town, very much as if he wasn't quite good enough for them. It was odd that at the time these points had mattered most to him he never allowed himself to even think of them, let alone mention them. Now he had it right out, and to tell the truth, it hardly bothered him at all any more. The only thing that had been on his mind lately was what was Trina Kameray doing when out of his sight, and how soon could he get out of whatever he was doing and join her. A woman on your mind did have its advantages that way, he had to admit it, you might not sleep and you might lose your grip on some things because of it, but at least it wiped out a lot of more important worries.

Having made his complaint there wasn't any way of backing out when Mary produced the dinner invitation with personal messages from the Judge and Aunt Felicia. It was something he could mention next week in New York when he saw the Major. He had that to think of. Over the martinis (with tomato juice for the Judge, Aunt Felicia, Mary, and Mrs. Sweeney)—Lou had launched into the Castles-in-the-Woods project, since Mary had told him the Judge wanted to . hear.

"The land is right near our place," the Judge explained to the others, "so that the project is of peculiar interest to, hmm, yes, hmm."

"But surely, Mr. Donovan," said Mrs. Sweeney with a menacing smile, "you can't mean you're having neon lights all through that lovely woods and all down the roads!"

"That's just one of the improvements," said Lou. "We're going to put that place on the map as the last word in modernity."

"But I thought the people there had been petitioning the government to make the town into another Williamsburg," said Mrs. Sweeney, looking to Mrs. Harrod for confirmation. "I thought there was an old tavern there with historical relics and a whole group of Revolutionary buildings. It was to be like Williamsburg, wasn't it?"

"Nothing about that in our contract," said Lou.

"Neon lights!" murmured Mrs. Sweeney.

"Same thing happened to us," said Mr. Sweeney. "Last year I went downstate to visit the old Sweeney homestead. Nephew lives there now. Imagine how I felt when instead of the old rolling acres with cows and horse grazing there were derricks. Oil there now."

"We just wept, literally," said Mrs. Sweeney. "And the young people just sitting around the porch, rocking, watching the oil-drilling."

"How awful!" sympathized Aunt Felicia.

"You mean you didn't have any interest in the property any more?" Lou inquired. "All that oil going to your nephew?"

"Very good," politely laughed Mr. Sweeney. "Incidentally, do you realize that Illinois ranks ninth in petroleum production this year?"

All right, there was something about the Castles business that rubbed these people the wrong way, and as usual they were brushing him off. Lou was about to crash right through again but there was no loophole. Aunt Felicia was giving out an ecstatic description of the gardens at Williamsburg, aided by Mary's memory, and they were getting into the Revolutionary chamber music revivals and how perfectly enchanting they were. Mary actually got excited over this subject, and Lou, rebuffed, watched her with hostile curiosity. He saw how much she looked like Aunt Felicia and it was funny he never noticed that before. Old Felicia was a lean old giraffe, her smiling, smug blonde pinhead stuck on a lean old neck with attached arms and legs. What was she doing with that old diamond dog-collar, when with a neck like that she needed a giraffe collar? Her eyes were still wide and dewy like Mary's and had never seen anything they didn't want to see, you could tell that. Watching them together, Mary's strained eager face a young replica of her aunt's, Lou couldn't understand how the resemblance had not frightened him before, had not, indeed, scared him off when he first met Mary.

It was after Aunt Felicia had assiduously devoted herself to him during the shrimps and soup that the suspicion struck Lou that this evening was all framed up by the Harrod family to make him more tractable. Mary had spent her time in the

Southwest confiding in Aunt Felicia all of the little things that had been giving her headaches lately, and Aunt Felicia was doing her best to patch it all up for her little pet niece. Or did those two congenitally cold women confide in each other actually? Probably they had some silent wigwagging signals of distress, understood only by each other and unaccompanied by any indecent revelation of emotion. Whatever it was, old Felicia, instead of the sour reflective smile with which she usually listened to her nephew-in-law's conversation, was giving him the full battery of her graciousness. This obvious resolution to pacify him with undivided attention did not include listening to what he said, so that he had to answer the same question half a dozen times, finally noting the eager glassy old eye shifting around the table during his answers, and noting, also, Mary's anxious gaze on him from time to time as if to see if this attention didn't make him happy.

"I had no idea you were a university man, Louis," said Aunt Felicia. "Princeton, you say?"

"I said Michigan," Lou repeated for the third time, "and just for the football season, if you call four months being a university man. I guess I learned as much as most of them did."

"I had a nephew who went to Princeton," said Aunt Felicia, with the gusty intensity with which she rode all conversation. "Perhaps you knew him when you were there. Farwell Lease, Junior."

Lou gave up.

"No," he said. "He wasn't there when I was there."

He sank into gloomy silence while Mrs. Carver, the ex-governor's third wife, a little bird-woman with darting head and bright little robin-eyes, twittered about life in Washington and how, really, there was nothing to compare with it in America. Oh the cherry-blossoms, cried Aunt Felicia and Mary in a breath, the wonderful Japanese cherry-blossoms! And Arlington! Perfectly beautiful! Lou looked at Mary's and old Felicia's suddenly animated faces and wondered again at what brought that quick rapture to their eyes—cherry-blossoms, music, a view. His lips curled. That was supposed to be culture, maybe that was supposed to be "sensitivity." Give him the sudden narrowing of the eyes, the intent frown, the suspended breath, that marked Trina Kameray when his hand sought her knee under a table. His glance travelled around the table and he thought of how little they knew of real magic, all this talk of stars over Mexico, fog over the Potomac, tunes from a harpsichord.

Mary must have observed his restlessness for she bent and whispered something to her uncle. Lou shrugged. So now the shoe was on the other foot. Instead of Mary whispering him to please ask uncle this or that, please be nice to Aunt Felicia, please don't monopolize the conversation, here she was urging them all to be nice to her husband. Well, he wasn't sure he liked it any better this way.

"Ah, um, Louis, hmm, I understand the New York office is a great step forward," said the Judge. "I understand you have contracts for the New York Fair and the San Francisco as well. It's not quite clear to me what your particular contribution, hmm, I should say, hmm."

"It's the Castles-in-the-Woods," Lou said. "I've been in business for ten years and I swear this is the most interesting proposition I ever came up against. You take the property itself, now——"

"Supposing we ladies go up to the living-room for our coffee," suggested Aunt Felicia, and in the little flurry of exits Mr. Sweeney took charge of the conversation, and Lou gloomily retreated into his own thoughts, emerging only now and then to say, "Yes, sir, that's about right, sir," and "That's about the size of it," and other vague disgruntled little comments. Mr. Grahame, wedging his vast bulk against the table, his watch-chain resting almost horizontally on his bay-window, dozed happily over his cigar; the Judge chewed at his cigar without smoking it, as per health regime, Mr. Sweeney was reminded of a dozen and one anecdotes peppered with statistics and spiced with the great names of banking and international politics. The ex-Governor of the nearby state came in with his war prophecies and went to the trouble of demonstrating on the tablecloth with the handle of his coffee spoon possible military maneuvers for the Spanish warlords. By this time Aunt Felicia upstairs was peremptorily tapping on the floor with some weapon or other, and the Judge signalled the butler.

"Tell Mother we'll be up directly," he said. "Go on, Sweeney."

Mr. Sweeney did not need to be told to go on, having gone on so long now that nothing short of a stroke would stop him. Lou, on whom he turned the full battery of his well-informed mind, had long since stopped worrying whether his face looked interested, since the tribute was not necessary at all.

"Mind you, two hundred thousand Chinese in San Francisco," repeated Mr. Sweeney, "one third of the population of Nanking, China. An unassimilated foreign group, you see."

"Is that a fact?" said Lou, and quietly noted that it was now ten-ten. It was funny he had made such a fuss all these years about the privilege of being bored by his wife's family. What was the matter with him, anyway, boasting of having been kicked around by these old big shots? Like saying, "Believe it or not, I had my evening spoiled last night by a personal friend of J. P. Morgan!" Or "I was fortunate enough to have a second cousin of the President bore me to death last night."

There was another message from the ladies. Mrs. Harrod was impatiently waiting to regale the gentlemen with a recorded concert beginning with Stravinsky's "Peter and the Wolf" which Mr. Grahame had never heard. Mr. Grahame, roused from his spasmodic napping by hearing his name, pushed the table away from his stomach and extracted his body from the chair.

"Come on, old boy," he urged Sweeney. "Mustn't inconvenience our hostess. You and Cassidy can have this out some other time."

On the way upstairs Lou figured what he would say. He had to get out quick because he could never tell what Trina Kameray was likely to do. She could be brilliantly discreet in public, sometimes, but on the other hand she could be alarmingly high-handed if her little caprices were not given proper consideration. She called up his house whenever she pleased, she wrote whatever she felt like, often quite naughty little notes, and when Lou tactfully tried to correct this sort of mischief, she shrugged.

"Either you are a man or you are not a man," she said. "Either you are afraid of our friendship or you are unafraid. If it is an inconvenience to you I have many other friends."

She never said it but he knew what she meant. It was that there was always Mr. Rosebush. Such a dear, such a valued friend, and she had been so unkind to him, giving him up for Lou, who wished she would not telephone him or speak to him in public, or show her friendship for him. It made one sad to think of giving up a loyal friend like Mr. Rosebush for a man who found her preference merely an embarrassment. In fact, she really ought to be meeting Mr. Rosebush in Baltimore this very minute instead of loitering around the West this way, within meeting distance of such an unappreciative man as Louis.

That persistent little threat usually brought Lou desperately out in the open, and unable to say more about the danger to his home life. They would have a home together some day, Trina said, so what did it matter how soon his present arrangements were blasted? Lou never answered this, for the immediate urgency of being with her always blinded him to future complications.

"Sorry, but I have to see a party from Rochester at ten thirty," Lou said to Aunt Felicia, upstairs, while Mary looked at him questioningly.

"Yes," said Aunt Felicia graciously, "I believe someone did call a few minutes ago inquiring if you had left."

Can you imagine that? That little Kameray had even had the nerve to call him at his wife's old home. That was the sort of arrogance that left a man breathless.

Lou got into his coat and hat in the hall, trying to act pained at this business intrusion of his social life. In the living-room Mr. Grahame settled in the largest chair with a loud creaking of indignant springs, the Judge adjusted the great phonograph, Mrs. Sweeney and Mrs. Carver arranged their velvet skirts on a small loveseat in reverent silence, the ex-Governor stood gazing gloomily into the fire, and Mr. Sweeney took up a safe position in a corner retreat where he adjusted his reading glasses for a refreshing glance through the *World Almanac*, handily placed in a magazine rack.

"You'll be back for me, dear?" Mary asked in a low voice. She knew he wouldn't. She knew he was meeting a woman at the Evanshire bar in Evanston because the operator had called from the Evanshire first. She only wished she had the courage to say she knew. The psychoanalyst—as she had justly feared —had done nothing to give her the simple everyday courage to make a scene. He had done nothing for her with this suggestion to draw Lou into her family's life. And when she had told him, with bursting temples and trembling hands, about the unmistakable evidence of another woman in her very bed during her Southwest trip, the stupid man had merely given her sedatives, and told her such a tiny catastophe was not the end of the world.

"I'm sure the Carvers can drop you," Lou said to her. "And by the by, there's a chance I may not drive back out tonight. Have to meet an early train downtown in the morning, so I may stay downtown. Night, dear."

He hurried out. Aunt Felicia and the Judge exchanged a look. Every one knew he was going to meet a woman. It would have been better if he had not come at all, Mary realized. She wished she dared rush out and follow him, see the woman, accuse her, flaunt the hairpins and handkerchief (shamelessly left under the pillow) and the hoop earring. She wished she was as bold as this woman, whoever she was, who brazenly visited her house. She stood waving to Lou in the door for a moment, then came back to take her seat on the sofa beside the fire. The music began. Aunt Felicia and the Judge were looking at her, so she kept her own eyes on the leaping fire, her long thin fingers interlaced in her lap, and in the pause while the records changed she murmured "Isn't it charming?" just like anyone else.

It couldn't have been her fault, Mary thought over and over, it couldn't, it couldn't. All the things he had admired when he first saw her, had shown so clearly how much he admired them, were still hers, she had not changed, even her feeling for Lou had not changed, her appearance had not changed, nothing was any different from the moment he met her on the ship coming from Honolulu when the Captain gave her a birthday dance. And Lou had made her uncle and aunt furious by taking her away from the dance out on the rainy deck where they sat not saying much, not even holding hands, but when she rose to go back to the others he said, "Believe it or not, I'm going to marry you or your sister." "I haven't any sister," she said, laughing. "Then it's going to be you," he said. So that was her love affair, her only one, the only one she ever wanted—six years of having someone demand more than she could give, of having him look steadily at her when they were out together until her gaze fluttered to meet his, of having her own happiness consist in curbing his desire, in finding that her protests could control his impetuosity. It was the way she was, it was her own version of passion, denying more than she gave, for the charm of her love was what she withheld, just as the basic force of Lou's love was in demanding what would be denied, wanting more, no matter what, than would be given. It was all part of their own special love that she should want him to make approaches so that she could say, "Oh no, no, Lou, you mustn't, you mustn't," and so keep the process within the strictest bounds, no intimate fumbling over her body, which after all was her own, and no reason why marriage in spite of its implicit obligations should give the lover complete and outright ownership to it. That was the sort of quaint daintiness which Lou had found intriguing from the very first, and nothing had happened since to make her bolder or more adventurous in sex. What made her head spin now with curious indignation was the faint suspicion that other women allowed and even encouraged this worst side of him; there might be dreadful creatures like the naked girls at the Spinning Top, like the woman he must have in New York, like the one he was meeting tonight in Evanston, dreadful women who pretended to like it just to trap him and so betray her, make her refusals seem wrong, his cajoling demands right. Puzzling over these doubts Mary cried all night, and she didn't know which was her greatest woe—his probable unfaithfulness, or the possibility that these other women were right to surrender completely and she was wrong. Even so she knew that what she wanted was for him to go through life wresting love from her, and being perpetually denied full abandonment.

It was frightening to wake up in the morning and know that love did not last, no matter how it was treated. Even a shrew, nagging, ragging, bullying and deprecating the husband out of sheer discontent with her own dream of him, must believe it can go on forever, and must be bewildered when, at a kind glance from some gentler woman, he leaves. People think relationships are made of rubber and stretch and give to every crisis, and it is a shock to find they can snap in two like a glass thermometer. Why should anyone feel that a great truth is hidden from him when it is written all over the sky that nothing is permanent? Mary reasoned it all out, rationalized the way the doctor had told her, but what good is reason when the heart is out of order? Just so many sheep to count till the brain got numb, that was all, and then the old heart could go ahead hurting, even exploding, for all the good reason could do.

The worst part was the half-dream before waking, the half-dream that everything was the same as it used to be. She could see herself and Lou dancing, walking, dining in little lovely corners, the way it was when he told her every day he was going to marry her, whether she liked it or not, and whether Aunt Felicia liked it or not. She thought of the way he kept looking at her until she was forced to look up and see the shock of desire in his eyes, and the way in a little while he would be striving for some excuse to touch her, to put her coat on for her, to help her get into her car. And then when she was home, undressing for bed and thinking of this resolute suitor, the phone would ring and he would say, "Mary? All right? I just wanted to make sure. Sweet dreams." And now Lou was calling up someone else, waiting for someone else to look up and meet his eye, calling up someone else to make sure she was all right. And there was no reason for it, no right to it, but there was nothing to be done.

No, there was nothing to be done, no questions to be asked and answered. She tried to do what the doctor had suggested, to think of the man's side, to realize that it is as sad to stop loving as it is to stop being loved. Sad to look at the back of a neck, the slope of a cheek that once gave quick pleasure, and here was the same curve, the same gesture—no change except that no joy, no love was inspired, object and eye were two unconnected telephones. Poor curve, sad gesture, void of all magic, powerless to convey life to expired love. The way she rumpled the back of her hair, once so dear to him, was just the way she rumpled her hair and no more. Her slender foot squirming around when she was embar-

rassed was just an annoying habit, not an endearingly childish
trick. His looking at the menu to see if her favorite duck was
on it, not because he wanted to give her pleasure, but to see
if there wasn't something he could find to mollify her outside
of a caress. Oh, of course, it was a sad role, the lover no
longer loving. But once the perfunctory sympathy was given
him the heart went out fully to oneself, the real victim, the
unloved.

If she was at fault, and she might be, then the fault had
been with her at the very start. If all the things he first loved
were still there and he no longer loved, then these must now
be all the things he hated. She would have to be different, she
would be like Flo Oliver, like the women at that night-club,
she would get up with the orchestra and beat the drums, she
would talk to strange men, she would drop in at bars by herself the way that Mrs. Kameray did, and ask other women's
escorts to join her at her own table. Those were all the things
she was *not* and therefore they must be the things he wanted
of women since those other women seemed to know him better than she did.

She knew, of course, that he wouldn't come home that
night. She knew that Aunt Felicia thought the same. That was
the drawback to confession. After the consolation of confessing, the confessor knows the facts and can offer no blind consolations. Mary slowly undressed, knowing he would not
come back and knowing she would not sleep. Knowing that if
and when he came home tomorrow she would not ask.

The telephone rang suddenly, unbelievably. Mary picked it
up with trembling fingers.

"Hello, Mary? All right?"

It was Aunt Felicia.

"Of course," she said. Aunt Felicia didn't ask if Lou was
home but that was what she meant.

"Sweet dreams, child," said Aunt Felicia.

"Bless you," said Mary, but after she got into bed she lay
there hating Aunt Felicia for thinking, indeed for knowing,
that Lou was not home.

XVIII

Mrs. Kameray lay on her stomach in the hot white sand and shaded her eyes with her hand to squint up at Lou.

"You have a very pretty figure," she said. "I don't know why it is you are always so cross."

Lou would not be flattered.

"What do you mean, a pretty figure?" he said. "I'm getting a pot like that old boy over there in the water."

"I like a pot," said Mrs. Kameray. "I think a pot is very nice for a man. A man at forty should have a pot. How old are you?"

"Forty-one," said Lou.

"Seventeen years older than me?" Mrs. Kameray sighed. "You forty-one and me twenty-four!"

Lou didn't answer. She was twenty-eight, he knew. She had started being twenty-four a week or two ago and he suspected it had something to do with the young Cuban band-leader she had found in Havana. He was still mad about it, mad especially that she had flown to Havana without telling him, so that when he arrived in Miami, and with considerable trouble about arrangements, too, he had to wait two days for her to come back. Two days when you worked on a high pressure basis such as Lou did meant a lot of explaining, to the different clients he was supposed to be seeing in New York and Washington. But he didn't dare scold Trina or she would quietly pack up and leave. He had gotten rooms for them at one of the town hotels, but as soon as Trina arrived she had announced they must stay at one of the Beach hotels. So they were at the Roney Plaza, and, awkwardly enough for Lou, as Mr. and Mrs. Donovan, since Trina declared she was not to be regarded as a mistress but as a wife. It was not nice, she said, tiptoeing back and forth across halls in the night. They should have a nice little suite together like a honeymoon couple, and if she wanted to scold a waiter or maid she could do so with perfect freedom and not have them give her that insulting "mistress" look.

"Besides I am your true wife," she stated. "I am the one who should be Mrs. Donovan. What are you doing about that, Louie? You promised me you would fix it all up."

Lou avoided her earnest inquiring gaze. God knows what he said in the tantalizing circumstances under which Trina extorted promises. It was unwise of him not to have handled the marriage thing better, however, because that came up all the time and she was getting very insistent about it.

"Don't let her tie up all your money, Louie," warned Trina. "You must let me help you with the settlement or she will want to take it all."

"You can't hurry those things," Lou mumbled.

"No? Not even for me? Not even to keep me from going back to Europe?" Trina raised her voice and Lou looked uneasily around them to see who might be listening. "You mean you would like me to go back into a burning building? That's how much you love me?"

For the first time Lou was glad to see the beautiful young Cuban lad coming up to them, for Trina at once was all smiles and demure charm. He was a slight, bronzed young Latin Apollo with little black moustache and sleek black hair. Mrs. Kameray swore that she had been instructed by the Major himself to find a suitable band-leader for the Castles-in-the-Woods ballroom orchestra and Tommy Padilla was one of the very first names she had been told to investigate. It was fortunate that, popular as he was in Cuba and Palm Beach, he still was able to spend all the time in the world at Miami getting acquainted with Mr. Donovan and talking things over so they could make a nice start that very summer. As soon as the young man joined them, Lou became acutely conscious of the brazenness of Trina's white bathing suit, the mere figment of a halter over the fine little bosom, a scant frill for a skirt, the pretty little navel all but out. Since she never under any circumstances went in the water she permitted herself quite an elaborate beach get-up, with a garland of red flowers in her flowing long brown hair, and a little red parasol.

"I love that little mole!" said Tommy gazing at the little brown flaw on Trina's bare diaphragm.

"Naughty!" said Trina primly. "Run along now, Tommy, let us see how beautifully you swim."

Tommy sprinted out to the water and flashed into the waves. Lou watched stonily. This was supposed to be the happy life, having your sweetheart on the beach of some tropic paradise, lolling in the sand, idling away the late winter days, not a care in the world but trying to hold on to your houri and watching other younger men exhibit their superior strength and beauty before her far too appreciative eyes.

"I still don't see why you had to stay a week in Havana just to get a bandleader," Lou said.

Trina reached out a small hand to clasp his. This was another gesture that made him uncomfortable in public, but when he rebuffed it she revenged herself by rebuffing his private advances. So he returned the pressure of her little fingers.

"I like Havana," said Trina dreamily. "It is like a little live heart beating away in the ocean. How it sways and beats with the maracas and the dancing feet. Like a little live heart."

"No town for a woman, alone," said Lou sternly.

"I have friends," said Trina. "I have a great many friends all over. There are many Russians in Havana. If there were no Russians there would still be the friends from Berlin and Vienna. You have friends I do not know. I have friends you do not know. Why not?"

Trina, pouting, was as irresistible to him as Trina, smiling, and he always felt a wave of frantic love for her when she made him feel guilty. She was reminding him now of the many times they had encountered business friends of his in the West and even these few days in Florida when he was obliged to pretend he was not with her. He knew that it was a scurvy thing to do, especially with a high class girl like Trina, but in every friend's eye he saw the image of Mary and for the life of him he could not ignore that image. It was thoroughly stupid of him, too, since on other occasions with other casual ladies he had arrogantly brazened it through. It was because this was different, that he had to mess it up. He knew Trina would behave with the most exquisite discretion before strangers—that is almost always—but she never failed to reproach him afterwards. He was ashamed of her? He was sorry he had made her love him? Very well, she would go back when the government made her. She was not a citizen, anyway. She would have to go unless some American man married her. No one would. So she would go back and very likely be killed. Certainly she would be killed. In Russia she was not a Communist. In Germany she was not a Gentile. Very well, she would be killed. It did not matter. Her poor little life meant nothing to no one, no one—expect Mr. Rosebush. Dear Mr. Rosebush. How wickedly she had treated him! He had been so good to her, had paid her whole passage back and forth to America two or three times. Such a good friend. Until Louie had made her fall in love with him and forget all her loyalty. For Louie's sake she must give up all her friends and her loyalties and for Louie's sake she must be treated like some bad common woman, someone not to be introduced to one's friends. Of course she could go back to Paris, but then her old husband Kameray would try to get her to come back to him, and then she would starve for he had no money.

"I thought you said he had money in a New York bank," said Lou. He hated to have her talk of other men, other husbands, other friends.

"A few thousand dollars," shrugged Trina. "It was really mine anyway because he had never made any divorce settlement. And if I had sent it to him in Europe Hitler would have taken it away from him. It could do him no good."

"I guess he's not starving," said Lou, uncomfortably. Trina's little allusions to the discomforts of her friends and relatives still in Europe made him bad-humored. Friends in concentration camps, grandfathers chased across Siberia by bloodhounds for all he knew, an ex-husband living like a rat in a Paris cellar, none of these seemed to stir Trina's emotion so much as the fact that European difficulties made her allowance from her grandpa in Geneva so slow in coming. Lou wanted to write out a check to end his pangs of conscience over the little pictures Trina's occasional remarks evoked in him. Why it should bother him, he didn't know, since she seemed philosophical about it. It bothered him, though, that it didn't seem to affect her. Or maybe it did. She was so mature, not like the American women he knew, she disguised her feelings since there was nothing to be gained by showing them. She was really braver than she seemed. Thinking this made Lou feel better.

"You've seen a lot of trouble, haven't you, Trina?" he said, moved.

Trina's hand gripped his.

"Some people are born for trouble," she sighed. "All my mother's people have had trouble in Russia, so why not me? And a little drop of the wrong blood in my husband causes us both more suffering! I am not born to be happy, Louie. Do you blame me I want everything, everything, quick, before it is too late?"

Her dark brown eyes welling with sudden tears had their usual effect on Lou. He would, that minute, have made a fine clean break with Mary, told her in ringing language that although she could get along beautifully, even better, without him in her life, there were other women who could not, women, or rather *a* woman, who had been through enough hell in her life to appreciate the protection of a man like Lou Donovan. He had one of his secret tempting visions of how sweet it would be to possess once and for all the charming little creature, to have this secret pleasure permanently instead of spasmodically and uncertainly. The image of Mary and the pride in the Harrod connection vanished with his quick longing to take Trina in his arms and hold her forever. These fleeting resolutions were lost, usually, in his sound later reflection that with Trina as his wife, who would there be for the little secret outings that were so much a part of his zest in life? A wife on a business trip, for instance, was just a wife, a poor piece of business, a dangerous exhibition of fatuity, very different indeed from the favorable impression of being independent.

"Tommy is not married," said Trina, sitting up and hugging her knees. The young man was still flashing sinewy brown arms through the sparkling water, occasionally pausing to wave to Trina.

"At twenty-one that shouldn't bother him," said Lou. "What I want to know is how he can spend thirty dollars a day for his room when he hasn't had a regular job for a year? I don't see how he can afford to stay in this hotel."

"He is like me," said Trina. "He likes the peacocks and the flamingoes. And the pretty fish in the dining-room. Everyone is not like you, Louie, seeing only the beefsteaks and the turtle soup."

It was a blonde day on the hotel beach and it may have been a surfeit of blondes in ice-blue bathing suits, or white shorts, that caused eyes to turn to Trina's flowing brown hair and swaggering little figure when she walked down to the water's edge to meet Tommy. Lou's appreciation of her curves was marred by his knowledge that it was shared by many. Trina used very little make-up and her public conduct was elaborately discreet; she never permitted her eyes to roam, and lowered them rebukingly when some crass stranger tried to stare her down. Her modesty and seeming fear of masculine attack gave an added piquancy to her merely average good looks, so that Lou was frequently disturbed by finding that her appeal was so general. For a man like Lou who did not like to be tied in any affair, it was harassing to realize that his little friend could not safely be neglected. Right this minute if he had to leave her Tommy would probably take over, or at least try to. Just as he was savoring this irritating thought a hotel boy came out on the beach and handed him a telegram.

"CAN YOU MEET ME HOTEL MAYFLOWER WASHINGTON TUESDAY CASTLES COMPLICATIONS CONFERENCE NEW YORK THURSDAY STOP ROSENBAUM."

The wire was forwarded from the Lord Baltimore in Baltimore where he was scheduled to be. Trina, coming up with Tommy, looked at him inquiringly.

"Have to fly north right away," Lou said briefly.

Trina's face fell.

"Can't we wait till tomorrow?" she begged. "It's our only really true vacation, Louie, you and me. Like a honeymoon. Don't you like to be on a honeymoon with me, Louie?"

"Yes," Lou said.

Trina took his arm.

"Our real one will be much better, you wait," she said. "We must go talk it over, Tommy. When you are dressed come and have champagne with us."

Back in their room Lou tried to be peremptory with her. Rosenbaum said he should be in Washington at a certain time and it was his duty to be there. He sat on the edge of the bed waggling the telephone receiver to convey that very message, but Trina flung herself down on the bed and wriggling on his lap took away the telephone.

"If you have to see him anyway in New York on Thursday, why must you go to Washington first?" she pouted.

There was something in what she said but in business you cannot point out the customer's mistake, just for your own convenience. However, what the customer doesn't know won't hurt him and Mrs. Kameray persuaded him to spend the hour pleasantly enough, both of them laughing at the idea of the Cuban Apollo patiently waiting for them below.

"Poor Tommy," sighed Mrs. Kameray, her eyes dancing. "He will be so worried about us."

The telephone rang.

"If that's Rosenbaum, I'll say I can't get out till tomorrow," Lou said, but the call was not from Rosenbaum at all. It was from Mrs. Donovan in Chicago. She wanted to speak directly to Mr. Donovan and, said the operator, *not* to Mrs. Donovan. This message, overheard by Trina Kameray, amused her almost as much as the idea of Tommy waiting. It alarmed Lou enough to make him decide to leave at once. For all he knew Mary might pull a 'Flo' on him and descend in Miami to meet this false Mrs. Donovan. He knew Trina was coldly unsympathetic about his alarm over Mary.

"Tell her at once you want a divorce to marry me," she said. "Do you want me to get another husband? If I don't have a husband I must go back to Europe. You want me to be killed, Louie, or is it you want me to make love to another husband?"

"Tell Chicago Mr. Donovan has left," Lou told the operator.

They went downstairs in silence, Lou stony-faced, Trina's cameo skin dewy, and looking fresh and smart in her trim little white flannel suit, her brown eyes sad, the full lips tremulous. The young Cuban did not find his friends very gay even over the champagne. He wanted to know why.

"It is because Louie's wife makes so much trouble for us," Trina explained gravely. "She does not want him to be happy one minute. I'll bet she would be nicer if you took her a present sometime, Louie, eh?"

"Oh, sure," Lou said gloomily. It did not make him happy to hear Trina talk, as she constantly did, about Mary. He had no intention of having anything out with Mary, but on the other hand he had not dared face her for weeks alone. All you could do in complications like this was to mark time. The hint about presents gave him a thought.

"Tell you what, I'll ship you on to New York and I'd better stop off in Washington," he suggested. "You can do a little shopping in New York."

"What kind of presents do you give your sweethearts, Tommy?" Trina gayly asked the young bandman, whose adoring gaze never left her face. He seemed astonished at the question.

"But what would the man give presents for?" he exclaimed. "It should be the lady who gives the presents. The lady always gives the present. It is much better that way."

The waiter brought the timetable and Lou glanced through it. Trina was content, now, to have him plan whatever he wished for them. She could go to New York and report directly to Lou's office on the result of her tour. She might well contact the Major himself, Lou thought. Meantime he, Lou, would see Rosenbaum in Washington and find out what was what; he would even, he graciously told Tommy, discuss the importance of having Tommy Padilla's Band. Tommy was delighted.

"Tell Mr. Rosenbaum it was my band he liked so much at El Dorado last Monday," he said. "Tell Mr. Rosenbaum that."

Lou did not flicker an eyelash.

"I will," he said.

He did not look at Mrs. Kameray, and she went on sipping her champagne unconcernedly.

"So old Rosebush was in Havana last week, too," he muttered.

"Didn't I mention it?" Trina lifted pretty brown eyes frankly. "But then I told you I had so many friends in Havana. In Porto Rico I have friends, too. But I love Cuba best. I like the way the airplanes swoop down flying over the city, like in a circus when the rider swoops down to pick up the handkerchief in his teeth, oh, it is thrilling!"

"Threeling?" Lou mocked her.

"And the cars that go so fast, whiz, whiz, coasting so fast down hill, and guns and masquerades with fighting, always, I love it."

"Life is cheap with Cubans," admitted Tommy, beaming.

"I could leeve forever in Cuba," sighed Trina. "To me it is like a little live heart, you know, beating and dancing like a little heart."

"Exactly!" exclaimed Tommy. "That is Havana to me, too."

To Lou, Havana was a place where Trina Kameray had casually spent a week with Rosenbaum and kept Lou waiting for her in Miami. The only way he could ever keep her away from Rosenbaum was to marry her, and he knew the reason she was not the least disturbed by his finding out was that she knew far too well that this would serve her purpose better than anything else. He wanted to upbraid her, but he had no threats to offer. It was she who held the whip, talking so affectingly with Tommy about the simple joys of swimming at La Playa, and dancing in the peaceful tropic night at Sans Souci. Dancing with Rosebush? Swimming with Rosebush? Lou dared not even ask.

XIX

Lou had dinner in Rosenbaum's suite at the Mayflower with Mrs. Rosenbaum, Rosenbaum, and their little niece, Hilda, and a dark, pinched, intense spinster sister of Mrs. Rosenbaum's, named Liza. In the course of the dinner a thin spectacled student at medical college, the Rosenbaum heir, paid a short visit and at his mother's earnest behest, ate her banana cream pie dessert, then departed. That was Everett. The entire Rosenbaum family seemed to have transported itself to Washington from Park Avenue for the purpose of attending some school function in which Everett was taking a proud part. Mrs. Rosenbaum was a fading Valkyrie, large, blonde, and domineering, with very little conversation, achieving her points by a commanding gesture, or merely by calling out a name as if the duties of each member of her group were so automatic that the sound of his or her name released a set program of action.

"Hilda!" she called out and the plain little ten-year-old with sandy pigtails immediately finished up her vegetables.

"Liza!" she called. "Liza!"

And poor Liza, who was called most often, rushed to pull down the shades, answer the door, pick up Hilda's napkin, answer Mr. Donovan's question, pass the butter, or show Everett the congratulatory telegrams from other relatives. Most of these brief commands seemed to be not for her own satisfaction but to save annoyance to her husband who broodingly sat through the five courses, making very little effort to draw out his guest, and crumbling his rolls into little balls on the tablecloth, an annoying gesture which Mrs. Rosenbaum's attentive blue eye caught.

"My husband is very tired," she said to Lou. "He has no appetite. He gives his life's blood for the Major. He's a family man and it's hard for him to spend so much time away from us."

"He sees more of Everett than he does of us," said Liza. Her thin dried face glowed with worship when she looked at Rosenbaum, as indeed it had glowed for the twenty-five years she had been privileged to assist her brother's wife in making him comfortable.

"Well, an only son, of course," said Rosenbaum.

"Our two daughters are on a cruise for the spring holidays," explained Mrs. Rosenbaum. "They are sixteen and eighteen. To Central America. They wanted to postpone it till summer and go abroad, but Father says Europe is too unsettled."

There was no mention of Castles-in-the-Woods and Lou grew restless. The waiters removed the dinner, Rosenbaum offered him a cigar, Hilda and Liza turned on the radio in the corner of the living-room and listened with somber unsmiling attention to Major Bowes' Amateur Hour. Mrs. Rosenbaum got out her knitting bag and sat down on the sofa beside Lou.

"Everett has to prepare an article tonight, so he couldn't stay with us," she said. "He'll take us to his fraternity house to tea tomorrow and then we won't see him again till he comes home in June."

"We're comfortable here," her husband reminded her. "It's a nice change for you. I wish I could stay over tomorrow night myself."

"If this is your last night," Lou made a stab at escape, "supposing we go downstairs and have a brandy, listen to the orchestra. Or we might drive down and catch part of the show at the National."

Mrs. Rosenbaum shook her head, smiling, her needles flying.

"We don't like public dining-rooms," she said. "We always like to have it seem like home. After all we came down here to see our son, not the city. You go out with him, Father, go ahead."

Lou was relieved to see that this suggestion was approved by the master. He went into his bedroom for a hat.

"Liza! Hilda!" commanded Mrs. Rosenbaum, and the two hurriedly came out to say good night to the guest. The little girl curtsied.

"She can speak English when she wants to," said Liza fondly, "but she is shy. She is so glad to be over here."

Lou didn't know what to say.

"Somebody ought to blast that guy, Hitler," he said. "He's a bad man, eh, girlie?"

Hilda burst into tears and hid her face behind her aunt Liza.

"She can't stand to have anyone say anything bad about anyone," explained Liza, apologetically. "She doesn't want anyone to be unkind to anyone, she says. It makes her cry."

"I'm sorry," said Lou, awkwardly.

Something in the little girl's brown eyes reminded him of Trina and they both seemed sad figures, sad kind figures, for Trina did not like any unkindness either, it seemed to him. Yes, that was what made her different from a fleeting affair, Trina was sad and kind and lonely, just like little Hilda. Maybe Rosenbaum noticed that, too. It reminded Lou that Trina had other characteristics that did not exactly apply to Hilda and doubtless never would, but now they were mixed up in his mind, and he thought he would make up to Hilda for making her cry by buying Trina a bracelet.

The World's Fair deal was off on Castles, Rosenbaum told Lou in the Occidental, where they went for a highball. The San Francisco contract hinged on the New York one, so that too was off.

"But it was all settled," said Lou. "What went wrong?"

Rosenbaum shrugged.

"The world," he said. "You can't pin down parties to contracts when politics get into it. Besides both ventures were prestige more than profit. We lose nothing."

"We?" Lou laughed mirthlessly. "You mean you and the Major lose nothing. I lose. The firms I contracted for lose. Whittleby Cotton, for instance, loses."

Rosenbaum smoked quietly. The fellow got on Lou's nerves. Getting him to jump to Washington just to let him have the bad news. As easy as that, it was. The World's Fair deal off, he says, and smokes his cigar and looks down at the table, dead-pan, nobody could tell what he was thinking, but you knew he was in the clear all right, the Major's old right-hand man didn't have any worries.

"How does the Major take it?" Lou asked.

He wouldn't give the fellow the satisfaction of showing how much the loss meant to him, personally, the little slices here and there he'd cut for himself that were now shrunk or out of the picture.

"The Major doesn't know, yet," said Rosenbaum gravely. "As a matter of fact the Major is a very sick man. We've kept it out of the papers and it would be bad policy to let it go further—all of his commitments, you see—but the Major suffered a stroke two days ago."

"But he couldn't have—he can't do that!" Lou cried out in frank indignation. "Where are we going to be without the Major?"

That damn cigar of Rosenbaum's. He sucked away on it as if it was piping him the right answers.

"It was wife trouble, mostly," Rosenbaum said, after a proper consultation with his cigar, "The Major's not too self-controlled in the home, and moreover he's a very jealous man. His wife usually leaves him after a row, they divorce or separate, then remarry, then he has a jealous fit again, and the same thing over. Last time was too much for the heart."

"That's too bad," said Lou bitterly. "That's just too damn bad."

All right, what if the World's Fair was out, that wasn't the biggest thing on their programs. It had helped publicize the idea of the Castles, and had been a feather in their cap, but hell, it wasn't everything. What made him sore, though, was that a millionaire, just because he has the world by the tail, could just calmly step out of the picture and say, "Things are getting a little complicated around here, boys, I guess I'll treat myself to a little stroke."

"You have a tan since I last saw you," Rosenbaum said, suddenly looking straight at Lou.

Lou gave it straight back.

"So have you," he said.

"I didn't realize you were spending that much time in the South," Rosenbaum said. "You were lucky to be able to play a little."

"I've always been lucky," said Lou and knocked wood.

"Perhaps opening your New York office is what has brought you luck," said Rosenbaum. "I understand this has been your most successful year."

"I'll make enough to pay my last year's income tax," said Lou, watching him, not knowing what jump was coming next. "That's all I can ask."

"So last year was good, too." Rosenbaum nodded thoughtfully.

"You're damn right last year was good," said Lou. "After all, I do know my business, old fellow."

"You're a clever man, Donovan," Rosenbaum agreed. "You've got a lot on the ball."

But—? Lou waited.

"All right, what's the tag?" he asked, smiling.

Rosenbaum studied the photographs on the wall beside them thoughtfully. Maybe they worked with the cigar to feed him his answers. Lou couldn't figure out what he was getting at, half friendly, half sinister, and so oppressively gloomy, like some big operator waiting for the D.A. to catch up with him.

"You give me the tag," said Rosenbaum. "I mean, where you heading for? What's next? Do you vision a chain of branch offices all over the country, thousands of people working for you, consultants for hotels on a big scale, investigating, even buying and selling instead of just recommending?"

"Not for me," said Lou. "I go faster travelling light. I got to be flexible, change my position at a minute's notice. I'm doing all right handling a half dozen big outfits. You can't delegate my kind of work. Small but personal and selective, that's my angle."

"That's right," Rosenbaum approved. "It's your personality, of course. You're a lucky guy, Donovan."

"I never trust to luck," said Lou. "I work hard and use the bean every minute. You can't go wrong on that formula. It's these fellows that trust to luck that lose out. Me, I'm studying all the time. New angles. New twists. You got to keep at it."

"I wouldn't play down luck," said Rosenbaum. "You can work hard and use the bean and still lose."

"Not the way I work," Lou grinned. "I take no chances."

"Take the war in Spain, the hurricane, the political purges," Rosenbaum went on reflectively. God knows what he was getting at, but Lou kept his eye on the ball. "There must have been plenty of clever business men whose brains didn't help them there. The Major's brains didn't keep him from blowing up over a little wife trouble. No, you need luck. Maybe that's all anybody does need."

A crack in there somewhere, all right, but Lou didn't pick it up. If Rosenbaum wanted to insinuate that his success in

business was pure luck, no brains, okay, there were other times for a comeback. You have to wait for a really good comeback. Keep 'em wondering when it's coming.

"I don't know, I don't know," Rosenbaum shook his head wearily. Liver, thought Lou, it must be a bad liver that made a man as glum as Rosenbaum. "For instance, supposing the Major should die. It turns out the entire Maryland estate goes to the Government for retired army men and their families. The Major was sentimental about the army."

"If the Major dies—what?"

Lou stared at him in blank consternation.

Rosenbaum nodded.

"That's the will. I didn't know it myself till I talked to his lawyers yesterday."

Lou drummed on the table, thinking.

"Then the Castles work would all be scrapped the minute he conks out?"

"If he conks out," assented Rosenbaum. "He probably won't. But we might as well know where we stand. It's all luck now."

"You're a cheerful bastard," Lou said. "After all the work we've put in on that job. You've seen my reports. You've seen the plans."

"I know. You get your fee just the same," Rosenbaum said. "The estate will have to settle the contracts broken as best it can."

Lou smiled wryly. Rosenbaum must know perfectly well that the fee was the least part of the Donovan profits. It was the side bets that made him the dough.

"It's going to help me a lot on new business with a lot of litigation about broken contracts hanging over," he said. "That's going to be just great."

"Adjustments can be made," Rosenbaum said. "You won't lose."

You bet he wouldn't. He'd stick a price on wasted services that would make them wince, all right.

"Did Mrs. Kameray's work seem satisfactory?" Rosenbaum asked. He didn't look at Lou, just kept his eyes on the table-cloth.

"Perfectly. Mrs. Kameray is a very intelligent woman, and

made a very good impression. So far as her work went, it couldn't have been improved upon. Made some excellent contacts and did some very good field work."

All right, how do you like that? If you want to find out something, Lou thought, go ahead, you won't get anywhere beating around the bush. The same thought must have struck Rosenbaum for he suddenly clasped his hands together and looked at Lou directly for a minute in silence.

"I know all about you and Mrs. Kameray," he said. "I knew she was probably going to meet you in Miami, just as she met you in St. Louis and on the coast. I don't know you, but I do know Trina. Trina's out to get married. Trina's out for safety and security, and she's going to get an American husband. You can't blame her. A person that's been kicked around, one country to another, through revolution, politics, war—that kind of thing makes a person determined to save his own hide at any cost. Security, that's all. You can't blame Trina."

It was Lou, now, who looked down at the table and then at the photographs on the wall hunting for answers.

"No one could blame her," was all he could get out.

Rosenbaum didn't care about answers, anyway. He seemed to know them.

"I've known Trina off and on for five years. In London, Paris. Her visits here. I've done more for her than anyone else. I can always do more for her than anyone else. All right, the one thing I can't do is marry her."

Lou busied himself with his drink. It was the last kind of conversation he liked. If Rosenbaum wanted to show his cards, go ahead, but he'd be damned if he, Donovan, would. He wasn't sure what they were himself, anyway. He was marking time, that was all.

"You saw my situation, tonight. I'm a family man. I have feelings. I love my wife and my girls, my son. Even if I didn't— . . . You don't have my feelings. You can walk out of your marriage and take Trina without a pang. I can't stop you."

"There's nothing the matter with my marriage, either," Lou said slowly. "It's not as easy as that."

Rosenbaum threw out his hands.

"Talk about happy marriages! It's the man with wife trou-

bles that is the luckiest. He can walk out, with justice. But what about the rest of us with the wives that stood by us when we got started, and then we change, we grow, and they don't, they just go along, bewildered, watching us change, get rich, get smart, and they're hurt and puzzled and even angry that they can no longer name our favorite dishes, even, we don't eat the jelly rolls they make, but they can't see why our taste should have changed. And we feel sorry because we loved them once so we must go on. We don't like to cut off our own memories, and our habits, the habits we don't know we have till they're disturbed."

It was not especially pleasant to know that Mrs. Kameray had been heckling Rosenbaum to marry her, too, all these years. Somehow Lou had gathered from her that he had offered to do this himself, but that she had thrown away this opportunity for Lou Donovan. She had indeed given up everyone for him because, she said, her little tiny love affairs had been so unsatisfactory up till the moment she met him. There was no doubt about her double-crossing, maybe, a little bit with Rosenbaum, but it was not really double-crossing, it was a little show of power, to make him do what she wanted. Well, it worked.

"But you are getting a divorce, I understand," said Rosenbaum. "I can't. You saw that I couldn't. I wanted you to see my situation, so you would see that it wasn't just that I didn't care enough about Trina. It's—well, you saw."

So that was what was weighing him down all this time, trying to make up his mind to meet Trina's terms. And she had given him the "or else." The "or else" was Lou. Well, it must have given the old boy a kick to knock the bottom out of his business while he was handing over his former love. That must have been a compensation to him. No wonder he wasn't worried about the Major dying and leaving Castles up in the air.

"You'll marry her, I can't meet that," Rosenbaum mused. "Maybe you don't want to cut up your home, either, but you will to keep hold of Trina."

"Maybe," said Lou. "I'm not sure."

Rosenbaum signalled the waiter for the check.

"If you're catching that plane we'd better leave," he suggested. They got their hats, both of them somber-faced, unsure of each other. Lou got a cab but Rosenbaum decided to walk a while before he went back to his hotel.

"I might as well tell you that marrying Trina won't settle your future," Rosenbaum said quietly. "Trina never gives up anything. And even married to you, she won't be able to do without me. Good night."

XX

WHAT a lousy town, what a two-timing, ungrateful, ugly, crooked, stinking town New York was, Lou thought, on his way to meet Jay Oliver at the Biltmore. You spend your life, the best years, working to help New York get richer, yes, that's what it amounts to, and as soon as you decide to put your stakes in and stay, then it turns on you. You could almost say that as soon as he got his name in the New York phone book with that good address and the Fifth Avenue office the city put the Indian sign on him. The contacts that he had worked so easily from the Chicago office melted away as soon as he was right around the corner, or at least his office was. It made no sense. The big hotel chain that he had been consultant for these ten years got cagey and talked about paying out too many commissions, their new general manager could handle everything, thank you. The New York receptionist was no Miss Frye, she kept her own hours and if the office was instituted just for the prestige of a New York address the whole point was worse than lost when occasional callers found nobody in, implying vaguely that Louis Donovan Service was out of business. What made Lou sore was that he was working as hard as he ever was, he knew his job even better, he was trimming for the shifts in European affairs, working ahead on propositions for railroad lines and continental air lines to build American playgrounds to take the place of the now problematical foreign resorts, places like Sun Valley to keep the traveller's dough at home instead of Mexico and South America where the trend now was. It made him boil, now that the Major had deliberately gone and died, to think of the winter wasted on Castles-in-the-Woods. He had his fee, all right, but that was only a drop in the bucket to what he had expected to make. And these New York business men. Fine fellows, till it came to a little need for co-operation, and then it was them against the out-of-town fellows, like himself. Rosenbaum, for instance. Nothing hostile, nothing you could object to, all on the level, but just a calm cool brush-off. No chance of even a show-down. "You have your fee," he says.

"Your contracts will be settled by the estate with the firms involved. Present your statements. Too bad. Regrets."

He had not run into Jay Oliver recently and he didn't know what had happened since Truesdale had located Ebie for him. There was some talk of Whittleby Cotton merging with a Delaware firm and that might leave Jay out on a limb. All right, they'd have a hard times session. That was one thing about a pal like Jay, you didn't have to put up a front with him.

Jay was in the bar working on a Scotch and soda.

"When did you start?" Lou asked, taking the seat beside him.

"Did I ever stop?" Jay countered. "Hi ya, Lou."

"God, how I hate this town," said Lou and signalled the bartender for the same.

"What about coming out to Ebie's with me on the two ten?" Jay suggested. "Do you good to get out in the country."

"I'd like to see Ebie," said Lou, "even in the country, but I got to see Bill Massey up at Florabella at three. Every god dam thing has gone wrong since I landed in this lousy town."

"What you needed is to relax," Jay counselled. "I been meaning to speak to you, Lou. You act as if everything stops when you stop and it just doesn't. Why, they tell me you been jumping all over the country like a Mexican bean this last year, and look where it gets you."

"That's right," said Lou. "Where?"

"Still you look good, Lou." Jay looked him over approvingly. "That suit must have set you back some."

It was a brown worsted with a faintly shaded darker stripe. Mrs. Kameray liked him in stripes. He wore a mahoghany tie with it, a beauty, that Jay eyed enviously.

"I got a new tailor," said Lou. "I'll send you there."

"The hell with it," said Jay. "What good is a suit when you've lost your shirt? What a fellow needs then is a drink."

It was as good an idea as any and they had a lot of things to talk over. The cancellation of the Castles order, Jay thought, was too bad, but only too bad. The merging of his company with the Delaware firm was ominous, sure, but there were other firms. He was thinking of getting in the hat business. He'd had some propositions. He'd rather make less money and live in the East. Anyway he wasn't going to worry now about anything but catching the two-ten to Danbury.

"I got to take a dog out to Ebie," he said. "I bought her a pup."

"Where is it?" Lou asked, looking around.

"I got a Western Union boy walking him around," Jay said, "I got him at eleven o'clock and I can't get in anywhere with him, so I got this lad to walk him. He'll be back."

"See Rosenbaum?"

"Sure I saw him," said Jay candidly. "He was playing footy-footy with little Kameray in the Versailles last night. The Major checking out didn't seem to upset his plans any."

Lou thought of Mrs. Kameray's tremulous voice on the phone yesterday, saying that such a nice man as the Major dying made her feel too too bad, Louie, she must cry and cry, her nose was red, she could not let him see her. It must have been just the right color for old Rosebush. Lou had suspected something but dared not accuse, instead he took out one of the Florabella show-room girls, but he was blue, it wasn't any fun. He knew Rosenbaum hated to go out to night places, so the price Mrs. Kameray was demanding of him was that, if he didn't marry her, at least he must take her out to nice places, he must not act so ashamed of her that it made her feel bad. And she was a stranger, she wanted to get acquainted with her new country, it was her own dear country, yes it was, even if she did have to go back quick because no American man would marry her and the nasty government wanted her to go back to burning Europe. Lou could hear her coaxing Rosenbaum, and it didn't make him feel any better. It was no comfort to think Rosenbaum being out celebrating the night his boss died wouldn't look good to people. Rosenbaum could look after that part all right. Nobody needed to worry about Rosebush.

He ordered a double Scotch and knew that he was on his way to pinning one on, but Jay was right, there were complications that only a drink could straighten out.

"Tell you what, Lou," said Jay, "I'd like to have you look over this pup of Ebie's. I don't know. I may be wrong."

They had a couple for the road and then went out to look

for the pup. The Western Union boy was returning him from
Central Park and Jay waved to him. It was an English shepherd dog, enormous and unwieldy.

"You call that a dog?" Lou demanded. It looked as if two
men were working it, like a vaudeville act. That was the pup
Jay was taking out to Ebie. It struck Lou as funny and the
two of them went down to Grand Central Station, laughing,
the dog pulling them along. There was difficulty getting the
dog on the train but with a drawing room it was arranged and
they sneaked him in. The dog sat with an enormous mournful gray face looking from one to the other. It was the best
time they'd had since they'd gotten into the Castles' big
money, and they slapped each other on the back and shouted
with laughter.

Lou took his coat off and carefully hung it in the closet and
Jay kicked his shoes off and they ordered three rounds of
highballs so they wouldn't have to wait. It was like old times.
When the train started Jay rang for the porter.

"Who's the engineer on this train?" he demanded.

The porter shook his head.

"Tell him I'd like to drive the engine from Stamford on,"
said Jay. "Here's my card."

The porter took it doubtfully.

"You tell him," urged Jay. "Tell him I'll call the General
Passenger Agent if he doesn't. It's Mr. Oliver."

The porter was still doubtful.

"Before you put Mr. Oliver in the engine will you send
back a pair of medium sized blondes from Car Number 856?"
Lou asked seriously. "Here's my card."

The porter, for another dollar, was willing to be amazed and
after he left Lou and Jay laughed again. The dog looked anxiously from one to the other. It was funny thinking of Ebie's face
when she saw the pony-sized puppy that Jay was bringing her.

"No kidding, how did Truesdale find Ebie?" Lou asked.

"He sold her a farm," said Jay. "It was easy. Then she got
sick and was stuck there. Ebie's all right. Ebie doesn't give a
damn where she is so long as I get there once in a while."

"Where's Flo?" asked Lou and then chuckled. "Or do you
know?"

"Sure I know," said Jay. "When Whittleby got shaky so did

Flo. Seemed to think it was my fault. Christ, nothing I could do. So she kept reminding me everything was in her name, God knows she had me there, and I'd better not count on her, so by the time Whittleby went under there were no surprises. She threw a fit and I walked out."

"Jesus, Jay, she's got everything sewed up," Lou exclaimed.

"That's the nice part," Jay chuckled. "She can't complain. She was so scared of being left out that she hung herself. Told me she'd been putting everything away in her own name for years. Her mother told her. Her mother says, on her wedding day, 'Looky, Flo, you're very happily married, but you must learn to put all the savings in your name against the day he runs out on you, the bastard.' Something like that. So she did. So I says, 'Okay, then you're all right,' and then I says, 'Could you loan me fifty thousand to get back on my feet?' and she says, 'You don't get any of my savings, don't kid yourself, they're mine' so I says, 'All right, then, I'm a bum, I'd only be using up your money' and I walked out. It's a wonderful thing, having a smart wife."

"You mean you're living with Ebie?"

"Sure, I'm living with Ebie," said Jay. "Ebie doesn't care whether we eat or not so long as I'm there. Those two play right into each other's hands."

Lou thought of Mary and of Mrs. Kameray and how they would never play into each other's hands. He was irritated at Jay for thinking that the answer to everything was just throwing the pot of gold to the injured party and walking out. All right with Flo, but what did you do with a wife like Mary? And what did you do when you didn't want to leave her, when she was the kind of wife you knew you wanted, the kind you should have, and you didn't know what to do about it?

"What'll you bet you're in the same old noose?" he said.

Jay didn't get mad.

"Listen," he said. "A noose is what everybody goes for. Soon as they get out of one they look around. 'Where's my new noose,' they say, and nobody's happy till they got the new one, love, business, it's all the same; everybody's got to have the neck in the old noose, it's better than nothing. They call it a place to rest their neck. Everybody's got to have a place to rest their neck, so long as it's always out, anyway."

The dog knocked over two of the waiting highballs lined up on the the windowsill, so they rang again for the porter.

"How big is Danbury when we get there?" asked Lou.

"It's a hat town," said Jay. "They make hats."

"I don't give a damn what they make," said Lou, "I'm just getting information. How big is the place?"

"All right," said Jay. "It's about seven and three-quarters."

"I'm sorry, sir," said the porter, "but the conductor says you got to wire New York for permission to run the engine."

"Did you tell him it was Mr. Oliver?" asked Jay.

"Did you tell him he was with Mr. Donovan?" asked Lou.

"Are you the Lou Donovan that used to manage the Olympia Motion Picture Theatre in Rahway?" asked the porter.

He was. He was indeed. And the porter was the very same porter.

"How's Mrs. Donovan?" asked the porter. "She sure used to play the organ nice. I certainly enjoyed Mrs. Donovan playing that there organ. The only high class feature we had."

"That's right," said Lou, and suddenly it all came back, the old days in the afternoon, the run through of the film of the evening, Francie playing the organ to feel out what pieces to play, the colored porter pausing in his scrubbing to say how good it was, and Francie afterward in the beer place remembering that the porter had said he liked 'I Loved You Truly' particularly. And it made him feel very old to suddenly think of Francie with kindness, it made him feel old to want to remind her of those days, days she was always reminding him of, it was queer being in the other position. He thought, maybe that's all Francie wants, not to sleep with me, just to talk over the same things, on the other hand he never had wanted to even talk over the same memories before this very instant.

"You sure put that movie house on the map," said the porter fondly. "Don't you remember how you used to always be yelling out for William, Mr. Lou?"

"I certainly do," said Lou and slipped him a bill, feeling queer. It was the first and only time he had ever thought of any part of his past before Chicago as if it was a normal pleasant past, and a wave of surprise came over him that it hadn't been a bad past at all. He'd had fun there in little towns with

Francie, they hadn't made a lot of dough, but when they did they enjoyed it. He couldn't, at this moment, figure out just when he stepped out of his past and became a different man, despising his past and everything connected with it, but he would remember this moment as the time he went back and looked at his past freely, and saw it was as good as anybody else's. Sure it was. Maybe it was in this present insecure period he was trying to catch on to anything that was solid, and if your past wasn't solid, what was? Maybe that was all it was, but suddenly he felt that it was nothing to be ashamed of, years of scramming in and out of boarding houses, bills half-paid, jobs not paid for, no, it was part of something. And there was old Francie, sticking by like mad. Now that he thought of it he'd never had anybody stick to him like that. When he got going good that was what threw him, it made him feel as if he *needed* someone sticking to him. Well. . . .

"Tell the conductor to go ahead with the same engineer," he said to the porter. "Act like nothing has happened."

Jay looked at him.

"So the fluzy was your wife," he said.

"Any objection?" said Lou.

Jay whistled.

"I'm just beginning to get you, pal," he said. "You're smarter than I thought. You know when I saw you going under for that Kameray phony I began thinking you were not so bright. I see now it was a gag to get Rosenbaum."

Lou lit a cigarette. The big dog came over and put his feet on Lou's lap. He had to laugh.

"I was going to give you a piece of advice," said Jay. "I was going to tell you to stick to the gals at the Spinning Top or the hostesses there on Fifty-fourth Street. Same as you told me. The Kameray is a phoney. She even gets a per cent on the suit you just bought. She calls up the store every time you buy anything and gets her per cent. Ebie told me."

Lou drank the second drink from the end. The dog watched him anxiously.

"Ebie's a great girl," said Lou, sore.

"Ebie's crazy about you, too," said Jay, pleased. "I used to wonder if you pulled anything on me when I was away, but I guess I was too suspicious."

"I hope, I hope," said Lou.

That was the way to look at it. Everybody was phoney, it made it better that way. The unbearable ache at the things he kept hearing about Trina was nothing but growing pains. You had to be a phoney to get anywhere in this world. Trina had to step faster than some because she'd had it tougher, that was all. You had to feel sorry for somebody like that, somebody that had to keep playing a game every minute just to get along.

"William," Jay opened the door and yelled out, "bring me the funnies, will you, Mr. Donovan wants to see where Lil Abner is today."

Ebie's pup looked worriedly from one man to the other. It had a naturally woebegone face, its drooping whiskers adding to the funereal effect. Jay sprawled out on the seat and chuckled.

"Look at Handsome, will you? No kidding, Lou, did you ever see a dog with as much on his mind as old Handsome, here? Listen, Handsome, while you're on your feet, hand me that last drink over there, will you? Might as well train you while I got this time on my hands."

The porter came in with the papers which Jay decided to read aloud. Every time the porter came in Lou was reminded of some long forgotten remnant of his past. Come to think of it he and Francie had had a hell of a good time bumming around the country in those days. If anybody had any better time they hadn't known about it. Tiptoeing out of that rooming house in Albany at two A.M. wearing all the belongings they could get on since the installment people had taken the wardrobe trunk back that day anyway; having to take the car going north instead of the one going south because they were afraid to wait. Breakfasting in the next town, worn out and punch drunk from all night riding and no sleep, and reading the ad in the paper that landed them his best job, the management of a Newark hotel. Then the fire that wiped out that job, then the free rent somebody gave them way out in the Jersey wilds and Francie got a job in some roadhouse, and some guy, maybe it was the manager, kept trying to make her, and one night Lou was waiting for her out in the dump where they lived, miles from nowhere, and when she was late, he got jealous, imagine that, jealous over old Francie, yes, jealous as all get-out, and what does he do but start walking the ten miles to the roadhouse just to see if that guy is keeping her there, and all of a sudden he remembers some kid down the road with a bicycle and he steals it and rides to the roadhouse, pedalling away against a wind for an hour and a half, his calves hurt still just remembering it, and when he got there he saw Francie playing for a big crowd of customers and like a fool he'd forgotten it was the night of some firemen's banquet and the place was keeping open all night, and he felt like such a fool he didn't even let her know he was there, but turned around and wheeled back home. She was there when he got home, the boss' bus took all the help home, and she was worried sick not finding him, and they had a fight because he wouldn't tell her where he'd been, and by God he never did, either.

"William," Jay called the porter, "will you step up to the engine again and say Mr. Oliver will take over as soon as we pass South Norwalk?"

"William," said Lou," will you furbish up these glasses? There are four of us here."

"Sure is good to see you again, Mr. Lou," said William.

"I got held up here last fall in the hurricane," said Jay. "Train from Boston got stuck just ahead of Providence and by golly we sat there for hours. Ferry boat sailed right up past the window. A couple of old bags and I got out and hired a brokendown taxi to drive us to South Norwalk. Fifty bucks. Took all day, what with roads washed up, trees floating around."

"I was in the Biltmore in Providence afterward," said Lou. "They showed me where the water came up in the Falstaff Room there."

The porter brought the fresh supply of drinks and lined them up on the windowsill. The dog immediately knocked one over, and this set Jay off into roars of laughter.

"Look at that face, Lou. Won't Ebie die when she sees him? Looks like my old man, I mean that. By God the old man used to come home from the road on four legs, too, just the same as Handsome here. Used to hear him coming up the steps on his hands and knees, fried to the gills, and the old lady right behind him giving it to him. 'So that's what you do with your expense account? So that's where the money goes? So that's how you wear out your new clothes!' and 'Where'd you get that carnation in your buttonhole, you old bastard?' I used to lie in bed, scared stiff, sorry for the old boy, you know. I was just a kid."

"My old man was in insurance," said Lou. "We used to move every spring. Akron, Erie, Buffalo, Evansville, Lansing —big houses, little houses, boarding houses, mansions—we never knew how we'd land."

Lou looked at his watch. It was four o'clock.

"Say, what am I doing on this train?" he wanted to know. "I had a date with Florabella an hour ago. Where we going?"

"Take it easy, Lou," Jay soothed him, "you got to relax, now, I mean that. We're just running out to say hello to Ebie. You like Ebie. Ebie likes you. Then there's Handsome. I couldn't very well take an animal that size out there alone, could I?"

"Why me?" Lou asked. "Why didn't you get Frank Buck?"

Jay yawned and pulled a newspaper over his face.

"Do me a favor, Handsome," he instructed the dog, with a weary sigh, "entertain Donovan while I catch a nap."

"How'm I going to get back?" Lou asked. "I can't take time out like this with things the way they are."

"Relax, Lou, for Christ's sake. You got nothing to worry about but money and that'll be gone in no time. Relax, old man."

Resigned, Lou stretched out on his seat. He pulled the funnies over his eyes, and the old days, the old hard luck days came dancing past like an old flicker, and for some reason they didn't seem bad at all, they seemed real, even fun, the panics and the triumphs seemed realer now than anything else, he couldn't understand why that was unless it was age, with all its sentimental fog, creeping up on him. Or maybe it was just his brain trying to keep from thinking about Trina and Rosenbaum and Mary and the kid back in Chicago, and a winter's work gone to pieces. Maybe that was it. Anyway, the whirring of the wheels was soothing. The dog, Handsome, looked anxiously from one paper-covered face to the other, then back to the remaining highballs poised on the window-sill and moaned lugubriously.

XXI

EBIE was in her studio over the garage, having such breakfast as Buck Kinley, her colored handy man, was in the
mood to serve. There was only warmed-over biscuits, bacon
and coffee, so Ebie judged that neither Buck nor his wife
Minelda was feeling very well this morning after their night in
town.

"Where's the cream?" she asked, not caring much.

"Minelda used it up this mawning," Buck said, yawning.
"She say she jes' felt like drinkin' some cream this mawning."

Nothing to be done about that. Minelda was boss of this
place. If something didn't suit Minelda she was likely to take
Buck and march right back to Asheville, leaving Ebie all alone
on this godforsaken farm. Serve her right, too. You ought
to be satisfied to let little-gray-home-down-by-the-old-mill-
stream-and-so-on be a tenor solo, your own fault if you bought
the property. Your own fault, too, if you were fool enough to try
to live in it and prove something or other about yourself
that didn't matter to anyone but you, and besides you got sick
proving it. She couldn't complain, really, about the getting
sick part, because that was where Jay had suddenly showed
up as the big protector. You'd think that finding her in bed
with pneumonia was all he'd ever been waiting for. Now she
was well and sick of the place, but it was Jay's dream home, now,
and she had to stay and be part of the song, me-and-you-in-the-
little-home-down-by-the-old-millstream. That was what she
always wanted, all right, then, what was she kicking about?

"Mis' Vane, where'd you put that gin?" Buck asked.

"Buck, you're not going to have gin before breakfast?"
Ebie protested.

"Yessum," said Buck, "that's what I'm gonna have. Where
is it?"

Ebie, resigned, motioned to the cupboard beside the stove
and Buck hastened to help himself. He poured out a tum-
blerful and started downstairs with it.

"I better take some to Minelda, she don't feel so hot," he
explained. "The way she's feelin' this mawning she's ready to

pick up and go. Say she's got on her travellin' shoes, heels afore and heels behind."

"What's the trouble now?" Ebie asked.

"Minelda's settin' to retire," Buck said. "She say she's gonna get outa the washin' and ironin' racket."

"Better hustle over with that gin," Ebie advised.

After he went she sat by the stove with her coffee, her back to the work-in-progress on the easel, said work being a "Haunted House" item that after three weeks fussing still looked like an ad for a new residental section, just as the "Old White Church" canvas in the corner looked like a bride's silverware ad, and the "Old Village Character" portrait would be well set-off by a caption "What This Fellow Needs is a Knox Hat." They didn't look so much worse than anyone else's, if she weren't so darned realistic she could believe they were even better than average. That was what you needed to be a genuine artist, vanity, and vanity on a terrific scale. You could talk all you wanted about the virtues of stick-to-it-iveness, faith-in-yourself, but nobody but an egotistical dumb-bell would have such blind faith in himself that he'd stick to it for years, not noticing he was no better than anybody else. Well, she was good in her own line. She could get an odd job now and then if she went back to town. Rosenbaum had called her on a couple. But Jay liked her better out here, waiting for him to show up. He had called her up last night from some tavern around town, she couldn't make out where, and she didn't ask or demand that he come right out, because you can't do that when you're trying to show how much more understanding you are than the other woman. You're on a spot, there. It's no wonder a man takes advantage of it. On the other hand, Jay wasn't required to understand or forgive anything. He'd walked out on a wife for her sake, so now he had permanent privileges to do as he liked and be forgiven.

"Never mind where I am," he kidded her over the phone, "the point is, where are you?" So he was on a bender. All right, then, he was on a bender. "I want you to tell me and tell me right, what the hell are you doing?"

"I'm listening to the radio, darling," Ebie said. "I've listened to Fibber and Molly and I'm almost ready for Raymond Gram Swing. Any objections?"

"I get it, you're in no condition to see Lou and me, then," Jay said. She could tell he must have spent the day on this one, and she could hear dance music behind him so he was still having fun. If Lou was with him they had some girls, too, those two never wasted their time running around alone. Jay would tell her all about it, they would laugh together about it later, and he would say how well she understood him. Well, she had to. "Sure, I run around," he'd tell her, "it's my nature, but you know you're the one I always come back to, you're the one I have to have, you understand that, Ebie."

"I know, darling," she would say.

The trouble was she had too much time to think out here in the country, waiting for him to pop in and out. It was a little scary getting your heart's desire after getting used to a life of just wishing for it. Here was Jay, all set to marry her as soon as he got his divorce, and also all set for her to forgive him legally the rest of his life. Any fool could see that was no improvement over their old situation, so far as she was concerned. She'd just have to sit home waiting to hear his confessions and forgive him. That was the trap she had been begging for. That was all everybody fought for, worked for, demanded as their right—traps. There was Lou Donovan, getting along fine, free, arrogant, sitting pretty, when he notices he has no trap so he hunts around for a super-duper-trap, little Trina Kameray. And here was she, Ebie, smart girl, for ten years chasing after a man who was pure poison to her career, to any career, made her business success seem silly because *he* was all she wanted, made this whim of hers for a farm a permanent cage for herself because it suddenly struck *him* just right. Talk about learning through your own mistakes, all you ever learned was, "This thing I'm after, this thing I'm going to do is a mistake and I'll always regret it, but that isn't going to stop me now." That was the value of experience. Experience told you not to lose your temper when the man you'd been wanting for ten years called up for the third time long after midnight and cordially invited you to hop in a car and bring Fibber and Molly and Swing over to Billy's Back Room somewhere on the road between Danbury and Brewster. Experience told you that was where the other woman lost out, nagging him to death, accusing, raising Cain, so it was up to you to be sweet, so what do you do? You lose your temper.

"But I tell you we can't leave now, Ebie," Jay patiently explained. "Listen, honey, will you just keep your trousers on while I explain? I'm in a game, I tell you, I just got a dream hand, I can't leave. I——"

So she hung up. Sweet, that was what she was. Now she was sorry, because there it was, she'd rather have Jay driving her crazy the rest of her life, than anything else. She put on the sweater hanging on the hook under the eaves and went downstairs, through the dark garage into the bright April sun. There was the old red barn where her mother was always storing her auction treasures, there was the elegant chicken house, the only modern, well-heated, well-roofed building on the place, now made available to Buck and Minelda by the fortuitous demise of the last chicken. Ebie crossed the road and opened the little white gate to the house proper, a jolly enough little house except that the roof leaked and it was cold as Greenland in every room but the kitchen. Minelda was in the kitchen, large, black and bossy, whipping up a cake, and plainly benefitted by the potion Buck had brought her.

"Mr. Oliver coming out today, Miss Vane?" she asked. "I thought he was bringing you a dawg this week."

Ebie was just explaining that Mr. Oliver must have forgotten about the dog when there was a loud honk-honking out in front from a yellow taxicab, an unfamiliar sight on these deserted roads. Ebie went out, with Buck running behind her, and saw a large gray doleful face peering out the window. It was handsome, unhappy beneath a pink paper hat. The driver leaned out to ask if this was Miss Vane.

"The gentlemen kept me waiting all night there and then they thought the dog had better come home," he explained. "Get out, there, Handsome."

It was such an unhappy, dignified beast, that Ebie began to laugh, as she patted him. It was plain to see that being sent home from a bar at this hour in the morning was a mortifying experience for him. A Scottie was what she'd asked for.

"Would you mind telling me what happened to the gentlemen?" she inquired.

The driver was willing to tell anything he knew. The two gentlemen had asked him to summon two other cabs, one to take one of the gentlemen out here later on presumably, the other to drive the other gentleman to New York. Personally he had no idea when they were leaving Bill's Back Room, but maybe they had started right after he left.

"Tell Minelda to feed him, will you, Buck?" Ebie ordered.

She was sick with disappointment. That was the way it would be, she'd be stuck out here waiting for him, and he'd be some place else having a good time, forgetting to let her know, just being sure that anything was all right with old Ebie. She'd just like to show him. She thought she had when she came out here but it hadn't worked out that way. It would be just like him to go back to New York with Lou, without even coming out to the farm. She ought to be braced for anything after all these years. Well, she had her work. She'd just put him out of her mind, forget about him till he walked in, paint like mad, bad or good, and just show that women could forget the same as men. She started back to the studio, while Handsome loped into the kitchen with Buck. At the bottom of the studio stairs she turned and came back. She looked down the road after the vanishing taxi, and after a moment's hesitation started walking rapidly in that direction. If Jay *had* started—and the taxi man said he might have—he'd come this way. She'd walk along to meet him and—if he *did* come, if he *hadn't* gone on to New York with Lou, she could ride back with him.

That was the kind of sap she was.

XXII

M R. LOWRY paused on the way to the bar to cast a furtive
look of admiration at himself in the mirror, observing
once again how exquisitely his beige shirt set off the rich chestnut waves of his toupée. Two young ladies, emerging from
the elevator, bowed to him with what he felt was more than
their customary warmth and he thought that next time he saw
them having a drink in the bar it would do no harm, as manager, to suggest their having a drink on the house. He smiled
gently picturing their astonished, happy faces, their grateful
cries of joy, and he was mentally offering them a second round
and what-about-dashing down to Barney's for a third (the
dark one decided to go home here and he was left with the
red-haired one, who made no bones about the terrific physical
pull he had for her) when he actually did get to the bar and had
to readjust to the somewhat drab reality of old Mrs. Vane.

"Well, well, my dear child," he said in the fatherly tone he
used with the old ladies, "you're looking fifteen years younger
today."

Mrs. Vane, who was going over some pink slips at the bar,
and lecturing Albert, the bartender, on the outrageous indifference of America to the poetry of Emily Dickinson, looked
sharply at Mr. Lowry through her lorgnette.

"Nonsense," she stated, "that toupée seems to have gone
to your head, Mr. Lowry. Here's a message from Four A. Says
the butterfly sofa I brought her from Pittsfield was filled with
baby mice. Ridiculous on the face of it."

"Must have been a mother mouse there somewhere,"
agreed Albert.

"Sit down, Mr. Lowry," commanded Mrs. Vane. "I was just
telling Albert that Emily Dickinson used to carry a little scrap
of poem in her apron pocket for days, days, mind you."

"Absent-minded, I guess," Albert said understandingly, and
swiped up the bar before placing Mrs. Vane's brandy before her.

Mrs. Vane leafed over her pink telephone slips, studied
them through her lorgnette, finally straightened them out
fondly and with a deep sigh of responsibility tucked them

away in a special corner of her large plaid handbag. Since the maw of the bag revealed a delirious tangle of goggles, cough-drops, aspirin, bank-books, post-cards, timetables, road-maps, memorandum pads, and spirits of ammonia, the careful consideration Mrs. Vane gave to the correct filing of her telephone slip seemed, even to the amiable Albert, a perfectly unreasonable waste of time.

"How's the antique business?" inquired Mr. Lowry, now studying his image in the mirror behind the bar. "Our little manicurist tells me you're branching out wonderfully."

Mrs. Vane nodded with a preoccupied air, then fixed the eagle eye intently on Mr. Lowry.

"Mr. Lowry," she asked. "How would you like a gun?"

Mr. Lowry blinked, and stammered that it was not his heart's desire that moment, but——

"We have a beautiful piece," she interrupted, "a Revolutionary musket that was used by General Washington. The thing for you to do is to put it on the wall in the lobby, with a photograph of Washington."

"Ah, yes," said Mr. Lowry, looking vague. "That might be a good suggestion. Still——"

"Listen to this, Albert," said Mrs. Vane, and held a small volume close to her nose, "this is the stanza I was telling you about yesterday——"

Albert, drawing a beer for the glum man in the derby at the end of the bar, hastily delivered same and leaned on his elbows respectfully, but Mr. Lowry escaped to the doorway, where suddenly a smile of visible ecstasy came over his face. He opened the door and held it open with something approaching a salaam, while a sharp draft whizzed in and enlivened the customers at the bar, indeed obliging Mrs. Vane's camphorated velvet drapes to flutter about her shoulders. The cause of Mr. Lowry's pleasure was soon evident. A shining new station wagon with a slight dusting of snow on the roof to testify to its voyaging had stopped in front of the Ellery, and from this emerged a middle-aged figure in checked brown trousers and swaggering polo coat, brief-case in hand. He was about to pull another bit of luggage from the car, but Mr. Lowry anticipated this by snapping his fingers at the venerable porter now delivering a fresh pink slip to Mrs. Vane.

"Get that luggage, there, boy," ordered Mr. Lowry, and then called out the door, "The boy will take it in, don't trouble about it, Mr. Truesdale."

Mr. Truesdale nodded briefly, acknowledging this, and came in the bar pulling off great woolen mittens so busily he ignored the manager's outstretched hand.

"Howja do, Lowry," he murmured, glancing around the bar.

"Well, well, well, Mr. Truesdale," boomed Lowry, beaming. "Hope your trip was successful."

"Get that front suite for me, Lowry?" Truesdale demanded. "I'm too exhausted to put up with that noisy hole you gave me last month."

"Everything's arranged, Mr. Truesdale," said Lowry, happily. "We moved the Peppers out of the corner suite and it's yours. That back suite was a mistake, very regrettable, I had no idea those people in the next room were so undesirable."

"Hope you put 'em out," said Truesdale. "Can't have that sort of thing in here."

"Exactly," agreed Lowry, tiptoeing behind Truesdale to the bar. "I said to them, 'See here,' I said, 'Mr. Truesdale is one of our oldest and most valued guests. Anyone he complains of in this hotel must go,' so—they went. I said, 'The Prince George or the Seville are up the street or the Lafayette further down,' I said——"

Truesdale waved his hand, frowning.

"Never mind, never mind, Lowry," he said. "I have to talk to Mrs. Vane here, no time for horseplay."

Mrs. Vane tucked away her reading glass and book in her bag at sight of Truesdale.

"We'd better take the booth," she said significantly. "Did you look at the choir-pew?"

Truesdale nodded.

"Beautiful piece," he informed Mr. Lowry. "Victorian pew, you see. Found it in an old barn outside Pawtucket. Ideal piece for the bar here, as a matter of fact, unique doncha know, especially with the stained glass window."

"He wouldn't take the gun," Mrs. Vane accused.

"I have to consider," Mr. Lowry protested, "I'm only the manager."

Mr. Truesdale took out a pencil and envelope and scribbled something.

"I'll speak to one of the better places, if you like, Mrs. Vane," he said patronizingly. "Of coss, only a rally fust claws place would be interested in a choir-pew bar corner."

Mr. Lowry looked unhappily down at his nails. He was not comforted by the appearance of the two pretty girls in the bar-room who this time definitely gave him the eye.

"I'm sorry you don't consider the Ellery a first class hotel, Mr. Truesdale," he said. "We're not big, we're not the newest hotel in the world, but we try to keep up our own little standard."

"I dassay, I dassay," impatiently retorted Truesdale. "Come, Mrs. Vane, let's take the booth where we won't be annoyed."

Mr. Lowry hastened ahead to the corner booth and flicked his handkerchief over the table, lifted the ashtray and set it down again, stepped aside with a bow after these preparations to allow the seating of the couple. Mr. Truesdale looked over the manager, frowning. The manager smiled, waiting for the comment, and finally ventured it himself.

"I know what you mean," he giggled. "It's the toupée. Do you notice it? It does take a little off the age, doesn't it?"

"Maybe so," conceded Truesdale, and added reminiscently to Mrs. Vane, "I recall the same remark was made to me at one time by the late Lord Hawkins, personal friend, of coss, we'd been to India together, Tanganyka, too, for that matter, great hunter, of coss, but bald as an owl. 'Truesdale,' he said, 'do you think a toupée of some sort would make me look a bit younger?' and I said, 'Hawkins, does a baby need a toupée to look younger?'"

"Ha, ha," guffawed Mr. Lowry. "That's good, that's damn good. Ha ha ha!"

He went away, wiping tears of laughter from his eyes, and was still shaking his head at the irresponsible wit of Mr. Truesdale as he passed the two young ladies smiling at him from the bar. He was not too overcome to note their eager eyes and reflected that if they thought their youth and looks entitled them to any extra favors from the manager they had another guess coming. If he looked as good as that to them he must look good enough to get younger and prettier women than they, by Gad, no use fussing around your own territory, getting into trouble, getting the other guests talking. In the hotel lobby, behind the desk, he adjusted his face into its normal gravity, picked up some letters for Mr. Truesdale in the "To Be Held" compartment of the mailbox, weighed them thoughtfully, and muttered, "The bastard! Wouldn't you know a little pipsqueak like that would come out on top while hardworking people like me are always in the hole?"

The ancient bellboy shuffled up to the desk.

"Now, what?" snapped Mr. Lowry.

"Everybody keeps asking me when the new management starts," apologetically explained the fellow. "They keeps sending me down to find out. I don't know what to tell them."

"Everything will go on as usual," said Mr. Lowry with restrained annoyance. "The raise in rates is effective next week. Guests will be notified of further changes as they take place."

"Some of them wants to know if the rates will go down after the World's Fair closes," the fellow went on inquiringly.

"How do I know?" barked Mr. Lowry. "Everything possible will be done to keep our standard the same as always, even if we have to double our prices to accomplish this. Everything!"

The sale of the Ellery Hotel had been a shock to Mr. Lowry, but nothing like the shock it had been to discover that Mr. Vernon Truesdale had been the guiding spirit in this transaction. In pointing out the possibilities of the Hotel Ellery to Lou Donovan as a quick profit-maker, Mr. Truesdale had noted the convenience of the hotel to World's Fair bus and subway facilities, the cheapness with which the place was run, and the ease with which a Guest Shopping Service could modestly capitalize on the needs of guests, even to World's Fair escort facilities. Mr. Donovan had, with no trouble at all, persuaded Mr. Grahame, head of the midwestern hotel chain, that this modest little New York hotel could be utilized as an adjunct to his more elaborate western establishments, be exploited, as a club, for the New York use of all of these western hotel customers. Vernon Truesdale was now Mr. Grahame's direct representative at the Ellery Hotel (through

the Louis Donovan Service) and it was only a matter of days
before he recommended that Mr. Lowry be thrown out on
his ear as too snobbishly eastern and—as he expressed it in his
last report to the Chicago office—"a genuine Midwestern
type of man be placed in charge here with a staff of same
types, in order to inspire feeling of homeyness and trust."

Mr. Truesdale, thinking of this surprise in store for Mr.
Lowry, permitted himself a slight wry smile as he seated himself in the corner booth opposite Mrs. Vane. Mrs. Vane, with
an air of tremendous importance, adjusted her flowing drapes,
recaptured from the floor the decayed morsel of imitation
leopard which she wore as ornament more than protection
against drafts, and after a sharp glance around for possible spies,
leaned toward Mr. Truesdale and hissed, "Must have some
advice, that's why I sent word to you. It's about my property."

"My advice is to sell it," said Mr. Truesdale with conviction. "Run down neighborhood, repairs required, money in
the bank a much better proposition right now, my dear
woman."

Mrs. Vane's eyes glistened with approval at this advice
which fortunately coincided with the action she had just
taken. She opened her bag, a dreamy expression playing
about her otherwise ferocious old face, and produced a folded
paper which she put in front of Mr. Truesdale. She looked
around cautiously again and then spoke in the reverent, loving murmur with which young mothers speak of their new-
born and old women speak of money.

"The money's already in the bank," she confided. "Plus the
deed stock and collateral. What do you think of Eastman Ko-
dak as my next buy?"

It is amazing how those three little words, "money in bank"
can bring the dewy sparkle of first love to old ladies' eyes. Little voices crying "grandma" do not tug at the old heart-strings
as do those sweet words "collateral," "stocks and bonds,"
"piece of property" and dearest of all "money in the bank,"
and no one who has seen a woman over sixty dress up to whisper these soft words to her banker or broker can doubt that
woman's final love must be negotiable. Mrs. Vane, having
passed through her affairs with woman suffrage, poetry, social
work and current events, had arrived at the usual triangle, her

passion for food and her true love for the Guarantee Trust. It did not matter how small the sums were that passed through her hands, the point was that sums were passing, the little things piled up in the cunningest way imaginable, and what could be more heartwarming than talking about them in rapt murmurs over a glass of brandy? Mrs. Vane had flirted with "property" and "profits" for years without ever being sure whether she was ahead or behind, the main thing was the sense of power, but in the last winter her resolute forays into the old barns and chickenhouses of the Eastern seaboard had unearthed unexpected little profits. Tenants in her "property" were bullied into buying these treasures, and if these deals were merely spasmodic adventures there was a healthy honest satisfaction in getting paid even a modest sum for something quite worthless. It had thoroughly revitalized Mrs. Vane, and while her literary prejudices were as vigorous as ever she was not blind to the even fresher thrills Mr. Truesdale had brought into her life in assisting her "antique" business. Mr. Truesdale had sold Ebie the house in Connecticut which had set off Mrs. Vane, he had tipped her on how to get the customer first before the object, if possible. Mr. Truesdale would long since have wriggled out of Mrs. Vane's clutches except for an exaggerated conception of the old lady's finances, and a pride in her resorting to him for final judgments on matters her bank and broker had already advised her. It was astounding to Mr. Truesdale to find his authoritative words to Mrs. Vane often turn out perfectly sound, and thinking of the profit some word of his had brought her he would mutter to himself, "Well, I'll be damned, what do you know? It really worked, by Gad, it really did. Well, I'll be damned."

"Have you consulted your daughter?" he now remembered to ask.

Mrs. Vane looked pained.

"Vernon, you know perfectly well I never consult any one but you. Ebie doesn't have a brain in her head, and besides I never see her."

"She's still on the farm, of coss," Mr. Truesdale said tentatively.

"I haven't the faintest idea," said Mrs. Vane with candid indifference. "Very likely so. Ebie's just like her father, no spirit

of adventure at all. Wanted me to stay out there in that god-
forsaken place. Ridiculous. I have to be in touch with affairs.
Let the young people stay out in the country and rot their
brains, if that's all they ask. Personally, a woman of my intelligence has to be right here in the center of things, looking
after my affairs. You know that, Vernon."

"The art work," said Mr. Truesdale, "does she continue
with it?"

The subject plainly bored Mrs. Vane for she tapped the
table nervously, impatient to get back to her romance with
property.

"Ebie's throwing herself away," she said. "She doesn't
make a cent—just paints around the place. Then she cries.
Absolutely ridiculous. I can't be around people crying, I told
her. No go. I have my own life to live."

"I understand she was sick quite a while," ventured Mr.
Truesdale.

"Is that so?" Mrs. Vane rattled the paper in front of him.
"See if that sounds legal to you, Vernon. I don't trust any one
but you."

"Hmm, let's see," Mr. Truesdale stroked his chin.
"Hmmm. Yes. Hmm. I see."

He was about ready to make a stab in the dark, having no
knowledge of deeds or mortgages, and okay the paper, when
he was relieved to be called to the telephone by the bellboy.
It was a call from Lou Donovan, asking if he could locate
Mrs. Kameray for him, who should be at the office that afternoon. Mr. Truesdale had not been keeping his eyes and ears
open for fifty years for nothing and he could have given a
fairly sound guess on Mrs. Kameray's whereabouts, if not the
exact place at least the company in which she could be found
most any time she was not with Mr. Donovan; it seemed
more professional, however, to merely accept the duty and say
nothing. It was a good way to clear himself of an evening listening to Mrs. Vane so he went back to the bar with a lighter
heart. She was frowning over her volume of Emily Dickinson
when he got back with his excuses.

"I'm sorry you have to go, Vernon," she said. "You're the
only intelligent person I know, the only person I can discuss
poetry with."

XXIII

"D O YOU want me to call the house?" Miss Frye asked.
    She stood in the door of the office bar, looking at him
curiously. Her hat was on, ready to go.

"I know, I heard you before," Lou muttered, just sitting
there staring out the window at the summer sun glittering
on the blue lake beyond. His bag was on the chromium-
trimmed bar chair just as he had left it, half-opened, the
new dull rose shirt on top. He knew Miss Frye was giving
him those funny looks just as she had ever since he came
in, and it got on his nerves. You can't keep up a front
every minute, and Frye ought to be smart enough by this
time not to show surprise when things seemed a little unusual.

"I checked over the liquor supply last week," said Miss
Frye, finally getting the idea that routine details of the business were all the boss cared to hear at this minute. "We're low
on Ballantines and Black and White and I reordered. Short on
brandy, too, but I didn't know what kind you wanted. What's
that stuff on the end there?"

"Sloe gin," said Lou. "It's the old honkytonk dish."

"You'd know," said Miss Frye, and he grinned. That was a
little more like it, she thought, but she still hated to leave him
there without doing something for him.

"How many you got coming in?" she asked.

"There's two or three hundred of them over at the Blackstone," he said. "The Western hotel men. They're all looking
for something for tonight and without wanting to brag about
my city I think, by God, they'll find it. So probably only a
dozen or so will turn up here."

"I guess there's plenty for that many, then," she said.
"They couldn't have used up that six thousand dollars worth
of liquor here in just a year. Look, Mr. Donovan, do you want
me to say anything to Mrs. Donovan? Tell her you're not
back yet or something like that?"

Lou whirled around at her.

"Miss Frye, for God's sake what do you want to know? I'm here. You got your salary. It's six o'clock. Why don't you go home?"

Miss Frye's mouth opened.

"All right, all right," Lou shouted, "if you want to know, I've already been home. I saw my wife. I saw my wife's room, too, with some guy's fifty-cent necktie hanging up over the dresser, and a bottle of ten-cent-store hair grease in the bathroom, a lousy bottle of hair grease in my bathroom! Carnation Hair Oil! That was the kind of guy my wife picked to put her to bed! A five- and ten-cent store gigolo!"

"I know," Miss Frye murmured, "it was that Spaniard she picked up the night she showed up at the Spinning Top! It was awful."

"You know so much, what do you hang around asking questions for?" Lou snarled. "I suppose you know all about her showing up there that night, plastered, all alone, playing the drums with the orchestra, asking this lousy foreigner to dance with her, taking him home——"

"Listen, Mr. Donovan, she wasn't herself, she was just getting even," Miss Frye cried out, "honestly, Mr. Donovan, you can't blame a woman, when you never are home any more and you do have somebody else——"

"Shut up!"

Miss Frye shut up. Lou was ashamed.

"All right, I was a bastard, myself. All right. But when a man's wife, the woman he has a right to expect something from, maybe not faithfulness but at least good taste, breeding, for Christ's sake, when she takes on a phoney with a fifty-cent tie and Carnation Hair Oil—even the pajamas, mind you, were there—imitation black silk pajamas, this sheik, this phoney Valentino——"

"Maybe you left some imitation lace panties around her room yourself once," Miss Frye, nettled, rose to defend her sex. "I don't notice you men always picking your social equals for bed, either."

It was ridiculous taking it out on Miss Frye. Old Frye, the only woman he could ever really count on, so far as that went. She would do anything for him, he knew that. Loyal. Still, there was nothing like loyalty to get on a person's nerves. Funny, but there it was.

"Frankly, Miss Frye, if you want to know the truth, I think my wife is going nuts," Lou said, more calmly. "That's all I can figure out. Takes this guy out to the black and tan every night, flaunts him in front of my business friends——"

"I know," said Miss Frye, "I didn't want to tell you before. That's why the Harrods kept trying to find you. The idea is it's all your fault starting her off with your divorce talk."

"Oh, sure," said Lou. "Everything's my fault. Oh, sure."

"Well, if you wanted to get out, now's your chance," Miss Frye said hopefully. "At least everybody knows now you got a reason. Everybody's seen her tooting around town with that heel."

"Oh, sure, it's all simple as that," Lou said bitterly. "I can walk out and leave a wife that's going nuts, sure, that's easy. What kind of piker would that look like? How long do you think I would be in business when that little news got around?"

"Lots of women doing what she's doing," Miss Frye said. "They're not nuts, either."

Lou didn't answer. He wasn't going to tell about Mary taking her clothes off the minute he got in the house and imitating the Spinning Top hootch dancer, yelling out, "This is what you like, isn't it? This is why you always leave me. This is what you're crazy about, all right, give me time, I'll be the kind of woman you like. Why don't you kiss me? Make love to me, go on, show me how the other woman does, I'll learn—" Lou had backed out of the room, his blood congealing, he had run down the hall to get the baby's nurse. The nurse only looked at him with cold hostile eyes.

"Mrs. Donovan's perfectly all right. She drinks by herself now, that's all," said the nurse. "It's your fault, Mr. Donovan. I don't need to tell you that."

"Well, go look after her, anyway," Lou had ordered. "Call her aunt. Call a doctor."

"Mrs. Donovan doesn't need a doctor," the nurse said harshly. "I'll give her a sedative myself. A doctor can't do anything about a woman being so unhappy she don't know what she's doing."

Lou had quietly picked up his bag and driven back to town. No point in telling these things to Miss Frye. No point in even thinking about them. No point in remembering that cheap perfume smell, that lousy hair-oil—that sheik, that dime-a-dancer——

"I'll stay at the Stevens till things settle," he said to Miss Frye. "Stock up the cognac tomorrow. And don't say anything."

Jay Oliver stuck his head in the door.

"What—no dames?" he exclaimed. "I was told you'd ordered a fresh lot from the Spinning Top for six o'clock maneuvers."

"What are you doing in town?" Lou demanded. "You old son-of-a-gun, they told me you never gave us a tumble since you switched to the Eastern office."

It was fine seeing Jay again. You got so used to getting Jay out of hot water that you missed him more than anybody else when he wasn't around needing help.

Jay threw an arm over Lou's shoulder.

"I sneak in," he whispered in his ear, mysteriously. "I creep in in the middle of the night and creep out. But I heard the gang was coming in over here so I thought I'd drop around."

"Flo still raising Cain?" Lou asked.

Jay nodded sorrowfully.

"When I don't catch it from Flo I get it from Ebie," he confided. "I just choose which hell I want to take. I usually take Ebie's but I get Flo's long distance, then."

"Why don't you hang up?"

Jay looked grieved.

"Listen, can't I catch hell if I want to? Anyway, with Ebie I like it because then we make up. Make a note of that, will you, Miss Frye? You got to fight to make-up."

"Tell our friend here about Mrs. Oliver," Lou urged Miss Frye. "It's a panic."

"She calls up here all the time," Miss Frye obediently revealed. "She says 'You can just tell Lou Donovan I hope he's good and satisfied now that he's ruined a home.'"

"Can you beat it?" Lou exclaimed. "Can you beat that, no kidding? A woman spends a lifetime ruining her own home and then blames it on somebody else. Me. Old Lou Donovan."

"She blames everything on you, Mr. Donovan," Miss Frye giggled. "You're the boy that taught Mr. Oliver to drink, you forced his first drop down his throat, you're the one that made him gamble and chase skirts and be a bum."

"That's right," Lou admitted. "I remember the trouble I had teaching Jay to like women. We had to tie him, he was that wild, but by God, we drove the lesson home."

"I'll leave you to give him another lesson," said Miss Frye. "I'll leave the door open for those little tramps."

"Tessie and Marie and Bobby tramps?" Lou reproached her indignantly. "Hell, they all live with their mothers."

"Then I'll leave it wide open," said Miss Frye, "in case they bring the mothers."

After she went Jay pulled a chair up beside Lou.

"What burns Flo up is that she can't get me back to give me hell to my face," he explained. "That's all a wife wants a guy to come back for. Either that or she wants to remind him all the rest of his life of how she forgave him that time. Flo's got everything sewed up in her name and it makes her boil that Ebie doesn't give a whoop. It makes her sore that she can't say the other woman is after my money."

"She got me on the phone once," Lou said. "She says, 'If you happen to see that so-and-so husband of mine you can just tell him I'm suing for plenty alimony, and what's more I'm taking a trip to Hawaii after I leave Reno. You can just tell him I'm the one that's got the pocketbook, and don't he wish he could take that woman of his some place.' I said, 'O.K., Flo, if I see him I'll tell him.' "

"That mother of hers!" Jay shook his head in gloomy recollection. " 'That's right, Florence,' she'd say to Flo, 'go ahead and make him give it to you. If you don't get it, Number Two will.' Not much left for Number Two when those two harpies get through with a fellow. Not that Flo hasn't got some good qualities."

"Doesn't Ebie get sore at all you got to pay out to Flo?"

"Ebie don't care about anything but having me around," Jay said complacently. "She says, 'Go ahead, give her everything, we'll get along. I can always go back to work. Give her all the alimony she wants. All I want is you.' That's the way Ebie feels."

Give her time, Lou thought, give her five, ten years and then ask her how she feels about Number One getting all the money, while Number Two has to do her own housework. Give her time.

"I hope marrying Ebie won't spoil things," Jay meditated, frowning. "I kinda hate to get hooked again. This way suits me, but you know women."

Maybe, Lou granted.

"Jesus, Lou, you're too damn smart, that's what makes me mad," Jay said. "You chase but you never get caught. I thought for a while you were letting the Kameray dame play you against Rosenbaum but I guess you didn't let yourself get in as deep there as I thought."

"That's how much you know," Lou commented silently.

"I used to see that little devil putting the screws on you, flashing Rosenbaum's bracelet around, asking your advice in that little phoney shy way she had about going back to her husband or marrying some band leader since she couldn't get any extension on her passport, and I'd think, well, look at old Lou squirming around in the old trap, old Wise Guy Donovan right on the old hook." Jay smiled at the idea of his own mistake. "I might have known you'd get out of that one if any man could. Stringing her along, letting her give you a little more line, and then getting away. Old son of a gun, I wish I had your technic."

Technic. That must be what it was to lie awake nights wondering how soon you could see her again, wondering how to keep from killing the men you knew she slept with, wondering how to give her more than Rosenbaum could give her, Rosenbaum who was so crazy about her he'd give her anything but marriage, but that was the thing she wanted most, and if Lou could only manage it— Now his back was to the wall. How much longer he could mark time with her he didn't know, the game had been getting sharper and sharper lately. Then just as he was giving in, this thing about Mary throws everything out. He couldn't tell that to Trina. Trina had had enough excuses. You couldn't blame Trina.

"I don't know whether it's brains or just fool luck that you never run into trouble," Jay sighed. "I sure envy you, though, old boy."

"I'll change spots with you any day you say," Lou offered.

There was the sound of voices in the adjoining office. It was no treat, in his present mood, for Lou to recognize old man Grahame coming in, and in a condition that his great friend Judge Harrod would not approve. The old boy was tacking in the wind like an old sailboat and a smile of vast good will illuminated his moon face. It was the first time he'd ever done Lou the honor of a social call, but it took more than that to cheer up Lou this day. Pritchard was with him and to add the last touch to a fine day who should be hanging on his arm but old Francie, all dressed up in white with a big straw hat that gave her more than she was entitled to in the way of looks.

"I brought my friend," Pritchard said. "This is Mrs. Thompson, Lou. Have you met?"

"Oh, sure," Lou said. Francie kept looking at him warily as if she thought he was going to bawl her out for coming along, but that was all right. She hadn't bothered him since the night at the Spinning Top months ago, and even though Mary had found out about the first marriage it wasn't Francie but Flo that had told her. You had to be fair, even if it didn't get you anywhere.

"How long do we wait for a drink in this joint?" Jay complained. He got behind the bar with Lou and they fixed up a round. Some more of the men came in and Lou was busy filling glasses. Keep busy, that was the trick, keep doing something, if it was only drinking, till the old brain quieted down. Noise was good, too, noise was wonderful, and there was so much noise in the place suddenly that Lou didn't hear Francie call him, just saw the hundred dollar bill she slid across the bar to him.

"That's the lucky hundred, Lou," she said. "It brought us luck. Frank never had such a run of luck. He's in Saratoga now, waiting for the track to open there. He told me to give you this and gee, Lou, he's so grateful."

"Ah, keep it, Francie," Lou said, but she shook her head and pushed it toward him. If it made her feel better, okay. Nothing could make him feel better, one way or the other.

"I understand you been doing a lot of running around, Francie," he said, in an undertone. "What's the idea? You got a good guy now, why don't you stick to him? You liked him well enough to marry him."

Francie's eyes filled.

"You're the only person for me, Lou," she whispered. "You know that's the only reason I'm running around. Just so damned miserable that's all, ever since you left. It's always you, Lou. I just happen to stay crazy about you."

It was too bad. You can't go around making a fellow feel like hell for not loving you any more. It isn't right. It isn't fair. When Lou didn't say anything Francie dashed a handkerchief across her eyes and turned abruptly to old Grahame who was hanging on to the bar to keep from tipping over like a leaded inkstand.

"Can a fellow get a little drinkie here?" Grahame asked with a little difficulty, then he rather adventurely let go of the bar and thrust his hand across it at Lou. "Great seeing you, old man. Shake hands. Always glad to see you, Donovan, my boy."

Now wasn't that a break for you!

"Thanks," said Lou, "but Cassidy's the name."

A TIME TO BE BORN

To Coburn Gilman

I

THIS WAS no time to cry over one broken heart. It was no time to worry about Vicky Haven or indeed any other young lady crossed in love, for now the universe, nothing less, was your problem. You woke in the morning with the weight of doom on your head. You lay with eyes shut wondering why you dreaded the day; was it a debt, was it a lost love?—and then you remembered the nightmare. It was a dream, you said, nothing but a dream, and the covers were thrown aside, the dream was over, now for the day. Then, fully awake, you remembered that it was no dream. Paris was gone, London was under fire, the Atlantic was now a drop of water between the flame on one side and the waiting dynamite on the other. This was a time of waiting, of marking time till ready, of not knowing what to expect or what to want either for yourself or for the world, private triumph or failure lost in the world's failure. The longed-for letter, the telephone ringing at last, the familiar knock at the door—very well, but there was still something to await—something unknown, something fantastic, perhaps the stone statue from *Don Giovanni* marching in or the gods of the mountain. Day's duties were performed to the metronome of Extras, radio broadcasts, committee conferences on war orphans, benefits for Britain, send a telegram to your congressman, watch your neighbor for free speech, vote for Willkie or for Roosevelt and banish care from the land.

This was certainly no time for Vicky Haven to engage your thoughts, for you were concerned with great nations, with war itself. This was a time when the true signs of war were the lavish plumage of the women; Fifth Avenue dress-shops and the finer restaurants were filled with these vanguards of war. Look at the jewels, the rare pelts, the gaudy birds on elaborate hair-dress, and know that the war was here; already the women had inherited the earth. The ominous smell of gunpowder was matched by a rising cloud of Schiaparelli's *Shocking*. The women were once more armed, and their happy voices sang of destruction to come. Off to the relief offices they rode in their beautiful new cars, off to knit, to sew, to take part in the charade, anything to help Lady Bertrand's cause; off they rode in the new car, the new mink, the new emerald bracelet, the new electrically treated complexion, presented by or extorted from the loving-hearted gentlemen who make both women and wars possible. Off to the front with a new permanent and enough specially blended night creams to last three months dashed the intrepid girl reporters. Unable to cope with competition on the home field, failing with the rhumbas and screen tests of peacetime, they quiver for the easy drama of the trenches; they can at least play lead in these amateur theatricals.

This was a time when the artists, the intellectuals, sat in cafés and in country homes and accused each other over their brandies or their California vintages of traitorous tendencies. This was a time for them to band together in mutual antagonism, a time to bury the professional hatchet, if possible in each other, a time to stare at their Flower Arrangements, Children Bathing, and privately to weep, "What good is it? Who cares now?" The poet, disgusted with the flight of skylarks in perfect sonnet form, declaimed the power of song against brutality and raised hollow voice in feeble proof. This was no time for beauty, for love, or private future; this was the time for ideals and quick profits on them before the world returned to reality and the drabber opportunities. What good for new sopranos to sing *"Vici d'arte, vici d'amore,"* what good for eager young students to make their bows? There was no future; every one waited, marked time, waited. For what? On Fifth Avenue and Fifty-fifth Street hundreds waited for a man on a hotel window ledge to jump; hundreds waited with craning necks and thirsty faces as if this single person's final gesture would solve the riddle of the world. Civilization stood on a ledge, and in the tension of waiting it was a relief to have one little man jump.

This was a time when writers dared not write of Vicky Haven or of simple young women like her. They wrote with shut eyes and deaf ears of other days, wise days they boasted, of horse-and-buggy men and covered-wagon Cinderellas; they glorified the necessities of their ancestors who had laid ground for the present confusion; they made ignorance shine

as native wit, the barrenness of other years and other simpler
men was made a talent, their austerity and the bold compul-
sions of their avarice a glorious virtue. In the Gold Rush to
the past they left no record of the present. Drowning men,
they remembered words their grandmothers told them, forgot today and tomorrow in the drug of memories. A curtain
of stars and stripes was hung over today and tomorrow and
over the awful lessons of other days. It was a sucker age, an
age for any propaganda, any cause, any lie, any gadget, and
scorning this susceptibility chroniclers sang the stubborn cynicism of past heroes who would not believe the earth was
round. It was an age of explosions, hurricanes, wrecks, strikes,
lies, corruption, and unbridled female exploitation. Unable to
find reason for this madness people looked to historical figures and ancient events for the pat answers. Amanda Keeler's
Such Is the Legend swept the bookstores as if this sword-and-
lace romance could comfort a public about to be bombed.
Such fabulous profits from this confection piled up for the
pretty author that her random thoughts on economics and
military strategy became automatically incontrovertible.
Broadcasting companies read her income tax figures and at
once begged her to prophesy the future of France; editors saw
audiences sob over little Missy Lulu's death scene in the
movie version of the romance and immediately ordered definitive articles from the gifted author on What's Wrong with
England, What's Wrong with Russia, What is the Future of
America. Ladies' clubs saw the label on her coat and the quality of her bracelet and at once begged her to instruct them in
politics.

This was an age for Amanda Keelers to spring up by the
dozen, level-eyed handsome young women with nothing to
lose, least of all a heart, so there they were holding it aloft
with spotlights playing on it from all corners of the world, a
beautiful heart bleeding for war and woe at tremendous financial advantage. No international disaster was too small to
receive endorsed photographs and publicity releases from
Miss Keeler or her imitators, no microphone too obscure to
scatter her clarion call to arms. Presented with a mind the
very moment her annual income hit a hundred thousand dollars, the pretty creature was urged to pass her counterfeit

perceptions at full face value, and being as grimly ambitious as the age was gullible, she made a heyday of the world's confusion.

This was the time Vicky Haven had elected to sniffle into her pillow for six months solid merely over her own unfortunate love life, in contrast to her old friend, Amanda Keeler, who rode the world's debacle as if it was her own yacht and saved her tears for Finland and the photographers.

This was certainly no time for a provincial young woman from Lakeville, Ohio, a certain Ethel Carey, to venture into Amanda Keeler's celebrated presence with pleas for Vicky Haven's salvation. Yet, the good-hearted emissary from Lakeville had the effrontery to justify her call on the grounds that there were thousands and thousands of Vickys all over the country, deserted by their lovers, and unable to find the crash of governments as fit a cause for tears as their own selfish little heartbreak. The good-hearted emissary, pondering all these matters on the train to New York, decided that even in this educated age there are little people who cannot ride the wars or if they do are only humble coach passengers, not the leaders or the float-riders; there are the little people who can only think that they are hungry, they haven't eaten, they have no money, they have lost their babies, their loves, their homes, and their sons mock them from prisons and insane asylums, so that rain or sun or snow or battles cannot stir their selfish personal absorption. If their picture was to be taken with their little woe seated on their lap like Morgan's midget it would not matter to them. These little people had no news value and therein was their crime. In their little wars there were no promotions, no parades, no dress uniforms, no regimental dances—no radio speeches, no interviews, no splendid conferences. What unimportant people they were, certainly, in this important age! In a time of oratory how inarticulate they were, in an age where every cause had its own beautiful blonde figurehead, how plain these little individual women were! The good-hearted emissary, Miss Carey, taking Vicky's unimportant sorrow to Amanda, thought about these things hard all the way from Grand Central to her hotel, and finally solved her indecision by having a facial at Arden's to gird her for the fray.

2

The house was Number Twenty-nine all right, and it was East not West but the young lady in the Checker Cab refused to be convinced. There was a mistake somewhere. Of course every one knew that Amanda had done very well for herself in New York, finally landing no less a prize than Julian Evans himself, but somehow this graystone mansion off Fifth Avenue was far grander than one had imagined. The young lady in the taxi couldn't quite picture Amanda in such a fabulous setting and, what was more, she didn't *want* to picture Amanda there. As an old friend from way back she naturally wanted Amanda to get ahead but not out of sight.

"She would!" Ethel thought grimly. "Trust Amanda."

All the way to New York, Ethel had been thinking benevolently of her old school friend's success, flattering herself on her great-hearted lack of envy, but this elegant monument to Amanda's shrewdness threw her right back into her old bitterness. Still, it wasn't exactly bitterness, call it rather a normal sense of justice. Why did Amanda Keeler get everything out of life and not Ethel Carey? The mood lasted but a moment, for Ethel hated to do any one the favor of being jealous. After all, it wasn't such a palace as all that, this Evans house. And fortunately Ethel was not the sort of person to be over-awed by a little material splendor, for the simple reason that the Careys were all bankers back in Lakeville and could hold their own socially or financially with anybody. Another thing, Amanda had not won all the prizes in school; Ethel had had her share. It was not Amanda who was voted "Most Likely to Succeed" but Ethel. Amanda would certainly be fair enough to admit that. Indeed, Ethel felt sure that Amanda would give respectful ear to her old friend's unfavorable reaction to The Book, regardless of the critical raves and the big sale. Amanda knew well enough that Ethel had as good a mind as she had. The book, Ethel was going to say quite frankly, is twice as long as it should have been and—you wouldn't want me to lie to you—perfectly lousy. If it hadn't been for Julian Evans' sixteen newspapers it would never have been such a sensation. And if it hadn't been for Amanda snatching Julian from under his first wife's nose—Ethel pulled herself together sternly. This was no frame of mind in which to ask favors. A few more such animadversions and she'd be ringing the bell and challenging Amanda with, "So you think you're smart, eh?"

Ethel paid the driver and got out of the cab. Facing the imposing five-story house with its gargoyles, its twin stone sphinxes guarding the iron-grilled doorway, a fresh wave of uncertainty came over her. What in heaven's name made her so sure Amanda would not snub her as she was said to snub all her old Middle Western friends? How could she ever restore her self-confidence if Amanda sent word, "Not in"? If it were not for the imperative necessity of doing something about Vicky Haven and her own brilliant plan to make Amanda the means of working Vicky's salvation, Ethel would have given up that very minute and dashed back to the St. Regis. But it was for Vicky she had come to New York, it was for Vicky's sake she was undergoing this severe test of good nature, it was for Vicky she must risk a butler's lifted eyebrow. Dear, dear Vicky, Ethel reminded herself, who had not the faintest notion of the good angels soon to bear her off to felicity and avenge her wrongs for her. Dear Vicky, the most unlucky girl in Lakeville just as Amanda had been the most lucky. Ethel braced herself with these reminders, thoroughly annoyed with herself at her fluttering heart and quaking knees. Here she was, as well dressed as any woman in New York (she was a fanatic about good clothes), money in her pocket, boat acquaintances with the best names in the travelling universe, a cosmopolitan woman in spite of the provincial roots; yet the mere sight of the mansion that Amanda Keeler's carefully milked fame and shrewd marriage had won made her stand there gawking and trembling like any World's Fair tourist. Her head swam with the doubts she tried to deny. Supposing Amanda said, "Ethel Who? Oh, but I meet so many people, and of course I haven't been back in Lakeville for years. You say you want me to do something about Vicky? Vicky Who? Oh, the little thing that had the crush on me in boarding-school? But, my dear Ethel, or is it Edna, you can't expect busy important *me* to give my time to a little sentimental duty like this Vicky What's-her-name when my days are filled with my war committees and my refugee children and my radio talks? Who would print my picture, I ask you, merely as some one who helped out an old friend? And why do you assume I would take up any suggestion of yours anyway? Really, my dear Edna, or Ella, or—"

These morbid anticipations were no whit dispelled by seeing two gentlemen emerge from Twenty-nine, one of them the celebrated liberal Senator—(the leonine, snow-white head and black loose tie were too often cartooned not to be easily recognized)—and the other a square-jawed young man whose face at the head of a political column was syndicated all over America. Yes, these were the people who were entitled to Amanda's time, these distinguished gentlemen now getting into a fine black town-car with grave faces as if they had just listened to the President himself instead of to nobody but Ethel's old friend Amanda who would never have made the best sorority if Ethel hadn't sponsored her. (The Keelers were *nobody* in Lakeville!)

The door was open, the butler stood there waiting for her to utter her business and there was no retreat now.

"Mrs. Evans," she demanded in a ringing voice, for she had just recalled that her own father had been president of the Lakeville Third National when Amanda Keeler's father was clerk in a haberdashery. Little things like that did bring reassurance, and so she was able to enter the reception hall with head high, her handsome foxes tossed proudly over her left shoulder.

The marble-floored, marble-benched foyer was as darkly reassuring as Grant's Tomb. A little appalled, Ethel's eyes, accustoming themselves to the dim light, saw grim Roman tapestries on the walls (or was that horn-of-plenty a Flemish trick?) and urns of enormous chrysanthemums at the foot of the broad staircase. From the hush of this place it might have been a small hospital. Perhaps, Ethel decided, if you were a public institution your home eventually came to look like one.

Of course, in all fairness, you couldn't blame Amanda for this pompous austerity since the house had been Julian Evans' home during his former marriage. Still, after two years, the new wife, if she wanted or knew how, could certainly have altered the style and set her own stamp upon it.

"She still has no taste, thank God," Ethel thought, comfortingly, but the truth was that Amanda was too successful, too arrogantly on top, to even *need* good taste. Good taste was the consolation of people who had nothing else, people like her own self, Ethel thought, inferiority feelings leaping back at her like great barn dogs trying to be pets.

The butler vanished. There she stood, alone with her doubts. She should have telephoned or written a note. It was presumptuous for any one, worst of all an old and quite un-valued friend, to drop in on this national figure, Amanda Keeler Evans, without appointment, expecting her to fly down the banister in an old kimono, hair in curlpapers, arms out-stretched in frantic welcome. It was presumptuous and worse—it was small-town. Yes, that is exactly the way Amanda would react to it, and this—as if Amanda had already made the accusation—made Ethel burn up. After all, Ethel Carey had been visiting New York from the year she was born, she had *always* been at home in New York; long before Amanda Keeler ever heard of the place, even; it was indeed she, Ethel Carey, who had brought the New York scandals and fashions back home to Amanda and the girls at Miss Doxey's, and now New York belonged to Amanda while Ethel was still just a transient from Lakeville. It was not pleasant to think of all the things about New York that Amanda knew now and Ethel had still to learn. For instance, she had never dreamed that these private stone houses had their own private elevators like an apartment house, yet Amanda had one, and there must be many other casual facts of New York life that Ethel had still to learn.

"Mrs. Evans is working," the butler reported, "but you may come up with me to her living-room."

Mrs. Evans' working quarters were on the fourth floor and Ethel was soothed to find that the living-room into which she was ushered up there was refreshingly impossible. Velvet theatrical curtains, more bad tapestries, fur rugs, great ugly vases, gold-framed expensive and enormous paintings by *Saturday Evening Post* cover artists, huge fringed floor-lamps and overstuffed armchairs were benignly smiled upon by a marble bust of possibly Sappho on a corner pedestal. Mr. Evans' former wife or even his mother (the papers said he owed everything to his mother) must be responsible for this décor, and Ethel felt a little fonder of Amanda for this daily cross. There was an ancestor in a great gold frame over the fireplace, a lady ancestor with the hooked beak and chin common to New England and the Old Testament. Her long neck leapt hungrily out of a rather rowdy décolletage. Ethel wondered if Amanda had finally been able to locate an ancestor or if this was one of Evans' prides. On the mantel were twin vases filled with varnished wheat, and a similar pastoral touch freshened a gnarled Chinese vase on an ebony-lacquered console. In a gilded mirror above this console Ethel saw her own face sneering. She had just been thinking that all the place needed was a Southern Methodist pennant and a rubber-plant, but she did not propose to have her expression betray such cynical comments. She was here, after all, to get something from Amanda, to arouse old loyalties, and you couldn't stir up sentiment with your mind stained with envious mockery. The mirror, too, reminded her that her silver foxes looked glaringly new, as if she'd bought them expressly for this visit, her eyebrows were plucked too thin, her suit skirt was too skimpy over the behind, and the new white silk blouse was too white. One thing about *you*, every one in Lakeville always said to Ethel, you always look smart, you've taken care of your figure and your complexion, you keep up, you can hold your own anywhere. Ethel, grimacing at herself with her new uneasiness, thought that what she really looked like was a woman grown pinched and desperate-eyed in the frantic effort to "keep up." She was thirty-two but she looked like a woman of forty so well-preserved she could pass for thirty-two. She had that frustrated-in-the-provinces look, that I-am-the-only-cosmopolite-in-all-Toledo-or-whatever look. It was too desperate. She tried a smile as heart-warming as a dentist's. All right, she was stage-struck and likely to forget her whole mission, if she didn't pull herself together. Remember, she told herself, the visit had nothing to do with her, it was all concerned with poor darling Vicky, who was in such a mess. Yes, she said reviving her ego, she must keep in mind that she and Amanda were two securely placed women about to lift a less fortunate sister out of the morass. The thought sustained her and she was able to take out a cigarette and puff at it with an air of elegant confidence.

On the other side of the center foyer were two doors and from one of these there now emerged a stout, fat-jowled woman with bristling black brows, slick black hair, and wearing a poison-green knitted dress to set off her bulging curves. This figure helped Ethel at once to complacency by its unaffected ugliness.

"I'm Mrs. Evans' assistant," the voice was a well-placed baritone. "Mrs. Evans is working in bed today. Come in."

The rear room was a large and sunny bedroom and surprisingly enough, done in the Hollywood modern style of white rugs, glass tables, and chromium touches quite out of period with the rest of the house. A great white satin-tufted bed fitted into a white-curtained alcove with a half-moon window above it. Here lay Amanda, propped up on cushions in some sort of high-necked Chinese bed coat. Her long blond hair fell to her shoulders in a long bob and her good looks, which consisted chiefly in the contrast of dark olive skin with angel gold hair, were definitely impaired by no make-up and thick-rimmed glasses. Believe me, she needs them, too, Ethel thought with a fresh surge of friendliness, the poor darling is blind as a bat without them. Papers, notebooks, cream jars, a deck of cards and a ten-cent-store dream book were scattered over the pretty coverlet, and Amanda's bed-desk appeared to be nothing less than a ouija board with a big YES in one corner and a big NO in the other. Through her thick glasses Amanda squinted up at Ethel, then held out a left hand, her right still clutching her pen.

"My dear, why on earth didn't you phone first?" she exclaimed. "I'm up to my ears today, but if I'd known I could have cancelled one interview. I had no *idea*! I thought it was that Carey woman from the Czech Relief."

"I should have wired," Ethel admitted, and sat down gingerly on the side of the bed.

The enormous green bosom that seemed to be convoying Miss Bemel's body appeared nearer to the bed, and the baritone voice croaked an interruption.

"I will make a summary of what the Senator just said for your article," said Miss Bemel. "Shall it be necessary to put it in quotes?"

Amanda squinted up at Miss Bemel.

"Certainly not," she said sharply. "After all it's my article, not his; no reason I should give him all that publicity."

"We'll need an additional paragraph to fill the column," said Miss Bemel.

"Put in some statistics about something," Amanda suggested, frowning. "Those Chamber of Commerce reports lying around there. Federal Housing figures for Savannah, maybe. You know. What time is the *Digest* interview?"

"Five," said Miss Bemel, giving Ethel a cold look. "In twenty minutes."

"Ethel, you won't mind popping off when they come, will you?" Amanda asked. Ah, how important little Amanda from Lakeville had become, Ethel inwardly mocked, all these Senators, and columns and *Digest* interviews! And above all these Miss Bemels!

The thing was to pave the way with flattery, and Ethel plunged.

"Every one in Lakeville is so proud of you. They read about you and the *Gazette* reprints all your speeches and all of your letters from London. It must have been frightful during the air raids. I don't see how you had the guts—I mean really, just sticking it out, that way. At the school reunion the girls at Miss Doxey's simply raved about how brave you were."

"My word, I'd rather have been in a few air raids than at the school reunion," exclaimed Amanda, rather ungraciously, Ethel thought.

One thing Amanda's war experience had given her was a brand new English accent that occasionally slipped down like a tiresome shoulderstrap and showed a Middle Western pinning. This was no time to be critical, however, so Ethel went on with the soothing oils.

"Every one talks about the book, naturally," she pursued, and then could not resist a little crack since Amanda's sudden glance at her wrist watch was a bit galling. "Personally I simply cannot read any historical novel, not even for love of you, darling."

Miss Ethel Carey's personal apathy toward Amanda Keeler's best-seller, *Such Is the Legend*, stirred the author to no reaction beyond a faintly complacent smile which made Ethel redden. All right, if Amanda liked to think all unfavorable criticism was mere jealousy, then by all means return to flattery. For a moment Ethel was tempted to insult by exaggerated praise but her instinct informed her that the most burlesque adulation was accepted as sound by some happy egos, and Amanda was one of those. She must, however, feed this appetite until she won her cause, so once more she set out.

"Every one in Lakeville turned out for your wedding in the newsreel," she pursued. "You should have heard them buzz when the close-up came. Right along with the 'Beauty of the Yukon' and 'Pinocchio'! You'd never dream Mr. Evans is forty-eight from his picture. How in the world did you meet him, Amanda?"

Amanda shrugged and then looked at Ethel with faintly surprised curiosity as if wondering why on earth she should be expected to confide a trade secret to an humble old schoolmate when she kept it even from her own self.

"Oh, the usual way, my dear," she said.

The usual way, my eye, thought Ethel, who had heard the story last year in Miami and confirmed a dozen times since. The story was that two years ago when Amanda's novel was merely being considered by a publisher, Amanda wangled an interview with Julian Evans, the great newspaper magnate. When the Evanses went to Miami, Amanda went, too, and hung around his hotel reminding him at every encounter with him of their previous meeting. He went to Rio alone and Amanda managed to follow and get on the same boat coming back. She struck up an intimacy with him in the bar, persuaded him to wire approval of her manuscript to her publisher, and so got it published. This feat, according to Ethel's informants, was accomplished in Amanda's last stronghold, the bed. But you had to give Amanda credit for actually getting a prissy family man like Julian Evans to bed. After that, of course, it was easy, since he was so pious and unaccustomed to affairs that he believed divorce and remarriage automatically followed any infidelity.

"The usual way," Amanda now said, with a yawn. At that it must have given her a kick to have the people who snubbed her for years and rejected her book now start fawning over her because she was Julian Evans' literary protégée and eventually his bride. Then when the power of his newspapers and syndicate swept the book to sensational triumph—oh, yes, Amanda must have permitted herself a secret smile. Ethel found it in her heart to feel a sympathetic pleasure in her old chum's success—yes, they really had been chums, the three of them, Ethel and Amanda, with little Vicky as their mutual charge. At Miss Doxey's they had been inseparable. Amanda could never deny it.

"Amanda, I came to talk to you about Vicky," she said. "A terrible thing has happened to Vicky."

"Little Vicky Haven?" Amanda was roused to interest, for little Vicky had been her slave. "A man?"

Ethel nodded.

"Tom Turner."

"That old sot?" Amanda frowned. "Is he still beauing all the Lakeville virgins?"

"But Vicky took him seriously," said Ethel. "It went on for four or five years, and every one gave up trying to talk her out of it. She did everything for him, apologized for his drinking, cleaned his flat, painted his bookshelves, made his curtains, made an absolute fool of herself. Then six months ago he eloped with her partner."

"Louse," admitted Amanda. "But how dumb of Vicky!"

"You'd feel sorry if you saw her," said Ethel. "The poor kid! All the work she did starting her little real estate business there, making a go of it, then taking that horrible widow, Mrs. Brown, in as her partner. And then having everything go to pieces at once—her lover and her partner."

Miss Bemel stuck her head in the door with a significant nod.

"It's all right, Bemel," Amanda said. "I'll receive them right here. They can wait."

"Imagine having to keep going to your little office every morning after the elopement, with everybody in town knowing you've been jilted," Ethel went on, getting excited. "Imagine having to go over your mail and your business deals with the woman who's got your man, the woman who's just been enjoying *your* bookshelves and *your* curtains in the apartment *you* fixed up. And Lakeville being so small, everybody talked and Vicky hasn't dared go anywhere because people either laugh about it or pity her, so she just cries and gets thin and has to go on with the business because she doesn't have any money but that. And you see her day after day just breaking her heart and not daring to ask Mrs. Brown to get out of the business. But that isn't the worst."

"I can't really be sorry for anybody dumb enough to fall for an old soak like Tom Turner," said Amanda.

"But now, Amanda, they're going to have a baby!" cried Ethel. "Vicky doesn't know it yet, but if she's suffered already just picture what their having a baby is going to do to her."

"Why in God's name doesn't she clear out?" Amanda asked impatiently. "Nobody *has* to stay in Lakeville."

"She's afraid to gamble on making a living any place else," Ethel explained. "And she doesn't want the town to think she can't take it, see. But if somebody in New York offered her a job, all secure, and sent for her—"

"Oh," said Amanda.

"I thought you'd understand," Ethel said, relieved. "You and Mr. Evans have all the contacts here. And it would be sort of a triumph for you to send for her, you being so famous now. It would help make up."

"I'll consult Julian tonight," Amanda said. She was relieved because this was less of a favor than she had expected to be asked. For a while she had feared Ethel wanted a loan. She was really quite free with Julian's money, mischievously so, knowing how sacred it was to him, almost as sacred as it had been to herself when she earned her own living writing advertising for Burdley's Department Store. But, as she often said, she did not like to be asked for loans because it made such embarrassing moments in conversation and afterward such awkward relations. A job for little Vicky was easy to manage, providing no personal contact was expected. Amanda didn't want her fine present life cluttered up with her undistinguished past.

"Julian can wangle something," said Amanda. "I'll wire her right away and then Julian can fix it up."

She looked at her watch again and Ethel obediently leaped up.

"I knew you'd be the one to fix it," she said. "She simply would never listen to any of us back there, but if you invited her on—after all you've always been her idol—"

Amanda's mouth tightened.

"I only trust I'll have time to entertain her while she's in town," she said carefully. "Anyway I'll see that she gets a job, even if I can't lead her around personally. Oh, Bemel!"

Ethel was so pleased with the happy result of her call that she did not mind being brushed out by Miss Bemel. She was shunted down the elevator and out the front door in a pleasant haze, thinking only of how clever she had been to invent this plan, and how fine it was to be able to put one's friend's successes to some good use.

"But wasn't she bitchy about the idea of Vicky visiting her," Ethel reflected, now free to be critical. "She absolutely turned livid at the mere thought of helping Vicky get the social breaks that *she* had. She probably is scared to death to introduce Vicky to old Julian Evans for fear Vicky will turn out as smart as she herself was. God, how I wish I had that vanity of hers! It's absolutely bullet-proof."

She walked over to Madison to look in the shops, and at the corner paused to look at the headlines spelled out in Julian Evans' afternoon paper. Same old stuff. The Germans doing the same old thing. It would be a relief to get this war over and get back to murder and the decent privileges of peacetime. No use buying a paper any more, really. She paused before a telegraph office, tempted to wire Vicky mysterious hints of glad news to come, but that might spoil everything. No, better leave it all to Amanda and her powerful husband now. With a sigh for her relinquished responsibility, Ethel went her way.

3

Amanda's Miss Bemel in the fourth floor chambers sent Mr. Evans' Mr. Castor in the third floor library a brief memorandum: "Place Victoria Haven, childhood friend of Mrs. Evans. Real estate experience. About $200." Mr. Evans, conferring on the day's private mail with Mr. Castor while waiting for the dinner guests to arrive, frowned over this memo, dictated a couple of telegrams and sent a memo back up to Mrs. Evans' Miss Bemel: "Have instructed Peabody Publishing Company to hire Victoria Haven in real estate news at fifty per week on her arrival in New York. Check with them on date."

This brief correspondence would have settled the little matter under ordinary conditions. Miss Bemel would have telegraphed the proposition—nay, the command—to Vicky in Lakeville, and arranged a luncheon date at a small restaurant for the two old friends (this would relieve Amanda of further intimacies), perhaps put the Haven name on the third guest list for one of the larger cocktail parties during the winter, and then friendship demands could be considered fulfilled. Julian might remember the name some evening when they were alone and might inquire whatever happened about that Peabody business and who was that girl anyway? Had she ever arrived? Had he met her? Amanda would have explained that she was the little quiet one in the corner at the Sunday party two weeks ago, that she was a school friend from Lakeville. This would have silenced Julian, for reminders of his wife's obscure past irritated him, perhaps because pasts were something even his power could not manipulate. It was not jealousy of what might have happened to Amanda's heart in those simpler days, either, at least he didn't think it was. But the contrast of his new wife's nondescript background with his former wife's august ancestry was not very gratifying, for it implied a step backward. He didn't like to have any one refer to Lakeville for fear mention would be made of Amanda's father having run a men's clothing store, her stepmother, née Jansen, of Norway, having been a "beautician." Heaven knows Amanda never brought her family into any conversation, and it was seldom indeed that she requested favors for old Lakeville associates.

The memos having been exchanged, things were about to take their usual course, with Vicky Haven's future put through the chutes and forgotten by the Evanses. Julian fussed with some press clippings, had a tomato juice by himself, pinned up a Benson etching on the mantel to get the effect (he fancied himself an authority on wild bird pictures and made consistent purchases along that line to confound his enemies who said he was blind to art), called his wife's bedroom three times to ask if she was ready yet, was snapped at properly for his impatience, decided to drop in on her to hasten her dressing, changed his mind recalling her icy sarcasm over his occasional invasion of her privacy, had another tomato juice and then put on his glasses to read for the eighth time his own editorial in his evening paper. This being a period when no one knew which way the cat would jump, either in Europe or in home politics, Julian was reserving his ammunition for the most powerful bidder and marked time till ready with stinging criticisms of the medical profession for having no cure for the common cold, stern admonitions to childless parents (he fortunately had two children by his former marriage), and articles on Predestination, pro and con. In history's dangerous hour Julian thus offered the world an aspirin.

It was Julian's custom to spend his mornings in conferences and writing in his home, in his dark-panelled red-carpeted study, and then go downtown at noon for important lunches and an afternoon in his office. Mr. Castor, working at home, conferred by telephone with a Mr. Harnett, the office secretary, and routed Julian from place to place as if he was a valuable freight car. Before dinner the master once again resorted to the home library and home affairs, usually in a disagreeable mood because he was hungry as could be at six-thirty and always had to wait for the half-past-eight dinner, one of the cruelties of the rich.

"Who's coming to dinner tonight, did you say?" he asked Mr. Castor again, and the little man—Julian could not have endured a secretary taller than himself—patiently answered that the guests would be an ex-president, an international banker, a future ambassador—possibly to St. James's—and a celebrated French titled exile. The point was, Julian fretfully wanted to know, could he get away at eleven to meet his London chief, newly arrived, and fraught with confidential information for his employer? Mr. Castor telephoned Miss Bemel on the floor above as to this point and advised his master that not only would the engagement with the London chief be feasible, but that Mrs. Evans would go with him. Mrs. Evans, according to Miss Bemel's report, believed that she could "get something" from meeting the gentleman.

"Good," said Julian, face falling at the thought of his resolute young wife's intrusion into his private kingdom. "Tell her we meet him at eleven at NBC right after his broadcast. We'll go on from there."

The first Mrs. Evans had kept in discreet shadow during Julian's life with her, and her ignorance of his business was, he sometimes thought, not such a fault after all, in spite of his initial delight at Second Wife's keen interest. At least in those days he could talk to people without interruption.

Julian Evans was five feet six, five feet seven with his built-in soles which gave him half an inch over the second Mrs. Evans (in her stocking feet), and a good four inches over the first Mrs. Evans, a stout little body who had, in her late forties, done him the favor of shrinking an extra inch, but it was too late to comfort him, for he was already in Amanda's web. He had been an earnest, ambitious young man, aided on the path to fame and fortune more by Mrs. Evans' family connections than his own sharp wits. At forty-eight he was personable enough, though bald, for he had no pot at all due to his Yogi exercises and lack of bad habits, and he was what is known as a very fine dresser. He had small hazel eyes that appeared, erroneously, to twinkle with humor and perspicacity. Very impressive, too, were his beetling iron-gray brows, firm big mouth over big white teeth, big jaw and a big commanding nose. He was positive of his importance but was beset by the fear of ridicule, and this led him to quite ridiculous extremes. If he lost his temper in the office he must, half an hour later, tiptoe down the corridor to listen for derisive accounts of the scene, and wherever laughter sounded he marked that office for future punishment, so certain was he that all laughter was insubordination and never innocent joviality. In his home he had a way of excusing himself from the guests, then standing outside the door listening for insults. The gratifying thing about this procedure was that if he did not actually hear anything he could always be sure that some crack or other had been whispered out of his hearing. He would return to the group and study one face after the other to see if a blush, a drooping glance, or a nervous gesture would not betray the mocker. One refreshing trait in Amanda was that she gave him the insult direct so he had no secret misapprehensions and could fight back, fight back in his own devious way. If Amanda privately berated him he merely smiled proudly in silence, saving his retort for the dinner table where he could retell the accusation as if it were the naïve remark of a child, and here, before their celebrated guests, Amanda was obliged to accept defeat with a smiling shrug, lest a show of shrewishness give pleasure to her rivals.

Amanda could always annoy him by her laughing deprecation that "Julian, of course, has *no* humor, no humor at all," but it was she who was most enraged when important guests turned from her earnestly informed conversation to exchange nonsense with each other, nonsense which she was unable as she was unwilling to follow.

Julian was still proud of his wife's unparalleled success and had specially bound copies of her book *Such Is the Legend* to present his business friends and their house guests, and he had instructed his staff to refer to this masterpiece, either in its book or movie version, on every possible occasion. This pleased Amanda for the first year. But after a while it embarrassed her to have him boast of how he had ordered this or that "profile" of her, and how it was he who had decided she should have a weekly column or some definitive article somewhere, instead of letting it appear that these honors were the result of public demand. She could not understand, on her part, why he sulked whenever she joined him in his engagements with national figures. Julian preferred to give her these interviews secondhand, straining the story through his own vanity so that she must credit him, instead of the other person.

Julian sat scowling at his paper, pride in today's editorial spoiled by the knowledge that now his evening with old Cheever would be spoiled by Amanda taking it over. It was to his interest as editor and publisher to feature Cheever in all his papers, but after Amanda had extracted Cheever's opinions it would be his loyal duty, as husband, to feature Amanda's articles at Cheever's expense. Cheever would be sore, and as appeasement he'd probably have to raise his salary. Julian was shrewd enough to foresee the whole situation in advance and it was enough to spoil his dinner.

Amanda's dress rustled outside and she came in, looking very beautiful in gold lamé with a wristlet of fragrant Parma violets, and smiling radiantly at him as if they were on the sweetest of terms. Julian was impressionable, almost foolishly so, as many pious upright men are where beauty is concerned, and Amanda had only to exploit her blonde good looks with an arresting costume to make his blood turn to water. Almost out of perversity Amanda sometimes preferred to play the rôle of bohemian, and except for the benefit of special males, not her husband, affected smart tweeds, loose fur coats over flannel slacks, very Hepburn, very collegiate, and arrogantly unmade-up as to face. Tonight was a very special favor which touched him.

"My darling," gulped Julian, forgiving everything now, and Amanda permitted him a little kiss. At thirty Amanda had all the beauty, fame and wit that money could buy, and she had another advantage over her rivals, that whereas they were sometimes in doubt of their aims, she knew exactly what she wanted from life, which was, in a word, everything. She was at this period bored with two years of fidelity, but she dared not risk her marriage just yet. Julian was necessary for at least another few years, and it would be folly to risk losing him. Julian was almost pathologically jealous of her, fearing the final indignity of horns, and never able to forget that she had surrendered to him before he even asked the favor, a fact that did not reassure him of her future fidelity. He queried chauffeurs about her movements, put sly questions to her friends, but Amanda's conduct was so far impeccable. If she was restless now, it was not that she wanted an affair for lust's sake, for she had a genuine distaste for sexual intimacy and hated to sacrifice a facial appointment for a mere frolic in bed; but there were so many things to be gained by trading on sex and she thought so little of the process that she itched to use it as currency once again, trading a half-hour in bed for a flattering friendship, a royal invitation; power of whatever sort appealed to her.

Julian was suspicious of just such a state of mind as this and now speculated which one of their dinner guests had inspired Amanda to put out her glamour-girl side. He made a mental note to keep an eye on which man she played up to during the evening. Amanda, though, had no definite plan. The idea of going out to a café—something Julian strongly disliked doing—had roused her interest much more than the anticipation of a distinguished dinner party. It was not enough that these

international names shone at her table; she wanted to stage
such triumphs in the middle of a smart restaurant for all the
world to envy. It was too bad Julian disliked restaurants,
though Amanda was obliged to admit their devotion to home
was socially more impressive.

She could not be at her best at dinner, figuring out as she
was, which restaurant to lead Cheever to, later on, some place
where the people would be whom she wanted to impress. The
newspaper crowd had never quite accepted her, since she had
won all the rewards without the customary groundwork;
Amanda could not resist temptations to further bait their
envy, since their good will was out of the question. She wondered if her purpose would be served best by Twenty One,
the Stork, or the little French place every one had taken up
lately. The last was the best bet, for recently the columnists
mentioned it every day. She was suddenly impatient to get the
dinner over and get out; the game of being lady of the house,
the grand hostess, seemed unbearably tedious tonight, and in
her boredom Amanda forgot to ask the ambassador some of
the questions Miss Bemel had instructed her to ask. Julian
was didactic and told the ambassador what an ambassador's
life was like, told the banker all about banking, explained the
refugee problem to the famous refugee, and informed the labor leader on labor problems and their solution. It was the
privilege of being a host and Julian never failed to exercise it
to the full. Nor did any guests ever contradict his superior
opinions, since this would have been not only rude but un-
practical. One never knew when this little man could be extremely helpful and the few who had dared to question his
omniscience with argument had paid for their valor in one
way or another. So it was Julian's evening, with no gainsaying
from Amanda, who merely smiled, received compliments, au-
tographed her book for the titled refugee who forgot to take
it with him, and finally manipulated the group (minus the labor leader and ambassador but plus Mr. Cheever of London)
to the little French place for a friendly nightcap.

"Is this really Jean's?" she exclaimed, puzzled, as they entered the café. "Isn't it—?"

She did not finish her question, for now she saw what a
mistake she had made to suggest this place. "Jean's," the new

little *boite*, was none other than her old secret meeting place
with Ken Saunders. Then it was *"Chez Papa"* with red-
checked tablecloths and a sixty-five cent dinner, the virtues of
which they had quarrelled over constantly. Ken always said it
didn't matter about the low price; it was as good as the Waldorf. He would never admit, just because he was fond of old
Papa, that the food was only passable. Not that she minded
much, not then, anyway, but she wanted Ken to admit it was
just sentiment, not quality, that made him like the place. Here
was the spot she had confessed she was marrying Julian, and
Ken had gotten up quietly, as if he was going to telephone,
and never come back. She waited half an hour, all ready with
her defenses—("But Ken," she was going to say to him, "we
always knew it would have to end sometime. We never intended to get married, you know that.") But he never gave
her a chance to explain, just walked out, not even good-bye.
She had not been back here since, and even though it was
made over into quite an elegant little spot, it was still *Chez
Papa* even to the picture of the Papa's Acrobatic Troupe over
the bar. Amanda felt queer. She had never regretted giving up
Ken; she had given him little thought since the parting, because she could stop thinking about a person at will, thank
God, but right now he seemed all over the place. It did not
even surprise her to see him actually standing at the bar, but
what did surprise her was the wave of exultation that this unexpected sight of him brought. Imagine feeling this way
about any one! It must be something in the air, some secret
restlessness she had not known, some craving for adventure
beyond war fronts; it couldn't possibly be just seeing Ken
again after three years, old Ken who had passed almost unheeded out of her life.

She knew perfectly well that he would not speak to her and
even though he saw her he did not permit any gleam of recognition to shine in his eye. She half-smiled at him, as bait, but
he turned away. The headwaiter was ushering the Evans party
into the dining-room and Amanda, chattering to Mr. Cheever
about nothing, wondered how she could manage to force Ken
to speak to her. She could not let him have the last insult. Besides there were all those defenses she had prepared for his accusations, and while she had no sense of guilt in the way she

had broken off with him, she was baffled by his quiet acceptance of her action as if it was the cheap sort of thing he had always expected her to do. She was intrigued, too, by her thoroughly ridiculous but urgent desire to justify herself to some one of so little consequence as Ken Saunders. It had nothing to do with love, she was sure of that. It was more because of that odd hold he used to have on her because he knew her better than any one. If he knew her so well, why hadn't he understood her marriage to Julian? What else had he expected of her? She wished he would tell her. Thinking fast, she did not sit down with the guests but went back through the bar, ostensibly to the powder room. It was an added challenge to find him no longer at the bar, as if her passing had been enough to send him away. He was in the hallway, putting on his coat—the same coat of three years ago, so he couldn't have done too well wherever he was. She caught his arm with a little cry of delight. He stiffened, then bowed.

"How do you do, Mrs. Evans?" he said calmly.

"But, Ken, what are you doing in town? I thought you were in Washington or Brazil or some place."

"I'll have to fire my press agent, that's all," Ken answered, still not looking at her. He was with that old pal of his, Dennis Orphen, who stood waiting in the doorway, hat in hand. Amanda always disliked Ken's friends; they were always too clever and too arrogant and invariably acted as if she were poisoning Ken's life. Orphen she particularly resented, for he had once pilloried her one literary idol, Andrew Callingham, in a novel. Now Orphen had his back to them as if he was not going to see That Woman make a Fool of his Pal again. It incited Amanda to be more insistent.

"Aren't you glad to see your old friends?"

"Friends, oh sure," he said. He was going to be difficult, maybe because Orphen was there. It was mean of him to resent her success, or maybe it was her marriage that bothered him the most.

"Aren't you going to say you liked the book?" She challenged him to show his envy.

"Like it? Of course I liked it. Just mad that it isn't mine, that's all." He was being disagreeable, but Amanda was determined to be kind, this once.

"Ken, you know you're too much of a procrastinator, that's all," she reproached him. "That's why I got there first."

She kept her hand on his sleeve and she could tell he wanted to be able to shake it off but was still affected by her. She had been sure he would be, but she had not expected any fluttering of the heart on her own part. It amused her to have this faint remnant of girlish romanticism. It must be what she had been needing. Yes, this was Fate always attending to her wants at the right time.

"Let's not be enemies, Ken," she said, cajolingly. "We were such friends for so long. Let's have lunch and you tell me where you've been and everything that's happened."

He was not to be had that easy.

"Can't be having affairs with people's wives," he said, "and that's the way it would have to be."

Amanda thought rapidly. It was reckless, of course it was reckless, but she felt she simply must find out if she could win him back again, or if he still hated her. Even if she had to sacrifice a little . . . oh, she had been a bitch before, they both knew it, but she had *had* to be in order to get anywhere. She would like to explain it to him, make him see how it had worked out so much better this way. She couldn't understand why his contempt should bother her, for he was only Ken Saunders, an attractive nobody, a luxury an ambitious woman could not afford. She knew he despised her for always playing safe, never risking an inch of her advantage. But now she wanted to surprise him, make amends. It could be done somehow. This must be the mischief she had been seeking, and since here it was, offered so patly the very day she sought it, then she must make the best of it.

"Supposing we lunch at my studio on Friday?" she said.

Reluctantly he surrendered to this half promise.

"All right. I'm staying at the Wharton. Where is your studio?"

Amanda had no studio. She had, up to this moment, never had the faintest notion of having a studio. Now, she reflected that an outside working place might answer a great deal of her domestic discontent. It would have to be managed discreetly, of course, and explained so carefully to Julian that there would be no danger of tattlers ruining it.

"I'll call you tomorrow and tell you the address," she said.

She was very gay when she rejoined her table. Amanda's gayety consisted in laughing a great deal whether the conversation merited it or not. She was really excited and thinking busily under this merry front, thinking of what would be the best neighborhood, far from or near to the house, and she was thinking that this was one of the situations for which she should have prepared long ago, the way plausibly paved, protection arranged in advance. She permitted Julian to have Cheever all to himself, much to his relief. On the way home Julian had the great satisfaction of repeating and interpreting everything Cheever had reported on England's condition and he gave a flattering account of what England felt (according to Cheever) about the great Julian Evans, and how, had England such a man to control its public opinion, conditions would be far, far happier. Having been able to reconstruct Cheever's remarks in such a pleasant light without her interruption or denial, Julian felt very tender toward his wife and recalled that she had not acted her usual rôle tonight. He racked his brain for a moment, wondering what had occurred during the evening to change her idea of Cheever's importance to her own work. He suddenly recollected the exchange of memos.

"I'm getting a job for some girl," he said, frowning. "Some old friend of yours. Who is she?"

"It's Victoria Haven," said Amanda, and took the plunge. "I'm afraid we'll have to get a place for her to live, too, darling, for she hasn't a penny."

"Hmm, don't want her staying with us, of course," Julian agreed. "How about it, will she let us give her an apartment?"

Amanda turned a face of sweet concern toward him.

"That's just it, we'll have to be careful not to let it seem charity," she said. "I wonder if we couldn't lease a little place as an outside studio for me. After all I do sometimes want to get off by myself. Then I could tell Vicky to live there since I only use it occasionally in the daytime when she'll be at her office. It's just to save her pride, you see. We'll have to say the place is just going to waste most of the time, so it's no bother."

Julian regarded his wife with admiration. She often surprised him with some trait he had never suspected, but it was most frequently not such an agreeable surprise as this present revelation. In the light from the street-lamp shining through the car window on her golden hair and frock she looked angelically appealing. It was an effort to remember from experience that if he should try to embrace her now her body would stiffen in chilly protest.

"You do have a heart," he said, and he was quite choked up about it. "Just don't let it run away with you, my dear."

"I won't," promised Amanda gently.

4

In the middle of the night Amanda gave up trying to sleep and slipped on robe and slippers for a smoke before her study fire, still smoldering in the grate. She drew the curtains carefully so that Julian, whose bedroom was directly beneath, would not see the light streaming out and come up for a "chat." Julian only slept in snatches, and until trained out of it by her temper, liked to tap on her door and say, "Are you awake, too, dear? Can I come in for a chat?" He would carry around his Swedish health bread, and the sight and sound of his fine big teeth crunching constantly was more than Amanda's nerves could stand. He had learned not to knock on the door, but he would be apt to tiptoe upstairs and listen outside her door for a possible call. Amanda was accustomed, on the rare occasions when she could not sleep, to sit clenching her hands as she listened to the crunching outside her door, the waiting for her welcome. Lately she would get angry in the night thinking she heard the crunching through the walls, and the sound of this blameless, non-fattening, health-giving habit was as infuriating to her as the ripple of liquid in a glass is to a dipsomaniac's wife.

What made sleep impossible tonight was the unwilling surge of memories about the past brought up by Vicky Haven's coming to New York. There was the other part of her past brought up by Ken Saunders, too, but with this she was prepared to cope. Seeing Ken again was exactly what it had been before, exasperation at his insolence mingled with exasperation at herself for tolerating him, for being teased by some one she was sure she neither loved nor admired, but for some reason could not dismiss. All right, it was unbelievably stupid of her to turn the affair on once again, but that was what she was headed for. She had such good reasons for doing whatever she did, such faith in the eventual rightness of whatever she wanted, that she could not really admit taking Ken on again was a mistake. It would do *something* for her— that first hunch she had was surely right. Not being cursed with hot Latin blood, she did not mind the Cæsar's wife rôle expected of her by the world, nor did she miss the casual passes of admirers; admirers were too conscious of Julian's power to make advances to his wife, and this was a relief to her. Still, any woman needs testimony that she *can* command the male senses, or after awhile she begins asking herself, uneasily, "Is it really because they're afraid of Julian? Or is it that I'm losing my looks or that intellectual success scares men and freezes your magnetism?" Doubts like that interfered with one's general efficiency, so surely the Ken Saunders business was justifiable. But Vicky Haven, and the re-opening of those childhood chapters?

Amanda poked the fire, sitting on a little stool before it. She picked up the last Andrew Callingham book, for he was her idol, the one person she worshiped but had unaccountably never managed to meet. But even this master prose would not distract her or soothe her into sleepiness. If it weren't for Julian's wakefulness and the kind of thoughts she had, insomnia would not be so bad, for at least it was time spent alone, time stolen from Miss Bemel, from work, from conferences, time to waste, really. But when insomnia meant thinking about long-ago frustrations, about days when you had no power over your life, then insomnia was an enemy. Retrospection was a vice, Amanda felt, an unnecessary weakening of your powers, for how could you remember the past without being afraid of the future? She knew and didn't care that people from Lakeville must think she was the cruelest of snobs, dismissing all affectionate offers of home-town distinctions, and rudely ignoring friendly calls or visits from old Lakeville neighbors. But Lakeville was not home-town to Amanda, it was childhood, and childhood was something to be forgotten, like a long sentence in prison. Amanda had succeeded very well in snipping off the years that still smarted,

but the name of Vicky Haven had brought them all back
again. In *Who's Who* and in her other public biographies
Amanda conceded only her birth in Lakeville, did not mention Miss Doxey's, but referred to France and Switzerland as
the scenes of her early education, with a bow to Columbia for
a brief course in journalism. But in the middle of the night,
shivering before the dying fire, bare feet slipping out of fur
mules, Lakeville was all too clear, childhood was a crime
painfully remembered.

"If your father thinks *I'm* going to buy your winter coat
just because he bought you your shoes, then he's very much
mistaken," this was her mother's sharp voice on the train
after they left her father in the station, at Cleveland. Mother
was taking her to Columbus for her legal six months' responsibility. Amanda was handed to her like a suitcase in the
Union Station in Cleveland by Father. "Hello, Floy," said
Father. "Hello, Howard," said Mother, and then Amanda
changed hands, and the heckling began. Even at five years old
Amanda had learned to let this slide off her back, to keep a
glass wall around her nerves and feelings. If they thought they
could make her cry they were very much mistaken! She was
not partial to either parent, since they ignored her before the
divorce to carry on their own quarrels over finance and fidelity, and after the divorce Mother carried on the quarrels,
taking both parts herself since Father was of course absent. At
least her father didn't talk about the demerits of his lost mate
the way Mother always did, always accusingly as if the child
was somehow to blame for this, and the child's sulky silence
seemed proof of loyalty to the other. Definitely the father was
in the wrong, any five-year-old would know that, since he did
not defend himself and it was evidently true he expected Mrs.
Keeler's small income from her first husband's insurance to
support Amanda in full, his own little salary being spent on
himself and his lady friends. At that time, too, he was a big
poker player, and there were often times, during his period of
parental grace, when he was gone for forty-eight hours, involved in a game somewhere. It was perfectly possible that
during these absences Amanda would be left alone in the
apartment over the store in Lakeville with neither money nor
food. This seemed to the child Amanda not so much hardship

as social stigma, and she haughtily refused sandwiches sent up
by neighbors who suspected this state of affairs, though she
was quite willing to take all the candy the Greek candy
kitchen man offered her.

"No underwear, no comb and brush, no decent sweater!"
her mother would go on, unpacking her bags later. "And
what's this? Yard material? Good Lord, does he expect me to
sew for you, too? No good stockings, of course. What? A red
satin kimono? A fine thing for a six-year-old! Some sweetie of
his gave you that, I suppose."

Mother always asked questions like this, but Amanda never
told on her father. She resented her mother's incessant inquiries quite as much as she resented her father's stinginess.
She knew that it was a toss-up between her mother's inquisition and her father's sly dipping into her birthday money
when she got back to Lakeville.

Amanda could not remember ever being hurt at this time,
merely angry at things denied her. She had considered herself
from very infancy as merely an impatient guest of her parents;
their authority was only a matter of their superior size; they
were an inferior couple whose company she would tolerate,
together or separately, only until she could make a better contact. As a child she could not remember having any child feelings, but only a sense of outrage at the indignity of a superior
person, a full-grown princess, like herself being doomed by
some mean witch to what seemed endless imprisonment in
the form of a child, suffering all the humiliations of smallness,
dependence, tumbles, discipline. It disgusted her to be buttoned into leggings on some one's lap and to be afraid alone
in the dark and to hurt when she fell down when her mental
inferiors, namely her parents, suffered none of these things.
Obeying no discipline so far as bedtime, spinach, and manners
were concerned, it was galling to have adult hands take the
liberty of administering the hair brush. At five she perfected
her own practical philosophy about corporal punishment. It
was clear that loud sobs of pain and remorse were the required response to punishment, but little Amanda would give
her guardians no such satisfaction. Instead she shut her eyes
and pretended the victim was some one else, her cousin, or
her playmate, and that she herself was a calm onlooker. This

secret weapon of detaching her feelings from her body gave her parents infinite discouragement and gave Amanda herself a sense of magic power.

"You can spank her and spank her but she just won't cry," she would hear her mother complain wearily. "How can you make her behave if she won't be punished?"

At ten she had a perfectly adult jealousy of her mother's independence, of her mother's fur coat and pocket-money and ability to buy things she wanted. Why should Mrs. Eva Keeler be entitled to more than little Amanda? She was older and bigger, that was all. Amanda knew she herself had more brains than any of these grown-ups who tried to tell her things. She did not know exactly what she knew (she hadn't *learned* it yet) but it was there, close to her but unshaped; one thing was certain, and that was the wrongness of whatever these outlanders said or did. You didn't need to be grown-up to know that much.

The death of her mother meant nothing more to Amanda than a new black outfit and a gratifying visit to the Careys in Florida. It was the nicest thing her mother had ever done for her, though the Southern trip necessitated playing with Ethel, at that time a fat, bossy little girl with all her sensibility yet to be acquired.

"Why, she isn't even crying!" she heard people say at her mother's funeral, as if it was for this moist tribute that people died. People were always wanting children to cry and prove again and again their helplessness, so that they might take advantage of it. She did cry a little, quite suddenly, when she remembered that now she would not get the red snow suit her mother had promised. She certainly wouldn't get it from her father, and she'd get as little equipment as possible, too. Her father did not mean to be stingy, but he didn't think it mattered what children wore. You gave them an orange or some candy once in a while, or a dollar. He thought when Amanda insisted on shoes or underwear or textbooks for school that she had simply been spoiled by her mother. Her tantrums, and later her chilly days of silent accusation, were proof of it, he thought, and so did his lady love, Miss Jansen, at the beauty shop, though she stolidly provided out of her own savings.

Besides the gift of detaching herself from bodily pain, Amanda had another magic secret. This was the secret of looking confident, and she'd learned this so long ago it seemed her own invention. It had begun by discovering that if you took long deep breaths you didn't get rattled in games or examinations. In piano recitals it always seemed that the persons who walked leisurely across the stage, adjusted the seat calmly, idled a moment to glance at the audience or adjust a sleeve, were the ones who played the best, even before they touched the piano. Success was in the take-off, in the initial appearance of complete confidence in one's adequacy. Amanda carefully studied the external manners of all experts, in dancing, talking, playing, and if she had insufficient cause for external poise, she believed the careful aping of the external effect would eventually stir the inner fire. It worked out in many cases. She studied the casual manner of the trained horseman, so her first ride did not betray her ignorance. Body straight, but not too straight, heels at proper angle, knees exactly flexed, reins between proper fingers, face nonchalant, Amanda was credited with good horsemanship before she'd even started.

With these private secrets at her command Amanda had finally broken through the cage of childhood into independence and the privileges of maturity. One of these privileges was to drop your childhood into a wastebasket, forget it, burn it, destroy all evidence of past weakness. Another privilege—and this, she arrogantly felt, was her special right—was unlimited power. To deny the first was to forego the latter.

Amanda suddenly flung her cigarette in the fireplace, thinking of how Lakeville was creeping in on her in the shape of Vicky Haven. It had to be, of course, if her plans for Ken Saunders were to be plausibly covered. But it fretted her, as if, even this long after her escape, there was chance of Fate shrinking her into helpless childhood again and denying her everything she wanted once again, just because she was too little to get it. The shame of dependence, of weakness, of not knowing things! It came over her in a great surge of anger. The time she had hidden under the table and bumped her head on it when she stood up, an indignity, she raged at the time, that would never have been visited on an adult! At least she had sufficiently awed her betters to discourage pet names. She had always been Amanda, never Baby, never Mandy, never Tootsie. She rather suspected that Julian had always been Editor Evans, too, judging from his grave infant portraits. This did not endear him to her. The thin, precocious little face in those early pictures seemed ridiculously naïve to her. It was all very well for your Amandas to have been born grown-up, but a man, to be a great man, should have once been a boy.

This reflection gratified Amanda so much that when she heard the inevitable crunching of Swedish toast outside her door she flattered Julian by asking him in for a smoke, though it was actually for the sole purpose of twitting him with this observation.

"I was always precocious, yes, my dear," Julian said, frowning over the effort to be fair, "but I don't think your conclusions could really be proved in a census."

But it nagged at him all night, as Amanda's little pin-pricks always did, for here, like ancestry or race, was something neither money nor power could correct.

II

VICTORIA HAVEN, at twenty-six, was considered one of Lakeville's brighter young women. She had a nice little growing business of her own (real estate), an office in the newest and tallest building on Market Street, two bank accounts, one with $462.83 in it (the office account), and one with $44.67 (personal), an annual full-page ad in the Chamber of Commerce booklet and an annual interview, sometimes even a speech at her college Alumnae Day. Vicky, like everybody, was sure she was far smarter than the average and it sometimes surprised her that she was so dumb about the simplest things, such as understanding politics, treaties, who was who, the use of oyster forks, service plates, back garters on girdles, the difference between Republicans and Democrats, and the management of a lover.

"There's no doubt about it, the female mind can't hold anything very long," she reflected sometimes, blaming her own shortcomings on the entire sex. There she was, an honor student at Miss Doxey's and for two years at the nearest college, yet knowledge had scampered through her brain as if it had been warned to get out within twenty-four hours. Yes, Vicky decided, the female mind, in its eagerness to shine afresh every day, had to have a very rapid turnover. There was no attic treasure chest or ice box where the good education was stored, moth-proof, mouse-proof, and shrink-proof. There was only a top dresser drawer where names, dates, fragments of facts were flung without mates as the information hurtled through. Vicky sometimes examined her own top drawer, horrified at these things she once knew but now only recognized the face; names like Bunsen burners, retorts, grids, Wagner Act, Robinson-Patman Act, Seabury Investigation, Diet of Worms, *pons asinorum*, Catiline, Hatshepsut, Munich, Chapman's Homer—or was it Homer's Chapman— egg-and-dart, Smoot-Hawley Bill, Muscle Shoals, Boulder Dam, plum circulio, Brook Farm, Kerensky, Glazounov, geometric progression, Javanese scale, pituitary, and five hundred rags and tags that must have belonged to a whole fact at one time but in their present futile tangle were nothing more than cues in a quiz program. Vicky, embarrassed by her own confused background, wondered if that wizard of the ages, her good friend Amanda Keeler, really assimilated the stiff facts of her own articles. Since Amanda, in the old days, had been concerned largely with wangling smart vacation invitations and devices for getting faculty favors without too much work, it was only reasonable to wonder if ten years had actually transformed the opportunist into the scholar.

As for love, Vicky had bungled that from the very first grade right up to the present time. She had one boy friend from the age of ten till nineteen, the basis of their attraction being that they were next-door neighbors. As soon as he was twenty-one he was dazzled by the mystery of a girl who lived seven blocks away and had impetuously placed her under a long engagement contract till he finished college, medical school, and hospital training. Vicky realized at the time that her ten years of spirited disagreement with everything he said, and articulate impatience with his plodding nature, may have had something to do with his final departure. She was inconvenienced by this break more than she was crushed. And then she did fall desperately in love with Tom Turner, fifteen years older than she was, an architectural engineer, when his drinking permitted, and exciting enough to the young women of the town.

"I shouldn't have tried to reform him," she lamented, wisely enough, in the aching months after he ran off with her more sophisticated partner, Mrs. Brown. She should have tried to be at least as sympathetic as his favorite bartender if she was to compete with the latter. Mrs. Brown had been. When Tom went on a bender to celebrate his appointment to a most eminent advisory staff, he called up Vicky to join the spree.

"Darling," Vicky had said, getting maternal at the hint of what this advancement might mean to their relationship, "don't you think you'd better go home and sleep, so as to be ready for your conference tomorrow?"

Mr. Turner, in turn, gave her a piece of advice which she forgave, being certain he would be sorry for it tomorrow, but this turned out not to be the case. Eager for feminine companionship and remembering a few pleasant nights with the sharp-faced Eudora Brown, Vicky's business partner, Tom had no difficulty in getting her merry assistance in painting the town. They showed up at the conference, married for no reason at all, and it was a gala occasion. It was a good lesson, Vicky tearfully admitted to herself, that reform was something to attempt after the ceremony, never before.

But if she was so smart, and if an education was any good at all, why didn't it teach a jilted lady how to recover her poise, how to win back the will to live, to dance, to love? Her top dresser drawer information was as useless here as in any other crisis. All Vicky could do was to read the women's magazines and discover how other heroines had solved this problem. The favorite solution, according to these experts, was to take your little savings out of the bank, buy a bathing-suit, some smart luggage, put on a little lipstick, throw away your ugly glasses and go to Palm Beach or Miami for two weeks. There you lay on the beach doggedly in rain or shine, your glasses hidden in a secret compartment of the hotel cellar, and a not-at-all-dangerous hair tint bringing out the highlights in your new permanent and the smart but inexpensive bathing-suit bringing out other highlights in your figure. On the fourteenth day, if not before, a tall bronzed Texas oil man would appear and be bowled over by your unaffected passion for peppermint sticks, unlike the snobbish society women he knew, and if you turned to page 114 you would find yourself, as heroine, bumbling down the church aisles without your glasses led by the Texas oil king and possibly a Seeing Eye dog.

Vicky was not convinced by this remedy, nor even certain she wanted to live in Texas, or that the sight of her rather thin figure in a smart but inexpensive bathing-suit would knock a millionaire off his feet. In fact she was pretty sure that the bathing-suit would have to be pretty expensive and very carefully cut indeed to "do things for her." Furthermore, the stories of How to Get Over a Broken Heart by Getting Another Man were invariably followed by other stories on what to do after you lost him again, after, say, ten years' marriage. The expert story-tellers appeared to be as certain you would lose him as they were that you would get him. You usually lost him on your tenth wedding anniversary to some girl in a bathing-suit lying on a Miami beach with a lipstick and no glasses. The way you gained him back was to take your savings, put them into a new hair-dye do and permanent, take a Figure-Reducing Course and erase that middle-aged spread which is the only thing that's holding you back, call up an old beau who is always waiting for you at the nearest hotel and who sends you orchids at this faint beckon from you, and by getting a little flushed with champagne (instead of disagreeable over gin) and learning the newer dance steps, your husband is re-fascinated and comes whizzing back for a second honeymoon. Vicky deduced that it was just as well for you to start saving again, however, since there was no permanent way of keeping your man outside of nailing him to the floor. The lesson of all the stories boiled down to saving your money, since all the secret solutions devolved on dipping into this ever-present savings account. And that was the trouble with Vicky's comeback after Tom had run out. The profits of her six years in business had been steadily put back into the business, new office equipment, printing, one thing and another, so that the personal savings account that was to see her to Palm Beach and Prince Charming was scarcely enough for the train fare, let alone two weeks of glamorous idleness. The thing was to make money, and in Lakeville money was made by a slow fairly honest process that might, after ten years, enable you to turn in your car every two years for a new one and have a little house just around the corner from next-to-the-smartest neighborhood. If she could only get to New York—if she could only find some excuse for dumping the business on her partner, now the wife of her lover, instead of this perpetual chin-upping about their wretched triangle.

"I suppose you wish I'd get out," Mrs. Brown had candidly said the day after the wedding. "I know that would be the decent thing to do, but the truth is I need this money coming in till Tommy gets his bills paid."

"No need to leave," Vicky stonily answered. "I couldn't afford to buy you out right now, anyway, and I'd have to train somebody else. We can manage. Providing you don't let your husband hang around the office."

"Oh, goodness, he wouldn't dream of it," Mrs. Brown's laughter pealed out richly. "He's simply scared to death of you."

So day by day they kept up the illusion of an amiable business partnership and the sight of Mrs. Brown's disposition
slowly souring under the effects of marriage to the man Vicky
loved did not keep Vicky from wishing to God she was in the
other woman's shoes.

"I'll get over it," she said to herself grimly. "It may take a
couple hundred years but I'll get over it."

And then Ethel Carey got back from New York with exciting stories of plays, nightclubs, brilliant parties, gossip about
Amanda, and sly hints that there were Texas oil men in New
York as well as Florida, just waiting to heal broken hearts.
Vicky was obliged to wearily declare that she did *not* want any
man, none at all, all she wanted was to get out of this hateful
town of Lakeville and make some money. Almost at once
Amanda's wire came, and then a letter about the idle studio
waiting for her to move in, and next, as Amanda was an impatient woman, a letter with a ticket for the following Tuesday.

"Never mind about the office," Ethel insisted. "I'll get
Papa to manage the whole thing, talk to Eudora and make all
the arrangements. Your job begins and you have to leave. It's
an emergency."

Having warned Vicky not to expect any friendly or personal
gestures from Amanda, who, don't forget, was a very busy
and a very important person nowadays, Ethel was dumfounded at the offer of hospitality in Amanda's own studio,
hints of a welcoming dinner the first night in town, and all
Ethel could conclude was that it was her own description of
Vicky's plight that had won these favors. She only hoped both
of them would remember this and not sit around the fire in
the long New York nights ganging up on her the way old
friends generally did.

"I know how you feel about our friendship now, Vicky,"
she said wistfully. "But what if you turn out as successful as
Amanda? Then you'll forget all about poor old Ethel."

Vicky warmly denied this. Ethel had been her only friend,
her only confidante in these trying months and she would
never, never forget it in the almost certain glory of her future
New York success.

"I only hope you'll stay the same," said Ethel, "only not
such a fool next time, dear, I hope."

At home Vicky met with more difficulty than she had anticipated. She rented a room from her brother's family in a pretty little house on the lake and had lived here at his suggestion ever since she left college. It had often occurred to her that for the same money she could get a little place in town, but her brother's family had gotten to count on her little contribution with their three children growing up. Brother Ted, who was ten years older than Vicky, liked to act smug about "giving Vicky a home now that Mother was gone," and the exchange of money for this kindness was never mentioned. Vicky had expected, from veiled remarks overheard in the last two years, that her room could be put to good use with the children growing, and even as it was she shared her bed with Joan, the oldest. So she imparted the good news of her departure with every expectation of hearty rejoicing. Instead the news met with shocked silence, brother and wife looking at each other significantly, the baby's burst into sobs quite ignored. Little Joan, age thirteen, scrawny, freckled, but happy in a "permanent" caught the cue of disapproval from her parents and looked from one face to the other, eager for Aunt Vicky to get scolded.

"I didn't think you'd do a thing like that, Vicky," her brother said, ladling out the veal pot-pie with careful justice. "You got a nice little business started and then you drop it and run wild."

"But I'm not running wild," Vicky protested. "I have a job and Amanda's giving me her studio to live in—it's the chance of a lifetime."

"You give a person a home and what thanks do you get?" observed the brother's wife.

Brother was more fair.

"I wouldn't say that, honey, I wouldn't put it just that way," he said. "Vicky's always paid a nominal rent and I know she would have raised it when she got to making more, of her own accord."

Vicky, who had been secretly contemplating moving and had no intention of paying more for the privilege of sharing her brother's expenses, stared in astonishment from one face to the other. The three little faces on the other side of the table, from Joan to Junior to Baby, frowned back in harmony with their parents.

"Can I call up Gertrude and tell her about Aunt Vicky going?" Joan asked.

"Hush, children! The point is, what do you want to go bumming around New York for," Brother continued judicially, "that's no kind of life for a nice girl, a girl as well thought of in Lakeville as you are."

"Aunt Vicky's afraid of being an old maid," bitterly offered Brother's wife, and the children tittered.

"Now, honey," appeased Brother again, "you can't blame Vicky for wanting to marry some day. But that's just the point. Maybe she did lose a beau or two here, true enough, but that don't mean there aren't other fellows here in Lakeville. Good solid boys she went to school with, know the family. That's what Vicky wants. You can't blame her for that, honey, and wanting some kids of her own like ours."

"Well, I'm not so sure that's what I want," Vicky flared back, looking with sudden dislike at the three smug little faces. "What do I want with kids when I'm trying to earn a living?"

"Vicky wants to have all that salary to spend on herself," again Brother's wife was accusing. "Every penny to put on her own back, I suppose."

"I've stayed with them too long," Vicky thought with immense perspicacity. "They want to own me as if I was a government bond that paid a nice little dividend all the time. In another year or so they'd be suing me for breach of promise if I left."

"I can have a room to myself if Aunt Vicky goes," said Joan. "I can have Gertrude come and stay all night whenever I like."

"If Vicky feels that she wants to let a good business slide and go fool around with strangers, I won't stop her," Brother went on gravely. "She knows all she owes to us, and she'll find out what it means to pay strangers for all the little comforts she gets here without thinking. Piano, radio, use of the car—"

"The car's half mine, after all," Vicky said in a small voice.

"All right then, go," said Brother's wife, losing her temper. "I suppose it means nothing to you that we'll have to let Bobby go to public school next year, then, instead of to the Academy, and Joanie will have to put off boarding school another year

("But Mama!" wailed Joanie, "Gertrude and all my bunch are going!") Oh, no, you'll be putting your good money on a fur coat, something for yourself, maybe a diamond wrist watch. Take a cruise, why don't you? We won't be even able to go to Canada for August like we planned. And a lot you care."

Vicky sat very still. She had not really given much thought to her fifty dollars a month contribution. It was no bargain as Lakeville prices went, but it was all in the family. Brother earned a fair enough salary at the printing company, but it was plain that that little extra fifty was what Belle counted on as gravy. It was Belle's little private windfall and she never thought that it would cease or that its donor had first rights to it. Brother, even trying to be fair, could not help a look of somber disapproval.

"We're thinking of your own good, Vicky," he said.

"Fun's all she's thinking of," cried Belle. "Fun and fur coats."

Junior, aged nine, brightened.

"Can I have Aunt Vicky's typewriter when she goes?" he asked.

"I want it," said Joan. "I'm the oldest. You can have her radio."

"The radio's broke," howled Junior. "I don't want an old broke radio, I want a typewriter to make writing on. Mama says I can have it."

"Hush!" cried their mother, and this set the baby to screaming convulsively. "It would be just like your Aunt Vicky to take them along to New York with her."

Vicky pushed aside her plate.

"Oh, Mama, look, I've broken off my fingernail!" exclaimed Joan dolefully. "And I've been growing them all winter so they'd be longer than Gertrude's. Just look."

"Well, you'll just have to cut them all off," snapped her mother.

"But, Mama, they'll look perfectly awful!" wailed Joan, holding out the maimed hand with its long red talons. "I'll just have to paste it back on or *something*! It's just a whole winter's work ruined, that's all it is."

"Shut up, we're talking about Aunt Vicky!" barked her father.

"But look!" sobbed Joanie. "How can I wear my *formal* and have nasty old sawed-off fingernails like Aunt Vicky? You've got to do something about it, Mama, honestly, you just got to!"

"I think I'll start packing," said Vicky.

As she left the room to the tune of Joan's quiet sobbing, she was not consoled by hearing her brother say, "Now, honey, we mustn't be too hard on Vicky, even if we do need that little extra help she gives. Don't forget Vicky's been through a lot having Tom throw her over and then everybody in town kidding about it behind her back. That takes a lot out of a girl, and Vicky's getting on, so she's got to get somebody quick. After all, Vicky's twenty-six!"

"But, Mama, just look," Joanie's voice rose in despair. "You won't even look at that nail! You don't care how I look, that's all. You want me to grow up and be an old maid like Aunt Vicky, that's what!"

2

The Tuesday she was leaving Lakeville, Vicky drove into town after breakfast with her brother Ted and little Joan. Usually she dropped Ted at the station to take a train into Cleveland, where most of his business was transacted, and she continued by the lake road, dropping Joan at school and then driving on to her office. But today Ted's business was right in Lakeville, besides it was his brotherly duty to take care of Vicky's trunk and ticket. Vicky would rather have driven in all by herself this morning, for she loved the car, and she loved the lake road, having thrashed out most of her problems in the last few years while driving along the blue water to work. Ted was not the natural driver that she was, either, so you could not relax and dream with him at the wheel, but must be constantly jarred by his nervous exclamations at every red light and every other car. "Look at that turn, will you? License ought to be taken away from him. Ah, of course. A *woman* driver. Might have known."

Vicky kept her eyes out the window, thinking, "This is the last time. Good-bye, Lake Erie, good-bye lake road, good-bye all the morning thoughts I used to have driving along this road to work, wondering if I'd be able to pick up Tom at the car tracks, wondering if we'd dare get married with all his debts and his drinking. Then after a while wondering how I could manage to *duck* seeing him at the tracks, and how I could get through the day with *her*. When we get up to the crossroads up here I'll look the other way so I don't see our special secret beach with the old burnt pavilion where we used to have our Saturday night suppers. Anyhow Eudora doesn't like that kind of thing, so they don't go there together. That's something."

Ted would never put the top down when he drove, and he resented having the windows open, too, for fear the dust would spoil the new upholstering, so that even on the hottest days the car was filled with his after-breakfast-cigar smoke, while a mere pane's width away lay the crisp azure lake air, as tantalizing as the crown jewels behind the jewellers' invisible glass window. Vicky opened her window this morning, defying Ted's customary argument about economy.

"It's the last time I'll smell Lake Erie," she said, and drew a long breath of the tingling freshness of lake winds, steamer-smoke, fish, and automobile gas—all the things that made up a Lakeville autumn morning. This is what she would miss, she thought.

"Last time for a month or so, maybe," chuckled Ted.

They were so sure the great city would throw her back here. They were fond of her, certainly, but part of the family fondness was in knowing that nobody else would ever like you or excuse your faults as they did. It would have been the same, had her mother lived, because Mother had been devoted to her son and her best wish for Vicky was that there would always be Ted on hand to protect her from her own folly. "Don't let Amanda Keeler's leaving town put ideas in your head, Vicky, my girl," Mother had warned her when Vicky had wanted to leave Miss Doxey's and go to New York just because Amanda had done so. "Our family has never liked big cities. We're country people and don't like to show off. Our women aren't show-offs like Amanda Keeler. We're just simple folks, marry the boys we grow up with, raise our families in the same town. No use your talking about being a

newspaper writer, because none of our family has ever been
writers. You can talk about times changing, blood don't
change. When you get out of Miss Doxey's, you'll find something to do right here in Lakeville or maybe Cleveland, doing
something quiet the way we like to do. Any of our family in
New York City would be like fish out of water. You stay here
where Ted can help you out when you need help."

Families could give you a fine inferiority, out of their affection for you, all right. Very likely if Mother was still alive,
Vicky would never dare take off, at all.

They came to the old Haven house just outside the town
limits. It was in good shape, but the lawn around it was
overgrown, and the porch covered with brown autumn
leaves, fluttering around the boarded-up windows. Vicky remembered her mother and Aunt Tessie sitting on the porch
watching the buildings going up all around them, as the
town extended. The city's extension program beat the depression by a few months and left the Haven house, relic of
1900, wedged in between rows of two-story, tax-paying
business buildings. In twelve years the town hadn't gotten
enough money together to continue its project so the
Haven house, owned by the city, stood idle and the new
buildings flanking it remained half-untenanted, Mother
died, and Aunt Tessie lived in Cleveland. There was her
childhood home, Vicky told herself. Take another look and
say good-bye.

"Belle's going to get Aunt Tessie to take your room," Ted
said.

So they had sat up late last night making their plans.

"She can help with the kids," he pursued. "She lives alone
there at the Willerton, so Belle thinks it would do her good
to have a little home life. You want a family around you when
you're getting on like she is. Somebody handy in case you get
sick."

Her income will come in handy, too, Vicky thought.

"But you promised I could have Aunt Vicky's room!"
Joan's eyes were wide with hurt surprise.

"I guess you won't mind sleeping with your Aunt Tessie,"
her father said.

"I *do* mind!" cried Joan. "Sleeping with an older person takes away your strength. Mrs. Murphy said so. It's hygiene."

"Course, when Vicky comes back we'll just have to throw Aunt Tessie out," Ted said, with a hearty laugh. "Can't have an old maids' home."

"You could do worse," Vicky said.

She cast a backward look at the lake, twinkling blue and clear in the morning sun, and there, in spite of all her care not to see it, was the end of the car-line where she used to pick up Tom. There was a man standing there, now, and she was so sure it was Tom that she turned around hastily and looked straight ahead. It couldn't be, of course, but it was enough to remind her that she must get away as fast as possible.

"Will you send me autographs of any movie actors you meet?" Joan asked urgently.

Again Ted laughed.

"I guess your Aunt Vicky won't be meeting any more movie stars than you will, toots," he said.

"You'd better send me *your* autographs," Vicky said.

She must have looked unusually serious, for Ted patted her shoulder.

"Don't worry about Aunt Tessie taking up your room," he comforted her. "The little bit she'll bring in doesn't count that much. We'll put you up, any time, broke or not."

Of course Ted was fond of her and wanted to be kind. But in her present supersensitive state she hated his clumsy references to losing her rent money rather than her company. Families were so damnably commercial. At your very christening they were already quarrelling over who would get your locket if you died.

They dropped Joan at her school. Joan leaned out of the car and saw that the school-yard was almost deserted and this brought from her a wail of disappointment.

"Gertrude and the bunch have already gone in!" she cried. "And I wanted to tell them about my aunt going to live in New York City! Oh, dear!"

Vicky laughingly kissed her, and in the embrace noticed that Joan was not only wearing her best perfume but had "borrowed" the chiffon scarf Vicky had tried to find that morning. It would be a trial for the child to have Aunt

Vicky's nice things supplanted by Aunt Tessie's ancient scrap box. Evidently thinking about this or about Aunt Tessie taking away her strength in the night like some poison-flower, Joan's pretty eyes filled with tears. Vicky was touched.

"Stay in New York City till I get through school, Aunt Vicky," Joan begged, waving her handkerchief after the car. "Then I'll get married and come live with you."

Ted took her trunks to the station and then brought Vicky back to her office in the Bank Building. They stood by the elevator, neither knowing what to say. He was her big brother, all the family she had left, but now he was his wife's family, and not a big brother any more. It was high time she broke off from this symbol of the old nest, but Vicky had a feeling of panic, that even if this nest became more and more thorny, it would still be better than the great bare world into which she was going. Here was the bulletin board of the City Bank Building, with her name on it—"Victoria Haven, Room 652–653," and there it was again, "Haven and Brown, Real Estate, Room 652–653." The second mention was what straightened out her wobbling sentiments and stiffened her chin. The "Brown" stood for Mrs. Eudora Brown who had married Tom Turner that cruel day, and whose presence every day in 652–653 was eternal reminder that Tom was gone, love was gone, four years of adoration mocked away.

"I guess you'll miss having your own business, Vicky," Ted said, looking at the bulletin board. "Not many kids your age ever got that far in Lakeville. It was too bad—"

He would say something about Tom Turner, now, and she couldn't bear it, so Vicky threw her arms around him and kissed him, feeling, as she ran into the elevator, as if she was Little Eva floating off to a land far-off and bleak.

Her own name on the door was a fact more immediate than the chilly Paradise waiting a bare seven hundred miles away. Vicky braced herself, as she did these days, to say "good morning" to her partner and to hear whatever stabbing anecdotes of the Turner honeymoon Eudora cared to reveal. Fortunately Vicky had begun to smile, even though wryly, at the silver-framed portrait of Tom over Eudora's desk, since for four years this very picture had hung three feet to the left

over the Haven desk. That the man should have travelled so
slowly in four years did begin to seem funny.

Eudora looked pinched and red-eyed, as if she and Tom
had been quarrelling. A bender with somebody else's
boyfriend was usually a gay, reckless occasion, but a bender
with your own husband, if he was a man like Tom, was likely
to end up in a fight, especially if the bender money was provided by the bride. It was easy to read the Turners' career.

"I don't know whether I can swing this office by myself or
not," Eudora said, plaintively. "It takes two, really. I doubt if
Caroline is going to work out."

Vicky sat with her hat on at her desk, emptying drawers,
looking over memorandum pads, little reminders of how
much this office had meant to her.

"Of course Tom thinks I'm silly to worry," Eudora said.
"After all, I did a good job selling bonds before I ever came
in with you."

"Sure," said Vicky.

She was trying to keep her mind on the necessity to be fair.
After all, it wasn't exactly Eudora's fault that she liked a party
with other girls' men, and if the men liked her best and one
of them did marry her, that wasn't her fault, either. The person at fault was, obviously, the man. Having cleared this matter up once and for all, Vicky was assailed by a fresh wave of
dislike for Eudora and a passionate desire to be in her shoes
as Mrs. Turner, red-eyed, unrespected, and all.

"Is that what you're going to wear to New York?" Eudora
inquired, critically.

"It's the only suit I've got," Vicky said curtly.

What did Eudora think a woman should wear on a train—
that black satin, low-bosomed, picture-hat outfit that she got
herself up in for city street wear?

"I saw Howard Keeler standing in front of the store,"
Eudora said, after a moment, still watching Vicky as if she expected her to give up these departing arrangements at the last
moment, and say the whole thing was a joke. Eudora did feel
that Vicky's leaving was an open reproach to her for taking
her man, and probably the town would feel the same way.
Impossible as the present cozy situation was, it would be
worse with Vicky flown.

"Did you tell him I'd be seeing Amanda?" Vicky asked.

"I did, but he didn't say anything. Didn't send any message or anything." Eudora meditated on this, her sharp eyes still following Vicky. "I think he's still so glad to have Amanda out of his hair that he doesn't care whether she's on top or on relief. Tom says he thinks Keeler doesn't have any feeling about Amanda at all, except that she always nagged him when she was a kid for things he couldn't give her."

So Tom didn't think Keeler had any feelings! A fine one to talk about feelings!

Vicky began dawdling, because she wanted to put off the words of farewell to Eudora, words that must sound natural and calm, and even friendly. She had to wait, though, because if she was taken off-guard she might say, "Good-bye, Eudora, good-bye because I can't stand being in the same office with you any more. And good luck, Eudora, because women like you always have good luck anyway, because you aren't afraid to hurt anybody. Yes, good-bye, Eudora, and if you'd had any decency you would have been the one to go instead of sending me to a big lonely city where I'll very likely die of loneliness."

Eudora stopped looking over the mail and began fiddling with her fingernails.

It was time to go. There were a million and one things to be attended to around town before she went to the train, and she would not be back in the office at all. It would be silly to say good-bye to Tom, Vicky thought, or would it be sillier to *avoid* saying it?

"I suppose you think you've left me a pretty good thing here," Eudora said, trying to keep the bitterness out of her voice. "You march off to New York, and it's my luck to be left with *this*. Oh, never mind, I know it's better than what I was doing when you met me, and there's money to be made in it. But why should it always be *you* that gets everything?"

Vicky was dumfounded, particularly since Eudora then put her head down on the desk and started sobbing. You would have thought it was Vicky who had won the husband, and not Eudora. Vicky had wept too often herself over Eudora's piracy, not to be steeled against her now. She took a firm grip on the doorknob to make sure of a quick exit if emotions got too high.

"You've got your husband, Eudora," Vicky said weakly.

Eudora lifted her face, shaking her wavy red hair impatiently.

"I don't need a husband!" she exclaimed. "It's too much responsibility! I want to go places, and lead my own life, and have a little pleasure out of life!"

She blew her nose, choked back further sobs, and said, in a restrained voice, "Good-bye, Vicky. Hope you have a good time."

Vicky hurried out and down the elevator once more, confused and unhappy over this mixing up of cards. She wished the train left at once instead of hours later, for the longer the delay the greater chance there was of seeing Tom Turner and breaking down. Later, when she actually got to the station she saw his battered Buick parked by the depot, and her heart failed her. She managed to get on the train without turning around, even when she heard his familiar voice calling, "Vicky! Hi, Vicky, good-bye!"

III

No sooner had Amanda started the strings working for Vicky than the idea seemed a brilliant life-saving inspiration. This younger protégée from the Middle West would be a springboard to freedom for her, Amanda thought, a perpetual alibi, a private cause that Julian could not touch. She had not dreamed, until she saw Ken Saunders again, how restricted her life as a public figure and public wife was becoming. She had been complacently certain that she was a person to be envied by thousands, men and women alike, and this knowledge had sustained her to such an extent she had given little thought to whether she enjoyed her position herself or not. But then the meeting with Ken Saunders opened a whole cage of gagged, imprisoned thoughts, the desire to be loved for herself alone— what nonsense, but there it was!—the wish to gratify perfectly idle, time-wasting whims. From this long-concealed cage was also released an astonishing reserve of resentment at being denied the simpler rights of an average woman; she did not dare flirt, have little adventures that the most ordinary pretty waitress might have, yield to a first impulse, over-eat, make a fool of herself, play with the wrong people, in short she was actually underprivileged as a female. Amanda wanted to conquer the established world rather than rebel against it, so she was not prepared to kick over her crown for a peasant frolic. She wanted both. And she was obsessed with the idea that Vicky could be manipulated to provide her with these lost rights. It wasn't really as if she was preferring the careless pleasures of the average woman to the prerogatives of her lofty position; it was simply, so Amanda told herself, that in order to be a really great person you must have all the experiences of the *simple* person! This was very much what Julian had told himself when he divorced his first wife for Amanda; he had assuaged his genuinely painful remorse by telling himself that a man, to give the full power of his genius to the public, must be sexually well adjusted. So Amanda, planning secret consolations, assured herself that it all came under the heading of "the full life making the full human being."

Amanda kept Miss Bemel so busy with little memoranda about her arriving friend from Lakeville, that the secretary took an active dislike to the newcomer. Miss Bemel admired more than anything else the ruthlessness of her employer, and in the case of this Miss Haven, Amanda appeared to be acting like an almost normal, if not sentimental, person. Why should Mrs. Evans, having made a point of silence regarding her Ohio background, implying usually that this had been a mere taking-off place for foreign travel and a most sheltered convent life abroad, suddenly risk this desirable picture by sponsoring a schoolmate who was certain to be no credit in any way to the household? Miss Bemel hoped this was not the beginning of philanthropic symptoms on her employer's part, for that she scorned. As a woman who from birth had been ridiculed for bulk, hairiness, varicosities and greed, Miss Bemel had always been forced to humble herself, not merely to win friends, but to keep people from loathing her on sight. Thirty sordid years had been spent in placating those richer, prettier, kinder, wittier, older, younger, than she. Therefore her position with Amanda Keeler offered heavenly release to Carrie Bemel, sweet vengeance for all those years. As the great lady's personal, private secret-keeper and buffer, Miss Bemel was allowed to insult at least a dozen people a day, and to enjoy immeasurably the spectacle of her superiors fawning over her as representative of a great name. Boys having left her strictly alone during the formative years, she had been permitted leisure to acquire an excellent education and to develop her brain to a point where its outcome was well worthy of Amanda Keeler Evans' signature. She even enjoyed the arrogance with which Amanda mentioned "*my* articles," "*my* opinion." To have confessed to being more than Amanda's patient secretary would have lowered Amanda's prestige, and would have done herself no good. So Miss Bemel gloried in Amanda's insolence and multiplied it, herself, by a hundred.

Every morning Miss Bemel turned in a complete digest of the dinner conversations or chance comments of important officials who had visited the house. Miss Bemel had taken all these words down in shorthand in her unseen chamber outside the dining-room or from invisible vantage grounds elsewhere in the house, and these were then checked with other information, and eventually woven into the printed words as the brilliant findings of Amanda Keeler Evans. Miss Bemel saw nothing the matter with this arrangement, since her own rise to power accompanied her mistress' ascension.

To tell the truth, Amanda would have been genuinely surprised to learn that any writer of consequence had any other method of creation. There were a number of minor scribes on liberal weeklies who were unable to afford a secretary, that she knew, but she had no idea that this was anything more than the necessary handicap of poverty. The tragedy of the attic poets, Keats, Shelley, Burns, was not that they died young but that they were obliged by poverty to do all their own writing. Amanda was reasonably confident that in a day of stress she would be quite able to do her own writing, but until that day she saw no need, and in fact should a day of stress arrive she would not be stupid enough to keep to a writing career at all, but would set about finding some more convenient means of getting money.

Even if the public had discovered, through malicious enemies, that Amanda's first knowledge of what she thought about Britain's labor problem, Spanish Rehabilitation, South American Co-operation, America First, War with the Far East, was the moment she read Miss Bemel's "report" above her own signature, no one would have thought the less of her intelligence, for the system was blessed by pragmatic success. The most successful playwrights, the most powerful columnists, the most popular magazine writers, seldom had any idea of how to throw a paragraph together, let alone a story, and hired various little unknown scribblers to attend to the "technical details." The technical details usually consisted of providing characters, dialogue and construction, if the plot was outlined for them, as well as the labor of writing. Sometimes the plot itself was assembled by this technical staff, for individuals were far too busy in this day and age to waste time on the petty groundwork of a work of genius; it was enough that they signed their full name to it and discharged the social obligations attendant upon its success. The public, querulous as it was with the impractical gyrations of the unknown artist, made up for this by being magnanimously understanding of the problems of the successful man, so it all evened up in the long run. Amanda was just as entitled to her "genius" as any of the other boys on Broadway or in the public prints.

Miss Bemel was going over the dinner list with a frown.

"It won't be necessary to include this Haven woman in the Wednesday dinner, will it?" Miss Bemel asked.

Amanda was in a devilish temper today, and Miss Bemel had noted the temper seemed to have sprung itself simultaneously with the wave of big-sister sentimentality for her friend from Lakeville. It was another mark against the coming visitor.

"Certainly, Miss Haven will be invited," snapped Amanda. "Her name's there, isn't it? Does that usually mean the person is to be omitted? Am I in the habit of giving you a list of people NOT to ask, Bemel? For God's sake, Bemel!"

"But she is only arriving that day," said Miss Bemel. "Perhaps she will be tired."

Amanda flung a cigarette into the ashtray at Miss Bemel's elbow, clearly hoping that the still burning ash might set the too assiduous creature on fire. Part of Amanda's nervousness was due to the unexpected effort of doing considerable arranging on her own hook, for she had selected and made all the plans for the "studio" she was presenting Vicky. She had done this because she intended to keep this secret from Miss Bemel—from Julian, too—who merely knew such a place existed and that Amanda had no interest in it beyond a gracious means of helping her protégée.

"Never mind your private thoughts, Bemel. Who's next?"

"I don't recognize the name of Saunders," pursued Miss Bemel, gnawing the end of her pencil thoughtfully. "Refugee?"

Refugees had been perfectly acceptable on Amanda's invitation list for some time, inasmuch as they were in her line of public work and those on dinner lists were in no unpleasant *need* of dinner. But Miss Bemel suspected the name "Saunders" was merely another Mid Western refugee, and consequent cause for alarm.

"Mr. Saunders is for Miss Haven," Amanda said with forced patience. "You can't expect a girl that doesn't know a soul in town to have any fun with those old bores we're having. The least I can do is furnish her some one young enough to beau her around."

Miss Bemel's eyebrows lifted in silent sarcasm. Fun? Who expected fun at an Evans dinner? Bores? Ambassadors, princes, congressmen, movie stars—bores? Not when their informal chitchat kept Amanda's name before the public. Miss Bemel shrugged pointedly and returned to her memorandum book.

"You're to be at the Welcome Home at twelve for two hours' auctioning," said she. "The child evacuées from the London slums will be there and the proceeds will go to their Jersey farm project."

Bemel was getting on her nerves.

"Telephone them that I can't possibly," Amanda said. "I'm worn to the bone with that thing. Tell Mr. Castor to tell Mr. Evans to send them a check."

"You might drop in for a minute," said Miss Bemel. "The photographers will be there promptly at twelve and you could leave right after."

"All right," granted Amanda more calmly. "I suppose I could spare a few minutes. I ought to do that."

"Where can I reach you if Washington calls?" inquired Bemel.

"My God, can't I have ten minutes to walk around the park?" cried Amanda.

"It's raining," answered Miss Bemel practically.

"For God's sake, stop carping," said Amanda. "Where's that damned elevator? Who's using it all this time? All right, all right, I'll walk down. Let the servants ride up and down all day, I don't care."

Miss Bemel shrugged and returned to her duties as Amanda, by way of punishing every one, including herself, started tearing down the four flights of stairs.

This did not prove a wise move, for she collided with her husband on the library floor and he led her inside. He was wearing the black Chinese robe in which he fancied himself, as it gave a dignified Oriental effect to his bald head. He had a telegram in his hand, and Amanda, bursting with impatience to get out, saw that he was in one of his Personal Discussion moods.

"I was about to send Castor up with this," he said, seating himself pontifically behind the great desk so that she sat, like a respectful employee, in the less majestic chair on the other side. "Then I decided to bring it up myself. We can get Florello."

"Florello?" Amanda made no effect to disguise her complete lack of interest in her husband's portentous news.

"Florello, my dear child," he said, smiling, "is the greatest fencing master of the present day. Does that mean nothing to you?"

"No," said Amanda.

Her husband took off his glasses and waggled them back and forth as he beamed fondly at her. He was always fondest of her when she confessed ignorance to something, and this was seldom enough, so he made the most of his advantage.

"Your publishers, I believe, are waiting for the sequel to *Such Is the Legend*," he said, and Amanda realized he was going to be a bore about it, but she could not stop him since it was, after all, being a bore about her own work, which excused the fault. "They suggested, if you recall it, my dear, and of course you do, that you take the further fortunes of your leading character, Raoul Le Maz, carry him through his Virginia adventures and through the Revolutionary War. As the story would naturally require research, I have had the advice of a number of experts on what facts should be checked, *et cetera*."

"I wish you wouldn't say that," Amanda said.

Julian looked mystified and a little hurt.

"I mean *et cetera*," said Amanda, a little ashamed, "I mean it sounds like a salesman's pep talk."

"I'm sorry if my language offends your ears," Julian said, still smiling but with a little aloofness, now. "As an editor and publisher of thirty years' standing—(Editor, publisher and office boy first, Amanda thought)—I am glad to receive any suggestions on language from a young author."

"Now, Julie," Amanda said, giving him a conciliatory pat on the knee. "Go on."

"Very well. Since Le Maz was a great duellist, I have hired Florello to supply you with information on that subject for two hours a week." Julian ticked off his words on his short, pudgy fingers. "For a historical survey of the period, I have engaged Doctor Pudkin, of Columbia University, to talk to you one hour a week and provide you with suitable inside stuff. For sketching out the plot I suggest Hervey Allen, say, or, if his price is too steep, possibly this fellow, Stark Young, since I understand their work is something along your line."

"Oh, Julian," Amanda exclaimed, "you can't get people like that to work for other writers. You simply can't."

"Who can't and why not?" Julian demanded. "We are not poor, my dear, and where the matter of your creative work is concerned I will gladly pay anything. Anything."

"You just can't even suggest it to well-known people," Amanda went on. "You just can't."

"But you don't want Mr. Thirer again," Julian reminded her. "He needs the money and would be glad to do it but after the last book you said you couldn't stand him."

"Oh, he's all right," Amanda said, reluctantly, "it's just that he acts so possessive about the thing. Not anything he *says*—just the way he acts."

"We'll discuss that part later, then, my dear," said Julian. "I only wanted you to know that in the press of all these foreign affairs I don't forget my wife has a career to forge. Do you want Castor to send a note out to the press, that you are engaged on the new book?"

If Julian would only stop acting as if her career was a project of his own and she was only a departmental head in charge of its execution! It was woeful the way he could take the fun out of everything. It was fine having his power behind her, but if he only had a faint touch of humor about it! On the other hand, who ever heard of humor as an asset to power?

"Please, Julian, don't heckle me about that book," she pleaded. "I'll do it—oh, of course I'll do it some time—but what's the hurry? Margaret Mitchell hasn't written a thing since *Gone With the Wind* and that's been years. And it isn't as if I wasn't busy all the time. For that matter people are still talking about the old one. Look."

She opened her bag and drew out a clipping, from some Johannesburg paper. Julian adjusted his glasses and read it, with a quiet smile.

"Greatest novel of this or perhaps any other generation," he read aloud, and then handed it back with a nod. "Sounds all right, doesn't it, for a man that says *et cetera*?"

Amanda's face fell.

"Oh, Julian, you didn't! It wasn't you again!"

"Couldn't trust Boggs out there to do it right so I wrote it myself and cabled it to him direct," Julian said, pleased even yet at the idea.

Spoiled. Everything spoiled by having it bought or bribed. Tears sprang to Amanda's eyes. If he were only not so brutal about it! But he acted as if the only possible way her work could get applause was by buying it. And he couldn't understand, since the results were just the same either bought or freely given, why she should make any fuss about it. All right, let him spoil everything.

"I suppose you arranged that article about me in *Letters* this quarter," she said sarcastically. "I suppose you take a bow on that, too."

Julian looked at her in silent reproach.

"My dear child, I would have given a fortune to have known about that article in advance," he said, tenderly. "I would have bought the magazine outright just to stop it. By God, I'll do it yet. Castor!"

The idea was too pleasing to Amanda to resist. A literary magazine has the nerve to ridicule her work with highbrow arrogance, and now it would be bought by Julian and brought to its knees. She could see next month's issue devoted to praising words about her by Julian's own private brain trust, while the former editors ground their teeth. Yes, in a way she could forgive this fault of Julian's in leading her career by a leash. It had its points.

Somber, little Mr. Castor materialized from the shadows of the cubbyhole adjoining the dark library and Amanda rose to go.

"By the way, this list for Wednesday's dinner," Julian fumbled through the papers on his desk till he found the pink memorandum from Miss Bemel. "Who is this Saunders? Is he Saunders steel?"

"No, darling, he's just a newspaper man like yourself," said Amanda. "Young, presentable, quite dull, but we have to have an extra man around for my little girl friend. After all, you can't expect her to be as interested in ideas as we are. Let's try to get her a beau while she's here."

"Hmm, yes," agreed Julian, still examining the list. "Better brush up on our dancing young men friends—if we have any."

"We'll just have to shop around for some," said Amanda.

"Another name here," said Julian, "Victoria Haven. Who's she?"

"She's the girl we're talking about, for God's sake!" Julian really could get you down by that stupid way he had, but the sharpness in her voice caused him now to look up. He saw the new hat, the orchids on her sable jacket.

"A rendezvous?" he inquired. "My, my, we do look fancy." Amanda drew on her gloves carefully.

"Photographers," she said. "The Welcome Home with me holding London slum kiddies on one knee and my American flag on the other."

"Ought to be at least a paragraph in it for Sunday," approved Julian.

"Stingy," teased Amanda and patted his hand. It was Julian's after-thought that she never caressed him any more except in the safe company of a third person or on her way somewhere. As he was by nature a faithful husband, no matter who the wife might be, this apathy of Amanda's was often very inconvenient for him. He would never for the world have thought that perhaps this second marriage was not a complete success, because of course it was a success, or at least had been right up to the wedding day.

2

"Aren't you taking on a little more than you should with this schoolmate of yours?" Julian gently inquired of Amanda, the day of Vicky's arrival. "People don't appreciate it, you know. They expect all the more. Very likely the poor girl thinks you'll be at the train to meet her."

"Naturally I'm meeting her," Amanda said coldly, though she had had no idea of doing so until Julian spoke. "After all, I am the one who suggested she come to New York."

"But time—time—time!" exclaimed Julian, for they both hoarded time, respecting it as if it was the stockholders' money, not to be spent on anything but the highest-paying, most reliable securities. In their reports to these mythical stockholders they were honor-bound to account for every split second, classifying their expenditures something like this: SLEEP (for efficiency purposes) 7 hrs. 18 min.; CONVERSATION WITH STAFF (for goodwill and *esprit de corps* purposes) 12 min.; TALK WITH BARBER OR MANICURIST (for purpose of man-in-the-street comments on affairs) 15 min.; JOKE with store-keeper (for aid to digestion) 3 min., *et cetera*. So Julian expected to remind Amanda that although he did not question her money expenditures, the time account was in both their names and it was not quite cricket for her to overdraw on a mere whim. Anything in the way of a human outlay excited his jealousy, for the one consolation in his wife's lack of warmth toward him was that nothing else drew fire from her, either. Already he was a little jealous about a past that was being rewarded in the person of this Miss Haven. Quite aware of this, Amanda now instructed Miss Bemel to have the car ready to meet Miss Haven's train, and to cancel the luncheon engagement with her new research man. Julian was getting far too possessive about her career, Amanda thought, restlessly; it made it rather a lark to annoy him by this little waste of time.

Half-way to Grand Central Amanda began to regret her decision. To annoy Julian was one thing, but to plant future annoyance for herself was something else. It would mean very little to Vicky that an extremely busy woman troubled herself to meet a train. Probably the child would take it for granted and assume that further personal gestures were quite in order. It would have been much wiser to start out on a different basis, let the first meeting be at dinner tonight when Vicky would see the sort of life Amanda now led and have the consequent tact to keep her distance. Amanda hated to doubt her own decisions, and she frowned now over the two sides to this question. If she was too remote with Vicky, then her new friendliness with Ken Saunders would stand out too conspicuously, because God knows there was no legitimate reason for taking him up—no reason that would bear weight with Julian or Miss Bemel. All right, here she was, great lady being welcome committee to visiting Cinderella. Amanda left the car impatiently and entered the station.

She did not know whether it was because she travelled so seldom by train these days that a railroad station was strange to her, or whether it was because it was unusual for so many people to look at her without recognition. At any rate she had an odd feeling of being stripped of herself, of being either lost or dead. She could hear her heels clack on the stone floor of the great mausoleum, but people hurrying by seemed strangely noiseless and ghostly, whatever cries they gave melted into one dull, muted motor noise. Daylight, dingy, diluted, sunless daylight coming through the skylight far up caught the moving figures in its pale web, permitting them to circle around until dark passageways opened up and offered escape. In this vault where seconds and minutes were treasured, Amanda had a sense of loneliness and fear she had never experienced. All these unseeing faces were testimony to a world still unconquered by her. Fear suddenly gave way to impatience at the stupidity of crowds who reacted only to accidents, freaks, movie stars, kings. There was so much she had yet to do, Amanda thought almost with self-pity, so many worlds yet to be subjugated; it was Julian's failure, not her own, she thought, that he was not able to buy *all* of them.

She resented being jostled, and though she was used to her good looks attracting attention she resented the approving eyes of strange men, as if she was a dish not only to their taste but well within their reach; above all she resented Vicky's train being half an hour late which made Julian right. Oh, definitely. She should never fritter away her time with these unnecessary little gestures. She used to rebel against Julian's counsel on her career; nowadays she rebelled against his *making* her rebel merely suggesting something she knew was wise.

"Ken," she suddenly thought, for Ken's hotel was just a block away. At least he would give her back her identity, raise her from crowd level to her proper eminence.

She telephoned him from a booth, and asked him to meet her in the Commodore Bar, a concession to his habits that brought an unexpected laugh from him. As soon as she hung up she was cross at the feeling of guilt, which she thought was in some obscure fashion the fault of Julian or of Ken or of Vicky Haven, these people who cluttered her path and made

her do things not in her plan. Why should she add mistake to
mistake by calling up Ken? A gaunt black-eyed girl with
Garbo as her model and a big red patent-leather purse caught
Amanda's arm.

"Could you give me two nickels for a dime? I gotta
'phone," she said. This sort of familiarity irritated Amanda, always, not for snobbish reasons but because it obliged her to
give priceless time to the trivial uses of worthless people.
Frowning, she drew two nickels from her bag and handed
them over in silence.

"My boy friend's waiting to hear if I got here," the girl explained, as if this linked her with all other women calling boy
friends, and entitled her to the courtesies of the club. Amanda
nodded silently and went on to the Commodore entrance
across the aisle. A man coming out looked at her twice and
tipped his hat. The square Irish face under the derby hat, and
the natty Chesterfield coat, paisley-patterned scarf, seemed familiar enough but Amanda did not place him.

"Haven't seen you for a long time," he said to her, looking
her over with pleasure. "A mink coat, too! Burdley's must be
paying better than when I was there."

Burdley's. That was the department store where Amanda
had worked for two years as advertising copy-writer. Searching her memory not too willingly, she remembered this man
was in Burdley's lamp department just outside the executive
offices. He had never seemed to know there was anything
special about her beyond her looks, anything any different
from the cash girls, for he asked them all for dates with complete lack of discrimination.

"How do you do," she murmured, with her usual dismissing smile.

The old friend was not so easily dismissed.

"It's been six, seven years, hasn't it?" he said genially.
"Where you going? Commute? I'm married now. Live in Pel-
ham. That wouldn't prevent my buying you lunch some day
if you say when. Where do I get you—still at Burdley's?"

What triumph was there in her work if the people from her
past whom she wanted to "show" simply would not be
shown? This man thought she was still punching a time clock
at Burdley's, taking orders from a dozen departmental heads,

arguing over raises and bonuses, fending off dates with buyers and bosses. In the station, mixing with this nondescript crowd, there was nothing to mark her as different from the black-eyed girl with the red purse; there were still hundreds of people, probably, who thought she was still working in Burdley's, people who read Amanda Keeler Evans and thought, "I knew a girl by that name once. In fact the girl I knew looked just like this woman's picture." But they were positive it was not the same person. The person they remembered could not *possibly* have written this great book or married this great man. With a faint thought of revenge, Amanda said, "Yes, do call me at Burdley's," but it was the man who had the last word, for he said, "Let's see—what's that name again? Mary —Mary—Mary—don't tell me, it'll come to me."

"Smith," said Amanda icily, and went through the door.

Already Julian had proved how necessary he was to her, a reminder that Amanda did not at all relish. She sat down at a table and waited for Ken, angry at herself for increasing her nonentity by waiting for another nonentity. It did not improve her temper to have him tweak her hair as he came up behind her. She wanted to have the privileges of any other woman, but she didn't want to be *treated* like any other woman.

"All right, you've proved it. I'm still on a leash," he said, sitting down. "Wasn't that all you wanted to know?"

"Stop saying things like that," she said curtly. "You spoil everything."

"Double whiskey sour," he said to the waiter.

"Coffee," said Amanda. It took her aback that the waiter showed no sign of recognizing her, nor did the couple at the next table whisper her name. She was so accustomed to go only to those places where she was known that this anonymity was a new experience. She didn't like it. She had resented it for all the years before she married Julian, the years she wrote perfume copy in Paris, unsigned, bitterly envying every name that brought nods of respect, envying the Hemingways, Hepburns, Windsors, and Edens equally, without regard for the nature of their achievements, merely envying the applause. Ken used to be her applause, assuring her she could do anything she set her mind to. He hated it, though, when she proved he was right. He still hated her, even though they were lovers again. Maybe he was just being clever. Maybe he sensed that once he gave in completely to her again she would be through with the game.

"I can't stand your drinking in the morning," she said suddenly, looking at his drink. "It's so weak of you."

"Another whiskey sour," Ken said to the waiter. "Double."

He looked at her with cold hostility.

"Why am I honored by your summons today?" he asked. "You proved I would come back running when you whistled. You proved that yesterday. Twenty-four minutes of glorious abandonment, by the clock—"

"Hush!"

"—not that I didn't appreciate the favor. Not that I don't want you in the same bed this very minute—"

"Ken—please!" She was really angry. "I might have known you'd be like this. I want to be nice, and you hate me for it."

He looked stonily at his drink.

"Why not, for Christ's sake? You kick me around for three years, you kick me out, then you want to see if I'm damn fool enough to come back. Just for the fun of it. You never had anybody love you the way I did, knowing all about you, knowing what a five letter woman you are and always will be, and still being fool enough to love you."

Amanda did not hush him now, for this soothed her, brought back her power, reminded her that she was Amanda, the Amanda that nothing could hurt except anonymity. She was soothed, but she was curious, too, that any one should care so much about any one, and be so affected physically by any other human being. She looked at his face surprised and gratified that it should show pain, because this was a tribute to her of a sort she could not understand.

"So you call me up and say you have sixteen minutes and two seconds with no one to walk over, and I'm fool enough to come." He tossed his drink down, and beckoned for the check. In the silence she glanced at her watch and he caught it.

"Have you found out what you want? Is my time up, now?" he mocked.

Amanda had found out what she wanted and his time was up, true enough, if truth was what he wanted. She felt warmed and satisfied, the little bruises of a few moments before quite forgotten. Now she was ready for Vicky, at least as soon as Ken would humble himself to ask for the next meeting. He would. He might try to be stubborn but she knew he would have to ask before they got to the door, and she was not going to make it easy for him. He surprised her by keeping grimly silent to the very moment of their parting at the train gates. He was doing it on purpose, she thought, because he knew she was too sure. It was clever of him, she admitted, for now she wondered about him and wondered if she really dared be sure again.

"Good-bye," he said resolutely.

"Dinner tonight, you remember," she said.

He nodded, still refusing to ask for another secret date, and now she was put out because she had taken the studio for no other reason but that. He was holding off to make her presumption seem silly, and a pleasurable sense of panic came over her. How stimulating it was to be uncertain of him! How clever, how terribly clever of him to tease her this way— unless he did mean a little bit of it. . . .

"Tuesday—between three and four," she murmured, plunging.

He gave no indication of agreeing. She wouldn't know until she had made all sorts of complicated arrangements with Bemel to cover her movements for that day. But of course he would be there. Of course she was right to be sure of him. Disappointed at the game losing its charm Amanda watched the crowd pouring through the gate. She hadn't seen Vicky for ten years but she recognized the slight figure in the brown suit, the eager, restless walk, and the shining eyes. She was glad to see her, she was surprised to find, but even before Vicky had caught her eye Amanda was beginning to wonder how much would be expected of her. So her greeting was a shade less warm than Vicky's, managing subtly to hint that the old intimacy was not to be counted upon.

"Why, it looks like any other city," Vicky exclaimed, looking around the station. "It might be anywhere."

Some one behind them laughed, and Amanda colored. She had never found provincialism refreshing and was impatient already with her protégée. She did not like it any better when Vicky gave an audible gasp at sight of the limousine.

"Oh, Amanda! How wonderful!"

"I'll drop you at the studio and see you tonight at dinner," Amanda cut in brusquely, and Vicky, accustomed to taking any uncomplimentary hint as specially made for her, did not find much more to say during the drive, nor did there seem any way of crossing the gulf of their long separation. Amanda clearly was not at all interested in any Lakeville news, and by a detached polite manner conveyed the idea that the Amanda of the old days was no more. Vicky was more subdued by this politeness than by any snub, and changed her manner immediately to the tactful taciturnity evidently required.

"Dinner tonight, as I said," Amanda said in parting. "I'll send for you."

Vicky was too awed, this time, to even thank her friend. Thanks were probably highly provincial, she gathered.

Amanda drove on home in a state of rising irritation. Now she had started something, she thought, but no one need think her time or friendship would be commanded. No matter to what use she might put others, they would soon find Amanda Keeler was not to be used.

IV

THE EVANSES knew every one, and by "every one" I certainly do not mean you or me or any one *we* know. This meant that they had no time for friendships or personalities, since "every one" shifted and "everybody" became "nobody" so often that it was silly even to remember first names. Neither Amanda nor Julian liked society, except as they could manipulate it in their own home. They knew whom they had there and what they expected to get out of them. At other people's dinners half the time you were wasting your time just because the host wasn't clear in his explanation of who his guests were.

"So that Craver chap was Southern Textiles," Julian would bitterly complain to Amanda, reading the paper next day. "And I wasted the whole evening talking diamonds to that Hindu. Damn the Thorps, anyway, I'm too busy to waste time at their dinners!"

"I spent half an hour being nice to that Corrigan," Amanda indignantly responded. "I thought he was Pictures, and all the time he was just Little Theatre."

This wanton waste of their time by other people was the cross Mr. and Mrs. Julian Evans shared in common, and they felt so completely justified in their complaint that they admitted it freely to would-be hostesses. It was as if they had to make up for the first twenty years of their existence which had been wasted in marbles, dolls, hoop-rolling, and scooter-racing. They might have spent those years building a social trust fund of Contacts and Culture instead of dawdling away at the maternal breast. No more idle fudge-making or agate-swapping; every smile, every "hello" must pay. At last, confining their social life to their own home as much as possible, the Evanses still regretted that they missed so much by lack of proper cooperation from their friends.

"Mr. Evans, Mr. Harris," hostesses said, and when Julian impatiently whispered his inquiry, "Who is Harris?" he only received the bright reply that Mr. Harris was from the Middle West, and had a very handsome wife. Who in heaven's name

wanted to know that Mr. Harris was Zeke Harris, a bright
Lutheran boy from Indianapolis who ran away from home
to be a brakeman on the B.&O. Railway, became dispatcher,
married a million, had a tough time all around before he
reached the top, but always idolized his mother? Mr. Harris
was, in the Evanses' labor-saving shorthand, "Wall Street."
Elva Macroy was not just a stunning blonde who never got
the man she wanted so ran through four marriages to forget
him. No. Elva Macroy was not that unhappy individual, she
was "Washington"! The insignificant little man with the careful English was not Mama Felder's little boy Izzy, but "Pictures, Inc.," and here and there, annoyingly disguised as
human beings, were The Theatre, Bethlehem Steel, Education, Palm Beach, Southern Pine, Racquet Club, The Ballet,
and of course Russia. Naturally the persons symbolizing these
matters changed from time to time and for that reason it always seemed a waste to Julian to learn their names. A few
names, if sufficiently in the public prints, naturally did stick
but no one felt more cheated than Julian, if after remembering for years that Hawkins was Public Utilities, and Public
Utilities was Hawkins, suddenly Hawkins became Cotton,
and Public Utilities was Purvis.

In their own home, however, the problem resolved itself
easily, with Miss Bemel and Mr. Castor providing guest-lists
with their social value in parentheses. In the case of Vicky
Haven, the parentheses enclosed the terse apology "(school-
friend)" and in the case of Ken Saunders, Miss Bemel had not
even considered his name in journalism of sufficient importance to mention but merely said "(escort)," adequate excuse
for any male guest.

Having been instructed by Amanda, before Wednesday's
dinner party, that he was to take a paternal interest in her
young friend, Julian remembered to direct a look of keen
concern in Vicky's direction during the cocktails, occasionally
stepping to her side and asking, "Well, Betty, are you having
a good time?" but being set straight on the name remembered to call her "Verna" the rest of the time. Since this was
the only personal attention Vicky received during the cocktail
period she was grateful to him, and tried to act very much at
ease by taking a martini every time it was offered and refusing

the canapés. This was because what she really wanted was the canapés, having had nothing but coffee since she got off the train, but she had learned long ago that whatever she wanted was certain to be bad form or in some way wrong. So, when she wanted a highball, she took a martini, and when she didn't want to smoke she took a cigarette. She was not helped in poise by her inner astonishment at actually being in New York, actually being here at a fabulous dinner party at the Julian Evanses', hobnobbing with all these great names, for she knew they must be great names even if she couldn't quite catch them.

At Amanda's dinners the gentlemen were never permitted to have their brandy alone because Amanda had a pathological horror of being left alone with women, particularly wives. Life was too short, she felt, to waste on these creatures of her own sex who had nothing to add to either her glory or her information. For the same reason neither Amanda nor Julian dared injure their acquisitive faculties by drinking. While guests had martinis, the Evanses had tomato juice; at table they permitted themselves only a solitary glass of champagne during the wine course, this as a concession only to the dignity of the vintage, and during the liqueurs they sipped at ice water. For some reason this temperate example made the guests go to extremes of thirst, and it was rumored around town that although the Evanses' dinners usually ended before midnight the sedate worth-whileness of the event sent the guests afterward to dens of ripest vulgarity. Taxi-drivers hung about the corner watchfully when the Evanses entertained, well aware that at least one elegant group, emerging from the mansion, would demand Harlem, even Coney Island, while others, restrained for hours in intellectual converse, would demand a tough waterfront dive or Third Avenue beerhall.

Vicky, without knowing the legend, felt the same way and found herself getting slightly fuzzy during the dinner, which made the affair seem even more wonderful than before. It was true she had as yet found no way of cracking the conversation, and so far as the party went she was positive she was a great dud, but it was a fine thing to sit between a genuine Lord and a millionaire banker, having them talk monumental matters across your face for six courses. It made her realize how insignificant a small-town nobody like Tom Turner was, and she could look back and marvel that she had ever wept over such a trivial person. Of course dinner with a trivial person like Tom used to be fun, no element of which ever intruded into the Evanses' dinner. But fun and glamour, perhaps, didn't mix, and at least this was something to write Ethel Carey about for home-town gossip. Vicky felt very pleased anticipating how this would sound in a letter and how it would chagrin the Tom Turners. For some reason women, flouted in love, invariably find an incomprehensibly satisfying revenge in soaring socially. "I will give a white-tie dinner for eighteen," they promise themselves. "How he will burn up when he hears about it." Or else they will be the guest at such functions. The idea that the defaulting lover will be hopelessly chagrined by this social soaring (no matter how he may abhor such a formal life) is as fixed in the female mind as is the child's dream of avenging itself on Teacher by slowly flying around the room with smiling ease. The net effect on both teacher and lover is more apt to be merely a mild astonishment tinctured with irritation rather than remorse. But Vicky treasured the thought that Tom would realize what a superior person he had thoughtlessly tossed away when he heard that she was being sponsored by the great Julian Evans and the famous Amanda. It might make him a little discontented with the ordinariness of his present wife, who could never possibly achieve such distinction.

Vicky watched her old school friend with awe and admiration. There was Amanda conducting the dinner as a symposium, herself the leader, extracting facts, data, opinions, and then repeating the routine in the after-dinner coffee hour, during which Amanda and Julian refreshed their minds on what they had learned at dinner with further discussion, Julian giving out a good deal of it as his own original thought and Amanda repeating the best she had heard without quotes. It was as if anything that went in her ear forthwith belonged to her by the laws of nature, and the lives or opinions of her guests belonged to her in the same way. Amanda's very lips seemed to move simultaneously with the lofty statements of her experts; she signed the words the second they left the other speaker's lips. Vicky saw no harm in this but only cause for despair that she herself had nothing to contribute to Amanda's store. While the Lord Somebody on her right told one on Churchill, Vicky combed her mind desperately for some comparable tidbit, but what Uncle Charlie said to the new farmhand back in Lakeville did not seem appropriate, or what Amanda's daddy said when he sold the Howard suit to the candy store man next door.

It was not, Vicky thought, that she was embarrassed by being present in such distinguished company; it was worse than that—it was that she wasn't even present. She was surprised when one of the master minds spoke to her, so certain was she that she must be invisible. It was like having actors in a film suddenly talk back to you. She saw herself in a mirror and said, "Well, I am here all right, that dowdy little thing must be me." The new dinner dress had seemed a treasure till she set foot in the Evanses' house and then Amanda's trailing cloth of gold made everything else seem the dullest of rags. Vicky had, in her first uneasy effort to establish the old girlish intimacy with Amanda, asked if she looked all right—should she wear the little gray capelet in back like a cowl or in front over her bare bosom?

"Either way you like, dear," Amanda had graciously advised with an appreciative glance at herself in the mirror. "You look sweet just as it is."

Then with a final fond stroke of her hip line and a tender pat to her blonde hair Amanda turned from the mirror and led the way to her other guests, leaving Vicky with the conviction that Amanda's eyes saw so little but Amanda that she wouldn't have known if other women's dresses were wrong-side out or upside down.

Thinking of how to describe to Ethel Carey this thrilling debut into New York life, Vicky looked carefully at the men. There must be some one among them on whom she could fasten as a possible suitor, mentally if not in reality. She hadn't really expected, after the weeping, worry and fatigue of packing of the last few weeks, to look her best, but she had expected to get at least a polite flicker of interest. Up to the second round of liqueurs no one had fallen at her feet, and Vicky was obliged to console herself with the thought that they were mostly so old that such a fall might prove fatal

anyway, and no girl's charm is enhanced by a flock of elderly
corpses around her hem. The one young man who looked
possibly human sat in a corner staring stonily into space and
addressing no one. This was the Mr. Saunders Amanda had
explained she had invited for Vicky's exclusive delight. Vicky,
casting a hopeful glance at him from time to time, saw nothing to encourage her, but for the sake of her letter to Ethel
made private notes on his appearance, and the manner in
which he divided his looks between Amanda, Julian, and the
opposite wall, with gloomy intensity.

"He must be *somebody*," Vicky thought. "He couldn't be
here without being *somebody*."

He was dressed correctly—or at least like the other men—
his shoes gleamed, his white tie was in place, his large squar-
ish hands manicured, but this made his unshaven blond face
more baffling. His thick fair hair was very pretty, Vicky
thought, but his large quarrelsome nose was certainly no
beauty. The heavy brows over his blue eyes were very dark
and his lashes, considering the square masculine lines of his
face, were ridiculously long, curling up like any glamour
girl's, and giving a look of bright innocence to his face. His
mouth was large and his chin was thrust out sulkily, adding to
the pugnacious effect of his thick shoulders. His silence and
immobility seemed to disturb his hostess not one whit, but
Vicky caught Julian occasionally studying this silent guest
with a thoughtful look. After a while, Vicky noticed, he took
to repeating whatever he had said to the others in a louder
voice in the direction of the silent Mr. Saunders, who continued to reward this graciousness with a glazed, hopeless eye.

"I was just telling Mr. Shebus," Julian bent toward the
backward guest and raised his voice, "that I have Andy Callingham covering Finland for me."

"Andy Callingham, think of it!" Amanda turned brightly to
Saunders. "Isn't that wonderful for Julian to get Callingham
himself?"

Mr. Saunders rose at this and walked gravely across the
room and grasped Mr. Evans' hand in congratulation. He
proceeded then to Amanda and grasped her hand. Without
speaking he resumed his seat in the corner and looked at the
wall. The guests looked at him uneasily.

Vicky ventured to show interest.

"I thought Andrew Callingham *had* to go to all the wars," she said in a voice she had never heard herself have before, though it may have become a little rusty from disuse this evening. "I mean—what I mean is—I thought he had to be seen at all the wars." As the guests turned courteous uncomprehending faces toward her she floundered on, "I mean the way Peggy Joyce has to be seen at all the—er—the night clubs."

In the silence following this inadvertent reflection on a public hero Vicky seized her drink wildly and gulped it, and Mr. Saunders rose, walked over and shook her limp hand. Why, he's tight, of course, thought Vicky in surprise, he's as tight as a mink. This time he carefully parted his tails and took the seat beside her on the sofa. It was embarrassing because now it was quite clear to every one that here were two interlopers in the club. Mr. Saunders, Vicky thought, is nobody, but nobody. It made her feel a little better, even though Amanda, she was sure, was now actively displeased with her, and Julian had dismissed both of the nobodies by showing the book of his collected editorials to the banker Shebus and the visiting baronet.

"The foreword, you see, is by Callingham himself," he explained. "See here—'the greatest editor of our time, Julian Evans'—I care more about that little remark from Callingham than I do about any compliment I've ever had. A great man himself, Callingham."

"I missed him in London," Amanda said. "Of course we saw all the same things, the same people—Churchill, Beaverbrook, de Gaulle."

Julian laughed patronizingly. There were few advantages that Amanda would grant him, but Callingham was his own, not hers.

"I doubt very much, my dear, if even you could command the interviews Andrew Callingham could," he said tenderly. "After all, he's been an international idol for years—he could wangle contacts that even I couldn't possibly arrange for you."

Amanda's frown of irritation deepened.

"I believe my last book sold about twice as much as the last Callingham book," she said quietly.

Mr. Saunders again rose and was about to congratulate her but Vicky hastily pulled him back by the coat-tails. As this gesture was even more strange than Mr. Saunders' motion, Vicky blushed and shrank back.

Amanda laughed, without amusement.

"I'm afraid we all frighten Miss Haven," she said. "Victoria is from Ohio, you know."

Mr. Saunders leaned forward with intense interest.

"Then of course you knew Churchill," he said.

Vicky shook her head, inarticulate.

"De Gaulle? Is de Gaulle the darling he seems really, Miss Haven?" pursued Mr. Saunders eagerly. "And you must have some first-hand stories about Eden."

"Ken, please," Amanda cried out, definitely angry.

Mr. Saunders sank back.

"Confidential, I suppose," he murmured. Vicky moved away from him a few inches. That would be her luck, to be snuggling in a sofa corner with the man who was insulting the rest of the party. That was the way Tom Turner used to be. That was the way she always ended up—with the outcasts, apologizing for them the next day, explaining that they were really too intelligent for their own good. At least she hadn't brought him there. Amanda couldn't hold that against her anyway. And when she left it would be clear enough that they did not come boxed together like Amos and Andy, or the Dead End Kids. Mr. Saunders' brief exhibition had brought about a lull in the conversation, and while Julian was rather awkwardly holding his book, waiting to revive interest in it, the banker and his Mexican wife rose to go. The alacrity with which host and hostess leaped to the adieux was indication that eleven o'clock was departure time at the Evanses, and others straggled to the door.

"Too bad we had no chance to hear the Signora sing," said Julian. "We do so much talk here we forget we have musical guests."

"Her gaucho song would have interested you, I think," said the banker, quite as anxious to exhibit his exotic wife's talents as Evans was to set off his own.

"I hope it's as interesting as her moustache," Mr. Saunders said pleasantly to Vicky in an alarmingly loud whisper. Vicky looked beseechingly toward Amanda but that young woman was at the door with her other guests, an example to all in how to handle a difficult situation. Vicky got up to go, since that seemed to be expected. She had had chance for no more than a few words with Amanda, and after tonight's demonstration of her inadequacy she was certain there would be little chance of reviving the old friendship. Amanda was loaning her her studio and securing her a job, but there seemed no warmth in the kindness, rather just a sense of duty. Well, sighed Vicky, she would have to find her circle elsewhere, wondrous as it would have been to bask in this golden light. Amanda had not even asked her how she liked her place, and outside of a note explaining the place and her further appointment with a Mr. Peabody, Vicky was afraid she was to be left quite on her own.

"Everything all right at your place, Vicky?" Amanda now remembered to ask lightly, as the wraps were brought. "Call the superintendent if anything's wrong."

"Will Mr. Saunders see that she gets home?" Julian asked.

Mr. Saunders was at the moment frankly helping himself to a Scotch and soda from the table.

"Oh, I'll get there all right," Vicky said quickly.

"Of course she can," Amanda said. "Why don't you take her to the street, Julian, and get a cab?"

"I thought—" hesitated Julian with a puzzled look toward the one remaining guest, Saunders, who was now dreamily gazing at the lady ancestor above the fireplace. The look seemed to rouse him for he said, "You know in my family we have mooseheads over the fireplace. Real ones, I mean, not just the picture."

No one said anything. Julian rang for the elevator and Amanda looked at her beautiful hands. Saunders turned and looked at her, put his glass down, and came out to them.

"I'll tell you all about it on the way home, Miss Haven," he said. "Good night, Amanda. Good night, Evans, old snort."

Vicky was still murmuring confused thank-yous and goodbyes as the door closed on Julian and Amanda standing there in silence. She could not understand why Saunders had fastened on her as a fellow rebel, and she could not understand why, if Amanda had asked him on her account, she seemed so displeased when they left together. She could not understand, too, why she was so glad to have his protection, especially since she had to hold his arm going down the street to keep him from swaying, if that's what you call protection. In the cab he lapsed into silent gloom once again.

"You shouldn't have called him snort," Vicky finally ventured. "You really shouldn't have done that."

Mr. Saunders looked pained.

"I rather thought it would please him," he said. "Do you think I should go back and explain?"

"No, no, no," Vicky said. In front of the florist shop on Lexington the cab stopped and Vicky said, "Good night." Saunders suddenly leaped out of the car and stared at the shop and the twin windows just above where Vicky was to live.

"So this is it," he said slowly, still staring upward. "So this is it."

He was still staring up at her windows when she went inside.

2

There was a Mr. Peabody in the Peabody Company and this was only one of many things to distinguish it from other Peabody Companies. The Mr. Peabody in this case—Otto Erasmus Peabody—even had a small, a very small percentage in the business, but otherwise was the patient moderator and representative of a temperamental board of directors whose success in other fields led them to consider themselves experts in managing a smart monthly magazine. As Mr. Peabody, in addition to his tiny percentage, drew a good salary from the company, he was tolerant with his board's eccentricities, faithfully carrying out whim after whim and refraining from comment when this week's loss exceeded last week's loss. When the magazine gained subscribers it lost the most money, according to a rule of publishing economics too complex to discuss here, yet it was constantly launching expensive campaigns for this very purpose. Mr. Peabody had grown not only gray but absolutely yellow (this was as to face) in the work of cooking up such circulation ideas. After fifteen years of listening to his directors shout and scream at each other his own voice had dropped permanently to a weary whisper, which, in its own way, was quite effective in calming the shredded nerves.

He was a tired fat man with a motherly face and a rather mother hubbard figure, that is, it was unmarked by waistline, and neck and knees had conspired to merge in a loose bundle that was shapeless without being actually gross. Other men— take his contemporary and friend Julian Evans, for instance, contrived to retain their masculine charm through forties, even fifties and sixties, but it was difficult to believe that Mr. Peabody had ever, even twenty years ago, appealed to any woman as anything but a sympathetic uncle. Yet he had a family which lived quite fashionably somewhere in Greenwich and in his cups, which was rare, he was as able as anybody else to lure some pretty thing to his anonymous lap. He had a way of combing his long back hair over his pate to conceal his baldness, which was the only thing that worried him about his appearance. The loose jowls, and anxious furrows in his yellow brow and cheek, the weary eye pouches, the uncomfortable upper dental plates, even the surprisingly red hair that sprouted gaily from his ears, were no concern at all. On the whole it was a round friendly face, the gray eye as kind as it was shrewd, and if there was any bitterness in his soul after all these years of preserving his inner honesty in a wicked world, such a thing had left no record in his appearance.

Mr. Peabody was the first person, and for some time was the only person, with whom Vicky Haven felt at home in New York. The outer reception room where she had waited for him had been terrifyingly impressive, and the young women employees who dashed in and out, a few with their dogs on leash, all exchanging elegant remarks in a diction so full of mystifying gargles and squeals that Vicky knew it must come from the best finishing schools. She began to wonder uneasily what would be expected of her and how she could ever compete with these poised beautiful young creatures, none of whom, she was sure, had ever had a moment's doubt of her place in the world. You wouldn't catch any of these competent young things permitting another woman to take away their Tom Turner or any other man. Vicky couldn't picture them permitting even desk space to a stranger. She was sure Mr. Peabody would be an exquisitely groomed man of fashion, a cross between Cary Grant and Roland Young, and with neither type had she ever been a pet.

Mr. Peabody therefore, smiling at her from his unpretentious personal office, was a great relief, and to Mr. Peabody, used to demands from his directors for distribution of favors in unworthy directions, Vicky was a relief. They sat beaming at each other across the desk without saying anything for a full minute and then Mr. Peabody remembered to welcome her, so he reached across to shake her warmly by the hand, repeating, "That's fine, that's fine, yes, that's just fine," until Vicky felt quite happy, without knowing what he meant at all.

"Not from New York?" he asked.

"Ohio," she said.

Mr. Peabody nodded as if he had known at once that brown eyes, sandy hair, and a tan sport suit could only come from Ohio, or that particular state's borderlines with Kentucky or Indiana. To be recognized at once as provincial was not her dream of dreams but Vicky was pleased now because Mr. Peabody seemed pleased. It might be, she reflected, that he too came from Ohio. This turned out not to be the case, and she was to discover later on that this was all the better, for there is something more annoying than pleasant in finding neighbors from back home chiselling in on your own exclusive New York. It mitigates your triumph in having conquered the great city and brings home the ungratifying truth that anybody can do it. Mr. Peabody was from Maine and the Peabody place near Bangor had been a showplace for three generations, housing Peabody senators, cabinet officials, university heads, and being an eternal inspiration to younger Peabodys that a penny saved is a penny earned, save the pennies and the dollars will take care of themselves. This bone-deep tradition was why our Mr. Peabody at fifty thousand a year, bought only one newspaper a day, no matter how curious he was to see what another paper had to say about a subject, and why he could not bring himself to spend more than a dollar for a tie, though the cost of sending a few of his office boys to business school or college never seemed to cause him a second's hesitation.

"What is my job?" Vicky asked, knowing now that of course she could do it, because Mr. Peabody looked at her as if she could.

"The magazine has started a real estate service," said Mr. Peabody, "and that's your work here. Julian tells me you did that before. You will visit country places and apartments that we advertise and have a shopper's guide sort of page."

It sounded simple enough. The only thing that worried Vicky was the thought of those other girls brushing past her in the reception room.

"Do I bring my dog to work?" she asked.

Mr. Peabody chuckled.

"That's our Social Register front," he explained. "We try to staff the fringe of the magazine with Junior League girls—the better names in society from a publicity point of view. Pretty, too, because we use them in photograph releases. Jockeys up our advertising value for luxury stuff."

Across the glass-paned wall to the next office Vicky saw two flawless coiffures of the "up-do" type, nothing that could be contrived in one's own bathroom mirror on the way to work. The two girls were gesturing—Mr. Peabody was happily sound-protected in his office—over what seemed at first a rose on a ribbon as they passed it back and forth, but then as they each tried it on over the two wonderful heads became a hat. Peabody's eye followed Vicky's.

"That's what I'm scared of," Vicky confessed. "Girls like that. They make me feel as if I had hay in my hair."

"I've worked in this business for twenty years," said Mr. Peabody. "And I still have hay in my hair. It's a business asset, Miss Haven."

"I'd still rather have false eyelashes," said Vicky.

"You will," sighed Mr. Peabody. He had been doodling with a red crayon on the pile of papers on his desk, and now saw that he had defaced a newly typed report with the same hour-glass ladies' figures that had marked the margins of his Third Reader. He hastily threw down the pencil and looked sternly into the next room.

"That's one of the Elroy girls, the tall one," he said. "She does something on the fashion end. The other is one of the Trays, the Newport Trays."

"I suppose business experience never can quite make up for your picture in the Sunday rotogravure," Vicky said ruefully.

"Now, now," soothed Mr. Peabody. "It wasn't your experience, it was Julian Evans, that got you this job. Just as bad as social background, you know. Same thing."

He telephoned for a Miss Myers to show her to her office. More girls appeared in the glass office next door, laughing, trying on the silly bonnet, all of them testifying to three hours a day spent on their hair, unless the blue-haired one took another hour on hers. Like some girls' school, Vicky thought, some snobbish up-the-Hudson school, instead of like a business office. The walnut panelling cut them off below the shoulders and the soundproofing cut off their voices, so she had a curious impression of being in a Buck Rogers strip, invisible herself, and gazing into another planet.

"Don't worry about those girls," Mr. Peabody admonished. "They are our front, but then we have a basic staff of professionals. The only thing is that they all get so they talk and act like this. It's hard to tell the difference unless you know the names.

"Another thing," he added as he padded down the narrow hall—why, Vicky thought, he wears high laced black shoes like some old lady with varicosities—"the professionals get paid, to make up for their lack of family. They won't bother you much, really, those girls. I hope you don't try to be like them, though," he gave a long sigh, "but I suppose you will. It won't be long."

They came to the main hall and here were the two signs Vicky was to remember, one with the arrow pointing left was marked "EDITORIAL: FASHIONS: EXECUTIVE:" and the one to the right was marked "BUSINESS." Even in the brief moment necessary for Mr. Peabody to greet a man coming out of the elevator Vicky could see that one was the front door and Business was the Delivery entrance. Her office was the Delivery Entrance. Glamour belonged in the other end.

Nevertheless the young woman seated in the little two-desk office when they reached it was gotten up very much like the girls Vicky had seen next to the Peabody office. She was, if anything, even more lacquered. Her black glossy hair was brushed up to an impeccable topknot of curls, her eyebrows were thin pencilled arcs of perpetual surprise, her mouth was wide and not too noticeably rebuilt, while her skin was a masterpiece of beige wax that looked more like a glossy magazine cover than human skin. She wore a severe, elegant green tweed dress with a row of wooden charms around the neck, and all that could be said of her legs, stretched out in sandalled "wedgies," was that at least they were freely exposed.

She acknowledged Mr. Peabody's introduction with a cool measuring eye. Miss Haven and Miss Finkelstein were to work together on real estate. Miss Finkelstein had been with the company twelve years. Miss Finkelstein knew the ropes. Miss Finkelstein could show the ropes to Miss Haven, who was an expert real estate woman previously employed by Julian Evans in an out-of-town advisory capacity. It was Miss Finkelstein's steely reception of her new co-worker that must have prompted Mr. Peabody to throw out the magic Evans name, for she visibly softened at it and, except for a patronizingly cultivated accent, cultivated, like the other girls to the point of intranslatableness, was quite pleasant in explaining the files, and the general system. She clearly enjoyed pressing buttons for typists, file clerks, and other underlings, by way of impressing the newcomer with the importance of her office. Vicky watched her busy activities quite humbly, hoping that Miss Finkelstein would not be too severe a chief.

"I adore Amanda Keeler Evans' work," said Miss Finkelstein, pausing from her exhibition of efficiency to do a little work on her amazingly long red nails. "Do you know her personally?"

"Oh, yes," said Vicky and explained the relationship. It was as if she had said she knew Windsor himself, for Miss F. leaned on her desk with her long enamelled face cupped in her two hands, charm bracelets silenced for a moment, in enthralled attention.

"She must be an absolute Movvel," said Miss F. "Absolutely too heavenly. How does she wear her hair now? Up?"

"Up," said Vicky. "No, down."

"I can weah mine down, you know," said Miss Finkelstein. "I must say I'm rahthah surprised that Amanda Keeler does. Oh deah, I mustn't forget that beastly dinnah at the Plaza! These frightful press-agents. As if any one wanted to meet Bette Davis."

Vicky was uncomfortably aware of Miss Finkelstein's eagle eyes putting price tags on her suit, her hair, her shoes, and was relieved when a dolorous, undersized office boy appeared with a batch of mail.

"We use George at this end mostly," Miss Finkelstein said, "I don't know why they're giving us Irving today. Please, Irving, tell Mr. Fiske we must have George back. Really. I mean. Really."

Irving stood gaping at Vicky.

"She taking Miss Moiphy's place?" he inquired.

"Yes, she is," snapped Miss Finkelstein.

"I thought you was gonna be permoted to Miss Moiphy's place," said Irving. "I didn't know you was gettin' a new boss. You said next you was gonna be boss."

It was the first Vicky had heard that Miss Finkelstein, far from being her chief, was to be her secretary. It was frightening news for her.

"Nevah mind what I said, boy," said Miss Finkelstein. "Please."

"I'm your brudder, ain't I?" inquired Irving. "I should tink if you stay here all dis time you'd get a break instead of always getting somebody shoved in over you."

"Irving, please!" remonstrated Miss Finkelstein, only she gave it a very agreeable "Uvving" sound. "Oh, yes, tell Mummy I won't be home for dinnah. I'm dashing up to the Plaza for some horrible affaiah."

"Mama'll be sore," said Irving. "She made meatloaf. When'll you get in?"

"Latish," said Miss Finkelstein, patting her perfect mouth with her flawless hand.

"How late?"

"Elevenish," yawned Miss Finkelstein. "Twelvish. Maybe oneish."

"Don't forget ya gotta three-dollar taxi bill all the way home from the Plaza," Irving said severely. "Mama's waitin' for ya to give her last week's dough anyway."

"Don't be vomitish, Irving!" Miss Finkelstein said coldly. "IF you don't mind."

"AHH!" Irving cried out in helpless irritation. "Ahh!"

He ran out of the office tearing his hair. Vicky, somewhat baffled by the little scene, stole a look at Miss Finkelstein to see if she was at all perturbed, but her secretary was calmly dialling the telephone.

"I must call Mummy," she murmured. "I hope you don't mind my having this desk. It was Miss Murphy's but really, I think the other is quite as good. If you don't mind sitting by the door."

Vicky didn't mind. She was too astonished by her new work to mind anything. She realized now that Miss Finkelstein, in her efforts to model herself after the debutante members of the office, had gone a little overboard on some things but it might all even up some day.

"Imagine Amanda Keeler still wearing her hair down," mused Miss Finkelstein, gracefully hanging over the telephone, awaiting her number. "I must tell Mummy. Irving is horrible, but Mummy is rather an old deah, you know. A complete peasant, you know. You wouldn't believe!"

Vicky found her head nodding dumbly. She rather wished she had Ethel Carey here now to tell her what to do next.

V

A MANDA'S furnished "studio" in which Vicky was free to
live from 5 P.M. to 11 A.M., so Amanda stated, was in the
Murray Hill section just off Park. Vicky was delighted with it
and pried out of the janitor the discouraging news that it was
$135 a month. This meant that she must dismiss the idea of
having anything of the same sort on her own salary. It was as
full of balconies, staircases, and doors as a regular house, so
that it was surprising to find it technically a one-room apartment. There was the foyer with its four doors that might lead
to four other chambers but in reality led only to a vast closet,
service entrance, kitchen, and bath-dressing-room. An iron
railing separated the foyer from the studio which was four
steps down and in this "dropped living-room" were more
doors leading to cedar closets, linen closets, wood closets, and
here were French doors leading to a small balcony of no
earthly good except to keep the happy tenant from falling out
of her room. The furniture was simple, the original owner
having left only the barest living necessities, and there was little to indicate Amanda's creative work here beyond typewriter
supplies, a few reference books and a few toilet trifles in the
dressing-room. Vicky was careful to conceal as much of her
own personal effects as possible, since evidence of a foreign
presence might disturb Amanda's working moods. It was
really Amanda's, after all, and she must try not to feel too
much at home.

"The place is too heavenly for words," she wrote Ethel
Carey. "New York is wonderful, the Peabody Company is
marvellous, Amanda has been so good to me, and I am so
happy to be away from Lakeville."

She found it wise to include in her glowing report a sly insinuation that there was a Mr. Kenneth Saunders who seemed
frightfully interested in her, so that Ethel would let it be
known in Lakeville that Vicky had a New York beau already.
Having posted the good news Vicky then cried some more
over Lakeville and Tom Turner, sniffled some over her mistakes at the Peabody office and the misfortune of having a

telephone that evidently had no bell. It is one thing to forget the old love in the triumph of new fortunes, but it is another matter indeed to try forgetting him wandering by yourself around a great strange city, neglected by the new world so that the happy lost past is inevitably thrust on your thoughts. At least in Lakeville people said hello.

On her solitary evening ventures to the Newsreel or to Radio City to see Melvyn Douglas or Cary Grant, her favorites, or bus-riding to the Cloisters on a Sunday, window-shopping at twilight up and down Lexington or Madison, Vicky puzzled constantly over what she had done at Amanda's dinner party to annoy her sponsor. She must have done something wrong, since Amanda never called her. The fact that Amanda had left theatre tickets twice with a brief note was no comfort, for there was an implication in the gift that Vicky could expect no personal contact with the donor. Once Vicky had taken Miss Finkelstein to see "The Male Animal" but the overbearing airs of that competent young woman luxuriating in an orchestra seat had ruined the evening for Vicky. With Amanda's next tickets Vicky had gone alone, certain that in New York going alone to a theatre was next thing to going on the streets. Her agonized Alice Adams efforts to act as if she were reserving the other seat for a most distinguished but delayed escort, spoiled that evening too for her.

She saw Ken Saunders in the Peabody building one rainy noon, but she was wearing rubbers and a fearful raincoat and hat that looked as if she anticipated a tidal wave, an ensemble in fact that had been suitable enough for a Lakeville storm but was a drab contrast to the smart, filmy inadequacies worn by the Peabody glamour girls as they dashed from taxi to marquee and marquee to taxi. Vicky had been conscious of her error as soon as she saw Miss Finkelstein's eye on her that morning and had prayed for the clouds to burst and torrents to come just so her hurricane precautions might be justified. But noon had reduced the shower to the merest drizzle and Vicky was trying to scuttle, invisibly, out of the building when Ken Saunders yelled at her, "Hiya, neighbor, going fishing?"

"No," said Vicky sourly, "I'm off for the Embassy Ball."

He was coming out of the drugstore on the street floor and in his battered hat and trench coat did not look elegant enough to be so sarcastic, Vicky thought, but then with men appearances don't matter. Vicky saw he was about to catch up with her and in a wave of wounded pride ran out the door with a furtive farewell nod to him. Then she dashed madly back to her apartment to change into something that would look pretty, at least until the first drop of rain should ruin it. But once prepared, naturally, she did not encounter Saunders again, though she looked in the drugstore hopefully on her return. Opportunity, clearly, never knocks at the right moment.

It was the same thing with Amanda. Twice she got up courage to call Amanda to thank her for tickets but both times Miss Bemel took the message because the brilliant girl was in conference. Expecting rebuffs as she did, Vicky was not at all surprised. "In conference," "at dinner," "in her bath," oh certainly, that was what the great always said to the mob.

Losing a lover does to a woman what losing a job does to a man; all confidence in self vanishes. There is the overwhelming conviction that you alone are singled out as unfit for the simplest privileges of life, and the days are filled with tiny testimony to this—the salesgirl's rudeness, the invitation denied, the luncheon Special crossed out when you arrive. Everything happens to you. So it was that Vicky was in no frame of mind to storm past her friend's neglect with sunny insouciance. Two "in conferences" from Amanda and she gave up all hope of ever seeing her friend again. When she ran into Amanda by accident one day in Saks Fifth Avenue she was half-impelled to slink into a corner, thus saving herself the embarrassment of being cut. But Amanda did rescue her this time so that once again Vicky became her admiring slave.

It was a Red Letter day for Vicky in many ways. For one thing it was the day she had decided to Do Something about Everything. Instead of squirming under Miss Finkelstein's critical eye every day and creeping along back halls to avoid contrast with the glamorous editorial staff, she would Do Something. She would plunge into glamour herself, and so rebuild her faltering ego. She would get a hat as much like Miss Elroy's as was decent, a coat like Miss Gray's with large pearl buttons and accessories similar to the dashing items affected by the Peabody "front" staff. There was no use in seeking an orig-

inal style for herself because what she wanted right now was to
look exactly like everybody else, so that no one would look at
her twice. That was what a crippled vanity did to you—a man
following you made you certain he merely wanted to say, "Pardon me, lady, your slip is showing," and his glance at your legs
only convinced you that your new stocking had sprung a run.
Yes, Vicky intended to use her first month's paycheck to begin
the new Vicky, the New York Vicky Haven. She was going to
do something perfectly wonderful about her hair, too. It was
sandy and she had been for many years perfectly pleased with
it, until she saw what breath-taking things the "front" girls did
to their hair—bars of dyed gold in brown hair, blue-gray tuft
over the left temple, scrolls of curls as carefully designed as a
permanent work of art . . . yes, she too would have her hair
made to look suitably artificial. When Ethel Carey arrived next
month from Lakeville Vicky was determined to show her how
marvellously New York had changed her. She would like to
have some new friends to show off, too, but in New York that
appeared to take time.

In the elevator at Saks, when Vicky caught a glimpse of her
benefactor, Amanda Evans did not really look so superior to
any other shopper. She wore no diadem and the valuable
body appeared to be quite unguarded. Here was a simple
everyday young woman going about her simple errand of
buying a few dozen boxes of hose or matching a lost glove.
Her black felt tailored hat was pulled over her blonde hair in
rather collegiate style, and her simple sport suit was un-
adorned by any of her furs. In fact, Amanda's costume was so
startlingly simple as to seem almost gaudy, and the other
ladies in the elevator, furred and feathered as they were,
shrank back from this lesson in elegance. Vicky, too, shrank
back, but Amanda caught sight of her and snatched her arm
with unexpected warmth.

"I'm having a hair trim," stated Amanda, "but let's have
some tea afterward. I want to hear all about you. Where will
you be?"

"Millinery," said Vicky, beaming under Amanda's sudden
friendliness.

"Do get something nice," said Amanda. "Wait, I'll go
along."

Flattered as she was at Amanda's interest, Vicky was uncertain whether she wanted this witness to her intended economies. She foresaw what would happen and what did happen—with Amanda near by she dared not ask prices but must consider only preferences. Amanda was as fussy and absorbed in the proper selection of Vicky's hat as even Ethel Carey would have been, and this sudden interest so flattered and confused Vicky that she forgot all about Miss Elroy's hat and decided on the only one that the saleslady and Amanda agreed was a "must." It was a tall black business with a snood effect and demanded an entirely new wardrobe to go with it. Dazed, Vicky began counting out the necessary twenty-seven dollars until she felt Amanda's hand closing over hers.

"My dear, you're not paying cash!" The incredulity in Amanda's voice had such a touch of horror in it that Vicky hastily pushed her money back in the bag.

"You never get any service paying cash, darling," Amanda, now amused at Vicky's consternation, explained. "I'll have Bemel arrange for your charge accounts around town and meantime charge things to me. Cash is simply money thrown away, so do put it back. I'll meet you in Suits when I get through. Tell Miss Blandet to fix you up."

Miss Blandet "fixed" Vicky up with a hundred dollar suit and a twenty dollar blouse but these were all quite free as they were charged to Amanda, subject to changing to Vicky's account later. A feeling of helplessness handicapped Vicky's choice of purchases and she feared that between Amanda and Miss Blandet she would be mesmerized into buying out the whole store. When Amanda came back Vicky was sitting down trying to figure out how much she had spent and how long it would take her to pay it. She hadn't gotten one thing she wanted, just the things Amanda and Miss Blandet wanted. It was probably much better for her but it rather spoiled the fun. She was a little silent as she and Amanda waited for the elevator. Then she felt some one's hand on her arm and saw none other than Miss Elroy from the front office in the very hat she had coveted, smiling happily at her.

"My dear, how wonderful running into you here!" cried Miss Elroy radiantly, who had up to this time never spoken to

Vicky beyond the exigencies of office demands. "I do want you to meet Mother. Mother—"

An elderly well-groomed woman was thrust between Miss Elroy and Vicky, whose name, in spite of her interest in her, Miss Elroy had obviously forgotten. They shook hands, murmuring.

"Mother and I are quarrelling over every stitch of my trousseau," laughed Miss Elroy gaily, and then Vicky saw that both Miss Elroy and her mother were staring fixedly at Amanda. She hurriedly introduced them and was disconcerted to find both Elroys fairly pouncing on Amanda's reluctant hand. Clearly, it had been for the sake of this introduction the young Miss Elroy had been so happy to see Vicky.

"You know the Carsons, the Beverly Carsons," Miss Elroy cried to Amanda. "They're simply mad, but mad, about you!"

"Oh, do you know Bev and Madge?" Amanda said.

Vicky, at first pleased at having been able to introduce any one, especially some one from the "front" office, to Amanda, realized that in New York introductions were like cash, and were not to be thrown about but used only when absolutely necessary. Amanda was cool and the cooler she became the more pressing the Elroys became. Wouldn't Amanda and Vicky join them for a spot of tea this minute—shopping was so exhausting? Or perhaps they would drop around the corner to the Elroys' apartment a little later. Vicky dumbly accepted. Amanda said it would be terribly nice but made no promises.

"We don't know Bev and Madge so well," said Miss Elroy, "but we know cousins of theirs very, *very* intimately. The Crosley Carsons."

"We've known the Crosley Carsons for years," Mrs. Elroy said benignly to Vicky who murmured that they were fortunate indeed.

By the time they had reached the street floor Vicky was aware that the prized nod from Miss Elroy was due completely to the Elroys' desire to meet Amanda Keeler Evans, either for her own or her husband's sake. It was astonishing to see what lengths these well-bred ladies were willing to go in order to clinch some future contact. Vicky found their anxiety contagious and tried to ease their feelings by babbling away to Amanda how effective was the full page color ad of Miss Nancy Elroy smoking a Felicity cigarette before the portrait of her old grandmother. Both Elroys brushed this faltering support aside, for to tell the truth they loved the feeling that they were meeting and conquering wonderfully superior people. It gave them a feeling of accomplishment and progress to wear down snubbing, and they felt there was something secretly the matter with any one who did not make use of his or her position to be arrogant. The merest Astor had only to step on them firmly to utterly enslave them, challenging them to further humble gestures. As this type of social masochism was unknown to Vicky, she thought Amanda's coolness was wounding the Elroys instead of tantalizing them.

"If Mrs. Evans can't come this afternoon, at least you will, won't you, Vicky?" begged Miss Elroy, having apparently caught at least the first name from Amanda. "Do come over around five, Vicky. We have so little chance to get acquainted at our sweat-shop."

The friendly gesture touched Vicky enormously, for she fully expected Amanda's refusal to cancel her own invitation. Of course she would come. This would be something to tell Ethel Carey, she thought happily, and she would certainly illustrate the letter with one of the printed pictures of Nancy Elroy to further impress Lakeville. She had a little matter to attend to on her job first, but she would surely be there at five. Having beamingly parted with the Elroys, Vicky waited with a defensive air for Amanda's comment on them. She was prepared for Amanda to make some subtly sardonic reference to the Elroys' eager play for her, but Amanda said nothing. They paused at the glove counter for some purchases and still Amanda kept a discreet silence about the Elroys.

"Isn't she attractive?" Vicky finally murmured.

"Very," said Amanda, and it was another lesson for Vicky in how certain women preserve their own importance. Amanda's silence was more damning than a contemptuous remark, for it implied that the people were of so little importance that they were unworthy of discussion. Vicky, in this case, knew that the Elroys were at least socially, if not financially, better placed than Amanda, but she was affected by Amanda's dismissal of them anyway. Amanda believed in honoring no rival by her envy, nor decorating any other woman by a witty jibe. She determinedly fought off any instinctive outbursts of malice, being aware that they often gave the object unexpected importance, for persons may build into public monuments merely by the stones hurled at them.

Vicky, at first prepared to defend the Elroys from Amanda's scorn, missed it when it was not forthcoming as a simple gesture of feminine equality. She was increasingly confused by Amanda; first there was Amanda's unexpected friendliness today, her warm interest in her younger friend's clothes, and the next moment she was making it clear that their worlds were far apart. No further words at all about meeting again. Not even an inquiry about the apartment which never bore any trace of Amanda's work, though cigarette butts, a small cellar of sherry and Scotch, and a smart housecoat, testified that she dropped in occasionally at least.

"Four-ten!" Amanda now exclaimed, glancing at her watch. "I should have been home at four. Bemel will be on her ear!"

Vicky thanked her for her help in shopping.

Amanda shrugged.

"After all, darling, somebody has to help you, you must know that," she observed unflatteringly. "Remember me to Ethel when you write."

She nipped into a taxicab, leaving Vicky in her usual state of wondering what wrong thing she had done to change the mood from warm friendship to the chilly stay-in-your-place parting atmosphere. The Elroys had helped destroy that first fine rapport, that was plain enough, but there must have been something else.

"I probably acted too friendly with the Elroys," Vicky decided. "I shouldn't burble over people that she is trying to snub. That's it."

Nevertheless she was excited at the thought of seeing the home and background of one of the "front" office girls, even if her obvious pleasure did annoy Amanda. She spent the next three-quarters of an hour in hastening through the work she had sacrificed for shopping. This was the investigation of a

house for sale on East Forty-ninth Street for her page in
Peabody's. She made her notes briskly and jotted down her
opening paragraph. "The death last month of Mrs.
Humphrey Zoom IV, in Palm Beach, has resulted in the dis-
mantling of the fine old Zoom mansion on East Forty-ninth
Street. Except for the drawing-room walls, the furnace, and
the upstairs floors, the house is in excellent shape for a future
owner. Either for residential purposes in its present form or
remodelled into smaller apartments for modern demands, the
Zoom property offers a fair opportunity, etc., etc., etc."

This brilliant item would be illustrated by a picture of the
house itself, and with the connivance of the advertising and
glamour departments, there would probably be a photograph
of one of the elegant older girls examining the house's garden
and wearing a costume and holding a pedigreed pup, both
advertised elsewhere in the magazine. Having disposed of this
little duty, Vicky powdered her nose and hastened with great
anticipation over to the Elroys' address.

At last, she thought complacently, she was getting a toe-
hold on the city.

2

The Elroys lived at the Marguery in a spacious suite that
was yet not spacious enough to keep the little family from
getting frightfully on each other's nerves. Papa—Beaver
Chauncey Elroy that was—had been dead some time, so it
was a household of women. Mrs. Elroy always allowed people
to believe it was the crash of '29 that broke her husband
down, but it had really been his liver, an organ the late Mr.
Elroy had kept dancing from the very moment he had disgraced himself at his own wedding reception. The Elroys
were all famed as gourmets and Beaver was said to have the
most fastidious palate in the family, taste buds so exquisitely
developed as to recognize the most mysterious of herbs in the
most complicated of sauces. There was a legend that once
Beaver had confounded the very Sabatini himself, in London,
when he leapt to his feet in the middle of the Savoy's most
brilliant banquet and cried out the proportions of basil over
dill—("basted with a Swiss *fendant*," he had declared)—in a

certain roast of veal. There were less reverent tales, too, concerning the time he had gone into Cavanagh's kitchen and selected with lordly arrogance the steaks for his party. "How
will you have them, Mr. Elroy?" respectfully asked the chef.
"Raw," declared the epicure imperiously, and at once astounded the kitchen by proceeding to devour all the cuts then
and there. The fact was that on his expeditions into
gourmetism Mr. Elroy basted his stomach with such a solid
coating of any old whiskey that a thoughtfully ordered dinner
with cautiously plotted wines, might just as well have been
pork chops and Doctor Pepper, since the diner was already
stupefied. Furthermore the career of gourmet cost a fortune
and Beaver was one Elroy who had started piling up debts almost the instant his voice had started changing. It was this
snarling pack of debts which speeded Beaver into the first
World War and unquestionably caused him to become quite a
military hero. He distinguished himself at Belleau Wood, and
in Château-Thierry he went over the top as if he were chased
by six process servers.

Mrs. Elroy had spent a good part of their married days
voicing just such crass derogation of his character that it must
have been quite a relief to escape her cultivated voice by
rolling into a soundproof grave. Mrs. Elroy had been a
Chivers from Columbus and felt that Park Avenue offered
nothing that could not be bettered by the exclusive social life
of her native city. Nancy and her young sister Tuffy had had
the Chivers' superiority so drilled into them from infancy that
they had actually come to believe in it, and in the Social Register put down their homes as New York, Palm Beach, and
Columbus. They were convinced that although the Elroys
were regarded as top-drawer in New York they would never
have made the Chivers' set in Columbus, a little conceit that
the Elroys politely ignored. When Mrs. Elroy heard of her
daughters being in Harlem or going about with dubious persons she would gasp, "It's not that I mind myself, but supposing some one from Columbus had seen you!" It was a
source of regret to the gentlewoman that both her daughters
merely came out at an Assembly dance instead of in the old
Chivers' home near Columbus. She only forgave Nancy's
connection with Peabody's because nowadays all the League

girls were doing odd things, and competed with each other by nightclub singing, screen tests, and gown shops instead of keeping within the honorable limits of social functions. They even did this in Columbus nowadays, so it must be all right, and certainly it gave Nancy a great deal of pleasant publicity, without the expense of lavish entertaining. The pity was that this publicity had gone so much to Nancy's head that she had allowed several promising young men to go their way and was finally obliged to settle on something less than top-drawer. He was not bad considering the times. He worked in an architect's office, there was money and a polo tradition somewhere in the family, and he was second cousin of somebody who was somebody in Canada. Harry Jones wasn't much of a name in itself, but when you put Cosgrove in the middle and a Roman IV at the end you had something that would look presentable enough on a wedding invitation. Nancy didn't mind him very much; he was taller than she was for dancing, which was nice, and his ears were laid neatly to his head, a point on which Mrs. Elroy was extremely insistent. As Nancy had been out ten seasons and had expected too much of her good looks, the Harry Jones offer seemed almost a last chance, especially since Tuffy was about to come out and was going to be a problem. At least with her plainness and ill health it was going to take a lot of money to put Tuffy over, both Nancy and her mother felt. Uncle Rockman Elroy, who was paying for the launching of Tuffy, was of the opinion that Tuffy would sweep the younger set off its feet by differing so conspicuously from the type. So far he was wrong but fond of Tuffy, so he paid willingly.

Uncle Rockman, a bachelor of fifty, a scholar of some note and a thoroughly unworldly man to all appearances, had offered his home to his brother's widow and daughters, and then had had the admirable taste to move out himself, maintaining only a nominal residence in the apartment, a maid's room in fact. He lived at the Gotham Hotel with the privacy and comfort that his habits required and popped in to his "home" with his brother's family as little as was required. He paid their expenses and unless some designing woman got her clutches on him first, was expected to leave his money to his sister-in-law and nieces, a prospect that added to his happiness since it gained him their love and respect. Mrs. Elroy was constantly calling him up to augment her authority with the girls, or writing him messages which he ignored as often as possible. ("Dear Rockman: I do wish you'd give Tuffy a talk. She insists on using her birthday money to take flying lessons instead of making herself look decent with a mink jacket Nancy and I ordered for her—")

Mrs. Elroy was still a handsome woman with a girlish figure and a well-chiselled face, features arranged in an expression of indefatigable sweetness and gentility. Nancy looked like her mother, only of course with a youthful sheen and radiance. She had her mother's beautiful clear blue eyes, widely spaced, the composed brow, the lovely mouth and corner dimples, all belying the nasty temper and selfishness that Mrs. Elroy felt were the rightful prerogatives of pretty young women. The breakfast table was a bedlam of feminine snarlings, rages, taunts, with Tuffy, Nancy and their mother going at each other furiously, wrangling over their mentions in the newspaper columns or over abuses of charge accounts. Yet their public manners were charming, even to each other, and probably kept in all the finer condition by not being wasted in private.

The Elroys, mother and daughters, knew cousins of practically everybody ever mentioned in Cholly Knickerbocker's column. They had the curious conviction that *cousins* of somebodies sounded much more impressive than the somebodies themselves, just as vice-president or brigadier-general sounds finer than mere "president" or "general."

"No, we don't know the Smith-Gareys, but we know their cousins very well, indeed," they would cry proudly as if this was much better. This crowing over cousins was so imbedded in the Elroy conversational routine that if they had a duke in their drawing-room they must add to the triumph by boasting that he was more than that, he was a second cousin of a very dear friend of Mrs. Elroy's sister in Columbus. There must have been some secret logic in this preference for the inferior connection; perhaps the intimate life and soul secrets of the great person were more clearly revealed by the gossip than by actual presence. It was certainly true that Mrs. Elroy had a perfect storehouse of libellous material on most prominent figures, all the information coming from cousins or assistants to cousins. Mrs. Elroy was not a gossip herself and not even malicious, but she read so few books that she found innocent substitute in seeing the lives of the somebodies put together by little tidbits from out-of-the-way sources.

So it was that Vicky Haven was genuinely welcomed to the Elroy family bosom since the unexpected discovery that she was a minor connection of Mrs. Julian Evans.

"I had no idea she was anybody," Nancy exclaimed to her mother, "until I saw her shopping with Amanda Evans! She looks very nice of course, but I never *dreamed!*"

"She probably knows all there is to know about Amanda," meditated Mrs. Elroy, taking out the old knitting bag and assuming the fixed benevolent smile she wore for charity knitting. "Poor Margaret Evans! But then the first wife always has to pay! You remember what her sister told us at the British Relief the other day—she hasn't gone to a single function since the divorce!"

"Oh, Mama, she never did!" Nancy exclaimed impatiently. "The first Mrs. Evans was an old Boston fud from the beginning. The Peabodys knew her. They were utter fuds, Mr. Peabody said. What would she do if she did go out—she's fifty if she's a day."

"She could do the Lambeth Walk," suggested Tuffy.

"Shut up, Tuffy," said her mother pleasantly, "and when Nancy's friend comes take your beau in Uncle Rockman's study."

"Beau!" mocked Nancy. "Beau, my foot. He's only coming here to borrow Tuffy's banjo. Tuffy couldn't get a boy here unless she promised him a reward or something."

Tuffy lay on the love seat in a torn dirty white sweater and paint-smattered slacks, with her legs thrown over the end. Her scant mousy hair had already lost the reasonably neat if not glamorous swirl which Robert of the Plaza had put into it for her dinner dance two nights ago. Her complexion was sallow and bad and, what was worse, Tuffy didn't care. It kept her mother and sister conversationally occupied which permitted Tuffy to think about other matters such as boys, for she was definitely boystruck. She waggled her small dirty feet in their incredibly battered little brown sandals in complete comfort and thought dreamily of having a terrific love affair

with some fiendishly sophisticated older man. This was a perfectly practicable dream since her one charm—and that was
completely undeniable—was that she was fifteen, and often
that in itself is enough to entice an elderly beau.

"I can't take my callers into Uncle Rockman's study," Tuffy
said calmly, "because Uncle Rockman is in there taking a nap.
As for whether I can get a beau or not, Miss Nancy, I could
get yours away if I cared to sleep with them."

"Tuffy!" gasped her mother. "Please."

"Now you know what I mean, Mother," said Nancy. "We
simply can't have her around when we have guests. She's simply impossible."

"I must have Rockman speak to her," said Mrs. Elroy.

Tuffy languidly collected her arms and legs and stood up,
yawning.

"Okay, I'll go wake up Uncle Rockman," she said obligingly. "He can clap a sermon round me if he likes."

She wandered away, head high, happily conscious that she
was a constant source of irritation to her mother and sister.

"Is any one else coming besides Mrs. Evans' friend?" asked
Mrs. Elroy, needles now flying piously for Britain.

"Probably Harry," Nancy answered with a slight frown.
She could hardly wait to marry Harry so she could be rude to
him legally and prevent him intruding on her social life.

"I didn't realize Rockman had come in today," pensively
remarked Mrs. Elroy. "He can pay cook."

Uncle Rockman gave his sister-in-law a large allowance sufficient to cover all expenses, but Mrs. Elroy found it more
convenient to use the money as ready cash and send all bills
to him. In spite of this caution she was sometimes trapped
into paying a servant herself so she tried to prepare against
such a mischance. With Nancy's wedding coming on she was
certain to be caught with all sorts of unforeseen little expenses
so she closed in on Rockman on every occasion now. She met
little resistance from him because for many years the wary
man had suspected she would like to marry him and he was
glad to placate her with money instead of his freedom, having
observed her disciplinary measures with his late brother.

The news of Uncle Rockman's rare presence in the
apartment caused Nancy to be thoughtfully silent for a few

moments, too, for she had a few favors to ask herself. She frowned impatiently when banjo thumpings were heard from the direction of Uncle Rockman's "study."

"Uncle Rockman isn't scolding Tuffy at all," she exclaimed angrily. "What's happening is that Tuffy has tapped him for a car of her own. Honestly, Mama, nobody can get anything out of Uncle if you let Tuffy always get at him first! You make me furious, Mama, honestly."

"Oh, shut up, Nancy," her good mother answered, for she knew what Nancy said was true, and that Tuffy had once again taken unfair advantage of her uncle's preference for her and made other demands unseasonable. Never mind, she had guided herself through Rockman's pockets before with perfect grace—she could do it again.

3

It was unkind of Amanda, Vicky kept thinking, to deprive the Elroys of the simple favor of her company. No matter how grand she herself might become she was certain that she would always be grateful to her admirers; if they found her presence inspiring, then she would be present; on no account would she dismiss their fond regard with a haughty shrug.

"But probably Amanda is quite right," she reflected after this noble resolution. "The public really doesn't like its idols to be folksy. Probably you get knocked off your pedestal soon enough without jumping down of your own accord."

The Elroy apartment had just been done over by an interior decorator, in preparation for Nancy's wedding, and it seemed to Vicky far more impressive than the Julian Evanses' home. The drawing-room had an air of blithe informality with flowered taffeta drapes, white wool rugs, glass tables, bowls of flowers and ferns everywhere, and an array of modern paintings that were gay and expert. Mrs. Elroy had arranged herself and her tea-table with the care she always took for strangers or cousins of strangers, and looked regal in her flowing pink teagown. The first chill of November was in the air so that in spite of the fire her aristocratic nose was tinted lavender with her seasonal sinus trouble, a disorder that

kept her dabbing daintily at her nose from time to time, until the gesture took on interesting punctuation value.

"My dear! How darling of you to come!" Nancy cried on
greeting Vicky and much to the confusion of both of them
started to kiss her warmly, but as Vicky was unprepared for
such a welcome it merely knocked her hat off, leaving both
girls breathless with apologetic murmurs.

"Mother! Vicky Haven's here!" Nancy cried out as if this
was the happiest news the house had ever had and Mrs. Elroy
looked up with a benevolent smile, her slender jewelled hand
outstretched.

It simply showed that your real New Yorkers were as
friendly as anybody else, Vicky thought, taking the low chair
beside Mrs. Elroy. Nancy, radiant in a green corduroy dinner
suit, seated herself gracefully on the footstool, hands clasped
girlishly about her knees.

"Don't let Mama force tea on you if you really want a cocktail," she advised. "Or how about sherry?"

Vicky looked uncertainly from the sherry in Nancy's hand
to the teacup in Mrs. Elroy's and was about to solve this
problem by having neither, but Nancy answered for her.

"We'll warm up on tea," she decided, "and then we'll clap
our tongues around a martini."

"Does Amanda Keeler Evans drink martinis?" queried Mrs.
Elroy. "I believe we read some place that she drank nothing
but a single pony of armagnac a day, and that before breakfast."

"The first Mrs. Evans never drank," Nancy said. "Unless of
course she was a dipsomaniac and did it in secret the way so
many women used to do. Didn't they, Mama?"

"Even so, I doubt if they were any worse than the young
girls nowadays drinking like sailors almost before they're
out," Mrs. Elroy sighed, her pretty hands fluttering over
lemon, cinnamon sticks, and blackberry jam, a bit in each
cup. "I sometimes wonder what sort of mothers they have to
bring them up that way."

"Were her people—well—top-drawer?" Nancy asked, and
Vicky saw that her visit was to be spent in giving guarded answers to this quiz on her friend's private habits. Even if she
told all she knew she was certain it would in no way throw

light on Amanda or damage her, either. It would please these people mightily to be told a few little stories about Amanda's pre-famous life, and as there was nothing derogatory in them Vicky decided to earn her welcome by being as garrulous as she knew how. She told about Amanda's brave gesture in taking over the Keeler Haberdashery for a summer when her father was too sick to work, and she told about Amanda's amusing habit of always getting engaged every semester at Miss Doxey's to somebody new and she told about Amanda going to Cleveland to study pastry-cooking for six weeks when she was sixteen because she was going to run a tea-room.

"How do the people in Lakeville feel about their famous representative now?" Mrs. Elroy asked.

"Oh, they're very proud of her," Vicky loyally exclaimed. "And they respect her for paying off every cent of her father's debts because so often children don't feel responsible, you know."

"Yes," said Mrs. Elroy thoughtfully. "That's quite true."

Something must have sounded a little wrong about the little anecdotes, for Vicky saw mother and daughter exchanging quiet glances that must have meant something. It was plain that what the home town found as virtues in Amanda were regarded by the metropolitan-minded as mere proof of inferior background. Vicky grew suddenly silent, her face very red.

Voices from the back of the apartment announced the coming of Tuffy and Uncle Rockman, and once again Nancy and Mrs. Elroy exchanged a look of meaning.

"That Tuffy!" bitterly muttered Nancy. "Mama, I wish you'd talk Uncle into sending her some place. College or New Mexico or any place. I'll bet she's talked Uncle out of a car and that means we won't dare ask him for anything else for months!"

Tuffy appeared carrying a bottle of Scotch under her arm and two glasses in her hand. Uncle Rockman followed her, chuckling, in bright red lounging coat and pipe.

"I knew there'd be nothing but those foul martinis," Tuffy said. "Uncle and I can't stand anything but Scotch. Who's that?"

"Tuffy, please!" her mother implored. "This is Miss Haven, a friend of Amanda Evans. And Vicky, this is Rockman, my husband's brother. Soda, Rockman?"

"How do you do," said Rockman, sitting down. "Water."

"Ah, don't let Mama mix it, she puts it in with an eye-dropper," said Tuffy, seizing the water carafe and at some danger to her mother's tea-table mixing her uncle's highball. "I'm the only one that can make a decent drink around this house. Clap your face around this, Uncle Rockman."

"Uncle Rockman writes for the scientific magazines," Nancy said to Vicky. "Are you home for a few days, Uncle?"

"Does that question sound ominous or inviting to you, young lady?" Uncle Rockman inquired, turning to Vicky. "My family here gets along so mighty well without my presence that I'm afraid Nancy only means to warn me off."

"Now, Uncle!" said Nancy. "You know Julian Evans, Uncle. Vicky is a great friend of the family. She says that Amanda Evans' father runs a haberdashery store back in the Middle West and owed so much money Amanda had to pay it off herself."

"She studied to be a pastry cook, it seems," Mrs. Elroy added. "What could have gotten into Julian after being married to poor Margaret—one of the best families in Boston, really!"

"Dozens of lovers before she met Julian, so Vicky says," brightly added Nancy.

"She didn't nail him till she was nearly thirty," Tuffy exclaimed. "God, Nancy, you wouldn't expect her to stay a virgin that long."

"Don't use the name of the Lord, Tuffy—how many times must I tell you?" Mrs. Elroy protested gently.

"You merely told me not to say 'Jesus,'" Tuffy defended herself. "What else did you find out about the lady?"

Vicky, during these lurid interpretations of what had seemed to her merely friendly gossip, had a hideous sensation of sinking through the floor. She couldn't imagine how her hostesses had been able to find so many dark meanings to her remarks and she wondered fearsomely how soon all this would be spread through the town, all carefully attributed to Vicky Haven. She gripped her teacup grimly as if it were her sole support and wondered how she could clear herself of having so unwittingly smirched her friend's name. If she talked about Peabody's office, she would appear to have no interest except business and that would not do. Casting her eyes about uneasily she encountered Uncle Rockman's kindly bright blue eyes.

"Amanda has really been awfully good to me," she said apologetically.

"Who is she?" politely inquired Uncle Rockman.

"Julian Evans' new wife—you know," impatiently explained his sister-in-law. "Amanda Keeler Evans."

Uncle Rockman sipped a highball in silent thought, then shook his head.

"Never heard of her," he said. "Any relation of Doctor Vestry Keeler at Leland Stanford?"

"Oh, *uncle!*" Nancy cried, with an apologetic smile at Vicky. "Of course you've heard of Amanda Keeler!"

"Oh, leave Uncle be," said Tuffy. "If you want to work on somebody's education, you got your future husband. They don't come any dumber."

"Mama!" Nancy exclaimed, flushing helplessly. "Uncle, please!"

"Harry is the all-time low in the male animal," Tuffy turned graciously to explain to Vicky. "If he can even braid a basket, I'll eat it."

Uncle Rockman was chuckling in fond appreciation of his ugly duckling's remarks so that Nancy proudly shook the tears from her eyes and set out to stir a martini. Vicky tried to keep a fixed happy look on her face though she had not been so embarrassed by a family gathering since she left her brother's roof. Mrs. Elroy frowned sternly at her younger daughter. She had always considered it a pretty woman's right to be a fiend in private, but to balance this state of society it was up to the plain girls to rigorously uphold the banner of breeding and constant good nature. Unfortunately Tuffy had never seen eye to eye with her on this and had the audacity to have all the selfishness and ill-temper of a belle. The awkward silence while Nancy sulkily poured martinis, Mrs. Elroy silently frowned, and Vicky squirmed, was broken by the maid's announcement that Mr. Plung had arrived to see Miss Tuffy.

"Don't let him in here," said Nancy. "Take him straight to the nursery."

This remark was sufficient to slay Miss Tuffy, who turned an angry red.

"It's not the nursery any more, damn you," she exclaimed. "Mama, she's got to stop calling it the nursery now!"

"It's always been the nursery, Tuffy," Mrs. Elroy said calmly. "I agree with Nancy. Take your caller to the nursery."

Tuffy stood up, her fists clenched, eyes flashing.

"I can't take a man with a beard to the nursery!" she wailed. "I can't, can I, Uncle Rockman?"

Uncle Rockman was sputtering over his highball in a fit of silent mirth and only shook his head at Vicky helplessly. The caller announced as Mr. Plung marched into the living-room without further warning, and it was quite true that by some extraordinary miracle his pasty young face had managed to accumulate enough red fuzz on the chin to pass as a beard. This feat appeared to have exhausted the young man to the point of being unable to speak or bow, for he stood in the doorway in soiled tan raincoat and most elaborately mottled sport shoes, quite as if he were frozen there.

"Run along, you two," Mrs. Elroy said imperiously.

"And don't start murdering that banjo again," added Nancy.

This humiliation in front of her bearded friend crushed Tuffy sufficiently for her to stalk out of the room very near tears.

"Come on, Plung," she said in a stifled voice. "We're to go to the nursery. With Nancy getting married, God knows it may be our last chance to see it."

"Mama!" Nancy said tensely. "Uncle Rockman!"

Uncle Rockman, by this time, had adjusted his expression to one of innocent vagueness. He shook his ice around in his glass thoughtfully until his older niece, in some irritation, took his glass and refilled it.

"Doctor Vestry Keeler was a very fine scholar," he observed. "Perhaps you read his book on 'Light.' Most illuminating—ha, ha—excuse the pun. Yes, I worked with Doctor Keeler at the University of Chicago a few years ago."

"I didn't know that," Vicky said quite truly, adding, with less conviction, "that must have been very interesting."

Uncle Rockman's round plump face glowed rosily out of his frame of curly gray hair. He had bright childish blue eyes, not too honest, the innocent eyes of a man who lied to himself in all the realities of human behavior, but was radiantly fearless in the face of Cosmic Theories. He considered Vicky now with interest, as if she had just made a rather profound remark.

"No, I can't say it was interesting," he reflected. "Nothing to the fun of working with Shapley. I suppose you recall his delightfully audacious statement that not only could the Finite be measured but that he personally could give the exact number of atoms. Ha, ha."

"Ha, ha," said Vicky, and she was so relieved at the switch from personalities to the abstract that she laughed as heartily as if Uncle Rockman had been quoting Jack Benny. She was hushed by the look of astonishment exchanged by the Elroy mother and daughter, but Uncle Rockman's further conversation, encouraged as he was by his unheralded success, obliged her to continue in her new rôle of the merry savant. Mrs. Elroy took up her knitting, Nancy sipped a martini and Uncle Rockman described many a pedantic roguery, gasping with merriment over Sir William Bragg's delightful *mot* on light theories. ("On Monday, Wednesday, Friday one must teach the corpuscle theory, and on Tuesday, Thursday, Saturday the wave theory.") How brilliant of Edison, he added, to name the unit a "wavicle."

"A wavicle," repeated Vicky with a burst of laughter.

"Rockman, are you quite sure you want another highball?" gently reproached Mrs. Elroy as her brother-in-law's plump fingers encircled the pinch-bottle again, tenderly.

"Quite," answered Rockman firmly and poured a rather mighty blast into his glass. In this pause Nancy sprang into action with a long discussion of Amanda Keeler's wedding, which she had only heard described, and Mrs. Elroy probed Vicky on the matter of whether Amanda's Lakeville family had been represented at the function, and whether it would look too imitative if Nancy were to follow Amanda's custom of having the Calypso singers at the wedding reception. Vicky answered very guardedly on both these points, and Mrs. Elroy then discoursed favorably on the beauty of her own

Columbus wedding. During this talk Uncle Rockman appeared to be listening attentively but betrayed himself in the high point of Mrs. Elroy's anecdote by absently humming a snatch of Gilbert and Sullivan. This was a baffling habit in such a courtly gentleman, a habit so revealing of his utter lack of interest in any conversation but his own that he would have been horrified to learn of it. It would have been far better had he interrupted, but he was too polite to do this; he merely fixed his attention on the speaker and presently his light preoccupied hum would rise louder and louder till the speaker would be practically drowned out.

"I'm afraid," said Mrs. Elroy, drily, "that Rockman has heard all this before."

"No, no—no, no, go on, my dear," Rockman blandly replied, quite above sarcasm.

Sounds of a banjo came from the other end of the hall.

"I suppose that's going to go on all during the wedding," Nancy said in a stifled voice, pacing proudly up and down the room. "I suppose Maury Paul will have quite a nice item about it in the paper. I imagine the photographers will have a perfect riot getting *that* in the picture."

"Oh, Nancy, do shut up," said Mrs. Elroy patiently. "I don't know why my children should both turn out so nasty-natured. It probably comes from my letting them spend their summers with their father's family."

"Of course it does, my dear," agreed Uncle Rockman amiably. He drank his third highball at a gulp and rose. "Well, I must be off. Dinner with Doctor Falman at the Faculty Club."

"Another martini, Miss Haven?" Mrs. Elroy graciously inquired. "Nancy, do look after your guests. I don't know how in the world you're going to manage in your own home."

"I must go," Vicky said.

"What do you mean, how will I manage?" Nancy laughed. "I daresay I'll manage all right until you decide to come and live with us, Mama."

Vicky, seeing Uncle Rockman rise, was afraid to spend any more time with her two new friends, and hastily made for the door.

"Since you're all alone in the city, you must let us share our home with you, my dear," benevolently urged Mrs. Elroy, dabbing at her patrician nostrils with a delicate handkerchief. "We can't let a friend of Amanda Evans get homesick, you know."

"Thank you," said Vicky. "It *is* a lot like home, Mrs. Elroy."

"Let's have lunch tomorrow," begged Nancy, following her to the door. "I have loads of things I want to ask you. And everybody else in the office is so horrible, don't you think?"

"Oh, yes," Vicky agreed, anxious only to get away from the charming fireside and get back to her harmonious solitude.

Waiting in the little vestibule for the elevator she was surprised to see Mr. Rockman Elroy suddenly emerge from the apartment door. He was tugging at his topcoat, a somewhat sportive tan checked affair, and panting a great deal as if his haste to escape from the home was quite equal to Vicky's.

In the elevator he said nothing although his kindly regard indicated approval of her. In the lobby the doorman rushed to get them a cab.

"Can I drop you anywhere going up?" inquired Uncle Rockman.

"No, thank you," Vicky said.

Mr. Elroy appeared to have something else on his mind, for he stood with one foot on the cab step and a finger thoughtfully placed beside his nose. Vicky, looking about her, would have liked to ask him something too, for she saw they were in a huge square courtyard with no apparent exit, and she fully expected to be beating around the palm-fringed colonnade all night hunting for escape.

"Miss Haven," Mr. Elroy finally found courage to inquire, "are you interested at all in the atom-smasher?"

"I am, indeed," she answered with enthusiasm. "Is that how you get out of here, Mr. Elroy?"

"Hop in, and I'll drive you where you're going," said Uncle Rockman. "I can't tell you how much I've enjoyed our conversation, Miss Haven."

Vicky was afraid to ruin this fine impression by a spoken word and her silence spoke so well for her that after a ten-minute monologue on the atom Uncle Rockman left her, repeating the compliment again and again.

VI

THE CHIEF problem in Ken Saunders' life for the past three years had been the putting off of tomorrow. Ever since Amanda's desertion he had devoted himself to not-thinking, to taking whatever trains or boats were leaving at whatever station he happened to be. It struck him with some bitterness that at no point in his career had he ever arrived at any station in time for the Grand Orient Express; his voyages were never first-class, his destinations never glamorous, his duties never poetic. He was no good-will-spreader in South America, no brave digger for secrets of the Aztec in Mexico; —no, he was merely compiling fruit statistics for an export journal. In Brazil he had no secret mission from the government to investigate the spy rings and unmask the Nazi agents—he was pamphleteer for a commercial hotel. In China he saw the war but nary a Soong sister, for his undistinguished duties there were in connection with a second-hand typewriting concern, and his social contacts more bibulous than political. This definite marking time in the career of such a promising journalist as Mr. Saunders had its penalties, for the Tomorrow he had postponed was bigger and blacker for the postponement. Saunders had usually pictured Tomorrow armed with a large club crouching behind night's corner ready to pounce, and the greedy ogre was all the more blood-thirsty for the delay. There was Tomorrow waiting at the boat for him the instant he landed back in New York. Serious work to be taken up again, and a benumbed heart brought properly back to the pain of living. You would have thought, since travel is educational, that three years of it would have brought the young man to a better understanding of life's burdens, but the truth was he had even less heart for them than before. The ambition to write novels seemed the silliest work in the world for a grown man, with war on every side; and the postures necessary for the new type of journalist were quite out of his nature. The fact that Amanda had made such a success of both these careers did not make them any more appealing to him, so that he ended up as Assistant Home Editor for no less a periodical than Peabody's. Peabody's had only recently taken an interest in the Home, but since the world of fashion seemed cracking up, smart editors were frantically trying to substitute interest in the hearth for interest in the pencil silhouette. Mr. Saunders, having been raised in an Oklahoma boarding house and being singularly uninformed on the mechanical and decorative equipment of any home, had at least a novel approach to his task and the recommendation of his friend Dennis Orphen. It was well-paying and left his mind free for the friendly discussions of the tavern and resulting erudite arguments on international affairs. To tell the truth, drink seemed the only protection against the lacerations of his mind, now that he was back in New York, his foot rocking away once more on the much touted ladder of success. At this time the famous ladder was propped against nothing and led nowhere, and any one foolish enough to make the world his oyster was courting ptomaine; yet the ladder tradition was still observed, and until the flames reached them young people were still found going through the motions of climbing.

Saunders was thirty-three, old enough to have been disappointed a thousand times, but still young enough to be surprised. He knew the world was filled with lies but he was always expecting the truth to pop up triumphant; its delay angered but did not disillusion him. In his hotel rooms he had the rejected manuscripts of the books he had written after his first eager, rather bad little novel. He and Amanda used to talk about how bad it was and how astonishing its success. Then they talked about how good the rejected books were and how astonishing their rejection. They talked, went to bed, argued, took each other for granted, then out of a blue sky Amanda married Julian Evans. Then Ken lost his job on a morning paper. Then he tried in vain to sell his old stories. Then he wrote a play that did not sell. Then he wrote a series of articles for a magazine that promptly went bankrupt. Then he looked out his hotel window and saw, as the final blow, that there was no use jumping, because a bare ten feet below was a roof for sunbathers from MacKinney's Turkish Bath House. Suicide there was impossible and murder—for he would have flattened a few toasting fat men— was not to his fancy. So his wanderings began, and the not-thinking. Back in New York, every ache was back with compound interest.

Seeing Amanda was worse than not seeing her. Everything in his nature recoiled from what she now represented. He resented the years he had mistaken her cool indifference for restraint. Her life seemed monstrous to him, and the fact that he was still in love with her was as frightening to him as if he found himself in bed with General Motors. Failure frightened him, looming up all the sharper by Amanda's success. He seldom slept. He wondered if he was through. He was thirty-three. Sometimes people were through at thirty-three. Thirty even. They became old drunks. The world was full of old drunken failures. Has-beens. Warnings. Men who didn't realize they were never any good anyway—just lucky enough to hold a job a few years and then—zoom! He, at least, had been wise enough to take whatever job had come up, a thought that was at least a comfort on payday no matter how unpleasant such compromises were the rest of the week. But, unless he went to bed tight, he stared at the ceiling all night, smoking cigarettes, waiting for Tomorrow to spring.

What did other men do whose lives suddenly came apart like a cheap ukulele? What did they do when they realized that perhaps there would be no second chance, no reconsidering, no retrieving? What did they do when the hopes that push the wheel stopped, when magic failed, and fear alone remained, rusting the soul; when the days rattled off like dried beans with no native juice, no hope of flavor; when fears, batted out the door like flies, left only to return by window? What did other men do, suspecting that what was for them had been served—no further helping, no more love, no more triumph; for them labor without joy or profit, for them a passport to nowhere, free ticket to the grim consolations of Age? Was it true, then, that this world was filled with men and women merely marking time before their cemetery? When did courage's lease expire, was there no renewal possible? What specialist in mediocrity determined the prize-winners and ruled what measure of banality was required for success? These were the thoughts that brightened Ken's nights, and since they were very similar to the dark queries that clustered around Vicky Haven's pillow, it was the most natural thing in the world for them, these two frightened people, to have the merriest lunches together in the Peabody Building. Since neither Ken nor Vicky was the sort to reveal private problems, each found the other most comforting, and almost disgustingly carefree.

"You're even beginning to look like a Peabody front girl," Ken accused her, one noon at Chez Jean. "Have you done something to yourself or is it just that propinquity has opened my eyes?"

Vicky pretended this question was merely academic and shrugged her shoulders.

"I mean it," Ken insisted, frowning at her. "I ask you out because Miss Finkelstein tells me you're the type girl who's very deep. I try to talk to you about life in the large and all you do is waggle your little peepers and look seductive."

"I wasn't trying to look seductive," Vicky maintained. "I was only trying to look interested. I'm the type girl that tries to give everything to what the gentleman is saying. Later I mull it over in my mind and can't make head nor tail of it."

Ken continued to study her in some perplexity.

"What have you done? Either you're fatter or thinner or you've had your hair dyed. It's always something like that when women change."

"Not dyed. High-lighted is the new word," said Vicky. "Can't I have any secrets? It's this hat, too. And new clothes. Now I spend every cent on my back."

"A fine thing in times like these," rebuked Ken.

"It gives me all the more to donate to Bundles for Britain," said Vicky stoutly. "Nancy Elroy told me so. And then I charge everything because, with inflation, money won't be worth anything anyway. So that leaves me cash for massages and rhumba lessons and perfume that drives men mad."

Ken looked at her with unmistakable pleasure.

"If you were twenty years younger I'd make a play for you, no fooling," he admitted.

"I wasn't always the girl that I am now," Vicky warned him. "I was fat and freckled and bald. Typhoid. I was crazy about the boys and I let them cheat off my quiz papers. I giggled all the time, too."

"Youth is all I demand of a woman," said Ken. "Too bad you're too late to get me. I would have been your man. Have dinner with me."

It was one thing to go out to lunch with some one from your office, man or woman, and it was quite another to have any one desire these contacts prolonged into the private hours after five. Vicky was as delighted as she had been when Nancy Elroy had promoted her to the lofty level of personal and family friend. Mr. Saunders had never made any overtures toward her outside the office, beyond escorting her home from the occasional parties to which Amanda invited them. Vicky alone got a secret kick out of Julian's taking for granted that Ken was her beau, but Mr. Saunders did not seem to realize this attitude of Julian's. The couple was plainly enough linked together by being the two nobodies in a drawing-room of notables, all uttering notable remarks. Taking her home, Saunders usually made caustic comments on the group or else was moodily silent; in either case left her at her door most impersonally. Vicky might have thought it odd she was never asked to the Evanses' without Ken, except for the fact that she liked that part about the evening the best, counting on him for support.

Today, after his offer, she was suddenly emboldened to make an advance herself. She had secretly thought of doing so, ever since she first met him, but his manner, genial but impersonal, had discouraged her, heretofore. Ethel Carey had wired that she was coming to New York that day. What fun it would be to exhibit apartment and new man to friend from home all in same blow!

"Why don't you come to my apartment?" she now invited him. "I'll make a curry. Besides I have a friend from home coming."

Mr. Saunders did not seem at all appalled at the brazenness of the suggestion. He even declared that he personally would make the rice. He was such a superb ricemaker, he stated, that he could, if necessary, make rice for fifty to a hundred guests at the drop of a hat. This offer decided Vicky to make a real party of it. She would invite Nancy Elroy and her fiancé. She was so puffed up at the prospect of her first social undertaking, that it was all she could do to keep from inviting the entire Peabody staff, from Mr. Peabody right down to Irving Finkelstein. She was even more set up when Ken walked down the corridor to visit her office, on the way back from lunch.

There Miss Finkelstein, in a brand new sleek Dorothy Lamour hair-do and a great deal of clanking jewelry to which she referred as "Spanish Barbaric," gave Mr. Saunders a gracious nod. Vicky saw that her own stock had risen with her secretary because of being lunched by a young male member of the staff. Even the front office girls and models seldom had Big Dates at noon; they clustered around the drug-store lunch counter downstairs in the building, feasting on tuna fish sandwiches and malties.

"Some one has been trying to get you on this telephone, Mr. Saunders," Miss Finkelstein informed him, and handed him the receiver.

Vicky hung up her hat and combed her hair. She would send Irving out for supplies, she decided, and then carry them home herself in a taxi. She would order some wine—but before that she must send Miss Finkelstein up to Nancy's desk with the invitation for dinner. This would be a big night, maybe the real beginning. And then Vicky saw that Kenneth was stammering over the telephone looking embarrassed.

"It's Amanda," he said to Vicky. "She wants you."

Very well, she would invite Amanda, too. Julian, Miss Bemel—anybody.

"Darling," Amanda rushed to speak before Vicky could begin. "Ken tells me he had some sort of tentative engagement with you tonight. The thing is, I want you both here. Julian has to fly to Washington and there will just be three or four of us."

"But I can't," Vicky said. "Ethel Carey's coming for dinner, and perhaps some other people."

There was a shocked pause.

"You can get out of that," Amanda said curtly. "Simply leave a note for Ethel."

If she'd said to bring Ethel, too, it would have been easier, Vicky afterwards reflected, but Amanda was taking no chances on old friends outside of Vicky.

"I'm sure Ken would rather come here," Amanda said, with a short laugh. "Your cooking may be better than my Pedro's, but I swear your liquor isn't, and that's what counts with Mr. Saunders. So, just leave a note for Ethel and I'll see you around eight."

"But I haven't seen Ethel for months," Vicky protested. "No, Amanda, I'm sorry."

"We might as well go," Ken murmured.

This decided Vicky. Whatever she had to offer was nothing in the face of a royal command from Amanda, in Mr. Saunders' eyes. Very well, let him go there. But that was no reason for letting Ethel down.

"I'm sure I'd like to, Amanda," Vicky continued carefully. "Ken will probably come up, but I couldn't possibly."

"Oh, the hell with Ethel Carey!" Amanda's voice was impatient, almost shrill. "There isn't a reason in the world you can't do me this little favor. You don't need to go through life being kind to Lakeville!"

Vicky was puzzled by being wanted so much, but she was adamant. If Amanda let down old friends, she, Vicky, didn't have to. Amanda was genuinely angry with her for being so stubborn, and after she hung up Vicky saw that Ken Saunders was looking silently at the floor with an expression she didn't understand, but which must mean disappointment. He must have thought she would actually hold him to their engagement, so she quickly set him right.

"I'll ask you another night," she said, trying to sound very cheerful. "You go up to Amanda's."

He stood there, lighting a cigarette, looking as if he was about to say something. Then he shrugged his shoulders and smiled. "All right," he said. "We'll make ours some other time."

Miss Finkelstein, gliding back in, looked sharply from one to the other. Silent partings always looked like romance, but whatever romance there was in this scene must have ended unsatisfactorily, for Miss Finkelstein's keen eyes did not miss the fact that Vicky was dabbing at her nose with a handkerchief and trying to hide her face by picking up invisible matters from the floor.

"Miss Haven!" Miss Finkelstein exclaimed, in awe. "Did something happen? Did he—Miss Haven, you're not *crying*!"

Vicky took a firm grip on herself.

"Hay fever," she explained. "I always get it this time of year. I think it's the martinis."

With this baffling remark she blew her nose so many times you would have thought she had to test the instrument thoroughly before permitting it to leave the factory.

2

No sooner had Ken Saunders disappointed her and Amanda gotten mad than Vicky knew that there would be more grief to come. Some people's nerves react to approaching evil or approaching beneficence as to temperature changes. They have a sense at night of danger rolling up like rain clouds, a sense, too, when the danger has passed. Something clutches the heart, a cold wind blows by, the thing is about to strike. This faculty is not connected with the intellect nor is it a supernatural power, but a gift as simple as a good sense of smell.

"There will be a letter," Vicky prophesied gloomily as she walked home that night. "Or maybe it will be a telephone call, somebody at the door."

Passing a gypsy tea-room she was almost tempted to go in and try to draw mysterious information from the fortune-teller, but she remembered that the last time she had done this, the gypsy had foretold an unpleasantness that had immediately come true. No use running out to meet trouble. A gypsy should be required to be wrong, or else she became an affront to science.

If she was to lose her job such news would surely have reached her at the office before she left, so it could scarcely be that. At the newsstand on her corner, Vicky surrendered to an Astrology magazine, and rather guiltily looked up Virgo's chances for today and tomorrow. Today, advised the journal, Virgo was under Saturn. Up till 1:30 P.M. she should have travelled, concluded arrangements to stabilize finances, collected outstanding debts, sold property, settled domestic issues, challenged life, increased earning power, made personal contacts; 1:30 to midnight should be devoted to getting at basic facts, postponing journeys, forming ideas, making personal adjustments and saving money. Tomorrow, under Neptune, she was to travel, write, speak her mind freely, take a long walk, and avoid gambling. After 1:30 journeys should again be avoided, investments made, old debts collected, responsibilities accepted and temper held in check.

Reeling at the generosity of the advice given, Vicky hastily replaced the magazine on the rack. Evidently, to please the stars, millions of Virgos, if that was their plural term, were racing around on journeys all A.M. and trying to get back to base in time to postpone any P.M. journeys. Her own muddled hunches were far more reliable, she decided, and since whatever was to be was bound to be bad from the chilly feeling down her spine, she might as well go straight home and get it over.

No mail in the mailbox, however. The janitor denied that any telegram had been delivered. But no sooner had she gotten in her apartment than the telephone rang and there was mischief itself on the other end of the wire. It was Ethel Carey, just arrived in New York.

"Come right up, dear." Vicky managed to sound convincingly happy over the telephone. "I can't wait to see you."

There was a pregnant pause and then the blow fell.

"Vicky, I can't." A sigh. "Darling, can you stand some bad news?"

So this was where it was coming from.

"That's what I live for," Vicky encouraged her.

Ethel plunged into the worst.

"Tom Turner and Eudora were on the same train with me. They insisted on coming to my hotel—we're at the Barclay—and now I'm tied up for dinner with them."

Vicky opened her mouth to speak but words did not come. The very thought that Tom was within a dozen blocks of her this minute made her head start swimming exactly the way it used to do, and every drop of common sense in her system seemed to evaporate that very second. Vicky reached for a chair with trembling fingers and sat down. What were Tom and Eudora doing in New York? He'd never made enough money to come here before.

"The awful thing is that Eudora suggested you come along to dinner with us," Ethel wailed. "Can you imagine the nerve of her? She's here buying an outfit for the baby—it's due in three months—and she actually thinks you'll shop with her. She thinks that working on Peabody's, you'd get a discount."

For some reason this did not seem as outrageous to Vicky as it did to Ethel. At least the Turners seemed to be certain Vicky was no longer sensitive about them, and that was an advantage. She couldn't have stood having them consider her feelings.

"I'd come down and see you all," she lied with fine calm, "but I have friends coming in so perhaps we can meet tomorrow."

Ethel seemed relieved at Vicky's matter-of-fact attitude.

"You're over it, aren't you, Vicky? That's wonderful. . . . Maybe we might even drop in tonight and see you. It would serve them right to see you with your New York friends. It would just serve them right."

Hanging up, Vicky thought, yes and it served herself right for lying about friends coming in. She couldn't bear to have them see her the way they were going to—all alone, depressed, quite dateless. She thought desperately of calling Amanda, but then Amanda was having a dinner, a dinner that required Ken Saunders. She thought again of Nancy Elroy, but Nancy had said she had another engagement.

Vicky's head buzzed so busily with the necessity for doing something devilishly shrewd and effective that movement was practically paralyzed, suggestions popping up so fast they cancelled each other. A dozen courses of action flashed through her mind and she set about following them all at once, painting two fingernails a victorious red, then drawing a bath but forgetting the stopper; ordering chrysanthemums from the florist, then remembering there was no vase big enough unless you counted the umbrella stand; shaping one eyebrow then deciding to eat dinner first. She ordered a reckless dinner for one sent over from the nearest Longchamps as the solution to her confusion, then remembered her tub and sat in it while the dinner got cold. The one thought that completely numbed all normal processes was the thought of Tom Turner. It is possible that a gentleman who leaves one love to run off with another feels wretchedly at the mercy of both the rest of his life, and is not at all complacent at the implication two women have found him irresistible. It is possible that whatever disgraceful situation his lack of chivalry has induced, is as painful to him as it is to his jilted love and even to his favored new one. But the general conviction has always been that here is a man gloating over his double triumph—one lady left sobbing with heartbreak over him, another revelling in the magic of his touch. That was the way Vicky thought of Tom Turner and it made her furious with him, first that he should be so conceited, and second that he should be so nearly right. After all she *had* cried a good deal over him. For all she knew she would burst into tears at sight of him again. Supposing he sat and held Eudora Brown's hand. Very likely he would. Married people were always doing that in front of their unmarried friends. Alone they might spit and snarl at each other, but there was some law, apparently, which required a public exhibition of satisfaction with the married state.

How should she act before them? Hysterically happy—that was the usual pose for the jilted one—or proudly reticent? All she could decide offhand was to be glamorous, and she set to work studiously on the routine approved by the Peabody beauties. Her new dress, when shaken out of the box and slipped on, astonished her by fitting, at least in most places; and her hair done up in its new way looked encouragingly Peabodyish except for a few wisps at the back of her neck that no polite person would notice unless they were snooping around behind her. She was particularly pleased with the new earrings she had copied from Nancy. These were in the shape of javelins and, though only clipped on, were cunningly devised to give an impression of stabbing through the upper to the lower lobes of the ear, a picture of self-torture that magnetized every eye and was very smart that month.

Vicky sat down to the coffee table where her dinner was spread, still undecided which façade she should present to the Turners. One thing was certain, whether she was haughty or whether she was effusively friendly, she must show that Manhattan was her natural background, and if anything had gone wrong in her Lakeville career it was merely because she was too big a person for the place.

The doorbell rang and Vicky, with a deep breath, prepared to face it. But instead of Ethel Carey and the Turners there stood Ken Saunders, looking rather sheepish.

"I took a walk around the Evanses' diggings," he said. "I decided I couldn't make it. I like this place better anyway."

Vicky was beaming, though she tried to look reproachful at the man who dared to defy her friend Amanda.

"But you've never been here before," she reminded him.

Ken reflected on this.

"That's so," he agreed. "Put your coat on, we're going out to dinner."

Vicky pointed to her dinner, just begun. Ken eyed it with a revulsion.

"Smelts! Fried oysters! Shrimp salad!" he exclaimed incredulously. "What did you do—go straight down the fish list?"

"I suppose so," Vicky said. "I thought it saved time."

"You can't eat that horrible stuff. Come on, get your hat, we'll go and get a real dinner."

He jerked his thumb toward the door and Vicky very happily ran to powder and get her things. If the Turners came they would see that in New York, Vicky Haven was too popular to be kept waiting. Too many men were eager to take her out. When she returned, she was astonished to find her guest seated at the coffee table busily finishing the last crumb of her dinner.

"I'm ready," she said. "I see you've already had dinner."

Ken looked at the table.

"So I have," he said. "I was thinking of something else. I'm such a busy man."

"It's all right," said Vicky. "I wasn't awfully hungry. I'll bet Amanda's mad at you for not coming there."

"I couldn't go there alone," said Ken. "Amanda would hate that."

Vicky was puzzled by this remark. Why couldn't he go to the Evanses alone? Other men did. Important gentlemen, of course. Ken kicked at the fire with his shoe and appeared to forget that Vicky was waiting to be taken out. When he turned to speak to her she was sure he was going to explain his curious insinuation that he was only welcome at the Evanses when properly escorted by a lady—in this case, Vicky.

"Smelts," he stated, "are a nasty little fish. I'm surprised at you. I would have said 'now there is a girl who orders venison with the best of them.' But no. Smelts. Smelts. Fried oysters. Shrimps."

"You can't judge by a girl's face, after all," Vicky said humbly.

Mr. Saunders suddenly reached in the wood cupboard where Amanda kept her cellar and extracted a bottle of rum. He appeared to have a rather uncanny sense of direction, for Vicky herself had not discovered this supply till a few weeks ago. Not knowing exactly what to do with a man who had first made a date, then cancelled it, then honored her by retrieving it, then eaten her dinner, Vicky sat down humbly on the ottoman to wait his lead. He opened the bottle and poured two drinks, one of which she obediently took and sipped. He drank his swiftly without speaking. He drank another, and then the bell rang.

This time it was not the Turners but none other than Mr. Rockman Elroy, who stood on the threshold. Her amazement made Mr. Elroy back away in embarrassment.

"Nancy told me you had invited her to dine tonight," he said, as if this would at once explain his unprecedented visit. "Inasmuch as she could not come I thought I myself would pay a call. Here."

With the "Here" he thrust a large coffinlike box in her arms.

More chrysanthemums, of course, and no place to put them. Mr. Elroy stood uncomfortably watching his flowers being carried tentatively from cocktail glass to double boiler and finally stuffed into a tall wastebasket with an ash tray of water at its feet.

"Thank you, Mr. Elroy," said Vicky, flushed from these clumsy maneuvers. "And this is Mr. Saunders."

"Of course," said Mr. Elroy, bowing stiffly.

Ken looked cross at the intrusion.

"When I bring violets, they *have* violets," Mr. Elroy ruefully observed. "When I bring these big things they have no place to put them but in an eye cup."

"It's the same with me," Vicky admitted. "When they bring me violets I don't know where to pin them and when they bring me these I end up parking them in the bathtub, for days. I've taken more baths with chrysanthemums."

"White tie!" observed Saunders, looking coldly at Mr. Elroy. "I'm afraid I'm not dressed for this call, Miss Haven."

"My goodness, I *am* flattered," Vicky exclaimed.

Uncle Rockman looked at his evening splendour with the puzzled expression of a man looking at one of nature's wonders for the first time. Then a light dawned.

"I'm giving a speech tonight," he said. "The associated paper men."

"So paper is your subject," said Saunders with a certain belligerence, Vicky felt.

"Not at all," Mr. Elroy said. "I am going to talk about the concern felt by Earth over the receding of the stars. That is closer to people's lives than mere paper."

"Of course," said Vicky. "I'm Virgo myself. September 3rd. So far the stars haven't done me much good."

"Give them another million years," advised Uncle Rockman. "By that time they will have receded indefinitely to Red and the universe will or will not be blown up."

"Two gets you five that it won't," said Ken.

He was being unnecessarily aggressive. And Uncle Rockman was being unnecessarily pompous. They couldn't have disliked each other more if they had been brothers. Vicky was very distressed because she was enormously touched by Uncle Rockman's visit. What could be handsomer, too, than a man of fifty with a fine glowing nose, crown of silver curls, and a body sufficiently weighted to keep him squarely on his feet in the stiffest of winds! She was disappointed that Ken did not appreciate Uncle Rockman's fine points.

"This paper banquet must be an elegant affair," she said, admiring his snowy shirtfront and glittering studs.

Uncle Rockman stroked his chin doubtfully.

"As a matter of fact the dinner is right in the factory and I recall being warned against dressing," he said. "But I always wear tails when I speak. It gives me something to wave about when I get stuck. I forget a point so I walk up and down the platform flapping my coat-tails till the thought comes back."

"Isn't that brilliant?" Vicky appealed to Ken.

Mr. Saunders merely gave Mr. Elroy a bleak nod, the hostility of which was not lost on Uncle Rockman. He sat down resolutely, however, and Vicky poured him a drink. The slight difficulty he had in coordinating the quivering of his fingers with his excitement over the drink hinted at his already high alcoholic content. That, of course, explained the boldness of his visit. Inasmuch as Saunders' visit was equally unprecedented Vicky began thinking that he too had been propelled there by over-stimulation. Her sudden popularity seemed less and less flattering. And the way the two men disliked each other was a problem for any hostess to handle, especially one with no dinner. In vain Vicky sought to find them a common ground but Mr. Saunders was sarcastic and curt, Mr. Elroy was courteous but silent. Vicky talked busily about the office, about her friends from Lakeville, about anything, but her two guests refused to use her words as a springboard to general talk.

Somewhat desperately Vicky plied them with rum and on the moment she was opening the second bottle a slight thaw began to take place. By the time the bell rang to admit Ethel and the Turners, Uncle Rockman was nestling back half-asleep on the sofa laughing fondly at everything Ken Saunders said. Ken had taken off his coat and necktie and was deeply engrossed in the task of proving that Extra-Sensory-Perception, as explained by Uncle Rockman, was nothing more nor less than a poor man's version of the match game. Both gentlemen were too absorbed in their new friendship to pay any heed to the entrance of Vicky's guests, or to be aware of the startling impression they created.

3

So here was Tom Turner, who had broken Vicky's heart to run away with her business partner, Eudora Brown. Here was Eudora, once a bosom friend, now holding her hands over her convex lap, looking enviously around Vicky's living-room. Desire makes its object worthy of desire, and for four years Tom Turner had been the worthy object of Vicky's affection. Now he belonged to somebody else and desire had been shocked by frustration into a numb despair, which Vicky discovered was modulating into a hostile disparagement of the man. All right, it was sour grapes to sit there silently criticizing everything about him—what was the matter with sour grapes? Sour grapes was as comforting a philosophy as any other, and a lot better than tearing your heart out with undying passion. He was as handsome as ever, in his dissipated ham actor way, and his voice was as richly effective as ever, but both of these hollow charms irritated the new Vicky. And how did he dare talk about Labor problems in the Middle West, having spent most of his time dodging hard work (unless there was no connection between these two fields)! She saw that she was by way of curing herself the moment she found herself being more tolerant of Eudora than she had dreamed possible. Even when Eudora shocked every one by her sarcastic cracks at her husband, "That's what *you* think! . . . Oh, listen to the expert! . . . Isn't it wonderful to know everything. . . ." and so on. Vicky merely laughed as if this was good-natured fun that needed no apology. She could tell, too, that Tom was impressed as was Eudora over the new background, new friends, and apparent happy recovery of their victim. That was why he wanted to argue about every subject that came up.

"You're quite wrong there, old man," he stated disagreeably at every remark made by the other two men. He was one of those men who betray their secret frustration in this way: taken into a handsome mansion they fall silent, coming slowly to an indignant mental boiling point of "This should be mine!" until out of a clear sky they start to shower insults on the innocent host. Married to a plain wife they take it as a personal grievance when they meet a single beauty, and cannot forbear pecking at the beauty with criticisms of her left thumb, her necklace, her accent, as if destruction by bits will ease the outrage of not being able to have her. Unemployed, they jeer at the stupidity of an envied friend working so hard for so little pay. In the unexpected presence of an admired or celebrated person they are reminded gallingly of their own inferior qualities and humiliate themselves by inadequate sarcasm, showing clearly how impressed they are and how irrevocably inferior they know themselves to be.

Vicky found herself seeing her late adored with such a clear unsympathetic eye that she brought herself up sharply. It was no truer that he was terrible now than that he was wonderful before. And if she had any stability at all she would not be disloyal to her old feelings. It would be much more to her credit, she admonished herself, to have her senses thrown in disorder by his presence in the room. This callous hostility brought on by being jilted merely proved she was a girl incapable of a deathless love—a scatter-brained emotional butterfly. Seeing through old lost lovers was not a gracious talent.

"Let me make the drinks," he said to her. "Unless of course your New York men friends have a special knack for mixing that us backwoodsmen don't get."

"Vicky looks like a new person, doesn't she, Tom?" Eudora asked urgently.

Tom would not compliment anything that was out of his reach so he merely smiled and shrugged.

"I don't see any difference. Hair looks a little funny, maybe. No, New York hasn't done much to Vicky."

This was naturally a remark intended to discipline any young woman who thought she was transformed into a beauty by loss of a lover.

Vicky finally decided that her nervous irritation was pure hunger, and ordered an immense supply of sandwiches from the delicatessen. She nibbled away while Ethel Carey and Eudora endeavored to supply her with the latest reports on Lakeville life. Her brother Ted had informed every one he expected her back for good by spring. The children had been kept home for a few days during the infantile paralysis scare and had set fire to the house in their boredom, involving Ted in some legalities about collecting insurance. The Haven-Brown Real Estate office was affected by the imminence of war and it was Ethel's whispered suspicion that Eudora might have to give up the office and come down to mere desk space in the bank.

"You were the brains of that office, anyway," Ethel whispered in the privacy of the bathroom, to Vicky. "Eudora as good as admits it. She flies off the handle too fast and antagonizes people. Especially now, of course."

Tom was considering building a government base somewhere in the Pacific islands, but again Ethel whispered to Vicky that this was all big talk and Mr. Turner had no intention of leaving Lakeville unless it got bombed. Other news was that Howard Keeler and wife had left haberdashery and beauty parlor to gypsy down the Florida coast in a second-hand trailer, with a pack of grocers, plumbers and other

Lakeville creditors about to gypsy down after them. Ethel's
own papa had been summoned to an important advisory post
in Washington and had promised Ethel a lunch at the White
House one of these days, though every one in Lakeville was
still Republican and called F.D. "that man in the White
House." Every girl in town had Amanda Keeler Evans scrap-
books (except for a rebel group called the Joan Crawford Fan
Club, of which Vicky's niece was the president), and items
about Amanda or her husband were in great demand. Eudora
Brown had been assured by her physician that a glass of wine
could not possibly injure her coming heir, and on the
strength of this medical support was drinking straight Bacardi
whenever she could get the bottle out of Mr. Elroy's or Ken
Saunders' hands. After her initial hearty but shamefaced
greeting of Vicky, she allowed her conversation to lapse into
one chief word, which was "stinks."

Even if Tom Turner had not been there the little group
would have been a difficult one for any hostess to organize.
Ethel carried on a constant flow of gossip about characters
Uncle Rockman and Ken did not know, Vicky ate sandwiches
and tried to avoid Tom Turner's urgent, curious gaze, Eudora
drank and made sardonic exclamations, and Uncle Rockman
and Ken talked feverishly of the atom. In occasional efforts at
general conversation Tom Turner described the Lakeville
Country Club inner politics to Uncle Rockman, who vanquished him with learned commentary on the splendid work
on the Soul being done at the Yale Institute of Human Relations by somebody named Burr. Swinging lightly out of this,
Uncle Rockman dealt with the Inverse Square Law, and finding his audience quite crushed he was able to take up the
atom again, of which he spoke fondly as if it was a dear little
Cupid flying through space making statistics for every good
child. Ken Saunders eagerly encouraged this monologue as a
means of freezing out Tom Turner, and Uncle had somehow
gotten into quantum this and quantum that when a final sip
at his drink made him slide farther down into the corner of
the cushioned sofa and fall asleep.

Ethel Carey nudged Vicky.

"Is he keeping you?" she whispered. "I mean I don't see how
anybody would let him go on like that unless he paid the rent."

Marriage had not improved Eudora Brown nor had pregnancy given a dewy light to her eyes. There was little that pleased her in the world or in the present evening. Her bridegroom, inheriting the floor on Uncle Rockman's fade-out, talked so instructively of current events, the war, and secret white papers, that Vicky concluded he must have no job; such vastly informed men usually had their time to themselves. This turned out to be something like the case, for Eudora cornered Vicky in the course of the evening.

"Could you loan us five hundred bucks?" she whispered. "You see this war is ruining Tom's business—and I'm going to have to let the office go after next month. Ethel says you've been doing so well—"

Vicky was too bewildered to answer at first and Eudora took this confusion as a criticism.

"After all, the way I look at it is this," she said. "If it hadn't been for me, it would be you in this spot right now, so I feel you owe me a *little* something!"

Vicky was so embarrassed that if she had had any money at all she would have poured it at once in Eudora's hat. Instead she gulped out something about "maybe later on," which angered Eudora.

"You're just like Amanda," she declared. "I wrote Amanda and she high-hatted me, too. Said she was doing all she could for refugees. Hell, I could have been a refugee if I'd gone abroad when every one else went."

Eudora's last remark was overheard by Ethel Carey, who was so shocked at the idea of asking Amanda for money that the two women were soon snapping at each other.

"Amanda stinks," Eudora repeated several times. "Amanda stinks on ice."

Mr. Saunders took offense at this.

"Say what you will about Amanda," he stated. "Let us not forget that she is the lawfully wedded wife of that great leader, Julian Evans."

Eudora observed that Mr. Evans also stank on ice.

"Possibly," admitted Ken. "At least he will bear watching."

"Sixteen papers and not one of them first-rate," stated Tom Turner. "A joint circulation of over—well roughly, let's say ten million readers—"

Suddenly Mr. Elroy struggled to his feet from the depths of the sofa.

"Did some one mention paper?" he inquired, blue eyes wide with anxiety. "I must talk to the paper men. Excuse me, please."

He waddled hastily to the door, Vicky running after him with coat and hat. Ken Saunders hurried ahead to get a cab and assist his new chum, but Uncle Rockman would have no assistance. He was in his own car and his own chauffeur knew exactly what was to be done. He was gone as swiftly as any fairy godmother, leaving Vicky's friends with the impression that he was something more than an elderly adviser, particularly since she could give little information about him or his reasons for calling on her. Even Ken Saunders seemed baffled.

Eudora Brown declared that any man that age who ran after a girl Vicky's age really did stink on ice. She said that was why she and Tom had gotten on so well, they were the right age for each other. Her husband caustically suggested that she stop being a damned fool but added that he really did not expect any such luck.

"Go ahead, say what you're going to say," said Eudora shrilly. "Tell everybody right in front of me that you're still crazy about Vicky. I don't care. Go ahead. Go on."

Ethel Carey grew white at this and suggested that they all leave. They could see Vicky tomorrow, maybe, unless she was as busy as she should be.

"Certainly I'm crazy about Vicky," said Tom Turner coldly, without looking at Vicky. "I always have been—always will be."

"There—that's all you wanted to hear, isn't it?" Eudora sobbed. "God knows I hear it often enough—*you* might as well."

Tom Turner planted himself in front of his wife.

"All right, let her hear!" he shouted. "I couldn't get Vicky to sleep with me—that was the only reason I walked out on her. No trouble like that with you. So what are you kicking about?"

"Tom! Eudora!" pleaded Ethel, holding their wraps in her arms. "Mr. Saunders, do get us a cab. We can't have this go on."

Vicky sat stonily in a chair, too numb to say good-bye. Ethel, with mixed feelings of horror and shocked delight, herded her two friends out, Eudora still weeping angrily and Tom haughtily removed from the lot of them. It was the worst evening she'd ever spent, Vicky thought. It was as if her one-time love for Tom must spoil even the tiniest hours of pleasure in her life forever. Anyway Uncle Rockman had missed the worst of it. And Nancy Elroy hadn't been there, that was something. But Ken Saunders had. He might tell Amanda and Julian. Or worse yet, he would just look at her and be scornful of any one involved in such a sordid mess.

Ken Saunders came back, rumpling his fair hair in utter perplexity.

"Do I gather what I just gathered?" he asked. "You don't need to tell me if you don't want to."

Vicky nodded.

"And the guy is still crazy about you?" he wanted to know.

Vicky wanted to say yes, for that was after all what Eudora had insisted and what Tom had said, too. But the instant they began torturing each other before her she had sensed that the truth was much less flattering—they only used her as the whip for their relationship. Eudora and Tom understood each other, counted on no nobility in each other, relied affectionately on each other's vulgarity, lashed at each other's weaknesses and bound themselves together by these. They belonged together. She had always been left out. They hadn't even looked at her when they were shouting about Tom's continued love for her. They didn't think of her as a person, hardly, but merely a name they used to excite themselves with. If Tom had really still been in love with her, Vicky thought, he would never have said so. But she couldn't explain this to Ken Saunders. She did tell him most of the story, though she did not like him to know how stubbornly she had held out against an affair with Tom, nor even how glad she was now that she had refused. Men always seemed to think this showed a serious flaw in a girl's character, a wilfulness that might prove further acquaintance most unprofitable. It was best to keep this wilfulness a secret.

"We do know how to pick out trouble for ourselves," Ken said. "Here we are, both of us in the prime of life, all messed up because we picked the wrong people. If we had any sense we'd have picked people like each other. But oh, no."

"Oh, no," said Vicky. So he had been in love with the wrong person, too!

They sat up in her kitchen till four o'clock comparing mistakes in their lives, holding hands and bewailing the thought that they could not fall in love with each other. Later he scrambled eggs with anchovies sprinkled over them and made coffee most competently. He had a knack for knowing where everything was—cigarettes, liquor, salt, coffee. In fact, Vicky wondered about it after he left. She decided that either his lost love's place must be very much like hers, or else there were a lot of apartments around New York fitted exactly like this one.

VII

J ULIAN EVANS felt that he was big enough to carry the world's problems with almost godlike dignity. He did not lose his temper over Russia as many men his junior did; he saw both sides of Chamberlain, found a calm word for Lindbergh, was thoughtful—not shrill—in his devotion to Roosevelt. In conferences with the nation's leaders, he did not permit himself to go "off the deep end" over politics, but preserved—at least publicly—a tolerance that would have done honor to the Supreme Court bench. This, at least, was his own secret conviction. But with the problem of Amanda he was in a state bordering on hysteria. Scarcely an hour in the day passed now that something she said, did, or indirectly caused, did not pop up to vex him. Fundamentally, there was the matter of sex; the manner in which she stiffened at his touch, as if he were some monster, as if, indeed, he was attempting something that was outside his lawful rights and even outside his ability. And then there was her open ingratitude at his management of her career, a career which God knows was becoming increasingly embarrassing to him. It was on this he was pondering as he sat in his study scowling at a carafe of orange juice. Mr. Cheever, his London man, stood at the window smoking his pipe and contributing not a little to Julian's vexation.

"Understand, Evans, I am not reflecting in the least on your wife's talents," Cheever said in measured tones. "Amanda Keeler Evans is unquestionably one of the finest minds of our times, a real force. I'm not denying that. I merely ask to be given first crack at my own territory, and if the stuff is printable at all, let it be under my by-line. I don't see the logic of scrapping my stuff and then letting Amanda spill it as hers. I feel there's a certain amount of injustice in that."

His superior moodily sipped his orange juice. He had known this was coming for some time. He had seen the signs months ago when Amanda flew to London and Cheever had gallantly placed his material at her disposal, to her credit and implicitly to his loss. A beautiful young woman spends two weeks in London and is magically able to give an accurate and complete survey of the whole situation, when the regular correspondent had spent twenty years there apparently unable to grasp things. It would never be understood by the public that Mr. Evans had permitted Amanda a freedom of opinion that was denied Cheever. More of this sort of thing was happening constantly since Cheever's stay in New York. Amanda took the cream, still. Julian had wanted to give it to her, but there should have been a little more discretion in it, so as not to lose Cheever. Being a pretty egotistical man in his own right, once his gallantry had worn off, Mr. Cheever was unquestionably in a mood to make trouble over his rights. He would be a hard man to replace. Certainly no newcomer would be able to supply Amanda with the historical and social documentation that Cheever had done. It was a moment for the utmost tact, Julian knew, just as he knew Cheever was in the right. But a consciousness of being in the wrong seldom puts a man in good humor, so he flew into a childish rage.

"Damn it, Cheever, the war isn't copyrighted!" he shouted, banging the desk, but not too hard, as it was easily marred. "The stuff is there—anybody with eyes can get it, and anybody with brains can sum it up! I can't be bothered with personal feelings in a public crisis like this! I've got my responsibilities to my papers, and the American public! By God, Cheever, if you want to be picayune about this when millions of men are being killed—"

He drank down a glass of orange juice and then mopped his brow. There were moments when he wished for some heart ailment which would oblige people to take care of crossing him. As it was, he managed, by clutching at his heart and then wiping his brow, to convey the effect of a strong man about to crack up. Cheever looked at him dispassionately over his pipe and said nothing, which irritated Julian even more. He would have liked Cheever to be in a temper and he, the chief, to be patronizingly calm. All this trouble was Amanda's fault. He had created this public figure and it was getting to be a bigger responsibility than anything he had hitherto taken on, and he was a man who had bought railroads and even mountains. The angrier he was at Amanda the angrier he was at Cheever, since rage with Amanda was a confession of her superiority.

"This is no time for personal vanity," Julian sputtered. "By-line! A fine thing to be worrying about, with children being bombed, homes wrecked. By God, Cheever, I'm too big a man to be subjected to this sort of thing! You can't expect me to waste time worrying over whose name is signed to what paragraph, with Europe burning!"

"If it's so trivial as all that, why do you insist, then, that full credit on my material be given to Amanda Evans?" Mr. Cheever inquired in an insultingly calm tone. "If the paper ever made a slip-up on *that* by-line there'd be hell to pay and you know it, damn you."

In the twenty years Amos Cheever had worked for Julian he had never been guilty of such open insubordination. Julian was shocked almost out of his anger, and his first instinct was that Cheever would never have dared take this stand unless he had some bigger job around the corner. All the rumors he had been hearing lately of a great Western syndicate combining with his nearest Eastern rival now catapulted through Julian's mind. The rumor must be true, and Cheever must have been offered more money there. The increased power of a rival did not alarm Julian very much for he would bide his time to outstrip that move. A little shrewd planning, a few conferences with bankers, lawyers, gamblers—a little discreet hi-jacking possibly—and Evans would be on top again as usual. What did disturb him was the damage Cheever could do him by leaving him. A man who had worked for him for twenty years, knew all about his family, Margaret and the children, had been cited for international dignities because of his journalistic work, knew England as well as he knew America —a man with such professional prestige Julian naturally felt was completely an Evans creation—and his moving to another employer would not fail to create inquiry. And Cheever, being angry, would talk. He would make a fool out of his only employer. He would say Julian Evans ran his business as a convenience to his wife's career. He might even say Amanda Keeler was the power behind the throne, edging out any employee who challenged her authority. How would that make Julian Evans look? Every one would whisper when they saw him, every one would laugh at him. The king lets his old prime minister be executed because the new queen is really king.

Such thoughts scampered through Julian's brain, scattering fear, and Julian's face was even pale when he turned again to Cheever.

"Let's not quarrel, Cheever," he said, with such a change of manner that Cheever looked at him in utter bewilderment. "We've been together too long, old man. As a matter of fact, the thing that bothers you is going to be cleared up in no time, anyway. Amanda is getting far too busy with her new book and of course, her work with the refugee children, to have time for editorial comment, either on the air or in our pages. We'll have to depend pretty much on you, old man."

The "old man" overture did not relax the grimness of Cheever's expression. He tapped his pipe on the huge Abalone shell Mr. Evans used as an ash tray.

"Hasn't she got all the publicity out of that child adoption committee that she needs?" he asked. Again this insolence was so unprecedented as to convince Julian that Cheever was as good as laughing at him over at the rival office this very minute. He would not permit himself to be annoyed, though he knew that he would be in a private fury about all this all night long.

"My dear Cheever, do you realize Amanda has—with my help—placed over two hundred children from England, France, even Czechoslovakia? Good homes, mind you, homes of friends of ours, often. Homes that never had a child and didn't want one, but by God, Amanda got them in and she deserves credit."

It was a nice point and Julian sat back, continuing to nod his head convincingly.

"I notice you have never inconvenienced your own home with any of these little visitors," Mr. Cheever answered thoughtfully.

Julian's cigar dropped from his fingers at this final bomb-shell. Here again were implications that were far more dis-turbing than the mere impudence of the remark. Cheever was saying something that other people must be saying, and what other people were saying could roll into a tremendous scan-

dal. Being a clever man, Julian saw at once how fatal was this
discrepancy between Amanda's public good works and her
private selfishness. He was perfectly aware of the important
connection between preaching and practice, and in his publicized campaigns tried to exhibit proper regard for this. But
Amanda was different. Amanda was a phenomenon. Julian
blamed himself now for being too lax with her. He should
have put her on guard against this sort of criticism. It was still
not too late.

"As I told you, Cheever, Amanda's time is taken up more
and more with her book. With her relief work and other
public activities, she has scarcely a minute even for me." Julian was feeling his ground very carefully and dared not allow
Cheever's cool gaze to dismay him. "If we were to take the
responsibility for any of these children Amanda would insist
on giving them her entire time and, of course, she serves our
cause far better by giving us her talents. So—"

"So her time is her own," Mr. Cheever observed with an
unpleasant smile. "No matter what else is going on in the
world, at least the Evanses are at peace. They sleep under a
roof, they eat four meals a day, they count their money, they
collect. Whatever happens the Evanses collect, and never pay.
God's pets."

Julian's secretary, Castor, had crept in and out during this
discussion, with letters, memoranda, and at one point with a
pair of glowing Northern Spy apples—a four o'clock habit of
Julian's which he was always willing to share with a guest.
The tenor of the talk had plainly given the little secretary
tremendous concern, for he was accustomed to see Julian in a
rage and the visitor in the proper state of dignified but servile
silence. Here was Julian Evans trying to propitiate an indignant employee and the employee refusing to be smoothed.
The saffron face of Mr. Castor was flushed with excitement,
even terror, over this unexpected turn. Even if Cheever had
not been mad, Castor would have been alarmed to see Mr.
Evans anything but majestically patronizing to an employee.
The secretary could not help feeling that in a moment perhaps the caller would whip out a revolver, as God knows
many enemies had threatened to do, and there would Julian
Evans be, making news in his own home, body stretched

across the floor, while Ernest Castor took charge of the investigators.

"I was typing Mr. Evans's editorial on 'Eyes Front, not Backward,' for the Sunday magazine, officer," Castor heard himself already explaining with quiet authority, "when I heard voices. I came in to the library and found Cheever, our London man, cursing Mr. Evans and waving a revolver. As it is up to me to protect not only Mr. Evans's private interests but his own person, I sprang at Cheever, a much larger man than I. I had the advantage of him by a certain elementary knowledge of *jiu jitsu* as well as a cool head. However, he had a gun. In a flash, I saw Mr. Evans on the floor, and the smoking revolver lay beside him. I saw at once that he was beyond hope. Blood was streaming—"

It was something of a disappointment for the imaginative little man to see that there was no gun, and that Cheever's anger was so far confined to cold statements which Mr. Evans found himself obliged to defend. Castor's secret passion for the theatrical was frustrated by Julian's namby-pamby handling of the rebellious employee. Like Miss Bemel, his great compensation for the indignities of his position was to see his employer inflict worse indignities on better men. But here was Julian almost apologizing to Cheever for the Evanses' not taking on the responsibilities Amanda's propaganda inflicted on other people. Castor stood just outside Julian's door in his own little cubbyhole and gnawed his fingernails desperately. He had a sudden daring inspiration when he heard Julian speak.

"That's quite an accusation you are trying to make there, Cheever," Julian was saying in a grave, shocked voice. "I gather you are trying to say that my wife and I do not live by the things we preach."

"*Trying* to say? I *did* say, for God's sake!" Mr. Cheever cried out in exasperation, and then Castor tiptoed into the room with a sheet of paper which he laid before Julian with a preoccupied air, as if he had no inkling of the argument he was interrupting.

"It's rather important, sir," Castor said meekly. "Mrs. Evans wants to know whether you wish the new boy brought here directly from the train or whether he is to go to your country place with the other refugees. He's in Montreal, waiting further instructions."

For a moment Julian looked blankly at his secretary, and then, as was his custom, took as his own work this gift from Providence.

"We'll keep him here as long as he's happy," he commanded briskly, and then said to Cheever with an air of grieved patience, "Do you really mean, Cheever, that you think Amanda should keep her personal charges here in the city with her just for the publicity value, when the country air is what their health demands?"

Cheever shrugged. However it had been done, Julian had as usual turned the tables in his own favor. He had made it appear that Amanda's personal sacrifices were never mentioned, and that such crass critics as Cheever objected not so much to her failure to inconvenience herself, as to her failure to advertise her private goodness. Julian himself believed this as soon as Castor had given him the opportunity. He would make it true. He would, if necessary, put his foot down with Amanda as he did with his staff. She must see it as he did. They must take on the burden of a refugee child in the home.

Castor tiptoed out of the room, his elation at his diplomacy not for an instant showing in his yellow sharp little face.

Cheever put his pipe in his pocket. It was turning out like all of his other interviews with Julian Evans, as long as he had known him. There was no defeating such a man. You raised an issue over a major point and Julian cleverly sidetracked you to some trivial complaint which he then settled in a noble way. He had come to settle with Evans over the matter of Amanda stealing his stuff, and the discussion ended with Julian triumphantly declaring that Amanda was nobly and modestly adopting a war refugee. You couldn't beat Julian because he refused to meet you with your own weapons on your own field.

Through the half-opened door little Castor watched Cheever leave and could see that the man was resigned momentarily, though he might still be hostile. For a moment Castor felt a little pity for the vanquished Cheever and a secret antagonism to Julian Evans, who signed this little minor triumph as if it had been his own instead of his secretary's.

Julian had a hundred people to sing his virtues, but Castor had only Castor to admire Castor's astuteness. He admired himself now, silently, for that hunch about Mr. Evans's letter. The Mrs. Evans mentioned, of course, was Julian's former wife, Margaret. Poor, stolid Margaret still followed her husband's advice on good works faithfully, shifting from longshoremen to sharecroppers, opening her home to the underhoused or the undersexed, whichever campaign Julian was fomenting at the moment. Now her big home on the Hudson was filled with dozens of left-overs from Julian's various public causes. Even her bitterness toward Julian's new wife did not prevent her from earnestly doing her Christian duty in the Amanda Keeler Evans adoption plan. Few people knew of this, however, so Castor was justly proud of saving the second Mrs. Evans at the expense of the first. He stood for a moment in the doorway to Julian's study, half-expecting his employer to commend his quick thinking. But as soon as Cheever had left, Julian was on the telephone sending for Miss Bemel, since his wife was not to be found. The next moment he was telephoning his downtown secretary, Harnett, to start working on a *New York Times* man, now in Geneva, as a potential successor to Cheever.

"Promise him anything he likes," Julian was saying. "Don't commit me to anything. Act on your own. If he won't play ball, then he can't go around saying he turned down Evans. Feel him out. I want to be protected just in case. Cheever's getting too damn troublesome."

Even Castor marvelled at the efficiency of his master. He had saved Cheever whom he needed, but the danger of losing him was already insulting Mr. Evans. Men didn't leave him. He fired them. Cheever wasn't going to be able to say he walked out on Evans because his wife ran the paper and took all the gravy. Evans was going to be able to say, on the contrary, that he let Cheever go because he was a troublemaker. His flash of mild pity for Cheever as he saw the bearded distinguished figure go down the hall immediately vanished. All Castor thought was, "The poor fool! If he is sap enough to let this happen, then he deserves it!"

2

Amanda had this in common with Julian—the belief that any calamity befalling some one else was simply in the course of nature, whereas the merest hitch in their own arrangements was the fault of some one in their service. The rain of complaints suddenly falling on Amanda for her refugee work was clearly due to Miss Bemel's inefficiency, or, to be fair, the joint inefficiency of Miss Bemel and the relief headquarters' secretary. Castor's memo from Julian urging immediate if temporary adoption of one or more refugee children was distinctly traceable to the stupidity of Amos Cheever. No matter whose fault, however, it was Amanda who must suffer this injustice, and what with these and many other matters she was in a state of high nervous tension. Ken Saunders, instead of proving a solace to her feminine vanity, was undermining her perpetually by breaking dates, quite as if his time were as important as hers, and that therefore he had the same justification that she had for such behavior. In spite of their new restless relationship, he obliged her to think about him, to wonder what he meant by this and that; no sooner had he convinced her he was again infatuated with her than he upset her assurance by ignoring her for days. Assurance of her sexual fascination was increasingly important to her other work, and Amanda was furious with Ken for interfering with her career by his capriciousness. As if, she thought in astonishment, she was just a woman, just *any* woman. She would call him to say that if she could finish an appointment with a congressman and dispose of a delegation of admirers from Argentina *and* shorten her luncheon engagement with a Burmese correspondent, she would meet him at the usual place sometime between two and three-thirty. It was incredible that, on arriving at the spot promptly at three-fifteen, Ken should not be there, yet this happened many times. It was the sort of minor annoyance that was most disturbing to Amanda's larger work. It was equally disturbing to find herself more anxious than ever to see him, to find out again if there were power in her caress, to wonder if indeed it was not she herself who was intrigued this time instead of vice versa.

Ethel Carey, visiting New York once again, contributed to Amanda's bad temper.

"I just want to be sure that man is all right for Vicky," Ethel said over the phone when Miss Bemel finally allowed the connection to be made.

Amanda, busy with all her other matters, was not in the least interested in Vicky's beaux. She resented being regarded by Lakeville as responsible for Vicky's progress in the city, so she was curt with Ethel.

"I'm sure Vicky can pick out her own boy-friends, my dear," she said. "She's a big girl now, Ethel."

"The *old* one, that Rockman Elroy, she says is just a friend," Ethel said confidentially. "I finally believed her on that. But the young one—the Saunders one—certainly knows his way around her apartment."

"Saunders? Did you say Saunders?" Amanda repeated blankly.

Ethel was pleased to finally capture her friend's attention.

"He's been there two or three times when I've been there," she went on eagerly. "I don't know how far things have gone but I can tell that Vicky's sort of crazy about him. So I thought I'd find out what sort of person he was. Is he married?"

The idea of Saunders seeing Vicky except under her command or in the necessary routine of their office, was beyond Amanda's comprehension. It was scarcely worth considering. But it was not agreeable to have Vicky's friends taking it seriously.

"I don't really know whether Saunders is married or not," she told Ethel. "I'm sure he's not the sort of person to be interested in Vicky, so she's foolish to get it into her head. Heavens, that girl deliberately makes trouble for herself, I'm afraid. I'm beginning to wonder how she can get on at all, if she stays so naïve."

"Oh, dear!" Ethel sighed. "I suppose it's going to be another one of those things. I hope she isn't having an affair with him! Rebound, you know."

Amanda was chilled at the mere idea.

"Vicky doesn't appeal to men that way, my dear," she said. "Do stop worrying about her. I'm sure Saunders isn't inter-

ested in her, so the best thing you can do is to straighten her
out about him. She's such an idiot about those things, really,
now."

Even to herself Amanda sounded unconvincing, which
made her even more annoyed with Ethel Carey, and with
Vicky Haven, too. These simple-minded females who thought
the important thing in life—even in such times as these—was
to make a suitable marriage, find a new beau, prove their fe-
maleness. It was not the first time Amanda had been contemptuous of her entire sex with their insistent devotion to
the trivia of life. She brushed off Ethel's hint of an invitation
to lunch or tea, and sailed into her refugee correspondence
with savage briskness.

"Mrs. Corpen thinks she has the nicest refugees of all the
women in her organization," Miss Bemel reported, reading
off the stack of mail with her new harlequin glasses, green-
rimmed, giving her thick, dark face a somewhat hippo effect.
"The children are dears, so she says, but now that their
mother has arrived she is having trouble. The mother is a very
charming young woman only she's been having affairs with all
the husbands in the neighborhood. Mrs. Corpen says here she
is rather suspicious of her own husband and she knows about
the gardener and the chauffeur for certain. So she wants the
committee to do something."

"What does she think I am—Dorothy Dix?" Amanda cried,
exasperated. "The woman's just a jealous old thing, that's all.
I can't be bothered."

Miss Bemel continued to look at Mrs. Corpen's plaintive
letter with a speculative expression, no doubt thinking that
the young refugee mother must be having a far better and
gayer time than Miss Bemel was having, and being protected
at it, too. A furtive seed of rebellion was sown in Miss Bemel's
soul that very moment, and she was not content to drop the
matter.

"After all, Mrs. Corpen is in a spot, Mrs. Evans," she said
doggedly. "She can't send the woman away, can she, without
people saying she's a Fascist or something. She's got to go on
and let her take her husband or every one will say she's unfair
to England."

"I'm sick of women being so trivial," Amanda said sharply.

Miss Bemel laid the letter reluctantly aside, half deciding to solve Mrs. Corpen's problem on her own hook. She wouldn't quite dare but it was a temptation, for these ruthless refugee women were a constant burn-up to the loveless Miss Bemel.

"Here's another request from that woman's magazine asking for an article on how you personally handle your little war charges," pursued Miss Bemel. "That makes the tenth such request."

Amanda's pretty brows met in a frown.

"I don't understand why every one is jumping on me right now," she said plaintively. "What's a person expected to do—outside of working on one novel and a dozen speeches and articles? Next they'll be at me for not doing my own cooking! You can send a memo to Mr. Evans that he can do anything he likes about this matter, I'm far too busy."

Miss Bemel bowed over her typewriter, happily. It was always a pleasure to send the ball back to Mr. Castor. While she typed, Amanda drummed on the desk, frowning. In half an hour the young man who was assisting her in writing her new book would arrive for two hours' conference. After that came a vital interview with an international banker. A round-table discussion with six foreign correspondents was booked for a six o'clock broadcast. It was a very full day for even Amanda, a day that required her to be on her toes even more than usual. It was unfair in every way that her mind should be unable to throw off the matter of Ken Saunders. It was outrageous that she should, in this busy hour, be speculating how she could manage to see him during the day in order to scold him for allowing girls like Vicky Haven to fall in love with him.

"It's all Ethel Carey's fault," Amanda muttered to herself. But as soon as she had delegated the blame for her own confusion on some one, she felt a little better, and was fairly civil to Miss Bemel for quite a while. This civility enabled Miss Bemel to snub the morning's callers with double vengeance, for it took only a kind word to give her her head. The entire household gathered, by Miss Bemel's high-handedness, that at last her mistress must be in a calmer mood, and proceeded accordingly.

3

Ethel Carey was able to assume a friendly detachment about Amanda's success while she remained in Lakeville, but no sooner did she set foot in New York than she was thrown into a stew of exasperation. Everything that used to stimulate her about New York now seemed to gently remind her that this was Amanda's own kingdom, and nobodies from Lakeville, no matter how well dressed, would be regarded as interlopers, here. To shop in Jay Thorpe's or Bergdorf's— once Ethel's greatest joy—was to yearn desperately for a never-to-be-won invitation to Amanda's elegant soirées. To buy a newspaper here was to see that even the war belonged to Amanda and her husband. Annoying above all was the sacred manner in which Amanda's staff protected her from contact with mere old friends. It was Ethel's firm resolve to batter down this reverence if she had to telephone the Evanses' house a dozen times a day.

"Good heavens, she's bound to have a few human traits like anybody else!" Ethel exclaimed to Vicky over their lunch at Chez Jean. "The way everybody acts about her you'd think she was above even going to the bathroom! Why shouldn't I drop in on her if I feel like it? Why is she any different than you or me except for being richer? When I asked her to lunch you would have thought I'd touched for actual money."

Vicky looked uneasily around the restaurant, fearful that by some chance Amanda might be in the next booth. She felt guilty that Amanda should have favored her with more personal attention than she granted to Ethel, especially after Ethel had confessed to first stirring up Amanda's interest in Vicky. It was true, too, that Vicky was quite as horrified as Miss Bemel herself at Ethel's debonair proposal to "drop in" on Amanda, and when Ethel was inspired to telephone Amanda to "come on down for a hen session" Vicky could have died of shame, just as if it was every one's duty to keep out of the royal path, cower in the background as much as possible lest the goddess be sullied by some ordinary human touch. It was disgusting to be a toady, Vicky thought, but that was what Amanda made of every one, except of course Ethel Carey.

"I know of course why she doesn't ask me to her parties," Ethel said, attacking her dainty squab with a savagery that might indicate the bird had pulled a knife on her first. "It's because I might say something about her stepmother's beauty shop back home, or about her father being a good-for-nothing. After all those little allusions she makes to her sheltered childhood, never exactly saying so, but just sort of implying that Daddy was a Southern colonel, and mummy was a lady, and the Keelers in England were all dukes. I'd let fly with something, you can be sure of that."

Vicky honestly couldn't see why Amanda would want to risk having Ethel Carey reveal her lowly past, or why Ethel thought of that privilege as her lawful right, but she dared not say so for Ethel would certainly accuse her of toadyism. It would be a fine thing to be like Ethel, to look every one from king to Garbo, straight in the eye and say, "Move over, there, I'm on this street, too."

"You know of course who paid for her tuition at Miss Doxey's," Ethel said and whipped out her lipstick for the purpose of readjusting her mouth after the scuffle with the squab. The manner in which she levelled this crimson trifle was so resolute, so ominous, that it foreboded a reloading of her guns, and Vicky resigned herself to further bombing of the Amanda legend.

"Wasn't it her father?" murmured Vicky.

Ethel twisted her newly-made lips to an unpretty pucker which involved a sardonic wrinkling of the nostrils, as well.

"Where would Howard Keeler get a thousand dollars?" she gently mocked. "Not that it's such a sum. Goodness knows Miss Doxey's is the cheapest school in the territory, and I wish to goodness I had followed Daddy's advice and gone East, but I was always so homesick. But at least I *could* have gone to Dobbs Ferry or Spence and none of the rest of you could."

"That's quite true, Ethel," Vicky was glad to agree on anything that might calm Ethel's ruffled vanity. "I know I could never have gone if my brother hadn't loaned me the money, and even he had to borrow it, so—"

"Howard Keeler's girl friend, the beautician, paid it, believe it or not!" Ethel whispered dramatically. "I know on account of Daddy's bank. All the time he was running around with her, Howard was devilled to death by Amanda. She didn't want to live over the store, naturally, even as a kid. And you know how snooty she was, not with you, maybe, because you were so much younger, but with all the rest of us. It burned her up to be just nobody that way. So she just raised perpetual Cain with her father. His girl-friend hated her and thought it was worth her while to send her away."

"Amanda didn't want her father to marry again, I know," Vicky cautiously admitted.

"Well, after all the woman did for his child, the poor man had to!" Ethel exclaimed. "She knew what she was doing, all right. She got Amanda out of the picture and then she marched her man straight down to City Hall and nailed him. It cost her all her savings, but at least she got him."

"Amanda couldn't stand her," Vicky recalled. "Remember how she used to hide when they came to school for visits?"

"That was because the second Mrs. Keeler said 'ain't'," said Ethel with some satisfaction. "So did the first, for that matter. They said 'ain't' from morning till night like mad. It killed Amanda."

The spectacle of the buxom blonde stepmother sending this naughty elision echoing over Miss Doxey's formal gardens, baying it from the chapel steps, writing it a hundred times a minute on the heavens, made Vicky break into hysterical laughter.

"What gets me," said Ethel, with vast bitterness, "is the way all this fuss about Amanda has made even Lakeville take her say-so about her family. They *know* Mrs. Keeler still has the beauty shop, they *know* Howard Keeler still has a dinky haberdashery store. They know Amanda was brought up over the store and went to Miss Doxey's lousy little school. But they think they must all be mistaken because it says in all the papers that Amanda had convent training abroad and her folks were 'land poor.' I can't tell them any different. 'Look,' they say, 'it says all this right here in black and white.' "

Vicky wanted to be sympathetic to Ethel, who after all had not been received by her old friend as warmly as she should have been, no doubt about that; however, in all fairness she did not see how Amanda could be blamed for not wishing to be reminded of the humble past Ethel was only too eager to recall. She saw Ethel picking up her salad fork with the air of marshalling new forces, and sought to sidetrack her.

"Lakeville is such a stupid town, anyway," she said. "I don't blame you for getting mad at it."

This was not a wise thought, it appeared, for Ethel held her fork poised in air a moment to give Vicky a level, haughty look.

"My dear Vicky, don't *you* go New York on me!" she exclaimed. "After all, if I wished to, I could live here, too. Personally I prefer Lakeville. My home, you must admit, is one of the prettier homes in the state. It's Frank Lloyd Wright! They don't come any better, you know. I travel. I hear all the best concerts in Cleveland. I go to hunting parties in Virginia. And Lakeville is *not* a slum."

"I know," Vicky nodded.

"We do quite as much for war relief as Amanda does, I assure you," Ethel went on proudly. "We have our adopted refugees just the same as anybody. We have our Bundles. You're not fair to Lakeville because you had an unfortunate experience there—"

Ethel could not forgive Vicky for appearing to recover from her "unfortunate experience" so easily. It seemed a personal affront to one who had devoted herself to ameliorating the "experience." The least Vicky could do was to need more sympathy.

"And now she has to write a sequel!" Ethel recalled her special grievance with access of fresh spleen. "Now she's announcing a trilogy, just because that's the one thing she's never tried! She *must* have everything!" With this thought she made an innocent-looking watercress salad the victim of her avenging fork. "Of course that will be a hit. How can it fail? Actually they tell me Julian has the reviews made up already and in type, all ready to spring on his readers. Almost before it's written, mind you, it's a hit."

Vicky squirmed under Ethel's rising voice. It was a pity, she thought, that any one who admired outspokenness and candor the way she did, was always so terrified when she actually heard it, and must always suffer this anguish that it was being overheard. It must be, she gloomily reflected, that she came of a long line of downstairs ancestors, governesses, chimney-sweeps, stablehands, housekeepers. Obviously Ethel, on the other hand, acquired her fine arrogance from forefathers who were squires, landed gentry. You wouldn't catch Ethel looking around apologetically at possible eavesdroppers, putting out an extra coin hastily when the waiter frowned at the tip, trying to smile at the policeman scolding you for crossing the street. Even while she admired Ethel's high-handedness, Vicky was plotting to distract Ethel from her subject by some wily feminine confidence.

"I was really glad to see Tom Turner and Eudora the other night," she said artlessly the moment she could break in. "I knew the minute that he stepped in the door it was all over, and I really in a way didn't want it to be. I just didn't want to find out I was that superficial. I was disgusted with myself for not having the guts to go on having a broken heart, honestly I was."

Ethel was only momentarily put off the trail.

"Honey, you're young yet. Besides, it would have been different, believe me, if it had been a real affair. I always thought, *of course*, that it was. I had no idea of anything else."

Again Vicky felt guilty. She should never have confided the sordid fact of her chastity to Ethel. Nowadays you didn't dare tell a thing like that to your own mother, or she'd have you analyzed to see what made you so backward. Certainly, it was proof of arrested development in any one over twenty, and Vicky blushed to think of it. Ever since she'd told Ethel, the latter kept pondering over the strange fact, acting a little resentful about it, as if her sympathy had been extracted under false circumstances. At least Vicky knew enough now to try in the future to give an impression of a proper background of adult love affairs.

"I think Amanda doesn't like the idea of your seeing that Saunders man," Ethel said. "Thinks he's too good for you, I suppose. I told her I thought you were falling for him in a big way."

"Oh, Ethel!" protested Vicky. "I told you not to tell!"

"What of it? I can read you like a book. You think every word he says is the most brilliant thing you ever heard. You sit there gawping at him like some little goon. Even Tom

Turner talked about it. Said he didn't see much in that fellow.
Of course that brought Eudora down on him in a big way.
'What's it to you, if she's got somebody else?' she said. 'All
right, go back to her. You got me in this condition, now you
want to leave me and go back to Vicky. All right, all right, I
can stand it.' You know. The usual."

Never, never would she tell Ethel another secret, Vicky
vowed, it was worse than telling all Lakeville and her own
family.

"Don't act so snooty, honey," Ethel laughed, in great
amusement over Vicky's suddenly stern countenance. "You
are crazy about Kenneth Saunders, and that's all there is to
it."

"Supposing I am," Vicky burst out in a flash of anger. "You
don't have to tell the world! Amanda, Eudora—everybody in
this restaurant!"

With this Vicky looked boldly around, fully expecting to
see the entire staff of her office as well as Amanda Evans
bending courteous ears to this broadcast of her weaknesses.
When she actually did catch a horrifying glimpse of a bushy
blond male head in the booth behind her, her heart failed her.
It would have to be Ken Saunders, of course. And he must
have heard every word.

"Oh, Ethel, how could you?" groaned Vicky. "Now I
daren't even leave this place, I'm so embarrassed!"

Ethel's teasing smile changed suddenly to a look of blank
consternation. She peered gingerly around the wall of the
booth, and had the grace to cover her eyes with a cry of remorse.

"Oh, Vicky, I didn't mean—oh, how awful! It just couldn't
happen!"

At this point Ken Saunders rose and stood beside their
table.

"If you think it isn't just as bad for me!" he said, very red-
faced. "Of course I missed the first part and that was probably the best. But now I suppose you're going to hate me for
hearing that last. It's not my fault." He had a sudden idea and
looked from Vicky's downcast face to Ethel's. "Say, you saw
me there and were doing it on purpose, weren't you. Of all
the dirty tricks! And I fell for it!"

"We just wondered how much more we had to feed you before you'd get on to it," Ethel laughed, with a triumphant look at Vicky. "You didn't actually think it was on the level, did you?"

Ken looked doubtfully at them.

"I do have a normal supply of vanity, I suppose," he said. "It never has seemed a screaming joke that any lady should be 'falling for me' as you put it. I won't forgive this for a long time."

Vicky managed to draw a breath of relief.

"It was the only way we could get you to talk to us," she said.

They walked back to the office together, and Ken reproached her again for playing such a shameful trick on his vanity. Vicky was so relieved at this happy misunderstanding that she did not think, until late that night, that perhaps Ken was only tactfully trying to save the situation. He didn't *want* her to be falling in love with him, and he refused to let it be said. He was deliberately pretending it had been a joke so he wouldn't have to cope with a love he didn't want. Having destroyed her sleep with this unpleasant thought Vicky got up and lit a cigarette.

"I wish there was some way to keep from seeing through things," she thought savagely. "I wish there was some pill like an aspirin that could stop your common sense. Common sense never did anybody any good."

VIII

EVEN AS astute a publisher as Mr. Peabody had difficulty keeping his magazine a nose ahead of the public taste in these confused days. A "far-seeing" editor can only live up to his name when the future looks pretty much like the past, and the public is reacting as it has before. Now surprises lay waiting in every corner, and *Peabody's* was obliged to be guided not by an editor and a board of advisors, but by a committee of circumstances. It could be reasonably assumed that so long as there were women there would be safety in Fashions, but this department, old as it was, had the most desperate of scrambles to keep up. In the early days of the war the Paris correspondents sent back helpful sketches of what milady should wear to a bombing, what combinations of color and fabric were advisable for the matron, the dowager, the debutante, for the arousing of patriotism, bravery, undying love, or respect. Forward-thinking readers at once sent in angry letters, cancelling subscriptions, berating Mr. Peabody personally for assuming that the fair sex were interested in anything in war times except target practice and tank driving. Compromising with these objections, the magazine showed pictures of the smarter *abris* in Paris, and made suggestions for uplifting military morale by a show of orchids, costume jewelry and lace stockings. This, too, was roundly criticized as too frivolous for the hour. Indignant women's organizations sent letters of protest at this insult to the gravity of the feminine mind; committees approached and even picketed Mr. Peabody's home, declaring that his publication was an affront to American womanhood, now massing its strength for war and not for fun. It was hard to steer a profitable course between these groups and the actual facts, which continued to prove soaring sales in furs, nail polish, lipsticks, perfumes, wrinkle creams, and other peace-time consolations. Mr. Peabody and his associates finally solved the problem by throwing their weight almost entirely on the Home and America, two blameless subjects for editorial reflection. If it was wrong to admit interest in bodily adornment, then

Peabody's would instruct its readers how to make their little homes into inexpensive castles of great beauty; if it was un-patriotic to praise Capri skies or to photograph Mediterranean resort activities, then *Peabody's* would loyally devote them-selves to the hidden charms of Route 21, the bouquet of western vintages, the decorative possibilities of gilding horse-chestnuts.

Peabody's "Home in America" department became an in-stant success. Past frivolities were forgiven. Other fashion magazines and women's periodicals tried vainly to keep up with this noble lead. The real estate advertising department took on fresh life, and a somewhat woolen note crept into the hitherto shimmering copy. Economy was a word fraught with imaginative nuances. Many of the Peabody League girls and their illustrious mothers were absolutely refusing to wear their jewels or sables for the duration, and mere working girls were easily detected now by their fur coats, having no alternative of well-cut cloth wraps as their richer sisters did.

Vicky Haven, with her real estate page, profited by the new homespun policy of the magazine and found commissions and bonuses added to her fifty dollar salary. Ken Saunders, in charge of the actual research into the American Home, was the gratified recipient of all manner of bribes, from electric ra-zors to vacuum cleaners. He moved from his hotel to an apartment which he was able to furnish almost completely with "gravy"—sofas, mattresses, gadgets pressed on him by earnest manufacturers in hopes of public mention of their product.

"Here is the charming home of the Bumbys in Plymouth, Ohio," the Home in America section would begin. "If the Bumbys can live this well in our great country on only $30 a week, surely you too can."

"Taxes are higher, wages are less, jobs are fewer," another issue would declare. "But see how pleasantly the Carmichaels live in a rented house in Bayonne, New Jersey, on the fruits of Father Carmichael's endowment insurance."

Photographs of the happy family would be included, menus of their simple but tasty fare, lists of books read by Sonny in the Knights of Columbus clubrooms, patterns for sweaters knitted by Mama after she had deftly put the wash to soak and the pot roast in the oven and was waiting for her Red Cross home work to arrive. It was a splendid means of building the American morale in time of fear and waiting, and it was even more profitable than the magazine's former luxury propaganda. True, the idea was not without its financial complications. Families on $30 a week had a tendency not to make the most of their native opportunities, so that in order to make them photographically appealing, *Peabody's* frequently had to send advance men to the locale to furnish and decorate a house themselves into which they popped the surprised and delighted typical Americans. Sonny and Sister had to be outfitted by the magazine, Daddy had to be calmed with a cash down payment, Junior had to be allowed to keep the bicycle which he, for photographic purposes, was supposed to have bought by saving money from lawn-mowing jobs. Sometimes, after the Peabody photographers and reporters had left the scene, the typical family found it impossible to take up their typical lives as they had lived them before being singled out for the honor of publicity. There were even suits brought against the magazine for loss of wives, husbands, jobs, when the publicity and unprecedented domestic conveniences were gone. However, *Peabody's* increased its legal staff and took care of these cases as they came up, insisting fairly enough that each was a typical American family only as long as that particular issue was on the stands, and it was now some one else's turn to be typical.

The "Home in America" research men made monthly expeditions into darkest America, under the instructions of Kenneth Saunders, departmental editor. The findings were even used, with proper payment, by the government and by educational and advertising agencies, and inasmuch as such august patrons could not be denied, there was oftentimes need for witchery. That is, if a typical home in Florida was promised for a certain issue, but Florida was under rains, then the camera staff and research writers must fly to southern California or even Alabama to capture the typical Florida home. These hazards were all in the game and very likely the less said about them, the better. Ken Saunders grew horrified as he saw his little brain-child blossom into this smiling Frankenstein, and begged to be let off. Mr. Peabody reasoned with him.

"It will rattle down to something worth while eventually," Mr. Peabody prophesied, solemnly doodling away with a red pencil on the outgoing mail his secretary had just brought him. "What worries you about it, Saunders?"

Ken stamped out a cigarette butt on the office floor, and lit another. He felt, under Peabody's kindly paternal gaze, like some little Lord Fauntleroy who had just found out there were rotters in the world. ("Peabody," he might as well have cried, "we chaps just don't *do* those things at Greyfriars!") It was a squirmy feeling and reminded Ken again that at thirty-three the carapace should be a little thicker.

"I think we should go overboard and make it complete fiction," he floundered, quite disgusted to find himself in the rôle of Decent Chap with Certain Standards. "Or else we ought to print the straight facts."

Mr. Peabody sighed and without looking up began carefully to erase his doodling. This involved moistening a large India rubber eraser and making a deal of a mess on his vest front and tie, a matter which brought his clean kerchief into play as dustmop.

"Print the straight facts!" he repeated with another deep sigh. "I've been in this business twenty-five years, Saunders, and one thing I can assure you from experience. A fact changes into a lie the instant it hits print. I can't explain it, but there it is. No, it isn't the time-lag. It's words. Printed words. You're lucky to siphon off ten per cent of the truth from any printed word. The most documented statements in the world. *World Almanac.* The printed word, speaking as an old editor, Saunders, is *ipso facto*, a lie."

Saunders laughed. Mr. Peabody, however, was not only serious but deeply moved by his own words. He was so accustomed to listening to other people, his employees, his trustees, and his family, and keeping his opinions pretty much to himself, that in his rare moments of garrulity he was as fascinated as any one else to hear what he had to say. The words he now heard himself saying were news to himself, and he could not keep a look of pleased surprise from his face as he spoke.

"It's the print that does it," Saunders suggested. "Maybe truth lies only in the fountain pen."

Mr. Peabody shook his head.

"It's not print, it's the word," he declared. "The spoken word, too. The lie forms as soon as the breath of thought hits air. You hear your own words and you say—'*That's* not what I mean.' And you go on and on, qualifying, groping, remembering a case that already cancels what you're saying."

Ken was impressed.

"That's absolutely true," he said thoughtfully.

Mr. Peabody's momentary elation vanished. He scratched his head, frowning.

"I doubt it," he said. "Every word is a lie, probably. However, I'm as good a word-eater as any one else. I daresay I have enough to nibble on the rest of the week. Anyway, don't take this job so hard, Saunders. If it makes you feel any better, call your department another name."

"The 'American Fantasy,' maybe," Ken said.

"All right, all right," Mr. Peabody shrugged his shoulders. "This is war-time. National fantasy is necessary."

Mr. Peabody stroked the long lock that covered his bald head very carefully. He saw by Ken's expression that the young man was impressed by his argument and this seemed to disturb him. For years he had thought of himself as an honest man in the midst of shrewd traders and well protected scoundrels. It shocked him now, listening to his counsel to Saunders, to find he was very likely as discreet a trader as the next one. He was buying the young man's confidence with a few seemingly honest confessions. That was just one more method of corruption. Finding cause to scold himself was one of Peabody's favorite occupations. It was a means, as he very well knew, of maintaining his high opinion of the rest of the human race. Whenever he stumbled on something evil in an associate, something that could not be denied or overlooked, he examined himself and usually was able to find some faint trace of a similar vice, so that he was in all honor forced to condone it in someone else. Since he knew himself to be a decent, kindly man, it followed that these suspect associates must also be. He found himself wavering between "All men are scoundrels" and "All men are saints," finally arriving at "All men are all men." He thought of himself as an almost too complacent optimist, but the proof of his cynicism was that although he was never shocked by the depths of human sin, he was constantly staggered by the slightest evidence of human civility. He was even astonished that the necessary evasiveness of the magazine should worry any one.

"This Saunders must be a remarkable fellow," he could not help thinking, and at once berated himself for being surprised at a simple show of candor from an employee. Good God, what had happened in his life that he was surprised when a servant didn't steal and when a child didn't lie? Mr. Peabody, who rarely wrestled with his soul, continued to stare at Ken Saunders, whose simple complaint about his department had brought about this psychic dredging. The latter was no dewy-eyed choir-boy, certainly, and he bore no evidence of having been tenderly nurtured in a cellophane vacuum.

"Where were you before you came here?" Peabody inquired.

"Travelling. Odd jobs in China, Mexico, and Chile. Before that I was on the *Express* here."

"Let's see," Mr. Peabody tried to recall the letter he associated with the name of Saunders. "Oh, yes, you were sent here by Julian Evans."

Ken whirled around.

"I beg pardon, I came here on my own, sir."

Mr. Peabody was certain now of his data.

"Evans asked me to take you on. That's right." He pushed a bell. "I'll get the letter right now, if you like."

Ken stared at him, knowing at once it was all too true.

"All right, but I didn't know he had done it," he said. "I have been boasting to my friends that I just walked in here and made a niche for myself. All on my own."

His face was scarlet with suppressed anger. He might have known that Amanda would find some way of deflating him. He couldn't have the tiny triumph of getting a job on his own. Amanda had to wangle it by waving her husband's name. Ken knew that if he had the support of just one drink he would throw up the job that minute. But there were debts, and above that, the old fears that kept you tied to what miserable security you had. He wished with all his heart that he really *was* drunk, and dared shout his hatred for his so-called sponsor, Julian Evans, and deny him the honor of being able

to get any man a job by the mere use of his magic name. After all, was the reckless honesty of the inebriated so much
worse than the sly caution of the sober-headed? The answer
depended, of course, on which you were.

"Miss Haven is here on Evans's account, too," reflected
Mr. Peabody. "I shouldn't be at all surprised if Julian thinks
he's the genius behind our Home campaign since he placed
you two people."

He chuckled silently, but since Julian Evans's opportunism
was no laughing matter to Ken, he scowled into space. He
thought of how arrogantly he had boasted to Amanda that
he could always get a job by just walking into a place, and he
thought of his secret, shamefaced pride that the thing was going so much better than he even wanted it to go. All the time
she knew exactly how he had gotten the chance. If she'd only
told him, flaunted in his face! Anything was better than this
secret use of her damned power, smiling silently at the little
starved buds of a masculine ego shooting up.

"He's one of the stockholders, so I suppose he might as
well think he guides our policy," Mr. Peabody went on,
highly amused. "Well, carry on, Saunders. It won't be for
long, anyway. We're staving off our bomb-proof home department as long as we can."

Saunders managed a smile and said good night. His head
was still burning with contempt for himself. He might as well
be a sleek-haired gigolo and give up working altogether.
Amanda was getting jobs for him through her illustrious husband and saying nothing about it as if it was the most natural
thing in the world. Especially for a man as incompetent as
Kenneth Saunders. Oh, certainly, some woman had to look
out for such a failure, or at least she must ask her husband to
do so.

"Damn her hide!" Ken muttered with clenched fists, as he
went down the corridor to his office. "Oh, damn, damn her
hide!"

There must be some way to put an end to loving some one
you hated. There must be some drug, some herb slipped
under your pillow, some incantation, that immediately
stopped another's power to destroy you. Another love, of
course, but that was not so easy. The gestures of love were

easy enough to simulate, but the counter-agent had to be as strong as the poison itself. Who could ever match the poison of loving Amanda? He hadn't really tried before to love any one else, Ken told himself, but now he must, if there was to be anything left of himself.

"Damn her, damn her," he was still softly muttering, so concentrated on this futile prayer that he passed Vicky Haven without even seeing her, a circumstance that brought a surprisingly similar remark to that lady's lips.

"What have I done that he doesn't speak?" she murmured, resentfully. "Now he knows I like him. Now he knows, so he's brushing me off. Oh, *damn* Ethel Carey!"

2

The manœuvering required for a meeting with Ken Saunders was a source of gnawing irritation to Amanda. She refused to go to his new apartment since certain ladies from her Bundles' committee lived in the building. She was afraid to telephone him at his office for fear some one might recognize her voice, so that arrangements were dependent on his telephoning her or upon telegraph communication. Once agreed on the time, she must take some circuitous route to Vicky's apartment, faking a profound interest in a honey and maple syrup shop across the street, so that her excuses would be ready if any one chanced to see her. There was, in addition to other difficulties, the possibility that he would not or could not come, after all these precautions had been taken. It was the first time in many years that Amanda had permitted herself the luxury of indiscretion, and she did not like it at all, but was perversely unable to put a stop to it.

Picking her way across the slushy street one day, her feet in toeless, heelless sandals disagreeably wet, and a raw February wind blowing her newly done hair into disarray, Amanda felt a burst of indignation that at this peak in her career she should still be victim of the same little torments that troubled any shopgirl. Here she was, supposedly in her right mind, making a fool of herself over an old lover, just because his contempt made her doggedly determined to win him in some other way, and because she could not give him up until she had revived completely his former infatuation. What did it matter, she demanded of herself in extreme exasperation, whether a merely average young man saw in her nothing but a merely average young woman? You would have thought, from this insistent sting to her vanity, that her whole career was planned in hope of pleasing Ken Saunders. It was exactly like the horrid little literary monthly (a journal surely no one ever saw, so why should it matter), that made her stay awake raging at night over its patronizing dismissal of her writing. That one miserable, utterly unimportant, minority voice became the one voice she must have sing her praise. So she must have Ken Saunders forced to admit she was important, something special.

As she was about to enter the building, she saw the Roumanian count who was due for dinner that very night, coming out of the adjoining house. Amanda walked hurriedly on, head bent, until the man was whisked off in a taxicab.

"Stupid!" she scolded herself, and for a minute had half a notion to give up the whole thing, take a cab and dash home where she belonged. "Why in heaven's name do I let myself in for this?"

But then Ken would mock at her for being so cowardly. Afraid she might make a social error, afraid she might lose her reputation or her husband by one little false move. She could not understand for the life of her just how Ken had won this terrible advantage over her, obliging her to apologize to him for her success, keeping her in this silly, footling state of trying to placate him, trying to make him yield completely once again. If he ever did—she would not admit this openly to herself but she knew it was true—she could be through with him, and go on about her life happily relieved of this maddening thorn. She was certainly not fool enough to be in love with him, she despised his arrogance toward money and power, the things that mattered, and what seemed to her his adolescent rebelliousness at Things as They Are. She disagreed with his point of view on everything, she always felt ruffled and humiliated when she left him, and why did she keep up this dangerous, unsatisfactory, but somehow compelling game?

"This is the last time, the very last," Amanda vowed, and let herself into her "studio."

Ken was already there, with a drink. Amanda braced herself. They always began by quarrelling.

"I see you have to dull the pain of our meetings with alcohol," she said, drawing off her gloves. She had beautiful hands, long and slender, but she no longer expected him to praise them. She saw by the mirror that the cold rain had really damaged her coiffure, and she bit her lip, annoyed that she had been foolish enough to have had it done especially for Ken, and doubly annoyed that it should be hanging now in damp blonde wisps against her cheek.

"Your hair looks charming," Ken perversely remarked. "You appeal to me most when something has gone wrong with your perfection."

Amanda looked around the apartment, frowning.

"Who do you suppose Vicky entertains?" she speculated with mild curiosity. "Every time I come here now I see new dishes, cocktail mixers, flowers."

Ken had something on his mind, she saw.

"You're worrying about her coming in, again," Amanda guessed.

"I would rather we were at my place," Ken admitted.

"I've told you a dozen times our arrangement. The place is mine—except week-ends—till five. Vicky wouldn't dream of breaking the rule unless I'm out of town."

Ken poured her a drink. Amanda shook her head, then saw Ken lift his eyebrow in that exasperating way he had.

"That cautious regard for the liver is such an endearing trait!" he remarked. "Imagine what might happen if you took a drink and said or did something quite unrehearsed!"

Amanda picked up the glass and drank it down. She rarely drank whiskey, certainly never except when it was socially necessary, but here was Ken, as usual, making a fault of a harmless virtue. The sharp tingling produced by the drink was unexpectedly agreeable. When she reached for another, Ken laughed, pleased with the collapse of this minor fortress. That was what he wanted of her, Amanda thought bitterly, he wanted her to lose everything she had ever gained, he wanted her to be poor and degraded and ugly, so that he could have the whip hand. The only way to really make him happy would be to forget a speech, break down and cry, fumble an article, make a public show of her feelings. Then he would step in and be the hero and protect her. Or would he then walk off and leave her?

"I have to be home to work with Emerson on my book," she said. This also was part of the game, pretending that to-day was to make an end of all intimacies, no time for that sort of thing today. Amanda was particularly savage in her tone this time, to show that whatever effect he thought the liquor might have on her, he was going to be badly fooled.

"Ralph Waldo?" Ken asked. She hated him when he joked. She was quite aware he thought she had no sense of humor, for he liked to make little jokes just to prove this lack. What of it? What was so wonderful about a sense of humor? You didn't see any of the big people going around giggling, did you?

"I'm very interested in this new book of yours, my dear," Ken said. "From what you tell me, you have managed to combine the characters from *The Three Sisters*, with the plot of the *Three Musketeers*. I like that little variation of *Anna Karenina* too. That will read very well. This man Emerson seems a very good little collaborator, indeed."

"Just because only one of your books was ever printed," Amanda said smiling at him steadily. "Darling, don't you think your jealousy of my work is just the least bit cheap?"

"It's all I can afford," Ken answered. He looked away from her, afraid she might be right. Maybe he was jealous, not just scornful of mediocrity too lavishly rewarded. Even now, he could not stop baiting her, as if this was the only relief from the endless torment of his chains.

"I wonder what field you will tackle next," he said. "After all you haven't been the first white woman in Lhasa—you haven't invented a new death-ray, you haven't designed a new type of bomber—you haven't done a mural, God forbid. Doesn't that burn you up to think of all those things you have left undone? Maybe things that even *you* can't do. Fancy!"

Amanda's smooth olive face did not change expression. She saw him pouring her another drink, challenging her to say she must conserve herself for her work. Stonily, she picked up the drink and drank it. She was seething with anger, but when words came, they were the plaintive apologetic phrases that he somehow managed to drag out of her.

"Of course I realize the millions of things I can't do, Ken, dear." Really, she could not understand herself with this man. "I've had more than my share of luck in some things. I do know you're much more brilliant than I am. You know I always said you had ten times the talent of a man like Andrew Callingham. You know I did, Ken."

"I know," said Ken. "That's because you want to minimize Callingham. He's the only person you can't even compete with yourself, so you're willing to let me have the bulge on him. Thanks."

Amanda stood up quickly, eyes flashing. She picked up her hat, and gloves. She would not stand it. It was fantastic she should go to all this trouble twice a week to be beaten down by this man who was nothing, literally nothing to her.

"Good-bye," Ken said calmly.

She went and put her arms around him.

"Ken, we mustn't go on doing these horrible things to each other!" she gasped, looking imploringly into his face. "As if we hated each other!"

"We do," Ken muttered. "I hate you for everything you've done and you hate me for all the things I haven't done. It's no go. Why do you come here? Why do you want me? You ruined everything once. What in God's name do you want of me now?"

Amanda looked at him, almost frightened. He was pale and beads of perspiration stood on his forehead. His clenched hands were trembling. It astonished her that any one should have such violent feelings, and she felt a surge of excitement to think she had caused it. She even felt her own body trembling, as if by contagion. It was a strange experience for her. Why, your body really can act quite separately from your mind or your intention, she thought, interested in this new discovery, quite as if she had suddenly found a talent for magic.

"But you love me, Ken!" she said. "You know you love me!"

"No," said Ken.

He stood up, trying to push her aside.

"You'd better go," he said.

"You can't treat me this way, Ken!" Now she was even saying things that surprised herself, pulling at his folded arms, trying to press her face to his. "You've no right to make me meet you this way and then send me away—you know you haven't! I can't stand it!"

Why, I'm actually crying, she thought, feeling a warm tear on her cheek.

"You're the only person, Ken, you know that—" There were even more of these unexpected words tumbling from her. "I am the only person you've ever loved, you know that, Ken, you've got to say it. I can't bear any one else to touch me—I—"

He forced himself free of her and stood gripping the table.

"You don't want me or any one else to touch you," he said bitterly. "You've only kept me on all this time because you got a kick out of seeing how much it meant to me. If you can keep me under your feet just by letting me make love to you once in a while, you're willing to endure it. That's all. And it's not good enough for me, my dear. Do you hear me? It's not damn good enough for me!"

Amanda again felt the curious wave of excitement at seeing this show of feeling. She wanted to fling herself in his arms, surrender desperately to love, somehow capture for herself this luxury of feeling. It was oddly agreeable to have these little sympathetic tremors going down her spine, and it was a new sensation not to be repelled by seeing a man lose control of himself, in fact to be curiously captivated by it, wanting more and more of it, wanting—yet not daring to be wanting—tears, surrender, collapse complete. In her elation Amanda grew flushed and breathless. She stood on tiptoe, head thrown back, eyes closed, waiting to be kissed, demanding to be kissed.

"No go," Ken said. "It's no go, old dear. I can't bear it any more. I can't, I tell you."

Amanda stepped back, drawing a long breath. Ken would not look at her. Awkwardly he picked up his hat, and walked toward the door, still not looking or else not daring to look at her.

"I'd better go first," he mumbled.

The door closed behind him.

Amanda stared incredulously at the door as if this object was somehow to blame, as if the door must be lying, it had not closed, it had not shut out this person she wanted. It could not be. If any one was to do any denying, surely it should have been she. She sat down, holding her hot temples tightly, wondering what had happened to her, how this tumult had unloosed itself in her brain, so that she couldn't remember what it was she had planned for the next hour. It was unthinkable that there was anything she wanted as much as she wanted Ken Saunders, that she could not have. It was wicked that she should be denied, denied in the very way she denied Julian. She began combing her hair very carefully, as if this external tidying up would serve some inner purpose as well. She thought if Ken had gone home to his apartment she would go there, too, wait in the hall till he got there. It didn't matter who saw her. Nothing mattered but getting him back, forcing him to give in to her. She would promise anything, she thought. If he wanted promises, he could have them. Why, she thought, I'm talking out loud. Which was true. She must be going crazy. She went on combing her hair, carefully. Her lipstick was still a smooth rich cherry line. He hadn't kissed her once. Not once. That ought to bring back her senses, she told herself. She put on her hat and then her gloves. She went out, closing the door quietly behind her, and in the street she did not allow herself to look westward to see if he might be still in sight, but climbed into a taxicab very calmly. It occurred to her that she might run into Julian when she got home, and he might notice that she was nervous.

"As if he would notice anything but himself!" Amanda answered herself sarcastically. She wondered what it would be like if she got home and found that Julian had dropped dead. Things like that happened in books. It was only fair that they should happen in real life, too. By the time she reached her door Amanda was fully composed, having occupied herself pleasantly with the definitely attractive possibilities of Julian being dead.

"It's not as if I made it a wish," she told herself, a little shocked at how far the idea had carried her. "It's just that I can't get the idea out of my head!"

IX

It was sheer luck that Amos Cheever's lady friend from London was unexpectedly granted entry into the United States, a matter which kept the rebellious man in a state of dazed calm while Julian Evans pulled his forces together. As Mr. Cheever had a wife in America, there were complications to be ironed out, all very much to the advantage of the foreign visitor inasmuch as she was much stronger, younger and newer than Mrs. Cheever. She had, furthermore, the whip hand of a surprise attack, and the good sense to know that it was now or never with Cheever. Mrs. Cheever, whose domestic nagging had made Cheever what he was, a fine foreign correspondent, was stunned into a divorce agreement and Cheever catapulted into a permanent arrangement with his Dody, something he had never really craved. Dody's firm intention was to stay in the States for good, and so Cheever found himself in the embarrassing position of backing down in his demands on Julian Evans, as gracefully as he dared, and hinting at a permanent New York post.

Evans's staff was well aware of Cheever's personal predicament and kept the master informed on its nice points, and presently Julian came to feel that it was his own brilliant strategy that had adjusted his difficulties with Cheever. As long as Cheever had London, there would be complications with Amanda, complications that would expose Julian to ridicule as an editor and as a tame husband. It worked out much better for him to shift his former Geneva man to London. The latter was happy to have the new post and for a while would not know just how his material was being plucked by Amanda. It was, perhaps, rather a pity that his work was greatly inferior to his predecessor's, so that Amanda's weekly articles were forced to suffer. But this circumstance was not really remarked on for some time, and meanwhile Amanda was distracted by other matters. This period was the beginning of the faintest possible cleavage between Julian's interests and his wife's career. Amanda was still obsessed by the Wagnerian spectacle of the world in flames and herself leading the warriors into Valhalla. Julian's shrewd eye was turning homeward more and more. Exploiting American problems for circulation purposes was a publishing gamble that did not interest Amanda since there was no star role in it for her, so Julian, with his new game all to himself, was all the more engrossed.

Julian had two New York papers, one for the Big Man, and one for the Little Man. The paper for the Big Man had been slowly in retreat since its unattractive stand during the Spanish War, but the paper for the Little Man had been snowballing to what seemed unlimited success. Julian himself was astonished one day to look over the figures of its meteoric rise, and at once decided to make a big change in the management of it, since its appointed editor had had the bad grace to take credit to himself for the achievement. Obviously Cheever was the man for this work. Cheever was not sure of himself on home ground and would therefore permit Julian's dictation, and besides, Cheever was in a spot. It was all most fortunate, or as Julian believed, most clever of himself to have manipulated Destiny in this fashion.

The Little Man now became Julian's obsession. You would have thought the Little Man was a wonderful new boy doll to hear Julian's fond talk of him. No toy steamboat, no pet pony, no first-born child, even, was ever as cherished by Julian as was his dear entrancing Little Man, a wistful little chap about two feet high looking appealingly like Paul Dombey, perhaps, a little on the tubercular side, very underprivileged, very underhoused, very dependent on Big Man Julian for spiritual guidance. The Little Man's newspaper cost two cents more than the Big Man's newspaper, but this was because there was so many of him, and it was true that the reporters on the Little Man's paper received higher wages than the Big Man's reporters. For a slightly less wage Amos Cheever was glad to help Julian lead the Little Man out of darkness and to pamper him with platitudes, vague fight talk, and somewhat defeatist exhortations to be proud of being a Little Man or a Little Man's wife or a Little Man's family.

There was one trouble Julian found in his *Little American.* That was the irritating habit some little men had of not admitting they were little men, of acting and even proclaiming that they were big men, on their way up out of Julian's jurisdiction. This did not happen often, but it made Julian's blood boil to have a taxi driver speak with lofty complacency of his independent business and his patronizing pity for the underdog, the little fellow.

"You're a little fellow, yourself!" Julian wanted to shout angrily, because there's no reasoning with a man who doesn't know he's an underprivileged, underhoused, underdog, but then Julian would think the taxi driver might look over his five-foot-six of fare and make some insulting comeback. So he confined his wisdom to the printed page and glowed over his clippings as tenderly as if they were a set of Dolly Dimple paper dolls.

These setbacks were minor, however, and *Little American* was lauded by the President himself for its fair play and four-square talk, and many intellectual weeklies began referring to Julian as an intellectual equal because of his pithy interviews with the Little People. The Little People were not, of course, the folks that poured down the mountain in pointed shoes at stroke of midnight, but Julian's conception of them was quite as extravagant.

Julian had, in fact, fallen in love with the superstition that any non-technical worker or any uneducated human being was automatically endowed with a rare and incontrovertible well of wisdom. Every day he ran interviews with truck drivers, cops, waiters, dock hands, busboys, janitors, and street cleaners, and their explanations of the government problems was God's own word, unless they spoiled the effect by mentioning a book or some source of documentation. Julian did not like it at all if it developed that the simple sage had been corrupted by an average education, or if he betrayed a normal interest in reading. The subjects of his research must be one-syllable little men, not articulate literates, as if lying, confusion, bigotry and corruption never came in one syllables, and in book-learning alone was there sin and woe. This reverence for ignorance was apparently so deep-seated in the public, as vouched for by *Little American* circulation, that it seems astonishing citizens continued to support colleges and schools. It would have been logical to assume that the serious parents would raise their children to be oracles of ignorance, uncorrupted by the nuances of language, able to couch their primitive impressions in as simple a form as "Ug."

Mr. Cheever, uncertainly happy with his new Dody, tried to forget the more dignified privileges of a London correspondent in war-time, in delving with Julian into the world of Little People. Being more of an adventurer than Julian, he was able, to his own surprise, to work up considerable enthusiasm for the new world. The collaboration brought Julian and Cheever closer together than they had ever been, for in one way it was a conspiracy against Amanda. It was the first step Julian had taken since his marriage without Amanda's profit in view. Each day that found Amanda still preoccupied with her own chosen fields gave Julian a sense of guilty elation. The Little Man was all his. Cheever had a little corner of him, maybe, but in name only. It was as exciting as a secret, which, in some ways it was, for Amanda did not quite realize the quiet rocketing to success of Julian's venture. While it was not theatrical or international enough to appeal to her, she would very likely have found some means to spoil Julian's pleasure. As it was, he spent less and less time at home, leaving Castor to fuss with the home correpondence, while the master hurried downtown, sometimes even by subway, to play with his new darling.

There was a change in Julian, too, observed even by his most indifferent associates. He now said good morning occasionally to the elevator-man, and when he upbraided a waiter for bad service he spoke to the headwaiter, too, so that there was no discrimination.

"The test of a publishing genius, Cheever," he said to his newly reconciled friend, "is the ability to keep ahead of the times, to change your whole set of standards, overnight, if needs be."

As he seemed pleased with this thought, it could only be deduced that Mr. Evans had passed his own test satisfactorily.

2

Julian had a secret from Amanda. He felt very guilty about this secret, but on the other hand it enabled him to shrug off Amanda's little thrusts which had formerly kept him in a constant state of hopeless wrath. Amanda had noticed with relief that he was not so inquisitive about her every minute spent away from the house, nor did he insist on his usual long lectures on the conduct of her future. It must be his increasing devotion to his *Little American*, she thought, and was grateful.

Miss Bemel finally got on to the secret quite by accident, if you could call Miss Bemel's methods ever accidental. Devoted as she was to Amanda's interests, there were many times when she was jealous of Mr. Castor's opportunities. He heard more gossip around the house, for one thing, and the servants were far too distrustful of Miss Bemel to share their little tidbits. In the three years she had worked for Amanda, she had taken great care not to let the staff think she was on their level; no, she was an official in the establishment, not a servant. In spite of her satisfaction in her position, it irked her that she was denied the duty of hiring and firing chauffeurs, cooks, and other dictatorial privileges enjoyed by little Mr. Castor for no reason except that he had done it for years before Amanda was on the scene. No one liked him, downstairs, but at least they were used to him and he was quiet.

Yes, there were times when Miss Bemel regretted the pedestal on which she had planted herself, some feet below her mistress's pedestal. Times when she went down to the kitchen with some instructions from Amanda and found the chef, the maids, chauffeur, and sometimes even Castor, laughing together over something, and then shutting up as soon as she entered. And then there were the times she asked for a cup of tea, knowing the others were having it around the kitchen stove in friendly fashion, and the butler would say, "You want it sent upstairs, of course, Miss Bemel." If she wanted it upstairs it would have been simple enough to make it in her samovar, and drink it by herself. But even a Bemel had her moments of yearning for conviviality, exchanging a complaint or two, maybe, letting out a little steam. No one was going to be foolish enough to make complaints around Miss Bemel, however, for she was certain to carry them straight to Amanda. It was a matter of chagrin to the staff when the cat got out of the bag, the day Miss Bemel came down to discuss the evening's dinner with the chef's wife. The chef was Swiss and pretended not to understand, though Miss Bemel had reason to believe this was only to protect himself from the lectures she liked to administer, since he looked equally blank when she tried them in French or German. Mrs. Pons was her husband's assistant and interpreter, her interpreting consisting of levelling a cool eye at Miss Bemel during her speech and keeping silent until the very end when she summed it up in one pithy word for her husband, the word invariably accompanied by a disdainful shrug. Today Miss Bemel was a tiny bit lonesome; she would have liked to unbend just a little, to make a joking offer of opening some sherry for the kitchen, because she had scolded one day about their tippling. So she stood at the pantry doorway, slowly sipping a glass of water, wondering what the chauffeur had been telling them that talk must stop while she was there.

"When you come back from taking Mr. Evans to the station, will you drive me up to the Bronx to see my sister?" Miss Bemel asked of the chauffeur, cocking her head coyly at him, to show her request was woman to man rather than Private Secretary to Menial.

The chauffeur, a young Irishman, looked at her sulkily, and then bit into a thick sandwich he held in one gloved hand.

"Goodness, didn't you have any lunch?" Miss Bemel laughed, pointing to his sandwich, a bit of joviality that brought only scowls to the others' faces.

As the chauffeur, Robert, continued to be silent, and Miss Bemel's face was slowly reddening, a sign of either embarrassment or future revenge, Mrs. Pons took it on herself to answer, with a minimum of grace.

"How can Robert drive to Hudson and back in time to take you uptown?"

"That's right," said Robert.

"Oh, I didn't know Mr. Evans was driving to Hudson," Miss Bemel murmured, confused for a moment, since she hated to have the staff think she was not informed on every little movement of the family. She recovered her poise by advising Mrs. Pons to change the dining-table center-piece, and chided her, smilingly, not to let Robert have any beer before his long drive, and so was able to make a respectable exit. She heard a muffled titter as she left, but refused to be disconcerted.

Hudson, she thought! Why was Mr. Evans going to Hudson when he had indicated, through Mr. Castor, that he was taking the train to Albany on business? And then the answer came to her. Far Off Hills, the first Mrs. Evans's estate, was somewhere around the town of Hudson, this side of Albany. Neither Mrs. Margaret Evans nor her two grown children were on friendly terms with Julian since he married Amanda. It was understood that their affairs were conducted completely through their lawyer, and that the two children harbored undying resentment toward their father. Miss Bemel pondered this matter on the way upstairs, and seeing Castor in the hallway decided to take the bull by the horns.

"Since when has he been visiting Number One?" she inquired, eyebrows beetling as if this ugly look would terrify the little man into a proper state of subordination. Mr. Castor, having for once the inside track, was not to be conquered so easily, but threw back his little head and pursed up his lips proudly.

"Since when has our department been any concern of yours?" he nipped back, and could not resist adding as he took his important little tin letter file into the door of his own little cubbyhole, keeping it well behind his back as if the Bemel eye could bore through any metal. "Must Mr. Evans have written permission from you to visit his own family? Perhaps you want him to report to you when he gets back."

Amanda's bell ringing prevented Miss Bemel from putting the little man in his place, which she could not have done very well being so astonished at this news. Why should Julian Evans be visiting his first wife, and what if there should be a reconciliation? Some mischief must be going on or it would not be kept secret.

"Does Mr. Evans ever see his family?" Miss Bemel could not help but ask of Amanda when she got back to the study. She wanted to see if Amanda knew of this infidelity, but it was perfectly plain that Amanda was only bored by such a question.

"What a question, Bemel!" Amanda exclaimed. "You know how nervous that whole outfit makes him! Certainly not."

So Miss Bemel knew that her apprehensions were right. If Amanda was in the dark, and the whole household knew it, then there was mischief. Once on the scent Miss Bemel did not spare herself. There were many things you could find out by pretending you knew them already, so she was able to extract a little bit here and a little there, from the parlor maid, the garage, and a fortunate bit of eavesdropping on Mr. Castor's telephone extension. Mr. Julian Evans was going up to Hudson at least once a week. Stores were calling up to ask if Mr. Evans had not made a slip in ordering certain purchases sent to his old address, Far Off Hills. (So he was sending gifts up there!) The mail contained two notes from Hudson, showing that the family had taken up writing to its former head once again. Miss Bemel could only figure out that something was going on which she could not yet get at. Perhaps Amanda's increasing bursts of temper were evidence of new friction, and Mr. Evans was returning to his peaceful, if drabber former ways. Miss Bemel began to worry about the security of her own position if the present marriage should break up. She made little efforts to put Amanda on guard.

"Is Mr. Evans going up to Albany again this week?" she inquired craftily, but Amanda merely exclaimed, "I'm sure I don't know, Bemel, but it's too late to cancel that dinner party, anyway."

So Amanda refused to be warned, and Miss Bemel continued to puzzle, until a maid from the Far Off Hills told Miss Bemel's cousin, who was a dressmaker in Troy, that poor Julian Evans had taken to visiting his ex-wife in order to pour out his troubles to her. He was a lonely man these days, he was reported to have said, and while he had not exactly said that Amanda did not understand him, his behavior indicated just that. It was his custom for the past three or four weeks to drop in on his first wife after conferences in the State Capitol, and recite in a loud voice the entire business while Mrs. Margaret Evans, stout little gray-haired woman of fifty, sat and nodded over her knitting, and agreed with him that he was indeed a wonder. The children, aged twenty and twenty-four, were not completely won over but were beginning to be tolerant of their father. Having delivered himself of his troubles the great man then looked over his kennels, talked to the various refugees, reformed convicts and war orphans that his preaching had caused Mrs. Evans to take on, and then leaped in his car and rode back to town, a freer, happier man. If Mrs. Evans seemed troubled about these visits, finding this demand on her sympathy a painful reminder of other days, it was too bad, but then some one is bound to suffer for the good of others, and Mrs. Evans had already proved that she could suffer nicely.

If Miss Bemel could not fathom the wherefore of this new routine of Mr. Evans, she could at least act as if she knew. "If anything comes up tonight about the White House appointment, can we reach Mr. Evans at Far Off Hills?" she would ask Castor calmly over the phone, knowing this would take the wind out of his sails, since Castor enjoyed his secrets as much as she did prying into them.

3

One thing Amanda would not permit in Vicky, was any expression of gratitude. Vicky knew the studio which she shared with Amanda was a hideaway from publicity so she must not mention Amanda's sponsoring it, in public. But that was no reason it should be brushed curtly aside when the two of them were alone. Besides Vicky could perfectly well afford her own place now, and she was wondering how to break this to Amanda. If Amanda would not be thanked for the place, then it was even harder to tell her that her generosity was no longer necessary. In her own home Amanda's talk was on such a lofty political plane, that there was little chance of breaking into the mood with "Speaking of housing, Amanda, I appreciate your letting me use your studio, but if you don't mind I'd like to have my own place now, and not have to feel gratitude to you. For that matter, I'd like to be able to run in and out all day without being afraid of interrupting one of your creative moods there, and I'd like to be able to break things, and be a hostess, not a permanent guest. I do appreciate it, but I want my freedom now."

Having been dismissed whenever she started to say something along these lines, Vicky had finally settled the matter by leasing an apartment on West Thirteenth Street, and with the lease in her pocket was prepared to make short work of her news. "I've moved," she would say, and Amanda might even be relieved to know her responsibility was over.

The evening seemed propitious for introducing a personal note, for the guests were merely a minor Eastern college president, Mr. Cheever and his Dody, and Mr. Peabody, as near a family group as the Evans dining-room ever achieved. Ken Saunders was not present, but he had not been present at the office, either, recently, so Vicky concluded he must be away on one of his routine research trips. She was sorry because she had wanted to ask his advice about this problem of gracefully returning a present such as an apartment. When he was around she did not feel so much like an Extra Woman in a city full of extra women. Mr. Peabody would do, of course, but Mr. Peabody was still Boss, and no matter how friendly your relations with him were, Boss was still Boss. Vicky bided her time during the dinner for an opportune moment to catch Amanda's eye and ear. Meantime her head swivelled back and forth from the college president to Editor Cheever and Editor Peabody as they sounded forth their worthier thoughts for Amanda's approval. Even the lightest conversations at Amanda's seemed to Vicky like baccalaureate speeches, and she had learned to keep a bright glazed look while pursuing her own trivial thoughts. Sometimes, of course, as tonight, people kept popping their faces in front of yours, and demanding, "Don't you agree, Miss Haven?" and then you were obliged to tie up your wandering fancies and attend to other people's facts.

The college president was the loudest tonight, crowding Amos Cheever and even Amanda into silent corners with his resonant chapel voice, and his "Ah-ah-aha—ah—er-e-er—" hemming by which he kept his place in the conversation when other words failed him. He was a vigorous, ruddy, massive man with iron-gray hair, an iron-gray moustache, and hard, black eyes that must have seriously dented all the objects at which they aimed. The outside world was protected from these dangerous rays by unrimmed bifocal glasses, doubtless crash-proof, since he levelled his glance straight at people as if he neither knew nor cared that it was loaded. Vicky kept leaning as far away from him as she could when he singled her out for target, though when his eyes missed you his booming voice could always find you.

"I'm theoretically anti-Nazi, of course," he roared, "but still I can't help feeling grateful to the régime. Look at the faculty board I got together last year! Carler of Vienna, Chasen of Munich, Lieber of the Sorbonne, Steinbrock of Berlin! Our little college could never afford such men in a hundred years! But Hitler shakes the tree and I get the plums! So I say Heil Hitler! He's done more for our college in ten years than all the trustees and alumni have been able to do in a hundred years!"

Julian Evans did not like such opportunistic talk, especially if it was true. He believed that inner chicanery should be balanced if not completely excused by lofty utterances from the tongue. A little reproof was in order.

"You actually feel, Doctor Swick, that it's civilized procedure to ravish three fourths of the world for the enrichment of one nation? You say every time Hitler has a pogrom and five thousand people are killed or expelled from their homes, we win one first-rate teacher?"

"We're the Byzantium of the future," boomed Doctor Swick. "The Byzantium of the twentieth and twenty-first century. You agree, Miss Haven?"

"I—" answered Vicky.

"What kind of a teacher could I get for the salary I pay Chasen?" Doctor Swick pounded on the table, making a surf in his wine glass, which Vicky watched apprehensively for fear it would add to the other dangers of his proximity. "I have to run my college on very little money. I want the best. I'm in the market for bargains. What do you say, Miss Haven?"

"I—" said Vicky, and was saved by a small baptism of wine from Doctor Swick's glass.

"That's nothing," apologized the doctor, bruskly. "Just put salt on it. What do you say, Miss Keeler, or rather Mrs. Evans?"

Amanda pensively drew her hand over her shining golden locks and leaned her chin on her hand. As this gesture brought the curve of her slim breasts into focus, Doctor Swick bent forward and waited with renewed voracity for her answer. Cheever and lady exchanged a frown, Mr. Evans coughed, and Vicky gazed raptly at her lap, which was now mottled with a mixture of claret and salt which the doctor had impulsively dumped there.

"Naturally Amanda feels as I do," Julian said in a strident tone of rebuke. "What you're saying is that American colleges can make money on Hitler's triumphs. Really, Doctor Swick!"

Amanda now lifted her dark, gold-framed face from her wrist, thus releasing Doctor Swick from an ocular spell, and permitted her pansy blue eyes to travel over the bowl of floating gardenias to her husband.

" 'Really, Doctor Swick!' " she mocked Julian with a musical laugh. "Really, Mr. Evans, you might say! Haven't your newspapers made a lot of money out of the war, Julian? Millions, of course—not just a few hundred dollars saved the way Doctor Swick means!"

Julian looked at his wife, jaw drooping, wounded surprise radiating from every fiber of his being.

"Exactly, exactly!" shouted Doctor Swick. "And exactly the way you have, too, Miss Keeler, I'm sure you were about to say."

As Amanda had had no intention of saying or thinking any such thing, she drew up rather frostily. Julian was relieved at this qualification from the doctor and relaxed, very slightly. Mr. Peabody dropped a fork and hid under the table gratefully for an alarmingly long time trying to recapture it, knocking heads with the butler who was down there for the same purpose. Mr. Cheever, at a nudge from his Dody, a silent square-jawed Scotch girl, leapt into the service of his master. His heart was not in it wholly, for as long as the master had known Cheever, he had known of Cheever's chronic indigestion, but made no concessions to this disability when he invited him to dinner, so that Cheever must either eat oysters Rockefeller and Roquefort salad dressing or starve. Tonight he had chosen to starve, permitting himself only a nibble of Swedish health bread, and he longed to end the dinner so that he might go to a Childs restaurant and stuff himself on his approved diet. He dabbed his napkin daintily over his handsome brown beard, which he doubtless wore to conceal not a weak mouth but a weak stomach, for he'd had both the indigestion and beard the same length of time.

"Whatever profit any of us here make out of the war is accidental," he said soothingly. "If Amanda Keeler's public work makes her a profit, it also profits the right cause. That

goes for the Evans's newspapers, and for Mr. Peabody's magazine, I'm sure. After all, Doctor Swick couldn't accuse us of
warmongering. That I'm sure."

Doctor Swick machine-gunned the circle with his glittering
eyes, his final ocular bullet piercing Vicky's quivering form.

"Ha! I don't know what your All-Out for Britain is if it isn't
warmongering! And if there was prestige as well as more
money in isolationism, I'll bet you'd all be on that side." He
roared at this friendly joke and was quite undaunted by the
silent response. "Come on now, I speak frankly, why can't we
all do the same? We're among friends," he added, though
never was this statement less supported. He took this silence
as encouragement to continue, and Vicky found herself
wishing guiltily for Ken since he would have revelled in this
catastrophic attack on the castle, and in the doctor's innocent
belief that he was making a splendid impression.

"No, no, I'm not moron public," chuckled Doctor Swick,
nudging Vicky quite brutally in the ribs, and appalling host
and Cheever by this insult to their Little Man. "I see the
whole picture. You war ladies, for instance, who lunch with
Ciano and Goering and Pétain, Daladier—all the rest, dance
with them, have a good time with them. You write or talk
about them with an anti-fascist flavor, but you played up
enough to them personally so that you could make a graceful
pirouette backwards if the ball goes their way. They know it,
too. They don't care about your little pieces, because they
know it's all a matter of who's in fashion. You ladies weren't
radical until it was chic, ha, ha—isn't that right, Cheever?"

"I—" choked Cheever, who unfortunately believed exactly
as Doctor Swick did on this one point, but disliked the man,
and moreover was duty-bound to stand by the two Evanses.

"Right, eh, Miss Haven?" nudged the doctor, and Vicky
murmured, "Oh, I—I mean—"

"Vicky's not doing anything about the war, Doctor Swick,
so she can't very well speak for or against you," Amanda said
coolly, and rose. "Shall we go?"

In the drawing-room with coffee and brandy, Doctor Swick
was rather thoughtful, though he still had no sensation of
walking around with a cut throat, something Cheever could
have warned him about if they were better friends. Any favors

Doctor Swick had hoped to wangle from the Evans syndicate were as good as scrapped already, but he would never know why.

"Well, Vicky," Amanda said, turning her back deliberately to Doctor Swick, who saw in the gesture merely an invitation to admire the satiny olive texture of her skin, "what's new in your life?"

"I'm moving," Vicky blurted out, knowing this was her only chance to break the news. "I want to thank you for the studio, of course, I do thank you for being so good to me, but now there's no reason why you should, so I've taken another place—"

Amanda's face glowed a dull red, and to Vicky's surprise she looked as if she had received an uncalled-for slap in the face.

"What? You're moving?" cried Amanda, unheeding the expressions of mild wonder about her. "You know perfectly well I got that place expressly for you, and you daren't walk out of it like that."

"I thought it might be more convenient for you—for me— I mean—" Vicky was so disturbed by Amanda's strange indignation that she found her throat choking up ominously.

"It's absolutely ridiculous for you to move any place else," Amanda rushed on warmly. "The place is there, why should you leave it? You can't just take a person's apartment when you find it convenient and then jump out when it suits you, without even consulting—without—it's perfectly nasty of you! Vicky, I'm disappointed in you!"

Not knowing what she had done that was so horrible Vicky was unable to know how to justify herself. She sat twisting her hands, opening her mouth to protest, then closing it helplessly.

"Is it so necessary to give up your present place, Victoria?" Julian intervened in his judicial manner. "Let's talk this over first. After all, you are more or less our charge, you know, and it may be the wiser thing to stay just where you are."

"I won't have it!" cried Amanda, seizing Vicky's wrist. "You're just doing this to hurt me, I know. Ken Saunders put you up to it. Didn't he? Didn't he, now?"

Vicky was startled by the violence of Amanda's manner, her flashing eyes and her far too firm grip on her wrist, and could think of no answer to excuse her little declaration of independence. Doctor Swick and Mr. Peabody were busily pretending to look over Julian's latest etchings in a big folder in the corner of the room, while Mr. Cheever and Dody, being on the same davenport with Vicky, were forced to tone down their expressions of utter amazement to polite interest.

"Why should any one put her up to it, as you say, Amanda?" Julian inquired sharply. "If Vicky wants to move, she doesn't need putting up to it. I don't understand you, Amanda—I—are you sure you're feeling all right, my dear?"

Amanda rose precipitately and flung her cigarette into the fireplace.

"All right, then, move. I don't give a damn, you little stupid! But why do you have to make a public scene about it?" And bursting into tears which she refused to brush aside, Amanda rushed out of the room, leaving a silence that must have reverberated around the block. Vicky had been afraid when Amanda first attacked her that she would burst into tears herself, but Amanda's unexpected breakdown steadied her. She felt calm in a numb sort of way, as if there was something final in this scene and something she would never understand. Amanda must hate her, she thought, yet she could think of no reason for this, or why, hating her, Amanda felt duty bound to invite her there. There was nothing to do but to get out of the house as quickly as possible, and when she started to go, murmuring something to the Cheevers, Julian made no effort to stop her but sat gripping a glass of ice water without moving, staring straight ahead.

"I'll drop you, Vicky," Mr. Peabody said. "I'm going on down to the station, anyway, for my train."

Vicky heard Julian's voice behind her as she got into her wrap.

"Sorry Amanda's in such a nervous state tonight. This war is affecting all of us, you know—don't know when it will strike here—and Amanda has put her whole heart into it. Then she's working very hard on her new book—ah, must you go too, Amos? Doctor Swick has to catch his train, I realize that. . . ."

And the house was emptied as if Amanda's outburst had been a raid alarm, guests tumbling over each other to get into the safety of a taxi, leaving Julian staring at an Audubon painting of the booby gannet, his latest purchase, pinned up on the wall. After a while he tiptoed back to Amanda's quarters and rapped gently on the door. There was no answer and he went thoughtfully back to the drawing-room. His eye fell on a cigar, half smoked, smoldering in the saucer by Doctor Swick's chair. For some reason this seemed the last straw. "Damned pedants!" he growled through clenched teeth. "Ought to be in jail, every one of them!" For the whole unpleasantness was, of course, the fault of no one but Doctor Swick.

4

Mr. Peabody and Vicky rode down Park Avenue in stunned silence. Maybe Mr. Peabody thought she was in some way guilty, Vicky reflected uneasily, for no one would believe Amanda's outburst was completely uncalled for. It was a wild night with the wind whipping raindrops across the taxicab windows and rattling ash-barrels along the areaways till it sounded like a bombardment. A fine night for Cinderella to be sent home from the ball in rags and disgrace.

"I suppose when people give you something they feel outraged that you shouldn't keep it forever," she ventured, presently. "I don't see what difference it makes to Amanda whether I stay in her studio or not."

"Evidently it does make a difference," said Mr. Peabody, guardedly. "Frightful night, isn't it?"

"I couldn't stay after what she said tonight, anyway. You can see that, Mr. Peabody, can't you?" Vicky went on. "I couldn't keep the place another minute."

Mr. Peabody rubbed a clearing on the windowpane to see the street signs before answering.

"When I was a boy in New England I used to run to my grandfather who was blind and deaf, always sitting by the stove in a shawl, and I'd tell him everything that was going on. 'Grandpa, it's raining,' I'd shout at him, and I remember he'd always shout back, 'Let 'er rain! We're in the dry!' "

Vicky managed a weak laugh, but refused to be distracted from her problem.

"Why should she call me a little stupid?" she murmured, puzzled and hurt. "Why should she say Ken Saunders put me up to it?"

Mr. Peabody peered out the window again.

"Would you like to dash in here for a nightcap? There's a canopy."

"No," said Vicky. "Why should he put me up to anything?"

Mr. Peabody gave up his efforts to change the subject reluctantly.

"Maybe she doesn't like Saunders. Or maybe she does. Or maybe Saunders doesn't like her any more. He seemed pretty upset about finding out she got him his job. That's why he resigned."

Vicky was startled at these tidings.

"So he's gone for good! Oh, dear!"

Mr. Peabody sighed.

"It was pretty sudden." He pondered a moment. "I wonder where he went. He threw up the job the day after I told him Amanda had recommended him. Haven't you heard from him?"

"No," said Vicky in a low voice, for it would be a calamity to lose Ken. Thinking of the possibility of never hearing from him again, her heart slid to her boots. It was a possibility, too, for she was certain she liked him better than he did her. She had tried not to fall in love again, but here she was, liking him much too much, thinking about him all day, dreaming about him at night, trying to meet him in the office hallways, running like mad to make the elevator he was strolling towards, in short, making a fool of herself all over again. So now he had vanished. And while she was wondering about everything else, why had he been so upset at learning it was Amanda who had sponsored his job? And did Amanda know he had quit?

"Why should Amanda care whether he put me up to this or not?" Vicky's thoughts went around in a circle, and she kept appealing to Mr. Peabody as if this motherly soul must know everything. "After all he's nothing in her life."

"They're old friends," Mr. Peabody said absently. "I used to see them around together before her marriage."

For some reason this surprised Vicky enormously. It was odd Ken never had mentioned knowing Amanda before, all the time he had asked questions about the old Amanda whom Vicky knew. You would have thought he might have contributed a few anecdotes himself.

"Doctor Swick was a curious specimen, wasn't he?" Mr. Peabody said cheerfully. "No wonder he's not able to wangle money for his college. Wonder what he wanted of Julian."

Mr. Peabody was determined to be of no help; it was almost as if he knew exactly how Vicky had offended Amanda and was too much of a gentleman to tell, if she was so stupid as not to guess of her own accord. Vicky was irritated with his attitude and was glad when he left her, though she'd forgotten her keys and had to wake up the janitor to get in the house, scampering in the rain to the basement entrance and adding water-spots to the claret stains on her best dinner dress.

In the studio she looked around, hating it now that it had made this trouble for her with Amanda. If it hadn't been raining, she thought, she would get out that very night, bag and baggage. Leaving here was as bad as when she had left her brother's house and had been reproached for it. Neither time did they want her to stay because they were fond of her, it was something else in both cases. For that matter nobody seemed to care enough about her to help her when she was in trouble like this. Except Ethel Carey, of course, but Ethel couldn't cope with this sort of mysterious trouble. Vicky sat on the couch and wrung her hands. If Ken Saunders only liked her a little better. . . . Suddenly she decided to call him up. It was eleven o'clock and she knew perfectly well it was an Eudora Brown sort of gesture, but you had to have somebody to whom you could turn.

Mr. Saunders was in. Mr. Saunders said further that he had just begun on a fresh bottle of crystal clear gin freshened up with the merest sprig of tonic. He would like nothing better than to share this dainty refreshment with a lady, since he had been confined to his room with a hangover for the past forty-eight hours and had no contact with the outside world.

"I only wanted to tell you I want to move out of this place tonight," said Vicky, confused by his intimate manner, his "darlings" and "Vicky, dears," even though she knew it meant only that he was drinking. "And when I told Amanda she got furious."

There was a pause and then Ken said, "I'm glad you moved, Vicky. I didn't like you there."

"I'm glad," Vicky said with relief. "I mean I'm glad somebody's glad. Thank you."

There was another pause and then Ken said, "Look here, Vicky, why don't you try and fall in love with me?"

"Why," stammered Vicky, "I suppose it's the difference in our religion. Your being a Moslem and me an Eastern Star."

"I'm not kidding," said Ken. "Don't you hear that tremolo in my voice? That's strong-man-choked with feeling."

"Spiritual or animal?" Vicky asked wildly.

"Animal. I can even name it. It's an ant-eater. Look, I've made my offer. Put on that sou'wester of yours and come over and fall in love with me. I know you've got it in you. Why aren't you over here pitching?"

"I'd only break your heart," said Vicky, "and then go round laughing about it behind your back. Why did you quit your job?"

"Never mind about that. What I'm saying is that you've led me on long enough. Honestly, Vicky, you're a sweet girl and I'm going to fall in love with you if it takes ten years. Why don't you do the same? Just set your teeth and start going. Come on. I'll give you advice and l'amour and gin and tonic and all my loose change and a copy of *Shropshire Lad* with marginal doodlings by my own hand."

"I'll be over," Vicky heard her own voice saying, to her utmost astonishment and even terror, for it's a terrifying thing to hear your voice saying things before you've even had the thought. "It's too rainy to stay at home, isn't it?"

"You *are* a darling."

At daybreak Vicky woke up with her head nuzzling somehow in Ken Saunders's neck and their arms twined around each other. She looked at his beautiful long baby lashes and his tousled blond hair and she listened to him breathe, smiling a little to herself, as if breathing was a very special talent. She was happier than she had ever been in her life. She wanted to wake him and tell him so.

"Ken," she whispered in his ear.

He murmured something without waking, and Vicky decided to let him sleep on. She was almost asleep again herself when the word he had murmured clicked in her mind. Amanda. He had said "Amanda" in his sleep. Vicky was suddenly as wide awake as if he had shouted the name. So that was it. He had been in love and wished he wasn't, he had said to her once. Amanda. Mr. Peabody used to see them together. Ken knew all the things about her apartment the first time he came there. He came there to see Amanda. That was it. That was why Amanda was angry tonight to have no more cover-up for the affair. That was why he was glad she was moving. "I didn't like you in there, Vicky," he had said. Slowly the pattern fitted together.

"This is awful," Vicky thought numbly. "This is awful. What will Amanda do to me now?"

She got up and dressed very softly, but hoping he would wake up and stop her, and say nothing was true but last night. But he didn't. She tiptoed down the stairs and into the gray daybreak. Buildings, trees, sky and street were ghost-gray and rain still hung in the air waiting for the wind to shake it out. An alley cat stalked up the basement stairs, and it, too, was gray. No cabs were in sight on Fifty-sixth Street, so she had to walk to Sixth Avenue to find one. Then she kept it waiting for half an hour in front of her apartment while she packed her things, flinging them into the trunk pell mell, panting a little, and whispering under her breath over and over, "Oh, dear, oh, dear, oh, dear!"

X

"Y OU'RE SURE you feel all right, Miss Haven?" Miss Finkelstein asked for the tenth time, staring fixedly at her office chief.

"I must look awful to have you keep asking that," Vicky answered.

Miss Finkelstein cocked her head critically.

"We-ell—" she admitted.

She ruffled through the card index box with glittering red talons, and after a moment's thought decided on the proper way to couch her criticism.

"You look like you did when you first came here, sort of," she observed enigmatically. "I don't mean your hair, because of course you've done wonders with that. Why don't you try it in a pompadour like Miss Elroy's and mine?"

True enough, Miss Finkelstein, following the Front Office lead, had swept her sleek black locks into a Gibson girl pompadour, though hers was, as usual, at least two inches higher than the others'. Vicky looked wanly at this example of the latest hairdressing and had a fleeting vision of her own small face haloed by a terrific tire, amber-colored instead of black like Miss Finkelstein's, but just as formidable. Maybe the starch in such a coiffure would favorably affect her whole being. Maybe it was little things like these that gave you the stamina to face the world.

"I like Miss Tray's Defense Hair-do," pursued Miss Finkelstein, favoring Vicky with a more intensive examination of her possibilities. "It's more off the face. Maybe that would suit you better. Or that Foreign Correspondent's Coiffure that they say Antoine invented for girls on assignments in India and China and those places where they can't get a wave-set. The picture looked frightfully attractive."

"I like mine this way," Vicky was goaded into reply. "Spectator style."

It seemed to Vicky that everything had happened to her in the last two weeks, and that furthermore it showed. She'd broken with Amanda, or Amanda, rather, had broken with

948

her, she'd spent the night accidentally with Amanda's lover and fallen fatally in love with him, Ethel Carey had wired her that the Tom Turner heir had arrived, and lastly she'd moved for no reason at all, had no telephone so she didn't know whether Ken wanted to see her again or not. These fourteen cataclysmic days had resulted in a feeling of numb impotence. It didn't matter whether her stockings, or even her shoes, were properly matched, whether she found the belt to her dress or not, whether the hat she idly clapped on her head was straw or felt, what she ate or when. Discrepancies, as indicated by Miss Finkelstein's eagle eye, were beyond her power to correct, just as it required more mental effort than she possessed to read her own proofs for next issue of *Peabody's*.

"I suppose moving takes it out of you," Miss Finkelstein said, understandingly. She opened her right-hand desk drawer and took out a beauty-kit. Opening her mouth wide as for a dental examination she applied a lipstick brush tenderly, mapping out first a rich curve considerably outside her natural lip-line, then filling it in as reverently as if she were restoring an old master. Vicky watched this process with gloomy fascination, wondering why it was Miss Finkelstein abandoned herself completely and wholeheartedly to only one thing, the trail of glamour. Maybe she, too, had made mistakes in love, and maybe this absorption was quite as satisfying as any other escape. For a second Vicky considered going to the beauty-shop across the street and getting a shampoo, a facial, a manicure, or all of them at once. This was how girls like Miss Finkelstein and Amanda kept in trim for their separate battles.

"Mr. Chatham is taking Mr. Saunders's place on Home Research," observed Miss Finkelstein. "They say Mr. Saunders is that sort. Never stays long in one job. Why do you suppose he never married? I think it's so *funny*."

What was so funny, Vicky wondered, though she knew Miss Finkelstein's use of the word "funny" covered many situations but never anything humorous.

"Probably in love with some married woman," mused Miss Finkelstein, now applying a minute brush to her eyelashes, sweeping them with a vigorous upstroke as if they were the glory of the Seven Sutherland Sisters. "That's always the way.

Mr. Chatham is really more for us, really, I mean. He's in the
Register, of course. Mr. Saunders—well, I know he's a friend
of yours, but honestly, didn't you have the feeling he was
not—well—not quite top-drawah?"

"I don't see why," Vicky answered perversely. "The top
drawer seems awfully big. So does the Social Register."

"I see what you mean," politely disagreed Miss Finkelstein.

Vicky wondered what Miss Finkelstein would think of a
person who went to bed with a man who wasn't in the Register. Miss Finkelstein, though, gave no evidence of ever regarding men as anything but means of social advancement.
There was a Sam who called up every day or two and received
frowning discouragement from Miss Finkelstein. ("Oh, Sam,
don't be a *sil*! How could I get to your mother's birthday
party when I had to go on with the crowd? . . . Oh, you
know. The usual. Well, you know what Saturday night at the
Stork is . . . Frightfully sorry, Samuel, but it was just one of
those things . . ." She called him "Samuel" with a special,
teasing inflection, as if using the full name was both witty and
coquettish.) There were also "this man from out of town,"
which signified something rather swell to a girl born and
brought up in New York, and various press agents and advertising men in close contact with the socially favored, who
took out Miss Finkelstein, but only roused her emotions by
letting her meet wonderful other people from the Front Office set. Evidently poor Samuel had nothing to offer but his
second-hand roadster and School of Dentistry dances, but
Miss Finkelstein did not quite want to lose him since most of
the fun in "getting around" is in the boasting to your old, less
fortunate friends.

Very likely Miss Finkelstein was right about Ken. Very likely
his ineligibility was the whole secret of Vicky's present
wretchedness. You wouldn't catch a Social Register man making love to a girl and then not calling her up, no matter where
she was, to see if she was sorry or glad or what. You wouldn't
find Racquet Club men getting a girl crazy about them and
then dropping her. Ah no, these *faux pas* were made only by
the commoners.

The telephone rang and Vicky snatched it with a leap of her
heart. If it really should be Ken, what should she say, how

should she act? If she acted casual, he would think what happened was the usual thing with her. If she acted all choked-up, as she was afraid she might be, then he would be afraid she was going to claim him for a husband. She said "hello" before she had made up her mind.

"Mr. Evans?" she repeated, stupidly. "Mr. Evans Who?"

"Mr. Evans!" exclaimed Miss Finkelstein, eyes wide. "My *dear*!"

"Oh. Oh, Julian, of course," Vicky finally grasped the name and pulled herself together. Julian had never called her. Neither had President Roosevelt for that matter. It seemed ominous.

"Victoria, you spoke of moving the other evening," said Julian, in the patient, fatherly, but pressed-for-time voice he assumed for the Little People. "Have you taken steps yet?"

"Steps? Oh . . . Yes, I've already moved, Julian."

"Good, then I'll have Harnett go over and make arrangements to close the place. Amanda, of course, doesn't use it."

"Well . . ." Vicky answered for there was an inquiry in his inflection. "I wouldn't know about that, you see, because I didn't realize she'd gotten it just for me until the other night."

She was saying too much, probably, but what was she supposed to say?

"Just a minute while I write down that address, Victoria."

She waited, puzzled, until she heard his impatient, "Yes?"

"What?" she asked stupidly.

"The address, my dear, the address."

She gave it to him, feeling dimly that there was something odd about all this, but nothing she could do about it.

"Thank you. I'll have Harnett go right over. Amanda's too rushed right now to attend to these details and apparently Miss Bemel knows nothing about it. How's your new quarters? Good neighborhood, I trust. See you soon, child. Good-bye."

It seemed odd that he should not have gone directly to Amanda for the address. Odd, too, that he made no mention of Amanda's rude behavior the other evening. Vicky pressed her hands to her head, dizzy with the whirl of events and conduct that she could not understand. She tried to concentrate on the proofsheets before her. House in Sutton Place for sale or rent, former home of Whatsis Whosis, now active in Washington. Photograph of Miss Nancy Elroy, soon to marry Harry Cosgrove Jones, IV, cousin of Sir Henry Cosgrove Jones of Toronto, examining the attractive view from the terrace of the new Cattleby Towers, rents beginning at $2200, ready July 1st. The letters in Cosgrove *montaged* into Cattleby and Nancy's satiny five-color face smiled, frowned, smiled, frowned, like the spectacle advertisements in opticians' windows. Vicky was conscious of Miss Finkelstein's steady scrutiny.

"You really do look sick, Miss Haven," said the young woman earnestly. "You didn't go out to lunch, either. Why don't you dash along?"

Miss Finkelstein was always "dashing," though her movements were better described as "springing," for she modelled her carriage on Nancy Elroy's, a lithe springing from the toes, head balancing imaginary book, shoulders pulling up torso. Vicky, far from a desire to dash along, thought she would be lucky to merely crawl along, so low were her spirits.

"I'd rather not get to my place before I have to," she said gloomily. "There's only a studio couch and a percolator and a lot of things to unpack. I can't bear the idea. I expect it will stay that way, too."

Miss Finkelstein pursed up her new lips speculatively.

"You poor angel!" she finally exclaimed. "I know what I'll do. I'll run you home myself and fix you up. I *love* fixing up apartments."

Vicky was too beaten to protest, although Miss Finkelstein terrified her as much as Amanda did. But first Miss Finkelstein must call up Mummy and explain the situation.

"Angel, I won't be home for perfect hours," Miss Finkelstein gurgled into the telephone. "Miss Haven isn't well and I'm looking after her."

Vicky watched Miss Finkelstein's preparations to take charge of her and felt herself growing smaller and weaker in comparison, for no matter how modest Miss Finkelstein's contribution to *Peabody's* was from nine to five, from five on till her bedtime she WAS *Peabody's*. Vicky saw the five o'clock metamorphosis coming over her, a dawning of arrogance held in check during the day, a summoning of all the Front Office airs and the complacency of all the de luxe subscribers. Looking at herself intently in the office mirror Miss Finkelstein tenderly okayed her pompadour, checked on her Chinese yellow foundation make-up which left a rim of pollen on her suit collar. Then she adjusted her smart little toasted straw sailor with floating pink veil on the top of her pompadour, a fitting crown for this monument to glamour. With a finger gloved in dusty pink suede Miss Finkelstein pressed a button.

"I'll tell the boy"—she always called the office-boy the boy even though it was usually her brother Irving,—"that I'm taking you home because you're ill. By the by, you want Mrs. Evans to know, don't you?"

Vicky realized by the eager glint in her eye that Miss Finkelstein's gesture was more a means of contacting Amanda Evans personally than helping Miss Haven.

"No, no," she answered hastily.

"Come on," urged Miss Finkelstein gayly. "You need looking after, and I'm going to do it."

Vicky smiled wan gratitude mingled with feeble alarm. Amanda used to look after her. Now Miss Finkelstein was taking over. Maybe that was progress.

2

"West Thirteenth?" Miss Finkelstein frowned, on their way downtown. "Are you sure that's a good neighborhood?"

Good neighborhood again. She sounded so exactly like Amanda and Julian that Vicky felt it was the voice of the whole world.

"I don't know why any one in New York worries about good neighborhoods," she said. "They never see their neighbors anyway so it might as well be a bad neighborhood."

She had signed up for the apartment one lunch hour, visiting it and leasing it very fast for fear her resolution would change. She had chosen the neighborhood because Ken Saunders spent a great deal of time down there with his friends the Orphens, and she was reduced to these shameless bids for his attention. She had figured so craftily on how far her apartment was from the Orphens' on Fifth Avenue and

Eleventh, that she had paid very little attention to the apartment she had leased. She now saw that, of all the blocks in
the district, the one she had selected was least savory, since it
was filled with department store trucks backing and snorting
into their slips on one side and a vast publishing house
spewed out arithmetics and *Gone with the Wind*s on the other,
so the progress of their taxi was as cautious as if on some
Alpine footpath. Miss Finkelstein's face betrayed her disappointment as they threaded their way through these dangers
to the new address.

"I like the trees downtown," Vicky feebly apologized.

"Trees?" queried Miss Finkelstein, quite rightly, since Thirteenth in this block was largely warehouse, and instead of the
charming trees that graced neighboring blocks its sidewalks
and curbs grew three piece tapestry living-room sets, floor
lamps, and porch-swings all in brown paper waiting for surly
men to shunt them onto vans and out to the hungry bare
rooms of Astoria and points west.

"I should have brought my *Cue*," mused Miss Finkelstein
further, as if that little magazine guide-book to the pleasures
of Manhattan would solve all their problems.

The cab driver kept thrusting his head out of the side window like an inquisitive turtle, finally pausing at a small brick
house before which jingled a tin sign-card bearing on a white
background the cheerful picture of a black puppy having its
ears boxed by a black kitten.

"A bar!" Miss Finkelstein exclaimed, in a low, wounded
voice.

"No," said Vicky, reassuringly. "It's just a pet-shop."

"A pet-shop on the first floor? But Miss Haven! Really!"
gasped Miss Finkelstein. "How *icky!*"

The pet-shop explained the group standing transfixed on
the sidewalk as Vicky and her friend got out of the cab, for
the enlarged first-floor window permitted a half dozen new-
born Scotties to exhibit their vivacity on one side, while on
the other side of the wire a Siamese cat regarded the passerby
with impartial scorn. On either side of the little brick house
were three-story houses of similar vintage but evidently given
up years ago as anything but wrecking material, for their
dingy windows were broken, and the paint trim of windows

and doors scaled to what might have been solid soot. On these Miss Finkelstein's eye rested, even while Vicky was admiring the tiny geranium beds on either side of the steps of her own residence, and the other evidences of special care in the polished brass knocker and freshly painted white door.

"I hope you're going to like this district," said Miss Finkelstein, shaking her head doubtfully.

Miss Finkelstein's hostility gave Vicky perverse satisfaction, convincing her that here was at last her very own niche, a place unrecommended by any one of her more aggressive friends. The steps and indeed the whole house listed with antiquity. Inside, the walls burst through their flowered wallpaper with plaster secrets; the tiny hallway downstairs had barely enough room for a marble-topped reception table without crowding the visitors to the pet-shop, and if the place bore ever so faintly the fragrance of the caravan it was due to little runaways from the pet-shop, who staggered with little mews and squeals up and down the staircase, poking their heads through every aperture and between every rail at greatly enjoyed risk to their lives. From the ceiling hung tipsy chandeliers, the cockeyed doorways had doors swinging on them at odd angles, pulling at the upper hinges like little boys at Mother's apron. All it needed to make Vicky love it with a warm joy of recognition—"This, now *this* is really *me*!"—was Miss Finkelstein's puzzled frown and delicate twitch of the nostrils.

"I'm on the top floor," Vicky said, running ahead with her key.

"A walk-up!" said Miss Finkelstein. "How quaint!"

The stairs were as crooked as the rest of the house, and the bends looked like an accordion, one end caving in and the other stretching out to full width. At each landing was the conventional old-time niche designed for easing the passage of coffins up and down stairs, though this grim function was camouflaged by little pots of trailing vines, their blossoms and leaves largely chewed off by visitations from the little pets below. The handrailing was to all intents and purposes made of taffy, certainly nothing to be relied upon, for it swung out at the slightest touch. On the third floor a square skylight lit up a square hallway which managed as many changes of level as

the sea bottom, and was further complicated by large bundles
of bedding in brown paper from Macy's for Miss Haven and
a small radio in a carton. There was a Western Union envelope slipped under the door, and Vicky opened it.

"PLEASE INFORM JULIAN IMMEDIATELY THAT YOU ARE
RETAINING STUDIO ON RECONSIDERATION. AMANDA."

Too late now, Amanda, Vicky thought, not without satisfaction. Whatever purpose she had served Amanda by using
her studio was lost now, and the good thing about Amanda's
attack on her was that it left her free to do as she liked, no
need for eternal gratitude now that Amanda had revealed her
cards. Vicky saw Miss Finkelstein's inky eyes fastened on the
yellow slip.

"It's from Amanda," Vicky was about to say, knowing this
would please her, but suddenly she didn't want to please Miss
Finkelstein, or to excuse herself to her. She only wanted to be
alone with her new house so definitely hers, because nobody,
Amanda, Ethel, brother Ted, Eudora Brown, Ethel Carey,
nobody would ever have selected it for her, and so it was the
beginning of her own life. The doubting look in her companion's eye only reassured her that she was on the right
path.

"I really should be at my Red Cross tonight," Miss Finkelstein said when she saw the little apartment with the swaying
floor, the dinky bathroom, and the clothesline across the back
window. "You could have gotten modern conveniences for
the same money."

"I know," said Vicky. She saw the studio couch, her sole
piece of furniture, neatly shoved in a corner by the fireplace.

"I think I'll lie down till I feel better, so why don't you
run?" she said, and apparently Miss Finkelstein was almost
ready to be persuaded, for she stood looking about the two
rooms, so definitely shabby, so definitely Greenwich Village
and shaking her head. She had pulled off her pink gloves and
picked up a broom with a conscientious determination to "fix
up" the apartment as she had threatened, but there seemed
no place to start. Vicky lay back on the uncovered green mattress, her felt hat and shoes tossed to one side, her arms
clasped behind her head. Through the two little back win-

dows she could see the budding tops of trees in the afternoon sunlight and she thought of how pleasant it would be to wake up in the morning to the sight of green leaves and birds. The roar of trucks on Thirteenth Street made the little house shake and hum, but this too was something Amanda would never have permitted and therefore it had a special charm. There was a fireplace in each of the two rooms, their marble mantels sinking into the walls at an angle, their little black grates heaped with cannel coal and bulging out of the narrow little arched fireplace. She would have charcoal steaks, Vicky thought dreamily, but that reminded her of those Saturday night shore picnics with Tom Turner, and she shivered.

"I really don't know where to begin, Miss Haven," Miss Finkelstein admitted, and after another moment's thought removed the jacket of her brown covertcloth suit, hanging it carefully in the closet, then adjusting her pink sweater so that it clung properly to the seductive curves of her Gay Deceivers. As if I gave a damn, marvelled Vicky, as if there was any one around to admire a fine bosom, however false, but its owner. (Then she was ashamed of herself for not appreciating the girl's kind intentions!)

"In a way, maybe I should have taken you over to Mummy," reflected Miss Finkelstein, gingerly sweeping. She gave a merry lilting laugh. "I was just thinking how surprised Mummy would be to see me fixing up some place when I'm so *awful*, really, about my own room. But I couldn't help thinking when Mr. Evans called you, that *they* might come down to see you and you looked too absolutely shot to do anything yourself. Do you think they might come? Oh, *shucks!* I meant to bring my *Such Is the Legend* along for her to autograph!"

It struck Vicky quite unfairly that she might well be at death's door, but Miss Finkelstein would play Florence Nightingale only long enough to get Amanda's autograph.

"She won't come," she said. Wasn't she anything at all, she wondered, without Amanda's protective name? Mice, that's what she was, she thought, chased around by her brother's family and Eudora and Ethel Carey and then Amanda. It would be almost better to be a nuisance, a bad girl, anything but this mousy nonentity colored only by Amanda Evans's sponsorship. Even Ken Saunders had been presented to her by Amanda, true, not for love, but as a suitable companion. All these months in New York and she wasn't even as free as she had been in Lakeville. She was Amanda's little pawn, a Miss Nobody-but-Friend-of-Amanda Keeler Evans to even Miss Finkelstein. She ought to leave *Peabody's* at once, cut the whole tie, even if she starved.

"She might come, of course," Miss Finkelstein said slowly, and put the broom carefully in the little kitchen cabinet. "I should think she would, really, when she finds out you're sick."

Vicky lay still, her face slowly reddening.

"You didn't—" she began in a low voice.

"Oh, yes, I called her," Miss Finkelstein said brightly, holding out her brilliant fingernails for a last fond examination. "You said not to, but after all, she is your best friend. I left word with her secretary."

Vicky felt a growing sense of defeat.

"What did you tell her?"

"I said you'd had an attack in the office," obliged Miss Finkelstein, now getting into her jacket, and carefully dusting off the British War Relief pin so that Amanda, if she came, might recognize a fellow-worker at once. "My dear, if she sees this place! I wish now I'd worn my fox scarf."

"That telegram was from her, saying she wasn't able to come," Vicky said, after a little thought.

Miss Finkelstein's face fell.

"It would have been *grand* meeting her at last," she sighed.

"Thanks ever so much for bringing me home, because I did feel faint," Vicky went on, resolutely determined to dispose of her eager assistant. "There really isn't anything to do, though, and I'll just go to sleep."

"You're sure I can't get you anything to eat?"

"Oh, no. The superintendent will bring up something," impatiently lied Vicky.

"Well," hesitated Miss Finkelstein, drawing on her gloves once more. "If you're sure there isn't anything—"

In another minute Vicky was sure she would have to scream, "For God's sake, leave me alone," but Miss Finkelstein made her exit just in time.

Vicky sat on the bed quietly, torn between such bitterness as she had seldom known and a desire to cry her eyes out. She wished she'd never come to New York. She wished she'd never known Amanda. She wished she'd never been born. Or if she must be born, why couldn't she have been Amanda Keeler, or Eudora Brown, or Miss Finkelstein, or Nancy Elroy, or any of the other women who knew what they wanted and knew how to go after it? Anger prevailed finally over self-pity and she had a sudden inspiration. She had backed out precipitately when Eudora took Tom Turner away. She had backed out again when she found she was falling in love with Amanda's lover. Of course, there were other factors in the latter situation—her shock at discovering how shrewdly she had been used by Amanda, for one thing. But the truth was she really *was* mice, never fighting for anything she wanted, always bowing out with a weak little apology, giving way to these stronger women. That's the way she might do all her life, and what would it get her?

"It must be this place is taking the hex off me," Vicky thought, amazed at the surge of energy and resolution coming over her. "It's the first time since I've been in New York that I feel myself. I know what I want. I want Ken Saunders. Maybe he's still in love with Amanda. Maybe she still wants him. It looks as if she does. But I don't care. I have a right to fight for what I want. It's more respectable than scramming all the time to keep out of people's way."

She put her shoes back on and made up her face as elaborately as Miss Finkelstein herself, though some of the freckles over her nose were still visible, on one side, and her beautifully carmined lips had the same cockeyed lilt to the left as the doors of her new apartment. She examined herself in the gilt mirror between her front windows, and except for her usual chagrin that no matter what she wore or did to herself she always looked like nobody but Vicky Haven, she decided she was presentable enough for the plan she had just formed, which was to track down Ken Saunders and try to win him completely from Amanda. She was quite aware that one word would send her flying back to cover, but still it was something to have even a teaspoonful of courage.

In the hallway she stumbled over a small black kitten which

was investigating her radio battery with an inquisitive yellow paw. Black cats were unlucky but nobody said anything about a very small black one with yellow paws to take the curse off, did they? In fact, Vicky thought, she would ask the janitor tomorrow if she couldn't keep it.

She thought of the neighborhood bars Ken had mentioned, as she went downstairs. He was spending his days, after leaving *Peabody's*, in steady drinking and in the company mostly of his friend Dennis Orphen. There was a bar near the Orphens' which he talked about. Martin's. That was it. Vicky set her face boldly toward Fifth Avenue. This was the way Amanda had gone after Julian. This was the way Eudora had gone after Tom. She began swinging along in a lithe, springy manner very like Miss Finkelstein's, a sense of power and immense resourcefulness surging through her veins like the very spirit of spring. This was the way, all right.

3

Washington Square Arch loomed up at the foot of Fifth Avenue like a gate to freedom. Vicky was not familiar with this end of Manhattan, but there was a spaciousness and tranquillity about it that charmed her, just as the cozy antiquity of her new apartment had done. Ambitious, frantic New York faded into soft leisurely twilight here, student lovers from the University strolled along, hatless, arms around each other; stately old churches embroidered the sky with Gothic ramparts and steeples, their arched open doorways revealed hushed candle-lit altars glittering through the plush darkness like ornaments in a jewel-box. A flock of planes whirred far overhead in the dusky blue, guardians of this peace, and the rim of a new moon hung over the Jefferson Market spire. High up a penthouse roof was fringed with an architectural moustache of budding hedge. That must be where Ken's friend, Dennis Orphen, lived. Vicky hesitated in front of the apartment house, half minded to go in and ask for Ken. It would be easier to look for him in the cafe, though, and easier to explain. Walking briskly toward Martin's Café, Vicky thought of how startled Miss Finkelstein would be to see her sprinting along without the slightest sign of illness. She was counting so blindly on finding Ken that she stopped short outside the bar, realizing how foolish was this confidence. People were never where you wanted them to be at the time you wanted them there, at the time you had found the courage to be your real self with them.

In the bright daylight, Martin's dark interior looked almost sinister, though no more so than the score of other dim-lit cafés in this area. Indeed there was no more reason why Ken Saunders and his downtown friends should have thrown Martin's their special favor rather than Tony's, or Marta's, or Tom's, or Bill's, or Frank's. But drinking men have peculiar fancies, and they swear that the fragrance of Martin's front room is entirely superior to and different from the conditions of an exactly similar room across the street called Bill's. It is impossible for them to savor a martini in this rival spot, it is quite out of the question for them to have any pleasure whatever outside the glamorous confines of their particular little haven. Drinking, to the devoted habitués of Martin's, was a homey, laudable occupation around the little pine bar of the front room, and even intoxication here had the stamp of respectability for it was Martin's martinis, under Martin's roof, and an agreeable, friendly manner of helping Martin support his family. You would have thought, from the loyalty the patrons bore whatever host they favored, that the man had particular qualities of sympathy and generosity that made special appeal. But this was seldom the case, and Martin was as sharp-faced, shrewd and cold a fish as any of his rivals, despite the tenderness with which his customers asked for Martin, Martin's health, Martin's wife, family, and future. On the credit side, Martin's endearing qualities must have been that he seldom if ever bought anybody any drinks, he freshened up his liquor stock each night with a little more neutral spirits than the law allowed, he charged ten cents more for old-fashioneds than Bill's did, and although he permitted old customers to charge food and drinks, he sent them duns at such frequent intervals that they were harrassed with guilt over the burden they were putting on good old Martin's generosity, and either showed their remorse by increasing their bill lavishly or by creeping around the corner to hang their heads and bills in less desirable taverns.

Inasmuch as Dennis Orphen spent a large part of his life in Martin's, it was quite reasonable to expect to find him there, and since he was Ken Saunders' bosom pal, it was logical to assume Ken too might be found here, and such was the case this afternoon. Mr. Orphen, his lady friend, Corinne Barrows, and Mr. Saunders had dropped into Martin's at noon for medicinal treatment of sorts, and by a fortunate chance had found themselves conveniently at the bar when the cocktail hour came on, a circumstance they were making the best of. They had profited by the afternoon in striking up conversation with a couple of soldiers on leave from Fort Dix, so that they felt quite rightly that their time could not have been spent more patriotically. The two uniformed strangers further served a good purpose of stopping a budding argument between Dennis and Corinne which would have in time flowered into a threesome, with Ken taking Corinne's part, then Dennis', and eventually being kicked out by the two as a trouble-maker. At least that was the pattern these intimate little parties usually took.

"I think this time I will have a daiquiri," stated Corinne, a plump, honey-colored little creature doing her best to look tweedy in a dark green suit and hat, but somehow betrayed by ruffled blouse, red fox furs and a bracelet of tiny topaz hearts. She had considered leaving her husband for Dennis Orphen for two or three years, and during her delay her grave, business-minded husband had unexpectedly been taken with an affair of his own, which resulted in divorce all around, with Corinne still confused by this turn of events. She loved Dennis as wildly as ever, she kept assuring him, but somehow it didn't seem like real love without a husband in the offing. She wanted a little more time to consider marrying Dennis, she felt, and since she was at heart an extremely affectionate, friendly little creature, thought it would be less lonely living with Dennis while she made up her mind. Whenever she drank she remembered that she was a deserted wife and grew very sad and abused, sorrowfully accusing Dennis of future infidelities.

"You can't change to daiquiris," said Dennis firmly. "You had martinis and scotch and you can't change to daiquiris."

"I always change," Corinne declared. "It makes me feel that I'm just beginning, so of course then I don't get tight. I pretend I'm just coming in."

"That's all right, what the hell?" agreed Martin, with a shrug, wiping off the bar where the soldiers had just spilled their beer.

"Have I got to stick to beer when I join up?" Ken asked.

"We shouldn't let Ken join up," Corinne protested to Dennis. "Darling, tell him there might be a war and then think how he'd feel!"

"She doesn't know there's already a war," Dennis informed Ken. "She thinks you could get a little soldier suit up at Schwartz's Toy Shop and have just as much fun playing here at Martin's."

"Are they all C.C.C. boys at Fort Dix?" Ken asked the soldiers.

"Sure. And they're all named Moe, Bo, and Maxie," said one.

"That's a big lie," said the other.

"Nothing like getting information," Ken said.

He had been drinking so steadily ever since he left *Peabody's* that his system had reached a stage of amiable saturation that transcended drunkenness and offered a façade of exaggerated sobriety. His decision to enlist had come about three o'clock and had been supported by earnest telephone calls to a lawyer friend, an army doctor friend, and a fireman buddy from the firehouse near his hotel. By four-thirty, Dennis and Corinne were addressing him as Corporal, and at six he had been promoted to Colonel. He was already upbraiding his friend Dennis as a slacker, in spite of Corinne's protests that Dennis simply did not have Ken's warlike nature but was a sweet-natured, lovable little fellow who might well bring about peace between nations merely by his sunny smile. She wanted to go home, but was afraid to leave the two men for fear Dennis would be persuaded to march out of Martin's straight into the United States Marines, or worse yet, the two of them would find feminine admiration for their military natures elsewhere. When Vicky Haven came into Martin's, Corinne was very glad she had stayed, not being quite sure whether this new face belonged to Ken or to her own Dennis, always a problem. Taking the realistic approach she acknowledged Ken's introduction very warily. You never knew when a new woman was going to snatch away your lover, so it was wisest to start right off being enemies.

"Can you beat this for coincidence?" Ken asked the world. "The very person in all the world I wanted to walk in here, and by God she does."

"Maybe she heard your regiment was on the march," Corinne suggested. She put her hand in Dennis' pocket very tenderly so that the new girl would know who was whose. She was not to be fooled by Vicky's radiant absorption in Ken, and besides Dennis did keep looking at the girl.

"Bastard never mentioned this one," he muttered in an undertone to Corinne. "Must be serious for her to track him down here."

Vicky was delighted with the stained glass illuminated portraits above the bar of a saintly faced Beatrice demurely holding her robe up above the knee while a lecherous-looking Dante leered. She was charmed by bald, fish-faced Martin himself, by the beauty of the yellow pine bar, and the extraordinary bouquet of her old-fashioneds. She found the conversation of the two soldiers and of Ken's two friends brilliant beyond words, and she remembered the titles of Dennis Orphen's novels, and after a third drink could almost swear she had read them and found them surpassingly good. This generous frame of mind was due, unquestionably to her new purpose in life, and her delight over actually having found Ken at the very moment she wanted him most. She didn't care a bit that his flattering devotion to her was due to drink, just as it must have been the other night. So long as he was glad to see her and called her darling, she was not going to inquire into the reasons.

Dennis Orphen, on the strength of selling his last novel to Hollywood, was buying highballs for the soldiers, but this did not promote the good feeling anticipated. Moe and Bo were deciding that the army was a rather exclusive affair which had no room for amateurs like Ken and Dennis. Even if we got into the war, they were certain that the two stinkers now buying them drinks would never be wanted.

Corinne put a quarter in the juke-box to play "Let's Be Buddies" five times, and having provided this treat for the others, beckoned Vicky to the Powder Room, otherwise ladies' confession chamber.

"I don't like politics, do you?" she began. She took her green hat off and began combing her long brown gold hair before the little vanity mirror. "Personally I wouldn't advise Ken to join up just because he's at loose ends. Supposing this country gets in the war and he'd actually have to *fight?*"

"I suppose you people have known him a long time," Vicky said.

Corinne nodded.

"Years. All the time he was crazy about Amanda Keeler, or maybe I shouldn't have said that."

"Oh, no," Vicky said. "I know about it."

"I can tell when he's started it up again, because he's ashamed to see Dennis and me then because we don't like her. Then when it's all off again he comes down all the time. Did you know Amanda?"

"Yes, but—" Vicky felt the name choking her, for it seemed to her that her whole happiness lay in cutting Amanda out of her life.

"Dennis thinks she ruined Ken for anybody else," Corinne confided. "You know. She put him through so much. Every one says she's so beautiful. Pooh. If you call a stick of wood beautiful!"

Vicky was afraid of a reply that might be too unfair to her old friend Amanda, so she became reserved in her answers and as haughty as being slightly sick over her old-fashioneds would permit. When they got back to the bar the soldiers had gone off to Trenton, quarreling with each other, and Dennis and Ken were wrangling over mighty world problems with which they now felt in perfect condition to deal. Ken was spilling his drinks and now Vicky could tell by his eyes that he didn't know whether she was there or not; he felt sociable enough, but he wasn't Ken any more.

"I want to go home," Corinne said plaintively. "I don't want to have to stay here all night just to keep Dennis from going home with somebody else."

"Have another daiquiri," invited Dennis. "Or change to a stinger and pretend you're just coming in."

"I don't want anything more to drink," Corinne said resolutely. "I'm the home type. Let's go home and I'll cook some old-fashioneds for supper, sort of a buffet."

"We could go to my new apartment," Vicky said. "There isn't any furniture, of course, but it's homey."

"I never look at people's furniture when I'm invited into a private home," stated Dennis. "I just look at their books."

"He wants to see if his are there," Corinne said.

"I turned down plenty of women just because they didn't have a book in the house," pursued Dennis confidentially. "Not even the Holy Writ."

"I turned down plenty because they didn't have a drink in the house," Ken Saunders said. "Not even a small pocket rye."

"I like a house with no furniture," Corinne said. "Let's go to her house and furnish it up with something. If we go to our house the maid will bark at us. Have you got a maid?"

"No," Vicky assured her. "I think I've got a cat, though."

"Six-thirty-five," said Dennis, consulting his watch. "This is the hour my animal love comes out. Let's go to this place."

"What the hell?" Martin cried, genially. "Joining up right now? I was just buying a drink."

As this was such a rare occurrence, they were bound to take advantage of the miracle and have the same all around except for Corinne, who decided to try a side-car because she'd had them on a Bermuda boat once and had a very gay time. The effect was not the same this time, however, for she suddenly began to weep, dabbing at her eyes with her yellow suede gloves in a most pitiful manner.

"I can't bear Dennis going off to war," she said tremulously. "You know you ought not to go 'way and leave me in this condition, darling."

"Are you in a condition?" Dennis asked, startled.

Corinne dried her eyes.

"It's just luck that I'm not," she murmured, sadly.

"It's Ken that's going," Vicky reminded her. "Don't you remember Dennis has to finish a novel first?"

"First we have to furnish your apartment," Ken said, with a burst of efficiency and after a few struggles with his legs and wallet and hat and the law of gravity, managed to lead the way to the great outdoors. This accomplished, he decided he must go back in and telephone.

"No, you don't," said Dennis. "He thinks he's going to call Amanda and it's over my dead body."

"Please stop him," Corinne begged Vicky. "He gets this way every time he's tight."

Vicky remembered to keep smiling.

"I have a message for her," said Ken, patiently. "I wanted to remind her to go to hell."

"I thought she told *you* that," said Dennis. He looked at Corinne and shrugged his shoulders. "Ah, what can you do? Maybe he'd better join up, by God. He couldn't make any worse fool of himself. By the time this country gets in he might be a general."

"What are we going to do with him?" Corinne wailed. "He gets started on Amanda and it's like a cat fit—!"

"I'll look after him," Vicky said brightly. "I won't let him telephone anybody."

They started up Sixth Avenue in the gathering darkness, Dennis and Vicky keeping a firm grasp on Ken's arms, and Corinne, mysterious grief forgotten, giggling behind Ken, pushing him along smartly. At the liquor store Dennis stopped and got a bottle of rye, at Corinne's inspiration, and at the delicatessen Vicky stopped and bought sandwiches.

Ken was now being marched around the corner by his three friends in the manner of a victim just rescued from death by freezing.

"What'll we do if he passes out in your place?" Corinne asked.

"I'll look after him," said Vicky.

Maybe she would come to her senses next day, next week, next year, and realize she was being a fool to go after a man who was still in love with somebody else, and who only made love to her when he was tight. But she didn't care. You had to take leavings, if you didn't get served the first time. You had to fight for even those.

They marched up the cockeyed stairs of the little house and into the bare, jolly little room. Mr. Saunders was deposited at once on the bed, and Corinne made a housewifely search for bitters and glasses, both of which were missing.

"I can see why you don't need chairs," she said reproachfully, "but your folks should have told you about glasses and bitters."

"No ice," Dennis observed, after an inspection of his own. He looked at the sandwiches, spread out neatly on the mattress beside Ken's sleeping frame. He shuddered.

"Sandwiches without mustard," he exclaimed, incredulously. "Oh, no, Vicky. No, no. Drinks without ice, maybe, or
without bitters, but sandwiches without mustard! Come on,
let's go back to Martin's."

"Martin's, of course!" echoed Corinne.

"We can park the general here, can't we?" Dennis asked.

Vicky looked at Ken, who was resting with what seemed an
air of finality, with his hat as pillow. If she went he might wake
up and call Amanda.

"You two go ahead," she advised. "I'll stay here and guard
the body."

Ken stirred as the door banged behind them, and he
reached for Vicky's hand. "Don't you go, Vicky," he begged.
"Don't you ever go."

4

Invitation to the Elroys for Sunday night supper again left
Vicky with mixed feelings. First she was comforted to think
that at least somebody liked her and was kind to her, and then
came the crushing reminder that the Elroys liked her only for
her contact with Amanda. Maybe she should tell them,
"Thank you for asking me, but Amanda is mad at me now so
naturally you will want to withdraw the invitation." But she
was unhappy and lonesome in her new bare little apartment,
feeling guilty because Amanda had treated her as if she *was*
guilty, and she was sick and stunned over her discovery of Ken
and Amanda. She was entitled to a little pleasure, even if it
was under false pretenses.

"Do come early," Nancy begged. "We're having cocktails
for a raft of people first, but just family for supper."

The cocktail party was in no sense a reassuring occasion to
Vicky, for Mrs. Elroy insisted on introducing Vicky to every
one as the friend of Amanda Keeler Evans, who, Mrs. Elroy
intimated, had also been invited and might drop in at any
moment. After a while Vicky cowered in a corner talking
feverishly to Tuffy's inarticulate young man named Plung
who was equally overpowered by the Elroys and anxious only
for oblivion. New faces were a menace, for Mrs. Elroy must
present them at once to her special prize. She would send a

smiling glance around the room, spot Vicky crouching behind little Mr. Plung, and would swoop down upon her
gracefully, drawing the new guest.

"You don't know Nancy's friend, Vicky Haven, do you?
Vicky is one of our pets. Well, Vicky, have you seen Amanda
recently?" Then, to the other guest, "Vicky and Amanda
Keeler Evans are devoted friends. Grew up together."

"Really?" the guest was bound to exclaim. "Oh, do tell us
about her! What a woman!"

There was nothing to do but to smile desperate assent or
else to make a fool of her hostess by saying this great friendship was no more.

Once Vicky thought wildly of saving Mrs. Elroy the trouble of introduction by pouncing on each guest as they entered
and saying, "How do you do? I'm a personal friend of
Amanda Evans. Isn't that perfectly wonderful of me?" Then
let Mrs. Elroy face the embarrassment! Well, she must either
stay away from the Elroys from now on, or else accept the
character they gave her. Not such a flattering character, at
that. Mrs. Elroy was saying, in essence, "Here is a young
woman of no consequence as you can readily see. But she has
justified her existence and her presence in our home by the
virtue of personal acquaintance with the great lady of our
time, Amanda Evans. If there is any other charm to be found
in Miss Haven greater than this one we mention, we have
failed to perceive it."

Miss Finkelstein all over, Vicky thought savagely. She began
to yearn for Uncle Rockman's kindly red face, but Uncle
plainly would have none of the younger set collected by
Nancy and Tuffy.

"He'll come in for supper, though," Tuffy answered
Vicky's inquiry. "He won't come to any of these pre-wedding
parties and besides he can't stand Nancy's beau. God, who
can?"

"I'll betcha he gives Nancy a whacking good check for a
wedding present," mused young Plung, thoughtfully fondling
his fragile beard.

Tuffy laughed raucously.

"Don't be an idiot, Plungy. If it wasn't for that wedding
check Nancy would call the whole thing off in a minute. The

man's a complete drip! But Nancy's passed up too many chances already, and besides she can't hold anybody very long."

It was a fact that although Nancy had had many men fall for her violently at first sight, she had no hold-overs, either among beaux or women friends. She took up with people quickly and was immediately dissatisfied, feeling vaguely cheated. She brushed them off with such callous rudeness there could be little fondness left for her, then snatched hungrily at some new casual acquaintance and repeated the whole process. She was like a child taking one greedy bite from every bonbon in the box, restlessly searching for some unpredictable sensation, spoiling the lot for herself and for others.

"Old Nancy's pretty fickle all right," agreed Plung wisely.

Vicky felt called upon to make some defense of her friend.

"I think you're unfair to Nancy," she began, but Tuffy brushed aside this protestation.

"Oh, she and Mama hang on to you because you've started Uncle Rockman coming to the house again. He always asks first if you're coming, so Nancy and Mama ask you to keep him in good humor."

"You sure need Uncle Rockman," chuckled young Plung.

At that moment Nancy spied the little group in the corner and hurried over.

"Vicky, don't run away right after supper, because Harry and I are going out for a little nightcap. You'll come along, won't you, angel?"

Chaperoning an engaged couple was not the most fun in the world, or being an extra woman, but Vicky was touched by this evidence of Nancy's affection.

"Don't do it," Tuffy nudged her. "Why should you be stuck with him just because Nancy has to be?"

This remark irritated Nancy so much that she rushed to her mother immediately, imploring her to make Tuffy behave at parties, for she ruined everything by her talk and bad manners and insinuations about Harry.

"It's not that I don't like Harry, Mother," Nancy said plaintively. "It's just that we don't have the same interests, Mother. He's a terrible bore, but Tuffy has no right saying so."

Mrs. Elroy looked alarmed, and glanced hastily around to see if such naughty words had been heard in the clamor of the party.

"Nancy, you mustn't say such things about your fiancé!" she exclaimed in a hushed voice. "Not until you're married!"

"At least Vicky will come along with us tonight," Nancy sighed, for the only possible way to get through evenings with Harry was to have an affair with him or have a sweet, harmless person like Vicky along to share the burden of boredom. An affair was out of the question, for no matter how free a girl might be with other men she had certain moral scruples about sleeping with the man she intended to marry. She had managed to get through the courtship period by dragging Harry to Twenty-One or the Stork Club or the many other places Manhattan provides for couples who hate to be alone together. In such noisy surroundings it was possible to sit for hours with no more conversational expenditure than a word to the waiter or the little grunts necessary to a game of gin rummy. Occasionally they would see another bride-and-groom-to-be showing open affection for each other and this was a cue for Harry and Nancy, too, to hold hands. Neither one had close friends to join them, and it made Nancy cross to find that people left an engaged couple alone as if the condition was dangerously contagious.

There was really nothing wrong with Harry's manners or looks, and that was against him from the start, for having nothing offensive about him was an offense in itself. He had a clean, round face with neat little features and neat little ears and brows. He took care that his hands were nicely kept with lotions and immaculate manicures, since hands were so important in card playing. No over-fragrant fumes rose from his sleek brown hair, and his toilet water had only a tang of blameless pine about it. Ears and nose were free of vagabond hirsutae, and his teeth were as faultless as if they were false. As for his clothes they were purchased at the proper places and unobtrusive, for Harry was convinced that everything conspicuous was bad taste and everything inconspicuous good taste. His voice was pitched to a soothing monotone, and his language suspiciously genteel. You would have thought from his careful diction and proper grammar that he had never

been to college at all, but had been brought up by some
menial with a vulgar reverence for the dictionary. He said
"Agreed!" and "Surely!" and "in that regard," and "aren't I?"
If he witnessed some restaurant brawl he was pained. "You
just don't do those things, you know!" he would say. "You
just don't!" and Nancy sighed with annoyance, because Fate
had sent her a would-be-gentleman in the season all the girls
were marrying roughnecks!

"After the wedding it won't be so bad around here,
maybe," Tuffy said hopefully. "Mama and Nancy are trying to
make Harry join the Canadian Air Force so he can have his
uniform in time for the wedding. He won't look so sappy,
then. And it will give Nancy a chance to fly back and forth to
Canada to visit him the way the other girls are doing. Plungy,
why don't you do that? Nancy'll burn up if I get a chance like
that too."

Mr. Plung seemed extremely infantile to be of any value as
a warrior, but for that matter so did all the other little fellows,
barely in long trousers, chattering blithely of their preference
for the navy because of this, or the engineers because of that.
Mr. Plung put an end to Tuffy's hopes by stating that he
didn't like Canada much from camping trips he'd spent there,
and furthermore he didn't like camping. He thought he'd go
ahead with his plans to study percussion, and if he had to,
he'd play in the Army band at a summons from his country.
"Oh, yes, percussion!" Vicky said, utterly mystified. It seemed
a noble enough course to Tuffy, judging by her grave nods of
agreement, but it did ruin her plans of annoying her sister. A
more immediate means of effecting this end suggested itself,
however, and she suddenly led Plung and two undersized,
eczematic lads off to the "nursery" to listen to some Bix
Beiderbecke records with appropriate stampings. Vicky was
drawn again into Mrs. Elroy's little circle, and urged to tell
the amusing story about Amanda Keeler Evans running away
from home that time, which showed what a really human side
the girl had, you know, so different from her public impression.

"This is awful," Vicky thought desperately, squirming out
of her task as gracefully as was possible. "I've got to tell them
I am not Amanda's friend any more and it's no good being

nice to me on that score because I never can produce her here, never could have and certainly can't now."

The few guests Nancy had permitted Tuffy to ask from the very young set were now being herded out by the carefully instructed Tuffy to Hamburger Heaven. Tuffy was not required for the family supper this Sunday because Uncle Rockman was bringing an elderly gentleman friend, and naturally the talk would be on a lofty mature plane which would not brook juvenile interruption.

"I am really quite flattered that Rockman is favoring us by bringing a friend," Mrs. Elroy confided in Vicky, as the departure of guests gave her a moment for her own tea. "I've told him over and over again that I should—all of us should—be delighted to meet his friends here. I want him to feel that the place is still his home, and his friends are welcome. He knows I am perfectly willing to be his hostess at any time he cares to entertain, but he always takes his friends to his clubs or the Gotham and we practically never meet them. They must think, really, that we're to be ashamed of!"

She fetched a wry smile at this and shook her beautifully built coiffure so that the lavender gleamed in its shining surface like amethyst. Vicky murmured her congratulations at family feeling finally overcoming Uncle Rockman's bachelor eccentricities, and almost at once the two gentlemen arrived, bringing a heady scent of cigars and fresh newspapers and manly Scotch, welcome change from the Spearmint and coca-cola atmosphere they were replacing. Mrs. Elroy resumed her sweet, genteel smile, tilting her fine head at a more queenly angle, and welcomed her brother-in-law's friend with arch reproaches for their tardiness, and for Rockman's naughtiness in not bringing his friends oftener to what was really his home. Nancy placed a daughterly right arm around her mother's blue lace back, leaving her engagement hand free for an informal but glittering handclasp.

"And here is Nancy's friend, Vicky Haven," Mrs. Elroy said in fluty tones, drawing Vicky to her side. "Perhaps Rockman mentioned her."

The stranger looked piercingly at Vicky.

"Oh, so this is the gal you spoke of, Rocky?" he asked, mysteriously enough.

"Vicky is a childhood friend of Amanda Keeler Evans, you know," Mrs. Elroy went on, while Vicky found her knees slowly melting beneath her. "Vicky is more or less Amanda's protégée, aren't you, my dear? You must tell Doctor Swick some of your amusing stories about Amanda."

"Fine," said Doctor Swick. "As a matter of fact I met the young lady at the Evanses home just a week or two ago."

The familiar black bullet-eyes once more shot through rimless lenses at Vicky, giving her once again the burning picture of that whole dreadful evening. She had a frantic impulse to shriek out, "All right, go ahead and tell what happened, you old monster. Tell how I was insulted and humiliated, and maybe that will stop Mrs. Elroy from making it all the worse right now."

But nothing would stop Mrs. Elroy, now, for if both her guests had met at the Evanses table, then she was all the more honored to have them her guests, and she urged the quailing Vicky to give Doctor Swick all her data on Amanda, her doting friend. Vicky escaped by getting Nancy to go to the bedroom with her, an exit gladly accepted by Nancy who was annoyed by her mother's elegant efforts to be coy. Smoking a cigarette and gulping down some martini left on the dressing-table, Vicky decided to confide in Nancy a little of her problem.

"I can't go through with supper facing that awful man, Nancy," she blurted out. "You see—well—he was there when Amanda said some things to me, and—well, he just looks at me as if he knew all about me. You see—"

It was even harder to tell than she thought but Nancy unexpectedly helped her, by being almost ominously interested.

"You mean you've quarrelled with Amanda?" Nancy broke in, after a brief silence. "You're not on good terms with her?"

"No, you see—it was about the apartment. You see—I guess I told you I lived in her—well, what she used for an outside workroom. So—"

"I didn't know that," Nancy said, in almost an offended tone. Vicky recalled that the reason she'd never mentioned it here was that the Elroys were sure to make conversational capital of such an arrangement, stressing the intimacy of the thing. But Nancy now saw another meaning.

"You mean she paid for the apartment?"

"Yes, but she never used it at night—"

By Nancy's cold intent eyes Vicky knew she was putting her foot in it, implicitly confessing that she had never been anything but a charity to Amanda and had boasted of equality in order to win the Elroy friendship. She stumbled on, trying to explain without telling really anything, but only succeeding in making herself sound like the most unscrupulous of imposters. Nancy fell silent, ominously, and only said, "Come on, we'd better be going out. Supper will be ready."

There was nothing to do but pray for strength to get through the meal, drinking as much as she could get of the martinis in case heavenly support was not enough. Uncle Rockman beamed rosily at her and won a wave of love from her by his dogged insistence that he'd never heard of any Amanda Keeler Evans since she was no connection of his great friend Doctor Keeler of Leland Stanford, and by discoursing weightily on the Dobler effect and various scientific phenomena; and just as Mrs. Elroy resolutely snatched the conversation to speak of a violet at the Flower Show being named the Amanda Evans, Uncle Rockman triumphantly snatched it back by declaring that the violet was the shrillest color in the spectrum, an octave higher than any other color as Doctor Swick himself could testify. Mrs. Elroy's voice rose higher and higher in her efforts to keep the conversation within her own gracious bounds, but a word was enough to set Doctor Swick off on war, and a fresh drink was enough to make Uncle Rockman interrupt, with renewed radiance on his own joyous world of the abstract. His eyes sparkled, he flushed, he positively bubbled with joy in his own fountain of youth, the atom, the electron, the measuring of the soul, the surveying of infinity. Vicky alone was entranced by his words, for Doctor Swick wanted to talk and Mrs. Elroy wanted to please. Nancy was silent and as usual Harry Cosgrove Jones, IV merely agreed or exclaimed and obliged every one but pleased nobody by his tact.

"Rockman, dear," Mrs. Elroy finally interrupted, when a dish of crab meat ravigote stopped the philosopher's tongue temporarily, "won't you let Doctor Swick finish his sentence?"

"All right, call me a bore," chuckled Uncle Rockman, with a wink at Vicky. "Victoria likes to hear me, don't you, girl? Victoria's the only intelligent woman I ever met. I told you so, Swick."

"Yes," said Doctor Swick, staring at Vicky. "You told me."

"I don't think any of us have realized how very intelligent Vicky *is*," said Nancy slowly.

Doctor Swick was her evil genius, Vicky thought. Wherever he went he made trouble for her, just by being present. She wanted to make him squirm, too, and so she said, courageously, "Doctor Swick finds much to admire in Hitler, don't you, Doctor Swick?"

"Oh, no, Doctor Swick!" Mrs. Elroy was definitely shocked, and Vicky was pleased to see that the doctor grew red, and flustered.

"I may have made some remark in a satirical sense," he said stiffly. "Naturally I have no respect for the Nazi régime."

Mrs. Elroy looked reproachfully at Vicky.

"Of course not. How could any one respect people who are willing to be led by such an upstart as Adolf Hitler? The Kaiser was at least a gentleman, an aristocrat, but imagine letting yourself be led by a common hoodlum."

As this special reason for discounting nazism was a fresh twist to the problem, every one was silent, and Mrs. Elroy eagerly strove to persuade Doctor Swick of her political awareness.

"He used to sit around in cafés with other hoodlums in Munich, or Berlin or wherever it was," she said, daintily brushing crumbs away from her plate. "They sang songs and actually walked from one café to another in the middle of the streets, singing and playing instruments. Hoodlums."

The picture of Hitler as a musical hoodlum was the only appealing thing Vicky ever heard about him, but this vulgar unconventionality seemed to have aroused the Elroy political conscience as no other atrocities could, and Mrs. Elroy went on in this vein, repeating what a cousin of an attaché in Germany had told her personally about Hindenburg's dinner for his new Chancellor years ago, when all the ambassadors simply ignored the upstart, who did not know his way around among the noble glasses and cutlery, and who was snubbed by every one naturally, since in those days no one ever dreamed the common people would consent to be led by a wrong-fork-user, a café-sitter.

So that's why people like the Elroys are against Hitler, Vicky thought, getting angry. They would stand for any barbarism but mean birth and bad manners, and it was a cruel trick for them to make a Cinderella of the monster just by their contempt for him. How dared people like the Elroys and Julian Evanses be on *our* side, besmirching it with their snide reasons? Making country club of a great cause, joining it only because its membership was above reproach, its parties and privileges the most superior, its officers all the best people? Why didn't they stay on the oppressor side where they belonged and where their tastes actually were? They did in the Spanish War, and for the same reasons that they switched over in this war. Vicky was aware of a wave of indignation bringing unexpected strength to her spirits.

"You don't object to cannibalism, then," she said. "It's the table manners they use, isn't it, Mrs. Elroy?"

Uncle Rockman was staring at his sister-in-law with a peculiar hostility.

"I actually believe you'd excuse the bastard if he was a Groton boy," he said in a choked voice. "Louise, you're talking like a damned fool. Isn't that so, Victoria? I've a good mind to get up and walk out of this house, by God."

"He's joking, of course," Harry Cosgrove Jones smilingly explained to Nancy, who was looking at her uncle in alarm, naturally enough, since she had never before seen him as anything but a benign, hoodwinked Santa.

"Come, now, Rocky," Doctor Swick said, showing a row of big white teeth and rubbing his hands as if he expected a fine cannibal treat himself. "Individuals are for or against nazis for a million reasons, most of them foolish, or personal."

"You know it's true, he's nobody," Nancy addressed her uncle defensively.

This made Uncle Rockman throw his napkin on the table.

"Of course he's nobody!" he exploded. "He's nobody because he's got neither brains nor humanity, not for your reasons! I won't listen to another word! Not another word!"

"Let her talk, Rocky, it's an angle," Doctor Swick urged, winking at Nancy. "I like all the angles. It's a hobby of mine."

"There's only one angle," said Uncle Rockman with such biting dignity that his family looked at him in complete bewilderment.

"Rockman, you're being a tiny bit rude, I believe," Mrs. Elroy said tremulously, her handkerchief springing to her fine blue nose in readiness for the eyes to well over.

"I think what your Uncle Rockman means—" pacifically interposed Harry Jones, apparently under the impression that handling an eccentric uncle was the duty of the groom-to-be.

This was the last straw to the thoroughly aroused gentleman.

"You don't have any idea of what I mean, young man, and you never could, I don't care if you marched out to war tomorrow! Swick, if you can stand listening to such gabble, the brains of a wasp, the—the—" Choking, Uncle Rockman backed his chair from the table and rose. "I said I'd leave. By God, I will!"

"Nancy, say something to your uncle!" wailed Mrs. Elroy. "Dr. Swick, I assure you there must be something the matter with him. I said nothing at all. I can't understand you, Rockman, really—when you know you're all I've got—all *we've* got—"

Uncle Rockman was in the hall picking up his stick and derby in ominous silence. They heard his grim, four-square footsteps marching toward the door as if he was leaving the house forever, an inconvenience frightening in its possibilities, so that Nancy and mother exchanged looks of dawning horror. Doctor Swick scratched his head thoughtfully, and Harry Jones, IV murmured inadequately. "You just don't *do* those things, you know." Vicky felt that she was left in a den of wolves, and without a second's reflection was on her feet, dashing after Uncle Rockman, breathlessly.

"Wait!" she cried, as the front door started to close. "I understand what you mean, Mr. Elroy."

Silently he stepped back and brought her hat and gloves from the closet, and with a red, angry face whisked her to the elevator.

"Of course you do, Vicky, my girl," he said. "Naturally, Vicky, my girl."

In the dining-room confusion broke forth.

"How dare she run after Uncle Rocky?" Nancy cried out.

"But what did I say?" Mrs. Elroy begged of Doctor Swick. "Did I say anything?"

Doctor Swick beat on the table with his square-tipped, thick fingers, and his eyes roved from mother to daughter.

"Rocky's too intolerant for a scientist and philosopher," he observed. "He ought to be more interested in all the angles. So that's the girl he wants to marry, eh?"

Nancy and her mother gave a single cry of pain.

"Doctor Swick! Is that what Rockman told you? Good heavens!"

"I can't stand hearing another word! Mother, when I think how that girl has tricked us! So it was just to get Uncle Rockman! And turning him against us!"

"Oh, he wants her all right," Doctor Swick said, comfortably. "Fed up facing old age alone, you know. Usual bachelor type of thing. Pretty face, youth, sort of daughter business."

His words seemed to strike straight to the hearts, for both mother and daughter burst openly into tears, and Harry Jones patted Nancy helplessly on the back as if she'd swallowed a foreign object. Doctor Swick himself was puzzled by the effect Rockman's exit and his own words was having on the others and tried to distract them with a little gossip.

"Funny thing happened the other night at the Julian Evanses when that girl was there. Maybe she *is* some sort of adventuress, if that's what you think. It happened this way—"

XI

AMANDA had not slept for so long now that she wondered how she ever had. Allanol, veronal, luminol, and the whole battery of sedatives did no more than induce a half-dozing state in which her thoughts raced even faster. It was ridiculous that with all the money and influence at her command she couldn't buy or wangle a simple thing like sleep. Bemel slept. The servants slept. If you went down to the basement at night you could hear their triumphant snores. True, Julian was an insomniac, and when she complained to him he merely said, "People who deal in the affairs of nations seldom sleep, my dear. Very likely you won't rest well until the war is over." The war! The war was getting too big for Amanda, it was no longer her private property, it was beyond one person's signature. It was like a club that had finally been opened to the public, the original members lost in the scuffle. The time for the amateurs was over, the pretty prologue was over, the play proper was to begin. The Amandas were almost at the end of their function, which was to entertain the audience until the professionals arrived. Never caring for any game in which she was not the leader, Amanda cast about in her mind for ways of easing out before she became *used* by the war instead of using it. There were other games where she could be the star. Without Julian Evans, too, God willing. It was hatred that was keeping her awake, Amanda thought, as if you couldn't hate somebody and forget it. But her feeling for Julian was like some flowering nightshade, a dark, growing thing that stood between her and every sensation. It was beyond all reason, now, so that she shuddered to pick up a newspaper he had just touched; she winced at his breakfast kiss so rudely that he stopped the little ceremony, and in her relief she did not care that he now seemed fully as hostile to her as she to him. The faintest possible suspicion that she might be pregnant occurred to her, but it was too soon to worry and moreover she was supposed to be sterile. The thought that she might have to sleep with Julian to cover up the slip was as odious as the galling knowledge that the lover in the case had left her like some village cavalier. No, this was too outrageous a trick for Fate to play, and Amanda would have none of it.

Sometimes she gave up even trying to sleep and paced restlessly around the study, reading a page or two of Malraux, Hemingway, or her favorite Callingham, for these were the only three writers she considered her peers. But underneath the surface level of her thoughts ran her furious desire for Ken Saunders, the absolute necessity for subjugating him and so restore her lost complacency. If she were in love with him, she kept wailing to herself, there would be some excuse for this obsession, but she could not possibly be in love with any one so far beneath her in every way.

In the morning it was Bemel. Opening her eyes Amanda would think of Miss Bemel and clench her teeth. Bemel epitomized everything that was going wrong in her life, and worse, Bemel knew things were going wrong. Things wouldn't really be going wrong, perhaps, if it wasn't for Bemel *knowing* they were and making them come out that way. At nine Miss Bemel came into the bedroom with the mail, pouncing on the new day as if it were a runaway horse to be yanked into control. She would stand behind Mrs. Pons as she was serving Amanda's breakfast tray, impatiently watching this brief rite, tapping her teeth with her pencil in her anxiety to get going, or get her machine, namely Amanda, going.

"That coffee doesn't look hot, Mrs. Pons," she would say, frowning. "Take it out and heat it up. Can't expect Mrs. Evans to begin the day on cold coffee."

This sort of thing made Amanda immediately declare she liked cold coffee or quince preserve instead of marmalade or whatever it was Bemel was so sure she did not like. Once the tray was out of the way, Bemel's performance began. There was the appointment pad to be recited, the hours cut into tiniest little wedges like a poorhouse pie with Miss Bemel presiding over the distribution. There was the mail to be summarized and the choice bits served to the mistress, the rest handled imperiously by Miss Bemel as she chose. It was only natural that such grave responsibilities should in time go to Miss Bemel's head, since they were the sole source of her importance. As the quantity of correspondence increased, Miss

Bemel's arrogance mounted until she was permitting herself the same tantrums around the other servants with which Amanda favored her. Such busy, important creatures as Amanda and Miss Bemel had no time for curbing tempers or smoothing out other people's feelings. The old days when Miss Bemel had grovelled in her devotion, and gloried in having her brains picked for Amanda's dear use, were well-nigh over, for Miss Bemel was being recognized now on her own. She had been interviewed for a great magazine as "The Woman Behind the Scenes" along with other famous secretaries in the White House and Wall Street. She was invited to join a Discussion Group where she sounded forth with authority on matters Amanda had not yet put into print, both on literature and politics, and when the ladies brought to her their arguments on Amanda's magazine and newspaper pieces Miss Bemel patronizingly explained the whole matter, not hesitating to use the pronoun "I" instead of "we," or better, "she." It was only natural that the rising glory of her private life should reveal itself in added self-satisfaction which could not be disguised even for policy's sake with Amanda herself.

"Mrs. Evans will probably go to China again very soon," she told the Discussion Group, mysteriously. "I haven't said anything definite about it to her, but the situation there is changing so fast I'm going to talk to her about going very soon."

The more Miss Bemel revealed herself as the Brains and Conscience of her employer in public, the more was she treated as the Pest and Whipping Boy of her employer in private, and there was brewing in the loyal secretary's heart the first seed of sedition, though it might take years to really mature. It was aggravating to have her vanity advanced two feet by night and then penalized three feet by day, like some arithmetic problem with no answer. At present all she could do was persevere doggedly in her efforts to keep control of Amanda.

"You really must make up your mind about the trip to China," she said, waving a telegram under Amanda's nose this morning. "It means postponing your novel, but it will mean infinitely more than that in the long run. I wired the Recorder that you were delaying in order to discuss it further with Mr. Evans."

"I make my own decisions, please, Bemel," Amanda said. "Is the hairdresser coming here this morning?"

"I cancelled him," Miss Bemel said. "In fact, you have so much more correspondence and people to see now that things are happening, I've spoken to Mr. Castor about an office away from the house for general details. War work, charity, and lectures. Keep the home free for your creative work."

Amanda handed Bemel the phone quietly.

"Call the hairdresser and tell him to be here as soon as possible," she said.

Miss Bemel looked affronted, then bit her lip, and took the phone reluctantly.

"Damn it, do as I say!" Amanda suddenly shouted, unable to bear more.

In the early days of their relationship Miss Bemel would have lowered her head and butted out of the room, lips trembling, prepared to scold every servant in the house by way of balancing her blood pressure. The Discussion Group, however, had given her poise.

"I should think with the war creeping in on us, you would have less time than ever for hair and massage and clothes," she said gravely. "The worse things get the more time you spend at fittings, and Arden's. I'm only saying this because it's been commented upon by the columnists."

Amanda controlled herself with difficulty.

"Thank you for reminding me," she said. "Call the hairdresser."

Miss Bemel's bushy brows met in a tangle of disapproval. God, she's an ugly female, thought Amanda, and even if she had a heart of valuable priorities her appearance in itself was a crime against mankind. As she swivelled around on her bovine rump to pick up the telephone, Amanda saw that she was getting bigger than ever, and it was not only in flesh but an increase in muscle and bone with a bosom as formidable and as sexless as a German general's. This rocky treasure taxed the capacity of whatever blouse she wore, especially the pock-marked yellow print now gracing her form, strained in a taut line across her back and then across her front so that bosoms popped out behind and before, above and below as if there were dozens of them, all crying for freedom. Certainly no man had ever touched her and no man ever would, reflected Amanda sourly. Frustration was what made the woman so detestable. But what about herself, then, Amanda thought, stunned. Wasn't she in the same boat as Bemel? She, too, was undesired. Ken Saunders had walked away from her open arms. Even Julian no longer approached her. She and Bemel, two frustrated women, and how do you like that? Instead of being softened by this link with her loyal slave, Amanda found her temper mounting to murderous heights, doubled by her disgust with herself.

"Emerson ten to eleven," Miss Bemel said, consulting her pad. "He's up to page 176 of the novel and is waiting for your okay on the fencing scene he has outlined. He worked with Signor Florelle over the details last night. They were both very much pleased with it, but it seemed a little weak to me."

Oh, so it seemed weak to Miss Bemel's superbly informed mind, did it?

"Hereafter, it won't be necessary for you to go over the novel," Amanda said. "I will deal with Mr. Emerson directly on that."

"But you haven't talked over the revised structure, yet, and I have," Miss Bemel protested. "You'd better let me sit in on it when he comes today."

Amanda's eyes blazed.

"Keep out of that novel, do you hear? You're not hired to tinker with that end of things."

Miss Bemel was shaken but not to be swerved.

"Well, I can tell you you'll never get it done with Emerson alone," she started. "He's not the worker Thirer used to be."

"All right, I'll fire him and do it all myself," Amanda shouted.

She snatched at the letters Miss Bemel still held in her hand, seething at the annotations Miss Bemel had made for reply on each one. The presumption of her, thought Amanda! The cheek! And furthermore the cheek of her fine assistant, young Emerson, in planning Amanda Keeler Evans's novel with the lady's secretary! All Julian's fault, Amanda concluded, dividing her bitterness now. By day Miss Bemel and by night Julian, driving her in the road that they chose. It was as if they and their helpers had built her tower for her to rule the world and then locked her in. What had once seemed getting her own way now was *their* way, she had no choice any more.

Miss Bemel tramped into the next room, her head lowered, her square back conveying wounded sensitivity.

"For God's sake, Bemel, go out and get yourself a girdle!" Amanda cried after her, unable to endure the sight of the creature.

"I wear a foundation garment, Mrs. Evans." Miss Bemel, now utterly at bay, turned to her tormentor with quivering lips.

"Garment! I hate calling things *garments!*" Amanda said savagely. "A lovely garment, a useful garment. God, how genteel!"

To this Miss Bemel proudly made no answer. She comforted her wounded pride with the note on her spindle from Mr. Castor stating that Mr. Evans would not be in for dinner as he was due at a conference upstate with his syndicate chief. Conference indeed! The first Mrs. Evans, of course! Small wonder with the present Mrs. Evans letting her hair down over the slightest thing. Not so clever, after all, was this Number Two who still hadn't caught on to what her husband was doing. Miss Bemel permitted herself a spiteful little smile as she sat down to the typewriter.

Amanda lay in bed for a moment considering the chances of running down Ken Saunders. She hadn't seen him since the day he walked out of the studio. His hotel said he'd given up his apartment there and left no address. One night in the middle of dinner he had telephoned her, very drunk, but she was entertaining a Free French official and a Facts and Figures man, so she could not talk. Five minutes later she had called frantically all the places he might be, but he was not to be found. The nerve of him, she thought passionately, the cheek of all these people, these Bemels, these Vickys, these Kens, who dared to clutter the smooth pattern of her life! If she went over to her studio, she thought, she might find a message from him there. It was absolute nonsense that this one little man's rejection of her should be ruining her life, making her brain a constant whirl of rage and futile storming. She got

up and went into the study. Seeing the pile of papers beside
Miss Bemel, it occurred to her that she might revenge herself
on this officious creature by handling her own mail and reducing the other to merest office boy. She frowned through
her glasses at a few of the letters and realized with vague bewilderment that her public life was so completely in Miss
Bemel's hands that she herself knew scarcely anything about
it. She could no more pick up the professional correspondence of this Amanda Evans than she could any stranger's.

"I'm a dummy. They've made a dummy of me," she
thought. "They own me, Bemel and Julian."

There was a note acknowledging Mr. Evans' check in settling the broken lease for the Murray Hill studio. Amanda
gave a little gasp. The note had been routed from Julian to
Castor to Bemel. There was something ominous in Julian
cancelling that lease without a word to her. What had he
found out? Had Vicky given him the address after the night
here? Why hadn't Miss Bemel mentioned it, or did she too
suspect something when she found out about the place which
had been kept pointedly secret from her? What if Julian had
found some clue there? She saw that Miss Bemel would not
give any satisfaction on these queries, for she was far too hurt
that the business had been conducted without her knowledge. Thoughtfully Amanda picked up the manuscript of her
new novel, and began reading it from the very beginning.
There were many passages she had never even glanced at, sections of her own rewritten by Mr. Emerson in a richly florid
style quite different from the style she had used, with Mr.
Thirer's help, in *Such Is the Legend*. She had given Emerson
too much leeway, that was clear, and as she read her face darkened with new indignation.

"He's changed this all around, Bemel," she said slowly.
"Where'd he get the idea of having Le Maz come to New
York after he left Virginia?"

"Mr. Evans suggested that," said Miss Bemel. "He thought
a chapter or two on the New York of that period would give
a little variety, and then it would appeal more to the motion
pictures."

"Mr. Evans might have spoken to me about it," said
Amanda stiffly.

"He didn't want to disturb you until Emerson had worked it out a little more," said Miss Bemel. "He did talk it over with the publishers and some picture people and they agreed with him."

Amanda sat still waiting for her rage to permit her to speak.

"Settle with Emerson when he comes," she said, finally. "The book is off."

"Off?" Miss Bemel said blankly, jaw dropping. "Off?"

"That's right. Write my publishers. I have decided to abandon the Le Maz story. Whatever I do next will be entirely different."

As soon as she saw Miss Bemel's horrified expression, a feeling of triumphant exaltation came over Amanda. She saw herself deliberately destroying the figurehead Julian had created and avenging herself by making herself a new Amanda, an Amanda who was none of their doing, none of their business. She wasn't sure how she was going to do this, but a sense of limitless power surged through her, a high elation. Chains would be cast off, she would be free again as she was when she first conquered Julian; she would be free of Julian, Bemel, Ken, just as she had freed herself once of her family and Lakeville. What had been done, could be done again.

Miss Bemel was staring at her helplessly, as if she sensed the change in the woman she was so certain she knew completely.

"You can't mean it, Mrs. Evans," she said weakly. "You can't mean you're dropping the book. Do wait till Mr. Evans comes back."

"This is no one's concern but mine," said Amanda coldly, and then she picked up the newspaper with the picture of Andrew Callingham on the front page, just back from Lisbon. It was a sign from heaven. The one person she admired more than any one else, the great man of the age, the one for whom she was really destined. Not a little Julian Evans, but a genius, a brave man, really worthy of being conquered by an Amanda. Fleetingly Amanda saw the two of them, the two greatest of their kind, sweeping through the world together, enriching each other, fulfilling each other, worthy of each other.

"Call Mr. Callingham at his hotel and tell him we are expecting him for dinner," said Amanda.

She was calm, again, the way she was when there was a challenge ahead she knew she could meet, and great rewards to be won. A man who could stir her physically as Ken had done, without the after-feeling of being trapped by an inferior! A man whose very name could swing her to unheard of glories, so that she would be fulfilled as woman and honored as queen! Amanda took a swift glance at herself in the mirror, examining herself as she always did, not with vanity in her beauty for itself but appraising it for what it could buy. Her blonde hair needed the hairdresser, certainly, for it hung about her shoulders, straight and careless as if she had walked through the woods in the rain. But that was right, thought Amanda, that was exactly right for the man who was supposed to hate civilized women!

"Cancel the hairdresser," she said briefly.

Miss Bemel looked at her without expression.

"Very well," she said. "But Mr. Evans won't be here for dinner, you know."

"You don't need to mention that to Mr. Callingham," said Amanda, realizing that only Julian could make these regal demands on his contributors. To get Callingham she still needed Julian. She ruffled through her papers, knowing Miss Bemel was looking at her strangely.

"What's this about Mrs. Elroy calling?" she asked.

"Mrs. Beaver Elroy. She's telephoned several times for an appointment, but would not tell me what it was about," Miss Bemel said. "It didn't seem important enough to call to your attention before."

"Perhaps it was personal," Amanda said softly. "Something you know nothing about."

"It was something about Miss Haven, she said," Miss Bemel said, wincing at the implication of secrets withheld from her.

Amanda frowned. She was glad to have Vicky and her last link with Lakeville off the records, though their last encounter still made her flush. But through this friend she might find something about Ken Saunders. Before she could wholeheartedly set out for Callingham she must clear it up once and for all with Saunders that it was she who was having the final word. She could not leave it that he had been the one to get out. She owed herself that satisfaction.

"Call her and make an appointment," she said coldly.

2

Mrs. Beaver Elroy had never in her whole fifty-one years been so distraught as she found herself on learning of her brother-in-law's sinister plans against her happiness. The Elroy home, never a model of contentment, now was a hornet's nest, with its members in such a dangerous state of hysterics that they might well have been quarantined as victims of the Vicky Haven Disease. It was Nancy's fault for ever bringing her to the house, it was Mother's fault for encouraging her, it was Tuffy's fault for not telling them what Uncle Rocky had confided in her regarding his admiration for Miss Haven. It was all their faults and they blamed each other without reserve, but most of all they blamed the designing, artful way in which the gold-digger from Lakeville had wormed herself into their confidence and taken away their only means of support, their father-advisor, their bank, their moral guide, Uncle Rockman. It was a tribute to that gentleman's foxiness in never permitting them to possess him that they did not allow their indignation to touch him. He was the object of pity and regret for having his innocent affections preyed upon by the Lakeville vixen, he was a poor lost angel whose mind was being poisoned by this interloper so that he neither answered Mrs. Elroy's letters nor appeared inside their door since the fateful night the truth had been revealed.

Nancy indicated that Vicky's treachery hastened her resignation from *Peabody's* since, she informed Mr. Peabody, it was impossible for her to work for the organization that harbored Miss Haven. It was a wicked interruption to the pre-wedding festivities, casting as it did a veil of doubt on whether Uncle Rockman would try to use some of his money on his bride-to-be rather than on those worthy and deserving of it. Nancy's low angry voice went on all night in the bedroom with her mother, and was stopped only when her mother, wishing to go to sleep, would tell her it was all her own fault for mixing with girls from offices, and indeed her fault for ever going into Business against her mother's wishes. Tuffy made things worse by cluttering up the house with her crowd so that free discussion of the family catastrophe was hampered. She did cry a great deal at the idea of being supplanted by a wife as Uncle's pet, but then she was crying also over the stormy path of her own love life which was far from satisfactory. The real sufferer in the case was Mrs. Elroy, for, as she told them, she was first of all a mother and stricken by any danger to her babies' well-being. Secondly she had given up her entire life to making a home for her brother-in-law, as a sort of monument to Beaver. It was regrettable, but not a diminishing fact, that Rockman had seldom made use of her sacrifice. She had, as she looked back on it, given up very good marriages with reputable widowers, to give Rockman the entire wealth of her heart. Now these years of patient, selfless devotion were proved unappreciated. A Miss Nobody, pretending to be a friend of Amanda Evans instead of a charity, had bemused the innocent man with her youth and wiles. The long cherished hopes of Mrs. Elroy to finally put Rockman into Beaver's shoes was dashed to bits, and moreover no one, not even Nancy, had ever shared this secret. A mother is above all a mother, but there are times when she is just a woman, and Mrs. Elroy was in that anguished condition.

She consulted her astrologer, a marvellous woman who had actually brought about Nancy's engagement by her timely advice, but this time the lady failed her by promising a new man, a Taurus with a heart condition. Mrs. Elroy would have no part of a Taurus with a heart condition. She wanted Rockman or nothing. She worked at the planchette with a spiritualistic friend from Columbus, hoping to receive guidance from Beaver. The friend may have done a little pushing, but as Mrs. Elroy said to herself in all fairness, if somebody didn't push, the thing wouldn't move. The two ladies worked feverishly over the board all one evening and contacted some of the most exclusive dead, including Edward VII and President Polk, but none offered wisdom to Mrs. Elroy in the problem of saving her brother-in-law. It occurred to her later that Beaver might have deliberately held off out of jealousy. Mrs. Elroy and her friend sat at the ouija board, finger-tips meeting, eyes closed, summoning Beaver's ghost from the Beyond, but Beaver was quite as undependable dead as he had been alive. Mrs. Elroy pictured him with life-like vividness leaning over the golden bar of heaven, while the telephone rang and rang, his wife's urgent messages unheeded by the celestial bartender. Mrs. Elroy gave up the little séance with a resigned shrug.

"Beaver always let me down," she sighed bravely to her friend. "Now Rockman lets us down. Something in the Elroy blood."

She had counted so completely on this graceful flowering of her connection with Rockman that she now felt as betrayed as if vows had been exchanged, and it was hard to remember that Rockman had never encouraged any such hopes. It had begun almost at Beaver's funeral. After the children grew up and married, then she would turn to the waiting Rockman and say, "Now, Rockman. Now is our reward." But no such thing. And since she dared not mention this special blow to her pride, it wounded her that the fitness of the thing had never occurred to the children any more than to Rockman. They prattled on about their own deprivation and their own selfish little lives with no regard for the private anguish of their mother.

In her trying hour Mrs. Elroy had the inspiration of using the calamity as a wedge into Amanda Evans' home. Her engagements, like her perfumes, furs, and handkerchiefs, were so much family property that it was an exciting adventure to lie about a "fitting" to Nancy, and then make her dignified dash for the Evans' home. According to Doctor Swick, Amanda had as good as ordered Vicky out of her house, so that she was certain to meet sympathy and support here. Otherwise, indeed, the appointment would not have been granted, since goodness knows all the Elroy previous invitations had been most coldly received.

Mrs. Elroy, gotten up for this tremendous occasion, was quite a job. An hour Pick-Me-Up facial at Rubenstein's had erased the troubled lines in her broad brow; a saucer of violets in a swirl of blue veiling served as crown for her fine new permanent; blue kid slippers tipped the still handsome slender legs, with "matching accessories" as *Peabody's* always said, including an enormous fine bag with silver trimmings large enough to carry the complete file of all the Elroy enemies. Her gray coat was both proper and feminine, allowing a ruffle of chiffon scarf to soften the betraying throat sag. There was not a doubt in the world that here was a lady, one well equipped by birth and appearance to visit the Evans' mansion. Mrs. Elroy had none of Ethel Carey's misapprehensions as she entered the marble foyer that afternoon, for she was a Chivers from Columbus and her proud memory had marbleized the entire family tree. But her heart did beat fast, thinking of the years spent in trying to bring about this contact, and it was no less a triumph that tragedy had effected what her social strategy had failed to do. And Amanda's immediate appearance in the drawing-room confused her to a point where she was actually gushing out something about "we have a little friend in common—Victoria—er—er—" before she recollected that it was more an enemy in common.

Amanda, never one to waste time on the pretty little amenities, confused Mrs. Elroy even further by conducting the interview on a bald businesslike basis quite different from the suave interchange Mrs. Elroy had dreamed.

"You see we accepted her as your protégée," Mrs. Elroy said, with a pained sweet smile. "Naturally any one would be proud to accept your recommendation, Mrs. Evans. But when she used our house to conduct a campaign on poor brother Rockman! Isn't there anything you can do, Mrs. Evans, to stop her? Isn't there some one in her family back home who could talk to her? I assure you, we are all heart-broken. She seemed so simple. And all the time setting out to marry poor Rockman, twice her age, and completely blind so far as women are concerned. There's no talking to him."

Amanda listened to her caller attentively, with a little frown.

"But you haven't said anything about Vicky accepting him," she interrupted. "How do you know she's going through with it?"

This question absolutely floored Mrs. Elroy. Her jaw drooped and she stared helplessly at Amanda.

"But of course she will!" she finally stammered. "That's the whole thing. She wouldn't have gotten him to that stage without intending to go through with it."

Amanda looked skeptical, and Mrs. Elroy began to feel foolish and a little angry. A woman of Mrs. Evans's brains should know that any one would marry Rockman Elroy who had a chance. Amanda's next query ruffled her even more.

"What's your objection to her marrying him?"

For this Mrs. Elroy mustered all her resources, her voice rising to a mildly querulous pitch in spite of her efforts to keep it low and silvery.

"The difference in their ages. And their class. But it's more than that, Mrs. Evans." Here Mrs. Elroy looked around to make sure that the dark room concealed no eavesdroppers. "She has a young man on the side, Nancy tells me. Mr. Saunders, who used to be at *Peabody's*. Of course she thinks she will get Rockman's name and his money and then keep up with her lover. It's plain as the nose on your face. And Mrs. Evans, one can't sit back and see one's brother, a fine wonderful man like Rockman, made a monkey of that way! That's why I came here."

That's it, Amanda thought. Ken had dared to leave her for little Vicky. He had made her leave the studio because it reminded him of Amanda. It was Ken's doing, all of it. Vicky couldn't know about them, Amanda was certain of that. Girls like Vicky had no flair for sensing undercurrents. She felt color coming into her face, thinking of being left for a little mouse like Vicky. Ken had planned it deliberately to humiliate her, to revenge himself for the years she had teased him. Excitement began burning inside her, knowing that through Vicky she could get back at him, recapture him, and then throw him back, always the sportsman's privilege. Of course, Vicky had no intention of marrying this old bachelor of Mrs. Elroy's. It would be a good job if she did. A plan formed in Amanda's mind swiftly.

"I can't promise anything will come of my talking to Vicky," she said carefully, stabbing her cigarette out in the ash tray. "Maybe she has made up her mind. I'll talk to her, in any case."

The interview was over, but it took Mrs. Elroy, unused to harsh business manners, a moment or two to realize the fact. She had expected to have a little polite chat to cover up the crude purpose of her call, but Amanda would have none of it.

She stood in the doorway, unsmiling, uncivil, really, Mrs.
Elroy thought, until the latter had collected her gloves and
bag. Amanda rang for some one to see the lady out, and waiting beside the elevator, looked sharply at her guest.

"It's your brother-in-law, not your brother, isn't it?" she
asked.

Mrs. Elroy nodded.

"About your age, you said," Amanda pursued, reflectively.
"Oh. Now, I see."

The implications of what she saw made Mrs. Elroy's sus-
ceptible nose assume a delicate heliotrope shade, and shat-
tered for the moment her satisfaction in the interview. Mrs.
Elroy shuddered as she felt the heavy doors of Twenty-nine
swing shut behind her, thinking of Amanda's cryptic "Oh,
now I see." She had not said a word to suggest such a thing,
but after all her trouble Amanda had merely thought the lady
was only anxious to get Rockman for herself. Walking gracefully down Fifth Avenue the liquid spring air revived Mrs.
Elroy's confidence. It didn't really matter what Amanda
Evans thought if she could restore Rockman to his rightful
owners. Yes, she really had accomplished something.

XII

EVERYWHERE people were whispering to each other, "I've just got back from Washington," with mysterious, significant looks as if now they knew the secrets of all nations. Merely by buying a round trip ticket to the nation's capital they acquired special powers of divination into the country's future, which on no account would they reveal. At every gathering a murmur fraught with spy-papers, secret missions, dangerous responsibilities, would sweep the room—"He's leaving for Washington tonight!" Heads would turn, every one would stare eagerly at whatever man had been so honorably mentioned, as if out of the whole world the President himself had decided here is the one most able to advise him. The mere name of the city, hitherto evoking only images of cherry blossoms and grisly state banquets, now invested whoever mentioned it with curious, enviable knowledge, and so trains and planes were packed with citizens rushing to Washington with their letters to some one high-up, their queries, their suggestions, their data. Initials of various departments and organizations buzzed up and down train corridors, hotel lobbies, club-rooms, bars—OCD, COI, OFF, and any one confessing bewilderment at these alphabetical symbols was socially as undesirable as any college freshman unable to grasp the fundamental difference between a Deke and a Beta. Brief-cases shot back and forth bulging with state secrets, plans for making ploughs out of bent paper clips, paper clips out of bent ploughs, bullets out of iambic pentameters and tea out of poison ivy. Artists knocked each other down in their stampede to the Mayflower with a Functional Canvas, columnists thought up five-word slogans for civilian morale and rushed to headquarters for their proper medals; civilians wore uniforms to denote they were civilians; men in action wore civilian clothes to denote they were in the service, possibly too important for the obscurity of full military trappings. It was a time to be just back, just going, or to know some one who was just back or just going to Washington. Like any other holy city, the mere pilgrimage was in itself enough to insure respect from one's fellows.

Mr. Julian Evans flew back and forth to Washington in a private plane with his business secretary, Harnett, Amos Cheever, four minor secretaries, a photographer and public relations man, in short, with a suitable staff for a leading public-opinion molder. He had a five-room suite at the proper hotel where he conferred in the greatest secrecy (except for the secretaries, dictaphone, and reporters) with dignitaries too high up to be even named here; reports of these conferences were then photostated, mimeographed, and mailed for further protection of their sacred contents, copies filed in a steel trunk which accompanied Julian on all his trips like a gagman's joke box. In the city of Washington itself the rest of the country faded away; Washington was America, the rest of the country was spoken of as "the field," as if its acres and population were the testing laboratory for the myriad experiments being discussed in the Capitol.

Amanda Keeler Evans, in this constant shuffling of events and public names, was less in the public eye on her own merits and more as the charming young wife of the great Julian, who, it was rumored was wanted by the President's closest chiefs for a post of unparallelled importance. In the magazines, the Washington hostesses took precedence over individual achievements by the Amandas; women volunteers and their organizers were publicized, and Amanda had neglected to get into this game. Unknown female patriots were springing up, their greatest value in their earnest anonymity. Amanda was confused by the masses of women too simple to be rivals, too numerous to be dismissed, and too mass-minded in their ambitions to be even faintly understood by her, let alone led.

"I'm afraid Amanda has missed the boat somewhere in these last crises," Julian confided candidly to Amos Cheever.

In the midst of all his new dignities and his new hostility towards her, Julian was in no mood to smooth out his wife's problems or to advise her career. Amanda, conscious of her own recent deficiencies and jealous of Julian's rising star, jeered at his new honors and ambitions, since they were tacit evidence of who was now top-man. She and Julian shouted at each other, disagreeing over the smallest trifle, they banged doors and carried on their wrangling even before the servants and guests, rather than be left alone with each other.

"At the most important period in my entire career," Julian gravely complained to Cheever, "the person I've done the most for in the whole world, the woman I have actually created—"

"You have, you have!" Cheever agreed, shaking his head sympathetically. "No one would ever deny it."

"—the woman I have not only made the queen of her field but honored with my name, turns against me and mocks me! What would the public say if they could see the torment she causes me? Incredible, Cheever! Incredible! People would laugh at me. They would! Oh, yes, they would! I would be ruined so far as public respect goes. No, no, Cheever, she must be curbed before she ruins us. I don't see how just yet, but I'll work it out. Ah, these human problems! They're the ones that defeat a man!"

It was only natural that hints of such domestic turmoil should reach the gossips, and if Amanda had been in a more perceptive state she might have observed that faint change in the responses of trades people, servants, and opportunistic friends always visible when a separation is in the air and it is not yet known which side is buttered. The abject loyalty, the humble adulation, dwindles to merely respectful attention in preparation for a graceful retreat in case the rich husband is now grooming a new bride. At the same time no open rudeness must be betrayed, for there is always the chance that the retiring wife may have wangled the bulk of the fortune.

Amanda observed none of these changes of wind, absorbed in her own private confusion. She had manipulated her course so far by complete self-confidence, remaining cool and in constant control of her reactions. Now panic was upon her, and she could think of no way to solve it but by destroying everything around her. She fought with her committees, broke lecture engagements, wept all night because she could not sleep, neglected social duties recklessly, allowed Julian to entertain dinner guests alone while she had tea in bed and sulked or else wrote furiously in her new book, which was to be none of Julian's or Miss Bemel's business. She telephoned

Andrew Callingham every night, just as she had once done Julian, and would not be dismissed or hurt by his suave apologies. If he had not yet married that Swedish dancer with whom he travelled, then there was a fair chance he never would, and Amanda was staking her claim in advance.

"I'm working on an entirely different line, now," she confided in him. "You're the one person in the world to understand what I'm attempting. It's—well, it's your kind of thing."

But Mr. Callingham, charmed as he was by her good looks and the power she had over Julian Evans, would not take her literary aspirations seriously. Julian had been too easy game for her, Amanda admitted to herself. His extreme morality had made him a born gull, with no defense against a wily woman. Other men, real men like Callingham with a thousand women after them every minute, wanted to be the pursuers and put up a valiant defense against ladies who took away their hunting licenses. This resistance did not discourage Amanda, but rather gave her added zest for the game. But other matters troubled her, and made her life a nightmare. What was Julian's talk of being governor or cabinet minister or ambassador, what was a new country dragged into war, what were the new problems of her refugee groups to her own unbelievable dilemma? She might as well have been some debutante virgin, for the complicated horror of her condition. In all her sophisticated life she had never faced such a problem, and since she had never regarded women friends as anything but a burden, she had no one to trust. Here was a situation no lunch with a steel millionaire could adjust, no flattery from a visiting king could settle, this was a problem for the woman friend. Amanda thought fleetingly of Ethel Carey, but Ethel was far away and not likely to be won back to intimacy after Amanda's recent snubs. Even knowing this, Amanda wired her an invitation to lunch next time she was in New York. It was insulting to be answered, not by wire, but by letter from Miss Carey's housekeeper in Lakeville, stating that Miss Carey was now in residence in Washington as an official in the A.W.V.O.

"They can't do this to me," Amanda thought, indignantly, just as she would have blamed "they" for cancer or old age.

Catastrophes happened to people, certainly, because people were stupid, emotional foolish animals. But they did not happen to Amanda. They *shouldn't*. If they seemed to be happening to her now, it must be some one's fault; some dolt had left a door open, some fool had given the wrong address. God himself must have gotten the name wrong. You would have thought that God was accustomed by this time to breaking the backs of those with already broken backs; it wasn't His way to inconvenience His own special hothouse flowers. He usually shipped them efficiently through life with the warning to all "Fragile. This Side Up." Yet here He was, bungling up His own special Amanda Evans' nice plans with the most reverent inefficiency. Possibly He had been too long with the firm and had delusions of grandeur. The Board of Directors would hear of this. Send a memo, Miss Bemel, that one more mistake like the last one and out He'd go, without his pension, too. Mr. and Mrs. Julian Evans would not tolerate impudence, even from their Maker.

2

In front of Vicky's apartment Amanda looked out of the cab curiously. A moving van was backed up to the curb and an entire home was being transferred from truck to sidewalk. A butterfly sofa with a worn Paisley covering went out first, its bottom spilling wire coils and stuffing; a small, old-fashioned pine cupboard with roses and violins painted on its broken doors; an uneven, teetering cherry chest; a needlepoint footstool on beetle legs, and a bushel basket of clay dishes. Why any one should bother to transfer these treasures from one tenement to another, Amanda could not imagine. She stepped out gingerly among this collection and opened her purse.

"You're Amanda Keeler Evans," grinned the driver.

Amanda gave a start, not prepared for recognition in this section.

"Knew you by those News Reels," said the driver, making change for her. He was beaming over his cleverness in having recognized her from such a vague clue as her picture in constant circulation. Amanda acknowledged his remark with a nervous nod, for she had no desire to be seen making this particular visit. When the man called after her if she'd like him to wait, she hurried on with bent head, pretending she hadn't heard. As she followed the sofa up the stone steps to the pet-shop entrance, she heard the voice of another cabby, "Hey, Mac, wasn't that Amanda Evans?" and her own driver's proud assent. It was not easy living in a glass house. There were no provisions for an occasional black-out, and Amanda wanted a black-out for a little while. She had gone to some trouble to pick up a cab far from her own neighborhood, changing to another one later on, but she seemed to carry her notoriety around with her like a hump. This was Vicky's fault for not being in the *Peabody* office when Amanda needed her, and for not answering telegrams. It was small-minded of Vicky to stay wounded over that last dinner, small-minded and extremely inconvenient for Amanda.

The moving man, a large red lobster of a fellow with white bristles sprinkled over head, nostrils, wattles and ears, stood in the tiny vestibule pressing a bell while his gaunt gray assistant stared at Amanda and stroked his unshaven cheek reflectively. Likely enough, they knew her too, Amanda thought, disturbed. Propinquity to the masses she championed in public always annoyed her in private, and she let them go ahead with their freight before entering. Then she climbed the stairs slowly, and absently picked up a kitten scampering in the path of the moving men. She heard Vicky's voice from the hall above.

"Here, Amanda!"

A little surprised Amanda looked up and saw Vicky's face looking down over the banisters.

"I meant the cat," Vicky said, embarrassed. "Her name's Amanda, too. Come on up."

Amanda handed the cat to Vicky and followed her into the apartment, bracing herself for what she was going to say. The low-ceilinged little apartment was like nothing she knew, and the wonder of why Vicky had thrown over the luxury of the Murray Hill studio for this funny little place made her realize how far removed they were from each other's understanding. Vicky covered whatever feelings she may have had at this un-expected call, by directing the moving men in placing the furniture.

"I bought out an apartment from a woman on MacDougal Street," she said, talking rapidly as if a pause between words might allow a real thought to be revealed. "Her husband's left her for some one else and so she's going to Africa with the Free French to be a nurse. It's exactly the kind of stuff I need, and it was quite cheap."

"I could have sent you furniture," said Amanda, sitting down in a little slipper chair and lighting a cigarette. "You could have had all the stuff in the studio. Modern stuff."

Vicky was pushing the little sofa against the wall.

"This is the kind I like, thanks," she answered. "I like furniture and houses all warm and used and kind. Old wood. I like old chairs and I like old houses. It's—well, they're friendlier."

Vicky looked confident and blooming in her candy-striped red apron and housecleaning gloves. Sometimes shy, uneasy girls bloomed this way in their own homes or on their own subjects.

"You weren't at *Peabody's*," Amanda began. "I do think you might have called me."

Vicky bent her head over the kitten, her hands stroking its black, furry neck. Then she looked up at her visitor with a troubled face.

"What do you want of me, Amanda?" she blurted out. "You want something or you wouldn't have followed me here. What is it?"

Amanda pressed her hands together tightly, and drew a long breath.

"Vicky, I'm in a ghastly mess. You're actually the only person who can do anything. Maybe, even you—but you've got to. You see, I was told I was sterile and I've never given it a thought, but now—" Her voice took on a strange hoarseness, as if confidences were so rare coming from her that they had to pass a dozen censors in her vocal chords before they could come out, and then they came out in a rusty creak with all the hidden corrosion clinging to them. She didn't look at Vicky who sat on the edge of the couch, staring blankly at her.

"Can you imagine! Like that idiot girl on the other side of the Lakeville Cemetery that everybody made fun of! Like those factory girls at that Fallen Women's Home outside

Cleveland! Here I am—all the money in the world—thirty-two years old—and as helpless as some farm girl in trouble. Not a soul to help me—no one I dare ask!" Once the dam burst, the bitter words poured out, heedless of the effect on Vicky, Amanda being conscious only of the unbearable pressure that was forcing them out. "Half a dozen of the best doctors on Julian's pay roll, but how dare I trust them? They'll go straight and tell him. He's tops right now. You'd think I could ask some women, but I don't gossip with any women. When I try to bring up the subject, they freeze up as if I was accusing them of something. What is it they all do, for God's sake? How do they get away with it? I know everything going on in the world but that one little matter of where a woman in my position can go for this sort of thing without being blackmailed. Think of it!" She gave a hard little laugh. "All this talk about birth control enlightenment, and what an advantage over the old dark ages! Nonsense! The professionals always knew what to do and still do. But right in the twentieth century a woman in a jam is still a woman in a jam! It's something to write about, isn't it?"

She got up and began slowly walking up and down, her slender hands hugging her elbows, her olive face pale and sick-yellow, with dark blue shadows under the eyes, and the eyes looking straight ahead, not seeing Vicky's numb, stricken figure.

"It's a joke, oh sure, I know it is," Amanda went on harshly. "Something cooked up to show me the only thing that matters is what's happening to you personally that very minute. Something to show me that if I know so much why don't I know how to get out of a jam that a million dumb clucks get out of every day without thinking. The admirable Crichton business! Knowing what the categorical imperative is, and five languages including Sanskrit, but no idea of how to open a can of beans. Certainly, it's a laugh! Oh, Vicky, don't sit there. Help me."

Suddenly tears began streaming down Amanda's face and she dropped on the bed, shoulders shaking, her arm across her face. Quite as suddenly the tears stopped though her face worked for self-control.

Vicky put her hand on her shoulder, unwillingly. The sight of Amanda in hysterics, strange and terrifying as it was, only left her numb. Some persons were suited only to triumph and they existed only in a blaze of glory; in descent they were not the same people, and must find new personalities for themselves. They needed their daily transfusions of victory for their blood and brain, and without this they had no corpuscles for defense, no philosophy for defeat. So Amanda, broken with her little misfortune, was not Amanda to Vicky but the curious awful spectacle of a statue in fragments. The events of the last two months had destroyed all her sentiment for her old idol; all she felt now was despair at the unhappiness Amanda continued to pour over her, mingled with the dreary conviction that once again she must throw herself on the tracks to save the fairy princess.

"I could telephone Corinne Barrows," she said.

"Dennis Orphen's girl. I remember. He wrote that satire on Andrew Callingham. I hate him!" cried Amanda. "Don't tell her I'm here."

"I'll ask her advice," Vicky said. "She's the only person I could ask. I won't say it's for you."

Fortunately Corinne was in, and being a warm, obliging little creature, was quite free with her information about a certain doctor in old Chelsea who could be obtained by mentioning her name. She would telephone him herself right away.

"You poor darling!" Corinne gasped. "Does Ken know?"

Vicky gulped.

"I haven't told him," she said, and hung up. "It's all right, Amanda. I'll make an appointment with the man. Or better still, we'll go right over."

This was all that Amanda needed to restore a little of her old self. It proved that she could still will things to come out smoothly, at no matter what cost to others. She began to make up her face.

"Why didn't you tell Julian?" Vicky asked, half-knowing the truth, but for some reason wanting it proved.

"My dear, I haven't slept with that toad in six months!" Amanda gave a short laugh, her hand on the doorknob. "No, my betrayer is another matter. That's the whole trouble."

It was Ken, then.

"Some one you're in love with—" Vicky heard her own words without wanting the answer.

Amanda did not answer at once, and Vicky could feel her withdrawing now that she had revealed herself so dangerously to another human being. The statue was endeavoring to assemble itself once again.

"Certainly not," said Amanda. "Some one in love with *me*."

Vicky looked at the lovely blonde head, the smooth shining waves gleaming under the tiny figment of ribbons Amanda wore as a hat, the darkly troubled blue eyes, the lips thin but prettily curved, the sleek gypsy brown skin. Nothing so beautiful as this could be so intentionally cruel, so brazen. There must be some excuse, or was it excuse enough that her beauty gave such pleasure to a million undeserving eyes? She must have something beyond that, some inner kindness maybe not for friends or for Ken, but for somebody. But the radiance she cast was deadly, no matter how you excused it, and Vicky felt her own new happiness withering under it like a leaf in the drought.

"I can't understand why you don't marry Rockman Elroy," Amanda said on their way downstairs. "After all there needn't be anything final about it. A year, and then Reno and a nice alimony. Really, Vicky, you haven't a grain of sense!"

"I know it," Vicky said. "I don't suppose I ever will have."

She dropped her keys in the mailbox for Ken, and the guilty clang seemed to reverberate up and down the streets like the crack of doom.

"You're not still in love with Tom Turner?" Amanda accused.

"No," said Vicky. "Some one else."

"Good," said Amanda.

What's good about it, Vicky thought? He's in love with you and you're in love with somebody who's in love with somebody else—oh, splendid. Perfectly ducky, in fact.

3

Vicky sat in the dark musty parlor in the brownstone house in Chelsea, with Julian Evans' newspaper in her hand. She read up and down the columns, the words piling on top of each other like coaches in a train wreck—Hitler—Churchill

—Gunther—Hess—Laval—Lindbergh—Knox—strike—plane crash—D.A.R.—Disney—Coughlin—all the matters of which Mr. Evans had complete knowledge—at the control of a button. For all the sense they made to Vicky they might have been a trail of "shrdlu etaoin's." She was thinking how strange it was for Julian to know everything in the world except what was going on in this insignificant little doctor's office in an obscure corner of Chelsea. There was Amanda's article, too, authoritatively explaining what would happen in industry, the home, the arts, when America was pulled into the war. Amanda knew everything, too, except how to handle an elementary human problem. Mr. and Mrs. Atlas, with the world lightly on their shoulders, but unequal to the burden of one straw.

"What will happen to me if Julian ever finds out?" Vicky wondered, although she knew for a certainty what would happen. Julian would blame Vicky for everything, and Amanda would manage to unload the whole misadventure on some one else.

Supposing the doctor, a grave, enormous young man, with huge white hands, should discover that his patient was Amanda Evans. He would certainly know that this was a blackmailing matter, for if it was above-board her husband would have arranged the operation, with his own physician, under the most decorous protection. On the other hand, supposing this silence from the inner office meant that Amanda had died on the operating table. Who would tell Julian but Vicky herself, and how would she explain it? Under these dark imaginings ran the sickening knowledge that it was Ken's child that was being denied birth, that although he had said he was free of Amanda's hold, he was bound to her by this, and that she, Vicky, loved him desperately and wanted above everything in the world to have a child, a dozen children by him. This was the way things always happened. Amanda could always have what Vicky wanted any time she liked. With a sick ache Vicky thought of how Amanda would use her to the end of her days, stepping into her life whenever she chose, taking what she liked. They were like the two ends of an hourglass that wouldn't work, the sand always staying in one, depriving the other. Amanda was the finest flower in the garden because she took the nourishment from all the other flowers, it was as natural and blameless as that.

"I knew he'd been in love with her and I know that's why he quit *Peabody's* and that's why he drinks all the time now so he can forget. I know that, even if I daren't let him know I do. But why must there always be more to know, one more little torment made especially for you?" Then Vicky shook her heard sternly, instructing her thoughts to stop their destructive work.

She fixed her eyes on the largest rose in the elaborately ugly carpet. It was a bloated saffron rose and it was shaded in green spots that made a face of it, a mouthless Oriental face against the bright blood red background. She would dream of that carpet face for a long time. Outside, through the stiff red rep window curtains, she could see a dark garden with a high board fence around it. Somewhere the afternoon June sun was shining, but over these dingy back courts a perpetual rain cloud spread like a circus top, veiling it in a strange antique twilight. There was an ailanthus tree quivering in some secret wind against the fence, and beyond that the stained blackened rear of a tenement on the next street with clothes lines stretched across its windows up to the fifth story like a musical score with a pair of ragged pink cotton bloomers as *do*, running up the scale of dishtowels, shirts, sheets, and slips to a faded blue apron for high *C*. The windows in this bleak memory of a house varied, some with white ruffled curtains, then a single piece of cretonne pinned up, then a crooked green shade. The grimy little yards were separated by rotting board fences into squares, and sharp-nosed, gaunt cats loped along the edges to vanish into garbage pails.

In the doctor's stone-paved yard with its single tree, a yellow cocker spaniel was chained to the fence. From the floor above where she sat Vicky could hear a woman's voice calling out, "Lie down, Penny! Down, I said. Down, Penny!" at which the pup would gaze alertly upward, lie down, jump up again, tail wagging, bark happily, thus prolonging the conversation to "Quiet, Penny! Stop that, Penny! . . . No, no, Penny. Stop, Penny. I said quiet, Penny. Good dog, Penny."

She would dream about that yellow dog, too, Vicky thought. She could shut her eyes and already see the nightmare, the carpet-rose blending into the dog-face. Somewhere, maybe from the window in the opposite tenement, the one with the ruffled curtains, she could hear another feminine voice, a voice with beer-bubbles in it, a broad rich sound that must come from a full belly and fat throat. You could hear its laughter burbling behind the curtains of history, warm, sensual, satiated. Another voice swelled it with deep, baritone chuckles and under this billow of laughter the small miseries of Vicky and the savage pain of Amanda were lost and buried.

Vicky watched the black onyx clock on the black marble mantelpiece. The clock's face was upheld by two golden fauns and its hands were fixed permanently at twelve-fifteen. Put that in the nightmare, too, Vicky told herself, put twelve-fifteen on the carpet-rose dog-face and give it the voice of the laughing woman. Put the whole dream in the unripe pickle green of these painted walls, and scent it with the combination of turpentine and disinfectant (either for bugs or anesthetic) that drifted through the air. This reminded Vicky to study once more the silent door behind which Amanda had vanished a half hour before. It occurred to her, with a shiver, that the inner room must be sound-proof, since not a murmur had come out of it.

Around the walls hung pictures heavily framed in brown or black wood; steel engravings of the *The Operation* (sinister looking doctors gathered around a skeletonic patient), *The Sick Child* (weeping, praying mother at bedside of dying boy), and enormous hand-tinted photographs of two eager, busty little girls in ruffled confirmation dress, their mature, knowing faces incongruously framed in frizzling black hair that repellantly resembled the doctor's. A small black walnut coffin on top of a too red mahogany-veneered console proved to be an old music-box. Vicky experimentally turned something which aroused a croaking and coughing and eventually a far-away forlorn tinkle of the *Last Rose of Summer*. This wheezed croupily into *The Scarf Dance, Ben Bolt*, and finally cackling *Dance of the Demons* that seemed to shake the ancient entrails of the box. Vicky tried to turn it off, but it went on and on, rattling through its repertoire endlessly like a garrulous witch.

Two girls came in the hall door, a drab blonde in a cheap flowery hat and black silk dress that disguised no bulge or cranny, and an older one with a variety of henna shades in her hair, ten-cent store ear-hoops and a paper knitting bag over her arm, from which she now took some brown yarn and needles.

"For God's sake, don't start knitting!" sharply cried the blonde, looking for support toward Vicky. "You'll drive me nuts if you start knitting now."

The older one paid no heed but calmly set to work on her socks.

"Ah, you're just nervy. You shoulda had it done sooner like I told you. Me, I get it done once a month regardless, just to be on the safe side."

"Where would I get that kinda money, kindly tell me?" muttered the other.

They both stared at Vicky with that combination of scorn and friendliness with which strange women are accustomed to regard each other when Fate throws them into the same situation. Sorority sisters, Vicky thought, Amanda's at that. But no, they were claiming her as their own, Amanda could always rise above them. Now she was thinking again, Vicky reproached herself, and there was no stopping the cruel process. She clenched her nails into her palms, trying to think of the woman laughing, the nightmare, anything to avoid her unhappy thoughts. If she only dared run away! . . . Then Amanda came out, white and angry. Indeed her indignation that such things could happen to her had anesthetized her to the pain of the operation. She kept her head high, refusing to look at the doctor whose pasty face was arranged in an expression of kindly professional concern. He motioned the other two women into the inner office, and followed Vicky and Amanda to the door.

"Walk a block or so before you take a cab," he instructed them in an undertone.

"Won't that be bad for her?" Vicky asked.

"It'll be bad for me if you don't," said the doctor, ironically.

On the street Amanda signalled at once for a cab.

"Let him protect his own dirty business," she said. "I paid him. I don't need to keep him out of jail."

Yes, he got her out of her trouble, and that was all he was put here for. Let other women whistle for help. None of Amanda's concern.

"You'll have to take me to your place for a couple of hours," Amanda said, lips set whitely. "I can't face Bemel, and I don't want to faint."

Vicky looked out the window, not knowing what to say. Ken might come in. He had said he would come in. He had told her he was happier with her than with any one else. He had told her Amanda had been a poison in his life that had run its course. But already she had begun tainting it again.

"I should hate her," Vicky thought, puzzled. "But it's like hating a hurricane or the sea. It can't be helped."

"What will I do about the house?" Amanda murmured. "The best thing is for you to call Bemel and cancel everything I have arranged for tonight. Tell her you're sick and need me. Tell her anything."

When they got to Vicky's address, the taxicab which had followed theirs from the doctor's slowed up for a moment, then swung sharply onward and around the corner uptown.

"What's that guy looking for?" growled their own driver, looking after the other car. "What's the matter with these mugs?"

Vicky took her change and helped Amanda up the outer stone steps. In front of the pet-shop window a man stood watching half a dozen infant Siamese kittens roll over each other.

"How funny for you to call your cat Amanda," said Amanda, remembering.

Vicky fumbled in the mailbox for the keys, hoping Ken had not come, for this meeting she could not face. But the keys were still there. She put her arms around Amanda and helped her slowly up the two flights. She could tell by Amanda's set lips that the effort was more than she had bargained for, and at the top step she sat down weakly, leaning her head against the railing. Her hat fell down and her hands clutched her fair hair.

"What if I die?" she whispered chokily. "Oh, God, what if I die! A fine mess! Oh, Vicky, do something! You're the only person. . . . Vicky—" She buried her head in her hands and the words were hardly audible. "Get Ken Saunders, will you?"

Vicky drew a long breath.

"Come on inside," she said. "I'll see if I can find him."

She pulled off Amanda's shoes and laid her on the bed. This was the first time Amanda had ever needed anybody. It was the first time she had ever needed Ken in all the years he had needed her so badly. If he was here, that need of him might strike the bond once more, and some one would have to stand by him against the moment sure to come when Amanda would try to hurt him again. It would be she, Vicky, who would have to support him, sensing the pull of his old habit of love and help him not to be hurt again. It would be harder on Ken than on anybody, Vicky told herself. He'd been in love with Amanda a long, long time, and you couldn't cut it off sharp and clean the way he had tried to do. Vicky knew that. Old love hung on to you like thistles. Whenever you brushed past, the thistles clung once more to your clothes, whether you would have them or not. It might have been that way for her, too, if Tom Turner had suddenly made a fresh claim on her. The person who hurt you most always had first claim.

"Did you call Ken?" Amanda murmured. "You know where he is. I don't. Please."

Vicky wished she could find some comforting thought, something to ease the dreadful pain in her heart. She went to the telephone and called Miss Bemel, first, as Amanda had instructed. Then she dialed Chez Jean, knowing he wasn't there, but to give herself time.

"What shall I tell him, if I find him?" she asked.

"Don't tell him anything," Amanda said quickly. "Just— just say I'm here and want to see him."

Ken wasn't at Chez Jean's or at Martin's, but he was at Dennis Orphen's. Corinne answered the phone.

"Vicky, I didn't tell him what you asked me," Corinne said, excitedly. "Was it you that wanted the address? You know."

"No," said Vicky, unable to think of any satisfactory answer to Corinne's curiosity. Ken was working with Dennis on some valuable new drink formula called a Scotch Mist, Corinne explained with suitable reverence. But he wasn't tight, really—at least not yet. Usually Vicky did not mind when he was tight because it was then he was completely hers, the whole hard surface removed. But she was glad he was not in

the soft stage yet, because he needed his toughness now. She
did, too.

"Ken, can you come right over?" she asked urgently.
"Amanda is here."

There was a pause.

"Let me know when she leaves," Ken said.

"But it's better for you to come now," Vicky protested,
with an uneasy glance at Amanda. "Please hurry."

She couldn't tell by his silence whether he was disturbed
over the imminence of Amanda or merely angry with herself
for making any demand on him. Amanda's white, still face
impelled her to say more.

"Amanda is sick, Ken," she said. "Do come. She—she
wants you."

"I'll come," said Ken. "But, for God's sake, stay with me,
will you?"

Vicky went into the kitchen and poured herself a little
whiskey. If she could only get through this meeting of Ken
and Amanda. With shaking hands she poured one for
Amanda, and took it in to her.

"Drink this. You'll feel better."

"Is he coming?" Amanda asked. She sat up, so pale and
woebegone that Vicky wondered again, with a constricted
heart, what would happen if she should die there. She would
have to call Julian, she thought. But then Miss Bemel had
mentioned that Mr. Evans would not be back. The whole
problem was for one person to handle, and that inadequate
person was Vicky Haven, now so shaky that her only
thought was how to keep from crying, and how to keep
from begging Amanda to stop tormenting her with demands
for pity.

"You called Bemel?" Amanda weakly asked. "What did she
say?"

"That Mr. Evans wouldn't be home," Vicky answered.
"She said Mr. Callingham had telephoned that he was calling
at six-thirty, and when he came she would explain."

"Andrew?" Amanda exclaimed, new life in her voice. She
sat up now, and finished the whiskey with a wry grimace.
"Why didn't you tell me before? Call Bemel and tell her I'll

be right there. What time is it now? Six-ten. Call her and say
I'll be a few minutes late but be sure and tell him to wait."

She got to her feet.

"But, Amanda, you're too weak—" Vicky protested,
amazed at this transformation. "Can't you tell him another
time—"

Amanda laughed mirthlessly. She was struggling with her
sandals.

"You don't tell a man like Callingham—'another time,' "
she said. "Do I look queer? Get a cab for me, will you?"

With mingled relief and alarm Vicky saw the pale, wan creature of a moment before suddenly transformed into the
brittle, competent woman she was supposed to be. No,
Amanda would not tolerate being accompanied home by
Vicky, especially since she had said Vicky was sick. No, she
would permit only Vicky's help going down the stairs to the
taxi with the added support of another liqueur glass of Scotch.
Callingham had put her off for several days now and nothing
could stop her from meeting him now, even if she had to use
an ambulance to get to him. The challenge of this longed-for
encounter gave a flushed beauty to her cheeks and a soft
sparkle to her eyes. It was incredible, Vicky thought, bewildered. The woman was indestructible. She was ungrateful,
too, for she stepped into the taxi without a word for the gru-
elling afternoon she had given her old friend, merely a gay
wave of the handkerchief.

"I'll try to find time for lunch some day," she called out
blithely, "as soon as I can pull out of some of my war work.
I've been doing too much, really. Soon, then, dear!"

The car rolled away and Vicky thought this was the way she
wanted Amanda to be—triumphant, indestructible, selfish,
perhaps, but anything rather than the frightened, broken
creature of a little while before. Then she thought of Ken and
her heart sank. As soon as Amanda discovered she could pull
Ken back, she was satisfied. Now she was in the position once
again to humiliate him by commanding his presence, and
then running away for bigger game the way she always had
done. Poor Ken. Poor Vicky. Poor everybody in Amanda's
path, for that matter. But then, it took as much human
energy, blood and tears to produce an Amanda as it did to pro-

duce any other successful institution. She wondered how she could tell him to save his feelings. She didn't care what Amanda ever did to her, if she would only stop hurting Ken. She wished there was something she could do to make up to him for all the things Amanda had done to him, but no matter how desperately you tried there seemed no way of keeping Fate from striking out at the person you loved. All you asked was the simple pleasure of saying, "Here, darling, is the moon you were crying for. That makes up for everything else, doesn't it?" But instead of that you had to say, "Darling, more bad news!"

She was sitting at the telephone, wondering if she could catch him at Corinne's in time, for it would be easier to tell him over the telephone without the necessity of seeing the disappointment in his face. Before she could make up her mind what to say, the door burst open and Ken came in. Afterwards she remembered this, at times when she wanted to reassure herself of his love: he came straight to her without looking around for Amanda at all!

"Amanda really did send for you," she babbled. "But something happened—somebody called her—she wanted to see you but—"

"I don't give a damn whether she wanted to see me or not," Ken interrupted impatiently. "I came because your voice sounded as if sixteen parachutists had crashed through the roof right on your head. What in God's name was she doing to you? Pulling a gun on you?"

"In a way," Vicky said, with a great sigh of relief. He'd come on her account, not because Amanda needed him. It was too much to believe. It must be that he was tighter than Corinne said he was. She mustn't kid herself that his kindness to her was anything but that, because it couldn't possibly be love. Not after he'd been in love with a woman like Amanda.

"What made her track you down again after she kicked you out?" Ken asked. "Nothing good, I know that."

He lit a cigarette and put it in Vicky's mouth.

"Honey, you're all shaky. Don't tell me if it upsets you."

"I—I can't ever tell you, Ken," Vicky said, and then began to cry. "I'd rather just try to forget it all by myself."

Ken stroked her hair, then bent over and kissed her.

"Not enough for her to mess up my life but she has to start messing up the girl I'm crazy about," he muttered. "I don't give a damn what she does to me, but by God, she's got to leave you alone."

Of course he must be tight to say such sweet things to her, Vicky reminded herself. She mustn't let herself think it was anything else, because it would just be all the worse for her. But she didn't care what made him this way, so long as it made her happy at least for this minute.

"Mind if I have a drink?" he asked.

"Mind?" Vicky said happily. "Drink the whole bottle, darling!"

XIII

THE TRAIN trip from Canada turned out to be a frightful one for Julian. Soldiers and boys on their way to camps crowded the train, making his usual reservations out of the question, so he must squeeze his party into two compartments, and then when something went wrong with the air-conditioning in his car, he was obliged to go into the crowded lounge car and conduct his conferences in the middle of chattering mobs. His party was not one to blend well under any circumstances, for there was Harnett, his business secretary, and Amos Cheever, who disliked Harnett; a gentleman on extremely private business for Julian named Dupper; and a young English refugee named Nugent about to be officially adopted by Julian. Photographs had already been taken of Julian leading the child on to the train with a benign smile, but fortunately for all concerned none had been taken later when the little fellow's precocity had worn Julian down.

"Do you think your wife will like me, sir?" inquired the boy, following Julian through the cars to the lounge.

He was four feet tall, seraphic as to countenance except for some missing front teeth, wistful as became a war refugee newly torn from his mother's arms, and he was the son of a baronet, certainly enough to please any foster mother. Julian drew out a cigar and lit it, not prepared to inform his charge that Mrs. Evans was due for a surprise and could not be relied upon for a hundred per cent favorable reaction.

"None of that, sir," young Nugent's voice called out peremptorily. He pointed upward. "You can read, can't you sir? It says 'Smoking Only in the Lounge.' "

Julian heard Cheever's chuckle from behind the boy and silently put his cigar back into his pocket.

"You've got no hair at all, have you, sir?" Nugent's voice piped up above the rumble of the train, so that passengers in the coaches looked up, smiling as they passed. "What sort of house have you got? How big?"

"Big enough," Julian tried to sound kindly, though he was always at a loss with children and mosquitoes, neither of whom could be lectured successfully for their habits. "However, you'll be packed off to school soon enough."

Young Nugent considered this the length of one coach and then poked his patron firmly in the back with a small forefinger.

"No, I shan't go to any school," he stated resolutely, and once more to Julian's chagrin passengers leaned in the aisle, smiling to hear the clear little British accents. "I'm not going to be shuttled about any more, thank you. London, the country, back to London, Liverpool, back to London, back to Liverpool, Canada, and now New York, and New York is where I'm going to stay! I shall go straight to your house and stay. No school, thank you, sir."

Julian decided to waive this matter till arrival, and if possible delegate the entire responsibility for the child to some one else. Delegate was a word he often used, though in anything but an executive the expression would have been "passing the buck." Amos Cheever was more or less responsible for this step, so Cheever would have to figure out the answer, particularly since without looking around Julian could feel the mischievous smiles of his associate.

Arriving in the lounge, the only car in which air conditioning was working at the moment, Julian squeezed behind a small table with Harnett and Cheever, leaving Nugent to wander about, and Mr. Dupper, the mysterious stranger, to stand at the bar.

"What should I do, sir?" Nugent politely asked, just as Mr. Harnett had taken out pad and pencil to record Julian's instructions to Cheever for an editorial on the food at Fort Dix.

"Play bear," Julian snapped wearily, and the suggestion succeeded well enough to give the gentlemen a ten minute respite. At the end of this period a porter brought him back to his elders, saying that the other passengers were not prepared to cope with the little one, who had been really playing bear, crouching on all fours under tables and pouncing on people.

"You said to play bear, sir," Nugent stiffly answered Julian's admonition. "I don't see very well how a person can play bear without biting people. There's no fun to a game unless you play it properly, you know, sir."

Again, Julian felt Cheever's discreet smile behind his back. He had intended deliberately to confront Amanda with this living example of her written exhortations, calling her bluff, and if she objected to adopting the child, it would give him further excuse for certain plans he was making. But already he saw that the knife could cut both ways, and he had once again laid himself open to the secret infuriating amusement of his staff.

"Perhaps it would be wiser to take Nugent to Far Off Hills," Mr. Harnett thoughtfully suggested, and Julian would have promoted him at once, if he dared, for voicing his own thought. "I think the country might be better for him, and we can drop off at Hudson on our way down."

"Exactly," said Julian approvingly. "I'll leave it all to you, Harnett."

Nugent looked doubtfully from one face to the other.

"How am I going to spend my birthday money?" he asked. "If I'm on a farm it gives me no chance to buy my boat with my birthday money."

He took out his wallet and waved his twenty-five dollars in front of Cheever's beard.

"I'll get your boat and send it up to you," offered Cheever genially. "What sort of boat is it?"

Julian rapped his fingers nervously on the table during this interruption, nerves quivering with the effort to be patient, since his first wife had protected him from all this sort of thing when he was a father.

Young Nugent produced from his wallet a much-handled cutting from a catalogue showing a beautiful toy sailboat of most flawless design for the sum of two hundred and fifty dollars. This was a problem Julian felt able to deal with, so he gave a fatherly talk on the value of money, and the difference between two hundred and fifty dollars and twenty-five dollars, dwelling on the interesting fact that his present of twenty-five dollars was a very tidy sum for a ten-year-old lad, a sum that would keep a working man's family for a whole week.

"But I don't want to keep a working man's family, sir," young Nugent expostulated with some annoyance. "What sort of birthday present would that be for me, sir, I ask you?"

Julian, staring at Cheever in order to keep the man from

laughing at him, explained that he was not commanding the little fellow to support any one's family with his gift-money, merely suggesting that he select a present for himself within that figure. He reminded him that twenty-five dollars was a lot of money and that money did not grow on bushes.

"Twenty-five dollars won't buy my sailboat," Nugent replied coldly. "If I can't buy my sailboat then twenty-five dollars is no good to me. Keep it, sir. It may mean a lot to you, but it can't do anything for me."

With this haughty gesture, Nugent laid his wallet before Julian and stalked down to the end of the car where he stood staring steadily at Mr. Dupper, something that no one else ever cared to do since the man was of a remarkably unsavory appearance.

It was next to impossible for Julian to dictate an editorial on the general idea of the brotherhood of man, the Little Man in uniform and nothing being too good for him, with soldiers jostling him on every side and Little Men and their Little Women spilling highballs over him every time the train swung round a bend. Mr. Cheever was growing more dignified every minute, in a stern effort to keep half a dozen double-Scotches from betraying themselves to his chief, but occasionally his command of himself was lost and he burst into extremely loud laughter, pointing at little Nugent standing with legs wide apart before Dupper. His enemy, Harnett, was perfectly aware of the double-Scotches, and glanced warningly at him from time to time, but Julian was so absorbed in his own complicated worries that he wouldn't have known what ailed Cheever if he'd gone into delirium tremens.

"Tell the porter we must have that air-conditioning fixed by the next station," Julian shouted above the tumult at Harnett. "We took a train instead of flying so we could get this work done. It's perfectly outrageous. I'm a stockholder on this railroad. At least we might have more room."

"They have to cut down the cars, Mr. Evans," Harnett explained, and this was a mistake as Julian hated any one *explaining* as if he was a child.

"What's this man Dupper doing for us?" Cheever inquired. Julian frowned out the window.

"Certain private business," he said.

"Disagreeable looking chap," said Cheever.

"You don't have to look at him," peevishly said Julian. "I'll see him alone as soon as somebody gets this train in condition."

Rising majestically Julian strode out of the car, and Harnett and Cheever exchanged a look.

"He's probably going to call up the President," said Cheever, in a low voice. "He always thinks that accidents like this, or sunburn or seasickness can be fixed by getting through to the President. He gets worse every year."

"Mrs. Evans Number One gets the kid, all right," Harnett said. "I knew he didn't know what he was letting himself in for. In a way I'd like to see Number Two's face when she clapped eyes on what the mister was bringing home."

Cheever, with a cautious eye toward the door through which Julian had vanished, signalled the waiter quickly for further refreshment.

"Better make it cuba libre," advised Harnett. "I'll have one too. Looks like coca-cola so he can't tell."

"Who is that mug, Dupper?" pondered Cheever. "Is he pimping for the boss? Looks like the type."

Harnett shrugged.

"I can give a guess, but not out loud," he said.

It was true that Mr. Dupper, who had so strangely joined the party at a station en route, had the appearance of a man engaged in the worst of underworld activities. He was a short, thick man with boiled gray eyes and an empty moon face, moist-lipped, wide-nosed, and horribly disfigured by a skin disease of a venereal nature if one could judge by the shameless lasciviousness of eyes and mouth. Born both lecherous and ugly, his only relief from his obsession must have been the most depraved of prostitutes, since there could never have been any choice for him.

As soon as he sat down to a table people got up and left. "Is this seat taken?" he would ask, and people would nod dumbly, looking at the nightmare face, so he had to stand at the bar, drinking highballs very fast, his derby hat pushed back on his round head, his ape shoulders hunched over, his wet shapeless mouth grinning defiantly. Two gray-haired men had nowhere to go but stand beside him, so he began talking to them, forcing them to look at him, while he talked fast, told amazing things, jokes, obscenities, riddles, secrets, anything to distract the mind from his face. The train swept down the Hudson, and he talked on feverishly, buying them drinks they dared not refuse, drinking fast so as not to see the mirror of his own horror in their eyes. The men left, other men appeared, and he went on talking, joking, showing he had something in the way of humor and strange experience that unharmed men had not. His tongue must have become swollen, his throat dry and sore from his frantic defense of his ugliness, from his always smiling mask of good nature. Then the air-conditioning in the Pullmans was restored and the lounge emptied, people no longer had to stand near him, no one needed to listen, no one even needed to look if they could drag their fearing eyes away. In the late twilight they came upon him after a while in the dark of the platform, all alone, his boiled eyes shining with stark evil, his lips drawn in sinister revealed hate, silent, a living sore, enemy of all good and all beauty, a man to fear in dark alleys, murderous, unpitying. The man with the diseased face stood in the shadows, spreading fear, sorrow, panic, and even with no crime in his soul, is accused.

Julian Evans, returning to the lounge satisfied with the train mechanism finally obeying his will and operating again, passed Dupper without seeing him, until Dupper touched him on the shoulder.

"When do you want me?" asked Dupper.

Julian hesitated, and then jerked his head back toward his compartment. He had not been prepared for Dupper's looks, and it seemed to him that any one looking at the man could read his mission. Never mind, it had to be.

"The kid's playing rummy with some gob in there," Dupper reassured him, as if that was the only cause of Julian's hesitation.

In the compartment Dupper took out a paper from his pocket.

"On the twentieth she had Callingham at the house to dinner while you were in Washington," said Dupper. "They left the house together at ten-thirty and drove to N.B.C. studios where he broadcast short-wave to London, and later they went into the Rainbow Room and sat in a corner talking for about an hour. She came back in a cab alone about one o'clock."

Julian felt his throat swelling as if his heart was about to pop out, and his head rang with Dupper's hoarse rasping voice, as if each word was scratched on sandpaper. He remembered his blood pressure as his temples began pounding, and he got up to get a glass of water. At the same time he turned off the light as if the evil in Dupper's words would be softened by shutting out the evil of his face. But the blue dusk coming through the window enhanced both words and face so that Julian switched the light on once again, and sat down, grasping his glass of water.

"She fired Emerson as you know on the twenty-first," pursued Dupper. "She was in the lobby of the Waldorf at four-thirty that afternoon. The Waldorf is Callingham's hotel. Asta Lundgren, the dancer that Callingham's been tied up with for the last few years, took a train for the West, presumably Milwaukee, late that night. She seemed to be crying. We lost track of both Callingham and Mrs. Evans after that, and don't know whether they were together or not. We haven't seen them together but we have reports on her movements."

"What?" Julian asked with dry lips, his palms sweating.

"She took a cab to Greenwich Village, stopped at the apartment of Victoria Haven, the same person who covered up her last apartment, then drove to a quack doctor in Chelsea. When they came out she went to the Thirteenth Street apartment and stayed one hour. Miss Bemel was told this was due to a serious sickness of Miss Haven's. Miss Haven was at work next day at *Peabody's*, with no signs of being sick. Mrs. Evans spent the next two days in bed, you remember. Mr. Callingham had an appointment for tea there. He sent flowers."

Julian struggled to open the window, gasping for breath. Dupper obligingly turned on the electric fan, and started to help him unfasten his collar, but his touch was too much for Julian who pushed him aside.

"You think it's certainly Callingham, then?" he whispered.

Dupper stared at him.

"That's the only guy you told us to watch," he said, defensively. "We could just as well have got the goods on somebody else, I reckon."

"What do you mean?"

Dupper laughed raucously.

"Probably a dozen more, too. That's the way we usually find it. Probably something about this man Emerson, too. That's why she fired him, maybe. A woman like that's got plenty of chances, you know, and she don't pass up anything. Too easy for her."

"How dare you say that?" Julian choked.

Dupper's eyes widened in astonishment.

"What's the matter? If she wasn't that way you wouldn't have set us trailing her, would you? Don't get touchy, there, governor. You started this deal, you know. You knew what time it was. You weren't being kidded, now, were you? Don't give me this innocent stuff. Not after what you gave us to start with."

"Get out of here," whispered Julian. "Get out. Don't say another word. You're saying—God knows what you're saying."

A gleam of fury shone in Dupper's eye, but after a moment's silence he got up, and put his papers back in his vest.

"After all, you asked for it, darling," he said, grinning. "You pay the bill. Nobody else cares who your wife's sleeping with."

He went out, whistling, letting the door close softly behind him. Julian sipped his water slowly, as if it would cool the boiling in his head. A Western Union blank suggested an outlet to him and he drew it toward him and wrote a wire to his staff lawyer, instructing him to buy off the paper's contract with Andrew Callingham, and to inform the syndicate heads that the name of Callingham was never under any circumstances to be mentioned, in book columns, theatre, society, or foreign news no matter what he might do. The yellow slip in his hand made him feel better, even though it could not be sent till the next stop. He would go in to the lounge when he felt calmer and see Cheever next. Dupper would have to keep out of the way the rest of the journey. Little Nugent could be dropped off at Margaret's, and no one need know he had been intended as a test for Amanda. Poor Margaret. Dear Margaret. What in God's name had bewitched him into almost ruining his life for Amanda, when Margaret was his talisman, his refuge? Sex was a horrible thing for a man meant to lead people, Julian thought, especially if you couldn't get it anyway. His whole body tingled with the insult of being rejected by the woman he could swear he had created. At least he could break her, too. That was something she hadn't counted upon. Amandas were a dime a dozen this year. She'd find that out soon enough when she tried to get things on her own.

Julian sat in the dark, watching the lights of villages as the train flew along into a light summer rain. Inky puddles caught the headlights and glittered darkly in rhythmic swirls like the dark thoughts circling in Julian's pounding head. There was a sudden stop at some wayside, to signal. In the rain, men on the little platform swung their lamps, their raincoats dripping, their hats pulled down. Looking out Julian could see no village behind the lonely station at all, but a great building that stretched interminably across the sky, lit up brilliantly for the night.

"State Insane Asylum," some one in the corridor murmured.

As the train screamed by figures appeared in every barred doorway, shadows were at every iron window, every aperture of the Asylum was lined with the desolate prisoners. There they stood or crouched, hour after hour at doors or windows, like wild pets, knowing that this is the door and that the train whistle means escape, and some day the door will open to let them out as to let them in. In their torch-lit mad minds the train blazing and screaming past them in the night was no more real than the other images that shrieked through their minds, and when at bedtime the light would be dimmed for sleep, what did it matter, what peace was there in that silence for sleep? Darkness, four-footed, monstrous, blinked tiger-eyed in their minds, never sleeping, and at daylight the souls would wake to yesterday's torment, no pity or peace, no truce for them; the pursuit would continue, the demons yowling after their exhausted prey, tearing the shreds of poor brains to shake out one more wild cry of pain. This was the picture the passenger could see in the second's pause at the institution, this was the picture on his eye-balls, on the windowpanes, tattooed on the backs of people sitting ahead, so that the

Catskills sleeping in the soft June rain, the winding brooks, the arching trees, dozing village churches, silvery river, the whole quiet countryside for miles and miles around all cried of Murder.

Amos Cheever stood in the doorway of the compartment.

"State Insane Asylum," he said. "Signal stop. Awful thing, insanity. Mind if I turn on this light?"

"People let themselves go," said Julian testily. "People have no control, that's all. Unless, of course, it's genuinely pathological. As a rule, though, people give in to it too easily. Remind me to get an article on that, will you, for the Sunday magazine?"

"Sometimes circumstances are too much for one human being to handle," Cheever argued. "Things do pile up, you know, sometimes."

"A man can handle them if he's a real man," Julian said, already feeling the sweet relief of power at the thought of what he would do to both Callingham and Amanda. "No excuse for any one losing their grip."

Afterwards Cheever remembered this, because when they dropped off at Hudson to deliver little Nugent to Margaret Evans, the poor woman had just been taken to a sanitarium in a strait jacket, screaming hallelujahs and oaths you would have sworn she had never even heard. Julian would have driven off to see her, shocked as he was by this failure of Margaret's to support him in his own misfortunes, but the doctor warned him he must not go. Mrs. Evans, it seems, was obsessed with the desire to kill Julian.

Harnett left little Nugent at the farm, nevertheless, for there were nurses and servants in charge of all the other refugees Margaret had befriended. Julian and Cheever drove into New York that night in the rain, and neither spoke. Dupper had vanished with the train, his well-documented misinformation in his breast pocket.

2

Mr. Castor met Miss Bemel on the third floor landing. Each bore an open copy of *Peabody's* for August. Miss Bemel was frowning and her free hand appeared to be searching her skull for some worthy trophy. Mr. Castor, on the contrary, was in the throes of a semi-smile, if the faint twitching of his saffron face could be described as that.

"Now *this*," said Mr. Castor, pausing to tap the periodical significantly, "is the real thing. This is what she should have been doing right along. It fits in with Mr. Evans's *Little American* policy."

"I think it's a great mistake on her part. A very great mistake," said Miss Bemel, with controlled passion. "I can assure you if I had seen the article before it went to the magazine it would never have gone. Never! But she seems to feel she can do things like this over my head. Very well. She will see."

"Mr. Evans will like this very much," Mr. Castor said doggedly. "The snob appeal is no longer the approach. *She* didn't seem to realize that at first. But this—this is the stuff."

Miss Bemel, in the very act of stamping her foot, remembered where she was and brought the member down without a sound. This frustrated foot-stamping had the expected unfavorable reaction in that her rage found outlet in an indiscreet raising of the voice.

"What's good about telling the world she came of humble people? What's good about saying that her father ran a haberdashery that he didn't even own, and that sometimes as a child she never had enough to eat and lived over a store in some wretched little village? Nobody needs to tell things like that in order to get their public sympathy! Especially when all her interviews before have told about her royal blood, and being lonely in the big house on the hill, and all that!"

Mr. Castor, by way of subtle rebuke, lowered his own voice to a pitch of exquisite softness.

"Permit me to disagree with you *in toto*, Miss Bemel! The public is revolution-minded these days. They are massing against the favored few, the rich, the titled, the aristocrats. Nothing could have been more politic than building up herself as a woman of the people, at this stage of the game." He placed a forefinger on his lower lip as if this time to produce an organ note, though it actually turned out to be merely a qualification. "Unless of course she *is* a woman of the people. She isn't, is she?"

"How do I know?" bellowed Miss Bemel. "I thought at least I was working for a *lady*. I can tell you my family wouldn't have let me do the dirty work for some cloak-and-suit man's daughter. The Bemels are *somebody*! And now this—this"—she spanked the magazine sharply—"about having no pocket money at school, and wearing somebody else's clothes and being snubbed by the country clubs! What will my Discussion Group think of me, slaving away for that sort of person? I'll bet Mr. Evans won't like it! I'll bet he doesn't want people thinking he picked his wife out of some Woolworth counter!"

Mr. Castor permitted the echoes of Miss Bemel's blast to finish their last bounce before he assuaged the air with his gentle croon.

"Possibly she might have indicated that although her people were poor, they were land-poor only," he admitted graciously. "Or she might have hinted that her mother's family, say, was connected with the Biddles or Cabots or Whitneys. Something of that sort."

"Of course she should have!" boomed Miss Bemel, folding her arms across her chest and letting the offending magazine shiver down the stairs. "That's what other people do. No matter how poor they were in childhood, or what sort of tearoom or boarding-house their folks ran, they manage to find a grandmother who was a countess or an ancestor who ran for President! They don't have to go *all out* for being low class, like *she* does here!"

Noise was beginning to win out over discretion, and Mr. Castor strummed his lower lip again judiciously, regarding once again the full-length picture of Amanda which illustrated her article "I CAME FROM ACROSS THE TRACKS." The picture showed Amanda, bare-shouldered and bare-backed in fluid silver brocade, dripping emeralds and orchids, facing the mirror of her living-room with a proud proletarian smile.

"In a way the picture does something for her," Mr. Castor said. He weighed silently the chances of Miss Bemel being right in regard to Julian's reaction.

"No," he finally shook his head. "Mr. Evans is primarily a publishing genius. Even if he personally did not like the idea of his wife presenting herself as a vulgarian, he would recognize the timeliness of it. He might possibly be annoyed that he knew nothing of the piece till it came out."

"Nobody did!" Having won her point on noise, Miss Bemel now obliged Castor's ears with a windy whisper fraught, as whispers so frequently are, with memories of garlic. "She does these things at night! Ever since she fired Emerson she's been doing things like this. Right here it says this is the first of several autobiographical sketches from her. How does that make *me* look? Her private secretary!"

Mr. Castor picked up her magazine and restored it to her.

"There are a number of things going on around here of which you are unaware," he said, smiling. "Your work with Mrs. Evans is after all the least of the activities in this domicile."

Miss Bemel glared at him, her bosom heaving at this unfair taunt.

"That," she said majestically, "is a matter of opinion."

She pursued her path upstairs, head high while Mr. Castor crept softly and triumphantly on down-stairs, knowing that he had started an unendurable curiosity in Miss Bemel's avid brain. This was his little revenge for permitting her to persuade him about Julian's reaction to Amanda's article. He was glad that she was not on hand to see how right she proved to be when he laid the magazine before his master a few minutes later, for Julian turned livid as he looked at it.

"How dare she do this to me?" he sputtered, pounding the desk. "How dare she—get out of here, Castor! Get out! What do you mean bringing me this sort of thing! Who told her to do this? What sort of funny business is this? No wonder every one laughs at me! I pick a wife from the muck, do I? The wife of Julian Evans is from immigrant stock—illiterates—trash! God, why do people do these things to me? Get Peabody on the phone! Wait a minute. . . . This reads like Andrew Callingham! That traitor! He did this. Where's Mrs. Evans?"

Mr. Castor moistened his lips and looked around to see if he was safely near an exit in case the master attacked him.

"She's having tea with Mr. Callingham," he whispered bravely.

"Where?" thundered Julian.

Mr. Castor backed toward the door.

"At his hotel, I believe," he faintly intoned. "He's leaving for Libya tomorrow, you know. You remember we signed him for some articles."

Julian gripped the arms of his chair.

"That contract is cancelled," he said hoarsely. "Callingham is not to be mentioned or printed in any of my publications. Neither is Amanda Keeler Evans from now on."

Mr. Castor gulped.

"Those are your orders!" Julian shouted, trembling. "Get to work on them! You heard me! No more Callingham! No more Amanda Keeler in any Julian Evans publication!"

"Yes, sir," Mr. Castor gasped and fled into his office where he sat mopping his forehead feebly for a few minutes till he composed himself sufficiently to telephone Harnett.

Julian sat still for a while, his whole body trembling. He could feel his blood thudding away in his arteries, his heart knocking away in his chest, and he thought this is all very bad for me, very bad for my health, must call a doctor, get self in shape to cope with situation, must keep upper hand, getting mad no good. . . . He remembered his Yogi exercises suddenly, and the importance of changing the circulation in moments of anger or mental disturbance. When Castor peeked through the crack in the door two minutes later he shuddered to see the great man standing on his head. Then he remembered it was only Yogi and shrank back with a moan of relief.

3

Amanda did not like to think of Vicky Haven any more. Vicky was like everything connected with Lakeville, a carrier of calamity. That day with her was a precipice in her life, down which she had almost fallen, and she shuddered to think of it, and was slowly correcting it in her memory. It could not possibly have been true that she had felt a weak overwhelming need for Ken; it could not have been true that for a fleeting second she had wanted to promise him any-thing, even a divorce from Julian, to win him back. She must have had a fever, she explained to herself, she would under no other conditions have slipped into such a disgusting rôle of ordinary helpless female. Thank God, the mere mention of

Callingham had saved the day, reminding her that she was on her way up, not down.

The conquest of Callingham was no easy matter, either, and Amanda tackled the job with all the more zest. There was his love of the last five years, the Swedish dancer. There had been a little talk about her recently, and Amanda had even speculated on the chances of getting Julian to put the FBI onto her. It irked her that she needed Julian more than ever to get Callingham. She realized that her greatest danger was that her passionate loathing for Julian might lead her to break with him before she was through using him. She needed every resource of her own and Julian's to get Callingham. She was skipping her special war activities to take part in those which he favored, so that they could be together on radio programs, benefit dinners, and all possible occasions where they might leave together quite naturally. She knew he admired her, and the fact that she had no idea how much further she had gotten with him made her even more intrigued with the game. His extreme egotism and complete indifference to her own literary ambitions only piqued her, since he was the only writer she herself owned was her superior. He must eventually admit her talent, she promised herself, even if she had to model her style exactly on his, in order for him to approve it. They would do brave things together, sweeping through India and Africa, on just such intrepid adventures as had characterized his life before, none the less daring for their wire net precautions of money, prestige, and unlimited political protection.

So Amanda pursued Andrew Callingham as she had pursued Julian four years before, being aggressively feminine over the telephone with him since that was what he liked, and keeping her glamour side away and playing the direct, four-square type, since he seemed to prefer that. He saw a great deal of Free French officials, so she saw them, too. He liked to go bowling so she took up bowling, too. He liked to work or play all night, using the mornings for sleep, so Amanda upset her own schedule to take over his, which gave her excuse to telephone him all hours of the night or to meet him for daybreak breakfast at Childs', a hobby of his. He was a cagey man, accustomed to holding his own against women, and indicated only a jovial amusement in Amanda's siege, ignoring all her playful bids for intimacy. A worthy lover, Amanda thought! Not a misfit like Ken Saunders, not just a glorified merchant like Julian, but a genius and what was most important, a successful genius with all the charm of a normal male.

The fateful day on which her story in *Peabody's* had affected Julian so vitally, she had wangled tea with Callingham, and since his friend the dancer had gone west on a tour, and he himself was going to Libya the next day he was in a mood for celebration with whoever it might be. Dozens of reporters, photographers, soldiers, sailors, and ladies in uniform drifted in and out of his suite, drinking his champagne or Scotch, so that the affair was not the intimate matter that Amanda had wished. She stayed on, however, shrugging away her dinner engagement at home with a Western governor and the Chinese Consul. Let Julian handle the political side of things. She was concentrating on her artistic ambitions. Callingham broke all his own engagements recklessly, and despised any one ridden by a clock and appointment-book. So that was Amanda's way, now, too.

"What would you say if I turned up in Libya one of these days?" she asked him with seeming lightness, though the plan was already forming in her mind.

He would not be trapped into any indication of feeling.

"I'd probably say how-do-you-do," he countered, easily. "I'd try not to ask you if you were following me."

"That's what I'd be doing," said Amanda, firmly.

"Great mistake, I assure you," he laughed. "I'm a hard man to find when I start going. Like as not I'll nip off from Libya for Siam, or India."

"Leave word where you're going and I'll get there," Amanda said.

Callingham only smiled.

"I will, too," Amanda told herself. "He knows I will."

She would see some one tomorrow about an assignment in Libya. Julian would have to pave the way for her to go there. It would be the last thing he would ever be allowed to do for her, if everything worked out. Amanda dawdled over the champagne, trying to disguise her annoyance with the callers who came and went, preventing any privacy. She remembered that she had had to spend the night with Julian in order to clinch her conquest of him, and she should have managed the same thing with Callingham. He ought not to leave without her having established some claim on him. She disliked drinking, but she had no other excuse to stay on, so she drank more than she ever had done, trying to out-stay every one else. But at twelve he decided to go to Twenty-One with the last half dozen soldiers, and Amanda was obliged to admit defeat. She offered her lips in a farewell kiss, but he brushed his lips lightly over her cheek instead.

All the way coming home she made plans, calculating exactly what steps must be taken to make her pursuit plausible, just what angle to give Julian in order to insure his backing up to the moment when she dared dismiss it. One thing was certain—that no matter how elusive a man might be here in New York, he was easy prey on foreign soil for the girl from home. Say, she managed to get over there in the next month or so, she was positive they would be lovers soon after. He proposed staying abroad at least a year, this time, or even till the end of the war, if end there ever would be. Very well, she would stay, too. Let Julian be the one to ask for the divorce. Settle herself in Callingham's bed, first, then let matters take their proper course. The future looked so satisfactory to Amanda that it almost made up for her dissatisfaction at the way the evening had been taken away from her. She came in to the house in a glow of secret excitement, even humming to herself, as if the victory had already been won.

She went into her own suite at once and here was her first shock, for Julian sat in her bedroom looking like a thundercloud. He never before had taken such a liberty and surprise overcame her, surprise and a sense of guilt at the thoughts she felt must be printed clearly on her brow.

"Why, Julian! What is the matter?" she gasped.

He stood up and pointed his finger at her, his face distorted with such fury that for the first time she was terrified of him.

"Get out of this house, you tramp!" he choked. "I know all about you. I've had you watched these many months. I know the kind of slime you are, now! I've got the whole story—the whole record! Don't dare to deny it—I've got witnesses. You can't sleep with me—no, oh no. But everybody else! Callingham, that's the man. I'll break you both! I'll show you how puny you are. Both of you! I built him up. I made you. I can tear you both apart, like a toy, do you hear, like some toy!"

Amanda thought, "Oh, my God, he means murder! . . . He's gone crazy! . . . This is the end of me!"

She backed toward the door but Julian followed her, shaking a trembling finger at her, his eyes wild and bloodshot, his voice strange and shaking with hatred.

"You took that apartment with your sidekick Victoria Haven, so you could have men there. You roped me in. You made me believe your lies, your trickery. All right, but you're going to pay. You'll find out there are men that can beat you at your own tricky game! You forced me to marry you, ruin my good home, give you the greatest chance a girl ever had! Then you cheat and lie to pay me back. 'I Came from the Wrong Side of the Tracks'! You bet you did, and by God, you're going back there. That's where you belong, you—you tramp, you slut, you—" Suddenly Julian shook his fists at the futility of expressing his rage and his voice rose to a shrill cry. "Damn you! I'll kill you! Making fun of me—trying to wreck my life, using me to pimp for you, even, to bring you bigger and better men to cheat! Driving my poor wife mad! Get out—"

"Julian—please—" Amanda tried to get away from his reach but he seized her arms and forced her back to the bed, his hands closing on her throat so that her necklace broke and the pearls rolled over the floor. Amanda started to scream but his hand closed over her mouth, and this at least gave her respite from strangling. His fury had made him weak so that she managed to struggle out of his reach and run toward the door, trampling her hat under foot and trying to clasp together her dress where he had torn it. He came after her, panting, veins standing out on his head so that even in her fright she thought he must be going to drop dead of heart failure any minute.

"Get out of this house, do you hear me?" he screamed, and there was a sound of servants stirring somewhere outside, a sound Amanda did not know whether to welcome or fear. She stumbled over a chair and he caught at her dress, again, but she freed herself with a mighty wrench and made the door just as Mrs. Pons and her husband, both in night-clothes and white with fear, got to the hall. Amanda ran past them, Julian close behind her, and she heard a lamp crash past her as she flew down stairs, and the frightened cries of the servants. She got to the floor below, falling down on the landing, a slipper dropping off, which she dared not stop to retrieve. A vase crashed on the step behind her, just missing her, and she found herself crying out a prayer for help, though there seemed no hope, the servants paralyzed into futility.

"Curse you—curse you—" Julian was sobbing somewhere behind her. "Get out of here—get out of this house—damn you, damn you—oh, damn you!"

She reached the front door and by some miracle the lock worked at once and she was able to get outside into the midnight street before he could get to her. She ran, gasping and limping on her one shoe, holding her torn dress together, down the street. Some one must have managed to hold Julian in time, for the door did not open and she began murmuring, "Oh, thank God, thank God!" her forehead dripping with perspiration, her throat throbbing with the pain of his choking. There was a taxi on the corner and she sank into it, sobbing.

"Where to?" the driver asked. "Where to, Mrs. Evans?"

She was glad he knew her. At least, with her torn gown and one shoe off he did not mistake her for some one to be taken to the police station. Mrs. Julian Evans was still a name to protect the most suspicious circumstances. She sat still for a moment rocking back and forth with little gasping sobs, unable to think. It was something that Julian's detectives had never spotted the Ken Saunders affair. They had gotten the crime right but the man wrong. Then she remembered something, and gave the driver the address. At Twenty-One she sent him in to get Callingham, and presently he came out.

"What in heaven's name—" exclaimed Callingham.

"Take me to your hotel, please," she said.

He flung away his cigarette, and looked at her, frowning.

"I'll have to borrow some shoes for you first," he said. "What size?"

"Six," said Amanda.

He went back into the restaurant and came out, smiling, with a pair of blue pumps.

"Hope you don't mind blue with your gray dress. I'm not a good shopper. I took the first thing I could get. The driver can take them back."

He didn't say anything when she gasped out her story. If she had been more sensitized to other's reactions or less upset, she might have felt his bracing himself against her. But all she could think at the time was that she was out of Julian's murderous reach, and by some miracle was safe with Callingham.

"Take me with you, Andrew," she implored him. "You must take me with you."

"It's not as easy as all that," he said, almost irritably.

They reached his hotel and she managed to compose herself enough to enter. Now she began to wonder what he would do with her. No man could walk out on a lady in her own present plight. He took her arm, out of the elevator and led her to his suite. His valet was clearing up the ravages of the recent party.

"One thing, you can't stay here," he said, scowling. "Bad enough with Julian thinking all that rot, without giving him reason to believe it. He might even have his detectives here this minute."

"I don't care," said Amanda. "Nothing would convince him any differently anyway."

He looked away from her, still frowning.

"I can tell you it isn't going to help you or me," he said. "Julian says he's going to break us and he could almost do it. I doubt if he can ruin us but he can make a hell of a lot of trouble. Frankly, I don't like it at all."

"We'd be in it together," said Amanda. "We're already in it. It's too late to do anything about it."

He laughed, unwillingly.

"I'm in love with somebody else, you know, and I'm going to marry her some day."

"No, you're not," said Amanda. "You're going to marry me."

"How?" he fended. "You're still married, and I'm going to Africa tomorrow and may never set eyes on you again."

"I'm coming over on the next boat," said Amanda. "I'll fix everything, never fear."

Callingham looked at her reflectively.

"Has it occurred to you that you may find it harder 'fixing' everything once you break with Julian? I don't think you know yet what you're up against, my dear girl. Personally, I've gotten along damn well before without Julian Evans's backing, and I can do it again. But you've used the man up to the hilt. What makes you think you can do without him now?"

He was being difficult. It was going to be harder than she thought.

"You'll help me," Amanda said.

"Don't count on it!" He grinned at her. "I'm not risking my hide and reputation for anybody, even a lovely anybody like you. Another thing, I'd better get you out of here as quietly as possible before hell breaks loose again."

"I don't care if it does," said Amanda boldly. "I'm staying with you tonight."

He burst out laughing.

"Fine. I never pass up a pretty gift like that. It won't change my mind about anything, though."

"It might," Amanda said, tossing her head.

"The talk is that you're no good in the hay, my dear," Callingham chuckled. "But I like to be open to conviction."

It might still work, Amanda thought, just as it had with Julian. With this farewell memory she could count on winning him over completely when she reached him in Africa. This was the way she had planned it and this was the way it would have to be. Unless, for the first time, something went wrong for her. Unless he was a stronger man than she. Unless he, in his own egotistical way, had other plans. Unless Julian really could put a hex on her.

Even under Callingham's rough embrace there came, along with her usual annoyance at the damage to her permanent, Amanda's first doubts.

XIV

ROCKMAN ELROY had Vicky Haven on his mind to the point of inconvenience. He would be strolling through the park, swinging his cane, dodging kiddycars and admiring the amiable antics of the sea lions, when he would think of a nice fact about sea lions which he would like to impart to some willing ear, and Vicky's was the only willing ear he had ever found. He would turn into the Metropolitan Museum for distraction and there would be a Tibetan temple piece and some Egyptian funerary jewelry suggesting a dozen informative tid-bits certain to enchant his niece's friend. In the back room of the Plaza as soon afterward as modern conveniences could whisk him there he would contemplate the cathedral architecture of the sacred room, doubtless its appeal for the group of young curates drinking beer in the corner, and he would think that perhaps he would change his drinking habits to gayer surroundings, places more suited to a young woman. He had never been the problem drinker that his brother Beaver had been, inasmuch as he had never been provoked to such excesses by a good wife. Still, he would begin either tomorrow or day after tomorrow to moderate his requirements so as not to alarm a gentle little thing like Victoria. He supported these vows with an extra highball, but this only made him long for company, some one who liked good conversation which he felt bubbling up in him like a whistling tea-kettle about to blow.

"Victoria is the only good talker I've ever met in a woman," he told himself flatteringly enough, the picture of her charming young face coming before him, eyes fascinated, lips parted not in speech but in breathless interest. Yes, he admitted it, he would like nothing better than to offer his hand in marriage to the girl! It was not that he was at the age where youth excited him, for even in the often treacherous fifties it alarmed rather than intrigued him. The musical shows then popular with their rousing teen-age casts brought out the Scrooge rather than the lecher in him, and he would have preferred to send the kiddies packing off to bed while he listened to Fritzi Scheff, or better still, nobody. No, he reflected, little Miss Haven was the very woman he should have had twenty-five years ago, and the difference in their ages was Time's mistake, not his own.

Being a trained philosopher, he was accustomed to make his choices in life first and justify them afterward. Why had the thought of marriage never before struck him with anything but revulsion? Why did it suddenly occur to him as if the institution was his own invention, so pleased was he with the impulse? Even philosophers are naïvely astonished to find themselves subject to the ordinary rules for human behavior, and Rockman, having had a most enjoyable, self-indulgent bachelor life, was genuinely amazed at the strange, unexpected loneliness of the bachelor fifties, the middle age for which marriage was made. His indulgences now seemed his privations. Engagements for lunch or dinner with their pleasant absence of permanent responsibility, their casual "good-bye" restoring his privacy once again to him, now seemed insulting compromises to his need for constant companionship; they were fraught with the fear that in another moment, after one more night-cap, one more for the road, he would be alone again, his prized barriers safely up once more; but now they offered prison instead of freedom, and through their bars the chilly fingers of Age, gaunt and lonely, clutched at him.

Once his mind was made up Rockman was only impatient with his delay in informing Vicky. He chuckled at the picture of what consternation his move would bring to his brother's family! What a stew Nancy and her mother would be in when they found him married to their discarded friend! Hastening to the address Miss Finkelstein had given him, he entertained himself with another pleasing picture—a honeymoon of travel which enabled him to lecture on the scenery to his enthralled bride. A florist's shop reminded him of a bridegroom's duties, and he stopped to purchase a great box of roses. With this under one arm, his cane under the other, he arrived at the Thirteenth Street apartment. Delaying his happiness a little longer, he paused to admire the puppies in the pet-shop before ascending the steps to the entrance hall. Here he encountered a brisk young woman in a most imposing uniform.

"You're Mr. Elroy, I believe," she said. "I met you at Victoria Haven's other place. I'm Ethel Carey from her home town."

"Of course," said Rockman, who remembered neither faces nor names. "Are you—er—calling on her now?"

Ethel looked at him in surprise.

"Oh, no, I'm just here making arrangements about storage and subletting and all that for her, while I'm in town. The wedding was so unexpected, you see, it didn't leave her time to do anything, so she left it all to me."

"The—ah—you said the wedding?" Rockman asked dumbly.

"If you can call such a helter-skelter business a wedding!" Ethel exclaimed, with a shrug. She opened the mail-box, extracted some letters, dropped them in her purse. "Naturally, with Ken going into the Army, Vicky was too rattled to do anything ceremonial, so—"

Rockman shifted his roses to his other arm.

"She—she married Saunders, then?" He tried not to show the desolation in his heart.

Ethel nodded.

"Thank heavens, she's got something she wanted at last," she sighed. "Goodness knows how it will work out, what with him at camp, somewhere in the South, but she says she's going to follow him wherever he goes. Poor lamb is so crazy about him! I'm not sure, myself. Do you think he's good enough for her?"

Rockman set the box of flowers down, and mopped his forehead.

"Saunders? Ideal man for her, I would say," he said bravely. "Perfectly splendid chap. Couldn't have done any better. Certain to be happy. Best thing in the world for her. Wish 'em every happiness. Perfectly mated, I would say. Fine thing. Wonderful thing."

Ethel blinked as his enthusiasm mounted.

"I wish I was as optimistic as you about it, Mr. Elroy," she said, shaking her head. "But of course marriages aren't awfully important nowadays anyway. War makes love and all that sort of thing seem sort of silly, doesn't it?"

"It does, indeed," agreed Rockman. "I take it you're leaving here now? So am I. Er—would you care to have a drink with me, say at the Brevoort Terrace? I'm rather at loose ends."

"So am I," said Ethel. "Everything seems so haywire, lately. Vicky getting married out of a blue sky, Amanda Keeler Evans shooting off to Africa so mysteriously, and Julian making a fool of himself with all those statements about her. There must be something funny about it somewhere or he wouldn't go to such trouble to say there wasn't. Besides, everybody knows he's started the divorce proceedings. You knew Amanda Keeler, of course?"

Rockman followed her down the steps to the street, and in her preoccupation she did not notice that the florist's box had been left in the vestibule of the apartment.

"Keeler—Keeler—Amanda Keeler," he repeated, frowning. "Don't think I ever heard of her. Unless she was a kin to Doctor Vestry Keeler, of Leland Stanford. A very sound man, Vestry Keeler—a good scholar. I remember when I worked with him at the University of Chicago—"

2

"There isn't a thing in the papers about it," marvelled Vicky, sitting up in bed with her sandy topknot barely visible above the mound of Sunday papers. "How strange!"

Ken was pecking at a typewriter by the window, his fine new honeymoon dressing-gown belted with a rag of a neck-tie. He looked up in amazement.

"You're not looking for Cholly Knickerbocker's account of our wedding, are you, my love?" He came over and gave her a benign, pitying kiss on the forehead. "Haven't I explained to you, pet, that people like us don't make news? What were you expecting—front page headlines—'SAUNDERRS TAKES HILLBILLY BRIDE TO SHADY HOTEL'? No, dear, people like us have to push each other out the window before we're news. Even then we're only good for two sticks."

"I'm looking for Amanda, silly," Vicky answered, pulling him down beside her. "You never see a thing about her any more. Ethel Carey claims she followed Callingham to Africa, but here it says his fiancée, Asta Lundgren, has flown to Egypt to marry him."

"Never mind, Amanda will get along," Ken shrugged. "She may not get who or what she wants but she'll get something."

"But, darling, no dispatches from her in any paper, no more articles, no mention of her after that first flurry of Julian's!" Vicky argued. "Things must have gone wrong with her! Maybe she did have to have Julian, after all! Maybe he's got people to gang up against her."

Ken meditated on this, lighting two cigarettes, and putting one in Vicky's mouth.

"Well, one thing, if Julian's stacking the cards against her, Andrew Callingham isn't going to be anywhere around her, I can promise you that," he said. "Callingham made his name saving his own nose and blowing his own horn, not looking after beautiful ladies on skids."

They were both silent, Vicky thinking that she would have to do a lot of talking in their married life to cover up these silences when Ken might be remembering another love. She would begin right now.

"If we don't get pulled into the war, won't you be sorry you enlisted, Ken? Won't you be sorry you didn't stay on at *Peabody's* or else free-lance a while? I should think you'd get awfully embarrassed running around in your soldier suitie with no war."

"We'll be in all right," Ken said. "And if I wasn't in, think how proud of me you'd be, all the other boys fighting and me up at *Peabody's* all rosy from golf and roast beef, telling the boys how to brighten up their tanks with a pretty piece of chintz?"

"I suppose I'll feel the same way," Vicky confessed. "Of course I wouldn't dare knit, except for the enemy. I could drive a truck, though. I might even fly. You'd look up when you'd hear a whiz and there I'd be ferrying a bomber! You wait!"

"I'll bet you would do it, at that," Ken said, admiringly. "You wouldn't talk about it, you'd just go do it. I can't understand how an up and coming girl like you managed to wait this long for a lout like me. How'd you know I was your man?"

"A gypsy told me," Vicky said. Then she sighed because she knew she was going to ask that question.

"Ken—" she began haltingly, "if Amanda should ever come back again—I mean—would you—I mean—"

Ken kissed her.

"You're the one for me, darling. There couldn't ever be any Amanda in my life, now that I know about you. Never, never, again."

Vicky stroked his hair.

"Thank you for that, darling," she said gratefully.

But she was not at all sure whether he was speaking the truth or what he hoped was the truth.

For that matter, neither was Ken.

CHRONOLOGY

NOTE ON THE TEXTS

NOTES

Chronology

1896   Born in family home at 53 West North Street in Mt. Gilead, Ohio, on November 28, the second of three daughters of Roy King Powell and Hattie Sherman Powell. (In later years Powell habitually gives her birth year as 1897. Father, b. August 24, 1869, and mother, b. March 24, 1872, are both from the Mt. Gilead area. Father is of Welsh-Irish descent, while family tradition claims the mother's family, while mostly English, is also part Cherokee. Father works at series of jobs, including night manager of a local hotel and traveling salesman selling perfume, bedding, cherries, cookies, and coffins. Sister Mabel born July 11, 1895.)

1899   Sister Phyllis born December 29 at 115 Cherry Street.

1903   Mother dies, probably the result of a botched abortion, on December 6, in Shelby, Ohio.

1904–6   Lives with series of relatives in central Ohio, while father is on the road as traveling salesman. (Later remembers: "a year of farm life with this or that aunt, life in small-town boarding houses, life with very prim strict relatives, to rougher life in the middle of little factory towns.")

1907–9   Father marries Sabra Stearns, a former schoolteacher and cashier, in 1907. Family is reunited in a large farmhouse outside Cleveland. Stepmother proves to be abusive and is despised by Powell and her sisters, all of whom eventually run away from home. Becomes an early and precocious reader; favorite writers include Alexandre Dumas, Victor Hugo, and Charles Dickens. Begins to write stories, plays, and sketches.

1910–14   When stepmother burns some of her notebooks in the summer of 1910, runs off to live with her maternal aunt, Orpha May Sherman Steinbrueck, in Shelby. Aunt encourages Powell's literary ambitions. ("She gave me music lessons and thought I had genius and when I wrote crude little poems and stories, she cherished them, positive that I was another Jean Webster or Ella Wheeler Wilcox.") Attends Shelby High School, where she is made yearbook editor in her senior year.

1914–17   With the financial assistance of her aunt, neighbors, and the school itself, matriculates in the fall of 1914 at Lake Erie College in Painesville, Ohio. Publishes stories in the *Lake Erie Record*, beginning in early 1915. Works during summer of 1915 as maid and waitress at a resort near the college; writes diary addressed to a fictional friend named "Mr. Woggs." Proves a barely adequate student at Lake Erie, but distinguishes herself in extracurricular activities, serving as editor of the *Lake Erie Record* in her senior year, writing and performing her own plays, and playing the part of Puck in an outdoor production of *A Midsummer Night's Dream*. Spends the summer of 1916 as a counselor at Camp Caho in Michigan. Works for a Shelby newspaper, the *Globe*, for most of the summer of 1917.

1918   Graduates from Lake Erie College and moves to Pomfret, Connecticut, where she writes, works on a farm, and does some suffragist campaigning throughout the northeastern corner of the state. Studies seriously but informally with author and photographer Ella Boult, who also lives in Pomfret. Moves on September 2 to 353 West 85th Street in New York City. Attempts to enlist in the U.S. Navy in October, but is hospitalized for a month when physical examination indicates that she is suffering from Spanish influenza.

1919   Does extensive free-lance writing for a wide variety of magazines and newspapers, while working at a succession of jobs. Appears as an extra in *Footlights and Shadows*, a silent film starring Olive Thomas.

1920   Lives at 569 West End Avenue and is employed by the Interchurch World Movement, where her duties include working in support of Armenian famine relief. Early in the year, meets a co-worker, Joseph Roebuck Gousha (b. August 20, 1890), a poet and critic from Pittsburgh who has also recently arrived in New York City; they attend Broadway plays together and take long walks in Tarrytown and on Staten Island. Marries Gousha on November 20 at the Church of the Transfiguration on 29th Street in Manhattan. After a honeymoon at the Hotel Pennsylvania on Seventh Avenue near Pennsylvania Station, Powell and her husband decide to maintain separate households, but then move in together at 31 Riverside Drive.

1921   Son Joseph R. Gousha Jr., known as "Jojo," is born on August 22 at St. Luke's Hospital in Manhattan after difficult delivery. Powell remains in hospital with son for three weeks.

1922   Begins her first novel, *Whither*, an autobiographical work about her early days in New York; writes mostly in Central Park and in the Children's Room of the New York Public Library. Joseph abandons writing and begins successful career in advertising.

1923   It becomes obvious that Jojo is mentally impaired (possibly autistic, a condition then not identified; he will be classified and ministered to as "retarded" or "schizophrenic" throughout most of his life, although his capacity for memorization and certain intellectual tasks is on the genius level). Joseph's financial success permits the family to hire Louise Lee as nurse and caretaker for Jojo (Lee remains with the household until 1954). Family begins practice of renting a summer beach cottage in Mt. Sinai, Long Island.

1924   Moves with family to 46 West Ninth Street in Greenwich Village. *Whither* is accepted by the Boston publisher Small, Maynard.

1925   *Whither* is published and almost immediately disavowed by Powell. Writes a second novel, *She Walks In Beauty*, which she will always describe as her first. Begins novel *The Bride's House*. After disagreements with Joseph, spends several weeks in Ohio with her sisters and Orpha May Steinbrueck. Jojo's disturbances are increasingly blatant and alarming. Powell establishes a deeply devoted, and possibly romantic, friendship with the leftist playwright John Howard Lawson late in the year.

1926   *The Bride's House* is completed but remains unpublished
        along with *She Walks In Beauty*. Father dies in July after a
        paralytic stroke. Powell's social circle includes Charles
        Norman, Eugene Jolas, Jacques LeClercq, Esther An-
        drews, and Canby Chambers, and she becomes acquainted
        with Ernest Hemingway, John Dos Passos, and Theodore
        Dreiser. Begins writing book reviews for the New York
        Evening Post, to which she will contribute for more than
        three decades.

1927   Spends most of the year working on plays, short stories,
        and free-lance work for magazines, while trying to find a
        publisher for her two unpublished novels (later claims
        that *She Walks In Beauty* was turned down by 36 pub-
        lishers).

1928   Lives at 106 Perry Street in Greenwich Village. *She Walks
        In Beauty* is published by Brentano's, to generally favor-
        able reviews and unremarkable sales. Joseph is briefly un-
        employed in the fall and Powell responds by writing a first
        draft of "The Party," a play (later retitled *Big Night*) sat-
        irizing the advertising world, in a period of three weeks.
        Starts work on novel *Dance Night*.

1929   *The Bride's House* is published; it meets with less success
        than her previous book. Jojo, sporadically violent and out
        of control, is now confined to hospitals or special schools
        much of the time. Powell becomes a close friend of Mar-
        garet Burnham De Silver, a wealthy woman whose schiz-
        ophrenic daughter is resident in the same New Jersey
        institution as Jojo. Another close friend is the editor
        Coburn Gilman, who becomes Powell's favorite drinking
        companion. Late in the year, Powell has what is diag-
        nosed as a heart attack at the family vacation home on
        Long Island and is brought back by taxi to New York,
        where she is hospitalized for several weeks. (Attack is
        probably symptom of a chest teratoma that she will suffer
        from until 1949.)

1930   *Dance Night* is published by Farrar & Rinehart; its poor
        sales and negative reviews depress Powell, who will always
        consider this her finest novel. Visits Bermuda in the sum-
        mer with Margaret De Silver. Earns some of her living

collaborating with nightclub comedian Dwight Fiske on
bawdy song-stories. (Many of these are later published in
Fiske's collections *Without Music* in 1933 and *Why Should
Penguins Fly?* in 1934.)

1931   Begins work on two novels, *Come Back to Sorrento* and a
          book she originally calls the "Lila" novel, which becomes
          Turn, Magic Wheel. Begins keeping a detailed diary with
          some regularity, a practice she continues for the rest of
          her life. An early play, *Walking Down Broadway*, is pur-
          chased for $7,500 and loosely adapted into a film directed
          by Erich von Stroheim (the film, which is taken away
          from von Stroheim and partially reshot, is retitled *Hello,
          Sister!* and released in 1933). The family moves in October
          to 9 East Tenth Street.

1932   *Come Back to Sorrento* is published by Farrar & Rinehart,
          who against Powell's wishes retitle it *The Tenth Moon*.
          Spends beginning of the year in California, working as a
          screenwriter, but receives no film credits. *Big Night* is se-
          lected for production by the Group Theater, and Powell
          is anxious about what she calls the "heavy footed literal-
          ism" of their staging. The play is directed by Cheryl
          Crawford, then, late in the rehearsal period, by Harold
          Clurman; the cast includes Stella Adler, J. Edward Brom-
          berg, and Clifford Odets. Begins work on novel *The Story
          of a Country Boy*, based in part on memories of her ma-
          ternal cousin Charles Miller.

1933   *Big Night* opens in January; receives harsh reviews and
          closes after four days, although it is praised by Robert
          Benchley in *The New Yorker*. Powell begins work on an-
          other play, *Jig-Saw*. Completes *The Story of a Country
          Boy*. Forms friendship with Edmund Wilson; friendship
          with John Dos Passos deepens. At the end of the year,
          there is a rupture, apparently final, with John Howard
          Lawson.

1934   Begins work on satirical novel *Turn, Magic Wheel*. *Jig-
          Saw* is produced by the Theater Guild, with Spring By-
          ington, Ernest Truex, and Cora Witherspoon in leading
          roles; production is a modest success, and play is pub-
          lished by Farrar & Rinehart. *The Story of a Country Boy* is

published to poor sales and undistinguished reviews; film rights are sold to Warner Brothers and First National Pictures for $12,500.

1935   Continues work on *Turn, Magic Wheel*; Farrar & Rinehart are mystified by her self-proclaimed "new style" of urban comedy, and John Farrar suggests that she put the novel aside, "not necessarily destroy." Visits Havana and Key West with Joseph and old friend Harry Lissfelt. *Man of Iron*, a film loosely derived from *The Story of a Country Boy*, is released to poor reviews.

1936   *Turn, Magic Wheel* is published by Farrar & Rinehart, to excellent reviews and moderate sales. British edition is published by John Constable; the reviews are even more enthusiastic. (Powell will continue to have a small but avid following in England.) Moves again to Hollywood in the fall; earns a large salary as a screenwriter and is promised an extended contract, guaranteeing her up to $1500 a week; dislikes writing for the movies and returns to New York.

1937   Works on novel *The Happy Island* while taking amphetamine diet pills. Attempts to produce a play, *Red Dress*, based on *She Walks In Beauty*, with Norman Bel Geddes.

1938   *The Happy Island* is published; it is a critical and financial failure. Jojo is moved to Gladwyne Colony in Valley Forge, Pennsylvania, where he lives for most of the next 14 years.

1939   Signs with Scribner's, where her new editor is Max Perkins, famous for his work with F. Scott Fitzgerald, Ernest Hemingway, and Thomas Wolfe. Appears as a regular guest analyzing popular songs on radio program *Music and Manners*, featuring Ann Honeycutt. Briefly employed as book critic for *Mademoiselle*; describes the work as a "kindergarten" job. Through Dos Passos, becomes increasingly friendly with Gerald and Sara Murphy, and spends weekends with them at their homes in East Hampton and Snedens Landing, New York. Works much of the year on novel *Angels on Toast*, writing part of it in a Coney Island hotel.

1940 *Angels on Toast* published by Scribner's, to good reviews and marginal sales. Begins work on *A Time To Be Born*, based in part on the career of Clare Boothe Luce.

1941 After a dream about her childhood in late January starts to sketch out what becomes *My Home Is Far Away*, a novel closely based on childhood experiences. At year's end, she helps rewrite a musical comedy, *The Lady Comes Across*; other participants in the project include composer Vernon Duke, lyricist John Latouche, choreographer George Balanchine, and actors Jessie Matthews, Mischa Auer, Joe E. Lewis, and Gower Champion.

1942 *The Lady Comes Across* closes in January after two performances. John Latouche remains one of Powell's closest friends. *A Time To Be Born*, published by Scribner's, becomes Powell's best-selling book to date by far, and is reprinted four times in the first year. The family moves in September to duplex at 35 East Ninth Street.

1943 Works steadily on *My Home Is Far Away*, which she envisions as the beginning of a trilogy. Writes in her diary: "In the new book, I want to trace corruption, private and public, through innocence and love—possibly learning that only by being prepared for all evil can evil be met." Begins work on novel "The Destroyers," later retitled *The Locusts Have No King*.

1944 *My Home Is Far Away* is published; it is dedicated to her cousin John Franklin Sherman, who was also raised by Orpha May Steinbrueck and is serving overseas. Begins "Marcia," the second volume of her projected trilogy (the novel is never finished, and less than 100 pages of draft survive). Edmund Wilson publishes a mixed review of *My Home Is Far Away* in *The New Yorker* in November; it hurts Powell deeply and nearly ruptures their friendship.

1945 In the summer, visits Ohio for what will be the last reunion with her two sisters.

1946 Incorporates the fascination and horror she feels listening to radio broadcasts of the United States atomic bomb tests on Bikini Atoll into the final scene of *The Locusts*

Have No King, which she now plans as a deliberately "post-war" novel. Takes an automobile trip to Florida with Margaret De Silver, where they visit with Esther Andrews, Canby Chambers, and Pauline Pfeiffer Hemingway. Undergoes a hysterectomy in the fall; tells friends she has been "spayed." Works on *The Locusts Have No King* throughout the year.

1947   Meets Malcolm Lowry during his visit to Manhattan to promote his recently published novel *Under the Volcano*; the two become friends and correspondents. Max Perkins dies in June. Powell attends to John Dos Passos after an automobile accident in September on Cape Cod, which costs him an eye and kills his wife, Katy. Hospitalized for more than two weeks after being attacked and badly beaten by Jojo in November.

1948   *The Locusts Have No King* is published by Scribner's. Powell deems it an "admirable, superior work—no holes of plot as in other works—and a sustained intelligence dominating the farcical and exaggerated so that it had more unity and structural solidity than anything I ever did." The novel receives favorable reviews but sales are mediocre. To Powell's surprise, her English publisher, John Constable, rejects the book. Visits Haiti and Key West in March.

1949   Pressure within Powell's chest is finally diagnosed as a teratoma, a rare tumor that often includes fragments of hair and teeth, which has become so acute that her ribs are cracking from its pressure. Tumor is successfully removed in April. Powell believes the growth a "failed twin" and nicknames it "Terry Toma." Accepts a month-long residency during the summer at the MacDowell Colony, but is irritated by the colony's regulations and traditions and remains stymied in her work on "Marcia." Sister Mabel Powell Pocock dies in October.

1950   Unable to make headway with her new project, a "novel of Washington Square" entitled *The Wicked Pavilion*. Feeling the need for a drastic change, moves in October with financial aid from Margaret De Silver to Paris, where she lives at the Hotel Lutetia on the Left Bank. Renews old friendships with Eugene Jolas and Libby Holman, and meets Samuel Beckett, Jean-Paul Sartre, and Simone de Beauvoir; dislikes France and finds Parisians "the most moralizing people in the world." Cuts her stay short when Chinese intervention in the Korean War suggests to her that a global conflict may be imminent.

1951   Stays briefly in London in January before returning to New York. Jojo has an unusually good year and spends a considerable amount of time at home, encouraging parents' hopes for further improvement. Writes in her diary on July 29: "Incredible that after working steadily on this novel, with very few sidetracks except wretched and futile attempts at money . . . I have gotten no further than 12 pages or so." Cuts her ties with Scribner's when they refuse, after her repeated urgings, to bring out a collection of her short stories. Rosalind Baker Wilson (daughter of Edmund Wilson) brings Powell to Houghton Mifflin.

1952   *Sunday, Monday and Always*, a collection of short stories, is published in June by Houghton Mifflin and receives excellent notices, with many reviewers using the occasion to celebrate Powell's work in general. In the fall, London-based publisher W. H. Allen agrees to bring out *The Locusts Have No King*, *Sunday, Monday and Always*, and the forthcoming novel, *The Wicked Pavilion*, in England, restoring Powell to print there for the first time in several years. Becomes active supporter of Adlai Stevenson in his presidential campaign against Dwight D. Eisenhower. Works sporadically on "Yow," a children's book about cats, which she does not finish.

1953   The demolition of Powell's beloved Hotel Lafayette and the adjoining Hotel Brevoort helps provide impetus to complete *The Wicked Pavilion*. Powell takes photographs of the rubble and models the novel's "Café Julien" on the Lafayette. In her diary, lists the novels that have most influenced her: *Sister Carrie* (Dreiser), *Dodsworth* (Lewis), *Sentimental Education* (Flaubert), *Satyricon* (Petronius), *Daniel Deronda* (Eliot), *Dead Souls* (Gogol), *Lost Illusions* and *The Distinguished Provincial* (Balzac), *Our Mutual Friend* and *David Copperfield* (Dickens), and *Jenny* (Undset).

1954   Meets Gore Vidal in March and forms friendship. Frequents the Cedar, a bar on University Place, where she meets many artists, including Franz Kline. *The Wicked Pavilion* is published in October; it is reviewed on the front page of the New York *Herald Tribune* book review and appears for a week on the *New York Times* bestseller list. Afraid of Jojo's violence, she and Joseph look into the possibility of a prefrontal lobotomy; Dos Passos convinces them not to go ahead with the operation. Louise Lee suffers a debilitating stroke in March and does not return to the Gousha household; this upsets Jojo greatly and his parents reluctantly confine him more or less permanently to the New York state hospital system.

1955   Begins a residency in April at Yaddo, arts colony outside Saratoga Springs, New York, and is happier there than at the MacDowell Colony; begins a new novel, later published as *A Cage for Lovers*. Through the writer and bookstore owner Peter Martin, meets the young Jacqueline Miller (later Rice), who becomes one of her closest friends and later serves as her executor. In November, endures first in series of severe nosebleeds; she is told in December that she is suffering from anemia. Contributes book reviews regularly to the New York *Post*.

1956   Rewrites *Angels on Toast* as a paperback for Fawcett Books under the title *A Man's Affair*. Writes television script based on story "You Should Have Brought Your Mink."

1957   Completes novel *A Cage for Lovers*, after a long series of rewrites demanded by the publisher; the book is published in October with little fanfare or appreciation. Joseph is informed in December by his advertising agency that he will be retired on January 1, 1958.

1958   Family finances collapse after Joseph's retirement. By October, the family is forced to move from 35 East Ninth Street, and begins a series of residencies in hotels and sublets. Powell writes a great deal of free-lance work and searches for a job. At the suggestion of Malcolm Cowley, Viking Press contracts Powell for a novel that will become *The Golden Spur*.

1959   Margaret De Silver rescues Powell and Joseph from their
        poverty with a generous trust fund.

1960   Powell and Joseph move to 43 Fifth Avenue. Powell
        spends much of the spring at Yaddo, where she becomes
        close friends with novelist Hannah Green, but leaves after
        another violent nosebleed. Joseph is diagnosed with rec-
        tal cancer in May; an operation relieves pain but his health
        continues to deteriorate. Powell returns to Lake Erie Col-
        lege to receive an honorary doctorate.

1961   Powell is hospitalized for anemia; doctors suggest re-
        moval of a growth, which she refuses. Spends much of the
        year taking care of her husband.

1962   Joseph dies on February 14. Margaret De Silver dies
        on June 1. *The Golden Spur* is published by Viking in
        October. Edmund Wilson's "Dawn Powell: Greenwich
        Village in the Fifties," the most significant critical piece
        on Powell's work during her lifetime, is published in *The
        New Yorker*.

1963   *The Golden Spur* is nominated for the National Book
        Award but does not win. Powell works with Lee Adams
        and Charles Strouse on a musical comedy version of *The
        Golden Spur*. Moves to a penthouse at 95 Christopher
        Street, prompting a lawsuit from her former landlords at
        43 Fifth Avenue. Autobiographical sketch "What Are You
        Doing In My Dreams?" is published in *Vogue*. Begins
        work on "Summer Rose," a novel.

1964   Returns to Lake Erie College in May to lecture, meet
        with students, and deliver graduation address. The Amer-
        ican Academy of Arts and Letters presents her with the
        Marjorie Peabody Waite Award for lifetime achievement
        in literature. Powell finds herself in more professional de-
        mand than in the past, with regular offers for well-paid
        free-lance work and a significantly higher advance for her
        next novel. Her health is poor; she has begun to lose
        weight and suffers from anemia. Diagnosed with colon
        cancer in August, she realizes that she is probably mor-
        tally ill. *The Golden Spur* musical project is indefinitely
        postponed.

1965   Completes "Staten Island, I Love You" for *Esquire*, a rem-
            iniscence of her walks with Joseph Gousha 45 years earlier.
            Continues to work on "Summer Rose." Her weight drops
            to 105 pounds. Enters St. Luke's Hospital in September,
            where she refuses a colostomy. Returns to her home,
            where she is tended by Hannah Green and Jacqueline
            Miller Rice, and visited often by Coburn Gilman. Signs a
            hastily drawn will in which she donates her body to med-
            ical research; returns to St. Luke's by ambulance. Dies on
            the afternoon of November 14. (In 1970 the Cornell Med-
            ical Center contacts Jacqueline Miller Rice about the re-
            turn of Powell's remains; Rice gives Cornell authority to
            bury them in New York City Cemetery on Hart Island, the
            city's potter's field.)

Note on the Texts

This volume contains five novels by Dawn Powell that were first published between 1930 and 1942: *Dance Night* (1930), *Come Back to Sorrento* (under the title *The Tenth Moon*, 1932), *Turn, Magic Wheel* (1936), *Angels on Toast* (1940), and *A Time To Be Born* (1942). This volume prints the texts of the first American editions for each of these novels. Although *Turn, Magic Wheel, Angels on Toast*, and *A Time To Be Born* were published in England, Powell's involvement in the preparation of these editions was minimal, and her English editors made changes based on British conventions of spelling and usage.

Powell began writing *Dance Night*, her fourth published novel, in the summer of 1928, working steadily on the book throughout 1929 and the first half of 1930. While writing *Dance Night*, Powell considered it the most ambitious novel she had yet attempted; an entry from her diary dated February 17, 1930, reads: "Novel still not under control. Biggest job I ever tackled and not sure yet I can do it." On March 10, Powell wrote, "Hate novel as if it were a personal foe—it's so damn hard and moves so slow. I want to write plays that move fast. Can't conceive of having energy ever to attack a novel again. They're so damn huge and unwieldy." In April, Powell signed a contract with Farrar & Rinehart for *Dance Night* and two additional novels. She submitted her finished typescript of *Dance Night* to Farrar & Rinehart in early summer 1930, and the book was published in the fall. This volume prints the text of the 1930 Farrar & Rinehart edition.

Come Back to Sorrento was written in 1931 and 1932. The origin of the novel can be traced to a diary entry dated January 1, 1931, where Powell writes of "the tragedy of people who once were glamorous, now trying in mediocre stations to modestly refer to their past," and of a "grand relic" who brags, "You see me in this little town—but Bernhardt told me I was a great actress!" By March, she had begun "Madame Benjamin," the working title of *Come Back to Sorrento*. She submitted the novel on April 22, 1932, to Farrar & Rinehart, who suggested a new title, *The Tenth Moon*, taken from the book's epigraph. Although Powell agreed to the change, she expressed her dissatisfaction in a diary entry dated May 29, 1932: "How I wish they would have allowed me to call it 'Come Back to Sorrento'; since one gets so little else for one's work, a title that pleases the writer seems such a little boon to ask. . . . *The Tenth Moon*—how I hate the empty,

silly, pointless title! . . . " *The Tenth Moon* was published in the fall of
1932. This volume restores Powell's title *Come Back to Sorrento* but
otherwise prints the text of the 1932 Farrar & Rinehart edition of
The Tenth Moon.

Powell conceived *Turn, Magic Wheel* in 1931, at about the same
time she began writing *Come Back to Sorrento*. In diary entries of
1931, she calls it "the 'Lila' novel," referring to the original name of
the character Effie Thorne. Powell wrote an outline of the book and
completed more than 50 pages by July 1931, but in the fall she put
it aside to concentrate on other projects: "I did a little more on
Connie [*Come Back to Sorrento*] and decided to forget for the moment Lila's novel," Powell wrote on November 1, 1931. "I could not
understand why, with Lila's story so clearly and concisely mapped
out, I could not whiz right through it. Finally, it came to me that I
cannot work from factual knowledge. A novel must be a rich forest
known at the start only by instinct." She did not return to *Turn,
Magic Wheel* until February 1934, shortly after finishing reading
proofs for *The Story of a Country Boy* (1934), the last of the three
novels published under her first contract with Farrar & Rinehart. In
a diary entry dated February 12, 1934, Powell writes that the novel
"should not be a daylight book but intense and brilliant and fine like
night thoughts. No wandering but each detail should point to the
one far-off star and be keyed by Lila's own waiting excitement and
preserved youth." By December 1934, the novel, now called "The
Hunter's Wife," had evolved and Powell considered Dennis Orphen
its "central figure." She submitted a synopsis and part of the novel
to Carol Brandt, her agent, in February 1935. Although a new contract stipulated that Powell was to write two more books for Farrar
& Rinehart, the firm turned down "The Hunter's Wife" in April 1935
and gave her permission to publish the book elsewhere; Brandt was
turned down by several houses while Powell continued to work on
the novel throughout the summer and fall. The book, now titled
Turn, Magic Wheel, was finished on November 2, 1935. It was then
submitted to Farrar & Rinehart, which, despite its initial rejection of
"The Hunter's Wife" fragment, accepted and published *Turn,
Magic Wheel* in February 1936. The 1936 Farrar & Rinehart edition is
the text printed here.

Powell worked on *Angels on Toast* throughout 1939 and the first
half of 1940. It was the first of her novels to be brought out by
Scribner's, which assigned Maxwell Perkins to edit it; Powell expressed "pleasure over Max Perkins' editorial work" in a diary entry
dated September 18, 1940, shortly before the book was published. In
1956, a rewritten and radically cut version of *Angels on Toast*, titled

A Man's Affair, was published as a paperback original by Fawcett Books. Powell never expressed dissatisfaction with *Angels on Toast* as it had originally been written, and she appears to have agreed to the revision for exclusively financial reasons. This volume prints the text of the 1940 Scribner's edition of *Angels on Toast*.

Powell began to conceive *A Time To Be Born* in the fall of 1940, shortly after the publication of *Angels on Toast*. A diary entry dated October 29, 1940, contains preliminary notes for the novel's opening scene: "Book. New York during the invasion. Eggs thrown at Willkie in Detroit. Accents on the bus. Waking up with pressure on the head. In London there is bombing. 87 children lost. A story of ambition against a background that is constantly torn down. The young men—idle, poor, no jobs to look forward to, drinking a little beer—apathetic because what chances are there for optimism?" Powell worked on *A Time To Be Born* throughout 1941 and finished the novel on May 18, 1942. It was published by Scribner's on August 3, 1942. The 1942 Scribner's edition of *A Time To Be Born* is the text printed here.

This volume presents the texts listed here without change except for the correction of typographical errors; it does not, however, attempt to reproduce nontextual features of their typographic design. Spelling, punctuation, and capitalization are often expressive features and are not altered, even when inconsistent or irregular. The following is a list of typographical errors corrected, cited by page and line number: 11.39, Seventeen-year old; 22.31, serious stood; 27.39, fraility; 39.14, objected,; 44.28, before unlocked; 48.29, watchman; 49.19, Four'"; 51.35, sighed,; 52.35, 'Well; 63.8, peoples'; 67.20, Steve lit; 71.29, home; 97.16, said,; 101.9, sleep; 121.8, coffee."; 126.28, yet."; 133.30, what he; 141.33, larger,"; 143.15, is this; 151.17, nickle; 151.18, nickles; 156.28, Bauer's; 157.17, dresser-scarf,; 177.11, too."; 192.10, then.)"; 200.32, suiside; 210.27, Benjamin's; 211.22, school-music teacher; 218.34, Wedgewood; 227.25, Murell; 236.10, people,; 238.38, deefat; 238.40, Soldier's; 239.29, "Caro Nome"; 269.6, Benjamin's; 285.9, Mrs. Marshall; 285.12, sheperdess; 286.5, Eugenié; 292.10, night; 299.24, day; 306.9, Marshall owned; 312.15, realise; 324.25, bruskly; 337.36, figure; 342.16, dewey-eyed; 369.15, Benjamin's; 369.16–17, Benjaman; 393.35, Thorndyke; 395.16, even-ning's; 401.11, Mervin; 406.2, EVERYDAY DAY; 408.23–24, entra'acte; 415.20, man that; 422.12, masqureade; 423.37, Marain; 458.1, *Publishers*'; 498.5, "Mr.; 507.32, political; 517.34, anoyed; 528.20, upstairs'; 532.33, to wonder; 554.26, Bell; 569.25, twenty-year ago; 576.14, plants; 598.19, mate,; 621.38, wiscracker; 630.13, sternly.; 633.28, Rubenstein; 674.18, Barer; 683.20, Flo,; 695.10, sad; 696.1, word,; 707.22, Judge.; 708.3

Mrs.; 710.21, now——; 719.9, bandleader, "Lou; 719.16, maraccas; 741.27, cigarete; 744.33, him,; 746.4, said,; 746.14–15, anyone's else; 751.20, vague,; 753.22, giggled,; 756.22, Vane's; 762.27, place.'"; 785.18–19, secretary and; 795.21, Collingham; 840.11, De Gaulle; 846.20, names."; 846.30, Editorial; 884.7, so, he; 914.7, Peabody's; 928.31, predecessors; 957.20, ahamed; 986.14, Jullian; 1038.23, sighed!.

Notes

In the notes below, the reference numbers denote page and line of this volume. No note is made for material included in standard desk-reference books such as Webster's *Collegiate*, *Biographical*, and *Geographical* dictionaries. For further biographical information than is contained in the chronology, see Tim Page, *Dawn Powell: A Biography* (New York: Henry Holt, 1998); Tim Page, ed., *The Diaries of Dawn Powell: 1931–1965* (South Royalton, Vermont: Steerforth Press, 1995); Tim Page, ed., *Selected Letters of Dawn Powell: 1913–1965* (New York: Henry Holt, 1999).

DANCE NIGHT

24.6–15   "I would rather . . . Great."]   Cf. the lecture "What I Saw, and What I Didn't See, in England, Ireland, and France" (1875) by Robert Green Ingersoll (1833–99), lawyer and orator noted for his controversial agnosticism.

40.15–18   "Will someone . . . till I die—"]   From "A Lemon in the Garden of Love" (1906), song by M. E. Rourke and Richard Carle.

42.3   Lillian Russell]   American stage star and famous beauty (1861–1922) whose vehicles included *The Grand Duchess* (1890) and, with the burlesque team Weber and Fields, *Fiddle-dee-dee* and *Whoop-dee-doo*.

49.19   Big Four]   Local nickname for the midwestern railroad line that serviced Cleveland, Cincinnati, Chicago, and St. Louis.

64.20   Down Among the Sheltering Palms]   Song (1914) by James Brockman and Abe Olman.

83.20   Clara Kimball Young]   Stage and movie actress (1890–1960) whose films included *Trilby* (1915), *The Yellow Passport* (1916), and *The Price She Paid* (1917).

90.12   "Under the Double Eagle."]   March composed by Josef Franz Wagner.

94.2   the Eastern Stars]   Eastern Star, Masonic organization for women.

94.3–4   "Laddie . . . Kingdom Come"]   *Laddie: A True Blue Story* (1913) by Gene Stratton Porter; *The Little Shepherd of Kingdom Come* (1903) by John Fox Jr.

101.11–13   "Has anybody here . . . Kelly——"]   "Has Anybody Here Seen Kelly" (1909), song by C. W. Murphy and others, from the musical *The Jolly Bachelors*.

115.35   say]   Thin silk or woolen fabric similar to serge.

152.23–24   "Some of . . . your hon-ey——"]   "Some of These Days" (1910), song by Shelton Brooks, popularized by Sophie Tucker.

180.18   Larkin premiums]   The Larkin Company included souvenirs such as picture cards, handkerchiefs, and bath towels in packages of soap during the 1880s and 1890s.

183.39–40   Billie Burke . . . Anna Held]   American actress Billie Burke (1884–1970); Hungarian-born vaudeville twins Rosie Dolly (1892–1970) and Jenny Dolly (1892–1941); Austrian-American actress Anna Held (1872–1918).

COME BACK TO SORRENTO

205.1   COME BACK TO SORRENTO]   Neapolitan song (1902) by Ernesto di Curtis.

212.28   Marylinn Miller]   Marilyn Miller (1898–1936), musical comedy star of the 1920s who made her stage debut at the age of five.

227.30   "Un Bel Ami"]   *Bel-Ami* (1885), novel by Guy de Maupassant.

232.17–18   'Oh Dolores . . . pain.']   Cf. Algernon Charles Swinburne, "Dolores": "O splendid and sterile Dolores, / Our lady of pain."

234.38–235.2   "Toreador" . . . "The Spinning Song"]   "Toreador," the baritone aria in Act II of Georges Bizet's *Carmen* (1875); "The Spinning Song," chorus from Act II of Richard Wagner's *The Flying Dutchman* (1843).

235.23   "Caro Nome!"]   Soprano aria from Act I of Giuseppe Verdi's *Rigoletto* (1851).

238.40   "The Soldiers' Chorus"]   The chorus "Gloire immortelle" from Act IV of Charles Gounod's *Faust* (1859).

243.37–38   Tristan . . . Der Freischutz]   Richard Wagner's *Tristan und Isolde* (1859); Carl Maria von Weber's *Der Freischütz* (1821).

247.12   "La donna é mobile——"]   Tenor aria from Act I of Giuseppe Verdi's *Rigoletto* (1851).

261.36   Lou Tellegen]   Dutch-born actor (1881–1934) who toured with Sarah Bernhardt in America and subsequently starred in many films, including *The Woman and the Puppet* (1920), *Parisian Nights* (1925), and *Three Bad Men* (1926).

284.24–26   "My love . . . mel-o-dy——"]   Cf. Robert Burns, "A Red, Red Rose" (1787).

285.12–13   "The Rustle of Spring"]   Work for piano by the German composer Christian Sinding (1856–1941).

286.4   "On the road to Mandalay—"]   Poem (1907) by Rudyard Kipling, set to music by Oley Speaks.

286.5   "Eugénie Grandet"]   Novel (1833) by Honoré de Balzac.

314.13–19, 24–25   Blake . . . the waste——']   "The Garden of Love" appears in William Blake's *Songs of Innocence and of Experience* (1794); however, the six lines quoted are from an untitled poem in Blake's notebook.

315.35   Chautauqua concerts]   The Chautauqua community, founded in 1874 in Jamestown, New York, was designed to promote intellectual and spiritual development. Subsequently "Chautauqua" came to be used as a generic term for various troupes that traveled throughout the country presenting cultural and exotic entertainments.

334.24   Waldstein Sonata]   Piano sonata no. 21 in C Major, op. 53, by Ludwig van Beethoven.

347.15–16   "The Rosary"]   Song (1898) by Ethelbert Nevin and Robert Cameron Rogers.

347.30   "Fantasie Stücke."]   *Fantasiestücke* (1838), suite of piano compositions by Robert Schumann.

368.30   Military Polonaise]   The Polonaise in A Major, op. 40, no. 1, by Frédéric Chopin.

TURN, MAGIC WHEEL

383.8   Gieseking]   Walter Gieseking (1895–1956), German pianist.

389.27   Halliburton]   Richard Halliburton (1900–39), world traveler and best-selling author; his books included *The Royal Road to Romance* (1925) and *The Glorious Adventure* (1927).

389.30   Lillie Langtry]   Popular English stage actress (1853–1929), known as the Jersey Lily.

389.31   H. C. Bunner]   American author of humorous sketches and light verse (1855–96).

393.35   Dame Sybil Thorndike]   English actress (1882–1976) known for Shakespearean roles.

395.9   "*Geschichten aus dem Wiener Wald*,"]   "Tales from the Vienna Woods," waltz (1868) by Johann Strauss.

397.6   "*The Fortune-Teller*,"]   Light opera (1898) by Victor Herbert.

400.6   '*Dein ist mein ganzes Herz*,']   "All my heart is yours": tenor aria from Franz Lehár's operetta *The Land of Smiles* (1929).

401.11   Mervyn LeRoy]   Hollywood director (1900–87), best known for such Warner Brothers productions as *Little Caesar* (1931) and *I Am a Fugitive from a Chain Gang* (1932).

403.12   Lewis Gannett]   Editor and book reviewer (1891–1966), long associated with the New York *Herald Tribune*.

404.6–7 *Wien, Wien, Nur Du Allein*] "Vienna, Vienna, only you alone": opening line of "Wien, du stadt meiner Traüme" by Rudolf Sieczynski (1879–1952).

406.2 Dorothy Dix] Pseudonym used by Elizabeth Gilmer (1870–1951) for her advice column, which began running in the New York *Journal* in 1901 and was later syndicated.

408.24 *Biography*] Comedy (1933) by S. N. Behrman.

409.21 Erskine Caldwell] Best-selling novelist (1903–87) best known for *Tobacco Road* (1932) and *God's Little Acre* (1933).

409.27 *Three Soldiers*] Novel (1921) by John Dos Passos.

422.17–18 drums of Santerre . . . dying words] The French revolutionary commander Antoine-Joseph Santerre ordered a drum roll to render inaudible the final words of Louis XVI before his execution in 1793.

441.21 Flip . . . Little Nemo] In Winsor McCay's long-running comic strip *Little Nemo in Slumberland* (which appeared sporadically, sometimes as *In the Land of Wonderful Dreams*, between 1905 and 1927), the dreams of Little Nemo are invariably terminated when his friend Flip wakes him.

441.33–34 Max Eastman] American poet and radical editor (1883–1969); founder of *The Masses* (1913–18) and *The Liberator* (1919–22).

443.20 *The Wind in the Willows*] Children's book (1908) by Kenneth Grahame.

444.6 Gibson girl] Image of the fashionable young woman as popularized in the drawings of William Hamilton Gibson (1850–96).

451.11 *Face the Music*] Musical (1932) by Moss Hart and Irving Berlin.

451.15 F.P.A.] Franklin P. Adams (1881–1960), journalist and author of light verse who wrote for several New York newspapers over the course of his career. His syndicated weekly column "The Conning Tower" was widely read.

451.27 *Men of Good Will*] *Les Hommes de bonne volonté* (1932–46), 27-volume novel by Jules Romains (1885–1972).

451.39–40 John Reed Club] The John Reed Club was started in 1929 by the editorial board of *New Masses* in accordance with the principles of agitation, education, and propaganda enunciated the previous year by the Comintern (Communist International), with the aim of broadening the appeal of radical socialism; it was named in honor of the poet and journalist John Reed (1887–1920). By 1934, there were some thirty clubs in cities and towns across the United States.

451.40 John Strachey] English Socialist (1901–63) who served in Parliament and published books including *The Coming Struggle for Power* (1932).

452.8   Tiller girls] Dance troupe known for their high-stepping routines and synchronized movements.

452.21   *Sailors of Cattaro*] *Die Matrosen von Catarro* (1930), by the German Communist playwright Friedrich Wolf, was produced in New York in 1935.

455.7   Louis Bromfield] American novelist (1896–1956) whose books included *The Green Bay Tree* (1924) and *Early Autumn* (1926), for which he won the Pulitzer Prize. Bromfield and Dawn Powell attended the fourth grade together in Mansfield, Ohio.

455.10   Hugh Walpole's] English novelist (1884–1941), author of many books including *Fortitude* (1913) and *The Dark Forest* (1916).

471.39   *So Red the Rose*] Best-selling novel (1934) of the Civil War by Stark Young (1881–1963).

472.10   Ann Harding] Movie actress (1904–81) whose films included *Holiday* (1930), *The Animal Kingdom* (1932), and *When Ladies Meet* (1933).

474.17   *Reckless*] M-G-M movie (1935) starring Jean Harlow, William Powell, and Franchot Tone, and directed by Victor Fleming.

475.24   Captain Anthony Eden] Anthony Eden (1897–1977), British statesman, later prime minister; he served as minister without portfolio for League of Nations affairs (1935) and secretary of state for foreign affairs (1935–38).

495.11   *To a Wild Rose*] Piano miniature (1896) by Edward MacDowell.

497.30   Uncle Wiggly] Uncle Wiggily Longears, rabbit hero of a popular series of children's books created by Howard R. Garis (1872–1961) in 1910.

499.11   Red Lewis] Sinclair Lewis.

507.31   Gay-Pay-U] The GPU (Russian acronym for State Political Administration), designation for the Soviet secret police from 1922 to 1934.

511.2   *Trees*] Joyce Kilmer's poem "Trees" was set to music in 1922 by Oscar Rasbach.

515.26   *Isle of Capri*] Song (1934) by Jimmy Kennedy and Will Grosz.

517.37–38   "people . . . sex."] Cf. *Adolphe* (1815), Chapter 5.

ANGELS ON TOAST

574.13   Victor Moore] American vaudeville comedian and movie actor (1876–1962).

600.6   Royal Cortissoz or Jewell] Royall Cortissoz (1869–1948), art editor of the New York *Herald Tribune* and noted opponent of modernism; Edward Alden Jewell (1888–1947), art critic of *The New York Times* during the 1930s and 1940s.

600.11   Kenneth Hayes Miller] American realist painter (1876–1952), teacher of Edward Hopper and Reginald Marsh.

601.34   "I Can Dream, Can't I?"] Song (1937) by Irving Khaal and Sammy Fain.

602.39   David Graham Phillips] American novelist and social critic (1867–1911), author of *The Cost* (1904), *Susan Lenox: Her Fall and Rise* (1917), and other works; he was shot dead by Fitzhugh Coyle Goldsborough, a young musician who had previously sent the writer a series of threatening notes and who was apparently motivated by the delusion that Phillips had defamed the Goldsborough family in his novels.

603.11–12   "Kiss Me Again"] Song by Henry Blossom and Victor Herbert, from the comic opera *Mlle. Modiste* (1905).

604.31   Floyd Collins] William Floyd Collins (1887–1925), of Edmonson County, Kentucky, was trapped on January 30, 1925, in Sand Cave, which he was exploring for possible commercial exploitation. The attempt to rescue him drew large crowds to the scene, and eventually attracted national attention through the medium of radio. Collins was dead by the time rescuers reached him on February 16.

674.18   Simon Barere] Russian-American pianist (1886–1951).

689.6   "Begin the Beguine"] Song (1935) by Cole Porter.

692.28   "Give My Regards to Broadway,"] Song (1904) by George M. Cohan.

A TIME TO BE BORN

769.20   the stone statue from *Don Giovanni*] The statue of the Commendatore, killed by Don Giovanni, comes to life at the end of Mozart's opera to carry him to Hell.

770.26   *Vici d'arte, vici d'amore*] Cf. Puccini's *Tosca*, Act II: "Vissi d'arte, vissi d'amore" ("I lived for art, I lived for love").

772.27–28   Morgan's midget] In June 1933, a publicist for the Ringling Brothers Circus posed German circus performer Lea Graff on the lap of financier J. P. Morgan Jr. as he waited to answer questions before a Senate committee. The photograph was widely distributed.

784.35–36   Benson etching . . . wild bird pictures] The popular paintings and etchings of the American artist Frank W. Benson (1862–1951) often depicted wildlife and sporting and hunting scenes.

840.25–26   Amos and Andy . . . Dead End Kids] *Amos and Andy* was among the most popular radio programs of the 1930s and 1940s; the Dead End Kids were a group of young actors (including Leo Gorcey and Huntz Hall) who appeared in William Wyler's film *Dead End* (1937) and were subsequently featured in other films including *Crime School* (1938), *They Made Me a Criminal* (1939), and *Hell's Kitchen* (1939).

844.3 Roland Young] Comic character actor who appeared in such films as *Ruggles of Red Gap* (1935), *The Man Who Could Work Miracles* (1936), and *Topper* (1937).

846.14 Buck Rogers] Hero of long-running comic strip (1929–67) featuring 25th-century outer space adventures. Based on a 1928 pulp story by Philip Francis Nowlan, the strip was adapted into a movie serial in 1939.

851.17 "The Male Animal"] Successful comedy (1940) by James Thurber and Elliott Nugent.

851.22 Alice Adams] The title character of Booth Tarkington's 1921 novel makes elaborate efforts to disguise her family's lower-middle-class status in order to attract a wealthy young man.

858.38 *fendant*] A dry and slightly acidic white wine produced in the Valais region of Switzerland.

859.17–18 Belleau Wood . . . Château-Thierry] Sites of American victories in June 1918, about 40 miles east of Paris.

861.23 Cholly Knickerbocker] Pseudonymous by-line of a long-running society gossip column in the Hearst newspapers.

862.23 Lambeth Walk] English dance, said to have originated in the Limehouse district of London; it was popularized in 1938 through the song of the same name by Noel Gay and Douglas Furber.

870.22 Sir William Bragg] William L. Bragg (1890–1971), Australian-born English physicist.

871.19 Maury Paul] One of the writers of the Cholly Knickerbocker column.

873.16 Soong sister] The Soongs were a Chinese mercantile family who achieved major political influence; of the daughters of Soong Yao-ju, Soong Ch'ing-ling married Sun Yat-sen, and Soong Mei-ling married Chiang Kai-shek.

878.6–7 Dorothy Lamour] Movie actress (1914–96) known for exotic roles in such films as *The Jungle Princess* (1936), *The Hurricane* (1938), and *Her Jungle Love* (1938).

905.25 Dorothy Dix] See note 406.2.

914.22 *abris*] Shelters.

929.25 Paul Dombey] The titular son in Charles Dickens' *Dombey and Son* (1848), whose early death dashes his father's ambitions.

946.8 Eastern Star."] See note 94.2.

946.24   *Shropshire Lad*]   *A Shropshire Lad*, verse collection (1896) by A. E. Housman.

949.40   Seven Sutherland Sisters]   Singing group that toured under the auspices of P. T. Barnum in the 1880s, celebrated for their elaborate coiffures.

963.12   C.C.C.]   Civilian Conservation Corps.

964.35–36   "Let's Be Buddies"]   Song (1940) by Cole Porter, from the musical *Panama Hattie*.

995.21   OCD, COI, OFF]   The Office of Civilian Defense (OCD) and the Coordinator of Information (COI); OFF may be a joke.

1002.31   admirable Crichton]   In J. M. Barrie's play *The Admirable Crichton* (1902), a group of shipwrecked aristocrats prove unable to fend for themselves and must rely on their butler for survival.

1007.34–36   *Last Rose . . . of the Demons*]   "'Tis the Last Rose of Summer," song (1813) by Thomas Moore and Richard Alfred Milliken; "The Scarf Dance," from Cécile Chaminade's ballet *Callirhoë* (1888); "Ben Bolt," song (1848) by Thomas Dunn English and Nelson Kneass; "Dance of the Demons" (1906).

1037.1   Fritzi Scheff]   Soubrette soprano and operetta star (1882–1953).

Library of Congress Cataloging-in-Publication Data

Powell, Dawn, 1896–1965
    [Novels. Selections]
    Novels, 1930–1942 / Dawn Powell.
        p. cm.—(The Library of America ; 126)
    Contents: Dance night — Come back to Sorrento — Turn, magic wheel
— Angels on toast — A time to be born
    ISBN 1–931082–01–4 (alk. paper)
        1. New York (N.Y.)—Fiction. 2. Ohio—Fiction. I. Dance night.
II. Come back to Sorrento. III. Turn, magic wheel. IV. Angels on toast.
V. A time to be born. VI. Title. VII. Series.

PS3531.O936   A6   2001
813'.52—dc21   00–054595

THE LIBRARY OF AMERICA SERIES

The Library of America fosters appreciation and pride in America's literary heritage by publishing, and keeping permanently in print, authoritative editions of its best and most significant writing. An independent nonprofit organization, it was founded in 1979 with seed money from the National Endowment for the Humanities and the Ford Foundation.

1. Herman Melville, *Typee, Omoo, Mardi* (1982)
2. Nathaniel Hawthorne, *Tales and Sketches* (1982)
3. Walt Whitman, *Poetry and Prose* (1982)
4. Harriet Beecher Stowe, *Three Novels* (1982)
5. Mark Twain, *Mississippi Writings* (1982)
6. Jack London, *Novels and Stories* (1982)
7. Jack London, *Novels and Social Writings* (1982)
8. William Dean Howells, *Novels 1875–1886* (1982)
9. Herman Melville, *Redburn, White-Jacket, Moby-Dick* (1983)
10. Nathaniel Hawthorne, *Collected Novels* (1983)
11. Francis Parkman, *France and England in North America*, vol. I (1983)
12. Francis Parkman, *France and England in North America*, vol. II (1983)
13. Henry James, *Novels 1871–1880* (1983)
14. Henry Adams, *Novels, Mont Saint Michel, The Education* (1983)
15. Ralph Waldo Emerson, *Essays and Lectures* (1983)
16. Washington Irving, *History, Tales and Sketches* (1983)
17. Thomas Jefferson, *Writings* (1984)
18. Stephen Crane, *Prose and Poetry* (1984)
19. Edgar Allan Poe, *Poetry and Tales* (1984)
20. Edgar Allan Poe, *Essays and Reviews* (1984)
21. Mark Twain, *The Innocents Abroad, Roughing It* (1984)
22. Henry James, *Essays, American & English Writers* (1984)
23. Henry James, *European Writers & The Prefaces* (1984)
24. Herman Melville, *Pierre, Israel Potter, The Confidence-Man, Tales & Billy Budd* (1985)
25. William Faulkner, *Novels 1930–1935* (1985)
26. James Fenimore Cooper, *The Leatherstocking Tales*, vol. I (1985)
27. James Fenimore Cooper, *The Leatherstocking Tales*, vol. II (1985)
28. Henry David Thoreau, *A Week, Walden, The Maine Woods, Cape Cod* (1985)
29. Henry James, *Novels 1881–1886* (1985)
30. Edith Wharton, *Novels* (1986)
31. Henry Adams, *History of the United States during the Administrations of Jefferson* (1986)
32. Henry Adams, *History of the United States during the Administrations of Madison* (1986)
33. Frank Norris, *Novels and Essays* (1986)
34. W. E. B. Du Bois, *Writings* (1986)
35. Willa Cather, *Early Novels and Stories* (1987)
36. Theodore Dreiser, *Sister Carrie, Jennie Gerhardt, Twelve Men* (1987)
37. Benjamin Franklin, *Writings* (1987)
38. William James, *Writings 1902–1910* (1987)
39. Flannery O'Connor, *Collected Works* (1988)
40. Eugene O'Neill, *Complete Plays 1913–1920* (1988)
41. Eugene O'Neill, *Complete Plays 1920–1931* (1988)
42. Eugene O'Neill, *Complete Plays 1932–1943* (1988)
43. Henry James, *Novels 1886–1890* (1989)
44. William Dean Howells, *Novels 1886–1888* (1989)
45. Abraham Lincoln, *Speeches and Writings 1832–1858* (1989)
46. Abraham Lincoln, *Speeches and Writings 1859–1865* (1989)
47. Edith Wharton, *Novellas and Other Writings* (1990)
48. William Faulkner, *Novels 1936–1940* (1990)
49. Willa Cather, *Later Novels* (1990)
50. Ulysses S. Grant, *Personal Memoirs and Selected Letters* (1990)

*This book is set in 10 point Linotron Galliard,
a face designed for photocomposition by Matthew Carter
and based on the sixteenth-century face Granjon. The paper is
acid-free Ecusta Nyalite and meets the requirements for permanence
of the American National Standards Institute. The binding
material is Brillianta, a woven rayon cloth made by
Van Heek-Scholco Textielfabrieken, Holland.
The composition is by The Clarinda
Company. Printing and binding by
R.R.Donnelley & Sons Company.
Designed by Bruce Campbell.*